THE
COMPLETE OXFORD
SHAKESPEARE

Martin Droeshout's engraving of Shakespeare, first published on the title-page of the First Folio (1623)

To the Reader

This figure that thou here seest put,
It was for gentle Shakespeare cut,
Wherein the graver had a strife
With nature to outdo the life.
O, could he but have drawn his wit
As well in brass as he hath hit

His face, the print would then surpass
All that was ever writ in brass!
But since he cannot, reader, look
Not on his picture, but his book.

BEN JONSON

THE
COMPLETE OXFORD
SHAKESPEARE

VOLUME I · HISTORIES

General Editors
STANLEY WELLS AND GARY TAYLOR

Editors
STANLEY WELLS, GARY TAYLOR
JOHN JOWETT, AND WILLIAM MONTGOMERY

With Introductions by
STANLEY WELLS

OXFORD UNIVERSITY PRESS

Oxford University Press, Walton Street, Oxford OX2 6DP
Oxford New York Toronto
Delhi Bombay Calcutta Madras Karachi
Kuala Lumpur Singapore Hong Kong Tokyo
Nairobi Dar es Salaam Cape Town
Melbourne Auckland Madrid
and associated companies in
Berlin Ibadan

Oxford is a trade mark of Oxford University Press

Published in the United States
by Oxford University Press Inc., New York

© Oxford University Press 1987

First published 1987
Reprinted 1988, 1989 (twice), 1990
First published in paperback 1994

British Library Cataloguing in Publication Data
Shakespeare, William
[Works]. The Oxford library: the complete
works of William Shakespeare.
I. Title   II. Wells, Stanley, 1930–
III. Taylor, Gary   IV. William Shakespeare, the complete works
822.3'3   PR2754
ISBN 0–19–818272–4 (Pbk)

Library of Congress Cataloging in Publication Data
Shakespeare, William, 1564–1616.
The complete Oxford Shakespeare.
Contents: v. 1. The histories—v. 2. The comedies—v. 3. The tragedies.
I. Wells, Stanley, W., 1930– .   II. Taylor, Gary.
III. Title   IV. Series.
PR2754.W45 1987   822.3'3   87–7850
ISBN 0–19–818272–4 (Pbk)

Printed in Spain
by Printer Industria Gráfica SA

CONTENTS

WILLIAM SHAKESPEARE

THE COMPLETE WORKS

with a General Introduction, and Introductions to individual works, by
STANLEY WELLS

The Complete Works has been edited collaboratively under the General Editorship of Stanley Wells and Gary Taylor. Each editor has undertaken prime responsibility for certain works, as follows:

STANLEY WELLS *The Two Gentlemen of Verona*; *The Taming of the Shrew*; *Titus Andronicus*; *Venus and Adonis*; *The Rape of Lucrece*; *Love's Labour's Lost*; *Much Ado About Nothing*; *As You Like It*; *Twelfth Night*; The Sonnets and 'A Lover's Complaint'; Various Poems (printed); *Othello*; *Macbeth*; *Antony and Cleopatra*; *The Winter's Tale*

GARY TAYLOR *1 Henry VI*; *Richard III*; *The Comedy of Errors*; *A Midsummer Night's Dream*; *Henry V*; *Hamlet*; *Troilus and Cressida*; Various Poems (manuscript); *Sir Thomas More* (passages attributed to Shakespeare); *All's Well That Ends Well*; *King Lear*; *Pericles*; *Cymbeline*

JOHN JOWETT *Romeo and Juliet*; *Richard II*; *King John*; *1 Henry IV*; *The Merry Wives of Windsor*; *2 Henry IV*; *Julius Caesar*; *Measure for Measure*; *Timon of Athens*; *Coriolanus*; *The Tempest*

WILLIAM MONTGOMERY *The First Part of the Contention*; *Richard Duke of York*; *The Merchant of Venice*; *All Is True*; *The Two Noble Kinsmen*

American Advisory Editor · S. Schoenbaum
Textual Adviser · G. R. Proudfoot
Music Adviser · F. W. Sternfeld
Editorial Assistant · Christine Avern-Carr

ILLUSTRATIONS

LIST OF ILLUSTRATIONS

GENERAL INTRODUCTION

THIS volume contains all the known plays and poems of William Shakespeare, a writer, actor, and man of the theatre who lived from 1564 to 1616. He was successful and admired in his own time; major literary figures of the subsequent century, such as John Milton, John Dryden, and Alexander Pope, paid tribute to him, and some of his plays continued to be acted during the later seventeenth and earlier eighteenth centuries; but not until the dawn of Romanticism, in the later part of the eighteenth century, did he come to be looked upon as a universal genius who outshone all his fellows and even, some said, partook of the divine. Since then, no other secular imaginative writer has exerted so great an influence over so large a proportion of the world's population. Yet Shakespeare's work is firmly rooted in the circumstances of its conception and development. Its initial success depended entirely on its capacity to please the theatre-goers (and, to a far lesser extent, the readers) of its time; and its later, profound impact is due in great part to that in-built need for constant renewal and adaptation that belongs especially to those works of art that reach full realization only in performance. Shakespeare's power over generations later than his own has been transmitted in part by artists who have drawn on, interpreted, and restructured his texts as others have drawn on the myths of antiquity; but it is the texts as they were originally performed that are the sources of his power, and that we attempt here to present with as much fidelity to his intentions as the circumstances in which they have been preserved will allow.

Shakespeare's Life: Stratford-upon-Avon and London

Shakespeare's background was commonplace. His father, John, was a glover and wool-dealer in the small Midlands market-town of Stratford-upon-Avon who had married Mary Arden, daughter of a prosperous farmer, in or about 1557. During Shakespeare's childhood his father played a prominent part in local affairs, becoming bailiff (mayor) and justice of the peace in 1568; later his fortunes declined. Of his eight children, four sons and one daughter survived childhood. William, his third child and eldest son, was baptized in Holy Trinity Church, Stratford-upon-Avon, on 26 April 1564; his birthday is traditionally celebrated on 23 April—St. George's Day. The only other member of his family to take up the theatre as a profession was his youngest brother, Edmund, born sixteen years after William. He became an actor and died at the age of twenty-seven: on the last day of 1607 the sexton of St. Saviour's, Southwark, noted 'Edmund Shakspeare A player Buried in ye Church wth a forenoone knell of ye great bell, xxs.' The high cost of the funeral suggests that it may have been paid for by his prosperous brother.

John Shakespeare's position in Stratford-upon-Avon would have brought certain privileges to his family. When young William was four years old he could have had the excitement of seeing his father, dressed in furred scarlet robes and wearing the alderman's official thumb-ring, regularly attended by two mace-bearing sergeants in buff, presiding at fairs and markets. A little later, he would have begun to attend a 'petty school' to acquire the rudiments of an education that would be continued at the King's New School, an established grammar school with a well-qualified master, assisted by an usher to help with the younger pupils. We have no lists of the school's pupils in Shakespeare's time, but his father's position would have qualified him to attend, and the school offered the kind of education that lies behind the plays and poems. Its boy pupils, aged from about eight to fifteen, endured an arduous routine. Classes began early in the morning: at six, normally; hours were long, holidays infrequent. Education was centred on Latin; in the upper forms, the speaking of English was forbidden. A scene (4.1) in *The Merry Wives of Windsor* showing a schoolmaster taking a boy named William through his Latin grammar draws on the officially approved textbook, William Lily's *Short Introduction of Grammar*, and, no doubt, on Shakespeare's memories of his youth.

From grammar the boys progressed to studying works of classical and neo-classical literature. They might read anthologies of Latin sayings and Aesop's *Fables*, followed by the fairly easy plays of Terence and Plautus (on whose *Menaechmi* Shakespeare was to base *The Comedy of Errors*). They might even act scenes from Latin plays. As they progressed, they would improve their command of language by translating from Latin into English and back, by imitating approved models of style, and by studying manuals of composition, the ancient rules of rhetoric, and modern rules of letter-writing. Putting their training into practice, they would compose formal epistles, orations, and declamations. Their efforts at composition would be stimulated, too, by their reading of the most admired authors. Works that Shakespeare wrote throughout his career show the abiding influence of Virgil's *Aeneid* and of Ovid's *Metamorphoses* (both in the original and in Arthur Golding's translation of 1567). Certainly he developed a taste for books, both classical and modern: his plays show that he continued to read seriously and imaginatively for the whole of his working life.

After Shakespeare died, Ben Jonson accused him of knowing 'small Latin and less Greek'; but Jonson took pride in his classical knowledge: a boy educated at an Elizabethan grammar school would be more thoroughly trained in classical rhetoric and Roman (if not Greek) literature than most present-day holders of a university degree in classics. Modern languages would not normally be on the curriculum. Somehow Shakespeare seems to have picked up a working knowledge of French—which he expected audiences of *Henry V* to understand—and of Italian (the source of *Othello*, for instance, is an Italian tale that had not been published in translation when he wrote his play). We do not know whether he ever travelled outside England.

Shakespeare must have worked hard at school, but there was a life beyond the classroom. He lived in a beautiful and fertile part of the country, with rivers and fields at hand. He had the company of brothers and sisters. Each Sunday the family would go to Stratford's splendid parish church, as the law required; his father, by virtue of his dignified status, would sit in the front pew. There Shakespeare's receptive mind would be impressed by the sonorous phrases of the Bible, in either the Bishops' or the Geneva version, the Homilies, and the Book of Common Prayer. From time to time travelling players would visit Stratford. Shakespeare's father would have the duty of licensing them to perform; probably his son first saw plays professionally acted in the Guildhall below his schoolroom.

Shakespeare would have left school when he was about fifteen. What he did then is not known. One of the earliest legends about him, recorded by John Aubrey around 1681, is that 'he had been in his younger years a schoolmaster in the country'. John Cottom, who was master of the Stratford school between 1579 and 1581 or 1582, and may have taught Shakespeare, was a Lancashire man whose family home was close to that of a landowner, Alexander Houghton. Both Cottom and Houghton were Roman Catholics, and there is some reason to believe that John Shakespeare may have retained loyalties to the old religion. When Houghton died, in 1581, he mentioned in his will one William Shakeshafte, apparently a player. The name is a possible variant of Shakespeare; conceivably Cottom found employment in Lancashire for his talented pupil as a tutor who also acted. If so, Shakespeare was soon back home. On 28 November 1582 a bond was issued permitting him to marry Anne Hathaway of Shottery, a village close to Stratford. She was eight years his senior, and pregnant. Their daughter, Susanna, was baptized on 26 May 1583, and twins, Hamnet and Judith, on 2 February 1585. Though Shakespeare's professional career (described in the next section of this Introduction) was to centre on London, his family remained in Stratford, and he maintained his links with his birthplace till he died and was buried there.

One of the unfounded myths about Shakespeare is that all we know about his life could be written on the back of a postage stamp. In fact we know a lot about some of the less exciting aspects of his life, such as his business dealings and his tax debts (as may be seen from the list of Contemporary Allusions, pp. xxxviii-xl). Though we cannot tell how often he visited Stratford after he moved to London, clearly he felt that he belonged where he

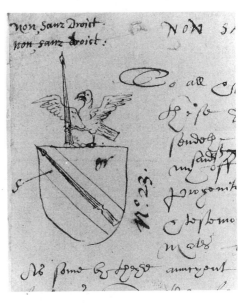

1. The Shakespeare coat of arms, from a draft dated 20 October 1596, prepared by Sir William Dethick, Garter King-of-Arms

was born. His success in his profession may be reflected in his father's application for a grant of arms in 1596, by which John Shakespeare acquired the official status of gentleman. In August of that year William's son, Hamnet, died, aged eleven and a half, and was buried in Stratford. Shakespeare was living in the Bishopsgate area of London, north of the river, in October of the same year, but in the following year showed that he looked on Stratford as his real home by buying a large house, New Place. It was demolished in 1759.

In October 1598 Richard Quiney, whose son was to marry Shakespeare's daughter Judith, travelled to London to plead with the Privy Council on behalf of Stratford Corporation, which was in financial trouble because of fires and bad weather. He wrote the only surviving letter addressed to Shakespeare; as it was found among Quiney's papers, it was presumably never delivered. It requested a loan of £30—a large sum, suggesting confidence in his friend's prosperity. In 1601 Shakespeare's father died, and was buried in Stratford. In May of the following year Shakespeare was able to invest £320 in 107 acres of arable land in Old Stratford. In the same year John Manningham, a London law student, recorded a piece of gossip that gives us a rare contemporary anecdote about the private life of Shakespeare and of Richard Burbage, the leading tragedian of his company:

Upon a time when Burbage played Richard III there was a citizen grew so far in liking with him that before she went from the play she appointed him to come that night unto her by the name of Richard the Third. Shakespeare, overhearing their conclusion, went before, was entertained, and at his game ere Burbage came. Then, message being brought that Richard the Third was at the door, Shakespeare caused return to be made that William the Conqueror was before Richard the Third.

In 1604 Shakespeare was lodging in north London with a Huguenot family called Mountjoy; in 1612 he was to testify in a court case relating to a marriage settlement on

2. Shakespeare's monument, designed by Gheerart Janssen, in Holy Trinity Church, Stratford-upon-Avon

the daughter of the house. The records of the case provide our only transcript of words actually spoken by Shakespeare; they are not characterful. In 1605 Shakespeare invested £440 in the Stratford tithes, which brought him in £60 a year; in June 1607 his elder daughter, Susanna, married a distinguished physician, John Hall, in Stratford, and there his only grandchild, their daughter Elizabeth, was baptized the following February. In 1609 his mother died there, and from about 1610 his increasing involvement with Stratford along with the reduction in his dramatic output suggests that he was withdrawing from his London responsibilities and spending more time at New Place. Perhaps he was deliberately devoting himself to his family's business interests; he was only forty-six years old: an age at which a healthy man was no more likely to retire then than now. If he was ill, he was not totally disabled, as he was in London in 1612 for the Mountjoy lawsuit. In March 1613 he bought a house in the Blackfriars area of London for £140: it seems to have been an investment rather than a home. Also in 1613 the last of his three brothers died. In late 1614 and 1615 he was involved in disputes about the enclosure of the land whose tithes he owned. In February 1616 his second daughter, Judith, married Thomas Quiney, causing William to make alterations to the draft of his will, which he signed on 25 March. His widow was entitled by law and local custom to part of his estate; he left most of the remainder to his elder daughter, Susanna, and her husband. He died on 23 April, and was buried two days later in a prominent position in the chancel of Holy Trinity Church. A monument was commissioned, presumably by members of his family, and was in position by 1623. The work of Gheerart Janssen, a stonemason whose shop was not far from the Globe Theatre, it incorporates a half-length effigy which is one of the only two surviving likenesses of Shakespeare with any strong claim to authenticity.

As this selective survey of the historical records shows, Shakespeare's life is at least as well documented as those of most of his contemporaries who did not belong to great families; we know more about him than about any other dramatist of his time except Ben Jonson. The inscription on the Stratford landowner's memorial links him with Socrates and Virgil; and in the far greater memorial of 1623, the First Folio edition of his plays, Jonson links this 'Star of poets' with his home town as the 'Sweet swan of Avon'. The Folio includes the second reliable likeness of Shakespeare, an engraving by Martin Droeshout which, we must assume, had been commissioned and approved by his friends and colleagues who put the volume together. In the Folio it faces the lines signed 'B.I.' (Ben Jonson) which we print beneath it. Shakespeare's widow died in 1623, and his last surviving descendant, Elizabeth Hall (who inherited New Place and married first a neighbour, Thomas Nash, and secondly John Bernard, knighted in 1661), in 1670.

Shakespeare's Professional Career

We do not know when Shakespeare joined the theatre after his marriage, or how he was employed in the mean time. In 1587 an actor of the Queen's Men—the most successful company of the 1580s—died as a result of manslaughter shortly before the company visited Stratford. That Shakespeare may have taken his place is an intriguing speculation. Nor do we know when he began to write. It seems likely (though not certain) that he became an actor before starting to write plays; at any rate, none of his extant writings certainly dates from his youth or early manhood. One of his less impressive sonnets—No. 145—apparently plays on the name 'Hathaway' (' "I hate" from hate away she threw'), and may be an early love poem; but this is his only surviving non-dramatic work that seems at all likely to have been written before he became a playwright. Possibly his earliest efforts in verse or drama are lost; just possibly some of them survive anonymously. It would have been very much in keeping with contemporary practice if he had worked in collaboration with other writers at this stage in his career. *1 Henry VI* is the only early play that we feel confident enough to identify as collaborative, but other writers' hands have also been plausibly suspected in *The First Part of the Contention* (*2 Henry VI*), *Richard, Duke of York* (*3 Henry VI*), and the opening scenes, in particular, of *Titus Andronicus*.

The first printed allusion to Shakespeare dates from 1592, in the pamphlet *Greene's Groatsworth of Wit*, published as the work of Robert Greene, writer of plays and prose romances, shortly after he died. Mention of an 'upstart crow' who 'supposes he is as well able to bombast out a blank verse as the best of you' and who 'is in his own conceit the only Shake-scene in a country' suggests rivalry; though parody of a line from *Richard, Duke of York* (*3 Henry VI*) shows that Shakespeare was already known on the London literary scene, the word 'upstart' does not suggest a long-established author.

It seems likely that Shakespeare's earliest surviving plays date from the late 1580s and the early 1590s: they include comedies (*The Two Gentlemen of Verona* and *The Taming of the Shrew*), history plays based on English chronicles (*The First Part of the Contention, Richard, Duke of York*), and a pseudo-classical tragedy (*Titus Andronicus*). We cannot say with any confidence which company (or companies) of players these were written for;

3. Henry Wriothesley, 3rd Earl of Southampton (1573–1624), at the age of twenty: a miniature by Nicholas Hilliard

Titus Andronicus, at least, seems to have gone from one company to another, since according to the title-page of the 1594 edition it had been acted by the Earl of Derby's, the Earl of Pembroke's, and the Earl of Sussex's Men. Early in his career, Shakespeare may have worked for more than one company. A watershed in his career was the devastating outbreak of plague which closed London's theatres almost entirely from June 1592 to May 1594. This seems to have turned Shakespeare's thoughts to the possibility of a literary career away from the theatre: in spring 1593 appeared his witty narrative poem *Venus and Adonis*, to be followed in 1594 by its tragic counterpart, *The Rape of Lucrece*. Both carry dedications over Shakespeare's name to Henry Wriothesley, third Earl of Southampton, who, though aged only twenty in 1593, was already making a name for himself as a patron of poets. Patrons could be important to Elizabethan writers; how Southampton rewarded Shakespeare for his dedications we do not know, but the affection with which Shakespeare speaks of him in the dedication to *Lucrece* suggests a strong personal connection and has encouraged the belief that Southampton may be the young man addressed so lovingly in Shakespeare's Sonnets.

Whether Shakespeare began to write the Sonnets at this time is a vexed question. Certainly it is the period at which his plays make most use of the formal characteristics of the sonnet: *Love's Labour's Lost* and *Romeo and Juliet*, for example, both incorporate sonnets into their structure; but *Henry V*, probably dating from 1599, has a sonnet as an Epilogue, and in *All's Well That Ends Well* (*c.*1604) a letter is cast in this form. Allusions within the

Sonnets suggest that they were written over a period of at least three years. At some later point they seem to have been rearranged into the order in which they were printed. Behind them—if indeed they are autobiographical at all—lies a tantalizingly elusive story of Shakespeare's personal life. Many attempts have been made to identify the poet's friend, the rival poet, and the dark woman who is both the poet's mistress and the seducer of his friend; none has achieved any degree of certainty.

After the epidemic of plague dwindled, a number of actors who had previously belonged to different companies amalgamated to form the Lord Chamberlain's Men. In the first official account that survives, Shakespeare is named, along with the famous comic actor Will Kemp and the tragedian Richard Burbage, as payee for performances at court during the previous Christmas season. The Chamberlain's Men rapidly became the leading dramatic company, though rivalled at first by the Admiral's Men, who had Edward Alleyn as their leading tragedian. Shakespeare stayed with the Chamberlain's (later King's) Men for the rest of his career as actor, playwright, and administrator. He is the only prominent playwright of his time to have had so stable a relationship with a single company.

With the founding of the Lord Chamberlain's Men, Shakespeare's career was placed upon a firm footing. It is not the purpose of this Introduction to describe his development as a dramatist, or to attempt a thorough discussion of the chronology of his writings. The Introductions to individual works state briefly what is known about when they were composed, and also name the principal literary sources on which Shakespeare drew in composing them. The works themselves are arranged in a conjectured order of composition. There are many uncertainties about this, especially in relation to the early plays. The most important single piece of evidence is a passage in a book called *Palladis Tamia: Wit's Treasury*, by a minor writer, Francis Meres, published in 1598. Meres wrote:

As Plautus and Seneca are accounted the best for comedy and tragedy among the Latins, so Shakespeare among the English is the most excellent in both kinds for the stage; for comedy, witness his *Gentlemen of Verona*, his *Errors*, his *Love Labour's Lost*, his *Love Labour's Won*, his *Midsummer's Night Dream*, and his *Merchant of Venice*; for tragedy, his *Richard II*, *Richard III*, *Henry IV*, *King John*, *Titus Andronicus*, and his *Romeo and Juliet*.

Some of the plays that Meres names had already been published or alluded to by 1598; but for others, he supplies a date by which they must have been written. Meres also alludes to Shakespeare's 'sugared sonnets among his private friends', which suggests that some, if not all, of the poems printed in 1609 as Shakespeare's Sonnets were circulating in manuscript by this date. Works not mentioned by Meres that are believed to have been written by 1598 are the three plays concerned with the reign of Henry VI, *The Taming of the Shrew*, and the narrative poems.

Shakespeare seems to have had less success as an actor than as a playwright. We cannot name for certain any of the parts that he played, though seventeenth-century traditions have it that he played Adam in *As You Like It*, and Hamlet's Ghost—and more generally that he had a penchant for 'kingly parts'. Ben Jonson listed him first among the 'principal comedians' in *Every Man in his Humour*, acted in 1598, when he reprinted it in the 1616 Folio, and Shakespeare is also listed among the performers of Jonson's tragedy *Sejanus* in 1603. He was certainly one of the leading administrators of the Chamberlain's Men. Until 1597, when their lease expired, they played mainly in the Theatre, London's first important playhouse, situated north of the River Thames in Shoreditch, outside the jurisdiction of the City fathers, who exercised a repressive influence on the drama. It had been built in 1576 by James Burbage, a joiner, the tragedian's father. Then they seem to have played mainly at the Curtain until some time in 1599. Shakespeare was a member of the syndicate

4. King James I
(1566-1625): a portrait
(1621) by Daniel Mytens

responsible for building the first Globe theatre, in Southwark, on the south bank of the Thames, out of the dismantled timbers of the Theatre in 1599. Initially he had a ten-per-cent financial interest in the enterprise, fluctuating as other shareholders joined or withdrew. It was a valuable share, for the Chamberlain's Men won great acclaim and made substantial profits. After Queen Elizabeth died, in 1603, they came under the patronage of the new king, James I; the royal patent of 19 May 1603 names Shakespeare along with other leaders of the company. London was in the grip of another severe epidemic of plague which caused a ban on playing till the following spring. The King's processional entry into London had to be delayed; when at last it took place, on 15 March 1604, each of the company's leaders was granted four and a half yards of scarlet cloth for his livery as one of the King's retainers; but the players seem not to have processed. Their association with the King was far from nominal; during the next thirteen years—up to the time of Shakespeare's death—they played at court more often than all the other theatre companies combined. Records are patchy, but we know, for instance, that they gave eleven plays at court between 1 November 1604 and 31 October 1605, and that seven of them were by Shakespeare: they included older plays—*The Comedy of Errors*, *Love's Labour's Lost*—and more recent ones—*Othello* and *Measure for Measure*. *The Merchant of Venice* was played twice.

Some measure of Shakespeare's personal success during this period may be gained from the ascription to him of works not now believed to be his; *Locrine* and *Thomas Lord Cromwell* were published in 1595 and 1602 respectively as by 'W.S.'; in 1599 a collection of poems, *The Passionate Pilgrim*, containing some poems certainly by other writers, appeared under his name; so, in 1606 and 1608, did *The London Prodigal* and *A Yorkshire Tragedy*. Since Shakespeare's time, too, many plays of the period, some published, some surviving only in manuscript, have been attributed to him. In modern times, the most plausible case has been made for parts, or all, of *Edward III*, which was entered in the registers of the Stationers' Company (a normal, but not invariable, way of setting in motion the publication process) in 1595 and published in 1596. It was first ascribed to Shakespeare in 1656. Certainly it displays links with some of his writings, but authorship problems are particularly acute during the part of his career when this play seems to have been written, and we cannot feel confident of the attribution.

In August 1608 the King's Men took up the lease of the smaller, 'private' indoor theatre, the Blackfriars; again, Shakespeare was one of the syndicate of owners. The company took possession in 1609; the Blackfriars served as a winter home; in better weather, performances continued to be given at the Globe. By now, Shakespeare was at a late stage in his career. Perhaps he realized it; he seems to have been willing to share his responsibilities as the company's resident dramatist with younger writers. *Timon of Athens*, tentatively dated around 1604-5, seems on internal evidence to be partly the work of Thomas Middleton (c.1570-1627). Another collaborative play, very successful in its time, was *Pericles* (c.1608), in which Shakespeare probably worked with George Wilkins, an unscrupulous character who gave up his brief career as a writer in favour of a longer one as a tavern (or brothel) keeper. But Shakespeare's most fruitful collaboration was with John Fletcher, his junior by fifteen years. Fletcher was collaborating with Francis Beaumont on plays for the King's Men by about 1608. Beaumont stopped writing plays when he married, in about 1613, and it is at this time that Fletcher seems to have collaborated with Shakespeare. A lost play, *Cardenio*, acted by the King's Men some time before 20 May 1613, was plausibly ascribed to Shakespeare and Fletcher in a document of 1653; *All is True* (*Henry VIII*), first acted about June 1613, is generally agreed on stylistic evidence to be another fruit of the same partnership; and *The Two Noble Kinsmen*, also dated 1613, which seems to be the last play in which Shakespeare had a hand, was ascribed to the pair on its publication in 1634. One of Shakespeare's last professional tasks seems to have been the minor one of devising an *impresa* for the Earl of Rutland to bear at a tournament held on 24 March 1613 to celebrate the tenth anniversary of the King's accession. An *impresa* was a paper or pasteboard shield painted with an emblematic device and motto which would be carried and interpreted for a knight by his squire; such a ceremony is portrayed in *Pericles* (Sc. 6). Shakespeare received forty-four shillings for his share in the work; Richard Burbage was paid the same sum 'for painting and making it'.

The Drama and Theatre of Shakespeare's Time

Shakespeare came upon the theatrical scene at an auspicious time. English drama and theatre had developed only slowly during the earlier part of the sixteenth century; during Shakespeare's youth they exploded into vigorous life. It was a period of secularization; previously, drama had been largely religious in subject matter and overtly didactic in treatment; as a boy of fifteen, Shakespeare could have seen one of the last performances of a great cycle of plays on religious themes at Coventry, not far from his home town. 1576 saw the building in London of the Theatre, to be rapidly followed by the Curtain: England's first important, custom-built playhouses. There was a sudden spurt in the development of all aspects of theatrical art: acting, production, playwriting, company organization, and administration. Within a few years the twin arts of drama and theatre entered upon a period of achievement whose brilliance remains unequalled.

The new drama was literary and rhetorical rather than scenic and spectacular: but its mainstream was theatrical too. Its writers were poets. Prose was only beginning to be used in plays during Shakespeare's youth; a playwright was often known as a 'poet', and most of the best playwrights of the period wrote with distinction in other forms. Shakespeare's most important predecessors and early contemporaries, from whom he learned much, were John Lyly (c.1554-1606), pre-eminent for courtly comedy and elegant prose, Robert Greene (1558-92), who helped particularly to develop the scope and language of romantic comedy, and Christopher Marlowe (1564-93), whose 'mighty line' put heroism excitingly on the stage and who shares with Shakespeare credit for establishing the English history play as a dramatic mode. As Shakespeare's career progressed, other dramatists displayed their talents and, doubtless, influenced and stimulated him. George Chapman (c.1560-1634) emerged as a dramatist in the mid-1590s and succeeded in both comedy and tragedy. He was deeply interested in classical themes, as was Ben Jonson (1572-1637), who became Shakespeare's chief rival. Jonson was a dominating personality, vocal about his accomplishments (and about Shakespeare, who, he said, 'wanted art'), and biting as a comic satirist. Thomas Dekker (c.1572-1632) wrote comedies that are more akin to Shakespeare's in their romantic warmth; the satirical plays of John Marston (c.1575-1634) are more sensational and cynical than Jonson's. Thomas Middleton brought a sharp wit to the portrayal of contemporary London life, and developed into a great tragic dramatist. Towards the end of Shakespeare's career, Francis Beaumont (1584-1616) and John Fletcher (1579-1625) came upon the scene; the affinity between Shakespeare's late tragicomedies and some of Fletcher's romances is reflected in their collaboration.

The companies for which these dramatists wrote were organized mainly from within. They were led by the sharers: eight in the Lord Chamberlain's Men at first, twelve by the end of Shakespeare's career. Collectively they owned the joint stock of play scripts, costumes, and properties; they shared both expenses and profits. All were working members of the company. Exceptionally, the sharers of Shakespeare's company owned the Globe theatre itself; more commonly, actors rented theatres from financial speculators such as Philip Henslowe, financier of the Admiral's Men. Subordinate to the sharers were the 'hired men'—lesser actors along with prompters ('bookholders'), stagekeepers, wardrobe keepers ('tiremen'), musicians, and money-collectors ('gatherers'). Even those not employed principally as actors might swell a scene at need. The hired men were paid by the week. Companies would need scribes to copy out actors' parts and to make fair copies from the playwrights' foul papers (working manuscripts), but they seem mainly to have been employed part-time. The other important group of company members are the apprentices. These were boys or youths each serving a formal term of apprenticeship to one of the sharers. They played female and juvenile roles.

The success of plays in the Elizabethan theatres depended almost entirely on the actors. They had to be talented, hard-working, and versatile. Plays were given in a repertory system on almost every afternoon of the week except during Lent. Only about two weeks could be allowed for rehearsal of a new play, and during that time the company would be regularly performing a variety of plays. Lacking printed copies, the actors worked from

5. Richard Burbage: reputedly a self-portrait

'parts' written out on scrolls giving only the cue lines from other characters' speeches. The bookholder, or prompter, had to make sure that actors entered at the right moment, properly equipped. Many of them would take several parts in the same play: doubling was a necessary practice. The strain on the memory was great, demanding a high degree of professionalism. Conditions of employment were carefully regulated: a contract of 1614 provides that an actor and sharer, Robert Dawes (not in Shakespeare's company), be fined one shilling for failure to turn up at the beginning of a rehearsal, two shillings for missing a rehearsal altogether, three shillings if he was not 'ready apparelled' for a performance, ten shillings if four other members of the company considered him to be 'overcome with drink' at the time he should be acting, and one pound if he simply failed to turn up for a performance without 'licence or just excuse of sickness'.

There can be no doubt that the best actors of Shakespeare's time would have been greatly admired in any age. English actors became famous abroad; some of the best surviving accounts are in letters written by visitors to England: the actors were literally 'something to write home about', and some of them performed (in English) on the Continent. Edward Alleyn, the leading tragedian of the Admiral's Men, renowned especially for his performances of Marlowe's heroes, made a fortune and founded Dulwich College. All too little is known about the actors of Shakespeare's company and the roles they played, but many testimonies survive to Richard Burbage's excellence in tragic roles. According to an elegy written after he died, in 1619,

> No more young Hamlet, old Hieronimo;
> Kind Lear, the grievèd Moor, and more beside
> That lived in him have now for ever died.

There is no reason to suppose that the boy actors lacked talent and skill; they were highly trained as apprentices to leading actors. Most plays of the period, including Shakespeare's,

6. The hall of the Middle Temple, London

have far fewer female than male roles, but some women's parts—such as Rosalind (in *As You Like It*) and Cleopatra—are long and important; Shakespeare must have had confidence in the boys who played them. Some of them later became sharers themselves.

The playwriting techniques of Shakespeare and his contemporaries were intimately bound up with the theatrical conditions to which they catered. Theatre buildings were virtually confined to London. Plays continued to be given in improvised circumstances when the companies toured the provinces and when they acted at court (that is, wherever the sovereign and his or her entourage happened to be—in London, usually Whitehall or Greenwich). In 1602, *Twelfth Night* was given in the still-surviving hall of one of London's Inns of Court, the Middle Temple. Acting companies could use guildhalls, the halls of great houses or of Oxford and Cambridge colleges, the yards of inns. (In 1608, *Richard II* and *Hamlet* were even performed by ships' crews at sea off the coast of Sierra Leone.) Many plays of the period require no more than an open space and the costumes and properties that the actors carried with them on their travels. Others made more use of the expanding facilities of the professional stage.

Permanent theatres were of two kinds, known now as public and private. Most important to Shakespeare were public theatres such as the Theatre, the Curtain, and the Globe. Unfortunately, the only surviving drawing (reproduced overleaf) portraying the interior of a public theatre in any detail is of the Swan, not used by Shakespeare's company. Though theatres were not uniform in design, they had important features in common. They were large wooden buildings, usually round or polygonal; the Globe, which was about 100 feet in diameter and 36 feet in height, could hold over three thousand spectators. Between the outer and inner walls—a space of about 12 feet—were three levels of tiered benches extending round most of the auditorium and roofed on top; after the Globe burnt down, in 1613, the roof, formerly thatched, was tiled. The surround of benches was broken on the lowest level by the stage, broad and deep, edged with palings, which jutted forth at a height of about 5 feet into the central yard, where spectators ('groundlings') could stand. Actors entered mainly, perhaps entirely, from openings in the wall at the back of the stage. At least two doors, one on each side, could be used; stage directions frequently call for characters to enter simultaneously from different doors, when the dramatic situation requires them to be meeting, and to leave 'severally' (separately) when they are parting. The depth of the stage meant that characters could enter through the stage doors some moments before other characters standing at the front of the stage might be expected to notice them.

Also in the wall at the rear of the stage there appears to have been some kind of central aperture which could be used for the disclosing and putting forth of Desdemona's bed (*Othello*, 5.2) or the concealment of the spying Polonius (*Hamlet*, 3.4) or of the sleeping Lear (*The History of King Lear*, Sc. 20). Behind the stage wall was the tiring-house—the actors' dressing area.

On the second level the seating facilities for spectators seem to have extended even to the back of the stage, forming a balcony which at the Globe was probably divided into five bays. Here was the 'lords' room', which could be taken over by the actors for plays in which action took place 'above' (or 'aloft'), as in Romeo's wooing of Juliet or the death of Mark Antony. It seems to have been possible for actors to move from the main stage to the upper level during the time taken to speak a few lines of verse, as we may see in *The Merchant of Venice* (2.6.51–70) or *Julius Caesar* (5.3.33–5). Somewhere above the lords' room was a window or platform known as 'the top'; Joan la Pucelle appears there briefly in *1 Henry VI* (3.3), and in *The Tempest*, Prospero is seen 'on the top, invisible' (3.3).

Above the stage, at a level higher than the second gallery, was a canopy, probably

tectum
porticus
orchestra
ingressus
mimorum
aedes
proscaenium
planities sive arena

7. The Swan Theatre: a copy, by Aernout van Buchel, of a drawing made about 1596 by Johannes de Witt, a Dutch visitor to London

supported by two pillars (which could themselves be used as hiding places) rising from the stage. One function of the canopy was to shelter the stage from the weather; it also formed the floor of one or more huts housing the machinery for special effects and its operators. Here cannon-balls could be rolled around a trough to imitate the sound of thunder, and fire crackers could be set off to simulate lightning. And from this area actors could descend in a chair operated by a winch. Shakespeare uses this facility mainly in his late plays: in *Cymbeline* for the descent of Jupiter (5.4), and, probably, in *Pericles* for the descent of Diana (Sc. 21) and in *The Tempest* for Juno's appearance in the masque (4.1). On the stage itself was a trap which could be opened to serve as Ophelia's grave (*Hamlet*, 5.1) or as Malvolio's dungeon (*Twelfth Night*, 4.2).

Somewhere in the backstage area, perhaps in or close to the gallery, must have been a space for the musicians who played a prominent part in many performances. No doubt then, as now, a single musician was capable of playing several instruments. Stringed instruments, plucked (such as the lute) and bowed (such as viols), were needed. Woodwind instruments included recorders (called for in *Hamlet* 3.2) and the stronger, shriller hautboys (ancestors of the modern oboe); trumpets and cornetts were needed for the many flourishes and sennets (more elaborate fanfares) played especially for the comings and goings of royal characters. Sometimes musicians would play on stage: entrances for trumpeters and drummers are common in battle scenes. More often they would be heard but not seen; from behind the stage (as, perhaps, at the opening of *Twelfth Night* or in the concluding dance of *Much Ado About Nothing*), or even occasionally under it (*Antony and Cleopatra*, 4.3). Some actors were themselves musicians: the performers of Feste (in *Twelfth Night*) and Ariel (in *The Tempest*) must sing and, probably, accompany themselves on lute and tabor (a small drum slung around the neck). Though traditional music has survived for some of the songs in Shakespeare's plays (such as Ophelia's mad songs, in *Hamlet*), we have little music which was certainly composed for them in his own time. The principal exception is two songs for *The Tempest* by Robert Johnson, a fine composer who was attached to the King's Men.

Shakespeare's plays require few substantial properties. A 'state', or throne on a dais, is sometimes called for, as are tables and chairs and, occasionally, a bed, a pair of stocks (*King Lear* Sc. 7/2.2), a cauldron (*Macbeth*, 4.1), a rose brier (*1 Henry VI*, 2.4), and a bush (*Two Noble Kinsmen*, 5.3). No doubt these and other such objects were pushed on and off the stage by attendants in full view of the audience. We know that Elizabethan companies spent lavishly on costumes, and some plays require special clothes; at the beginning of *2 Henry IV*, Rumour enters 'painted full of tongues'; regal personages, and supernatural figures such as Hymen in *As You Like It* (5.4) and the goddesses in *The Tempest* (4.1), must have been distinctively costumed; presumably a bear-skin was needed for *The Winter's Tale* (3.3). Probably no serious attempt was made at historical realism. The only surviving contemporary drawing of a scene from a Shakespeare play, illustrating *Titus Andronicus* (reproduced on the following page), shows the characters dressed in a mixture of Elizabethan and classical costumes, and this accords with the often anachronistic references to clothing in plays with a historical setting. The same drawing also illustrates the use of head-dresses, of varied weapons as properties—the guard to the left appears to be wearing a scimitar—of facial and bodily make-up for Aaron, the Moor, and of eloquent gestures. Extended passages of wordless action are not uncommon in Shakespeare's plays. Dumb shows feature prominently in earlier Elizabethan plays, and in Shakespeare the direction 'alarum' or 'alarums and excursions' may stand for lengthy and exciting passages of arms. Even in one of Shakespeare's latest plays, *Cymbeline*, important episodes are conducted in wordless mime (see, for example, 5.2–4).

8. A drawing, attributed to Henry Peacham, illustrating Shakespeare's *Titus Andronicus*

Towards the end of Shakespeare's career his company regularly performed in a private theatre, the Blackfriars, as well as at the Globe. Like other private theatres, this was an enclosed building, using artificial lighting, and so more suitable for winter performances. Private playhouses were smaller than the public ones—the Blackfriars held about 600 spectators—and admission prices were much higher—a minimum of sixpence at the Blackfriars against one penny at the Globe. Facilities at the Blackfriars must have been essentially similar to those at the Globe since some of the same plays were given at both theatres. But the sense of social occasion seems to have been different. Audiences were more elegant (though not necessarily better behaved); music featured more prominently.

It seems to have been under the influence of private-theatre practice that, from about 1609 onwards, performances of plays customarily marked the conventional five-act structure by a pause, graced with music, after each act. Previously, though dramatists often showed awareness of five-act structure (as Shakespeare conspicuously does in *Henry V*, with a Chorus before each act), public performances seem to have been continuous, making the scene the main structural unit. None of the editions of Shakespeare's plays printed in his lifetime (which do not include any written after 1609) marks either act or scene divisions. The innovation of act-pauses threw more emphasis on the act as a unit, and made it possible for dramatists to relax their observance of what has come to be known as 'the law of re-entry', according to which a character who had left the stage at the end of one scene would not normally make an immediate reappearance at the beginning of the next. Thus, if Shakespeare had been writing *The Tempest* before 1609, it is unlikely that Prospero and Ariel, having left the stage at the end of Act 4, would have instantly reappeared at the start of Act 5. We attempt to reflect this feature of Shakespeare's dramaturgy by making no special distinction between scene-breaks and act-breaks except in those later plays in which Shakespeare seems to have observed the new convention (and in *Titus Andronicus*, *Measure for Measure*, and *Macbeth*, since the texts of these plays apparently reflect theatre practice after they were first written, and in *The Comedy of Errors*, a neo-classically structured play in which the act-divisions appear to be authoritative, and to represent a private performance).

Dramatic conventions changed and developed considerably during Shakespeare's career.

Throughout it, they favoured self-evident artifice over naturalism. This is apparent in Shakespeare's dramatic language, with its soliloquies (sometimes addressed directly to the audience), its long, carefully structured speeches, its elaborate use of simile, metaphor, and rhetorical figures of speech (in prose as well as verse), its rhyme, and its patterned dialogue. It is evident in some aspects of behaviour and characterization: Oberon and Prospero have only to declare themselves invisible to become so; disguises can be instantly donned with an appearance of impenetrability, and as rapidly abandoned; some characters—Rumour at the opening of 2 Henry IV, Time in The Winter's Tale, even the Gardeners in Richard II—clearly serve a symbolic rather than a realistic function: and supernatural manifestations are common. The calculated positioning of characters on the stage may help to make a dramatic point, as in the scene in The Two Gentlemen of Verona (4.2) in which the disguised Julia overhears her faithless lover's serenade to her rival, Silvia; or, more complexly, that in Troilus and Cressida (5.2) in which Troilus and Ulysses observe Diomede's courtship of Cressida while they are themselves observed by the cynical Thersites. Not uncommonly, Shakespeare provokes his spectators into consciousness that they are watching a play, as when Cassius, in Julius Caesar, looks forward to the time when the conspirators' 'lofty scene' will be 'acted over | In states unborn and accents yet unknown' (3.1.112-14); or, in Troilus and Cressida, when Troilus, Cressida, and Pandarus reach out from the past tense of history to the present tense of theatrical performance in a ritualistic anticipation of what their names will come to signify (3.3.169-202).

Techniques such as these are closely related to the non-illusionistic nature of the Elizabethan stage, in which the mechanics of production were frequently visible. Many scenes take place nowhere in particular. Awareness of place was conveyed through dialogue and action rather than through scenery; location could change even within a scene (as, for example, in 2 Henry IV, where movement of the dying King's bed across the stage establishes the scene as 'some other chamber': 4.3.132). Sometimes Shakespeare uses conflicting reactions to an imagined place as a kind of shorthand guide to character: to the idealistic Gonzalo, Prospero's island is lush, lusty, and green; to the cynical Antonio, 'tawny' (The Tempest, 2.1.56-8): such an effect would have been dulled by scenery which proved one or the other right.

In some ways, the changes in Shakespeare's practice as his art develops favour naturalism: his verse becomes freer, metaphor predominates over simile, rhyme and other formalistic elements are reduced, the proportion of prose over verse increases to the middle of his career (but then decreases again), some of his most psychologically complex character portrayals—Coriolanus, Cleopatra—come late. But his drama remains rooted in the conventions of a rhetorical, non-scenic (though not unspectacular) theatre: the supernatural looms largest in his later plays—Macbeth, Pericles, Cymbeline, and The Tempest. The Tempest draws no less self-consciously on the neo-classical conventions of five-act structure than The Comedy of Errors, and Prospero's narration to Miranda (1.2) is as blatant a piece of dramatic exposition as Egeon's tale in the opening scene of the earlier play. Heroines of the late romances—Marina (in Pericles), Perdita (in The Winter's Tale), and Miranda (in The Tempest)—are portrayed with less concern for psychological realism than those of the romantic comedies—Viola (in Twelfth Night) and Rosalind (in As You Like It)—and the revelation to Leontes at the end of The Winter's Tale is both more improbable and more moving than the similar revelation made to Egeon at the end of The Comedy of Errors.

The theatre of Shakespeare's time was his most valuable collaborator. Its simplicity was one of its strengths. The actors of his company were the best in their kind. His audiences may not have been learned, or sophisticated, by modern standards; according to some accounts, they could be unruly; but they conferred popularity upon plays which for emotional power, range, and variety, for grandeur of conception and subtlety of execution, are among the most demanding, as well as the most entertaining, ever written. If we value Shakespeare's plays, we must also think well of the theatrical circumstances that permitted, and encouraged, his genius to flourish.

The Early Printing of Shakespeare's Plays

For all its literary distinction, drama in Shakespeare's time was an art of performance; many plays of the period never got into print: they were published by being acted. It is lucky for us that, so far as we know, all Shakespeare's finished plays except the collaborative *Cardenio* reached print. None of his plays that were printed in his time survives in even a fragment of his own handwriting; the only literary manuscript plausibly ascribed to him is a section of *Sir Thomas More*, a play not printed until the nineteenth century. The only works of Shakespeare that he himself seems to have cared about putting into print are the narrative poems *Venus and Adonis* and *The Rape of Lucrece*. A major reason for this is Shakespeare's exceptionally close involvement with the acting company for which he wrote. There was no effective dramatic copyright; acting companies commonly bought plays from their authors—as a resident playwright, Shakespeare was probably expected to write about two each year—and it was in the companies' interests that their plays should not get into print, when they could be acted by rival companies. Nevertheless, by one means and another, and in one form and another, about half of Shakespeare's plays were printed singly in his lifetime, almost all of them in the flimsy, paperback format of a quarto—a book made from sheets of paper that had been folded twice, and normally costing sixpence. Some of the plays were pirated: printed, that is, in unauthorized editions, from texts that seem to have been put together from memory by actors or even, perhaps, by spectators, perhaps primarily to create scripts for other companies, perhaps purely for publication. These are the so-called 'bad' quartos: bad not because they were, necessarily, badly printed, but because they did not descend in a direct line of written transmission from their author's manuscript. The reported texts of *The First Part of the Contention* and *Richard, Duke of York* (usually known by the titles under which they were printed in the First Folio—*2 Henry VI* and *3 Henry VI*) appeared in 1594 and 1595 respectively; they seem to have been made on the basis of London performances so that the plays could be acted by a company other than the one for which they were written. Also in 1594 appeared *The Taming of A Shrew*, perhaps better described as an imitation of Shakespeare's *The Taming of the Shrew* (the titles may have been regarded as interchangeable) than as a detailed reconstruction of it. The 1597 *Richard III* is perhaps the best of the reported texts; it seems to have been assembled from the company's collective memory, perhaps because they did not have access to the official prompt-book. The text of *Romeo and Juliet* printed in the same year seems to have been put together by a few actors exploiting a popular success. The 1600 quarto of *Henry V* probably presents a text made for a smaller company of actors than that for which it had been written. *The Merry Wives of Windsor* of 1602 seems to derive largely from the memory of the actor who played the Host of the Garter Inn—perhaps a hired man no longer employed by Shakespeare's company. Worst reported of all is the 1603 *Hamlet*, which also appears to derive from the memory of one or more actors in minor roles. Last printed of the 'bad' quartos is *Pericles*, of 1609.

The reported texts have many faults. Frequently they garble the verse and prose of the original—'To be or not to be; ay, there's the point', says the 1603 *Hamlet*; usually they abbreviate—the 1603 *Hamlet* has about 2,200 lines, compared to the 3,800 of the good quarto; sometimes they include lines from plays by other authors (especially Marlowe);

Ham. To be,or not to be, I there's the point,
To Die, to sleepe, is that all? I all:
No, to sleepe, to dreame, I mary there it goes,
For in that dreame of death, when wee awake,
And borne before an euerlasting Iudge,
From whence no passenger euer retur'nd,
The vndiscouered country, at whose sight
The happy smile, and the accursed damn'd.
But for this, the ioyfull hope of this,
Whol'd beare the scornes and flattery of the world,
Scorned by the right rich, the rich cursed of the poore?
The widow being opprest, the orphan wrong'd,
The taste of hunger, or a tirants raigne,
And thousand more calamities besides,
To grunt and sweate vnder this weary life,
When that he may his full *Quietus* make,
With a bare bodkin, who would this indure,
But for a hope of something after death?
Which pusles the braine, and doth confound the sence,
Which makes vs rather beare those euilles we haue,
Than flie to others that we know not of.
I that, O this conscience makes cowardes of vs all,
Lady in thy orizons, be all my sinnes remembred.

9. 'To be or not to be' as it appeared in the 'bad' quarto of 1603

sometimes they include passages clearly cobbled together to supply gaps in the reporter's memory. For all this, they are not without value in helping us to judge how Shakespeare's plays were originally performed. Their stage directions may give us more information about how the plays were staged than is available in other texts: for instance, the reported text of *Hamlet* has the direction '*Enter Ofelia playing on a lute, and her hair down, singing*'—far more vivid than the good Quarto's '*Enter Ophelia*', or even the Folio's '*Enter Ophelia distracted*'. Because these are post-performance texts, they may preserve, in the midst of corruption, authentically Shakespearian changes made to the play after it was first written and not recorded elsewhere. A particularly interesting case is *The Taming of the Shrew*: the play as printed in the Folio, in what is clearly, in general, the more authentic text, abandons early in its action the framework device which makes the story of Katherine and Petruccio a play within the play; the quarto continues this framework through the play, and provides an amusing little episode rounding it off. These passages may derive from ones written by Shakespeare but not printed in the Folio: we print them as Additional Passages at the end of the play. In general, we draw more liberally than most previous editors on the reported texts, in the belief that they can help us to come closer than before to the plays as they were acted by Shakespeare's company as well as by others.

Although in general it was to the advantage of the companies that owned play scripts not to allow them to be printed, some of Shakespeare's plays were printed from authentic manuscripts during his lifetime, and even while they were still being performed by his company; these are the 'good' quartos. First came *Titus Andronicus*, printed in 1594 from Shakespeare's own papers, probably because the company for which he wrote it had been disbanded. In 1597 *Richard II* was printed from Shakespeare's manuscript, minus the politically sensitive episode (4.1) in which Richard gives up his crown to Bolingbroke: a clear instance of censorship, whether self-imposed or not. The first play to be published in

Shakespeare's name is *Love's Labour's Lost*, in 1598. Several other quartos printed from good manuscripts appeared around the same time: *1 Henry IV* (probably from a scribal transcript) in 1598, and *A Midsummer Night's Dream*, *The Merchant of Venice*, *2 Henry IV*, and *Much Ado About Nothing* (all from Shakespeare's papers) in 1600. In 1604 appeared a text of *Hamlet* printed from Shakespeare's own papers and declaring itself to be 'Newly imprinted and enlarged to almost as much again as it was, according to the true and perfect copy': surely an attempt to replace a bad text by a good one. *King Lear* followed, in 1608, in a badly printed quarto whose status has been much disputed, but which we believe to derive from Shakespeare's own manuscript. In 1609 came *Troilus and Cressida*, probably from Shakespeare's own papers, in an edition which in the first-printed copies claims to present the play 'as it was acted by the King's majesty's servants at the Globe', but in later-printed ones declares that it has never been 'staled with the stage'. The only new play to appear between Shakespeare's death and the publication of the Folio in 1623 was *Othello*, printed in 1622 apparently from a transcript of Shakespeare's own papers.

It is clear that publishers found Shakespeare a valuable property—some of these quartos were several times reprinted—and easy to understand why some of his plays were pirated. It is less easy to see why Shakespeare and his colleagues released reliable texts of some plays for publication but not others. As a shareholder in the company to which the plays belonged, Shakespeare himself must have been a partner in its decisions, and it is difficult to believe that he was so lacking in personal vanity that he was happy to be represented in print by garbled texts; but he seems to have taken no interest in the progress of his plays through the press. Even some of those printed from authentic manuscripts—such as the 1604 *Hamlet*—are badly printed, and certainly not proof-read by the author; none of them bears an author's dedication or shows any sign of having been prepared for the press in the way that, for instance, Ben Jonson clearly prepared some of his plays. John Marston, introducing the printed text of his play *The Malcontent* in 1604, wrote: 'Only one thing afflicts me, to think that scenes invented merely to be spoken, should be enforcively published to be read'. Perhaps Shakespeare was similarly afflicted.

In 1616, the year of Shakespeare's death, Ben Jonson published his own collected plays in a handsome Folio. It was the first time that an English writer for the popular stage had been so honoured (or had so honoured himself), and it established a precedent by which Shakespeare's fellows could commemorate their colleague and friend. Principal responsibility for this ambitious enterprise was undertaken by John Heminges and Henry Condell, both long-established actors with Shakespeare's company; latterly, Heminges had been its business manager. They, along with Richard Burbage, had been the colleagues whom Shakespeare remembered in his will: he left each of them 26s. 8d. to buy a mourning ring. Although the Folio did not appear until 1623, they may have started work on it soon after Shakespeare died: big books take a long time to prepare. And they undertook their task with serious care. Most importantly, they printed eighteen plays that had not so far appeared in print, and which might otherwise have vanished. They omitted (so far as we can tell) only *Pericles*, *Cardenio* (now vanished), *The Two Noble Kinsmen*—perhaps because these three were collaborative—and the mysterious *Love's Labour's Won* (see p. 349). And they went to considerable pains to provide good texts. They had no previous experience as editors; they may have had help from others (including Ben Jonson, who wrote commendatory verses for the Folio): anyhow, although printers find it easier to set from print than from manuscript, they were not content simply to reprint quartos whenever they were available. In fact they seem to have made a conscious effort to identify and to avoid making use of the quartos now recognized as bad. In their introductory epistle addressed 'To the Great Variety of Readers', they declare that the public has been 'abused with divers stolen and surreptitious copies, maimed and deformed by the frauds and stealths of injurious impostors'. But now these plays are 'offered to your view cured, and perfect of their limbs; and all the rest absolute in their numbers, as he conceived them'.

None of the quartos believed by modern scholars to be unauthoritative was used unaltered as copy for the Folio. As men of the theatre, Heminges and Condell had access to prompt-books, and they made considerable use of them. For some plays, such as *Titus Andronicus* (which includes a whole scene not present in the quarto), and *A Midsummer Night's Dream*, the printers had a copy of a quarto (not necessarily the first) marked up with alterations made as the result of comparison with a theatre manuscript. For other plays (the first four to be printed in the Folio—*The Tempest*, *The Two Gentlemen of Verona*, *The Merry Wives of Windsor*, and *Measure for Measure*—along with *The Winter's Tale*) they employed a professional scribe, Ralph Crane, to transcribe papers in the theatre's possession. For others, such as *Henry V* and *All's Well That Ends Well*, they seem to have had authorial papers; and for yet others, such as *Macbeth*, a prompt-book. We cannot always be sure of the copy used by the printers, and sometimes it may have been mixed: for *Richard III* they seem to have used pages of the third quarto mixed with pages of the sixth quarto combined with passages in manuscript; a copy of the third quarto of *Richard II*, a copy of the fifth quarto, and a theatre manuscript all contributed to the Folio text of that play; the annotated third quarto of *Titus Andronicus* was supplemented by the 'fly' scene (3.2) which Shakespeare appears to have added after the play was first composed. Dedicating the Folio to the brother Earls of Pembroke and Montgomery, Heminges and Condell claimed that, in collecting Shakespeare's plays together, they had 'done an office to the dead, to procure his orphans guardians' (that is, to provide noble patrons for the works he had left behind), 'without ambition either of self-profit or fame, only to keep the memory of so worthy a friend and fellow alive as was our Shakespeare'. Certainly they deserve our gratitude.

The Modern Editor's Task

It will be clear from all this that the documents from which even the authoritative early editions of Shakespeare's plays were printed were of a very variable nature. Some were his own papers in a rough state, including loose ends, duplications, inconsistencies, and vaguenesses. At the other extreme were prompt-books representing the play as close to the state in which it appeared in Shakespeare's theatre as we can get; and there were various intermediate states. For those plays of which we have only one text—those first printed in the Folio, along with *Pericles* and *The Two Noble Kinsmen*—the editor is at least not faced with the problem of alternative choices. The surviving text of *Macbeth* gives every sign of being an adaptation: if so, there is no means of recovering what Shakespeare originally wrote. The scribe seems to have entirely expunged Shakespeare's stage directions from *The Two Gentlemen of Verona*: we must make do with what we have. Other plays, however, confront the editor with a problem of choice. Pared down to its essentials, it is this: should he offer his readers a text which is as close as possible to what Shakespeare originally wrote, or should he aim to formulate a text presenting the play as it appeared when performed by the company of which Shakespeare was a principal shareholder in the theatres that he helped to control and on whose success his livelihood depended? The problem exists in two different forms. For some plays, the changes made in the more theatrical text (always the Folio, if we discount the bad quartos) are relatively minor, consisting perhaps in a few reallocations of dialogue, the addition of music cues to the stage directions, and perhaps some cuts. So it is with, for example, *A Midsummer Night's*

Dream and *Richard II*. More acute—and more critically exciting—are the problems raised when the more theatrical version appears to represent, not merely the text as originally written after it had been prepared for theatrical use, but a more radical revision of that text made (in some cases) after the first version had been presented in its own terms. At least five of Shakespeare's plays exist in these states: they are *2 Henry IV*, *Hamlet*, *Troilus and Cressida*, *Othello*, and *King Lear*.

The editorial problem is compounded by the existence of conflicting theories to explain the divergences between the surviving texts of these plays. Until recently, it was generally believed that the differences resulted from imperfect transmission: that Shakespeare wrote only one version of each play, and that each variant text represents that original text in a more or less corrupt form. As a consequence of this belief, editors conflated the texts, adding to one passages present only in the other, and selecting among variants in wording in an effort to present what the editor regarded as the most 'Shakespearian' version possible. *Hamlet* provides an example. The 1604 quarto was set from Shakespeare's own papers (with some contamination from the reported text of 1603). The Folio includes about 80 lines that are not in the quarto, but omits about 230 that are there. The Folio was clearly influenced by, if not printed directly from, a theatre manuscript. There are hundreds of local variants. Editors invariably conflate the two texts, assuming that the absence of passages from each was the result either of accidental omission or of cuts made in the theatre against Shakespeare's wishes; they also reject a selection of the variant readings. It is at least arguable that this produces a version that never existed in Shakespeare's time. We believe that the 1604 quarto represents the play as Shakespeare first wrote it, before it was performed, and that the Folio represents a theatrical text of the play after he had revised it. Given this belief, it would be equally logical to base an edition on either text: one the more literary, the other the more theatrical. Both types of edition would be of interest; each would present within its proper context readings which editors who conflate the texts have to abandon.

It would be extravagant in a one-volume edition to present double texts of all the plays that exist in significantly variant form. The theatrical version is, inevitably, that which comes closest to the 'final' version of the play. We have ample testimony from the theatre at all periods, including our own, that play scripts undergo a process of, often, considerable modification on their way from the writing table to the stage. Occasionally, dramatists resent this process; we know that some of Shakespeare's contemporaries resented cuts made in some of their plays. But we know too that plays may be much improved by intelligent cutting, and that dramatists of great literary talent may benefit from the discipline of the theatre. It is, of course, possible that Shakespeare's colleagues occasionally overruled him, forcing him to omit cherished lines, or that practical circumstances—such as the incapacity of a particular actor to do justice to every aspect of his role—necessitated adjustments that Shakespeare would have preferred not to make. But he was himself, supremely, a man of the theatre. We have seen that he displayed no interest in how his plays were printed: in this he is at the opposite extreme from Ben Jonson, who was still in mid-career when he prepared the collected edition of his works. We know that Shakespeare was an actor and shareholder in the leading theatre company of its time, a major financial asset to that company, a man immersed in the life of that theatre and committed to its values. The concept of the director of a play did not exist in his time; but someone must have exercised some, at least, of the functions of the modern director, and there is good reason to believe that that person must have been Shakespeare himself, for his own plays. The very fact that those texts of his plays that contain cuts also give evidence of more 'literary' revision suggests that he was deeply involved in the process by which his plays came to be modified in performance. For these reasons, this edition chooses, when possible, to print the more theatrical version of each play. In some cases, this requires the omission from the body of the text of lines that Shakespeare certainly wrote; there is, of course, no suggestion that these lines are unworthy of their author; merely that, in some if not all performances, he and his company found that the play's overall structure and pace were better without them. All such lines are printed as Additional Passages at the end of the play.

In all but one of Shakespeare's plays the revisions are local—changes in the wording of individual phrases and lines—or else they are effected by additions and cuts. Essentially, then, the story line is not affected. But in *King Lear* the differences between the two texts are more radical. It is not simply that the 1608 quarto lacks over 100 lines that are in the Folio, or that the Folio lacks close on 300 lines that are in the Quarto, or that there are over 850 verbal variants, or that several speeches are assigned to different speakers. It is rather that the sum total of these differences amounts, in this play, to a substantial shift in the presentation and interpretation of the underlying action. The differences are particularly apparent in the military action of the last two acts. We believe, in short, that there are two distinct plays of *King Lear*, not merely two different texts of the same play; so we print edited versions of both the Quarto ('*The History of* . . .') and the Folio ('*The Tragedy of* . . .').

Though the editor's selection, when choice is available, of the edition that should form the basis of his text is fundamentally important, many other tasks remain. Elizabethan printers could do meticulously scholarly work, but they rarely expended their best efforts on plays, which—at least in quarto format—they treated as ephemeral publications. Moreover, dramatic manuscripts and heavily annotated quartos must have set them difficult problems. Scribal transcripts would have been easier for the printer, but scribes were themselves liable to introduce error in copying difficult manuscripts, and also had a habit of sophisticating what they copied—for example, by expanding colloquial contractions— in ways that would distort the dramatist's intentions. On the whole, the Folio is a rather well-printed volume; there are not a great many obvious misprints; but for all that, corruption is often discernible. A few quartos—notably *A Midsummer Night's Dream* (1600)—are exceptionally well printed, but others, such as the 1604 *Hamlet*, abound in obvious error, which is a sure sign that they also commit hidden corruptions. Generations of editors have tried to correct the texts; but possible corruptions are still being identified, and new attempts at correction are often made. The preparation of this edition has required a minutely detailed examination of the early texts. At many points we have adopted emendations suggested by previous editors; at other points we offer original readings; and occasionally we revert to the original text at points where it has often been emended.

Stage directions are a special problem, especially in a one-volume edition where some degree of uniformity may be thought desirable. The early editions are often deficient in directions for essential action, even in such basic matters as when characters enter and when they depart. Again, generations of editors have tried to supply such deficiencies, not always systematically. We try to remedy the deficiencies, always bearing in mind the conditions of Shakespeare's stage. At many points the requisite action is apparent from the dialogue; at other points precisely what should happen, or the precise point at which it should happen, is in doubt—and, perhaps, was never clearly determined even by the author. In our edition we use broken brackets—e.g. ⌈*He kneels*⌉—to identify dubious action or placing. Inevitably, this is to some extent a matter of individual interpretation; and, of course, modern directors may, and do, often depart freely from the original directions, both explicit and implicit. Our original-spelling edition, while including the added directions, stays somewhat closer to the wording of the original editions than our modern-spelling edition. Readers interested in the precise directions of the original texts on which ours are based will find them reprinted in *William Shakespeare: A Textual Companion*.

Ever since Shakespeare's plays began to be reprinted, their spelling and punctuation have been modernized. Often, however, this task has been left to the printer; many editors who have undertaken it themselves have merely marked up earlier edited texts, producing a palimpsest; there has been little discussion of the principles involved; and editors have been even less systematic in this area than in that of stage directions. Modernizing the spelling of earlier periods is not the simple business it may appear. Some words are easily handled: 'doe' becomes 'do', 'I' meaning 'yes' becomes 'ay', 'beutie' becomes 'beauty', and so on. But it is not always easy to distinguish between variant spellings and variant forms. It is not our aim to modernize Shakespeare's language: we do not change 'ay' to 'yes', 'ye' to 'you', 'eyne' to 'eyes', or 'hath' to 'has'; we retain obsolete inflections and prefixes. We aim not to make changes that would affect the metre of verse: when the early editions mark an elision—'know'st', 'ha'not', 'i'th'temple'—we do so, too; when scansion requires that an -ed ending be sounded, contrary to modern usage, we mark it with a grave accent—'formèd', 'movèd'. Older forms of words are often preserved when they are required for metre, rhyme, word-play, or characterization. But we do not retain old spellings simply because they may provide a clue to the way words were pronounced by some people in Shakespeare's time, because such clues may be misleading (we know, for instance, that 'boil' was often pronounced as 'bile', 'Rome' as 'room', and 'person' as 'parson'), and, more importantly, because many words which we spell in the same way as the Elizabethans have changed pronunciation in the mean time; it seems pointless to offer in a generally modern context a mere selection of spellings that may convey some of the varied pronunciations available in Shakespeare's time. Many words existed in indifferently variant spellings; we have sometimes preferred the more modern spelling, especially when the older one might mislead: thus, we spell 'beholden', not 'beholding', 'distraught' (when appropriate), not 'distract'.

Similar principles are applied to proper names: it is, for instance, meaningless to preserve the Folio's 'Petruchio' when this is clearly intended to represent the old (as well as the modern) pronunciation of the Italian name 'Petruccio'; failure to modernize adequately here results even in the theatre in the mistaken pedantry of 'Pet-rook-io'. For some words, the arguments for and against modernization are finely balanced. The generally French setting of *As You Like It* has led us to prefer 'Ardenne' to the more familiar 'Arden', though we would not argue that geographical consistency is Shakespeare's strongest point. Problematic too is the military rank of ensign; this appears in early texts of Shakespeare as 'ancient' (or 'aunciant', 'auncient', 'auntient', etc.). 'Ancient' in this sense, in its various forms, was originally a corruption of 'ensign', and from the sixteenth to the eighteenth centuries the forms were interchangeable. Shakespeare himself may well have used both. There is no question that the sense conveyed by modern 'ensign' is overwhelmingly dominant in Shakespeare's designation of Iago (in *Othello*) and Pistol (in *2 Henry IV*, *Henry V*, and *The Merry Wives of Windsor*), and it is equally clear that 'ancient' could be seriously misleading, so we prefer 'ensign'. This is contrary to the editorial tradition, but a parallel is afforded by the noun 'dolphin', which is the regular spelling in Shakespearian texts for the French 'dauphin'. Here tradition favours 'dauphin', although it did not become common in English until the later seventeenth century. It would be as misleading to imply that Iago and Pistol were ancient as that the Dauphin of France was an aquatic mammal.

Punctuation, too, poses problems. Judging by most of the early, 'good' quartos as well as the fragment of *Sir Thomas More*, Shakespeare himself punctuated lightly. The syntax of his time was in any case more fluid than ours; the imposition upon it of a precisely grammatical system of punctuation reduces ambiguity and imposes definition upon indefinition. But Elizabethan scribes and printers seem to have regarded punctuation as their prerogative; thus, the 1600 quarto of *A Midsummer Night's Dream* is far more precisely punctuated than any Shakespearian manuscript is likely to have been; and Ralph Crane clearly imposed his own system upon the texts he transcribed. So it is impossible to put much faith in the punctuation of the early texts. Additionally, their system is often ambiguous: the question mark could signal an exclamation, and parentheses were idiosyncratically employed. Modern editors, then, may justifiably replace the varying, often conflicting systems of the early texts by one which attempts to convey their sense to the modern reader. Working entirely from the early texts, we have tried to use comparatively light pointing which will not impose certain nuances upon the text at the expense of others. Readers interested in the punctuation of the original texts will find it reproduced with minimal alteration in our original-spelling edition.

Theatre is an endlessly fluid medium. Each performance of a play is unique, differing from others in pace, movement, gesture, audience response, and even—because of the fallibility of human memory—in the words spoken. It is likely too that in Shakespeare's time, as in ours, changes in the texts of plays were consciously made to suit varying circumstances: the characteristics of particular actors, the place in which the play was performed, the anticipated reactions of his audience, and so on. The circumstances by which Shakespeare's plays have been transmitted to us mean that it is impossible to recover exactly the form in which they stood either in his own original manuscripts or in those manuscripts, or transcripts of them, after they had been prepared for use in the theatre. Still less can we hope to pinpoint the words spoken in any particular performance. Nevertheless, it is in performance that the plays lived and had their being. Performance is the end to which they were created, and in this edition we have devoted our efforts to recovering and presenting texts of Shakespeare's plays as they were acted in the London playhouses which stood at the centre of his professional life.

CONTEMPORARY ALLUSIONS TO SHAKESPEARE

MANY contemporary documents, some manuscript, some printed, refer directly to Shakespeare and to members of his family. The following list (which is not exhaustive) briefly indicates the nature of the principal allusions to him and to his closest relatives. It does not include publication records of his plays (given in the *Textual Companion*), the appearances of his name on title-pages, unascribed allusions to his works, commendatory poems, epistles, and dedications printed elsewhere in the edition, or records of performances except for that of 1604–5, in which Shakespeare is named. The principal documents are discussed, and most of them reproduced, in S. Schoenbaum's *William Shakespeare: A Documentary Life* (1975).

26 April 1564	Baptism of 'Gulielmus filius Iohannes Shakspere' in Stratford-upon-Avon
27 November 1582	Entry of marriage licence at Worcester 'inter Wᵐ Shaxpere et Annō whateley'
28 November 1582	Marriage licence bond issued in Worcester for 'Willm Shagspere' and 'Anne Hathwey'
26 May 1583	Baptism of 'Susanna daughter to William Shakspere' in Stratford-upon-Avon
2 February 1585	Baptism of 'Hamnet & Iudeth sonne & daughter to Williā Shakspere' in Stratford-upon-Avon
1589	Reference to William Shakespeare in an earlier lawsuit brought by his parents against John Lambert concerning property at Wilmcote, near Stratford-upon-Avon
1592	Robert Greene's reference in *Greene's Groatsworth of Wit* to 'an vpstart Crow' who 'is in his owne conceit the onely Shake-scene in a countrey' (see p. xviii); Henry Chettle's (oblique) reference in *Kind-Harts Dreame* to Shakespeare's 'vprightnes of dealing, and fatious [= facetious?] grace in writting'.
1594	Reference to Shakespeare as author of *Lucrece* in Henry Willobie's *Willobie his Avisa*
1595	Allusion to 'Sweet Shakespeare' as author of *Lucrece* in William Covell's *Polimanteia*
15 March 1595	Shakespeare named as joint payee of the Lord Chamberlain's Men for performances at court
1596	A petition by William Wayte (in London) for sureties of the peace against 'Willm Shakspere' and others
11 August 1596	Burial of 'Hamnet filius William Shakspere' in Stratford-upon-Avon
October, 1596	Two draft grants of arms to John Shakespeare
4 May 1597, etc.	Documents recording William Shakespeare's purchase of New Place, Stratford-upon-Avon

15 November 1597	'William Shackspeare' of Bishopsgate ward, London, listed as not having paid taxes due in February
1598	Shakespeare one of the 'principall Comœdians' in Ben Jonson's *Every Man in his Humour* (according to a list printed in the 1616 Jonson Folio)
1598	Sale by 'mr shaxspere' of a load of stone in Stratford-upon-Avon
1598	Appearance of Shakespeare's name on title-pages of the second quartos of *Richard II* and *Richard III* and of the first (surviving) quarto of *Love's Labour's Lost*. (Later title-page ascriptions are not listed.)
1598	Praise of Shakespeare as author of *Venus and Adonis* and *Lucrece* in Richard Barnfield's *Poems in Divers Humours*
1598	Francis Meres's references in *Palladis Tamia* (see p. xix)
4 February 1598	'Wᵐ Shackespe' listed as holder of corn and malt in Stratford-upon-Avon
1 October 1598	'William Shakespeare' named as tax defaulter in Bishopsgate ward, London
15 October 1598	Letter from Richard Quiney asking 'mr Wᵐ Shackespe' for a loan of £30
1598–9	'Willm̄ Shakespeare' named in Enrolled Subsidy Account (London)
1598–1601	References to Shakespeare in *The Pilgrimage to Parnassus* and *The Return from Parnassus, Parts 1 and 2*, acted at St. John's College, Cambridge
1599	Draft of grant permitting John Shakespeare to impale his arms with those of the Arden family
16 May 1599	The newly built Globe theatre mentioned (in a London inventory) as being in the occupation of 'William Shakespeare and others'
6 October 1599	'Willmus Shakspere' named as owing money to the Exchequer (London)
6 October 1600	'Willmus Shakspeare' named as owing money to the Exchequer (London)
c.1601	References to Shakespeare as author of *Venus and Adonis*, *Lucrece*, and *Hamlet* in a manuscript note by Gabriel Harvey
8 September 1601	Burial of John Shakespeare in Stratford-upon-Avon
1602	Reconveyance of New Place to William Shakespeare
1602	Reference to 'Shakespear yᵉ Player' in York Herald's complaint
13 March 1602	John Manningham's diary entry of an anecdote about Burbage and Shakespeare (see pp. xv–xvi)
1 May 1602	Shakespeare paid William and John Combe £320 for land in Old Stratford
28 September 1602	Shakespeare bought a cottage in Chapel Lane, Stratford-upon-Avon
1603	Shakespeare listed among 'The principall Tragœdians' in Ben Jonson's *Sejanus*
1603	Shakespeare (and others) called on to lament the death of Queen Elizabeth in Henry Chettle's *A Mourneful Dittie, entituled Elizabeths Losse*
17 and 19 May 1603	Shakespeare named in documents conferring the title of King's Men on the former Lord Chamberlain's Men
c.1604	Shakespeare sued Philip Rogers of Stratford-upon-Avon for debt
1604	Anthony Scoloker, in *Diaphantus, or the Passions of Love*, mentions the popularity of *Hamlet* and refers to '*Friendly Shakespeare's Tragedies*'
15 March 1604	Shakespeare and his fellows granted scarlet cloth for King James's entry into London (see p. xx)
24 October 1604	Shakespeare recorded as owner of a cottage and garden in Rowington Manor
1604–5	'Shaxberd' named as author of several plays performed at court

1605	Passing reference to Shakespeare in William Camden's *Remaines of a greater Worke concerning Britaine*'
4 May 1605	Augustine Phillips (actor) bequeaths 'to my fellowe William Shakespeare a xxxˢ peece in gould'
24 July 1605	Shakespeare pays £440 for an interest in a lease of tithes in the Stratford-upon-Avon area
1607	Commendatory allusion to Shakespeare in William Barksted's *Myrrha, the Mother of Adonis*
5 June 1607	Marriage of Susanna Shakespeare to John Hall in Stratford-upon-Avon
9 September 1608	Burial of Shakespeare's mother, 'Mary Shaxspere wydowe', in Stratford-upon-Avon
1608-9	Documents recording Shakespeare's lawsuit for debt against John Addenbrooke of Stratford-upon-Avon
11 September 1611	Shakespeare subscribes to the cost of a bill for repairing highways
1612	Praise of 'the right happy and copious industry of M. *Shake-speare*' (and others) in John Webster's epistle to *The White Devil*
1612	Shakespeare testifies in Stephen Belott's suit against Christopher Mountjoy, in London (see pp. xvi–xvii)
*c.*1613	Leonard Digges, in a manuscript note, compares Shakespeare to Lope de Vega
28 January 1613	John Combe of Stratford-upon-Avon bequeaths £5 to 'mr William Shackspere'
10 March 1613	Shakespeare buys a gatehouse in Blackfriars for £140
31 March 1613	Payment to Shakespeare and Richard Burbage of 44 shillings for an *impresa* for the Earl of Rutland (see p. xxi)
1614	Passing reference to Shakespeare in an epistle by Richard Carew printed in the second edition of Camden's *Remaines*
5 September 1614, etc.	Documents recording Shakespeare's involvement in disputes concerning enclosures in the Stratford-upon-Avon area
*c.*1615	Complimentary reference to Shakespeare in a manuscript poem by Francis Beaumont
1615	Passing reference to Shakespeare by Edward Howes in fifth edition of John Stow's *Annales*
26 April 1615	Shakespeare engaged in litigation concerned with the Blackfriars gatehouse
10 February 1616	Marriage of Judith Shakespeare to Thomas Quiney in Stratford-upon-Avon
25 March 1616	Shakespeare's will drawn up in Stratford-upon-Avon
25 April 1616	Burial of William Shakespeare in Stratford-upon-Avon (his monument records that he died on 23 April)
8 August 1623	Burial of Anne Shakespeare in Stratford-upon-Avon
16 July 1649	Burial of Shakespeare's daughter, Susanna Hall, in Stratford-upon-Avon
9 February 1662	Burial of Shakespeare's daughter, Judith Quiney, in Stratford-upon-Avon
1670	Death of Shakespeare's last direct descendant, his granddaughter Elizabeth, who married Thomas Nash in 1626 and John (later Sir John) Bernard in 1649

COMMENDATORY POEMS AND PREFACES (1599-1640)

Ad Gulielmum Shakespeare

Honey-tongued Shakespeare, when I saw thine issue
I swore Apollo got them, and none other,
Their rosy-tainted features clothed in tissue,
Some heaven-born goddess said to be their mother.
Rose-cheeked Adonis with his amber tresses,   5
Fair fire-hot Venus charming him to love her,
Chaste Lucretia virgin-like her dresses,
Proud lust-stung Tarquin seeking still to prove her,
Romeo, Richard, more whose names I know not—
Their sugared tongues and power-attractive beauty   10
Say they are saints although that saints they show not,
For thousands vows to them subjective duty.
They burn in love, thy children; Shakespeare het them;
Go, woo thy muse more nymphish brood beget them.

> John Weever, *Epigrams* (1599)

A never writer to an ever
reader: news

Eternal reader, you have here a new play never staled
with the stage, never clapper-clawed with the palms of
the vulgar, and yet passing full of the palm comical, for
it is a birth of that brain that never undertook anything
comical vainly; and were but the vain names of comedies
changed for the titles of commodities, or of plays for pleas,
you should see all those grand censors that now style
them such vanities flock to them for the main grace of
their gravities, especially this author's comedies, that are
so framed to the life that they serve for the most common
commentaries of all the actions of our lives, showing such
a dexterity and power of wit that the most displeased
with plays are pleased with his comedies, and all such
dull and heavy-witted worldlings as were never capable
of the wit of a comedy, coming by report of them to his
representations, have found that wit there that they never
found in themselves, and have parted better witted than
they came, feeling an edge of wit set upon them more
than ever they dreamed they had brain to grind it on. So
much and such savoured salt of wit is in his comedies
that they seem, for their height of pleasure, to be born
in that sea that brought forth Venus. Amongst all there
is none more witty than this, and had I time I would
comment upon it, though I know it needs not for so
much as will make you think your testern well bestowed,

but for so much worth as even poor I know to be stuffed
in it. It deserves such a labour as well as the best comedy
in Terence or Plautus. And believe this, that when he is
gone and his comedies out of sale, you will scramble for
them, and set up a new English Inquisition. Take this for
a warning, and at the peril of your pleasure's loss and
judgement's, refuse not, nor like this the less for not being
sullied with the smoky breath of the multitude; but thank
fortune for the scape it hath made amongst you, since
by the grand possessors' wills I believe you should have
prayed for them rather than been prayed. And so I leave
all such to be prayed for, for the states of their
wits' healths, that will not praise it.
Vale.

> Anonymous, in *Troilus and Cressida* (1609)

To our English Terence, Master Will Shakespeare

Some say, good Will, which I in sport do sing,
Hadst thou not played some kingly parts in sport
Thou hadst been a companion for a king,
And been a king among the meaner sort.
Some others rail; but rail as they think fit,   5
Thou hast no railing but a reigning wit,
    And honesty thou sow'st, which they do reap
    So to increase their stock which they do keep.

> John Davies, *The Scourge of Folly* (1610)

To Master William Shakespeare

Shakespeare, that nimble Mercury, thy brain,
Lulls many hundred Argus-eyes asleep,
So fit for all thou fashionest thy vein;
At th'horse-foot fountain thou hast drunk full deep.
Virtue's or vice's theme to thee all one is.   5
Who loves chaste life, there's Lucrece for a teacher;
Who list read lust, there's Venus and Adonis,
True model of a most lascivious lecher.
Besides, in plays thy wit winds like Meander,
Whence needy new composers borrow more   10
Than Terence doth from Plautus or Menander.
But to praise thee aright, I want thy store.
    Then let thine own works thine own worth upraise,
    And help t'adorn thee with deservèd bays.

> Thomas Freeman, *Run and a Great Cast* (1614)

Inscriptions upon the Shakespeare monument, Stratford-upon-Avon

Iudicio Pylium, genio Socratem, arte Maronem,
Terra tegit, populus maeret, Olympus habet.

Stay, passenger, why goest thou by so fast?
Read, if thou canst, whom envious death hath placed
Within this monument: Shakespeare, with whom   5
Quick nature died; whose name doth deck this tomb
Far more than cost, sith all that he hath writ
Leaves living art but page to serve his wit.

Obiit anno domini 1616,
aetatis 53, *die* 23 *Aprilis*

On the death of William Shakespeare

Renownèd Spenser, lie a thought more nigh
To learnèd Chaucer; and rare Beaumont, lie
A little nearer Spenser, to make room
For Shakespeare in your threefold, fourfold tomb.
To lodge all four in one bed make a shift   5
Until doomsday, for hardly will a fifth
Betwixt this day and that by fate be slain
For whom your curtains need be drawn again.
But if precedency in death doth bar
A fourth place in your sacred sepulchre,   10
Under this carvèd marble of thine own,
Sleep, rare tragedian Shakespeare, sleep alone.
Thy unmolested peace, unsharèd cave,
Possess as lord, not tenant, of thy grave,
That unto us or others it may be   15
Honour hereafter to be laid by thee.

William Basse (*c.*1616-22), in Shakespeare's
Poems (1640)

The Stationer to the Reader
(in *The Tragedy of Othello*, 1622)

To set forth a book without an epistle were like to the
old English proverb, 'A blue coat without a badge', and
the author being dead, I thought good to take that piece
of work upon me. To commend it I will not, for that
which is good, I hope every man will commend without
entreaty; and I am the bolder because the author's name
is sufficient to vent his work. Thus, leaving everyone to
the liberty of judgement, I have ventured to print this
play, and leave it to the general censure.

Yours,   10
Thomas Walkley.

The Epistle Dedicatory
(in *Comedies, Histories, and Tragedies*, 1623)

TO THE MOST NOBLE
AND
INCOMPARABLE PAIR
OF BRETHREN

WILLIAM   5
Earl of Pembroke, &c., Lord Chamberlain to the
King's most excellent majesty,

AND

PHILIP   9
Earl of Montgomery, &c., gentleman of his majesty's
bedchamber; both Knights of the most noble Order
of the Garter, and our singular good
LORDS.

Right Honourable,

Whilst we study to be thankful in our particular for the
many favours we have received from your lordships, we
are fallen upon the ill fortune to mingle two the most
diverse things that can be: fear and rashness; rashness
in the enterprise, and fear of the success. For when we
value the places your highnesses sustain, we cannot but
know their dignity greater than to descend to the reading
of these trifles; and while we name them trifles we have
deprived ourselves of the defence of our dedication. But
since your lordships have been pleased to think these
trifles something heretofore, and have prosecuted both
them and their author, living, with so much favour, we
hope that, they outliving him, and he not having the
fate, common with some, to be executor to his own
writings, you will use the like indulgence toward them you
have done unto their parent. There is a great difference
whether any book choose his patrons, or find them. This
hath done both; for so much were your lordships' likings
of the several parts when they were acted as, before they
were published, the volume asked to be yours. We have
but collected them, and done an office to the dead to
procure his orphans guardians, without ambition either
of self-profit or fame, only to keep the memory of so
worthy a friend and fellow alive as was our Shakespeare,
by humble offer of his plays to your most noble patronage.
Wherein, as we have justly observed no man to come
near your lordships but with a kind of religious address,
it hath been the height of our care, who are the presenters,
to make the present worthy of your highnesses by the
perfection. But there we must also crave our abilities to
be considered, my lords. We cannot go beyond our own
powers. Country hands reach forth milk, cream, fruits,
or what they have; and many nations, we have heard,
that had not gums and incense, obtained their requests
with a leavened cake. It was no fault to approach their
gods by what means they could, and the most, though
meanest, of things are made more precious when they

are dedicated to temples. In that name, therefore, we most humbly consecrate to your highnesses these remains of your servant Shakespeare, that what delight is in them may be ever your lordships', the reputation his, and the faults ours, if any be committed by a pair so careful to show their gratitude both to the living and the dead as is

Your lordships' most bounden,
JOHN HEMINGES.
HENRY CONDELL.

———

To the Great Variety of Readers

From the most able to him that can but spell: there you are numbered; we had rather you were weighed, especially when the fate of all books depends upon your capacities, and not of your heads alone, but of your purses. Well, it is now public, and you will stand for your privileges, we know: to read and censure. Do so, but buy it first. That doth best commend a book, the stationer says. Then, how odd soever your brains be, or your wisdoms, make your licence the same, and spare not. Judge your six-penn'orth, your shilling's worth, your five shillings' worth at a time, or higher, so you rise to the just rates, and welcome. But whatever you do, buy. Censure will not drive a trade or make the jack go; and though you be a magistrate of wit, and sit on the stage at Blackfriars or the Cockpit to arraign plays daily, know, these plays have had their trial already, and stood out all appeals, and do now come forth quitted rather by a decree of court than any purchased letters of commendation. 19

It had been a thing, we confess, worthy to have been wished that the author himself had lived to have set forth and overseen his own writings. But since it hath been ordained otherwise, and he by death departed from that right, we pray you do not envy his friends the office of their care and pain to have collected and published them, and so to have published them as where, before, you were abused with divers stolen and surreptitious copies, maimed and deformed by the frauds and stealths of injurious impostors that exposed them, even those are now offered to your view cured and perfect of their limbs, and all the rest absolute in their numbers, as he conceived them; who, as he was a happy imitator of nature, was a most gentle expresser of it. His mind and hand went together, and what he thought he uttered with that easiness that we have scarce received from him a blot in his papers. But it is not our province, who only gather his works and give them you, to praise him; it is yours, that read him. And there we hope, to your diverse capacities, you will find enough both to draw and hold you; for his wit can no more lie hid than it could be lost. Read him, therefore, and again, and again, and if then you do not like him, surely you are in some manifest danger not to understand him. And so we leave you to other of his friends whom if you need can be your guides; if you need them not, you can lead yourselves and others. And such readers we wish him. 46

John Heminges, Henry Condell, in *Comedies, Histories, and Tragedies* (1623)

———

To the memory of my beloved,
The AUTHOR
Master William Shakespeare,
AND
what he hath left us

To draw no envy, Shakespeare, on thy name
Am I thus ample to thy book and fame;
While I confess thy writings to be such
As neither man nor muse can praise too much:
'Tis true, and all men's suffrage. But these ways   5
Were not the paths I meant unto thy praise,
For silliest ignorance on these may light,
Which, when it sounds at best, but echoes right;
Or blind affection, which doth ne'er advance
The truth, but gropes, and urgeth all by chance;   10
Or crafty malice might pretend this praise,
And think to ruin where it seemed to raise.
These are as some infamous bawd or whore
Should praise a matron: what could hurt her more?
But thou art proof against them, and indeed   15
Above th'ill fortune of them, or the need.
I therefore will begin. Soul of the age!
The applause, delight, the wonder of our stage!
My Shakespeare, rise. I will not lodge thee by
Chaucer or Spenser, or bid Beaumont lie   20
A little further to make thee a room.
Thou art a monument without a tomb,
And art alive still while thy book doth live
And we have wits to read and praise to give.
That I not mix thee so, my brain excuses: 25
I mean with great but disproportioned muses.
For if I thought my judgement were of years
I should commit thee surely with thy peers,
And tell how far thou didst our Lyly outshine,
Or sporting Kyd, or Marlowe's mighty line.   30
And though thou hadst small Latin and less Greek,
From thence to honour thee I would not seek
For names, but call forth thund'ring Aeschylus,
Euripides, and Sophocles to us,
Pacuvius, Accius, him of Cordova dead,   35
To life again, to hear thy buskin tread
And shake a stage; or, when thy socks were on,
Leave thee alone for the comparison
Of all that insolent Greece or haughty Rome
Sent forth, or since did from their ashes come.   40
Triumph, my Britain, thou hast one to show
To whom all scenes of Europe homage owe.
He was not of an age, but for all time,
And all the muses still were in their prime
When like Apollo he came forth to warm   45
Our ears, or like a Mercury to charm!

Nature herself was proud of his designs,
  And joyed to wear the dressing of his lines,
Which were so richly spun, and woven so fit,
  As since she will vouchsafe no other wit.   50
The merry Greek, tart Aristophanes,
  Neat Terence, witty Plautus, now not please,
But antiquated and deserted lie
  As they were not of nature's family.
Yet must I not give nature all; thy art,   55
  My gentle Shakespeare, must enjoy a part.
For though the poet's matter nature be,
  His art doth give the fashion; and that he
Who casts to write a living line must sweat—
  Such as thine are—and strike the second heat   60
Upon the muses' anvil, turn the same,
  And himself with it that he thinks to frame;
Or for the laurel he may gain a scorn,
  For a good poet's made as well as born.
And such wert thou. Look how the father's face   65
  Lives in his issue, even so the race
Of Shakespeare's mind and manners brightly shines
  In his well-turnèd and true-filèd lines,
In each of which he seems to shake a lance,
  As brandished at the eyes of ignorance.   70
Sweet swan of Avon! What a sight it were
  To see thee in our waters yet appear,
And make those flights upon the banks of Thames
  That so did take Eliza and our James!
But stay, I see thee in the hemisphere   75
  Advanced, and made a constellation there!
Shine forth, thou star of poets, and with rage
  Or influence chide or cheer the drooping stage,
Which, since thy flight from hence, hath mourned like
    night   80
  And despairs day, but for thy volume's light.
     Ben Jonson, in *Comedies, Histories, and Tragedies*
                                  (1623)

Upon the Lines and Life of the Famous Scenic Poet, Master William Shakespeare

Those hands which you so clapped go now and wring,
You Britons brave, for done are Shakespeare's days.
His days are done that made the dainty plays
Which made the globe of heav'n and earth to ring.
Dried is that vein, dried is the Thespian spring,   5
Turned all to tears, and Phoebus clouds his rays.
That corpse, that coffin now bestick those bays
Which crowned him poet first, then poets' king.
If tragedies might any prologue have,
All those he made would scarce make one to this,   10
Where fame, now that he gone is to the grave—
Death's public tiring-house—the *nuntius* is;
For though his line of life went soon about,
The life yet of his lines shall never out.
     Hugh Holland, in *Comedies, Histories, and Tragedies*
                                  (1623)

TO THE MEMORY
of the deceased author Master
William Shakespeare

Shakespeare, at length thy pious fellows give
The world thy works, thy works by which outlive
Thy tomb thy name must; when that stone is rent,
And time dissolves thy Stratford monument,
Here we alive shall view thee still. This book,   5
When brass and marble fade, shall make thee look
Fresh to all ages. When posterity
Shall loathe what's new, think all is prodigy
That is not Shakespeare's ev'ry line, each verse
Here shall revive, redeem thee from thy hearse.   10
Nor fire nor cank'ring age, as Naso said
Of his, thy wit-fraught book shall once invade;
Nor shall I e'er believe or think thee dead—
Though missed—until our bankrupt stage be sped—
Impossible—with some new strain t'outdo   15
Passions of Juliet and her Romeo,
Or till I hear a scene more nobly take
Than when thy half-sword parleying Romans spake.
Till these, till any of thy volume's rest
Shall with more fire, more feeling be expressed,   20
Be sure, our Shakespeare, thou canst never die,
But crowned with laurel, live eternally.
     Leonard Digges, in *Comedies, Histories, and Tragedies*
                                  (1623)

To the memory of Master William Shakespeare

We wondered, Shakespeare, that thou went'st so soon
From the world's stage to the grave's tiring-room.
We thought thee dead, but this thy printed worth
Tells thy spectators that thou went'st but forth
To enter with applause. An actor's art   5
Can die, and live to act a second part.
That's but an exit of mortality;
This, a re-entrance to a *plaudite*.
     James Mabbe, in *Comedies, Histories, and Tragedies*
                                  (1623)

The Names of the Principal Actors in all these Plays

William Shakespeare.	Samuel Gilburn.
Richard Burbage.	Robert Armin.
John Heminges.	William Ostler.
Augustine Phillips.	Nathan Field.
William Kempe.	John Underwood. 5
Thomas Pope.	Nicholas Tooley.
George Bryan.	William Ecclestone.
Henry Condell.	Joseph Taylor.
William Sly.	Robert Benfield.
Richard Cowley.	Robert Gough. 10
John Lowin.	Richard Robinson.
Samuel Cross.	John Shank.
Alexander Cook.	John Rice.

     In *Comedies, Histories, and Tragedies* (1623)

An Epitaph on the Admirable Dramatic Poet,
William Shakespeare

What need my Shakespeare for his honoured bones
The labour of an age in pilèd stones,
Or that his hallowed relics should be hid
Under a star-ypointing pyramid?
Dear son of memory, great heir of fame, 5
What need'st thou such dull witness of thy name?
Thou in our wonder and astonishment
Hast built thyself a lasting monument,
For whilst to th' shame of slow-endeavouring art
Thy easy numbers flow, and that each heart 10
Hath from the leaves of thy unvalued book
Those Delphic lines with deep impression took,
Then thou, our fancy of herself bereaving,
Dost make us marble with too much conceiving,
And so sepulchered in such pomp dost lie 15
That kings for such a tomb would wish to die.

John Milton (1630), in *Comedies, Histories, and Tragedies*
(1632)

———

Upon the Effigies of my Worthy
Friend, the Author Master William
Shakespeare, and his Works

Spectator, this life's shadow is. To see
The truer image and a livelier he,
Turn reader. But observe his comic vein,
Laugh; and proceed next to a tragic strain,
Then weep. So when thou find'st two contraries, 5
Two different passions from thy rapt soul rise,
Say—who alone effect such wonders could—
Rare Shakespeare to the life thou dost behold.

Anonymous, in *Comedies, Histories, and Tragedies* (1632)

———

On Worthy Master Shakespeare and his Poems

A mind reflecting ages past, whose clear
And equal surface can make things appear
Distant a thousand years, and represent
Them in their lively colours' just extent;
To outrun hasty time, retrieve the fates, 5
Roll back the heavens, blow ope the iron gates
Of death and Lethe, where confusèd lie
Great heaps of ruinous mortality;
In that deep dusky dungeon to discern
A royal ghost from churls; by art to learn 10
The physiognomy of shades, and give
Them sudden birth, wond'ring how oft they live;
What story coldly tells, what poets feign
At second hand, and picture without brain
Senseless and soulless shows; to give a stage, 15
Ample and true with life, voice, action, age,
As Plato's year and new scene of the world
Them unto us or us to them had hurled;
To raise our ancient sovereigns from their hearse,
Make kings his subjects; by exchanging verse 20
Enlive their pale trunks, that the present age

Joys in their joy, and trembles at their rage;
Yet so to temper passion that our ears
Take pleasure in their pain, and eyes in tears
Both weep and smile: fearful at plots so sad, 25
Then laughing at our fear; abused, and glad
To be abused, affected with that truth
Which we perceive is false; pleased in that ruth
At which we start, and by elaborate play
Tortured and tickled; by a crablike way 30
Time past made pastime, and in ugly sort
Disgorging up his ravin for our sport,
While the plebeian imp from lofty throne
Creates and rules a world, and works upon
Mankind by secret engines; now to move 35
A chilling pity, then a rigorous love;
To strike up and stroke down both joy and ire;
To steer th'affections, and by heavenly fire
Mould us anew; stol'n from ourselves—
This, and much more which cannot be expressed 40
But by himself, his tongue and his own breast,
Was Shakespeare's freehold, which his cunning brain
Improved by favour of the ninefold train.
The buskined muse, the comic queen, the grand
And louder tone of Clio; nimble hand 45
And nimbler foot of the melodious pair,
The silver-voicèd lady, the most fair
Calliope, whose speaking silence daunts,
And she whose praise the heavenly body chants.
These jointly wooed him, envying one another, 50
Obeyed by all as spouse, but loved as brother,
And wrought a curious robe of sable grave,
Fresh green, and pleasant yellow, red most brave,
And constant blue, rich purple, guiltless white,
The lowly russet, and the scarlet bright, 55
Branched and embroidered like the painted spring,
Each leaf matched with a flower, and each string
Of golden wire, each line of silk; there run
Italian works whose thread the sisters spun,
And there did sing, or seem to sing, the choice 60
Birds of a foreign note and various voice.
Here hangs a mossy rock, there plays a fair
But chiding fountain purlèd. Not the air
Nor clouds nor thunder but were living drawn
Not out of common tiffany or lawn, 65
But fine materials which the muses know,
And only know the countries where they grow.
Now when they could no longer him enjoy
In mortal garments pent: death may destroy,
They say, his body, but his verse shall live, 70
And more than nature takes our hands shall give.
In a less volume, but more strongly bound,
Shakespeare shall breathe and speak, with laurel crowned,
Which never fades; fed with Ambrosian meat
In a well-linèd vesture rich and neat. 75
So with this robe they clothe him, bid him wear it,
For time shall never stain, nor envy tear it.

'The friendly admirer of his endowments', I.M.S.,
in *Comedies, Histories, and Tragedies* (1632)

Upon Master WILLIAM SHAKESPEARE, the *Deceased Author, and his* POEMS

Poets are born, not made: when I would prove
This truth, the glad remembrance I must love
Of never-dying Shakespeare, who alone
Is argument enough to make that one.
First, that he was a poet none would doubt   5
That heard th'applause of what he sees set out
Imprinted, where thou hast—I will not say,
Reader, his works, for to contrive a play
To him 'twas none—the pattern of all wit,
Art without art unparalleled as yet.   10
Next, nature only helped him, for look thorough
This whole book, thou shalt find he doth not borrow
One phrase from Greeks, nor Latins imitate,
Nor once from vulgar languages translate,
Nor plagiary-like from others glean,   15
Nor begs he from each witty friend a scene
To piece his acts with. All that he doth write
Is pure his own—plot, language exquisite—
But O! what praise more powerful can we give
The dead than that by him the King's men live,   20
His players, which should they but have shared the fate,
All else expired within the short term's date,
How could the Globe have prospered, since through want
Of change the plays and poems had grown scant.
But, happy verse, thou shalt be sung and heard   25
When hungry quills shall be such honour barred.
Then vanish, upstart writers to each stage,
You needy poetasters of this age;
Where Shakespeare lived or spake, vermin, forbear;
Lest with your froth you spot them, come not near.   30
But if you needs must write, if poverty
So pinch that otherwise you starve and die,
On God's name may the Bull or Cockpit have
Your lame blank verse, to keep you from the grave,
Or let new Fortune's younger brethren see   35
What they can pick from your lean industry.
I do not wonder, when you offer at
Blackfriars, that you suffer; 'tis the fate
Of richer veins, prime judgements that have fared
The worse with this deceasèd man compared.   40
So have I seen, when Caesar would appear,
And on the stage at half-sword parley were
Brutus and Cassius; O, how the audience
Were ravished, with what wonder they went thence,
When some new day they would not brook a line   45
Of tedious though well-laboured *Catiline*.
Sejanus too was irksome, they prized more
Honest Iago, or the jealous Moor.
And though the Fox and subtle Alchemist,
Long intermitted, could not quite be missed,   50
Though these have shamed all the ancients, and might raise
Their author's merit with a crown of bays,
Yet these, sometimes, even at a friend's desire
Acted, have scarce defrayed the seacoal fire

And doorkeepers; when let but Falstaff come,   55
Hal, Poins, the rest, you scarce shall have a room,
All is so pestered. Let but Beatrice
And Benedick be seen, lo, in a trice
The Cockpit galleries, boxes, all are full
To hear Malvolio, that cross-gartered gull.   60
Brief, there is nothing in his wit-fraught book
Whose sound we would not hear, on whose worth look;
Like old-coined gold, whose lines in every page
Shall pass true current to succeeding age.
But why do I dead Shakespeare's praise recite?   65
Some second Shakespeare must of Shakespeare write;
For me 'tis needless, since an host of men
Will pay to clap his praise, to free my pen.

> Leonard Digges (before 1636), in Shakespeare's
> *Poems* (1640)

In remembrance of Master *William Shakespeare.*

ODE

1.

Beware, delighted poets, when you sing
To welcome nature in the early spring,
   Your num'rous feet not tread
The banks of Avon; for each flower
(As it ne'er knew a sun or shower)   5
   Hangs there the pensive head.

2.

Each tree, whose thick and spreading growth hath made
Rather a night beneath the boughs than shade,
   Unwilling now to grow,
Looks like the plume a captive wears,   10
Whose rifled falls are steeped i'th' tears
   Which from his last rage flow.

3.

The piteous river wept itself away
Long since, alas, to such a swift decay
   That, reach the map and look   15
If you a river there can spy,
And for a river your mocked eye
   Will find a shallow brook.

> Sir William Davenant, *Madagascar, with other
> Poems* (1637)

An Elegy on the death of that famous Writer and Actor, Master William Shakspeare

I dare not do thy memory that wrong
Unto our larger griefs to give a tongue;
I'll only sigh in earnest, and let fall
My solemn tears at thy great funeral,
For every eye that rains a show'r for thee   5
Laments thy loss in a sad elegy.
Nor is it fit each humble muse should have
Thy worth his subject, now thou'rt laid in grave;

No, it's a flight beyond the pitch of those
Whose worthless pamphlets are not sense in prose.   10
Let learnèd Jonson sing a dirge for thee,
And fill our orb with mournful harmony;
But we need no remembrancer; thy fame
Shall still accompany thy honoured name
To all posterity, and make us be   15
Sensible of what we lost in losing thee,
Being the age's wonder, whose smooth rhymes
Did more reform than lash the looser times.
Nature herself did her own self admire
As oft as thou wert pleasèd to attire   20
Her in her native lustre, and confess
Thy dressing was her chiefest comeliness.
How can we then forget thee, when the age
Her chiefest tutor, and the widowed stage
Her only favourite, in thee hath lost,   25
And nature's self what she did brag of most?
Sleep, then, rich soul of numbers, whilst poor we
Enjoy the profits of thy legacy,
And think it happiness enough we have
So much of thee redeemèd from the grave   30
As may suffice to enlighten future times
With the bright lustre of thy matchless rhymes.

Anonymous (before 1638), in Shakespeare's
Poems (1640)

To Shakespeare

Thy muse's sugared dainties seem to us
Like the famed apples of old Tantalus,
For we, admiring, see and hear thy strains,
But none I see or hear those sweets attains.

To the same

Thou hast so used thy pen, or shook thy spear,
That poets startle, nor thy wit come near.

Thomas Bancroft, Two Books of Epigrams and
Epitaphs (1639)

To Master William Shakespeare

Shakespeare, we must be silent in thy praise,
'Cause our encomiums will but blast thy bays,
Which envy could not, that thou didst so well;
Let thine own histories prove thy chronicle.

Anonymous, in Wit's Recreations (1640)

To the Reader

I here presume, under favour, to present to your view
some excellent and sweetly composed poems of Master
William Shakespeare, which in themselves appear of the
same purity the author himself, then living, avouched.
They had not the fortune, by reason of their infancy in
his death, to have the due accommodation of proportionable glory with the rest of his ever-living works,
yet the lines of themselves will afford you a more authentic
approbation than my assurance any way can; to invite
your allowance, in your perusal you shall find them
serene, clear, and elegantly plain, such gentle strains as
shall recreate and not perplex your brain, no intricate or
cloudy stuff to puzzle intellect, but perfect eloquence, such
as will raise your admiration to his praise. This assurance,
I know, will not differ from your acknowledgement; and
certain I am my opinion will be seconded by the sufficiency
of these ensuing lines. I have been somewhat solicitous
to bring this forth to the perfect view of all men, and in
so doing, glad to be serviceable for the continuance of
glory to the deserved author in these his poems.   20

John Benson, in Shakespeare's Poems (1640)

Of Master William Shakespeare

What, lofty Shakespeare, art again revived,
And Virbius-like now show'st thyself twice lived?
'Tis Benson's love that thus to thee is shown,
The labour's his, the glory still thine own.
These learnèd poems amongst thine after-birth,   5
That makes thy name immortal on the earth,
Will make the learnèd still admire to see
The muses' gifts so fully infused on thee.
Let carping Momus bark and bite his fill,
And ignorant Davus slight thy learnèd skill,   10
Yet those who know the worth of thy desert,
And with true judgement can discern thy art,
Will be admirers of thy high-tuned strain,
Amongst whose number let me still remain.

John Warren, in Shakespeare's Poems (1640)

THE FIRST PART OF THE
CONTENTION

(2 HENRY VI)

WHEN Shakespeare's history plays were gathered together in the 1623 Folio, seven years after he died, they were printed in the order of their historical events, each with a title naming the king in whose reign those events occurred. No one supposes that this is the order in which Shakespeare wrote them; and the Folio titles are demonstrably not, in all cases, those by which the plays were originally known. The three concerned with the reign of Henry VI are listed in the Folio, simply and unappealingly, as the *First*, *Second*, and *Third Parts of King Henry the Sixth*, and these are the names by which they have continued to be known. Versions of the *Second* and *Third* had appeared long before the Folio, in 1594 and 1595; their head titles read *The First Part of the Contention of the two Famous Houses of York and Lancaster with the Death of the Good Duke Humphrey* and *The True Tragedy of Richard, Duke of York, and the Good King Henry the Sixth*. These are, presumably, full versions of the plays' original titles, and we revert to them in preference to the Folio's historical listing.

A variety of internal evidence suggests that the Folio's *Part One* was composed after *The First Part of the Contention* and *Richard, Duke of York*, so we depart from the Folio order, though a reader wishing to read the plays in their narrative sequence will read *Henry VI, Part One* before the other two plays. The dates of all three are uncertain, but *Part One* is alluded to in 1592, when it was probably new. *The First Part of the Contention* probably belongs to 1590-1.

The play draws extensively on English chronicle history for its portrayal of the troubled state of England under Henry VI (1421-71). It dramatizes the touchingly weak King's powerlessness against the machinations of his nobles, especially Richard, Duke of York, himself ambitious for the throne. Richard engineers the Kentish rebellion, led by Jack Cade, which provides some of the play's liveliest episodes; and at the play's end Richard seems poised to take the throne.

Historical events of ten years (1445-55) are dramatized with comparative fidelity within a coherent structure that offers a wide variety of theatrical entertainment. Though the play employs old-fashioned conventions of language (particularly the recurrent classical references) and of dramaturgy (such as the horrors of severed heads), its bold characterization, its fundamentally serious but often ironically comic presentation of moral and political issues, the powerful rhetoric of its verse, and the vivid immediacy of its prose have proved highly effective in its rare modern revivals.

THE PERSONS OF THE PLAY

Of the King's Party

KING HENRY VI

QUEEN MARGARET

William de la Pole, Marquis, later Duke, of SUFFOLK, the Queen's lover

Duke Humphrey of GLOUCESTER, the Lord Protector, the King's uncle

Dame Eleanor Cobham, the DUCHESS of Gloucester

CARDINAL BEAUFORT, Bishop of Winchester, Gloucester's uncle and the King's great-uncle

Duke of BUCKINGHAM

Duke of SOMERSET

Old Lord CLIFFORD

YOUNG CLIFFORD, his son

Of the Duke of York's Party

Duke of YORK

EDWARD, Earl of March ⎫
Crookback RICHARD ⎭ his sons

Earl of SALISBURY

Earl of WARWICK, his son

The petitions and the combat

Two or three PETITIONERS

Thomas HORNER, an armourer

PETER Thump, his man

Three NEIGHBOURS, who drink to Horner

Three PRENTICES, who drink to Peter

The conjuration

Sir John HUME ⎫
John SOUTHWELL ⎭ priests

Margery Jordan, a WITCH

Roger BOLINGBROKE, a conjurer

ASNATH, a spirit

The false miracle

Simon SIMPCOX

SIMPCOX'S WIFE

The MAYOR of Saint Albans

Aldermen of Saint Albans

A BEADLE of Saint Albans

Townsmen of Saint Albans

Eleanor's penance

Gloucester's SERVANTS

Two SHERIFFS of London

Sir John STANLEY

HERALD

The murder of Gloucester

Two MURDERERS

COMMONS

The murder of Suffolk

CAPTAIN of a ship

MASTER of that ship

The Master's MATE

Walter WHITMORE

Two GENTLEMEN

The Cade Rebellion

Jack CADE, a Kentishman suborned by the Duke of York

Dick the BUTCHER ⎫
Smith the WEAVER ⎪
A Sawyer ⎬ Cade's followers
JOHN ⎪
REBELS ⎭

Emmanuel, the CLERK of Chatham ⎫
Sir Humphrey STAFFORD ⎪
STAFFORD'S BROTHER ⎪
Lord SAYE ⎬ those who die at the rebels' hands
Lord SCALES ⎪
Matthew Gough ⎪
A SERGEANT ⎭

Three or four CITIZENS of London

Alexander IDEN, an esquire of Kent, who kills Cade

Others

VAUX, a messenger

A POST

MESSENGERS

A SOLDIER

Attendants, guards, servants, soldiers, falconers

The First Part of the Contention
of the Two Famous Houses of York and Lancaster

1.1 *Flourish of trumpets, then hautboys. Enter, at one
door, King Henry and Humphrey Duke of
Gloucester, the Duke of Somerset, the Duke of
Buckingham, Cardinal Beaufort, ⌈and others⌉.
Enter, at the other door, the Duke of York, and the
Marquis of Suffolk, and Queen Margaret, and the
Earls of Salisbury and Warwick*

SUFFOLK (*kneeling before King Henry*)
As by your high imperial majesty
I had in charge at my depart for France,
As Procurator to your excellence,
To marry Princess Margaret for your grace,
So, in the famous ancient city Tours, 5
In presence of the Kings of France and Sicil,
The Dukes of Orléans, Calaber, Bretagne, and Alençon,
Seven earls, twelve barons, and twenty reverend
bishops,
I have performed my task and was espoused,
And humbly now upon my bended knee, 10
In sight of England and her lordly peers,
Deliver up my title in the Queen
To your most gracious hands, that are the substance
Of that great shadow I did represent—
The happiest gift that ever marquis gave, 15
The fairest queen that ever king received.

KING HENRY
Suffolk, arise. Welcome, Queen Margaret.
I can express no kinder sign of love
Than this kind kiss.
He kisses her
O Lord that lends me life,
Lend me a heart replete with thankfulness! 20
For thou hast given me in this beauteous face
A world of earthly blessings to my soul,
If sympathy of love unite our thoughts.

QUEEN MARGARET
Th'excess of love I bear unto your grace
Forbids me to be lavish of my tongue 25
Lest I should speak more than beseems a woman.
Let this suffice: my bliss is in your liking,
And naught can make poor Margaret miserable
Unless the frown of mighty England's King.

KING HENRY
Her sight did ravish, but her grace in speech, 30
Her words yclad with wisdom's majesty,
Makes me from wond'ring fall to weeping joys,
·Such is the fullness of my heart's content.
Lords, with one cheerful voice, welcome my love.

LORDS (*kneeling*)
Long live Queen Margaret, England's happiness. 35

QUEEN MARGARET We thank you all.

Flourish. ⌈They all rise⌉

SUFFOLK (*to Gloucester*)
My Lord Protector, so it please your grace,
Here are the articles of contracted peace
Between our sovereign and the French King Charles,
For eighteen months concluded by consent. 40

GLOUCESTER (*reads*) Imprimis: it is agreed between the
French King Charles and William de la Pole, Marquis
of Suffolk, ambassador for Henry, King of England, that
the said Henry shall espouse the Lady Margaret,
daughter unto René, King of Naples, Sicilia, and
Jerusalem, and crown her Queen of England, ere the
thirtieth of May next ensuing.

Item: it is further agreed between them that the
duchy of Anjou and the county of Maine shall be
released and delivered to the King her fa— 50
⌈Gloucester lets the paper fall⌉

KING HENRY
Uncle, how now?

GLOUCESTER Pardon me, gracious lord.
Some sudden qualm hath struck me at the heart
And dimmed mine eyes that I can read no further.

KING HENRY (*to Cardinal Beaufort*)
Uncle of Winchester, I pray read on. 54

CARDINAL BEAUFORT (*reads*) Item: it is further agreed
between them that the duchy of Anjou and the county
of Maine shall be released and delivered to the King
her father, and she sent over of the King of England's
own proper cost and charges, without dowry.

KING HENRY
They please us well. (*To Suffolk*) Lord Marquis, kneel
down. 60
Suffolk kneels
We here create thee first Duke of Suffolk,
And gird thee with the sword.
Suffolk rises
Cousin of York,
We here discharge your grace from being regent
I'th' parts of France till term of eighteen months
Be full expired. Thanks uncle Winchester, 65
Gloucester, York, and Buckingham, Somerset,
Salisbury, and Warwick.
We thank you all for this great favour done
In entertainment to my princely Queen.
Come, let us in, and with all speed provide 70
To see her coronation be performed.
*Exeunt King Henry, Queen Margaret, and
Suffolk. ⌈Gloucester stays⌉ all the rest*

GLOUCESTER
Brave peers of England, pillars of the state,
To you Duke Humphrey must unload his grief,

3

Your grief, the common grief of all the land.
What—did my brother Henry spend his youth, 75
His valour, coin, and people in the wars?
Did he so often lodge in open field
In winter's cold and summer's parching heat
To conquer France, his true inheritance?
And did my brother Bedford toil his wits 80
To keep by policy what Henry got?
Have you yourselves, Somerset, Buckingham,
Brave York, Salisbury, and victorious Warwick,
Received deep scars in France and Normandy?
Or hath mine uncle Beaufort and myself, 85
With all the learnèd Council of the realm,
Studied so long, sat in the Council House
Early and late, debating to and fro,
How France and Frenchmen might be kept in awe,
And had his highness in his infancy 90
Crownèd in Paris in despite of foes?
And shall these labours and these honours die?
Shall Henry's conquest, Bedford's vigilance,
Your deeds of war, and all our counsel die?
O peers of England, shameful is this league, 95
Fatal this marriage, cancelling your fame,
Blotting your names from books of memory,
Razing the characters of your renown,
Defacing monuments of conquered France,
Undoing all, as all had never been! 100

CARDINAL BEAUFORT
Nephew, what means this passionate discourse,
This peroration with such circumstance?
For France, 'tis ours; and we will keep it still.

GLOUCESTER
Ay, uncle, we will keep it if we can—
But now it is impossible we should. 105
Suffolk, the new-made duke that rules the roast,
Hath given the duchy of Anjou and Maine
Unto the poor King René, whose large style
Agrees not with the leanness of his purse.

SALISBURY
Now by the death of Him that died for all, 110
These counties were the keys of Normandy—
But wherefore weeps Warwick, my valiant son?

WARWICK
For grief that they are past recovery.
For were there hope to conquer them again
My sword should shed hot blood, mine eyes no tears.
Anjou and Maine? Myself did win them both!
Those provinces these arms of mine did conquer—
And are the cities that I got with wounds
Delivered up again with peaceful words?
Mort Dieu! 120

YORK
For Suffolk's duke, may he be suffocate,
That dims the honour of this warlike isle!
France should have torn and rent my very heart
Before I would have yielded to this league.
I never read but England's kings have had 125

Large sums of gold and dowries with their wives—
And our King Henry gives away his own,
To match with her that brings no vantages.

GLOUCESTER
A proper jest, and never heard before,
That Suffolk should demand a whole fifteenth 130
For costs and charges in transporting her!
She should have stayed in France and starved in France
Before—

CARDINAL BEAUFORT
My lord of Gloucester, now ye grow too hot!
It was the pleasure of my lord the King. 135

GLOUCESTER
My lord of Winchester, I know your mind.
'Tis not my speeches that you do mislike,
But 'tis my presence that doth trouble ye.
Rancour will out. Proud prelate, in thy face
I see thy fury. If I longer stay 140
We shall begin our ancient bickerings—
But I'll be gone, and give thee leave to speak.
Lordings, farewell, and say when I am gone,
I prophesied France will be lost ere long. *Exit*

CARDINAL BEAUFORT
So, there goes our Protector in a rage. 145
'Tis known to you he is mine enemy;
Nay more, an enemy unto you all,
And no great friend, I fear me, to the King.
Consider, lords, he is the next of blood
And heir apparent to the English crown. 150
Had Henry got an empire by his marriage,
And all the wealthy kingdoms of the west,
There's reason he should be displeased at it.
Look to it, lords—let not his smoothing words
Bewitch your hearts. Be wise and circumspect. 155
What though the common people favour him,
Calling him 'Humphrey, the good Duke of Gloucester',
Clapping their hands and crying with loud voice
'Jesu maintain your royal excellence!'
With 'God preserve the good Duke Humphrey!' 160
I fear me, lords, for all this flattering gloss,
He will be found a dangerous Protector.

BUCKINGHAM
Why should he then protect our sovereign,
He being of age to govern of himself?
Cousin of Somerset, join you with me, 165
And all together, with the Duke of Suffolk,
We'll quickly hoist Duke Humphrey from his seat.

CARDINAL BEAUFORT
This weighty business will not brook delay—
I'll to the Duke of Suffolk presently. *Exit*

SOMERSET
Cousin of Buckingham, though Humphrey's pride 170
And greatness of his place be grief to us,
Yet let us watch the haughty Cardinal;
His insolence is more intolerable
Than all the princes in the land beside.
If Gloucester be displaced, he'll be Protector. 175

BUCKINGHAM
Or thou or I, Somerset, will be Protector,
Despite Duke Humphrey or the Cardinal.
Exeunt Buckingham and Somerset
SALISBURY
Pride went before, ambition follows him.
While these do labour for their own preferment,
Behoves it us to labour for the realm.   180
I never saw but Humphrey Duke of Gloucester
Did bear him like a noble gentleman.
Oft have I seen the haughty Cardinal,
More like a soldier than a man o'th' church,
As stout and proud as he were lord of all,   185
Swear like a ruffian, and demean himself
Unlike the ruler of a commonweal.
Warwick, my son, the comfort of my age,
Thy deeds, thy plainness, and thy housekeeping
Hath won thee greatest favour of the commons,   190
Excepting none but good Duke Humphrey.
And, brother York, thy acts in Ireland,
In bringing them to civil discipline,
Thy late exploits done in the heart of France,
When thou wert Regent for our sovereign,   195
Have made thee feared and honoured of the people.
The reverence of mine age and Neville's name
Is of no little force if I command.
Join we together for the public good,
In what we can to bridle and suppress   200
The pride of Suffolk and the Cardinal
With Somerset's and Buckingham's ambition;
And, as we may, cherish Duke Humphrey's deeds
While they do tend the profit of the land.
WARWICK
So God help Warwick, as he loves the land,   205
And common profit of his country!
YORK
And so says York, *(aside)* for he hath greatest cause.
SALISBURY
Then let's away, and look unto the main.
WARWICK
Unto the main? O, father, Maine is lost!   209
That Maine which by main force Warwick did win,
And would have kept so long as breath did last!
Main chance, father, you meant—but I meant Maine,
Which I will win from France or else be slain.
Exeunt Warwick and Salisbury, leaving only
York
YORK
Anjou and Maine are given to the French,
Paris is lost, the state of Normandy   215
Stands on a tickle point now they are gone;
Suffolk concluded on the articles,
The peers agreed, and Henry was well pleased
To change two dukedoms for a duke's fair daughter.
I cannot blame them all—what is't to them?   220
'Tis thine they give away and not their own!
Pirates may make cheap pennyworths of their pillage,
And purchase friends, and give to courtesans,

Still revelling like lords till all be gone,
Whileas the seely owner of the goods   225
Weeps over them, and wrings his hapless hands,
And shakes his head, and, trembling, stands aloof,
While all is shared and all is borne away,
Ready to starve and dare not touch his own.
So York must sit and fret and bite his tongue,   230
While his own lands are bargained for and sold.
Methinks the realms of England, France, and Ireland
Bear that proportion to my flesh and blood
As did the fatal brand Althaea burnt
Unto the prince's heart of Calydon.   235
Anjou and Maine both given unto the French!
Cold news for me—for I had hope of France,
Even as I have of fertile England's soil.
A day will come when York shall claim his own,
And therefore I will take the Nevilles' parts,   240
And make a show of love to proud Duke Humphrey,
And, when I spy advantage, claim the crown,
For that's the golden mark I seek to hit.
Nor shall proud Lancaster usurp my right,
Nor hold the sceptre in his childish fist,   245
Nor wear the diadem upon his head
Whose church-like humours fits not for a crown.
Then, York, be still a while till time do serve.
Watch thou, and wake when others be asleep,
To pry into the secrets of the state—   250
Till Henry, surfeit in the joys of love
With his new bride and England's dear-bought queen,
And Humphrey with the peers be fall'n at jars.
Then will I raise aloft the milk-white rose,
With whose sweet smell the air shall be perfumed, 255
And in my standard bear the arms of York,
To grapple with the house of Lancaster;
And force perforce I'll make him yield the crown,
Whose bookish rule hath pulled fair England down.
Exit

1.2   *Enter Duke Humphrey of Gloucester and his wife*
         Eleanor, the Duchess
DUCHESS
Why droops my lord, like over-ripened corn
Hanging the head at Ceres' plenteous load?
Why doth the great Duke Humphrey knit his brows,
As frowning at the favours of the world?
Why are thine eyes fixed to the sullen earth,   5
Gazing on that which seems to dim thy sight?
What seest thou there? King Henry's diadem,
Enchased with all the honours of the world?
If so, gaze on, and grovel on thy face
Until thy head be circled with the same.   10
Put forth thy hand, reach at the glorious gold.
What, is't too short? I'll lengthen it with mine;
And having both together heaved it up,
We'll both together lift our heads to heaven
And never more abase our sight so low   15
As to vouchsafe one glance unto the ground.

GLOUCESTER

O Nell, sweet Nell, if thou dost love thy lord,
Banish the canker of ambitious thoughts!
And may that hour when I imagine ill
Against my king and nephew, virtuous Henry,   20
Be my last breathing in this mortal world!
My troublous dream this night doth make me sad.

DUCHESS

What dreamed my lord? Tell me and I'll requite it
With sweet rehearsal of my morning's dream.

GLOUCESTER

Methought this staff, mine office-badge in court,   25
Was broke in twain—by whom I have forgot,
But, as I think, it was by th' Cardinal—
And on the pieces of the broken wand
Were placed the heads of Edmund, Duke of Somerset,
And William de la Pole, first Duke of Suffolk.   30
This was my dream—what it doth bode, God knows.

DUCHESS

Tut, this was nothing but an argument
That he that breaks a stick of Gloucester's grove
Shall lose his head for his presumption.
But list to me, my Humphrey, my sweet duke: 35
Methought I sat in seat of majesty
In the cathedral church of Westminster,
And in that chair where kings and queens are
    crowned,
Where Henry and Dame Margaret kneeled to me,
And on my head did set the diadem.   40

GLOUCESTER

Nay, Eleanor, then must I chide outright.
Presumptuous dame! Ill-nurtured Eleanor!
Art thou not second woman in the realm,
And the Protector's wife beloved of him?
Hast thou not worldly pleasure at command   45
Above the reach or compass of thy thought?
And wilt thou still be hammering treachery
To tumble down thy husband and thyself
From top of honour to disgrace's feet?
Away from me, and let me hear no more!   50

DUCHESS

What, what, my lord? Are you so choleric
With Eleanor for telling but her dream?
Next time I'll keep my dreams unto myself
And not be checked.

GLOUCESTER

Nay, be not angry; I am pleased again.   55

Enter a Messenger

MESSENGER

My Lord Protector, 'tis his highness' pleasure
You do prepare to ride unto Saint Albans,
Whereas the King and Queen do mean to hawk.

GLOUCESTER

I go. Come, Nell, thou wilt ride with us?

DUCHESS

Yes, my good lord, I'll follow presently.   60

Exeunt Gloucester and the Messenger

Follow I must; I cannot go before
While Gloucester bears this base and humble mind.
Were I a man, a duke, and next of blood,
I would remove these tedious stumbling blocks
And smooth my way upon their headless necks.   65
And, being a woman, I will not be slack
To play my part in fortune's pageant.
(Calling within) Where are you there? Sir John! Nay,
    fear not man.
We are alone. Here's none but thee and I.

Enter Sir John Hume

HUME

Jesus preserve your royal majesty.   70

DUCHESS

What sayst thou? 'Majesty'? I am but 'grace'.

HUME

But by the grace of God and Hume's advice
Your grace's title shall be multiplied.

DUCHESS

What sayst thou, man? Hast thou as yet conferred
With Margery Jordan, the cunning witch of Eye,   75
With Roger Bolingbroke, the conjuror?
And will they undertake to do me good?

HUME

This they have promisèd: to show your highness
A spirit raised from depth of underground
That shall make answer to such questions   80
As by your Grace shall be propounded him.

DUCHESS

It is enough. I'll think upon the questions.
When from Saint Albans we do make return,
We'll see these things effected to the full.
Here, Hume *(giving him money)*, take this reward.
    Make merry, man,   85
With thy confederates in this weighty cause.   *Exit*

HUME

Hume must make merry with the Duchess' gold;
Marry, and shall. But how now, Sir John Hume?
Seal up your lips, and give no words but mum;
The business asketh silent secrecy.   90
Dame Eleanor gives gold to bring the witch.
Gold cannot come amiss were she a devil.
Yet have I gold flies from another coast—
I dare not say from the rich Cardinal
And from the great and new-made Duke of Suffolk,   95
Yet I do find it so; for, to be plain,
They, knowing Dame Eleanor's aspiring humour,
Have hired me to undermine the Duchess,
And buzz these conjurations in her brain.
They say 'A crafty knave does need no broker',   100
Yet am I Suffolk and the Cardinal's broker.
Hume, if you take not heed you shall go near
To call them both a pair of crafty knaves.
Well, so it stands; and thus, I fear, at last
Hume's knavery will be the Duchess' wrack,   105
And her attainture will be Humphrey's fall.
Sort how it will, I shall have gold for all.   *Exit*

1.3   *Enter Peter, the armourer's man, with two or three*
       other Petitioners

FIRST PETITIONER My masters, let's stand close. My Lord
Protector will come this way by and by and then we
may deliver our supplications in the quill.

SECOND PETITIONER Marry, the Lord protect him, for he's
a good man, Jesu bless him.   5

       Enter the Duke of Suffolk and Queen Margaret

⌈FIRST PETITIONER⌉ Here a comes, methinks, and the Queen
with him. I'll be the first, sure.

       He goes to meet Suffolk and the Queen

SECOND PETITIONER Come back, fool—this is the Duke of
Suffolk and not my Lord Protector.

SUFFOLK (*to the First Petitioner*)
How now, fellow—wouldst anything with me?   10

FIRST PETITIONER I pray, my lord, pardon me—I took ye
for my Lord Protector.

QUEEN MARGARET ⌈*seeing his supplication, she reads*⌉ 'To my
Lord Protector'—are your supplications to his lordship?
Let me see them.   15

       ⌈*She takes First Petitioner's supplication*⌉

What is thine?

FIRST PETITIONER Mine is, an't please your grace, against
John Goodman, my lord Cardinal's man, for keeping
my house and lands and wife and all from me.

SUFFOLK Thy wife too? That's some wrong indeed. ⌈*To the*
Second Petitioner⌉ What's yours?   21

       He takes the supplication

What's here? (*Reads*) 'Against the Duke of Suffolk for
enclosing the commons of Melford'! ⌈*To the Second*
Petitioner⌉ How now, Sir Knave?

SECOND PETITIONER Alas, sir, I am but a poor petitioner of
our whole township.   26

PETER ⌈*offering his petition*⌉ Against my master, Thomas
Horner, for saying that the Duke of York was rightful
heir to the crown.

QUEEN MARGARET What sayst thou? Did the Duke of York
say he was rightful heir to the crown?   31

PETER That my master was? No, forsooth, my master said
that he was and that the King was an usurer.

QUEEN MARGARET An usurper thou wouldst say.

PETER Ay, forsooth—an usurper.   35

SUFFOLK (*calling within*) Who is there?

       Enter a servant

Take this fellow in and send for his master with a
pursuivant presently. (*To Peter*) We'll hear more of your
matter before the King.   *Exit the servant with Peter*

QUEEN MARGARET (*to the Petitioners*)
And as for you that love to be protected   40
Under the wings of our Protector's grace,
Begin your suits anew and sue to him.

       ⌈*She*⌉ *tears the supplication*

Away, base cullions! Suffolk, let them go.

ALL PETITIONERS Come, let's be gone.

                                        Exeunt Petitioners

QUEEN MARGARET
My lord of Suffolk, say, is this the guise?   45
Is this the fashions in the court of England?

Is this the government of Britain's isle,
And this the royalty of Albion's king?
What, shall King Henry be a pupil still
Under the surly Gloucester's governance?   50
Am I a queen in title and in style,
And must be made a subject to a duke?
I tell thee, Pole, when in the city Tours
Thou rann'st a-tilt in honour of my love
And stol'st away the ladies' hearts of France,   55
I thought King Henry had resembled thee
In courage, courtship, and proportion.
But all his mind is bent to holiness,
To number Ave-Maries on his beads.
His champions are the prophets and apostles,   60
His weapons holy saws of sacred writ,
His study is his tilt-yard, and his loves
Are brazen images of canonizèd saints.
I would the college of the cardinals
Would choose him Pope, and carry him to Rome,   65
And set the triple crown upon his head—
That were a state fit for his holiness.

SUFFOLK
Madam, be patient—as I was cause
Your highness came to England, so will I
In England work your grace's full content.   70

QUEEN MARGARET
Beside the haught Protector have we Beaufort
The imperious churchman, Somerset, Buckingham,
And grumbling York; and not the least of these
But can do more in England than the King.

SUFFOLK
And he of these that can do most of all   75
Cannot do more in England than the Nevilles:
Salisbury and Warwick are no simple peers.

QUEEN MARGARET
Not all these lords do vex me half so much
As that proud dame, the Lord Protector's wife.
She sweeps it through the court with troops of ladies
More like an empress than Duke Humphrey's wife.   81
Strangers in court do take her for the queen.
She bears a duke's revenues on her back,
And in her heart she scorns our poverty.
Shall I not live to be avenged on her?   85
Contemptuous base-born callet as she is,
She vaunted 'mongst her minions t'other day
The very train of her worst-wearing gown
Was better worth than all my father's lands,
Till Suffolk gave two dukedoms for his daughter.   90

SUFFOLK
Madam, myself have limed a bush for her,
And placed a choir of such enticing birds
That she will light to listen to their lays,
And never mount to trouble you again.
So let her rest; and, madam, list to me,   95
For I am bold to counsel you in this:
Although we fancy not the Cardinal,
Yet must we join with him and with the lords

Till we have brought Duke Humphrey in disgrace.
As for the Duke of York, this late complaint   100
Will make but little for his benefit.
So one by one we'll weed them all at last,
And you yourself shall steer the happy helm.
          Sound a sennet. ⌈Enter King Henry with the Duke
          of York and the Duke of Somerset on either side of
          him whispering with him. Also enter Duke
          Humphrey of Gloucester, Dame Eleanor the
          Duchess of Gloucester, the Duke of Buckingham, the
          Earls of Salisbury and Warwick, and Cardinal
          Beaufort Bishop of Winchester⌉
KING HENRY
For my part, noble lords, I care not which:
Or Somerset or York, all's one to me.   105
YORK
If York have ill demeaned himself in France
Then let him be denied the regentship.
SOMERSET
If Somerset be unworthy of the place,
Let York be regent—I will yield to him.
WARWICK
Whether your grace be worthy, yea or no,   110
Dispute not that: York is the worthier.
CARDINAL BEAUFORT
Ambitious Warwick, let thy betters speak.
WARWICK
The Cardinal's not my better in the field.
BUCKINGHAM
All in this presence are thy betters, Warwick.
WARWICK
Warwick may live to be the best of all.   115
SALISBURY
Peace, son; (*to Buckingham*) and show some reason,
          Buckingham,
Why Somerset should be preferred in this.
QUEEN MARGARET
Because the King, forsooth, will have it so.
GLOUCESTER
Madam, the King is old enough himself
To give his censure. These are no women's matters.
QUEEN MARGARET
If he be old enough, what needs your grace   121
To be Protector of his excellence?
GLOUCESTER
Madam, I am Protector of the realm,
And at his pleasure will resign my place.
SUFFOLK
Resign it then, and leave thine insolence.   125
Since thou wert king—as who is king but thou?—
The commonwealth hath daily run to wrack,
The Dauphin hath prevailed beyond the seas,
And all the peers and nobles of the realm
Have been as bondmen to thy sovereignty.   130
CARDINAL BEAUFORT (*to Gloucester*)
The commons hast thou racked, the clergy's bags
Are lank and lean with thy extortions.

SOMERSET (*to Gloucester*)
Thy sumptuous buildings and thy wife's attire
Have cost a mass of public treasury.
BUCKINGHAM (*to Gloucester*)
Thy cruelty in execution   135
Upon offenders hath exceeded law
And left thee to the mercy of the law.
QUEEN MARGARET (*to Gloucester*)
Thy sale of offices and towns in France—
If they were known, as the suspect is great—
Would make thee quickly hop without thy head.   140
          Exit Gloucester
          Queen Margaret lets fall her fan
(*To the Duchess*)
Give me my fan—what, minion, can ye not?
          She gives the Duchess a box on the ear
I cry you mercy, madam! Was it you?
DUCHESS
Was't I? Yea, I it was, proud Frenchwoman!
Could I come near your beauty with my nails,
I'd set my ten commandments in your face.   145
KING HENRY
Sweet aunt, be quiet—'twas against her will.
DUCHESS
Against her will? Good King, look to't in time!
She'll pamper thee and dandle thee like a baby.
Though in this place most master wear no breeches,
She shall not strike Dame Eleanor unrevenged!   *Exit*
BUCKINGHAM (*aside to Cardinal Beaufort*)
Lord Cardinal, I will follow Eleanor   151
And listen after Humphrey how he proceeds.
She's tickled now, her fury needs no spurs—
She'll gallop far enough to her destruction.   *Exit*
          Enter Duke Humphrey of Gloucester
GLOUCESTER
Now, lords, my choler being overblown   155
With walking once about the quadrangle,
I come to talk of commonwealth affairs.
As for your spiteful false objections,
Prove them, and I lie open to the law.
But God in mercy so deal with my soul   160
As I in duty love my King and country.
But to the matter that we have in hand—
I say, my sovereign, York is meetest man
To be your regent in the realm of France.
SUFFOLK
Before we make election, give me leave   165
To show some reason of no little force
That York is most unmeet of any man.
YORK
I'll tell thee, Suffolk, why I am unmeet:
First, for I cannot flatter thee in pride;
Next, if I be appointed for the place,   170
My lord of Somerset will keep me here
Without discharge, money, or furniture,
Till France be won into the Dauphin's hands.
Last time I danced attendance on his will
Till Paris was besieged, famished, and lost.   175

WARWICK
That can I witness, and a fouler fact
Did never traitor in the land commit.

SUFFOLK Peace, headstrong Warwick.

WARWICK
Image of pride, why should I hold my peace?
Enter, guarded, Horner the armourer and Peter his
man

SUFFOLK
Because here is a man accused of treason —   180
Pray God the Duke of York excuse himself!

YORK
Doth anyone accuse York for a traitor?

KING HENRY
What mean'st thou, Suffolk? Tell me, what are these?

SUFFOLK
Please it your majesty, this is the man
He indicates Peter
That doth accuse his master (*indicating Horner*) of high
treason.   185
His words were these: that Richard Duke of York
Was rightful heir unto the English crown,
And that your majesty was an usurper.

KING HENRY (*to Horner*) Say, man, were these thy words?

HORNER An't shall please your majesty, I never said nor
thought any such matter. God is my witness, I am
falsely accused by the villain.

PETER [*raising his hands*] By these ten bones, my lords, he
did speak them to me in the garret one night as we
were scouring my lord of York's armour.   195

YORK
Base dunghill villain and mechanical,
I'll have thy head for this thy traitor's speech!
(*To King Henry*) I do beseech your royal majesty,
Let him have all the rigour of the law.   199

HORNER Alas, my lord, hang me if ever I spake the words.
My accuser is my prentice, and when I did correct him
for his fault the other day, he did vow upon his knees
he would be even with me. I have good witness of this,
therefore, I beseech your majesty, do not cast away an
honest man for a villain's accusation.   205

KING HENRY (*to Gloucester*)
Uncle, what shall we say to this in law?

GLOUCESTER
This doom, my lord, if I may judge by case:
Let Somerset be regent o'er the French,
Because in York this breeds suspicion.
(*Indicating Horner and Peter*)
And let these have a day appointed them   210
For single combat in convenient place,
For he (*indicating Horner*) hath witness of his servant's
malice.
This is the law, and this Duke Humphrey's doom.

KING HENRY
Then be it so. (*To Somerset*) My lord of Somerset,
We make you regent o'er the realm of France   215
There to defend our rights 'gainst foreign foes.

SOMERSET
I humbly thank your royal majesty.

HORNER
And I accept the combat willingly.

PETER [*to Gloucester*] Alas, my lord, I cannot fight; for
God's sake, pity my case! The spite of man prevaileth
against me. O Lord, have mercy upon me — I shall never
be able to fight a blow! O Lord, my heart!

GLOUCESTER
Sirrah, or you must fight or else be hanged.

KING HENRY
Away with them to prison, and the day
Of combat be the last of the next month.   225
Come, Somerset, we'll see thee sent away.
Flourish. Exeunt

1.4   *Enter Margery Jordan, a witch; Sir John Hume*
and John Southwell, two priests; and Roger
Bolingbroke, a conjuror

HUME Come, my masters, the Duchess, I tell you, expects
performance of your promises.

BOLINGBROKE Master Hume, we are therefore provided.
Will her ladyship behold and hear our exorcisms?

HUME Ay, what else? Fear you not her courage.   5

BOLINGBROKE I have heard her reported to be a woman
of an invincible spirit. But it shall be convenient, Master
Hume, that you be by her, aloft, while we be busy
below. And so, I pray you, go in God's name and leave
us.   *Exit Hume*
Mother Jordan, be you prostrate and grovel on the
earth.
She lies down upon her face.
[*Enter Eleanor, the Duchess of Gloucester, aloft*]
John Southwell, read you and let us to our work.

DUCHESS Well said, my masters, and welcome all. To this
gear the sooner the better.   15
[*Enter Hume aloft*]

BOLINGBROKE
Patience, good lady — wizards know their times.
Deep night, dark night, the silent of the night,
The time of night when Troy was set on fire,
The time when screech-owls cry and bandogs howl,
And spirits walk, and ghosts break up their graves —   20
That time best fits the work we have in hand.
Madam, sit you, and fear not. Whom we raise
We will make fast within a hallowed verge.
Here do the ceremonies belonging, and make the
circle. Southwell reads 'Coniuro te', &c. It
thunders and lightens terribly, then the spirit
Asnath riseth

ASNATH Adsum.

WITCH Asnath,   25
By the eternal God whose name and power
Thou tremblest at, answer that I shall ask,
For till thou speak, thou shalt not pass from hence.

ASNATH
Ask what thou wilt, that I had said and done.

BOLINGBROKE (*reads*)
'First, of the King: what shall of him become?'   30
ASNATH
The Duke yet lives that Henry shall depose,
But him outlive, and die a violent death.
            As the spirit speaks, ⌈Southwell⌉ writes the answer
BOLINGBROKE (*reads*)
'Tell me what fate awaits the Duke of Suffolk.'
ASNATH
By water shall he die, and take his end.
BOLINGBROKE (*reads*)
'What shall betide the Duke of Somerset?'   35
ASNATH
Let him shun castles. Safer shall he be
Upon the sandy plains than where castles mounted
    stand.
Have done—for more I hardly can endure.
BOLINGBROKE
Descend to darkness and the burning lake!
False fiend, avoid!   40
        Thunder and lightning. The spirit sinks down
            again
    Enter, breaking in, the Dukes of York and
    Buckingham with their guard, among them Sir
    Humphrey Stafford
YORK
Lay hands upon these traitors and their trash.
    ⌈*Bolingbroke, Southwell, and Jordan are taken*
    prisoner. Buckingham takes the writings from
    Bolingbroke and Southwell⌉
(*To Jordan*) Beldam, I think we watched you at an inch.
(*To the Duchess*) What, madam, are you there? The
    King and common weal
Are deep indebted for this piece of pains.
My lord Protector will, I doubt it not,   45
See you well guerdoned for these good deserts.
DUCHESS
Not half so bad as thine to England's king,
Injurious Duke, that threatest where's no cause.
BUCKINGHAM
True, madam, none at all—
    ⌈*He raises the writings*⌉
                    what call you this?
(*To his men*) Away with them. Let them be clapped up
    close   50
And kept asunder. (*To the Duchess*) You, madam, shall
    with us.
Stafford, take her to thee.
        Exeunt Stafford ⌈and others⌉ to the Duchess
            ⌈*and Hume⌉ above*
We'll see your trinkets here all forthcoming.
All away!
        Exeunt below Jordan, Southwell, and
        Bolingbroke, guarded, and, above, ⌈Hume and⌉
        the Duchess guarded by Stafford ⌈and others.
            York and Buckingham remain⌉
YORK
Lord Buckingham, methinks you watched her well.   55

A pretty plot, well chosen to build upon.
Now pray, my lord, let's see the devil's writ.
    ⌈*Buckingham gives him the writings*⌉
What have we here?
    He reads the writings
                Why, this is just
Aio Aeacidam, Romanos vincere posse.
These oracles are hardily attained   60
And hardly understood. Come, come, my lord,
The King is now in progress towards Saint Albans;
With him the husband of this lovely lady.
Thither goes these news as fast as horse can carry
    them—
A sorry breakfast for my lord Protector.   65
BUCKINGHAM
Your grace shall give me leave, my lord of York,
To be the post in hope of his reward.
YORK (*returning the writings to Buckingham*)
At your pleasure, my good lord.   ⌈*Exit Buckingham*⌉
(*Calling within*)   Who's within there, ho!
    Enter a servingman
Invite my lords of Salisbury and Warwick
To sup with me tomorrow night. Away.   70
            Exeunt severally

2.1   *Enter King Henry, Queen Margaret with her*
    hawk on her fist, Duke Humphrey of Gloucester,
    Cardinal Beaufort, and the Duke of Suffolk, with
    falconers hollering
QUEEN MARGARET
Believe me, lords, for flying at the brook
I saw not better sport these seven years' day;
Yet, by your leave, the wind was very high,
And, ten to one, old Joan had not gone out.
KING HENRY (*to Gloucester*)
But what a point, my lord, your falcon made,   5
And what a pitch she flew above the rest!
To see how God in all his creatures works!
Yea, man and birds are fain of climbing high.
SUFFOLK
No marvel, an it like your majesty,
My Lord Protector's hawks do tower so well;   10
They know their master loves to be aloft,
And bears his thoughts above his falcon's pitch.
GLOUCESTER
My lord, 'tis but a base ignoble mind
That mounts no higher than a bird can soar.
CARDINAL BEAUFORT
I thought as much; he would be above the clouds.   15
GLOUCESTER
Ay, my lord Cardinal, how think you by that?
Were it not good your grace could fly to heaven?
KING HENRY
The treasury of everlasting joy.
CARDINAL BEAUFORT (*to Gloucester*)
Thy heaven is on earth; thine eyes and thoughts
Beat on a crown, the treasure of thy heart,   20

Pernicious Protector, dangerous peer,
That smooth'st it so with King and common weal!
GLOUCESTER
What, Cardinal? Is your priesthood grown
    peremptory?
Tantaene animis caelestibus irae?
Churchmen so hot? Good uncle, hide such malice   25
With some holiness—can you do it?
SUFFOLK
No malice, sir, no more than well becomes
So good a quarrel and so bad a peer.
GLOUCESTER
As who, my lord?
SUFFOLK   Why, as you, my lord—
An't like your lordly Lord's Protectorship.   30
GLOUCESTER
Why, Suffolk, England knows thine insolence.
QUEEN MARGARET
And thy ambition, Gloucester.
KING HENRY   I prithee peace,
Good Queen, and whet not on these furious peers—
For blessèd are the peacemakers on earth.
CARDINAL BEAUFORT
Let me be blessèd for the peace I make   35
Against this proud Protector with my sword.
    ⌈*Gloucester and Cardinal Beaufort speak privately to
    one another*⌉
GLOUCESTER
Faith, holy uncle, would't were come to that.
CARDINAL BEAUFORT
Marry, when thou dar'st.
GLOUCESTER   Dare? I tell thee, priest,
Plantagenets could never brook the dare!
CARDINAL BEAUFORT
I am Plantagenet as well as thou,   40
And son to John of Gaunt.
GLOUCESTER In bastardy.
CARDINAL BEAUFORT I scorn thy words.
GLOUCESTER
Make up no factious numbers for the matter,
In thine own person answer thy abuse.   45
CARDINAL BEAUFORT
Ay, where thou dar'st not peep; an if thou dar'st,
This evening on the east side of the grove.
KING HENRY
How now, my lords?
CARDINAL BEAUFORT (*aloud*)
                Believe me, cousin Gloucester,
Had not your man put up the fowl so suddenly,
We had had more sport. (*Aside to Gloucester*) Come
    with thy two-hand sword.   50
GLOUCESTER (*aloud*) True, uncle.
    (*Aside to Cardinal Beaufort*)
Are ye advised? The east side of the grove.
CARDINAL BEAUFORT (*aside to Gloucester*)
I am with you.
KING HENRY   Why, how now, uncle Gloucester?

GLOUCESTER
Talking of hawking, nothing else, my lord.
    (*Aside to the Cardinal*)
Now, by God's mother, priest, I'll shave your crown
    for this,   55
Or all my fence shall fail.
CARDINAL BEAUFORT (*aside to Gloucester*)
                Medice, teipsum—
Protector, see to't well; protect yourself.
KING HENRY
The winds grow high; so do your stomachs, lords.
How irksome is this music to my heart!
When such strings jar, what hope of harmony?   60
I pray, my lords, let me compound this strife.
    Enter one crying 'a miracle'
GLOUCESTER What means this noise?
Fellow, what miracle dost thou proclaim?
ONE
A miracle, a miracle!
SUFFOLK
Come to the King—tell him what miracle.   65
ONE (*to King Henry*)
Forsooth, a blind man at Saint Alban's shrine
Within this half-hour hath received his sight—
A man that ne'er saw in his life before.
KING HENRY
Now God be praised, that to believing souls
Gives light in darkness, comfort in despair!   70
    *Enter the Mayor and aldermen of Saint Albans,
    with music, bearing the man, Simpcox, between two
    in a chair. Enter Simpcox's Wife ⌈and other
    townsmen⌉ with them*
CARDINAL BEAUFORT
Here comes the townsmen on procession
To present your highness with the man.
    ⌈*The townsmen kneel*⌉
KING HENRY
Great is his comfort in this earthly vale,
Although by sight his sin be multiplied.
GLOUCESTER (*to the townsmen*)
Stand by, my masters, bring him near the King.   75
His highness' pleasure is to talk with him.
    They ⌈rise and⌉ bear Simpcox before the King
KING HENRY (*to Simpcox*)
Good fellow, tell us here the circumstance,
That we for thee may glorify the Lord.
What, hast thou been long blind and now restored?
SIMPCOX
Born blind, an't please your grace.   80
SIMPCOX'S WIFE   Ay, indeed, was he.
SUFFOLK What woman is this?
SIMPCOX'S WIFE His wife, an't like your worship.
GLOUCESTER Hadst thou been his mother
Thou couldst have better told.
KING HENRY (*to Simpcox*)   Where wert thou born?
SIMPCOX
At Berwick, in the north, an't like your grace.   85

KING HENRY
Poor soul, God's goodness hath been great to thee.
Let never day nor night unhallowed pass,
But still remember what the Lord hath done.
QUEEN MARGARET (*to Simpcox*)
Tell me, good fellow, cam'st thou here by chance,
Or of devotion to this holy shrine?   90
SIMPCOX
God knows, of pure devotion, being called
A hundred times and oftener, in my sleep,
By good Saint Alban, who said, 'Simon, come;
Come offer at my shrine and I will help thee.'
SIMPCOX'S WIFE
Most true, forsooth, and many time and oft   95
Myself have heard a voice to call him so.
CARDINAL BEAUFORT (*to Simpcox*)
What, art thou lame?
SIMPCOX   Ay, God almighty help me.
SUFFOLK
How cam'st thou so?
SIMPCOX   A fall off of a tree.
SIMPCOX'S WIFE (*to Suffolk*)
A plum tree, master.
GLOUCESTER   How long hast thou been blind?
SIMPCOX
O, born so, master.
GLOUCESTER   What, and wouldst climb a tree?
SIMPCOX
But that in all my life, when I was a youth.   101
SIMPCOX'S WIFE (*to Gloucester*)
Too true—and bought his climbing very dear.
GLOUCESTER (*to Simpcox*)
Mass, thou loved'st plums well that wouldst venture
    so.
SIMPCOX
Alas, good master, my wife desired some damsons,
And made me climb with danger of my life.   105
GLOUCESTER ⌈*aside*⌉
A subtle knave, but yet it shall not serve.
(*To Simpcox*) Let me see thine eyes: wink now, now
    open them.
In my opinion yet thou seest not well.
SIMPCOX Yes, master, clear as day, I thank God and Saint
Alban.   110
GLOUCESTER (*pointing*)
Sayst thou me so? What colour is this cloak of?
SIMPCOX
Red, master; red as blood.
GLOUCESTER   Why, that's well said.
(*Pointing*) And his cloak?
SIMPCOX   Why, that's green.
GLOUCESTER (*pointing*)   And what colour's
His hose?
SIMPCOX   Yellow, master; yellow as gold.
GLOUCESTER
And what colour's my gown?
SIMPCOX   Black, sir; coal-black, as jet.
KING HENRY
Why, then, thou know'st what colour jet is of?   116

SUFFOLK
And yet I think jet did he never see.
GLOUCESTER
But cloaks and gowns before this day, a many.
SIMPCOX'S WIFE
Never before this day in all his life.
GLOUCESTER Tell me, sirrah, what's my name?   120
SIMPCOX Alas, master, I know not.
GLOUCESTER (*pointing*) What's his name?
SIMPCOX I know not.
GLOUCESTER (*pointing*) Nor his?
SIMPCOX No, truly, sir.   125
GLOUCESTER (*pointing*) Nor his name?
SIMPCOX No indeed, master.
GLOUCESTER What's thine own name?
SIMPCOX Simon Simpcox, an it please you, master.
GLOUCESTER
Then, Simon, sit thou there the lying'st knave   130
In Christendom. If thou hadst been born blind
Thou mightst as well have known our names as thus
To name the several colours we do wear.
Sight may distinguish colours, but suddenly
To nominate them all—it is impossible.   135
Saint Alban here hath done a miracle.
Would you not think his cunning to be great
That could restore this cripple to his legs again?
SIMPCOX O master, that you could!
GLOUCESTER (*to the Mayor and aldermen*)
My masters of Saint Albans, have you not   140
Beadles in your town, and things called whips?
MAYOR
We have, my lord, an if it please your grace.
GLOUCESTER Then send for one presently.
MAYOR (*to a townsman*)
Sirrah, go fetch the beadle hither straight.   *Exit one*
GLOUCESTER
Bring me a stool.
        A stool is brought
(*To Simpcox*)   Now, sirrah, if you mean   145
To save yourself from whipping, leap me o'er
This stool and run away.
SIMPCOX   Alas, master,
I am not able even to stand alone.
You go about to torture me in vain.
        Enter a Beadle with whips
GLOUCESTER
Well, sirrah, we must have you find your legs.   150
(*To the Beadle*) Whip him till he leap over that same
    stool.
BEADLE I will, my lord.
(*To Simpcox*) Come on, sirrah, off with your doublet
    quickly.
SIMPCOX Alas, master, what shall I do? I am not able to
stand.   155
        *After the Beadle hath hit him once, he leaps over
        the stool and runs away. ⌈Some of⌉ the townsmen
        follow and cry, 'A miracle! A miracle!'*
KING HENRY
O God, seest thou this and bear'st so long?

12

QUEEN MARGARET
  It made me laugh to see the villain run!
GLOUCESTER ⌈to the Beadle⌉
  Follow the knave, and take this drab away.
SIMPCOX'S WIFE
  Alas, sir, we did it for pure need.
                    ⌈Exit the Beadle with the Wife⌉
GLOUCESTER ⌈to the Mayor⌉
  Let them be whipped through every market-town   160
  Till they come to Berwick, from whence they came.
          Exeunt the Mayor ⌈and any remaining townsmen⌉
CARDINAL BEAUFORT
  Duke Humphrey has done a miracle today.
SUFFOLK
  True: made the lame to leap and fly away.
GLOUCESTER
  But you have done more miracles than I—
  You made, in a day, my lord, whole towns to fly.   165
          Enter the Duke of Buckingham
KING HENRY
  What tidings with our cousin Buckingham?
BUCKINGHAM
  Such as my heart doth tremble to unfold.
  A sort of naughty persons, lewdly bent,
  Under the countenance and confederacy
  Of Lady Eleanor, the Protector's wife,   170
  The ringleader and head of all this rout,
  Have practised dangerously against your state,
  Dealing with witches and with conjurors,
  Whom we have apprehended in the fact,
  Raising up wicked spirits from under ground,   175
  Demanding of King Henry's life and death
  And other of your highness' Privy Council.
  And here's the answer the devil did make to them.
          Buckingham gives King Henry the writings
⌈KING HENRY⌉ (reads)
  'First of the King: what shall of him become?
  The Duke yet lives that Henry shall depose,   180
  But him outlive and die a violent death.'
  God's will be done in all. Well, to the rest.
  (Reads) 'Tell me what fate awaits the Duke of Suffolk?
  By water shall he die, and take his end.'
SUFFOLK ⌈aside⌉
  By water must the Duke of Suffolk die?   185
  It must be so, or else the devil doth lie.
KING HENRY (reads)
  'What shall betide the Duke of Somerset?
  Let him shun castles. Safer shall he be
  Upon the sandy plains than where castles mounted
      stand.'
CARDINAL BEAUFORT (to Gloucester)
  And so, my Lord Protector, by this means   190
  Your lady is forthcoming yet at London.
  (Aside to Gloucester)
  This news, I think, hath turned your weapon's edge.
  'Tis like, my lord, you will not keep your hour.
GLOUCESTER
  Ambitious churchman, leave to afflict my heart.

  Sorrow and grief have vanquished all my powers,   195
  And, vanquished as I am, I yield to thee
  Or to the meanest groom.
KING HENRY
  O God, what mischiefs work the wicked ones,
  Heaping confusion on their own heads thereby!
QUEEN MARGARET
  Gloucester, see here the tainture of thy nest,   200
  And look thyself be faultless, thou wert best.
GLOUCESTER
  Madam, for myself, to heaven I do appeal,
  How I have loved my King and common weal;
  And for my wife, I know not how it stands.
  Sorry I am to hear what I have heard.   205
  Noble she is, but if she have forgot
  Honour and virtue and conversed with such
  As, like to pitch, defile nobility,
  I banish her my bed and company,
  And give her as a prey to law and shame   210
  That hath dishonoured Gloucester's honest name.
KING HENRY
  Well, for this night we will repose us here;
  Tomorrow toward London back again,
  To look into this business thoroughly,
  And call these foul offenders to their answers,   215
  And poise the cause in justice' equal scales,
  Whose beam stands sure, whose rightful cause
      prevails.   Flourish. Exeunt

2.2   Enter the Duke of York and the Earls of Salisbury
       and Warwick
YORK
  Now, my good lords of Salisbury and Warwick,
  Our simple supper ended, give me leave
  In this close walk to satisfy myself
  In craving your opinion of my title,
  Which is infallible, to England's crown.   5
SALISBURY
  My lord, I long to hear it out at full.
WARWICK
  Sweet York, begin, and if thy claim be good,
  The Nevilles are thy subjects to command.
YORK Then thus:
  Edward the Third, my lords, had seven sons: 10
  The first, Edward the Black Prince, Prince of Wales;
  The second, William of Hatfield; and the third,
  Lionel Duke of Clarence; next to whom
  Was John of Gaunt, the Duke of Lancaster;
  The fifth was Edmund Langley, Duke of York;   15
  The sixth was Thomas of Woodstock, Duke of
      Gloucester;
  William of Windsor was the seventh and last.
  Edward the Black Prince died before his father
  And left behind him Richard, his only son,
  Who, after Edward the Third's death, reigned as king
  Till Henry Bolingbroke, Duke of Lancaster,   21
  The eldest son and heir of John of Gaunt,
  Crowned by the name of Henry the Fourth,

Seized on the realm, deposed the rightful king,
Sent his poor queen to France from whence she came,
And him to Pomfret; where, as well you know,   26
Harmless Richard was murdered traitorously.
WARWICK (*to Salisbury*)
Father, the Duke of York hath told the truth;
Thus got the house of Lancaster the crown.
YORK
Which now they hold by force and not by right;   30
For Richard, the first son's heir, being dead,
The issue of the next son should have reigned.
SALISBURY
But William of Hatfield died without an heir.
YORK
The third son, Duke of Clarence, from whose line
I claim the crown, had issue Phillipe, a daughter,   35
Who married Edmund Mortimer, Earl of March;
Edmund had issue, Roger, Earl of March;
Roger had issue, Edmund, Anne and Eleanor.
SALISBURY
This Edmund, in the reign of Bolingbroke,
As I have read, laid claim unto the crown,   40
And, but for Owain Glyndŵr, had been king,
Who kept him in captivity till he died.
But to the rest.
YORK   His eldest sister, Anne,
My mother, being heir unto the crown,
Married Richard, Earl of Cambridge, who was son   45
To Edmund Langley, Edward the Third's fifth son.
By her I claim the kingdom: she was heir
To Roger, Earl of March, who was the son
Of Edmund Mortimer, who married Phillipe,
Sole daughter unto Lionel, Duke of Clarence.   50
So if the issue of the elder son
Succeed before the younger, I am king.
WARWICK
What plain proceedings is more plain than this?
Henry doth claim the crown from John of Gaunt,
The fourth son; York claims it from the third: 55
Till Lionel's issue fails, John's should not reign.
It fails not yet, but flourishes in thee
And in thy sons, fair slips of such a stock.
Then, father Salisbury, kneel we together,
And in this private plot be we the first   60
That shall salute our rightful sovereign
With honour of his birthright to the crown.
SALISBURY *and* WARWICK (*kneeling*)
Long live our sovereign Richard, England's king!
YORK
We thank you, lords;
⌜*Salisbury and Warwick rise*⌝
          but I am not your king
Till I be crowned, and that my sword be stained   65
With heart-blood of the house of Lancaster—
And that's not suddenly to be performed,
But with advice and silent secrecy.
Do you, as I do, in these dangerous days,
Wink at the Duke of Suffolk's insolence,   70
At Beaufort's pride, at Somerset's ambition,

At Buckingham, and all the crew of them,
Till they have snared the shepherd of the flock,
That virtuous prince, the good Duke Humphrey.
'Tis that they seek, and they, in seeking that,   75
Shall find their deaths, if York can prophesy.
SALISBURY
My lord, break off—we know your mind at full.
WARWICK
My heart assures me that the Earl of Warwick
Shall one day make the Duke of York a king.
YORK
And Neville, this I do assure myself—   80
Richard shall live to make the Earl of Warwick
The greatest man in England but the King.   *Exeunt*

2.3   *Sound trumpets. Enter King Henry and state, with
          guard, to banish the Duchess: King Henry and
          Queen Margaret, Duke Humphrey of Gloucester, the
          Duke of Suffolk ⌜and the Duke of Buckingham,
          Cardinal Beaufort⌝, and, led with officers, Dame
          Eleanor Cobham the Duchess, Margery Jordan the
          witch, John Southwell and Sir John Hume the two
          priests, and Roger Bolingbroke the conjuror; ⌜then
          enter to them⌝ the Duke of York and the Earls of
          Salisbury ⌜and Warwick⌝*
KING HENRY (*to the Duchess*)
Stand forth, Dame Eleanor Cobham, Gloucester's wife.
          She comes forward
In sight of God and us your guilt is great;
Receive the sentence of the law for sins
Such as by God's book are adjudged to death.
(*To the Witch, Southwell, Hume, and Bolingbroke*)
You four, from hence to prison back again;   5
From thence, unto the place of execution.
The witch in Smithfield shall be burned to ashes,
And you three shall be strangled on the gallows.
          ⌜*Exeunt Witch, Southwell, Hume, and
                    Bolingbroke, guarded*⌝
(*To the Duchess*)
You, madam, for you are more nobly born,
Despoilèd of your honour in your life,   10
Shall, after three days' open penance done,
Live in your country here in banishment
With Sir John Stanley in the Isle of Man.
DUCHESS
Welcome is banishment; welcome were my death.
GLOUCESTER
Eleanor, the law, thou seest, hath judgèd thee;   15
I cannot justify whom the law condemns.
          ⌜*Exit the Duchess, guarded*⌝
Mine eyes are full of tears, my heart of grief.
Ah, Humphrey, this dishonour in thine age
Will bring thy head with sorrow to the grave.
(*To King Henry*)
I beseech your majesty, give me leave to go.   20
Sorrow would solace, and mine age would ease.
KING HENRY
Stay, Humphrey Duke of Gloucester. Ere thou go,
Give up thy staff. Henry will to himself

14

Protector be; and God shall be my hope,
My stay, my guide, and lantern to my feet.   25
And go in peace, Humphrey, no less beloved
Than when thou wert Protector to thy King.

QUEEN MARGARET
I see no reason why a king of years
Should be to be protected like a child.
God and King Henry govern England's helm!   30
Give up your staff, sir, and the King his realm.

GLOUCESTER
My staff? Here, noble Henry, is my staff.
As willingly do I the same resign
As erst thy father Henry made it mine;
And even as willing at thy feet I leave it   35
As others would ambitiously receive it.
He lays the staff at King Henry's feet
Farewell, good King. When I am dead and gone,
May honourable peace attend thy throne.   *Exit*

QUEEN MARGARET
Why, now is Henry King and Margaret Queen,
And Humphrey Duke of Gloucester scarce himself,   40
That bears so shrewd a maim; two pulls at once—
His lady banished and a limb lopped off.
She picks up the staff
This staff of honour raught, there let it stand
Where it best fits to be, in Henry's hand.
She gives the staff to King Henry

SUFFOLK
Thus droops this lofty pine and hangs his sprays;   45
Thus Eleanor's pride dies in her youngest days.

YORK
Lords, let him go. Please it your majesty,
This is the day appointed for the combat,
And ready are the appellant and defendant—
The armourer and his man—to enter the lists,   50
So please your highness to behold the fight.

QUEEN MARGARET
Ay, good my lord, for purposely therefor
Left I the court to see this quarrel tried.

KING HENRY
A God's name, see the lists and all things fit;
Here let them end it, and God defend the right.   55

YORK
I never saw a fellow worse bestead,
Or more afraid to fight, than is the appellant,
The servant of this armourer, my lords.
Enter at one door Horner the armourer and his
Neighbours, drinking to him so much that he is
drunken; and he enters with a drummer before him
and ⌈carrying⌉ his staff with a sandbag fastened to
it. Enter at the other door Peter his man, also with
a drummer and a staff with sandbag, and Prentices
drinking to him

FIRST NEIGHBOUR (*offering drink to Horner*) Here, neighbour
Horner, I drink to you in a cup of sack, and fear not,
neighbour, you shall do well enough.   61

SECOND NEIGHBOUR (*offering drink to Horner*) And here,
neighbour, here's a cup of charneco.

THIRD NEIGHBOUR (*offering drink to Horner*) Here's a pot of
good double beer, neighbour, drink and be merry, and
fear not your man.   66

HORNER ⌈*accepting the offers of drink*⌉ Let it come, i'faith
I'll pledge you all, and a fig for Peter.

FIRST PRENTICE (*offering drink to Peter*) Here, Peter, I drink
to thee, and be not afeard.   70

SECOND PRENTICE (*offering drink to Peter*) Here, Peter, here's
a pint of claret wine for thee.

THIRD PRENTICE (*offering drink to Peter*) And here's a quart
for me, and be merry, Peter, and fear not thy master.
Fight for credit of the prentices!   75

PETER ⌈*refusing the offers of drink*⌉ I thank you all. Drink
and pray for me, I pray you, for I think I have taken
my last draught in this world. Here, Robin, an if I die,
I give thee my apron; and, Will, thou shalt have my
hammer; and here, Tom, take all the money that I
have. O Lord bless me, I pray God, for I am never able
to deal with my master, he hath learned so much fence
already.

SALISBURY Come, leave your drinking, and fall to blows.
(*To Peter*) Sirrah, what's thy name?   85

PETER Peter, forsooth.

SALISBURY Peter? What more?

PETER Thump.

SALISBURY Thump! Then see that thou thump thy master
well.   90

HORNER Masters, I am come hither, as it were, upon my
man's instigation, to prove him a knave and myself an
honest man; and touching the Duke of York, I will
take my death I never meant him any ill, nor the King,
nor the Queen; and therefore, Peter, have at thee with
a downright blow.   96

YORK
Dispatch; this knave's tongue begins to double.
Sound trumpets an alarum to the combatants. They
fight and Peter hits Horner on the head and strikes
him down

HORNER Hold, Peter, hold—I confess, I confess treason.
He dies

YORK (*to an attendant, pointing to Horner*) Take away his
weapon. (*To Peter*) Fellow, thank God and the good
wine in thy master's wame.   101

PETER ⌈*kneeling*⌉ O God, have I overcome mine enemy in
this presence? O, Peter, thou hast prevailed in right.

KING HENRY (*to attendants, pointing to Horner*)
Go, take hence that traitor from our sight,
For by his death we do perceive his guilt.   105
And God in justice hath revealed to us
The truth and innocence of this poor fellow,
Which he had thought to have murdered wrongfully.
(*To Peter*) Come, fellow, follow us for thy reward.
Sound a flourish. Exeunt, some carrying
Horner's body

2.4   *Enter Duke Humphrey of Gloucester and his men*
     in mourning cloaks

GLOUCESTER
Thus sometimes hath the brightest day a cloud;
And after summer evermore succeeds

Barren winter, with his wrathful nipping cold;
So cares and joys abound as seasons fleet.
Sirs, what's o'clock?   5
SERVANT Ten, my lord.
GLOUCESTER
    Ten is the hour that was appointed me
    To watch the coming of my punished Duchess;
    Uneath may she endure the flinty streets,
    To tread them with her tender-feeling feet.   10
    Sweet Nell, ill can thy noble mind abrook
    The abject people gazing on thy face
    With envious looks, laughing at thy shame,
    That erst did follow thy proud chariot wheels
    When thou didst ride in triumph through the streets.
    But soft, I think she comes; and I'll prepare   16
    My tear-stained eyes to see her miseries.
        Enter the Duchess, Dame Eleanor Cobham, barefoot,
        with a white sheet about her, written verses pinned
        on her back, and carrying a wax candle in her
        hand; she is accompanied by the ⌈two Sheriffs⌉ of
        London, and Sir John Stanley, and officers with bills
        and halberds
SERVANT (*to Gloucester*)
    So please your grace, we'll take her from the sheriffs.
GLOUCESTER
    No, stir not for your lives, let her pass by.
DUCHESS
    Come you, my lord, to see my open shame?   20
    Now thou dost penance too. Look how they gaze,
    See how the giddy multitude do point
    And nod their heads, and throw their eyes on thee.
    Ah, Gloucester, hide thee from their hateful looks,
    And, in thy closet pent up, rue my shame,   25
    And ban thine enemies—both mine and thine.
GLOUCESTER
    Be patient, gentle Nell; forget this grief.
DUCHESS
    Ah, Gloucester, teach me to forget myself;
    For whilst I think I am thy married wife,
    And thou a prince, Protector of this land,   30
    Methinks I should not thus be led along,
    Mailed up in shame, with papers on my back,
    And followed with a rabble that rejoice
    To see my tears and hear my deep-fet groans.
    The ruthless flint doth cut my tender feet,   35
    And when I start, the envious people laugh,
    And bid me be advisèd how I tread.
    Ah, Humphrey, can I bear this shameful yoke?
    Trowest thou that e'er I'll look upon the world,
    Or count them happy that enjoys the sun?   40
    No, dark shall be my light, and night my day;
    To think upon my pomp shall be my hell.
    Sometime I'll say I am Duke Humphrey's wife,
    And he a prince and ruler of the land;
    Yet so he ruled, and such a prince he was,   45
    As he stood by whilst I, his forlorn Duchess,
    Was made a wonder and a pointing stock
    To every idle rascal follower.

But be thou mild and blush not at my shame,
Nor stir at nothing till the axe of death   50
Hang over thee, as sure it shortly will.
For Suffolk, he that can do all in all
With her that hateth thee and hates us all,
And York, and impious Beaufort that false priest,
Have all limed bushes to betray thy wings,   55
And fly thou now thou canst, they'll tangle thee.
But fear not thou until thy foot be snared,
Nor never seek prevention of thy foes.
GLOUCESTER
    Ah, Nell, forbear; thou aimest all awry.
    I must offend before I be attainted,   60
    And had I twenty times so many foes,
    And each of them had twenty times their power,
    All these could not procure me any scathe
    So long as I am loyal, true, and crimeless.
    Wouldst have me rescue thee from this reproach?   65
    Why, yet thy scandal were not wiped away,
    But I in danger for the breach of law.
    Thy greatest help is quiet, gentle Nell.
    I pray thee sort thy heart to patience.
    These few days' wonder will be quickly worn.   70
        Enter a Herald
HERALD I summon your grace to his majesty's parliament
    holden at Bury the first of this next month.
GLOUCESTER
    And my consent ne'er asked herein before?
    This is close dealing. Well, I will be there.   *Exit Herald*
    My Nell, I take my leave; and, Master Sheriff,   75
    Let not her penance exceed the King's commission.
⌈FIRST⌉ SHERIFF
    An't please your grace, here my commission stays,
    And Sir John Stanley is appointed now
    To take her with him to the Isle of Man.
GLOUCESTER
    Must you, Sir John, protect my lady here?   80
STANLEY
    So am I given in charge, may't please your grace.
GLOUCESTER
    Entreat her not the worse in that I pray
    You use her well. The world may laugh again,
    And I may live to do you kindness if
    You do it her. And so, Sir John, farewell.   85
        ⌈*Gloucester begins to leave*⌉
DUCHESS
    What, gone, my lord, and bid me not farewell?
GLOUCESTER
    Witness my tears—I cannot stay to speak.
        Exeunt Gloucester and his men
DUCHESS
    Art thou gone too? All comfort go with thee,
    For none abides with me. My joy is death—
    Death, at whose name I oft have been afeard,   90
    Because I wished this world's eternity.
    Stanley, I prithee go and take me hence.
    I care not whither, for I beg no favour,
    Only convey me where thou art commanded.

STANLEY
  Why, madam, that is to the Isle of Man,   95
  There to be used according to your state.
DUCHESS
  That's bad enough, for I am but reproach;
  And shall I then be used reproachfully?
STANLEY
  Like to a duchess and Duke Humphrey's lady,
  According to that state you shall be used.   100
DUCHESS
  Sheriff, farewell, and better than I fare,
  Although thou hast been conduct of my shame.
⌈FIRST⌉ SHERIFF
  It is my office, and, madam, pardon me.
DUCHESS
  Ay, ay, farewell—thy office is discharged.
                         ⌈*Exeunt Sheriffs*⌉
  Come, Stanley, shall we go?   105
STANLEY
  Madam, your penance done, throw off this sheet,
  And go we to attire you for our journey.
DUCHESS
  My shame will not be shifted with my sheet—
  No, it will hang upon my richest robes
  And show itself, attire me how I can.   110
  Go, lead the way, I long to see my prison.   *Exeunt*

3.1   *Sound a sennet. Enter to the parliament: enter two*
      heralds before, then the Dukes of Buckingham and
      Suffolk, and then the Duke of York and Cardinal
      Beaufort, and then King Henry and Queen
      Margaret, and then the Earls of Salisbury and
      Warwick, ⌈*with attendants*⌉
KING HENRY
  I muse my lord of Gloucester is not come.
  'Tis not his wont to be the hindmost man,
  Whate'er occasion keeps him from us now.
QUEEN MARGARET
  Can you not see, or will ye not observe,
  The strangeness of his altered countenance?   5
  With what a majesty he bears himself?
  How insolent of late is he become?
  How proud, how peremptory, and unlike himself?
  We know the time since he was mild and affable,
  And if we did but glance a far-off look,   10
  Immediately he was upon his knee,
  That all the court admired him for submission.
  But meet him now, and be it in the morn
  When everyone will give the time of day,
  He knits his brow, and shows an angry eye,   15
  And passeth by with stiff unbowèd knee,
  Disdaining duty that to us belongs.
  Small curs are not regarded when they grin,
  But great men tremble when the lion roars—
  And Humphrey is no little man in England.   20
  First, note that he is near you in descent,
  And, should you fall, he is the next will mount.
  Meseemeth then it is no policy,
  Respecting what a rancorous mind he bears

  And his advantage following your decease,   25
  That he should come about your royal person,
  Or be admitted to your highness' Council.
  By flattery hath he won the commons' hearts,
  And when he please to make commotion,
  'Tis to be feared they all will follow him.   30
  Now 'tis the spring, and weeds are shallow-rooted;
  Suffer them now, and they'll o'ergrow the garden,
  And choke the herbs for want of husbandry.
  The reverent care I bear unto my lord
  Made me collect these dangers in the Duke.   35
  If it be fond, call it a woman's fear;
  Which fear, if better reasons can supplant,
  I will subscribe and say I wronged the Duke.
  My lord of Suffolk, Buckingham, and York,
  Reprove my allegation if you can,   40
  Or else conclude my words effectual.
SUFFOLK
  Well hath your highness seen into this Duke,
  And had I first been put to speak my mind,
  I think I should have told your grace's tale.
  The Duchess by his subornation,   45
  Upon my life, began her devilish practices;
  Or if he were not privy to those faults,
  Yet by reputing of his high descent,
  As next the King he was successive heir,
  And such high vaunts of his nobility,   50
  Did instigate the bedlam brainsick Duchess
  By wicked means to frame our sovereign's fall.
  Smooth runs the water where the brook is deep,
  And in his simple show he harbours treason.
  The fox barks not when he would steal the lamb.   55
  (*To King Henry*)
  No, no, my sovereign, Gloucester is a man
  Unsounded yet, and full of deep deceit.
CARDINAL BEAUFORT (*to King Henry*)
  Did he not, contrary to form of law,
  Devise strange deaths for small offences done?
YORK (*to King Henry*)
  And did he not, in his Protectorship,   60
  Levy great sums of money through the realm
  For soldiers' pay in France, and never sent it,
  By means whereof the towns each day revolted?
BUCKINGHAM (*to King Henry*)
  Tut, these are petty faults to faults unknown,
  Which time will bring to light in smooth Duke
      Humphrey.   65
KING HENRY
  My lords, at once: the care you have of us
  To mow down thorns that would annoy our foot
  Is worthy praise, but shall I speak my conscience?
  Our kinsman Gloucester is as innocent
  From meaning treason to our royal person   70
  As is the sucking lamb or harmless dove.
  The Duke is virtuous, mild, and too well given
  To dream on evil or to work my downfall.
QUEEN MARGARET
  Ah, what's more dangerous than this fond affiance?
  Seems he a dove? His feathers are but borrowed,   75

For he's disposèd as the hateful raven.
Is he a lamb? His skin is surely lent him,
For he's inclined as is the ravenous wolf.
Who cannot steal a shape that means deceit?
Take heed, my lord, the welfare of us all   80
Hangs on the cutting short that fraudful man.

Enter the Duke of Somerset

SOMERSET ⌈*kneeling before King Henry*⌉
All health unto my gracious sovereign.

KING HENRY
Welcome, Lord Somerset. What news from France?

SOMERSET
That all your interest in those territories
Is utterly bereft you—all is lost.   85

KING HENRY
Cold news, Lord Somerset; but God's will be done.
⌈*Somerset rises*⌉

YORK (*aside*)
Cold news for me, for I had hope of France,
As firmly as I hope for fertile England.
Thus are my blossoms blasted in the bud,
And caterpillars eat my leaves away.   90
But I will remedy this gear ere long,
Or sell my title for a glorious grave.

Enter Duke Humphrey of Gloucester

GLOUCESTER ⌈*kneeling before King Henry*⌉
All happiness unto my lord the King.
Pardon, my liege, that I have stayed so long.

SUFFOLK
Nay, Gloucester, know that thou art come too soon 95
Unless thou wert more loyal than thou art.
I do arrest thee of high treason here.

GLOUCESTER ⌈*rising*⌉
Well, Suffolk's Duke, thou shalt not see me blush,
Nor change my countenance for this arrest.
A heart unspotted is not easily daunted.   100
The purest spring is not so free from mud
As I am clear from treason to my sovereign.
Who can accuse me? Wherein am I guilty?

YORK
'Tis thought, my lord, that you took bribes of France,
And, being Protector, stayed the soldiers' pay,   105
By means whereof his highness hath lost France.

GLOUCESTER
Is it but thought so? What are they that think it?
I never robbed the soldiers of their pay,
Nor ever had one penny bribe from France.
So help me God, as I have watched the night,   110
Ay, night by night, in studying good for England,
That doit that e'er I wrested from the King,
Or any groat I hoarded to my use,
Be brought against me at my trial day!
No: many a pound of mine own proper store,   115
Because I would not tax the needy commons,
Have I dispursèd to the garrisons,
And never asked for restitution.

CARDINAL BEAUFORT
It serves you well, my lord, to say so much.

GLOUCESTER
I say no more than truth, so help me God.   120

YORK
In your Protectorship you did devise
Strange tortures for offenders, never heard of,
That England was defamed by tyranny.

GLOUCESTER
Why, 'tis well known that whiles I was Protector
Pity was all the fault that was in me,   125
For I should melt at an offender's tears,
And lowly words were ransom for their fault.
Unless it were a bloody murderer,
Or foul felonious thief that fleeced poor passengers,
I never gave them condign punishment.   130
Murder, indeed—that bloody sin—I tortured
Above the felon or what trespass else.

SUFFOLK
My lord, these faults are easy, quickly answerèd,
But mightier crimes are laid unto your charge
Whereof you cannot easily purge yourself.   135
I do arrest you in his highness' name,
And here commit you to my good lord Cardinal
To keep until your further time of trial.

KING HENRY
My lord of Gloucester, 'tis my special hope
That you will clear yourself from all suspense.   140
My conscience tells me you are innocent.

GLOUCESTER
Ah, gracious lord, these days are dangerous.
Virtue is choked with foul ambition,
And charity chased hence by rancour's hand.
Foul subornation is predominant,   145
And equity exiled your highness' land.
I know their complot is to have my life,
And if my death might make this island happy
And prove the period of their tyranny,
I would expend it with all willingness.   150
But mine is made the prologue to their play,
For thousands more that yet suspect no peril
Will not conclude their plotted tragedy.
Beaufort's red sparkling eyes blab his heart's malice,
And Suffolk's cloudy brow his stormy hate;   155
Sharp Buckingham unburdens with his tongue
The envious load that lies upon his heart;
And doggèd York that reaches at the moon,
Whose overweening arm I have plucked back,
By false accuse doth level at my life.   160
(*To Queen Margaret*)
And you, my sovereign lady, with the rest,
Causeless have laid disgraces on my head,
And with your best endeavour have stirred up
My liefest liege to be mine enemy.
Ay, all of you have laid your heads together—   165
Myself had notice of your conventicles—
And all to make away my guiltless life.
I shall not want false witness to condemn me,
Nor store of treasons to augment my guilt.
The ancient proverb will be well effected: 170
'A staff is quickly found to beat a dog'.

CARDINAL BEAUFORT (*to King Henry*)
My liege, his railing is intolerable.
If those that care to keep your royal person
From treason's secret knife and traitor's rage
Be thus upbraided, chid, and rated at,   175
And the offender granted scope of speech,
'Twill make them cool in zeal unto your grace.
SUFFOLK (*to King Henry*)
Hath he not twit our sovereign lady here
With ignominious words, though clerkly couched,
As if she had suborned some to swear   180
False allegations to o'erthrow his state?
QUEEN MARGARET
But I can give the loser leave to chide.
GLOUCESTER
Far truer spoke than meant. I lose indeed;
Beshrew the winners, for they played me false!
And well such losers may have leave to speak.   185
BUCKINGHAM (*to King Henry*)
He'll wrest the sense, and hold us here all day.
Lord Cardinal, he is your prisoner.
CARDINAL BEAUFORT (*to some of his attendants*)
Sirs, take away the Duke and guard him sure.
GLOUCESTER
Ah, thus King Henry throws away his crutch
Before his legs be firm to bear his body.   190
Thus is the shepherd beaten from thy side,
And wolves are gnarling who shall gnaw thee first.
Ah, that my fear were false; ah, that it were!
For, good King Henry, thy decay I fear.
Exit Gloucester, guarded by the Cardinal's men
KING HENRY
My lords, what to your wisdoms seemeth best   195
Do or undo, as if ourself were here.
QUEEN MARGARET
What, will your highness leave the Parliament?
KING HENRY
Ay, Margaret, my heart is drowned with grief,
Whose flood begins to flow within mine eyes,
My body round engirt with misery;   200
For what's more miserable than discontent?
Ah, uncle Humphrey, in thy face I see
The map of honour, truth, and loyalty;
And yet, good Humphrey, is the hour to come
That e'er I proved thee false, or feared thy faith.   205
What louring star now envies thy estate,
That these great lords and Margaret our Queen
Do seek subversion of thy harmless life?
Thou never didst them wrong, nor no man wrong.
And as the butcher takes away the calf,   210
And binds the wretch, and beats it when it strains,
Bearing it to the bloody slaughterhouse,
Even so remorseless have they borne him hence;
And as the dam runs lowing up and down,
Looking the way her harmless young one went,   215
And can do naught but wail her darling's loss;
Even so myself bewails good Gloucester's case
With sad unhelpful tears, and with dimmed eyes
Look after him, and cannot do him good,

So mighty are his vowèd enemies.   220
His fortunes I will weep, and 'twixt each groan,
Say 'Who's a traitor? Gloucester, he is none'.
Exit ⌈with Salisbury and Warwick⌉
QUEEN MARGARET
Free lords, cold snow melts with the sun's hot beams.
Henry my lord is cold in great affairs,
Too full of foolish pity; and Gloucester's show   225
Beguiles him as the mournful crocodile
With sorrow snares relenting passengers,
Or as the snake rolled in a flow'ring bank
With shining chequered slough doth sting a child
That for the beauty thinks it excellent.   230
Believe me, lords, were none more wise than I—
And yet herein I judge mine own wit good—
This Gloucester should be quickly rid the world
To rid us from the fear we have of him.
CARDINAL BEAUFORT
That he should die is worthy policy;   235
But yet we want a colour for his death.
'Tis meet he be condemned by course of law.
SUFFOLK
But, in my mind, that were no policy.
The King will labour still to save his life,
The commons haply rise to save his life;   240
And yet we have but trivial argument
More than mistrust that shows him worthy death.
YORK
So that, by this, you would not have him die?
SUFFOLK
Ah, York, no man alive so fain as I.
YORK (*aside*)
'Tis York that hath more reason for his death.   245
(*Aloud*) But my lord Cardinal, and you my lord of
    Suffolk,
Say as you think, and speak it from your souls.
Were't not all one an empty eagle were set
To guard the chicken from a hungry kite,
As place Duke Humphrey for the King's Protector?   250
QUEEN MARGARET
So the poor chicken should be sure of death.
SUFFOLK
Madam, 'tis true; and were't not madness then
To make the fox surveyor of the fold,
Who being accused a crafty murderer,
His guilt should be but idly posted over   255
Because his purpose is not executed?
No—let him die in that he is a fox,
By nature proved an enemy to the flock,
Before his chaps be stained with crimson blood,
As Humphrey, proved by reasons, to my liege.   260
And do not stand on quillets how to slay him;
Be it by gins, by snares, by subtlety,
Sleeping or waking, 'tis no matter how,
So he be dead; for that is good conceit
Which mates him first that first intends deceit.   265
QUEEN MARGARET
Thrice-noble Suffolk, 'tis resolutely spoke.

SUFFOLK
Not resolute, except so much were done;
For things are often spoke and seldom meant;
But that my heart accordeth with my tongue,
Seeing the deed is meritorious,　　　　　　　270
And to preserve my sovereign from his foe,
Say but the word and I will be his priest.

CARDINAL BEAUFORT
But I would have him dead, my lord of Suffolk,
Ere you can take due orders for a priest.
Say you consent and censure well the deed,　　275
And I'll provide his executioner;
I tender so the safety of my liege.

SUFFOLK
Here is my hand; the deed is worthy doing.

QUEEN MARGARET And so say I.

YORK
And I. And now we three have spoke it,　　　280
It skills not greatly who impugns our doom.
　　　Enter a Post

POST
Great lord, from Ireland am I come amain
To signify that rebels there are up
And put the Englishmen unto the sword.
Send succours, lords, and stop the rage betime,　285
Before the wound do grow uncurable;
For, being green, there is great hope of help.　[*Exit*]

CARDINAL BEAUFORT
A breach that craves a quick expedient stop!
What counsel give you in this weighty cause?

YORK
That Somerset be sent as regent thither.　　　290
'Tis meet that lucky ruler be employed—
Witness the fortune he hath had in France.

SOMERSET
If York, with all his far-fet policy,
Had been the regent there instead of me,
He never would have stayed in France so long.　295

YORK
No, not to lose it all as thou hast done.
I rather would have lost my life betimes
Than bring a burden of dishonour home
By staying there so long till all were lost.
Show me one scar charactered on thy skin.　　300
Men's flesh preserved so whole do seldom win.

QUEEN MARGARET
Nay, then, this spark will prove a raging fire
If wind and fuel be brought to feed it with.
No more, good York; sweet Somerset, be still.
Thy fortune, York, hadst thou been regent there,　305
Might happily have proved far worse than his.

YORK
What, worse than naught? Nay, then a shame take
　　all!

SOMERSET
And, in the number, thee that wishest shame.

CARDINAL BEAUFORT
My lord of York, try what your fortune is.

Th'uncivil kerns of Ireland are in arms　　　310
And temper clay with blood of Englishmen.
To Ireland will you lead a band of men
Collected choicely, from each county some,
And try your hap against the Irishmen?

YORK
I will, my lord, so please his majesty.　　　315

SUFFOLK
Why, our authority is his consent,
And what we do establish he confirms.
Then, noble York, take thou this task in hand.

YORK
I am content. Provide me soldiers, lords,
Whiles I take order for mine own affairs.　　320

SUFFOLK
A charge, Lord York, that I will see performed.
But now return we to the false Duke Humphrey.

CARDINAL BEAUFORT
No more of him—for I will deal with him
That henceforth he shall trouble us no more.
And so, break off; the day is almost spent.　　325
Lord Suffolk, you and I must talk of that event.

YORK
My lord of Suffolk, within fourteen days
At Bristol I expect my soldiers;
For there I'll ship them all for Ireland.

SUFFOLK
I'll see it truly done, my lord of York.　　　330
　　　　　　　　　　Exeunt all but York

YORK
Now, York, or never, steel thy fearful thoughts,
And change misdoubt to resolution.
Be that thou hop'st to be, or what thou art
Resign to death; it is not worth th'enjoying.
Let pale-faced fear keep with the mean-born man　335
And find no harbour in a royal heart.
Faster than springtime showers comes thought on
　　thought,
And not a thought but thinks on dignity.
My brain, more busy than the labouring spider,
Weaves tedious snares to trap mine enemies.　　340
Well, nobles, well: 'tis politicly done
To send me packing with an host of men.
I fear me you but warm the starvèd snake,
Who, cherished in your breasts, will sting your hearts.
'Twas men I lacked, and you will give them me.　345
I take it kindly. Yet be well assured
You put sharp weapons in a madman's hands.
Whiles I in Ireland nurse a mighty band,
I will stir up in England some black storm
Shall blow ten thousand souls to heaven or hell,　350
And this fell tempest shall not cease to rage
Until the golden circuit on my head
Like to the glorious sun's transparent beams
Do calm the fury of this mad-bred flaw.
And for a minister of my intent,　　　　　　355
I have seduced a headstrong Kentishman,
John Cade of Ashford,

To make commotion, as full well he can,
Under the title of John Mortimer.
In Ireland have I seen this stubborn Cade   360
Oppose himself against a troop of kerns,
And fought so long till that his thighs with darts
Were almost like a sharp-quilled porcupine;
And in the end, being rescued, I have seen
Him caper upright like a wild Morisco,   365
Shaking the bloody darts as he his bells.
Full often like a shag-haired crafty kern
Hath he conversèd with the enemy
And, undiscovered, come to me again
And given me notice of their villainies.   370
This devil here shall be my substitute,
For that John Mortimer, which now is dead,
In face, in gait, in speech, he doth resemble.
By this I shall perceive the commons' mind,
How they affect the house and claim of York.   375
Say he be taken, racked, and torturèd—
I know no pain they can inflict upon him
Will make him say I moved him to those arms.
Say that he thrive, as 'tis great like he will—
Why then from Ireland come I with my strength   380
And reap the harvest which that coistrel sowed.
For Humphrey being dead, as he shall be,
And Henry put apart, the next for me.   *Exit*

3.2   [*The curtains are drawn apart, revealing Duke*
        Humphrey of Gloucester in his bed with two men
        lying on his breast, smothering him in his bed]
FIRST MURDERER (*to the Second Murderer*)
   Run to my lord of Suffolk—let him know
   We have dispatched the Duke as he commanded.
SECOND MURDERER
   O that it were to do! What have we done?
   Didst ever hear a man so penitent?
        Enter the Duke of Suffolk
FIRST MURDERER   Here comes my lord.   5
SUFFOLK
   Now, sirs, have you dispatched this thing?
FIRST MURDERER   Ay, my good lord, he's dead.
SUFFOLK
   Why, that's well said. Go, get you to my house.
   I will reward you for this venturous deed.
   The King and all the peers are here at hand.   10
   Have you laid fair the bed? Is all things well,
   According as I gave directions?
FIRST MURDERER   'Tis, my good lord.
SUFFOLK
   Then draw the curtains close; away, be gone!
        Exeunt [*the Murderers, drawing the curtains as*
                        they leave]
        Sound trumpets, then enter King Henry and Queen
        Margaret, Cardinal Beaufort, the Duke of Somerset,
        and attendants
KING HENRY [*to Suffolk*]
   Go call our uncle to our presence straight.   15
   Say we intend to try his grace today
   If he be guilty, as 'tis publishèd.

SUFFOLK
   I'll call him presently, my noble lord.   *Exit*
KING HENRY
   Lords, take your places; and, I pray you all,
   Proceed no straiter 'gainst our uncle Gloucester 20
   Than from true evidence, of good esteem,
   He be approved in practice culpable.
QUEEN MARGARET
   God forbid any malice should prevail
   That faultless may condemn a noble man!
   Pray God he may acquit him of suspicion!   25
KING HENRY
   I thank thee, Meg. These words content me much.
        Enter Suffolk
   How now? Why look'st thou pale? Why tremblest
        thou?
   Where is our uncle? What's the matter, Suffolk?
SUFFOLK
   Dead in his bed, my lord—Gloucester is dead.
QUEEN MARGARET   Marry, God forfend!   30
CARDINAL BEAUFORT
   God's secret judgement. I did dream tonight
   The Duke was dumb and could not speak a word.
        King Henry falls to the ground
QUEEN MARGARET
   How fares my lord? Help, lords—the King is dead!
SOMERSET
   Rear up his body; wring him by the nose.
QUEEN MARGARET
   Run, go, help, help! O Henry, ope thine eyes!   35
SUFFOLK
   He doth revive again. Madam, be patient.
KING HENRY
   O heavenly God!
QUEEN MARGARET   How fares my gracious lord?
SUFFOLK
   Comfort, my sovereign; gracious Henry, comfort.
KING HENRY
   What, doth my lord of Suffolk comfort me?
   Came he right now to sing a raven's note   40
   Whose dismal tune bereft my vital powers;
   And thinks he that the chirping of a wren,
   By crying comfort from a hollow breast
   Can chase away the first-conceivèd sound?
   Hide not thy poison with such sugared words.   45
        [*He begins to rise. Suffolk offers to assist him*]
   Lay not thy hands on me—forbear, I say!
   Their touch affrights me as a serpent's sting.
   Thou baleful messenger, out of my sight!
   Upon thy eyeballs murderous tyranny
   Sits in grim majesty to fright the world.   50
   Look not upon me, for thine eyes are wounding—
   Yet do not go away. Come, basilisk,
   And kill the innocent gazer with thy sight.
   For in the shade of death I shall find joy;
   In life, but double death, now Gloucester's dead. 55
QUEEN MARGARET
   Why do you rate my lord of Suffolk thus?
   Although the Duke was enemy to him,

Yet he most Christian-like laments his death.
And for myself, foe as he was to me,
Might liquid tears, or heart-offending groans,   60
Or blood-consuming sighs recall his life,
I would be blind with weeping, sick with groans,
Look pale as primrose with blood-drinking sighs,
And all to have the noble Duke alive.
What know I how the world may deem of me?   65
For it is known we were but hollow friends,
It may be judged I made the Duke away.
So shall my name with slander's tongue be wounded
And princes' courts be filled with my reproach.
This get I by his death. Ay me, unhappy,   70
To be a queen, and crowned with infamy.

KING HENRY
Ah, woe is me for Gloucester, wretched man!

QUEEN MARGARET
Be woe for me, more wretched than he is.
What, dost thou turn away and hide thy face?
I am no loathsome leper—look on me!   75
What, art thou, like the adder, waxen deaf?
Be poisonous too and kill thy forlorn queen.
Is all thy comfort shut in Gloucester's tomb?
Why, then Queen Margaret was ne'er thy joy.
Erect his statuë and worship it,   80
And make my image but an alehouse sign.
Was I for this nigh wrecked upon the sea,
And twice by awkward winds from England's bank
Drove back again unto my native clime?
What boded this, but well forewarning winds   85
Did seem to say, 'Seek not a scorpion's nest,
Nor set no footing on this unkind shore'.
What did I then, but cursed the gentle gusts
And he that loosed them forth their brazen caves,
And bid them blow towards England's blessèd shore,
Or turn our stern upon a dreadful rock.   91
Yet Aeolus would not be a murderer,
But left that hateful office unto thee.
The pretty vaulting sea refused to drown me,
Knowing that thou wouldst have me drowned on
          shore   95
With tears as salt as sea through thy unkindness.
The splitting rocks cow'red in the sinking sands,
And would not dash me with their ragged sides,
Because thy flinty heart, more hard than they,
Might in thy palace perish Margaret.   100
As far as I could ken thy chalky cliffs,
When from thy shore the tempest beat us back,
I stood upon the hatches in the storm,
And when the dusky sky began to rob
My earnest-gaping sight of thy land's view,   105
I took a costly jewel from my neck—
A heart it was, bound in with diamonds—
And threw it towards thy land. The sea received it,
And so I wished thy body might my heart.
And even with this I lost fair England's view,   110
And bid mine eyes be packing with my heart,
And called them blind and dusky spectacles

For losing ken of Albion's wishèd coast.
How often have I tempted Suffolk's tongue—
The agent of thy foul inconstancy—   115
To sit and witch me, as Ascanius did,
When he to madding Dido would unfold
His father's acts, commenced in burning Troy!
Am I not witched like her? Or thou not false like him?
Ay me, I can no more. Die, Margaret,   120
For Henry weeps that thou dost live so long.
          *Noise within. Enter the Earls of Warwick and
          Salisbury with many commons*

WARWICK (*to King Henry*)
It is reported, mighty sovereign,
That good Duke Humphrey traitorously is murdered
By Suffolk and the Cardinal Beaufort's means.
The commons, like an angry hive of bees   125
That want their leader, scatter up and down
And care not who they sting in his revenge.
Myself have calmed their spleenful mutiny,
Until they hear the order of his death.

KING HENRY
That he is dead, good Warwick, 'tis too true.   130
But how he died God knows, not Henry.
Enter his chamber, view his breathless corpse,
And comment then upon his sudden death.

WARWICK
That shall I do, my liege.—Stay, Salisbury,
With the rude multitude till I return.   135
          ⌐*Exeunt Warwick at one door, Salisbury and
                    commons at another*⌐

KING HENRY
O thou that judgest all things, stay my thoughts,
My thoughts that labour to persuade my soul
Some violent hands were laid on Humphrey's life.
If my suspect be false, forgive me God,   140
For judgement only doth belong to thee.
Fain would I go to chafe his paly lips
With twenty thousand kisses, and to drain
Upon his face an ocean of salt tears,
To tell my love unto his dumb, deaf trunk,
And with my fingers feel his hand unfeeling.   145
But all in vain are these mean obsequies,
          ⌐*Enter Warwick who draws apart the curtains and
          shows*⌐ *Gloucester dead in his bed. Bed put forth*
And to survey his dead and earthy image,
What were it but to make my sorrow greater?

WARWICK
Come hither, gracious sovereign, view this body.

KING HENRY
That is to see how deep my grave is made: 150
For with his soul fled all my worldly solace,
For seeing him I see my life in death.

WARWICK
As surely as my soul intends to live
With that dread King that took our state upon Him
To free us from his Father's wrathful curse,   155
I do believe that violent hands were laid
Upon the life of this thrice-famèd Duke.

SUFFOLK
A dreadful oath, sworn with a solemn tongue!
What instance gives Lord Warwick for his vow?
WARWICK
See how the blood is settled in his face.   160
Oft have I seen a timely-parted ghost
Of ashy semblance, meagre, pale, and bloodless,
Being all descended to the labouring heart;
Who, in the conflict that it holds with death,
Attracts the same for aidance 'gainst the enemy;   165
Which, with the heart, there cools, and ne'er returneth
To blush and beautify the cheek again.
But see, his face is black and full of blood;
His eyeballs further out than when he lived,
Staring full ghastly like a strangled man;   170
His hair upreared; his nostrils stretched with
          struggling;
His hands abroad displayed, as one that grasped
And tugged for life and was by strength subdued.
Look on the sheets. His hair, you see, is sticking;
His well-proportioned beard made rough and rugged,
Like to the summer's corn by tempest lodged.   176
It cannot be but he was murdered here.
The least of all these signs were probable.
SUFFOLK
Why, Warwick, who should do the Duke to death?
Myself and Beaufort had him in protection,   180
And we, I hope, sir, are no murderers.
WARWICK
But both of you were vowed Duke Humphrey's foes,
(To Cardinal Beaufort)
And you, forsooth, had the good Duke to keep.
'Tis like you would not feast him like a friend;
And 'tis well seen he found an enemy.   185
QUEEN MARGARET
Then you, belike, suspect these noblemen
As guilty of Duke Humphrey's timeless death?
WARWICK
Who finds the heifer dead and bleeding fresh,
And sees fast by a butcher with an axe,
But will suspect 'twas he that made the slaughter?   190
Who finds the partridge in the puttock's nest
But may imagine how the bird was dead,
Although the kite soar with unbloodied beak?
Even so suspicious is this tragedy.
QUEEN MARGARET
Are you the butcher, Suffolk? Where's your knife?   195
Is Beaufort termed a kite? Where are his talons?
SUFFOLK
I wear no knife to slaughter sleeping men.
But here's a vengeful sword, rusted with ease,
That shall be scoured in his rancorous heart
That slanders me with murder's crimson badge.   200
Say, if thou dar'st, proud Lord of Warwickshire,
That I am faulty in Duke Humphrey's death.
          ⌐Exit Cardinal Beaufort assisted by Somerset⌐
WARWICK
What dares not Warwick, if false Suffolk dare him?

QUEEN MARGARET
He dares not calm his contumelious spirit,
Nor cease to be an arrogant controller,   205
Though Suffolk dare him twenty thousand times.
WARWICK
Madam, be still, with reverence may I say,
For every word you speak in his behalf
Is slander to your royal dignity.
SUFFOLK
Blunt-witted lord, ignoble in demeanour!   210
If ever lady wronged her lord so much,
Thy mother took into her blameful bed
Some stern untutored churl, and noble stock
Was graffed with crabtree slip, whose fruit thou art,
And never of the Nevilles' noble race.   215
WARWICK
But that the guilt of murder bucklers thee
And I should rob the deathsman of his fee,
Quitting thee thereby of ten thousand shames,
And that my sovereign's presence makes me mild,
I would, false murd'rous coward, on thy knee   220
Make thee beg pardon for thy passèd speech,
And say it was thy mother that thou meant'st—
That thou thyself wast born in bastardy!
And after all this fearful homage done,
Give thee thy hire and send thy soul to hell,   225
Pernicious blood-sucker of sleeping men!
SUFFOLK
Thou shalt be waking while I shed thy blood,
If from this presence thou dar'st go with me.
WARWICK
Away, even now, or I will drag thee hence.
Unworthy though thou art, I'll cope with thee,   230
And do some service to Duke Humphrey's ghost.
          Exeunt Suffolk and Warwick
KING HENRY
What stronger breastplate than a heart untainted?
Thrice is he armed that hath his quarrel just;
And he but naked, though locked up in steel,
Whose conscience with injustice is corrupted.   235
COMMONS (within) Down with Suffolk! Down with Suffolk!
QUEEN MARGARET What noise is this?
          Enter Suffolk and Warwick with their weapons
          drawn
KING HENRY
Why, how now, lords? Your wrathful weapons drawn
Here in our presence? Dare you be so bold?
Why, what tumultuous clamour have we here?   240
SUFFOLK
The trait'rous Warwick with the men of Bury
Set all upon me, mighty sovereign!
COMMONS (within) Down with Suffolk! Down with Suffolk!
          Enter from the commons the Earl of Salisbury
SALISBURY (to the commons, within)
Sirs, stand apart. The King shall know your mind.
(To King Henry)
Dread lord, the commons send you word by me   245
Unless Lord Suffolk straight be done to death,

23

Or banishèd fair England's territories,
They will by violence tear him from your palace
And torture him with grievous ling'ring death.
They say, by him the good Duke Humphrey died;   250
They say, in him they fear your highness' death;
And mere instinct of love and loyalty,
Free from a stubborn opposite intent,
As being thought to contradict your liking,
Makes them thus forward in his banishment.   255
They say, in care of your most royal person,
That if your highness should intend to sleep,
And charge that no man should disturb your rest
In pain of your dislike, or pain of death,
Yet, notwithstanding such a strait edict,   260
Were there a serpent seen with forkèd tongue,
That slily glided towards your majesty,
It were but necessary you were waked,
Lest, being suffered in that harmful slumber,
The mortal worm might make the sleep eternal.   265
And therefore do they cry, though you forbid,
That they will guard you, whe'er you will or no,
From such fell serpents as false Suffolk is,
With whose envenomèd and fatal sting
Your loving uncle, twenty times his worth,   270
They say, is shamefully bereft of life.

COMMONS (*within*) An answer from the King, my lord of
Salisbury!

SUFFOLK
'Tis like the commons, rude unpolished hinds,
Could send such message to their sovereign.   275
But you, my lord, were glad to be employed,
To show how quaint an orator you are.
But all the honour Salisbury hath won
Is that he was the Lord Ambassador
Sent from a sort of tinkers to the King.   280

COMMONS (*within*) An answer from the King, or we will
all break in!

KING HENRY
Go, Salisbury, and tell them all from me
I thank them for their tender loving care,
And had I not been 'cited so by them,   285
Yet did I purpose as they do entreat;
For sure my thoughts do hourly prophesy
Mischance unto my state by Suffolk's means.
And therefore by His majesty I swear,
Whose far unworthy deputy I am,   290
He shall not breathe infection in this air
But three days longer, on the pain of death.
                ⌈*Exit Salisbury*⌉

QUEEN MARGARET ⌈*kneeling*⌉
O Henry, let me plead for gentle Suffolk.

KING HENRY
Ungentle Queen, to call him gentle Suffolk.
No more, I say! If thou dost plead for him   295
Thou wilt but add increase unto my wrath.
Had I but said, I would have kept my word;
But when I swear, it is irrevocable.

(*To Suffolk*) If after three days' space thou here beest
     found
On any ground that I am ruler of,   300
The world shall not be ransom for thy life.
Come, Warwick; come, good Warwick, go with me.
I have great matters to impart to thee.
         Exeunt King Henry and Warwick with
         attendants ⌈*who draw the curtains as they*
         leave⌉. *Queen Margaret and Suffolk remain*

QUEEN MARGARET ⌈*rising*⌉
Mischance and sorrow go along with you!
Heart's discontent and sour affliction   305
Be playfellows to keep you company!
There's two of you, the devil make a third,
And threefold vengeance tend upon your steps!

SUFFOLK
Cease, gentle Queen, these execrations,
And let thy Suffolk take his heavy leave.   310

QUEEN MARGARET
Fie, coward woman and soft-hearted wretch!
Hast thou not spirit to curse thine enemies?

SUFFOLK
A plague upon them! Wherefore should I curse them?
Could curses kill, as doth the mandrake's groan,
I would invent as bitter searching terms,   315
As curst, as harsh, and horrible to hear,
Delivered strongly through my fixèd teeth,
With full as many signs of deadly hate,
As lean-faced envy in her loathsome cave.
My tongue should stumble in mine earnest words;   320
Mine eyes should sparkle like the beaten flint;
My hair be fixed on end, as one distraught;
Ay, every joint should seem to curse and ban.
And, even now, my burdened heart would break
Should I not curse them. Poison be their drink!   325
Gall, worse than gall, the daintiest that they taste!
Their sweetest shade a grove of cypress trees!
Their chiefest prospect murd'ring basilisks!
Their softest touch as smart as lizards' stings!
Their music frightful as the serpent's hiss,   330
And boding screech-owls make the consort full!
All the foul terrors in dark-seated hell—

QUEEN MARGARET
Enough, sweet Suffolk, thou torment'st thyself,
And these dread curses, like the sun 'gainst glass,
Or like an overchargèd gun, recoil   335
And turn the force of them upon thyself.

SUFFOLK
You bade me ban, and will you bid me leave?
Now by this ground that I am banished from,
Well could I curse away a winter's night,
Though standing naked on a mountain top,   340
Where biting cold would never let grass grow,
And think it but a minute spent in sport.

QUEEN MARGARET
O let me entreat thee cease. Give me thy hand,
That I may dew it with my mournful tears;
Nor let the rain of heaven wet this place   345

To wash away my woeful monuments.
⌈*She kisses his palm*⌉
O, could this kiss be printed in thy hand
That thou mightst think upon these lips by the seal,
Through whom a thousand sighs are breathed for
　　thee!
So get thee gone, that I may know my grief.　350
'Tis but surmised whiles thou art standing by,
As one that surfeits thinking on a want.
I will repeal thee, or, be well assured,
Adventure to be banishèd myself.
And banishèd I am, if but from thee.　　355
Go, speak not to me; even now be gone!
O, go not yet. Even thus two friends condemned
Embrace, and kiss, and take ten thousand leaves,
Loather a hundred times to part than die.
Yet now farewell, and farewell life with thee.　360

SUFFOLK
Thus is poor Suffolk ten times banishèd—
Once by the King, and three times thrice by thee.
'Tis not the land I care for, wert thou thence,
A wilderness is populous enough,
So Suffolk had thy heavenly company.　　365
For where thou art, there is the world itself,
With every several pleasure in the world;
And where thou art not, desolation.
I can no more. Live thou to joy thy life;
Myself no joy in naught but that thou liv'st.　370
　　Enter Vaux

QUEEN MARGARET
Whither goes Vaux so fast? What news, I prithee?

VAUX
To signify unto his majesty
That Cardinal Beaufort is at point of death.
For suddenly a grievous sickness took him
That makes him gasp, and stare, and catch the air, 375
Blaspheming God and cursing men on earth.
Sometime he talks as if Duke Humphrey's ghost
Were by his side; sometime he calls the King,
And whispers to his pillow as to him
The secrets of his over-chargèd soul;　　380
And I am sent to tell his majesty
That even now he cries aloud for him.

QUEEN MARGARET
Go tell this heavy message to the King.　*Exit Vaux*
Ay me! What is this world? What news are these?
But wherefore grieve I at an hour's poor loss　385
Omitting Suffolk's exile, my soul's treasure?
Why only, Suffolk, mourn I not for thee,
And with the southern clouds contend in tears—
Theirs for the earth's increase, mine for my sorrow's?
Now get thee hence. The King, thou know'st, is
　　coming.　　390
If thou be found by me, thou art but dead.

SUFFOLK
If I depart from thee, I cannot live.
And in thy sight to die, what were it else
But like a pleasant slumber in thy lap?

Here could I breathe my soul into the air,　395
As mild and gentle as the cradle babe
Dying with mother's dug between his lips;
Where, from thy sight, I should be raging mad,
And cry out for thee to close up mine eyes,
To have thee with thy lips to stop my mouth,　400
So shouldst thou either turn my flying soul
Or I should breathe it, so, into thy body—
　　⌈*He kisseth her*⌉
And then it lived in sweet Elysium.
By thee to die were but to die in jest;
From thee to die were torture more than death.　405
O, let me stay, befall what may befall!

QUEEN MARGARET
Away. Though parting be a fretful corrosive,
It is applièd to a deathful wound.
To France, sweet Suffolk. Let me hear from thee.
For wheresoe'er thou art in this world's Globe　410
I'll have an Iris that shall find thee out.

SUFFOLK
I go.

QUEEN MARGARET　And take my heart with thee.
　　⌈*She kisseth him*⌉

SUFFOLK
A jewel, locked into the woefull'st cask
That ever did contain a thing of worth.
Even as a splitted barque, so sunder we—　415
This way fall I to death.

QUEEN MARGARET　　　This way for me.
　　　　　　　　　　　　　　　Exeunt severally

3.3　*Enter King Henry and the Earls of Salisbury and*
　　Warwick. Then the curtains be drawn revealing
　　Cardinal Beaufort in his bed raving and staring as if
　　he were mad

KING HENRY (*to Cardinal Beaufort*)
How fares my lord? Speak, Beaufort, to thy sovereign.

CARDINAL BEAUFORT
If thou beest death, I'll give thee England's treasure
Enough to purchase such another island,
So thou wilt let me live and feel no pain.

KING HENRY
Ah, what a sign it is of evil life　　5
Where death's approach is seen so terrible.

WARWICK
Beaufort, it is thy sovereign speaks to thee.

CARDINAL BEAUFORT
Bring me unto my trial when you will.
Died he not in his bed? Where should he die?
Can I make men live whe'er they will or no?　10
O, torture me no more—I will confess.
Alive again? Then show me where he is.
I'll give a thousand pound to look upon him.
He hath no eyes! The dust hath blinded them.
Comb down his hair—look, look: it stands upright, 15
Like lime twigs set to catch my wingèd soul.
Give me some drink, and bid the apothecary
Bring the strong poison that I bought of him.

KING HENRY
  O Thou eternal mover of the heavens,
  Look with a gentle eye upon this wretch.   20
  O, beat away the busy meddling fiend
  That lays strong siege unto this wretch's soul,
  And from his bosom purge this black despair.
WARWICK
  See how the pangs of death do make him grin.
SALISBURY
  Disturb him not; let him pass peaceably.   25
KING HENRY
  Peace to his soul, if God's good pleasure be.
  Lord Card'nal, if thou think'st on heaven's bliss,
  Hold up thy hand, make signal of thy hope.
      Cardinal Beaufort dies
  He dies and makes no sign. O God, forgive him.
WARWICK
  So bad a death argues a monstrous life.   30
KING HENRY
  Forbear to judge, for we are sinners all.
  Close up his eyes and draw the curtain close,
  And let us all to meditation.
          Exeunt, ⌈drawing the curtains. The bed is
                                  removed⌉

4.1   *Alarums within, and the chambers be discharged*
      like as it were a fight at sea. And then enter the
      Captain of the ship, the Master, the Master's Mate,
      Walter Whitmore, ⌈and others⌉. With them, as
      their prisoners, the Duke of Suffolk, disguised, and
      two Gentlemen
CAPTAIN
  The gaudy, blabbing, and remorseful day
  Is crept into the bosom of the sea;
  And now loud-howling wolves arouse the jades
  That drag the tragic melancholy night;
  Who, with their drowsy, slow, and flagging wings   5
  Clip dead men's graves, and from their misty jaws
  Breathe foul contagious darkness in the air.
  Therefore bring forth the soldiers of our prize,
  For whilst our pinnace anchors in the downs,
  Here shall they make their ransom on the sand,   10
  Or with their blood stain this discoloured shore.
  Master, (*pointing to the First Gentleman*) this prisoner
      freely give I thee,
  (*To the Mate*)
  And thou, that art his mate, make boot of this.
      He points to the Second Gentleman
  (*To Walter Whitmore*)
  The other (*pointing to Suffolk*), Walter Whitmore, is
      thy share.
FIRST GENTLEMAN (*to the Master*)
  What is my ransom, Master, let me know.   15
MASTER
  A thousand crowns, or else lay down your head.
MATE (*to the Second Gentleman*)
  And so much shall you give, or off goes yours.

CAPTAIN (*to both the Gentlemen*)
  What, think you much to pay two thousand crowns,
  And bear the name and port of gentlemen?
⌈WHITMORE⌉
  Cut both the villains' throats! ⌈*To Suffolk*⌉ For die you
      shall.   20
  The lives of those which we have lost in fight
  ⌈   ⌉
  Be counterpoised with such a petty sum.
FIRST GENTLEMAN (*to the Master*)
  I'll give it, sir, and therefore spare my life.
SECOND GENTLEMAN (*to the Mate*)
  And so will I, and write home for it straight.   25
WHITMORE (*to Suffolk*)
  I lost mine eye in laying the prize aboard,
  And therefore to revenge it, shalt thou die—
  And so should these, if I might have my will.
CAPTAIN
  Be not so rash; take ransom; let him live.
SUFFOLK
  Look on my George—I am a gentleman.   30
  Rate me at what thou wilt, thou shalt be paid.
WHITMORE
  And so am I; my name is Walter Whitmore.
      Suffolk starteth
  How now—why starts thou? What doth thee affright?
SUFFOLK
  Thy name affrights me, in whose sound is death.
  A cunning man did calculate my birth,   35
  And told me that by 'water' I should die.
  Yet let not this make thee be bloody-minded;
  Thy name is Gualtier, being rightly sounded.
WHITMORE
  Gualtier or Walter—which it is I care not.
  Never yet did base dishonour blur our name   40
  But with our sword we wiped away the blot.
  Therefore, when merchant-like I sell revenge,
  Broke be my sword, my arms torn and defaced,
  And I proclaimed a coward through the world.
SUFFOLK
  Stay, Whitmore; for thy prisoner is a prince,   45
  The Duke of Suffolk, William de la Pole.
WHITMORE
  The Duke of Suffolk muffled up in rags?
SUFFOLK
  Ay, but these rags are no part of the Duke.
  Jove sometime went disguised, and why not I?
CAPTAIN
  But Jove was never slain as thou shalt be.   50
SUFFOLK
  Obscure and lousy swain, King Henry's blood,
  The honourable blood of Lancaster,
  Must not be shed by such a jady groom.
  Hast thou not kissed thy hand and held my stirrup?
  Bare-headed plodded by my foot-cloth mule   55
  And thought thee happy when I shook my head?
  How often hast thou waited at my cup,

Fed from my trencher, kneeled down at the board
When I have feasted with Queen Margaret?
Remember it, and let it make thee crestfall'n,   60
Ay, and allay this thy abortive pride,
How in our voiding lobby hast thou stood
And duly waited for my coming forth?
This hand of mine hath writ in thy behalf,
And therefore shall it charm thy riotous tongue.   65

WHITMORE
Speak, Captain—shall I stab the forlorn swain?

CAPTAIN
First let my words stab him as he hath me.

SUFFOLK
Base slave, thy words are blunt and so art thou.

CAPTAIN
Convey him hence and, on our longboat's side,
Strike off his head.

SUFFOLK   Thou dar'st not for thy own.   70

CAPTAIN
Pole—

⌜SUFFOLK⌝ Pole?

CAPTAIN   Ay, kennel, puddle, sink, whose filth and dirt
Troubles the silver spring where England drinks,
Now will I dam up this thy yawning mouth
For swallowing the treasure of the realm.
Thy lips that kissed the Queen shall sweep the ground,
And thou that smiledst at good Duke Humphrey's   76
          death
Against the senseless winds shalt grin in vain,
Who in contempt shall hiss at thee again.
And wedded be thou to the hags of hell,
For daring to affy a mighty lord   80
Unto the daughter of a worthless king,
Having neither subject, wealth, nor diadem,
By devilish policy art thou grown great,
And like ambitious Sylla, overgorged
With gobbets of thy mother's bleeding heart.   85
By thee Anjou and Maine were sold to France,
The false revolting Normans, thorough thee,
Disdain to call us lord, and Picardy
Hath slain their governors, surprised our forts,
And sent the ragged soldiers, wounded, home.   90
The princely Warwick, and the Nevilles all,
Whose dreadful swords were never drawn in vain,
As hating thee, are rising up in arms;
And now the house of York, thrust from the crown,
By shameful murder of a guiltless king   95
And lofty, proud, encroaching tyranny,
Burns with revenging fire, whose hopeful colours
Advance our half-faced sun, striving to shine,
Under the which is writ, 'Invitis nubibus'.
The commons here in Kent are up in arms,   100
And, to conclude, reproach and beggary
Is crept into the palace of our King,
And all by thee. (To Whitmore) Away, convey him
          hence.

SUFFOLK
O that I were a god, to shoot forth thunder
Upon these paltry, servile, abject drudges.   105

Small things make base men proud. This villain here,
Being captain of a pinnace, threatens more
Than Bargulus, the strong Illyrian pirate.
Drones suck not eagles' blood, but rob beehives.
It is impossible that I should die   110
By such a lowly vassal as thyself.
Thy words move rage, and not remorse in me.

⌜CAPTAIN⌝
But my deeds, Suffolk, soon shall stay thy rage.

SUFFOLK
I go of message from the Queen to France—
I charge thee, waft me safely cross the Channel!   115
CAPTAIN Walter—

WHITMORE
Come, Suffolk, I must waft thee to thy death.

SUFFOLK
Paene gelidus timor occupat artus—
It is thee I fear.

WHITMORE
Thou shalt have cause to fear before I leave thee.   120
What, are ye daunted now? Now will ye stoop?

FIRST GENTLEMAN (to Suffolk)
My gracious lord, entreat him—speak him fair.

SUFFOLK
Suffolk's imperial tongue is stern and rough,
Used to command, untaught to plead for favour.
Far be it we should honour such as these   125
With humble suit. No, rather let my head
Stoop to the block than these knees bow to any
Save to the God of heaven and to my king;
And sooner dance upon a bloody pole
Than stand uncovered to the vulgar groom.   130
True nobility is exempt from fear;
More can I bear than you dare execute.

CAPTAIN
Hale him away, and let him talk no more.

SUFFOLK
Come, 'soldiers', show what cruelty ye can,
That this my death may never be forgot.   135
Great men oft die by vile Besonians;
A Roman sworder and banditto slave
Murdered sweet Tully; Brutus' bastard hand
Stabbed Julius Caesar; savage islanders
Pompey the Great; and Suffolk dies by pirates.   140
          Exit Whitmore with Suffolk

CAPTAIN
And as for these whose ransom we have set,
It is our pleasure one of them depart.
(To the Second Gentleman)
Therefore, come you with us and (to his men, pointing
          to the First Gentleman) let him go.
          Exeunt all but the First Gentleman
          Enter Whitmore with Suffolk's head and body

WHITMORE
There let his head and lifeless body lie,   144
Until the Queen his mistress bury it.   Exit

FIRST GENTLEMAN
O barbarous and bloody spectacle!
His body will I bear unto the King.

If he revenge it not, yet will his friends;
So will the Queen, that living held him dear.

Exit with Suffolk's head and body

4.2   *Enter two Rebels ⌈with long staves⌉*

FIRST REBEL Come and get thee a sword, though made of
a lath; they have been up these two days.

SECOND REBEL They have the more need to sleep now
then.   4

FIRST REBEL I tell thee, Jack Cade the clothier means to
dress the commonwealth, and turn it, and set a new
nap upon it.

SECOND REBEL So he had need, for 'tis threadbare. Well, I
say it was never merry world in England since gentlemen came up.   10

FIRST REBEL O, miserable age! Virtue is not regarded in
handicraftsmen.

SECOND REBEL The nobility think scorn to go in leather
aprons.

FIRST REBEL Nay more, the King's Council are no good
workmen.   16

SECOND REBEL True; and yet it is said 'Labour in thy
vocation'; which is as much to say as 'Let the
magistrates be labouring men'; and therefore should
we be magistrates.   20

FIRST REBEL Thou hast hit it; for there's no better sign of
a brave mind than a hard hand.

SECOND REBEL I see them! I see them! There's Best's son,
the tanner of Wingham—

FIRST REBEL He shall have the skins of our enemies to
make dog's leather of.   26

SECOND REBEL And Dick the butcher—

FIRST REBEL Then is sin struck down like an ox, and
iniquity's throat cut like a calf.

SECOND REBEL And Smith the weaver—   30

FIRST REBEL Argo, their thread of life is spun.

SECOND REBEL Come, come, let's fall in with them.

*Enter Jack Cade, Dick the Butcher, Smith the
Weaver, a sawyer, ⌈and a drummer,⌉ with infinite
numbers, ⌈all with long staves⌉*

CADE We, John Cade, so termed of our supposed father—

BUTCHER (*to his fellows*) Or rather of stealing a cade of
herrings.   35

CADE For our enemies shall fall before us, inspired with
the spirit of putting down kings and princes—command
silence!

BUTCHER Silence!

CADE My father was a Mortimer—   40

BUTCHER (*to his fellows*) He was an honest man and a good
bricklayer.

CADE My mother a Plantagenet—

BUTCHER (*to his fellows*) I knew her well, she was a midwife.

CADE My wife descended of the Lacys—   45

BUTCHER (*to his fellows*) She was indeed a pedlar's daughter
and sold many laces.

WEAVER (*to his fellows*) But now of late, not able to travel
with her furred pack, she washes bucks here at home.

CADE Therefore am I of an honourable house.   50

BUTCHER (*to his fellows*) Ay, by my faith, the field is
honourable, and there was he born, under a hedge;
for his father had never a house but the cage.

CADE Valiant I am—

WEAVER (*to his fellows*) A must needs, for beggary is
valiant.   56

CADE I am able to endure much—

BUTCHER (*to his fellows*) No question of that, for I have
seen him whipped three market days together.

CADE I fear neither sword nor fire.   60

WEAVER (*to his fellows*) He need not fear the sword, for
his coat is of proof.

BUTCHER (*to his fellows*) But methinks he should stand in
fear of fire, being burned i'th' hand for stealing of
sheep.   65

CADE Be brave, then, for your captain is brave and vows
reformation. There shall be in England seven halfpenny
loaves sold for a penny, the three-hooped pot shall have
ten hoops, and I will make it felony to drink small beer.
All the realm shall be in common, and in Cheapside
shall my palfrey go to grass. And when I am king, as
king I will be—

ALL CADE'S FOLLOWERS God save your majesty!

CADE I thank you good people! —there shall be no money.
All shall eat and drink on my score, and I will apparel
them all in one livery that they may agree like brothers,
and worship me their lord.

BUTCHER The first thing we do let's kill all the lawyers.

CADE Nay, that I mean to do. Is not this a lamentable
thing that of the skin of an innocent lamb should be
made parchment? That parchment, being scribbled
o'er, should undo a man? Some say the bee stings, but
I say 'tis the bee's wax. For I did but seal once to a
thing, and I was never mine own man since. How
now? Who's there?   85

Enter some bringing forth the Clerk of Chatham

WEAVER The Clerk of Chatham—he can write and read
and cast account.

CADE O, monstrous!

WEAVER We took him setting of boys' copies.

CADE Here's a villain.   90

WEAVER He's a book in his pocket with red letters in't.

CADE Nay, then he is a conjuror!

BUTCHER Nay, he can make obligations and write court
hand.   94

CADE I am sorry for't. The man is a proper man, of mine
honour. Unless I find him guilty, he shall not die. Come
hither, sirrah, I must examine thee. What is thy name?

CLERK Emmanuel.

BUTCHER They use to write that on the top of letters—
'twill go hard with you.   100

CADE Let me alone. (*To the Clerk*) Dost thou use to write
thy name? Or hast thou a mark to thyself like an
honest plain-dealing man?

CLERK Sir, I thank God I have been so well brought up
that I can write my name.   105

ALL CADE'S FOLLOWERS He hath confessed—away with
him! He's a villain and a traitor.

CADE Away with him, I say, hang him with his pen and inkhorn about his neck.   *Exit one with the Clerk*
Enter a Messenger
MESSENGER Where's our general?   110
CADE Here I am, thou particular fellow.
MESSENGER Fly, fly, fly! Sir Humphrey Stafford and his brother are hard by with the King's forces.
CADE Stand, villain, stand—or I'll fell thee down. He shall be encountered with a man as good as himself. He is but a knight, is a?   116
MESSENGER No.
CADE To equal him I will make myself a knight presently.
He kneels and knights himself
Rise up, Sir John Mortimer.
He rises
Now have at him!   120
Enter Sir Humphrey Stafford and his brother, with a drummer and soldiers
STAFFORD (*to Cade's followers*)
Rebellious hinds, the filth and scum of Kent,
Marked for the gallows, lay your weapons down;
Home to your cottages, forsake this groom.
The King is merciful, if you revolt.
STAFFORD'S BROTHER (*to Cade's followers*)
But angry, wrathful, and inclined to blood,   125
If you go forward. Therefore, yield or die.
CADE (*to his followers*)
As for these silken-coated slaves, I pass not.
It is to you, good people, that I speak,
Over whom, in time to come, I hope to reign—
For I am rightful heir unto the crown.   130
STAFFORD
Villain, thy father was a plasterer
And thou thyself a shearman, art thou not?
CADE
And Adam was a gardener.
STAFFORD'S BROTHER   And what of that?
CADE
Marry, this: Edmund Mortimer, Earl of March,
Married the Duke of Clarence' daughter, did he not?
STAFFORD Ay, sir.   136
CADE
By her he had two children at one birth.
STAFFORD'S BROTHER That's false.
CADE
Ay, there's the question—but I say 'tis true.
The elder of them, being put to nurse,   140
Was by a beggar-woman stol'n away,
And, ignorant of his birth and parentage,
Became a bricklayer when he came to age.
His son am I—deny it an you can.
BUTCHER
Nay, 'tis too true—therefore he shall be king.   145
WEAVER Sir, he made a chimney in my father's house, and the bricks are alive at this day to testify. Therefore deny it not.
STAFFORD (*to Cade's followers*)
And will you credit this base drudge's words
That speaks he knows not what?   150

ALL CADE'S FOLLOWERS
Ay, marry, will we—therefore get ye gone.
STAFFORD'S BROTHER
Jack Cade, the Duke of York hath taught you this.
CADE (*aside*)
He lies, for I invented it myself.
(*Aloud*) Go to, sirrah—tell the King from me that for his father's sake, Henry the Fifth, in whose time boys went to span-counter for French crowns, I am content he shall reign; but I'll be Protector over him.
BUTCHER And, furthermore, we'll have the Lord Saye's head for selling the dukedom of Maine.   159
CADE And good reason, for thereby is England maimed, and fain to go with a staff, but that my puissance holds it up. Fellow-kings, I tell you that that Lord Saye hath gelded the commonwealth, and made it an eunuch, and, more than that, he can speak French, and therefore he is a traitor!   165
STAFFORD
O gross and miserable ignorance!
CADE Nay, answer if you can: the Frenchmen are our enemies; go to, then, I ask but this—can he that speaks with the tongue of an enemy be a good counsellor or no?   170
ALL CADE'S FOLLOWERS No, no—and therefore we'll have his head!
STAFFORD'S BROTHER (*to Stafford*)
Well, seeing gentle words will not prevail,
Assail them with the army of the King.
STAFFORD
Herald, away, and throughout every town   175
Proclaim them traitors that are up with Cade;
That those which fly before the battle ends
May, even in their wives' and children's sight,
Be hanged up for example at their doors.
And you that be the King's friends, follow me!   180
Exeunt ⌜the Staffords and their soldiers⌝
CADE
And you that love the commons, follow me!
Now show yourselves men—'tis for liberty.
We will not leave one lord, one gentleman—
Spare none but such as go in clouted shoon,
For they are thrifty honest men, and such   185
As would, but that they dare not, take our parts.
BUTCHER They are all in order, and march toward us.
CADE
But then are we in order when we are
Most out of order. Come, march forward!   ⌜*Exeunt*⌝

4.3   *Alarums to the fight; ⌜excursions,⌝ wherein both the Staffords are slain. Enter Jack Cade, Dick the Butcher, and the rest*
CADE Where's Dick, the butcher of Ashford?
BUTCHER Here, sir.
CADE They fell before thee like sheep and oxen, and thou behaved'st thyself as if thou hadst been in thine own slaughterhouse. Therefore, thus will I reward thee—the Lent shall be as long again as it is. Thou shalt have licence to kill for a hundred, lacking one.

BUTCHER I desire no more.

CADE And to speak truth, thou deserv'st no less.

[*He apparels himself in the Staffords' armour*]

This monument of the victory will I bear, and the
bodies shall be dragged at my horse heels till I do come
to London, where we will have the Mayor's sword
borne before us.

BUTCHER If we mean to thrive and do good, break open
the jails and let out the prisoners.   15

CADE Fear not that, I warrant thee. Come, let's march
towards London.

Exeunt, [dragging the Staffords' bodies]

4.4   *Enter King Henry [reading] a supplication, Queen*
      Margaret carrying Suffolk's head, the Duke of
      Buckingham, and the Lord Saye, [with others]

QUEEN MARGARET [*aside*]

Oft have I heard that grief softens the mind,
And makes it fearful and degenerate;
Think, therefore, on revenge, and cease to weep.
But who can cease to weep and look on this?
Here may his head lie on my throbbing breast,   5
But where's the body that I should embrace?

BUCKINGHAM (*to King Henry*)

What answer makes your grace to the rebels'
supplication?

KING HENRY

I'll send some holy bishop to entreat,
For God forbid so many simple souls
Should perish by the sword. And I myself,   10
Rather than bloody war shall cut them short,
Will parley with Jack Cade their general.
But stay, I'll read it over once again.

He reads

QUEEN MARGARET (*to Suffolk's head*)

Ah, barbarous villains! Hath this lovely face
Ruled like a wandering planet over me,   15
And could it not enforce them to relent,
That were unworthy to behold the same?

KING HENRY

Lord Saye, Jack Cade hath sworn to have thy head.

SAYE

Ay, but I hope your highness shall have his.

KING HENRY (*to Queen Margaret*)

How now, madam? Still lamenting and mourning   20
Suffolk's death?
I fear me, love, if that I had been dead,
Thou wouldest not have mourned so much for me.

QUEEN MARGARET

No, my love, I should not mourn, but die for thee.

Enter a Messenger, [in haste]

KING HENRY

How now? What news? Why com'st thou in such
haste?   25

MESSENGER

The rebels are in Southwark—fly, my lord!
Jack Cade proclaims himself Lord Mortimer,
Descended from the Duke of Clarence' house,

And calls your grace usurper, openly,
And vows to crown himself in Westminster.   30
His army is a ragged multitude
Of hinds and peasants, rude and merciless.
Sir Humphrey Stafford and his brother's death
Hath given them heart and courage to proceed.
All scholars, lawyers, courtiers, gentlemen,   35
They call false caterpillars and intend their death.

KING HENRY

O, graceless men; they know not what they do.

BUCKINGHAM

My gracious lord, retire to Kenilworth
Until a power be raised to put them down.

QUEEN MARGARET

Ah, were the Duke of Suffolk now alive   40
These Kentish rebels would be soon appeased!

KING HENRY

Lord Saye, the trait'rous rabble hateth thee—
Therefore away with us to Kenilworth.

SAYE

So might your grace's person be in danger.
The sight of me is odious in their eyes,   45
And therefore in this city will I stay
And live alone as secret as I may.

Enter another Messenger

SECOND MESSENGER (*to King Henry*)

Jack Cade hath almost gotten London Bridge;
The citizens fly and forsake their houses;
The rascal people, thirsting after prey,   50
Join with the traitor; and they jointly swear
To spoil the city and your royal court.

BUCKINGHAM (*to King Henry*)

Then linger not, my lord; away, take horse!

KING HENRY

Come, Margaret. God, our hope, will succour us.

QUEEN MARGARET [*aside*]

My hope is gone, now Suffolk is deceased.   55

KING HENRY (*to Saye*)

Farewell, my lord. Trust not the Kentish rebels.

BUCKINGHAM (*to Saye*)

Trust nobody, for fear you be betrayed.

SAYE

The trust I have is in mine innocence,
And therefore am I bold and resolute.

Exeunt [Saye at one door, the rest at another]

4.5   *Enter the Lord Scales upon the Tower, walking.*
      Enter three or four Citizens below

SCALES How now? Is Jack Cade slain?

FIRST CITIZEN No, my lord Scales, nor likely to be slain,
for he and his men have won the bridge, killing all
those that did withstand them. The Lord Mayor craveth
aid of your honour from the Tower to defend the city
from the rebels.   6

SCALES

Such aid as I can spare you shall command,
But I am troubled here with them myself.
The rebels have essayed to win the Tower.

Get you to Smithfield, there to gather head,   10
And thither will I send you Matthew Gough.
Fight for your king, your country, and your lives!
And so, farewell, for I must hence again.

Exeunt, Scales above, the Citizens below

4.6   *Enter Jack Cade, the Weaver, the Butcher, and the*
rest. Cade strikes his sword on London Stone

CADE Now is Mortimer lord of this city. And, here sitting
upon London Stone, I charge and command that, of
the city's cost, the Pissing Conduit run nothing but
claret wine this first year of our reign. And now
henceforward it shall be treason for any that calls me
otherwise than Lord Mortimer.   6

Enter a Soldier, running

SOLDIER Jack Cade, Jack Cade!
CADE Zounds, knock him down there!

They kill him

BUTCHER If this fellow be wise, he'll never call ye Jack
Cade more; I think he hath a very fair warning.   10

⌈*He takes a paper from the soldier's body*
and reads it⌉

My lord, there's an army gathered together in
Smithfield.
CADE Come then, let's go fight with them—but first, go
on and set London Bridge afire, and, if you can, burn
down the Tower too. Come, let's away.   *Exeunt*

4.7   *Alarums.* ⌈*Excursions, wherein*⌉ *Matthew Gough is*
slain, and all the rest of his men with him.
Then enter Jack Cade with his company, among
them the Butcher, the Weaver, and John, a rebel

CADE So, sirs, now go some and pull down the Savoy;
others to th' Inns of Court—down with them all.
BUTCHER I have a suit unto your lordship.
CADE Be it a lordship, thou shalt have it for that word.
BUTCHER Only that the laws of England may come out of
your mouth.   6
JOHN (*aside to his fellows*) Mass, 'twill be sore law then,
for he was thrust in the mouth with a spear, and 'tis
not whole yet.
WEAVER (*aside to John*) Nay, John, it will be stinking law,
for his breath stinks with eating toasted cheese.   11
CADE I have thought upon it—it shall be so. Away! Burn
all the records of the realm. My mouth shall be the
Parliament of England.
JOHN (*aside to his fellows*) Then we are like to have biting
statutes unless his teeth be pulled out.   16
CADE And henceforward all things shall be in common.

Enter a Messenger

MESSENGER My lord, a prize, a prize! Here's the Lord Saye
which sold the towns in France. He that made us pay
one-and-twenty fifteens and one shilling to the pound
the last subsidy.   21

Enter a rebel with the Lord Saye

CADE Well, he shall be beheaded for it ten times. (*To Saye*)
Ah, thou say, thou serge—nay, thou buckram lord!
Now art thou within point-blank of our jurisdiction
regal. What canst thou answer to my majesty for giving

up of Normandy unto Mounsieur Basimecu, the
Dauphin of France? Be it known unto thee by these
presence, even the presence of Lord Mortimer, that I
am the besom that must sweep the court clean of such
filth as thou art. Thou hast most traitorously corrupted
the youth of the realm in erecting a grammar school;
and, whereas before, our forefathers had no other books
but the score and the tally, thou hast caused printing
to be used and, contrary to the King his crown and
dignity, thou hast built a paper-mill. It will be proved
to thy face that thou hast men about thee that usually
talk of a noun and a verb and such abominable words
as no Christian ear can endure to hear. Thou hast
appointed justices of peace to call poor men before them
about matters they were not able to answer. Moreover,
thou hast put them in prison, and, because they could
not read, thou hast hanged them when indeed only for
that cause they have been most worthy to live. Thou
dost ride on a foot-cloth, dost thou not?
SAYE What of that?   45
CADE Marry, thou ought'st not to let thy horse wear a
cloak when honester men than thou go in their hose
and doublets.
BUTCHER And work in their shirts, too; as myself, for
example, that am a butcher.   50
SAYE You men of Kent.
BUTCHER What say you of Kent?
SAYE
Nothing but this—'tis *bona terra, mala gens.*
CADE *Bonum terrum*—zounds, what's that?
BUTCHER He speaks French.   55
⌈FIRST REBEL⌉ No, 'tis Dutch.
⌈SECOND REBEL⌉ No, 'tis Out-talian, I know it well enough.
SAYE
Hear me but speak, and bear me where you will.
Kent, in the commentaries Caesar writ,
Is termed the civil'st place of all this isle;   60
Sweet is the country, because full of riches;
The people liberal, valiant, active, wealthy;
Which makes me hope you are not void of pity.
I sold not Maine, I lost not Normandy;
Yet to recover them would lose my life.   65
Justice with favour have I always done,
Prayers and tears have moved me—gifts could never.
When have I aught exacted at your hands,
But to maintain the King, the realm, and you?
Large gifts have I bestowed on learnèd clerks   70
Because my book preferred me to the King,
And seeing ignorance is the curse of God,
Knowledge the wing wherewith we fly to heaven.
Unless you be possessed with devilish spirits,
You cannot but forbear to murder me.   75
This tongue hath parleyed unto foreign kings
For your behoof—
CADE Tut, when struck'st thou one blow in the field?
SAYE
Great men have reaching hands. Oft have I struck
Those that I never saw, and struck them dead.   80
REBEL O monstrous coward! What, to come behind folks?

SAYE
These cheeks are pale for watching for your good—
CADE Give him a box o'th' ear, and that will make 'em
red again.
   ⌈*One of the rebels strikes Saye*⌉
SAYE
Long sitting to determine poor men's causes   85
Hath made me full of sickness and diseases.
CADE Ye shall have a hempen caudle, then, and the
health o'th' hatchet.
BUTCHER (*to Saye*) Why dost thou quiver, man?
SAYE
The palsy, and not fear, provokes me.   90
CADE Nay, he nods at us as who should say 'I'll be even
with you'. I'll see if his head will stand steadier on a
pole or no. Take him away, and behead him.
SAYE
Tell me wherein have I offended most?
Have I affected wealth or honour? Speak.   95
Are my chests filled up with extorted gold?
Is my apparel sumptuous to behold?
Whom have I injured, that ye seek my death?
These hands are free from guiltless bloodshedding,
This breast from harbouring foul deceitful thoughts. 100
O let me live!
CADE (*aside*) I feel remorse in myself with his words, but
I'll bridle it. He shall die an it be but for pleading so
well for his life. (*Aloud*) Away with him—he has a
familiar under his tongue; he speaks not a God's name.
Go, take him away, I say, to the Standard in Cheapside,
and strike off his head presently; and then go to Mile
End Green—break into his son-in-law's house, Sir James
Cromer, and strike off his head, and bring them both
upon two poles hither.   110
ALL CADE'S FOLLOWERS It shall be done!
SAYE
Ah, countrymen, if, when you make your prayers,
God should be so obdurate as yourselves,
How would it fare with your departed souls?
And therefore yet relent and save my life!   115
CADE Away with him, and do as I command ye!
   Exeunt ⌈the Butcher and⌉ one or two with the
                            Lord Saye
The proudest peer in the realm shall not wear a head
on his shoulders unless he pay me tribute. There shall
not a maid be married but she shall pay to me her
maidenhead, ere they have it. Married men shall hold
of me *in capite*. And we charge and command that their
wives be as free as heart can wish or tongue can tell.
   Enter a Rebel
REBEL O captain, London Bridge is afire!
CADE Run to Billingsgate and fetch pitch and flax and
quench it.   125
   Enter the Butcher and a Sergeant
SERGEANT Justice, justice, I pray you, sir, let me have
justice of this fellow here.
CADE Why, what has he done?
SERGEANT Alas, sir, he has ravished my wife.
BUTCHER (*to Cade*) Why, my lord, he would have 'rested

me and I went and entered my action in his wife's
proper house.
CADE Dick, follow thy suit in her common place. (*To the
Sergeant*) You whoreson villain, you are a sergeant—
you'll take any man by the throat for twelve pence,
and 'rest a man when he's at dinner, and have him to
prison ere the meat be out of his mouth. (*To the Butcher*)
Go, Dick, take him hence: cut out his tongue for
cogging, hough him for running, and, to conclude,
brain him with his own mace.   140
   Exit the Butcher with the Sergeant
REBEL My lord, when shall we go to Cheapside and take
up commodities upon our bills?
CADE Marry, presently. He that will lustily stand to it
shall go with me and take up these commodities
following—item, a gown, a kirtle, a petticoat, and a
smock.   146
ALL CADE'S FOLLOWERS O brave!
   Enter two with the Lord Saye's head and Sir James
   Cromer's upon two poles
CADE But is not this braver? Let them kiss one another,
for they loved well when they were alive.   149
   ⌈*The two heads are made to kiss*⌉
Now part them again, lest they consult about the giving
up of some more towns in France. Soldiers, defer the
spoil of the city until night. For with these borne before
us instead of maces will we ride through the streets,
and at every corner have them kiss. Away!
   ⌈*Exeunt two with the heads. The others begin to*
                                    follow⌉
Up Fish Street! Down Saint Magnus' Corner! Kill and
knock down! Throw them into Thames!   156
   Sound a parley
What noise is this? Dare any be so bold to sound retreat
or parley when I command them kill?
   Enter the Duke of Buckingham and old Lord Clifford
BUCKINGHAM
Ay, here they be that dare and will disturb thee!
Know, Cade, we come ambassadors from the King   160
Unto the commons, whom thou hast misled,
And here pronounce free pardon to them all
That will forsake thee and go home in peace.
CLIFFORD
What say ye, countrymen, will ye relent
And yield to mercy whilst 'tis offered you,   165
Or let a rebel lead you to your deaths?
Who loves the King and will embrace his pardon,
Fling up his cap and say 'God save his majesty'.
Who hateth him and honours not his father,
Henry the Fifth, that made all France to quake,   170
Shake he his weapon at us, and pass by.
   They ⌈fling up their caps and⌉ forsake Cade
ALL CADE'S FOLLOWERS God save the King! God save the
King!
CADE What, Buckingham and Clifford, are ye so brave?
(*To the rabble*) And you, base peasants, do ye believe
him? Will you needs be hanged with your pardons
about your necks? Hath my sword, therefore, broke
through London gates that you should leave me at the

White Hart in Southwark? I thought ye would never
have given out these arms till you had recovered your
ancient freedom. But you are all recreants and dastards,
and delight to live in slavery to the nobility. Let them
break your backs with burdens, take your houses over
your heads, ravish your wives and daughters before
your faces. For me, I will make shift for one, and so
God's curse light upon you all.   186

ALL CADE'S FOLLOWERS We'll follow Cade! We'll follow
Cade!

They run to Cade again

CLIFFORD
Is Cade the son of Henry the Fifth
That thus you do exclaim you'll go with him?   190
Will he conduct you through the heart of France
And make the meanest of you earls and dukes?
Alas, he hath no home, no place to fly to,
Nor knows he how to live but by the spoil—
Unless by robbing of your friends and us.   195
Were't not a shame that whilst you live at jar
The fearful French, whom you late vanquishèd,
Should make a start o'er seas and vanquish you?
Methinks already in this civil broil
I see them lording it in London streets,   200
Crying '*Villiago!*' unto all they meet.
Better ten thousand base-born Cades miscarry
Than you should stoop unto a Frenchman's mercy.
To France! To France! And get what you have lost!
Spare England, for it is your native coast.   205
Henry hath money; you are strong and manly;
God on our side, doubt not of victory.

ALL CADE'S FOLLOWERS A Clifford! A Clifford! We'll follow
the King and Clifford!   209

They forsake Cade

CADE (*aside*) Was ever feather so lightly blown to and fro
as this multitude? The name of Henry the Fifth hales
them to an hundred mischiefs, and makes them leave
me desolate. I see them lay their heads together to
surprise me. My sword make way for me, for here is
no staying. (*Aloud*) In despite of the devils and hell,
have through the very middest of you! And heavens
and honour be witness that no want of resolution in
me, but only my followers' base and ignominious
treasons, makes me betake me to my heels.

*He runs through them with his staff, and flies
away*

BUCKINGHAM
What, is he fled? Go, some, and follow him,   220
And he that brings his head unto the King
Shall have a thousand crowns for his reward.

Exeunt some of them after Cade

(*To the remaining rebels*)
Follow me, soldiers, we'll devise a mean
To reconcile you all unto the King.   *Exeunt*

4.8   *Sound trumpets. Enter King Henry, Queen*
    Margaret, and the Duke of Somerset on the terrace

KING HENRY
Was ever King that joyed an earthly throne

And could command no more content than I?
No sooner was I crept out of my cradle
But I was made a king at nine months old.
Was never subject longed to be a king   5
As I do long and wish to be a subject.

*Enter the Duke of Buckingham and Lord Clifford ⌈on
the terrace⌉*

BUCKINGHAM (*to King Henry*)
Health and glad tidings to your majesty.

KING HENRY
Why, Buckingham, is the traitor Cade surprised?
Or is he but retired to make him strong?

*Enter, below, multitudes with halters about their
necks*

CLIFFORD
He is fled, my lord, and all his powers do yield,   10
And humbly thus with halters on their necks
Expect your highness' doom of life or death.

KING HENRY
Then, heaven, set ope thy everlasting gates
To entertain my vows of thanks and praise.
(*To the multitudes below*)
Soldiers, this day have you redeemed your lives,   15
And showed how well you love your prince and
country.
Continue still in this so good a mind,
And Henry, though he be infortunate,
Assure yourselves will never be unkind.
And so, with thanks and pardon to you all,   20
I do dismiss you to your several countries.

ALL CADE'S FORMER FOLLOWERS God save the King! God
save the King!   ⌈*Exeunt multitudes below*⌉

Enter a Messenger ⌈on the terrace⌉

MESSENGER (*to King Henry*)
Please it your grace to be advertisèd
The Duke of York is newly come from Ireland,   25
And with a puissant and a mighty power
Of galloglasses and stout Irish kerns
Is marching hitherward in proud array,
And still proclaimeth, as he comes along,
His arms are only to remove from thee   30
The Duke of Somerset, whom he terms a traitor.

KING HENRY
Thus stands my state, 'twixt Cade and York distressed,
Like to a ship that, having scaped a tempest,
Is straightway calmed and boarded with a pirate.
But now is Cade driven back, his men dispersed,   35
And now is York in arms to second him.
I pray thee, Buckingham, go and meet him,
And ask him what's the reason of these arms.
Tell him I'll send Duke Edmund to the Tower;
And, Somerset, we will commit thee thither,   40
Until his army is dismissed from him.

SOMERSET
My lord, I'll yield myself to prison willingly,
Or unto death, to do my country good.

KING HENRY (*to Buckingham*)
In any case, be not too rough in terms,
For he is fierce and cannot brook hard language.   45

BUCKINGHAM

I will, my lord, and doubt not so to deal
As all things shall redound unto your good.

KING HENRY

Come, wife, let's in and learn to govern better;
For yet may England curse my wretched reign.

Flourish. Exeunt

4.9   *Enter Jack Cade*

CADE Fie on ambitions; fie on myself that have a sword
and yet am ready to famish. These five days have I hid
me in these woods and durst not peep out, for all the
country is laid for me. But now am I so hungry that if
I might have a lease of my life for a thousand years, I
could stay no longer. Wherefore o'er a brick wall have
I climbed into this garden to see if I can eat grass or
pick a sallet another while, which is not amiss to cool
a man's stomach this hot weather. And I think this
word 'sallet' was born to do me good; for many a time,
but for a sallet, my brain-pan had been cleft with a
brown bill; and many a time, when I have been dry,
and bravely marching, it hath served me instead of a
quart pot to drink in; and now the word 'sallet' must
serve me to feed on.   15

⌈*He lies down picking of herbs and eating them.*⌉
Enter Sir Alexander Iden ⌈*and five of his men*⌉

IDEN

Lord, who would live turmoilèd in the court
And may enjoy such quiet walks as these?
This small inheritance my father left me
Contenteth me, and worth a monarchy.
I seek not to wax great by others' waning,   20
Or gather wealth I care not with what envy;
Sufficeth that I have maintains my state,
And sends the poor well pleasèd from my gate.

⌈*Cade rises to his knees*⌉

CADE (*aside*) Zounds, here's the lord of the soil come to
seize me for a stray for entering his fee-simple without
leave. (*To Iden*) A villain, thou wilt betray me and get
a thousand crowns of the king by carrying my head
to him; but I'll make thee eat iron like an ostrich and
swallow my sword like a great pin, ere thou and I part.

IDEN

Why, rude companion, whatsoe'er thou be,   30
I know thee not. Why then should I betray thee?
Is't not enough to break into my garden,
And, like a thief, to come to rob my grounds,
Climbing my walls in spite of me the owner,
But thou wilt brave me with these saucy terms?   35

CADE Brave thee? Ay, by the best blood that ever was
broached—and beard thee too! Look on me well—I
have eat no meat these five days, yet come thou and
thy five men, an if I do not leave you all as dead as a
doornail I pray God I may never eat grass more.   40

IDEN

Nay, it shall ne'er be said while England stands
That Alexander Iden, an esquire of Kent,

Took odds to combat a poor famished man.
Oppose thy steadfast gazing eyes to mine—
See if thou canst outface me with thy looks.   45
Set limb to limb, and thou art far the lesser—
Thy hand is but a finger to my fist,
Thy leg a stick comparèd with this truncheon.
My foot shall fight with all the strength thou hast,
And if mine arm be heavèd in the air,   50
Thy grave is digged already in the earth.
As for words, whose greatness answers words,
Let this my sword report what speech forbears.
(*To his men*) Stand you all aside.   54

CADE By my valour, the most complete champion that
ever I heard. (*To his sword*) Steel, if thou turn the edge
or cut not out the burly-boned clown in chines of beef
ere thou sleep in thy sheath, I beseech God on my
knees thou mayst be turned to hobnails.   59

⌈*Cade stands.*⌉ Here they fight, and Cade falls down

O, I am slain! Famine and no other hath slain me! Let
ten thousand devils come against me, and give me but
the ten meals I have lost, and I'd defy them all. Wither,
garden, and be henceforth a burying place to all that
do dwell in this house, because the unconquered soul
of Cade is fled.   65

IDEN

Is't Cade that I have slain, that monstrous traitor?
Sword, I will hallow thee for this thy deed
And hang thee o'er my tomb when I am dead.
Ne'er shall this blood be wipèd from thy point
But thou shalt wear it as a herald's coat   70
To emblaze the honour that thy master got.

CADE Iden, farewell, and be proud of thy victory. Tell
Kent from me she hath lost her best man, and exhort
all the world to be cowards. For I, that never feared
any, am vanquished by famine, not by valour.   75

He dies

IDEN

How much thou wrong'st me, heaven be my judge.
Die, damnèd wretch, the curse of her that bore thee!
And ⌈*stabbing him again*⌉ as I thrust thy body in with
my sword,
So wish I I might thrust thy soul to hell.
Hence will I drag thee headlong by the heels   80
Unto a dunghill, which shall be thy grave,
And there cut off thy most ungracious head,
Which I will bear in triumph to the King,
Leaving thy trunk for crows to feed upon.

Exeunt with the body

5.1   *Enter the Duke of York and his army of Irish with
a drummer and soldiers bearing colours*

YORK

From Ireland thus comes York to claim his right,
And pluck the crown from feeble Henry's head.
Ring, bells, aloud; burn, bonfires, clear and bright,
To entertain great England's lawful king.
Ah, *sancta maiestas*! Who would not buy thee dear? 5

Let them obey that knows not how to rule;
This hand was made to handle naught but gold.
I cannot give due action to my words,
Except a sword or sceptre balance it.
A sceptre shall it have, have I a sword,   10
On which I'll toss the fleur-de-lis of France.
        Enter the Duke of Buckingham
(*Aside*) Whom have we here? Buckingham to disturb
me?
The King hath sent him sure—I must dissemble.
BUCKINGHAM
York, if thou meanest well, I greet thee well.
YORK
Humphrey of Buckingham, I accept thy greeting.   15
Art thou a messenger, or come of pleasure?
BUCKINGHAM
A messenger from Henry, our dread liege,
To know the reason of these arms in peace;
Or why thou, being a subject as I am,
Against thy oath and true allegiance sworn,   20
Should raise so great a power without his leave,
Or dare to bring thy force so near the court?
YORK (*aside*)
Scarce can I speak, my choler is so great.
O, I could hew up rocks and fight with flint,
I am so angry at these abject terms;   25
And now, like Ajax Telamonius,
On sheep or oxen could I spend my fury.
I am far better born than is the King,
More like a king, more kingly in my thoughts;
But I must make fair weather yet a while,   30
Till Henry be more weak and I more strong.
(*Aloud*) Buckingham, I prithee pardon me,
That I have given no answer all this while;
My mind was troubled with deep melancholy.
The cause why I have brought this army hither   35
Is to remove proud Somerset from the King,
Seditious to his grace and to the state.
BUCKINGHAM
That is too much presumption on thy part;
But if thy arms be to no other end,
The King hath yielded unto thy demand: 40
The Duke of Somerset is in the Tower.
YORK
Upon thine honour, is he prisoner?
BUCKINGHAM
Upon mine honour, he is prisoner.
YORK
Then, Buckingham, I do dismiss my powers.
Soldiers, I thank you all; disperse yourselves;   45
Meet me tomorrow in Saint George's field.
You shall have pay and everything you wish.
                        Exeunt soldiers
(*To Buckingham*) And let my sovereign, virtuous
        Henry,
Command my eldest son—nay, all my sons—
As pledges of my fealty and love.   50
I'll send them all as willing as I live.

Lands, goods, horse, armour, anything I have
Is his to use, so Somerset may die.
BUCKINGHAM
York, I commend this kind submission.
We twain will go into his highness' tent.   55
        Enter King Henry and attendants
KING HENRY
Buckingham, doth York intend no harm to us,
That thus he marcheth with thee arm in arm?
YORK
In all submission and humility
York doth present himself unto your highness.
KING HENRY
Then what intends these forces thou dost bring?   60
YORK
To heave the traitor Somerset from hence,
And fight against that monstrous rebel Cade,
Who since I heard to be discomfited.
        Enter Iden with Cade's head
IDEN
If one so rude and of so mean condition
May pass into the presence of a king,   65
⌈*Kneeling*⌉ Lo, I present your grace a traitor's head,
The head of Cade, whom I in combat slew.
KING HENRY
The head of Cade? Great God, how just art thou!
O let me view his visage, being dead,
That living wrought me such exceeding trouble.   70
Tell me, my friend, art thou the man that slew him?
IDEN ⌈*rising*⌉
Iwis, an't like your majesty.
KING HENRY
How art thou called? And what is thy degree?
IDEN
Alexander Iden, that's my name;
A poor esquire of Kent that loves his king.   75
BUCKINGHAM (*to King Henry*)
So please it you, my lord, 'twere not amiss
He were created knight for his good service.
KING HENRY
Iden, kneel down.
        Iden kneels and King Henry knights him
                        Rise up a knight.
        Iden rises
We give thee for reward a thousand marks,
And will that thou henceforth attend on us.   80
IDEN
May Iden live to merit such a bounty,
And never live but true unto his liege.   ⌈*Exit*⌉
        Enter Queen Margaret and the Duke of Somerset
KING HENRY
See, Buckingham, Somerset comes wi'th' Queen.
Go bid her hide him quickly from the Duke.
QUEEN MARGARET
For thousand Yorks he shall not hide his head,   85
But boldly stand and front him to his face.
YORK
How now? Is Somerset at liberty?

Then, York, unloose thy long imprisoned thoughts,
And let thy tongue be equal with thy heart.
Shall I endure the sight of Somerset?   90
False King, why hast thou broken faith with me,
Knowing how hardly I can brook abuse?
'King' did I call thee? No, thou art not king;
Not fit to govern and rule multitudes,
Which dar'st not—no, nor canst not—rule a traitor. 95
That head of thine doth not become a crown;
Thy hand is made to grasp a palmer's staff,
And not to grace an aweful princely sceptre.
That gold must round engird these brows of mine,
Whose smile and frown, like to Achilles' spear,   100
Is able with the change to kill and cure.
Here is a hand to hold a sceptre up,
And with the same to act controlling laws.
Give place! By heaven, thou shalt rule no more
O'er him whom heaven created for thy ruler.   105

SOMERSET
O monstrous traitor! I arrest thee, York,
Of capital treason 'gainst the King and crown.
Obey, audacious traitor; kneel for grace.

YORK (*to an attendant*)
Sirrah, call in my sons to be my bail.   *Exit attendant*
I know, ere they will have me go to ward,   110
They'll pawn their swords for my enfranchisement.

QUEEN MARGARET ⌈*to Buckingham*⌉
Call hither Clifford; bid him come amain,
To say if that the bastard boys of York
Shall be the surety for their traitor father.
Exit ⌈Buckingham⌉

YORK
O blood-bespotted Neapolitan,   115
Outcast of Naples, England's bloody scourge!
The sons of York, thy betters in their birth,
Shall be their father's bail, and bane to those
That for my surety will refuse the boys.
*Enter ⌈at one door⌉ York's sons Edward and
crookback Richard ⌈with a drummer and soldiers⌉*
See where they come. I'll warrant they'll make it good.
*Enter ⌈at the other door⌉ Clifford ⌈and his son, with
a drummer and soldiers⌉*

QUEEN MARGARET
And here comes Clifford to deny their bail.   121

CLIFFORD (*kneeling before King Henry*)
Health and all happiness to my lord the King.
He rises

YORK
I thank thee, Clifford. Say, what news with thee?
Nay, do not fright us with an angry look—
We are thy sovereign, Clifford; kneel again.   125
For thy mistaking so, we pardon thee.

CLIFFORD
This is my king, York; I do not mistake.
But thou mistakes me much to think I do.
(*To King Henry*)
To Bedlam with him! Is the man grown mad?

KING HENRY
Ay, Clifford, a bedlam and ambitious humour   130
Makes him oppose himself against his king.

CLIFFORD
He is a traitor; let him to the Tower,
And chop away that factious pate of his.

QUEEN MARGARET
He is arrested, but will not obey.
His sons, he says, shall give their words for him.   135

YORK (*to Edward and Richard*) Will you not, sons?

EDWARD
Ay, noble father, if our words will serve.

RICHARD
And if words will not, then our weapons shall.

CLIFFORD
Why, what a brood of traitors have we here!

YORK
Look in a glass, and call thy image so.   140
I am thy king, and thou a false-heart traitor.
Call hither to the stake my two brave bears,
That with the very shaking of their chains,
They may astonish these fell-lurking curs.
(*To an attendant*)
Bid Salisbury and Warwick come to me.   145
Exit attendant
*Enter the Earls of Warwick and Salisbury ⌈with a
drummer and soldiers⌉*

CLIFFORD
Are these thy bears? We'll bait thy bears to death,
And manacle the bearherd in their chains,
If thou dar'st bring them to the baiting place.

RICHARD
Oft have I seen a hot o'erweening cur
Run back and bite, because he was withheld;   150
Who, being suffered with the bear's fell paw,
Hath clapped his tail between his legs and cried;
And such a piece of service will you do,
If you oppose yourselves to match Lord Warwick.

CLIFFORD
Hence, heap of wrath, foul indigested lump,   155
As crooked in thy manners as thy shape!

YORK
Nay, we shall heat you thoroughly anon.

CLIFFORD
Take heed, lest by your heat you burn yourselves.

KING HENRY
Why, Warwick, hath thy knee forgot to bow?
Old Salisbury, shame to thy silver hair,   160
Thou mad misleader of thy brainsick son!
What, wilt thou on thy deathbed play the ruffian,
And seek for sorrow with thy spectacles?
O, where is faith? O, where is loyalty?
If it be banished from the frosty head,   165
Where shall it find a harbour in the earth?
Wilt thou go dig a grave to find out war,
And shame thine honourable age with blood?
Why, art thou old and want'st experience?

Or wherefore dost abuse it if thou hast it?
For shame in duty bend thy knee to me,
That bows unto the grave with mickle age.

SALISBURY
My lord, I have considered with myself
The title of this most renownèd Duke,
And in my conscience do repute his grace   175
The rightful heir to England's royal seat.

KING HENRY
Hast thou not sworn allegiance unto me?

SALISBURY I have.

KING HENRY
Canst thou dispense with heaven for such an oath?

SALISBURY
It is great sin to swear unto a sin,   180
But greater sin to keep a sinful oath.
Who can be bound by any solemn vow
To do a murd'rous deed, to rob a man,
To force a spotless virgin's chastity,
To reave the orphan of his patrimony,   185
To wring the widow from her customed right,
And have no other reason for this wrong
But that he was bound by a solemn oath?

QUEEN MARGARET
A subtle traitor needs no sophister.

KING HENRY (to an attendant)
Call Buckingham, and bid him arm himself.   190
                                                              Exit attendant

YORK (to King Henry)
Call Buckingham and all the friends thou hast,
I am resolved for death or dignity.

CLIFFORD
The first, I warrant thee, if dreams prove true.

WARWICK
You were best to go to bed and dream again,
To keep you from the tempest of the field.   195

CLIFFORD
I am resolved to bear a greater storm
Than any thou canst conjure up today—
And that I'll write upon thy burgonet
Might I but know thee by thy household badge.

WARWICK
Now by my father's badge, old Neville's crest,   200
The rampant bear chained to the ragged staff,
This day I'll wear aloft my burgonet,
As on a mountain top the cedar shows
That keeps his leaves in spite of any storm,
Even to affright thee with the view thereof.   205

CLIFFORD
And from thy burgonet I'll rend thy bear,
And tread it under foot with all contempt,
Despite the bearherd that protects the bear.

YOUNG CLIFFORD
And so to arms, victorious father,
To quell the rebels and their complices.   210

RICHARD
Fie, charity, for shame! Speak not in spite—
For you shall sup with Jesu Christ tonight.

YOUNG CLIFFORD
Foul stigmatic, that's more than thou canst tell.

RICHARD
If not in heaven, you'll surely sup in hell.
                                                              Exeunt severally

5.2 ⌜An alehouse sign: a castle.⌝ Alarums to the battle.
        Then enter the Duke of Somerset and Richard
        fighting. Richard kills Somerset ⌜under the sign⌝

RICHARD So lie thou there—
For underneath an alehouse' paltry sign,
The Castle in Saint Albans, Somerset
Hath made the wizard famous in his death.
Sword, hold thy temper; heart, be wrathfull still—   5
Priests pray for enemies, but princes kill.
                                Exit ⌜with Somerset's body. The sign is
                                                                    removed⌝

5.3 ⌜Alarum again.⌝ Enter the Earl of Warwick

WARWICK
Clifford of Cumberland, 'tis Warwick calls!
An if thou dost not hide thee from the bear,
Now, when the angry trumpet sounds alarum,
And dead men's cries do fill the empty air,
Clifford I say, come forth and fight with me!   5
Proud northern lord, Clifford of Cumberland,
Warwick is hoarse with calling thee to arms!

CLIFFORD (within)
Warwick, stand still; and stir not till I come.
                Enter the Duke of York

WARWICK
How now, my noble lord? What, all afoot?

YORK
The deadly-handed Clifford slew my steed.   10
But match to match I have encountered him,
And made a prey for carrion kites and crows
Even of the bonny beast he loved so well.
                Enter Lord Clifford

WARWICK (to Clifford)
Of one or both of us the time is come.

YORK
Hold, Warwick—seek thee out some other chase,   15
For I myself must hunt this deer to death.

WARWICK
Then nobly, York; 'tis for a crown thou fight'st.
(To Clifford) As I intend, Clifford, to thrive today,
It grieves my soul to leave thee unassailed.   Exit

YORK
Clifford, since we are singled here alone,   20
Be this the day of doom to one of us.
For know my heart hath sworn immortal hate
To thee and all the house of Lancaster.

CLIFFORD
And here I stand and pitch my foot to thine,
Vowing not to stir till thou or I be slain.   25
For never shall my heart be safe at rest
Till I have spoiled the hateful house of York.

Alarums. They fight. York kills Clifford

YORK

Now, Lancaster, sit sure—thy sinews shrink.

Come, fearful Henry, grovelling on thy face—   29

Yield up thy crown unto the prince of York.   *Exit*

Alarums, then enter Young Clifford

YOUNG CLIFFORD

Shame and confusion, all is on the rout!

Fear frames disorder, and disorder wounds

Where it should guard. O, war, thou son of hell,

Whom angry heavens do make their minister,

Throw in the frozen bosoms of our part   35

Hot coals of vengeance! Let no soldier fly!

He that is truly dedicate to war

Hath no self-love; nor he that loves himself

Hath not essentially, but by circumstance,

The name of valour.

He sees his father's body

O, let the vile world end,   40

And the premisèd flames of the last day

Knit earth and heaven together.

Now let the general trumpet blow his blast,

Particularities and petty sounds

To cease! Wast thou ordainèd, dear father,   45

To lose thy youth in peace, and to achieve

The silver livery of advisèd age,

And in thy reverence and thy chair-days, thus

To die in ruffian battle? Even at this sight

My heart is turned to stone, and while 'tis mine   50

It shall be stony. York not our old men spares;

No more will I their babes. Tears virginal

Shall be to me even as the dew to fire,

And beauty that the tyrant oft reclaims

Shall to my flaming wrath be oil and flax.   55

Henceforth I will not have to do with pity.

Meet I an infant of the house of York,

Into as many gobbets will I cut it

As wild Medea young Absyrtus did.

In cruelty will I seek out my fame.   60

Come, thou new ruin of old Clifford's house,

He takes his father's body up on his back

As did Aeneas old Anchises bear,

So bear I thee upon my manly shoulders.

But then Aeneas bare a living load,

Nothing so heavy as these woes of mine.   65

Exit with the body

5.4   ⌈*Alarums again. Then enter three or four bearing*
       the Duke of Buckingham wounded to his tent.⌉
       Alarums still. Enter King Henry, Queen Margaret,
       and others

QUEEN MARGARET

Away, my lord! You are slow. For shame, away!

KING HENRY

Can we outrun the heavens? Good Margaret, stay.

QUEEN MARGARET

What are you made of? You'll nor fight nor fly.

Now is it manhood, wisdom, and defence,

To give the enemy way, and to secure us   5

By what we can, which can no more but fly.

Alarum afar off

If you be ta'en, we then should see the bottom

Of all our fortunes; but if we haply scape—

As well we may if not through your neglect—

We shall to London get where you are loved,   10

And where this breach now in our fortunes made

May readily be stopped.

Enter Young Clifford

YOUNG CLIFFORD (*to King Henry*)

But that my heart's on future mischief set,

I would speak blasphemy ere bid you fly;

But fly you must; uncurable discomfit   15

Reigns in the hearts of all our present parts.

Away for your relief, and we will live

To see their day and them our fortune give.

Away, my lord, away!   *Exeunt*

5.5   *Alarum. Retreat. Enter the Duke of York, his*
       sons Edward and Richard, and soldiers, including a
       drummer and some bearing colours

YORK (*to Edward and Richard*)

How now, boys! Fortunate this fight hath been,

I hope, to us and ours for England's good

And our great honour, that so long we lost

Whilst faint-heart Henry did usurp our rights.

Of Salisbury, who can report of him?   5

That winter lion who in rage forgets

Agèd contusions and all brush of time,

And, like a gallant in the brow of youth,

Repairs him with occasion. This happy day

Is not itself, nor have we won one foot   10

If Salisbury be lost.

RICHARD   My noble father,

Three times today I holp him to his horse;

Three times bestrid him; thrice I led him off,

Persuaded him from any further act;

But still where danger was, still there I met him,   15

And like rich hangings in a homely house,

So was his will in his old feeble body.

Enter the Earls of Salisbury and Warwick

EDWARD (*to York*)

See, noble father, where they both do come—

The only props unto the house of York!

SALISBURY

Now, by my sword, well hast thou fought today;   20

By th' mass, so did we all. I thank you, Richard.

God knows how long it is I have to live,

And it hath pleased him that three times today

You have defended me from imminent death.

Well, lords, we have not got that which we have—   25

'Tis not enough our foes are this time fled,

Being opposites of such repairing nature.

YORK

I know our safety is to follow them,

For, as I hear, the King is fled to London,

To call a present court of Parliament.   30

Let us pursue him ere the writs go forth.
What says Lord Warwick, shall we after them?
WARWICK
After them? Nay, before them if we can!
Now by my hand, lords, 'twas a glorious day!

Saint Albans battle won by famous York   35
Shall be eternized in all age to come.
Sound drums and trumpets, and to London all,
And more such days as these to us befall!
                                    ⌐Flourish.⌐ Exeunt

ADDITIONAL PASSAGES

A. We adopt the 1594 Quarto version of the Queen's
initial speech, 1.1.24–9; the Folio version, which follows,
is probably the author's original draft.

QUEEN MARGARET
Great King of England, and my gracious lord,
The mutual conference that my mind hath had—
By day, by night; waking, and in my dreams;
In courtly company, or at my beads—
With you, mine alder liefest sovereign,   5
Makes me the bolder to salute my king
With ruder terms, such as my wit affords
And overjoy of heart doth minister.

B. For 1.4.39–40.2 the Quarto substitutes the following;
it may report a revision made in rehearsal to cover the
Spirit's descent.

                              The Spirit sinks down again
BOLINGBROKE
Then down, I say, unto the damnèd pool
Where Pluto in his fiery wagon sits
Riding, amidst the singed and parchèd smokes,
The road of Ditis by the River Styx.
There howl and burn for ever in those flames.   5
Rise, Jordan, rise, and stay thy charming spells—
Zounds, we are betrayed!

C. The entire debate on Duke Humphrey's death in 3.1 is
handled differently by the Quarto from the Folio. We retain
the Folio version of the debate, but the Quarto version may
represent authorial revision. The following Q lines, roughly
corresponding to 3.1.310–30.1, are of particular interest
because they supply Buckingham with speeches for this
latter part of the scene.

[YORK]
Let me have some bands of chosen soldiers,
And York shall try his fortune 'gainst those kerns.
QUEEN MARGARET
York, thou shalt. My lord of Buckingham,
Let it be your charge to muster up such soldiers
As shall suffice him in these needful wars.   5

BUCKINGHAM
Madam, I will, and levy such a band
As soon shall overcome those Irish rebels.
But, York, where shall those soldiers stay for thee?
YORK
At Bristol I will expect them ten days hence.   9
BUCKINGHAM
Then thither shall they come, and so farewell.   *Exit*
YORK
Adieu, my lord of Buckingham.
QUEEN MARGARET
Suffolk, remember what you have to do—
And you, Lord Cardinal—concerning Duke Humphrey.
'Twere good that you did see to it in time.
Come, let us go, that it may be performed.   15
                                Exeunt all but York

D. We adopt the Quarto version of the confrontation
between Clifford and York at 5.3.20–30; the Folio version,
an edited text of which follows, is probably the author's
original draft.

CLIFFORD
What seest thou in me, York? Why dost thou pause?
YORK
With thy brave bearing should I be in love,
But that thou art so fast mine enemy.
CLIFFORD
Nor should thy prowess want praise and esteem,
But that 'tis shown ignobly and in treason.   5
YORK
So let it help me now against thy sword,
As I in justice and true right express it.
CLIFFORD
My soul and body on the action, both.
YORK
A dreadful lay. Address thee instantly.
CLIFFORD
La fin couronne les oeuvres.   10
        Alarms. They fight. York kills Clifford
YORK
Thus war hath given thee peace, for thou art still.
Peace with his soul, heaven, if it be thy will.   *Exit*

RICHARD DUKE OF YORK
(3 HENRY VI)

THE play printed in the 1623 Folio as *The Third Part of Henry the Sixth, with the Death of the Duke of York* was described on the title-page of its first, unauthoritative publication in 1595 as *The True Tragedy of Richard, Duke of York, and the Death of Good King Henry the Sixth, with the whole Contention between the two houses Lancaster and York*. It is clearly a continuation of *The First Part of the Contention*, taking up the story where that play had ended, with the aspirations of Richard, Duke of York to the English throne, and was probably composed immediately afterwards.

The final scenes of *The First Part of the Contention* briefly introduce two of York's sons, Edward (the eldest) and Richard (already described as a 'foul, indigested lump, | As crooked in . . . manners as [in] shape'). They, along with their brothers Edmund, Earl of Rutland, and George (later Duke of Clarence), figure more prominently in *Richard Duke of York*. The first scenes show York apparently fulfilling his ambition, as Henry VI weakly cedes his rights to the throne after his death; but Queen Margaret leads an army against York, and, when he is captured, personally taunts him with news of the murder of his youngest son, stabs York to death, and commands that his head be 'set on York gates'. (This powerful scene includes the line 'O tiger's heart wrapped in a woman's hide', paraphrased by Robert Greene before September 1592, which establishes the upward limit of the play's date.)

Though Richard of York dies early in the action, the remainder of the play centres on his sons' efforts (aided by Warwick's politic schemings) to avenge his death and to establish the dominance of Yorkists over Lancastrians. The balance of power shifts frequently, and the brothers' alliance crumbles, but finally Queen Margaret, with her French allies, is defeated and captured, and Richard of York's surviving sons avenge their father's death by killing her son, Edward, before her eyes. Richard of Gloucester starts to clear his way to the throne by murdering 'Good King Henry' in the Tower, and the play ends with the new King Edward IV exulting in his 'country's peace and brothers' loves' while Richard makes clear to the audience that Edward's self-confidence is ill-founded.

Though the play is loud and strife-ridden with war, power politics, and personal ambition, a concern with humane values emerges in the subtle and touching continuing portrayal of the quietist Henry VI, a saintly fool who meditates on the superiority of humble contentment to regal misery in an emblematic scene (2.5) that epitomizes the tragedy of civil strife.

Richard Duke of York, like *The First Part of the Contention*, draws extensively on English chronicle history. Historically, the period of the action covers about sixteen years (1455 to 1471), but events are telescoped and rearranged; for instance, the opening scenes move rapidly from the Battle of St Albans (1445) to York's death (1450); the future Richard III was only three years old, and living abroad, at the time of this opening battle in which he takes an active part; and Richard's murder of Henry owes more to legend than to fact.

THE PERSONS OF THE PLAY

Of the King's Party

KING HENRY VI

QUEEN MARGARET

PRINCE EDWARD, their son

Duke of SOMERSET

Duke of EXETER

Earl of NORTHUMBERLAND

Earl of WESTMORLAND

Lord CLIFFORD

Lord Stafford

SOMERVILLE

Henry, young Earl of Richmond

A SOLDIER who has killed his father

A HUNTSMAN who guards King Edward

The Divided House of Neville

Earl of WARWICK, first of York's party, later of Lancaster's

Marquis of MONTAGUE, his brother, of York's party

Earl of OXFORD, their brother-in-law, of Lancaster's party

Lord HASTINGS, their brother-in-law, of York's party

Of the Duke of York's Party

Richard Plantagenet, Duke of YORK

EDWARD, Earl of March, his son, later Duke of York and KING EDWARD IV

LADY GRAY, a widow, later Edward's wife and queen

Earl RIVERS, her brother

GEORGE, Edward's brother, later Duke OF CLARENCE

RICHARD, Edward's brother, later Duke OF GLOUCESTER

Earl of RUTLAND, Edward's brother

Rutland's TUTOR, a chaplain

SIR JOHN Mortimer, York's uncle

Sir Hugh Mortimer, his brother

Duke of NORFOLK

Sir William Stanley

Earl of Pembroke

Sir John MONTGOMERY

A NOBLEMAN

Two GAMEKEEPERS

Three WATCHMEN, who guard King Edward's tent

LIEUTENANT of the Tower

The French

KING LOUIS

LADY BONA, his sister-in-law

Lord Bourbon, the French High Admiral

Others

A SOLDIER who has killed his son

Mayor of Coventry

MAYOR of York

Aldermen of York

Soldiers, messengers, and attendants

42

The True Tragedy of Richard Duke of York and the Good King Henry the Sixth

1.1 *A chair of state. Alarum. Enter Richard*
Plantagenet, Duke of York, his two sons Edward,
Earl of March, and Crookback Richard, the Duke of
Norfolk, the Marquis of Montague, and the Earl of
Warwick, ⌜with drummers⌝ and soldiers. ⌜They all
wear white roses in their hats⌝

WARWICK
I wonder how the King escaped our hands?

YORK
While we pursued the horsemen of the north,
He slyly stole away and left his men;
Whereat the great lord of Northumberland,
Whose warlike ears could never brook retreat,
Cheered up the drooping army; and himself,   5
Lord Clifford, and Lord Stafford, all abreast,
Charged our main battle's front, and, breaking in,
Were by the swords of common soldiers slain.

EDWARD
Lord Stafford's father, Duke of Buckingham,   10
Is either slain or wounded dangerous.
I cleft his beaver with a downright blow.
That this is true, father, behold his blood.
He shows a bloody sword

MONTAGUE ⌜to York⌝
And, brother, here's the Earl of Wiltshire's blood,
He shows a bloody sword
Whom I encountered as the battles joined.   15

RICHARD (*to Somerset's head, which he shows*)
Speak thou for me, and tell them what I did.

YORK
Richard hath best deserved of all my sons.
(*To the head*) But is your grace dead, my lord of
Somerset?

NORFOLK
Such hap have all the line of John of Gaunt.

RICHARD
Thus do I hope to shake King Henry's head.   20
⌜*He holds aloft the head, then throws it down*⌝

WARWICK
And so do I, victorious prince of York.
Before I see thee seated in that throne
Which now the house of Lancaster usurps,
I vow by heaven these eyes shall never close.
This is the palace of the fearful King,   25
And this (*pointing to the chair of state*), the regal
seat—possess it, York,
For this is thine, and not King Henry's heirs'.

YORK
Assist me then, sweet Warwick, and I will,
For hither we have broken in by force.

NORFOLK
We'll all assist you—he that flies shall die.   30

YORK
Thanks, gentle Norfolk. Stay by me, my lords
And soldiers—stay, and lodge by me this night.
They go up upon the state

WARWICK
And when the King comes, offer him no violence
Unless he seek to thrust you out perforce.
⌜*The soldiers withdraw*⌝

YORK
The Queen this day here holds her Parliament,   35
But little thinks we shall be of her council;
By words or blows here let us win our right.

RICHARD
Armed as we are, let's stay within this house.

WARWICK
'The Bloody Parliament' shall this be called,
Unless Plantagenet, Duke of York, be king,   40
And bashful Henry deposed, whose cowardice
Hath made us bywords to our enemies.

YORK
Then leave me not, my lords. Be resolute—
I mean to take possession of my right.

WARWICK
Neither the King nor he that loves him best—   45
The proudest he that holds up Lancaster—
Dares stir a wing if Warwick shake his bells.
I'll plant Plantagenet, root him up who dares.
Resolve thee, Richard—claim the English crown.
⌜*York sits in the chair.*⌝
Flourish. Enter King Henry, Lord Clifford, the Earls
of Northumberland and Westmorland, the Duke of
Exeter, and the rest. ⌜They all wear red roses in
their hats⌝

KING HENRY
My lords, look where the sturdy rebel sits—   50
Even in the chair of state! Belike he means,
Backed by the power of Warwick, that false peer,
To aspire unto the crown and reign as king.
Earl of Northumberland, he slew thy father—
And thine, Lord Clifford—and you both have vowed
revenge   55
On him, his sons, his favourites, and his friends.

NORTHUMBERLAND
If I be not, heavens be revenged on me.

CLIFFORD
The hope thereof makes Clifford mourn in steel.

WESTMORLAND
What, shall we suffer this? Let's pluck him down.
My heart for anger burns—I cannot brook it.   60

KING HENRY
Be patient, gentle Earl of Westmorland.

CLIFFORD
Patience is for poltroons, such as he (*indicating York*).
He durst not sit there had your father lived.
My gracious lord, here in the Parliament
Let us assail the family of York.   65
NORTHUMBERLAND
Well hast thou spoken, cousin, be it so.
KING HENRY
Ah, know you not the city favours them,
And they have troops of soldiers at their beck?
EXETER
But when the Duke is slain, they'll quickly fly.
KING HENRY
Far be the thought of this from Henry's heart,   70
To make a shambles of the Parliament House.
Cousin of Exeter, frowns, words, and threats
Shall be the war that Henry means to use.
(*To York*) Thou factious Duke of York, descend my
      throne
And kneel for grace and mercy at my feet.   75
I am thy sovereign.
YORK   I am thine.
EXETER
For shame, come down—he made thee Duke of York.
YORK
It was mine inheritance, as the earldom was.
EXETER
Thy father was a traitor to the crown.
WARWICK
Exeter, thou art a traitor to the crown   80
In following this usurping Henry.
CLIFFORD
Whom should he follow but his natural king?
WARWICK
True, Clifford, and that's Richard Duke of York.
KING HENRY (*to York*)
And shall I stand and thou sit in my throne?
YORK
It must and shall be so—content thyself.   85
WARWICK (*to King Henry*)
Be Duke of Lancaster, let him be king.
WESTMORLAND
He is both king and Duke of Lancaster—
And that, the Lord of Westmorland shall maintain.
WARWICK
And Warwick shall disprove it. You forget
That we are those which chased you from the field,   90
And slew your fathers, and, with colours spread,
Marched through the city to the palace gates.
NORTHUMBERLAND
Yes, Warwick, I remember it to my grief,
And, by his soul, thou and thy house shall rue it.
WESTMORLAND (*to York*)
Plantagenet, of thee, and these thy sons,   95
Thy kinsmen, and thy friends, I'll have more lives
Than drops of blood were in my father's veins.
CLIFFORD (*to Warwick*)
Urge it no more, lest that, instead of words,

I send thee, Warwick, such a messenger
As shall revenge his death before I stir.   100
WARWICK ⌈*to York*⌉
Poor Clifford, how I scorn his worthless threats.
YORK ⌈*to King Henry*⌉
Will you we show our title to the crown?
If not, our swords shall plead it in the field.
KING HENRY
What title hast thou, traitor, to the crown?
Thy father was, as thou art, Duke of York;   105
Thy grandfather, Roger Mortimer, Earl of March.
I am the son of Henry the Fifth,
Who made the Dauphin and the French to stoop
And seized upon their towns and provinces.
WARWICK
Talk not of France, sith thou hast lost it all.   110
KING HENRY
The Lord Protector lost it, and not I.
When I was crowned, I was but nine months old.
RICHARD
You are old enough now, and yet, methinks, you lose.
(*To York*) Father, tear the crown from the usurper's
      head.
EDWARD (*to York*)
Sweet father, do so—set it on your head.   115
MONTAGUE (*to York*)
Good brother, as thou lov'st and honour'st arms,
Let's fight it out and not stand cavilling thus.
RICHARD
Sound drums and trumpets, and the King will fly.
YORK Sons, peace!
⌈NORTHUMBERLAND⌉
Peace, thou—and give King Henry leave to speak.   120
KING HENRY
Ah, York, why seekest thou to depose me?
Are we not both Plantagenets by birth,
And from two brothers lineally descent?
Suppose by right and equity thou be king—
Think'st thou that I will leave my kingly throne,   125
Wherein my grandsire and my father sat?
No—first shall war unpeople this my realm;
Ay, and their colours, often borne in France,
And now in England to our heart's great sorrow,
Shall be my winding-sheet. Why faint you, lords?   130
My title's good, and better far than his.
WARWICK
Prove it, Henry, and thou shalt be king.
KING HENRY
Henry the Fourth by conquest got the crown.
YORK
'Twas by rebellion against his king.
KING HENRY ⌈*aside*⌉
I know not what to say—my title's weak.   135
(*To York*) Tell me, may not a king adopt an heir?
YORK What then?
KING HENRY
An if he may, then am I lawful king—
For Richard, in the view of many lords,

44

Resigned the crown to Henry the Fourth,   140
Whose heir my father was, and I am his.
YORK
He rose against him, being his sovereign,
And made him to resign his crown perforce.
WARWICK
Suppose, my lords, he did it unconstrained—
Think you 'twere prejudicial to his crown?   145
EXETER
No, for he could not so resign his crown
But that the next heir should succeed and reign.
KING HENRY
Art thou against us, Duke of Exeter?
EXETER
His is the right, and therefore pardon me.
YORK
Why whisper you, my lords, and answer not?   150
EXETER ⌜*to King Henry*⌝
My conscience tells me he is lawful king.
KING HENRY ⌜*aside*⌝
All will revolt from me and turn to him.
NORTHUMBERLAND (*to York*)
Plantagenet, for all the claim thou lay'st,
Think not that Henry shall be so deposed.
WARWICK
Deposed he shall be, in despite of all.   155
NORTHUMBERLAND
Thou art deceived—'tis not thy southern power
Of Essex, Norfolk, Suffolk, nor of Kent,
Which makes thee thus presumptuous and proud,
Can set the Duke up in despite of me.
CLIFFORD
King Henry, be thy title right or wrong,   160
Lord Clifford vows to fight in thy defence.
May that ground gape and swallow me alive
Where I shall kneel to him that slew my father.
KING HENRY
O, Clifford, how thy words revive my heart!
YORK
Henry of Lancaster, resign thy crown.   165
What mutter you, or what conspire you, lords?
WARWICK
Do right unto this princely Duke of York,
Or I will fill the house with armèd men
And over the chair of state, where now he sits,
Write up his title with usurping blood.   170
          He stamps with his foot and the soldiers show
          themselves
KING HENRY
My lord of Warwick, hear me but one word—
Let me for this my lifetime reign as king.
YORK
Confirm the crown to me and to mine heirs,
And thou shalt reign in quiet while thou liv'st.
KING HENRY
I am content. Richard Plantagenet,   175
Enjoy the kingdom after my decease.
CLIFFORD
What wrong is this unto the prince your son?

WARWICK
What good is this to England and himself?
WESTMORLAND
Base, fearful, and despairing Henry.
CLIFFORD
How hast thou injured both thyself and us?   180
WESTMORLAND
I cannot stay to hear these articles.
NORTHUMBERLAND Nor I.
CLIFFORD
Come, cousin, let us tell the Queen these news.
WESTMORLAND (*to King Henry*)
Farewell, faint-hearted and degenerate king,
In whose cold blood no spark of honour bides.   185
          ⌜*Exit with his soldiers*⌝
NORTHUMBERLAND (*to King Henry*)
Be thou a prey unto the house of York,
And die in bands for this unmanly deed.
          ⌜*Exit with his soldiers*⌝
CLIFFORD (*to King Henry*)
In dreadful war mayst thou be overcome,
Or live in peace, abandoned and despised.
          Exit ⌜*with his soldiers*⌝
WARWICK (*to King Henry*)
Turn this way, Henry, and regard them not.   190
EXETER (*to King Henry*)
They seek revenge and therefore will not yield.
KING HENRY
Ah, Exeter.
WARWICK   Why should you sigh, my lord?
KING HENRY
Not for myself, Lord Warwick, but my son,
Whom I unnaturally shall disinherit.
But be it as it may. (*To York*) I here entail   195
The crown to thee and to thine heirs for ever,
Conditionally, that here thou take thine oath
To cease this civil war, and whilst I live
To honour me as thy king and sovereign,
And nor by treason nor hostility   200
To seek to put me down and reign thyself.
YORK
This oath I willingly take and will perform.
WARWICK
Long live King Henry. (*To York*) Plantagenet, embrace
him.
          ⌜*York descends.*⌝ *Henry and York embrace*
KING HENRY (*to York*)
And long live thou, and these thy forward sons.
YORK
Now York and Lancaster are reconciled.   205
EXETER
Accursèd be he that seeks to make them foes.
          Sennet. Here York's train comes down from the
          state
YORK (*to King Henry*)
Farewell, my gracious lord, I'll to my castle.
          Exeunt York, Edward, and Richard, ⌜*with*
                                        soldiers⌝

WARWICK
And I'll keep London with my soldiers.

Exit ⌈with soldiers⌉

NORFOLK
And I to Norfolk with my followers.

Exit ⌈with soldiers⌉

MONTAGUE
And I unto the sea from whence I came.   210

Exit ⌈with soldiers⌉

KING HENRY
And I with grief and sorrow to the court.

⌈*King Henry and Exeter turn to leave.*⌉
Enter Queen Margaret and Prince Edward

EXETER
Here comes the Queen, whose looks bewray her anger.
I'll steal away.

KING HENRY   Exeter, so will I.

QUEEN MARGARET
Nay, go not from me—I will follow thee.

KING HENRY
Be patient, gentle Queen, and I will stay.   215

QUEEN MARGARET
Who can be patient in such extremes?
Ah, wretched man, would I had died a maid
And never seen thee, never borne thee son,
Seeing thou hast proved so unnatural a father.
Hath he deserved to lose his birthright thus?   220
Hadst thou but loved him half so well as I,
Or felt that pain which I did for him once,
Or nourished him as I did with my blood,
Thou wouldst have left thy dearest heart-blood there
Rather than have made that savage Duke thine heir
And disinherited thine only son.   226

PRINCE EDWARD
Father, you cannot disinherit me.
If you be king, why should not I succeed?

KING HENRY
Pardon me, Margaret; pardon me, sweet son—
The Earl of Warwick and the Duke enforced me.   230

QUEEN MARGARET
Enforced thee? Art thou king, and wilt be forced?
I shame to hear thee speak! Ah, timorous wretch,
Thou hast undone thyself, thy son, and me,
And giv'n unto the house of York such head
As thou shalt reign but by their sufferance.   235
To entail him and his heirs unto the crown—
What is it, but to make thy sepulchre
And creep into it far before thy time?
Warwick is Chancellor and the Lord of Calais;
Stern Falconbridge commands the narrow seas;   240
The Duke is made Protector of the Realm;
And yet shalt thou be safe? Such safety finds
The trembling lamb environèd with wolves.
Had I been there, which am a seely woman,
The soldiers should have tossed me on their pikes   245
Before I would have granted to that act.
But thou preferr'st thy life before thine honour.
And seeing thou dost, I here divorce myself
Both from thy table, Henry, and thy bed,

Until that act of Parliament be repealed   250
Whereby my son is disinherited.
The northern lords that have forsworn thy colours
Will follow mine, if once they see them spread—
And spread they shall be, to thy foul disgrace
And the utter ruin of the house of York.   255
Thus do I leave thee. (*To Prince Edward*) Come, son,
          let's away.
Our army is ready—come, we'll after them.

KING HENRY
Stay, gentle Margaret, and hear me speak.

QUEEN MARGARET
Thou hast spoke too much already.

⌈*To Prince Edward*⌉   Get thee gone.

KING HENRY
Gentle son Edward, thou wilt stay with me?   260

QUEEN MARGARET
Ay, to be murdered by his enemies.

PRINCE EDWARD (*to King Henry*)
When I return with victory from the field,
I'll see your grace. Till then, I'll follow her.

QUEEN MARGARET
Come, son, away—we may not linger thus.

Exit with Prince Edward

KING HENRY
Poor Queen, how love to me and to her son   265
Hath made her break out into terms of rage.
Revenged may she be on that hateful Duke,
Whose haughty spirit, wingèd with desire,
Will coast my crown, and, like an empty eagle,
Tire on the flesh of me and of my son.   270
The loss of those three lords torments my heart.
I'll write unto them and entreat them fair.
Come, cousin, you shall be the messenger.

EXETER
And I, I hope, shall reconcile them all.

Flourish. Exeunt

1.2   *Enter Richard, Edward Earl of March, and the*
          Marquis of Montague

RICHARD
Brother, though I be youngest give me leave.

EDWARD
No, I can better play the orator.

MONTAGUE
But I have reasons strong and forcible.

Enter the Duke of York

YORK
Why, how now, sons and brother—at a strife?
What is your quarrel? How began it first?   5

EDWARD
No quarrel, but a slight contention.

YORK About what?

RICHARD
About that which concerns your grace and us—
The crown of England, father, which is yours.

YORK
Mine, boy? Not till King Henry be dead.   10

RICHARD
Your right depends not on his life or death.

EDWARD
Now you are heir—therefore enjoy it now.
By giving the house of Lancaster leave to breathe,
It will outrun you, father, in the end.

YORK
I took an oath that he should quietly reign.   15

EDWARD
But for a kingdom any oath may be broken.
I would break a thousand oaths to reign one year.

RICHARD (to York)
No—God forbid your grace should be forsworn.

YORK
I shall be if I claim by open war.

RICHARD
I'll prove the contrary, if you'll hear me speak.   20

YORK
Thou canst not, son—it is impossible.

RICHARD
An oath is of no moment being not took
Before a true and lawful magistrate
That hath authority over him that swears.
Henry had none, but did usurp the place.   25
Then, seeing 'twas he that made you to depose,
Your oath, my lord, is vain and frivolous.
Therefore to arms—and, father, do but think
How sweet a thing it is to wear a crown,
Within whose circuit is Elysium   30
And all that poets feign of bliss and joy.
Why do we linger thus? I cannot rest
Until the white rose that I wear be dyed
Even in the luke-warm blood of Henry's heart.

YORK
Richard, enough! I will be king or die.   35
(To Montague) Brother, thou shalt to London presently
And whet on Warwick to this enterprise.
Thou, Richard, shalt to the Duke of Norfolk
And tell him privily of our intent.
You, Edward, shall to Edmund Brook, Lord Cobham,
With whom the Kentishmen will willingly rise.   41
In them I trust, for they are soldiers
Witty, courteous, liberal, full of spirit.
While you are thus employed, what resteth more
But that I seek occasion how to rise,   45
And yet the King not privy to my drift,
Nor any of the house of Lancaster.

Enter a Messenger
But stay, what news? Why com'st thou in such post?

MESSENGER
The Queen, with all the northern earls and lords,
Intend here to besiege you in your castle.   50
She is hard by with twenty thousand men,
And therefore fortify your hold, my lord.

YORK
Ay, with my sword. What—think'st thou that we fear
    them?
Edward and Richard, you shall stay with me;
My brother Montague shall post to London.   55

Let noble Warwick, Cobham, and the rest,
Whom we have left protectors of the King,
With powerful policy strengthen themselves,
And trust not simple Henry nor his oaths.

MONTAGUE
Brother, I go—I'll win them, fear it not.   60
And thus most humbly I do take my leave.   _Exit_

Enter Sir John Mortimer and his brother Sir Hugh

YORK
Sir John and Sir Hugh Mortimer, mine uncles,
You are come to Sandal in a happy hour.
The army of the Queen mean to besiege us.

SIR JOHN
She shall not need, we'll meet her in the field.   65

YORK What, with five thousand men?

RICHARD
Ay, with five hundred, father, for a need.
A woman's general—what should we fear?

A march sounds afar off

EDWARD
I hear their drums. Let's set our men in order,
And issue forth and bid them battle straight.   70

YORK ⌐to Sir John and Sir Hugh¬
Five men to twenty—though the odds be great,
I doubt not, uncles, of our victory.
Many a battle have I won in France
Whenas the enemy hath been ten to one—
Why should I not now have the like success?   _Exeunt_

1.3   _Alarums, and then enter the young Earl of Rutland
        and his Tutor, a chaplain_

RUTLAND
Ah, whither shall I fly to scape their hands?

Enter Lord Clifford with soldiers
Ah, tutor, look where bloody Clifford comes.

CLIFFORD (to the Tutor)
Chaplain, away—thy priesthood saves thy life.
As for the brat of this accursèd duke,
Whose father slew my father—he shall die.   5

TUTOR
And I, my lord, will bear him company.

CLIFFORD Soldiers, away with him.

TUTOR
Ah, Clifford, murder not this innocent child
Lest thou be hated both of God and man.

                                    Exit, guarded

⌐_Rutland falls to the ground_¬

CLIFFORD
How now—is he dead already?   10
Or is it fear that makes him close his eyes?
I'll open them.

RUTLAND ⌐_reviving_¬
So looks the pent-up lion o'er the wretch
That trembles under his devouring paws,
And so he walks, insulting o'er his prey,   15
And so he comes to rend his limbs asunder.
Ah, gentle Clifford, kill me with thy sword
And not with such a cruel threat'ning look.
Sweet Clifford, hear me speak before I die.

I am too mean a subject for thy wrath. 20
Be thou revenged on men, and let me live.

CLIFFORD
In vain thou speak'st, poor boy. My father's blood
Hath stopped the passage where thy words should
    enter.

RUTLAND
Then let my father's blood open it again.
He is a man, and, Clifford, cope with him. 25

CLIFFORD
Had I thy brethren here, their lives and thine
Were not revenge sufficient for me.
No—if I digged up thy forefathers' graves,
And hung their rotten coffins up in chains,
It could not slake mine ire nor ease my heart. 30
The sight of any of the house of York
Is as a fury to torment my soul.
And till I root out their accursèd line,
And leave not one alive, I live in hell.
Therefore— 35

RUTLAND
O, let me pray before I take my death.
⌈Kneeling⌉ To thee I pray: sweet Clifford, pity me.

CLIFFORD
Such pity as my rapier's point affords.

RUTLAND
I never did thee harm—why wilt thou slay me?

CLIFFORD
Thy father hath.

RUTLAND   But 'twas ere I was born. 40
Thou hast one son—for his sake pity me,
Lest in revenge thereof, sith God is just,
He be as miserably slain as I.
Ah, let me live in prison all my days,
And when I give occasion of offence, 45
Then let me die, for now thou hast no cause.

CLIFFORD
No cause? Thy father slew my father, therefore die.
    He stabs him

RUTLAND
Dii faciant laudis summa sit ista tuae.   *He dies*

CLIFFORD
Plantagenet—I come, Plantagenet!
And this thy son's blood cleaving to my blade 50
Shall rust upon my weapon till thy blood,
Congealed with this, do make me wipe off both.
    Exit with Rutland's body ⌈and soldiers⌉

1.4   *Alarum. Enter Richard Duke of York*

YORK
The army of the Queen hath got the field;
My uncles both are slain in rescuing me;
And all my followers to the eager foe
Turn back, and fly like ships before the wind,
Or lambs pursued by hunger-starvèd wolves. 5
My sons—God knows what hath bechancèd them.
But this I know—they have demeaned themselves
Like men born to renown by life or death.

Three times did Richard make a lane to me,
And thrice cried, 'Courage, father, fight it out!' 10
And full as oft came Edward to my side,
With purple falchion painted to the hilt
In blood of those that had encountered him.
And when the hardiest warriors did retire,
Richard cried, 'Charge and give no foot of ground!' 15
⌈   ⌉
And cried 'A crown or else a glorious tomb!
A sceptre or an earthly sepulchre!'
With this, we charged again—but out, alas—
We bodged again, as I have seen a swan 20
With bootless labour swim against the tide
And spend her strength with over-matching waves.
    A short alarum within
Ah, hark—the fatal followers do pursue,
And I am faint and cannot fly their fury;
And were I strong, I would not shun their fury. 25
The sands are numbered that makes up my life.
Here must I stay, and here my life must end.
    Enter Queen Margaret, Lord Clifford, the Earl of
    Northumberland, and the young Prince Edward,
    with soldiers
Come bloody Clifford, rough Northumberland—
I dare your quenchless fury to more rage!
I am your butt, and I abide your shot. 30

NORTHUMBERLAND
Yield to our mercy, proud Plantagenet.

CLIFFORD
Ay, to such mercy as his ruthless arm,
With downright payment, showed unto my father.
Now Phaëton hath tumbled from his car,
And made an evening at the noontide prick. 35

YORK
My ashes, as the phoenix, may bring forth
A bird that will revenge upon you all,
And in that hope I throw mine eyes to heaven,
Scorning whate'er you can afflict me with.
Why come you not? What—multitudes, and fear? 40

CLIFFORD
So cowards fight when they can fly no further;
So doves do peck the falcon's piercing talons;
So desperate thieves, all hopeless of their lives,
Breathe out invectives 'gainst the officers.

YORK
O, Clifford, but bethink thee once again, 45
And in thy thought o'errun my former time,
And, if thou canst for blushing, view this face
And bite thy tongue, that slanders him with cowardice
Whose frown hath made thee faint and fly ere this.

CLIFFORD
I will not bandy with thee word for word, 50
But buckle with thee blows twice two for one.
    ⌈He draws his sword⌉

QUEEN MARGARET
Hold, valiant Clifford: for a thousand causes
I would prolong a while the traitor's life.
Wrath makes him deaf—speak thou, Northumberland.

NORTHUMBERLAND
  Hold, Clifford—do not honour him so much   55
  To prick thy finger though to wound his heart.
  What valour were it when a cur doth grin
  For one to thrust his hand between his teeth
  When he might spurn him with his foot away?
  It is war's prize to take all vantages,   60
  And ten to one is no impeach of valour.
        They [fight and] take York
CLIFFORD
  Ay, ay, so strives the woodcock with the gin.
NORTHUMBERLAND
  So doth the cony struggle in the net.
YORK
  So triumph thieves upon their conquered booty,
  So true men yield, with robbers so o'ermatched.   65
NORTHUMBERLAND (*to the Queen*)
  What would your grace have done unto him now?
QUEEN MARGARET
  Brave warriors, Clifford and Northumberland,
  Come make him stand upon this molehill here,
  That wrought at mountains with outstretchèd arms
  Yet parted but the shadow with his hand.   70
  (*To York*) What—was it you that would be England's
        king?
  Was't you that revelled in our Parliament,
  And made a preachment of your high descent?
  Where are your mess of sons to back you now?
  The wanton Edward and the lusty George?   75
  And where's that valiant crookback prodigy,
  Dickie, your boy, that with his grumbling voice
  Was wont to cheer his dad in mutinies?
  Or with the rest where is your darling Rutland?
  Look, York, I stained this napkin with the blood   80
  That valiant Clifford with his rapier's point
  Made issue from the bosom of thy boy.
  And if thine eyes can water for his death,
  I give thee this to dry thy cheeks withal.
  Alas, poor York, but that I hate thee deadly   85
  I should lament thy miserable state.
  I prithee, grieve, to make me merry, York.
  What—hath thy fiery heart so parched thine entrails
  That not a tear can fall for Rutland's death?
  Why art thou patient, man? Thou shouldst be mad, 90
  And I, to make thee mad, do mock thee thus.
  Stamp, rave, and fret, that I may sing and dance.
  Thou wouldst be fee'd, I see, to make me sport.
  York cannot speak unless he wear a crown.
  (*To her men*) A crown for York, and, lords, bow low to
        him.   95
  Hold you his hands whilst I do set it on.
        She puts a paper crown on York's head
  Ay, marry, sir, now looks he like a king,
  Ay, this is he that took King Henry's chair,
  And this is he was his adopted heir.
  But how is it that great Plantagenet   100
  Is crowned so soon and broke his solemn oath?

  As I bethink me, you should not be king
  Till our King Henry had shook hands with death.
  And will you pale your head in Henry's glory,
  And rob his temples of the diadem   105
  Now, in his life, against your holy oath?
  O 'tis a fault too, too, unpardonable.
  Off with the crown,
        [*She knocks it from his head*]
                          and with the crown his head,
  And whilst we breathe, take time to do him dead.
CLIFFORD
  That is my office for my father's sake.   110
QUEEN MARGARET
  Nay, stay—let's hear the orisons he makes.
YORK
  She-wolf of France, but worse than wolves of France,
  Whose tongue more poisons than the adder's tooth—
  How ill-beseeming is it in thy sex
  To triumph like an Amazonian trull   115
  Upon their woes whom fortune captivates!
  But that thy face is visor-like, unchanging,
  Made impudent with use of evil deeds,
  I would essay, proud Queen, to make thee blush.   119
  To tell thee whence thou cam'st, of whom derived,
  Were shame enough to shame thee—wert thou not
        shameless
  Thy father bears the type of King of Naples,
  Of both the Sicils, and Jerusalem—
  Yet not so wealthy as an English yeoman.
  Hath that poor monarch taught thee to insult?   125
  It needs not, nor it boots thee not, proud Queen,
  Unless the adage must be verified
  That beggars mounted run their horse to death.
  'Tis beauty that doth oft make women proud—
  But, God he knows, thy share thereof is small;   130
  'Tis virtue that doth make them most admired—
  The contrary doth make thee wondered at;
  'Tis government that makes them seem divine—
  The want thereof makes thee abominable.
  Thou art as opposite to every good   135
  As the antipodes are unto us,
  Or as the south to the septentrion.
  O tiger's heart wrapped in a woman's hide!
  How couldst thou drain the life-blood of the child
  To bid the father wipe his eyes withal,   140
  And yet be seen to bear a woman's face?
  Women are soft, mild, pitiful, and flexible—
  Thou stern, obdurate, flinty, rough, remorseless.
  Bidd'st thou me rage? Why, now thou hast thy wish.
  Wouldst have me weep? Why, now thou hast thy will.
  For raging wind blows up incessant showers,   146
  And when the rage allays the rain begins.
  These tears are my sweet Rutland's obsequies,
  And every drop cries vengeance for his death
  'Gainst thee, fell Clifford, and thee, false Frenchwoman.
NORTHUMBERLAND
  Beshrew me, but his passions move me so   151
  That hardly can I check my eyes from tears.

YORK
That face of his the hungry cannibals
Would not have touched, would not have stained
    with blood—
But you are more inhuman, more inexorable,   155
O, ten times more than tigers of Hyrcania.
See, ruthless Queen, a hapless father's tears.
This cloth thou dipped'st in blood of my sweet boy,
And I with tears do wash the blood away.
Keep thou the napkin and go boast of this,   160
And if thou tell'st the heavy story right,
Upon my soul the hearers will shed tears,
Yea, even my foes will shed fast-falling tears
And say, 'Alas, it was a piteous deed'.
There, take the crown—and with the crown, my
    curse: 165
And in thy need such comfort come to thee
As now I reap at thy too cruel hand.
Hard-hearted Clifford, take me from the world.
My soul to heaven, my blood upon your heads.
NORTHUMBERLAND
Had he been slaughter-man to all my kin,   170
I should not, for my life, but weep with him,
To see how inly sorrow gripes his soul.
QUEEN MARGARET
What—weeping-ripe, my lord Northumberland?
Think but upon the wrong he did us all,
And that will quickly dry thy melting tears.   175
CLIFFORD
Here's for my oath, here's for my father's death.
    He stabs York
QUEEN MARGARET
And here's to right our gentle-hearted King.
    She stabs York
YORK
Open thy gate of mercy, gracious God—
My soul flies through these wounds to seek out thee.
    ⌈*He dies*⌉
QUEEN MARGARET
Off with his head and set it on York gates,   180
So York may overlook the town of York.
    Flourish. Exeunt with York's body

2.1   *A march. Enter Edward Earl of March and Richard,*
    ⌈*with a drummer and soldiers*⌉
EDWARD
I wonder how our princely father scaped,
Or whether he be scaped away or no
From Clifford's and Northumberland's pursuit.
Had he been ta'en we should have heard the news;
Had he been slain we should have heard the news;   5
Or had he scaped, methinks we should have heard
The happy tidings of his good escape.
How fares my brother? Why is he so sad?
RICHARD
I cannot joy until I be resolved
Where our right valiant father is become.   10
I saw him in the battle range about,

And watched him how he singled Clifford forth.
Methought he bore him in the thickest troop,
As doth a lion in a herd of neat;
Or as a bear encompassed round with dogs,   15
Who having pinched a few and made them cry,
The rest stand all aloof and bark at him.
So fared our father with his enemies;
So fled his enemies my warlike father.
Methinks 'tis prize enough to be his son.   20
    ⌈*Three suns appear in the air*⌉
See how the morning opes her golden gates
And takes her farewell of the glorious sun.
How well resembles it the prime of youth,
Trimmed like a younker prancing to his love!
EDWARD
Dazzle mine eyes, or do I see three suns?   25
RICHARD
Three glorious suns, each one a perfect sun;
Not separated with the racking clouds,
But severed in a pale clear-shining sky.
    ⌈*The three suns begin to join*⌉
See, see—they join, embrace, and seem to kiss,
As if they vowed some league inviolable.   30
Now are they but one lamp, one light, one sun.
In this the heaven figures some event.
EDWARD
'Tis wondrous strange, the like yet never heard of.
I think it cites us, brother, to the field,
That we, the sons of brave Plantagenet,   35
Each one already blazing by our meeds,
Should notwithstanding join our lights together
And over-shine the earth as this the world.
Whate'er it bodes, henceforward will I bear
Upon my target three fair-shining suns.   40
RICHARD
Nay, bear three daughters—by your leave I speak it—
You love the breeder better than the male.
    Enter one blowing
But what art thou whose heavy looks foretell
Some dreadful story hanging on thy tongue?
MESSENGER
Ah, one that was a woeful looker-on   45
Whenas the noble Duke of York was slain—
Your princely father and my loving lord.
EDWARD
O, speak no more, for I have heard too much.
RICHARD
Say how he died, for I will hear it all.
MESSENGER
Environèd he was with many foes,   50
And stood against them as the hope of Troy
Against the Greeks that would have entered Troy.
But Hercules himself must yield to odds;
And many strokes, though with a little axe,
Hews down and fells the hardest-timbered oak.   55
By many hands your father was subdued,
But only slaughtered by the ireful arm
Of unrelenting Clifford and the Queen,

Who crowned the gracious Duke in high despite,
Laughed in his face, and when with grief he wept,   60
The ruthless Queen gave him to dry his cheeks
A napkin steepèd in the harmless blood
Of sweet young Rutland, by rough Clifford slain;
And after many scorns, many foul taunts,
They took his head, and on the gates of York   65
They set the same; and there it doth remain,
The saddest spectacle that e'er I viewed.

EDWARD

Sweet Duke of York, our prop to lean upon,
Now thou art gone, we have no staff, no stay.
O Clifford, boist'rous Clifford—thou hast slain   70
The flower of Europe for his chivalry,
And treacherously hast thou vanquished him—
For hand to hand he would have vanquished thee.
Now my soul's palace is become a prison.
Ah, would she break from hence that this my body   75
Might in the ground be closèd up in rest.
For never henceforth shall I joy again—
Never, O never, shall I see more joy.

RICHARD

I cannot weep, for all my body's moisture
Scarce serves to quench my furnace-burning heart;   80
Nor can my tongue unload my heart's great burden,
For selfsame wind that I should speak withal
Is kindling coals that fires all my breast,
And burns me up with flames that tears would quench.
To weep is to make less the depth of grief;   85
Tears, then, for babes—blows and revenge for me!
Richard, I bear thy name; I'll venge thy death
Or die renownèd by attempting it.

EDWARD

His name that valiant Duke hath left with thee,
His dukedom and his chair with me is left.   90

RICHARD

Nay, if thou be that princely eagle's bird,
Show thy descent by gazing 'gainst the sun:
For 'chair and dukedom', 'throne and kingdom' say—
Either that is thine or else thou wert not his.

March. Enter the Earl of Warwick and the Marquis
of Montague ⌈with drummers, an ensign, and
soldiers⌉

WARWICK

How now, fair lords? What fare? What news abroad?

RICHARD

Great lord of Warwick, if we should recount   96
Our baleful news, and at each word's deliverance
Stab poniards in our flesh till all were told,
The words would add more anguish than the wounds.
O valiant lord, the Duke of York is slain.   100

EDWARD

O Warwick, Warwick! That Plantagenet,
Which held thee dearly as his soul's redemption,
Is by the stern Lord Clifford done to death.

WARWICK

Ten days ago I drowned these news in tears.
And now, to add more measure to your woes,   105

I come to tell you things sith then befall'n.
After the bloody fray at Wakefield fought,
Where your brave father breathed his latest gasp,
Tidings, as swiftly as the posts could run,
Were brought me of your loss and his depart.   110
I then in London, keeper of the King,
Mustered my soldiers, gathered flocks of friends,
And, very well appointed as I thought,
Marched toward Saint Albans to intercept the Queen,
Bearing the King in my behalf along—   115
For by my scouts I was advertisèd
That she was coming with a full intent
To dash our late decree in Parliament
Touching King Henry's oath and your succession.
Short tale to make, we at Saint Albans met,   120
Our battles joined, and both sides fiercely fought;
But whether 'twas the coldness of the King,
Who looked full gently on his warlike queen,
That robbed my soldiers of their heated spleen,
Or whether 'twas report of her success,   125
Or more than common fear of Clifford's rigour—
Who thunders to his captains blood and death—
I cannot judge; but, to conclude with truth,
Their weapons like to lightning came and went;
Our soldiers', like the night-owl's lazy flight,   130
Or like an idle thresher with a flail,
Fell gently down, as if they struck their friends.
I cheered them up with justice of our cause,
With promise of high pay, and great rewards.
But all in vain. They had no heart to fight,   135
And we in them no hope to win the day.
So that we fled—the King unto the Queen,
Lord George your brother, Norfolk, and myself
In haste, post-haste, are come to join with you.
For in the Marches here we heard you were,   140
Making another head to fight again.

EDWARD

Where is the Duke of Norfolk, gentle Warwick?
And when came George from Burgundy to England?

WARWICK

Some six miles off the Duke is with his soldiers;
And for your brother—he was lately sent   145
From your kind aunt, Duchess of Burgundy,
With aid of soldiers to this needful war.

RICHARD

'Twas odd belike when valiant Warwick fled.
Oft have I heard his praises in pursuit,
But ne'er till now his scandal of retire.   150

WARWICK

Nor now my scandal, Richard, dost thou hear—
For thou shalt know this strong right hand of mine
Can pluck the diadem from faint Henry's head
And wring the aweful sceptre from his fist,
Were he as famous and as bold in war   155
As he is famed for mildness, peace, and prayer.

RICHARD

I know it well, Lord Warwick—blame me not.
'Tis love I bear thy glories make me speak.

But in this troublous time what's to be done?
Shall we go throw away our coats of steel,   160
And wrap our bodies in black mourning gowns,
Numb'ring our Ave-Maries with our beads?
Or shall we on the helmets of our foes
Tell our devotion with revengeful arms?
If for the last, say 'ay', and to it, lords.   165
WARWICK
Why, therefore Warwick came to seek you out,
And therefore comes my brother Montague.
Attend me, lords. The proud insulting Queen,
With Clifford and the haught Northumberland,
And of their feather many more proud birds,   170
Have wrought the easy-melting King like wax.
(*To Edward*) He swore consent to your succession,
His oath enrollèd in the Parliament.
And now to London all the crew are gone,
To frustrate both his oath and what beside   175
May make against the house of Lancaster.
Their power, I think, is thirty thousand strong.
Now, if the help of Norfolk and myself,
With all the friends that thou, brave Earl of March,
Amongst the loving Welshmen canst procure,   180
Will but amount to five-and-twenty thousand,
Why, *via*, to London will we march,
And once again bestride our foaming steeds,
And once again cry 'Charge!' upon our foes—
But never once again turn back and fly.   185
RICHARD
Ay, now methinks I hear great Warwick speak.
Ne'er may he live to see a sunshine day
That cries 'Retire!' if Warwick bid him stay.
EDWARD
Lord Warwick, on thy shoulder will I lean,
And when thou fail'st—as God forbid the hour—   190
Must Edward fall, which peril heaven forfend!
WARWICK
No longer Earl of March, but Duke of York;
The next degree is England's royal throne—
For King of England shalt thou be proclaimed
In every borough as we pass along,   195
And he that throws not up his cap for joy,
Shall for the fault make forfeit of his head.
King Edward, valiant Richard, Montague—
Stay we no longer dreaming of renown,
But sound the trumpets and about our task.   200
RICHARD
Then, Clifford, were thy heart as hard as steel,
As thou hast shown it flinty by thy deeds,
I come to pierce it or to give thee mine.
EDWARD
Then strike up drums—God and Saint George for us!
Enter a Messenger
WARWICK How now? What news?   205
MESSENGER
The Duke of Norfolk sends you word by me
The Queen is coming with a puissant host,
And craves your company for speedy counsel.

WARWICK
Why then it sorts. Brave warriors, let's away.
                              ⌜*March.*⌝ *Exeunt*

2.2 ⌜*York's head is thrust out, above.*⌝
       Flourish. Enter King Henry, Queen Margaret, Lord
       Clifford, the Earl of Northumberland, and young
       Prince Edward, with a drummer and trumpeters
QUEEN MARGARET
Welcome, my lord, to this brave town of York.
Yonder's the head of that arch-enemy
That sought to be encompassed with your crown.
Doth not the object cheer your heart, my lord?
KING HENRY
Ay, as the rocks cheer them that fear their wreck.   5
To see this sight, it irks my very soul.
Withhold revenge, dear God—'tis not my fault,
Nor wittingly have I infringed my vow.
CLIFFORD
My gracious liege, this too much lenity
And harmful pity must be laid aside.   10
To whom do lions cast their gentle looks?
Not to the beast that would usurp their den.
Whose hand is that the forest bear doth lick?
Not his that spoils her young before her face.
Who scapes the lurking serpent's mortal sting?   15
Not he that sets his foot upon her back.
The smallest worm will turn, being trodden on,
And doves will peck in safeguard of their brood.
Ambitious York did level at thy crown,
Thou smiling while he knit his angry brows.   20
He, but a duke, would have his son a king,
And raise his issue like a loving sire;
Thou, being a king, blest with a goodly son,
Didst yield consent to disinherit him,
Which argued thee a most unloving father.   25
Unreasonable creatures feed their young,
And though man's face be fearful to their eyes,
Yet, in protection of their tender ones,
Who hath not seen them, even with those wings
Which sometime they have used with fearful flight,   30
Make war with him that climbed unto their nest,
Offering their own lives in their young's defence?
For shame, my liege, make them your precedent!
Were it not pity that this goodly boy
Should lose his birthright by his father's fault,   35
And long hereafter say unto his child
'What my great-grandfather and grandsire got
My careless father fondly gave away'?
Ah, what a shame were this! Look on the boy,
And let his manly face, which promiseth   40
Successful fortune, steel thy melting heart
To hold thine own and leave thine own with him.
KING HENRY
Full well hath Clifford played the orator,
Inferring arguments of mighty force.
But, Clifford, tell me—didst thou never hear   45
That things ill got had ever bad success?

And happy always was it for that son
Whose father for his hoarding went to hell?
I'll leave my son my virtuous deeds behind,
And would my father had left me no more.   50
For all the rest is held at such a rate
As brings a thousandfold more care to keep
Than in possession any jot of pleasure.
Ah, cousin York, would thy best friends did know
How it doth grieve me that thy head is here.   55

QUEEN MARGARET
My lord, cheer up your spirits—our foes are nigh,
And this soft courage makes your followers faint.
You promised knighthood to our forward son.
Unsheathe your sword and dub him presently.
Edward, kneel down.   60
Prince Edward kneels

KING HENRY
Edward Plantagenet, arise a knight—
And learn this lesson: draw thy sword in right.

PRINCE EDWARD (*rising*)
My gracious father, by your kingly leave,
I'll draw it as apparent to the crown,
And in that quarrel use it to the death.   65

CLIFFORD
Why, that is spoken like a toward prince.
Enter a Messenger

MESSENGER
Royal commanders, be in readiness—
For with a band of thirty thousand men
Comes Warwick backing of the Duke of York;
And in the towns, as they do march along,   70
Proclaims him king, and many fly to him.
Darraign your battle, for they are at hand.

CLIFFORD (*to King Henry*)
I would your highness would depart the field—
The Queen hath best success when you are absent.

QUEEN MARGARET (*to King Henry*)
Ay, good my lord, and leave us to our fortune.   75

KING HENRY
Why, that's my fortune too—therefore I'll stay.

NORTHUMBERLAND
Be it with resolution then to fight.

PRINCE EDWARD (*to King Henry*)
My royal father, cheer these noble lords
And hearten those that fight in your defence.
Unsheathe your sword, good father; cry 'Saint George!'
*March. Enter Edward Duke of York, the Earl of
Warwick, Richard, George, the Duke of Norfolk, the
Marquis of Montague, and soldiers*

EDWARD
Now, perjured Henry, wilt thou kneel for grace,   81
And set thy diadem upon my head—
Or bide the mortal fortune of the field?

QUEEN MARGARET
Go rate thy minions, proud insulting boy!
Becomes it thee to be thus bold in terms   85
Before thy sovereign and thy lawful king?

EDWARD
I am his king, and he should bow his knee.
I was adopted heir by his consent.

GEORGE (*to Queen Margaret*)
Since when his oath is broke—for, as I hear,
You that are king, though he do wear the crown,   90
Have caused him by new act of Parliament
To blot our brother out, and put his own son in.

CLIFFORD And reason too—
Who should succeed the father but the son?

RICHARD
Are you there, butcher? O, I cannot speak!   95

CLIFFORD
Ay, crookback, here I stand to answer thee,
Or any he the proudest of thy sort.

RICHARD
'Twas you that killed young Rutland, was it not?

CLIFFORD
Ay, and old York, and yet not satisfied.

RICHARD
For God's sake, lords, give signal to the fight.   100

WARWICK
What sayst thou, Henry, wilt thou yield the crown?

QUEEN MARGARET
Why, how now, long-tongued Warwick, dare you
    speak?
When you and I met at Saint Albans last,
Your legs did better service than your hands.

WARWICK
Then 'twas my turn to fly—and now 'tis thine.   105

CLIFFORD
You said so much before, and yet you fled.

WARWICK
'Twas not your valour, Clifford, drove me thence.

NORTHUMBERLAND
No, nor your manhood that durst make you stay.

RICHARD
Northumberland, I hold thee reverently.
Break off the parley, for scarce I can refrain   110
The execution of my big-swoll'n heart
Upon that Clifford, that cruel child-killer.

CLIFFORD
I slew thy father—call'st thou him a child?

RICHARD
Ay, like a dastard and a treacherous coward,
As thou didst kill our tender brother Rutland.   115
But ere sun set I'll make thee curse the deed.

KING HENRY
Have done with words, my lords, and hear me speak.

QUEEN MARGARET
Defy them, then, or else hold close thy lips.

KING HENRY
I prithee give no limits to my tongue—
I am a king, and privileged to speak.   120

CLIFFORD
My liege, the wound that bred this meeting here
Cannot be cured by words—therefore be still.

RICHARD
Then, executioner, unsheathe thy sword.
By him that made us all, I am resolved
That Clifford's manhood lies upon his tongue.   125
EDWARD
Say, Henry, shall I have my right or no?
A thousand men have broke their fasts today
That ne'er shall dine unless thou yield the crown.
WARWICK (to King Henry)
If thou deny, their blood upon thy head;
For York in justice puts his armour on.   130
PRINCE EDWARD
If that be right which Warwick says is right,
There is no wrong, but everything is right.
RICHARD
Whoever got thee, there thy mother stands—
For, well I wot, thou hast thy mother's tongue.
QUEEN MARGARET
But thou art neither like thy sire nor dam,   135
But like a foul misshapen stigmatic,
Marked by the destinies to be avoided,
As venom toads or lizards' dreadful stings.
RICHARD
Iron of Naples, hid with English gilt,
Whose father bears the title of a king—   140
As if a channel should be called the sea—
Sham'st thou not, knowing whence thou art
          extraught,
To let thy tongue detect thy base-born heart?
EDWARD
A wisp of straw were worth a thousand crowns
To make this shameless callet know herself.   145
Helen of Greece was fairer far than thou,
Although thy husband may be Menelaus;
And ne'er was Agamemnon's brother wronged
By that false woman, as this king by thee.
His father revelled in the heart of France,   150
And tamed the King, and made the Dauphin stoop;
And had he matched according to his state,
He might have kept that glory to this day.
But when he took a beggar to his bed,
And graced thy poor sire with his bridal day,   155
Even then that sunshine brewed a shower for him
That washed his father's fortunes forth of France,
And heaped sedition on his crown at home.
For what hath broached this tumult but thy pride?
Hadst thou been meek, our title still had slept,   160
And we, in pity of the gentle King,
Had slipped our claim until another age.
GEORGE (to Queen Margaret)
But when we saw our sunshine made thy spring,
And that thy summer bred us no increase,
We set the axe to thy usurping root.   165
And though the edge hath something hit ourselves,
Yet know thou, since we have begun to strike,
We'll never leave till we have hewn thee down,
Or bathed thy growing with our heated bloods.

EDWARD (to Queen Margaret)
And in this resolution I defy thee,   170
Not willing any longer conference
Since thou deniest the gentle King to speak.
Sound trumpets—let our bloody colours wave!
And either victory, or else a grave!
QUEEN MARGARET Stay, Edward.   175
EDWARD
No, wrangling woman, we'll no longer stay—
These words will cost ten thousand lives this day.
          ⌈Flourish. March. Exeunt Edward and his men
          at one door and Queen Margaret and her men
          at another door⌉

2.3   *Alarum. Excursions. Enter the Earl of Warwick*
WARWICK
Forespent with toil, as runners with a race,
I lay me down a little while to breathe;
For strokes received, and many blows repaid,
Have robbed my strong-knit sinews of their strength,
And, spite of spite, needs must I rest a while.   5
          Enter Edward, the Duke of York, running
EDWARD
Smile, gentle heaven, or strike, ungentle death!
For this world frowns, and Edward's sun is clouded.
WARWICK
How now, my lord, what hap? What hope of good?
          Enter George, ⌈running⌉
GEORGE
Our hap is loss, our hope but sad despair;
Our ranks are broke, and ruin follows us.   10
What counsel give you? Whither shall we fly?
EDWARD
Bootless is flight—they follow us with wings,
And weak we are, and cannot shun pursuit.
          Enter Richard, ⌈running⌉
RICHARD
Ah, Warwick, why hast thou withdrawn thyself?
Thy brother's blood the thirsty earth hath drunk,   15
Broached with the steely point of Clifford's lance.
And in the very pangs of death he cried,
Like to a dismal clangour heard from far,
'Warwick, revenge—brother, revenge my death!'
So, underneath the belly of their steeds   20
That stained their fetlocks in his smoking blood,
The noble gentleman gave up the ghost.
WARWICK
Then let the earth be drunken with our blood.
I'll kill my horse, because I will not fly.
Why stand we like soft-hearted women here,   25
Wailing our losses, whiles the foe doth rage;
And look upon, as if the tragedy
Were played in jest by counterfeiting actors?
(Kneeling) Here, on my knee, I vow to God above
I'll never pause again, never stand still,   30
Till either death hath closed these eyes of mine
Or fortune given me measure of revenge.

EDWARD (*kneeling*)
O, Warwick, I do bend my knee with thine,
And in this vow do chain my soul to thine.
And, ere my knee rise from the earth's cold face, 35
I throw my hands, mine eyes, my heart to Thee,
Thou setter up and plucker down of kings,
Beseeching Thee, if with Thy will it stands
That to my foes this body must be prey,
Yet that Thy brazen gates of heaven may ope 40
And give sweet passage to my sinful soul.
   ⌜*They rise*⌝
Now, lords, take leave until we meet again,
Where'er it be, in heaven or in earth.

RICHARD
Brother, give me thy hand; and, gentle Warwick,
Let me embrace thee in my weary arms. 45
I, that did never weep, now melt with woe
That winter should cut off our springtime so.

WARWICK
Away, away! Once more, sweet lords, farewell.

GEORGE
Yet let us all together to our troops,
And give them leave to fly that will not stay; 50
And call them pillars that will stand to us;
And, if we thrive, promise them such rewards
As victors wear at the Olympian games.
This may plant courage in their quailing breasts,
For yet is hope of life and victory. 55
Forslow no longer—make we hence amain.   *Exeunt*

2.4   ⌜*Alarums.*⌝ *Excursions. Enter Richard* ⌜*at one door*⌝
      and Lord Clifford ⌜*at the other*⌝

RICHARD
Now, Clifford, I have singled thee alone.
Suppose this arm is for the Duke of York,
And this for Rutland, both bound to revenge,
Wert thou environed with a brazen wall.

CLIFFORD
Now, Richard, I am with thee here alone. 5
This is the hand that stabbed thy father York,
And this the hand that slew thy brother Rutland,
And here's the heart that triumphs in their death
And cheers these hands that slew thy sire and brother
To execute the like upon thyself— 10
And so, have at thee!
   They fight. The Earl of Warwick comes and rescues
   Richard. Lord Clifford flies

RICHARD
Nay, Warwick, single out some other chase—
For I myself will hunt this wolf to death.   *Exeunt*

2.5   *Alarum. Enter King Henry*

KING HENRY
This battle fares like to the morning's war,
   When dying clouds contend with growing light,
What time the shepherd, blowing of his nails,
   Can neither call it perfect day nor night.

Now sways it this way like a mighty sea 5
   Forced by the tide to combat with the wind,
Now sways it that way like the selfsame sea
   Forced to retire by fury of the wind.
Sometime the flood prevails, and then the wind;
Now one the better, then another best— 10
Both tugging to be victors, breast to breast,
Yet neither conqueror nor conquerèd.
So is the equal poise of this fell war.
Here on this molehill will I sit me down.
To whom God will, there be the victory. 15
For Margaret my queen, and Clifford, too,
Have chid me from the battle, swearing both
They prosper best of all when I am thence.
Would I were dead, if God's good will were so—
For what is in this world but grief and woe? 20
O God! Methinks it were a happy life
To be no better than a homely swain.
To sit upon a hill, as I do now;
To carve out dials quaintly, point by point,
Thereby to see the minutes how they run: 25
How many makes the hour full complete,
How many hours brings about the day,
How many days will finish up the year,
How many years a mortal man may live.
When this is known, then to divide the times: 30
So many hours must I tend my flock,
So many hours must I take my rest,
So many hours must I contemplate,
So many hours must I sport myself,
So many days my ewes have been with young, 35
So many weeks ere the poor fools will ean,
So many years ere I shall shear the fleece.
So minutes, hours, days, weeks, months, and years,
Passed over to the end they were created,
Would bring white hairs unto a quiet grave. 40
Ah, what a life were this! How sweet! How lovely!
Gives not the hawthorn bush a sweeter shade
To shepherds looking on their seely sheep
Than doth a rich embroidered canopy
To kings that fear their subjects' treachery? 45
O yes, it doth—a thousandfold it doth.
And to conclude, the shepherd's homely curds,
His cold thin drink out of his leather bottle,
His wonted sleep under a fresh tree's shade,
All which secure and sweetly he enjoys, 50
Is far beyond a prince's delicates,
His viands sparkling in a golden cup,
His body couchèd in a curious bed,
When care, mistrust, and treason waits on him.
   Alarum. Enter ⌜*at one door*⌝ *a Soldier with a dead*
   man in his arms. King Henry stands apart

SOLDIER
Ill blows the wind that profits nobody. 55
This man, whom hand to hand I slew in fight,
May be possessèd with some store of crowns;
And I, that haply take them from him now,

May yet ere night yield both my life and them
To some man else, as this dead man doth me.   60
          [*He removes the dead man's helmet*]
Who's this? O God! It is my father's face
Whom in this conflict I, unwares, have killed.
O, heavy times, begetting such events!
From London by the King was I pressed forth;
My father, being the Earl of Warwick's man,   65
Came on the part of York, pressed by his master;
And I, who at his hands received my life,
Have by my hands of life bereavèd him.
Pardon me, God, I knew not what I did;
And pardon, father, for I knew not thee.   70
My tears shall wipe away these bloody marks,
And no more words till they have flowed their fill.
          He weeps
KING HENRY
O piteous spectacle! O bloody times!
Whiles lions war and battle for their dens,
Poor harmless lambs abide their enmity.   75
Weep, wretched man, I'll aid thee tear for tear;
And let our hearts and eyes, like civil war,
Be blind with tears, and break, o'ercharged with grief.
          Enter [at another door] another Soldier with a dead
          man [in his arms]
SECOND SOLDIER
Thou that so stoutly hath resisted me,
Give me thy gold, if thou hast any gold—   80
For I have bought it with an hundred blows.
          [*He removes the dead man's helmet*]
But let me see: is this our foeman's face?
Ah, no, no, no—it is mine only son!
Ah, boy, if any life be left in thee,
Throw up thine eye! (*Weeping*) See, see, what showers
          arise,   85
Blown with the windy tempest of my heart,
Upon thy wounds, that kills mine eye and heart!
O, pity, God, this miserable age!
What stratagems, how fell, how butcherly,
Erroneous, mutinous, and unnatural,   90
This deadly quarrel daily doth beget!
O boy, thy father gave thee life too soon,
And hath bereft thee of thy life too late!
KING HENRY
Woe above woe! Grief more than common grief!
O that my death would stay these ruthful deeds!   95
O, pity, pity, gentle heaven, pity!
The red rose and the white are on his face,
The fatal colours of our striving houses;
The one his purple blood right well resembles,
The other his pale cheeks, methinks, presentent.   100
Wither one rose, and let the other flourish—
If you contend, a thousand lives must wither.
FIRST SOLDIER
How will my mother for a father's death
Take on with me, and ne'er be satisfied!
SECOND SOLDIER
How will my wife for slaughter of my son   105
Shed seas of tears, and ne'er be satisfied!

KING HENRY
How will the country for these woeful chances
Misthink the King, and not be satisfied!
FIRST SOLDIER
Was ever son so rued a father's death?
SECOND SOLDIER
Was ever father so bemoaned his son?   110
KING HENRY
Was ever king so grieved for subjects' woe?
Much is your sorrow, mine ten times so much.
FIRST SOLDIER (*to his father's body*)
I'll bear thee hence where I may weep my fill.
          Exit [at one door] with the body of his father
SECOND SOLDIER (*to his son's body*)
These arms of mine shall be thy winding sheet;
My heart, sweet boy, shall be thy sepulchre,   115
For from my heart thine image ne'er shall go.
My sighing breast shall be thy funeral bell,
And so obsequious will thy father be,
E'en for the loss of thee, having no more,
As Priam was for all his valiant sons.   120
I'll bear thee hence, and let them fight that will—
For I have murdered where I should not kill.
          Exit [at another door] with the body of his son
KING HENRY
Sad-hearted men, much overgone with care,
Here sits a king more woeful than you are.
          Alarums. Excursions. Enter Prince Edward
PRINCE EDWARD
Fly, father, fly—for all your friends are fled,   125
And Warwick rages like a chafèd bull!
Away—for death doth hold us in pursuit!
          [*Enter Queen Margaret*]
QUEEN MARGARET
Mount you, my lord—towards Berwick post amain.
Edward and Richard, like a brace of greyhounds
Having the fearful flying hare in sight,   130
With fiery eyes sparkling for very wrath,
And bloody steel grasped in their ireful hands,
Are at our backs—and therefore hence amain.
          [*Enter Exeter*]
EXETER
Away—for vengeance comes along with them!
Nay—stay not to expostulate—make speed—   135
Or else come after. I'll away before.
KING HENRY
Nay, take me with thee, good sweet Exeter.
Not that I fear to stay, but love to go
Whither the Queen intends. Forward, away.   *Exeunt*

2.6   *A loud alarum. Enter Lord Clifford, wounded*
          [*with an arrow in his neck*]
CLIFFORD
Here burns my candle out—ay, here it dies,
Which, whiles it lasted, gave King Henry light.
O Lancaster, I fear thy overthrow
More than my body's parting with my soul!
My love and fear glued many friends to thee—   5
And, now I fall, thy tough commixture melts,

Impairing Henry, strength'ning misproud York.
The common people swarm like summer flies,
And whither fly the gnats but to the sun?
And who shines now but Henry's enemies?   10
O Phoebus, hadst thou never given consent
That Phaëton should check thy fiery steeds,
Thy burning car never had scorched the earth!
And, Henry, hadst thou swayed as kings should do,
Or as thy father and his father did,   15
Giving no ground unto the house of York,
They never then had sprung like summer flies;
I and ten thousand in this luckless realm
Had left no mourning widows for our death;
And thou this day hadst kept thy chair in peace.   20
For what doth cherish weeds, but gentle air?
And what makes robbers bold, but too much lenity?
Bootless are plaints, and cureless are my wounds;
No way to fly, nor strength to hold out flight;
The foe is merciless and will not pity,   25
For at their hands I have deserved no pity.
The air hath got into my deadly wounds,
And much effuse of blood doth make me faint.
Come York and Richard, Warwick and the rest—
I stabbed your fathers' bosoms; split my breast.   30
    ⌜He faints.⌝
    Alarum and retreat. Enter Edward Duke of York,
    his brothers George and Richard, the Earl of
    Warwick, ⌜the Marquis of Montague,⌝ and soldiers
EDWARD
Now breathe we, lords—good fortune bids us pause,
And smooth the frowns of war with peaceful looks.
Some troops pursue the bloody-minded Queen,
That led calm Henry, though he were a king,
As doth a sail filled with a fretting gust   35
Command an argosy to stem the waves.
But think you, lords, that Clifford fled with them?
WARWICK
No—'tis impossible he should escape;
For, though before his face I speak the words,
Your brother Richard marked him for the grave.   40
And whereso'er he is, he's surely dead.
    Clifford groans
⌜EDWARD⌝
Whose soul is that which takes her heavy leave?
⌜RICHARD⌝
A deadly groan, like life and death's departing.
⌜EDWARD⌝ ⌜to Richard⌝
See who it is.
    ⌜Richard goes to Clifford⌝
                    And now the battle's ended,
If friend or foe, let him be gently used.   45
RICHARD
Revoke that doom of mercy, for 'tis Clifford;
Who not contented that he lopped the branch
In hewing Rutland when his leaves put forth,
But set his murd'ring knife unto the root
From whence that tender spray did sweetly spring—   50
I mean our princely father, Duke of York.

WARWICK
From off the gates of York fetch down the head,
Your father's head, which Clifford placèd there.
Instead whereof let this supply the room—
Measure for measure must be answerèd.   55
EDWARD
Bring forth that fatal screech-owl to our house,
That nothing sung but death to us and ours.
    ⌜Clifford is dragged forward⌝
Now death shall stop his dismal threat'ning sound
And his ill-boding tongue no more shall speak.
WARWICK
I think his understanding is bereft.   60
Speak, Clifford, dost thou know who speaks to thee?
Dark cloudy death o'ershades his beams of life,
And he nor sees nor hears us what we say.
RICHARD
O, would he did—and so perhaps he doth.
'Tis but his policy to counterfeit,   65
Because he would avoid such bitter taunts
Which in the time of death he gave our father.
GEORGE
If so thou think'st, vex him with eager words.
RICHARD
Clifford, ask mercy and obtain no grace.
EDWARD
Clifford, repent in bootless penitence.   70
WARWICK
Clifford, devise excuses for thy faults.
GEORGE
While we devise fell tortures for thy faults.
RICHARD
Thou didst love York, and I am son to York.
EDWARD
Thou pitied'st Rutland—I will pity thee.
GEORGE
Where's Captain Margaret to fence you now?   75
WARWICK
They mock thee, Clifford—swear as thou wast wont.
RICHARD
What, not an oath? Nay, then, the world goes hard
When Clifford cannot spare his friends an oath.
I know by that he's dead—and, by my soul,
If this right hand would buy but two hours' life   80
That I, in all despite, might rail at him,
This hand should chop it off, and with the issuing
    blood
Stifle the villain whose unstanchèd thirst
York and young Rutland could not satisfy.
WARWICK
Ay, but he's dead. Off with the traitor's head,   85
And rear it in the place your father's stands.
And now to London with triumphant march,
There to be crownèd England's royal king;
From whence shall Warwick cut the sea to France,
And ask the Lady Bona for thy queen.   90
So shalt thou sinew both these lands together.
And, having France thy friend, thou shalt not dread

The scattered foe that hopes to rise again,
For though they cannot greatly sting to hurt,
Yet look to have them buzz to offend thine ears.   95
First will I see the coronation,
And then to Brittany I'll cross the sea
To effect this marriage, so it please my lord.
EDWARD
Even as thou wilt, sweet Warwick, let it be.
For in thy shoulder do I build my seat,   100
And never will I undertake the thing
Wherein thy counsel and consent is wanting.
Richard, I will create thee Duke of Gloucester,
And George, of Clarence; Warwick, as ourself,
Shall do and undo as him pleaseth best.   105
RICHARD
Let me be Duke of Clarence, George of Gloucester—
For Gloucester's dukedom is too ominous.
WARWICK
Tut, that's a foolish observation—
Richard, be Duke of Gloucester. Now to London
To see these honours in possession.   110
          Exeunt. ⌈*York's head is removed*⌉

3.1   *Enter two Gamekeepers, with crossbows in their*
          hands
FIRST GAMEKEEPER
Under this thick-grown brake we'll shroud ourselves,
For through this laund anon the deer will come,
And in this covert will we make our stand,
Culling the principal of all the deer.
SECOND GAMEKEEPER
I'll stay above the hill, so both may shoot.   5
FIRST GAMEKEEPER
That cannot be—the noise of thy crossbow
Will scare the herd, and so my shoot is lost.
Here stand we both, and aim we at the best.
And, for the time shall not seem tedious,
I'll tell thee what befell me on a day   10
In this self place where now we mean to stand.
FIRST GAMEKEEPER
Here comes a man—let's stay till he be past.
          They stand apart.
          Enter King Henry, disguised, carrying a prayer-book
KING HENRY
From Scotland am I stolen, even of pure love,
To greet mine own land with my wishful sight.
No, Harry, Harry—'tis no land of thine.   15
Thy place is filled, thy sceptre wrung from thee,
Thy balm washed off wherewith thou wast anointed.
No bending knee will call thee Caesar now,
No humble suitors press to speak for right,
No, not a man comes for redress of thee—   20
For how can I help them and not myself?
FIRST GAMEKEEPER (*to the Second Gamekeeper*)
Ay, here's a deer whose skin's a keeper's fee:
This is the quondam king—let's seize upon him.
KING HENRY
Let me embrace thee, sour adversity,
For wise men say it is the wisest course.   25

SECOND GAMEKEEPER (*to the First Gamekeeper*)
Why linger we? Let us lay hands upon him.
FIRST GAMEKEEPER (*to the Second Gamekeeper*)
Forbear awhile—we'll hear a little more.
KING HENRY
My queen and son are gone to France for aid,
And, as I hear, the great commanding Warwick
Is thither gone to crave the French King's sister   30
To wife for Edward. If this news be true,
Poor Queen and son, your labour is but lost—
For Warwick is a subtle orator,
And Louis a prince soon won with moving words.
By this account, then, Margaret may win him—   35
For she's a woman to be pitied much.
Her sighs will make a batt'ry in his breast,
Her tears will pierce into a marble heart,
The tiger will be mild whiles she doth mourn,
And Nero will be tainted with remorse   40
To hear and see her plaints, her brinish tears.
Ay, but she's come to beg; Warwick to give.
She on his left side, craving aid for Henry;
He on his right, asking a wife for Edward.
She weeps and says her Henry is deposed,   45
He smiles and says his Edward is installed;
That she, poor wretch, for grief can speak no more,
Whiles Warwick tells his title, smooths the wrong,
Inferreth arguments of mighty strength,
And in conclusion wins the King from her   50
With promise of his sister and what else
To strengthen and support King Edward's place.
O, Margaret, thus 'twill be; and thou, poor soul,
Art then forsaken, as thou went'st forlorn.
SECOND GAMEKEEPER (*coming forward*)
Say, what art thou that talk'st of kings and queens?   55
KING HENRY
More than I seem, and less than I was born to:
A man at least, for less I should not be;
And men may talk of kings, and why not I?
SECOND GAMEKEEPER
Ay, but thou talk'st as if thou wert a king.
KING HENRY
Why, so I am, in mind—and that's enough.   60
SECOND GAMEKEEPER
But if thou be a king, where is thy crown?
KING HENRY
My crown is in my heart, not on my head;
Not decked with diamonds and Indian stones,
Nor to be seen. My crown is called content—
A crown it is that seldom kings enjoy.   65
SECOND GAMEKEEPER
Well, if you be a king crowned with content,
Your crown content and you must be contented
To go along with us—for, as we think,
You are the king King Edward hath deposed,
And we his subjects sworn in all allegiance   70
Will apprehend you as his enemy.
KING HENRY
But did you never swear and break an oath?

SECOND GAMEKEEPER
No—never such an oath, nor will not now.
KING HENRY
Where did you dwell when I was King of England?
SECOND GAMEKEEPER
Here in this country, where we now remain.   75
KING HENRY
I was anointed king at nine months old,
My father and my grandfather were kings,
And you were sworn true subjects unto me—
And tell me, then, have you not broke your oaths?
FIRST GAMEKEEPER
No, for we were subjects but while you were king.   80
KING HENRY
Why, am I dead? Do I not breathe a man?
Ah, simple men, you know not what you swear.
Look as I blow this feather from my face,
And as the air blows it to me again,
Obeying with my wind when I do blow,   85
And yielding to another when it blows,
Commanded always by the greater gust—
Such is the lightness of you common men.
But do not break your oaths, for of that sin
My mild entreaty shall not make you guilty.   90
Go where you will, the King shall be commanded;
And be you kings, command, and I'll obey.
FIRST GAMEKEEPER
We are true subjects to the King, King Edward.
KING HENRY
So would you be again to Henry,
If he were seated as King Edward is.   95
FIRST GAMEKEEPER
We charge you, in God's name and in the King's,
To go with us unto the officers.
KING HENRY
In God's name, lead; your king's name be obeyed;
And what God will, that let your king perform;   99
And what he will I humbly yield unto.   *Exeunt*

3.2   *Enter King Edward, Richard Duke of Gloucester,*
          George Duke of Clarence, and the Lady Gray
KING EDWARD
Brother of Gloucester, at Saint Albans field
This lady's husband, Sir Richard Gray, was slain,
His lands then seized on by the conqueror.
Her suit is now to repossess those lands,
Which we in justice cannot well deny,   5
Because in quarrel of the house of York
The worthy gentleman did lose his life.
RICHARD OF GLOUCESTER
Your highness shall do well to grant her suit—
It were dishonour to deny it her.
KING EDWARD
It were no less; but yet I'll make a pause.   10
RICHARD OF GLOUCESTER (*aside to George*) Yea, is it so?
I see the lady hath a thing to grant
Before the King will grant her humble suit.
GEORGE OF CLARENCE (*aside to Richard*)
He knows the game; how true he keeps the wind!

RICHARD OF GLOUCESTER (*aside to George*) Silence.   15
KING EDWARD (*to Lady Gray*)
Widow, we will consider of your suit;
And come some other time to know our mind.
LADY GRAY
Right gracious lord, I cannot brook delay.
May it please your highness to resolve me now,
And what your pleasure is shall satisfy me.   20
RICHARD OF GLOUCESTER (*aside to George*)
Ay, widow? Then I'll warrant you all your lands
An if what pleases him shall pleasure you.
Fight closer, or, good faith, you'll catch a blow.
GEORGE OF CLARENCE (*aside to Richard*)
I fear her not unless she chance to fall.
RICHARD OF GLOUCESTER (*aside to George*)
God forbid that! For he'll take vantages.   25
KING EDWARD (*to Lady Gray*)
How many children hast thou, widow? Tell me.
GEORGE OF CLARENCE (*aside to Richard*)
I think he means to beg a child of her.
RICHARD OF GLOUCESTER (*aside to George*)
Nay, whip me then—he'll rather give her two.
LADY GRAY (*to King Edward*) Three, my most gracious lord.
RICHARD OF GLOUCESTER (*aside*)
You shall have four, an you'll be ruled by him.   30
KING EDWARD (*to Lady Gray*)
'Twere pity they should lose their father's lands.
LADY GRAY
Be pitiful, dread lord, and grant it them.
KING EDWARD (*to Richard and George*)
Lords, give us leave—I'll try this widow's wit.
RICHARD OF GLOUCESTER ⌈*aside to George*⌉
Ay, good leave have you; for you will have leave,
Till youth take leave and leave you to the crutch. 35
          Richard and George stand apart
KING EDWARD (*to Lady Gray*)
Now tell me, madam, do you love your children?
LADY GRAY
Ay, full as dearly as I love myself.
KING EDWARD
And would you not do much to do them good?
LADY GRAY
To do them good I would sustain some harm.
KING EDWARD
Then get your husband's lands, to do them good.   40
LADY GRAY
Therefore I came unto your majesty.
KING EDWARD
I'll tell you how these lands are to be got.
LADY GRAY
So shall you bind me to your highness' service.
KING EDWARD
What service wilt thou do me, if I give them?
LADY GRAY
What you command, that rests in me to do.   45
KING EDWARD
But you will take exceptions to my boon.
LADY GRAY
No, gracious lord, except I cannot do it.

KING EDWARD
Ay, but thou canst do what I mean to ask.
LADY GRAY
Why, then, I will do what your grace commands.
RICHARD OF GLOUCESTER (*to George*)
He plies her hard, and much rain wears the marble. 50
GEORGE OF CLARENCE
As red as fire! Nay, then her wax must melt.
LADY GRAY (*to King Edward*)
Why stops my lord? Shall I not hear my task?
KING EDWARD
An easy task—'tis but to love a king.
LADY GRAY
That's soon performed, because I am a subject.
KING EDWARD
Why, then, thy husband's lands I freely give thee. 55
LADY GRAY (*curtsies*)
I take my leave, with many thousand thanks.
RICHARD OF GLOUCESTER (*to George*)
The match is made—she seals it with a curtsy.
KING EDWARD (*to Lady Gray*)
But stay thee—'tis the fruits of love I mean.
LADY GRAY
The fruits of love I mean, my loving liege.
KING EDWARD
Ay, but I fear me in another sense.   60
What love think'st thou I sue so much to get?
LADY GRAY
My love till death, my humble thanks, my prayers—
That love which virtue begs and virtue grants.
KING EDWARD
No, by my troth, I did not mean such love.
LADY GRAY
Why, then, you mean not as I thought you did.   65
KING EDWARD
But now you partly may perceive my mind.
LADY GRAY
My mind will never grant what I perceive
Your highness aims at, if I aim aright.
KING EDWARD
To tell thee plain, I aim to lie with thee.
LADY GRAY
To tell you plain, I had rather lie in prison.   70
KING EDWARD
Why, then, thou shalt not have thy husband's lands.
LADY GRAY
Why, then, mine honesty shall be my dower;
For by that loss I will not purchase them.
KING EDWARD
Therein thou wrong'st thy children mightily.
LADY GRAY
Herein your highness wrongs both them and me.   75
But, mighty lord, this merry inclination
Accords not with the sadness of my suit.
Please you dismiss me either with ay or no.
KING EDWARD
Ay, if thou wilt say 'ay' to my request;
No, if thou dost say 'no' to my demand.   80

LADY GRAY
Then, no, my lord—my suit is at an end.
RICHARD OF GLOUCESTER (*to George*)
The widow likes him not—she knits her brows.
GEORGE OF CLARENCE
He is the bluntest wooer in Christendom.
KING EDWARD (*aside*)
Her looks doth argue her replete with modesty;
Her words doth show her wit incomparable;   85
All her perfections challenge sovereignty.
One way or other, she is for a king;
And she shall be my love or else my queen.
(*To Lady Gray*) Say that King Edward take thee for his
     queen?
LADY GRAY
'Tis better said than done, my gracious lord.   90
I am a subject fit to jest withal,
But far unfit to be a sovereign.
KING EDWARD
Sweet widow, by my state I swear to thee
I speak no more than what my soul intends,
And that is to enjoy thee for my love.   95
LADY GRAY
And that is more than I will yield unto.
I know I am too mean to be your queen,
And yet too good to be your concubine.
KING EDWARD
You cavil, widow—I did mean my queen.   99
LADY GRAY
'Twill grieve your grace my sons should call you father.
KING EDWARD
No more than when my daughters call thee mother.
Thou art a widow and thou hast some children;
And, by God's mother, I, being but a bachelor,
Have other some. Why, 'tis a happy thing
To be the father unto many sons.   105
Answer no more, for thou shalt be my queen.
RICHARD OF GLOUCESTER (*to George*)
The ghostly father now hath done his shrift.
GEORGE OF CLARENCE
When he was made a shriver, 'twas for shift.
KING EDWARD (*to Richard and George*)
Brothers, you muse what chat we two have had.
     Richard and George come forward
RICHARD OF GLOUCESTER
The widow likes it not, for she looks very sad.   110
KING EDWARD
You'd think it strange if I should marry her.
GEORGE OF CLARENCE
To who, my lord?
KING EDWARD   Why, Clarence, to myself.
RICHARD OF GLOUCESTER
That would be ten days' wonder at the least.
GEORGE OF CLARENCE
That's a day longer than a wonder lasts.
RICHARD OF GLOUCESTER
By so much is the wonder in extremes.   115

KING EDWARD
Well, jest on, brothers—I can tell you both
Her suit is granted for her husband's lands.
    Enter a Nobleman

NOBLEMAN
My gracious lord, Henry your foe is taken
And brought as prisoner to your palace gate.

KING EDWARD
See that he be conveyed unto the Tower—   120
(*To Richard and George*)
And go we, brothers, to the man that took him,
To question of his apprehension.
(*To Lady Gray*) Widow, go you along. ⌐*To Richard and
    George*⌐ Lords, use her honourably.
                   Exeunt all but Richard

RICHARD OF GLOUCESTER
Ay, Edward will use women honourably.
Would he were wasted, marrow, bones, and all,   125
That from his loins no hopeful branch may spring
To cross me from the golden time I look for.
And yet, between my soul's desire and me—
The lustful Edward's title burièd—
Is Clarence, Henry, and his son young Edward,   130
And all the unlooked-for issue of their bodies,
To take their rooms ere I can place myself.
A cold premeditation for my purpose.
Why, then, I do but dream on sovereignty
Like one that stands upon a promontory   135
And spies a far-off shore where he would tread,
Wishing his foot were equal with his eye,
And chides the sea that sunders him from thence,
Saying he'll lade it dry to have his way—
So do I wish the crown being so far off,   140
And so I chide the means that keeps me from it,
And so I say I'll cut the causes off,
Flattering me with impossibilities.
My eye's too quick, my heart o'erweens too much,
Unless my hand and strength could equal them.   145
Well, say there is no kingdom then for Richard—
What other pleasure can the world afford?
I'll make my heaven in a lady's lap,
And deck my body in gay ornaments,
And 'witch sweet ladies with my words and looks.   150
O, miserable thought! And more unlikely
Than to accomplish twenty golden crowns.
Why, love forswore me in my mother's womb,
And, for I should not deal in her soft laws,
She did corrupt frail nature with some bribe   155
To shrink mine arm up like a withered shrub,
To make an envious mountain on my back—
Where sits deformity to mock my body—
To shape my legs of an unequal size,
To disproportion me in every part,   160
Like to a chaos, or an unlicked bear whelp
That carries no impression like the dam.
And am I then a man to be beloved?
O, monstrous fault, to harbour such a thought!

Then, since this earth affords no joy to me   165
But to command, to check, to o'erbear such
As are of better person than myself,
I'll make my heaven to dream upon the crown,
And whiles I live, t'account this world but hell,
Until my misshaped trunk that bears this head   170
Be round impalèd with a glorious crown.
And yet I know not how to get the crown,
For many lives stand between me and home.
And I—like one lost in a thorny wood,
That rends the thorns and is rent with the thorns,   175
Seeking a way and straying from the way,
Not knowing how to find the open air,
But toiling desperately to find it out—
Torment myself to catch the English crown.
And from that torment I will free myself,   180
Or hew my way out with a bloody axe.
Why, I can smile, and murder whiles I smile,
And cry 'Content!' to that which grieves my heart,
And wet my cheeks with artificial tears,
And frame my face to all occasions.   185
I'll drown more sailors than the mermaid shall;
I'll slay more gazers than the basilisk;
I'll play the orator as well as Nestor,
Deceive more slyly than Ulysses could,
And, like a Sinon, take another Troy.   190
I can add colours to the chameleon,
Change shapes with Proteus for advantages,
And set the murderous Machiavel to school.
Can I do this, and cannot get a crown?
Tut, were it farther off, I'll pluck it down.   *Exit*

3.3   ⌐*Two*⌐ *chairs of state. Flourish. Enter King Louis
      of France, his sister the Lady Bona, Lord Bourbon
      his admiral, Prince Edward, Queen Margaret, and
      the Earl of Oxford. Louis goes up upon the state,
      sits, and riseth up again*

KING LOUIS
Fair Queen of England, worthy Margaret,
Sit down with us. It ill befits thy state
And birth that thou shouldst stand while Louis
    doth sit.

QUEEN MARGARET
No, mighty King of France, now Margaret
Must strike her sail and learn a while to serve   5
Where kings command. I was, I must confess,
Great Albion's queen in former golden days,
But now mischance hath trod my title down,
And with dishonour laid me on the ground,
Where I must take like seat unto my fortune   10
And to my humble state conform myself.

KING LOUIS
Why, say, fair Queen, whence springs this deep
    despair?

QUEEN MARGARET
From such a cause as fills mine eyes with tears
And stops my tongue, while heart is drowned in cares.

KING LOUIS
Whate'er it be, be thou still like thyself,   15
And sit thee by our side.
   Seats her by him
                      Yield not thy neck
To fortune's yoke, but let thy dauntless mind
Still ride in triumph over all mischance.
Be plain, Queen Margaret, and tell thy grief.
It shall be eased if France can yield relief.   20
QUEEN MARGARET
Those gracious words revive my drooping thoughts,
And give my tongue-tied sorrows leave to speak.
Now, therefore, be it known to noble Louis
That Henry, sole possessor of my love,
Is of a king become a banishèd man,   25
And forced to live in Scotland a forlorn,
While proud ambitious Edward, Duke of York,
Usurps the regal title and the seat
Of England's true-anointed lawful King.
This is the cause that I, poor Margaret,   30
With this my son, Prince Edward, Henry's heir,
Am come to crave thy just and lawful aid.
An if thou fail us all our hope is done.
Scotland hath will to help, but cannot help;
Our people and our peers are both misled,   35
Our treasure seized, our soldiers put to flight,
And, as thou seest, ourselves in heavy plight.
KING LOUIS
Renownèd Queen, with patience calm the storm,
While we bethink a means to break it off.
QUEEN MARGARET
The more we stay, the stronger grows our foe.   40
KING LOUIS
The more I stay, the more I'll succour thee.
QUEEN MARGARET
O, but impatience waiteth on true sorrow.
   Enter the Earl of Warwick
And see where comes the breeder of my sorrow.
KING LOUIS
What's he approacheth boldly to our presence?
QUEEN MARGARET
Our Earl of Warwick, Edward's greatest friend.   45
KING LOUIS
Welcome, brave Warwick. What brings thee to France?
   He descends. She ariseth
QUEEN MARGARET (*aside*)
Ay, now begins a second storm to rise,
For this is he that moves both wind and tide.
WARWICK (*to King Louis*)
From worthy Edward, King of Albion,
My lord and sovereign, and thy vowèd friend,   50
I come in kindness and unfeignèd love,
First, to do greetings to thy royal person,
And then, to crave a league of amity,
And lastly, to confirm that amity
With nuptial knot, if thou vouchsafe to grant   55
That virtuous Lady Bona, thy fair sister,
To England's King in lawful marriage.

QUEEN MARGARET (*aside*)
If that go forward, Henry's hope is done.
WARWICK (*to Lady Bona*)
And, gracious madam, in our King's behalf
I am commanded, with your leave and favour,   60
Humbly to kiss your hand, and with my tongue
To tell the passion of my sovereign's heart,
Where fame, late ent'ring at his heedful ears,
Hath placed thy beauty's image and thy virtue.
QUEEN MARGARET
King Louis and Lady Bona, hear me speak   65
Before you answer Warwick. His demand
Springs not from Edward's well-meant honest love,
But from deceit, bred by necessity.
For how can tyrants safely govern home
Unless abroad they purchase great alliance?   70
To prove him tyrant this reason may suffice—
That Henry liveth still; but were he dead,
Yet here Prince Edward stands, King Henry's son.
Look, therefore, Louis, that by this league and
    marriage
Thou draw not on thy danger and dishonour,   75
For though usurpers sway the rule a while,
Yet heav'ns are just and time suppresseth wrongs.
WARWICK
Injurious Margaret.
PRINCE EDWARD   And why not 'Queen'?
WARWICK
Because thy father Henry did usurp,
And thou no more art prince than she is queen.   80
OXFORD
Then Warwick disannuls great John of Gaunt,
Which did subdue the greatest part of Spain;
And, after John of Gaunt, Henry the Fourth,
Whose wisdom was a mirror to the wisest;
And, after that wise prince, Henry the Fifth,   85
Who by his prowess conquerèd all France.
From these our Henry lineally descends.
WARWICK
Oxford, how haps it in this smooth discourse
You told not how Henry the Sixth hath lost
All that which Henry the Fifth had gotten?   90
Methinks these peers of France should smile at that.
But for the rest, you tell a pedigree
Of threescore and two years—a silly time
To make prescription for a kingdom's worth.
OXFORD
Why, Warwick, canst thou speak against thy liege,   95
Whom thou obeyedest thirty and six years,
And not bewray thy treason with a blush?
WARWICK
Can Oxford, that did ever fence the right,
Now buckler falsehood with a pedigree?
For shame—leave Henry, and call Edward king.   100
OXFORD
Call him my king by whose injurious doom
My elder brother, the Lord Aubrey Vere,
Was done to death? And more than so, my father,

Even in the downfall of his mellowed years,
When nature brought him to the door of death?   105
No, Warwick, no—while life upholds this arm,
This arm upholds the house of Lancaster.
WARWICK And I the house of York.
KING LOUIS
Queen Margaret, Prince Edward, and Oxford,
Vouchsafe, at our request, to stand aside   110
While I use further conference with Warwick.
      Queen Margaret ⌜comes down from the state and⌝,
            with Prince Edward and Oxford, stands apart
QUEEN MARGARET
Heavens grant that Warwick's words bewitch him not.
KING LOUIS
Now, Warwick, tell me even upon thy conscience,
Is Edward your true king? For I were loath
To link with him that were not lawful chosen.   115
WARWICK
Thereon I pawn my credit and mine honour.
KING LOUIS
But is he gracious in the people's eye?
WARWICK
The more that Henry was unfortunate.
KING LOUIS
Then further, all dissembling set aside,
Tell me for truth the measure of his love   120
Unto our sister Bona.
WARWICK   Such it seems
As may beseem a monarch like himself.
Myself have often heard him say and swear
That this his love was an eternal plant,
Whereof the root was fixed in virtue's ground,   125
The leaves and fruit maintained with beauty's sun,
Exempt from envy, but not from disdain,
Unless the Lady Bona quit his pain.
KING LOUIS (*to Lady Bona*)
Now, sister, let us hear your firm resolve.
LADY BONA
Your grant, or your denial, shall be mine.   130
(*To Warwick*) Yet I confess that often ere this day,
When I have heard your king's desert recounted,
Mine ear hath tempted judgement to desire.
KING LOUIS (*to Warwick*)
Then, Warwick, thus—our sister shall be Edward's.
And now, forthwith, shall articles be drawn   135
Touching the jointure that your king must make,
Which with her dowry shall be counterpoised.
(*To Queen Margaret*) Draw near, Queen Margaret, and
      be a witness
That Bona shall be wife to the English king.
      Queen Margaret, Prince Edward, ⌜and Oxford⌝ come
            forward
PRINCE EDWARD
To Edward, but not to the English king.   140
QUEEN MARGARET
Deceitful Warwick—it was thy device
By this alliance to make void my suit!
Before thy coming Louis was Henry's friend.

KING LOUIS
And still is friend to him and Margaret.
But if your title to the crown be weak,   145
As may appear by Edward's good success,
Then 'tis but reason that I be released
From giving aid which late I promisèd.
Yet shall you have all kindness at my hand
That your estate requires and mine can yield.   150
WARWICK (*to Queen Margaret*)
Henry now lives in Scotland at his ease,
Where having nothing, nothing can he lose.
And as for you yourself, our quondam queen,
You have a father able to maintain you,
And better 'twere you troubled him than France.   155
QUEEN MARGARET
Peace, impudent and shameless Warwick, peace!
Proud setter-up and puller-down of kings!
I will not hence till, with my talk and tears,
Both full of truth, I make King Louis behold
Thy sly conveyance and thy lord's false love,   160
      Post blowing a horn within
For both of you are birds of selfsame feather.
KING LOUIS
Warwick, this is some post to us or thee.
      Enter the Post
POST (*to Warwick*)
My lord ambassador, these letters are for you,
Sent from your brother Marquis Montague;
(*To Louis*) These from our King unto your majesty; 165
(*To Queen Margaret*)
And, madam, these for you, from whom I know not.
      They all read their letters
OXFORD (*to Prince Edward*)
I like it well that our fair Queen and mistress
Smiles at her news, while Warwick frowns at his.
PRINCE EDWARD
Nay, mark how Louis stamps as he were nettled.
I hope all's for the best.   170
KING LOUIS
Warwick, what are thy news? And yours, fair Queen?
QUEEN MARGARET
Mine, such as fill my heart with unhoped joys.
WARWICK
Mine, full of sorrow and heart's discontent.
KING LOUIS
What! Has your king married the Lady Gray?
And now to soothe your forgery and his,   175
Sends me a paper to persuade me patience?
Is this th'alliance that he seeks with France?
Dare he presume to scorn us in this manner?
QUEEN MARGARET
I told your majesty as much before—
This proveth Edward's love and Warwick's honesty.
WARWICK
King Louis, I here protest in sight of heaven   181
And by the hope I have of heavenly bliss,
That I am clear from this misdeed of Edward's,
No more my king, for he dishonours me,

But most himself, if he could see his shame.   185
Did I forget that by the house of York
My father came untimely to his death?
Did I let pass th'abuse done to my niece?
Did I impale him with the regal crown?
Did I put Henry from his native right?   190
And am I guerdoned at the last with shame?
Shame on himself, for my desert is honour.
And to repair my honour, lost for him,
I here renounce him and return to Henry.
(*To Queen Margaret*) My noble Queen, let former
    grudges pass,   195
And henceforth I am thy true servitor.
I will revenge his wrong to Lady Bona
And replant Henry in his former state.

QUEEN MARGARET
Warwick, these words have turned my hate to love,
And I forgive and quite forget old faults,   200
And joy that thou becom'st King Henry's friend.

WARWICK
So much his friend, ay, his unfeignèd friend,
That if King Louis vouchsafe to furnish us
With some few bands of chosen soldiers,
I'll undertake to land them on our coast   205
And force the tyrant from his seat by war.
'Tis not his new-made bride shall succour him.
And as for Clarence, as my letters tell me,
He's very likely now to fall from him
For matching more for wanton lust than honour,   210
Or than for strength and safety of our country.

LADY BONA (*to King Louis*)
Dear brother, how shall Bona be revenged,
But by thy help to this distressèd Queen?

QUEEN MARGARET (*to King Louis*)
Renownèd Prince, how shall poor Henry live
Unless thou rescue him from foul despair?   215

LADY BONA (*to King Louis*)
My quarrel and this English Queen's are one.

WARWICK
And mine, fair Lady Bona, joins with yours.

KING LOUIS
And mine with hers, and thine, and Margaret's.
Therefore at last I firmly am resolved:
You shall have aid.   220

QUEEN MARGARET
Let me give humble thanks for all at once.

KING LOUIS (*to the Post*)
Then, England's messenger, return in post
And tell false Edward, thy supposèd king,
That Louis of France is sending over masquers
To revel it with him and his new bride.   225
Thou seest what's passed, go fear thy king withal.

LADY BONA (*to the Post*)
Tell him, in hope he'll prove a widower shortly,
I'll wear the willow garland for his sake.

QUEEN MARGARET (*to the Post*)
Tell him my mourning weeds are laid aside,
And I am ready to put armour on.   230

WARWICK (*to the Post*)
Tell him from me that he hath done me wrong,
And therefore I'll uncrown him ere't be long.
(*Giving money*) There's thy reward—be gone.
    Exit Post

KING LOUIS
But, Warwick, thou and Oxford, with five thousand
    men,
Shall cross the seas and bid false Edward battle;   235
And, as occasion serves, this noble Queen
And Prince shall follow with a fresh supply.
Yet, ere thou go, but answer me one doubt:
What pledge have we of thy firm loyalty?

WARWICK
This shall assure my constant loyalty: 240
That if our Queen and this young Prince agree,
I'll join mine eldest daughter and my joy
To him forthwith in holy wedlock bands.

QUEEN MARGARET
Yes, I agree, and thank you for your motion.
(*To Prince Edward*) Son Edward, she is fair and
    virtuous,   245
Therefore delay not. Give thy hand to Warwick,
And with thy hand thy faith irrevocable
That only Warwick's daughter shall be thine.

PRINCE EDWARD
Yes, I accept her, for she well deserves it,
And here to pledge my vow I give my hand.   250
    He and Warwick clasp hands

KING LOUIS
Why stay we now? These soldiers shall be levied,
And thou, Lord Bourbon, our high admiral,
Shall waft them over with our royal fleet.
I long till Edward fall by war's mischance
For mocking marriage with a dame of France.   255
    Exeunt all but Warwick

WARWICK
I came from Edward as ambassador,
But I return his sworn and mortal foe.
Matter of marriage was the charge he gave me,
But dreadful war shall answer his demand.
Had he none else to make a stale but me?   260
Then none but I shall turn his jest to sorrow.
I was the chief that raised him to the crown,
And I'll be chief to bring him down again.
Not that I pity Henry's misery,
But seek revenge on Edward's mockery.   *Exit*

4.1   *Enter Richard Duke of Gloucester, George Duke*
    of Clarence, the Duke of Somerset, and the Marquis
    of Montague

RICHARD OF GLOUCESTER
Now tell me, brother Clarence, what think you
Of this new marriage with the Lady Gray?
Hath not our brother made a worthy choice?

GEORGE OF CLARENCE
Alas, you know 'tis far from hence to France;
How could he stay till Warwick made return?   5

SOMERSET
My lords, forbear this talk—here comes the King.
Flourish. Enter King Edward, the Lady Gray his
Queen, the Earl of Pembroke, and the Lords
Stafford and Hastings. Four stand on one side ⌐of
the King⌐, and four on the other
RICHARD OF GLOUCESTER And his well-chosen bride.
GEORGE OF CLARENCE
I mind to tell him plainly what I think.
KING EDWARD
Now, brother of Clarence, how like you our choice,
That you stand pensive, as half-malcontent?   10
GEORGE OF CLARENCE
As well as Louis of France, or the Earl of Warwick,
Which are so weak of courage and in judgement
That they'll take no offence at our abuse.   •
KING EDWARD
Suppose they take offence without a cause—
They are but Louis and Warwick; I am Edward,   15
Your king and Warwick's, and must have my will.
RICHARD OF GLOUCESTER
And you shall have your will, because our king.
Yet hasty marriage seldom proveth well.
KING EDWARD
Yea, brother Richard, are you offended too?   19
RICHARD OF GLOUCESTER
Not I, no—God forbid that I should wish them severed
Whom God hath joined together. Ay, and 'twere pity
To sunder them that yoke so well together.
KING EDWARD
Setting your scorns and your mislike aside,
Tell me some reason why the Lady Gray
Should not become my wife and England's queen.   25
And you too, Somerset and Montague,
Speak freely what you think.
GEORGE OF CLARENCE
Then this is my opinion: that King Louis
Becomes your enemy for mocking him
About the marriage of the Lady Bona.   30
RICHARD OF GLOUCESTER
And Warwick, doing what you gave in charge,
Is now dishonourèd by this new marriage.
KING EDWARD
What if both Louis and Warwick be appeased
By such invention as I can devise?
MONTAGUE
Yet, to have joined with France in such alliance   35
Would more have strengthened this our
          commonwealth
'Gainst foreign storms than any home-bred marriage.
HASTINGS
Why, knows not Montague that of itself
England is safe, if true within itself?
MONTAGUE
But the safer when 'tis backed with France.   40
HASTINGS
'Tis better using France than trusting France.
Let us be backed with God and with the seas

Which he hath giv'n for fence impregnable,
And with their helps only defend ourselves.
In them and in ourselves our safety lies.   45
GEORGE OF CLARENCE
For this one speech Lord Hastings well deserves
To have the heir of the Lord Hungerford.
KING EDWARD
Ay, what of that? It was my will and grant—
And for this once my will shall stand for law.
RICHARD OF GLOUCESTER
And yet, methinks, your grace hath not done well   50
To give the heir and daughter of Lord Scales
Unto the brother of your loving bride.
She better would have fitted me or Clarence,
But in your bride you bury brotherhood.
GEORGE OF CLARENCE
Or else you would not have bestowed the heir   55
Of the Lord Bonville on your new wife's son,
And leave your brothers to go speed elsewhere.
KING EDWARD
Alas, poor Clarence, is it for a wife
That thou art malcontent? I will provide thee.
GEORGE OF CLARENCE
In choosing for yourself you showed your judgement,
Which being shallow, you shall give me leave   61
To play the broker in mine own behalf,
And to that end I shortly mind to leave you.
KING EDWARD
Leave me, or tarry. Edward will be king,
And not be tied unto his brother's will.   65
LADY GRAY
My lords, before it pleased his majesty
To raise my state to title of a queen,
Do me but right, and you must all confess
That I was not ignoble of descent—
And meaner than myself have had like fortune.   70
But as this title honours me and mine,
So your dislikes, to whom I would be pleasing,
Doth cloud my joys with danger and with sorrow.
KING EDWARD
My love, forbear to fawn upon their frowns.
What danger or what sorrow can befall thee   75
So long as Edward is thy constant friend,
And their true sovereign, whom they must obey?
Nay, whom they shall obey, and love thee too—
Unless they seek for hatred at my hands,
Which if they do, yet will I keep thee safe,   80
And they shall feel the vengeance of my wrath.
RICHARD OF GLOUCESTER *(aside)*
I hear, yet say not much, but think the more.
Enter the Post from France
KING EDWARD
Now, messenger, what letters or what news from
          France?
POST
My sovereign liege, no letters and few words,
But such as I, without your special pardon,   85
Dare not relate.

KING EDWARD
Go to, we pardon thee. Therefore, in brief,
Tell me their words as near as thou canst guess them.
What answer makes King Louis unto our letters?
POST
At my depart these were his very words: 90
'Go tell false Edward, thy supposèd king,
That Louis of France is sending over masquers
To revel it with him and his new bride.'
KING EDWARD
Is Louis so brave? Belike he thinks me Henry.
But what said Lady Bona to my marriage?   95
POST
These were her words, uttered with mild disdain:
'Tell him in hope he'll prove a widower shortly,
I'll wear the willow garland for his sake.'
KING EDWARD
I blame not her, she could say little less;
She had the wrong. But what said Henry's queen?   100
For I have heard that she was there in place.
POST
'Tell him', quoth she, 'my mourning weeds are done,
And I am ready to put armour on.'
KING EDWARD
Belike she minds to play the Amazon.
But what said Warwick to these injuries?   105
POST
He, more incensed against your majesty
Than all the rest, discharged me with these words:
'Tell him from me that he hath done me wrong,
And therefore I'll uncrown him ere't be long.'
KING EDWARD
Ha! Durst the traitor breathe out so proud words?   110
Well, I will arm me, being thus forewarned.
They shall have wars and pay for their presumption.
But say, is Warwick friends with Margaret?
POST
Ay, gracious sovereign, they are so linked in friendship
That young Prince Edward marries Warwick's daughter.
GEORGE OF CLARENCE
Belike the elder; Clarence will have the younger.   116
Now, brother King, farewell, and sit you fast,
For I will hence to Warwick's other daughter,
That, though I want a kingdom, yet in marriage
I may not prove inferior to yourself.   120
You that love me and Warwick, follow me.
                    Exit Clarence, and Somerset follows
RICHARD OF GLOUCESTER
Not I—⌈*aside*⌉ my thoughts aim at a further matter.
I stay not for the love of Edward, but the crown.
KING EDWARD
Clarence and Somerset both gone to Warwick?
Yet am I armed against the worst can happen,   125
And haste is needful in this desp'rate case.
Pembroke and Stafford, you in our behalf
Go levy men and make prepare for war.
They are already, or quickly will be, landed.
Myself in person will straight follow you.   130
                    Exeunt Pembroke and Stafford

But ere I go, Hastings and Montague,
Resolve my doubt. You twain, of all the rest,
Are near'st to Warwick by blood and by alliance.
Tell me if you love Warwick more than me.
If it be so, then both depart to him—   135
I rather wish you foes than hollow friends.
But if you mind to hold your true obedience,
Give me assurance with some friendly vow
That I may never have you in suspect.
MONTAGUE
So God help Montague as he proves true.   140
HASTINGS
And Hastings as he favours Edward's cause.
KING EDWARD
Now, brother Richard, will you stand by us?
RICHARD OF GLOUCESTER
Ay, in despite of all that shall withstand you.
KING EDWARD
Why, so. Then am I sure of victory.
Now, therefore, let us hence and lose no hour   145
Till we meet Warwick with his foreign power.   *Exeunt*

4.2   *Enter the Earls of Warwick and Oxford in England,*
       with French soldiers
WARWICK
Trust me, my lord, all hitherto goes well.
The common sort by numbers swarm to us.
       Enter the Dukes of Clarence and Somerset
But see where Somerset and Clarence comes.
Speak suddenly, my lords, are we all friends?
GEORGE OF CLARENCE Fear not that, my lord.   5
WARWICK
Then, gentle Clarence, welcome unto Warwick—
And welcome, Somerset. I hold it cowardice
To rest mistrustful where a noble heart
Hath pawned an open hand in sign of love,
Else might I think that Clarence, Edward's brother,   10
Were but a feignèd friend to our proceedings.
But come, sweet Clarence, my daughter shall be thine.
And now what rests but, in night's coverture,
Thy brother being carelessly encamped,
His soldiers lurking in the towns about,   15
And but attended by a simple guard,
We may surprise and take him at our pleasure?
Our scouts have found the adventure very easy;
That, as Ulysses and stout Diomed
With sleight and manhood stole to Rhesus' tents   20
And brought from thence the Thracian fatal steeds,
So we, well covered with the night's black mantle,
At unawares may beat down Edward's guard
And seize himself—I say not 'slaughter him',
For I intend but only to surprise him.   25
You that will follow me to this attempt,
Applaud the name of Henry with your leader.
       They all cry 'Henry'
Why, then, let's on our way in silent sort,
For Warwick and his friends, God and Saint George!
                                              Exeunt

4.3 *Enter three Watchmen, to guard King Edward's tent*

FIRST WATCHMAN
Come on, my masters, each man take his stand.
The King by this is set him down to sleep.

SECOND WATCHMAN What, will he not to bed?

FIRST WATCHMAN
Why, no—for he hath made a solemn vow
Never to lie and take his natural rest   5
Till Warwick or himself be quite suppressed.

SECOND WATCHMAN
Tomorrow then belike shall be the day,
If Warwick be so near as men report.

THIRD WATCHMAN
But say, I pray, what nobleman is that
That with the King here resteth in his tent?   10

FIRST WATCHMAN
'Tis the Lord Hastings, the King's chiefest friend.

THIRD WATCHMAN
O, is it so? But why commands the King
That his chief followers lodge in towns about him,
While he himself keeps in the cold field?

SECOND WATCHMAN
'Tis the more honour, because more dangerous.   15

THIRD WATCHMAN
Ay, but give me worship and quietness—
I like it better than a dangerous honour.
If Warwick knew in what estate he stands,
'Tis to be doubted he would waken him.

FIRST WATCHMAN
Unless our halberds did shut up his passage.   20

SECOND WATCHMAN
Ay, wherefore else guard we his royal tent
But to defend his person from night-foes?
   Enter silently the Earl of Warwick, George Duke of
   Clarence, the Earl of Oxford, and the Duke of
   Somerset, with French soldiers

WARWICK
This is his tent—and see where stand his guard.
Courage, my masters—honour now or never!
But follow me, and Edward shall be ours.   25

FIRST WATCHMAN Who goes there?

SECOND WATCHMAN Stay or thou diest.
   Warwick and the rest all cry 'Warwick, Warwick!'
   and set upon the guard, who fly, crying 'Arm,
   arm!' Warwick and the rest follow them

4.4 *With the drummer playing and trumpeter sounding,*
   enter the Earl of Warwick, the Duke of Somerset,
   and the rest bringing King Edward out in his gown,
   sitting in a chair. Richard Duke of Gloucester and
   Lord Hastings flies over the stage

SOMERSET What are they that fly there?

WARWICK
Richard and Hastings—let them go. Here is the Duke.

KING EDWARD
'The Duke'! Why, Warwick, when we parted,
Thou calledst me king.

WARWICK   Ay, but the case is altered.

When you disgraced me in my embassade,   5
Then I degraded you from being king,
And come now to create you Duke of York.
Alas, how should you govern any kingdom
That know not how to use ambassadors,
Nor how to be contented with one wife,   10
Nor how to use your brothers brotherly,
Nor how to study for the people's welfare,
Nor how to shroud yourself from enemies?

KING EDWARD (*seeing George*)
Yea, brother of Clarence, art thou here too?
Nay, then, I see that Edward needs must down.   15
Yet, Warwick, in despite of all mischance,
Of thee thyself and all thy complices,
Edward will always bear himself as king.
Though fortune's malice overthrow my state,
My mind exceeds the compass of her wheel.   20

WARWICK
Then, for his mind, be Edward England's king.
   Warwick takes off Edward's crown
But Henry now shall wear the English crown,
And be true king indeed, thou but the shadow.
My lord of Somerset, at my request,
See that, forthwith, Duke Edward be conveyed   25
Unto my brother, Archbishop of York.
When I have fought with Pembroke and his fellows,
I'll follow you, and tell what answer
Louis and the Lady Bona send to him.
Now for a while farewell, good Duke of York.   30
   They begin to lead Edward out forcibly

KING EDWARD
What fates impose, that men must needs abide.
It boots not to resist both wind and tide.
                         Exeunt some with Edward

OXFORD
What now remains, my lords, for us to do
But march to London with our soldiers?

WARWICK
Ay, that's the first thing that we have to do—   35
To free King Henry from imprisonment
And see him seated in the regal throne.   *Exeunt*

4.5 *Enter Earl Rivers and his sister, Lady Gray,*
   Edward's queen

RIVERS
Madam, what makes you in this sudden change?

LADY GRAY
Why, brother Rivers, are you yet to learn
What late misfortune is befall'n King Edward?

RIVERS
What? Loss of some pitched battle against Warwick?

LADY GRAY
No, but the loss of his own royal person.   5

RIVERS Then is my sovereign slain?

LADY GRAY
Ay, almost slain—for he is taken prisoner,
Either betrayed by falsehood of his guard
Or by his foe surprised at unawares,

And, as I further have to understand,   10
Is new committed to the Bishop of York,
Fell Warwick's brother, and by that our foe.
RIVERS
These news, I must confess, are full of grief.
Yet, gracious madam, bear it as you may.
Warwick may lose, that now hath won the day.   15
LADY GRAY
Till then fair hope must hinder life's decay,
And I the rather wean me from despair
For love of Edward's offspring in my womb.
This is it that makes me bridle passion
And bear with mildness my misfortune's cross.   20
Ay, ay, for this I draw in many a tear
And stop the rising of blood-sucking sighs,
Lest with my sighs or tears I blast or drown
King Edward's fruit, true heir to th'English crown.
RIVERS
But, madam, where is Warwick then become?   25
LADY GRAY
I am informèd that he comes towards London
To set the crown once more on Henry's head.
Guess thou the rest—King Edward's friends must down.
But to prevent the tyrant's violence—
For trust not him that hath once broken faith—   30
I'll hence forthwith unto the sanctuary,
To save at least the heir of Edward's right.
There shall I rest secure from force and fraud.
Come, therefore, let us fly while we may fly.
If Warwick take us, we are sure to die.   *Exeunt*

4.6 *Enter Richard Duke of Gloucester, Lord Hastings,*
        and Sir William Stanley, ⌈with soldiers⌉
RICHARD OF GLOUCESTER
Now my lord Hastings and Sir William Stanley,
Leave off to wonder why I drew you hither
Into this chiefest thicket of the park.
Thus stands the case: you know our King, my brother,
Is prisoner to the Bishop here, at whose hands   5
He hath good usage and great liberty,
And, often but attended with weak guard,
Comes hunting this way to disport himself.
I have advertised him by secret means
That if about this hour he make this way   10
Under the colour of his usual game,
He shall here find his friends with horse and men
To set him free from his captivity.
        Enter King Edward and a Huntsman with him
HUNTSMAN
This way, my lord—for this way lies the game.
KING EDWARD
Nay, this way, man—see where the huntsmen stand.
Now, brother of Gloucester, Lord Hastings, and the
        rest,   16
Stand you thus close to steal the Bishop's deer?
RICHARD OF GLOUCESTER
Brother, the time and case requireth haste.
Your horse stands ready at the park corner.

KING EDWARD But whither shall we then?   20
HASTINGS To Lynn, my lord,
And shipped from thence to Flanders.
RICHARD OF GLOUCESTER ⌈*aside*⌉
Well guessed, believe me—for that was my meaning.
KING EDWARD
Stanley, I will requite thy forwardness.
RICHARD OF GLOUCESTER
But wherefore stay we? 'Tis no time to talk.   25
KING EDWARD
Huntsman, what sayst thou? Wilt thou go along?
HUNTSMAN
Better do so than tarry and be hanged.
RICHARD OF GLOUCESTER
Come then, away—let's have no more ado.
KING EDWARD
Bishop, farewell—shield thee from Warwick's frown,
And pray that I may repossess the crown.   *Exeunt*

4.7 *Flourish. Enter the Earl of Warwick and George*
        Duke of Clarence ⌈with the crown⌉. Then enter
        King Henry, the Earl of Oxford, the Duke of
        Somerset ⌈with⌉ young Henry Earl of Richmond,
        the Marquis of Montague, and the Lieutenant of the
        Tower
KING HENRY
Master Lieutenant, now that God and friends
Have shaken Edward from the regal seat
And turned my captive state to liberty,
My fear to hope, my sorrows unto joys,
At our enlargement what are thy due fees?   5
LIEUTENANT
Subjects may challenge nothing of their sovereigns—
But if an humble prayer may prevail,
I then crave pardon of your majesty.
KING HENRY
For what, Lieutenant? For well using me?
Nay, be thou sure I'll well requite thy kindness,   10
For that it made my prisonment a pleasure—
Ay, such a pleasure as encagèd birds
Conceive when, after many moody thoughts,
At last by notes of household harmony
They quite forget their loss of liberty.   15
But, Warwick, after God, thou sett'st me free,
And chiefly therefore I thank God and thee.
He was the author, thou the instrument.
Therefore, that I may conquer fortune's spite
By living low, where fortune cannot hurt me,   20
And that the people of this blessèd land
May not be punished with my thwarting stars,
Warwick, although my head still wear the crown,
I here resign my government to thee,
For thou art fortunate in all thy deeds.   25
WARWICK
Your grace hath still been famed for virtuous,
And now may seem as wise as virtuous
By spying and avoiding fortune's malice,
For few men rightly temper with the stars.

Yet in this one thing let me blame your grace: 30
For choosing me when Clarence is in place.

GEORGE OF CLARENCE
No, Warwick, thou art worthy of the sway,
To whom the heav'ns in thy nativity
Adjudged an olive branch and laurel crown,
As likely to be blest in peace and war.   35
And therefore I yield thee my free consent.

WARWICK
And I choose Clarence only for Protector.

KING HENRY
Warwick and Clarence, give me both your hands.
Now join your hands, and with your hands your
  hearts,
That no dissension hinder government.   40
I make you both Protectors of this land,
While I myself will lead a private life
And in devotion spend my latter days,
To sin's rebuke and my creator's praise.

WARWICK
What answers Clarence to his sovereign's will?   45

GEORGE OF CLARENCE
That he consents, if Warwick yield consent,
For on thy fortune I repose myself.

WARWICK
Why, then, though loath, yet must I be content.
We'll yoke together, like a double shadow
To Henry's body, and supply his place—   50
I mean in bearing weight of government—
While he enjoys the honour and his ease.
And, Clarence, now then it is more than needful
Forthwith that Edward be pronounced a traitor,
And all his lands and goods be confiscate.   55

GEORGE OF CLARENCE
What else? And that succession be determined.

WARWICK
Ay, therein Clarence shall not want his part.

KING HENRY
But with the first of all your chief affairs,
Let me entreat—for I command no more—
That Margaret your queen and my son Edward   60
Be sent for, to return from France with speed.
For, till I see them here, by doubtful fear
My joy of liberty is half eclipsed.

GEORGE OF CLARENCE
It shall be done, my sovereign, with all speed.

KING HENRY
My lord of Somerset, what youth is that   65
Of whom you seem to have so tender care?

SOMERSET
My liege, it is young Henry, Earl of Richmond.

KING HENRY
Come hither, England's hope.
  King Henry lays his hand on Richmond's head
        If secret powers
Suggest but truth to my divining thoughts,
This pretty lad will prove our country's bliss.   70
His looks are full of peaceful majesty,

His head by nature framed to wear a crown,
His hand to wield a sceptre, and himself
Likely in time to bless a regal throne.
Make much of him, my lords, for this is he   75
Must help you more than you are hurt by me.
  Enter a Post

WARWICK What news, my friend?

POST
That Edward is escapèd from your brother
And fled, as he hears since, to Burgundy.

WARWICK
Unsavoury news—but how made he escape?   80

POST
He was conveyed by Richard Duke of Gloucester
And the Lord Hastings, who attended him
In secret ambush on the forest side
And from the Bishop's huntsmen rescued him—
For hunting was his daily exercise.   85

WARWICK
My brother was too careless of his charge.
(*To King Henry*) But let us hence, my sovereign, to
  provide
A salve for any sore that may betide.
  Exeunt all but Somerset, Richmond, and Oxford

SOMERSET (*to Oxford*)
My lord, I like not of this flight of Edward's,
For doubtless Burgundy will yield him help,   90
And we shall have more wars before't be long.
As Henry's late presaging prophecy
Did glad my heart with hope of this young Richmond,
So doth my heart misgive me, in these conflicts,
What may befall him, to his harm and ours.   95
Therefore, Lord Oxford, to prevent the worst,
Forthwith we'll send him hence to Brittany,
Till storms be past of civil enmity.

OXFORD
Ay, for if Edward repossess the crown,
'Tis like that Richmond with the rest shall down.   100

SOMERSET
It shall be so—he shall to Brittany.
Come, therefore, let's about it speedily.   *Exeunt*

4.8 *Flourish. Enter King Edward, Richard Duke of*
  Gloucester, and Lord Hastings, ⌜with a troop of
  Hollanders⌝

KING EDWARD
Now, brother Richard, Lord Hastings, and the rest,
Yet thus far fortune maketh us amends,
And says that once more I shall interchange
My wanèd state for Henry's regal crown.
Well have we passed and now repassed the seas   5
And brought desirèd help from Burgundy.
What then remains, we being thus arrived
From Ravenspurgh haven before the gates of York,
But that we enter, as into our dukedom?
  ⌜*Hastings⌝ knocks at the gates of York*

RICHARD OF GLOUCESTER
The gates made fast? Brother, I like not this.   10

For many men that stumble at the threshold
Are well foretold that danger lurks within.
KING EDWARD
Tush, man, abodements must not now affright us.
By fair or foul means we must enter in,
For hither will our friends repair to us.   15
HASTINGS
My liege, I'll knock once more to summon them.
   He knocks.
   Enter, on the walls, the Mayor and aldermen of York
MAYOR
My lords, we were forewarnèd of your coming,
And shut the gates for safety of ourselves—
For now we owe allegiance unto Henry.
KING EDWARD
But, Master Mayor, if Henry be your king,   20
Yet Edward at the least is Duke of York.
MAYOR
True, my good lord, I know you for no less.
KING EDWARD
Why, and I challenge nothing but my dukedom,
As being well content with that alone.
RICHARD OF GLOUCESTER (*aside*)
But when the fox hath once got in his nose,   25
He'll soon find means to make the body follow.
HASTINGS
Why, Master Mayor, why stand you in a doubt?
Open the gates—we are King Henry's friends.
MAYOR
Ay, say you so? The gates shall then be opened.
   They descend
RICHARD OF GLOUCESTER
A wise stout captain, and soon persuaded.   30
HASTINGS
The good old man would fain that all were well,
So 'twere not long of him; but being entered,
I doubt not, I, but we shall soon persuade
Both him and all his brothers unto reason.
   Enter below the Mayor and two aldermen
KING EDWARD
So, Master Mayor, these gates must not be shut   35
But in the night or in the time of war.
What—fear not, man, but yield me up the keys,
   King Edward takes some keys from the Mayor
For Edward will defend the town and thee,
And all those friends that deign to follow me.
   March. Enter Sir John Montgomery with a
   drummer and soldiers
RICHARD OF GLOUCESTER
Brother, this is Sir John Montgomery,   40
Our trusty friend, unless I be deceived.
KING EDWARD
Welcome, Sir John—but why come you in arms?
MONTGOMERY
To help King Edward in his time of storm,
As every loyal subject ought to do.
KING EDWARD
Thanks, good Montgomery, but we now forget   45

Our title to the crown, and only claim
Our dukedom till God please to send the rest.
MONTGOMERY
Then fare you well, for I will hence again.
I came to serve a king and not a duke.
Drummer, strike up, and let us march away.   50
   The drummer begins to sound a march
KING EDWARD
Nay, stay, Sir John, a while, and we'll debate
By what safe means the crown may be recovered.
MONTGOMERY
What talk you of debating? In few words,
If you'll not here proclaim yourself our king
I'll leave you to your fortune and be gone   55
To keep them back that come to succour you.
Why shall we fight, if you pretend no title?
RICHARD OF GLOUCESTER (*to King Edward*)
Why, brother, wherefore stand you on nice points?
KING EDWARD
When we grow stronger, then we'll make our claim.
Till then 'tis wisdom to conceal our meaning.   60
HASTINGS
Away with scrupulous wit! Now arms must rule.
RICHARD OF GLOUCESTER
And fearless minds climb soonest unto crowns.
Brother, we will proclaim you out of hand,
The bruit thereof will bring you many friends.
KING EDWARD
Then be it as you will, for 'tis my right,   65
And Henry but usurps the diadem.
MONTGOMERY
Ay, now my sovereign speaketh like himself,
And now will I be Edward's champion.
HASTINGS
Sound trumpet, Edward shall be here proclaimed.
   ⌈*To Montgomery*⌉
Come, fellow soldier, make thou proclamation.   70
   Flourish
⌈MONTGOMERY⌉ Edward the Fourth, by the grace of God
King of England and France, and Lord of Ireland—
And whosoe'er gainsays King Edward's right,
By this I challenge him to single fight.
   He throws down his gauntlet
ALL Long live Edward the Fourth!   75
KING EDWARD
Thanks, brave Montgomery, and thanks unto you all.
If fortune serve me I'll requite this kindness.
Now, for this night, let's harbour here in York;
And when the morning sun shall raise his car
Above the border of this horizon,   80
We'll forward towards Warwick and his mates.
For well I wot that Henry is no soldier.
Ah, froward Clarence, how evil it beseems thee
To flatter Henry and forsake thy brother!
Yet, as we may, we'll meet both thee and Warwick.   85
Come on, brave soldiers—doubt not of the day
And, that once gotten, doubt not of large pay.
   Exeunt

4.9 *Flourish. Enter King Henry, the Earl of Warwick,*
the Marquis of Montague, George Duke of
Clarence, and the Earl of Oxford

WARWICK

What counsel, lords? Edward from Belgia,
With hasty Germans and blunt Hollanders,
Hath passed in safety through the narrow seas,
And with his troops doth march amain to London,
And many giddy people flock to him.   5

KING HENRY

Let's levy men and beat him back again.

GEORGE OF CLARENCE

A little fire is quickly trodden out,
Which, being suffered, rivers cannot quench.

WARWICK

In Warwickshire I have true-hearted friends,
Not mutinous in peace, yet bold in war.   10
Those will I muster up. And thou, son Clarence,
Shalt stir in Suffolk, Norfolk, and in Kent,
The knights and gentlemen to come with thee.
Thou, brother Montague, in Buckingham,
Northampton, and in Leicestershire shalt find   15
Men well inclined to hear what thou command'st.
And thou, brave Oxford, wondrous well beloved
In Oxfordshire, shalt muster up thy friends.
My sovereign, with the loving citizens,
Like to his island girt in with the ocean,   20
Or modest Dian circled with her nymphs,
Shall rest in London till we come to him.
Fair lords, take leave and stand not to reply.
Farewell, my sovereign.

KING HENRY

Farewell, my Hector, and my Troy's true hope.   25

GEORGE OF CLARENCE

In sign of truth, I kiss your highness' hand.
He kisses King Henry's hand

KING HENRY

Well-minded Clarence, be thou fortunate.

MONTAGUE

Comfort, my lord, and so I take my leave.
⌈*He kisses King Henry's hand*⌉

OXFORD

And thus I seal my truth and bid adieu.
⌈*He kisses King Henry's hand*⌉

KING HENRY

Sweet Oxford, and my loving Montague,   30
And all at once, once more a happy farewell.   ⌈*Exit*⌉

WARWICK

Farewell, sweet lords—let's meet at Coventry.
Exeunt ⌈*severally*⌉

4.10 ⌈*Enter King Henry and the Duke of Exeter*⌉

KING HENRY

Here at the palace will I rest a while.
Cousin of Exeter, what thinks your lordship?
Methinks the power that Edward hath in field
Should not be able to encounter mine.

EXETER

The doubt is that he will seduce the rest.   5

KING HENRY

That's not my fear. My meed hath got me fame.
I have not stopped mine ears to their demands,
Nor posted off their suits with slow delays.
My pity hath been balm to heal their wounds,
My mildness hath allayed their swelling griefs,   10
My mercy dried their water-flowing tears.
I have not been desirous of their wealth,
Nor much oppressed them with great subsidies,
Nor forward of revenge, though they much erred.
Then why should they love Edward more than me?   15
No, Exeter, these graces challenge grace;
And when the lion fawns upon the lamb,
The lamb will never cease to follow him.
Shout within 'A Lancaster', ⌈*'A York'*⌉

EXETER

Hark, hark, my lord—what shouts are these?
Enter King Edward and Richard Duke of Gloucester,
with soldiers

KING EDWARD

Seize on the shame-faced Henry—bear him hence,   20
And once again proclaim us King of England.
You are the fount that makes small brooks to flow.
Now stops thy spring—my sea shall suck them dry,
And swell so much the higher by their ebb.
Hence with him to the Tower—let him not speak.   25
Exeunt some with King Henry and Exeter
And lords, towards Coventry bend we our course,
Where peremptory Warwick now remains.
The sun shines hot, and, if we use delay,
Cold biting winter mars our hoped-for hay.

RICHARD OF GLOUCESTER

Away betimes, before his forces join,   30
And take the great-grown traitor unawares.
Brave warriors, march amain towards Coventry.
Exeunt

5.1 *Enter the Earl of Warwick, the Mayor of Coventry,*
two Messengers, and others upon the walls

WARWICK

Where is the post that came from valiant Oxford?
⌈*The First Messenger steps forward*⌉
How far hence is thy lord, mine honest fellow?

FIRST MESSENGER

By this at Dunsmore, marching hitherward.

WARWICK

How far off is our brother Montague?
Where is the post that came from Montague?   5
⌈*The Second Messenger steps forward*⌉

SECOND MESSENGER

By this at Da'ntry, with a puissant troop.
Enter Somerville ⌈*to them, above*⌉

WARWICK

Say, Somerville—what says my loving son?
And, by thy guess, how nigh is Clarence now?

SOMERVILLE
At Southam I did leave him with his forces,
And do expect him here some two hours hence.   10
A march afar off
WARWICK
Then Clarence is at hand—I hear his drum.
SOMERVILLE
It is not his, my lord. Here Southam lies.
The drum your honour hears marcheth from Warwick.
WARWICK
Who should that be? Belike, unlooked-for friends.
SOMERVILLE
They are at hand, and you shall quickly know.   15
Flourish. Enter below King Edward and Richard
Duke of Gloucester, with soldiers
KING EDWARD
Go, trumpet, to the walls, and sound a parley.
⌈*Sound a parley*⌉
RICHARD OF GLOUCESTER
See how the surly Warwick mans the wall.
WARWICK
O, unbid spite—is sportful Edward come?
Where slept our scouts, or how are they seduced,
That we could hear no news of his repair?   20
KING EDWARD
Now, Warwick, wilt thou ope the city gates,
Speak gentle words, and humbly bend thy knee,
Call Edward king, and at his hands beg mercy?
And he shall pardon thee these outrages.
WARWICK
Nay, rather, wilt thou draw thy forces hence,   25
Confess who set thee up and plucked thee down,
Call Warwick patron, and be penitent?
And thou shalt still remain the Duke of York.
RICHARD OF GLOUCESTER
I thought at least he would have said 'the King'.
Or did he make the jest against his will?   30
WARWICK
Is not a dukedom, sir, a goodly gift?
RICHARD OF GLOUCESTER
Ay, by my faith, for a poor earl to give.
I'll do thee service for so good a gift.
WARWICK
'Twas I that gave the kingdom to thy brother.
KING EDWARD
Why then, 'tis mine, if but by Warwick's gift.   35
WARWICK
Thou art no Atlas for so great a weight;
And, weakling, Warwick takes his gift again;
And Henry is my king, Warwick his subject.
KING EDWARD
But Warwick's king is Edward's prisoner,
And, gallant Warwick, do but answer this: 40
What is the body when the head is off?
RICHARD OF GLOUCESTER
Alas, that Warwick had no more forecast,
But whiles he thought to steal the single ten,
The king was slyly fingered from the deck.

⌈*To Warwick*⌉ You left poor Henry at the Bishop's
palace,   45
And ten to one you'll meet him in the Tower.
KING EDWARD
'Tis even so—⌈*to Warwick*⌉ yet you are Warwick still.
RICHARD OF GLOUCESTER
Come, Warwick, take the time—kneel down, kneel
down.
Nay, when? Strike now, or else the iron cools.
WARWICK
I had rather chop this hand off at a blow,   50
And with the other fling it at thy face,
Than bear so low a sail to strike to thee.
KING EDWARD
Sail how thou canst, have wind and tide thy friend,
This hand, fast wound about thy coal-black hair,
Shall, whiles thy head is warm and new cut off,   55
Write in the dust this sentence with thy blood:
'Wind-changing Warwick now can change no more'.
Enter the Earl of Oxford, with a drummer and
⌈*soldiers bearing*⌉ *colours*
WARWICK
O cheerful colours! See where Oxford comes.
OXFORD
Oxford, Oxford, for Lancaster!
⌈*Oxford and his men pass over the stage and*
exeunt into the city⌉
RICHARD OF GLOUCESTER (*to King Edward*)
The gates are open—let us enter too.   60
KING EDWARD
So other foes may set upon our backs?
Stand we in good array, for they no doubt
Will issue out again and bid us battle.
If not, the city being but of small defence,
We'll quickly rouse the traitors in the same.   65
WARWICK ⌈*to Oxford, within*⌉
O, welcome, Oxford, for we want thy help.
Enter the Marquis of Montague with a drummer
and ⌈*soldiers bearing*⌉ *colours*
MONTAGUE
Montague, Montague, for Lancaster!
⌈*Montague and his men pass over the stage and*
exeunt into the city⌉
RICHARD OF GLOUCESTER
Thou and thy brother both shall bye this treason
Even with the dearest blood your bodies bear.
KING EDWARD
The harder matched, the greater victory.   70
My mind presageth happy gain and conquest.
Enter the Duke of Somerset with a drummer and
⌈*soldiers bearing*⌉ *colours*
SOMERSET
Somerset, Somerset, for Lancaster!
⌈*Somerset and his men pass over the stage and*
exeunt into the city⌉
RICHARD OF GLOUCESTER
Two of thy name, both dukes of Somerset,
Have sold their lives unto the house of York—
And thou shalt be the third, an this sword hold.   75

Enter George Duke of Clarence with a drummer and
⌈*soldiers bearing*⌉ *colours*

WARWICK
And lo, where George of Clarence sweeps along,
Of force enough to bid his brother battle;
With whom an upright zeal to right prevails
More than the nature of a brother's love.
GEORGE OF CLARENCE
Clarence, Clarence, for Lancaster!   80
KING EDWARD
Et tu, Brute—wilt thou stab Caesar too?
(*To a trumpeter*) A parley, sirra, to George of Clarence.
Sound a parley. Richard of Gloucester and George of
Clarence whisper together
WARWICK
Come, Clarence, come—thou wilt if Warwick call.
GEORGE OF CLARENCE
Father of Warwick, know you what this means?
⌈*He takes his red rose out of his hat and throws it*
at Warwick⌉
Look—here I throw my infamy at thee!   85
I will not ruinate my father's house,
Who gave his blood to lime the stones together,
And set up Lancaster. Why, trowest thou, Warwick,
That Clarence is so harsh, so blunt, unnatural,
To bend the fatal instruments of war   90
Against his brother and his lawful king?
Perhaps thou wilt object my holy oath.
To keep that oath were more impiety
Than Jephthah, when he sacrificed his daughter.
I am so sorry for my trespass made   95
That, to deserve well at my brothers' hands,
I here proclaim myself thy mortal foe,
With resolution, wheresoe'er I meet thee—
As I will meet thee, if thou stir abroad—
To plague thee for thy foul misleading me.   100
And so, proud-hearted Warwick, I defy thee,
And to my brothers turn my blushing cheeks.
(*To King Edward*)
Pardon me, Edward—I will make amends.
(*To Richard*)
And, Richard, do not frown upon my faults,
For I will henceforth be no more unconstant.   105
KING EDWARD
Now welcome more, and ten times more beloved,
Than if thou never hadst deserved our hate.
RICHARD OF GLOUCESTER (*to George*)
Welcome, good Clarence—this is brother-like.
WARWICK (*to George*)
O, passing traitor—perjured and unjust!
KING EDWARD
What, Warwick, wilt thou leave the town and fight?
Or shall we beat the stones about thine ears?   111
WARWICK ⌈*aside*⌉
Alas, I am not cooped here for defence.
(*To King Edward*)
I will away towards Barnet presently,
And bid thee battle, Edward, if thou dar'st.

KING EDWARD
Yes, Warwick—Edward dares, and leads the way.   115
Lords, to the field—Saint George and victory!
Exeunt below King Edward and his company.
March. The Earl of Warwick and his company
descend and follow

5.2   *Alarum and excursions. Enter King Edward*
bringing forth the Earl of Warwick, wounded
KING EDWARD
So lie thou there. Die thou, and die our fear—
For Warwick was a bug that feared us all.
Now, Montague, sit fast—I seek for thee
That Warwick's bones may keep thine company.   *Exit*
WARWICK
Ah, who is nigh? Come to me, friend or foe,   5
And tell me who is victor, York or Warwick?
Why ask I that? My mangled body shows,
My blood, my want of strength, my sick heart shows,
That I must yield my body to the earth
And by my fall the conquest to my foe.   10
Thus yields the cedar to the axe's edge,
Whose arms gave shelter to the princely eagle,
Under whose shade the ramping lion slept,
Whose top-branch over-peered Jove's spreading tree
And kept low shrubs from winter's powerful wind.   15
These eyes, that now are dimmed with death's black
        veil,
Have been as piercing as the midday sun
To search the secret treasons of the world.
The wrinkles in my brows, now filled with blood,
Were likened oft to kingly sepulchres—   20
For who lived king, but I could dig his grave?
And who durst smile when Warwick bent his brow?
Lo now my glory smeared in dust and blood.
My parks, my walks, my manors that I had,
Even now forsake me, and of all my lands   25
Is nothing left me but my body's length.
Why, what is pomp, rule, reign, but earth and dust?
And, live we how we can, yet die we must.
Enter the Earl of Oxford and the Duke of Somerset
SOMERSET
Ah, Warwick, Warwick—wert thou as we are,
We might recover all our loss again.   30
The Queen from France hath brought a puissant
        power.
Even now we heard the news. Ah, couldst thou fly!
WARWICK
Why, then I would not fly. Ah, Montague,
If thou be there, sweet brother, take my hand,
And with thy lips keep in my soul a while.   35
Thou lov'st me not—for, brother, if thou didst,
Thy tears would wash this cold congealèd blood
That glues my lips and will not let me speak.
Come quickly, Montague, or I am dead.
SOMERSET
Ah, Warwick—Montague hath breathed his last,   40
And to the latest gasp cried out for Warwick,

And said 'Commend me to my valiant brother.'
And more he would have said, and more he spoke,
Which sounded like a canon in a vault,
That mote not be distinguished; but at last   45
I well might hear, delivered with a groan,
'O, farewell, Warwick.'

WARWICK
Sweet rest his soul. Fly, lords, and save yourselves—
For Warwick bids you all farewell, to meet in heaven.
                                      He dies

OXFORD
Away, away—to meet the Queen's great power!   50
    Here they bear away Warwick's body. Exeunt

5.3   *Flourish. Enter King Edward in triumph, with*
      Richard Duke of Gloucester, George Duke of
      Clarence, and ⌈soldiers⌉

KING EDWARD
Thus far our fortune keeps an upward course,
And we are graced with wreaths of victory.
But in the midst of this bright-shining day
I spy a black suspicious threatening cloud
That will encounter with our glorious sun   5
Ere he attain his easeful western bed.
I mean, my lords, those powers that the Queen
Hath raised in Gallia have arrived our coast,
And, as we hear, march on to fight with us.

GEORGE OF CLARENCE
A little gale will soon disperse that cloud,   10
And blow it to the source from whence it came.
Thy very beams will dry those vapours up,
For every cloud engenders not a storm.

RICHARD OF GLOUCESTER
The Queen is valued thirty thousand strong,
And Somerset, with Oxford, fled to her.   15
If she have time to breathe, be well assured,
Her faction will be full as strong as ours.

KING EDWARD
We are advertised by our loving friends
That they do hold their course toward Tewkesbury.
We, having now the best at Barnet field,   20
Will thither straight, for willingness rids way—
And, as we march, our strength will be augmented
In every county as we go along.
Strike up the drum, cry 'Courage!'; and away.
                  ⌈Flourish. March.⌉ Exeunt

5.4   *Flourish. March. Enter Queen Margaret, Prince*
      Edward, the Duke of Somerset, the Earl of Oxford,
      and soldiers

QUEEN MARGARET
Great lords, wise men ne'er sit and wail their loss,
But cheerly seek how to redress their harms.
What though the mast be now blown overboard,
The cable broke, the holding-anchor lost,
And half our sailors swallowed in the flood?   5
Yet lives our pilot still. Is't meet that he
Should leave the helm and, like a fearful lad,

With tearful eyes add water to the sea,
And give more strength to that which hath too much,
Whiles, in his moan, the ship splits on the rock   10
Which industry and courage might have saved?
Ah, what a shame; ah, what a fault were this.
Say Warwick was our anchor—what of that?
And Montague our top-mast—what of him?
Our slaughtered friends the tackles—what of these?   15
Why, is not Oxford here another anchor?
And Somerset another goodly mast?
The friends of France our shrouds and tacklings?
And, though unskilful, why not Ned and I
For once allowed the skilful pilot's charge?   20
We will not from the helm to sit and weep,
But keep our course, though the rough wind say no,
From shelves and rocks that threaten us with wreck.
As good to chide the waves as speak them fair.
And what is Edward but a ruthless sea?   25
What Clarence but a quicksand of deceit?
And Richard but a raggèd fatal rock?
All these the enemies to our poor barque.
Say you can swim—alas, 'tis but a while;
Tread on the sand—why, there you quickly sink;   30
Bestride the rock—the tide will wash you off,
Or else you famish. That's a threefold death.
This speak I, lords, to let you understand,
If case some one of you would fly from us,   34
That there's no hoped-for mercy with the brothers York
More than with ruthless waves, with sands, and rocks.
Why, courage then—what cannot be avoided
'Twere childish weakness to lament or fear.

PRINCE EDWARD
Methinks a woman of this valiant spirit
Should, if a coward heard her speak these words,   40
Infuse his breast with magnanimity
And make him, naked, foil a man at arms.
I speak not this as doubting any here—
For did I but suspect a fearful man,
He should have leave to go away betimes,   45
Lest in our need he might infect another
And make him of like spirit to himself.
If any such be here—as God forbid—
Let him depart before we need his help.

OXFORD
Women and children of so high a courage,   50
And warriors faint—why, 'twere perpetual shame!
O brave young Prince, thy famous grandfather
Doth live again in thee! Long mayst thou live
To bear his image and renew his glories!

SOMERSET
And he that will not fight for such a hope,   55
Go home to bed, and like the owl by day,
If he arise, be mocked and wondered at.

QUEEN MARGARET
Thanks, gentle Somerset; sweet Oxford, thanks.

PRINCE EDWARD
And take his thanks that yet hath nothing else.

Enter a Messenger

MESSENGER

Prepare you, lords, for Edward is at hand   60
Ready to fight—therefore be resolute.

OXFORD

I thought no less. It is his policy
To haste thus fast to find us unprovided.

SOMERSET

But he's deceived; we are in readiness.

QUEEN MARGARET

This cheers my heart, to see your forwardness.   65

OXFORD

Here pitch our battle—hence we will not budge.
*Flourish and march. Enter King Edward, Richard
Duke of Gloucester, and George Duke of Clarence,
with soldiers*

KING EDWARD (*to his followers*)

Brave followers, yonder stands the thorny wood
Which, by the heavens' assistance and your strength,
Must by the roots be hewn up yet ere night.
I need not add more fuel to your fire,   70
For well I wot ye blaze to burn them out.
Give signal to the fight, and to it, lords.

QUEEN MARGARET (*to her followers*)

Lords, knights, and gentlemen—what I should say
My tears gainsay; for every word I speak
Ye see I drink the water of my eye.   75
Therefore, no more but this: Henry your sovereign
Is prisoner to the foe, his state usurped,
His realm a slaughter-house, his subjects slain,
His statutes cancelled, and his treasure spent—
And yonder is the wolf that makes this spoil.   80
You fight in justice; then in God's name, lords,
Be valiant, and give signal to the fight.
Alarum, retreat, excursions. Exeunt

5.5   *Flourish. Enter King Edward, Richard Duke of
Gloucester, and George Duke of Clarence with
Queen Margaret, the Earl of Oxford, and the Duke
of Somerset, guarded*

KING EDWARD

Now here a period of tumultuous broils.
Away with Oxford to Hames Castle straight;
For Somerset, off with his guilty head.
Go bear them hence—I will not hear them speak.

OXFORD

For my part, I'll not trouble thee with words.   5
                  Exit, guarded

SOMERSET

Nor I, but stoop with patience to my fortune.
                  Exit, guarded

QUEEN MARGARET

So part we sadly in this troublous world
To meet with joy in sweet Jerusalem.

KING EDWARD

Is proclamation made that who finds Edward
Shall have a high reward and he his life?   10

RICHARD OF GLOUCESTER

It is, and lo where youthful Edward comes.
Enter Prince Edward, guarded

KING EDWARD

Bring forth the gallant—let us hear him speak.
What, can so young a thorn begin to prick?
Edward, what satisfaction canst thou make
For bearing arms, for stirring up my subjects,   15
And all the trouble thou hast turned me to?

PRINCE EDWARD

Speak like a subject, proud ambitious York.
Suppose that I am now my father's mouth—
Resign thy chair, and where I stand, kneel thou,
Whilst I propose the self-same words to thee,   20
Which, traitor, thou wouldst have me answer to.

QUEEN MARGARET

Ah, that thy father had been so resolved.

RICHARD OF GLOUCESTER

That you might still have worn the petticoat
And ne'er have stolen the breech from Lancaster.

PRINCE EDWARD

Let Aesop fable in a winter's night—   25
His currish riddles sorts not with this place.

RICHARD OF GLOUCESTER

By heaven, brat, I'll plague ye for that word.

QUEEN MARGARET

Ay, thou wast born to be a plague to men.

RICHARD OF GLOUCESTER

For God's sake take away this captive scold.

PRINCE EDWARD

Nay, take away this scolding crookback rather.   30

KING EDWARD

Peace, wilful boy, or I will charm your tongue.

GEORGE OF CLARENCE (*to Prince Edward*)

Untutored lad, thou art too malapert.

PRINCE EDWARD

I know my duty—you are all undutiful.
Lascivious Edward, and thou, perjured George,
And thou, misshapen Dick—I tell ye all   35
I am your better, traitors as ye are,
And thou usurp'st my father's right and mine.

KING EDWARD

Take that, the likeness of this railer here.
King Edward stabs Prince Edward

RICHARD OF GLOUCESTER

Sprawl'st thou? Take that, to end thy agony.
Richard stabs Prince Edward

GEORGE OF CLARENCE

And there's for twitting me with perjury.   40
George stabs Prince Edward, ⌈who dies⌉

QUEEN MARGARET

O, kill me too!

RICHARD OF GLOUCESTER   Marry, and shall.
He offers to kill her

KING EDWARD

Hold, Richard, hold—for we have done too much.

RICHARD OF GLOUCESTER

Why should she live to fill the world with words?

Queen Margaret faints

KING EDWARD

What—doth she swoon? Use means for her recovery.

RICHARD OF GLOUCESTER (*aside to George*)

Clarence, excuse me to the King my brother.   45

I'll hence to London on a serious matter.

Ere ye come there, be sure to hear some news.

GEORGE OF CLARENCE (*aside to Richard*) What? What?

RICHARD OF GLOUCESTER (*aside to George*)

The Tower, the Tower.   *Exit*

QUEEN MARGARET

O Ned, sweet Ned—speak to thy mother, boy.   50

Canst thou not speak? O traitors, murderers!

They that stabbed Caesar shed no blood at all,

Did not offend, nor were not worthy blame,

If this foul deed were by to equal it.

He was a man—this, in respect, a child;   55

And men ne'er spend their fury on a child.

What's worse than murderer that I may name it?

No, no, my heart will burst an if I speak;

And I will speak that so my heart may burst.

Butchers and villains! Bloody cannibals!   60

How sweet a plant have you untimely cropped!

You have no children, butchers; if you had,

The thought of them would have stirred up remorse.

But if you ever chance to have a child,

Look in his youth to have him so cut off   65

As, deathsmen, you have rid this sweet young Prince!

KING EDWARD

Away with her—go, bear her hence perforce.

QUEEN MARGARET

Nay, never bear me hence—dispatch me here.

Here sheathe thy sword—I'll pardon thee my death.

What? Wilt thou not? Then, Clarence, do it thou.   70

GEORGE OF CLARENCE

By heaven, I will not do thee so much ease.

QUEEN MARGARET

Good Clarence, do; sweet Clarence, do thou do it.

GEORGE OF CLARENCE

Didst thou not hear me swear I would not do it?

QUEEN MARGARET

Ay, but thou usest to forswear thyself.

'Twas sin before, but now 'tis charity.   75

What, wilt thou not? Where is that devil's butcher,

Hard-favoured Richard? Richard, where art thou?

Thou art not here. Murder is thy alms-deed—

Petitioners for blood thou ne'er putt'st back.

KING EDWARD

Away, I say—I charge ye, bear her hence.   80

QUEEN MARGARET

So come to you and yours as to this Prince!

Exit, guarded

KING EDWARD Where's Richard gone?

GEORGE OF CLARENCE

To London all in post—⌈*aside*⌉ and as I guess,

To make a bloody supper in the Tower.

KING EDWARD

He's sudden if a thing comes in his head.   85

Now march we hence. Discharge the common sort

With pay and thanks, and let's away to London,

And see our gentle Queen how well she fares.

By this I hope she hath a son for me.   *Exeunt*

5.6   *Enter on the walls King Henry the Sixth, reading*

a book, Richard Duke of Gloucester, and the

Lieutenant of the Tower

RICHARD OF GLOUCESTER

Good day, my lord. What, at your book so hard?

KING HENRY

Ay, my good lord—'my lord', I should say, rather.

'Tis sin to flatter; 'good' was little better.

'Good Gloucester' and 'good devil' were alike,

And both preposterous—therefore not 'good lord'.   5

RICHARD OF GLOUCESTER (*to the Lieutenant*)

Sirrah, leave us to ourselves. We must confer.

Exit Lieutenant

KING HENRY

So flies the reckless shepherd from the wolf;

So first the harmless sheep doth yield his fleece,

And next his throat unto the butcher's knife.

What scene of death hath Roscius now to act?   10

RICHARD OF GLOUCESTER

Suspicion always haunts the guilty mind;

The thief doth fear each bush an officer.

KING HENRY

The bird that hath been limèd in a bush

With trembling wings misdoubteth every bush.

And I, the hapless male to one sweet bird,   15

Have now the fatal object in my eye

Where my poor young was limed, was caught and

killed.

RICHARD OF GLOUCESTER

Why, what a peevish fool was that of Crete,

That taught his son the office of a fowl!

And yet, for all his wings, the fool was drowned.   20

KING HENRY

I, Daedalus; my poor boy, Icarus;

Thy father, Minos, that denied our course;

The sun that seared the wings of my sweet boy,

Thy brother Edward; and thyself, the sea,

Whose envious gulf did swallow up his life.   25

Ah, kill me with thy weapon, not with words!

My breast can better brook thy dagger's point

Than can my ears that tragic history.

But wherefore dost thou come? Is't for my life?

RICHARD OF GLOUCESTER

Think'st thou I am an executioner?   30

KING HENRY

A persecutor I am sure thou art;

If murdering innocents be executing,

Why, then thou art an executioner.

RICHARD OF GLOUCESTER

Thy son I killed for his presumption.

KING HENRY

Hadst thou been killed when first thou didst presume,

Thou hadst not lived to kill a son of mine.   36

And thus I prophesy: that many a thousand
Which now mistrust no parcel of my fear,
And many an old man's sigh, and many a widow's,
And many an orphan's water-standing eye—   40
Men for their sons', wives for their husbands',
Orphans for their parents' timeless death—
Shall rue the hour that ever thou wast born.
The owl shrieked at thy birth—an evil sign;
The night-crow cried, aboding luckless time;   45
Dogs howled, and hideous tempests shook down trees;
The raven rooked her on the chimney's top;
And chatt'ring pies in dismal discords sung.
Thy mother felt more than a mother's pain,
And yet brought forth less than a mother's hope—   50
To wit, an indigested and deformèd lump,
Not like the fruit of such a goodly tree.
Teeth hadst thou in thy head when thou wast born,
To signify thou cam'st to bite the world;
And if the rest be true which I have heard   55
Thou cam'st—

RICHARD
I'll hear no more. Die, prophet, in thy speech,
   He stabs him
For this, amongst the rest, was I ordained.

KING HENRY
Ay, and for much more slaughter after this.
O, God forgive my sins, and pardon thee.   *He dies*

RICHARD OF GLOUCESTER
What—will the aspiring blood of Lancaster   61
Sink in the ground? I thought it would have mounted.
See how my sword weeps for the poor King's death.
O, may such purple tears be alway shed
From those that wish the downfall of our house!   65
If any spark of life be yet remaining,
Down, down to hell, and say I sent thee thither—
   He stabs him again
I that have neither pity, love, nor fear.
Indeed, 'tis true that Henry told me of,
For I have often heard my mother say   70
I came into the world with my legs forward.
Had I not reason, think ye, to make haste,
And seek their ruin that usurped our right?
The midwife wondered and the women cried
'O, Jesus bless us, he is born with teeth!'—   75
And so I was, which plainly signified
That I should snarl and bite and play the dog.
Then, since the heavens have shaped my body so,
Let hell make crooked my mind to answer it.
I had no father, I am like no father;   80
I have no brother, I am like no brother;
And this word, 'love', which greybeards call divine,
Be resident in men like one another
And not in me—I am myself alone.
Clarence, beware; thou kept'st me from the light—   85
But I will sort a pitchy day for thee.
For I will buzz abroad such prophecies
That Edward shall be fearful of his life,
And then, to purge his fear, I'll be thy death.

Henry and his son are gone; thou, Clarence, art next;
And by one and one I will dispatch the rest,   91
Counting myself but bad till I be best.
I'll throw thy body in another room
And triumph, Henry, in thy day of doom.
   Exit with the body

5.7   ⌈*A chair of state.*⌉ *Flourish. Enter King Edward,*
    Lady Gray his Queen, George Duke of Clarence,
    Richard Duke of Gloucester, the Lord Hastings, a
    nurse carrying the infant Prince Edward, and
    attendants

KING EDWARD
Once more we sit in England's royal throne,
Repurchased with the blood of enemies.
What valiant foemen, like to autumn's corn,
Have we mowed down in tops of all their pride!
Three dukes of Somerset, threefold renowned   5
For hardy and undoubted champions;
Two Cliffords, as the father and the son;
And two Northumberlands—two braver men
Ne'er spurred their coursers at the trumpet's sound.
With them, the two brave bears, Warwick and
     Montague,   10
That in their chains fettered the kingly lion
And made the forest tremble when they roared.
Thus have we swept suspicion from our seat
And made our footstool of security.
   (*To Lady Gray*)
Come hither, Bess, and let me kiss my boy.   15
   The nurse brings forth the infant prince. King
   Edward kisses him
Young Ned, for thee, thine uncles and myself
Have in our armours watched the winter's night,
Went all afoot in summer's scalding heat,
That thou mightst repossess the crown in peace;
And of our labours thou shalt reap the gain.   20

RICHARD OF GLOUCESTER (*aside*)
I'll blast his harvest, an your head were laid;
For yet I am not looked on in the world.
This shoulder was ordained so thick to heave;
And heave it shall some weight or break my back.
Work thou the way, and thou shalt execute.   25

KING EDWARD
Clarence and Gloucester, love my lovely queen;
And kiss your princely nephew, brothers, both.

GEORGE OF CLARENCE
The duty that I owe unto your majesty
I seal upon the lips of this sweet babe.
   He kisses the infant prince

LADY GRAY
Thanks, noble Clarence—worthy brother, thanks.   30

RICHARD OF GLOUCESTER
And that I love the tree from whence thou sprang'st,
Witness the loving kiss I give the fruit.
   He kisses the infant prince
(*Aside*) To say the truth, so Judas kissed his master,
And cried 'All hail!' whenas he meant all harm.

KING EDWARD

   Now am I seated as my soul delights,   35

   Having my country's peace and brothers' loves.

GEORGE OF CLARENCE

   What will your grace have done with Margaret?

   René her father to the King of France

   Hath pawned the Sicils and Jerusalem,

   And hither have they sent it for her ransom.   40

KING EDWARD

   Away with her, and waft her hence to France.

   And now what rests but that we spend the time

   With stately triumphs, mirthful comic shows,

   Such as befits the pleasure of the court?

   Sound drums and trumpets—farewell, sour annoy! 45

   For here, I hope, begins our lasting joy.

                   ⌈*Flourish.*⌉ *Exeunt*

ADDITIONAL PASSAGES

A. Our edition adopts the 1595 version of 1.1.120-5 in the belief that it reflects an authorial revision; an edited text of the Folio alternative follows.

KING HENRY

   Peace, thou—and give King Henry leave to speak.

WARWICK

   Plantagenet shall speak first—hear him, lords,

   And be you silent and attentive too,

   For he that interrupts him shall not live.

KING HENRY ⌈*to York*⌉

   Think'st thou that I will leave my kingly throne,   5

B. The 1595 text abridges 5.4.82.1–5.5.17 and may reflect authorial revision. An edited text of the abridged passage follows:

ALL THE LANCASTER PARTY

   Saint George for Lancaster!

      Alarums to the battle. ⌈*The house of*⌉ *York flies, then*

      the chambers are discharged. Then enter King Edward,

      George of Clarence, and Richard of Gloucester, and their

followers: they make a great shout, and cry 'For York!

For York!' Then Queen Margaret, Prince Edward,

Oxford and Somerset are all taken prisoner. Flourish,

and enter all again

KING EDWARD

   Now here a period of tumultuous broils.

   Away with Oxford to Hames Castle straight;

   For Somerset, off with his guilty head.

   Go, bear them hence—I will not hear them speak.   5

OXFORD

   For my part, I'll not trouble thee with words.

                     Exit, guarded

SOMERSET

   Nor I, but stoop with patience to my death.

                     Exit, guarded

KING EDWARD (*to Prince Edward*)

   Edward, what satisfaction canst thou make

   For stirring up my subjects to rebellion?

PRINCE EDWARD

   Speak like a subject, proud ambitious York.   10

HENRY VI PART ONE

BY WILLIAM SHAKESPEARE AND OTHERS

THE play printed here first appeared in the 1623 Folio, as *The First Part of Henry VI*; it tells the beginning of the story that is continued in *The First Part of the Contention* and in *Richard Duke of York*. Although in narrative sequence it belongs before those plays, there is good reason to believe that it was written after them. It is probably the 'new' play referred to as 'harey the vj' in the record of its performance on 3 March 1592 by Lord Strange's Men. The box-office takings of £3 16s. 8d. were a record for the season, and the play was acted another fifteen times during the following ten months. Its success is mentioned in Thomas Nashe's satirical pamphlet *Piers Penniless*, published later in 1592. Defending the drama against moralistic attacks, Nashe claims that plays based on 'our English chronicles' celebrate 'our forefathers' valiant acts' and set them up as a 'reproof to these degenerate effeminate days of ours'. By way of illustration he alludes specifically to the exploits of Lord Talbot, the principal English warrior in *Henry VI Part One*: 'How would it have joyed brave Talbot, the terror of the French, to think that after he had lain two hundred years in his tomb he should triumph again on the stage, and have his bones new-embalmed with the tears of ten thousand spectators at least, at several times, who in the tragedian that represents his person imagine they behold him fresh bleeding!' Nashe may have had personal reasons to puff this play: a variety of evidence suggests that Shakespeare wrote it in collaboration with at least two other authors; Nashe himself was probably responsible for Act 1. The passages most confidently attributed to Shakespeare are Act 2, Scene 4 and Act 4, Scene 2 to the death of Talbot at 4.7.32.

A mass of material, some derived from 'English chronicles', some invented, is packed into this play. It opens impressively with the funeral of Henry V, celebrated for unifying England and subjugating France; but his nobles are at loggerheads even over his coffin, and news rapidly arrives of serious losses in France. The rivalry displayed here between Humphrey, Duke of Gloucester—Protector of the infant Henry VI—and Henry Beaufort, Bishop of Winchester, plays an important part in both this play and *The Contention*, as does the conflict between Richard, Duke of York, and the houses of Somerset and Suffolk; in the Temple Garden scene (2.4), invented by Shakespeare, York's and Somerset's supporters symbolize their respective loyalties by plucking white and red roses. Their dissension weakens England's military strength, but she has a great hero in Lord Talbot, whose nobility as a warrior is pitted against the treachery of the French, led by King Charles and Joan la Pucelle (Joan of Arc), here—following the chronicles—portrayed as a witch and a whore. Historical facts are freely manipulated: Joan was burnt in 1431, though the play's authors have her take part in a battle of 1451 in which Talbot's death is brought forward by two years. The play ends with an uneasy peace between England and France.

THE PERSONS OF THE PLAY

The English

KING Henry VI

Duke of GLOUCESTER, Lord Protector, uncle of King Henry

Duke of BEDFORD, Regent of France

Duke of EXETER

Bishop of WINCHESTER (later Cardinal), uncle of King Henry

Duke of SOMERSET

RICHARD PLANTAGENET, later DUKE OF YORK, and Regent of France

Earl of WARWICK

Earl of SALISBURY

Earl of SUFFOLK

Lord TALBOT

JOHN Talbot

Edmund MORTIMER

Sir William GLASDALE

Sir Thomas GARGRAVE

Sir John FASTOLF

Sir William LUCY

WOODVILLE, Lieutenant of the Tower of London

MAYOR of London

VERNON

BASSET

A LAWYER

A LEGATE

Messengers, warders and keepers of the Tower of London, servingmen, officers, captains, soldiers, herald, watch

The French

CHARLES, Dauphin of France

RENÉ, Duke of Anjou, King of Naples

MARGARET, his daughter

Duke of ALENÇON

BASTARD of Orléans

Duke of BURGUNDY, uncle of King Henry

GENERAL of the French garrison at Bordeaux

COUNTESS of Auvergne

MASTER GUNNER of Orléans

A BOY, his son

JOAN la Pucelle

A SHEPHERD, father of Joan

Porter, French sergeant, French sentinels, French scout, French herald, the Governor of Paris, fiends, and soldiers

The First Part of Henry the Sixth

1.1 *Dead march. Enter the funeral of King Henry the*
Fifth, attended on by the Duke of Bedford (Regent
of France), the Duke of Gloucester (Protector), the
Duke of Exeter, the Earl of Warwick, the Bishop of
Winchester, and the Duke of Somerset

BEDFORD
Hung be the heavens with black! Yield, day, to night!
Comets, importing change of times and states,
Brandish your crystal tresses in the sky,
And with them scourge the bad revolting stars
That have consented unto Henry's death—   5
King Henry the Fifth, too famous to live long.
England ne'er lost a king of so much worth.

GLOUCESTER
England ne'er had a king until his time.
Virtue he had, deserving to command.
His brandished sword did blind men with his beams. 10
His arms spread wider than a dragon's wings.
His sparkling eyes, replete with wrathful fire,
More dazzled and drove back his enemies
Than midday sun, fierce bent against their faces.
What should I say? His deeds exceed all speech.   15
He ne'er lift up his hand but conquerèd.

EXETER
We mourn in black; why mourn we not in blood?
Henry is dead, and never shall revive.
Upon a wooden coffin we attend,
And death's dishonourable victory   20
We with our stately presence glorify,
Like captives bound to a triumphant car.
What, shall we curse the planets of mishap,
That plotted thus our glory's overthrow?
Or shall we think the subtle-witted French   25
Conjurers and sorcerers, that, afraid of him,
By magic verses have contrived his end?

WINCHESTER
He was a king blest of the King of Kings.
Unto the French, the dreadful judgement day
So dreadful will not be as was his sight.   30
The battles of the Lord of Hosts he fought.
The Church's prayers made him so prosperous.

GLOUCESTER
The Church? Where is it? Had not churchmen prayed,
His thread of life had not so soon decayed.
None do you like but an effeminate prince,   35
Whom like a schoolboy you may overawe.

WINCHESTER
Gloucester, whate'er we like, thou art Protector,
And lookest to command the Prince and realm.
Thy wife is proud: she holdeth thee in awe,
More than God or religious churchmen may.   40

GLOUCESTER
Name not religion, for thou lov'st the flesh,

And ne'er throughout the year to church thou go'st,
Except it be to pray against thy foes.

BEDFORD
Cease, cease these jars, and rest your minds in peace.
Let's to the altar. Heralds, wait on us.   45
⌐*Exeunt Warwick, Somerset, and heralds*
with coffin⌐
Instead of gold, we'll offer up our arms—
Since arms avail not, now that Henry's dead.
Posterity, await for wretched years,
When, at their mothers' moistened eyes, babes shall
        suck,
Our isle be made a marish of salt tears,   50
And none but women left to wail the dead.
Henry the Fifth, thy ghost I invocate:
Prosper this realm; keep it from civil broils;
Combat with adverse planets in the heavens.
A far more glorious star thy soul will make   55
Than Julius Caesar or bright—
        Enter a Messenger

MESSENGER
My honourable lords, health to you all.
Sad tidings bring I to you out of France,
Of loss, of slaughter, and discomfiture.
Guyenne, Compiègne, Rouen, Rheims, Orléans,   60
Paris, Gisors, Poitiers are all quite lost.

BEDFORD
What sayst thou, man, before dead Henry's corpse?
Speak softly, or the loss of those great towns
Will make him burst his lead and rise from death.

GLOUCESTER (*to the Messenger*)
Is Paris lost? Is Rouen yielded up?   65
If Henry were recalled to life again,
These news would cause him once more yield the
        ghost.

EXETER (*to the Messenger*)
How were they lost? What treachery was used?

MESSENGER
No treachery, but want of men and money.
Amongst the soldiers this is mutterèd: 70
That here you maintain several factions,
And whilst a field should be dispatched and fought,
You are disputing of your generals.
One would have ling'ring wars, with little cost;
Another would fly swift, but wanteth wings;   75
A third thinks, without expense at all,
By guileful fair words peace may be obtained.
Awake, awake, English nobility!
Let not sloth dim your honours new-begot.
Cropped are the flower-de-luces in your arms;   80
Of England's coat, one half is cut away.   ⌐*Exit*⌐

EXETER
Were our tears wanting to this funeral,
These tidings would call forth her flowing tides.

81

BEDFORD
Me they concern; Regent I am of France.
Give me my steelèd coat. I'll fight for France.   85
Away with these disgraceful wailing robes!
⌈He removes his mourning robe⌉
Wounds will I lend the French, instead of eyes,
To weep their intermissive miseries.
Enter to them another Messenger with letters
SECOND MESSENGER
Lords, view these letters, full of bad mischance.
France is revolted from the English quite,   90
Except some petty towns of no import.
The Dauphin Charles is crownèd king in Rheims;
The Bastard of Orléans with him is joined;
René, Duke of Anjou, doth take his part;
The Duke of Alençon flyeth to his side.   *Exit*
EXETER
The Dauphin crownèd King? All fly to him?   96
O whither shall *we* fly from this reproach?
GLOUCESTER
We will not fly, but to our enemies' throats.
Bedford, if thou be slack, I'll fight it out.
BEDFORD
Gloucester, why doubt'st thou of my forwardness?   100
An army have I mustered in my thoughts,
Wherewith already France is overrun.
Enter another Messenger
THIRD MESSENGER
My gracious lords, to add to your laments,
Wherewith you now bedew King Henry's hearse,
I must inform you of a dismal fight   105
Betwixt the stout Lord Talbot and the French.
WINCHESTER
What, wherein Talbot overcame—is't so?
THIRD MESSENGER
O no, wherein Lord Talbot was o'erthrown.
The circumstance I'll tell you more at large.
The tenth of August last, this dreadful lord,   110
Retiring from the siege of Orléans,
Having full scarce six thousand in his troop,
By three-and-twenty thousand of the French
Was round encompassèd and set upon.
No leisure had he to enrank his men.   115
He wanted pikes to set before his archers—
Instead whereof, sharp stakes plucked out of hedges
They pitchèd in the ground confusèdly,
To keep the horsemen off from breaking in.
More than three hours the fight continuèd,   120
Where valiant Talbot above human thought
Enacted wonders with his sword and lance.
Hundreds he sent to hell, and none durst stand him;
Here, there, and everywhere, enraged he slew.
The French exclaimed the devil was in arms: 125
All the whole army stood agazed on him.
His soldiers, spying his undaunted spirit,
'A Talbot! A Talbot!' cried out amain,
And rushed into the bowels of the battle.

Here had the conquest fully been sealed up,   130
If Sir John Fastolf had not played the coward.
He, being in the vanguard placed behind,
With purpose to relieve and follow them,
Cowardly fled, not having struck one stroke.
Hence grew the general wrack and massacre.   135
Enclosèd were they with their enemies.
A base Walloon, to win the Dauphin's grace,
Thrust Talbot with a spear into the back—
Whom all France, with their chief assembled strength,
Durst not presume to look once in the face.   140
BEDFORD
Is Talbot slain then? I will slay myself,
For living idly here in pomp and ease
Whilst such a worthy leader, wanting aid,
Unto his dastard foemen is betrayed.
THIRD MESSENGER
O no, he lives, but is took prisoner,   145
And Lord Scales with him, and Lord Hungerford;
Most of the rest slaughtered, or took likewise.
BEDFORD
His ransom there is none but I shall pay.
I'll hale the Dauphin headlong from his throne;
His crown shall be the ransom of my friend;   150
Four of their lords I'll change for one of ours.
Farewell, my masters; to my task will I.
Bonfires in France forthwith I am to make,
To keep our great Saint George's feast withal.
Ten thousand soldiers with me I will take,   155
Whose bloody deeds shall make all Europe quake.
THIRD MESSENGER
So you had need. Fore Orléans, besieged,
The English army is grown weak and faint.
The Earl of Salisbury craveth supply,
And hardly keeps his men from mutiny,   160
Since they, so few, watch such a multitude.   ⌈*Exit*⌉
EXETER
Remember, lords, your oaths to Henry sworn:
Either to quell the Dauphin utterly,
Or bring him in obedience to your yoke.
BEDFORD
I do remember it, and here take my leave   165
To go about my preparation.   *Exit*
GLOUCESTER
I'll to the Tower with all the haste I can,
To view th'artillery and munition,
And then I will proclaim young Henry king.   *Exit*
EXETER
To Eltham will I, where the young King is,   170
Being ordained his special governor,
And for his safety there I'll best devise.   *Exit*
WINCHESTER
Each hath his place and function to attend;
I am left out; for me, nothing remains.
But long I will not be Jack-out-of-office.   175
The King from Eltham I intend to steal,
And sit at chiefest stern of public weal.   *Exit*

1.2   *Sound a flourish. Enter Charles the Dauphin, the*
       Duke of Alençon, and René Duke of Anjou,
       marching with drummer and soldiers
CHARLES
    Mars his true moving—even as in the heavens,
    So in the earth—to this day is not known.
    Late did he shine upon the English side;
    Now we are victors: upon us he smiles.
    What towns of any moment but we have?   5
    At pleasure here we lie near Orléans
    Otherwhiles the famished English, like pale ghosts,
    Faintly besiege us one hour in a month.
ALENÇON
    They want their porrage and their fat bull beeves.
    Either they must be dieted like mules,   10
    And have their provender tied to their mouths,
    Or piteous they will look, like drownèd mice.
RENÉ
    Let's raise the siege. Why live we idly here?
    Talbot is taken, whom we wont to fear.
    Remaineth none but mad-brained Salisbury,   15
    And he may well in fretting spend his gall:
    Nor men nor money hath he to make war.
CHARLES
    Sound, sound, alarum! We will rush on them.
    Now for the honour of the forlorn French,
    Him I forgive my death that killeth me   20
    When he sees me go back one foot or flee.   *Exeunt*

1.3   *Here alarum. The French are beaten back by the*
       English with great loss. Enter Charles the Dauphin,
       the Duke of Alençon, and René Duke of Anjou
CHARLES
    Who ever saw the like? What men have I?
    Dogs, cowards, dastards! I would ne'er have fled,
    But that they left me 'midst my enemies.
RENÉ
    Salisbury is a desperate homicide.
    He fighteth as one weary of his life.   5
    The other lords, like lions wanting food,
    Do rush upon us as their hungry prey.
ALENÇON
    Froissart, a countryman of ours, records
    England all Olivers and Rolands bred
    During the time Edward the Third did reign.   10
    More truly now may this be verified,
    For none but Samsons and Goliases
    It sendeth forth to skirmish. One to ten?
    Lean raw-boned rascals, who would e'er suppose
    They had such courage and audacity?   15
CHARLES
    Let's leave this town, for they are hare-brained slaves,
    And hunger will enforce them to be more eager.
    Of old I know them: rather with their teeth
    The walls they'll tear down, than forsake the siege.
RENÉ
    I think by some odd gimmers or device   20
    Their arms are set, like clocks, still to strike on,

    Else ne'er could they hold out so as they do.
    By my consent we'll even let them alone.
ALENÇON Be it so.
           Enter the Bastard of Orléans
BASTARD
    Where's the Prince Dauphin? I have news for him.   25
CHARLES
    Bastard of Orléans, thrice welcome to us.
BASTARD
    Methinks your looks are sad, your cheer appalled.
    Hath the late overthrow wrought this offence?
    Be not dismayed, for succour is at hand.
    A holy maid hither with me I bring,   30
    Which, by a vision sent to her from heaven,
    Ordainèd is to raise this tedious siege
    And drive the English forth the bounds of France.
    The spirit of deep prophecy she hath,
    Exceeding the nine sibyls of old Rome.   35
    What's past and what's to come she can descry.
    Speak: shall I call her in? Believe my words,
    For they are certain and unfallible.
CHARLES
    Go call her in.   *Exit Bastard*
              But first, to try her skill,
    René stand thou as Dauphin in my place.   40
    Question her proudly; let thy looks be stern.
    By this means shall we sound what skill she hath.
         Enter ⌈the Bastard of Orléans with⌉ Joan la Pucelle,
         armed
RENÉ (*as Charles*)
    Fair maid, is't thou wilt do these wondrous feats?
JOAN
    René, is't thou that thinkest to beguile me?
    Where is the Dauphin? (*To Charles*) Come, come from
         behind.   45
    I know thee well, though never seen before.
    Be not amazed. There's nothing hid from me.
    In private will I talk with thee apart.
    Stand back you lords, and give us leave awhile.
         René, Alençon ⌈and Bastard⌉ stand apart
RENÉ ⌈*to Alençon and Bastard*⌉
    She takes upon her bravely, at first dash.   50
JOAN
    Dauphin, I am by birth a shepherd's daughter,
    My wit untrained in any kind of art.
    Heaven and our Lady gracious hath it pleased
    To shine on my contemptible estate.
    Lo, whilst I waited on my tender lambs,   55
    And to sun's parching heat displayed my cheeks,
    God's mother deignèd to appear to me,
    And in a vision, full of majesty,
    Willed me to leave my base vocation
    And free my country from calamity.   60
    Her aid she promised, and assured success.
    In complete glory she revealed herself—
    And whereas I was black and swart before,
    With those clear rays which she infused on me
    That beauty am I blest with, which you may see.   65

Ask me what question thou canst possible,
And I will answer unpremeditated.
My courage try by combat, if thou dar'st,
And thou shalt find that I exceed my sex.
Resolve on this: thou shalt be fortunate,   70
If thou receive me for thy warlike mate.

CHARLES
Thou hast astonished me with thy high terms.
Only this proof I'll of thy valour make:
In single combat thou shalt buckle with me.
An if thou vanquishest, thy words are true;   75
Otherwise, I renounce all confidence.

JOAN
I am prepared. Here is my keen-edged sword,
Decked with five flower-de-luces on each side—
The which at Touraine, in Saint Katherine's
        churchyard,
Out of a great deal of old iron I chose forth.   80

CHARLES
Then come a God's name. I fear no woman.

JOAN
And while I live, I'll ne'er fly from a man.
        Here they fight and Joan la Pucelle overcomes

CHARLES
Stay, stay thy hands! Thou art an Amazon,
And fightest with the sword of Deborah.

JOAN
Christ's mother helps me, else I were too weak.   85

CHARLES
Whoe'er helps thee, 'tis thou that must help me.
Impatiently I burn with thy desire.
My heart and hands thou hast at once subdued.
Excellent Pucelle if thy name be so,
Let me thy servant, and not sovereign be.   90
'Tis the French Dauphin sueth to thee thus.

JOAN
I must not yield to any rites of love,
For my profession's sacred from above.
When I have chasèd all thy foes from hence,
Then will I think upon a recompense.   95

CHARLES
Meantime, look gracious on thy prostrate thrall.

RENÉ [*to the other lords apart*]
My lord, methinks, is very long in talk.

ALENÇON
Doubtless he shrives this woman to her smock,
Else ne'er could he so long protract his speech.

RENÉ
Shall we disturb him, since he keeps no mean?   100

ALENÇON
He may mean more than we poor men do know.
These women are shrewd tempters with their tongues.

RENÉ (*to Charles*)
My lord, where are you? What devise you on?
Shall we give o'er Orléans, or no?

JOAN
Why, no, I say. Distrustful recreants,   105
Fight till the last gasp; I'll be your guard.

CHARLES
What she says, I'll confirm. We'll fight it out.

JOAN
Assigned am I to be the English scourge.
This night the siege assurèdly I'll raise.
Expect Saint Martin's summer, halcyon's days,   110
Since I have entered into these wars.
Glory is like a circle in the water,
Which never ceaseth to enlarge itself
Till, by broad spreading, it disperse to naught.
With Henry's death, the English circle ends.   115
Dispersèd are the glories it included.
Now am I like that proud insulting ship
Which Caesar and his fortune bore at once.

CHARLES
Was Mohammed inspirèd with a dove?
Thou with an eagle art inspirèd then.   120
Helen, the mother of great Constantine,
Nor yet Saint Philip's daughters were like thee.
Bright star of Venus, fall'n down on the earth,
How may I reverently worship thee enough?

ALENÇON
Leave off delays, and let us raise the siege.   125

RENÉ
Woman, do what thou canst to save our honours.
Drive them from Orléans, and be immortalized.

CHARLES
Presently we'll try. Come, let's away about it.
No prophet will I trust, if she prove false.   *Exeunt*

1.4   *Enter the Duke of Gloucester, with his Servingmen
        in blue coats*

GLOUCESTER
I am come to survey the Tower this day.
Since Henry's death, I fear there is conveyance.
Where be these warders, that they wait not here?
        [*A Servingman*] *knocketh on the gates*
Open the gates: 'tis Gloucester that calls.

FIRST WARDER [*within the Tower*]
Who's there that knocketh so imperiously?   5

GLOUCESTER'S FIRST MAN
It is the noble Duke of Gloucester.

SECOND WARDER [*within the Tower*]
Whoe'er he be, you may not be let in.

GLOUCESTER'S FIRST MAN
Villains, answer you so the Lord Protector?

FIRST WARDER [*within the Tower*]
The Lord protect him, so we answer him.
We do no otherwise than we are willed.   10

GLOUCESTER
Who willed you? Or whose will stands, but mine?
There's none Protector of the realm but I.
(*To Servingmen*) Break up the gates. I'll be your
        warrantize.
Shall I be flouted thus by dunghill grooms?
        Gloucester's men rush at the Tower gates

WOODVILLE [*within the Tower*]
What noise is this? What traitors have we here?   15

GLOUCESTER
Lieutenant, is it you whose voice I hear?
Open the gates! Here's Gloucester, that would enter.
WOODVILLE [within the Tower]
Have patience, noble duke: I may not open.
My lord of Winchester forbids.
From him I have express commandëment   20
That thou, nor none of thine, shall be let in.
GLOUCESTER
Faint-hearted Woodville! Prizest him fore me?—
Arrogant Winchester, that haughty prelate,
Whom Henry, our late sovereign, ne'er could brook?
Thou art no friend to God or to the King.   25
Open the gates, or I'll shut thee out shortly.
SERVINGMEN
Open the gates unto the Lord Protector,
Or we'll burst them open, if that you come not
    quickly.
    Enter, to the Lord Protector at the Tower gates, the
    Bishop of Winchester and his men in tawny coats
WINCHESTER
How now, ambitious vizier! What means this?
GLOUCESTER
Peeled priest, dost thou command me to be shut out?
WINCHESTER
I do, thou most usurping proditor,   31
And not 'Protector', of the King or realm.
GLOUCESTER
Stand back, thou manifest conspirator.
Thou that contrived'st to murder our dead lord,
Thou that giv'st whores indulgences to sin,   35
If thou proceed in this thy insolence—
WINCHESTER
Nay, stand thou back! I will not budge a foot.
This be Damascus, be thou cursèd Cain,
To slay thy brother Abel, if thou wilt.
GLOUCESTER
I will not slay thee, but I'll drive thee back.   40
Thy purple robes, as a child's bearing-cloth,
I'll use to carry thee out of this place.
WINCHESTER
Do what thou dar'st, I beard thee to thy face.
GLOUCESTER
What, am I dared and bearded to my face?
Draw, men, for all this privilegèd place.   45
    All draw their swords
Blue coats to tawny coats!—Priest, beware your
    beard.
I mean to tug it, and to cuff you soundly.
Under my feet I'll stamp thy bishop's mitre.
In spite of Pope, or dignities of church,
Here by the cheeks I'll drag thee up and down.   50
WINCHESTER
Gloucester, thou wilt answer this before the Pope.
GLOUCESTER
Winchester goose! I cry, 'A rope, a rope!'
(To his Servingmen)
Now beat them hence. Why do you let them stay?

(To Winchester)
Thee I'll chase hence, thou wolf in sheep's array.
Out, tawny coats! Out, cloakèd hypocrite!   55
    Here Gloucester's men beat out the Bishop's men.
    Enter in the hurly-burly the Mayor of London and
    his Officers
MAYOR
Fie, lords!—that you, being supreme magistrates,
Thus contumeliously should break the peace.
GLOUCESTER
Peace, mayor, thou know'st little of my wrongs.
Here's Beaufort—that regards nor God nor king—
Hath here distrained the Tower to his use.   60
WINCHESTER (to Mayor)
Here's Gloucester—a foe to citizens,
One that still motions war, and never peace,
O'ercharging your free purses with large fines—
That seeks to overthrow religion,
Because he is Protector of the realm,   65
And would have armour here out of the Tower
To crown himself king and suppress the Prince.
GLOUCESTER
I will not answer thee with words but blows.
    Here the factions skirmish again
MAYOR
Naught rests for me, in this tumultuous strife,
But to make open proclamation.   70
Come, officer, as loud as e'er thou canst, cry.
OFFICER All manner of men, assembled here in arms this
    day against God's peace and the King's, we charge and
    command you in his highness' name to repair to your
    several dwelling places, and not to wear, handle, or
    use any sword, weapon, or dagger henceforward, upon
    pain of death.
    The skirmishes cease
GLOUCESTER
Bishop, I'll be no breaker of the law.
But we shall meet and break our minds at large.
WINCHESTER
Gloucester, we'll meet to thy cost, be sure.   80
Thy heart-blood I will have for this day's work.
MAYOR
I'll call for clubs, if you will not away.
(Aside) This bishop is more haughty than the devil.
GLOUCESTER
Mayor, farewell. Thou dost but what thou mayst.
WINCHESTER
Abominable Gloucester, guard thy head,   85
For I intend to have it ere long.
                    Exeunt both factions severally
MAYOR (to Officers)
See the coast cleared, and then we will depart.—
Good God, these nobles should such stomachs bear!
I myself fight not once in forty year.   Exeunt

1.5   Enter the Master Gunner of Orléans with his Boy
MASTER GUNNER
Sirrah, thou know'st how Orléans is besieged,
And how the English have the suburbs won.

BOY

Father, I know, and oft have shot at them;
Howe'er, unfortunate, I missed my aim.

MASTER GUNNER

But now thou shalt not. Be thou ruled by me.   5
Chief Master Gunner am I of this town;
Something I must do to procure me grace.
The Prince's spials have informèd me
How the English, in the suburbs close entrenched,
Wont, through a secret grate of iron bars   10
In yonder tower, to overpeer the city,
And thence discover how with most advantage
They may vex us with shot or with assault.
To intercept this inconvenience,
A piece of ordnance 'gainst it I have placed,   15
And even these three days have I watched, if I could
     see them.
Now do thou watch, for I can stay no longer.
If thou spy'st any, run and bring me word,
And thou shalt find me at the governor's.

BOY

Father, I warrant you, take you no care—   20
          ⌈Exit Master Gunner at one door⌉
I'll never trouble you, if I may spy them.
          Exit ⌈at the other door⌉

1.6   Enter the Earl of Salisbury and Lord Talbot above
        on the turrets with others, among them Sir
        Thomas Gargrave and Sir William Glasdale

SALISBURY

Talbot, my life, my joy, again returned?
How wert thou handled, being prisoner?
Or by what means got'st thou to be released?
Discourse, I prithee, on this turret's top.

TALBOT

The Duke of Bedford had a prisoner,   5
Called the brave Lord Ponton de Santrailles;
For him was I exchanged and ransomèd.
But with a baser man-of-arms by far
Once in contempt they would have bartered me—
Which I, disdaining, scorned, and cravèd death   10
Rather than I would be so pilled esteemed.
In fine, redeemed I was, as I desired.
But O, the treacherous Fastolf wounds my heart,
Whom with my bare fists I would execute
If I now had him brought into my power.   15

SALISBURY

Yet tell'st thou not how thou wert entertained.

TALBOT

With scoffs and scorns and contumelious taunts.
In open market place produced they me,
To be a public spectacle to all.
'Here', said they, 'is the terror of the French,   20
The scarecrow that affrights our children so.'
Then broke I from the officers that led me
And with my nails digged stones out of the ground
To hurl at the beholders of my shame.
My grisly countenance made others fly.   25

None durst come near, for fear of sudden death.
In iron walls they deemed me not secure:
So great fear of my name 'mongst them were spread
That they supposed I could rend bars of steel
And spurn in pieces posts of adamant.   30
Wherefore a guard of chosen shot I had
That walked about me every minute while;
And if I did but stir out of my bed,
Ready they were to shoot me to the heart.
          The Boy ⌈passes over the stage⌉ with a linstock

SALISBURY

I grieve to hear what torments you endured.   35
But we will be revenged sufficiently.
Now is it supper time in Orléans.
Here, through this grate, I count each one,
And view the Frenchmen how they fortify.
Let us look in: the sight will much delight thee.—   40
Sir Thomas Gargrave and Sir William Glasdale,
Let me have your express opinions
Where is best place to make our batt'ry next.
          ⌈They look through the grate⌉

GARGRAVE

I think at the north gate, for there stands Lou.

GLASDALE

And I here, at the bulwark of the Bridge.   45

TALBOT

For aught I see, this city must be famished
Or with light skirmishes enfeeblèd.
          Here they shoot off chambers ⌈within⌉ and Salisbury
          and Gargrave fall down

SALISBURY

O Lord have mercy on us, wretched sinners!

GARGRAVE

O Lord have mercy on me, woeful man!

TALBOT

What chance is this that suddenly hath crossed us?   50
Speak, Salisbury—at least, if thou canst, speak.
How far'st thou, mirror of all martial men?
One of thy eyes and thy cheek's side struck off?
Accursèd tower! Accursèd fatal hand
That hath contrived this woeful tragedy!   55
In thirteen battles Salisbury o'ercame;
Henry the Fifth he first trained to the wars;
Whilst any trump did sound or drum struck up
His sword did ne'er leave striking in the field.
Yet liv'st thou, Salisbury? Though thy speech doth
     fail,   60
One eye thou hast to look to heaven for grace.
The sun with one eye vieweth all the world.
Heaven, be thou gracious to none alive
If Salisbury wants mercy at thy hands.—
Sir Thomas Gargrave, hast thou any life?   65
Speak unto Talbot. Nay, look up to him.—
Bear hence his body; I will help to bury it.
          ⌈Exit one with Gargrave's body⌉
Salisbury, cheer thy spirit with this comfort:
Thou shalt not die whiles—
He beckons with his hand, and smiles on me,   70

As who should say, 'When I am dead and gone,
Remember to avenge me on the French.'
Plantagenet, I will—and like thee, Nero,
Play on the lute, beholding the towns burn.
Wretched shall France be only in my name. 75
   Here an alarum, and it thunders and lightens
What stir is this? What tumult's in the heavens?
Whence cometh this alarum and the noise?
   Enter a Messenger

MESSENGER
My lord, my lord, the French have gathered head.
The Dauphin, with one Joan la Pucelle joined,
A holy prophetess new risen up, 80
Is come with a great power to raise the siege.
   Here Salisbury lifteth himself up and groans

TALBOT
Hear, hear, how dying Salisbury doth groan!
It irks his heart he cannot be revenged.
Frenchmen, I'll be a Salisbury to you.
Pucelle or pucelle, Dauphin or dog-fish, 85
Your hearts I'll stamp out with my horse's heels
And make a quagmire of your mingled brains.—
Convey me Salisbury into his tent,
And then we'll try what these dastard Frenchmen
   dare.   *Alarum. Exeunt carrying Salisbury*

1.7 *Here an alarum again, and Lord Talbot pursueth the*
   Dauphin and driveth him. Then enter Joan la
   Pucelle driving Englishmen before her and ⌈exeunt⌉.
   Then enter Lord Talbot

TALBOT
Where is my strength, my valour, and my force?
Our English troops retire; I cannot stay them.
A woman clad in armour chaseth men.
   Enter Joan la Pucelle
Here, here she comes. (*To Joan*) I'll have a bout with
   thee.
Devil or devil's dam, I'll conjure thee. 5
Blood will I draw on thee—thou art a witch—
And straightway give thy soul to him thou serv'st.

JOAN
Come, come, 'tis only I that must disgrace thee.
   Here they fight

TALBOT
Heavens, can you suffer hell so to prevail?
My breast I'll burst with straining of my courage 10
And from my shoulders crack my arms asunder
But I will chastise this high-minded strumpet.
   They fight again

JOAN
Talbot, farewell. Thy hour is not yet come.
I must go victual Orléans forthwith.
   A short alarum, then ⌈the French pass over the
   stage and⌉ enter the town with soldiers
O'ertake me if thou canst. I scorn thy strength. 15
Go, go, cheer up thy hungry-starvèd men.
Help Salisbury to make his testament.
This day is ours, as many more shall be.
   Exit into the town

TALBOT
My thoughts are whirlèd like a potter's wheel.
I know not where I am nor what I do. 20
A witch by fear, not force, like Hannibal
Drives back our troops and conquers as she lists.
So bees with smoke and doves with noisome stench
Are from their hives and houses driven away.
They called us, for our fierceness, English dogs; 25
Now, like to whelps, we crying run away.
   A short alarum. ⌈Enter English soldiers⌉
Hark, countrymen: either renew the fight
Or tear the lions out of England's coat.
Renounce your style; give sheep in lions' stead.
Sheep run not half so treacherous from the wolf, 30
Or horse or oxen from the leopard,
As you fly from your oft-subduèd slaves.
   Alarum. Here another skirmish
It will not be. Retire into your trenches.
You all consented unto Salisbury's death,
For none would strike a stroke in his revenge. 35
Pucelle is entered into Orléans
In spite of us or aught that we could do.
                  ⌈Exeunt Soldiers⌉
O would I were to die with Salisbury!
The shame hereof will make me hide my head.
          Exit. Alarum. Retreat

1.8 *Flourish. Enter on the walls Joan la Pucelle,*
   Charles the Dauphin, René Duke of Anjou, the Duke
   of Alençon and French Soldiers ⌈with colours⌉

JOAN
Advance our waving colours on the walls;
Rescued is Orléans from the English.
Thus Joan la Pucelle hath performed her word.

CHARLES
Divinest creature, Astraea's daughter,
How shall I honour thee for this success? 5
Thy promises are like Adonis' garden,
That one day bloomed and fruitful were the next.
France, triumph in thy glorious prophetess!
Recovered is the town of Orléans.
More blessèd hap did ne'er befall our state. 10

RENÉ
Why ring not out the bells aloud throughout the
   town?
Dauphin, command the citizens make bonfires
And feast and banquet in the open streets
To celebrate the joy that God hath given us.

ALENÇON
All France will be replete with mirth and joy 15
When they shall hear how we have played the men.

CHARLES
'Tis Joan, not we, by whom the day is won—
For which I will divide my crown with her,
And all the priests and friars in my realm
Shall in procession sing her endless praise. 20
A statelier pyramid to her I'll rear
Than Rhodope's of Memphis ever was.
In memory of her, when she is dead

Her ashes, in an urn more precious
Than the rich-jewelled coffer of Darius,   25
Transported shall be at high festivals
Before the kings and queens of France.
No longer on Saint Denis will we cry,
But Joan la Pucelle shall be France's saint.
Come in, and let us banquet royally   30
After this golden day of victory.   *Flourish. Exeunt*

2.1   *Enter ⌐on the walls⌐ a French Sergeant of a band,*
           with two Sentinels
SERGEANT
Sirs, take your places and be vigilant.
If any noise or soldier you perceive
Near to the walls, by some apparent sign
Let us have knowledge at the court of guard.
⌐A SENTINEL⌐
Sergeant, you shall.   *Exit Sergeant*
                Thus are poor servitors,   5
When others sleep upon their quiet beds,
Constrained to watch in darkness, rain, and cold.
      Enter Lord Talbot, the Dukes of Bedford and
      Burgundy, and soldiers with scaling ladders, their
      drums beating a dead march
TALBOT
Lord regent, and redoubted Burgundy—
By whose approach the regions of Artois,
Wallon, and Picardy are friends to us—   10
This happy night the Frenchmen are secure,
Having all day caroused and banqueted.
Embrace we then this opportunity,
As fitting best to quittance their deceit,
Contrived by art and baleful sorcery.   15
BEDFORD
Coward of France! How much he wrongs his fame,
Despairing of his own arms' fortitude,
To join with witches and the help of hell.
BURGUNDY
Traitors have never other company.
But what's that 'Pucelle' whom they term so pure?   20
TALBOT
A maid, they say.
BEDFORD   A maid? And be so martial?
BURGUNDY
Pray God she prove not masculine ere long.
If underneath the standard of the French
She carry armour as she hath begun—
TALBOT
Well, let them practise and converse with spirits.   25
God is our fortress, in whose conquering name
Let us resolve to scale their flinty bulwarks.
BEDFORD
Ascend, brave Talbot. We will follow thee.
TALBOT
Not all together. Better far, I guess,
That we do make our entrance several ways—   30
That, if it chance the one of us do fail,
The other yet may rise against their force.

BEDFORD
Agreed. I'll to yon corner.
BURGUNDY   And I to this.
      ⌐Exeunt severally Bedford and Burgundy with
                        some soldiers⌐
TALBOT
And here will Talbot mount, or make his grave.
Now, Salisbury, for thee, and for the right   35
Of English Henry, shall this night appear
How much in duty I am bound to both.
      ⌐Talbot and his soldiers⌐ scale the walls
⌐SENTINELS⌐
Arm! Arm! The enemy doth make assault!
ENGLISH SOLDIERS Saint George! A Talbot!
                              Exeunt above
      ⌐Alarum.⌐ The French ⌐soldiers⌐ leap o'er the walls
      in their shirts ⌐and exeunt⌐. Enter several ways the
      Bastard of Orléans, the Duke of Alençon, and René
      Duke of Anjou, half ready and half unready
ALENÇON
How now, my lords? What, all unready so?   40
BASTARD
Unready? Ay, and glad we scaped so well.
RENÉ
'Twas time, I trow, to wake and leave our beds,
Hearing alarums at our chamber doors.
ALENÇON
Of all exploits since first I followed arms
Ne'er heard I of a warlike enterprise   45
More venturous or desperate than this.
BASTARD
I think this Talbot be a fiend of hell.
RENÉ
If not of hell, the heavens sure favour him.
ALENÇON
Here cometh Charles. I marvel how he sped.
      Enter Charles the Dauphin and Joan la Pucelle
BASTARD
Tut, holy Joan was his defensive guard.   50
CHARLES (*to Joan*)
Is this thy cunning, thou deceitful dame?
Didst thou at first, to flatter us withal,
Make us partakers of a little gain
That now our loss might be ten times so much?
JOAN
Wherefore is Charles impatient with his friend?   55
At all times will you have my power alike?
Sleeping or waking must I still prevail,
Or will you blame and lay the fault on me?—
Improvident soldiers, had your watch been good,
This sudden mischief never could have fall'n.   60
CHARLES
Duke of Alençon, this was your default,
That, being captain of the watch tonight,
Did look no better to that weighty charge.
ALENÇON
Had all your quarters been as safely kept
As that whereof I had the government,   65
We had not been thus shamefully surprised.

BASTARD
Mine was secure.

RENÉ   And so was mine, my lord.

CHARLES
And for myself, most part of all this night
Within her quarter and mine own precinct
I was employed in passing to and fro   70
About relieving of the sentinels.
Then how or which way should they first break in?

JOAN
Question, my lords, no further of the case,
How or which way. 'Tis sure they found some place
But weakly guarded, where the breach was made. 75
And now there rests no other shift but this—
To gather our soldiers, scattered and dispersed,
And lay new platforms to endamage them.
    Alarum. Enter an English Soldier
ENGLISH SOLDIER A Talbot! A Talbot!
    The French fly, leaving their clothes behind
ENGLISH SOLDIER
I'll be so bold to take what they have left.   80
The cry of 'Talbot' serves me for a sword,
For I have loaden me with many spoils,
Using no other weapon but his name. *Exit with spoils*

2.2   *Enter Lord Talbot, the Dukes of Bedford and*
       Burgundy, a Captain, ⌈and soldiers⌉

BEDFORD
The day begins to break and night is fled,
Whose pitchy mantle overveiled the earth.
Here sound retreat and cease our hot pursuit.
    Retreat is sounded
TALBOT
Bring forth the body of old Salisbury
And here advance it in the market place,   5
The middle centre of this cursèd town.
                        ⌈*Exit one or more*⌉
Now have I paid my vow unto his soul:
For every drop of blood was drawn from him
There hath at least five Frenchmen died tonight.
And that hereafter ages may behold   10
What ruin happened in revenge of him,
Within their chiefest temple I'll erect
A tomb, wherein his corpse shall be interred—
Upon the which, that everyone may read,
Shall be engraved the sack of Orléans,   15
The treacherous manner of his mournful death,
And what a terror he had been to France.
But, lords, in all our bloody massacre
I muse we met not with the Dauphin's grace,
His new-come champion, virtuous Joan of Arc,   20
Nor any of his false confederates.

BEDFORD
'Tis thought, Lord Talbot, when the fight began,
Roused on the sudden from their drowsy beds,
They did amongst the troops of armèd men
Leap o'er the walls for refuge in the field.   25

BURGUNDY
Myself, as far as I could well discern
For smoke and dusky vapours of the night,
Am sure I scared the Dauphin and his trull,
When arm-in-arm they both came swiftly running,
Like to a pair of loving turtle-doves   30
That could not live asunder day or night.
After that things are set in order here,
We'll follow them with all the power we have.
    Enter a Messenger
MESSENGER
All hail, my lords! Which of this princely train
Call ye the warlike Talbot, for his acts   35
So much applauded through the realm of France?
TALBOT
Here is the Talbot. Who would speak with him?
MESSENGER
The virtuous lady, Countess of Auvergne,
With modesty admiring thy renown,
By me entreats, great lord, thou wouldst vouchsafe 40
To visit her poor castle where she lies,
That she may boast she hath beheld the man
Whose glory fills the world with loud report.
BURGUNDY
Is it even so? Nay, then I see our wars
Will turn unto a peaceful comic sport,   45
When ladies crave to be encountered with.
You may not, my lord, despise her gentle suit.
TALBOT
Ne'er trust me then, for when a world of men
Could not prevail with all their oratory,
Yet hath a woman's kindness overruled.—   50
And therefore tell her I return great thanks,
And in submission will attend on her.—
Will not your honours bear me company?
BEDFORD
No, truly, 'tis more than manners will.
And I have heard it said, 'Unbidden guests   55
Are often welcomest when they are gone'.
TALBOT
Well then, alone—since there's no remedy—
I mean to prove this lady's courtesy.
Come hither, captain.
    He whispers
                        You perceive my mind?
CAPTAIN
I do, my lord, and mean accordingly.   60
                        Exeunt ⌈severally⌉

2.3   *Enter the Countess of Auvergne and her Porter*
COUNTESS
Porter, remember what I gave in charge,
And when you have done so, bring the keys to me.
PORTER Madam, I will.   *Exit*
COUNTESS
The plot is laid. If all things fall out right,
I shall as famous be by this exploit   5
As Scythian Tomyris by Cyrus' death.

Great is the rumour of this dreadful knight,
And his achievements of no less account.
Fain would mine eyes be witness with mine ears,
To give their censure of these rare reports. 10
Enter Messenger and Lord Talbot

MESSENGER
Madam, according as your ladyship desired,
By message craved, so is Lord Talbot come.

COUNTESS
And he is welcome. What, is this the man?

MESSENGER
Madam, it is.

COUNTESS   Is this the scourge of France?
Is this the Talbot, so much feared abroad 15
That with his name the mothers still their babes?
I see report is fabulous and false.
I thought I should have seen some Hercules,
A second Hector, for his grim aspect
And large proportion of his strong-knit limbs. 20
Alas, this is a child, a seely dwarf.
It cannot be this weak and writhled shrimp
Should strike such terror to his enemies.

TALBOT
Madam, I have been bold to trouble you.
But since your ladyship is not at leisure, 25
I'll sort some other time to visit you.
He is going

COUNTESS *(to Messenger)*
What means he now? Go ask him whither he goes.

MESSENGER
Stay, my Lord Talbot, for my lady craves
To know the cause of your abrupt departure.

TALBOT
Marry, for that she's in a wrong belief, 30
I go to certify her Talbot's here.
Enter Porter with keys

COUNTESS
If thou be he, then art thou prisoner.

TALBOT
Prisoner? To whom?

COUNTESS   To me, bloodthirsty lord;
And for that cause I trained thee to my house.
Long time thy shadow hath been thrall to me, 35
For in my gallery thy picture hangs;
But now the substance shall endure the like,
And I will chain these legs and arms of thine
That hast by tyranny these many years
Wasted our country, slain our citizens, 40
And sent our sons and husbands captivate—

TALBOT Ha, ha, ha!

COUNTESS
Laughest thou, wretch? Thy mirth shall turn to
     moan.

TALBOT
I laugh to see your ladyship so fond
To think that you have aught but Talbot's shadow 45
Whereon to practise your severity.

COUNTESS Why? Art not thou the man?

TALBOT I am indeed.

COUNTESS Then have I substance too.

TALBOT
No, no, I am but shadow of myself. 50
You are deceived; my substance is not here.
For what you see is but the smallest part
And least proportion of humanity.
I tell you, madam, were the whole frame here,
It is of such a spacious lofty pitch 55
Your roof were not sufficient to contain't.

COUNTESS
This is a riddling merchant for the nonce.
He will be here, and yet he is not here.
How can these contrarieties agree?

TALBOT
That will I show you presently. 60
*He winds his horn. Within, drums strike up; a peal
of ordnance. Enter English soldiers*
How say you, madam? Are you now persuaded
That Talbot is but shadow of himself?
These are his substance, sinews, arms, and strength,
With which he yoketh your rebellious necks,
Razeth your cities and subverts your towns, 65
And in a moment makes them desolate.

COUNTESS
Victorious Talbot, pardon my abuse.
I find thou art no less than fame hath bruited,
And more than may be gathered by thy shape.
Let my presumption not provoke thy wrath, 70
For I am sorry that with reverence
I did not entertain thee as thou art.

TALBOT
Be not dismayed, fair lady, nor misconster
The mind of Talbot, as you did mistake
The outward composition of his body. 75
What you have done hath not offended me;
Nor other satisfaction do I crave
But only, with your patience, that we may
Taste of your wine and see what cates you have:
For soldiers' stomachs always serve them well. 80

COUNTESS
With all my heart; and think me honourèd
To feast so great a warrior in my house.   *Exeunt*

2.4   *A rose brier. Enter Richard Plantagenet, the Earl of
       Warwick, the Duke of Somerset, William de la Pole
       (the Earl of Suffolk), Vernon, and a Lawyer*

RICHARD PLANTAGENET
Great lords and gentlemen, what means this silence?
Dare no man answer in a case of truth?

SUFFOLK
Within the Temple hall we were too loud.
The garden here is more convenient.

RICHARD PLANTAGENET
Then say at once if I maintained the truth; 5
Or else was wrangling Somerset in th'error?

SUFFOLK
Faith, I have been a truant in the law,
And never yet could frame my will to it,
And therefore frame the law unto my will.

SOMERSET
Judge you, my lord of Warwick, then between us.   10
WARWICK
Between two hawks, which flies the higher pitch,
Between two dogs, which hath the deeper mouth,
Between two blades, which bears the better temper,
Between two horses, which doth bear him best,
Between two girls, which hath the merriest eye,   15
I have perhaps some shallow spirit of judgement;
But in these nice sharp quillets of the law,
Good faith, I am no wiser than a daw.
RICHARD PLANTAGENET
Tut, tut, here is a mannerly forbearance.
The truth appears so naked on my side   20
That any purblind eye may find it out.
SOMERSET
And on my side it is so well apparelled,
So clear, so shining, and so evident,
That it will glimmer through a blind man's eye.
RICHARD PLANTAGENET
Since you are tongue-tied and so loath to speak,   25
In dumb significants proclaim your thoughts.
Let him that is a true-born gentleman
And stands upon the honour of his birth,
If he suppose that I have pleaded truth,
From off this briar pluck a white rose with me.   30
He plucks a white rose
SOMERSET
Let him that is no coward nor no flatterer,
But dare maintain the party of the truth,
Pluck a red rose from off this thorn with me.
He plucks a red rose
WARWICK
I love no colours, and without all colour
Of base insinuating flattery   35
I pluck this white rose with Plantagenet.
SUFFOLK
I pluck this red rose with young Somerset,
And say withal I think he held the right.
VERNON
Stay, lords and gentlemen, and pluck no more
Till you conclude that he upon whose side   40
The fewest roses from the tree are cropped
Shall yield the other in the right opinion.
SOMERSET
Good Master Vernon, it is well objected.
If I have fewest, I subscribe in silence.
RICHARD PLANTAGENET And I.   45
VERNON
Then for the truth and plainness of the case
I pluck this pale and maiden blossom here,
Giving my verdict on the white rose' side.
SOMERSET
Prick not your finger as you pluck it off,
Lest, bleeding, you do paint the white rose red,   50
And fall on my side so against your will.
VERNON
If I, my lord, for my opinion bleed,

Opinion shall be surgeon to my hurt
And keep me on the side where still I am.
SOMERSET Well, well, come on! Who else?   55
LAWYER
Unless my study and my books be false,
The argument you held was wrong in law;
In sign whereof I pluck a white rose too.
RICHARD PLANTAGENET
Now Somerset, where is your argument?
SOMERSET
Here in my scabbard, meditating that   60
Shall dye your white rose in a bloody red.
RICHARD PLANTAGENET
Meantime your cheeks do counterfeit our roses,
For pale they look with fear, as witnessing
The truth on our side.
SOMERSET   No, Plantagenet,
'Tis not for fear, but anger, that thy cheeks   65
Blush for pure shame to counterfeit our roses,
And yet thy tongue will not confess thy error.
RICHARD PLANTAGENET
Hath not thy rose a canker, Somerset?
SOMERSET
Hath not thy rose a thorn, Plantagenet?
RICHARD PLANTAGENET
Ay, sharp and piercing, to maintain his truth,   70
Whiles thy consuming canker eats his falsehood.
SOMERSET
Well, I'll find friends to wear my bleeding roses,
That shall maintain what I have said is true,
Where false Plantagenet dare not be seen.
RICHARD PLANTAGENET
Now, by this maiden blossom in my hand,   75
I scorn thee and thy fashion, peevish boy.
SUFFOLK
Turn not thy scorns this way, Plantagenet.
RICHARD PLANTAGENET
Proud Pole, I will, and scorn both him and thee.
SUFFOLK
I'll turn my part thereof into thy throat.
SOMERSET
Away, away, good William de la Pole.   80
We grace the yeoman by conversing with him.
WARWICK
Now, by God's will, thou wrong'st him, Somerset.
His grandfather was Lionel Duke of Clarence,
Third son to the third Edward, King of England.
Spring crestless yeomen from so deep a root?   85
RICHARD PLANTAGENET
He bears him on the place's privilege,
Or durst not for his craven heart say thus.
SOMERSET
By him that made me, I'll maintain my words
On any plot of ground in Christendom.
Was not thy father, Richard Earl of Cambridge,   90
For treason executed in our late king's days?
And by his treason stand'st not thou attainted,
Corrupted, and exempt from ancient gentry?

His trespass yet lives guilty in thy blood,
And till thou be restored thou art a yeoman.   95
RICHARD PLANTAGENET
My father was attachèd, not attainted;
Condemned to die for treason, but no traitor—
And that I'll prove on better men than Somerset,
Were growing time once ripened to my will.
For your partaker Pole, and you yourself,   100
I'll note you in my book of memory,
To scourge you for this apprehension.
Look to it well, and say you are well warned.
SOMERSET
Ah, thou shalt find us ready for thee still,
And know us by these colours for thy foes,   105
For these my friends, in spite of thee, shall wear.
RICHARD PLANTAGENET
And, by my soul, this pale and angry rose,
As cognizance of my blood-drinking hate,
Will I forever, and my faction, wear
Until it wither with me to my grave,   110
Or flourish to the height of my degree.
SUFFOLK
Go forward, and be choked with thy ambition.
And so farewell until I meet thee next.   *Exit*
SOMERSET
Have with thee, Pole.—Farewell, ambitious Richard.
                                                    Exit
RICHARD PLANTAGENET
How I am braved, and must perforce endure it!   115
WARWICK
This blot that they object against your house
Shall be wiped out in the next parliament,
Called for the truce of Winchester and Gloucester.
An if thou be not then created York,
I will not live to be accounted Warwick.   120
Meantime, in signal of my love to thee,
Against proud Somerset and William Pole,
Will I upon thy party wear this rose.
And here I prophesy: this brawl today,
Grown to this faction in the Temple garden,   125
Shall send, between the red rose and the white,
A thousand souls to death and deadly night.
RICHARD PLANTAGENET
Good Master Vernon, I am bound to you,
That you on my behalf would pluck a flower.
VERNON
In your behalf still will I wear the same.   130
LAWYER And so will I.
RICHARD PLANTAGENET Thanks, gentles.
Come, let us four to dinner. I dare say
This quarrel will drink blood another day.
                    Exeunt. The rose brier is removed

2.5   *Enter Edmund Mortimer, brought in a chair ⌈by⌉ his
          Keepers*
MORTIMER
Kind keepers of my weak decaying age,
Let dying Mortimer here rest himself.

Even like a man new-halèd from the rack,
So fare my limbs with long imprisonment;
And these grey locks, the pursuivants of death,   5
Argue the end of Edmund Mortimer,
Nestor-like agèd in an age of care.
These eyes, like lamps whose wasting oil is spent,
Wax dim, as drawing to their exigent;
Weak shoulders, overborne with burdening grief,   10
And pithless arms, like to a withered vine
That droops his sapless branches to the ground.
Yet are these feet—whose strengthless stay is numb,
Unable to support this lump of clay—
Swift-wingèd with desire to get a grave,   15
As witting I no other comfort have.
But tell me, keeper, will my nephew come?
KEEPER
Richard Plantagenet, my lord, will come.
We sent unto the Temple, unto his chamber,
And answer was returned that he will come.   20
MORTIMER
Enough. My soul shall then be satisfied.
Poor gentleman, his wrong doth equal mine.
Since Henry Monmouth first began to reign—
Before whose glory I was great in arms—
This loathsome sequestration have I had;   25
And even since then hath Richard been obscured,
Deprived of honour and inheritance.
But now the arbitrator of despairs,
Just Death, kind umpire of men's miseries,
With sweet enlargement doth dismiss me hence.   30
I would his troubles likewise were expired,
That so he might recover what was lost.
              Enter Richard Plantagenet
KEEPER
My lord, your loving nephew now is come.
MORTIMER
Richard Plantagenet, my friend, is he come?
RICHARD PLANTAGENET
Ay, noble uncle, thus ignobly used: 35
Your nephew, late despisèd Richard, comes.
MORTIMER (*to Keepers*)
Direct mine arms I may embrace his neck
And in his bosom spend my latter gasp.
O tell me when my lips do touch his cheeks,
That I may kindly give one fainting kiss.   40
              He embraces Richard
And now declare, sweet stem from York's great stock,
Why didst thou say of late thou wert despised?
RICHARD PLANTAGENET
First lean thine agèd back against mine arm,
And in that ease I'll tell thee my dis-ease.
This day in argument upon a case   45
Some words there grew 'twixt Somerset and me;
Among which terms he used his lavish tongue
And did upbraid me with my father's death;
Which obloquy set bars before my tongue,
Else with the like I had requited him.   50
Therefore, good uncle, for my father's sake,

In honour of a true Plantagenet,
And for alliance' sake, declare the cause
My father, Earl of Cambridge, lost his head.
MORTIMER
That cause, fair nephew, that imprisoned me,   55
And hath detained me all my flow'ring youth
Within a loathsome dungeon, there to pine,
Was cursèd instrument of his decease.
RICHARD PLANTAGENET
Discover more at large what cause that was,
For I am ignorant and cannot guess.   60
MORTIMER
I will, if that my fading breath permit
And death approach not ere my tale be done.
Henry the Fourth, grandfather to this King,
Deposed his nephew Richard, Edward's son,
The first begotten and the lawful heir   65
Of Edward king, the third of that descent;
During whose reign the Percies of the north,
Finding his usurpation most unjust,
Endeavoured my advancement to the throne.
The reason moved these warlike lords to this   70
Was for that—young King Richard thus removed,
Leaving no heir begotten of his body—
I was the next by birth and parentage,
For by my mother I derivèd am
From Lionel Duke of Clarence, the third son   75
To King Edward the Third—whereas the King
From John of Gaunt doth bring his pedigree,
Being but fourth of that heroic line.
But mark: as in this haughty great attempt
They labourèd to plant the rightful heir,   80
I lost my liberty, and they their lives.
Long after this, when Henry the Fifth,
Succeeding his father Bolingbroke, did reign,
Thy father, Earl of Cambridge then, derived
From famous Edmund Langley, Duke of York,   85
Marrying my sister that thy mother was,
Again, in pity of my hard distress,
Levied an army, weening to redeem
And have installed me in the diadem;
But, as the rest, so fell that noble earl,   90
And was beheaded. Thus the Mortimers,
In whom the title rested, were suppressed.
RICHARD PLANTAGENET
Of which, my lord, your honour is the last.
MORTIMER
True, and thou seest that I no issue have,
And that my fainting words do warrant death.   95
Thou art my heir. The rest I wish thee gather—
But yet be wary in thy studious care.
RICHARD PLANTAGENET
Thy grave admonishments prevail with me.
But yet methinks my father's execution
Was nothing less than bloody tyranny.   100
MORTIMER
With silence, nephew, be thou politic.
Strong-fixèd is the house of Lancaster,

And like a mountain, not to be removed.
But now thy uncle is removing hence,
As princes do their courts, when they are cloyed   105
With long continuance in a settled place.
RICHARD PLANTAGENET
O uncle, would some part of my young years
Might but redeem the passage of your age.
MORTIMER
Thou dost then wrong me, as that slaughterer doth
Which giveth many wounds when one will kill.   110
Mourn not, except thou sorrow for my good.
Only give order for my funeral.
And so farewell, and fair be all thy hopes,
And prosperous be thy life in peace and war.   *Dies*
RICHARD PLANTAGENET
And peace, no war, befall thy parting soul.   115
In prison hast thou spent a pilgrimage,
And like a hermit overpassed thy days.
Well, I will lock his counsel in my breast,
And what I do imagine, let that rest.
Keepers, convey him hence, and I myself   120
Will see his burial better than his life.
                    Exeunt Keepers with Mortimer's body
Here dies the dusky torch of Mortimer,
Choked with ambition of the meaner sort.
And for those wrongs, those bitter injuries,
Which Somerset hath offered to my house,   125
I doubt not but with honour to redress.
And therefore haste I to the Parliament,
Either to be restorèd to my blood,
Or make mine ill th'advantage of my good.   *Exit*

3.1   *Flourish. Enter young King Henry, the Dukes of*
          Exeter and Gloucester, the Bishop of Winchester;
          the Duke of Somerset and the Earl of Suffolk ⌈with
          red roses⌉; the Earl of Warwick and Richard
          Plantagenet ⌈with white roses⌉. Gloucester offers to
          put up a bill; Winchester snatches it, tears it
WINCHESTER
Com'st thou with deep premeditated lines?
With written pamphlets studiously devised?
Humphrey of Gloucester, if thou canst accuse,
Or aught intend'st to lay unto my charge,
Do it without invention, suddenly,   5
As I with sudden and extemporal speech
Purpose to answer what thou canst object.
GLOUCESTER
Presumptuous priest, this place commands my
          patience,
Or thou shouldst find thou hast dishonoured me.
Think not, although in writing I preferred   10
The manner of thy vile outrageous crimes,
That therefore I have forged, or am not able
Verbatim to rehearse the method of my pen.
No, prelate, such is thy audacious wickedness,
Thy lewd, pestiferous, and dissentious pranks,   15
As very infants prattle of thy pride.
Thou art a most pernicious usurer,

Froward by nature, enemy to peace,
Lascivious, wanton, more than well beseems
A man of thy profession and degree.   20
And for thy treachery, what's more manifest?—
In that thou laid'st a trap to take my life,
As well at London Bridge as at the Tower.
Beside, I fear me, if thy thoughts were sifted,
The King thy sovereign is not quite exempt   25
From envious malice of thy swelling heart.

WINCHESTER
Gloucester, I do defy thee.—Lords, vouchsafe
To give me hearing what I shall reply.
If I were covetous, ambitious, or perverse,
As he will have me, how am I so poor?   30
Or how haps it I seek not to advance
Or raise myself, but keep my wonted calling?
And for dissension, who preferreth peace
More than I do?—except I be provoked.
No, my good lords, it is not that offends;   35
It is not that that hath incensed the Duke.
It is because no one should sway but he,
No one but he should be about the King—
And that engenders thunder in his breast
And makes him roar these accusations forth.   40
But he shall know I am as good—

GLOUCESTER   As good?—
Thou bastard of my grandfather.

WINCHESTER
Ay, lordly sir; for what are you, I pray,
But one imperious in another's throne?   45

GLOUCESTER
Am I not Protector, saucy priest?

WINCHESTER
And am not I a prelate of the Church?

GLOUCESTER
Yes—as an outlaw in a castle keeps
And useth it to patronage his theft.

WINCHESTER
Unreverent Gloucester.

GLOUCESTER   Thou art reverend   50
Touching thy spiritual function, not thy life.

WINCHESTER
Rome shall remedy this.

⌈GLOUCESTER⌉   Roam thither then.
⌈WARWICK⌉ (to Winchester)
My lord, it were your duty to forbear.

SOMERSET
Ay, so the bishop be not overborne:
Methinks my lord should be religious,   55
And know the office that belongs to such.

WARWICK
Methinks his lordship should be humbler.
It fitteth not a prelate so to plead.

SOMERSET
Yes, when his holy state is touched so near.

WARWICK
State holy or unhallowed, what of that?   60
Is not his grace Protector to the King?

RICHARD PLANTAGENET (aside)
Plantagenet, I see, must hold his tongue,
Lest it be said, 'Speak, sirrah, when you should;
Must your bold verdict intertalk with lords?'
Else would I have a fling at Winchester.   65

KING HENRY
Uncles of Gloucester and of Winchester,
The special watchmen of our English weal,
I would prevail, if prayers might prevail,
To join your hearts in love and amity.
O what a scandal is it to our crown   70
That two such noble peers as ye should jar!
Believe me, lords, my tender years can tell
Civil dissension is a viperous worm
That gnaws the bowels of the commonwealth.
A noise within

⌈SERVINGMEN⌉ (within) Down with the tawny coats!   75

KING HENRY
What tumult's this?

WARWICK   An uproar, I dare warrant,
Begun through malice of the Bishop's men.
A noise again

⌈SERVINGMEN⌉ (within) Stones, stones!
Enter the Mayor of London

MAYOR
O my good lords, and virtuous Henry,
Pity the city of London, pity us!   80
The Bishop and the Duke of Gloucester's men,
Forbidden late to carry any weapon,
Have filled their pockets full of pebble stones
And, banding themselves in contrary parts,
Do pelt so fast at one another's pate   85
That many have their giddy brains knocked out.
Our windows are broke down in every street,
And we for fear compelled to shut our shops.
Enter in skirmish, with bloody pates, Winchester's
Servingmen in tawny coats and Gloucester's in blue
coats

KING HENRY
We charge you, on allegiance to ourself,
To hold your slaught'ring hands and keep the peace.
⌈The skirmish ceases⌉
Pray, Uncle Gloucester, mitigate this strife.   91

FIRST SERVINGMAN Nay, if we be forbidden stones, we'll
fall to it with our teeth.

SECOND SERVINGMAN
Do what ye dare, we are as resolute.
Skirmish again

GLOUCESTER
You of my household, leave this peevish broil,   95
And set this unaccustomed fight aside.

THIRD SERVINGMAN
My lord, we know your grace to be a man
Just and upright and, for your royal birth,
Inferior to none but to his majesty;
And ere that we will suffer such a prince,   100
So kind a father of the commonweal,
To be disgracèd by an inkhorn mate,

We and our wives and children all will fight
And have our bodies slaughtered by thy foes.

FIRST SERVINGMAN
Ay, and the very parings of our nails   105
Shall pitch a field when we are dead.
They begin to skirmish again

GLOUCESTER   Stay, stay, I say!
An if you love me as you say you do,
Let me persuade you to forbear a while.

KING HENRY
O how this discord doth afflict my soul!
Can you, my lord of Winchester, behold   110
My sighs and tears, and will not once relent?
Who should be pitiful if you be not?
Or who should study to prefer a peace,
If holy churchmen take delight in broils?

WARWICK
Yield, my lord Protector; yield, Winchester—   115
Except you mean with obstinate repulse
To slay your sovereign and destroy the realm.
You see what mischief—and what murder, too—
Hath been enacted through your enmity.
Then be at peace, except ye thirst for blood.   120

WINCHESTER
He shall submit, or I will never yield.

GLOUCESTER
Compassion on the King commands me stoop,
Or I would see his heart out ere the priest
Should ever get that privilege of me.

WARWICK
Behold, my lord of Winchester, the Duke   125
Hath banished moody discontented fury,
As by his smoothèd brows it doth appear.
Why look you still so stern and tragical?

GLOUCESTER
Here, Winchester, I offer thee my hand.

KING HENRY (*to Winchester*)
Fie, Uncle Beaufort! I have heard you preach   130
That malice was a great and grievous sin;
And will not you maintain the thing you teach,
But prove a chief offender in the same?

WARWICK
Sweet King! The Bishop hath a kindly gird.
For shame, my lord of Winchester, relent.
What, shall a child instruct you what to do?   135

WINCHESTER
Well, Duke of Gloucester, I will yield to thee
Love for thy love, and hand for hand I give.

GLOUCESTER (*aside*)
Ay, but I fear me with a hollow heart.
(*To the others*) See here, my friends and loving
   countrymen,   140
This token serveth for a flag of truce
Betwixt ourselves and all our followers.
So help me God, as I dissemble not.

WINCHESTER
So help me God (*aside*) as I intend it not.

KING HENRY
O loving uncle, kind Duke of Gloucester,   145
How joyful am I made by this contract!
(*To Servingmen*) Away, my masters, trouble us no
   more,
But join in friendship as your lords have done.

FIRST SERVINGMAN Content. I'll to the surgeon's.

SECOND SERVINGMAN And so will I.   150

THIRD SERVINGMAN And I will see what physic the tavern
   affords.   *Exeunt the Mayor and Servingmen*

WARWICK
Accept this scroll, most gracious sovereign,
Which in the right of Richard Plantagenet
We do exhibit to your majesty.   155

GLOUCESTER
Well urged, my lord of Warwick—for, sweet prince,
An if your grace mark every circumstance,
You have great reason to do Richard right,
Especially for those occasions
At Eltham Place I told your majesty.   160

KING HENRY
And those occasions, uncle, were of force.—
Therefore, my loving lords, our pleasure is
That Richard be restorèd to his blood.

WARWICK
Let Richard be restorèd to his blood.
So shall his father's wrongs be recompensed.   165

WINCHESTER
As will the rest, so willeth Winchester.

KING HENRY
If Richard will be true, not that alone
But all the whole inheritance I give
That doth belong unto the house of York,
From whence you spring by lineal descent.   170

RICHARD PLANTAGENET
Thy humble servant vows obedience
And humble service till the point of death.

KING HENRY
Stoop then, and set your knee against my foot.
Richard kneels
And in reguerdon of that duty done,
I gird thee with the valiant sword of York.   175
Rise, Richard, like a true Plantagenet,
And rise created princely Duke of York.

RICHARD DUKE OF YORK (*rising*)
And so thrive Richard, as thy foes may fall;
And as my duty springs, so perish they
That grudge one thought against your majesty.   180

ALL BUT RICHARD AND SOMERSET
Welcome, high prince, the mighty Duke of York!

SOMERSET (*aside*)
Perish, base prince, ignoble Duke of York!

GLOUCESTER
Now will it best avail your majesty
To cross the seas and to be crowned in France.
The presence of a king engenders love   185
Amongst his subjects and his loyal friends,
As it disanimates his enemies.

KING HENRY
When Gloucester says the word, King Henry goes,
For friendly counsel cuts off many foes.
GLOUCESTER
Your ships already are in readiness.   190
Sennet. Exeunt all but Exeter
EXETER
Ay, we may march in England or in France,
Not seeing what is likely to ensue.
This late dissension grown betwixt the peers
Burns under feignèd ashes of forged love,
And will at last break out into a flame.   195
As festered members rot but by degree
Till bones and flesh and sinews fall away,
So will this base and envious discord breed.
And now I fear that fatal prophecy
Which, in the time of Henry named the Fifth,   200
Was in the mouth of every sucking babe:
That 'Henry born at Monmouth should win all,
And Henry born at Windsor should lose all'—
Which is so plain that Exeter doth wish
His days may finish, ere that hapless time.   *Exit*

3.2   *Enter Joan la Pucelle, disguised, with four French*
        Soldiers with sacks upon their backs
JOAN
These are the city gates, the gates of Rouen,
Through which our policy must make a breach.
Take heed. Be wary how you place your words.
Talk like the vulgar sort of market men
That come to gather money for their corn.   5
If we have entrance, as I hope we shall,
And that we find the slothful watch but weak,
I'll by a sign give notice to our friends,
That Charles the Dauphin may encounter them.
A SOLDIER
Our sacks shall be a mean to sack the city,   10
And we be lords and rulers over Rouen.
Therefore we'll knock.
        They knock
WATCH (*within*)
        Qui là?
JOAN   *Paysans, la pauvre gens de France:*
Poor market folks that come to sell their corn.
WATCH (*opening the gates*)
Enter, go in. The market bell is rung.   15
JOAN (*aside*)
Now, Rouen, I'll shake thy bulwarks to the ground.
        Exeunt

3.3   *Enter Charles the Dauphin, the Bastard of Orléans,*
        ⌈*the Duke of Alençon, René Duke of Anjou, and*
        French soldiers⌉
CHARLES
Saint Denis bless this happy stratagem,
And once again we'll sleep secure in Rouen.
BASTARD
Here entered Pucelle and her practisants.

Now she is there, how will she specify
'Here is the best and safest passage in'?   5
RENÉ
By thrusting out a torch from yonder tower—
Which, once discerned, shows that her meaning is:
No way to that, for weakness, which she entered.
        Enter Joan la Pucelle on the top, thrusting out a
        torch burning
JOAN
Behold, this is the happy wedding torch
That joineth Rouen unto her countrymen,   10
But burning fatal to the Talbonites.
BASTARD
See, noble Charles, the beacon of our friend.
The burning torch in yonder turret stands.
CHARLES
Now shine it like a comet of revenge,
A prophet to the fall of all our foes!   15
RENÉ
Defer no time; delays have dangerous ends.
Enter and cry, 'The Dauphin!', presently,
And then do execution on the watch.
        Alarum. Exeunt

3.4   *An alarum. Enter Lord Talbot in an excursion*
TALBOT
France, thou shalt rue this treason with thy tears,
If Talbot but survive thy treachery.
Pucelle, that witch, that damnèd sorceress,
Hath wrought this hellish mischief unawares,
That hardly we escaped the pride of France.   *Exit*

3.5   *An alarum. Excursions. The Duke of Bedford*
        brought in sick, in a chair. Enter Lord Talbot and
        the Duke of Burgundy, without; within, Joan la
        Pucelle, Charles the Dauphin, the Bastard of
        Orléans, ⌈*the Duke of Alençon, and René Duke of*
        Anjou⌉ *on the walls*
JOAN
Good morrow gallants. Want ye corn for bread?
I think the Duke of Burgundy will fast
Before he'll buy again at such a rate.
'Twas full of darnel. Do you like the taste?
BURGUNDY
Scoff on, vile fiend and shameless courtesan.   5
I trust ere long to choke thee with thine own,
And make thee curse the harvest of that corn.
CHARLES
Your grace may starve, perhaps, before that time.
BEDFORD
O let no words, but deeds, revenge this treason.
JOAN
What will you do, good graybeard? Break a lance   10
And run a-tilt at death within a chair?
TALBOT
Foul fiend of France, and hag of all despite,
Encompassed with thy lustful paramours,
Becomes it thee to taunt his valiant age

And twit with cowardice a man half dead?   15
Damsel, I'll have a bout with you again,
Or else let Talbot perish with this shame.

JOAN
Are ye so hot, sir?—Yet, Pucelle, hold thy peace.
If Talbot do but thunder, rain will follow.
   The English whisper together in counsel
God speed the parliament; who shall be the Speaker?

TALBOT
Dare ye come forth and meet us in the field?   21

JOAN
Belike your lordship takes us then for fools,
To try if that our own be ours or no.

TALBOT
I speak not to that railing Hecate
But unto thee, Alençon, and the rest.   25
Will ye, like soldiers, come and fight it out?

ALENÇON
Seignieur, no.

TALBOT   Seignieur, hang! Base muleteers of France,
Like peasant footboys do they keep the walls
And dare not take up arms like gentlemen.

JOAN
Away, captains, let's get us from the walls,   30
For Talbot means no goodness by his looks.
Goodbye, my lord. We came but to tell you
That we are here.   *Exeunt French from the walls*

TALBOT
And there will we be, too, ere it be long,
Or else reproach be Talbot's greatest fame.   35
Vow Burgundy, by honour of thy house,
Pricked on by public wrongs sustained in France,
Either to get the town again or die.
And I—as sure as English Henry lives,
And as his father here was conqueror;   40
As sure as in this late betrayèd town
Great Cœur-de-lion's heart was buried—
So sure I swear to get the town or die.

BURGUNDY
My vows are equal partners with thy vows.

TALBOT
But ere we go, regard this dying prince,   45
The valiant Duke of Bedford. (*To Bedford*) Come, my
   lord,
We will bestow you in some better place,
Fitter for sickness and for crazy age.

BEDFORD
Lord Talbot, do not so dishonour me.
Here will I sit before the walls of Rouen,   50
And will be partner of your weal or woe.

BURGUNDY
Courageous Bedford, let us now persuade you.

BEDFORD
Not to be gone from hence; for once I read
That stout Pendragon, in his litter sick,
Came to the field and vanquishèd his foes.   55
Methinks I should revive the soldiers' hearts,
Because I ever found them as myself.

TALBOT
Undaunted spirit in a dying breast!
Then be it so; heavens keep old Bedford safe.
And now no more ado, brave Burgundy,   60
But gather we our forces out of hand,
And set upon our boasting enemy.
                      Exit with Burgundy
   An alarum. Excursions. Enter Sir John Fastolf and a
   Captain

CAPTAIN
Whither away, Sir John Fastolf, in such haste?

FASTOLF
Whither away? To save myself by flight.
We are like to have the overthrow again.   65

CAPTAIN
What, will you fly, and leave Lord Talbot?

FASTOLF
Ay, all the Talbots in the world, to save my life.   *Exit*

CAPTAIN
Cowardly knight, ill fortune follow thee!   *Exit*
   Retreat. Excursions. Joan, Alençon, and Charles fly

BEDFORD
Now, quiet soul, depart when heaven please,
For I have seen our enemies' overthrow.   70
What is the trust or strength of foolish man?
They that of late were daring with their scoffs
Are glad and fain by flight to save themselves.
   Bedford dies, and is carried in by two in his chair

3.6   *An alarum. Enter Lord Talbot, the Duke of*
       Burgundy, and the rest of the English soldiers

TALBOT
Lost and recovered in a day again!
This is a double honour, Burgundy;
Yet heavens have glory for this victory!

BURGUNDY
Warlike and martial Talbot, Burgundy
Enshrines thee in his heart, and there erects   5
Thy noble deeds as valour's monuments.

TALBOT
Thanks, gentle Duke. But where is Pucelle now?
I think her old familiar is asleep.
Now where's the Bastard's braves, and Charles his
   gleeks?
What, all amort? Rouen hangs her head for grief   10
That such a valiant company are fled.
Now will we take some order in the town,
Placing therein some expert officers,
And then depart to Paris, to the King,
For there young Henry with his nobles lie.   15

BURGUNDY
What wills Lord Talbot pleaseth Burgundy.

TALBOT
But yet, before we go, let's not forget
The noble Duke of Bedford late deceased,
But see his exequies fulfilled in Rouen.
A braver soldier never couchèd lance;   20
A gentler heart did never sway in court.

But kings and mightiest potentates must die,
For that's the end of human misery.   *Exeunt*

3.7   *Enter Charles the Dauphin, the Bastard of Orléans,*
          the Duke of Alençon, Joan la Pucelle, ⌈and French
          soldiers⌉

JOAN
Dismay not, princes, at this accident,
Nor grieve that Rouen is so recoverèd.
Care is no cure, but rather corrosive,
For things that are not to be remedied.
Let frantic Talbot triumph for a while,   5
And like a peacock sweep along his tail;
We'll pull his plumes and take away his train,
If Dauphin and the rest will be but ruled.

CHARLES
We have been guided by thee hitherto,
And of thy cunning had no diffidence.   10
One sudden foil shall never breed distrust.

BASTARD (*to Joan*)
Search out thy wit for secret policies,
And we will make thee famous through the world.

ALENÇON (*to Joan*)
We'll set thy statue in some holy place
And have thee reverenced like a blessèd saint.   15
Employ thee then, sweet virgin, for our good.

JOAN
Then thus it must be; this doth Joan devise:
By fair persuasions mixed with sugared words
We will entice the Duke of Burgundy
To leave the Talbot and to follow us.   20

CHARLES
Ay, marry, sweeting, if we could do that
France were no place for Henry's warriors,
Nor should that nation boast it so with us,
But be extirpèd from our provinces.

ALENÇON
For ever should they be expulsed from France   25
And not have title of an earldom here.

JOAN
Your honours shall perceive how I will work
To bring this matter to the wishèd end.
          Drum sounds afar off
Hark, by the sound of drum you may perceive
Their powers are marching unto Paris-ward.   30
          Here sound an English march
There goes the Talbot, with his colours spread,
And all the troops of English after him.
          Here sound a French march
Now in the rearward comes the Duke and his;
Fortune in favour makes him lag behind.
Summon a parley. We will talk with him.   35
          Trumpets sound a parley

CHARLES ⌈*calling*⌉
A parley with the Duke of Burgundy.
          ⌈*Enter the Duke of Burgundy*⌉

BURGUNDY
Who craves a parley with the Burgundy?

JOAN
The princely Charles of France, thy countryman.

BURGUNDY
What sayst thou, Charles?—for I am marching hence.

CHARLES
Speak, Pucelle, and enchant him with thy words.   40

JOAN
Brave Burgundy, undoubted hope of France,
Stay. Let thy humble handmaid speak to thee.

BURGUNDY
Speak on, but be not over-tedious.

JOAN
Look on thy country, look on fertile France,
And see the cities and the towns defaced   45
By wasting ruin of the cruel foe.
As looks the mother on her lowly babe
When death doth close his tender-dying eyes,
See, see the pining malady of France;
Behold the wounds, the most unnatural wounds,   50
Which thou thyself hast given her woeful breast.
O turn thy edgèd sword another way,
Strike those that hurt, and hurt not those that help.
One drop of blood drawn from thy country's bosom
Should grieve thee more than streams of foreign gore.
Return thee, therefore, with a flood of tears,   56
And wash away thy country's stainèd spots.

BURGUNDY ⌈*aside*⌉
Either she hath bewitched me with her words,
Or nature makes me suddenly relent.

JOAN
Besides, all French and France exclaims on thee,   60
Doubting thy birth and lawful progeny.
Who join'st thou with but with a lordly nation
That will not trust thee but for profit's sake?
When Talbot hath set footing once in France
And fashioned thee that instrument of ill,   65
Who then but English Henry will be lord,
And thou be thrust out like a fugitive?
Call we to mind, and mark but this for proof:
Was not the Duke of Orléans thy foe?
And was he not in England prisoner?   70
But when they heard he was thine enemy
They set him free, without his ransom paid,
In spite of Burgundy and all his friends.
See, then, thou fight'st against thy countrymen,
And join'st with them will be thy slaughtermen.   75
Come, come, return; return, thou wandering lord,
Charles and the rest will take thee in their arms.

BURGUNDY ⌈*aside*⌉
I am vanquishèd. These haughty words of hers
Have battered me like roaring cannon-shot
And made me almost yield upon my knees.   80
(*To the others*) Forgive me, country, and sweet
          countrymen;
And lords, accept this hearty kind embrace.
My forces and my power of men are yours.
So farewell, Talbot. I'll no longer trust thee.   84

98

JOAN
Done like a Frenchman—⌈*aside*⌉ turn and turn again.
CHARLES
Welcome, brave Duke. Thy friendship makes us fresh.
BASTARD
And doth beget new courage in our breasts.
ALENÇON
Pucelle hath bravely played her part in this,
And doth deserve a coronet of gold.
CHARLES
Now let us on, my lords, and join our powers,   90
And seek how we may prejudice the foe.   *Exeunt*

3.8   ⌈*Flourish.*⌉ *Enter King Henry, the Duke of*
     Gloucester, the Bishop of Winchester, the Duke of
     Exeter ; Richard Duke of York, the Earl of
     Warwick, and Vernon ⌈*with white roses*⌉*; the Earl*
     of Suffolk, the Duke of Somerset, and Basset ⌈*with*
     red roses⌉*. To them, with his soldiers, enter Lord*
     Talbot
TALBOT
My gracious prince and honourable peers,
Hearing of your arrival in this realm
I have a while given truce unto my wars
To do my duty to my sovereign;
In sign whereof, this arm that hath reclaimed   5
To your obedience fifty fortresses,
Twelve cities, and seven walled towns of strength,
Beside five hundred prisoners of esteem,
Lets fall his sword before your highness' feet,
And with submissive loyalty of heart   10
Ascribes the glory of his conquest got
First to my God, and next unto your grace.
     ⌈*He kneels*⌉
KING HENRY
Is this the Lord Talbot, uncle Gloucester,
That hath so long been resident in France?
GLOUCESTER
Yes, if it please your majesty, my liege.   15
KING HENRY (*to Talbot*)
Welcome, brave captain and victorious lord.
When I was young—as yet I am not old—
I do remember how my father said
A stouter champion never handled sword.
Long since we were resolvèd of your truth,   20
Your faithful service and your toil in war,
Yet never have you tasted our reward,
Or been reguerdoned with so much as thanks,
Because till now we never saw your face.
Therefore stand up,
     Talbot rises
               and for these good deserts   25
We here create you Earl of Shrewsbury;
And in our coronation take your place.
     Sennet. Exeunt all but Vernon and Basset
VERNON
Now sir, to you that were so hot at sea,

Disgracing of these colours that I wear
In honour of my noble lord of York,   30
Dar'st thou maintain the former words thou spak'st?
BASSET
Yes, sir, as well as you dare patronage
The envious barking of your saucy tongue
Against my lord the Duke of Somerset.
VERNON
Sirrah, thy lord I honour as he is.   35
BASSET
Why, what is he?—as good a man as York.
VERNON
Hark ye, not so. In witness, take ye that.
     Vernon strikes him
BASSET
Villain, thou know'st the law of arms is such
That whoso draws a sword 'tis present death,
Or else this blow should broach thy dearest blood.   40
But I'll unto his majesty and crave
I may have liberty to venge this wrong,
When thou shalt see I'll meet thee to thy cost.
VERNON
Well, miscreant, I'll be there as soon as you,
And after meet you sooner than you would.   *Exeunt*

4.1   ⌈*Flourish.*⌉ *Enter King Henry, the Duke of*
     Gloucester, the Bishop of Winchester, the Duke of
     Exeter ; Richard Duke of York, and the Earl of
     Warwick with white roses ; the Earl of Suffolk and
     the Duke of Somerset with red roses ; Lord Talbot,
     and the Governor of Paris
GLOUCESTER
Lord Bishop, set the crown upon his head.
WINCHESTER
God save King Henry, of that name the sixth!
     Winchester crowns the King
GLOUCESTER
Now, Governor of Paris, take your oath
That you elect no other king but him;
Esteem none friends but such as are his friends,   5
And none your foes but such as shall pretend
Malicious practices against his state.
This shall ye do, so help you righteous God.
     Enter Sir John Fastolf with a letter
FASTOLF
My gracious sovereign, as I rode from Calais
To haste unto your coronation   10
A letter was delivered to my hands,
     ⌈*He presents the letter*⌉
Writ to your grace from th' Duke of Burgundy.
TALBOT
Shame to the Duke of Burgundy and thee!
I vowed, base knight, when I did meet thee next,
To tear the Garter from thy craven's leg,   15
     He tears it off
Which I have done because unworthily
Thou wast installèd in that high degree.—
Pardon me, princely Henry and the rest.

This dastard at the battle of Patay
When but in all I was six thousand strong,   20
And that the French were almost ten to one,
Before we met, or that a stroke was given,
Like to a trusty squire did run away;
In which assault we lost twelve hundred men.
Myself and divers gentlemen beside   25
Were there surprised and taken prisoners.
Then judge, great lords, if I have done amiss,
Or whether that such cowards ought to wear
This ornament of knighthood: yea or no?

GLOUCESTER
To say the truth, this fact was infamous   30
And ill beseeming any common man,
Much more a knight, a captain and a leader.

TALBOT
When first this order was ordained, my lords,
Knights of the Garter were of noble birth,
Valiant and virtuous, full of haughty courage,   35
Such as were grown to credit by the wars;
Not fearing death nor shrinking for distress,
But always resolute in most extremes.
He then that is not furnished in this sort
Doth but usurp the sacred name of knight,   40
Profaning this most honourable order,
And should—if I were worthy to be judge—
Be quite degraded, like a hedge-born swain
That doth presume to boast of gentle blood.

KING HENRY (to Fastolf)
Stain to thy countrymen, thou hear'st thy doom.   45
Be packing, therefore, thou that wast a knight.
Henceforth we banish thee on pain of death.
                                        Exit Fastolf
And now, my Lord Protector, view the letter
Sent from our uncle, Duke of Burgundy.

GLOUCESTER
What means his grace that he hath changed his
    style?   50
No more but plain and bluntly 'To the King'?
Hath he forgot he is his sovereign?
Or doth this churlish superscription
Pretend some alteration in good will?
What's here? 'I have upon especial cause,   55
Moved with compassion of my country's wrack
Together with the pitiful complaints
Of such as your oppression feeds upon,
Forsaken your pernicious faction
And joined with Charles, the rightful King of France.'
O monstrous treachery! Can this be so?   61
That in alliance, amity, and oaths
There should be found such false dissembling guile?

KING HENRY
What? Doth my uncle Burgundy revolt?

GLOUCESTER
He doth, my lord, and is become your foe.   65

KING HENRY
Is that the worst this letter doth contain?

GLOUCESTER
It is the worst, and all, my lord, he writes.

KING HENRY
Why then, Lord Talbot there shall talk with him
And give him chastisement for this abuse.
(To Talbot) How say you, my lord? Are you not
    content?   70

TALBOT
Content, my liege? Yes. But that I am prevented,
I should have begged I might have been employed.

KING HENRY
Then gather strength and march unto him straight.
Let him perceive how ill we brook his treason,
And what offence it is to flout his friends.   75

TALBOT
I go, my lord, in heart desiring still
You may behold confusion of your foes.   Exit
    Enter Vernon wearing a white rose, and Basset
    wearing a red rose

VERNON (to King Henry)
Grant me the combat, gracious sovereign.

BASSET (to King Henry)
And me, my lord; grant me the combat, too.

RICHARD DUKE OF YORK (to King Henry, pointing to Vernon)
This is my servant; hear him, noble Prince.   80

SOMERSET (to King Henry, pointing to Basset)
And this is mine, sweet Henry; favour him.

KING HENRY
Be patient, lords, and give them leave to speak.
Say, gentlemen, what makes you thus exclaim,
And wherefore crave you combat, or with whom?

VERNON
With him, my lord; for he hath done me wrong.   85

BASSET
And I with him; for he hath done me wrong.

KING HENRY
What is that wrong whereof you both complain?
First let me know, and then I'll answer you.

BASSET
Crossing the sea from England into France,
This fellow here with envious carping tongue   90
Upbraided me about the rose I wear,
Saying the sanguine colour of the leaves
Did represent my master's blushing cheeks
When stubbornly he did repugn the truth
About a certain question in the law   95
Argued betwixt the Duke of York and him,
With other vile and ignominious terms;
In confutation of which rude reproach,
And in defence of my lord's worthiness,
I crave the benefit of law of arms.   100

VERNON
And that is my petition, noble lord;
For though he seem with forgèd quaint conceit
To set a gloss upon his bold intent,
Yet know, my lord, I was provoked by him,
And he first took exceptions at this badge,   105
Pronouncing that the paleness of this flower

Bewrayed the faintness of my master's heart.

RICHARD DUKE OF YORK
Will not this malice, Somerset, be left?

SOMERSET
Your private grudge, my lord of York, will out,
Though ne'er so cunningly you smother it.   110

KING HENRY
Good Lord, what madness rules in brainsick men
When for so slight and frivolous a cause
Such factious emulations shall arise?
Good cousins both of York and Somerset,
Quiet yourselves, I pray, and be at peace.   115

RICHARD DUKE OF YORK
Let this dissension first be tried by fight,
And then your highness shall command a peace.

SOMERSET
The quarrel toucheth none but us alone;
Betwixt ourselves let us decide it then.

RICHARD DUKE OF YORK
There is my pledge. Accept it, Somerset.   120

VERNON (to King Henry)
Nay, let it rest where it began at first.

BASSET (to King Henry)
Confirm it so, mine honourable lord.

GLOUCESTER
Confirm it so? Confounded be your strife,
And perish ye with your audacious prate!
Presumptuous vassals, are you not ashamed   125
With this immodest clamorous outrage
To trouble and disturb the King and us?
And you, my lords, methinks you do not well
To bear with their perverse objections,
Much less to take occasion from their mouths   130
To raise a mutiny betwixt yourselves.
Let me persuade you take a better course.

EXETER
It grieves his highness. Good my lords, be friends.

KING HENRY
Come hither, you that would be combatants.
Henceforth I charge you, as you love our favour,   135
Quite to forget this quarrel and the cause.
And you, my lords, remember where we are—
In France, amongst a fickle wavering nation.
If they perceive dissension in our looks,
And that within ourselves we disagree,   140
How will their grudging stomachs be provoked
To wilful disobedience, and rebel!
Beside, what infamy will there arise
When foreign princes shall be certified
That for a toy, a thing of no regard,   145
King Henry's peers and chief nobility
Destroyed themselves and lost the realm of France!
O, think upon the conquest of my father,
My tender years, and let us not forgo
That for a trifle that was bought with blood.   150
Let me be umpire in this doubtful strife.
I see no reason, if I wear this rose,

He takes a red rose

That anyone should therefore be suspicious
I more incline to Somerset than York.
Both are my kinsmen, and I love them both.   155
As well they may upbraid me with my crown
Because, forsooth, the King of Scots is crowned.
But your discretions better can persuade
Than I am able to instruct or teach,
And therefore, as we hither came in peace,   160
So let us still continue peace and love.
Cousin of York, we institute your grace
To be our regent in these parts of France;
And good my lord of Somerset, unite
Your troops of horsemen with his bands of foot,   165
And like true subjects, sons of your progenitors,
Go cheerfully together and digest
Your angry choler on your enemies.
Ourself, my Lord Protector, and the rest,
After some respite, will return to Calais,   170
From thence to England, where I hope ere long
To be presented by your victories
With Charles, Alençon, and that traitorous rout.

Flourish. Exeunt all but York, Warwick,
Vernon, and Exeter

WARWICK
My lord of York, I promise you, the King
Prettily, methought, did play the orator.   175

RICHARD DUKE OF YORK
And so he did; but yet I like it not
In that he wears the badge of Somerset.

WARWICK
Tush, that was but his fancy; blame him not.
I dare presume, sweet Prince, he thought no harm.

RICHARD DUKE OF YORK
An if I wist he did—but let it rest.   180
Other affairs must now be managèd.

Exeunt all but Exeter

EXETER
Well didst thou, Richard, to suppress thy voice;
For had the passions of thy heart burst out
I fear we should have seen deciphered there
More rancorous spite, more furious raging broils,   185
Than yet can be imagined or supposed.
But howsoe'er, no simple man that sees
This jarring discord of nobility,
This shouldering of each other in the court,
This factious bandying of their favourites,   190
But that it doth presage some ill event.
'Tis much when sceptres are in children's hands,
But more when envy breeds unkind division:
There comes the ruin, there begins confusion.   *Exit*

4.2   *Enter Lord Talbot with a trumpeter and drummer*
      and soldiers before Bordeaux

TALBOT
Go to the gates of Bordeaux, trumpeter.
Summon their general unto the wall.

The trumpeter sounds a parley. Enter French
General, aloft

English John Talbot, captain, calls you forth,

Servant in arms to Harry King of England;
And thus he would: open your city gates,   5
Be humble to us, call my sovereign yours
And do him homage as obedient subjects,
And I'll withdraw me and my bloody power.
But if you frown upon this proffered peace,
You tempt the fury of my three attendants—   10
Lean famine, quartering steel, and climbing fire—
Who in a moment even with the earth
Shall lay your stately and air-braving towers
If you forsake the offer of their love.

GENERAL
Thou ominous and fearful owl of death,   15
Our nation's terror and their bloody scourge,
The period of thy tyranny approacheth.
On us thou canst not enter but by death,
For I protest we are well fortified
And strong enough to issue out and fight.   20
If thou retire, the Dauphin well appointed
Stands with the snares of war to tangle thee.
On either hand thee there are squadrons pitched
To wall thee from the liberty of flight,
And no way canst thou turn thee for redress   25
But death doth front thee with apparent spoil,
And pale destruction meets thee in the face.
Ten thousand French have ta'en the sacrament
To fire their dangerous artillery
Upon no Christian soul but English Talbot.   30
Lo, there thou stand'st, a breathing valiant man
Of an invincible unconquered spirit.
This is the latest glory of thy praise,
That I thy enemy due thee withal,
For ere the glass that now begins to run   35
Finish the process of his sandy hour,
These eyes that see thee now well colourèd
Shall see thee withered, bloody, pale, and dead.
        Drum afar off
Hark, hark, the Dauphin's drum, a warning bell,
Sings heavy music to thy timorous soul,   40
And mine shall ring thy dire departure out.   *Exit*

TALBOT
He fables not. I hear the enemy.
Out, some light horsemen, and peruse their wings.
                                    ⌈*Exit one or more*⌉
O negligent and heedless discipline,
How are we parked and bounded in a pale!—   45
A little herd of England's timorous deer
Mazed with a yelping kennel of French curs.
If we be English deer, be then in blood,
Not rascal-like to fall down with a pinch,
But rather, moody-mad and desperate stags,   50
Turn on the bloody hounds with heads of steel
And make the cowards stand aloof at bay.
Sell every man his life as dear as mine
And they shall find dear deer of us, my friends.
God and Saint George, Talbot and England's right, 55
Prosper our colours in this dangerous fight!   *Exeunt*

4.3   *Enter a Messenger that meets the Duke of York.*
        Enter Richard Duke of York with a trumpeter and
        many soldiers
RICHARD DUKE OF YORK
Are not the speedy scouts returned again
That dogged the mighty army of the Dauphin?
MESSENGER
They are returned, my lord, and give it out
That he is marched to Bordeaux with his power
To fight with Talbot. As he marched along,   5
By your espials were discoverèd
Two mightier troops than that the Dauphin led,
Which joined with him and made their march for
        Bordeaux.
RICHARD DUKE OF YORK
A plague upon that villain Somerset
That thus delays my promisèd supply   10
Of horsemen that were levied for this siege!
Renownèd Talbot doth expect my aid,
And I am louted by a traitor villain
And cannot help the noble chevalier.
God comfort him in this necessity;   15
If he miscarry, farewell wars in France!
        Enter another messenger, Sir William Lucy
LUCY
Thou princely leader of our English strength,
Never so needful on the earth of France,
Spur to the rescue of the noble Talbot,
Who now is girdled with a waste of iron   20
And hemmed about with grim destruction.
To Bordeaux, warlike Duke; to Bordeaux, York,
Else farewell Talbot, France, and England's honour.
RICHARD DUKE OF YORK
O God, that Somerset, who in proud heart
Doth stop my cornets, were in Talbot's place!   25
So should we save a valiant gentleman
By forfeiting a traitor and a coward.
Mad ire and wrathful fury makes me weep,
That thus we die while remiss traitors sleep.
LUCY
O, send some succour to the distressed lord.   30
RICHARD DUKE OF YORK
He dies, we lose; I break my warlike word;
We mourn, France smiles; we lose, they daily get,
All 'long of this vile traitor Somerset.
LUCY
Then God take mercy on brave Talbot's soul,
And on his son young John, who two hours since   35
I met in travel toward his warlike father.
This seven years did not Talbot see his son,
And now they meet where both their lives are done.
RICHARD DUKE OF YORK
Alas, what joy shall noble Talbot have
To bid his young son welcome to his grave?   40
Away—vexation almost stops my breath
That sundered friends greet in the hour of death.
Lucy, farewell. No more my fortune can

But curse the cause I cannot aid the man.
Maine, Blois, Poitiers, and Tours are won away   45
'Long all of Somerset and his delay.
                Exeunt all but Lucy
LUCY
Thus while the vulture of sedition
Feeds in the bosom of such great commanders,
Sleeping neglection doth betray to loss
The conquest of our scarce-cold conqueror,   50
That ever-living man of memory
Henry the Fifth. Whiles they each other cross,
Lives, honours, lands, and all hurry to loss.   ⌜*Exit*⌝

4.4   *Enter the Duke of Somerset with his army*
SOMERSET (*to a Captain*)
It is too late, I cannot send them now.
This expedition was by York and Talbot
Too rashly plotted. All our general force
Might with a sally of the very town
Be buckled with. The over-daring Talbot   5
Hath sullied all his gloss of former honour
By this unheedful, desperate, wild adventure.
York set him on to fight and die in shame
That, Talbot dead, great York might bear the name.
        ⌜*Enter Lucy*⌝
CAPTAIN
Here is Sir William Lucy, who with me   10
Set from our o'ermatched forces forth for aid.
SOMERSET
How now, Sir William, whither were you sent?
LUCY
Whither, my lord? From bought and sold Lord Talbot,
Who, ringed about with bold adversity,
Cries out for noble York and Somerset   15
To beat assailing death from his weak legions;
And whiles the honourable captain there
Drops bloody sweat from his war-wearied limbs
And, unadvantaged, ling'ring looks for rescue,
You his false hopes, the trust of England's honour,   20
Keep off aloof with worthless emulation.
Let not your private discord keep away
The levied succours that should lend him aid,
While he, renownèd noble gentleman,
Yield up his life unto a world of odds.   25
Orléans the Bastard, Charles, and Burgundy,
Alençon, René, compass him about,
And Talbot perisheth by your default.
SOMERSET
York set him on; York should have sent him aid.
LUCY
And York as fast upon your grace exclaims,   30
Swearing that you withhold his levied horse
Collected for this expedition.
SOMERSET
York lies. He might have sent and had the horse.
I owe him little duty and less love,
And take foul scorn to fawn on him by sending.   35

LUCY
The fraud of England, not the force of France,
Hath now entrapped the noble-minded Talbot.
Never to England shall he bear his life,
But dies betrayed to fortune by your strife.
SOMERSET
Come, go. I will dispatch the horsemen straight.   40
Within six hours they will be at his aid.
LUCY
Too late comes rescue. He is ta'en or slain,
For fly he could not if he would have fled,
And fly would Talbot never, though he might.
SOMERSET
If he be dead, brave Talbot, then adieu.   45
LUCY
His fame lives in the world, his shame in you.
                Exeunt ⌜*severally*⌝

4.5   *Enter Lord Talbot and his son John*
TALBOT
O young John Talbot, I did send for thee
To tutor thee in stratagems of war,
That Talbot's name might be in thee revived
When sapless age and weak unable limbs
Should bring thy father to his drooping chair.   5
But O—malignant and ill-boding stars!—
Now thou art come unto a feast of death,
A terrible and unavoided danger.
Therefore, dear boy, mount on my swiftest horse,
And I'll direct thee how thou shalt escape   10
By sudden flight. Come, dally not, be gone.
JOHN
Is my name Talbot, and am I your son,
And shall I fly? O, if you love my mother,
Dishonour not her honourable name
To make a bastard and a slave of me.   15
The world will say he is not Talbot's blood
That basely fled when noble Talbot stood.
TALBOT
Fly to revenge my death if I be slain.
JOHN
He that flies so will ne'er return again.
TALBOT
If we both stay, we both are sure to die.   20
JOHN
Then let me stay and, father, do you fly.
Your loss is great; so your regard should be.
My worth unknown, no loss is known in me.
Upon my death the French can little boast;
In yours they will: in you all hopes are lost.   25
Flight cannot stain the honour you have won,
But mine it will, that no exploit have done.
You fled for vantage, everyone will swear,
But if I bow, they'll say it was for fear.
There is no hope that ever I will stay   30
If the first hour I shrink and run away.
Here on my knee I beg mortality
Rather than life preserved with infamy.

TALBOT
Shall all thy mother's hopes lie in one tomb?
JOHN
Ay, rather than I'll shame my mother's womb.   35
TALBOT
Upon my blessing I command thee go.
JOHN
To fight I will, but not to fly the foe.
TALBOT
Part of thy father may be saved in thee.
JOHN
No part of him but will be shamed in me.
TALBOT
Thou never hadst renown, nor canst not lose it.   40
JOHN
Yes, your renownèd name—shall flight abuse it?
TALBOT
Thy father's charge shall clear thee from that stain.
JOHN
You cannot witness for me, being slain.
If death be so apparent, then both fly.
TALBOT
And leave my followers here to fight and die?   45
My age was never tainted with such shame.
JOHN
And shall my youth be guilty of such blame?
No more can I be severed from your side
Than can yourself your self in twain divide.
Stay, go, do what you will: the like do I,   50
For live I will not if my father die.
TALBOT
Then here I take my leave of thee, fair son,
Born to eclipse thy life this afternoon.
Come, side by side together live and die,
And soul with soul from France to heaven fly.   55
                                        Exeunt

4.6 *Alarum. Excursions, wherein Lord Talbot's son John*
        is hemmed about by French soldiers and Talbot
        rescues him. ⌈*The English drive off the French*⌉
TALBOT
Saint George and victory! Fight, soldiers, fight!
The Regent hath with Talbot broke his word,
And left us to the rage of France his sword.
Where is John Talbot? (*To John*) Pause and take thy
     breath.
I gave thee life, and rescued thee from death.   5
JOHN
O twice my father, twice am I thy son:
The life thou gav'st me first was lost and done
Till with thy warlike sword, despite of fate,
To my determined time thou gav'st new date.
TALBOT
When from the Dauphin's crest thy sword struck fire
It warmed thy father's heart with proud desire   11
Of bold-faced victory. Then leaden age,
Quickened with youthful spleen and warlike rage,
Beat down Alençon, Orléans, Burgundy,

And from the pride of Gallia rescued thee.   15
The ireful Bastard Orléans, that drew blood
From thee, my boy, and had the maidenhood
Of thy first fight, I soon encounterèd,
And interchanging blows, I quickly shed
Some of his bastard blood, and in disgrace   20
Bespoke him thus: 'Contaminated, base,
And misbegotten blood I spill of thine,
Mean and right poor, for that pure blood of mine
Which thou didst force from Talbot, my brave boy.'
Here, purposing the Bastard to destroy,   25
Came in strong rescue. Speak thy father's care:
Art thou not weary, John? How dost thou fare?
Wilt thou yet leave the battle, boy, and fly,
Now thou art sealed the son of chivalry?
Fly to revenge my death when I am dead;   30
The help of one stands me in little stead.
O, too much folly is it, well I wot,
To hazard all our lives in one small boat.
If I today die not with Frenchmen's rage,
Tomorrow I shall die with mickle age.   35
By me they nothing gain, and if I stay
'Tis but the short'ning of my life one day.
In thee thy mother dies, our household's name,
My death's revenge, thy youth, and England's fame.
All these and more we hazard by thy stay;   40
All these are saved if thou wilt fly away.
JOHN
The sword of Orléans hath not made me smart;
These words of yours draw life-blood from my heart.
On that advantage, bought with such a shame,
To save a paltry life and slay bright fame,   45
Before young Talbot from old Talbot fly
The coward horse that bears me fall and die;
And like me to the peasant boys of France,
To be shame's scorn and subject of mischance!
Surely, by all the glory you have won,   50
An if I fly I am not Talbot's son.
Then talk no more of flight; it is no boot.
If son to Talbot, die at Talbot's foot.
TALBOT
Then follow thou thy desp'rate sire of Crete,
Thou Icarus; thy life to me is sweet.   55
If thou wilt fight, fight by thy father's side,
And commendable proved, let's die in pride.   *Exeunt*

4.7 *Alarum. Excursions. Enter old Lord Talbot led by*
        a Servant
TALBOT
Where is my other life? Mine own is gone.
O where's young Talbot, where is valiant John?
Triumphant death smeared with captivity,
Young Talbot's valour makes me smile at thee.
When he perceived me shrink and on my knee,   5
His bloody sword he brandished over me,
And like a hungry lion did commence
Rough deeds of rage and stern impatience.
But when my angry guardant stood alone,

Tend'ring my ruin and assailed of none,   10
Dizzy-eyed fury and great rage of heart
Suddenly made him from my side to start
Into the clust'ring battle of the French,
And in that sea of blood my boy did drench
His over-mounting spirit; and there died   15
My Icarus, my blossom, in his pride.
Enter English soldiers with John Talbot's body,
borne
SERVANT
O my dear lord, lo where your son is borne.
TALBOT
Thou antic death, which laugh'st us here to scorn,
Anon from thy insulting tyranny,
Coupled in bonds of perpetuity,   20
Two Talbots wingèd through the lither sky
In thy despite shall scape mortality.
(*To John*) O thou whose wounds become hard-favoured
death,
Speak to thy father ere thou yield thy breath.
Brave death by speaking, whether he will or no;   25
Imagine him a Frenchman and thy foe.—
Poor boy, he smiles, methinks, as who should say
'Had death been French, then death had died today'.
Come, come, and lay him in his father's arms.
Soldiers lay John in Talbot's arms
My spirit can no longer bear these harms.   30
Soldiers, adieu. I have what I would have,
Now my old arms are young John Talbot's grave.
He dies. ⌈*Alarum.*⌉ *Exeunt soldiers leaving the*
bodies
Enter Charles the Dauphin, the dukes of Alençon
and Burgundy, the Bastard of Orléans, and Joan la
Pucelle
CHARLES
Had York and Somerset brought rescue in,
We should have found a bloody day of this.
BASTARD
How the young whelp of Talbot's, raging wood,   35
Did flesh his puny sword in Frenchmen's blood!
JOAN
Once I encountered him, and thus I said:
'Thou maiden youth, be vanquished by a maid.'
But with a proud, majestical high scorn
He answered thus: 'Young Talbot was not born   40
To be the pillage of a giglot wench.'
So rushing in the bowels of the French,
He left me proudly, as unworthy fight.
BURGUNDY
Doubtless he would have made a noble knight.
See where he lies inhearsèd in the arms   45
Of the most bloody nurser of his harms.
BASTARD
Hew them to pieces, hack their bones asunder,
Whose life was England's glory, Gallia's wonder.
CHARLES
O no, forbear; for that which we have fled
During the life, let us not wrong it dead.   50

Enter Sir William Lucy ⌈*with a French herald*⌉
LUCY
Herald, conduct me to the Dauphin's tent
To know who hath obtained the glory of the day.
CHARLES
On what submissive message art thou sent?
LUCY
Submission, Dauphin? 'Tis a mere French word.
We English warriors wot not what it means.   55
I come to know what prisoners thou hast ta'en,
And to survey the bodies of the dead.
CHARLES
For prisoners ask'st thou? Hell our prison is.
But tell me whom thou seek'st.
LUCY
But where's the great Alcides of the field,   60
Valiant Lord Talbot, Earl of Shrewsbury,
Created for his rare success in arms
Great Earl of Wexford, Waterford, and Valence,
Lord Talbot of Goodrich and Urchinfield,
Lord Strange of Blackmere, Lord Verdun of Alton,   65
Lord Cromwell of Wingfield, Lord Furnival of Sheffield,
The thrice victorious lord of Falconbridge,
Knight of the noble order of Saint George,
Worthy Saint Michael and the Golden Fleece,
Great *Maréchal* to Henry the Sixth   70
Of all his wars within the realm of France?
JOAN
Here's a silly, stately style indeed.
The Turk, that two-and-fifty kingdoms hath,
Writes not so tedious a style as this.
Him that thou magnifi'st with all these titles   75
Stinking and flyblown lies here at our feet.
LUCY
Is Talbot slain, the Frenchmen's only scourge,
Your kingdom's terror and black Nemesis?
O, were mine eye-balls into bullets turned,
That I in rage might shoot them at your faces!   80
O, that I could but call these dead to life!—
It were enough to fright the realm of France.
Were but his picture left amongst you here
It would amaze the proudest of you all.
Give me their bodies, that I may bear them hence   85
And give them burial as beseems their worth.
JOAN (*to Charles*)
I think this upstart is old Talbot's ghost,
He speaks with such a proud commanding spirit.
For God's sake let him have them. To keep them here
They would but stink and putrefy the air.   90
CHARLES Go, take their bodies hence.
LUCY
I'll bear them hence, but from their ashes shall be
reared
A phoenix that shall make all France afeard.
CHARLES
So we be rid of them, do with them what thou wilt.
⌈*Exeunt Lucy and herald with the bodies*⌉
And now to Paris in this conquering vein.   95
All will be ours, now bloody Talbot's slain.   *Exeunt*

5.1   *Sennet. Enter King Henry, the Dukes of Gloucester*
      and Exeter, ⌈and others⌉

KING HENRY (*to Gloucester*)
  Have you perused the letters from the Pope,
  The Emperor, and the Earl of Armagnac?
GLOUCESTER
  I have, my lord, and their intent is this:
  They humbly sue unto your excellence
  To have a godly peace concluded of   5
  Between the realms of England and of France.
KING HENRY
  How doth your grace affect their motion?
GLOUCESTER
  Well, my good lord, and as the only means
  To stop effusion of our Christian blood
  And 'stablish quietness on every side.   10
KING HENRY
  Ay, marry, uncle; for I always thought
  It was both impious and unnatural
  That such immanity and bloody strife
  Should reign among professors of one faith.
GLOUCESTER
  Beside, my lord, the sooner to effect   15
  And surer bind this knot of amity,
  The Earl of Armagnac, near knit to Charles—
  A man of great authority in France—
  Proffers his only daughter to your grace
  In marriage, with a large and sumptuous dowry. 20
KING HENRY
  Marriage, uncle? Alas, my years are young,
  And fitter is my study and my books
  Than wanton dalliance with a paramour.
  Yet call th'ambassadors,   ⌈*Exit one or more*⌉
                          and as you please,
  So let them have their answers every one.   25
  I shall be well content with any choice
  Tends to God's glory and my country's weal.
      Enter the Bishop of Winchester, now in cardinal's
      habit, and three ambassadors, one a Papal Legate
EXETER (*aside*)
  What, is my lord of Winchester installed
  And called unto a cardinal's degree?
  Then I perceive that will be verified   30
  Henry the Fifth did sometime prophesy:
  'If once he come to be a cardinal,
  He'll make his cap co-equal with the crown.'
KING HENRY
  My lords ambassadors, your several suits
  Have been considered and debated on.   35
  Your purpose is both good and reasonable,
  And therefore are we certainly resolved
  To draw conditions of a friendly peace,
  Which by my lord of Winchester we mean
  Shall be transported presently to France.   40
GLOUCESTER ⌈*to ambassadors*⌉
  And for the proffer of my lord your master,
  I have informed his highness so at large
  As, liking of the lady's virtuous gifts,

  Her beauty, and the value of her dower,
  He doth intend she shall be England's queen.   45
KING HENRY ⌈*to ambassadors*⌉
  In argument and proof of which contract
  Bear her this jewel, pledge of my affection.
  (*To Gloucester*) And so, my lord Protector, see them
                          guarded
  And safely brought to Dover, wherein shipped,
  Commit them to the fortune of the sea.   50
      Exeunt ⌈severally⌉ all but Winchester and
                                        ⌈*Legate*⌉
WINCHESTER
  Stay, my lord legate; you shall first receive
  The sum of money which I promisèd
  Should be delivered to his holiness
  For clothing me in these grave ornaments.   54
LEGATE
  I will attend upon your lordship's leisure. ⌈*Exit*⌉
WINCHESTER
  Now Winchester will not submit, I trow,
  Or be inferior to the proudest peer.
  Humphrey of Gloucester, thou shalt well perceive
  That nor in birth or for authority
  The Bishop will be overborne by thee.   60
  I'll either make thee stoop and bend thy knee,
  Or sack this country with a mutiny.   ⌈*Exit*⌉

5.2   *Enter Charles the Dauphin ⌈reading a letter⌉, the*
      Dukes of Burgundy and Alençon, the Bastard of
      Orléans, René Duke of Anjou, and Joan la Pucelle
CHARLES
  These news, my lords, may cheer our drooping spirits.
  'Tis said the stout Parisians do revolt
  And turn again unto the warlike French.
ALENÇON
  Then march to Paris, royal Charles of France,
  And keep not back your powers in dalliance.   5
JOAN
  Peace be amongst them if they turn to us;
  Else, ruin combat with their palaces!
      Enter a Scout
SCOUT
  Success unto our valiant general,
  And happiness to his accomplices.
CHARLES
  What tidings send our scouts? I prithee speak. 10
SCOUT
  The English army, that divided was
  Into two parties, is now conjoined in one,
  And means to give you battle presently.
CHARLES
  Somewhat too sudden, sirs, the warning is;
  But we will presently provide for them.   15
BURGUNDY
  I trust the ghost of Talbot is not there.
⌈JOAN⌉
  Now he is gone, my lord, you need not fear.
  Of all base passions, fear is most accursed.

Command the conquest, Charles, it shall be thine;
Let Henry fret and all the world repine.   20
CHARLES
Then on, my lords; and France be fortunate!   Exeunt

5.3   *Alarum. Excursions. Enter Joan la Pucelle*
JOAN
The Regent conquers, and the Frenchmen fly.
Now help, ye charming spells and periapts,
And ye choice spirits that admonish me
And give me signs of future accidents.
    Thunder
You speedy helpers, that are substitutes   5
Under the lordly monarch of the north,
Appear, and aid me in this enterprise.
    Enter Fiends
This speed and quick appearance argues proof
Of your accustomed diligence to me.
Now, ye familiar spirits that are culled   10
Out of the powerful regions under earth,
Help me this once, that France may get the field.
    They walk and speak not
O, hold me not with silence overlong!
Where I was wont to feed you with my blood,
I'll lop a member off and give it you   15
In earnest of a further benefit,
So you do condescend to help me now.
    They hang their heads
No hope to have redress? My body shall
Pay recompense if you will grant my suit.
    They shake their heads
Cannot my body nor blood-sacrifice   20
Entreat you to your wonted furtherance?
Then take my soul—my body, soul, and all—
Before that England give the French the foil.
    They depart
See, they forsake me. Now the time is come
That France must vail her lofty-plumèd crest   25
And let her head fall into England's lap.
My ancient incantations are too weak,
And hell too strong for me to buckle with.
Now, France, thy glory droopeth to the dust.   Exit

5.4   *Excursions. The Dukes of Burgundy and York fight*
       hand to hand. The French fly. Joan la Pucelle is
       taken
RICHARD DUKE OF YORK
Damsel of France, I think I have you fast.
Unchain your spirits now with spelling charms,
And try if they can gain your liberty.
A goodly prize, fit for the devil's grace!
⌜*To his soldiers*⌝ See how the ugly witch doth bend her
    brows,   5
As if with Circe she would change my shape.
JOAN
Changed to a worser shape thou canst not be.
RICHARD DUKE OF YORK
O, Charles the Dauphin is a proper man.
No shape but his can please your dainty eye.

JOAN
A plaguing mischief light on Charles and thee,   10
And may ye both be suddenly surprised
By bloody hands in sleeping on your beds!
RICHARD DUKE OF YORK
Fell banning hag, enchantress, hold thy tongue.
JOAN
I prithee give me leave to curse awhile.
RICHARD DUKE OF YORK
Curse, miscreant, when thou comest to the stake.   15
                                                   Exeunt

5.5   *Alarum. Enter the Earl of Suffolk with Margaret*
       in his hand
SUFFOLK
Be what thou wilt, thou art my prisoner.
    He gazes on her
O fairest beauty, do not fear nor fly,
For I will touch thee but with reverent hands,
And lay them gently on thy tender side.
I kiss these fingers for eternal peace.   5
Who art thou? Say, that I may honour thee.
MARGARET
Margaret my name, and daughter to a king,
The King of Naples, whosoe'er thou art.
SUFFOLK
An earl I am, and Suffolk am I called.
Be not offended, nature's miracle,   10
Thou art allotted to be ta'en by me.
So doth the swan his downy cygnets save,
Keeping them prisoner underneath his wings.
Yet if this servile usage once offend,
Go, and be free again, as Suffolk's friend.   15
    She is going
O stay! (*Aside*) I have no power to let her pass.
My hand would free her, but my heart says no.
As plays the sun upon the glassy stream,
Twinkling another-counterfeited beam,
So seems this gorgeous beauty to mine eyes.   20
Fain would I woo her, yet I dare not speak.
I'll call for pen and ink, and write my mind.
Fie, de la Pole, disable not thyself!
Hast not a tongue? Is she not here to hear?
Wilt thou be daunted at a woman's sight?   25
Ay, beauty's princely majesty is such
Confounds the tongue, and makes the senses rough.
MARGARET
Say, Earl of Suffolk—if thy name be so—
What ransom must I pay before I pass?
For I perceive I am thy prisoner.   30
SUFFOLK (*aside*)
How canst thou tell she will deny thy suit
Before thou make a trial of her love?
MARGARET
Why speak'st thou not? What ransom must I pay?
SUFFOLK (*aside*)
She's beautiful, and therefore to be wooed;
She is a woman, therefore to be won.   35

MARGARET
Wilt thou accept of ransom, yea or no?
SUFFOLK (aside)
Fond man, remember that thou hast a wife;
Then how can Margaret be thy paramour?
MARGARET (aside)
I were best to leave him, for he will not hear.
SUFFOLK (aside)
There all is marred; there lies a cooling card.   40
MARGARET (aside)
He talks at random; sure the man is mad.
SUFFOLK (aside)
And yet a dispensation may be had.
MARGARET
And yet I would that you would answer me.
SUFFOLK (aside)
I'll win this Lady Margaret. For whom?
Why, for my king—tush, that's a wooden thing.   45
MARGARET (aside)
He talks of wood. It is some carpenter.
SUFFOLK (aside)
Yet so my fancy may be satisfied,
And peace establishèd between these realms.
But there remains a scruple in that too,
For though her father be the King of Naples,   50
Duke of Anjou and Maine, yet is he poor,
And our nobility will scorn the match.
MARGARET
Hear ye, captain? Are you not at leisure?
SUFFOLK (aside)
It shall be so, disdain they ne'er so much.
Henry is youthful, and will quickly yield.   55
(To Margaret) Madam, I have a secret to reveal.
MARGARET (aside)
What though I be enthralled, he seems a knight
And will not any way dishonour me.
SUFFOLK
Lady, vouchsafe to listen what I say.
MARGARET (aside)
Perhaps I shall be rescued by the French,   60
And then I need not crave his courtesy.
SUFFOLK
Sweet madam, give me hearing in a cause.
MARGARET (aside)
Tush, women have been captivate ere now.
SUFFOLK Lady, wherefore talk you so?
MARGARET
I cry you mercy, 'tis but *quid* for *quo*.   65
SUFFOLK
Say, gentle Princess, would you not suppose
Your bondage happy to be made a queen?
MARGARET
To be a queen in bondage is more vile
Than is a slave in base servility,
For princes should be free.
SUFFOLK   And so shall you,   70
If happy England's royal king be free.
MARGARET
Why, what concerns his freedom unto me?

SUFFOLK
I'll undertake to make thee Henry's queen,
To put a golden sceptre in thy hand,
And set a precious crown upon thy head,   75
If thou wilt condescend to be my—
MARGARET   What?
SUFFOLK His love.
MARGARET
I am unworthy to be Henry's wife.
SUFFOLK
No, gentle madam, I unworthy am
To woo so fair a dame to be his wife   80
(Aside) And have no portion in the choice myself.—
How say you, madam; are ye so content?
MARGARET
An if my father please, I am content.
SUFFOLK
Then call our captains and our colours forth,
⌈Enter captains, colours, and trumpeters⌉
And, madam, at your father's castle walls   85
We'll crave a parley to confer with him.
Sound a parley. Enter René Duke of Anjou on the
walls
See, René, see thy daughter prisoner.
RENÉ
To whom?
SUFFOLK   To me.
RENÉ   Suffolk, what remedy?
I am a soldier, and unapt to weep
Or to exclaim on fortune's fickleness.   90
SUFFOLK
Yes, there is remedy enough, my lord.
Assent, and for thy honour give consent
Thy daughter shall be wedded to my king,
Whom I with pain have wooed and won thereto;
And this her easy-held imprisonment   95
Hath gained thy daughter princely liberty.
RENÉ
Speaks Suffolk as he thinks?
SUFFOLK   Fair Margaret knows
That Suffolk doth not flatter, face or feign.
RENÉ
Upon thy princely warrant I descend
To give thee answer of thy just demand.   100
SUFFOLK
And here I will expect thy coming.   ⌈Exit René above⌉
Trumpets sound. Enter René
RENÉ
Welcome, brave Earl, into our territories.
Command in Anjou what your honour pleases.
SUFFOLK
Thanks, René, happy for so sweet a child,
Fit to be made companion with a king.   105
What answer makes your grace unto my suit?
RENÉ
Since thou dost deign to woo her little worth
To be the princely bride of such a lord,
Upon condition I may quietly

Enjoy mine own, the countries Maine and Anjou,   110
Free from oppression or the stroke of war,
My daughter shall be Henry's, if he please.

SUFFOLK
That is her ransom. I deliver her,
And those two counties I will undertake
Your grace shall well and quietly enjoy.   115

RENÉ
And I again in Henry's royal name,
As deputy unto that gracious king,
Give thee her hand for sign of plighted faith.

SUFFOLK
René of France, I give thee kingly thanks,
Because this is in traffic of a king.   120
(*Aside*) And yet methinks I could be well content
To be mine own attorney in this case.
(*To René*) I'll over then to England with this news,
And make this marriage to be solemnized.
So farewell, René; set this diamond safe   125
In golden palaces, as it becomes.

RENÉ
I do embrace thee as I would embrace
The Christian prince King Henry, were he here.

MARGARET (*to Suffolk*)
Farewell, my lord. Good wishes, praise, and prayers
Shall Suffolk ever have of Margaret.   130
     She is going

SUFFOLK
Farewell, sweet madam; but hark you, Margaret—
No princely commendations to my king?

MARGARET
Such commendations as becomes a maid,
A virgin, and his servant, say to him.

SUFFOLK
Words sweetly placed, and modestly directed.   135
     ⌐*She is going*⌐
But madam, I must trouble you again—
No loving token to his majesty?

MARGARET
Yes, my good lord: a pure unspotted heart,
Never yet taint with love, I send the King.

SUFFOLK And this withal.   140
     He kisses her

MARGARET
That for thyself; I will not so presume
To send such peevish tokens to a king.
     ⌐*Exeunt René and Margaret*⌐

SUFFOLK ⌐*aside*⌐
O, wert thou for myself!—but Suffolk, stay.
Thou mayst not wander in that labyrinth.
There Minotaurs and ugly treasons lurk.   145
Solicit Henry with her wondrous praise.
Bethink thee on her virtues that surmount,
Mad natural graces that extinguish art.
Repeat their semblance often on the seas,
That when thou com'st to kneel at Henry's feet   150
Thou mayst bereave him of his wits with wonder.
     ⌐*Exeunt*⌐

5.6   *Enter Richard Duke of York, the Earl of Warwick,*
     and a Shepherd

RICHARD DUKE OF YORK
Bring forth that sorceress condemned to burn.
     ⌐*Enter Joan la Pucelle guarded*⌐

SHEPHERD
Ah, Joan, this kills thy father's heart outright.
Have I sought every country far and near,
And now it is my chance to find thee out
Must I behold thy timeless cruel death?   5
Ah Joan, sweet daughter Joan, I'll die with thee.

JOAN
Decrepit miser, base ignoble wretch,
I am descended of a gentler blood.
Thou art no father nor no friend of mine.

SHEPHERD
Out, out!—My lords, an't please you, 'tis not so.   10
I did beget her, all the parish knows.
Her mother liveth yet, can testify
She was the first fruit of my bach'lorship.

WARWICK (*to Joan*)
Graceless, wilt thou deny thy parentage?

RICHARD DUKE OF YORK
This argues what her kind of life hath been—   15
Wicked and vile; and so her death concludes.

SHEPHERD
Fie, Joan, that thou wilt be so obstacle.
God knows thou art a collop of my flesh,
And for thy sake have I shed many a tear.
Deny me not, I prithee, gentle Joan.   20

JOAN
Peasant, avaunt! (*To the English*) You have suborned
     this man
Of purpose to obscure my noble birth.

SHEPHERD (*to the English*)
'Tis true I gave a noble to the priest
The morn that I was wedded to her mother.
(*To Joan*) Kneel down, and take my blessing, good my
     girl.   25
Wilt thou not stoop? Now cursèd be the time
Of thy nativity. I would the milk
Thy mother gave thee when thou sucked'st her breast
Had been a little ratsbane for thy sake.
Or else, when thou didst keep my lambs afield,   30
I wish some ravenous wolf had eaten thee.
Dost thou deny thy father, cursèd drab?
(*To the English*) O burn her, burn her! Hanging is too
     good.   *Exit*

RICHARD DUKE OF YORK (*to guards*)
Take her away, for she hath lived too long,
To fill the world with vicious qualities.   35

JOAN
First let me tell you whom you have condemned:
Not one begotten of a shepherd swain,
But issued from the progeny of kings;
Virtuous and holy, chosen from above
By inspiration of celestial grace   40
To work exceeding miracles on earth.

I never had to do with wicked spirits;
But you that are polluted with your lusts,
Stained with the guiltless blood of innocents,
Corrupt and tainted with a thousand vices—   45
Because you want the grace that others have,
You judge it straight a thing impossible
To compass wonders but by help of devils.
No, misconceivèd Joan of Arc hath been
A virgin from her tender infancy,   50
Chaste and immaculate in very thought,
Whose maiden-blood thus rigorously effused
Will cry for vengeance at the gates of heaven.

RICHARD DUKE OF YORK
Ay, ay, (to guards) away with her to execution.

WARWICK (to guards)
And hark ye, sirs: because she is a maid,   55
Spare for no faggots. Let there be enough.
Place barrels of pitch upon the fatal stake,
That so her torture may be shortenèd.

JOAN
Will nothing turn your unrelenting hearts?
Then Joan, discover thine infirmity,   60
That warranteth by law to be thy privilege:
I am with child, ye bloody homicides.
Murder not then the fruit within my womb,
Although ye hale me to a violent death.

RICHARD DUKE OF YORK
Now heaven forfend—the holy maid with child?   65

WARWICK (to Joan)
The greatest miracle that e'er ye wrought.
Is all your strict preciseness come to this?

RICHARD DUKE OF YORK
She and the Dauphin have been ingling.
I did imagine what would be her refuge.

WARWICK
Well, go to, we will have no bastards live,   70
Especially since Charles must father it.

JOAN
You are deceived. My child is none of his.
It was Alençon that enjoyed my love.

RICHARD DUKE OF YORK
Alençon, that notorious Machiavel?
It dies an if it had a thousand lives.   75

JOAN
O give me leave, I have deluded you.
'Twas neither Charles nor yet the Duke I named,
But René King of Naples that prevailed.

WARWICK
A married man?—That's most intolerable.

RICHARD DUKE OF YORK
Why, here's a girl; I think she knows not well—   80
There were so many—whom she may accuse.

WARWICK
It's sign she hath been liberal and free.

RICHARD DUKE OF YORK
And yet forsooth she is a virgin pure!
(To Joan) Strumpet, thy words condemn thy brat and
thee.
Use no entreaty, for it is in vain.   85

JOAN
Then lead me hence; with whom I leave my curse.
May never glorious sun reflex his beams
Upon the country where you make abode,
But darkness and the gloomy shade of death
Environ you till mischief and despair   90
Drive you to break your necks or hang yourselves.
Enter the Bishop of Winchester, now Cardinal

RICHARD DUKE OF YORK (to Joan)
Break thou in pieces, and consume to ashes,
Thou foul accursèd minister of hell.
⌈Exit Joan, guarded⌉

WINCHESTER
Lord Regent, I do greet your excellence
With letters of commission from the King.   95
For know, my lords, the states of Christendom,
Moved with remorse of these outrageous broils,
Have earnestly implored a general peace
Betwixt our nation and the aspiring French,
And here at hand the Dauphin and his train   100
Approacheth to confer about some matter.

RICHARD DUKE OF YORK
Is all our travail turned to this effect?
After the slaughter of so many peers,
So many captains, gentlemen, and soldiers
That in this quarrel have been overthrown   105
And sold their bodies for their country's benefit,
Shall we at last conclude effeminate peace?
Have we not lost most part of all the towns
By treason, falsehood, and by treachery,
Our great progenitors had conquerèd?   110
O Warwick, Warwick, I foresee with grief
The utter loss of all the realm of France!

WARWICK
Be patient, York. If we conclude a peace
It shall be with such strict and severe covenants
As little shall the Frenchmen gain thereby.   115
Enter Charles the Dauphin, the Duke of Alençon,
the Bastard of Orléans, and René Duke of Anjou

CHARLES
Since, lords of England, it is thus agreed
That peaceful truce shall be proclaimed in France,
We come to be informèd by yourselves
What the conditions of that league must be.

RICHARD DUKE OF YORK
Speak, Winchester; for boiling choler chokes   120
The hollow passage of my poisoned voice
By sight of these our baleful enemies.

WINCHESTER
Charles and the rest, it is enacted thus:
That, in regard King Henry gives consent,
Of mere compassion and of lenity,   125
To ease your country of distressful war
And suffer you to breathe in fruitful peace,
You shall become true liegemen to his crown.
And, Charles, upon condition thou wilt swear
To pay him tribute and submit thyself,   130
Thou shalt be placed as viceroy under him,
And still enjoy thy regal dignity.

ALENÇON
  Must he be then as shadow of himself?—
  Adorn his temples with a coronet,
  And yet in substance and authority   135
  Retain but privilege of a private man?
  This proffer is absurd and reasonless.
CHARLES
  'Tis known already that I am possessed
  With more than half the Gallian territories,
  And therein reverenced for their lawful king.   140
  Shall I, for lucre of the rest unvanquished,
  Detract so much from that prerogative
  As to be called but viceroy of the whole?
  No, lord ambassador, I'll rather keep
  That which I have than, coveting for more,   145
  Be cast from possibility of all.
RICHARD DUKE OF YORK
  Insulting Charles, hast thou by secret means
  Used intercession to obtain a league
  And, now the matter grows to compromise,
  Stand'st thou aloof upon comparison?   150
  Either accept the title thou usurp'st,
  Of benefit proceeding from our king
  And not of any challenge of desert,
  Or we will plague thee with incessant wars.
RENÉ (aside to Charles)
  My lord, you do not well in obstinacy   155
  To cavil in the course of this contract.
  If once it be neglected, ten to one
  We shall not find like opportunity.
ALENÇON (aside to Charles)
  To say the truth, it is your policy
  To save your subjects from such massacre   160
  And ruthless slaughters as are daily seen
  By our proceeding in hostility;
  And therefore take this compact of a truce,
  Although you break it when your pleasure serves. 164
WARWICK
  How sayst thou, Charles? Shall our condition stand?
CHARLES It shall,
  Only reserved you claim no interest
  In any of our towns of garrison.
RICHARD DUKE OF YORK
  Then swear allegiance to his majesty,
  As thou art knight, never to disobey   170
  Nor be rebellious to the crown of England,
  Thou nor thy nobles, to the crown of England.
  ⌈They swear⌉
  So, now dismiss your army when ye please.
  Hang up your ensigns, let your drums be still;   174
  For here we entertain a solemn peace.   Exeunt

5.7   Enter the Earl of Suffolk, in conference with King
      Henry, and the Dukes of Gloucester and Exeter
KING HENRY (to Suffolk)
  Your wondrous rare description, noble Earl,
  Of beauteous Margaret hath astonished me.
  Her virtues gracèd with external gifts

  Do breed love's settled passions in my heart,
  And like as rigour of tempestuous gusts   5
  Provokes the mightiest hulk against the tide,
  So am I driven by breath of her renown
  Either to suffer shipwreck or arrive
  Where I may have fruition of her love.
SUFFOLK
  Tush, my good lord, this superficial tale   10
  Is but a preface of her worthy praise.
  The chief perfections of that lovely dame,
  Had I sufficient skill to utter them,
  Would make a volume of enticing lines
  Able to ravish any dull conceit;   15
  And, which is more, she is not so divine,
  So full replete with choice of all delights,
  But with as humble lowliness of mind
  She is content to be at your command—
  Command, I mean, of virtuous chaste intents,   20
  To love and honour Henry as her lord.
KING HENRY
  And otherwise will Henry ne'er presume.
  (To Gloucester) Therefore, my lord Protector, give
    consent
  That Marg'ret may be England's royal queen.
GLOUCESTER
  So should I give consent to flatter sin.   25
  You know, my lord, your highness is betrothed
  Unto another lady of esteem.
  How shall we then dispense with that contract
  And not deface your honour with reproach?
SUFFOLK
  As doth a ruler with unlawful oaths,   30
  Or one that, at a triumph having vowed
  To try his strength, forsaketh yet the lists
  By reason of his adversary's odds.
  A poor earl's daughter is unequal odds,
  And therefore may be broke without offence.   35
GLOUCESTER
  Why, what, I pray, is Margaret more than that?
  Her father is no better than an earl,
  Although in glorious titles he excel.
SUFFOLK
  Yes, my lord; her father is a king,
  The King of Naples and Jerusalem,   40
  And of such great authority in France
  As his alliance will confirm our peace
  And keep the Frenchmen in allegiance.
GLOUCESTER
  And so the Earl of Armagnac may do,
  Because he is near kinsman unto Charles.   45
EXETER
  Beside, his wealth doth warrant a liberal dower,
  Where René sooner will receive than give.
SUFFOLK
  A dower, my lords? Disgrace not so your King
  That he should be so abject, base, and poor
  To choose for wealth and not for perfect love.   50
  Henry is able to enrich his queen,

And not to seek a queen to make him rich.
So worthless peasants bargain for their wives,
As market men for oxen, sheep, or horse.
Marriage is a matter of more worth   55
Than to be dealt in by attorneyship.
Not whom *we* will but whom his grace affects
Must be companion of his nuptial bed.
And therefore, lords, since he affects her most,
That most of all these reasons bindeth us: 60
In our opinions she should be preferred.
For what is wedlock forcèd but a hell,
An age of discord and continual strife,
Whereas the contrary bringeth bliss,
And is a pattern of celestial peace.   65
Whom should we match with Henry, being a king,
But Margaret, that is daughter to a king?
Her peerless feature joinèd with her birth
Approves her fit for none but for a king.
Her valiant courage and undaunted spirit,   70
More than in women commonly is seen,
Will answer our hope in issue of a king.
For Henry, son unto a conqueror,
Is likely to beget more conquerors
If with a lady of so high resolve   75
As is fair Margaret he be linked in love.
Then yield, my lords, and here conclude with me:
That Margaret shall be queen, and none but she.
KING HENRY
Whether it be through force of your report,
My noble lord of Suffolk, or for that   80
My tender youth was never yet attaint

With any passion of inflaming love,
I cannot tell; but this I am assured:
I feel such sharp dissension in my breast,
Such fierce alarums both of hope and fear,   85
As I am sick with working of my thoughts.
Take therefore shipping; post, my lord, to France;
Agree to any covenants, and procure
That Lady Margaret do vouchsafe to come
To cross the seas to England and be crowned   90
King Henry's faithful and anointed queen.
For your expenses and sufficient charge,
Among the people gather up a tenth.
Be gone, I say; for till you do return
I rest perplexèd with a thousand cares.   95
(*To Gloucester*) And you, good uncle, banish all offence.
If you do censure me by what you were,
Not what you are, I know it will excuse
This sudden execution of my will.
And so conduct me where from company   100
I may revolve and ruminate my grief.
                                   Exit ⌈*with Exeter*⌉
GLOUCESTER
Ay, grief, I fear me, both at first and last.   *Exit*
SUFFOLK
Thus Suffolk hath prevailed, and thus he goes
As did the youthful Paris once to Greece,
With hope to find the like event in love,   105
But prosper better than the Trojan did.
Margaret shall now be queen and rule the King;
But I will rule both her, the King, and realm.   *Exit*

RICHARD III

IN narrative sequence, *Richard III* follows directly after *Richard Duke of York*, and that play's closing scenes, in which Richard of Gloucester expresses his ambitions for the crown, suggest that Shakespeare had a sequel in mind. But he seems to have gone back to tell the beginning of the story of Henry VI's reign before covering the events from Henry VI's death (in 1471) to the Battle of Bosworth (1485). We have no record of the first performance of *Richard III* (probably in late 1592 or early 1593, outside London); it was printed in 1597, with five reprints before its inclusion in the 1623 Folio.

The principal source of information about Richard III available to Shakespeare was Sir Thomas More's *History of King Richard III* as incorporated in chronicle histories by Edward Hall (1542) and Raphael Holinshed (1577, revised in 1587), both of which Shakespeare seems to have used. His artistic influences include the tragedies of the Roman dramatist Seneca (who was born about 4 BC and died in AD 65), with their ghosts, their rhetorical style, their prominent choruses, and their indirect, highly formal presentation of violent events. (Except for the stabbing of Clarence (1.4) there is no on-stage violence in *Richard III* until the final battle scenes.)

In this play, Shakespeare demonstrates a more complete artistic control of his historical material than in its predecessors: Richard himself is a more dominating central figure than is to be found in any of the earlier plays, historical events are freely manipulated in the interests of an overriding design, and the play's language is more highly patterned and rhetorically unified. That part of the play which shows Richard's bloody progress to the throne is based on the events of some twelve years; the remainder covers the two years of his reign. Shakespeare omits some important events, but invents Richard's wooing of Lady Anne over her father-in-law's coffin, and causes Queen Margaret, who had returned to France in 1476 and who died before Richard became king, to remain in England as a choric figure of grief and retribution. The characterization of Richard as a self-delighting ironist builds upon More. The episodes in which the older women of the play—the Duchess of York, Queen Elizabeth, and Queen Margaret—bemoan their losses, and the climactic procession of ghosts before the final confrontation of Richard with the idealized figure of Richmond, the future Henry VII, help to make *Richard III* the culmination of a tetralogy as well as a masterly poetic drama in its own right. The final speech, in which Richmond, heir to the house of Lancaster and grandfather of Queen Elizabeth I, proclaims the union of 'the white rose and the red' in his marriage to Elizabeth of York, provides a patriotic climax which must have been immensely stirring to the play's early audiences.

Colley Cibber's adaptation (1700) of *Richard III*, incorporating the death of Henry VI, shortening and adapting the play, and making the central role (played by Cibber) even more dominant than it had originally been, held the stage with great success until the late nineteenth century. Since then, Shakespeare's text has been restored (though usually abbreviated—next to *Hamlet*, this is Shakespeare's longest play), and the role of Richard has continued to present a rewarding challenge to leading actors.

THE PERSONS OF THE PLAY

KING EDWARD IV

DUCHESS OF YORK, his mother

PRINCE EDWARD ⎫
Richard, the young Duke of YORK ⎭ his sons

George, Duke of CLARENCE ⎫
RICHARD, Duke of GLOUCESTER, later KING ⎭ his brothers
   RICHARD

Clarence's SON

Clarence's DAUGHTER

QUEEN ELIZABETH, King Edward's wife

Anthony Woodville, Earl RIVERS, her brother

Marquis of DORSET ⎫
Lord GRAY ⎭ her sons

Sir Thomas VAUGHAN

GHOST OF KING HENRY the Sixth

QUEEN MARGARET, his widow

GHOST OF PRINCE EDWARD, his son

LADY ANNE, Prince Edward's widow

William, LORD HASTINGS, Lord Chamberlain

Lord STANLEY, Earl of Derby, his friend

HENRY EARL OF RICHMOND, later KING HENRY VII, Stanley's
   son-in-law

Earl of OXFORD ⎫
Sir James BLUNT ⎬ Richmond's followers
Sir Walter HERBERT ⎭

Duke of BUCKINGHAM ⎫
Duke of NORFOLK ⎪
Sir Richard RATCLIFF ⎪
Sir William CATESBY ⎬ Richard Gloucester's follower
Sir James TIRREL ⎪
Two MURDERERS ⎪
A PAGE ⎭

CARDINAL

Bishop of ELY

John, a PRIEST

CHRISTOPHER, a Priest

Sir Robert BRACKENBURY, Lieutenant of the Tower of Londo

Lord MAYOR of London

A SCRIVENER

Hastings, a PURSUIVANT

SHERIFF

Aldermen and Citizens

Attendants, two bishops, messengers, soldiers

114

The Tragedy of King Richard the Third

1.1 *Enter Richard Duke of Gloucester*

RICHARD GLOUCESTER

Now is the winter of our discontent
Made glorious summer by this son of York;
And all the clouds that loured upon our house
In the deep bosom of the ocean buried.
Now are our brows bound with victorious wreaths, 5
Our bruisèd arms hung up for monuments,
Our stern alarums changed to merry meetings,
Our dreadful marches to delightful measures.
Grim-visaged war hath smoothed his wrinkled front,
And now—instead of mounting barbèd steeds 10
To fright the souls of fearful adversaries—
He capers nimbly in a lady's chamber
To the lascivious pleasing of a lute.
But I, that am not shaped for sportive tricks
Nor made to court an amorous looking-glass, 15
I that am rudely stamped and want love's majesty
To strut before a wanton ambling nymph,
I that am curtailed of this fair proportion,
Cheated of feature by dissembling nature,
Deformed, unfinished, sent before my time 20
Into this breathing world scarce half made up—
And that so lamely and unfashionable
That dogs bark at me as I halt by them—
Why, I in this weak piping time of peace
Have no delight to pass away the time, 25
Unless to spy my shadow in the sun
And descant on mine own deformity.
And therefore since I cannot prove a lover
To entertain these fair well-spoken days,
I am determinèd to prove a villain 30
And hate the idle pleasures of these days.
Plots have I laid, inductions dangerous,
By drunken prophecies, libels and dreams
To set my brother Clarence and the King
In deadly hate the one against the other. 35
And if King Edward be as true and just
As I am subtle false and treacherous,
This day should Clarence closely be mewed up
About a prophecy which says that 'G'
Of Edward's heirs the murderer shall be. 40

*Enter George Duke of Clarence, guarded, and Sir
Robert Brackenbury*

Dive, thoughts, down to my soul: here Clarence comes.
Brother, good day. What means this armèd guard
That waits upon your grace?

CLARENCE   His majesty,
Tend'ring my person's safety, hath appointed
This conduct to convey me to the Tower. 45

RICHARD GLOUCESTER

Upon what cause?

CLARENCE   Because my name is George.

RICHARD GLOUCESTER

Alack, my lord, that fault is none of yours.
He should for that commit your godfathers.
Belike his majesty hath some intent
That you should be new-christened in the Tower. 50
But what's the matter, Clarence? May I know?

CLARENCE

Yea, Richard, when I know—for I protest
As yet I do not. But as I can learn
He hearkens after prophecies and dreams,
And from the cross-row plucks the letter 'G' 55
And says a wizard told him that by 'G'
His issue disinherited should be.
And for my name of George begins with 'G',
It follows in his thought that I am he.
These, as I learn, and suchlike toys as these, 60
Hath moved his highness to commit me now.

RICHARD GLOUCESTER

Why, this it is when men are ruled by women.
'Tis not the King that sends you to the Tower;
My Lady Gray, his wife—Clarence, 'tis she
That tempts him to this harsh extremity. 65
Was it not she, and that good man of worship
Anthony Woodeville her brother there,
That made him send Lord Hastings to the Tower,
From whence this present day he is delivered?
We are not safe, Clarence; we are not safe. 70

CLARENCE

By heaven, I think there is no man secure
But the Queen's kindred, and night-walking heralds
That trudge betwixt the King and Mrs Shore.
Heard ye not what an humble suppliant
Lord Hastings was for his delivery? 75

RICHARD GLOUCESTER

Humbly complaining to her deity
Got my Lord Chamberlain his liberty.
I'll tell you what: I think it is our way,
If we will keep in favour with the King,
To be her men and wear her livery. 80
The jealous, o'erworn widow and herself,
Since that our brother dubbed them gentlewomen,
Are mighty gossips in our monarchy.

BRACKENBURY

I beseech your graces both to pardon me.
His majesty hath straitly given in charge 85
That no man shall have private conference,
Of what degree soever, with your brother.

RICHARD GLOUCESTER

Even so. An't please your worship, Brackenbury,
You may partake of anything we say.
We speak no treason, man. We say the King 90
Is wise and virtuous, and his noble Queen
Well struck in years, fair, and not jealous.

We say that Shore's wife hath a pretty foot,
A cherry lip,
A bonny eye, a passing pleasing tongue,   95
And that the Queen's kin are made gentlefolks.
How say you, sir? Can you deny all this?
BRACKENBURY
With this, my lord, myself have naught to do.
RICHARD GLOUCESTER
Naught to do with Mrs Shore? I tell thee, fellow:
He that doth naught with her—excepting one—   100
Were best to do it secretly alone.
BRACKENBURY What one, my lord?
RICHARD GLOUCESTER
Her husband, knave. Wouldst thou betray me?
BRACKENBURY
I beseech your grace to pardon me, and do withal
Forbear your conference with the noble Duke.   105
CLARENCE
We know thy charge, Brackenbury, and will obey.
RICHARD GLOUCESTER
We are the Queen's abjects, and must obey.
Brother, farewell. I will unto the King,
And whatsoe'er you will employ me in—
Were it to call King Edward's widow 'sister'—   110
I will perform it to enfranchise you.
Meantime, this deep disgrace in brotherhood
Touches me dearer than you can imagine.
CLARENCE
I know it pleaseth neither of us well.
RICHARD GLOUCESTER
Well, your imprisonment shall not be long.   115
I will deliver you or lie for you.
Meantime, have patience.
CLARENCE   I must perforce. Farewell.
    Exeunt Clarence, Brackenbury, and guard, to
                                          the Tower
RICHARD GLOUCESTER
Go tread the path that thou shalt ne'er return.
Simple plain Clarence, I do love thee so
That I will shortly send thy soul to heaven,   120
If heaven will take the present at our hands.
But who comes here? The new-delivered Hastings?
    Enter Lord Hastings from the Tower
LORD HASTINGS
Good time of day unto my gracious lord.
RICHARD GLOUCESTER
As much unto my good Lord Chamberlain.
Well are you welcome to the open air.   125
How hath your lordship brooked imprisonment?
LORD HASTINGS
With patience, noble lord, as prisoners must.
But I shall live, my lord, to give them thanks
That were the cause of my imprisonment.
RICHARD GLOUCESTER
No doubt, no doubt—and so shall Clarence too,   130
For they that were your enemies are his,
And have prevailed as much on him as you.

LORD HASTINGS
More pity that the eagles should be mewed
While kites and buzzards prey at liberty.
RICHARD GLOUCESTER What news abroad?   135
LORD HASTINGS
No news so bad abroad as this at home:
The King is sickly, weak, and melancholy,
And his physicians fear him mightily.
RICHARD GLOUCESTER
Now by Saint Paul, that news is bad indeed.
O he hath kept an evil diet long,   140
And overmuch consumed his royal person.
'Tis very grievous to be thought upon.
Where is he? In his bed?
LORD HASTINGS   He is.
RICHARD GLOUCESTER
Go you before and I will follow you.   *Exit Hastings*
He cannot live, I hope, and must not die   145
Till George be packed with post-haste up to heaven.
I'll in to urge his hatred more to Clarence,
With lies well steeled with weighty arguments.
And if I fail not in my deep intent,
Clarence hath not another day to live—   150
Which done, God take King Edward to his mercy
And leave the world for me to bustle in.
For then I'll marry Warwick's youngest daughter.
What though I killed her husband and her father?
The readiest way to make the wench amends   155
Is to become her husband and her father,
The which will I: not all so much for love,
As for another secret close intent,
By marrying her, which I must reach unto.
But yet I run before my horse to market.   160
Clarence still breathes, Edward still lives and reigns;
When they are gone, then must I count my gains.
                                                     Exit

1.2   *Enter gentlemen, bearing the corpse of King Henry*
        the Sixth in an open coffin, with halberdiers to
        guard it, Lady Anne being the mourner
LADY ANNE
Set down, set down your honourable load,
If honour may be shrouded in a hearse,
Whilst I a while obsequiously lament
Th'untimely fall of virtuous Lancaster.
    They set the coffin down
Poor key-cold figure of a holy king,   5
Pale ashes of the house of Lancaster,
Thou bloodless remnant of that royal blood:
Be it lawful that I invocate thy ghost
To hear the lamentations of poor Anne,
Wife to thy Edward, to thy slaughtered son,   10
Stabbed by the selfsame hand that made these wounds.
Lo, in these windows that let forth thy life,
I pour the helpless balm of my poor eyes.
O cursèd be the hand that made these holes,
Cursèd the blood that let this blood from hence,   15

Cursèd the heart that had the heart to do it.
More direful hap betide that hated wretch
That makes us wretched by the death of thee
Than I can wish to wolves, to spiders, toads,
Or any creeping venomed thing that lives.   20
If ever he have child, abortive be it,
Prodigious, and untimely brought to light,
Whose ugly and unnatural aspect
May fright the hopeful mother at the view,
And that be heir to his unhappiness.   25
If ever he have wife, let her be made
More miserable by the death of him
Than I am made by my young lord and thee.—
Come now towards Chertsey with your holy load,
Taken from Paul's to be interrèd there,   30
　　　⌈*The gentlemen lift the coffin*⌉
And still as you are weary of this weight
Rest you, whiles I lament King Henry's corpse.
　　Enter Richard Duke of Gloucester
RICHARD GLOUCESTER (*to the gentlemen*)
Stay, you that bear the corpse, and set it down.
LADY ANNE
What black magician conjures up this fiend
To stop devoted charitable deeds?   35
RICHARD GLOUCESTER (*to the gentlemen*)
Villains, set down the corpse, or by Saint Paul
I'll make a corpse of him that disobeys.
⌈HALBERDIER⌉
My lord, stand back and let the coffin pass.
RICHARD GLOUCESTER
Unmannered dog, stand thou when I command.
Advance thy halberd higher than my breast,   40
Or by Saint Paul I'll strike thee to my foot
And spurn upon thee, beggar, for thy boldness.
　　They set the coffin down
LADY ANNE (*to gentlemen and halberdiers*)
What, do you tremble? Are you all afraid?
Alas, I blame you not, for you are mortal,
And mortal eyes cannot endure the devil.—   45
Avaunt, thou dreadful minister of hell.
Thou hadst but power over his mortal body;
His soul thou canst not have; therefore be gone.
RICHARD GLOUCESTER
Sweet saint, for charity be not so cursed.
LADY ANNE
Foul devil, for God's sake hence and trouble us not, 50
For thou hast made the happy earth thy hell,
Filled it with cursing cries and deep exclaims.
If thou delight to view thy heinous deeds,
Behold this pattern of thy butcheries.—
O gentlemen, see, see! Dead Henry's wounds   55
Ope their congealèd mouths and bleed afresh.—
Blush, blush, thou lump of foul deformity,
For 'tis thy presence that ex-hales this blood
From cold and empty veins where no blood dwells.
Thy deed, inhuman and unnatural,   60
Provokes this deluge supernatural.
O God, which this blood mad'st, revenge his death.

O earth, which this blood drink'st, revenge his death.
Either heav'n with lightning strike the murd'rer dead,
Or earth gape open wide and eat him quick   65
As thou dost swallow up this good king's blood,
Which his hell-governed arm hath butcherèd.
RICHARD GLOUCESTER
Lady, you know no rules of charity,
Which renders good for bad, blessings for curses.
LADY ANNE
Villain, thou know'st no law of God nor man.   70
No beast so fierce but knows some touch of pity.
RICHARD GLOUCESTER
But I know none, and therefore am no beast.
LADY ANNE
O wonderful, when devils tell the truth!
RICHARD GLOUCESTER
More wonderful, when angels are so angry.
Vouchsafe, divine perfection of a woman,   75
Of these supposèd crimes to give me leave
By circumstance but to acquit myself.
LADY ANNE
Vouchsafe, diffused infection of a man,
Of these known evils but to give me leave
By circumstance t'accuse thy cursèd self.   80
RICHARD GLOUCESTER
Fairer than tongue can name thee, let me have
Some patient leisure to excuse myself.
LADY ANNE
Fouler than heart can think thee, thou canst make
No excuse current but to hang thyself.
RICHARD GLOUCESTER
By such despair I should accuse myself.   85
LADY ANNE
And by despairing shalt thou stand excused,
For doing worthy vengeance on thyself
That didst unworthy slaughter upon others.
RICHARD GLOUCESTER
Say that I slew them not.
LADY ANNE　　　　　　　　Then say they were not slain.
But dead they are—and, devilish slave, by thee.   90
RICHARD GLOUCESTER
I did not kill your husband.
LADY ANNE　　　　　　　　Why, then he is alive.
RICHARD GLOUCESTER
Nay, he is dead, and slain by Edward's hand.
LADY ANNE
In thy foul throat thou liest. Queen Margaret saw
Thy murd'rous falchion smoking in his blood,
The which thou once didst bend against her breast, 95
But that thy brothers beat aside the point.
RICHARD GLOUCESTER
I was provokèd by her sland'rous tongue,
That laid their guilt upon my guiltless shoulders.
LADY ANNE
Thou wast provokèd by thy bloody mind,
That never dream'st on aught but butcheries.   100
Didst thou not kill this king?
RICHARD GLOUCESTER　　　　　　I grant ye.

LADY ANNE
  Dost grant me, hedgehog? Then God grant me, too,
  Thou mayst be damnèd for that wicked deed.
  O he was gentle, mild, and virtuous.
RICHARD GLOUCESTER
  The better for the King of Heaven that hath him.   105
LADY ANNE
  He *is* in heaven, where thou shalt never come.
RICHARD GLOUCESTER
  Let him thank me that holp to send him thither,
  For he was fitter for that place than earth.
LADY ANNE
  And thou unfit for any place but hell.
RICHARD GLOUCESTER
  Yes, one place else, if you will hear me name it.   110
LADY ANNE
  Some dungeon.
RICHARD GLOUCESTER Your bedchamber.
LADY ANNE
  Ill rest betide the chamber where thou liest.
RICHARD GLOUCESTER
  So will it, madam, till I lie with you.
LADY ANNE
  I hope so.
RICHARD GLOUCESTER I know so. But gentle Lady Anne,
  To leave this keen encounter of our wits   115
  And fall something into a slower method,
  Is not the causer of the timeless deaths
  Of these Plantagenets, Henry and Edward,
  As blameful as the executioner?
LADY ANNE
  Thou wast the cause of that accursed effect.   120
RICHARD GLOUCESTER
  Your beauty was the cause of that effect—
  Your beauty that did haunt me in my sleep
  To undertake the death of all the world
  So I might live one hour in your sweet bosom.
LADY ANNE
  If I thought that, I tell thee, homicide,   125
  These nails should rend that beauty from my cheeks.
RICHARD GLOUCESTER
  These eyes could not endure sweet beauty's wreck.
  You should not blemish it if I stood by.
  As all the world is cheerèd by the sun,
  So I by that: it is my day, my life.   130
LADY ANNE
  Black night o'ershade thy day, and death thy life.
RICHARD GLOUCESTER
  Curse not thyself, fair creature: thou art both.
LADY ANNE
  I would I were, to be revenged on thee.
RICHARD GLOUCESTER
  It is a quarrel most unnatural,
  To be revenged on him that loveth you.   135
LADY ANNE
  It is a quarrel just and reasonable,
  To be revenged on him that killed my husband.

RICHARD GLOUCESTER
  He that bereft thee, lady, of thy husband,
  Did it to help thee to a better husband.
LADY ANNE
  His better doth not breathe upon the earth.   140
RICHARD GLOUCESTER
  He lives that loves thee better than he could.
LADY ANNE
  Name him.
RICHARD GLOUCESTER Plantagenet.
LADY ANNE   Why, that was he.
RICHARD GLOUCESTER
  The selfsame name, but one of better nature.
LADY ANNE
  Where is he?
RICHARD GLOUCESTER Here.
                    She spits at him
                                Why dost thou spit at me?
LADY ANNE
  Would it were mortal poison for thy sake.   145
RICHARD GLOUCESTER
  Never came poison from so sweet a place.
LADY ANNE
  Never hung poison on a fouler toad.
  Out of my sight! Thou dost infect mine eyes.
RICHARD GLOUCESTER
  Thine eyes, sweet lady, have infected mine.
LADY ANNE
  Would they were basilisks to strike thee dead.   150
RICHARD GLOUCESTER
  I would they were, that I might die at once,
  For now they kill me with a living death.
  Those eyes of thine from mine have drawn salt tears,
  Shamed their aspects with store of childish drops.
  I never sued to friend nor enemy;   155
  My tongue could never learn sweet smoothing word;
  But now thy beauty is proposed my fee,
  My proud heart sues and prompts my tongue to speak.
                    She looks scornfully at him
  Teach not thy lip such scorn, for it was made
  For kissing, lady, not for such contempt.   160
  If thy revengeful heart cannot forgive,
        ⌈*He kneels and offers her his sword*⌉
  Lo, here I lend thee this sharp-pointed sword,
  Which if thou please to hide in this true breast
  And let the soul forth that adoreth thee,
  I lay it naked to the deadly stroke   165
  And humbly beg the death upon my knee.
        He lays his breast open; she offers at it with his
        sword
  Nay, do not pause, for I did kill King Henry;
  But 'twas thy beauty that provokèd me.
  Nay, now dispatch: 'twas I that stabbed young
        Edward;
  But 'twas thy heavenly face that set me on.   170
        She drops the sword
  Take up the sword again, or take up me.

LADY ANNE
  Arise, dissembler.
                    ⌐He rises⌐
                          Though I wish thy death,
  I will not be thy executioner.
RICHARD GLOUCESTER
  Then bid me kill myself, and I will do it.
LADY ANNE
  I have already.
RICHARD GLOUCESTER That was in thy rage.   175
  Speak it again, and even with the word
  This hand—which for thy love did kill thy love—
  Shall, for thy love, kill a far truer love.
  To both their deaths shalt thou be accessary.
LADY ANNE I would I knew thy heart.   180
RICHARD GLOUCESTER 'Tis figured in my tongue.
LADY ANNE I fear me both are false.
RICHARD GLOUCESTER Then never man was true.
LADY ANNE Well, well, put up your sword.
RICHARD GLOUCESTER Say then my peace is made.   185
LADY ANNE That shalt thou know hereafter.
RICHARD GLOUCESTER But shall I live in hope?
LADY ANNE All men, I hope, live so.
RICHARD GLOUCESTER Vouchsafe to wear this ring.
LADY ANNE To take is not to give.   190
RICHARD GLOUCESTER
  Look how my ring encompasseth thy finger;
  Even so thy breast encloseth my poor heart.
  Wear both of them, for both of them are thine.
  And if thy poor devoted servant may
  But beg one favour at thy gracious hand,   195
  Thou dost confirm his happiness for ever.
LADY ANNE What is it?
RICHARD GLOUCESTER
  That it may please you leave these sad designs
  To him that hath most cause to be a mourner,
  And presently repair to Crosby House,   200
  Where—after I have solemnly interred
  At Chertsey monast'ry this noble king,
  And wet his grave with my repentant tears—
  I will with all expedient duty see you.
  For divers unknown reasons, I beseech you   205
  Grant me this boon.
LADY ANNE
  With all my heart—and much it joys me, too,
  To see you are become so penitent.
  Tressell and Berkeley, go along with me.
RICHARD GLOUCESTER
  Bid me farewell.
LADY ANNE   'Tis more than you deserve.   210
  But since you teach me how to flatter you,
  Imagine I have said farewell already.
                              Exeunt two with Anne
RICHARD GLOUCESTER
  Sirs, take up the corpse.
GENTLEMAN   Towards Chertsey, noble lord?
RICHARD GLOUCESTER
  No, to Blackfriars; there attend my coming.
                    Exeunt with corpse all but Gloucester

Was ever woman in this humour wooed?   215
Was ever woman in this humour won?
I'll have her, but I will not keep her long.
What, I that killed her husband and his father,
To take her in her heart's extremest hate,
With curses in her mouth, tears in her eyes,   220
The bleeding witness of my hatred by,
Having God, her conscience, and these bars against
     me,
And I no friends to back my suit withal
But the plain devil and dissembling looks—
And yet to win her, all the world to nothing? Ha! 225
Hath she forgot already that brave prince,
Edward her lord, whom I some three months since
Stabbed in my angry mood at Tewkesbury?
A sweeter and a lovelier gentleman,
Framed in the prodigality of nature,   230
Young, valiant, wise, and no doubt right royal,
The spacious world cannot again afford—
And will she yet abase her eyes on me,
That cropped the golden prime of this sweet prince
And made her widow to a woeful bed?   235
On me, whose all not equals Edward's moiety?
On me, that halts and am misshapen thus?
My dukedom to a beggarly *denier*,
I do mistake my person all this while.
Upon my life she finds, although I cannot,   240
Myself to be a marv'lous proper man.
I'll be at charges for a looking-glass
And entertain a score or two of tailors
To study fashions to adorn my body.
Since I am crept in favour with myself,   245
I will maintain it with some little cost.
But first I'll turn yon fellow in his grave,
And then return lamenting to my love.
Shine out, fair sun, till I have bought a glass,   249
That I may see my shadow as I pass.   *Exit*

1.3   *Enter Queen Elizabeth, Lord Rivers, ⌐Marquis*
         Dorset⌐, and Lord Gray
RIVERS (*to Elizabeth*)
  Have patience, madam. There's no doubt his majesty
  Will soon recover his accustomed health.
GRAY (*to Elizabeth*)
  In that you brook it ill, it makes him worse.
  Therefore, for God's sake entertain good comfort,
  And cheer his grace with quick and merry eyes.   5
QUEEN ELIZABETH
  If he were dead, what would betide on me?
⌐RIVERS⌐
  No other harm but loss of such a lord.
QUEEN ELIZABETH
  The loss of such a lord includes all harms.
GRAY
  The heavens have blessed you with a goodly son
  To be your comforter when he is gone.   10
QUEEN ELIZABETH
  Ah, he is young, and his minority

Is put unto the trust of Richard Gloucester,
A man that loves not me—nor none of you.

RIVERS
Is it concluded he shall be Protector?

QUEEN ELIZABETH
It is determined, not concluded yet;　　　　　　15
But so it must be, if the King miscarry.

Enter the Duke of Buckingham and Lord Stanley
Earl of Derby

GRAY
Here come the Lords of Buckingham and Derby.

BUCKINGHAM (*to Elizabeth*)
Good time of day unto your royal grace.

STANLEY (*to Elizabeth*)
God make your majesty joyful, as you have been.

QUEEN ELIZABETH
The Countess Richmond, good my lord of Derby,　　20
To your good prayer will scarcely say 'Amen'.
Yet, Derby—notwithstanding she's your wife,
And loves not me—be you, good lord, assured
I hate not you for her proud arrogance.

STANLEY
I do beseech you, either not believe　　　　　　25
The envious slanders of her false accusers
Or, if she be accused on true report,
Bear with her weakness, which I think proceeds
From wayward sickness, and no grounded malice.

⌈RIVERS⌉
Saw you the King today, my lord of Derby?　　　30

STANLEY
But now the Duke of Buckingham and I
Are come from visiting his majesty.

QUEEN ELIZABETH
With likelihood of his amendment, lords?

BUCKINGHAM
Madam, good hope: his grace speaks cheerfully.

QUEEN ELIZABETH
God grant him health. Did you confer with him?　　35

BUCKINGHAM
Ay, madam. He desires to make atonement
Between the Duke of Gloucester and your brothers,
And between them and my Lord Chamberlain,
And sent to warn them to his royal presence.

QUEEN ELIZABETH
Would all were well! But that will never be.　　　40
I fear our happiness is at the height.

Enter Richard Duke of Gloucester and Lord Hastings

RICHARD GLOUCESTER
They do me wrong, and I will not endure it.
Who are they that complain unto the King
That I forsooth am stern and love them not?
By holy Paul, they love his grace but lightly　　　45
That fill his ears with such dissentious rumours.
Because I cannot flatter and look fair,
Smile in men's faces, smooth, deceive, and cog,
Duck with French nods and apish courtesy,
I must be held a rancorous enemy.　　　　　　　50
Cannot a plain man live and think no harm,

But thus his simple truth must be abused
With silken, sly, insinuating jacks?

⌈RIVERS⌉
To whom in all this presence speaks your grace?

RICHARD GLOUCESTER
To thee, that hast nor honesty nor grace.　　　　55
When have I injured thee? When done thee wrong?
Or thee? Or thee? Or any of your faction?
A plague upon you all! His royal grace—
Whom God preserve better than you would wish—
Cannot be quiet scarce a breathing while　　　60
But you must trouble him with lewd complaints.

QUEEN ELIZABETH
Brother of Gloucester, you mistake the matter.
The King—on his own royal disposition,
And not provoked by any suitor else—
Aiming belike at your interior hatred,　　　　65
That in your outward action shows itself
Against my children, brothers, and myself,
Makes him to send, that he may learn the ground
Of your ill will, and thereby to remove it.

RICHARD GLOUCESTER
I cannot tell. The world is grown so bad　　　70
That wrens make prey where eagles dare not perch.
Since every jack became a gentleman,
There's many a gentle person made a jack.

QUEEN ELIZABETH
Come, come, we know your meaning, brother
Gloucester.
You envy my advancement, and my friends'.　　　75
God grant we never may have need of you.

RICHARD GLOUCESTER
Meantime, God grants that I have need of you.
Our brother is imprisoned by your means,
Myself disgraced, and the nobility
Held in contempt, while great promotions　　　80
Are daily given to ennoble those
That scarce some two days since were worth a noble.

QUEEN ELIZABETH
By him that raised me to this care-full height
From that contented hap which I enjoyed,
I never did incense his majesty　　　　　　85
Against the Duke of Clarence, but have been
An earnest advocate to plead for him.
My lord, you do me shameful injury
Falsely to draw me in these vile suspects.

RICHARD GLOUCESTER
You may deny that you were not the mean　　90
Of my Lord Hastings' late imprisonment.

RIVERS She may, my lord, for—

RICHARD GLOUCESTER
She may, Lord Rivers; why, who knows not so?
She may do more, sir, than denying that.
She may help you to many fair preferments,　　95
And then deny her aiding hand therein,
And lay those honours on your high desert.
What may she not? She may—ay, marry, may she.

RIVERS What 'marry, may she'?

RICHARD GLOUCESTER
What marry, may she? Marry with a king: 100
A bachelor, and a handsome stripling, too.
Iwis your grandam had a worser match.

QUEEN ELIZABETH
My lord of Gloucester, I have too long borne
Your blunt upbraidings and your bitter scoffs.
By heaven, I will acquaint his majesty 105
Of those gross taunts that oft I have endured.
I had rather be a country servant-maid
Than a great queen, with this condition:
To be so baited, scorned, and stormèd at.

Enter old Queen Margaret, unseen behind them
Small joy have I in being England's queen. 110

QUEEN MARGARET (*aside*)
And lessened be that small, God I beseech him.
Thy honour, state, and seat is due to me.

RICHARD GLOUCESTER (*to Elizabeth*)
What? Threat you me with telling of the King?
Tell him, and spare not. Look what I have said,
I will avouch't in presence of the King. 115
I dare adventure to be sent to th' Tower.
'Tis time to speak; my pains are quite forgot.

QUEEN MARGARET (*aside*)
Out, devil! I remember them too well.
Thou killed'st my husband Henry in the Tower,
And Edward, my poor son, at Tewkesbury. 120

RICHARD GLOUCESTER (*to Elizabeth*)
Ere you were queen—ay, or your husband king—
I was a packhorse in his great affairs,
A weeder-out of his proud adversaries,
A liberal rewarder of his friends.
To royalize his blood, I spent mine own. 125

QUEEN MARGARET (*aside*)
Ay, and much better blood than his or thine.

RICHARD GLOUCESTER (*to Elizabeth*)
In all which time you and your husband Gray
Were factious for the house of Lancaster;
And Rivers, so were you.—Was not your husband
In Margaret's battle at Saint Albans slain? 130
Let me put in your minds, if you forget,
What you have been ere this, and what you are;
Withal, what I have been, and what I am.

QUEEN MARGARET (*aside*)
A murd'rous villain, and so still thou art.

RICHARD GLOUCESTER
Poor Clarence did forsake his father Warwick— 135
Ay, and forswore himself, which Jesu pardon—

QUEEN MARGARET (*aside*) Which God revenge!

RICHARD GLOUCESTER
To fight on Edward's party for the crown,
And for his meed, poor lord, he is mewed up.
I would to God my heart were flint like Edward's, 140
Or Edward's soft and pitiful like mine.
I am too childish-foolish for this world.

QUEEN MARGARET (*aside*)
Hie thee to hell for shame, and leave this world,
Thou cacodemon; there thy kingdom is.

RIVERS
My lord of Gloucester, in those busy days 145
Which here you urge to prove us enemies,
We followed then our lord, our sovereign king.
So should we you, if you should be our king.

RICHARD GLOUCESTER
If I should be? I had rather be a pedlar.
Far be it from my heart, the thought thereof. 150

QUEEN ELIZABETH
As little joy, my lord, as you suppose
You should enjoy, were you this country's king,
As little joy may you suppose in me,
That I enjoy being the queen thereof.

QUEEN MARGARET (*aside*)
Ah, little joy enjoys the queen thereof, 155
For I am she, and altogether joyless.
I can no longer hold me patient.

She comes forward
Hear me, you wrangling pirates, that fall out
In sharing that which you have pilled from me.
Which of you trembles not that looks on me? 160
If not that I am Queen, you bow like subjects;
Yet that by you deposed, you quake like rebels.
(*To Richard*) Ah, gentle villain, do not turn away.

RICHARD GLOUCESTER
Foul wrinkled witch, what mak'st thou in my sight?

QUEEN MARGARET
But repetition of what thou hast marred: 165
That will I make before I let thee go.
A husband and a son thou ow'st to me,
(*To Elizabeth*) And thou a kingdom; (*to the rest*) all of
 you allegiance.
This sorrow that I have by right is yours,
And all the pleasures you usurp are mine. 170

RICHARD GLOUCESTER
The curse my noble father laid on thee—
When thou didst crown his warlike brows with paper,
And with thy scorns drew'st rivers from his eyes,
And then, to dry them, gav'st the duke a clout
Steeped in the faultless blood of pretty Rutland— 175
His curses then, from bitterness of soul
Denounced against thee, are all fall'n upon thee,
And God, not we, hath plagued thy bloody deed.

QUEEN ELIZABETH (*to Margaret*)
So just is God to right the innocent.

LORD HASTINGS (*to Margaret*)
O 'twas the foulest deed to slay that babe, 180
And the most merciless that e'er was heard of.

RIVERS (*to Margaret*)
Tyrants themselves wept when it was reported.

DORSET (*to Margaret*)
No man but prophesied revenge for it.

BUCKINGHAM (*to Margaret*)
Northumberland, then present, wept to see it.

QUEEN MARGARET
What? Were you snarling all before I came, 185
Ready to catch each other by the throat,
And turn you all your hatred now on me?

Did York's dread curse prevail so much with heaven
That Henry's death, my lovely Edward's death,
Their kingdom's loss, my woeful banishment,   190
Should all but answer for that peevish brat?
Can curses pierce the clouds and enter heaven?
Why then, give way, dull clouds, to my quick curses!
Though not by war, by surfeit die your king,
As ours by murder to make him a king.   195
(*To Elizabeth*) Edward thy son, that now is Prince of
  Wales,
For Edward my son, that was Prince of Wales,
Die in his youth by like untimely violence.
Thyself, a queen, for me that was a queen,
Outlive thy glory like my wretched self.   200
Long mayst thou live—to wail thy children's death,
And see another, as I see thee now,
Decked in thy rights, as thou art 'stalled in mine.
Long die thy happy days before thy death,
And after many lengthened hours of grief   205
Die, neither mother, wife, nor England's queen.—
Rivers and Dorset, you were standers-by,
And so wast thou, Lord Hastings, when my son
Was stabbed with bloody daggers. God I pray him,
That none of you may live his natural age,   210
But by some unlooked accident cut off.

RICHARD GLOUCESTER
Have done thy charm, thou hateful, withered hag.

QUEEN MARGARET
And leave out thee? Stay, dog, for thou shalt hear me.
If heaven have any grievous plague in store
Exceeding those that I can wish upon thee,   215
O let them keep it till thy sins be ripe,
And then hurl down their indignation
On thee, the troubler of the poor world's peace.
The worm of conscience still begnaw thy soul.
Thy friends suspect for traitors while thou liv'st,   220
And take deep traitors for thy dearest friends.
No sleep close up that deadly eye of thine,
Unless it be while some tormenting dream
Affrights thee with a hell of ugly devils.
Thou elvish-marked, abortive, rooting hog,   225
Thou that wast sealed in thy nativity
The slave of nature and the son of hell,
Thou slander of thy heavy mother's womb,
Thou loathèd issue of thy father's loins,
Thou rag of honour, thou detested—   230

RICHARD GLOUCESTER Margaret.

QUEEN MARGARET
  Richard.

RICHARD GLOUCESTER Ha?

QUEEN MARGARET   I call thee not.

RICHARD GLOUCESTER
I cry thee mercy then, for I did think
That thou hadst called me all these bitter names.

QUEEN MARGARET
Why so I did, but looked for no reply.   235
O let me make the period to my curse.

RICHARD GLOUCESTER
'Tis done by me, and ends in 'Margaret'.

QUEEN ELIZABETH (*to Margaret*)
Thus have you breathed your curse against yourself.

QUEEN MARGARET
Poor painted Queen, vain flourish of my fortune,
Why strew'st thou sugar on that bottled spider   240
Whose deadly web ensnareth thee about?
Fool, fool, thou whet'st a knife to kill thyself.
The day will come that thou shalt wish for me
To help thee curse this poisonous bunch-backed toad.

LORD HASTINGS
False-boding woman, end thy frantic curse,   245
Lest to thy harm thou move our patience.

QUEEN MARGARET
Foul shame upon you, you have all moved mine.

RIVERS
Were you well served, you would be taught your duty.

QUEEN MARGARET
To serve me well you all should do me duty.
Teach me to be your queen, and you my subjects: 250
O serve me well, and teach yourselves that duty.

DORSET
Dispute not with her: she is lunatic.

QUEEN MARGARET
Peace, master Marquis, you are malapert.
Your fire-new stamp of honour is scarce current.
O that your young nobility could judge   255
What 'twere to lose it and be miserable.
They that stand high have many blasts to shake them,
And if they fall they dash themselves to pieces.

RICHARD GLOUCESTER
Good counsel, marry!—Learn it, learn it, Marquis.

DORSET
It touches you, my lord, as much as me.   260

RICHARD GLOUCESTER
Ay, and much more; but I was born so high.
Our eyrie buildeth in the cedar's top,
And dallies with the wind, and scorns the sun.

QUEEN MARGARET
And turns the sun to shade. Alas, alas!
Witness my son, now in the shade of death,   265
Whose bright outshining beams thy cloudy wrath
Hath in eternal darkness folded up.
Your eyrie buildeth in our eyrie's nest.—
O God that seest it, do not suffer it;
As it was won with blood, lost be it so.   270

⌜RICHARD GLOUCESTER⌝
Peace, peace! For shame, if not for charity.

QUEEN MARGARET
Urge neither charity nor shame to me.
Uncharitably with me have you dealt,
And shamefully my hopes by you are butchered.
My charity is outrage; life, my shame;   275
And in that shame still live my sorrow's rage.

BUCKINGHAM Have done, have done.

QUEEN MARGARET
O princely Buckingham, I'll kiss thy hand

In sign of league and amity with thee.
Now fair befall thee and thy noble house!   280
Thy garments are not spotted with our blood,
Nor thou within the compass of my curse.

BUCKINGHAM
Nor no one here, for curses never pass
The lips of those that breathe them in the air.

QUEEN MARGARET
I will not think but they ascend the sky   285
And there awake God's gentle sleeping peace.
O Buckingham, take heed of yonder dog.
    She points at Richard
Look when he fawns, he bites; and when he bites,
His venom tooth will rankle to the death.
Have naught to do with him; beware of him;   290
Sin, death, and hell have set their marks on him,
And all their ministers attend on him.

RICHARD GLOUCESTER
What doth she say, my lord of Buckingham?

BUCKINGHAM
Nothing that I respect, my gracious lord.

QUEEN MARGARET
What, dost thou scorn me for my gentle counsel,   295
And soothe the devil that I warn thee from?
O but remember this another day,
When he shall split thy very heart with sorrow,
And say, 'Poor Margaret was a prophetess'.—
Live each of you the subjects to his hate,   300
And he to yours, and all of you to God's.   *Exit*

⌈HASTINGS⌉
My hair doth stand on end to hear her curses.

RIVERS
And so doth mine. I muse why she's at liberty.

RICHARD GLOUCESTER
I cannot blame her, by God's holy mother.
She hath had too much wrong, and I repent   305
My part thereof that I have done to her.

QUEEN ELIZABETH
I never did her any, to my knowledge.

RICHARD GLOUCESTER
Yet you have all the vantage of her wrong.
I was too hot to do somebody good,
That is too cold in thinking of it now.   310
Marry, as for Clarence, he is well repaid:
He is franked up to fatting for his pains.
God pardon them that are the cause thereof.

RIVERS
A virtuous and a Christian-like conclusion,
To pray for them that have done scathe to us.   315

RICHARD GLOUCESTER
So do I ever— (*speaks to himself*) being well advised:
For had I cursed now, I had cursed myself.
    Enter Sir William Catesby

CATESBY
Madam, his majesty doth call for you,
And for your grace, and you my gracious lords.

QUEEN ELIZABETH
Catesby, I come.—Lords, will you go with me?   320

RIVERS We wait upon your grace.
    Exeunt all but Richard

RICHARD GLOUCESTER
I do the wrong, and first begin to brawl.
The secret mischiefs that I set abroach
I lay unto the grievous charge of others.
Clarence, whom I indeed have cast in darkness,   325
I do beweep to many simple gulls—
Namely to Derby, Hastings, Buckingham—
And tell them, ''Tis the Queen and her allies
That stir the King against the Duke my brother'.
Now they believe it, and withal whet me   330
To be revenged on Rivers, Dorset, Gray;
But then I sigh, and with a piece of scripture
Tell them that God bids us do good for evil;
And thus I clothe my naked villainy
With odd old ends, stol'n forth of Holy Writ,   335
And seem a saint when most I play the devil.
    Enter two Murderers
But soft, here come my executioners.—
How now, my hardy, stout, resolvèd mates!
Are you now going to dispatch this thing?

A MURDERER
We are, my lord, and come to have the warrant,   340
That we may be admitted where he is.

RICHARD GLOUCESTER
Well thought upon; I have it here about me.
    He gives them the warrant
When you have done, repair to Crosby Place.
But sirs, be sudden in the execution,
Withal obdurate; do not hear him plead,   345
For Clarence is well spoken, and perhaps
May move your hearts to pity, if you mark him.

A MURDERER
Tut, tut, my lord, we will not stand to prate.
Talkers are no good doers. Be assured,
We go to use our hands, and not our tongues.   350

RICHARD GLOUCESTER
Your eyes drop millstones when fools' eyes fall tears.
I like you, lads. About your business straight.
Go, go, dispatch.

⌈MURDERERS⌉   We will, my noble lord.
    Exeunt Richard at one door, the Murderers at
                           another

1.4   *Enter George Duke of Clarence and ⌈Sir Robert*
        Brackenbury⌉

⌈BRACKENBURY⌉
Why looks your grace so heavily today?

CLARENCE
O I have passed a miserable night,
So full of fearful dreams, of ugly sights,
That as I am a Christian faithful man,
I would not spend another such a night   5
Though 'twere to buy a world of happy days,
So full of dismal terror was the time.

⌈BRACKENBURY⌉
What was your dream, my lord? I pray you, tell me.

CLARENCE

Methoughts that I had broken from the Tower,
And was embarked to cross to Burgundy,   10
And in my company my brother Gloucester,
Who from my cabin tempted me to walk
Upon the hatches; there we looked toward England,
And cited up a thousand heavy times
During the wars of York and Lancaster   15
That had befall'n us. As we paced along
Upon the giddy footing of the hatches,
Methought that Gloucester stumbled, and in falling
Struck me—that sought to stay him—overboard
Into the tumbling billows of the main.   20
O Lord! Methought what pain it was to drown,
What dreadful noise of waters in my ears,
What sights of ugly death within my eyes.
Methoughts I saw a thousand fearful wrecks,
Ten thousand men that fishes gnawed upon,   25
Wedges of gold, great ouches, heaps of pearl,
Inestimable stones, unvalued jewels,
All scattered in the bottom of the sea.
Some lay in dead men's skulls; and in those holes
Where eyes did once inhabit, there were crept—   30
As 'twere in scorn of eyes—reflecting gems,
Which wooed the slimy bottom of the deep
And mocked the dead bones that lay scattered by.

⌈BRACKENBURY⌉

Had you such leisure in the time of death,
To gaze upon these secrets of the deep?   35

CLARENCE

Methought I had, and often did I strive
To yield the ghost, but still the envious flood
Stopped-in my soul and would not let it forth
To find the empty, vast, and wand'ring air,
But smothered it within my panting bulk,   40
Who almost burst to belch it in the sea.

⌈BRACKENBURY⌉

Awaked you not in this sore agony?

CLARENCE

No, no, my dream was lengthened after life.
O then began the tempest to my soul!
I passed, methought, the melancholy flood,   45
With that sour ferryman which poets write of,
Unto the kingdom of perpetual night.
The first that there did greet my stranger soul
Was my great father-in-law, renownèd Warwick,
Who cried aloud, 'What scourge for perjury   50
Can this dark monarchy afford false Clarence?'
And so he vanished. Then came wand'ring by
A shadow like an angel, with bright hair,
Dabbled in blood, and he shrieked out aloud,
'Clarence is come: false, fleeting, perjured Clarence,   55
That stabbed me in the field by Tewkesbury.
Seize on him, furies! Take him unto torment!'
With that, methoughts a legion of foul fiends
Environed me, and howlèd in mine ears
Such hideous cries that with the very noise   60
I trembling waked, and for a season after

Could not believe but that I was in hell,
Such terrible impression made my dream.

⌈BRACKENBURY⌉

No marvel, lord, though it affrighted you;
I am afraid, methinks, to hear you tell it.   65

CLARENCE

Ah, Brackenbury, I have done these things,
That now give evidence against my soul,
For Edward's sake; and see how he requites me.
Keeper, I pray thee, sit by me awhile.
My soul is heavy, and I fain would sleep.   70

⌈BRACKENBURY⌉

I will, my lord. God give your grace good rest.

Clarence sleeps

Sorrow breaks seasons and reposing hours,
Makes the night morning and the noontide night.
Princes have but their titles for their glories,
An outward honour for an inward toil,   75
And for unfelt imaginations
They often feel a world of restless cares;
So that, between their titles and low name,
There's nothing differs but the outward fame.

Enter two Murderers

FIRST MURDERER Ho, who's here?   80

BRACKENBURY

What wouldst thou, fellow? And how cam'st thou
hither?

SECOND MURDERER I would speak with Clarence, and I
came hither on my legs.

BRACKENBURY What, so brief?   84

FIRST MURDERER 'Tis better, sir, than to be tedious. (*To
Second Murderer*) Let him see our commission, and talk
no more.

Brackenbury reads

BRACKENBURY

I am in this commanded to deliver
The noble Duke of Clarence to your hands.
I will not reason what is meant hereby,   90
Because I will be guiltless of the meaning.
There lies the Duke asleep, and there the keys.
⌈*He throws down the keys*⌉
I'll to the King and signify to him
That thus I have resigned to you my charge.   94

FIRST MURDERER You may, sir; 'tis a point of wisdom.
Fare you well.   *Exit Brackenbury*

SECOND MURDERER What, shall I stab him as he sleeps?

FIRST MURDERER No. He'll say 'twas done cowardly, when
he wakes.

SECOND MURDERER Why, he shall never wake until the
great judgement day.   101

FIRST MURDERER Why, then he'll say we stabbed him
sleeping.

SECOND MURDERER The urging of that word 'judgement'
hath bred a kind of remorse in me.   105

FIRST MURDERER What, art thou afraid?

SECOND MURDERER Not to kill him, having a warrant, but
to be damned for killing him, from the which no
warrant can defend me.

FIRST MURDERER I thought thou hadst been resolute. 110
SECOND MURDERER So I am—to let him live.
FIRST MURDERER I'll back to the Duke of Gloucester and
tell him so.
SECOND MURDERER Nay, I pray thee. Stay a little. I hope
this passionate humour of mine will change. It was
wont to hold me but while one tells twenty. 116
⌈He counts to twenty⌉
FIRST MURDERER How dost thou feel thyself now?
SECOND MURDERER Some certain dregs of conscience are
yet within me.
FIRST MURDERER Remember our reward, when the deed's
done. 121
SECOND MURDERER 'Swounds, he dies. I had forgot the
reward.
FIRST MURDERER Where's thy conscience now? 124
SECOND MURDERER O, in the Duke of Gloucester's purse.
FIRST MURDERER When he opens his purse to give us our
reward, thy conscience flies out.
SECOND MURDERER 'Tis no matter. Let it go. There's few
or none will entertain it.
FIRST MURDERER What if it come to thee again? 130
SECOND MURDERER I'll not meddle with it. It makes a man
a coward. A man cannot steal but it accuseth him. A
man cannot swear but it checks him. A man cannot
lie with his neighbour's wife but it detects him. 'Tis a
blushing, shamefaced spirit, that mutinies in a man's
bosom. It fills a man full of obstacles. It made me once
restore a purse of gold that by chance I found. It
beggars any man that keeps it. It is turned out of towns
and cities for a dangerous thing, and every man that
means to live well endeavours to trust to himself and
live without it. 141
FIRST MURDERER 'Swounds, 'tis even now at my elbow,
persuading me not to kill the Duke.
SECOND MURDERER Take the devil in thy mind, and believe
him not: he would insinuate with thee but to make
thee sigh. 146
FIRST MURDERER I am strong framed; he cannot prevail
with me.
SECOND MURDERER Spoke like a tall man that respects thy
reputation. Come, shall we fall to work? 150
FIRST MURDERER Take him on the costard with the hilts
of thy sword, and then throw him into the malmsey
butt in the next room.
SECOND MURDERER O excellent device!—and make a sop
of him. 155
FIRST MURDERER Soft, he wakes.
SECOND MURDERER Strike!
FIRST MURDERER No, we'll reason with him.
CLARENCE
Where art thou, keeper? Give me a cup of wine.
SECOND MURDERER
You shall have wine enough, my lord, anon. 160
CLARENCE
In God's name, what art thou?
FIRST MURDERER   A man, as you are.
CLARENCE But not as I am, royal.

FIRST MURDERER Nor you as we are, loyal.
CLARENCE
Thy voice is thunder, but thy looks are humble.
FIRST MURDERER
My voice is now the King's; my looks, mine own. 165
CLARENCE
How darkly and how deadly dost thou speak.
Your eyes do menace me. Why look you pale?
Who sent you hither? Wherefore do you come?
SECOND MURDERER
To, to, to—
CLARENCE   To murder me.
BOTH MURDERERS   Ay, ay.
CLARENCE
You scarcely have the hearts to tell me so, 170
And therefore cannot have the hearts to do it.
Wherein, my friends, have I offended you?
FIRST MURDERER
Offended us you have not, but the King.
CLARENCE
I shall be reconciled to him again.
SECOND MURDERER
Never, my lord; therefore prepare to die. 175
CLARENCE
Are you drawn forth among a world of men
To slay the innocent? What is my offence?
Where is the evidence that doth accuse me?
What lawful quest have given their verdict up
Unto the frowning judge, or who pronounced 180
The bitter sentence of poor Clarence' death?
Before I be convict by course of law,
To threaten me with death is most unlawful.
I charge you, as you hope to have redemption
By Christ's dear blood, shed for our grievous sins, 185
That you depart and lay no hands on me.
The deed you undertake is damnable.
FIRST MURDERER
What we will do, we do upon command.
SECOND MURDERER
And he that hath commanded is our king.
CLARENCE
Erroneous vassals, the great King of Kings 190
Hath in the table of his law commanded
That thou shalt do no murder. Will you then
Spurn at his edict, and fulfil a man's?
Take heed, for he holds vengeance in his hand
To hurl upon their heads that break his law. 195
SECOND MURDERER
And that same vengeance doth he hurl on thee,
For false forswearing, and for murder too.
Thou didst receive the sacrament to fight
In quarrel of the house of Lancaster.
FIRST MURDERER
And, like a traitor to the name of God, 200
Didst break that vow, and with thy treacherous blade
Unripped'st the bowels of thy sov'reign's son.
SECOND MURDERER
Whom thou wast sworn to cherish and defend.

FIRST MURDERER
How canst thou urge God's dreadful law to us,
When thou hast broke it in such dear degree?   205
CLARENCE
Alas, for whose sake did I that ill deed?
For Edward, for my brother, for his sake.
He sends ye not to murder me for this,
For in that sin he is as deep as I.
If God will be avengèd for the deed,   210
O know you yet, he doth it publicly.
Take not the quarrel from his pow'rful arm;
He needs no indirect or lawless course
To cut off those that have offended him.
FIRST MURDERER
Who made thee then a bloody minister   215
When gallant springing brave Plantagenet,
That princely novice, was struck dead by thee?
CLARENCE
My brother's love, the devil, and my rage.
FIRST MURDERER
Thy brother's love, our duty, and thy faults
Provoke us hither now to slaughter thee.   220
CLARENCE
If you do love my brother, hate not me.
I am his brother, and I love him well.
If you are hired for meed, go back again,
And I will send you to my brother Gloucester,
Who shall reward you better for my life   225
Than Edward will for tidings of my death.
SECOND MURDERER
You are deceived. Your brother Gloucester hates you.
CLARENCE
O no, he loves me, and he holds me dear.
Go you to him from me.
FIRST MURDERER   Ay, so we will.
CLARENCE
Tell him, when that our princely father York   230
Blessed his three sons with his victorious arm,
And charged us from his soul to love each other,
He little thought of this divided friendship.
Bid Gloucester think of this, and he will weep.
FIRST MURDERER
Ay, millstones, as he lessoned us to weep.   235
CLARENCE
O do not slander him, for he is kind.
FIRST MURDERER
As snow in harvest. Come, you deceive yourself.
'Tis he that sends us to destroy you here.
CLARENCE
It cannot be, for he bewept my fortune,
And hugged me in his arms, and swore with sobs 240
That he would labour my delivery.
FIRST MURDERER
Why, so he doth, when he delivers you
From this earth's thraldom to the joys of heaven.
SECOND MURDERER
Make peace with God, for you must die, my lord.
CLARENCE
Have you that holy feeling in your souls   245

To counsel me to make my peace with God,
And are you yet to your own souls so blind
That you will war with God by murd'ring me?
O sirs, consider: they that set you on
To do this deed will hate you for the deed.   250
SECOND MURDERER (to First)
What shall we do?
CLARENCE   Relent, and save your souls.
FIRST MURDERER
Relent? No. 'Tis cowardly and womanish.
CLARENCE
Not to relent is beastly, savage, devilish.—
My friend, I spy some pity in thy looks.
O if thine eye be not a flatterer,   255
Come thou on my side, and entreat for me.
A begging prince, what beggar pities not?
Which of you, if you were a prince's son,
Being pent from liberty as I am now,
If two such murderers as yourselves came to you, 260
Would not entreat for life? As you would beg
Were you in my distress—
SECOND MURDERER Look behind you, my lord!
FIRST MURDERER (stabbing Clarence)
Take that, and that! If all this will not serve,
I'll drown you in the malmsey butt within.   265
                        Exit with Clarence's body
SECOND MURDERER
A bloody deed, and desperately dispatched!
How fain, like Pilate, would I wash my hands
Of this most grievous, guilty murder done.
        Enter First Murderer
FIRST MURDERER
How now? What mean'st thou, that thou help'st me
    not?
By heaven, the Duke shall know how slack you have
    been.   270
SECOND MURDERER
I would he knew that I had saved his brother.
Take thou the fee, and tell him what I say,
For I repent me that the Duke is slain.   Exit
FIRST MURDERER
So do not I. Go, coward as thou art.—
Well, I'll go hide the body in some hole   275
Till that the Duke give order for his burial.
And, when I have my meed, I will away,
For this will out, and then I must not stay.   Exit

2.1   Flourish. Enter King Edward, sick, Queen Elizabeth,
      Lord Marquis Dorset, Lord Rivers, Lord Hastings,
      Sir William Catesby, the Duke of Buckingham ⌐and
      Lord Gray⌐
KING EDWARD
Why, so! Now have I done a good day's work.
You peers, continue this united league.
I every day expect an embassage
From my redeemer to redeem me hence,
And more in peace my soul shall part to heaven   5
Since I have made my friends at peace on earth.

Hastings and Rivers, take each other's hand.
Dissemble not your hatred; swear your love.

RIVERS
By heaven, my soul is purged from grudging hate,
And with my hand I seal my true heart's love.   10
⌈*He takes Hastings' hand*⌉

LORD HASTINGS
So thrive I, as I truly swear the like.

KING EDWARD
Take heed you dally not before your king,
Lest he that is the supreme King of Kings
Confound your hidden falsehood, and award
Either of you to be the other's end.   15

LORD HASTINGS
So prosper I, as I swear perfect love.

RIVERS
And I, as I love Hastings with my heart.

KING EDWARD (*to Elizabeth*)
Madam, yourself is not exempt from this,
Nor your son Dorset;—Buckingham, nor you.
You have been factious one against the other.   20
Wife, love Lord Hastings, let him kiss your hand—
And what you do, do it unfeignedly.

QUEEN ELIZABETH (*giving Hastings her hand to kiss*)
There, Hastings. I will never more remember
Our former hatred: so thrive I, and mine.

KING EDWARD
Dorset, embrace him. Hastings, love Lord Marquis.   25

DORSET
This interchange of love, I here protest,
Upon my part shall be inviolable.

LORD HASTINGS And so swear I.
They embrace

KING EDWARD
Now, princely Buckingham, seal thou this league
With thy embracements to my wife's allies,   30
And make me happy in your unity.

BUCKINGHAM (*to Elizabeth*)
Whenever Buckingham doth turn his hate
Upon your grace, but with all duteous love
Doth cherish you and yours, God punish me
With hate in those where I expect most love.   35
When I have most need to employ a friend,
And most assurèd that he is a friend,
Deep, hollow, treacherous, and full of guile
Be he unto me. This do I beg of heaven,
When I am cold in love to you or yours.   40
They embrace

KING EDWARD
A pleasing cordial, princely Buckingham,
Is this thy vow unto my sickly heart.
There wanteth now our brother Gloucester here,
To make the blessèd period of this peace.
Enter Sir Richard Ratcliffe and Richard Duke of
Gloucester

BUCKINGHAM And in good time,   45
Here comes Sir Richard Ratcliffe and the Duke.

RICHARD GLOUCESTER
Good morrow to my sovereign King and Queen.—
And princely peers, a happy time of day.

KING EDWARD
Happy indeed, as we have spent the day.
Brother, we have done deeds of charity,   50
Made peace of enmity, fair love of hate,
Between these swelling wrong-incensèd peers.

RICHARD GLOUCESTER
A blessèd labour, my most sovereign lord.
Among this princely heap if any here,
By false intelligence or wrong surmise,   55
Hold me a foe,
If I unwittingly or in my rage
Have aught committed that is hardly borne
By any in this presence, I desire
To reconcile me to his friendly peace.   60
'Tis death to me to be at enmity.
I hate it, and desire all good men's love.—
First, madam, I entreat true peace of you,
Which I will purchase with my duteous service.—
Of you, my noble cousin Buckingham,   65
If ever any grudge were lodged between us.—
Of you, Lord Rivers, and Lord Gray of you,
That all without desert have frowned on me.—
Dukes, earls, lords, gentlemen, indeed of all!
I do not know that Englishman alive   70
With whom my soul is any jot at odds
More than the infant that is born tonight.
I thank my God for my humility.

QUEEN ELIZABETH
A holy day shall this be kept hereafter.
I would to God all strifes were well compounded.—   75
My sovereign lord, I do beseech your highness
To take our brother Clarence to your grace.

RICHARD GLOUCESTER
Why, madam, have I offered love for this,
To be so flouted in this royal presence?
Who knows not that the gentle Duke is dead?   80
The others all start
You do him injury to scorn his corpse.

⌈RIVERS⌉
Who knows not he is dead? Who knows he is?

QUEEN ELIZABETH
All-seeing heaven, what a world is this?

BUCKINGHAM
Look I so pale, Lord Dorset, as the rest?

DORSET
Ay, my good lord, and no one in the presence   85
But his red colour hath forsook his cheeks.

KING EDWARD
Is Clarence dead? The order was reversed.

RICHARD GLOUCESTER
But he, poor man, by your first order died,
And that a wingèd Mercury did bear;
Some tardy cripple bore the countermand,   90
That came too lag to see him burièd.

God grant that some, less noble and less loyal,
Nearer in bloody thoughts, but not in blood,
Deserve not worse than wretched Clarence did,
And yet go current from suspicion.   95
Enter Lord Stanley Earl of Derby
STANLEY (*kneeling*)
A boon, my sovereign, for my service done.
KING EDWARD
I pray thee, peace! My soul is full of sorrow.
STANLEY
I will not rise, unless your highness hear me.
KING EDWARD
Then say at once, what is it thou requests?
STANLEY
The forfeit, sovereign, of my servant's life,   100
Who slew today a riotous gentleman,
Lately attendant on the Duke of Norfolk.
KING EDWARD
Have I a tongue to doom my brother's death,
And shall that tongue give pardon to a slave?
My brother slew no man; his fault was thought;   105
And yet his punishment was bitter death.
Who sued to me for him? Who in my wrath
Kneeled at my feet, and bid me be advised?
Who spoke of brotherhood? Who spoke of love?
Who told me how the poor soul did forsake   110
The mighty Warwick and did fight for me?
Who told me, in the field at Tewkesbury,
When Oxford had me down, he rescued me,
And said, 'Dear brother, live, and be a king'?
Who told me, when we both lay in the field,   115
Frozen almost to death, how he did lap me
Even in his garments, and did give himself
All thin and naked to the numb-cold night?
All this from my remembrance brutish wrath
Sinfully plucked, and not a man of you   120
Had so much grace to put it in my mind.
But when your carters or your waiting vassals
Have done a drunken slaughter, and defaced
The precious image of our dear redeemer,
You straight are on your knees for 'Pardon, pardon!'—
And I, unjustly too, must grant it you.   126
But, for my brother, not a man would speak,
Nor I, ungracious, speak unto myself
For him, poor soul. The proudest of you all
Have been beholden to him in his life,   130
Yet none of you would once beg for his life.
O God, I fear thy justice will take hold
On me—and you, and mine, and yours, for this.—
Come, Hastings, help me to my closet.
Ah, poor Clarence!   135
Exeunt some with King and Queen
RICHARD GLOUCESTER
This is the fruits of rashness. Marked you not
How that the guilty kindred of the Queen
Looked pale, when they did hear of Clarence' death?
O, they did urge it still unto the King.

God will revenge it. Come, lords, will you go   140
To comfort Edward with our company?
BUCKINGHAM We wait upon your grace.   *Exeunt*

2.2   *Enter the old Duchess of York with the two children*
        of Clarence
BOY
Good grannam, tell us, is our father dead?
DUCHESS No, boy.
GIRL
Why do you weep so oft, and beat your breast,
And cry, 'O Clarence, my unhappy son'?
BOY
Why do you look on us and shake your head,   5
And call us orphans, wretches, castaways,
If that our noble father were alive?
DUCHESS OF YORK
My pretty cousins, you mistake me both.
I do lament the sickness of the King,
As loath to lose him, not your father's death.   10
It were lost sorrow to wail one that's lost.
BOY
Then you conclude, my grannam, he is dead.
The King mine uncle is to blame for this.
God will revenge it—whom I will importune
With earnest prayers, all to that effect.   15
GIRL And so will I.
DUCHESS OF YORK
Peace, children, peace! The King doth love you well.
Incapable and shallow innocents,
You cannot guess who caused your father's death.
BOY
Grannam, we can. For my good uncle Gloucester   20
Told me the King, provoked to it by the Queen,
Devised impeachments to imprison him,
And when my uncle told me so he wept,
And pitied me, and kindly kissed my cheek,
Bade me rely on him as on my father,   25
And he would love me dearly as his child.
DUCHESS OF YORK
Ah, that deceit should steal such gentle shapes,
And with a virtuous visor hide deep vice!
He is my son, ay, and therein my shame;
Yet from my dugs he drew not this deceit.   30
BOY
Think you my uncle did dissemble, grannam?
DUCHESS OF YORK Ay, boy.
BOY
I cannot think it. Hark, what noise is this?
Enter Queen Elizabeth with her hair about her ears
QUEEN ELIZABETH
Ah, who shall hinder me to wail and weep?
To chide my fortune, and torment myself?   35
I'll join with black despair against my soul,
And to myself become an enemy.
DUCHESS OF YORK
What means this scene of rude impatience?

QUEEN ELIZABETH
  To mark an act of tragic violence.
  Edward, my lord, thy son, our king, is dead.   40
  Why grow the branches when the root is gone?
  Why wither not the leaves that want their sap?
  If you will live, lament; if die, be brief,
  That our swift-wingèd souls may catch the King's,
  Or like obedient subjects follow him   45
  To his new kingdom of ne'er-changing night.
DUCHESS OF YORK
  Ah, so much interest have I in thy sorrow
  As I had title in thy noble husband.
  I have bewept a worthy husband's death,
  And lived with looking on his images.   50
  But now two mirrors of his princely semblance
  Are cracked in pieces by malignant death,
  And I for comfort have but one false glass,
  That grieves me when I see my shame in him.
  Thou art a widow, yet thou art a mother,   55
  And hast the comfort of thy children left.
  But death hath snatched my husband from mine arms
  And plucked two crutches from my feeble hands,
  Clarence and Edward. O what cause have I,
  Thine being but a moiety of my moan,   60
  To overgo thy woes, and drown thy cries?
BOY (to Elizabeth)
  Ah, aunt, you wept not for our father's death.
  How can we aid you with our kindred tears?
DAUGHTER (to Elizabeth)
  Our fatherless distress was left unmoaned;
  Your widow-dolour likewise be unwept.   65
QUEEN ELIZABETH
  Give me no help in lamentation.
  I am not barren to bring forth complaints.
  All springs reduce their currents to mine eyes,
  That I, being governed by the wat'ry moon,
  May send forth plenteous tears to drown the world.   70
  Ah, for my husband, for my dear Lord Edward!
CHILDREN
  Ah, for our father, for our dear Lord Clarence!
DUCHESS OF YORK
  Alas, for both, both mine, Edward and Clarence!
QUEEN ELIZABETH
  What stay had I but Edward, and he's gone?
CHILDREN
  What stay had we but Clarence, and he's gone?   75
DUCHESS OF YORK
  What stays had I but they, and they are gone?
QUEEN ELIZABETH
  Was never widow had so dear a loss!
CHILDREN
  Were never orphans had so dear a loss!
DUCHESS OF YORK
  Was never mother had so dear a loss!
  Alas, I am the mother of these griefs.   80
  Their woes are parcelled; mine is general.
  She for an Edward weeps, and so do I;
  I for a Clarence weep, so doth not she.

  These babes for Clarence weep, and so do I;
  I for an Edward weep, so do not they.   85
  Alas, you three on me, threefold distressed,
  Pour all your tears. I am your sorrow's nurse,
  And I will pamper it with lamentation.
     Enter Richard Duke of Gloucester, the Duke of
     Buckingham, Lord Stanley Earl of Derby, Lord
     Hastings, and Sir Richard Ratcliffe
RICHARD GLOUCESTER (to Elizabeth)
  Sister, have comfort. All of us have cause
  To wail the dimming of our shining star,   90
  But none can help our harms by wailing them.—
  Madam, my mother, I do cry you mercy.
  I did not see your grace. Humbly on my knee
  I crave your blessing.
DUCHESS OF YORK
  God bless thee, and put meekness in thy breast,   95
  Love, charity, obedience, and true duty.
RICHARD GLOUCESTER
  Amen. (*Aside*) 'And make me die a good old man.'
  That is the butt-end of a mother's blessing;
  I marvel that her grace did leave it out.
BUCKINGHAM
  You cloudy princes and heart-sorrowing peers   100
  That bear this heavy mutual load of moan,
  Now cheer each other in each other's love.
  Though we have spent our harvest of this king,
  We are to reap the harvest of his son.
  The broken rancour of your high-swoll'n hearts   105
  But lately splinted, knit, and joined together,
  Must gently be preserved, cherished, and kept.
  Meseemeth good that, with some little train,
  Forthwith from Ludlow the young Prince be fet
  Hither to London to be crowned our king.   110
RICHARD GLOUCESTER
  Then be it so, and go we to determine
  Who they shall be that straight shall post to Ludlow.—
  Madam, and you my sister, will you go
  To give your censures in this weighty business?   114
QUEEN ELIZABETH *and* DUCHESS OF YORK With all our hearts.
     Exeunt all but Richard and Buckingham
BUCKINGHAM
  My lord, whoever journeys to the Prince,
  For God's sake let not us two stay at home,
  For by the way I'll sort occasion,
  As index to the story we late talked of,
  To part the Queen's proud kindred from the Prince. 120
RICHARD GLOUCESTER
  My other self, my counsel's consistory,
  My oracle, my prophet, my dear cousin!
  I, as a child, will go by thy direction.
  Towards Ludlow then, for we'll not stay behind.
     Exeunt

2.3   *Enter one Citizen at one door and another at the*
     other
FIRST CITIZEN
  Good morrow, neighbour. Whither away so fast?

SECOND CITIZEN
  I promise you, I scarcely know myself.
  Hear you the news abroad?
FIRST CITIZEN   Yes, that the King is dead.
SECOND CITIZEN
  Ill news, by'r Lady; seldom comes the better.
  I fear, I fear, 'twill prove a giddy world.   5
      Enter another Citizen
THIRD CITIZEN
  Neighbours, God speed.
FIRST CITIZEN   Give you good morrow, sir.
THIRD CITIZEN
  Doth the news hold of good King Edward's death?
SECOND CITIZEN
  Ay, sir, it is too true. God help the while.
THIRD CITIZEN
  Then, masters, look to see a troublous world.
FIRST CITIZEN
  No, no, by God's good grace his son shall reign.   10
THIRD CITIZEN
  Woe to that land that's governed by a child.
SECOND CITIZEN
  In him there is a hope of government,
  Which in his nonage council under him,
  And in his full and ripened years himself,
  No doubt shall then, and till then, govern well.   15
FIRST CITIZEN
  So stood the state when Henry the Sixth
  Was crowned in Paris but at nine months old.
THIRD CITIZEN
  Stood the state so? No, no, good friends, God wot.
  For then this land was famously enriched
  With politic, grave counsel; then the King   20
  Had virtuous uncles to protect his grace.
FIRST CITIZEN
  Why, so hath this, both by his father and mother.
THIRD CITIZEN
  Better it were they all came by his father,
  Or by his father there were none at all.
  For emulation who shall now be near'st   25
  Will touch us all too near, if God prevent not.
  O full of danger is the Duke of Gloucester,
  And the Queen's sons and brothers haught and proud.
  And were they to be ruled, and not to rule,
  This sickly land might solace as before.   30
FIRST CITIZEN
  Come, come, we fear the worst. All will be well.
THIRD CITIZEN
  When clouds are seen, wise men put on their cloaks;
  When great leaves fall, then winter is at hand;
  When the sun sets, who doth not look for night?
  Untimely storms make men expect a dearth.   35
  All may be well, but if God sort it so
  'Tis more than we deserve, or I expect.
SECOND CITIZEN
  Truly the hearts of men are full of fear.
  You cannot reason almost with a man
  That looks not heavily and full of dread.   40

THIRD CITIZEN
  Before the days of change still is it so.
  By a divine instinct men's minds mistrust
  Ensuing danger, as by proof we see
  The water swell before a boist'rous storm.
  But leave it all to God. Whither away?   45
SECOND CITIZEN
  Marry, we were sent for to the justices.
THIRD CITIZEN
  And so was I. I'll bear you company.   *Exeunt*

2.4   *Enter* ⌈*Lord Cardinal*⌉, *young Duke of York, Queen
       Elizabeth, and the old Duchess of York*
⌈CARDINAL⌉
  Last night, I hear, they lay them at Northampton.
  At Stony Stratford they do rest tonight.
  Tomorrow, or next day, they will be here.
DUCHESS OF YORK
  I long with all my heart to see the Prince.
  I hope he is much grown since last I saw him.   5
QUEEN ELIZABETH
  But I hear, no. They say my son of York
  Has almost overta'en him in his growth.
YORK
  Ay, mother, but I would not have it so.
DUCHESS OF YORK
  Why, my young cousin, it is good to grow.
YORK
  Grandam, one night as we did sit at supper,   10
  My uncle Rivers talked how I did grow
  More than my brother. 'Ay', quoth my nuncle
      Gloucester,
  'Small herbs have grace; gross weeds do grow apace'.
  And since, methinks I would not grow so fast,
  Because sweet flow'rs are slow, and weeds make
      haste.   15
DUCHESS OF YORK
  Good faith, good faith, the saying did not hold
  In him that did object the same to thee.
  He was the wretched'st thing when he was young,
  So long a-growing, and so leisurely,
  That if his rule were true he should be gracious.   20
⌈CARDINAL⌉
  Why, so no doubt he is, my gracious madam.
DUCHESS OF YORK
  I hope he is, but yet let mothers doubt.
YORK
  Now, by my troth, if I had been remembered,
  I could have given my uncle's grace a flout
  To touch his growth, nearer than he touched mine.   25
DUCHESS OF YORK
  How, my young York? I pray thee, let me hear it.
YORK
  Marry, they say my uncle grew so fast
  That he could gnaw a crust at two hours old.
  'Twas full two years ere I could get a tooth.
  Grannam, this would have been a biting jest.   30

DUCHESS OF YORK
I pray thee, pretty York, who told thee this?
YORK Grannam, his nurse.
DUCHESS OF YORK
His nurse? Why, she was dead ere thou wast born.
YORK
If 'twere not she, I cannot tell who told me.
QUEEN ELIZABETH
A parlous boy! Go to, you are too shrewd.   35
⌜CARDINAL⌝
Good madam, be not angry with the child.
QUEEN ELIZABETH
Pitchers have ears.
          Enter ⌜Marquis Dorset⌝
⌜CARDINAL⌝   Here comes your son, Lord Dorset.
What news, Lord Marquis?
⌜DORSET⌝   Such news, my lord,
As grieves me to report.
QUEEN ELIZABETH   How doth the Prince?
⌜DORSET⌝
Well, madam, and in health.
DUCHESS OF YORK   What is thy news then?
⌜DORSET⌝
Lord Rivers and Lord Gray are sent to Pomfret,   41
And with them Thomas Vaughan, prisoners.
DUCHESS OF YORK
Who hath committed them?
⌜DORSET⌝   The mighty dukes,
Gloucester and Buckingham.
⌜CARDINAL⌝   For what offence?
⌜DORSET⌝
The sum of all I can, I have disclosed.   45
Why or for what the nobles were committed
Is all unknown to me, my gracious lord.
QUEEN ELIZABETH
Ay me! I see the ruin of our house.
The tiger now hath seized the gentle hind.
Insulting tyranny begins to jet   50
Upon the innocent and aweless throne.
Welcome destruction, blood, and massacre!
I see, as in a map, the end of all.
DUCHESS OF YORK
Accursèd and unquiet wrangling days,
How many of you have mine eyes beheld?   55
My husband lost his life to get the crown,
And often up and down my sons were tossed,
For me to joy and weep their gain and loss.
And being seated, and domestic broils
Clean overblown, themselves the conquerors   60
Make war upon themselves, brother to brother,
Blood to blood, self against self. O preposterous
And frantic outrage, end thy damnèd spleen,
Or let me die, to look on death no more.
QUEEN ELIZABETH *(to York)*
Come, come, my boy, we will to sanctuary.—   65
Madam, farewell.
DUCHESS OF YORK   Stay, I will go with you.

QUEEN ELIZABETH
You have no cause.
⌜CARDINAL⌝ *(to Elizabeth)* My gracious lady, go,
And thither bear your treasure and your goods.
For my part, I'll resign unto your grace
The seal I keep, and so betide to me   70
As well I tender you and all of yours.
Go, I'll conduct you to the sanctuary.   *Exeunt*

3.1   *The Trumpets sound. Enter young Prince Edward,*
          the Dukes of Gloucester and Buckingham, Lord
          Cardinal, with others, including ⌜Lord Stanley Earl
          of Derby and⌝ Sir William Catesby
BUCKINGHAM
Welcome, sweet Prince, to London, to your chamber.
RICHARD GLOUCESTER *(to Prince Edward)*
Welcome, dear cousin, my thoughts' sovereign.
The weary way hath made you melancholy.
PRINCE EDWARD
No, uncle, but our crosses on the way
Have made it tedious, wearisome, and heavy.   5
I want more uncles here to welcome me.
RICHARD GLOUCESTER
Sweet Prince, the untainted virtue of your years
Hath not yet dived into the world's deceit,
Nor more can you distinguish of a man
Than of his outward show, which God he knows   10
Seldom or never jumpeth with the heart.
Those uncles which you want were dangerous.
Your grace attended to their sugared words,
But looked not on the poison of their hearts.   14
God keep you from them, and from such false friends.
PRINCE EDWARD
God keep me from false friends; but they were none.
          Enter Lord Mayor ⌜and his train⌝
RICHARD GLOUCESTER
My lord, the Mayor of London comes to greet you.
MAYOR *(kneeling to Prince Edward)*
God bless your grace with health and happy days.
PRINCE EDWARD
I thank you, good my lord, and thank you all.—
I thought my mother and my brother York   20
Would long ere this have met us on the way.
Fie, what a slug is Hastings, that he hastes not
To tell us whether they will come or no.
          Enter Lord Hastings
BUCKINGHAM
In happy time here comes the sweating lord.
PRINCE EDWARD *(to Hastings)*
Welcome, my lord. What, will our mother come?   25
LORD HASTINGS
On what occasion God he knows, not I,
The Queen your mother, and your brother York,
Have taken sanctuary. The tender Prince
Would fain have come with me to meet your grace,
But by his mother was perforce withheld.   30
BUCKINGHAM
Fie, what an indirect and peevish course

Is this of hers!—Lord Cardinal, will your grace
Persuade the Queen to send the Duke of York
Unto his princely brother presently?—
If she deny, Lord Hastings, go with him,   35
And from her jealous arms pluck him perforce.

CARDINAL
My lord of Buckingham, if my weak oratory
Can from his mother win the Duke of York,
Anon expect him. But if she be obdurate
To mild entreaties, God in heaven forbid   40
We should infringe the sacred privilege
Of blessèd sanctuary. Not for all this land
Would I be guilty of so deep a sin.

BUCKINGHAM
You are too senseless-obstinate, my lord,
Too ceremonious and traditional.   45
Weigh it not with the grossness of this age.
You break not sanctuary in seizing him.
The benefit thereof is always granted
To those whose dealings have deserved the place,
And those who have the wit to claim the place.   50
This prince hath neither claimed it nor deserved it,
And therefore, in my mind, he cannot have it.
Then taking him from thence that 'longs not there,
You break thereby no privilege nor charter.
Oft have I heard of 'sanctuary men',   55
But 'sanctuary children' ne'er till now.

CARDINAL
My lord, you shall o'errule my mind for once.—
Come on, Lord Hastings, will you go with me?

LORD HASTINGS I come, my lord.

PRINCE EDWARD
Good lords, make all the speedy haste you may.—   60
                    Exeunt Cardinal and Hastings
Say, uncle Gloucester, if our brother come,
Where shall we sojourn till our coronation?

RICHARD GLOUCESTER
Where it seems best unto your royal self.
If I may counsel you, some day or two
Your highness shall repose you at the Tower,   65
Then where you please and shall be thought most fit
For your best health and recreation.

PRINCE EDWARD
I do not like the Tower of any place.—
Did Julius Caesar build that place, my lord?

BUCKINGHAM
He did, my gracious lord, begin that place,   70
Which since succeeding ages have re-edified.

PRINCE EDWARD
Is it upon record, or else reported
Successively from age to age, he built it?

BUCKINGHAM
Upon record, my gracious liege.

PRINCE EDWARD
But say, my lord, it were not registered,   75
Methinks the truth should live from age to age,
As 'twere retailed to all posterity
Even to the general all-ending day.

RICHARD GLOUCESTER (aside)
So wise so young, they say, do never live long.

PRINCE EDWARD What say you, uncle?   80

RICHARD GLOUCESTER
I say, 'Without characters fame lives long'.
(Aside) Thus like the formal Vice, Iniquity,
I moralize two meanings in one word.

PRINCE EDWARD
That Julius Caesar was a famous man:
With what his valour did t'enrich his wit,   85
His wit set down to make his valour live.
Death made no conquest of this conqueror,
For yet he lives in fame though not in life.
I'll tell you what, my cousin Buckingham.

BUCKINGHAM What, my good lord?   90

PRINCE EDWARD
An if I live until I be a man,
I'll win our ancient right in France again,
Or die a soldier, as I lived a king.

RICHARD GLOUCESTER (aside)
Short summers lightly have a forward spring.
        Enter young Duke of York, Lord Hastings, and Lord
        Cardinal

BUCKINGHAM
Now in good time, here comes the Duke of York.   95

PRINCE EDWARD
Richard of York, how fares our loving brother?

YORK
Well, my dread lord—so must I call you now.

PRINCE EDWARD
Ay, brother, to our grief, as it is yours.
Too late he died that might have kept that title,
Which by his death hath lost much majesty.   100

RICHARD GLOUCESTER
How fares our noble cousin, Lord of York?

YORK
I thank you, gentle uncle, well. O, my lord,
You said that idle weeds are fast in growth;
The Prince, my brother, hath outgrown me far.

RICHARD GLOUCESTER
He hath, my lord.

YORK   And therefore is he idle?   105

RICHARD GLOUCESTER
O my fair cousin, I must not say so.

YORK
He is more beholden to you then than I.

RICHARD GLOUCESTER
He may command me as my sovereign,
But you have power in me as a kinsman.

YORK
I pray you, uncle, render me this dagger.   110

RICHARD GLOUCESTER
My dagger, little cousin? With all my heart.

PRINCE EDWARD A beggar, brother?

YORK
Of my kind uncle that I know will give,
It being but a toy which is no grief to give.

RICHARD GLOUCESTER
A greater gift than that I'll give my cousin.   115

YORK
A greater gift? O, that's the sword to it.
RICHARD GLOUCESTER
Ay, gentle cousin, were it light enough.
YORK
O, then I see you will part but with light gifts.
In weightier things you'll say a beggar nay.
RICHARD GLOUCESTER
It is too heavy for your grace to wear.   120
YORK
I'd weigh it lightly, were it heavier.
RICHARD GLOUCESTER
What, would you have my weapon, little lord?
YORK
I would, that I might thank you as you call me.
RICHARD GLOUCESTER How?
YORK Little.   125
PRINCE EDWARD
My lord of York will still be cross in talk.—
Uncle, your grace knows how to bear with him.
YORK
You mean to bear me, not to bear with me.—
Uncle, my brother mocks both you and me.
Because that I am little like an ape,   130
He thinks that you should bear me on your shoulders.
BUCKINGHAM
With what a sharp, prodigal wit he reasons.
To mitigate the scorn he gives his uncle,
He prettily and aptly taunts himself.
So cunning and so young is wonderful.   135
RICHARD GLOUCESTER (to Prince Edward)
My lord, will't please you pass along?
Myself and my good cousin Buckingham
Will to your mother to entreat of her
To meet you at the Tower and welcome you.
YORK (to Prince Edward)
What, will you go unto the Tower, my lord?   140
PRINCE EDWARD
My Lord Protector needs will have it so.
YORK
I shall not sleep in quiet at the Tower.
RICHARD GLOUCESTER Why, what should you fear there?
YORK
Marry, my uncle Clarence' angry ghost.
My grannam told me he was murdered there.   145
PRINCE EDWARD
I fear no uncles dead.
RICHARD GLOUCESTER   Nor none that live, I hope.
PRINCE EDWARD
An if they live, I hope I need not fear.
(To York) But come, my lord, and with a heavy heart,
Thinking on them, go we unto the Tower.
              A Sennet. Exeunt all but Richard, Buckingham,
                                                and Catesby
BUCKINGHAM (to Richard)
Think you, my lord, this little prating York   150
Was not incensèd by his subtle mother
To taunt and scorn you thus opprobriously?

RICHARD GLOUCESTER
No doubt, no doubt. O, 'tis a parlous boy,
Bold, quick, ingenious, forward, capable.
He is all the mother's, from the top to toe.   155
BUCKINGHAM
Well, let them rest.—Come hither, Catesby. Thou art
  sworn
As deeply to effect what we intend
As closely to conceal what we impart.
Thou know'st our reasons, urged upon the way.
What think'st thou? Is it not an easy matter   160
To make Lord William Hastings of our mind,
For the instalment of this noble duke
In the seat royal of this famous isle?
CATESBY
He for his father's sake so loves the Prince
That he will not be won to aught against him.   165
BUCKINGHAM
What think'st thou then of Stanley? Will not he?
CATESBY
He will do all-in-all as Hastings doth.
BUCKINGHAM
Well then, no more but this. Go, gentle Catesby,
And, as it were far off, sound thou Lord Hastings
How he doth stand affected to our purpose.   170
If thou dost find him tractable to us,
Encourage him, and tell him all our reasons.
If he be leaden, icy, cold, unwilling,
Be thou so too, and so break off your talk,
And give us notice of his inclination,   175
For we tomorrow hold divided counsels,
Wherein thyself shalt highly be employed.
RICHARD GLOUCESTER
Commend me to Lord William. Tell him, Catesby,
His ancient knot of dangerous adversaries
Tomorrow are let blood at Pomfret Castle,   180
And bid my lord, for joy of this good news,
Give Mrs Shore one gentle kiss the more.
BUCKINGHAM
Good Catesby, go effect this business soundly.
CATESBY
My good lords both, with all the heed I can.
RICHARD GLOUCESTER
Shall we hear from you, Catesby, ere we sleep?   185
CATESBY You shall, my lord.
RICHARD GLOUCESTER
At Crosby House, there shall you find us both.
                                          Exit Catesby
BUCKINGHAM
My lord, what shall we do if we perceive
Lord Hastings will not yield to our complots?
RICHARD GLOUCESTER
Chop off his head. Something we will determine.   190
And look when I am king, claim thou of me
The earldom of Hereford, and all the movables
Whereof the King my brother was possessed.
BUCKINGHAM
I'll claim that promise at your grace's hand.

RICHARD GLOUCESTER
And look to have it yielded with all kindness.   195
Come, let us sup betimes, that afterwards
We may digest our complots in some form.   *Exeunt*

3.2   *Enter a Messenger to the door of Lord Hastings*
MESSENGER (*knocking*)
My lord, my lord!
LORD HASTINGS ⌈*within*⌉ Who knocks?
MESSENGER   One from Lord Stanley.
     ⌈*Enter Lord Hastings*⌉
LORD HASTINGS
What is't o'clock?
MESSENGER   Upon the stroke of four.
LORD HASTINGS
Cannot my Lord Stanley sleep these tedious nights?
MESSENGER
So it appears by that I have to say.
First he commends him to your noble self.   5
LORD HASTINGS   What then?
MESSENGER
Then certifies your lordship that this night
He dreamt the boar had razèd off his helm.
Besides, he says there are two councils kept,
And that may be determined at the one   10
Which may make you and him to rue at th'other.
Therefore he sends to know your lordship's pleasure,
If you will presently take horse with him,
And with all speed post with him toward the north
To shun the danger that his soul divines.   15
LORD HASTINGS
Go, fellow, go, return unto thy lord.
Bid him not fear the separated councils.
His honour and myself are at the one,
And at the other is my good friend Catesby,
Where nothing can proceed that toucheth us   20
Whereof I shall not have intelligence.
Tell him his fears are shallow, without instance.
And for his dreams, I wonder he's so simple,
To trust the mock'ry of unquiet slumbers.
To fly the boar before the boar pursues   25
Were to incense the boar to follow us,
And make pursuit where he did mean no chase.
Go, bid thy master rise, and come to me,
And we will both together to the Tower,
Where he shall see the boar will use us kindly.   30
MESSENGER
I'll go, my lord, and tell him what you say.   *Exit*
     Enter Catesby
CATESBY
Many good morrows to my noble lord.
LORD HASTINGS
Good morrow, Catesby. You are early stirring.
What news, what news, in this our tott'ring state?
CATESBY
It is a reeling world indeed, my lord,   35
And I believe will never stand upright
Till Richard wear the garland of the realm.

LORD HASTINGS
How? 'Wear the garland'? Dost thou mean the crown?
CATESBY Ay, my good lord.
LORD HASTINGS
I'll have this crown of mine cut from my shoulders   40
Before I'll see the crown so foul misplaced.
But canst thou guess that he doth aim at it?
CATESBY
Ay, on my life, and hopes to find you forward
Upon his party for the gain thereof—
And thereupon he sends you this good news: 45
That this same very day your enemies,
The kindred of the Queen, must die at Pomfret.
LORD HASTINGS
Indeed I am no mourner for that news,
Because they have been still my adversaries.
But that I'll give my voice on Richard's side   50
To bar my master's heirs in true descent,
God knows I will not do it, to the death.
CATESBY
God keep your lordship in that gracious mind!
LORD HASTINGS
But I shall laugh at this a twelvemonth hence:
That they which brought me in my master's hate,   55
I live to look upon their tragedy.
Well, Catesby, ere a fortnight make me older,
I'll send some packing that yet think not on't.
CATESBY
'Tis a vile thing to die, my gracious lord,
When men are unprepared, and look not for it.   60
LORD HASTINGS
O monstrous, monstrous! And so falls it out
With Rivers, Vaughan, Gray—and so 'twill do
With some men else, that think themselves as safe
As thou and I, who as thou know'st are dear
To princely Richard and to Buckingham.   65
CATESBY
The Princes both make high account of you—
(*Aside*) For they account his head upon the bridge.
LORD HASTINGS
I know they do, and I have well deserved it.
     Enter Lord Stanley
Come on, come on, where is your boar-spear, man?
Fear you the boar, and go so unprovided?   70
STANLEY
My lord, good morrow.—Good morrow, Catesby.—
You may jest on, but by the Holy Rood
I do not like these several councils, I.
LORD HASTINGS
My lord, I hold my life as dear as you do yours,
And never in my days, I do protest,   75
Was it so precious to me as 'tis now.
Think you, but that I know our state secure,
I would be so triumphant as I am?
STANLEY
The lords at Pomfret, when they rode from London,
Were jocund, and supposed their states were sure,   80
And they indeed had no cause to mistrust;
But yet you see how soon the day o'ercast.

This sudden stab of rancour I misdoubt.
Pray God, I say, I prove a needless coward.   84
What, shall we toward the Tower? The day is spent.
LORD HASTINGS
Come, come, have with you! Wot you what, my lord?
Today the lords you talked of are beheaded.
STANLEY
They for their truth might better wear their heads
Than some that have accused them wear their hats.
But come, my lord, let us away.   90
        Enter a Pursuivant named ⌈Hastings⌉
LORD HASTINGS
Go on before; I'll follow presently.
                        Exeunt Stanley and Catesby
Well met, Hastings. How goes the world with thee?
PURSUIVANT
The better that your lordship please to ask.
LORD HASTINGS
I tell thee, man, 'tis better with me now
Than when I met thee last, where now we meet.   95
Then was I going prisoner to the Tower,
By the suggestion of the Queen's allies;
But now, I tell thee—keep it to thyself—
This day those enemies are put to death,
And I in better state than e'er I was.   100
PURSUIVANT
God hold it to your honour's good content.
LORD HASTINGS
Gramercy, Hastings. There, drink that for me.
        He throws him his purse
PURSUIVANT God save your lordship.   *Exit*
        Enter a Priest
PRIEST
Well met, my lord. I am glad to see your honour.
LORD HASTINGS
I thank thee, good Sir John, with all my heart.   105
I am in your debt for your last exercise.
Come the next sabbath, and I will content you.
        ⌈*He whispers in his ear.*⌉
        Enter Buckingham
BUCKINGHAM
What, talking with a priest, Lord Chamberlain?
Your friends at Pomfret, they do need the priest;
Your honour hath no shriving work in hand.   110
LORD HASTINGS
Good faith, and when I met this holy man
The men you talk of came into my mind.
What, go you toward the Tower?
BUCKINGHAM
I do, my lord, but long I cannot stay there;
I shall return before your lordship thence.   115
LORD HASTINGS
Nay, like enough, for I stay dinner there.
BUCKINGHAM (*aside*)
And supper too, although thou know'st it not.
Come, will you go?
LORD HASTINGS   I'll wait upon your lordship.
                                              Exeunt

3.3   *Enter Sir Richard Ratcliffe with Halberdiers taking*
       Lord Rivers, Lord Gray, and Sir Thomas Vaughan
       to death at Pomfret
RIVERS
Sir Richard Ratcliffe, let me tell thee this:
Today shalt thou behold a subject die
For truth, for duty, and for loyalty.
GRAY (*to Ratcliffe*)
God bless the Prince from all the pack of you!
A knot you are of damnèd bloodsuckers.   5
VAUGHAN (*to Ratcliffe*)
You live, that shall cry woe for this hereafter.
RATCLIFFE
Dispatch. The limit of your lives is out.
RIVERS
O Pomfret, Pomfret! O thou bloody prison,
Fatal and ominous to noble peers!
Within the guilty closure of thy walls,   10
Richard the Second here was hacked to death,
And, for more slander to thy dismal seat,
We give to thee our guiltless blood to drink.
GRAY
Now Margaret's curse is fall'n upon our heads,
For standing by when Richard stabbed her son.   15
RIVERS
Then cursed she Hastings; then cursed she
        Buckingham;
Then cursed she Richard. O remember, God,
To hear her prayer for them as now for us.
And for my sister and her princely sons,
Be satisfied, dear God, with our true blood,   20
Which, as thou know'st, unjustly must be spilt.
RATCLIFFE
Make haste: the hour of death is expiate.
RIVERS
Come, Gray; come, Vaughan; let us here embrace.
Farewell, until we meet again in heaven.   *Exeunt*

3.4   *Enter the Duke of Buckingham, Lord Stanley Earl of*
       Derby, Lord Hastings, Bishop of Ely, the Duke of
       Norfolk, ⌈Sir William Catesby⌉, with others at a table
LORD HASTINGS
Now, noble peers, the cause why we are met
Is to determine of the coronation.
In God's name, speak: when is the royal day?
BUCKINGHAM
Is all things ready for that solemn time?
STANLEY
It is, and wants but nomination.   5
BISHOP OF ELY
Tomorrow, then, I judge a happy day.
BUCKINGHAM
Who knows the Lord Protector's mind herein?
Who is most inward with the noble Duke?
BISHOP OF ELY
Your grace, methinks, should soonest know his mind.
BUCKINGHAM
We know each other's faces. For our hearts,   10
He knows no more of mine than I of yours,

Or I of his, my lord, than you of mine.—
Lord Hastings, you and he are near in love.

LORD HASTINGS
I thank his grace; I know he loves me well.
But for his purpose in the coronation,   15
I have not sounded him, nor he delivered
His gracious pleasure any way therein.
But you, my honourable lords, may name the time,
And in the Duke's behalf I'll give my voice,
Which I presume he'll take in gentle part.   20

Enter Richard Duke of Gloucester

BISHOP OF ELY
In happy time, here comes the Duke himself.

RICHARD GLOUCESTER
My noble lords, and cousins all, good morrow.
I have been long a sleeper, but I trust
My absence doth neglect no great design
Which by my presence might have been concluded. 25

BUCKINGHAM
Had not you come upon your cue, my lord,
William Lord Hastings had pronounced your part—
I mean, your voice, for crowning of the King.

RICHARD GLOUCESTER
Than my Lord Hastings no man might be bolder.
His lordship knows me well, and loves me well.—   30
My lord of Ely, when I was last in Holborn
I saw good strawberries in your garden there.
I do beseech you send for some of them.

BISHOP OF ELY
Marry, and will, my lord, with all my heart.   *Exit*

RICHARD GLOUCESTER
Cousin of Buckingham, a word with you.   35
(*Aside*) Catesby hath sounded Hastings in our business,
And finds the testy gentleman so hot
That he will lose his head ere give consent
His 'master's child'—as worshipful he terms it—
Shall lose the royalty of England's throne.   40

BUCKINGHAM
Withdraw yourself a while; I'll go with you.

Exeunt Richard ⌐and Buckingham⌐

STANLEY
We have not yet set down this day of triumph.
Tomorrow, in my judgement, is too sudden,
For I myself am not so well provided
As else I would be, were the day prolonged.   45

Enter Bishop of Ely

BISHOP OF ELY
Where is my lord, the Duke of Gloucester?
I have sent for these strawberries.

LORD HASTINGS
His grace looks cheerfully and smooth this morning.
There's some conceit or other likes him well,
When that he bids good morrow with such spirit.   50
I think there's never a man in Christendom
Can lesser hide his love or hate than he,
For by his face straight shall you know his heart.

STANLEY
What of his heart perceive you in his face
By any likelihood he showed today?   55

LORD HASTINGS
Marry, that with no man here he is offended—
For were he, he had shown it in his looks.

STANLEY I pray God he be not.

Enter Richard ⌐and Buckingham⌐

RICHARD GLOUCESTER
I pray you all, tell me what they deserve
That do conspire my death with devilish plots   60
Of damnèd witchcraft, and that have prevailed
Upon my body with their hellish charms?

LORD HASTINGS
The tender love I bear your grace, my lord,
Makes me most forward in this princely presence
To doom th'offenders, whatsoe'er they be.   65
I say, my lord, they have deservèd death.

RICHARD GLOUCESTER
Then be your eyes the witness of their evil:
See how I am bewitched. Behold, mine arm
Is like a blasted sapling withered up.
And this is Edward's wife, that monstrous witch,   70
Consorted with that harlot, strumpet Shore,
That by their witchcraft thus have markèd me.

LORD HASTINGS
If they have done this deed, my noble lord—

RICHARD GLOUCESTER
'If'? Thou protector of this damnèd strumpet,
Talk'st thou to me of 'ifs'? Thou art a traitor.— 75
Off with his head. Now, by Saint Paul I swear,
I will not dine until I see the same.
Some see it done.
The rest that love me, rise and follow me.

Exeunt all but ⌐Catesby⌐ and Hastings

LORD HASTINGS
Woe, woe for England! Not a whit for me,   80
For I, too fond, might have prevented this.
Stanley did dream the boar did raze our helms,
But I did scorn it and disdain to fly.
Three times today my footcloth horse did stumble,
And started when he looked upon the Tower,   85
As loath to bear me to the slaughterhouse.
O now I need the priest that spake to me.
I now repent I told the pursuivant,
As too triumphing, how mine enemies
Today at Pomfret bloodily were butchered,   90
And I myself secure in grace and favour.
O Margaret, Margaret! Now thy heavy curse
Is lighted on poor Hastings' wretched head.

⌐CATESBY⌐
Come, come, dispatch: the Duke would be at dinner.
Make a short shrift; he longs to see your head.   95

LORD HASTINGS
O momentary grace of mortal men,
Which we more hunt for than the grace of God.
Who builds his hope in th'air of your good looks
Lives like a drunken sailor on a mast,
Ready with every nod to tumble down   100
Into the fatal bowels of the deep.

⌐CATESBY⌐
Come, come, dispatch. 'Tis bootless to exclaim.

LORD HASTINGS
O bloody Richard! Miserable England!
I prophesy the fearful'st time to thee
That ever wretched age hath looked upon.—   105
Come lead me to the block; bear him my head.
They smile at me, who shortly shall be dead.   *Exeunt*

3.5   *Enter Richard Duke of Gloucester and the Duke of*
     Buckingham in rotten armour, marvellous ill-
     favoured
RICHARD GLOUCESTER
Come, cousin, canst thou quake and change thy
    colour?
Murder thy breath in middle of a word?
And then again begin, and stop again,
As if thou wert distraught and mad with terror?
BUCKINGHAM
Tut, I can counterfeit the deep tragedian,   5
Tremble and start at wagging of a straw,
Speak, and look back, and pry on every side,
Intending deep suspicion; ghastly looks
Are at my service, like enforcèd smiles,
And both are ready in their offices   10
At any time to grace my stratagems.
     Enter the Lord Mayor
RICHARD GLOUCESTER (*aside to Buckingham*) Here comes
    the Mayor.
BUCKINGHAM (*aside to Richard*)
Let me alone to entertain him.—Lord Mayor—
RICHARD GLOUCESTER ⌜*calling as to one within*⌝
Look to the drawbridge there!
BUCKINGHAM Hark, a drum!   15
RICHARD GLOUCESTER ⌜*calling as to one within*⌝
Catesby, o'erlook the walls!
BUCKINGHAM Lord Mayor, the reason we have sent—
RICHARD GLOUCESTER
Look back, defend thee! Here are enemies.
BUCKINGHAM
God and our innocence defend and guard us.
     Enter ⌜*Sir William Catesby*⌝ *with Hastings' head*
RICHARD GLOUCESTER
O, O, be quiet! It is Catesby.   20
CATESBY
Here is the head of that ignoble traitor,
The dangerous and unsuspected Hastings.
RICHARD GLOUCESTER
So dear I loved the man that I must weep.
I took him for the plainest harmless creature
That breathed upon the earth, a Christian,   25
Made him my book wherein my soul recorded
The history of all her secret thoughts.
So smooth he daubed his vice with show of virtue
That, his apparent open guilt omitted—
I mean, his conversation with Shore's wife—   30
He lived from all attainture of suspect.
BUCKINGHAM
The covert'st sheltered traitor that ever lived.
(*To the Mayor*) Would you imagine, or almost believe—

Were't not that, by great preservation,
We live to tell it—that the subtle traitor   35
This day had plotted in the Council house
To murder me and my good lord of Gloucester?
MAYOR Had he done so?
RICHARD GLOUCESTER
What, think you we are Turks or infidels,
Or that we would against the form of law   40
Proceed thus rashly in the villain's death
But that the extreme peril of the case,
The peace of England, and our persons' safety,
Enforced us to this execution?
MAYOR
Now fair befall you, he deserved his death,   45
And your good graces both have well proceeded,
To warn false traitors from the like attempts.
I never looked for better at his hands
After he once fell in with Mrs Shore.
⌜RICHARD GLOUCESTER⌝
Yet had not we determined he should die,   50
Until your lordship came to see his end,
Which now the loving haste of these our friends—
Something against our meanings—have prevented;
Because, my lord, we would have had you hear
The traitor speak, and timorously confess   55
The manner and the purpose of his treason,
That you might well have signified the same
Unto the citizens, who haply may
Misconster us in him, and wail his death.
MAYOR
But, my good lord, your graces' word shall serve   60
As well as I had seen and heard him speak.
And do not doubt, right noble princes both,
But I'll acquaint our duteous citizens
With all your just proceedings in this cause.
RICHARD GLOUCESTER
And to that end we wished your lordship here,   65
T'avoid the censures of the carping world.
BUCKINGHAM
Which, since you come too late of our intent,
Yet witness what you hear we did intend,
And so, my good Lord Mayor, we bid farewell.
     Exit Mayor
RICHARD GLOUCESTER
Go after; after, cousin Buckingham!   70
The Mayor towards Guildhall hies him in all post;
There, at your meetest vantage of the time,
Infer the bastardy of Edward's children.
Tell them how Edward put to death a citizen
Only for saying he would make his son   75
'Heir to the Crown'—meaning indeed, his house,
Which by the sign thereof was termèd so.
Moreover, urge his hateful luxury
And bestial appetite in change of lust,
Which stretched unto their servants, daughters, wives,
Even where his raging eye, or savage heart,   81
Without control, listed to make a prey.
Nay, for a need, thus far come near my person:

Tell them, when that my mother went with child
Of that insatiate Edward, noble York,   85
My princely father, then had wars in France,
And by true computation of the time
Found that the issue was not his begot—
Which well appearèd in his lineaments,
Being nothing like the noble Duke my father.   90
Yet touch this sparingly, as 'twere far off,
Because, my lord, you know my mother lives.
BUCKINGHAM
Doubt not, my lord, I'll play the orator
As if the golden fee for which I plead
Were for myself. And so, my lord, adieu.   95
                                    He starts to go
RICHARD GLOUCESTER
If you thrive well, bring them to Baynard's Castle,
Where you shall find me well accompanied
With reverend fathers and well-learnèd bishops.
BUCKINGHAM
I go, and towards three or four o'clock
Look for the news that the Guildhall affords.   *Exit*
RICHARD GLOUCESTER
Now will I in, to take some privy order   101
To draw the brats of Clarence out of sight,
And to give notice that no manner person
Have any time recourse unto the Princes.   *Exeunt*

3.6   *Enter a Scrivener with a paper in his hand*
SCRIVENER
Here is the indictment of the good Lord Hastings,
Which in a set hand fairly is engrossed,
That it may be today read o'er in Paul's—
And mark how well the sequel hangs together:
Eleven hours I have spent to write it over,   5
For yesternight by Catesby was it sent me;
The precedent was full as long a-doing;
And yet, within these five hours, Hastings lived,
Untainted, unexamined, free, at liberty.
Here's a good world the while! Who is so gross   10
That cannot see this palpable device?
Yet who so bold but says he sees it not?
Bad is the world, and all will come to naught,
When such ill dealing must be seen in thought.   *Exit*

3.7   *Enter Richard Duke of Gloucester at one door and*
          the Duke of Buckingham at another
RICHARD GLOUCESTER
How now, how now! What say the citizens?
BUCKINGHAM
Now, by the holy mother of our Lord,
The citizens are mum, say not a word.
RICHARD GLOUCESTER
Touched you the bastardy of Edward's children?
BUCKINGHAM
I did, with his contract with Lady Lucy,   5
And his contract by deputy in France,
Th'insatiate greediness of his desire,

And his enforcement of the city wives,
His tyranny for trifles, his own bastardy—
As being got your father then in France,   10
And his resemblance, being not like the Duke.
Withal, I did infer your lineaments—
Being the right idea of your father
Both in your face and nobleness of mind;
Laid open all your victories in Scotland,   15
Your discipline in war, wisdom in peace,
Your bounty, virtue, fair humility—
Indeed, left nothing fitting for your purpose
Untouched or slightly handled in discourse.
And when mine oratory grew toward end,   20
I bid them that did love their country's good
Cry 'God save Richard, England's royal king!'
RICHARD GLOUCESTER And did they so?
BUCKINGHAM
No, so God help me. They spake not a word,
But, like dumb statuas or breathing stones,   25
Stared each on other and looked deadly pale—
Which, when I saw, I reprehended them,
And asked the Mayor, what meant this wilful silence?
His answer was, the people were not used
To be spoke to but by the Recorder.   30
Then he was urged to tell my tale again:
'Thus saith the Duke . . . thus hath the Duke
     inferred'—
But nothing spoke in warrant from himself.
When he had done, some followers of mine own,
At lower end of the Hall, hurled up their caps,   35
And some ten voices cried 'God save King Richard!'
And thus I took the vantage of those few:
'Thanks, gentle citizens and friends', quoth I;
'This general applause and cheerful shout
Argues your wisdoms and your love to Richard'—   40
And even here brake off and came away.
RICHARD GLOUCESTER
What tongueless blocks were they! Would they not
     speak?
⌈BUCKINGHAM⌉ No, by my troth, my lord.
RICHARD GLOUCESTER
Will not the Mayor then, and his brethren, come?
BUCKINGHAM
The Mayor is here at hand. Intend some fear;   45
Be not you spoke with, but by mighty suit;
And look you get a prayer book in your hand,
And stand between two churchmen, good my lord,
For on that ground I'll build a holy descant.
And be not easily won to our request.   50
Play the maid's part: still answer 'nay'—and take it.
RICHARD GLOUCESTER
I go. An if you plead as well for them
As I can say nay to thee for myself,
No doubt we'll bring it to a happy issue.
                              One knocks within
BUCKINGHAM
Go, go, up to the leads! The Lord Mayor knocks.—   55
                                    Exit Richard

Enter the Lord Mayor, aldermen, and citizens
Welcome, my lord. I dance attendance here.
I think the Duke will not be spoke withal.
   Enter Catesby
Now Catesby, what says your lord to my request?
CATESBY
  He doth entreat your grace, my noble lord,
  To visit him tomorrow, or next day.   60
  He is within with two right reverend fathers,
  Divinely bent to meditation,
  And in no worldly suits would he be moved,
  To draw him from his holy exercise.
BUCKINGHAM
  Return, good Catesby, to the gracious Duke.   65
  Tell him myself, the Mayor, and aldermen,
  In deep designs, in matter of great moment,
  No less importing than our general good,
  Are come to have some conference with his grace.
CATESBY
  I'll signify so much unto him straight.   *Exit*
BUCKINGHAM
  Ah ha! My lord, this prince is not an Edward.   71
  He is not lolling on a lewd day-bed,
  But on his knees at meditation;
  Not dallying with a brace of courtesans,
  But meditating with two deep divines;   75
  Not sleeping to engross his idle body,
  But praying to enrich his watchful soul.
  Happy were England would this virtuous prince
  Take on his grace the sovereignty thereof.
  But, sure I fear, we shall not win him to it.   80
MAYOR
  Marry, God defend his grace should say us nay.
BUCKINGHAM
  I fear he will. Here Catesby comes again.
   Enter Catesby
Now Catesby, what says his grace?
CATESBY
  He wonders to what end you have assembled
  Such troops of citizens to come to him,   85
  His grace not being warned thereof before.
  He fears, my lord, you mean no good to him.
BUCKINGHAM
  Sorry I am my noble cousin should
  Suspect me that I mean no good to him.
  By heaven, we come to him in perfect love,   90
  And so once more return and tell his grace.
                     Exit Catesby
  When holy and devout religious men
  Are at their beads, 'tis much to draw them thence.
  So sweet is zealous contemplation.
   Enter Richard aloft, between two bishops. ⌈*Enter*
   Catesby below⌉
MAYOR
  See where his grace stands 'tween two clergymen. 95
BUCKINGHAM
  Two props of virtue for a Christian prince,
  To stay him from the fall of vanity;
  And see, a book of prayer in his hand—

True ornaments to know a holy man.—
Famous Plantagenet, most gracious prince,   100
Lend favourable ear to our request,
And pardon us the interruption
Of thy devotion and right Christian zeal.
RICHARD GLOUCESTER
  My lord, there needs no such apology.
  I do beseech your grace to pardon me,   105
  Who, earnest in the service of my God,
  Deferred the visitation of my friends.
  But leaving this, what is your grace's pleasure?
BUCKINGHAM
  Even that, I hope, which pleaseth God above,
  And all good men of this ungoverned isle.   110
RICHARD GLOUCESTER
  I do suspect I have done some offence
  That seems disgracious in the city's eye,
  And that you come to reprehend my ignorance.
BUCKINGHAM
  You have, my lord. Would it might please your grace
  On our entreaties to amend your fault.   115
RICHARD GLOUCESTER
  Else wherefore breathe I in a Christian land?
BUCKINGHAM
  Know then, it is your fault that you resign
  The supreme seat, the throne majestical,
  The sceptred office of your ancestors,
  Your state of fortune and your due of birth,   120
  The lineal glory of your royal house,
  To the corruption of a blemished stock,
  Whiles in the mildness of your sleepy thoughts—
  Which here we waken to our country's good—
  The noble isle doth want her proper limbs: 125
  Her face defaced with scars of infamy,
  Her royal stock graft with ignoble plants
  And almost shouldered in the swallowing gulf
  Of dark forgetfulness and deep oblivion,
  Which to recure we heartily solicit   130
  Your gracious self to take on you the charge
  And kingly government of this your land—
  Not as Protector, steward, substitute,
  Or lowly factor for another's gain,
  But as successively, from blood to blood,   135
  Your right of birth, your empery, your own.
  For this, consorted with the citizens,
  Your very worshipful and loving friends,
  And by their vehement instigation,
  In this just cause come I to move your grace.   140
RICHARD GLOUCESTER
  I cannot tell if to depart in silence
  Or bitterly to speak in your reproof
  Best fitteth my degree or your condition.
  Your love deserves my thanks; but my desert,
  Unmeritable, shuns your high request.   145
  First, if all obstacles were cut away
  And that my path were even to the crown,
  As the ripe revenue and due of birth,
  Yet so much is my poverty of spirit,
  So mighty and so many my defects,   150

That I would rather hide me from my greatness—
Being a barque to brook no mighty sea—
Than in my greatness covet to be hid,
And in the vapour of my glory smothered.
But God be thanked, there is no need of me,   155
And much I need to help you, were there need.
The royal tree hath left us royal fruit,
Which, mellowed by the stealing hours of time,
Will well become the seat of majesty
And make, no doubt, us happy by his reign.   160
On him I lay that you would lay on me,
The right and fortune of his happy stars,
Which God defend that I should wring from him.

BUCKINGHAM
My lord, this argues conscience in your grace,
But the respects thereof are nice and trivial,   165
All circumstances well considerèd.
You say that Edward is your brother's son;
So say we, too—but not by Edward's wife.
For first was he contract to Lady Lucy—
Your mother lives a witness to his vow—   170
And afterward, by substitute, betrothed
To Bona, sister to the King of France.
These both put off, a poor petitioner,
A care-crazed mother to a many sons,
A beauty-waning and distressèd widow   175
Even in the afternoon of her best days,
Made prize and purchase of his wanton eye,
Seduced the pitch and height of his degree
To base declension and loathed bigamy.
By her in his unlawful bed he got   180
This Edward, whom our manners call the Prince.
More bitterly could I expostulate,
Save that for reverence to some alive
I give a sparing limit to my tongue.
Then, good my lord, take to your royal self   185
This proffered benefit of dignity—
If not to bless us and the land withal,
Yet to draw forth your noble ancestry
From the corruption of abusing times,
Unto a lineal, true-derivèd course.   190

MAYOR (to Richard)
Do, good my lord; your citizens entreat you.

BUCKINGHAM (to Richard)
Refuse not, mighty lord, this proffered love.

CATESBY (to Richard)
O make them joyful: grant their lawful suit.

RICHARD GLOUCESTER
Alas, why would you heap this care on me?
I am unfit for state and majesty.   195
I do beseech you, take it not amiss.
I cannot, nor I will not, yield to you.

BUCKINGHAM
If you refuse it—as, in love and zeal,
Loath to depose the child, your brother's son,
As well we know your tenderness of heart   200
And gentle, kind, effeminate remorse,
Which we have noted in you to your kindred,

And equally indeed to all estates—
Yet know, whe'er you accept our suit or no,
Your brother's son shall never reign our king,   205
But we will plant some other in the throne,
To the disgrace and downfall of your house.
And in this resolution here we leave you.—
Come, citizens. 'Swounds, I'll entreat no more.

RICHARD GLOUCESTER
O do not swear, my lord of Buckingham.   210
⌈Exeunt Buckingham and some others⌉

CATESBY
Call him again, sweet prince. Accept their suit.

⌈ANOTHER⌉
If you deny them, all the land will rue it.

RICHARD GLOUCESTER
Will you enforce me to a world of cares?
Call them again.   Exit one or more
I am not made of stone,
But penetrable to your kind entreats,   215
Albeit against my conscience and my soul.

Enter Buckingham and the rest

Cousin of Buckingham, and sage, grave men,
Since you will buckle fortune on my back,
To bear her burden, whe'er I will or no,
I must have patience to endure the load.   220
But if black scandal or foul-faced reproach
Attend the sequel of your imposition,
Your mere enforcement shall acquittance me
From all the impure blots and stains thereof;
For God doth know, and you may partly see,   225
How far I am from the desire of this.

MAYOR
God bless your grace! We see it, and will say it.

RICHARD GLOUCESTER
In saying so, you shall but say the truth.

BUCKINGHAM
Then I salute you with this royal title:
Long live kind Richard, England's worthy king!   230

⌈ALL BUT RICHARD⌉ Amen.

BUCKINGHAM
Tomorrow may it please you to be crowned?

RICHARD GLOUCESTER
Even when you please, for you will have it so.

BUCKINGHAM
Tomorrow then, we will attend your grace.
And so, most joyfully, we take our leave.   235

RICHARD GLOUCESTER (to the bishops)
Come, let us to our holy work again.—
Farewell, my cousin. Farewell, gentle friends.
        Exeunt Richard and bishops above, the rest
                                below

4.1   Enter Queen Elizabeth, the old Duchess of York, and
        Marquis Dorset at one door; Lady Anne (Duchess
        of Gloucester) with Clarence's daughter at another
        door

DUCHESS OF YORK
Who meets us here? My niece Plantagenet,

Led in the hand of her kind aunt of Gloucester?
Now for my life, she's wand'ring to the Tower,
On pure heart's love, to greet the tender Prince.—
Daughter, well met.
LADY ANNE   God give your graces both   5
A happy and a joyful time of day.
QUEEN ELIZABETH
As much to you, good sister. Whither away?
LADY ANNE
No farther than the Tower, and—as I guess—
Upon the like devotion as yourselves:
To gratulate the gentle princes there.   10
QUEEN ELIZABETH
Kind sister, thanks. We'll enter all together—
    Enter from the Tower ⌈Brackenbury⌉ the Lieutenant
And in good time, here the Lieutenant comes.
Master Lieutenant, pray you by your leave,
How doth the Prince, and my young son of York?
BRACKENBURY
Right well, dear madam. By your patience,   15
I may not suffer you to visit them.
The King hath strictly charged the contrary.
QUEEN ELIZABETH
The King? Who's that?
BRACKENBURY   I mean, the Lord Protector.
QUEEN ELIZABETH
The Lord protect him from that kingly title.
Hath he set bounds between their love and me?   20
I am their mother; who shall bar me from them?
DUCHESS OF YORK
I am their father's mother; I will see them.
LADY ANNE
Their aunt I am in law, in love their mother;
Then bring me to their sights. I'll bear thy blame,
And take thy office from thee on my peril.   25
BRACKENBURY
No, madam, no; I may not leave it so.
I am bound by oath, and therefore pardon me.   *Exit*
    Enter Lord Stanley Earl of Derby
STANLEY
Let me but meet you ladies one hour hence,
And I'll salute your grace of York as mother
And reverend looker-on of two fair queens.   30
    (To Anne) Come, madam, you must straight to
        Westminster,
There to be crownèd Richard's royal queen.
QUEEN ELIZABETH
Ah, cut my lace asunder, that my pent heart
May have some scope to beat, or else I swoon
With this dead-killing news.   35
LADY ANNE
Despiteful tidings! O unpleasing news!
DORSET *(to Anne)*
Be of good cheer.—Mother, how fares your grace?
QUEEN ELIZABETH
O Dorset, speak not to me. Get thee gone.
Death and destruction dogs thee at thy heels.
Thy mother's name is ominous to children.   40

If thou wilt outstrip death, go cross the seas,
And live with Richmond from the reach of hell.
Go, hie thee! Hie thee from this slaughterhouse,
Lest thou increase the number of the dead,
And make me die the thrall of Margaret's curses: 45
'Nor mother, wife, nor counted England's Queen'.
STANLEY
Full of wise care is this your counsel, madam.
    (To Dorset) Take all the swift advantage of the hours.
You shall have letters from me to my son
In your behalf, to meet you on the way.   50
Be not ta'en tardy by unwise delay.
DUCHESS OF YORK
O ill-dispersing wind of misery!
O my accursèd womb, the bed of death!
A cockatrice hast thou hatched to the world,
Whose unavoided eye is murderous.   55
STANLEY *(to Anne)*
Come, madam, come. I in all haste was sent.
LADY ANNE
And I in all unwillingness will go.
O would to God that the inclusive verge
Of golden metal that must round my brow
Were red-hot steel, to sear me to the brains.   60
Anointed let me be with deadly venom,
And die ere men can say 'God save the Queen'.
QUEEN ELIZABETH
Go, go, poor soul. I envy not thy glory.
To feed my humour, wish thyself no harm.
LADY ANNE
No? Why? When he that is my husband now   65
Came to me as I followed Henry's corpse,
When scarce the blood was well washed from his
        hands,
Which issued from my other angel husband
And that dear saint which then I weeping followed—
O when, I say, I looked on Richard's face,   70
This was my wish: 'Be thou', quoth I, 'accursed
For making me, so young, so old a widow,
And when thou wedd'st, let sorrow haunt thy bed;
And be thy wife—if any be so mad—
More miserable made by the life of thee   75
Than thou hast made me by my dear lord's death.'
Lo, ere I can repeat this curse again,
Within so small a time, my woman's heart
Grossly grew captive to his honey words
And proved the subject of mine own soul's curse,   80
Which hitherto hath held mine eyes from rest—
For never yet one hour in his bed
Did I enjoy the golden dew of sleep,
But with his timorous dreams was still awaked.
Besides, he hates me for my father Warwick,   85
And will, no doubt, shortly be rid of me.
QUEEN ELIZABETH
Poor heart, adieu. I pity thy complaining.
LADY ANNE
No more than with my soul I mourn for yours.

DORSET
Farewell, thou woeful welcomer of glory.
LADY ANNE
Adieu, poor soul, that tak'st thy leave of it. 90
DUCHESS OF YORK
Go thou to Richmond, and good fortune guide thee.
⌈*Exit Dorset*⌉
Go thou to Richard, and good angels tend thee.
⌈*Exeunt Anne, Stanley, and Clarence's daughter*⌉
Go thou to sanctuary, and good thoughts possess thee.
⌈*Exit Elizabeth*⌉
I to my grave, where peace and rest lie with me.
Eighty odd years of sorrow have I seen, 95
And each hour's joy racked with a week of teen.
⌈*Exit*⌉

4.2   *Sound a sennet. Enter King Richard in pomp, the*
Duke of Buckingham, Sir William Catesby, ⌈other
nobles⌉, and a Page
KING RICHARD
Stand all apart.—Cousin of Buckingham.
BUCKINGHAM My gracious sovereign?
KING RICHARD Give me thy hand.
Sound ⌈a sennet⌉. Here Richard ascendeth the
throne
Thus high by thy advice
And thy assistance is King Richard seated. 5
But shall we wear these glories for a day?
Or shall they last, and we rejoice in them?
BUCKINGHAM
Still live they, and for ever let them last.
KING RICHARD
Ah, Buckingham, now do I play the touch,
To try if thou be current gold indeed. 10
Young Edward lives. Think now what I would speak.
BUCKINGHAM Say on, my loving lord.
KING RICHARD
Why, Buckingham, I say I would be king.
BUCKINGHAM
Why, so you are, my thrice-renownèd liege.
KING RICHARD
Ha? Am I king? 'Tis so. But Edward lives. 15
BUCKINGHAM
True, noble prince.
KING RICHARD   O bitter consequence,
That Edward still should live 'true noble prince'.
Cousin, thou wast not wont to be so dull.
Shall I be plain? I wish the bastards dead,
And I would have it immediately performed. 20
What sayst thou now? Speak suddenly, be brief.
BUCKINGHAM Your grace may do your pleasure.
KING RICHARD
Tut, tut, thou art all ice. Thy kindness freezes.
Say, have I thy consent that they shall die?
BUCKINGHAM
Give me some little breath, some pause, dear lord, 25
Before I positively speak in this.
I will resolve you herein presently.   *Exit*

CATESBY (*to another, aside*)
The King is angry. See, he gnaws his lip.
KING RICHARD (*aside*)
I will converse with iron-witted fools
And unrespective boys. None are for me 30
That look into me with considerate eyes.
High-reaching Buckingham grows circumspect.—
Boy.
PAGE My lord?
KING RICHARD
Know'st thou not any whom corrupting gold 35
Will tempt unto a close exploit of death?
PAGE
I know a discontented gentleman
Whose humble means match not his haughty spirit.
Gold were as good as twenty orators,
And will no doubt tempt him to anything. 40
KING RICHARD
What is his name?
PAGE   His name, my lord, is Tyrrell.
KING RICHARD
I partly know the man. Go call him hither, boy.
Exit Page
⌈*Aside*⌉ The deep-revolving, witty Buckingham
No more shall be the neighbour to my counsels.
Hath he so long held out with me untired, 45
And stops he now for breath? Well, be it so.
Enter Lord Stanley Earl of Derby
How now, Lord Stanley? What's the news?
STANLEY Know, my loving lord,
The Marquis Dorset, as I hear, is fled
To Richmond, in those parts beyond the seas 50
Where he abides.
KING RICHARD
Come hither, Catesby. (*Aside to Catesby*) Rumour it
abroad
That Anne, my wife, is very grievous sick.
I will take order for her keeping close.
Enquire me out some mean-born gentleman, 55
Whom I will marry straight to Clarence' daughter.
The boy is foolish, and I fear not him.
Look how thou dream'st. I say again, give out
That Anne, my queen, is sick, and like to die.
About it, for it stands me much upon 60
To stop all hopes whose growth may damage me.
⌈*Exit Catesby*⌉
(*Aside*) I must be married to my brother's daughter,
Or else my kingdom stands on brittle glass.
Murder her brothers, and then marry her?
Uncertain way of gain, but I am in 65
So far in blood that sin will pluck on sin.
Tear-falling pity dwells not in this eye.—
Enter Sir James Tyrrell; ⌈he kneels⌉
Is thy name Tyrrell?
TYRRELL
James Tyrrell, and your most obedient subject.
KING RICHARD
Art thou indeed?
TYRRELL   Prove me, my gracious lord. 70

KING RICHARD
Dar'st thou resolve to kill a friend of mine?
TYRRELL
Please you, but I had rather kill two enemies.
KING RICHARD
Why there thou hast it: two deep enemies,
Foes to my rest, and my sweet sleep's disturbers,
Are they that I would have thee deal upon.   75
Tyrrell, I mean those bastards in the Tower.
TYRRELL
Let me have open means to come to them,
And soon I'll rid you from the fear of them.
KING RICHARD
Thou sing'st sweet music. Hark, come hither, Tyrrell.
Go, by this token. Rise, and lend thine ear.   80
    Richard whispers in his ear
'Tis no more but so. Say it is done,
And I will love thee, and prefer thee for it.
TYRRELL I will dispatch it straight.
⌈KING RICHARD⌉
Shall we hear from thee, Tyrrell, ere we sleep?
    Enter Buckingham
⌈TYRRELL⌉ Ye shall, my lord.   *Exit*
BUCKINGHAM
My lord, I have considered in my mind   86
The late request that you did sound me in.
KING RICHARD
Well, let that rest. Dorset is fled to Richmond.
BUCKINGHAM I hear the news, my lord.
KING RICHARD
Stanley, he is your wife's son. Well, look to it.   90
BUCKINGHAM
My lord, I claim the gift, my due by promise,
For which your honour and your faith is pawned:
Th'earldom of Hereford, and the movables
Which you have promisèd I shall possess.
KING RICHARD
Stanley, look to your wife. If she convey   95
Letters to Richmond, you shall answer it.
BUCKINGHAM
What says your highness to my just request?
KING RICHARD
I do remember me, Henry the Sixth
Did prophesy that Richmond should be king,
When Richmond was a little peevish boy.   100
A king . . . perhaps . . . perhaps.
BUCKINGHAM   My lord?
KING RICHARD
How chance the prophet could not at that time
Have told me, I being by, that I should kill him?
BUCKINGHAM
My lord, your promise for the earldom.
KING RICHARD
Richmond? When last I was at Exeter,   105
The Mayor in courtesy showed me the castle,
And called it 'Ruge-mount'—at which name I started,
Because a bard of Ireland told me once
I should not live long after I saw 'Richmond'.

BUCKINGHAM My lord?   110
KING RICHARD Ay? What's o'clock?
BUCKINGHAM
I am thus bold to put your grace in mind
Of what you promised me.
KING RICHARD   But what's o'clock?
BUCKINGHAM Upon the stroke of ten.
KING RICHARD Well, let it strike!   115
BUCKINGHAM Why 'let it strike'?
KING RICHARD
Because that, like a jack, thou keep'st the stroke
Betwixt thy begging and my meditation.
I am not in the giving vein today.
BUCKINGHAM
Why then resolve me, whe'er you will or no?   120
KING RICHARD
Thou troublest me. I am not in the vein.
    Exit Richard, followed by all but Buckingham
BUCKINGHAM
And is it thus? Repays he my deep service
With such contempt? Made I him king for this?
O let me think on Hastings, and be gone
To Brecon, while my fearful head is on.   125
    Exit ⌈at another door⌉

4.3   *Enter Sir James Tyrrell*
TYRRELL
The tyrannous and bloody act is done—
The most arch deed of piteous massacre
That ever yet this land was guilty of.
Dighton and Forrest, whom I did suborn
To do this piece of ruthless butchery,   5
Albeit they were fleshed villains, bloody dogs,
Melted with tenderness and mild compassion,
Wept like two children in their deaths' sad story.
'O thus', quoth Dighton, 'lay the gentle babes';
'Thus, thus', quoth Forrest, 'girdling one another   10
Within their alabaster innocent arms.
Their lips were four red roses on a stalk,
And in their summer beauty kissed each other.
A book of prayers on their pillow lay,
'Which once', quoth Forrest, 'almost changed my mind.
But O, the devil'—there the villain stopped,   16
When Dighton thus told on, 'We smotherèd
The most replenishèd sweet work of nature,
That from the prime creation e'er she framed.'
Hence both are gone, with conscience and remorse.   20
They could not speak, and so I left them both,
To bear this tidings to the bloody king.
    Enter King Richard
And here he comes.—All health, my sovereign lord.
KING RICHARD
Kind Tyrrell, am I happy in thy news?
TYRRELL
If to have done the thing you gave in charge   25
Beget your happiness, be happy then,
For it is done.
KING RICHARD   But didst thou see them dead?

TYRRELL
  I did, my lord.
KING RICHARD   And buried, gentle Tyrrell?
TYRRELL
  The chaplain of the Tower hath buried them;
  But where, to say the truth, I do not know.   30
KING RICHARD
  Come to me, Tyrrell, soon, at after-supper,
  When thou shalt tell the process of their death.
  Meantime, but think how I may do thee good,
  And be inheritor of thy desire.
  Farewell till then.
TYRRELL   I humbly take my leave.   Exit
KING RICHARD
  The son of Clarence have I pent up close.   36
  His daughter meanly have I matched in marriage.
  The sons of Edward sleep in Abraham's bosom,
  And Anne, my wife, hath bid this world goodnight.
  Now, for I know the Breton Richmond aims   40
  At young Elizabeth, my brother's daughter,
  And by that knot looks proudly o'er the crown,
  To her go I, a jolly thriving wooer—
    Enter Sir Richard Ratcliffe, ⌈running⌉
RATCLIFFE My lord.
KING RICHARD
  Good news or bad, that thou com'st in so bluntly? 45
RATCLIFFE
  Bad news, my lord. Ely is fled to Richmond,
  And Buckingham, backed with the hardy Welshmen,
  Is in the field, and still his power increaseth.
KING RICHARD
  Ely with Richmond troubles me more near
  Than Buckingham and his rash-levied strength.   50
  Come, I have learned that fearful commenting
  Is leaden servitor to dull delay.
  Delay leads impotent and snail-paced beggary.
  Then fiery expedition be my wing:
  Jove's Mercury, an herald for a king.   55
  Go, muster men. My counsel is my shield.
  We must be brief, when traitors brave the field.
    Exeunt

4.4   *Enter old Queen Margaret*
QUEEN MARGARET
  So now prosperity begins to mellow
  And drop into the rotten mouth of death.
  Here in these confines slyly have I lurked
  To watch the waning of mine enemies.
  A dire induction am I witness to,   5
  And will to France, hoping the consequence
  Will prove as bitter, black, and tragical.
    ⌈*Enter the old Duchess of York and Queen Elizabeth*⌉
  Withdraw thee, wretched Margaret. Who comes
    here?
QUEEN ELIZABETH
  Ah, my poor princes! Ah, my tender babes!
  My unblown flowers, new-appearing sweets!   10
  If yet your gentle souls fly in the air,

  And be not fixed in doom perpetual,
  Hover about me with your airy wings
  And hear your mother's lamentation.
QUEEN MARGARET *(aside)*
  Hover about her, say that right for right   15
  Hath dimmed your infant morn to agèd night.
DUCHESS OF YORK
  So many miseries have crazed my voice
  That my woe-wearied tongue is still and mute.
  Edward Plantagenet, why art thou dead?
QUEEN MARGARET *(aside)*
  Plantagenet doth quit Plantagenet;   20
  Edward for Edward pays a dying debt.
QUEEN ELIZABETH
  Wilt thou, O God, fly from such gentle lambs
  And throw them in the entrails of the wolf?
  When didst thou sleep, when such a deed was done?
QUEEN MARGARET *(aside)*
  When holy Harry died, and my sweet son.   25
DUCHESS OF YORK
  Dead life, blind sight, poor mortal living ghost,
  Woe's scene, world's shame, grave's due by life
    usurped,
  Brief abstract and record of tedious days,
  Rest thy unrest on England's lawful earth,
  Unlawfully made drunk with innocents' blood.   30
    ⌈*They*⌉ *sit*
QUEEN ELIZABETH
  Ah that thou wouldst as soon afford a grave
  As thou canst yield a melancholy seat.
  Then would I hide my bones, not rest them here.
  Ah, who hath any cause to mourn but we?
QUEEN MARGARET *(coming forward)*
  If ancient sorrow be most reverend,   35
  Give mine the benefit of seniory,
  And let my griefs frown on the upper hand.
  If sorrow can admit society,
  Tell o'er your woes again by viewing mine.
  I had an Edward, till a Richard killed him;   40
  I had a husband, till a Richard killed him.
  (To Elizabeth) Thou hadst an Edward, till a Richard
    killed him;
  Thou hadst a Richard, till a Richard killed him.
DUCHESS OF YORK ⌈*rising*⌉
  I had a Richard too, and thou didst kill him;
  I had a Rutland too, thou holpst to kill him.   45
QUEEN MARGARET
  Thou hadst a Clarence too, and Richard killed him.
  From forth the kennel of thy womb hath crept
  A hell-hound that doth hunt us all to death:
  That dog that had his teeth before his eyes,
  To worry lambs and lap their gentle blood;   50
  That foul defacer of God's handiwork,
  That reigns in gallèd eyes of weeping souls;
  That excellent grand tyrant of the earth
  Thy womb let loose to chase us to our graves.
  O upright, just, and true-disposing God,   55
  How do I thank thee that this charnel cur

Preys on the issue of his mother's body,
And makes her pewfellow with others' moan.

DUCHESS OF YORK

O Harry's wife, triumph not in my woes.
God witness with me, I have wept for thine.   60

QUEEN MARGARET

Bear with me. I am hungry for revenge,
And now I cloy me with beholding it.
Thy Edward, he is dead, that killed my Edward;
Thy other Edward dead, to quite my Edward;
Young York, he is but boot, because both they   65
Matched not the high perfection of my loss;
Thy Clarence, he is dead, that stabbed my Edward,
And the beholders of this frantic play—
Th'adulterate Hastings, Rivers, Vaughan, Gray—
Untimely smothered in their dusky graves.   70
Richard yet lives, hell's black intelligencer,
Only reserved their factor to buy souls
And send them thither; but at hand, at hand
Ensues his piteous and unpitied end.
Earth gapes, hell burns, fiends roar, saints pray,   75
To have him suddenly conveyed from hence.
Cancel his bond of life, dear God, I plead,
That I may live and say, 'The dog is dead'.

QUEEN ELIZABETH

O thou didst prophesy the time would come
That I should wish for thee to help me curse   80
That bottled spider, that foul bunch-backed toad.

QUEEN MARGARET

I called thee then 'vain flourish of my fortune';
I called thee then, poor shadow, 'painted queen'—
The presentation of but what I was,
The flattering index of a direful pageant,   85
One heaved a-high to be hurled down below,
A mother only mocked with two fair babes,
A dream of what thou wast, a garish flag
To be the aim of every dangerous shot,
A sign of dignity, a breath, a bubble,   90
A queen in jest, only to fill the scene.
Where is thy husband now? Where be thy brothers?
Where are thy two sons? Wherein dost thou joy?
Who sues, and kneels, and says 'God save the Queen'?
Where be the bending peers that flattered thee?   95
Where be the thronging troops that followed thee?
Decline all this, and see what now thou art:
For happy wife, a most distressèd widow;
For joyful mother, one that wails the name;
For queen, a very caitiff, crowned with care;   100
For one being sued to, one that humbly sues;
For she that scorned at me, now scorned of me;
For she being feared of all, now fearing one;
For she commanding all, obeyed of none.
Thus hath the course of justice whirled about,   105
And left thee but a very prey to time,
Having no more but thought of what thou wert
To torture thee the more, being what thou art.
Thou didst usurp my place, and dost thou not
Usurp the just proportion of my sorrow?   110

Now thy proud neck bears half my burdened yoke—
From which, even here, I slip my weary head,
And leave the burden of it all on thee.
Farewell, York's wife, and queen of sad mischance.
These English woes shall make me smile in France.   115

QUEEN ELIZABETH (rising)

O thou, well skilled in curses, stay a while,
And teach me how to curse mine enemies.

QUEEN MARGARET

Forbear to sleep the nights, and fast the days;
Compare dead happiness with living woe;
Think that thy babes were sweeter than they were,   120
And he that slew them fouler than he is.
Bett'ring thy loss makes the bad causer worse.
Revolving this will teach thee how to curse.

QUEEN ELIZABETH

My words are dull. O quicken them with thine!

QUEEN MARGARET

Thy woes will make them sharp and pierce like mine.
                                         Exit

DUCHESS OF YORK

Why should calamity be full of words?   126

QUEEN ELIZABETH

Windy attorneys to their client woes,
Airy recorders of intestate joys,
Poor breathing orators of miseries.
Let them have scope. Though what they will impart
Help nothing else, yet do they ease the heart.   131

DUCHESS OF YORK

If so, then be not tongue-tied; go with me,
And in the breath of bitter words let's smother
My damnèd son, that thy two sweet sons smothered.
    A march within
The trumpet sounds. Be copious in exclaims.   135
    Enter King Richard and his train ⌈marching with
    drummers and trumpeters⌉

KING RICHARD

Who intercepts me in my expedition?

DUCHESS OF YORK

O, she that might have intercepted thee,
By strangling thee in her accursèd womb,
From all the slaughters, wretch, that thou hast done.

QUEEN ELIZABETH

Hid'st thou that forehead with a golden crown,   140
Where should be branded—if that right were right—
The slaughter of the prince that owed that crown,
And the dire death of my poor sons and brothers?
Tell me, thou villain-slave, where are my children?

DUCHESS OF YORK

Thou toad, thou toad, where is thy brother Clarence?
And little Ned Plantagenet his son?   146

QUEEN ELIZABETH

Where is the gentle Rivers, Vaughan, Gray?

DUCHESS OF YORK Where is kind Hastings?

KING RICHARD (to his train)

A flourish, trumpets! Strike alarum, drums!
Let not the heavens hear these tell-tale women   150
Rail on the Lord's anointed. Strike, I say!

Flourish. Alarums
(*To the women*) Either be patient and entreat me fair,
Or with the clamorous report of war
Thus will I drown your exclamations.
DUCHESS OF YORK　Art thou my son? 　　　　　　155
KING RICHARD
Ay, I thank God, my father, and yourself.
DUCHESS OF YORK
Then patiently hear my impatience.
KING RICHARD
Madam, I have a touch of your condition,
That cannot brook the accent of reproof.
DUCHESS OF YORK
O let me speak!
KING RICHARD　　Do, then; but I'll not hear. 　160
DUCHESS OF YORK
I will be mild and gentle in my words.
KING RICHARD
And brief, good mother, for I am in haste.
DUCHESS OF YORK
Art thou so hasty? I have stayed for thee,
God knows, in torment and in agony—
KING RICHARD
And came I not at last to comfort you? 　　165
DUCHESS OF YORK
No, by the Holy Rood, thou know'st it well.
Thou cam'st on earth to make the earth my hell.
A grievous burden was thy birth to me;
Tetchy and wayward was thy infancy; 　　　169
Thy schooldays frightful, desp'rate, wild, and furious;
Thy prime of manhood daring, bold, and venturous;
Thy age confirmed, proud, subtle, sly, and bloody;
More mild, but yet more harmful; kind in hatred.
What comfortable hour canst thou name
That ever graced me in thy company? 　　　175
KING RICHARD
Faith, none but Humphrey Hewer, that called your
　　grace
To breakfast once, forth of my company.
If I be so disgracious in your eye,
Let me march on, and not offend you, madam.—
Strike up the drum.
DUCHESS OF YORK　　I pray thee, hear me speak. 　180
KING RICHARD
You speak too bitterly.
DUCHESS OF YORK　　　　Hear me a word,
For I shall never speak to thee again.
KING RICHARD So.
DUCHESS OF YORK
Either thou wilt die by God's just ordinance
Ere from this war thou turn a conqueror, 　　185
Or I with grief and extreme age shall perish,
And never more behold thy face again.
Therefore take with thee my most heavy curse,
Which in the day of battle tire thee more
Than all the complete armour that thou wear'st. 　190
My prayers on the adverse party fight,
And there the little souls of Edward's children

Whisper the spirits of thine enemies,
And promise them success and victory.
Bloody thou art, bloody will be thy end; 　　195
Shame serves thy life, and doth thy death attend.
　　　　　　　　　　　　　　　　　　　Exit
QUEEN ELIZABETH
Though far more cause, yet much less spirit to curse
Abides in me; I say 'Amen' to all.
KING RICHARD
Stay, madam. I must talk a word with you.
QUEEN ELIZABETH
I have no more sons of the royal blood 　　200
For thee to slaughter. For my daughters, Richard,
They shall be praying nuns, not weeping queens,
And therefore level not to hit their lives.
KING RICHARD
You have a daughter called Elizabeth,
Virtuous and fair, royal and gracious. 　　205
QUEEN ELIZABETH
And must she die for this? O let her live,
And I'll corrupt her manners, stain her beauty,
Slander myself as false to Edward's bed,
Throw over her the veil of infamy.
So she may live unscarred of bleeding slaughter, 　210
I will confess she was not Edward's daughter.
KING RICHARD
Wrong not her birth. She is a royal princess.
QUEEN ELIZABETH
To save her life I'll say she is not so.
KING RICHARD
Her life is safest only in her birth.
QUEEN ELIZABETH
And only in that safety died her brothers. 　215
KING RICHARD
Lo, at their births good stars were opposite.
QUEEN ELIZABETH
No, to their lives ill friends were contrary.
KING RICHARD
All unavoided is the doom of destiny—
QUEEN ELIZABETH
True, when avoided grace makes destiny.
My babes were destined to a fairer death, 　220
If grace had blessed thee with a fairer life.
KING RICHARD
Madam, so thrive I in my enterprise
And dangerous success of bloody wars,
As I intend more good to you and yours
Than ever you or yours by me were harmed. 　225
QUEEN ELIZABETH
What good is covered with the face of heaven,
To be discovered, that can do me good?
KING RICHARD
Th'advancement of your children, gentle lady.
QUEEN ELIZABETH
Up to some scaffold, there to lose their heads.
KING RICHARD
Unto the dignity and height of fortune, 　230
The high imperial type of this earth's glory.

QUEEN ELIZABETH
Flatter my sorrow with report of it.
Tell me what state, what dignity, what honour,
Canst thou demise to any child of mine?
KING RICHARD
Even all I have—ay, and myself and all,   235
Will I withal endow a child of thine,
So in the Lethe of thy angry soul
Thou drown the sad remembrance of those wrongs,
Which thou supposest I have done to thee.
QUEEN ELIZABETH
Be brief, lest that the process of thy kindness   240
Last longer telling than thy kindness' date.
KING RICHARD
Then know that, from my soul, I love thy daughter.
QUEEN ELIZABETH
My daughter's mother thinks that with her soul.
KING RICHARD What do you think?
QUEEN ELIZABETH
That thou dost love my daughter *from* thy soul;   245
So *from* thy soul's love didst thou love her brothers,
And *from* my heart's love I do thank thee for it.
KING RICHARD
Be not so hasty to confound my meaning.
I mean, that *with* my soul I love thy daughter,
And do intend to make her queen of England.   250
QUEEN ELIZABETH
Well then, who dost thou mean shall be her king?
KING RICHARD
Even he that makes her queen. Who else should be?
QUEEN ELIZABETH
What, thou?
KING RICHARD Even so. How think you of it?
QUEEN ELIZABETH
How canst thou woo her?
KING RICHARD   That would I learn of you,
As one being best acquainted with her humour.   255
QUEEN ELIZABETH
And wilt thou learn of me?
KING RICHARD   Madam, with all my heart.
QUEEN ELIZABETH
Send to her, by the man that slew her brothers,
A pair of bleeding hearts; thereon engrave
'Edward' and 'York'; then haply will she weep.
Therefore present to her—as sometimes Margaret   260
Did to thy father, steeped in Rutland's blood—
A handkerchief which, say to her, did drain
The purple sap from her sweet brother's body,
And bid her wipe her weeping eyes withal.
If this inducement move her not to love,   265
Send her a letter of thy noble deeds.
Tell her thou mad'st away her uncle Clarence,
Her uncle Rivers—ay, and for her sake
Mad'st quick conveyance with her good aunt Anne.
KING RICHARD
You mock me, madam. This is not the way   270
To win your daughter.
QUEEN ELIZABETH   There is no other way,
Unless thou couldst put on some other shape,

And not be Richard, that hath done all this.
KING RICHARD
Infer fair England's peace by this alliance.
QUEEN ELIZABETH
Which she shall purchase with still-lasting war.   275
KING RICHARD
Tell her the King, that may command, entreats.
QUEEN ELIZABETH
That at her hands which the King's King forbids.
KING RICHARD
Say she shall be a high and mighty queen.
QUEEN ELIZABETH
To vail the title, as her mother doth.
KING RICHARD
Say I will love her everlastingly.   280
QUEEN ELIZABETH
But how long shall that title 'ever' last?
KING RICHARD
Sweetly in force unto her fair life's end.
QUEEN ELIZABETH
But how long fairly shall her sweet life last?
KING RICHARD
As long as heaven and nature lengthens it.
QUEEN ELIZABETH
As long as hell and Richard likes of it.   285
KING RICHARD
Say I, her sovereign, am her subject love.
QUEEN ELIZABETH
But she, your subject, loathes such sovereignty.
KING RICHARD
Be eloquent in my behalf to her.
QUEEN ELIZABETH
An honest tale speeds best being plainly told.
KING RICHARD
Then plainly to her tell my loving tale.   290
QUEEN ELIZABETH
Plain and not honest is too harsh a style.
KING RICHARD
Your reasons are too shallow and too quick.
QUEEN ELIZABETH
O no, my reasons are too deep and dead—
Too deep and dead, poor infants, in their graves.
KING RICHARD
Harp not on that string, madam. That is past.   295
QUEEN ELIZABETH
Harp on it still shall I, till heart-strings break.
KING RICHARD
Now by my George, my garter, and my crown—
QUEEN ELIZABETH
Profaned, dishonoured, and the third usurped.
KING RICHARD
I swear—
QUEEN ELIZABETH By nothing, for this is no oath.
Thy George, profaned, hath lost his holy honour;   300
Thy garter, blemished, pawned his lordly virtue;
Thy crown, usurped, disgraced his kingly glory.
If something thou wouldst swear to be believed,
Swear then by something that thou hast not wronged.

KING RICHARD
  Then by myself—
QUEEN ELIZABETH   Thy self is self-misused.   305
KING RICHARD
  Now by the world—
QUEEN ELIZABETH   'Tis full of thy foul wrongs.
KING RICHARD
  My father's death—
QUEEN ELIZABETH   Thy life hath that dishonoured.
KING RICHARD
  Why then, by God—
QUEEN ELIZABETH   God's wrong is most of all.
  If thou didst fear to break an oath with him,
  The unity the King my husband made   310
  Thou hadst not broken, nor my brothers died.
  If thou hadst feared to break an oath by him,
  Th'imperial metal circling now thy head
  Had graced the tender temples of my child,
  And both the princes had been breathing here,   315
  Which now—two tender bedfellows for dust—
  Thy broken faith hath made the prey for worms.
  What canst thou swear by now?
KING RICHARD   The time to come.
QUEEN ELIZABETH
  That thou hast wrongèd in the time o'erpast,
  For I myself have many tears to wash   320
  Hereafter time, for time past wronged by thee.
  The children live, whose fathers thou hast
        slaughtered—
  Ungoverned youth, to wail it in their age.
  The parents live, whose children thou hast
        butchered—
  Old barren plants, to wail it with their age.   325
  Swear not by time to come, for that thou hast
  Misused ere used, by times ill-used o'erpast.
KING RICHARD
  As I intend to prosper and repent,
  So thrive I in my dangerous affairs
  Of hostile arms—myself myself confound,   330
  Heaven and fortune bar me happy hours,
  Day yield me not thy light nor night thy rest;
  Be opposite, all planets of good luck,
  To my proceeding—if, with dear heart's love,
  Immaculate devotion, holy thoughts,   335
  I tender not thy beauteous, princely daughter.
  In her consists my happiness and thine.
  Without her follows—to myself and thee,
  Herself, the land, and many a Christian soul—
  Death, desolation, ruin, and decay.   340
  It cannot be avoided but by this;
  It will not be avoided but by this.
  Therefore, good-mother—I must call you so—
  Be the attorney of my love to her.
  Plead what I will be, not what I have been;   345
  Not my deserts, but what I will deserve.
  Urge the necessity and state of times,
  And be not peevish-fond in great designs.

QUEEN ELIZABETH
  Shall I be tempted of the devil thus?
KING RICHARD
  Ay, if the devil tempt you to do good.   350
QUEEN ELIZABETH
  Shall I forget myself to be myself?
KING RICHARD
  Ay, if yourself's remembrance wrong yourself.
QUEEN ELIZABETH Yet thou didst kill my children.
KING RICHARD
  But in your daughter's womb I bury them,
  Where, in that nest of spicery, they will breed   355
  Selves of themselves, to your recomfiture.
QUEEN ELIZABETH
  Shall I go win my daughter to thy will?
KING RICHARD
  And be a happy mother by the deed.
QUEEN ELIZABETH
  I go. Write to me very shortly,
  And you shall understand from me her mind.   360
KING RICHARD
  Bear her my true love's kiss,
        He kisses her
                          and so farewell—
                                    Exit Elizabeth
  Relenting fool, and shallow, changing woman.
        Enter Sir Richard Ratcliffe
  How now, what news?
RATCLIFFE
  Most mighty sovereign, on the western coast
  Rideth a puissant navy. To our shores   365
  Throng many doubtful, hollow-hearted friends,
  Unarmed and unresolved, to beat them back.
  'Tis thought that Richmond is their admiral,
  And there they hull, expecting but the aid
  Of Buckingham to welcome them ashore.   370
KING RICHARD
  Some light-foot friend post to the Duke of Norfolk.
  Ratcliffe thyself, or Catesby—where is he?
CATESBY
  Here, my good lord.
KING RICHARD   Catesby, fly to the Duke.
CATESBY
  I will, my lord, with all convenient haste.
KING RICHARD
  Ratcliffe, come hither. Post to Salisbury;   375
  When thou com'st thither— (*to Catesby*) dull,
        unmindful villain,
  Why stay'st thou here, and goest not to the Duke?
CATESBY
  First, mighty liege, tell me your highness' pleasure:
  What from your grace I shall deliver to him?
KING RICHARD
  O true, good Catesby. Bid him levy straight   380
  The greatest strength and power that he can make,
  And meet me suddenly at Salisbury.
CATESBY I go.   *Exit*

RATCLIFFE
What, may it please you, shall I do at Salisbury?
KING RICHARD
Why, what wouldst thou do there before I go?   385
RATCLIFFE
Your highness told me I should post before.
KING RICHARD
My mind is changed.
    Enter Lord Stanley
                 Stanley, what news with you?
STANLEY
None, good my liege, to please you with the hearing,
Nor none so bad but well may be reported.
KING RICHARD
Hoyday, a riddle! Neither good nor bad.   390
Why need'st thou run so many mile about
When thou mayst tell thy tale the nearest way?
Once more, what news?
STANLEY   Richmond is on the seas.
KING RICHARD
There let him sink, and be the seas on him.
White-livered renegade, what doth he there?   395
STANLEY
I know not, mighty sovereign, but by guess.
KING RICHARD Well, as you guess?
STANLEY
Stirred up by Dorset, Buckingham, and Ely,
He makes for England, here to claim the crown.
KING RICHARD
Is the chair empty? Is the sword unswayed?   400
Is the King dead? The empire unpossessed?
What heir of York is there alive but we?
And who is England's king but great York's heir?
Then tell me, what makes he upon the seas?
STANLEY
Unless for that, my liege, I cannot guess.   405
KING RICHARD
Unless for that he comes to be your liege,
You cannot guess wherefore the Welshman comes.
Thou wilt revolt and fly to him, I fear.
STANLEY
No, my good lord, therefore mistrust me not.
KING RICHARD
Where is thy power then? To beat him back,   410
Where be thy tenants and thy followers?
Are they not now upon the western shore,
Safe-conducting the rebels from their ships?
STANLEY
No, my good lord, my friends are in the north.
KING RICHARD
Cold friends to me. What do they in the north,   415
When they should serve their sovereign in the west?
STANLEY
They have not been commanded, mighty King.
Pleaseth your majesty to give me leave,
I'll muster up my friends and meet your grace
Where and what time your majesty shall please.   420

KING RICHARD
Ay, ay, thou wouldst be gone to join with Richmond.
But I'll not trust thee.
STANLEY   Most mighty sovereign,
You have no cause to hold my friendship doubtful.
I never was, nor never will be, false.
KING RICHARD
Go then and muster men—but leave behind   425
Your son George Stanley. Look your heart be firm,
Or else his head's assurance is but frail.
STANLEY
So deal with him as I prove true to you.   *Exit*
    Enter a Messenger
MESSENGER
My gracious sovereign, now in Devonshire,
As I by friends am well advertisèd,   430
Sir Edward Courtenay and the haughty prelate,
Bishop of Exeter, his elder brother,
With many more confederates are in arms.
    Enter another Messenger
SECOND MESSENGER
In Kent, my liege, the Guildfords are in arms,
And every hour more competitors   435
Flock to the rebels, and their power grows strong.
    Enter another Messenger
THIRD MESSENGER
My lord, the army of great Buckingham—
KING RICHARD
Out on ye, owls! Nothing but songs of death?
    He striketh him
There, take thou that, till thou bring better news.
THIRD MESSENGER
The news I have to tell your majesty   440
Is that, by sudden flood and fall of water,
Buckingham's army is dispersed and scattered,
And he himself wandered away alone,
No man knows whither.
KING RICHARD   I cry thee mercy.—
Ratcliffe, reward him for the blow I gave him.—   445
Hath any well-advisèd friend proclaimed
Reward to him that brings the traitor in?
THIRD MESSENGER
Such proclamation hath been made, my lord.
    Enter another Messenger
FOURTH MESSENGER
Sir Thomas Lovell and Lord Marquis Dorset—
'Tis said, my liege—in Yorkshire are in arms.   450
But this good comfort bring I to your highness:
The Breton navy is dispersed by tempest.
Richmond in Dorsetshire sent out a boat
Unto the shore, to ask those on the banks
If they were his assistants, yea or no?   455
Who answered him they came from Buckingham
Upon his party. He, mistrusting them,
Hoist sail and made his course again for Bretagne.
KING RICHARD
March on, march on, since we are up in arms,

If not to fight with foreign enemies,   460
Yet to beat down these rebels here at home.
Enter Catesby

CATESBY
My liege, the Duke of Buckingham is taken.
That is the best news. That the Earl of Richmond
Is with a mighty power landed at Milford
Is colder tidings, yet they must be told.   465

KING RICHARD
Away, towards Salisbury! While we reason here,
A royal battle might be won and lost.
Someone take order Buckingham be brought
To Salisbury. The rest march on with me.
Flourish. Exeunt

4.5 *Enter Lord Stanley Earl of Derby and Sir
Christopher, a priest*

STANLEY
Sir Christopher, tell Richmond this from me:
That in the sty of this most deadly boar
My son George Stanley is franked up in hold.
If I revolt, off goes young George's head.
The fear of that holds off my present aid.   5
But tell me, where is princely Richmond now?

SIR CHRISTOPHER
At Pembroke, or at Ha'rfordwest in Wales.

STANLEY
What men of name resort to him?

SIR CHRISTOPHER
Sir Walter Herbert, a renownèd soldier,
Sir Gilbert Talbot, Sir William Stanley,   10
Oxford, redoubted Pembroke, Sir James Blunt,
And Rhys-ap-Thomas with a valiant crew,
And many other of great name and worth—
And towards London do they bend their power,
If by the way they be not fought withal.   15

STANLEY
Well, hie thee to thy lord. Commend me to him.
Tell him the Queen hath heartily consented
He should espouse Elizabeth her daughter.
My letter will resolve him of my mind.   19
Farewell.   *Exeunt severally*

5.1 *Enter the Duke of Buckingham with halberdiers, led
by a Sheriff to execution*

BUCKINGHAM
Will not King Richard let me speak with him?

SHERIFF
No, my good lord, therefore be patient.

BUCKINGHAM
Hastings, and Edward's children, Gray and Rivers,
Holy King Henry and thy fair son Edward,
Vaughan, and all that have miscarrièd   5
By underhand, corrupted, foul injustice:
If that your moody, discontented souls
Do through the clouds behold this present hour,
Even for revenge mock my destruction.
This is All-Souls' day, fellow, is it not?   10

SHERIFF It is.

BUCKINGHAM
Why then All-Souls' day is my body's doomsday.
This is the day which, in King Edward's time,
I wished might fall on me, when I was found
False to his children and his wife's allies.   15
This is the day wherein I wished to fall
By the false faith of him whom most I trusted.
This, this All-Souls' day to my fearful soul
Is the determined respite of my wrongs.
That high all-seer which I dallied with   20
Hath turned my feignèd prayer on my head,
And given in earnest what I begged in jest.
Thus doth he force the swords of wicked men
To turn their own points in their masters' bosoms.
Thus Margaret's curse falls heavy on my neck.   25
'When he', quoth she, 'shall split thy heart with
        sorrow,
Remember Margaret was a prophetess'.
Come lead me, officers, to the block of shame.
Wrong hath but wrong, and blame the due of blame.
Exeunt

5.2 *Enter Henry Earl of Richmond with a letter, the
Earl of Oxford, Sir James Blunt, Sir Walter
Herbert, and others, with drum and colours*

HENRY EARL OF RICHMOND
Fellows in arms, and my most loving friends,
Bruised underneath the yoke of tyranny,
Thus far into the bowels of the land
Have we marched on without impediment,
And here receive we from our father Stanley   5
Lines of fair comfort and encouragement.
The wretched, bloody, and usurping boar,
That spoils your summer fields and fruitful vines,
Swills your warm blood like wash, and makes his
        trough
In your inbowelled bosoms, this foul swine   10
Lies now even in the centry of this isle,
Near to the town of Leicester, as we learn.
From Tamworth thither is but one day's march.
In God's name, cheerly on, courageous friends,
To reap the harvest of perpetual peace   15
By this one bloody trial of sharp war.

OXFORD
Every man's conscience is a thousand swords
To fight against this guilty homicide.

HERBERT
I doubt not but his friends will turn to us.

BLUNT
He hath no friends but what are friends for fear,   20
Which in his dearest need will fly from him.

HENRY EARL OF RICHMOND
All for our vantage. Then, in God's name, march.
True hope is swift, and flies with swallows' wings;
Kings it makes gods, and meaner creatures kings.
Exeunt ⌐marching⌐

5.3 *Enter King Richard in arms, with the Duke of*
Norfolk, Sir Richard Ratcliffe, ⌜Sir William
Catesby, and others⌝
KING RICHARD
Here pitch our tent, even here in Bosworth field.
Soldiers begin to pitch ⌜a tent⌝
Why, how now, Catesby? Why look you so sad?
⌜CATESBY⌝
My heart is ten times lighter than my looks.
KING RICHARD
My lord of Norfolk.
NORFOLK   Here, most gracious liege.
KING RICHARD
Norfolk, we must have knocks. Ha, must we not?   5
NORFOLK
We must both give and take, my loving lord.
KING RICHARD
Up with my tent! Here will I lie tonight.
But where tomorrow? Well, all's one for that.
Who hath descried the number of the traitors?
NORFOLK
Six or seven thousand is their utmost power.   10
KING RICHARD
Why, our battalia trebles that account.
Besides, the King's name is a tower of strength,
Which they upon the adverse faction want.
Up with the tent! Come, noble gentlemen,
Let us survey the vantage of the ground.   15
Call for some men of sound direction.
Let's lack no discipline, make no delay—
For, lords, tomorrow is a busy day.
                              Exeunt ⌜at one door⌝

5.4 *Enter ⌜at another door⌝ Henry Earl of Richmond,*
Sir James Blunt, Sir William Brandon, ⌜the Earl of
Oxford, Marquis Dorset, and others⌝
HENRY EARL OF RICHMOND
The weary sun hath made a golden set,
And by the bright track of his fiery car
Gives token of a goodly day tomorrow.
Sir William Brandon, you shall bear my standard.
The Earl of Pembroke keeps his regiment;   5
Good Captain Blunt, bear my good night to him,
And by the second hour in the morning
Desire the Earl to see me in my tent.
Yet one thing more, good Captain, do for me:
Where is Lord Stanley quartered, do you know?   10
BLUNT
Unless I have mista'en his colours much,
Which well I am assured I have not done,
His regiment lies half a mile, at least,
South from the mighty power of the King.
HENRY EARL OF RICHMOND
If without peril it be possible,   15
Sweet Blunt, make some good means to speak with
him,
And give him from me this most needful note.

BLUNT
Upon my life, my lord, I'll undertake it.
And so God give you quiet rest tonight.
HENRY EARL OF RICHMOND
Good night, good Captain Blunt.   *Exit Blunt*
Come, gentlemen.   20
Give me some ink and paper in my tent.
I'll draw the form and model of our battle,
Limit each leader to his several charge,
And part in just proportion our small power.
Let us consult upon tomorrow's business.   25
Into my tent: the dew is raw and cold.
                    They withdraw into the tent

5.5 ⌜*A table brought in.*⌝ *Enter King Richard, Sir*
Richard Ratcliffe, the Duke of Norfolk, Sir William
Catesby, and others
KING RICHARD What is't o'clock?
CATESBY
It's supper-time, my lord. It's nine o'clock.
KING RICHARD
I will not sup tonight. Give me some ink and paper.
What, is my beaver easier than it was?
And all my armour laid into my tent?   5
CATESBY
It is, my liege, and all things are in readiness.
KING RICHARD
Good Norfolk, hie thee to thy charge.
Use careful watch; choose trusty sentinels.
NORFOLK I go, my lord.
KING RICHARD
Stir with the lark tomorrow, gentle Norfolk.   10
NORFOLK
I warrant you, my lord.   *Exit*
KING RICHARD   Catesby.
CATESBY   My lord?
KING RICHARD
Send out a pursuivant-at-arms
To Stanley's regiment. Bid him bring his power
Before sun-rising, lest his son George fall
Into the blind cave of eternal night.   ⌜*Exit Catesby*⌝
Fill me a bowl of wine. Give me a watch.   16
Saddle white Surrey for the field tomorrow.
Look that my staves be sound, and not too heavy.
Ratcliffe.
RATCLIFFE My lord?   20
KING RICHARD
Saw'st thou the melancholy Lord Northumberland?
RATCLIFFE
Thomas the Earl of Surrey and himself,
Much about cockshut time, from troop to troop
Went through the army, cheering up the soldiers.
KING RICHARD
So, I am satisfied. Give me some wine.   25
I have not that alacrity of spirit,
Nor cheer of mind, that I was wont to have.
The wine is brought
Set it down. Is ink and paper ready?

RATCLIFFE

It is, my lord.

KING RICHARD   Leave me. Bid my guard watch.

About the mid of night come to my tent,   30

Ratcliffe, and help to arm me. Leave me, I say.

Exit Ratcliffe ⌈with others. Richard writes, and
later sleeps⌉
Enter Lord Stanley Earl of Derby to Henry Earl of
Richmond and the lords in his tent

STANLEY

Fortune and victory sit on thy helm!

HENRY EARL OF RICHMOND

All comfort that the dark night can afford

Be to thy person, noble father-in-law.

Tell me, how fares our loving mother?   35

STANLEY

I, by attorney, bless thee from thy mother,

Who prays continually for Richmond's good.

So much for that. The silent hours steal on,

And flaky darkness breaks within the east.

In brief—for so the season bids us be—   40

Prepare thy battle early in the morning,

And put thy fortune to th'arbitrement

Of bloody strokes and mortal-sharing war.

I, as I may—that which I would, I cannot—

With best advantage will deceive the time,   45

And aid thee in this doubtful shock of arms.

But on thy side I may not be too forward—

Lest, being seen, thy brother, tender George,

Be executed in his father's sight.

Farewell. The leisure and the fearful time   50

Cuts off the ceremonious vows of love

And ample interchange of sweet discourse,

Which so long sundered friends should dwell upon.

God give us leisure for these rights of love.

Once more, adieu. Be valiant, and speed well.   55

HENRY EARL OF RICHMOND

Good lords, conduct him to his regiment.

I'll strive with troubled thoughts to take a nap,

Lest leaden slumber peise me down tomorrow,

When I should mount with wings of victory.

Once more, good night, kind lords and gentlemen.   60

Exeunt Stanley and the lords

⌈*Richmond kneels*⌉

O thou, whose captain I account myself,

Look on my forces with a gracious eye.

Put in their hands thy bruising irons of wrath,

That they may crush down with a heavy fall

Th'usurping helmets of our adversaries.   65

Make us thy ministers of chastisement,

That we may praise thee in the victory.

To thee I do commend my watchful soul,

Ere I let fall the windows of mine eyes.

Sleeping and waking, O defend me still!   *He sleeps*

Enter the Ghost of young Prince Edward ⌈above⌉

GHOST OF PRINCE EDWARD *(to Richard)*

Let me sit heavy on thy soul tomorrow,   71

Prince Edward, son to Henry the Sixth.

Think how thou stabbedst me in my prime of youth

At Tewkesbury. Despair, therefore, and die.

(To Richmond) Be cheerful, Richmond, for the wrongèd

souls   75

Of butchered princes fight in thy behalf.

King Henry's issue, Richmond, comforts thee.   ⌈*Exit*⌉

Enter ⌈above⌉ the Ghost of King Henry the Sixth

GHOST OF KING HENRY *(to Richard)*

When I was mortal, my anointed body

By thee was punchèd full of deadly holes.

Think on the Tower and me. Despair and die.   80

Harry the Sixth bids thee despair and die.

(To Richmond) Virtuous and holy, be thou conqueror.

Harry that prophesied thou shouldst be king

Comforts thee in thy sleep. Live and flourish!   ⌈*Exit*⌉

Enter ⌈above⌉ the Ghost of George Duke of Clarence

GHOST OF CLARENCE *(to Richard)*

Let me sit heavy on thy soul tomorrow,   85

I that was washed to death with fulsome wine,

Poor Clarence, by thy guile betrayed to death.

Tomorrow in the battle think on me,

And fall thy edgeless sword. Despair and die.

(To Richmond) Thou offspring of the house of

Lancaster,   90

The wrongèd heirs of York do pray for thee.

Good angels guard thy battle. Live and flourish!

⌈*Exit*⌉

Enter ⌈above⌉ the Ghosts of Lord Rivers, Lord Gray,
and Sir Thomas Vaughan

GHOST OF RIVERS *(to Richard)*

Let me sit heavy on thy soul tomorrow,

Rivers that died at Pomfret. Despair and die.

GHOST OF GRAY *(to Richard)*

Think upon Gray, and let thy soul despair.   95

GHOST OF VAUGHAN *(to Richard)*

Think upon Vaughan, and with guilty fear

Let fall thy pointless lance. Despair and die.

ALL THREE *(to Richmond)*

Awake, and think our wrongs in Richard's bosom

Will conquer him. Awake, and win the day!

⌈*Exeunt Ghosts*⌉

Enter ⌈above⌉ the Ghosts of the two young Princes

⌈GHOSTS OF THE PRINCES⌉ *(to Richard)*

Dream on thy cousins, smothered in the Tower.   100

Let us be lead within thy bosom, Richard,

And weigh thee down to ruin, shame, and death.

Thy nephews' souls bid thee despair and die.

(To Richmond) Sleep, Richmond, sleep in peace and

wake in joy.

Good angels guard thee from the boar's annoy.   105

Live, and beget a happy race of kings!

Edward's unhappy sons do bid thee flourish.

⌈*Exeunt Ghosts*⌉

Enter ⌈above⌉ the Ghost of Lord Hastings

GHOST OF HASTINGS *(to Richard)*

Bloody and guilty, guiltily awake,

And in a bloody battle end thy days.

Think on Lord Hastings, then despair and die.   110

(To Richmond) Quiet, untroubled soul, awake, awake!
Arm, fight, and conquer for fair England's sake.
⌐*Exit*⌐

Enter ⌐*above*⌐ *the Ghost of Lady Anne*

GHOST OF LADY ANNE *(to Richard)*
Richard, thy wife, that wretched Anne thy wife,
That never slept a quiet hour with thee,
Now fills thy sleep with perturbations.   115
Tomorrow in the battle think on me,
And fall thy edgeless sword. Despair and die.
(To Richmond) Thou quiet soul, sleep thou a quiet
    sleep.
Dream of success and happy victory.
Thy adversary's wife doth pray for thee.   ⌐*Exit*⌐

Enter ⌐*above*⌐ *the Ghost of the Duke of Buckingham*

GHOST OF BUCKINGHAM *(to Richard)*
The first was I that helped thee to the crown;   121
The last was I that felt thy tyranny.
O in the battle think on Buckingham,
And die in terror of thy guiltiness!
Dream on, dream on, of bloody deeds and death; 125
Fainting, despair; despairing, yield thy breath.
(To Richmond) I died for hope ere I could lend thee aid.
But cheer thy heart, and be thou not dismayed.
God and good angels fight on Richmond's side,
And Richard falls in height of all his pride.   ⌐*Exit*⌐

Richard starteth up out of a dream

KING RICHARD
Give me another horse! Bind up my wounds!   131
Have mercy, Jesu!—Soft, I did but dream.
O coward conscience, how dost thou afflict me?
The lights burn blue. It is now dead midnight.
Cold fearful drops stand on my trembling flesh.   135
What do I fear? Myself? There's none else by.
Richard loves Richard; that is, I am I.
Is there a murderer here? No. Yes, I am.
Then fly! What, from myself? Great reason. Why?
Lest I revenge. Myself upon myself?   140
Alack, I love myself. Wherefore? For any good
That I myself have done unto myself?
O no, alas, I rather hate myself
For hateful deeds committed by myself.
I am a villain. Yet I lie: I am not.   145
Fool, of thyself speak well.—Fool, do not flatter.
My conscience hath a thousand several tongues,
And every tongue brings in a several tale,
And every tale condemns me for a villain.
Perjury, perjury, in the high'st degree!   150
Murder, stern murder, in the dir'st degree!
All several sins, all used in each degree,
Throng to the bar, crying all, 'Guilty, guilty!'
I shall despair. There is no creature loves me,
And if I die no soul will pity me.   155
Nay, wherefore should they?—Since that I myself
Find in myself no pity to myself.
Methought the souls of all that I had murdered
Came to my tent, and every one did threat
Tomorrow's vengeance on the head of Richard.   160

Enter Ratcliffe

RATCLIFFE My lord?
KING RICHARD 'Swounds, who is there?
RATCLIFFE
My lord, 'tis I. The early village cock
Hath twice done salutation to the morn.
Your friends are up, and buckle on their armour.   165
KING RICHARD
O Ratcliffe, I have dreamed a fearful dream.
What thinkest thou, will all our friends prove true?
RATCLIFFE
No doubt, my lord.
KING RICHARD   Ratcliffe, I fear, I fear.
RATCLIFFE
Nay, good my lord, be not afraid of shadows.
KING RICHARD
By the Apostle Paul, shadows tonight   170
Have struck more terror to the soul of Richard
Than can the substance of ten thousand soldiers
Armèd in proof and led by shallow Richmond.
'Tis not yet near day. Come, go with me.
Under our tents I'll play the eavesdropper,   175
To see if any mean to shrink from me.

                    Exeunt Richard and Ratcliffe

Enter the lords to Henry Earl of Richmond, sitting
    in his tent

⌐LORDS⌐ Good morrow, Richmond.
HENRY EARL OF RICHMOND
Cry mercy, lords and watchful gentlemen,
That you have ta'en a tardy sluggard here.
⌐A LORD⌐ How have you slept, my lord?   180
HENRY EARL OF RICHMOND
The sweetest sleep and fairest boding dreams
That ever entered in a drowsy head
Have I since your departure had, my lords.
Methought their souls whose bodies Richard murdered
Came to my tent and cried on victory.   185
I promise you, my soul is very jocund
In the remembrance of so fair a dream.
How far into the morning is it, lords?
⌐A LORD⌐ Upon the stroke of four.
HENRY EARL OF RICHMOND
Why then, 'tis time to arm, and give direction.   190

His oration to his soldiers

Much that I could say, loving countrymen,
The leisure and enforcement of the time
Forbids to dwell on. Yet remember this:
God and our good cause fight upon our side.
The prayers of holy saints and wrongèd souls,   195
Like high-reared bulwarks, stand before our forces.
Richard except, those whom we fight against
Had rather have us win than him they follow.
For what is he they follow? Truly, friends,
A bloody tyrant and a homicide;   200
One raised in blood, and one in blood established;
One that made means to come by what he hath,
And slaughtered those that were the means to help
    him;

A base, foul stone, made precious by the foil
Of England's chair, where he is falsely set; 205
One that hath ever been God's enemy.
Then if you fight against God's enemy,
God will, in justice, ward you as his soldiers.
If you do sweat to put a tyrant down,
You sleep in peace, the tyrant being slain. 210
If you do fight against your country's foes,
Your country's foison pays your pains the hire.
If you do fight in safeguard of your wives,
Your wives shall welcome home the conquerors.
If you do free your children from the sword, 215
Your children's children quites it in your age.
Then, in the name of God and all these rights,
Advance your standards! Draw your willing swords!
For me, the ransom of this bold attempt
Shall be my cold corpse on the earth's cold face; 220
But if I thrive, to gain of my attempt,
The least of you shall share his part thereof.
Sound, drums and trumpets, bold and cheerfully!
God and Saint George! Richmond and victory!
     ⌈*Exeunt to the sound of drums and trumpets*⌉

5.6   *Enter King Richard, Sir Richard Ratcliffe, Sir*
       William Catesby, and others

KING RICHARD
  What said Northumberland, as touching Richmond?
RATCLIFFE
  That he was never trainèd up in arms.
KING RICHARD
  He said the truth. And what said Surrey then?
RATCLIFFE
  He smiled and said, 'The better for our purpose'.
KING RICHARD
  He was in the right, and so indeed it is. 5
    Clock strikes
  Tell the clock there. Give me a calendar.
  Who saw the sun today?
    ⌈*A book is brought*⌉
RATCLIFFE   Not I, my lord.
KING RICHARD
  Then he disdains to shine, for by the book
  He should have braved the east an hour ago.
  A black day will it be to somebody. 10
  Ratcliffe.
RATCLIFFE
  My lord?
KING RICHARD The sun will not be seen today.
  The sky doth frown and lour upon our army.
  I would these dewy tears were from the ground.
  Not shine today—why, what is that to me 15
  More than to Richmond? For the selfsame heaven
  That frowns on me looks sadly upon him.
    Enter the Duke of Norfolk
NORFOLK
  Arm, arm, my lord! The foe vaunts in the field.
KING RICHARD
  Come, bustle, bustle! Caparison my horse.
    ⌈*Richard arms*⌉

Call up Lord Stanley, bid him bring his power. 20
                       Exit one
I will lead forth my soldiers to the plain,
And thus my battle shall be orderèd.
My forward shall be drawn out all in length,
Consisting equally of horse add foot,
Our archers placèd strongly in the midst. 25
John Duke of Norfolk, Thomas Earl of Surrey,
Shall have the leading of this multitude.
They thus directed, we ourself will follow
In the main battle, whose puissance on both sides
Shall be well wingèd with our chiefest horse. 30
This, and Saint George to boot! What think'st thou,
  Norfolk?
NORFOLK
  A good direction, warlike sovereign.
    He showeth him a paper
  This paper found I on my tent this morning.
  (*He reads*)
    'Jackie of Norfolk be not too bold,
    For Dickon thy master is bought and sold.' 35
KING RICHARD
  A thing devisèd by the enemy.—
  Go, gentlemen, each man unto his charge.
  Let not our babbling dreams affright our souls.
  Conscience is but a word that cowards use,
  Devised at first to keep the strong in awe. 40
  Our strong arms be our conscience; swords, our law.
  March on, join bravely! Let us to't, pell mell—
  If not to heaven, then hand in hand to hell.
    His oration to his army
  What shall I say, more than I have inferred?
  Remember whom you are to cope withal: 45
  A sort of vagabonds, rascals and runaways,
  A scum of Bretons and base lackey peasants,
  Whom their o'ercloyèd country vomits forth
  To desperate ventures and assured destruction.
  You sleeping safe, they bring to you unrest; 50
  You having lands and blessed with beauteous wives,
  They would distrain the one, distain the other.
  And who doth lead them, but a paltry fellow?
  Long kept in Bretagne at our mother's cost;
  A milksop; one that never in his life 55
  Felt so much cold as over shoes in snow.
  Let's whip these stragglers o'er the seas again,
  Lash hence these overweening rags of France,
  These famished beggars, weary of their lives,
  Who—but for dreaming on this fond exploit— 60
  For want of means, poor rats, had hanged themselves.
  If we be conquered, let *men* conquer us,
  And not these bastard Bretons, whom our·fathers
  Have in their own land beaten, bobbed, and thumped,
  And in record left them the heirs of shame. 65
  Shall these enjoy our lands? Lie with our wives?
  Ravish our daughters?
    Drum afar off
                Hark, I hear their drum.
  Fight, gentlemen of England! Fight, bold yeomen!
  Draw, archers, draw your arrows to the head!

Spur your proud horses hard, and ride in blood!   70
Amaze the welkin with your broken staves!
   Enter a Messenger
What says Lord Stanley? Will he bring his power?
MESSENGER
My lord, he doth deny to come.
KING RICHARD Off with young George's head!
NORFOLK
My lord, the enemy is past the marsh.   75
After the battle let George Stanley die.
KING RICHARD
A thousand hearts are great within my bosom.
Advance our standards! Set upon our foes!
Our ancient word of courage, fair Saint George,
Inspire us with the spleen of fiery dragons.   80
Upon them! Victory sits on our helms!   *Exeunt*

5.7   *Alarum. Excursions. Enter Sir William Catesby*
CATESBY ⌈*calling*⌉
Rescue, my lord of Norfolk! Rescue, rescue!
⌈*To a soldier*⌉ The King enacts more wonders than a
   man,
Daring an opposite to every danger.
His horse is slain, and all on foot he fights,
Seeking for Richmond in the throat of death.   5
⌈*Calling*⌉ Rescue, fair lord, or else the day is lost!
   Alarums. Enter King Richard
KING RICHARD
A horse! A horse! My kingdom for a horse!
CATESBY
Withdraw, my lord. I'll help you to a horse.
KING RICHARD
Slave, I have set my life upon a cast,
And I will stand the hazard of the die.   10
I think there be six Richmonds in the field.
Five have I slain today, instead of him.
A horse! A horse! My kingdom for a horse!   *Exeunt*

5.8   *Alarum. Enter King Richard* ⌈*at one door*⌉ *and*
   Henry Earl of Richmond ⌈*at another*⌉*. They fight.*
   Richard is slain. ⌈*Exit Richmond.*⌉ *Retreat and*
   flourish. Enter Henry Earl of Richmond and Lord
   Stanley Earl of Derby, with divers other lords and
   soldiers
HENRY EARL OF RICHMOND
God and your arms be praised, victorious friends!
The day is ours. The bloody dog is dead.

STANLEY (*bearing the crown*)
Courageous Richmond, well hast thou acquit thee.
Lo, here this long usurpèd royalty
From the dead temples of this bloody wretch   5
Have I plucked off, to grace thy brows withal.
Wear it, enjoy it, and make much of it.
   ⌈*He sets the crown on Henry's head*⌉
KING HENRY THE SEVENTH
Great God of heaven, say 'Amen' to all.
But tell me—young George Stanley, is he living?
STANLEY
He is, my lord, and safe in Leicester town,   10
Whither, if it please you, we may now withdraw us.
KING HENRY THE SEVENTH
What men of name are slain on either side?
⌈STANLEY⌉ (*reads*)
John Duke of Norfolk, Robert Brackenbury,
Walter Lord Ferrers, and Sir William Brandon.
KING HENRY THE SEVENTH
Inter their bodies as becomes their births.   15
Proclaim a pardon to the soldiers fled
That in submission will return to us.
And then—as we have ta'en the sacrament—
We will unite the white rose and the red.
Smile, heaven, upon this fair conjunction,   20
That long have frowned upon their enmity.
What traitor hears me and says not 'Amen'?
England hath long been mad, and scarred herself;
The brother blindly shed the brother's blood;
The father rashly slaughtered his own son;   25
The son, compelled, been butcher to the sire;
All that divided York and Lancaster,
United in their dire division.
O now let Richmond and Elizabeth,
The true succeeders of each royal house,   30
By God's fair ordinance conjoin together,
And let their heirs—God, if his will be so—
Enrich the time to come with smooth-faced peace,
With smiling plenty, and fair prosperous days.
Abate the edge of traitors, gracious Lord,   35
That would reduce these bloody days again
And make poor England weep forth streams of blood.
Let them not live to taste this land's increase,
That would with treason wound this fair land's peace.
Now civil wounds are stopped; peace lives again.   40
That she may long live here, God say 'Amen'.
   ⌈*Flourish.*⌉ *Exeunt*

ADDITIONAL PASSAGES

The following passages are contained in the Folio text, but not the Quarto; they were apparently omitted from performances.

A. AFTER 1.2.154

These eyes, which never shed remorseful tear—
No, when my father York and Edward wept
To hear the piteous moan that Rutland made
When black-faced Clifford shook his sword at him;
Nor when thy warlike father like a child   5
Told the sad story of my father's death
And twenty times made pause to sob and weep,
That all the standers-by had wet their cheeks
Like trees bedashed with rain. In that sad time
My manly eyes did scorn an humble tear,   10
And what these sorrows could not thence exhale
Thy beauty hath, and made them blind with weeping.

B. AFTER 1.3.166

RICHARD GLOUCESTER
Wert thou not banishèd on pain of death?
QUEEN MARGARET
I was, but I do find more pain in banishment
Than death can yield me here by my abode.

C. AFTER 1.4.68

O God! If my deep prayers cannot appease thee
But thou wilt be avenged on my misdeeds,
Yet execute thy wrath in me alone.
O spare my guiltless wife and my poor children.

D. AFTER 2.2.88

The Folio has Dorset and Rivers enter with Queen Elizabeth at 2.2.33.1.

DORSET
Comfort, dear mother. God is much displeased
That you take with unthankfulness his doing.
In common worldly things 'tis called ungrateful
With dull unwillingness to pay a debt
Which with a bounteous hand was kindly lent;   5
Much more to be thus opposite with heaven
For it requires the royal debt it lent you.
RIVERS
Madam, bethink you like a careful mother
Of the young Prince your son. Send straight for him;
Let him be crowned. In him your comfort lives.   10
Drown desperate sorrow in dead Edward's grave
And plant your joys in living Edward's throne.

E. AFTER 2.2.110

RIVERS
Why with some little train, my lord of Buckingham?

BUCKINGHAM
Marry, my lord, lest by a multitude
The new-healed wound of malice should break out,
Which would be so much the more dangerous
By how much the estate is green and yet ungoverned.   5
Where every horse bears his commanding rein
And may direct his course as please himself,
As well the fear of harm as harm apparent
In my opinion ought to be prevented.
RICHARD GLOUCESTER
I hope the King made peace with all of us,   10
And the compact is firm and true in me.
RIVERS
And so in me, and so I think in all.
Yet since it is but green, it should be put
To no apparent likelihood of breach,
Which haply by much company might be urged.   15
Therefore I say, with noble Buckingham,
That it is meet so few should fetch the Prince.
HASTINGS And so say I.

F. AFTER 3.1.170

And summon him tomorrow to the Tower
To sit about the coronation.

G. AFTER 3.5.100

Beginning Richard Gloucester's speech. The Folio brings on Lovell and Ratcliffe instead of Catesby at 3.5.19.1.

KING RICHARD
Go, Lovell, with all speed to Doctor Shaw;
(To Ratcliffe) Go thou to Friar Penker. Bid them both
Meet me within this hour at Baynard's Castle.
                                        Exeunt Lovell and Ratcliffe

H. AFTER 3.7.143

If not to answer, you might haply think
Tongue-tied ambition, not replying, yielded
To bear the golden yoke of sovereignty,
Which fondly you would here impose on me.
If to reprove you for this suit of yours,   5
So seasoned with your faithful love to me,
Then on the other side I checked my friends.
Therefore to speak, and to avoid the first,
And then in speaking not to incur the last,
Definitively thus I answer you.   10

I. AFTER 4.1.96

In the Folio, the characters do not exit during the Duchess of York's preceding speech.

QUEEN ELIZABETH
Stay: yet look back with me unto the Tower.—
Pity, you ancient stones, those tender babes,

Whom envy hath immured within your walls.
Rough cradle for such little pretty ones,
Rude ragged nurse, old sullen playfellow   5
For tender princes: use my babies well.
So foolish sorrow bids your stones farewell.   *Exeunt*

J. AFTER 4.4.221

KING RICHARD
  You speak as if that I had slain my cousins.
QUEEN ELIZABETH
  Cousins indeed, and by their uncle cozened
Of comfort, kingdom, kindred, freedom, life.
Whose hand soever lanced their tender hearts,
Thy head all indirectly gave direction.   5
No doubt the murd'rous knife was dull and blunt
Till it was whetted on thy stone-hard heart
To revel in the entrails of my lambs.
But that still use of grief makes wild grief tame,
My tongue should to thy ears not name my boys   10
Till that my nails were anchored in thine eyes—
And I in such a desp'rate bay of death,
Like a poor barque of sails and tackling reft,
Rush all to pieces on thy rocky bosom.

K. AFTER 4.4.273

KING RICHARD
  Say that I did all this for love of her.
QUEEN ELIZABETH
  Nay, then indeed she cannot choose but hate thee,
Having bought love with such a bloody spoil.
KING RICHARD
  Look what is done cannot be now amended.
Men shall deal unadvisedly sometimes,   5
Which after-hours gives leisure to repent.
If I did take the kingdom from your sons,
To make amends I'll give it to your daughter.
If I have killed the issue of your womb,
To quicken your increase I will beget   10
Mine issue of your blood upon your daughter.
A grandam's name is little less in love
Than is the doting title of a mother.

They are as children but one step below,
Even of your mettall, of your very blood: 15
Of all one pain, save for a night of groans
Endured of her for whom you bid like sorrow.
Your children were vexation to your youth,
But mine shall be a comfort to your age.
The loss you have is but a son being king,   20
And by that loss your daughter is made queen.
I cannot make you what amends I would,
Therefore accept such kindness as I can.
Dorset your son, that with a fearful soul
Leads discontented steps in foreign soil,   25
This fair alliance quickly shall call home
To high promotions and great dignity.
The king that calls your beauteous daughter wife,
Familiarly shall call thy Dorset brother.
Again shall you be mother to a king,   30
And all the ruins of distressful times
Repaired with double riches of content.
What? We have many goodly days to see.
The liquid drops of tears that you have shed
Shall come again, transformed to orient pearl,   35
Advantaging their loan with interest
Of ten times double gain of happiness.
Go then, my mother, to thy daughter go.
Make bold her bashful years with your experience.
Prepare her ears to hear a wooer's tale.   40
Put in her tender heart th'aspiring flame
Of golden sovereignty. Acquaint the Princess
With the sweet silent hours of marriage joys.
And when this arm of mine hath chastisèd
The petty rebel, dull-brained Buckingham,   45
Bound with triumphant garlands will I come
And lead thy daughter to a conqueror's bed—
To whom I will retail my conquest won,
And she shall be sole victoress: Caesar's Caesar.
QUEEN ELIZABETH
  What were I best to say? Her father's brother   50
Would be her lord? Or shall I say her uncle?
Or he that slew her brothers and her uncles?
Under what title shall I woo for thee,
That God, the law, my honour, and her love
Can make seem pleasing to her tender years?   55

VENUS AND ADONIS

WITH *Venus and Adonis*, Shakespeare made his debut in print: his signature appears at the end of the formal dedication to the Earl of Southampton in which the poem is described as 'the first heir of my invention'—though Shakespeare had already begun to make his mark as a playwright. A terrible outbreak of plague, which was to last for almost two years, began in the summer of 1592, and London's theatres were closed as a precaution against infection. Probably Shakespeare wrote his poem at this time, perhaps seeing a need for an alternative career. It is an early example of the Ovidian erotic narrative poems that were fashionable for about thirty years from 1589; the best known outside Shakespeare is Christopher Marlowe's *Hero and Leander*, written at about the same time.

Ovid, in Book 10 of the *Metamorphoses*, tells the story of Venus and Adonis in about seventy-five lines of verse; Shakespeare's poem—drawing, probably, on both the original Latin and Arthur Golding's English version (1565-7)—is 1,194 lines long. He modified Ovid's tale as well as expanding it. In Ovid, the handsome young mortal Adonis returns the love urged on him by Venus, the goddess of love. Shakespeare turns Adonis into a bashful teenager, unripe for love, who shies away from her advances. In Ovid, the lovers go hunting together (though Venus chases only relatively harmless beasts, and advises Adonis to do the same); in Shakespeare, Adonis takes to the hunt rather as a respite from Venus' remorseless attentions. Whereas Ovid's Venus flies off to Cyprus in her dove-drawn chariot and returns only after Adonis has been mortally wounded, Shakespeare's anxiously awaits the outcome of the chase. She hears the yelping of Adonis' hounds, sees a blood-stained boar, comes upon Adonis' defeated dogs, and at last finds his body. In Ovid, she metamorphoses him into an anemone; in Shakespeare, Adonis' body melts away, and Venus plucks the purple and white flower that springs up in its place.

Shakespeare's only addition to Ovid's narrative is the episode (259-324) in which Adonis' stallion lusts after a mare, so frustrating Adonis' attempt to escape Venus' embraces. But there are many rhetorical elaborations, such as Venus' speech of attempted seduction (95-174), her disquisition on the dangers of boar-hunting (613-714), her metaphysical explanation of why the night is dark (721-68), Adonis' reply (769-810), culminating in his eloquent contrast between lust and love, and Venus' lament over his body (1069-1164).

Venus and Adonis is a mythological poem whose landscape is inhabited by none but the lovers and those members of the animal kingdom—the lustful stallion, the timorous hare (679-708), the sensitive snail (1033-6), and the savage boar—which reflect their passions. The boar's disruption of the harmony that existed between Adonis and the animals will, says Venus, result in eternal discord: 'Sorrow on love hereafter shall attend' (1136).

In Shakespeare's own time, *Venus and Adonis* was his most frequently reprinted work, with at least ten editions during his life, and another half-dozen by 1636. After this it fell out of fashion until Coleridge wrote enthusiastically about it in *Biographia Literaria* (1817). Though its conscious artifice may limit its appeal, it is a brilliantly sophisticated erotic comedy, a counterpart in verbal ingenuity to *Love's Labour's Lost*; the comedy of the poem, like that of the play, is darkened and deepened in its later stages by the shadow of sudden death.

Vilia miretur vulgus ; mihi flavus Apollo
Pocula Castalia plena ministret aqua.

TO THE RIGHT HONOURABLE HENRY WRIOTHESLEY,
EARL OF SOUTHAMPTON, AND BARON OF TITCHFIELD

Right Honourable, I know not how I shall offend in dedicating my unpolished lines to your lordship, nor how the world will censure me for choosing so strong a prop to support so weak a burden. Only, if your honour seem but pleased, I account myself highly praised, and vow to take advantage of all idle hours till I have honoured you with some graver labour. But if the first heir of my invention prove deformed, I shall be sorry it had so noble a godfather, and never after ear so barren a land for fear it yield me still so bad a harvest. I leave it to your honourable survey, and your honour to your heart's content, which I wish may always answer your own wish and the world's hopeful expectation.

Your honour's in all duty,

William Shakespeare

Venus and Adonis

Even as the sun with purple-coloured face
Had ta'en his last leave of the weeping morn,
Rose-cheeked Adonis hied him to the chase.
Hunting he loved, but love he laughed to scorn.
  Sick-thoughted Venus makes amain unto him, 5
  And like a bold-faced suitor 'gins to woo him.

'Thrice fairer than myself,' thus she began,
'The fields' chief flower, sweet above compare,
Stain to all nymphs, more lovely than a man,
More white and red than doves or roses are— 10
  Nature that made thee with herself at strife
  Saith that the world hath ending with thy life.

'Vouchsafe, thou wonder, to alight thy steed
And rein his proud head to the saddle-bow;
If thou wilt deign this favour, for thy meed 15
A thousand honey secrets shalt thou know.
  Here come and sit where never serpent hisses;
  And, being sat, I'll smother thee with kisses,

'And yet not cloy thy lips with loathed satiety,
But rather famish them amid their plenty, 20
Making them red, and pale, with fresh variety;
Ten kisses short as one, one long as twenty.
  A summer's day will seem an hour but short,
  Being wasted in such time-beguiling sport.'

With this, she seizeth on his sweating palm, 25
The precedent of pith and livelihood,
And, trembling in her passion, calls it balm—
Earth's sovereign salve to do a goddess good.
  Being so enraged, desire doth lend her force
  Courageously to pluck him from his horse. 30

Over one arm, the lusty courser's rein;
Under her other was the tender boy,
Who blushed and pouted in a dull disdain
With leaden appetite, unapt to toy.
  She red and hot as coals of glowing fire; 35
  He red for shame, but frosty in desire.

The studded bridle on a ragged bough
Nimbly she fastens—O, how quick is love!
The steed is stallèd up, and even now
To tie the rider she begins to prove. 40
  Backward she pushed him, as she would be thrust,
  And governed him in strength, though not in lust.

So soon was she along as he was down,
Each leaning on their elbows and their hips.
Now doth she stroke his cheek, now doth he frown 45
And 'gins to chide, but soon she stops his lips,

And, kissing, speaks, with lustful language broken:
'If thou wilt chide, thy lips shall never open.'

He burns with bashful shame; she with her tears
Doth quench the maiden burning of his cheeks. 50
Then, with her windy sighs and golden hairs,
To fan and blow them dry again she seeks.
  He saith she is immodest, blames her miss;
  What follows more she murders with a kiss.

Even as an empty eagle, sharp by fast, 55
Tires with her beak on feathers, flesh, and bone,
Shaking her wings, devouring all in haste
Till either gorge be stuffed or prey be gone,
  Even so she kissed his brow, his cheek, his chin,
  And where she ends she doth anew begin. 60

Forced to content, but never to obey,
Panting he lies and breatheth in her face.
She feedeth on the steam as on a prey
And calls it heavenly moisture, air of grace,
  Wishing her cheeks were gardens full of flowers, 65
  So they were dewed with such distilling showers.

Look how a bird lies tangled in a net,
So fastened in her arms Adonis lies.
Pure shame and awed resistance made him fret,
Which bred more beauty in his angry eyes. 70
  Rain added to a river that is rank
  Perforce will force it overflow the bank.

Still she entreats, and prettily entreats,
For to a pretty ear she tunes her tale.
Still is he sullen, still he lours and frets 75
'Twixt crimson shame and anger ashy-pale.
  Being red, she loves him best; and being white,
  Her best is bettered with a more delight.

Look how he can, she cannot choose but love;
And by her fair immortal hand she swears 80
From his soft bosom never to remove
Till he take truce with her contending tears,
  Which long have rained, making her cheeks all wet;
  And one sweet kiss shall pay this countless debt.

Upon this promise did he raise his chin, 85
Like a divedapper peering through a wave
Who, being looked on, ducks as quickly in—
So offers he to give what she did crave.
  But when her lips were ready for his pay,
  He winks, and turns his lips another way. 90

Never did passenger in summer's heat
More thirst for drink than she for this good turn.
Her help she sees, but help she cannot get.
She bathes in water, yet her fire must burn.
    'O pity,' gan she cry, 'flint-hearted boy!   95
    'Tis but a kiss I beg—why art thou coy?

'I have been wooed as I entreat thee now
Even by the stern and direful god of war,
Whose sinewy neck in battle ne'er did bow,
Who conquers where he comes in every jar.   100
    Yet hath he been my captive and my slave,
    And begged for that which thou unasked shalt have.

'Over my altars hath he hung his lance,
His battered shield, his uncontrollèd crest,
And for my sake hath learned to sport and dance,   105
To toy, to wanton, dally, smile, and jest,
    Scorning his churlish drum and ensign red,
    Making my arms his field, his tent my bed.

'Thus he that over-ruled I overswayed,
Leading him prisoner in a red-rose chain.   110
Strong-tempered steel his stronger strength obeyed,
Yet was he servile to my coy disdain.
    O, be not proud, nor brag not of thy might,
    For mast'ring her that foiled the god of fight.

'Touch but my lips with those fair lips of thine—   115
Though mine be not so fair, yet are they red—
The kiss shall be thine own as well as mine.
What seest thou in the ground? Hold up thy head.
    Look in mine eyeballs: there thy beauty lies.
    Then why not lips on lips, since eyes in eyes?   120

'Art thou ashamed to kiss? Then wink again,
And I will wink. So shall the day seem night.
Love keeps his revels where there are but twain.
Be bold to play—our sport is not in sight.
    These blue-veined violets whereon we lean   125
    Never can blab, nor know not what we mean.

'The tender spring upon thy tempting lip
Shows thee unripe; yet mayst thou well be tasted.
Make use of time; let not advantage slip.
Beauty within itself should not be wasted.   130
    Fair flowers that are not gathered in their prime
    Rot, and consume themselves in little time.

'Were I hard-favoured, foul, or wrinkled-old,
Ill-nurtured, crooked, churlish, harsh in voice,
O'er-worn, despisèd, rheumatic, and cold,   135
Thick-sighted, barren, lean, and lacking juice,
    Then mightst thou pause, for then I were not for
        thee.
    But having no defects, why dost abhor me?

'Thou canst not see one wrinkle in my brow.
Mine eyes are grey, and bright, and quick in turning.   140
My beauty as the spring doth yearly grow.
My flesh is soft and plump, my marrow burning.
    My smooth moist hand, were it with thy hand felt,
    Would in thy palm dissolve, or seem to melt.

'Bid me discourse, I will enchant thine ear;   145
Or like a fairy, trip upon the green;
Or like a nymph, with long, dishevelled hair,
Dance on the sands, and yet no footing seen.
    Love is a spirit all compact of fire,
    Not gross to sink, but light, and will aspire.   150

'Witness this primrose bank whereon I lie:
These forceless flowers like sturdy trees support me.
Two strengthless doves will draw me through the sky
From morn till night, even where I list to sport me.
    Is love so light, sweet boy, and may it be   155
    That thou should think it heavy unto thee?

'Is thine own heart to thine own face affected?
Can thy right hand seize love upon thy left?
Then woo thyself, be of thyself rejected;
Steal thine own freedom, and complain on theft.   160
    Narcissus so himself himself forsook,
    And died to kiss his shadow in the brook.

'Torches are made to light, jewels to wear,
Dainties to taste, fresh beauty for the use,
Herbs for their smell, and sappy plants to bear.   165
Things growing to themselves are growth's abuse.
    Seeds spring from seeds, and beauty breedeth
        beauty:
    Thou wast begot; to get it is thy duty.

'Upon the earth's increase why shouldst thou feed
Unless the earth with thy increase be fed?   170
By law of nature thou art bound to breed,
That thine may live when thou thyself art dead;
    And so in spite of death thou dost survive,
    In that thy likeness still is left alive.'

By this, the lovesick queen began to sweat,   175
For where they lay the shadow had forsook them,
And Titan, tired in the midday heat,
With burning eye did hotly overlook them,
    Wishing Adonis had his team to guide
    So he were like him, and by Venus' side.   180

And now Adonis, with a lazy sprite
And with a heavy, dark, disliking eye,
His louring brows o'erwhelming his fair sight,
Like misty vapours when they blot the sky,
    Souring his cheeks, cries, 'Fie, no more of love!   185
    The sun doth burn my face; I must remove.'

'Ay me,' quoth Venus, 'young, and so unkind?
What bare excuses mak'st thou to be gone?
I'll sigh celestial breath, whose gentle wind
Shall cool the heat of this descending sun. 190
  I'll make a shadow for thee of my hairs;
  If they burn too, I'll quench them with my tears.

'The sun that shines from heaven shines but warm,
And lo, I lie between that sun and thee.
The heat I have from thence doth little harm; 195
Thine eye darts forth the fire that burneth me,
  And were I not immortal, life were done
  Between this heavenly and earthly sun.

'Art thou obdurate, flinty, hard as steel?
Nay, more than flint, for stone at rain relenteth. 200
Art thou a woman's son, and canst not feel
What 'tis to love, how want of love tormenteth?
  O, had thy mother borne so hard a mind,
  She had not brought forth thee, but died unkind.

'What am I, that thou shouldst contemn me this? 205
Or what great danger dwells upon my suit?
What were thy lips the worse for one poor kiss?
Speak, fair; but speak fair words, or else be mute.
  Give me one kiss, I'll give it thee again,
  And one for int'rest, if thou wilt have twain. 210

'Fie, lifeless picture, cold and senseless stone,
Well painted idol, image dull and dead,
Statue contenting but the eye alone,
Thing like a man, but of no woman bred:
  Thou art no man, though of a man's complexion, 215
  For men will kiss even by their own direction.'

This said, impatience chokes her pleading tongue,
And swelling passion doth provoke a pause.
Red cheeks and fiery eyes blaze forth her wrong.
Being judge in love, she cannot right her cause; 220
  And now she weeps, and now she fain would speak,
  And now her sobs do her intendments break.

Sometime she shakes her head, and then his hand;
Now gazeth she on him, now on the ground.
Sometime her arms enfold him like a band; 225
She would, he will not in her arms be bound.
  And when from thence he struggles to be gone,
  She locks her lily fingers one in one.

'Fondling,' she saith, 'since I have hemmed thee here
Within the circuit of this ivory pale, 230
I'll be a park, and thou shalt be my deer.
Feed where thou wilt, on mountain or in dale;
  Graze on my lips, and if those hills be dry,
  Stray lower, where the pleasant fountains lie.

'Within this limit is relief enough, 235
Sweet bottom-grass, and high delightful plain,
Round rising hillocks, brakes obscure and rough,
To shelter thee from tempest and from rain.
  Then be my deer, since I am such a park;
  No dog shall rouse thee, though a thousand bark.' 240

At this Adonis smiles as in disdain,
That in each cheek appears a pretty dimple.
Love made those hollows, if himself were slain,
He might be buried in a tomb so simple,
  Foreknowing well, if there he came to lie, 245
  Why, there love lived, and there he could not die.

These lovely caves, these round enchanting pits,
Opened their mouths to swallow Venus' liking.
Being mad before, how doth she now for wits?
Struck dead at first, what needs a second striking? 250
  Poor queen of love, in thine own law forlorn,
  To love a cheek that smiles at thee in scorn!

Now which way shall she turn? What shall she say?
Her words are done, her woes the more increasing.
The time is spent; her object will away, 255
And from her twining arms doth urge releasing.
  'Pity,' she cries; 'some favour, some remorse!'
  Away he springs, and hasteth to his horse.

But lo, from forth a copse that neighbours by
A breeding jennet, lusty, young, and proud, 260
Adonis' trampling courser doth espy,
And forth she rushes, snorts, and neighs aloud.
  The strong-necked steed, being tied unto a tree,
  Breaketh his rein, and to her straight goes he.

Imperiously he leaps, he neighs, he bounds, 265
And now his woven girths he breaks asunder.
The bearing earth with his hard hoof he wounds,
Whose hollow womb resounds like heaven's thunder.
  The iron bit he crusheth 'tween his teeth,
  Controlling what he was controllèd with. 270

His ears up-pricked, his braided hanging mane
Upon his compassed crest now stand on end;
His nostrils drink the air, and forth again,
As from a furnace, vapours doth he send.
  His eye, which scornfully glisters like fire, 275
  Shows his hot courage and his high desire.

Sometime he trots, as if he told the steps,
With gentle majesty and modest pride.
Anon he rears upright, curvets, and leaps,
As who should say, 'Lo, thus my strength is tried, 280
  And this I do to captivate the eye
  Of the fair breeder that is standing by.'

What recketh he his rider's angry stir,
His flattering 'Holla,' or his 'Stand, I say!'?
What cares he now for curb or pricking spur,   285
For rich caparisons or trappings gay?
   He sees his love, and nothing else he sees,
   For nothing else with his proud sight agrees.

Look when a painter would surpass the life
In limning out a well proportioned steed,   290
His art with nature's workmanship at strife,
As if the dead the living should exceed:
   So did this horse excel a common one
   In shape, in courage, colour, pace, and bone.

Round-hoofed, short-jointed, fetlocks shag and long,   295
Broad breast, full eye, small head, and nostril wide,
High crest, short ears, straight legs, and passing
   strong;
Thin mane, thick tail, broad buttock, tender hide—
   Look what a horse should have he did not lack,
   Save a proud rider on so proud a back.   300

Sometime he scuds far off, and there he stares;
Anon he starts at stirring of a feather.
To bid the wind a base he now prepares,
And whe'er he run or fly they know not whether;
   For through his mane and tail the high wind sings,
   Fanning the hairs, who wave like feathered wings.   306

He looks upon his love, and neighs unto her;
She answers him as if she knew his mind,
Being proud, as females are, to see him woo her,
She puts on outward strangeness, seems unkind,   310
   Spurns at his love, and scorns the heat he feels,
   Beating his kind embracements with her heels.

Then, like a melancholy malcontent,
He vails his tail that, like a falling plume,
Cool shadow to his melting buttock lent.   315
He stamps, and bites the poor flies in his fume.
   His love, perceiving how he was enraged,
   Grew kinder, and his fury was assuaged.

His testy master goeth about to take him,
When lo, the unbacked breeder, full of fear,   320
Jealous of catching, swiftly doth forsake him,
With her the horse, and left Adonis there.
   As they were mad unto the wood they hie them,
   Outstripping crows that strive to overfly them.

All swoll'n with chafing, down Adonis sits,   325
Banning his boist'rous and unruly beast;
And now the happy season once more fits
That lovesick love by pleading may be blessed;
   For lovers say the heart hath treble wrong
   When it is barred the aidance of the tongue.   330

An oven that is stopped, or river stayed,
Burneth more hotly, swelleth with more rage.
So of concealèd sorrow may be said
Free vent of words love's fire doth assuage.
   But when the heart's attorney once is mute,   335
   The client breaks, as desperate in his suit.

He sees her coming, and begins to glow,
Even as a dying coal revives with wind,
And with his bonnet hides his angry brow,
Looks on the dull earth with disturbèd mind,   340
   Taking no notice that she is so nigh,
   For all askance he holds her in his eye.

O, what a sight it was wistly to view
How she came stealing to the wayward boy,
To note the fighting conflict of her hue,   345
How white and red each other did destroy!
   But now her cheek was pale; and by and by
   It flashed forth fire, as lightning from the sky.

Now was she just before him as he sat,
And like a lowly lover down she kneels;   350
With one fair hand she heaveth up his hat;
Her other tender hand his fair cheek feels.
   His tend'rer cheek receives her soft hand's print
   As apt as new-fall'n snow takes any dint.

O, what a war of looks was then between them,   355
Her eyes petitioners to his eyes suing!
His eyes saw her eyes as they had not seen them;
Her eyes wooed still; his eyes disdained the wooing;
   And all this dumb play had his acts made plain
   With tears which, chorus-like, her eyes did rain.   360

Full gently now she takes him by the hand,
A lily prisoned in a jail of snow,
Or ivory in an alabaster band;
So white a friend engirds so white a foe.
   This beauteous combat, wilful and unwilling,   365
   Showed like two silver doves that sit a-billing.

Once more the engine of her thoughts began:
'O fairest mover on this mortal round,
Would thou wert as I am, and I a man,
My heart all whole as thine, thy heart my wound;   370
   For one sweet look thy help I would assure thee,
   Though nothing but my body's bane would cure
     thee.'

'Give me my hand,' saith he. 'Why dost thou feel it?'
'Give me my heart,' saith she, 'and thou shalt have it.
O, give it me, lest thy hard heart do steel it,   375
And, being steeled, soft sighs can never grave it;
   Then love's deep groans I never shall regard,
   Because Adonis' heart hath made mine hard.'

'For shame,' he cries, 'let go, and let me go!
My day's delight is past; my horse is gone,   380
And 'tis your fault I am bereft him so.
I pray you hence, and leave me here alone;
  For all my mind, my thought, my busy care
  Is how to get my palfrey from the mare.'

Thus she replies: 'Thy palfrey, as he should,   385
Welcomes the warm approach of sweet desire.
Affection is a coal that must be cooled,
Else, suffered, it will set the heart on fire.
  The sea hath bounds, but deep desire hath none;
  Therefore no marvel though thy horse be gone.   390

'How like a jade he stood tied to the tree,
Servilely mastered with a leathern rein!
But when he saw his love, his youth's fair fee,
He held such petty bondage in disdain,
  Throwing the base thong from his bending crest,   395
  Enfranchising his mouth, his back, his breast.

'Who sees his true-love in her naked bed,
Teaching the sheets a whiter hue than white,
But when his glutton eye so full hath fed
His other agents aim at like delight?   400
  Who is so faint that dares not be so bold
  To touch the fire, the weather being cold?

'Let me excuse thy courser, gentle boy;
And learn of him, I heartily beseech thee,
To take advantage on presented joy.   405
Though I were dumb, yet his proceedings teach thee.
  O, learn to love! The lesson is but plain,
  And, once made perfect, never lost again.'

'I know not love,' quoth he, 'nor will not know it,
Unless it be a boar, and then I chase it.   410
'Tis much to borrow, and I will not owe it.
My love to love is love but to disgrace it;
  For I have heard it is a life in death,
  That laughs and weeps, and all but with a breath.

'Who wears a garment shapeless and unfinished?   415
Who plucks the bud before one leaf put forth?
If springing things be any jot diminished,
They wither in their prime, prove nothing worth.
  The colt that's backed and burdened being young,
  Loseth his pride, and never waxeth strong.   420

'You hurt my hand with wringing. Let us part,
And leave this idle theme, this bootless chat.
Remove your siege from my unyielding heart;
To love's alarms it will not ope the gate.
  Dismiss your vows, your feignèd tears, your
    flatt'ry;   425
  For where a heart is hard they make no batt'ry.'

'What, canst thou talk?' quoth she. 'Hast thou a tongue?
O, would thou hadst not, or I had no hearing!   380
Thy mermaid's voice hath done me double wrong.
I had my load before, now pressed with bearing: 430
  Melodious discord, heavenly tune harsh sounding,
  Ears' deep-sweet music, and heart's deep-sore
    wounding.

'Had I no eyes but ears, my ears would love
That inward beauty and invisible;
Or were I deaf, thy outward parts would move   435
Each part in me that were but sensible.
  Though neither eyes nor ears to hear nor see,
  Yet should I be in love by touching thee.

'Say that the sense of feeling were bereft me,
And that I could not see, nor hear, nor touch,   440
And nothing but the very smell were left me,
Yet would my love to thee be still as much;
  For from the stillitory of thy face excelling
  Comes breath perfumed, that breedeth love by
    smelling.

'But O, what banquet wert thou to the taste,   445
Being nurse and feeder of the other four!
Would they not wish the feast might ever last
And bid suspicion double-lock the door
  Lest jealousy, that sour unwelcome guest,
  Should by his stealing-in disturb the feast?'   450

Once more the ruby-coloured portal opened
Which to his speech did honey passage yield,
Like a red morn that ever yet betokened
Wrack to the seaman, tempest to the field,
  Sorrow to shepherds, woe unto the birds,   455
  Gusts and foul flaws to herdmen and to herds.

This ill presage advisedly she marketh.
Even as the wind is hushed before it raineth,
Or as the wolf doth grin before he barketh,
Or as the berry breaks before it staineth,   460
  Or like the deadly bullet of a gun,
  His meaning struck her ere his words begun,

And at his look she flatly falleth down,
For looks kill love, and love by looks reviveth;
A smile recures the wounding of a frown,   465
But blessèd bankrupt that by loss so thriveth!
  The silly boy, believing she is dead,
  Claps her pale cheek till clapping makes it red,

And, all amazed, brake off his late intent,
For sharply he did think to reprehend her,   470
Which cunning love did wittily prevent.
Fair fall the wit that can so well defend her!
  For on the grass she lies as she were slain,
  Till his breath breatheth life in her again.

He wrings her nose, he strikes her on the cheeks, 475
He bends her fingers, holds her pulses hard;
He chafes her lips; a thousand ways he seeks
To mend the hurt that his unkindness marred.
    He kisses her; and she, by her good will,
    Will never rise, so he will kiss her still. 480

The night of sorrow now is turned to day.
Her two blue windows faintly she upheaveth,
Like the fair sun when, in his fresh array,
He cheers the morn, and all the earth relieveth;
    And as the bright sun glorifies the sky, 485
    So is her face illumined with her eye,

Whose beams upon his hairless face are fixed,
As if from thence they borrowed all their shine.
Were never four such lamps together mixed,
Had not his clouded with his brow's repine. 490
    But hers, which through the crystal tears gave light,
    Shone like the moon in water seen by night.

'O, where am I?' quoth she; 'in earth or heaven,
Or in the ocean drenched, or in the fire?
What hour is this: or morn or weary even? 495
Do I delight to die, or life desire?
    But now I lived, and life was death's annoy;
    But now I died, and death was lively joy.

'O, thou didst kill me; kill me once again!
Thy eyes' shrewd tutor, that hard heart of thine, 500
Hath taught them scornful tricks, and such disdain
That they have murdered this poor heart of mine,
    And these mine eyes, true leaders to their queen,
    But for thy piteous lips no more had seen.

'Long may they kiss each other, for this cure! 505
O, never let their crimson liveries wear,
And as they last, their verdure still endure
To drive infection from the dangerous year,
    That the star-gazers, having writ on death,
    May say the plague is banished by thy breath! 510

'Pure lips, sweet seals in my soft lips imprinted,
What bargains may I make still to be sealing?
To sell myself I can be well contented,
So thou wilt buy, and pay, and use good dealing;
    Which purchase if thou make, for fear of slips 515
    Set thy seal manual on my wax-red lips.

'A thousand kisses buys my heart from me;
And pay them at thy leisure, one by one.
What is ten hundred touches unto thee?
Are they not quickly told, and quickly gone? 520
    Say for non-payment that the debt should double,
    Is twenty hundred kisses such a trouble?'

'Fair queen,' quoth he, 'if any love you owe me,
Measure my strangeness with my unripe years.
Before I know myself, seek not to know me. 525
No fisher but the ungrown fry forbears.
    The mellow plum doth fall, the green sticks fast,
    Or, being early plucked, is sour to taste.

'Look, the world's comforter with weary gait
His day's hot task hath ended in the west. 530
The owl, night's herald, shrieks 'tis very late;
The sheep are gone to fold, birds to their nest,
    And coal-black clouds, that shadow heaven's light,
    Do summon us to part and bid good night.

'Now let me say good night, and so say you. 535
If you will say so, you shall have a kiss.'
'Good night,' quoth she; and ere he says adieu
The honey fee of parting tendered is.
    Her arms do lend his neck a sweet embrace.
    Incorporate then they seem; face grows to face, 540

Till breathless he disjoined, and backward drew
The heavenly moisture, that sweet coral mouth,
Whose precious taste her thirsty lips well knew,
Whereon they surfeit, yet complain on drought.
    He with her plenty pressed, she faint with dearth, 545
    Their lips together glued, fall to the earth.

Now quick desire hath caught the yielding prey,
And glutton-like she feeds, yet never filleth.
Her lips are conquerors, his lips obey,
Paying what ransom the insulter willeth; 550
    Whose vulture thought doth pitch the price so high
    That she will draw his lips' rich treasure dry,

And, having felt the sweetness of the spoil,
With blindfold fury she begins to forage.
Her face doth reek and smoke, her blood doth boil, 555
And careless lust stirs up a desperate courage,
    Planting oblivion, beating reason back,
    Forgetting shame's pure blush and honour's wrack.

Hot, faint, and weary with her hard embracing,
Like a wild bird being tamed with too much handling,
Or as the fleet-foot roe that's tired with chasing, 561
Or like the froward infant stilled with dandling,
    He now obeys, and now no more resisteth,
    While she takes all she can, not all she listeth.

What wax so frozen but dissolves with temp'ring 565
And yields at last to every light impression?
Things out of hope are compassed oft with vent'ring,
Chiefly in love, whose leave exceeds commission.
    Affection faints not, like a pale-faced coward,
    But then woos best when most his choice is froward.

When he did frown, O, had she then gave over,   571
Such nectar from his lips she had not sucked.
Foul words and frowns must not repel a lover.
What though the rose have prickles, yet 'tis plucked!
Were beauty under twenty locks kept fast,   575
Yet love breaks through, and picks them all at last.

For pity now she can no more detain him.
The poor fool prays her that he may depart.
She is resolved no longer to restrain him,
Bids him farewell, and look well to her heart,   580
The which, by Cupid's bow she doth protest,
He carries thence encagèd in his breast.

'Sweet boy,' she says, 'this night I'll waste in sorrow,
For my sick heart commands mine eyes to watch.
Tell me, love's master, shall we meet tomorrow?   585
Say, shall we, shall we? Wilt thou make the match?'
He tells her no, tomorrow he intends
To hunt the boar with certain of his friends.

'The boar!' quoth she; whereat a sudden pale,
Like lawn being spread upon the blushing rose,   590
Usurps her cheek. She trembles at his tale,
And on his neck her yoking arms she throws.
She sinketh down, still hanging by his neck.
He on her belly falls, she on her back.

Now is she in the very lists of love,   595
Her champion mounted for the hot encounter.
All is imaginary she doth prove.
He will not manage her, although he mount her,
That worse than Tantalus' is her annoy,
To clip Elysium, and to lack her joy.   600

Even so poor birds, deceived with painted grapes,
Do surfeit by the eye, and pine the maw;
Even so she languisheth in her mishaps
As those poor birds that helpless berries saw.
The warm effects which she in him finds missing   605
She seeks to kindle with continual kissing.

But all in vain, good queen! It will not be.
She hath assayed as much as may be proved;
Her pleading hath deserved a greater fee:
She's Love; she loves; and yet she is not loved.   610
'Fie, fie,' he says, 'you crush me. Let me go.
You have no reason to withhold me so.'

'Thou hadst been gone,' quoth she, 'sweet boy, ere this,
But that thou told'st me thou wouldst hunt the boar.
O, be advised; thou know'st not what it is   615
With javelin's point a churlish swine to gore,
Whose tushes, never sheathed, he whetteth still,
Like to a mortal butcher, bent to kill.

'On his bow-back he hath a battle set
Of bristly pikes that ever threat his foes.   620
His eyes like glow-worms shine; when he doth fret
His snout digs sepulchres where'er he goes.
Being moved, he strikes, whate'er is in his way,
And whom he strikes his crooked tushes slay.

'His brawny sides with hairy bristles armed   625
Are better proof than thy spear's point can enter.
His short thick neck cannot be easily harmed.
Being ireful, on the lion he will venture.
The thorny brambles and embracing bushes,
As fearful of him, part; through whom he rushes.   630

'Alas, he naught esteems that face of thine,
To which love's eyes pays tributary gazes,
Nor thy soft hands, sweet lips, and crystal eyne,
Whose full perfection all the world amazes;
But having thee at vantage—wondrous dread!—   635
Would root these beauties as he roots the mead.

'O, let him keep his loathsome cabin still.
Beauty hath naught to do with such foul fiends.
Come not within his danger by thy will.
They that thrive well take counsel of their friends.   640
When thou didst name the boar, not to dissemble,
I feared thy fortune, and my joints did tremble.

'Didst thou not mark my face? Was it not white?
Sawest thou not signs of fear lurk in mine eye?
Grew I not faint, and fell I not downright?   645
Within my bosom, whereon thou dost lie,
My boding heart pants, beats, and takes no rest,
But like an earthquake shakes thee on my breast.

'For where love reigns, disturbing jealousy
Doth call himself affection's sentinel,   650
Gives false alarms, suggesteth mutiny,
And in a peaceful hour doth cry, "Kill, kill!",
Distemp'ring gentle love in his desire,
As air and water do abate the fire.

'This sour informer, this bate-breeding spy,   655
This canker that eats up love's tender spring,
This carry-tale, dissentious jealousy,
That sometime true news, sometime false doth bring,
Knocks at my heart, and whispers in mine ear
That if I love thee, I thy death should fear;   660

'And, more than so, presenteth to mine eye
The picture of an angry chafing boar,
Under whose sharp fangs on his back doth lie
An image like thyself, all stained with gore,
Whose blood upon the fresh flowers being shed   665
Doth make them droop with grief, and hang the head.

'What should I do, seeing thee so indeed,
That tremble at th'imagination?
The thought of it doth make my faint heart bleed,
And fear doth teach it divination. 670
  I prophesy thy death, my living sorrow,
  If thou encounter with the boar tomorrow.

'But if thou needs wilt hunt, be ruled by me:
Uncouple at the timorous flying hare,
Or at the fox which lives by subtlety, 675
Or at the roe which no encounter dare.
  Pursue these fearful creatures o'er the downs,
  And on thy well-breathed horse keep with thy
    hounds.

'And when thou hast on foot the purblind hare,
Mark the poor wretch, to overshoot his troubles, 680
How he outruns the wind, and with what care
He cranks and crosses with a thousand doubles.
  The many musits through the which he goes
  Are like a labyrinth to amaze his foes.

'Sometime he runs among a flock of sheep 685
To make the cunning hounds mistake their smell,
And sometime where earth-delving conies keep,
To stop the loud pursuers in their yell;
  And sometime sorteth with a herd of deer.
  Danger deviseth shifts; wit waits on fear. 690

'For there his smell with others being mingled,
The hot scent-snuffing hounds are driven to doubt,
Ceasing their clamorous cry till they have singled,
With much ado, the cold fault cleanly out.
  Then do they spend their mouths. Echo replies, 695
  As if another chase were in the skies.

'By this, poor Wat, far off upon a hill,
Stands on his hinder legs with list'ning ear,
To hearken if his foes pursue him still.
Anon their loud alarums he doth hear, 700
  And now his grief may be comparèd well
  To one sore sick that hears the passing-bell.

'Then shalt thou see the dew-bedabbled wretch
Turn, and return, indenting with the way.
Each envious brier his weary legs do scratch; 705
Each shadow makes him stop, each murmur stay;
  For misery is trodden on by many,
  And, being low, never relieved by any.

'Lie quietly, and hear a little more;
Nay, do not struggle, for thou shalt not rise. 710
To make thee hate the hunting of the boar
Unlike myself thou hear'st me moralize,
  Applying this to that, and so to so,
  For love can comment upon every woe.

'Where did I leave?' 'No matter where,' quoth he; 715
'Leave me, and then the story aptly ends.
The night is spent.' 'Why what of that?' quoth she.
'I am,' quoth he, 'expected of my friends,
  And now 'tis dark, and going I shall fall.'
  'In night,' quoth she, 'desire sees best of all. 720

'But if thou fall, O, then imagine this:
The earth, in love with thee, thy footing trips,
And all is but to rob thee of a kiss.
Rich preys make true men thieves; so do thy lips
  Make modest Dian cloudy and forlorn 725
  Lest she should steal a kiss, and die forsworn.

'Now of this dark night I perceive the reason.
Cynthia, for shame, obscures her silver shine
Till forging nature be condemned of treason
For stealing moulds from heaven, that were divine, 730
  Wherein she framed thee, in high heaven's despite,
  To shame the sun by day and her by night.

'And therefore hath she bribed the destinies
To cross the curious workmanship of nature,
To mingle beauty with infirmities, 735
And pure perfection with impure defeature,
  Making it subject to the tyranny
  Of mad mischances and much misery;

'As burning fevers, agues pale and faint,
Life-poisoning pestilence, and frenzies wood, 740
The marrow-eating sickness whose attaint
Disorder breeds by heating of the blood;
  Surfeits, impostumes, grief, and damned despair
  Swear nature's death for framing thee so fair.

'And not the least of all these maladies 745
But in one minute's fight brings beauty under.
Both favour, savour, hue, and qualities,
Whereat th'impartial gazer late did wonder,
  Are on the sudden wasted, thawed, and done,
  As mountain snow melts with the midday sun. 750

'Therefore, despite of fruitless chastity,
Love-lacking vestals and self-loving nuns,
That on the earth would breed a scarcity
And barren dearth of daughters and of sons,
  Be prodigal. The lamp that burns by night 755
  Dries up his oil to lend the world his light.

'What is thy body but a swallowing grave,
Seeming to bury that posterity
Which, by the rights of time, thou needs must have
If thou destroy them not in dark obscurity? 760
  If so, the world will hold thee in disdain,
  Sith in thy pride so fair a hope is slain.

'So in thyself thyself art made away,
A mischief worse than civil, home-bred strife,
Or theirs whose desperate hands themselves do slay, 765
Or butcher sire that reaves his son of life.
    Foul cank'ring rust the hidden treasure frets,
    But gold that's put to use more gold begets.'

'Nay, then,' quoth Adon, 'You will fall again
Into your idle, over-handled theme. 770
The kiss I gave you is bestowed in vain,
And all in vain you strive against the stream;
    For, by this black-faced night, desire's foul nurse,
    Your treatise makes me like you worse and worse.

'If love have lent you twenty thousand tongues, 775
And every tongue more moving than your own,
Bewitching like the wanton mermaid's songs,
Yet from mine ear the tempting tune is blown;
    For know, my heart stands armèd in mine ear,
    And will not let a false sound enter there, 780

'Lest the deceiving harmony should run
Into the quiet closure of my breast,
And then my little heart were quite undone,
In his bedchamber to be barred of rest.
    No, lady, no. My heart longs not to groan, 785
    But soundly sleeps, while now it sleeps alone.

'What have you urged that I cannot reprove?
The path is smooth that leadeth on to danger.
I hate not love, but your device in love,
That lends embracements unto every stranger. 790
    You do it for increase—O strange excuse,
    When reason is the bawd to lust's abuse!

'Call it not love, for love to heaven is fled
Since sweating lust on earth usurped his name,
Under whose simple semblance he hath fed 795
Upon fresh beauty, blotting it with blame;
    Which the hot tyrant stains, and soon bereaves,
    As caterpillars do the tender leaves.

'Love comforteth, like sunshine after rain,
But lust's effect is tempest after sun. 800
Love's gentle spring doth always fresh remain;
Lust's winter comes ere summer half be done.
    Love surfeits not; lust like a glutton dies.
    Love is all truth, lust full of forgèd lies.

'More I could tell, but more I dare not say; 805
The text is old, the orator too green.
Therefore in sadness now I will away;
My face is full of shame, my heart of teen.
    Mine ears that to your wanton talk attended
    Do burn themselves for having so offended.' 810

With this he breaketh from the sweet embrace
Of those fair arms which bound him to her breast,
And homeward through the dark laund runs apace,
Leaves love upon her back, deeply distressed.
    Look how a bright star shooteth from the sky, 815
    So glides he in the night from Venus' eye,

Which after him she darts, as one on shore
Gazing upon a late-embarkèd friend 770
Till the wild waves will have him seen no more,
Whose ridges with the meeting clouds contend. 820
    So did the merciless and pitchy night
    Fold in the object that did feed her sight.

Whereat amazed, as one that unaware
Hath dropped a precious jewel in the flood,
Or stonished, as night wand'rers often are, 825
Their light blown out in some mistrustful wood:
    Even so, confounded in the dark she lay,
    Having lost the fair discovery of her way.

And now she beats her heart, whereat it groans,
That all the neighbour caves, as seeming troubled, 830
Make verbal repetition of her moans;
Passion on passion deeply is redoubled.
    'Ay me,' she cries, and twenty times 'Woe, woe!'
    And twenty echoes twenty times cry so.

She, marking them, begins a wailing note, 835
And sings extemporally a woeful ditty,
How love makes young men thrall, and old men dote,
How love is wise in folly, foolish-witty.
    Her heavy anthem still concludes in woe,
    And still the choir of echoes answer so. 840

Her song was tedious, and outwore the night;
For lovers' hours are long, though seeming short.
If pleased themselves, others, they think, delight
In such-like circumstance, with such-like sport.
    Their copious stories oftentimes begun 845
    End without audience, and are never done.

For who hath she to spend the night withal
But idle sounds resembling parasites,
Like shrill-tongued tapsters answering every call,
Soothing the humour of fantastic wits? 850
    She says ''Tis so'; they answer all ''Tis so',
    And would say after her, if she said 'No'.

Lo, here the gentle lark, weary of rest,
From his moist cabinet mounts up on high
And wakes the morning, from whose silver breast 855
The sun ariseth in his majesty,
    Who doth the world so gloriously behold
    That cedar tops and hills seem burnished gold.

Venus salutes him with this fair good-morrow:
'O thou clear god, and patron of all light, 860
From whom each lamp and shining star doth borrow
The beauteous influence that makes him bright:
  There lives a son that sucked an earthly mother
  May lend thee light, as thou dost lend to other.'

This said, she hasteth to a myrtle grove, 865
Musing the morning is so much o'erworn
And yet she hears no tidings of her love.
She hearkens for his hounds, and for his horn.
  Anon she hears them chant it lustily,
  And all in haste she coasteth to the cry. 870

And as she runs, the bushes in the way
Some catch her by the neck, some kiss her face,
Some twine about her thigh to make her stay.
She wildly breaketh from their strict embrace,
  Like a milch doe whose swelling dugs do ache, 875
  Hasting to feed her fawn hid in some brake.

By this she hears the hounds are at a bay,
Whereat she starts, like one that spies an adder
Wreathed up in fatal folds just in his way,
The fear whereof doth make him shake and shudder; 880
  Even so the timorous yelping of the hounds
  Appals her senses, and her spirit confounds.

For now she knows it is no gentle chase,
But the blunt boar, rough bear, or lion proud,
Because the cry remaineth in one place, 885
Where fearfully the dogs exclaim aloud.
  Finding their enemy to be so curst,
  They all strain court'sy who shall cope him first.

This dismal cry rings sadly in her ear,
Through which it enters to surprise her heart, 890
Who, overcome by doubt and bloodless fear,
With cold-pale weakness numbs each feeling part;
  Like soldiers when their captain once doth yield,
  They basely fly, and dare not stay the field.

Thus stands she in a trembling ecstasy, 895
Till, cheering up her senses all dismayed,
She tells them 'tis a causeless fantasy
And childish error that they are afraid;
  Bids them leave quaking, bids them fear no more;
  And with that word she spied the hunted boar, 900

Whose frothy mouth, bepainted all with red,
Like milk and blood being mingled both together,
A second fear through all her sinews spread,
Which madly hurries her, she knows not whither.
  This way she runs, and now she will no further, 905
  But back retires to rate the boar for murder.

A thousand spleens bear her a thousand ways.
She treads the path that she untreads again.
Her more than haste is mated with delays,
Like the proceedings of a drunken brain, 910
  Full of respects, yet naught at all respecting;
  In hand with all things, naught at all effecting.

Here kennelled in a brake she finds a hound,
And asks the weary caitiff for his master;
And there another licking of his wound, 915
'Gainst venomed sores the only sovereign plaster.
  And here she meets another, sadly scowling,
  To whom she speaks; and he replies with howling.

When he hath ceased his ill-resounding noise,
Another flap-mouthed mourner, black and grim, 920
Against the welkin volleys out his voice.
Another, and another, answer him,
  Clapping their proud tails to the ground below,
  Shaking their scratched ears, bleeding as they go.

Look how the world's poor people are amazed 925
At apparitions, signs, and prodigies,
Whereon with fearful eyes they long have gazed,
Infusing them with dreadful prophecies:
  So she at these sad signs draws up her breath,
  And, sighing it again, exclaims on death. 930

'Hard-favoured tyrant, ugly, meagre, lean,
Hateful divorce of love'—thus chides she death;
'Grim-grinning ghost, earth's worm: what dost thou
    mean
To stifle beauty, and to steal his breath
  Who, when he lived, his breath and beauty set 935
  Gloss on the rose, smell to the violet?

'If he be dead—O no, it cannot be,
Seeing his beauty, thou shouldst strike at it.
O yes, it may; thou hast no eyes to see,
But hatefully, at random dost thou hit. 940
  Thy mark is feeble age; but thy false dart
  Mistakes that aim, and cleaves an infant's heart.

'Hadst thou but bid beware, then he had spoke,
And, hearing him, thy power had lost his power.
The destinies will curse thee for this stroke. 945
They bid thee crop a weed; thou pluck'st a flower.
  Love's golden arrow at him should have fled,
  And not death's ebon dart to strike him dead.

'Dost thou drink tears, that thou provok'st such
    weeping?
What may a heavy groan advantage thee? 950
Why hast thou cast into eternal sleeping
Those eyes that taught all other eyes to see?
  Now nature cares not for thy mortal vigour,
  Since her best work is ruined with thy rigour.'

Here overcome, as one full of despair,   955
She vailed her eyelids, who like sluices stopped
The crystal tide that from her two cheeks fair
In the sweet channel of her bosom dropped.
　But through the flood-gates breaks the silver rain,
　And with his strong course opens them again.   960

O, how her eyes and tears did lend and borrow!
Her eye seen in the tears, tears in her eye,
Both crystals, where they viewed each other's sorrow:
Sorrow, that friendly sighs sought still to dry,
　But, like a stormy day, now wind, now rain,   965
　Sighs dry her cheeks, tears make them wet again.

Variable passions throng her constant woe,
As striving who should best become her grief.
All entertained, each passion labours so
That every present sorrow seemeth chief,   970
　But none is best. Then join they all together,
　Like many clouds consulting for foul weather.

By this, far off she hears some huntsman hollo;
A nurse's song ne'er pleased her babe so well.
The dire imagination she did follow   975
This sound of hope doth labour to expel;
　For now reviving joy bids her rejoice
　And flatters her it is Adonis' voice.

Whereat her tears began to turn their tide,
Being prisoned in her eye like pearls in glass;   980
Yet sometimes falls an orient drop beside,
Which her cheek melts, as scorning it should pass
　To wash the foul face of the sluttish ground,
　Who is but drunken when she seemeth drowned.

O hard-believing love—how strange it seems   985
Not to believe, and yet too credulous!
Thy weal and woe are both of them extremes.
Despair, and hope, makes thee ridiculous.
　The one doth flatter thee in thoughts unlikely;
　In likely thoughts the other kills thee quickly.   990

Now she unweaves the web that she hath wrought.
Adonis lives, and death is not to blame.
It was not she that called him all to naught.
Now she adds honours to his hateful name.
　She clepes him king of graves, and grave for kings, 995
　Imperious supreme of all mortal things.

'No, no,' quoth she, 'sweet death, I did but jest.
Yet pardon me, I felt a kind of fear
Whenas I met the boar, that bloody beast,
Which knows no pity, but is still severe.   1000
　Then, gentle shadow—truth I must confess—
　I railed on thee, fearing my love's decease.

''Tis not my fault; the boar provoked my tongue.
Be wreaked on him, invisible commander.
'Tis he, foul creature, that hath done thee wrong.   1005
I did but act; he's author of thy slander.
　Grief hath two tongues, and never woman yet
　Could rule them both, without ten women's wit.'

Thus, hoping that Adonis is alive,
Her rash suspect she doth extenuate,   1010
And, that his beauty may the better thrive,
With death she humbly doth insinuate;
　Tells him of trophies, statues, tombs; and stories
　His victories, his triumphs, and his glories.

'O Jove,' quoth she, 'how much a fool was I   1015
To be of such a weak and silly mind
To wail his death who lives, and must not die
Till mutual overthrow of mortal kind!
　For he being dead, with him is beauty slain,
　And beauty dead, black chaos comes again.   1020

'Fie, fie, fond love, thou art as full of fear
As one with treasure laden, hemmed with thieves.
Trifles unwitnessèd with eye or ear
Thy coward heart with false bethinking grieves.'
　Even at this word she hears a merry horn,   1025
　Whereat she leaps, that was but late forlorn.

As falcons to the lure, away she flies.
The grass stoops not, she treads on it so light;
And in her haste unfortunately spies
The foul boar's conquest on her fair delight;   1030
　Which seen, her eyes, as murdered with the view,
　Like stars ashamed of day, themselves withdrew.

Or as the snail, whose tender horns being hit
Shrinks backward in his shelly cave with pain,
And there, all smothered up, in shade doth sit,   1035
Long after fearing to creep forth again;
　So at his bloody view her eyes are fled
　Into the deep dark cabins of her head,

Where they resign their office and their light
To the disposing of her troubled brain,   1040
Who bids them still consort with ugly night,
And never wound the heart with looks again,
　Who, like a king perplexèd in his throne,
　By their suggestion gives a deadly groan,

Whereat each tributary subject quakes,   1045
As when the wind, imprisoned in the ground,
Struggling for passage, earth's foundation shakes,
Which with cold terror doth men's minds confound.
　This mutiny each part doth so surprise
　That from their dark beds once more leap her eyes,

And, being opened, threw unwilling light 1051
Upon the wide wound that the boar had trenched
In his soft flank, whose wonted lily-white
With purple tears that his wound wept was drenched.
No flower was nigh, no grass, herb, leaf, or weed, 1055
But stole his blood, and seemed with him to bleed.

This solemn sympathy poor Venus noteth.
Over one shoulder doth she hang her head.
Dumbly she passions, franticly she doteth.
She thinks he could not die, he is not dead. 1060
Her voice is stopped, her joints forget to bow,
Her eyes are mad that they have wept till now.

Upon his hurt she looks so steadfastly
That her sight, dazzling, makes the wound seem three;
And then she reprehends her mangling eye, 1065
That makes more gashes where no breach should be.
His face seems twain; each several limb is doubled;
For oft the eye mistakes, the brain being troubled.

'My tongue cannot express my grief for one,
And yet,' quoth she, 'behold two Adons dead! 1070
My sighs are blown away, my salt tears gone,
Mine eyes are turned to fire, my heart to lead.
Heavy heart's lead, melt at mine eyes' red fire!
So shall I die by drops of hot desire.

'Alas, poor world, what treasure hast thou lost, 1075
What face remains alive that's worth the viewing?
Whose tongue is music now? What canst thou boast
Of things long since, or anything ensuing?
The flowers are sweet, their colours fresh and trim;
But true sweet beauty lived and died with him. 1080

'Bonnet nor veil henceforth no creature wear:
Nor sun nor wind will ever strive to kiss you.
Having no fair to lose, you need not fear.
The sun doth scorn you, and the wind doth hiss you.
But when Adonis lived, sun and sharp air 1085
Lurked like two thieves to rob him of his fair;

'And therefore would he put his bonnet on,
Under whose brim the gaudy sun would peep.
The wind would blow it off, and, being gone,
Play with his locks; then would Adonis weep, 1090
And straight, in pity of his tender years,
They both would strive who first should dry his tears.

'To see his face the lion walked along
Behind some hedge, because he would not fear him.
To recreate himself when he hath sung, 1095
The tiger would be tame, and gently hear him.
If he had spoke, the wolf would leave his prey,
And never fright the silly lamb that day.

'When he beheld his shadow in the brook,
The fishes spread on it their golden gills. 1100
When he was by, the birds such pleasure took
That some would sing, some other in their bills
Would bring him mulberries and ripe-red cherries.
He fed them with his sight, they him with berries.

'But this foul, grim, and urchin-snouted boar, 1105
Whose downward eye still looketh for a grave,
Ne'er saw the beauteous livery that he wore:
Witness the entertainment that he gave.
If he did see his face, why then, I know
He thought to kiss him, and hath killed him so. 1110

''Tis true, 'tis true; thus was Adonis slain;
He ran upon the boar with his sharp spear,
Who did not whet his teeth at him again,
But by a kiss thought to persuade him there,
And, nuzzling in his flank, the loving swine 1115
Sheathed unaware the tusk in his soft groin.

'Had I been toothed like him, I must confess
With kissing him I should have killed him first;
But he is dead, and never did he bless
My youth with his, the more am I accursed.' 1120
With this she falleth in the place she stood,
And stains her face with his congealèd blood.

She looks upon his lips, and they are pale.
She takes him by the hand, and that is cold.
She whispers in his ears a heavy tale, 1125
As if they heard the woeful words she told.
She lifts the coffer-lids that close his eyes,
Where lo, two lamps burnt out in darkness lies;

Two glasses, where herself herself beheld
A thousand times, and now no more reflect, 1130
Their virtue lost, wherein they late excelled,
And every beauty robbed of his effect.
'Wonder of time,' quoth she, 'this is my spite,
That, thou being dead, the day should yet be light.

'Since thou art dead, lo, here I prophesy 1135
Sorrow on love hereafter shall attend.
It shall be waited on with jealousy,
Find sweet beginning, but unsavoury end;
Ne'er settled equally, but high or low,
That all love's pleasure shall not match his woe. 1140

'It shall be fickle, false, and full of fraud,
Bud, and be blasted, in a breathing-while:
The bottom poison, and the top o'erstrawed
With sweets that shall the truest sight beguile.
The strongest body shall it make most weak, 1145
Strike the wise dumb, and teach the fool to speak.

'It shall be sparing, and too full of riot,
Teaching decrepit age to tread the measures.
The staring ruffian shall it keep in quiet,
Pluck down the rich, enrich the poor with treasures; 1150
  It shall be raging-mad, and silly-mild;
  Make the young old, the old become a child.

'It shall suspect where is no cause of fear;
It shall not fear where it should most mistrust.
It shall be merciful, and too severe,   1155
And most deceiving when it seems most just.
  Perverse it shall be where it shows most toward,
  Put fear to valour, courage to the coward.

'It shall be cause of war and dire events,
And set dissension 'twixt the son and sire;   1160
Subject and servile to all discontents,
As dry combustious matter is to fire.
  Sith in his prime death doth my love destroy,
  They that love best their loves shall not enjoy.'

By this, the boy that by her side lay killed   1165
Was melted like a vapour from her sight,
And in his blood that on the ground lay spilled
A purple flower sprung up, chequered with white,
  Resembling well his pale cheeks, and the blood
  Which in round drops upon their whiteness stood. 1170

She bows her head the new-sprung flower to smell,
Comparing it to her Adonis' breath,
And says within her bosom it shall dwell,
Since he himself is reft from her by death.
  She crops the stalk, and in the breach appears   1175
  Green-dropping sap, which she compares to tears.

'Poor flower,' quoth she, 'this was thy father's guise—
Sweet issue of a more sweet-smelling sire—
For every little grief to wet his eyes.
To grow unto himself was his desire,   1180
  And so 'tis thine; but know it is as good
  To wither in my breast as in his blood.

'Here was thy father's bed, here in my breast.
Thou art the next of blood, and 'tis thy right.
Lo, in this hollow cradle take thy rest;   1185
My throbbing heart shall rock thee day and night.
  There shall not be one minute in an hour
  Wherein I will not kiss my sweet love's flower.'

Thus, weary of the world, away she hies,
And yokes her silver doves, by whose swift aid   1190
Their mistress, mounted, through the empty skies
In her light chariot quickly is conveyed,
  Holding their course to Paphos, where their queen
  Means to immure herself, and not be seen.

THE RAPE OF LUCRECE

DEDICATING *Venus and Adonis* to the Earl of Southampton in 1593, Shakespeare promised, if the poem pleased, to 'take advantage of all idle hours' to honour the Earl with 'some graver labour'. *The Rape of Lucrece*, also dedicated to Southampton, was entered in the Stationers' Register on 9 May 1594, and printed in the same year. The warmth of the dedication suggests that the Earl was by then a friend as well as a patron.

Like *Venus and Adonis*, *The Rape of Lucrece* is an erotic narrative based on Ovid, but this time the subject matter is historical, the tone tragic. The events took place in 509 BC, and were already legendary at the time of the first surviving account, by Livy in his history of Rome published between 27 and 25 BC. Shakespeare's main source was Ovid's *Fasti*, but he seems also to have known Livy's and other accounts.

Historically, Lucretia's rape had political consequences. Her ravisher, Tarquin, was a member of the tyrannical ruling family of Rome. During the siege of Ardea, a group of noblemen boasted of their wives' virtue, and rode home to test them; only Collatine's wife, Lucretia, lived up to her husband's claims, and Sextus Tarquinius was attracted to her. Failing to seduce her, he raped her and returned to Rome. Lucretia committed suicide, and her husband's friend, Lucius Junius Brutus, used the occasion as an opportunity to rouse the Roman people against Tarquinius' rule and to constitute themselves a republic.

Shakespeare concentrates on the private side of the story; Tarquin is lusting after Lucrece in the poem's opening lines, and the ending devotes only a few lines to the consequence of her suicide. As in *Venus and Adonis*, Shakespeare makes a little narrative material go a long way. At first, the focus is on Tarquin; after he has threatened Lucrece, it swings over to her. The opening sequence, with its marvellously dramatic account of Tarquin's tormented state of mind as he approaches Lucrece's chamber, is the more intense. Tarquin disappears from the action soon after the rape, when Lucrece delivers herself of a long complaint, apostrophizing night, opportunity, and time, and cursing Tarquin with rhetorical fervour, before deciding to kill herself. After summoning her husband, she seeks consolation in a painting of Troy which is described (1373-1442) in lines indebted to the first and second books of Virgil's *Aeneid* and to Book 13 of Ovid's *Metamorphoses*. After she dies, her husband and father mourn, but Brutus calls for deeds not words, and determines on revenge. The last lines of the poem look forward to the banishment of the Tarquins, but nothing is said of the establishment of a republic.

Like *Venus and Adonis*, *Lucrece*, initially popular (with six editions in Shakespeare's lifetime and another three by 1655), was later neglected. Coleridge admired it, and more recent criticism has recognized in it a profoundly dramatic quality combined with, if sometimes dissipated by, a remarkable force of rhetoric. The writing of the poem seems to have been a formative experience for Shakespeare. In it he not only laid the basis for his later plays on Roman history, but also explored themes that were to figure prominently in his later work. This is especially apparent in the portrayal of a man who 'still pursues his fear' (308), the relentless power of self-destructive evil that Shakespeare remembered when he made Macbeth, on his way to murder Duncan, speak of 'withered murder' which, 'With Tarquin's ravishing strides, towards his design | Moves like a ghost'.

TO THE RIGHT HONOURABLE HENRY WRIOTHESLEY,
EARL OF SOUTHAMPTON AND BARON OF TITCHFIELD

The love I dedicate to your lordship is without end, whereof this pamphlet without beginning is but a superfluous moiety. The warrant I have of your honourable disposition, not the worth of my untutored lines, makes it assured of acceptance. What I have done is yours; what I have to do is yours, being part in all I have, devoted yours. Were my worth greater my duty would show greater, meantime, as it is, it is bound to your lordship, to whom I wish long life still lengthened with all happiness.

Your lordship's in all duty,

William Shakespeare

THE ARGUMENT

Lucius Tarquinius (for his excessive pride surnamed Superbus), after he had caused his own father-in-law Servius Tullius to be cruelly murdered, and, contrary to the Roman laws and customs, not requiring or staying for the people's suffrages had possessed himself of the kingdom, went accompanied with his sons and other noblemen of Rome to besiege Ardea, during which siege the principal men of the army meeting one evening at the tent of Sextus Tarquinius, the King's son, in their discourses after supper everyone commended the virtues of his own wife, among whom Collatinus extolled the incomparable chastity of his wife, Lucretia. In that pleasant humour they all posted to Rome, and, intending by their secret and sudden arrival to make trial of that which everyone had before avouched, only Collatinus finds his wife (though it were late in the night) spinning amongst her maids. The other ladies were all found dancing, and revelling, or in several disports. Whereupon the noblemen yielded Collatinus the victory and his wife the fame. At that time Sextus Tarquinius, being enflamed with Lucrece' beauty, yet smothering his passions for the present, departed with the rest back to the camp, from whence he shortly after privily withdrew himself and was, according to his estate, royally entertained and lodged by Lucrece at Collatium. The same night he treacherously stealeth into her chamber, violently ravished her, and early in the morning speedeth away. Lucrece, in this lamentable plight, hastily dispatcheth messengers—one to Rome for her father, another to the camp for Collatine. They came, the one accompanied with Junius Brutus, the other with Publius Valerius, and, finding Lucrece attired in mourning habit, demanded the cause of her sorrow. She, first taking an oath of them for her revenge, revealed the actor and whole manner of his dealing, and withal suddenly stabbed herself. Which done, with one consent they all vowed to root out the whole hated family of the Tarquins, and, bearing the dead body to Rome, Brutus acquainted the people with the doer and manner of the vile deed, with a bitter invective against the tyranny of the King; wherewith the people were so moved that with one consent and a general acclamation the Tarquins were all exiled and the state government changed from kings to consuls.

The Rape of Lucrece

From the besieged Ardea all in post,
Borne by the trustless wings of false desire,
Lust-breathèd Tarquin leaves the Roman host
And to Collatium bears the lightless fire
Which, in pale embers hid, lurks to aspire   5
    And girdle with embracing flames the waist
    Of Collatine's fair love, Lucrece the chaste.

Haply that name of chaste unhapp'ly set
This bateless edge on his keen appetite,
When Collatine unwisely did not let   10
To praise the clear unmatchèd red and white
Which triumphed in that sky of his delight,
    Where mortal stars as bright as heaven's beauties
    With pure aspects did him peculiar duties.

For he the night before in Tarquin's tent   15
Unlocked the treasure of his happy state,
What priceless wealth the heavens had him lent
In the possession of his beauteous mate,
Reck'ning his fortune at such high-proud rate
    That kings might be espousèd to more fame,   20
    But king nor peer to such a peerless dame.

O happiness enjoyed but of a few,
And, if possessed, as soon decayed and done
As is the morning's silver melting dew
Against the golden splendour of the sun,   25
An expired date cancelled ere well begun!
    Honour and beauty in the owner's arms
    Are weakly fortressed from a world of harms.

Beauty itself doth of itself persuade
The eyes of men without an orator.   30
What needeth then apology be made
To set forth that which is so singular?
Or why is Collatine the publisher
    Of that rich jewel he should keep unknown
    From thievish ears, because it is his own?   35

Perchance his boast of Lucrece' sov'reignty
Suggested this proud issue of a king,
For by our ears our hearts oft tainted be.
Perchance that envy of so rich a thing,
Braving compare, disdainfully did sting   40
    His high-pitched thoughts, that meaner men should
        vaunt
    That golden hap which their superiors want.

But some untimely thought did instigate
His all-too-timeless speed, if none of those.
His honour, his affairs, his friends, his state   45
Neglected all, with swift intent he goes

To quench the coal which in his liver glows.
    O rash false heat, wrapped in repentant cold,
    Thy hasty spring still blasts and ne'er grows old!

When at Collatium this false lord arrived,   50
Well was he welcomed by the Roman dame,
Within whose face beauty and virtue strived
Which of them both should underprop her fame.
When virtue bragged, beauty would blush for shame;
    When beauty boasted blushes, in despite   55
    Virtue would stain that or with silver white.

But beauty, in that white entitulèd
From Venus' doves, doth challenge that fair field.
Then virtue claims from beauty beauty's red,
Which virtue gave the golden age to gild   60
    Their silver cheeks, and called it then their shield:
    Teaching them thus to use it in the fight:
    When shame assailed, the red should fence the
        white.

This heraldry in Lucrece' face was seen,
Argued by beauty's red and virtue's white.   65
Of either's colour was the other queen,
Proving from world's minority their right.
Yet their ambition makes them still to fight,
    The sovereignty of either being so great
    That oft they interchange each other's seat.   70

This silent war of lilies and of roses
Which Tarquin viewed in her fair face's field
In their pure ranks his traitor eye encloses,
Where, lest between them both it should be killed,
The coward captive vanquishèd doth yield   75
    To those two armies that would let him go
    Rather than triumph in so false a foe.

Now thinks he that her husband's shallow tongue,
The niggard prodigal that praised her so,
In that high task hath done her beauty wrong,   80
Which far exceeds his barren skill to show.
Therefore that praise which Collatine doth owe
    Enchanted Tarquin answers with surmise
    In silent wonder of still-gazing eyes.

This earthly saint adorèd by this devil   85
Little suspecteth the false worshipper,
For unstained thoughts do seldom dream on evil.
Birds never limed no secret bushes fear,
So guiltless she securely gives good cheer
    And reverent welcome to her princely guest,   90
    Whose inward ill no outward harm expressed,

For that he coloured with his high estate,
Hiding base sin in pleats of majesty,
That nothing in him seemed inordinate
Save sometime too much wonder of his eye,   95
Which, having all, all could not satisfy,
  But poorly rich so wanteth in his store
  That, cloyed with much, he pineth still for more.

But she that never coped with stranger eyes
Could pick no meaning from their parling looks,   100
Nor read the subtle shining secrecies
Writ in the glassy margins of such books.
She touched no unknown baits nor feared no hooks,
  Nor could she moralize his wanton sight
  More than his eyes were opened to the light.   105

He stories to her ears her husband's fame
Won in the fields of fruitful Italy,
And decks with praises Collatine's high name
Made glorious by his manly chivalry
With bruisèd arms and wreaths of victory.   110
  Her joy with heaved-up hand she doth express,
  And wordless so greets heaven for his success.

Far from the purpose of his coming thither
He makes excuses for his being there.
No cloudy show of stormy blust'ring weather   115
Doth yet in his fair welkin once appear
Till sable night, mother of dread and fear,
  Upon the world dim darkness doth display
  And in her vaulty prison stows the day.

For then is Tarquin brought unto his bed,   120
Intending weariness with heavy sprite;
For after supper long he questionèd
With modest Lucrece, and wore out the night.
Now leaden slumber with life's strength doth fight,
  And everyone to rest himself betakes   125
  Save thieves, and cares, and troubled minds that
    wakes.

As one of which doth Tarquin lie revolving
The sundry dangers of his will's obtaining,
Yet ever to obtain his will resolving,
Though weak-built hopes persuade him to abstaining.
  Despair to gain doth traffic oft for gaining,   131
  And when great treasure is the meed proposed,
  Though death be adjunct, there's no death supposed.

Those that much covet are with gain so fond
That what they have not, that which they possess, 135
They scatter and unloose it from their bond,
And so by hoping more they have but less,
Or, gaining more, the profit of excess
  Is but to surfeit and such griefs sustain
  That they prove bankrupt in this poor-rich gain. 140

The aim of all is but to nurse the life
With honour, wealth, and ease in waning age,
And in this aim there is such thwarting strife
That one for all, or all for one, we gage,
As life for honour in fell battle's rage,   145
  Honour for wealth; and oft that wealth doth cost
  The death of all, and all together lost.

So that, in vent'ring ill, we leave to be
The things we are for that which we expect,
And this ambitious foul infirmity   150
In having much, torments us with defect
Of that we have; so then we do neglect
  The thing we have, and all for want of wit
  Make something nothing by augmenting it.

Such hazard now must doting Tarquin make,   155
Pawning his honour to obtain his lust,
And for himself himself he must forsake.
Then where is truth if there be no self-trust?
When shall he think to find a stranger just
  When he himself himself confounds, betrays   160
  To sland'rous tongues and wretched hateful days?

Now stole upon the time the dead of night
When heavy sleep had closed up mortal eyes.
No comfortable star did lend his light,
No noise but owls' and wolves' death-boding cries 165
Now serves the season, that they may surprise
  The silly lambs. Pure thoughts are dead and still,
  While lust and murder wakes to stain and kill.

And now this lustful lord leapt from his bed,
Throwing his mantle rudely o'er his arm,   170
Is madly tossed between desire and dread.
Th'one sweetly flatters, th'other feareth harm,
But honest fear, bewitched with lust's foul charm,
  Doth too-too oft betake him to retire,
  Beaten away by brainsick rude desire.   175

His falchion on a flint he softly smiteth,
That from the cold stone sparks of fire do fly,
Whereat a waxen torch forthwith he lighteth,
Which must be lodestar to his lustful eye,
And to the flame thus speaks advisedly: 180
  'As from this cold flint I enforced this fire,
  So Lucrece must I force to my desire.'

Here pale with fear he doth premeditate
The dangers of his loathsome enterprise,
And in his inward mind he doth debate   185
What following sorrow may on this arise.
Then, looking scornfully, he doth despise
  His naked armour of still-slaughtered lust,
  And justly thus controls his thoughts unjust:

'Fair torch, burn out thy light, and lend it not   190
To darken her whose light excelleth thine;
And die, unhallowed thoughts, before you blot
With your uncleanness that which is divine.
Offer pure incense to so pure a shrine.
   Let fair humanity abhor the deed   195
   That spots and stains love's modest snow-white weed.

'O shame to knighthood and to shining arms!
O foul dishonour to my household's grave!
O impious act including all foul harms!
A martial man to be soft fancy's slave!   200
True valour still a true respect should have;
   Then my digression is so vile, so base,
   That it will live engraven in my face.

'Yea, though I die the scandal will survive
And be an eyesore in my golden coat.   205
Some loathsome dash the herald will contrive
To cipher me how fondly I did dote,
That my posterity, shamed with the note,
   Shall curse my bones and hold it for no sin
   To wish that I their father had not been.   210

'What win I if I gain the thing I seek?
A dream, a breath, a froth of fleeting joy.
Who buys a minute's mirth to wail a week,
Or sells eternity to get a toy?
For one sweet grape who will the vine destroy?   215
   Or what fond beggar, but to touch the crown,
   Would with the sceptre straight be strucken down?

'If Collatinus dream of my intent
Will he not wake, and in a desp'rate rage
Post hither this vile purpose to prevent?—   220
This siege that hath engirt his marriage,
This blur to youth, this sorrow to the sage,
   This dying virtue, this surviving shame,
   Whose crime will bear an ever-during blame.

'O what excuse can my invention make   225
When thou shalt charge me with so black a deed?
Will not my tongue be mute, my frail joints shake,
Mine eyes forgo their light, my false heart bleed?
The guilt being great, the fear doth still exceed,
   And extreme fear can neither fight nor fly,   230
   But coward-like with trembling terror die.

'Had Collatinus killed my son or sire,
Or lain in ambush to betray my life,
Or were he not my dear friend, this desire
Might have excuse to work upon his wife   235
As in revenge or quittal of such strife.
   But as he is my kinsman, my dear friend,
   The shame and fault finds no excuse nor end.

'Shameful it is—ay, if the fact be known.
Hateful it is—there is no hate in loving.
I'll beg her love—but she is not her own.   240
The worst is but denial and reproving;
My will is strong past reason's weak removing.
   Who fears a sentence or an old man's saw
   Shall by a painted cloth be kept in awe.'   245

Thus graceless holds he disputation
'Tween frozen conscience and hot-burning will,
And with good thoughts makes dispensation,
Urging the worser sense for vantage still;
Which in a moment doth confound and kill   250
   All pure effects, and doth so far proceed
   That what is vile shows like a virtuous deed.

Quoth he, 'She took me kindly by the hand,
And gazed for tidings in my eager eyes,
Fearing some hard news from the warlike band   255
Where her belovèd Collatinus lies.
O how her fear did make her colour rise!
   First red as roses that on lawn we lay,
   Then white as lawn, the roses took away.

'And how her hand, in my hand being locked,   260
Forced it to tremble with her loyal fear,
Which struck her sad, and then it faster rocked
Until her husband's welfare she did hear,
Whereat she smilèd with so sweet a cheer
   That had Narcissus seen her as she stood   265
   Self-love had never drowned him in the flood.

'Why hunt I then for colour or excuses?
All orators are dumb when beauty pleadeth.
Poor wretches have remorse in poor abuses;
Love thrives not in the heart that shadows dreadeth;   270
Affection is my captain, and he leadeth,
   And when his gaudy banner is displayed,
   The coward fights, and will not be dismayed.

'Then childish fear avaunt, debating die,
Respect and reason wait on wrinkled age!   275
My heart shall never countermand mine eye,
Sad pause and deep regard beseems the sage,
My part is youth, and beats these from the stage.
   Desire my pilot is, beauty my prize.
   Then who fears sinking where such treasure lies?'   280

As corn o'ergrown by weeds, so heedful fear
Is almost choked by unresisted lust.
Away he steals, with open list'ning ear,
Full of foul hope and full of fond mistrust,
Both which as servitors to the unjust   285
   So cross him with their opposite persuasion
   That now he vows a league, and now invasion.

Within his thought her heavenly image sits,
And in the selfsame seat sits Collatine.
That eye which looks on her confounds his wits,   290
That eye which him beholds, as more divine,
Unto a view so false will not incline,
  But with a pure appeal seeks to the heart,
  Which once corrupted, takes the worser part,

And therein heartens up his servile powers   295
Who, flattered by their leader's jocund show,
Stuff up his lust as minutes fill up hours,
And as their captain, so their pride doth grow,
Paying more slavish tribute than they owe.
  By reprobate desire thus madly led   300
  The Roman lord marcheth to Lucrece' bed.

The locks between her chamber and his will,
Each one by him enforced, retires his ward;
But as they open they all rate his ill,
Which drives the creeping thief to some regard.   305
  The threshold grates the door to have him heard,
  Night-wand'ring weasels shriek to see him there.
  They fright him, yet he still pursues his fear.

As each unwilling portal yields him way,
Through little vents and crannies of the place   310
The wind wars with his torch to make him stay,
And blows the smoke of it into his face,
Extinguishing his conduct in this case.
  But his hot heart, which fond desire doth scorch,
  Puffs forth another wind that fires the torch,   315

And being lighted, by the light he spies
Lucretia's glove wherein her needle sticks.
He takes it from the rushes where it lies,
And gripping it, the needle his finger pricks,
As who should say 'This glove to wanton tricks   320
  Is not inured. Return again in haste.
  Thou seest our mistress' ornaments are chaste.'

But all these poor forbiddings could not stay him;
He in the worst sense consters their denial.
The doors, the wind, the glove that did delay him   325
He takes for accidental things of trial,
Or as those bars which stop the hourly dial,
  Who with a ling'ring stay his course doth let
  Till every minute pays the hour his debt.

'So, so,' quoth he, 'these lets attend the time,   330
Like little frosts that sometime threat the spring
To add a more rejoicing to the prime,
And give the sneapèd birds more cause to sing.
Pain pays the income of each precious thing.
  Huge rocks, high winds, strong pirates, shelves, and
      sands   335
  The merchant fears, ere rich at home he lands.'

Now is he come unto the chamber door
That shuts him from the heaven of his thought,
Which with a yielding latch, and with no more,
Hath barred him from the blessèd thing he sought.   340
  So from himself impiety hath wrought
  That for his prey to pray he doth begin,
  As if the heavens should countenance his sin.

But in the midst of his unfruitful prayer
Having solicited th'eternal power   345
That his foul thoughts might compass his fair fair,
And they would stand auspicious to the hour,
Even there he starts. Quoth he, 'I must deflower.
  The powers to whom I pray abhor this fact;
  How can they then assist me in the act?   350

'Then love and fortune be my gods, my guide!
My will is backed with resolution.
Thoughts are but dreams till their effects be tried;
The blackest sin is cleared with absolution.
Against love's fire fear's frost hath dissolution.   355
  The eye of heaven is out, and misty night
  Covers the shame that follows sweet delight.'

This said, his guilty hand plucked up the latch,
And with his knee the door he opens wide.
The dove sleeps fast that this night-owl will catch.   360
Thus treason works ere traitors be espied.
Who sees the lurking serpent steps aside,
  But she, sound sleeping, fearing no such thing,
  Lies at the mercy of his mortal sting.

Into the chamber wickedly he stalks,   365
And gazeth on her yet-unstainèd bed.
The curtains being close, about he walks,
Rolling his greedy eye-balls in his head.
By their high treason is his heart misled,
  Which gives the watchword to his hand full soon   370
  To draw the cloud that hides the silver moon.

Look as the fair and fiery-pointed sun
Rushing from forth a cloud bereaves our sight,
Even so, the curtain drawn, his eyes begun
To wink, being blinded with a greater light.   375
Whether it is that she reflects so bright
  That dazzleth them, or else some shame supposed,
  But blind they are, and keep themselves enclosed.

O had they in that darksome prison died,
Then had they seen the period of their ill.   380
Then Collatine again by Lucrece' side
In his clear bed might have reposèd still.
But they must ope, this blessèd league to kill,
  And holy-thoughted Lucrece to their sight
  Must sell her joy, her life, her world's delight.   385

Her lily hand her rosy cheek lies under,
Coz'ning the pillow of a lawful kiss,
Who therefore angry seems to part in sunder,
Swelling on either side to want his bliss;
Between whose hills her head entombèd is,   390
  Where like a virtuous monument she lies
  To be admired of lewd unhallowed eyes.

Without the bed her other fair hand was,
On the green coverlet, whose perfect white
Showed like an April daisy on the grass,   395
With pearly sweat resembling dew of night.
Her eyes like marigolds had sheathed their light,
  And canopied in darkness sweetly lay
  Till they might open to adorn the day.

Her hair like golden threads played with her breath— 400
O modest wantons, wanton modesty!—
Showing life's triumph in the map of death,
And death's dim look in life's mortality.
Each in her sleep themselves so beautify
  As if between them twain there were no strife,   405
  But that life lived in death, and death in life.

Her breasts like ivory globes circled with blue,
A pair of maiden worlds unconquerèd,
Save of their lord no bearing yoke they knew,
And him by oath they truly honourèd.   410
These worlds in Tarquin new ambition bred,
  Who like a foul usurper went about
  From this fair throne to heave the owner out.

What could he see but mightily he noted?
What did he note but strongly he desired?   415
What he beheld, on that he firmly doted,
And in his will his wilful eye he tired.
With more than admiration he admired
  Her azure veins, her alabaster skin,
  Her coral lips, her snow-white dimpled chin.   420

As the grim lion fawneth o'er his prey,
Sharp hunger by the conquest satisfied,
So o'er this sleeping soul doth Tarquin stay,
His rage of lust by gazing qualified,
Slaked not suppressed for standing by her side.   425
  His eye which late this mutiny restrains
  Unto a greater uproar tempts his veins,

And they like straggling slaves for pillage fighting,
Obdurate vassals fell exploits effecting,
In bloody death and ravishment delighting,   430
Nor children's tears nor mothers' groans respecting,
Swell in their pride, the onset still expecting.
  Anon his beating heart, alarum striking,
  Gives the hot charge, and bids them do their liking.

His drumming heart cheers up his burning eye,   435
His eye commends the leading to his hand.
His hand, as proud of such a dignity,
Smoking with pride marched on to make his stand
On her bare breast, the heart of all her land,
  Whose ranks of blue veins as his hand did scale   440
  Left their round turrets destitute and pale.

They, must'ring to the quiet cabinet
Where their dear governess and lady lies,
Do tell her she is dreadfully beset,
And fright her with confusion of their cries.   445
She much amazed breaks ope her locked-up eyes,
  Who, peeping forth this tumult to behold,
  Are by his flaming torch dimmed and controlled.

Imagine her as one in dead of night
From forth dull sleep by dreadful fancy waking,   450
That thinks she hath beheld some ghastly sprite
Whose grim aspect sets every joint a-shaking.
What terror 'tis! But she in worser taking,
  From sleep disturbèd, heedfully doth view
  The sight which makes supposèd terror true.   455

Wrapped and confounded in a thousand fears,
Like to a new-killed bird she trembling lies,
She dares not look, yet, winking, there appears
Quick-shifting antics, ugly in her eyes.
Such shadows are the weak brain's forgeries,   460
  Who, angry that the eyes fly from their lights,
  In darkness daunts them with more dreadful sights.

His hand that yet remains upon her breast—
Rude ram, to batter such an ivory wall—
May feel her heart, poor citizen, distressed,   465
Wounding itself to death, rise up and fall,
Beating her bulk, that his hand shakes withal.
  This moves in him more rage and lesser pity
  To make the breach and enter this sweet city.

First like a trumpet doth his tongue begin   470
To sound a parley to his heartless foe,
Who o'er the white sheet peers her whiter chin,
The reason of this rash alarm to know,
Which he by dumb demeanour seeks to show.
  But she with vehement prayers urgeth still   475
  Under what colour he commits this ill.

Thus he replies: 'The colour in thy face,
That even for anger makes the lily pale
And the red rose blush at her own disgrace,
Shall plead for me and tell my loving tale.   480
Under that colour am I come to scale
  Thy never-conquered fort. The fault is thine,
  For those thine eyes betray thee unto mine.

'Thus I forestall thee, if thou mean to chide:
Thy beauty hath ensnared thee to this night,   485
Where thou with patience must my will abide,
My will that marks thee for my earth's delight,
Which I to conquer sought with all my might.
    But as reproof and reason beat it dead,
    By thy bright beauty was it newly bred.   490

'I see what crosses my attempt will bring,
I know what thorns the growing rose defends;
I think the honey guarded with a sting;
All this beforehand counsel comprehends.
But will is deaf, and hears no heedful friends.   495
    Only he hath an eye to gaze on beauty,
    And dotes on what he looks, 'gainst law or duty.

'I have debated even in my soul
What wrong, what shame, what sorrow I shall breed;
But nothing can affection's course control,   500
Or stop the headlong fury of his speed.
I know repentant tears ensue the deed,
    Reproach, disdain, and deadly enmity,
    Yet strive I to embrace mine infamy.'

This said, he shakes aloft his Roman blade,   505
Which like a falcon tow'ring in the skies
Coucheth the fowl below with his wings' shade
Whose crooked beak threats, if he mount he dies.
So under his insulting falchion lies
    Harmless Lucretia, marking what he tells   510
    With trembling fear, as fowl hear falcons' bells.

'Lucrece,' quoth he, 'this night I must enjoy thee.
If thou deny, then force must work my way,
For in thy bed I purpose to destroy thee.
That done, some worthless slave of thine I'll slay   515
To kill thine honour with thy life's decay;
    And in thy dead arms do I mean to place him,
    Swearing I slew him seeing thee embrace him.

'So thy surviving husband shall remain
The scornful mark of every open eye,   520
Thy kinsmen hang their heads at this disdain,
Thy issue blurred with nameless bastardy,
And thou, the author of their obloquy,
    Shalt have thy trespass cited up in rhymes
    And sung by children in succeeding times.   525

'But if thou yield, I rest thy secret friend.
The fault unknown is as a thought unacted.
A little harm done to a great good end
For lawful policy remains enacted.
The poisonous simple sometime is compacted   530
    In a pure compound; being so applied,
    His venom in effect is purified.

'Then for thy husband and thy children's sake
Tender my suit; bequeath not to their lot
The shame that from them no device can take,   535
The blemish that will never be forgot,
Worse than a slavish wipe or birth-hour's blot;
    For marks descried in men's nativity
    Are nature's faults, not their own infamy.'

Here with a cockatrice' dead-killing eye   540
He rouseth up himself, and makes a pause,
While she, the picture of pure piety,
Like a white hind under the gripe's sharp claws,
Pleads in a wilderness where are no laws
    To the rough beast that knows no gentle right,   545
    Nor aught obeys but his foul appetite.

But when a black-faced cloud the world doth threat,
In his dim mist th'aspiring mountains hiding,
From earth's dark womb some gentle gust doth get
Which blows these pitchy vapours from their biding,   550
Hind'ring their present fall by this dividing;
    So his unhallowed haste her words delays,
    And moody Pluto winks while Orpheus plays.

Yet, foul night-waking cat, he doth but dally
While in his holdfast foot the weak mouse panteth.   555
Her sad behaviour feeds his vulture folly,
A swallowing gulf that even in plenty wanteth.
His ear her prayers admits, but his heart granteth
    No penetrable entrance to her plaining.
    Tears harden lust, though marble wear with raining.

Her pity-pleading eyes are sadly fixed   561
In the remorseless wrinkles of his face.
Her modest eloquence with sighs is mixed,
Which to her oratory adds more grace.
She puts the period often from his place,   565
    And midst the sentence so her accent breaks
    That twice she doth begin ere once she speaks.

She conjures him by high almighty Jove,
By knighthood, gentry, and sweet friendship's oath,
By her untimely tears, her husband's love,   570
By holy human law and common troth,
By heaven and earth and all the power of both,
    That to his borrowed bed he make retire,
    And stoop to honour, not to foul desire.

Quoth she, 'Reward not hospitality   575
With such black payment as thou hast pretended.
Mud not the fountain that gave drink to thee;
Mar not the thing that cannot be amended;
End thy ill aim before thy shoot be ended.
    He is no woodman that doth bend his bow   580
    To strike a poor unseasonable doe.

'My husband is thy friend; for his sake spare me.
Thyself art mighty; for thine own sake leave me;
Myself a weakling; do not then ensnare me.
Thou look'st not like deceit; do not deceive me.   585
My sighs like whirlwinds labour hence to heave thee.
　If ever man were moved with woman's moans,
　Be movèd with my tears, my sighs, my groans.

'All which together, like a troubled ocean,
Beat at thy rocky and wreck-threat'ning heart   590
To soften it with their continual motion,
For stones dissolved to water do convert.
O, if no harder than a stone thou art,
　Melt at my tears, and be compassionate.
　Soft pity enters at an iron gate.   595

'In Tarquin's likeness I did entertain thee.
Hast thou put on his shape to do him shame?
To all the host of heaven I complain me.
Thou wrong'st his honour, wound'st his princely name.
Thou art not what thou seem'st, and if the same,   600
　Thou seem'st not what thou art, a god, a king,
　For kings like gods should govern everything.

'How will thy shame be seeded in thine age
When thus thy vices bud before thy spring?
If in thy hope thou dar'st do such outrage,   605
What dar'st thou not when once thou art a king?
O be remembered, no outrageous thing
　From vassal actors can be wiped away;
　Then kings' misdeeds cannot be hid in clay.

'This deed will make thee only loved for fear,   610
But happy monarchs still are feared for love.
With foul offenders thou perforce must bear
When they in thee the like offences prove.
If but for fear of this, thy will remove;
　For princes are the glass, the school, the book   615
　Where subjects' eyes do learn, do read, do look.

'And wilt thou be the school where lust shall learn?
Must he in thee read lectures of such shame?
Wilt thou be glass wherein it shall discern
Authority for sin, warrant for blame,   620
To privilege dishonour in thy name?
　Thou back'st reproach against long-living laud,
　And mak'st fair reputation but a bawd.

'Hast thou command? By him that gave it thee,
From a pure heart command thy rebel will.   625
Draw not thy sword to guard iniquity,
For it was lent thee all that brood to kill.
Thy princely office how canst thou fulfil
　When, patterned by thy fault, foul sin may say
　He learned to sin, and thou didst teach the way?   630

'Think but how vile a spectacle it were
To view thy present trespass in another.
Men's faults do seldom to themselves appear;
Their own transgressions partially they smother.
This guilt would seem death-worthy in thy brother.   635
　O, how are they wrapped in with infamies
　That from their own misdeeds askance their eyes!

'To thee, to thee my heaved-up hands appeal,
Not to seducing lust, thy rash relier.
I sue for exiled majesty's repeal;   640
Let him return, and flatt'ring thoughts retire.
His true respect will prison false desire,
　And wipe the dim mist from thy doting eyne,
　That thou shalt see thy state, and pity mine.'

'Have done,' quoth he; 'my uncontrollèd tide   645
Turns not, but swells the higher by this let.
Small lights are soon blown out; huge fires abide,
And with the wind in greater fury fret.
The petty streams, that pay a daily debt
　To their salt sovereign, with their fresh falls' haste   650
　Add to his flow, but alter not his taste.'

'Thou art,' quoth she, 'a sea, a sovereign king,
And lo, there falls into thy boundless flood
Black lust, dishonour, shame, misgoverning,
Who seek to stain the ocean of thy blood.   655
If all these petty ills shall change thy good,
　Thy sea within a puddle's womb is hearsed,
　And not the puddle in thy sea dispersed.

'So shall these slaves be king, and thou their slave;
Thou nobly base, they basely dignified;   660
Thou their fair life, and they thy fouler grave;
Thou loathèd in their shame, they in thy pride.
The lesser thing should not the greater hide.
　The cedar stoops not to the base shrub's foot,
　But low shrubs wither at the cedar's root.   665

'So let thy thoughts, low vassals to thy state'–
'No more,' quoth he, 'by heaven, I will not hear thee.
Yield to my love. If not, enforcèd hate
Instead of love's coy touch shall rudely tear thee.
That done, despitefully I mean to bear thee   670
　Unto the base bed of some rascal groom
　To be thy partner in this shameful doom.'

This said, he sets his foot upon the light;
For light and lust are deadly enemies.
Shame folded up in blind concealing night   675
When most unseen, then most doth tyrannize.
The wolf hath seized his prey, the poor lamb cries,
　Till with her own white fleece her voice controlled
　Entombs her outcry in her lips' sweet fold.

For with the nightly linen that she wears 680
He pens her piteous clamours in her head,
Cooling his hot face in the chastest tears
That ever modest eyes with sorrow shed.
O that prone lust should stain so pure a bed,
    The spots whereof could weeping purify, 685
    Her tears should drop on them perpetually!

But she hath lost a dearer thing than life,
And he hath won what he would lose again.
This forcèd league doth force a further strife,
This momentary joy breeds months of pain; 690
This hot desire converts to cold disdain.
    Pure chastity is rifled of her store,
    And lust, the thief, far poorer than before.

Look as the full-fed hound or gorgèd hawk,
Unapt for tender smell or speedy flight, 695
Make slow pursuit, or altogether balk
The prey wherein by nature they delight,
So surfeit-taking Tarquin fares this night.
    His taste delicious, in digestion souring,
    Devours his will that lived by foul devouring. 700

O deeper sin than bottomless conceit
Can comprehend in still imagination!
Drunken desire must vomit his receipt
Ere he can see his own abomination.
While lust is in his pride, no exclamation 705
    Can curb his heat or rein his rash desire,
    Till like a jade self-will himself doth tire.

And then with lank and lean discoloured cheek,
With heavy eye, knit brow, and strengthless pace,
Feeble desire, all recreant, poor, and meek, 710
Like to a bankrupt beggar wails his case.
The flesh being proud, desire doth fight with grace,
    For there it revels, and when that decays,
    The guilty rebel for remission prays.

So fares it with this faultful lord of Rome 715
Who this accomplishment so hotly chased;
For now against himself he sounds this doom,
That through the length of times he stands disgraced.
Besides, his soul's fair temple is defaced,
    To whose weak ruins muster troops of cares 720
    To ask the spotted princess how she fares.

She says her subjects with foul insurrection
Have battered down her consecrated wall,
And by their mortal fault brought in subjection
Her immortality, and made her thrall 725
To living death and pain perpetual,
    Which in her prescience she controllèd still,
    But her foresight could not forestall their will.

Ev'n in this thought through the dark night he
    stealeth,
A captive victor that hath lost in gain, 730
Bearing away the wound that nothing healeth,
The scar that will, despite of cure, remain;
Leaving his spoil perplexed in greater pain.
    She bears the load of lust he left behind,
    And he the burden of a guilty mind. 735

He like a thievish dog creeps sadly thence;
She like a wearied lamb lies panting there.
He scowls, and hates himself for his offence;
She, desperate, with her nails her flesh doth tear.
He faintly flies, sweating with guilty fear; 740
    She stays, exclaiming on the direful night.
    He runs, and chides his vanished loathed delight.

He thence departs, a heavy convertite;
She there remains, a hopeless castaway.
He in his speed looks for the morning light; 745
She prays she never may behold the day.
    'For day,' quoth she, 'night's scapes doth open lay,
    And my true eyes have never practised how
    To cloak offences with a cunning brow.

'They think not but that every eye can see 750
The same disgrace which they themselves behold,
And therefore would they still in darkness be,
To have their unseen sin remain untold.
For they their guilt with weeping will unfold,
    And grave, like water that doth eat in steel, 755
    Upon my cheeks what helpless shame I feel.'

Here she exclaims against repose and rest,
And bids her eyes hereafter still be blind.
She wakes her heart by beating on her breast,
And bids it leap from thence where it may find 760
Some purer chest to close so pure a mind.
    Frantic with grief, thus breathes she forth her spite
    Against the unseen secrecy of night:

'O comfort-killing night, image of hell,
Dim register and notary of shame, 765
Black stage for tragedies and murders fell,
Vast sin-concealing chaos, nurse of blame!
Blind muffled bawd, dark harbour for defame,
    Grim cave of death, whisp'ring conspirator
    With close-tongued treason and the ravisher! 770

'O hateful, vaporous, and foggy night,
Since thou art guilty of my cureless crime,
Muster thy mists to meet the eastern light,
Make war against proportioned course of time.
Or if thou wilt permit the sun to climb 775
    His wonted height, yet ere he go to bed
    Knit poisonous clouds about his golden head.

'With rotten damps ravish the morning air,
Let their exhaled unwholesome breaths make sick
The life of purity, the supreme fair,   780
Ere he arrive his weary noon-tide prick;
And let thy musty vapours march so thick
    That in their smoky ranks his smothered light
    May set at noon, and make perpetual night.

'Were Tarquin night, as he is but night's child,   785
The silver-shining queen he would distain;
Her twinkling handmaids too, by him defiled,
Through night's black bosom should not peep again.
So should I have co-partners in my pain,
    And fellowship in woe doth woe assuage,   790
    As palmers' chat makes short their pilgrimage.

'Where now I have no one to blush with me,
To cross their arms and hang their heads with mine,
To mask their brows and hide their infamy,
But I alone, alone must sit and pine,   795
Seasoning the earth with showers of silver brine,
    Mingling my talk with tears, my grief with groans,
    Poor wasting monuments of lasting moans.

'O night, thou furnace of foul reeking smoke,
Let not the jealous day behold that face   800
Which underneath thy black all-hiding cloak
Immodestly lies martyred with disgrace!
Keep still possession of thy gloomy place,
    That all the faults which in thy reign are made
    May likewise be sepulchred in thy shade.   805

'Make me not object to the tell-tale day:
The light will show charactered in my brow
The story of sweet chastity's decay,
The impious breach of holy wedlock vow.
Yea, the illiterate that know not how   810
    To cipher what is writ in learnèd books
    Will quote my loathsome trespass in my looks.

'The nurse to still her child will tell my story,
And fright her crying babe with Tarquin's name.
The orator to deck his oratory   815
Will couple my reproach to Tarquin's shame.
Feast-finding minstrels tuning my defame
    Will tie the hearers to attend each line,
    How Tarquin wrongèd me, I Collatine.

'Let my good name, that senseless reputation,   820
For Collatine's dear love be kept unspotted;
If that be made a theme for disputation,
The branches of another root are rotted,
And undeserved reproach to him allotted
    That is as clear from this attaint of mine   825
    As I ere this was pure to Collatine.

'O unseen shame, invisible disgrace!
O unfelt sore, crest-wounding private scar!
Reproach is stamped in Collatinus' face,
And Tarquin's eye may read the mot afar,   830
How he in peace is wounded, not in war.
    Alas, how many bear such shameful blows,
    Which not themselves but he that gives them knows!

'If, Collatine, thine honour lay in me,
From me by strong assault it is bereft;   835
My honey lost, and I, a drone-like bee,
Have no perfection of my summer left,
But robbed and ransacked by injurious theft.
    In thy weak hive a wandering wasp hath crept,
    And sucked the honey which thy chaste bee kept. 840

'Yet am I guilty of thy honour's wrack;
Yet for thy honour did I entertain him.
Coming from thee, I could not put him back,
For it had been dishonour to disdain him.
Besides, of weariness he did complain him,   845
    And talked of virtue—O unlooked-for evil,
    When virtue is profaned in such a devil!

'Why should the worm intrude the maiden bud,
Or hateful cuckoos hatch in sparrows' nests,
Or toads infect fair founts with venom mud,   850
Or tyrant folly lurk in gentle breasts,
Or kings be breakers of their own behests?
    But no perfection is so absolute
    That some impurity doth not pollute.

'The agèd man that coffers up his gold   855
Is plagued with cramps, and gouts, and painful fits,
And scarce hath eyes his treasure to behold,
But like still-pining Tantalus he sits,
And useless barns the harvest of his wits,
    Having no other pleasure of his gain   860
    But torment that it cannot cure his pain.

'So then he hath it when he cannot use it,
And leaves it to be mastered by his young,
Who in their pride do presently abuse it.
Their father was too weak and they too strong   865
To hold their cursèd-blessèd fortune long.
    The sweets we wish for turn to loathèd sours
    Even in the moment that we call them ours.

'Unruly blasts wait on the tender spring,
Unwholesome weeds take root with precious flowers, 870
The adder hisses where the sweet birds sing,
What virtue breeds, iniquity devours.
    We have no good that we can say is ours
    But ill-annexèd opportunity
    Or kills his life or else his quality.   875

'O opportunity, thy guilt is great!
'Tis thou that execut'st the traitor's treason;
Thou sets the wolf where he the lamb may get;
Whoever plots the sin, thou points the season.
'Tis thou that spurn'st at right, at law, at reason; 880
  And in thy shady cell where none may spy him
  Sits sin, to seize the souls that wander by him.

'Thou mak'st the vestal violate her oath,
Thou blow'st the fire when temperance is thawed,
Thou smother'st honesty, thou murd'rest troth, 885
Thou foul abettor, thou notorious bawd;
Thou plantest scandal and displacest laud.
  Thou ravisher, thou traitor, thou false thief,
  Thy honey turns to gall, thy joy to grief.

'Thy secret pleasure turns to open shame, 890
Thy private feasting to a public fast,
Thy smoothing titles to a ragged name,
Thy sugared tongue to bitter wormwood taste.
Thy violent vanities can never last.
  How comes it then, vile opportunity, 895
  Being so bad, such numbers seek for thee?

'When wilt thou be the humble suppliant's friend,
And bring him where his suit may be obtained?
When wilt thou sort an hour great strifes to end,
Or free that soul which wretchedness hath chained, 900
Give physic to the sick, ease to the pained?
  The poor, lame, blind, halt, creep, cry out for thee,
  But they ne'er meet with opportunity.

'The patient dies while the physician sleeps,
The orphan pines while the oppressor feeds, 905
Justice is feasting while the widow weeps,
Advice is sporting while infection breeds.
Thou grant'st no time for charitable deeds.
  Wrath, envy, treason, rape, and murder's rages,
  Thy heinous hours wait on them as their pages. 910

'When truth and virtue have to do with thee
A thousand crosses keep them from thy aid.
They buy thy help, but sin ne'er gives a fee;
He gratis comes, and thou art well appaid
As well to hear as grant what he hath said. 915
  My Collatine would else have come to me
  When Tarquin did, but he was stayed by thee.

'Guilty thou art of murder and of theft,
Guilty of perjury and subornation,
Guilty of treason, forgery, and shift, 920
Guilty of incest, that abomination:
An accessory by thine inclination
  To all sins past and all that are to come
  From the creation to the general doom.

'Misshapen time, copesmate of ugly night, 925
Swift subtle post, carrier of grisly care,
Eater of youth, false slave to false delight,
Base watch of woes, sin's pack-horse, virtue's snare,
Thou nursest all, and murd'rest all that are.
  O hear me then, injurious shifting time; 930
  Be guilty of my death, since of my crime.

'Why hath thy servant opportunity
Betrayed the hours thou gav'st me to repose,
Cancelled my fortunes, and enchainèd me
To endless date of never-ending woes? 935
Time's office is to fine the hate of foes,
  To eat up errors by opinion bred,
  Not spend the dowry of a lawful bed.

'Time's glory is to calm contending kings,
To unmask falsehood and bring truth to light, 940
To stamp the seal of time in agèd things,
To wake the morn and sentinel the night,
To wrong the wronger till he render right,
  To ruinate proud buildings with thy hours
  And smear with dust their glitt'ring golden towers; 945

'To fill with worm-holes stately monuments,
To feed oblivion with decay of things,
To blot old books and alter their contents,
To pluck the quills from ancient ravens' wings,
To dry the old oak's sap and blemish springs, 950
  To spoil antiquities of hammered steel,
  And turn the giddy round of fortune's wheel;

'To show the beldame daughters of her daughter,
To make the child a man, the man a child,
To slay the tiger that doth live by slaughter, 955
To tame the unicorn and lion wild,
To mock the subtle in themselves beguiled,
  To cheer the ploughman with increaseful crops,
  And waste huge stones with little water drops.

'Why work'st thou mischief in thy pilgrimage, 960
Unless thou couldst return to make amends?
One poor retiring minute in an age
Would purchase thee a thousand thousand friends,
Lending him wit that to bad debtors lends.
  O this dread night, wouldst thou one hour come
    back, 965
  I could prevent this storm and shun thy wrack!

'Thou ceaseless lackey to eternity,
With some mischance cross Tarquin in his flight.
Devise extremes beyond extremity
To make him curse this cursèd crimeful night. 970
Let ghastly shadows his lewd eyes affright,
  And the dire thought of his committed evil
  Shape every bush a hideous shapeless devil.

'Disturb his hours of rest with restless trances;
Afflict him in his bed with bedrid groans;
Let there bechance him pitiful mischances   975
To make him moan, but pity not his moans.
Stone him with hardened hearts harder than stones,
  And let mild women to him lose their mildness,
  Wilder to him than tigers in their wildness.   980

'Let him have time to tear his curlèd hair,
Let him have time against himself to rave,
Let him have time of time's help to despair,
Let him have time to live a loathèd slave,
Let him have time a beggar's orts to crave,   985
  And time to see one that by alms doth live
  Disdain to him disdainèd scraps to give.

'Let him have time to see his friends his foes,
And merry fools to mock at him resort.
Let him have time to mark how slow time goes   990
In time of sorrow, and how swift and short
His time of folly and his time of sport;
  And ever let his unrecalling crime
  Have time to wail th'abusing of his time.

'O time, thou tutor both to good and bad,   995
Teach me to curse him that thou taught'st this ill;
At his own shadow let the thief run mad,
Himself himself seek every hour to kill;
Such wretched hands such wretched blood should spill,
  For who so base would such an office have   1000
  As sland'rous deathsman to so base a slave?

'The baser is he, coming from a king,
To shame his hope with deeds degenerate.
The mightier man, the mightier is the thing
That makes him honoured or begets him hate,   1005
For greatest scandal waits on greatest state.
  The moon being clouded presently is missed,
  But little stars may hide them when they list.

'The crow may bathe his coal-black wings in mire
And unperceived fly with the filth away,   1010
But if the like the snow-white swan desire,
The stain upon his silver down will stay.
Poor grooms are sightless night, kings glorious day.
  Gnats are unnoted wheresoe'er they fly,
  But eagles gazed upon with every eye.   1015

'Out, idle words, servants to shallow fools,
Unprofitable sounds, weak arbitrators!
Busy yourselves in skill-contending schools,
Debate where leisure serves with dull debaters,
To trembling clients be you mediators;   1020
  For me, I force not argument a straw,
  Since that my case is past the help of law.

'In vain I rail at opportunity,
At time, at Tarquin, and uncheerful night.
In vain I cavil with mine infamy,   1025
In vain I spurn at my confirmed despite.
This helpless smoke of words doth me no right;
  The remedy indeed to do me good
  Is to let forth my foul defilèd blood.

'Poor hand, why quiver'st thou at this decree?   1030
Honour thyself to rid me of this shame,
For if I die, my honour lives in thee,
But if I live, thou liv'st in my defame.
Since thou couldst not defend thy loyal dame,
  And wast afeard to scratch her wicked foe,   1035
  Kill both thyself and her for yielding so.'

This said, from her betumbled couch she starteth,
To find some desp'rate instrument of death.
But this, no slaughterhouse, no tool imparteth
To make more vent for passage of her breath,   1040
Which thronging through her lips so vanisheth
  As smoke from Etna that in air consumes,
  Or that which from dischargèd cannon fumes.

'In vain,' quoth she, 'I live, and seek in vain
Some happy mean to end a hapless life.   1045
I feared by Tarquin's falchion to be slain,
Yet for the selfsame purpose seek a knife.
But when I feared I was a loyal wife;
  So am I now—O no, that cannot be,
  Of that true type hath Tarquin rifled me.   1050

'O, that is gone for which I sought to live,
And therefore now I need not fear to die.
To clear this spot by death, at least I give
A badge of fame to slander's livery,
A dying life to living infamy.   1055
  Poor helpless help, the treasure stol'n away,
  To burn the guiltless casket where it lay!

'Well, well, dear Collatine, thou shalt not know
The stainèd taste of violated troth.
I will not wrong thy true affection so   1060
To flatter thee with an infringèd oath.
This bastard graft shall never come to growth.
  He shall not boast, who did thy stock pollute,
  That thou art doting father of his fruit,

'Nor shall he smile at thee in secret thought,   1065
Nor laugh with his companions at thy state.
But thou shalt know thy int'rest was not bought
Basely with gold, but stol'n from forth thy gate.
For me, I am the mistress of my fate,
  And with my trespass never will dispense   1070
  Till life to death acquit my forced offence.

'I will not poison thee with my attaint,
Nor fold my fault in cleanly coined excuses.
My sable ground of sin I will not paint
To hide the truth of this false night's abuses.   1075
My tongue shall utter all; mine eyes, like sluices,
  As from a mountain spring that feeds a dale
  Shall gush pure streams to purge my impure tale.'

By this, lamenting Philomel had ended
The well-tuned warble of her nightly sorrow,   1080
And solemn night with slow sad gait descended
To ugly hell, when lo, the blushing morrow
Lends light to all fair eyes that light will borrow.
  But cloudy Lucrece shames herself to see,
  And therefore still in night would cloistered be.   1085

Revealing day through every cranny spies,
And seems to point her out where she sits weeping;
To whom she sobbing speaks, 'O eye of eyes,
Why pry'st thou through my window? Leave thy
  peeping,
Mock with thy tickling beams eyes that are sleeping, 1090
  Brand not my forehead with thy piercing light,
  For day hath naught to do what's done by night.'

Thus cavils she with everything she sees:
True grief is fond and testy as a child
Who, wayward once, his mood with naught agrees; 1095
Old woes, not infant sorrows, bear them mild.
Continuance tames the one; the other wild,
  Like an unpractised swimmer plunging still,
  With too much labour drowns for want of skill.

So she, deep drenchèd in a sea of care,   1100
Holds disputation with each thing she views,
And to herself all sorrow doth compare;
No object but her passion's strength renews,
And as one shifts, another straight ensues.
  Sometime her grief is dumb and hath no words,   1105
  Sometime 'tis mad and too much talk affords.

The little birds that tune their morning's joy
Make her moans mad with their sweet melody,
For mirth doth search the bottom of annoy;
Sad souls are slain in merry company;   1110
Grief best is pleased with grief's society.
  True sorrow then is feelingly sufficed
  When with like semblance it is sympathized.

'Tis double death to drown in ken of shore;
He ten times pines that pines beholding food;   1115
To see the salve doth make the wound ache more;
Great grief grieves most at that would do it good;
Deep woes roll forward like a gentle flood
  Who, being stopped, the bounding banks o'erflows.
  Grief dallied with nor law nor limit knows.   1120

'You mocking birds,' quoth she, 'your tunes entomb
Within your hollow-swelling feathered breasts,
And in my hearing be you mute and dumb;
My restless discord loves no stops nor rests;
A woeful hostess brooks not merry guests.   1125
  Relish your nimble notes to pleasing ears;
  Distress likes dumps when time is kept with tears.

'Come, Philomel, that sing'st of ravishment,
Make thy sad grove in my dishevelled hair.
As the dank earth weeps at thy languishment,   1130
So I at each sad strain will strain a tear,
And with deep groans the diapason bear;
  For burden-wise I'll hum on Tarquin still,
  While thou on Tereus descants better skill.

'And whiles against a thorn thou bear'st thy part   1135
To keep thy sharp woes waking, wretched I,
To imitate thee well, against my heart
Will fix a sharp knife to affright mine eye,
Who if it wink shall thereon fall and die.
  These means, as frets upon an instrument,   1140
  Shall tune our heart-strings to true languishment.

'And for, poor bird, thou sing'st not in the day,
As shaming any eye should thee behold,
Some dark deep desert seated from the way,
That knows not parching heat nor freezing cold,   1145
Will we find out, and there we will unfold
  To creatures stern sad tunes to change their kinds.
  Since men prove beasts, let beasts bear gentle minds.'

As the poor frighted deer that stands at gaze,
Wildly determining which way to fly,   1150
Or one encompassed with a winding maze,
That cannot tread the way out readily,
So with herself is she in mutiny,
  To live or die which of the twain were better
  When life is shamed and death reproach's debtor.   1155

'To kill myself,' quoth she, 'alack, what were it
But with my body my poor soul's pollution?
They that lose half with greater patience bear it
Than they whose whole is swallowed in confusion.
That mother tries a merciless conclusion   1160
  Who, having two sweet babes, when death takes one
  Will slay the other and be nurse to none.

'My body or my soul, which was the dearer,
When the one pure the other made divine?
Whose love of either to myself was nearer,   1165
When both were kept for heaven and Collatine?
Ay me, the bark peeled from the lofty pine
  His leaves will wither and his sap decay;
  So must my soul, her bark being peeled away.

'Her house is sacked, her quiet interrupted,
Her mansion battered by the enemy,
Her sacred temple spotted, spoiled, corrupted,
Grossly engirt with daring infamy.
Then let it not be called impiety
  If in this blemished fort I make some hole   1175
  Through which I may convey this troubled soul.

'Yet die I will not till my Collatine
Have heard the cause of my untimely death,
That he may vow in that sad hour of mine
Revenge on him that made me stop my breath.   1180
My stainèd blood to Tarquin I'll bequeath,
  Which by him tainted shall for him be spent,
  And as his due writ in my testament.

'My honour I'll bequeath unto the knife
That wounds my body so dishonourèd.   1185
'Tis honour to deprive dishonoured life;
The one will live, the other being dead.
So of shame's ashes shall my fame be bred,
  For in my death I murder shameful scorn;
  My shame so dead, mine honour is new born.   1190

'Dear lord of that dear jewel I have lost,
What legacy shall I bequeath to thee?
My resolution, love, shall be thy boast,
By whose example thou revenged mayst be.
How Tarquin must be used, read it in me.   1195
  Myself, thy friend, will kill myself, thy foe;
  And for my sake serve thou false Tarquin so.

'This brief abridgement of my will I make:
My soul and body to the skies and ground;
My resolution, husband, do thou take;   1200
Mine honour be the knife's that makes my wound;
My shame be his that did my fame confound;
  And all my fame that lives disbursèd be
  To those that live and think no shame of me.

'Thou, Collatine, shalt oversee this will.   1205
How was I overseen that thou shalt see it!
My blood shall wash the slander of mine ill;
My life's foul deed my life's fair end shall free it.
Faint not, faint heart, but stoutly say "So be it".
  Yield to my hand, my hand shall conquer thee;   1210
  Thou dead, both die, and both be victors be.'

This plot of death when sadly she had laid,
And wiped the brinish pearl from her bright eyes,
With untuned tongue she hoarsely calls her maid,
Whose swift obedience to her mistress hies;   1215
For fleet-winged duty with thought's feathers flies.
  Poor Lucrece' cheeks unto her maid seem so
  As winter meads when sun doth melt their snow.

Her mistress she doth give demure good-morrow   1170
With soft slow tongue, true mark of modesty,   1220
And sorts a sad look to her lady's sorrow,
For why her face wore sorrow's livery;
But durst not ask of her audaciously
  Why her two suns were cloud-eclipsèd so,
  Nor why her fair cheeks over-washed with woe.   1225

But as the earth doth weep, the sun being set,
Each flower moistened like a melting eye,
Even so the maid with swelling drops gan wet
Her circled eyne, enforced by sympathy   1180
Of those fair suns set in her mistress' sky,   1230
  Who in a salt-waved ocean quench their light;
  Which makes the maid weep like the dewy night.

A pretty while these pretty creatures stand,
Like ivory conduits coral cisterns filling.   1185
One justly weeps, the other takes in hand   1235
No cause but company of her drops' spilling.
Their gentle sex to weep are often willing,
  Grieving themselves to guess at others' smarts,
  And then they drown their eyes or break their hearts.

For men have marble, women waxen minds,   1240
And therefore are they formed as marble will.
The weak oppressed, th'impression of strange kinds
Is formed in them by force, by fraud, or skill.
Then call them not the authors of their ill,   1195
  No more than wax shall be accounted evil   1245
  Wherein is stamped the semblance of a devil.

Their smoothness like a goodly champaign plain
Lays open all the little worms that creep;
In men as in a rough-grown grove remain
Cave-keeping evils that obscurely sleep.   1250
Through crystal walls each little mote will peep;
  Though men can cover crimes with bold stern looks,
  Poor women's faces are their own faults' books.

No man inveigh against the withered flower,
But chide rough winter that the flower hath killed.   1255
Not that devoured, but that which doth devour
Is worthy blame. O, let it not be held
Poor women's faults that they are so full-filled
  With men's abuses. Those proud lords, to blame,
  Make weak-made women tenants to their shame.   1260

The precedent whereof in Lucrece view,
Assailed by night with circumstances strong
Of present death, and shame that might ensue
By that her death, to do her husband wrong.
Such danger to resistance did belong   1265
  That dying fear through all her body spread;
  And who cannot abuse a body dead?

By this, mild patience bid fair Lucrece speak
To the poor counterfeit of her complaining.
'My girl,' quoth she, 'on what occasion break   1270
Those tears from thee that down thy cheeks are
    raining?
If thou dost weep for grief of my sustaining,
  Know, gentle wench, it small avails my mood.
  If tears could help, mine own would do me good.

'But tell me, girl, when went'—and there she stayed,
Till after a deep groan—'Tarquin from hence?'   1276
'Madam, ere I was up,' replied the maid,
'The more to blame my sluggard negligence.
Yet with the fault I thus far can dispense:
  Myself was stirring ere the break of day,   1280
  And ere I rose was Tarquin gone away.

'But lady, if your maid may be so bold,
She would request to know your heaviness.'
'O, peace,' quoth Lucrece, 'if it should be told,
The repetition cannot make it less;   1285
For more it is than I can well express,
  And that deep torture may be called a hell
  When more is felt than one hath power to tell.

'Go, get me hither paper, ink, and pen;
Yet save that labour, for I have them here.   1290
What should I say? One of my husband's men
Bid thou be ready by and by to bear
A letter to my lord, my love, my dear.
  Bid him with speed prepare to carry it;
  The cause craves haste, and it will soon be writ.'   1295

Her maid is gone, and she prepares to write,
First hovering o'er the paper with her quill.
Conceit and grief an eager combat fight;
What wit sets down is blotted straight with will;
This is too curious-good, this blunt and ill.   1300
  Much like a press of people at a door
  Throng her inventions, which shall go before.

At last she thus begins: 'Thou worthy lord
Of that unworthy wife that greeteth thee,
Health to thy person! Next, vouchsafe t'afford—   1305
If ever, love, thy Lucrece thou wilt see—
Some present speed to come and visit me.
  So I commend me, from our house in grief;
  My woes are tedious, though my words are brief.'

Here folds she up the tenor of her woe,   1310
Her certain sorrow writ uncertainly.
By this short schedule Collatine may know
Her grief, but not her grief's true quality.
She dares not thereof make discovery,
  Lest he should hold it her own gross abuse,   1315
  Ere she with blood had stained her stain's excuse.

Besides, the life and feeling of her passion
She hoards, to spend when he is by to hear her,
When sighs and groans and tears may grace the
    fashion
Of her disgrace, the better so to clear her   1320
From that suspicion which the world might bear her.
  To shun this blot she would not blot the letter
  With words, till action might become them better.

To see sad sights moves more than hear them told,
For then the eye interprets to the ear   1325
The heavy motion that it doth behold,
When every part a part of woe doth bear.
'Tis but a part of sorrow that we hear;
  Deep sounds make lesser noise than shallow fords,
  And sorrow ebbs, being blown with wind of words.

Her letter now is sealed, and on it writ   1331
'At Ardea to my lord with more than haste'.
The post attends, and she delivers it,
Charging the sour-faced groom to hie as fast
As lagging fowls before the northern blast.   1335
  Speed more than speed but dull and slow she deems;
  Extremity still urgeth such extremes.

The homely villain curtsies to her low,
And blushing on her with a steadfast eye
Receives the scroll without or yea or no,   1340
And forth with bashful innocence doth hie.
But they whose guilt within their bosoms lie
  Imagine every eye beholds their blame,
  For Lucrece thought he blushed to see her shame,

When, silly groom, God wot, it was defect   1345
Of spirit, life, and bold audacity.
Such harmless creatures have a true respect
To talk in deeds, while others saucily
Promise more speed, but do it leisurely.
  Even so this pattern of the worn-out age   1350
  Pawned honest looks, but laid no words to gage.

His kindled duty kindled her mistrust,
That two red fires in both their faces blazed.
She thought he blushed as knowing Tarquin's lust,
And blushing with him, wistly on him gazed.   1355
Her earnest eye did make him more amazed.
  The more she saw the blood his cheeks replenish,
  The more she thought he spied in her some blemish.

But long she thinks till he return again,
And yet the duteous vassal scarce is gone.   1360
The weary time she cannot entertain,
For now 'tis stale to sigh, to weep, and groan.
So woe hath wearied woe, moan tired moan,
  That she her plaints a little while doth stay,
  Pausing for means to mourn some newer way.   1365

At last she calls to mind where hangs a piece
Of skilful painting made for Priam's Troy,
Before the which is drawn the power of Greece,
For Helen's rape the city to destroy,
Threat'ning cloud-kissing Ilion with annoy;   1370
    Which the conceited painter drew so proud
    As heaven, it seemed, to kiss the turrets bowed.

A thousand lamentable objects there,
In scorn of nature, art gave lifeless life.
Many a dry drop seemed a weeping tear   1375
Shed for the slaughtered husband by the wife.
The red blood reeked to show the painter's strife,
    And dying eyes gleamed forth their ashy lights
    Like dying coals burnt out in tedious nights.

There might you see the labouring pioneer   1380
Begrimed with sweat and smeared all with dust,
And from the towers of Troy there would appear
The very eyes of men through loop-holes thrust,
Gazing upon the Greeks with little lust.
    Such sweet observance in this work was had   1385
    That one might see those far-off eyes look sad.

In great commanders grace and majesty
You might behold, triumphing in their faces;
In youth, quick bearing and dexterity;
And here and there the painter interlaces   1390
Pale cowards marching on with trembling paces,
    Which heartless peasants did so well resemble
    That one would swear he saw them quake and
      tremble.

In Ajax and Ulysses, O what art
Of physiognomy might one behold!   1395
The face of either ciphered either's heart;
Their face their manners most expressly told.
In Ajax' eyes blunt rage and rigour rolled,
    But the mild glance that sly Ulysses lent
    Showed deep regard and smiling government.   1400

There pleading might you see grave Nestor stand,
As 'twere encouraging the Greeks to fight,
Making such sober action with his hand
That it beguiled attention, charmed the sight.
In speech it seemed his beard all silver-white   1405
    Wagged up and down, and from his lips did fly
    Thin winding breath which purled up to the sky.

About him were a press of gaping faces
Which seemed to swallow up his sound advice,
All jointly list'ning, but with several graces,   1410
As if some mermaid did their ears entice;
Some high, some low, the painter was so nice.
    The scalps of many, almost hid behind,
    To jump up higher seemed, to mock the mind.

Here one man's hand leaned on another's head,   1415
His nose being shadowed by his neighbour's ear;
Here one being thronged bears back, all boll'n and red;
Another, smothered, seems to pelt and swear,
And in their rage such signs of rage they bear
    As but for loss of Nestor's golden words   1420
    It seemed they would debate with angry swords.

For much imaginary work was there;
Conceit deceitful, so compact, so kind,
That for Achilles' image stood his spear
Gripped in an armèd hand; himself behind   1425
Was left unseen save to the eye of mind;
    A hand, a foot, a face, a leg, a head,
    Stood for the whole to be imaginèd.

And from the walls of strong-besiegèd Troy
When their brave hope, bold Hector, marched to field,
Stood many Trojan mothers sharing joy   1431
To see their youthful sons bright weapons wield;
And to their hope they such odd action yield
    That through their light joy seemèd to appear,
    Like bright things stained, a kind of heavy fear.   1435

And from the strand of Dardan where they fought
To Simois' reedy banks the red blood ran,
Whose waves to imitate the battle sought
With swelling ridges, and their ranks began
To break upon the gallèd shore, and then   1440
    Retire again, till meeting greater ranks
    They join, and shoot their foam at Simois' banks.

To this well painted piece is Lucrece come,
To find a face where all distress is stelled.
Many she sees where cares have carvèd some,   1445
But none where all distress and dolour dwelled
Till she despairing Hecuba beheld
    Staring on Priam's wounds with her old eyes,
    Which bleeding under Pyrrhus' proud foot lies.

In her the painter had anatomized   1450
Time's ruin, beauty's wreck, and grim care's reign.
Her cheeks with chaps and wrinkles were disguised;
Of what she was no semblance did remain.
Her blue blood changed to black in every vein,
    Wanting the spring that those shrunk pipes had fed,
    Showed life imprisoned in a body dead.   1456

On this sad shadow Lucrece spends her eyes,
And shapes her sorrow to the beldame's woes,
Who nothing wants to answer her but cries
And bitter words to ban her cruel foes.   1460
The painter was no god to lend her those,
    And therefore Lucrece swears he did her wrong
    To give her so much grief, and not a tongue.

'Poor instrument,' quoth she, 'without a sound,
I'll tune thy woes with my lamenting tongue,   1465
And drop sweet balm in Priam's painted wound,
And rail on Pyrrhus that hath done him wrong,
And with my tears quench Troy that burns so long,
    And with my knife scratch out the angry eyes
    Of all the Greeks that are thine enemies.   1470

'Show me the strumpet that began this stir,
That with my nails her beauty I may tear.
Thy heat of lust, fond Paris, did incur
This load of wrath that burning Troy doth bear;
Thine eye kindled the fire that burneth here,   1475
    And here in Troy, for trespass of thine eye,
    The sire, the son, the dame and daughter die.

'Why should the private pleasure of someone
Become the public plague of many moe?
Let sin alone committed light alone   1480
Upon his head that hath transgressèd so;
Let guiltless souls be freed from guilty woe.
    For one's offence why should so many fall,
    To plague a private sin in general?

'Lo, here weeps Hecuba, here Priam dies,   1485
Here manly Hector faints, here Troilus swoons,
Here friend by friend in bloody channel lies,
And friend to friend gives unadvisèd wounds,
And one man's lust these many lives confounds.
    Had doting Priam checked his son's desire,   1490
    Troy had been bright with fame, and not with fire.'

Here feelingly she weeps Troy's painted woes;
For sorrow, like a heavy hanging bell
Once set on ringing, with his own weight goes;
Then little strength rings out the doleful knell.   1495
So Lucrece, set a-work, sad tales doth tell
    To pencilled pensiveness and coloured sorrow.
    She lends them words, and she their looks doth
        borrow.

She throws her eyes about the painting round,
And who she finds forlorn she doth lament.   1500
At last she sees a wretched image bound,
That piteous looks to Phrygian shepherds lent.
His face, though full of cares, yet showed content.
    Onward to Troy with the blunt swains he goes,
    So mild that patience seemed to scorn his woes.   1505

In him the painter laboured with his skill
To hide deceit and give the harmless show
An humble gait, calm looks, eyes wailing still,
A brow unbent that seemed to welcome woe;
Cheeks neither red nor pale, but mingled so   1510
    That blushing red no guilty instance gave,
    Nor ashy pale the fear that false hearts have.

But like a constant and confirmèd devil
He entertained a show so seeming just,
And therein so ensconced his secret evil   1515
That jealousy itself could not mistrust
False creeping craft and perjury should thrust
    Into so bright a day such blackfaced storms,
    Or blot with hell-born sin such saint-like forms.

The well skilled workman this mild image drew   1520
For perjured Sinon, whose enchanting story
The credulous old Priam after slew;
Whose words like wildfire burnt the shining glory
Of rich-built Ilion, that the skies were sorry,
    And little stars shot from their fixèd places   1525
    When their glass fell wherein they viewed their faces.

This picture she advisedly perused,
And chid the painter for his wondrous skill,
Saying some shape in Sinon's was abused,
So fair a form lodged not a mind so ill;   1530
And still on him she gazed, and gazing still,
    Such signs of truth in his plain face she spied
    That she concludes the picture was belied.

'It cannot be,' quoth she, 'that so much guile'—
She would have said 'can lurk in such a look',   1535
But Tarquin's shape came in her mind the while,
And from her tongue 'can lurk' from 'cannot' took.
'It cannot be' she in that sense forsook,
    And turned it thus: 'It cannot be, I find,
    But such a face should bear a wicked mind.   1540

'For even as subtle Sinon here is painted,
So sober-sad, so weary, and so mild,
As if with grief or travail he had fainted,
To me came Tarquin armèd, too beguiled
With outward honesty, but yet defiled   1545
    With inward vice. As Priam him did cherish,
    So did I Tarquin, so my Troy did perish.

'Look, look, how list'ning Priam wets his eyes
To see those borrowed tears that Sinon sheds.
Priam, why art thou old and yet not wise?   1550
For every tear he falls a Trojan bleeds.
His eye drops fire, no water thence proceeds.
    Those round clear pearls of his that move thy pity
    Are balls of quenchless fire to burn thy city.

'Such devils steal effects from lightless hell,   1555
For Sinon in his fire doth quake with cold,
And in that cold hot-burning fire doth dwell.
These contraries such unity do hold
Only to flatter fools and make them bold;
    So Priam's trust false Sinon's tears doth flatter   1560
    That he finds means to burn his Troy with water.'

Here, all enraged, such passion her assails
That patience is quite beaten from her breast.
She tears the senseless Sinon with her nails,
Comparing him to that unhappy guest   1565
Whose deed hath made herself herself detest.
  At last she smilingly with this gives o'er:
  'Fool, fool,' quoth she, 'his wounds will not be sore.'

Thus ebbs and flows the current of her sorrow,
And time doth weary time with her complaining.   1570
She looks for night, and then she longs for morrow,
And both she thinks too long with her remaining.
Short time seems long in sorrow's sharp sustaining.
  Though woe be heavy, yet it seldom sleeps,
  And they that watch see time how slow it creeps. 1575

Which all this time hath overslipped her thought
That she with painted images hath spent,
Being from the feeling of her own grief brought
By deep surmise of others' detriment,
Losing her woes in shows of discontent.   1580
  It easeth some, though none it ever cured,
  To think their dolour others have endured.

But now the mindful messenger come back
Brings home his lord and other company,
Who finds his Lucrece clad in mourning black,   1585
And round about her tear-distainèd eye
Blue circles streamed, like rainbows in the sky.
  These water-galls in her dim element
  Foretell new storms to those already spent.

Which when her sad beholding husband saw,   1590
Amazedly in her sad face he stares.
Her eyes, though sod in tears, looked red and raw,
Her lively colour killed with deadly cares.
He hath no power to ask her how she fares.
  Both stood like old acquaintance in a trance,   1595
  Met far from home, wond'ring each other's chance.

At last he takes her by the bloodless hand,
And thus begins: 'What uncouth ill event
Hath thee befall'n, that thou dost trembling stand?
Sweet love, what spite hath thy fair colour spent? 1600
Why art thou thus attired in discontent?
  Unmask, dear dear, this moody heaviness,
  And tell thy grief, that we may give redress.'

Three times with sighs she gives her sorrow fire
Ere once she can discharge one word of woe.   1605
At length addressed to answer his desire,
She modestly prepares to let them know
Her honour is ta'en prisoner by the foe,
  While Collatine and his consorted lords
  With sad attention long to hear her words.   1610

And now this pale swan in her wat'ry nest
Begins the sad dirge of her certain ending.
'Few words,' quoth she, 'shall fit the trespass best,
Where no excuse can give the fault amending.
In me more woes than words are now depending,   1615
  And my laments would be drawn out too long
  To tell them all with one poor tired tongue.

'Then be this all the task it hath to say:
Dear husband, in the interest of thy bed
A stranger came, and on that pillow lay   1620
Where thou wast wont to rest thy weary head;
And what wrong else may be imaginèd
  By foul enforcement might be done to me,
  From that, alas, thy Lucrece is not free.

'For in the dreadful dead of dark midnight   1625
With shining falchion in my chamber came
A creeping creature with a flaming light,
And softly cried, "Awake, thou Roman dame,
And entertain my love; else lasting shame
  On thee and thine this night I will inflict,   1630
  If thou my love's desire do contradict.

' "For some hard-favoured groom of thine," quoth he,
"Unless thou yoke thy liking to my will,
I'll murder straight, and then I'll slaughter thee,
And swear I found you where you did fulfil   1635
The loathsome act of lust, and so did kill
  The lechers in their deed. This act will be
  My fame, and thy perpetual infamy." '

'With this I did begin to start and cry,
And then against my heart he set his sword,   1640
Swearing unless I took all patiently
I should not live to speak another word.
So should my shame still rest upon record,
  And never be forgot in mighty Rome
  Th'adulterate death of Lucrece and her groom.   1645

'Mine enemy was strong, my poor self weak,
And far the weaker with so strong a fear.
My bloody judge forbade my tongue to speak;
No rightful plea might plead for justice there.
His scarlet lust came evidence to swear   1650
  That my poor beauty had purloined his eyes;
  And when the judge is robbed, the prisoner dies.

'O teach me how to make mine own excuse,
Or at the least this refuge let me find:
Though my gross blood be stained with this abuse, 1655
Immaculate and spotless is my mind.
That was not forced, that never was inclined
  To accessory yieldings, but still pure
  Doth in her poisoned closet yet endure.'

Lo, here the hopeless merchant of this loss,   1660
With head declined and voice dammed up with woe,
With sad set eyes and wreathèd arms across,
From lips new waxen pale begins to blow
The grief away that stops his answer so;
    But wretched as he is, he strives in vain.   1665
    What he breathes out, his breath drinks up again.

As through an arch the violent roaring tide
Outruns the eye that doth behold his haste,
Yet in the eddy boundeth in his pride
Back to the strait that forced him on so fast,   1670
In rage sent out, recalled in rage being past;
    Even so his sighs, his sorrows, make a saw,
    To push grief on, and back the same grief draw.

Which speechless woe of his poor she attendeth,
And his untimely frenzy thus awaketh: 1675
'Dear lord, thy sorrow to my sorrow lendeth
Another power; no flood by raining slaketh.
My woe too sensible thy passion maketh,
    More feeling-painful. Let it then suffice
    To drown on woe one pair of weeping eyes.   1680

'And for my sake, when I might charm thee so,
For she that was thy Lucrece, now attend me.
Be suddenly revengèd on my foe—
Thine, mine, his own. Suppose thou dost defend me
From what is past. The help that thou shalt lend me 1685
    Comes all too late, yet let the traitor die,
    For sparing justice feeds iniquity.

'But ere I name him, you fair lords,' quoth she,
Speaking to those that came with Collatine,
'Shall plight your honourable faiths to me   1690
With swift pursuit to venge this wrong of mine;
For 'tis a meritorious fair design
    To chase injustice with revengeful arms.
    Knights, by their oaths, should right poor ladies'
    harms.'

At this request with noble disposition   1695
Each present lord began to promise aid,
As bound in knighthood to her imposition,
Longing to hear the hateful foe bewrayed.
But she that yet her sad task hath not said
    The protestation stops. 'O speak,' quoth she;   1700
    'How may this forcèd stain be wiped from me?

'What is the quality of my offence,
Being constrained with dreadful circumstance?
May my pure mind with the foul act dispense,
My low-declinèd honour to advance?   1705
May any terms acquit me from this chance?
    The poisoned fountain clears itself again,
    And why not I from this compellèd stain?'

With this they all at once began to say
Her body's stain her mind untainted clears,   1710
While with a joyless smile she turns away
The face, that map which deep impression bears
Of hard misfortune, carved in it with tears.
    'No, no,' quoth she, 'no dame hereafter living
    By my excuse shall claim excuse's giving.'   1715

Here with a sigh as if her heart would break
She throws forth Tarquin's name. 'He, he,' she says—
But more than he her poor tongue could not speak,
Till after many accents and delays,
Untimely breathings, sick and short essays,   1720
    She utters this: 'He, he, fair lords, 'tis he
    That guides this hand to give this wound to me.'

Even here she sheathèd in her harmless breast
A harmful knife, that thence her soul unsheathed.
That blow did bail it from the deep unrest   1725
Of that polluted prison where it breathed.
Her contrite sighs unto the clouds bequeathed
    Her wingèd sprite, and through her wounds doth fly
    Life's lasting date from cancelled destiny.

Stone-still, astonished with this deadly deed   1730
Stood Collatine and all his lordly crew,
Till Lucrece' father that beholds her bleed
Himself on her self-slaughtered body threw;
And from the purple fountain Brutus drew
    The murd'rous knife; and as it left the place   1735
    Her blood in poor revenge held it in chase,

And bubbling from her breast it doth divide
In two slow rivers, that the crimson blood
Circles her body in on every side,
Who like a late-sacked island vastly stood,   1740
Bare and unpeopled in this fearful flood.
    Some of her blood still pure and red remained,
    And some looked black, and that false Tarquin-
    stained.

About the mourning and congealèd face
Of that black blood a wat'ry rigol goes,   1745
Which seems to weep upon the tainted place;
And ever since, as pitying Lucrece' woes,
Corrupted blood some watery token shows;
    And blood untainted still doth red abide,
    Blushing at that which is so putrefied.   1750

'Daughter, dear daughter,' old Lucretius cries,
'That life was mine which thou hast here deprived.
If in the child the father's image lies,
Where shall I live now Lucrece is unlived?
Thou wast not to this end from me derived.   1755
    If children predecease progenitors,
    We are their offspring, and they none of ours.

'Poor broken glass, I often did behold
In thy sweet semblance my old age new born;
But now that fair fresh mirror, dim and old,   1760
Shows me a bare-boned death by time outworn.
O, from thy cheeks my image thou hast torn,
    And shivered all the beauty of my glass,
    That I no more can see what once I was.

'O time, cease thou thy course and last no longer,   1765
If they surcease to be that should survive!
Shall rotten death make conquest of the stronger,
And leave the falt'ring feeble souls alive?
The old bees die, the young possess their hive.
    Then live, sweet Lucrece, live again and see   1770
    Thy father die, and not thy father thee.'

By this starts Collatine as from a dream,
And bids Lucretius give his sorrow place;
And then in key-cold Lucrece' bleeding stream
He falls, and bathes the pale fear in his face,   1775
And counterfeits to die with her a space,
    Till manly shame bids him possess his breath,
    And live to be revengèd on her death.

The deep vexation of his inward soul
Hath served a dumb arrest upon his tongue,   1780
Who, mad that sorrow should his use control,
Or keep him from heart-easing words so long,
Begins to talk; but through his lips do throng
    Weak words, so thick come in his poor heart's aid
    That no man could distinguish what he said.   1785

Yet sometime 'Tarquin' was pronouncèd plain,
But through his teeth, as if the name he tore.
This windy tempest, till it blow up rain,
Held back his sorrow's tide to make it more.
At last it rains, and busy winds give o'er.   1790
    Then son and father weep with equal strife
    Who should weep most, for daughter or for wife.

The one doth call her his, the other his,
Yet neither may possess the claim they lay.
The father says 'She's mine'; 'O, mine she is,'   1795
Replies her husband, 'do not take away
My sorrow's interest; let no mourner say
    He weeps for her, for she was only mine,
    And only must be wailed by Collatine.'

'O,' quoth Lucretius, 'I did give that life   1800
Which she too early and too late hath spilled.'
'Woe, woe,' quoth Collatine, 'she was my wife.
I owed her, and 'tis mine that she hath killed.'
'My daughter' and 'my wife' with clamours filled
    The dispersed air, who, holding Lucrece' life,   1805
    Answered their cries, 'my daughter' and 'my wife'.

Brutus, who plucked the knife from Lucrece' side,
Seeing such emulation in their woe
Began to clothe his wit in state and pride,
Burying in Lucrece' wound his folly's show.   1810
He with the Romans was esteemèd so
    As silly jeering idiots are with kings,
    For sportive words and utt'ring foolish things.

But now he throws that shallow habit by
Wherein deep policy did him disguise,   1815
And armed his long-hid wits advisedly
To check the tears in Collatinus' eyes.
'Thou wrongèd lord of Rome,' quoth he, 'arise.
    Let my unsounded self, supposed a fool,
    Now set thy long-experienced wit to school.   1820

'Why, Collatine, is woe the cure for woe?
Do wounds help wounds, or grief help grievous deeds?
Is it revenge to give thyself a blow
For his foul act by whom thy fair wife bleeds?
Such childish humour from weak minds proceeds;   1825
    Thy wretched wife mistook the matter so
    To slay herself, that should have slain her foe.

'Courageous Roman, do not steep thy heart
In such relenting dew of lamentations,
But kneel with me, and help to bear thy part   1830
To rouse our Roman gods with invocations
That they will suffer these abominations—
    Since Rome herself in them doth stand disgraced—
    By our strong arms from forth her fair streets chased.

'Now by the Capitol that we adore,   1835
And by this chaste blood so unjustly stained,
By heaven's fair sun that breeds the fat earth's store,
By all our country rights in Rome maintained,
And by chaste Lucrece' soul that late complained
    Her wrongs to us, and by this bloody knife,   1840
    We will revenge the death of this true wife.'

This said, he struck his hand upon his breast,
And kissed the fatal knife to end his vow,
And to his protestation urged the rest,
Who, wond'ring at him, did his words allow.   1845
Then jointly to the ground their knees they bow,
    And that deep vow which Brutus made before
    He doth again repeat, and that they swore.

When they had sworn to this advisèd doom
They did conclude to bear dead Lucrece thence,   1850
To show her bleeding body thorough Rome,
And so to publish Tarquin's foul offence;
Which being done with speedy diligence,
    The Romans plausibly did give consent
    To Tarquin's everlasting banishment.   1855

RICHARD II

THE subject-matter of *Richard II* seemed inflammatorily topical to Shakespeare's contemporaries. Richard, who had notoriously indulged his favourites, had been compelled to yield his throne to Henry Bolingbroke, Earl of Hereford: like Richard, the ageing Queen Elizabeth had no obvious successor, and she too encouraged favourites—such as the Earl of Essex—who might aspire to the throne. When Shakespeare's play first appeared in print (in 1597), and in the two succeeding editions printed during Elizabeth's life, the episode (4.1.145-308) showing Richard yielding the crown was omitted; and in 1601, on the day before Essex led his ill-fated rebellion against Elizabeth, his fellow conspirators commissioned a special performance in the hope of arousing popular support, even though the play was said to be 'long out of use'—surprisingly, since it was probably written no earlier than 1595.

But Shakespeare introduced no obvious topicality into his dramatization of Richard's reign, for which he read widely while using Raphael Holinshed's *Chronicles* (1577, revised and enlarged in 1587) as his main source of information. In choosing to write about Richard II (1367-1400) he was returning to the beginning of the story whose ending he had staged in *Richard III*; for Bolingbroke's usurpation of the throne to which Richard's hereditary right was indisputable had set in train the series of events finally expiated only in the union of the houses of York and Lancaster celebrated in the last speech of *Richard III*. Like *Richard III*, this is a tragical history, focusing on a single character; but Richard II is a far more introverted and morally ambiguous figure than Richard III. In this play, written entirely in verse, Shakespeare forgoes stylistic variety in favour of an intense, plangent lyricism.

Our early impressions of Richard are unsympathetic. Having banished Mowbray and Bolingbroke, he behaves callously to Bolingbroke's father, John of Gaunt, a stern upholder of the old order to whose warning against his irresponsible behaviour he pays no attention, and upon Gaunt's death confiscates his property with no regard for Bolingbroke's rights. During Richard's absence on an Irish campaign, Bolingbroke returns to England and gains support in his efforts to claim his inheritance. Gradually, as the balance of power shifts, Richard makes deeper claims on the audience's sympathy. When he confronts Bolingbroke at Flint Castle (3.1) he eloquently laments his imminent deposition even though Bolingbroke insists that he comes only to claim what is his; soon afterwards (4.1.98-103) the Duke of York announces Richard's abdication. The transference of power is effected in a scene of lyrical expansiveness, and Richard becomes a pitiable figure as he is led to imprisonment in Pomfret (Pontefract) Castle while his former queen is banished to France. Richard's self-exploration reaches its climax in his soliloquy spoken shortly before his murder at the hands of Piers Exton; at the end of the play, Henry, anxious and guilt-laden, denies responsibility for the murder and plans an expiatory pilgrimage to the Holy Land.

THE PERSONS OF THE PLAY

KING RICHARD II

The QUEEN, his wife

JOHN OF GAUNT, Duke of Lancaster, Richard's uncle

Harry BOLINGBROKE, Duke of Hereford, John of Gaunt's son, later
   KING HENRY IV

DUCHESS OF GLOUCESTER, widow of Gaunt's and York's brother

Duke of YORK, King Richard's uncle

DUCHESS OF YORK

Duke of AUMERLE, their son

Thomas MOWBRAY, Duke of Norfolk

GREEN
BAGOT   } followers of King Richard
BUSHY

Percy, Earl of NORTHUMBERLAND
HARRY PERCY, his son
Lord ROSS   } of Bolingbroke's party
Lord WILLOUGHBY

Earl of SALISBURY
BISHOP OF CARLISLE   } of King Richard's party
Sir Stephen SCROPE

Lord BERKELEY

Lord FITZWATER

Duke of SURREY

ABBOT OF WESTMINSTER

Sir Piers EXTON

LORD MARSHAL

HERALDS

CAPTAIN of the Welsh army

LADIES attending the Queen

GARDENER

Gardener's MEN

Exton's MEN

KEEPER of the prison at Pomfret

GROOM of King Richard's stable

Lords, soldiers, attendants

The Tragedy of King Richard the Second

1.1 *Enter King Richard and John of Gaunt, with the*
Lord Marshal, other nobles, and attendants

KING RICHARD

Old John of Gaunt, time-honoured Lancaster,
Hast thou according to thy oath and bond
Brought hither Henry Hereford, thy bold son,
Here to make good the boist'rous late appeal,
Which then our leisure would not let us hear,   5
Against the Duke of Norfolk, Thomas Mowbray?

JOHN OF GAUNT   I have, my liege.

KING RICHARD

Tell me moreover, hast thou sounded him
If he appeal the Duke on ancient malice
Or worthily, as a good subject should,   10
On some known ground of treachery in him?

JOHN OF GAUNT

As near as I could sift him on that argument,
On some apparent danger seen in him
Aimed at your highness, no inveterate malice.

KING RICHARD

Then call them to our presence.   ⌈*Exit one or more*⌉
                 Face to face   15
And frowning brow to brow, ourselves will hear
The accuser and the accusèd freely speak.
High-stomached are they both and full of ire;
In rage, deaf as the sea, hasty as fire.

Enter Bolingbroke Duke of Hereford, and Mowbray
Duke of Norfolk

BOLINGBROKE

Many years of happy days befall   20
My gracious sovereign, my most loving liege!

MOWBRAY

Each day still better others' happiness,
Until the heavens, envying earth's good hap,
Add an immortal title to your crown!

KING RICHARD

We thank you both. Yet one but flatters us,   25
As well appeareth by the cause you come,
Namely, to appeal each other of high treason.
Cousin of Hereford, what dost thou object
Against the Duke of Norfolk, Thomas Mowbray?

BOLINGBROKE

First—heaven be the record to my speech—   30
In the devotion of a subject's love,
Tend'ring the precious safety of my Prince,
And free from other misbegotten hate,
Come I appellant to this princely presence.
Now, Thomas Mowbray, do I turn to thee;   35
And mark my greeting well, for what I speak
My body shall make good upon this earth,
Or my divine soul answer it in heaven.
Thou art a traitor and a miscreant,
Too good to be so, and too bad to live,   40

Since the more fair and crystal is the sky,
The uglier seem the clouds that in it fly.
Once more, the more to aggravate the note,
With a foul traitor's name stuff I thy throat,
And wish, so please my sovereign, ere I move   45
What my tongue speaks my right-drawn sword may
    prove.

MOWBRAY

Let not my cold words here accuse my zeal.
'Tis not the trial of a woman's war,
The bitter clamour of two eager tongues,
Can arbitrate this cause betwixt us twain.   50
The blood is hot that must be cooled for this.
Yet can I not of such tame patience boast
As to be hushed and naught at all to say.
First, the fair reverence of your highness curbs me
From giving reins and spurs to my free speech,   55
Which else would post until it had returned
These terms of treason doubled down his throat.
Setting aside his high blood's royalty,
And let him be no kinsman to my liege,
I do defy him, and I spit at him,   60
Call him a slanderous coward and a villain;
Which to maintain I would allow him odds,
And meet him, were I tied to run afoot
Even to the frozen ridges of the Alps,
Or any other ground inhabitable,   65
Wherever Englishman durst set his foot.
Meantime let this defend my loyalty:
By all my hopes, most falsely doth he lie.

BOLINGBROKE (*throwing down his gage*)

Pale trembling coward, there I throw my gage,
Disclaiming here the kindred of the King,   70
And lay aside my high blood's royalty,
Which fear, not reverence, makes thee to except.
If guilty dread have left thee so much strength
As to take up mine honour's pawn, then stoop.
By that, and all the rites of knighthood else,   75
Will I make good against thee, arm to arm,
What I have spoke or thou canst worse devise.

MOWBRAY (*taking up the gage*)

I take it up, and by that sword I swear
Which gently laid my knighthood on my shoulder,
I'll answer thee in any fair degree   80
Or chivalrous design of knightly trial;
And when I mount, alive may I not light
If I be traitor or unjustly fight!

KING RICHARD (*to Bolingbroke*)

What doth our cousin lay to Mowbray's charge?
It must be great that can inherit us   85
So much as of a thought of ill in him.

BOLINGBROKE

Look what I speak, my life shall prove it true:

That Mowbray hath received eight thousand nobles
In name of lendings for your highness' soldiers,
The which he hath detained for lewd employments, 90
Like a false traitor and injurious villain.
Besides I say, and will in battle prove,
Or here or elsewhere, to the furthest verge
That ever was surveyed by English eye,
That all the treasons for these eighteen years 95
Complotted and contrivèd in this land
Fetch from false Mowbray their first head and spring.
Further I say, and further will maintain
Upon his bad life, to make all this good,
That he did plot the Duke of Gloucester's death, 100
Suggest his soon-believing adversaries,
And consequently, like a traitor-coward,
Sluiced out his innocent soul through streams of blood;
Which blood, like sacrificing Abel's, cries
Even from the tongueless caverns of the earth 105
To me for justice and rough chastisement.
And, by the glorious worth of my descent,
This arm shall do it or this life be spent.

KING RICHARD
How high a pitch his resolution soars!
Thomas of Norfolk, what sayst thou to this? 110

MOWBRAY
O, let my sovereign turn away his face,
And bid his ears a little while be deaf,
Till I have told this slander of his blood
How God and good men hate so foul a liar!

KING RICHARD
Mowbray, impartial are our eyes and ears. 115
Were he my brother, nay, my kingdom's heir,
As he is but my father's brother's son,
Now by my sceptre's awe I make a vow
Such neighbour-nearness to our sacred blood
Should nothing privilege him, nor partialize 120
The unstooping firmness of my upright soul.
He is our subject, Mowbray; so art thou.
Free speech and fearless I to thee allow.

MOWBRAY
Then, Bolingbroke, as low as to thy heart
Through the false passage of thy throat thou liest! 125
Three parts of that receipt I had for Calais
Disbursed I duly to his highness' soldiers.
The other part reserved I by consent,
For that my sovereign liege was in my debt
Upon remainder of a dear account 130
Since last I went to France to fetch his queen.
Now swallow down that lie. For Gloucester's death,
I slew him not, but to my own disgrace
Neglected my sworn duty in that case.
For you, my noble lord of Lancaster, 135
The honourable father to my foe,
Once did I lay an ambush for your life,
A trespass that doth vex my grievèd soul;
But ere I last received the Sacrament
I did confess it, and exactly begged 140
Your grace's pardon, and I hope I had it.

This is my fault. As for the rest appealed,
It issues from the rancour of a villain,
A recreant and most degenerate traitor,
Which in myself I boldly will defend, 145

He throws down his gage
And interchangeably hurl down my gage
Upon this overweening traitor's foot,
To prove myself a loyal gentleman
Even in the best blood chambered in his bosom;
In haste whereof most heartily I pray 150
Your highness to assign our trial day.

⌈*Bolingbroke takes up the gage*⌉
KING RICHARD
Wrath-kindled gentlemen, be ruled by me.
Let's purge this choler without letting blood.
This we prescribe, though no physician:
Deep malice makes too deep incision; 155
Forget, forgive, conclude, and be agreed;
Our doctors say this is no time to bleed.
Good uncle, let this end where it begun.
We'll calm the Duke of Norfolk, you your son.

JOHN OF GAUNT
To be a make-peace shall become my age. 160
Throw down, my son, the Duke of Norfolk's gage.

KING RICHARD
And, Norfolk, throw down his.

JOHN OF GAUNT   When, Harry, when?
Obedience bids I should not bid again.

KING RICHARD
Norfolk, throw down! We bid; there is no boot.

MOWBRAY (*kneeling*)
Myself I throw, dread sovereign, at thy foot. 165
My life thou shalt command, but not my shame.
The one my duty owes, but my fair name,
Despite of death that lives upon my grave,
To dark dishonour's use thou shalt not have.
I am disgraced, impeached, and baffled here, 170
Pierced to the soul with slander's venomed spear,
The which no balm can cure but his heart blood
Which breathed this poison.

KING RICHARD   Rage must be withstood.
Give me his gage. Lions make leopards tame.

MOWBRAY ⌈*standing*⌉
Yea, but not change his spots. Take but my shame,
And I resign my gage. My dear dear lord, 176
The purest treasure mortal times afford
Is spotless reputation; that away,
Men are but gilded loam, or painted clay.
A jewel in a ten-times barred-up chest 180
Is a bold spirit in a loyal breast.
Mine honour is my life. Both grow in one.
Take honour from me, and my life is done.
Then, dear my liege, mine honour let me try.
In that I live, and for that will I die. 185

KING RICHARD
Cousin, throw down your gage. Do you begin.

BOLINGBROKE
O God defend my soul from such deep sin!

Shall I seem crest-fallen in my father's sight?
Or with pale beggar-fear impeach my height
Before this out-dared dastard? Ere my tongue 190
Shall wound my honour with such feeble wrong,
Or sound so base a parle, my teeth shall tear
The slavish motive of recanting fear,
And spit it bleeding in his high disgrace
Where shame doth harbour, even in Mowbray's face.

         Exit John of Gaunt

KING RICHARD
We were not born to sue, but to command; 196
Which since we cannot do to make you friends,
Be ready, as your lives shall answer it,
At Coventry upon Saint Lambert's day.
There shall your swords and lances arbitrate 200
The swelling difference of your settled hate.
Since we cannot atone you, we shall see
Justice design the victor's chivalry.
Lord Marshal, command our officers-at-arms 204
Be ready to direct these home alarms. *Exeunt*

1.2 *Enter John of Gaunt, Duke of Lancaster, with the*
   Duchess of Gloucester

JOHN OF GAUNT
Alas, the part I had in Gloucester's blood
Doth more solicit me than your exclaims
To stir against the butchers of his life.
But since correction lieth in those hands
Which made the fault that we cannot correct, 5
Put we our quarrel to the will of heaven,
Who, when they see the hours ripe on earth,
Will rain hot vengeance on offenders' heads.

DUCHESS OF GLOUCESTER
Finds brotherhood in thee no sharper spur?
Hath love in thy old blood no living fire? 10
Edward's seven sons, whereof thyself art one,
Were as seven vials of his sacred blood,
Or seven fair branches springing from one root.
Some of those seven are dried by nature's course,
Some of those branches by the destinies cut; 15
But Thomas, my dear lord, my life, my Gloucester,
One vial full of Edward's sacred blood,
One flourishing branch of his most royal root,
Is cracked, and all the precious liquor spilt;
Is hacked down, and his summer leaves all faded 20
By envy's hand and murder's bloody axe.
Ah, Gaunt, his blood was thine! That bed, that womb,
That mettle, that self mould that fashioned thee,
Made him a man; and though thou liv'st and
  breathest,
Yet art thou slain in him. Thou dost consent 25
In some large measure to thy father's death
In that thou seest thy wretched brother die,
Who was the model of thy father's life.
Call it not patience, Gaunt, it is despair.
In suff'ring thus thy brother to be slaughtered 30
Thou show'st the naked pathway to thy life,

Teaching stern murder how to butcher thee.
That which in mean men we entitle patience
Is pale cold cowardice in noble breasts.
What shall I say? To safeguard thine own life 35
The best way is to venge my Gloucester's death.

JOHN OF GAUNT
God's is the quarrel; for God's substitute,
His deputy anointed in his sight,
Hath caused his death; the which if wrongfully,
Let heaven revenge, for I may never lift 40
An angry arm against his minister.

DUCHESS OF GLOUCESTER
Where then, alas, may I complain myself?

JOHN OF GAUNT
To God, the widow's champion and defence.

DUCHESS OF GLOUCESTER
Why then, I will. Farewell, old Gaunt.
Thou goest to Coventry, there to behold 45
Our cousin Hereford and fell Mowbray fight.
O, set my husband's wrongs on Hereford's spear,
That it may enter butcher Mowbray's breast!
Or if misfortune miss the first career,
Be Mowbray's sins so heavy in his bosom 50
That they may break his foaming courser's back
And throw the rider headlong in the lists,
A caitiff, recreant to my cousin Hereford!
Farewell, old Gaunt. Thy sometimes brother's wife
With her companion, grief, must end her life. 55

JOHN OF GAUNT
Sister, farewell. I must to Coventry.
As much good stay with thee as go with me.

DUCHESS OF GLOUCESTER
Yet one word more. Grief boundeth where it falls,
Not with the empty hollowness, but weight.
I take my leave before I have begun, 60
For sorrow ends not when it seemeth done.
Commend me to thy brother, Edmund York.
Lo, this is all.—Nay, yet depart not so!
Though this be all, do not so quickly go.
I shall remember more. Bid him—ah, what?— 65
With all good speed at Pleshey visit me.
Alack, and what shall good old York there see
But empty lodgings and unfurnished walls,
Unpeopled offices, untrodden stones,
And what hear there for welcome but my groans? 70
Therefore commend me; let him not come there
To seek out sorrow that dwells everywhere.
Desolate, desolate will I hence and die.
The last leave of thee takes my weeping eye.

         Exeunt *severally*

1.3 *Enter Lord Marshal* *with officers setting out*
   chairs, *and the Duke of Aumerle*

LORD MARSHAL
My lord Aumerle, is Harry Hereford armed?

AUMERLE
Yea, at all points, and longs to enter in.

LORD MARSHAL
The Duke of Norfolk, sprightfully and bold,
Stays but the summons of the appellant's trumpet.

AUMERLE
Why then, the champions are prepared, and stay   5
For nothing but his majesty's approach.

*The trumpets sound, and King Richard enters, with
John of Gaunt, Duke of Lancaster, ⌈Bushy, Bagot,
Green,⌉ and other nobles. When they are set, enter
Mowbray Duke of Norfolk, defendant, in arms, ⌈and
a Herald⌉*

KING RICHARD
Marshal, demand of yonder champion
The cause of his arrival here in arms.
Ask him his name, and orderly proceed
To swear him in the justice of his cause.   10

LORD MARSHAL (to Mowbray)
In God's name and the King's, say who thou art,
And why thou com'st thus knightly clad in arms,
Against what man thou com'st, and what thy
    quarrel.
Speak truly on thy knighthood and thy oath,
As so defend thee heaven and thy valour!   15

MOWBRAY
My name is Thomas Mowbray, Duke of Norfolk,
Who hither come engagèd by my oath—
Which God defend a knight should violate—
Both to defend my loyalty and truth
To God, my king, and my succeeding issue,   20
Against the Duke of Hereford that appeals me;
And by the grace of God and this mine arm
To prove him, in defending of myself,
A traitor to my God, my king, and me.
And as I truly fight, defend me heaven!   25
⌈He sits.⌉

*The trumpets sound. Enter Bolingbroke Duke of
Hereford, appellant, in armour, ⌈and a Herald⌉*

KING RICHARD
Marshal, ask yonder knight in arms
Both who he is and why he cometh hither
Thus plated in habiliments of war;
And formally, according to our law,
Depose him in the justice of his cause.   30

LORD MARSHAL (to Bolingbroke)
What is thy name? And wherefore com'st thou hither
Before King Richard in his royal lists?
Against whom comest thou? And what's thy quarrel?
Speak like a true knight, so defend thee heaven!

BOLINGBROKE
Harry of Hereford, Lancaster, and Derby   35
Am I, who ready here do stand in arms
To prove by God's grace and my body's valour
In lists on Thomas Mowbray, Duke of Norfolk,
That he is a traitor foul and dangerous
To God of heaven, King Richard, and to me.   40
And as I truly fight, defend me heaven!
⌈He sits⌉

LORD MARSHAL
On pain of death, no person be so bold
Or daring-hardy as to touch the lists
Except the Marshal and such officers
Appointed to direct these fair designs.   45

BOLINGBROKE ⌈standing⌉
Lord Marshal, let me kiss my sovereign's hand
And bow my knee before his majesty,
For Mowbray and myself are like two men
That vow a long and weary pilgrimage;
Then let us take a ceremonious leave   50
And loving farewell of our several friends.

LORD MARSHAL (to King Richard)
The appellant in all duty greets your highness,
And craves to kiss your hand and take his leave.

KING RICHARD
We will descend and fold him in our arms.
He descends from his seat and embraces Bolingbroke
Cousin of Hereford, as thy cause is just,   55
So be thy fortune in this royal fight.
Farewell, my blood, which if today thou shed,
Lament we may, but not revenge thee dead.

BOLINGBROKE
O, let no noble eye profane a tear
For me if I be gored with Mowbray's spear.   60
As confident as is the falcon's flight
Against a bird do I with Mowbray fight.
(*To the Lord Marshal*) My loving lord, I take my leave
    of you;
(*To Aumerle*) Of you, my noble cousin, Lord Aumerle;
Not sick, although I have to do with death,   65
But lusty, young, and cheerly drawing breath.
Lo, as at English feasts, so I regreet
The daintiest last, to make the end most sweet.
(*To Gaunt, ⌈kneeling⌉*) O thou, the earthly author of my
    blood,
Whose youthful spirit in me regenerate   70
Doth with a two-fold vigour lift me up
To reach at victory above my head,
Add proof unto mine armour with thy prayers,
And with thy blessings steel my lance's point,
That it may enter Mowbray's waxen coat   75
And furbish new the name of John a Gaunt
Even in the lusty haviour of his son.

JOHN OF GAUNT
God in thy good cause make thee prosperous!
Be swift like lightning in the execution,
And let thy blows, doubly redoublèd,
Fall like amazing thunder on the casque   80
Of thy adverse pernicious enemy.
Rouse up thy youthful blood, be valiant, and live.

BOLINGBROKE ⌈standing⌉
Mine innocence and Saint George to thrive!

MOWBRAY ⌈standing⌉
However God or fortune cast my lot,   85
There lives or dies, true to King Richard's throne,
A loyal, just, and upright gentleman.

Never did captive with a freer heart
Cast off his chains of bondage and embrace
His golden uncontrolled enfranchisement   90
More than my dancing soul doth celebrate
This feast of battle with mine adversary.
Most mighty liege, and my companion peers,
Take from my mouth the wish of happy years.
As gentle and as jocund as to jest   95
Go I to fight. Truth hath a quiet breast.
KING RICHARD
Farewell, my lord. Securely I espy
Virtue with valour couchèd in thine eye.—
Order the trial, Marshal, and begin.
LORD MARSHAL
Harry of Hereford, Lancaster, and Derby,   100
Receive thy lance; and God defend the right!
⌈An officer bears a lance to Bolingbroke⌉
BOLINGBROKE
Strong as a tower in hope, I cry 'Amen!'
LORD MARSHAL (to an officer)
Go bear this lance to Thomas, Duke of Norfolk.
⌈An officer bears a lance to Mowbray⌉
FIRST HERALD
Harry of Hereford, Lancaster, and Derby
Stands here for God, his sovereign, and himself, 105
On pain to be found false and recreant,
To prove the Duke of Norfolk, Thomas Mowbray,
A traitor to his God, his king, and him,
And dares him to set forward to the fight.
SECOND HERALD
Here standeth Thomas Mowbray, Duke of Norfolk, 110
On pain to be found false and recreant,
Both to defend himself and to approve
Henry of Hereford, Lancaster, and Derby
To God his sovereign and to him disloyal,
Courageously and with a free desire   115
Attending but the signal to begin.
LORD MARSHAL
Sound trumpets, and set forward combatants!
⌈A charge is sounded.⌉
King Richard throws down his warder
Stay, the King hath thrown his warder down.
KING RICHARD
Let them lay by their helmets and their spears,
And both return back to their chairs again.   120
⌈Bolingbroke and Mowbray disarm and sit⌉
(To the nobles) Withdraw with us, and let the trumpets
    sound
While we return these dukes what we decree.
A long flourish, during which King Richard and his
    nobles withdraw and hold council, ⌈then come
    forward⌉. King Richard addresses Bolingbroke and
    Mowbray
Draw near, and list what with our council we have
    done.
For that our kingdom's earth should not be soiled
With that dear blood which it hath fosterèd,   125
And for our eyes do hate the dire aspect

Of civil wounds ploughed up with neighbours'
    swords,
Which, so roused up with boist'rous untuned drums,
With harsh-resounding trumpets' dreadful bray,
And grating shock of wrathful iron arms,   130
Might from our quiet confines fright fair peace
And make us wade even in our kindred's blood,
Therefore we banish you our territories.
You, cousin Hereford, upon pain of life,
Till twice five summers have enriched our fields 135
Shall not regreet our fair dominions,
But tread the stranger paths of banishment.
BOLINGBROKE
Your will be done. This must my comfort be:
That sun that warms you here shall shine on me,
And those his golden beams to you here lent   140
Shall point on me and gild my banishment.
KING RICHARD
Norfolk, for thee remains a heavier doom,
Which I with some unwillingness pronounce.
The sly slow hours shall not determinate
The dateless limit of thy dear exile.   145
The hopeless word of 'never to return'
Breathe I against thee, upon pain of life.
MOWBRAY
A heavy sentence, my most sovereign liege,
And all unlooked-for from your highness' mouth.
A dearer merit, not so deep a maim   150
As to be cast forth in the common air,
Have I deservèd at your highness' hands.
The language I have learnt these forty years,
My native English, now I must forgo,
And now my tongue's use is to me no more   155
Than an unstringèd viol or a harp,
Or like a cunning instrument cased up,
Or, being open, put into his hands
That knows no touch to tune the harmony.
Within my mouth you have enjailed my tongue,   160
Doubly portcullised with my teeth and lips,
And dull unfeeling barren ignorance
Is made my jailer to attend on me.
I am too old to fawn upon a nurse,
Too far in years to be a pupil now.   165
What is thy sentence then but speechless death,
Which robs my tongue from breathing native breath?
KING RICHARD
It boots thee not to be compassionate.
After our sentence, plaining comes too late.
MOWBRAY
Then thus I turn me from my country's light,   170
To dwell in solemn shades of endless night.
KING RICHARD
Return again, and take an oath with thee.
(To both) Lay on our royal sword your banished hands.
Swear by the duty that you owe to God—
Our part therein we banish with yourselves—   175
To keep the oath that we administer.
You never shall, so help you truth and God,

Embrace each other's love in banishment,
Nor never look upon each other's face,
Nor never write, regreet, nor reconcile   180
This low'ring tempest of your home-bred hate,
Nor never by advisèd purpose meet
To plot, contrive, or complot any ill
'Gainst us, our state, our subjects, or our land.
BOLINGBROKE
I swear.
MOWBRAY And I, to keep all this.   185
BOLINGBROKE
Norfolk, so far as to mine enemy:
By this time, had the King permitted us,
One of our souls had wandered in the air,
Banished this frail sepulchre of our flesh,
As now our flesh is banished from this land.   190
Confess thy treasons ere thou fly the realm.
Since thou hast far to go, bear not along
The clogging burden of a guilty soul.
MOWBRAY
No, Bolingbroke, if ever I were traitor,
My name be blotted from the book of life,   195
And I from heaven banished as from hence.
But what thou art, God, thou, and I do know,
And all too soon I fear the King shall rue.
Farewell, my liege. Now no way can I stray:.
Save back to England, all the world's my way.   Exit
KING RICHARD
Uncle, even in the glasses of thine eyes   201
I see thy grievèd heart. Thy sad aspect
Hath from the number of his banished years
Plucked four away. (To Bolingbroke) Six frozen winters
    spent,
Return with welcome home from banishment.   205
BOLINGBROKE
How long a time lies in one little word!
Four lagging winters and four wanton springs
End in a word: such is the breath of kings.
JOHN OF GAUNT
I thank my liege that in regard of me
He shortens four years of my son's exile.   210
But little vantage shall I reap thereby,
For ere the six years that he hath to spend
Can change their moons and bring their times about,
My oil-dried lamp and time-bewasted light
Shall be extinct with age and endless night.   215
My inch of taper will be burnt and done,
And blindfold death not let me see my son.
KING RICHARD
Why, uncle, thou hast many years to live.
JOHN OF GAUNT
But not a minute, King, that thou canst give.
Shorten my days thou canst with sudden sorrow, 220
And pluck nights from me, but not lend a morrow.
Thou canst help time to furrow me with age,
But stop no wrinkle in his pilgrimage.
Thy word is current with him for my death,
But dead, thy kingdom cannot buy my breath.   225

KING RICHARD
Thy son is banished upon good advice,
Whereto thy tongue a party verdict gave.
Why at our justice seem'st thou then to lour?
JOHN OF GAUNT
Things sweet to taste prove in digestion sour.
You urged me as a judge, but I had rather   230
You would have bid me argue like a father.
Alas, I looked when some of you should say
I was too strict to make mine own away,
But you gave leave to my unwilling tongue
Against my will to do myself this wrong.   235
KING RICHARD
Cousin, farewell; and uncle, bid him so.
Six years we banish him, and he shall go.
            ⌈Flourish.⌉ Exeunt all but Aumerle, the Lord
                    Marshal, John of Gaunt, and Bolingbroke
AUMERLE (to Bolingbroke)
Cousin, farewell. What presence must not know,
From where you do remain let paper show.   ⌈Exit⌉
LORD MARSHAL (to Bolingbroke)
My lord, no leave take I, for I will ride   240
As far as land will let me by your side.
JOHN OF GAUNT (to Bolingbroke)
O, to what purpose dost thou hoard thy words,
That thou return'st no greeting to thy friends?
BOLINGBROKE
I have too few to take my leave of you,
When the tongue's office should be prodigal   245
To breathe the abundant dolour of the heart.
JOHN OF GAUNT
Thy grief is but thy absence for a time.
BOLINGBROKE
Joy absent, grief is present for that time.
JOHN OF GAUNT
What is six winters? They are quickly gone.
BOLINGBROKE
To men in joy, but grief makes one hour ten.   250
JOHN OF GAUNT
Call it a travel that thou tak'st for pleasure.
BOLINGBROKE
My heart will sigh when I miscall it so,
Which finds it an enforcèd pilgrimage.
JOHN OF GAUNT
The sullen passage of thy weary steps
Esteem as foil wherein thou art to set   255
The precious jewel of thy home return.
BOLINGBROKE
O, who can hold a fire in his hand
By thinking on the frosty Caucasus,
Or cloy the hungry edge of appetite
By bare imagination of a feast,   260
Or wallow naked in December snow
By thinking on fantastic summer's heat?
O no, the apprehension of the good
Gives but the greater feeling to the worse.
Fell sorrow's tooth doth never rankle more   265
Than when he bites, but lanceth not the sore.

JOHN OF GAUNT
  Come, come, my son, I'll bring thee on thy way.
  Had I thy youth and cause, I would not stay.
BOLINGBROKE
  Then England's ground, farewell. Sweet soil, adieu,
  My mother and my nurse that bears me yet!   270
  Where'er I wander, boast of this I can:
  Though banished, yet a trueborn Englishman. *Exeunt*

1.4   *Enter King Richard with ⌈Green and Bagot⌉ at one*
       door, and the Lord Aumerle at another
KING RICHARD
  We did observe.—Cousin Aumerle,
  How far brought you high Hereford on his way?
AUMERLE
  I brought high Hereford, if you call him so,
  But to the next highway, and there I left him.
KING RICHARD
  And say, what store of parting tears were shed?   5
AUMERLE
  Faith, none for me, except the north-east wind,
  Which then grew bitterly against our faces,
  Awaked the sleeping rheum, and so by chance
  Did grace our hollow parting with a tear.
KING RICHARD
  What said our cousin when you parted with him? 10
AUMERLE
  'Farewell.' And for my heart disdainèd that my tongue
  Should so profane the word, that taught me craft
  To counterfeit oppression of such grief
  That words seemed buried in my sorrow's grave.
  Marry, would the word 'farewell' have lengthened
    hours   15
  And added years to his short banishment,
  He should have had a volume of farewells;
  But since it would not, he had none of me.
KING RICHARD
  He is our cousin, cousin; but 'tis doubt,
  When time shall call him home from banishment, 20
  Whether our kinsman come to see his friends.
  Ourself and Bushy, Bagot here, and Green
  Observed his courtship to the common people,
  How he did seem to dive into their hearts
  With humble and familiar courtesy,   25
  What reverence he did throw away on slaves,
  Wooing poor craftsmen with the craft of smiles
  And patient underbearing of his fortune,
  As 'twere to banish their affects with him.
  Off goes his bonnet to an oysterwench.   30
  A brace of draymen bid God speed him well,
  And had the tribute of his supple knee
  With 'Thanks, my countrymen, my loving friends',
  As were our England in reversion his,
  And he our subjects' next degree in hope.   35
GREEN
  Well, he is gone, and with him go these thoughts.
  Now for the rebels which stand out in Ireland.
  Expedient manage must be made, my liege,

Ere further leisure yield them further means
For their advantage and your highness' loss.   40
KING RICHARD
  We will ourself in person to this war,
  And for our coffers with too great a court
  And liberal largess are grown somewhat light,
  We are enforced to farm our royal realm,
  The revenue whereof shall furnish us   45
  For our affairs in hand. If that come short,
  Our substitutes at home shall have blank charters,
  Whereto, when they shall know what men are rich,
  They shall subscribe them for large sums of gold,
  And send them after to supply our wants;   50
  For we will make for Ireland presently.
    Enter Bushy
  Bushy, what news?
BUSHY
  Old John of Gaunt is grievous sick, my lord,
  Suddenly taken, and hath sent post-haste
  To entreat your majesty to visit him.   55
KING RICHARD Where lies he?
BUSHY At Ely House.
KING RICHARD
  Now put it, God, in his physician's mind
  To help him to his grave immediately.
  The lining of his coffers shall make coats   60
  To deck our soldiers for these Irish wars.
  Come, gentlemen, let's all go visit him.
  Pray God we may make haste and come too late!
                              Exeunt

2.1   *Enter John of Gaunt, Duke of Lancaster, sick,*
       ⌈carried in a chair,⌉ with the Duke of York
JOHN OF GAUNT
  Will the King come, that I may breathe my last
  In wholesome counsel to his unstaid youth?
YORK
  Vex not yourself, nor strive not with your breath,
  For all in vain comes counsel to his ear.
JOHN OF GAUNT
  O, but they say the tongues of dying men   5
  Enforce attention, like deep harmony.
  Where words are scarce they are seldom spent in
    vain,
  For they breathe truth that breathe their words in
    pain.
  He that no more must say is listened more
    Than they whom youth and ease have taught to
    glose.   10
  More are men's ends marked than their lives before.
    The setting sun, and music at the close,
  As the last taste of sweets, is sweetest last,
  Writ in remembrance more than things long past.
  Though Richard my life's counsel would not hear, 15
  My death's sad tale may yet undeaf his ear.
YORK
  No, it is stopped with other, flattering sounds,
  As praises of whose taste the wise are feared,

Lascivious metres to whose venom sound
The open ear of youth doth always listen,   20
Report of fashions in proud Italy,
Whose manners still our tardy-apish nation
Limps after in base imitation.
Where doth the world thrust forth a vanity—
So it be new there's no respect how vile—   25
That is not quickly buzzed into his ears?
Then all too late comes counsel, to be heard
Where will doth mutiny with wit's regard.
Direct not him whose way himself will choose:
'Tis breath thou lack'st, and that breath wilt thou lose.

JOHN OF GAUNT
Methinks I am a prophet new-inspired,   31
And thus, expiring, do foretell of him.
His rash, fierce blaze of riot cannot last,
For violent fires soon burn out themselves.
Small showers last long, but sudden storms are short.
He tires betimes that spurs too fast betimes.   36
With eager feeding food doth choke the feeder.
Light vanity, insatiate cormorant,
Consuming means, soon preys upon itself.
This royal throne of kings, this sceptred isle,   40
This earth of majesty, this seat of Mars,
This other Eden, demi-paradise,
This fortress built by nature for herself
Against infection and the hand of war,
This happy breed of men, this little world,   45
This precious stone set in the silver sea,
Which serves it in the office of a wall,
Or as a moat defensive to a house
Against the envy of less happier lands;
This blessèd plot, this earth, this realm, this England,
This teeming womb of royal kings,   51
Feared by their breed and famous by their birth,
Renownèd for their deeds as far from home
For Christian service and true chivalry
As is the sepulchre, in stubborn Jewry,   55
Of the world's ransom, blessèd Mary's son;
This land of such dear souls, this dear dear land,
Dear for her reputation through the world,
Is now leased out—I die pronouncing it—
Like to a tenement or pelting farm.   60
England, bound in with the triumphant sea,
Whose rocky shore beats back the envious siege
Of wat'ry Neptune, is now bound in with shame,
With inky blots and rotten parchment bonds.
That England that was wont to conquer others   65
Hath made a shameful conquest of itself.
Ah, would the scandal vanish with my life,
How happy then were my ensuing death!
Enter King Richard and the Queen; ⌈the Duke of
Aumerle,⌉ Bushy, ⌈Green, Bagot,⌉ Lord Ross, and
Lord Willoughby

YORK
The King is come. Deal mildly with his youth,
For young hot colts, being reined, do rage the more.70

QUEEN
How fares our noble uncle Lancaster?

KING RICHARD
What comfort, man? How is't with agèd Gaunt?

JOHN OF GAUNT
O, how that name befits my composition!
Old Gaunt indeed, and gaunt in being old.
Within me grief hath kept a tedious fast,   75
And who abstains from meat that is not gaunt?
For sleeping England long time have I watched.
Watching breeds leanness, leanness is all gaunt.
The pleasure that some fathers feed upon
Is my strict fast: I mean my children's looks.   80
And therein fasting, hast thou made me gaunt.
Gaunt am I for the grave, gaunt as a grave,
Whose hollow womb inherits naught but bones.

KING RICHARD
Can sick men play so nicely with their names?

JOHN OF GAUNT
No, misery makes sport to mock itself.   85
Since thou dost seek to kill my name in me,
I mock my name, great King, to flatter thee.

KING RICHARD
Should dying men flatter with those that live?

JOHN OF GAUNT
No, no, men living flatter those that die.

KING RICHARD
Thou now a-dying sayst thou flatt'rest me.   90

JOHN OF GAUNT
O no: thou diest, though I the sicker be.

KING RICHARD
I am in health; I breathe, and see thee ill.

JOHN OF GAUNT
Now He that made me knows I see thee ill:
Ill in myself to see, and in thee seeing ill.
Thy deathbed is no lesser than thy land,   95
Wherein thou liest in reputation sick;
And thou, too careless patient as thou art,
Committ'st thy anointed body to the cure
Of those physicians that first wounded thee.
A thousand flatterers sit within thy crown,   100
Whose compass is no bigger than thy head,
And yet, encagèd in so small a verge,
The waste is no whit lesser than thy land.
O, had thy grandsire with a prophet's eye
Seen how his son's son should destroy his sons,   105
From forth thy reach he would have laid thy shame,
Deposing thee before thou wert possessed,
Which art possessed now to depose thyself.
Why, cousin, wert thou regent of the world
It were a shame to let this land by lease.   110
But, for thy world, enjoying but this land,
Is it not more than shame to shame it so?
Landlord of England art thou now, not king.
Thy state of law is bondslave to the law,
And—   115

KING RICHARD
And thou, a lunatic lean-witted fool,
Presuming on an ague's privilege,
Dar'st with thy frozen admonition
Make pale our cheek, chasing the royal blood

With fury from his native residence.   120
Now by my seat's right royal majesty,
Wert thou not brother to great Edward's son,
This tongue that runs so roundly in thy head
Should run thy head from thy unreverent shoulders.

JOHN OF GAUNT
O, spare me not, my brother Edward's son,   125
For that I was his father Edward's son.
That blood already, like the pelican,
Hast thou tapped out and drunkenly caroused.
My brother Gloucester, plain well-meaning soul—
Whom fair befall in heaven 'mongst happy souls—   130
May be a precedent and witness good
That thou respect'st not spilling Edward's blood.
Join with the present sickness that I have,
And thy unkindness be like crookèd age,
To crop at once a too-long withered flower.   135
Live in thy shame, but die not shame with thee.
These words hereafter thy tormentors be.
(To attendants) Convey me to my bed, then to my
grave.
Love they to live that love and honour have.
                    Exit, ⌈carried in the chair⌉

KING RICHARD
And let them die that age and sullens have,   140
For both hast thou, and both become the grave.

YORK
I do beseech your majesty impute his words
To wayward sickliness and age in him.
He loves you, on my life, and holds you dear
As Harry Duke of Hereford, were he here.   145

KING RICHARD
Right, you say true: as Hereford's love, so his.
As theirs, so mine; and all be as it is.
                Enter the Earl of Northumberland

NORTHUMBERLAND
My liege, old Gaunt commends him to your majesty.

KING RICHARD
What says he?

NORTHUMBERLAND Nay, nothing: all is said.
His tongue is now a stringless instrument.   150
Words, life, and all, old Lancaster hath spent.

YORK
Be York the next that must be bankrupt so!
Though death be poor, it ends a mortal woe.

KING RICHARD
The ripest fruit first falls, and so doth he.
His time is spent; our pilgrimage must be.   155
So much for that. Now for our Irish wars.
We must supplant those rough rug-headed kerns,
Which live like venom where no venom else
But only they have privilege to live.
And for these great affairs do ask some charge,   160
Towards our assistance we do seize to us
The plate, coin, revenues, and movables
Whereof our uncle Gaunt did stand possessed.

YORK
How long shall I be patient? Ah, how long
Shall tender duty make me suffer wrong?   165

Not Gloucester's death, nor Hereford's banishment,
Nor Gaunt's rebukes, nor England's private wrongs,
Nor the prevention of poor Bolingbroke
About his marriage, nor my own disgrace,
Have ever made me sour my patient cheek,   170
Or bend one wrinkle on my sovereign's face.
I am the last of noble Edward's sons,
Of whom thy father, Prince of Wales, was first.
In war was never lion raged more fierce,
In peace was never gentle lamb more mild,   175
Than was that young and princely gentleman.
His face thou hast, for even so looked he,
Accomplished with the number of thy hours.
But when he frowned it was against the French,
And not against his friends. His noble hand   180
Did win what he did spend, and spent not that
Which his triumphant father's hand had won.
His hands were guilty of no kindred blood,
But bloody with the enemies of his kin.
O, Richard, York is too far gone with grief,   185
Or else he never would compare between.

KING RICHARD
Why uncle, what's the matter?

YORK   O my liege,
Pardon me if you please; if not, I, pleased
Not to be pardoned, am content withal.
Seek you to seize and grip into your hands   190
The royalties and rights of banished Hereford?
Is not Gaunt dead? And doth not Hereford live?
Was not Gaunt just? And is not Harry true?
Did not the one deserve to have an heir?
Is not his heir a well-deserving son?   195
Take Hereford's rights away, and take from Time
His charters and his customary rights:
Let not tomorrow then ensue today;
Be not thyself, for how art thou a king
But by fair sequence and succession?   200
Now afore God—God forbid I say true!—
If you do wrongfully seize Hereford's rights,
Call in the letters patents that he hath
By his attorneys general to sue
His livery, and deny his offered homage,   205
You pluck a thousand dangers on your head,
You lose a thousand well-disposèd hearts,
And prick my tender patience to those thoughts
Which honour and allegiance cannot think.

KING RICHARD
Think what you will, we seize into our hands   210
His plate, his goods, his money, and his lands.

YORK
I'll not be by the while. My liege, farewell.
What will ensue hereof there's none can tell.
But by bad courses may be understood
That their events can never fall out good.   Exit

KING RICHARD
Go, Bushy, to the Earl of Wiltshire straight.   216
Bid him repair to us to Ely House
To see this business. Tomorrow next
We will for Ireland, and 'tis time, I trow.

And we create, in absence of ourself,   220
Our uncle York Lord Governor of England;
For he is just and always loved us well.—
Come on, our Queen; tomorrow must we part.
Be merry, for our time of stay is short.
> [*Flourish.*] *Exeunt [Bushy at one door; King
> Richard, the Queen, Aumerle, Green, and
> Bagot at another door]. Northumberland,
> Willoughby, and Ross remain*

NORTHUMBERLAND
Well, lords, the Duke of Lancaster is dead.   225
ROSS
And living too, for now his son is Duke.
WILLOUGHBY
Barely in title, not in revenues.
NORTHUMBERLAND
Richly in both, if justice had her right.
ROSS
My heart is great, but it must break with silence
Ere't be disburdened with a liberal tongue.   230
NORTHUMBERLAND
Nay, speak thy mind, and let him ne'er speak more
That speaks thy words again to do thee harm.
WILLOUGHBY
Tends that that thou wouldst speak to the Duke of
    Hereford?
If it be so, out with it boldly, man.
Quick is mine ear to hear of good towards him.   235
ROSS
No good at all that I can do for him,
Unless you call it good to pity him,
Bereft and gelded of his patrimony.
NORTHUMBERLAND
Now afore God, 'tis shame such wrongs are borne
In him, a royal prince, and many more   240
Of noble blood in this declining land.
The King is not himself, but basely led
By flatterers; and what they will inform
Merely in hate 'gainst any of us all,
That will the King severely prosecute   245
'Gainst us, our lives, our children, and our heirs.
ROSS
The commons hath he pilled with grievous taxes,
And quite lost their hearts. The nobles hath he fined
For ancient quarrels, and quite lost their hearts.
WILLOUGHBY
And daily new exactions are devised,   250
As blanks, benevolences, and I wot not what.
But what, a' God's name, doth become of this?
NORTHUMBERLAND
Wars hath not wasted it; for warred he hath not,
But basely yielded upon compromise
That which his ancestors achieved with blows.   255
More hath he spent in peace than they in wars.
ROSS
The Earl of Wiltshire hath the realm in farm.
WILLOUGHBY
The King's grown bankrupt like a broken man.

NORTHUMBERLAND
Reproach and dissolution hangeth over him.
ROSS
He hath not money for these Irish wars,   260
His burdenous taxations notwithstanding,
But by the robbing of the banished Duke.
NORTHUMBERLAND
His noble kinsman. Most degenerate King!
But, lords, we hear this fearful tempest sing,
Yet seek no shelter to avoid the storm.   265
We see the wind sit sore upon our sails,
And yet we strike not, but securely perish.
ROSS
We see the very wreck that we must suffer,
And unavoided is the danger now
For suffering so the causes of our wreck.   270
NORTHUMBERLAND
Not so: even through the hollow eyes of death
I spy life peering; but I dare not say
How near the tidings of our comfort is.
WILLOUGHBY
Nay, let us share thy thoughts, as thou dost ours.
ROSS
Be confident to speak, Northumberland.   275
We three are but thyself, and, speaking so,
Thy words are but as thoughts. Therefore be bold.
NORTHUMBERLAND
Then thus. I have from Port le Blanc,
A bay in Brittaine, received intelligence
That Harry Duke of Hereford, Reinold Lord Cobham,
Thomas son and heir to the Earl of Arundel   281
That late broke from the Duke of Exeter,
His brother, Archbishop late of Canterbury,
Sir Thomas Erpingham, Sir Thomas Ramston,
Sir John Norbery,   285
Sir Robert Waterton, and Francis Coint,
All these well furnished by the Duke of Brittaine
With eight tall ships, three thousand men of war,
Are making hither with all due expedience,
And shortly mean to touch our northern shore.   290
Perhaps they had ere this, but that they stay
The first departing of the King for Ireland.
If then we shall shake off our slavish yoke,
Imp out our drooping country's broken wing,
Redeem from broking pawn the blemished crown,   295
Wipe off the dust that hides our sceptre's gilt,
And make high majesty look like itself,
Away with me in post to Ravenspurgh.
But if you faint, as fearing to do so,
Stay, and be secret, and myself will go.   300
ROSS
To horse, to horse! Urge doubts to them that fear.
WILLOUGHBY
Hold out my horse, and I will first be there.   *Exeunt*

2.2   *Enter the Queen, Bushy, and Bagot*
BUSHY
Madam, your majesty is too much sad.

You promised when you parted with the King
To lay aside life-harming heaviness
And entertain a cheerful disposition.

QUEEN
To please the King I did; to please myself 5
I cannot do it. Yet I know no cause
Why I should welcome such a guest as grief,
Save bidding farewell to so sweet a guest
As my sweet Richard. Yet again, methinks
Some unborn sorrow, ripe in fortune's womb, 10
Is coming towards me; and my inward soul
At nothing trembles. With something it grieves
More than with parting from my lord the King.

BUSHY
Each substance of a grief hath twenty shadows
Which shows like grief itself but is not so. 15
For sorrow's eye, glazèd with blinding tears,
Divides one thing entire to many objects—
Like perspectives, which, rightly gazed upon,
Show nothing but confusion; eyed awry,
Distinguish form. So your sweet majesty, 20
Looking awry upon your lord's departure,
Find shapes of grief more than himself to wail,
Which, looked on as it is, is naught but shadows
Of what it is not. Then, thrice-gracious Queen,
More than your lord's departure weep not: more is
     not seen, 25
Or if it be, 'tis with false sorrow's eye,
Which for things true weeps things imaginary.

QUEEN
It may be so, but yet my inward soul
Persuades me it is otherwise. Howe'er it be,
I cannot but be sad: so heavy-sad 30
As thought—on thinking on no thought I think—
Makes me with heavy nothing faint and shrink.

BUSHY
'Tis nothing but conceit, my gracious lady.

QUEEN
'Tis nothing less: conceit is still derived
From some forefather grief; mine is not so; 35
For nothing hath begot my something grief—
Or something hath the nothing that I grieve—
'Tis in reversion that I do possess—
But what it is that is not yet known what,
I cannot name; 'tis nameless woe, I wot. 40
     Enter Green

GREEN
God save your majesty, and well met, gentlemen.
I hope the King is not yet shipped for Ireland.

QUEEN
Why hop'st thou so? 'Tis better hope he is,
For his designs crave haste, his haste good hope.
Then wherefore dost thou hope he is not shipped? 45

GREEN
That he, our hope, might have retired his power,
And driven into despair an enemy's hope,
Who strongly hath set footing in this land.
The banished Bolingbroke repeals himself,

And with uplifted arms is safe arrived 50
At Ravenspurgh.

QUEEN   Now God in heaven forbid!

GREEN
Ah madam, 'tis too true! And, that is worse,
The Lord Northumberland, his son young Harry Percy,
The Lords of Ross, Beaumont, and Willoughby,
With all their powerful friends, are fled to him. 55

BUSHY
Why have you not proclaimed Northumberland,
And all the rest, revolted faction-traitors?

GREEN
We have; whereupon the Earl of Worcester
Hath broke his staff, resigned his stewardship,
And all the household servants fled with him 60
To Bolingbroke.

QUEEN
So, Green, thou art the midwife to my woe,
And Bolingbroke my sorrow's dismal heir.
Now hath my soul brought forth her prodigy,
And I, a gasping new-delivered mother, 65
Have woe to woe, sorrow to sorrow joined.

BUSHY
Despair not, madam.

QUEEN   Who shall hinder me?
I will despair, and be at enmity
With cozening hope. He is a flatterer,
A parasite, a keeper-back of death, 70
Who gently would dissolve the bonds of life,
Which false hope lingers in extremity.
     Enter the Duke of York, ⌈wearing a gorget⌉

GREEN Here comes the Duke of York.

QUEEN
With signs of war about his agèd neck.
O, full of careful business are his looks! 75
Uncle, for God's sake speak comfortable words.

YORK
Should I do so, I should belie my thoughts.
Comfort's in heaven, and we are on the earth,
Where nothing lives but crosses, cares, and grief.
Your husband, he is gone to save far off, 80
Whilst others come to make him lose at home.
Here am I, left to underprop his land,
Who, weak with age, cannot support myself.
Now comes the sick hour that his surfeit made.
Now shall he try his friends that flattered him. 85
     Enter a Servingman

SERVINGMAN
My lord, your son was gone before I came.

YORK
He was? Why so, go all which way it will.
The nobles they are fled. The commons they are cold,
And will, I fear, revolt on Hereford's side.
Sirrah, get thee to Pleshey, to my sister Gloucester. 90
Bid her send me presently a thousand pound—
Hold; take my ring.

SERVINGMAN
My lord, I had forgot to tell your lordship,

Today as I came by I callèd there—
But I shall grieve you to report the rest.   95
YORK What is't, knave?
SERVINGMAN
An hour before I came, the Duchess died.
YORK
God for his mercy, what a tide of woes
Comes rushing on this woeful land at once!
I know not what to do. I would to God,   100
So my untruth had not provoked him to it,
The King had cut off my head with my brother's.
What, are there no posts dispatched for Ireland?
How shall we do for money for these wars?
(To the Queen) Come, sister—cousin, I would say; pray
    pardon me.   105
(To the Servingman) Go, fellow, get thee home. Provide
    some carts,
And bring away the armour that is there.
                        ⌜Exit Servingman⌝
Gentlemen, will you go muster men?
If I know how or which way to order these affairs
Thus disorderly thrust into my hands,   110
Never believe me. Both are my kinsmen.
T'one is my sovereign, whom both my oath
And duty bids defend; t'other again
Is my kinsman, whom the King hath wronged,
Whom conscience and my kindred bids to right.   115
Well, somewhat we must do. (To the Queen) Come,
    cousin,
I'll dispose of you.—
Gentlemen, go muster up your men,
And meet me presently at Berkeley Castle.
I should to Pleshey too, but time will not permit.   120
All is uneven,
And everything is left at six and seven.
       Exeunt the Duke of York and the Queen. Bushy,
                   Bagot, and Green remain
BUSHY
The wind sits fair for news to go for Ireland,
But none returns. For us to levy power
Proportionable to the enemy   125
Is all unpossible.
GREEN
Besides, our nearness to the King in love
Is near the hate of those love not the King.
BAGOT
And that is the wavering commons; for their love
Lies in their purses, and whoso empties them   130
By so much fills their hearts with deadly hate.
BUSHY
Wherein the King stands generally condemned.
BAGOT
If judgement lie in them, then so do we,
Because we ever have been near the King.
GREEN
Well, I will for refuge straight to Bristol Castle.   135
The Earl of Wiltshire is already there.

BUSHY
Thither will I with you; for little office
Will the hateful commoners perform for us,
Except like curs to tear us all to pieces.
(To Bagot) Will you go along with us?   140
BAGOT
No, I will to Ireland, to his majesty.
Farewell: if heart's presages be not vain
We three here part that ne'er shall meet again.
BUSHY
That's as York thrives to beat back Bolingbroke.
GREEN
Alas, poor Duke, the task he undertakes   145
Is numb'ring sands and drinking oceans dry.
Where one on his side fights, thousands will fly.
⌜BAGOT⌝
Farewell at once, for once, for all and ever.
BUSHY
Well, we may meet again.
BAGOT   I fear me never.
       Exeunt ⌜Bushy and Green at one door, and
                   Bagot at another door⌝

2.3   *Enter Bolingbroke Duke of Lancaster and Hereford,*
        and the Earl of Northumberland
BOLINGBROKE
How far is it, my lord, to Berkeley now?
NORTHUMBERLAND Believe me, noble lord,
I am a stranger here in Gloucestershire.
These high wild hills and rough uneven ways
Draws out our miles and makes them wearisome;   5
And yet your fair discourse hath been as sugar,
Making the hard way sweet and delectable.
But I bethink me what a weary way
From Ravenspurgh to Cotswold will be found
In Ross and Willoughby, wanting your company,   10
Which I protest hath very much beguiled
The tediousness and process of my travel.
But theirs is sweetened with the hope to have
The present benefit which I possess;
And hope to joy is little less in joy   15
Than hope enjoyed. By this the weary lords
Shall make their way seem short as mine hath done
By sight of what I have: your noble company.
BOLINGBROKE
Of much less value is my company
Than your good words.
      Enter Harry Percy
                But who comes here?   20
NORTHUMBERLAND
It is my son, young Harry Percy,
Sent from my brother Worcester, whencesoever.
Harry, how fares your uncle?
HARRY PERCY
I had thought, my lord, to have learned his health of
    you.
NORTHUMBERLAND Why, is he not with the Queen?   25

HARRY PERCY
No, my good lord; he hath forsook the court,
Broken his staff of office, and dispersed
The household of the King.
NORTHUMBERLAND   What was his reason?
He was not so resolved when last we spake together.
HARRY PERCY
Because your lordship was proclaimèd traitor.   30
But he, my lord, is gone to Ravenspurgh
To offer service to the Duke of Hereford,
And sent me over by Berkeley to discover
What power the Duke of York had levied there,
Then with directions to repair to Ravenspurgh.   35
NORTHUMBERLAND
Have you forgot the Duke of Hereford, boy?
HARRY PERCY
No, my good lord, for that is not forgot
Which ne'er I did remember. To my knowledge,
I never in my life did look on him.
NORTHUMBERLAND
Then learn to know him now. This is the Duke.   40
HARRY PERCY
My gracious lord, I tender you my service,
Such as it is, being tender, raw, and young,
Which elder days shall ripen and confirm
To more approvèd service and desert.
BOLINGBROKE
I thank thee, gentle Percy, and be sure   45
I count myself in nothing else so happy
As in a soul rememb'ring my good friends;
And as my fortune ripens with thy love,
It shall be still thy true love's recompense.
My heart this covenant makes; my hand thus seals it.
He gives Percy his hand
NORTHUMBERLAND
How far is it to Berkeley, and what stir   51
Keeps good old York there with his men of war?
HARRY PERCY
There stands the castle, by yon tuft of trees,
Manned with three hundred men, as I have heard,
And in it are the Lords of York, Berkeley, and
    Seymour,
None else of name and noble estimate.   55
Enter Lord Ross and Lord Willoughby
NORTHUMBERLAND
Here come the Lords of Ross and Willoughby,
Bloody with spurring, fiery red with haste.
BOLINGBROKE
Welcome, my lords. I wot your love pursues
A banished traitor. All my treasury   60
Is yet but unfelt thanks, which, more enriched,
Shall be your love and labour's recompense.
ROSS
Your presence makes us rich, most noble lord.
WILLOUGHBY
And far surmounts our labour to attain it.
BOLINGBROKE
Evermore thank's the exchequer of the poor,   65

Which till my infant fortune comes to years
Stands for my bounty.
Enter Berkeley
                                But who comes here?
NORTHUMBERLAND
It is my lord of Berkeley, as I guess.
BERKELEY
My lord of Hereford, my message is to you.
BOLINGBROKE
My lord, my answer is to 'Lancaster',   70
And I am come to seek that name in England,
And I must find that title in your tongue
Before I make reply to aught you say.
BERKELEY
Mistake me not, my lord, 'tis not my meaning
To raze one title of your honour out.   75
To you, my lord, I come—what lord you will—
From the most gracious regent of this land,
The Duke of York, to know what pricks you on
To take advantage of the absent time
And fright our native peace with self-borne arms.   80
Enter the Duke of York
BOLINGBROKE
I shall not need transport my words by you.
Here comes his grace in person.—My noble uncle!
He kneels
YORK
Show me thy humble heart, and not thy knee,
Whose duty is deceivable and false.
BOLINGBROKE My gracious uncle—   85
YORK
Tut, tut, grace me no grace, nor uncle me no uncle.
I am no traitor's uncle, and that word 'grace'
In an ungracious mouth is but profane.
Why have those banished and forbidden legs
Dared once to touch a dust of England's ground?   90
But then more 'why': why have they dared to march
So many miles upon her peaceful bosom,
Frighting her pale-faced villages with war
And ostentation of despisèd arms?
Com'st thou because the anointed King is hence?   95
Why, foolish boy, the King is left behind,
And in my loyal bosom lies his power.
Were I but now the lord of such hot youth
As when brave Gaunt, thy father, and myself
Rescued the Black Prince, that young Mars of men, 100
From forth the ranks of many thousand French,
O then how quickly should this arm of mine,
Now prisoner to the palsy, chastise thee
And minister correction to thy fault!
BOLINGBROKE
My gracious uncle, let me know my fault.   105
On what condition stands it and wherein?
YORK
Even in condition of the worst degree:
In gross rebellion and detested treason.
Thou art a banished man, and here art come

Before the expiration of thy time   110
In braving arms against thy sovereign.
BOLINGBROKE ⌈standing⌉
As I was banished, I was banished Hereford;
But as I come, I come for Lancaster.
And, noble uncle, I beseech your grace,
Look on my wrongs with an indifferent eye.   115
You are my father, for methinks in you
I see old Gaunt alive. O then, my father,
Will you permit that I shall stand condemned
A wandering vagabond, my rights and royalties
Plucked from my arms perforce and given away   120
To upstart unthrifts? Wherefore was I born?
If that my cousin King be King in England,
It must be granted I am Duke of Lancaster.
You have a son, Aumerle my noble kinsman.
Had you first died and he been thus trod down,   125
He should have found his uncle Gaunt a father
To rouse his wrongs and chase them to the bay.
I am denied to sue my livery here,
And yet my letters patents give me leave.
My father's goods are all distrained and sold,   130
And these and all are all amiss employed.
What would you have me do? I am a subject,
And I challenge law; attorneys are denied me;
And therefore personally I lay my claim
To my inheritance of free descent.   135
NORTHUMBERLAND
The noble Duke hath been too much abused.
ROSS
It stands your grace upon to do him right.
WILLOUGHBY
Base men by his endowments are made great.
YORK
My lords of England, let me tell you this.
I have had feeling of my cousin's wrongs,   140
And laboured all I could to do him right.
But in this kind to come, in braving arms,
Be his own carver, and cut out his way
To find out right with wrong—it may not be.
And you that do abet him in this kind   145
Cherish rebellion, and are rebels all.
NORTHUMBERLAND
The noble Duke hath sworn his coming is
But for his own, and for the right of that
We all have strongly sworn to give him aid;
And let him never see joy that breaks that oath.   150
YORK
Well, well, I see the issue of these arms.
I cannot mend it, I must needs confess,
Because my power is weak and all ill-left.
But if I could, by Him that gave me life,
I would attach you all, and make you stoop   155
Unto the sovereign mercy of the King.
But since I cannot, be it known to you
I do remain as neuter. So fare you well—
Unless you please to enter in the castle
And there repose you for this night.   160

BOLINGBROKE   110
An offer, uncle, that we will accept.
But we must win your grace to go with us
To Bristol Castle, which they say is held
By Bushy, Bagot, and their complices,
The caterpillars of the commonwealth,   165
Which I have sworn to weed and pluck away.
YORK
It may be I will go with you—but yet I'll pause,
For I am loath to break our country's laws.
Nor friends nor foes, to me welcome you are.
Things past redress are now with me past care.   170
                                                                      Exeunt

2.4   Enter the Earl of Salisbury and a Welsh Captain
WELSH CAPTAIN
My lord of Salisbury, we have stayed ten days,
And hardly kept our countrymen together,
And yet we hear no tidings from the King.
Therefore we will disperse ourselves. Farewell.
SALISBURY
Stay yet another day, thou trusty Welshman.   5
The King reposeth all his confidence in thee.
WELSH CAPTAIN
'Tis thought the King is dead. We will not stay.
The bay trees in our country are all withered,
And meteors fright the fixèd stars of heaven.
The pale-faced moon looks bloody on the earth,   10
And lean-looked prophets whisper fearful change.
Rich men look sad, and ruffians dance and leap;
The one in fear to lose what they enjoy,
The other to enjoy by rage and war.
These signs forerun the death or fall of kings.   15
Farewell. Our countrymen are gone and fled,
As well assured Richard their king is dead.   Exit
SALISBURY
Ah, Richard! With the eyes of heavy mind
I see thy glory, like a shooting star,
Fall to the base earth from the firmament.   20
Thy sun sets weeping in the lowly west,
Witnessing storms to come, woe, and unrest.
Thy friends are fled to wait upon thy foes,
And crossly to thy good all fortune goes.   Exit

3.1   Enter Bolingbroke Duke of Lancaster and Hereford,
        the Duke of York, the Earl of Northumberland,
        ⌈Lord Ross, Harry Percy, and Lord Willoughby⌉
BOLINGBROKE Bring forth these men.
        Enter Bushy and Green, guarded as prisoners
Bushy and Green, I will not vex your souls,
Since presently your souls must part your bodies,
With too much urging your pernicious lives,
For 'twere no charity. Yet to wash your blood   5
From off my hands, here in the view of men
I will unfold some causes of your deaths.
You have misled a prince, a royal king,
A happy gentleman in blood and lineaments,
By you unhappied and disfigured clean.   10

You have, in manner, with your sinful hours
Made a divorce betwixt his queen and him,
Broke the possession of a royal bed,
And stained the beauty of a fair queen's cheeks
With tears drawn from her eyes by your foul wrongs.
Myself—a prince by fortune of my birth,   16
Near to the King in blood, and near in love
Till you did make him misinterpret me—
Have stooped my neck under your injuries,
And sighed my English breath in foreign clouds,   20
Eating the bitter bread of banishment,
Whilst you have fed upon my signories,
Disparked my parks and felled my forest woods,
From my own windows torn my household coat,
Razed out my imprese, leaving me no sign,   25
Save men's opinions and my living blood,
To show the world I am a gentleman.
This and much more, much more than twice all this,
Condemns you to the death.—See them delivered over
To execution and the hand of death.   30
BUSHY
More welcome is the stroke of death to me
Than Bolingbroke to England.
GREEN
My comfort is that heaven will take our souls,
And plague injustice with the pains of hell.
BOLINGBROKE
My lord Northumberland, see them dispatched.   35
        Exit Northumberland, with Bushy and Green,
                                        guarded
Uncle, you say the Queen is at your house.
For God's sake, fairly let her be intreated.
Tell her I send to her my kind commends.
Take special care my greetings be delivered.
YORK
A gentleman of mine I have dispatched   40
With letters of your love to her at large.
BOLINGBROKE
Thanks, gentle uncle.—Come, lords, away,
To fight with Glyndŵr and his complices.
A while to work, and after, holiday.   *Exeunt*

3.2   ⌈*Flourish.*⌉ *Enter King Richard, the Duke of*
       Aumerle, the Bishop of Carlisle, and ⌈*soldiers, with*
       drum and colours⌉
KING RICHARD
Harlechly Castle call they this at hand?
AUMERLE
Yea, my lord. How brooks your grace the air
After your late tossing on the breaking seas?
KING RICHARD
Needs must I like it well. I weep for joy
To stand upon my kingdom once again.   5
        He touches the ground
Dear earth, I do salute thee with my hand,
Though rebels wound thee with their horses' hoofs.
As a long-parted mother with her child
Plays fondly with her tears, and smiles in meeting,

So, weeping, smiling, greet I thee my earth,   10
And do thee favours with my royal hands.
Feed not thy sovereign's foe, my gentle earth,
Nor with thy sweets comfort his ravenous sense;
But let thy spiders that suck up thy venom
And heavy-gaited toads lie in their way,   15
Doing annoyance to the treacherous feet
Which with usurping steps do trample thee.
Yield stinging nettles to mine enemies,
And when they from thy bosom pluck a flower
Guard it, I pray thee, with a lurking adder,   20
Whose double tongue may with a mortal touch
Throw death upon thy sovereign's enemies.—
Mock not my senseless conjuration, lords.
This earth shall have a feeling, and these stones
Prove armèd soldiers, ere her native king   25
Shall falter under foul rebellion's arms.
BISHOP OF CARLISLE
Fear not, my lord. That power that made you king
Hath power to keep you king in spite of all.
AUMERLE
He means, my lord, that we are too remiss,
Whilst Bolingbroke, through our security,   30
Grows strong and great in substance and in friends.
KING RICHARD
Discomfortable cousin, know'st thou not
That when the searching eye of heaven is hid
Behind the globe, that lights the lower world,
Then thieves and robbers range abroad unseen   35
In murders and in outrage bloody here;
But when from under this terrestrial ball
He fires the proud tops of the eastern pines,
And darts his light through every guilty hole,
Then murders, treasons, and detested sins,   40
The cloak of night being plucked from off their backs,
Stand bare and naked, trembling at themselves?
So when this thief, this traitor, Bolingbroke,
Who all this while hath revelled in the night
Whilst we were wand'ring with the Antipodes,   45
Shall see us rising in our throne, the east,
His treasons will sit blushing in his face,
Not able to endure the sight of day,
But, self-affrighted, tremble at his sin.
Not all the water in the rough rude sea   50
Can wash the balm from an anointed king.
The breath of worldly men cannot depose
The deputy elected by the Lord.
For every man that Bolingbroke hath pressed
To lift shrewd steel against our golden crown,   55
God for his Richard hath in heavenly pay
A glorious angel. Then if angels fight,
Weak men must fall; for heaven still guards the right.
        Enter the Earl of Salisbury
Welcome, my lord. How far off lies your power?
SALISBURY
Nor nea'er nor farther off, my gracious lord,   60
Than this weak arm. Discomfort guides my tongue,

And bids me speak of nothing but despair.
One day too late, I fear me, noble lord,
Hath clouded all thy happy days on earth.
O, call back yesterday, bid time return,   65
And thou shalt have twelve thousand fighting men.
Today, today, unhappy day too late,
Overthrows thy joys, friends, fortune, and thy state;
For all the Welshmen, hearing thou wert dead,
Are gone to Bolingbroke, dispersed, and fled.   70
AUMERLE
Comfort, my liege. Why looks your grace so pale?
KING RICHARD
But now the blood of twenty thousand men
    Did triumph in my face, and they are fled;
And till so much blood thither come again
    Have I not reason to look pale and dead?   75
All souls that will be safe fly from my side,
For time hath set a blot upon my pride.
AUMERLE
Comfort, my liege. Remember who you are.
KING RICHARD
I had forgot myself. Am I not King?
Awake, thou sluggard majesty, thou sleep'st!   80
Is not the King's name forty thousand names?
Arm, arm, my name! A puny subject strikes
At thy great glory. Look not to the ground,
Ye favourites of a king: are we not high?
High be our thoughts. I know my uncle York   85
Hath power enough to serve our turn.
        Enter Scrope
                            But who comes here?
SCROPE
More health and happiness betide my liege
Than can my care-tuned tongue deliver him.
KING RICHARD
Mine ear is open and my heart prepared.
The worst is worldly loss thou canst unfold.   90
Say, is my kingdom lost? Why 'twas my care,
And what loss is it to be rid of care?
Strives Bolingbroke to be as great as we?
Greater he shall not be. If he serve God
We'll serve Him too, and be his fellow so.   95
Revolt our subjects? That we cannot mend.
They break their faith to God as well as us.
Cry woe, destruction, ruin, loss, decay:
The worst is death, and death will have his day.
SCROPE
Glad am I that your highness is so armed   100
To bear the tidings of calamity.
Like an unseasonable stormy day,
Which makes the silver rivers drown their shores
As if the world were all dissolved to tears,
So high above his limits swells the rage   105
Of Bolingbroke, covering your fearful land
With hard bright steel, and hearts harder than steel.
Whitebeards have armed their thin and hairless scalps
Against thy majesty. Boys with women's voices
Strive to speak big, and clap their female joints   110

In stiff unwieldy arms against thy crown.
Thy very beadsmen learn to bend their bows
Of double-fatal yew against thy state.
Yea, distaff-women manage rusty bills
Against thy seat. Both young and old rebel,   115
And all goes worse than I have power to tell.
KING RICHARD
Too well, too well thou tell'st a tale so ill.
Where is the Earl of Wiltshire? Where is Bagot?
What is become of Bushy, where is Green,
That they have let the dangerous enemy   120
Measure our confines with such peaceful steps?
If we prevail, their heads shall pay for it.
I warrant they have made peace with Bolingbroke.
SCROPE
Peace have they made with him indeed, my lord.
KING RICHARD
O villains, vipers damned without redemption!   125
Dogs easily won to fawn on any man!
Snakes in my heart-blood warmed, that sting my
        heart!
Three Judases, each one thrice-worse than Judas!
Would they make peace? Terrible hell make war
Upon their spotted souls for this offence!   130
SCROPE
Sweet love, I see, changing his property,
Turns to the sourest and most deadly hate.
Again uncurse their souls. Their peace is made
With heads, and not with hands. Those whom you
        curse
Have felt the worst of death's destroying wound,   135
And lie full low, graved in the hollow ground.
AUMERLE
Is Bushy, Green, and the Earl of Wiltshire dead?
SCROPE
Ay, all of them at Bristol lost their heads.
AUMERLE
Where is the Duke my father, with his power?
KING RICHARD
No matter where. Of comfort no man speak.   140
Let's talk of graves, of worms and epitaphs,
Make dust our paper, and with rainy eyes
Write sorrow on the bosom of the earth.
Let's choose executors and talk of wills—
And yet not so, for what can we bequeath   145
Save our deposèd bodies to the ground?
Our lands, our lives, and all are Bolingbroke's;
And nothing can we call our own but death,
And that small model of the barren earth
Which serves as paste and cover to our bones.   150
⌈*Sitting*⌉ For God's sake, let us sit upon the ground,
And tell sad stories of the death of kings—
How some have been deposed, some slain in war,
Some haunted by the ghosts they have deposed,
Some poisoned by their wives, some sleeping killed, 155
All murdered. For within the hollow crown
That rounds the mortal temples of a king
Keeps Death his court; and there the antic sits,

Scoffing his state and grinning at his pomp,
Allowing him a breath, a little scene,   160
To monarchize, be feared, and kill with looks,
Infusing him with self and vain conceit,
As if this flesh which walls about our life
Were brass impregnable; and humoured thus,
Comes at the last, and with a little pin   165
Bores through his castle wall; and farewell, king.
Cover your heads, and mock not flesh and blood
With solemn reverence. Throw away respect,
Tradition, form, and ceremonious duty,
For you have but mistook me all this while.   170
I live with bread, like you; feel want,
Taste grief, need friends. Subjected thus,
How can you say to me I am a king?

BISHOP OF CARLISLE
My lord, wise men ne'er wail their present woes,
But presently prevent the ways to wail.   175
To fear the foe, since fear oppresseth strength,
Gives in your weakness strength unto your foe;
And so your follies fight against yourself.
Fear, and be slain. No worse can come to fight;
And fight and die is death destroying death,   180
Where fearing dying pays death servile breath.

AUMERLE
My father hath a power. Enquire of him,
And learn to make a body of a limb.

KING RICHARD ⌈standing⌉
Thou chid'st me well. Proud Bolingbroke, I come
To change blows with thee for our day of doom.   185
This ague-fit of fear is overblown.
An easy task it is to win our own.
Say, Scrope, where lies our uncle with his power?
Speak sweetly, man, although thy looks be sour.

SCROPE
Men judge by the complexion of the sky   190
    The state and inclination of the day.
So may you by my dull and heavy eye
    My tongue hath but a heavier tale to say.
I play the torturer by small and small
To lengthen out the worst that must be spoken.   195
Your uncle York is joined with Bolingbroke,
And all your northern castles yielded up,
And all your southern gentlemen in arms
Upon his faction.

KING RICHARD   Thou hast said enough.
(To Aumerle) Beshrew thee, cousin, which didst lead
    me forth   200
Of that sweet way I was in to despair.
What say you now? What comfort have we now?
By heaven, I'll hate him everlastingly
That bids me be of comfort any more.
Go to Flint Castle; there I'll pine away.   205
A king, woe's slave, shall kingly woe obey.
That power I have, discharge, and let them go
To ear the land that hath some hope to grow;
For I have none. Let no man speak again
To alter this, for counsel is but vain.   210

AUMERLE
My liege, one word.

KING RICHARD   He does me double wrong
That wounds me with the flatteries of his tongue.
Discharge my followers. Let them hence away
From Richard's night to Bolingbroke's fair day.
                                                            Exeunt

3.3   *Enter Bolingbroke Duke of Lancaster and Hereford,*
           the Duke of York, the Earl of Northumberland,
           ⌈and soldiers, with drum and colours⌉

BOLINGBROKE
So that by this intelligence we learn
The Welshmen are dispersed, and Salisbury
Is gone to meet the King, who lately landed
With some few private friends upon this coast.

NORTHUMBERLAND
The news is very fair and good, my lord.   5
Richard not far from hence hath hid his head.

YORK
It would beseem the Lord Northumberland
To say 'King Richard'. Alack the heavy day
When such a sacred king should hide his head!

NORTHUMBERLAND
Your grace mistakes. Only to be brief   10
Left I his title out.

YORK   The time hath been,
Would you have been so brief with him, he would
Have been so brief with you to shorten you,
For taking so the head, your whole head's length.

BOLINGBROKE
Mistake not, uncle, further than you should.   15

YORK
Take not, good cousin, further than you should,
Lest you mistake the heavens are over our heads.

BOLINGBROKE
I know it, uncle, and oppose not myself
Against their will.
       Enter Harry Percy ⌈and a trumpeter⌉
                     But who comes here?
Welcome, Harry. What, will not this castle yield?   20

HARRY PERCY
The castle royally is manned, my lord,
Against thy entrance.

BOLINGBROKE   Royally?
Why, it contains no king.

HARRY PERCY   Yes, my good lord,
It doth contain a king. King Richard lies
Within the limits of yon lime and stone,   25
And with him are the Lord Aumerle, Lord Salisbury,
Sir Stephen Scrope, besides a clergyman
Of holy reverence; who, I cannot learn.

NORTHUMBERLAND
O, belike it is the Bishop of Carlisle.

BOLINGBROKE (to Northumberland) Noble lord,   30
Go to the rude ribs of that ancient castle;
Through brazen trumpet send the breath of parley
Into his ruined ears, and thus deliver.

Henry Bolingbroke
Upon his knees doth kiss King Richard's hand,　35
And sends allegiance and true faith of heart
To his most royal person, hither come
Even at his feet to lay my arms and power,
Provided that my banishment repealed
And lands restored again be freely granted.　40
If not, I'll use the advantage of my power,
And lay the summer's dust with showers of blood
Rained from the wounds of slaughtered Englishmen;
The which how far off from the mind of Bolingbroke
It is such crimson tempest should bedrench　45
The fresh green lap of fair King Richard's land,
My stooping duty tenderly shall show.
Go, signify as much, while here we march
Upon the grassy carpet of this plain.
Let's march without the noise of threat'ning drum,　50
That from this castle's tottered battlements
Our fair appointments may be well perused.
Methinks King Richard and myself should meet
With no less terror than the elements
Of fire and water when their thund'ring shock　55
At meeting tears the cloudy cheeks of heaven.
Be he the fire, I'll be the yielding water.
The rage be his, whilst on the earth I rain
My waters: on the earth, and not on him.—
March on, and mark King Richard, how he looks.　60
　　They march about the stage; then Bolingbroke,
　　York, Percy, and soldiers stand at a distance from
　　the walls; Northumberland and trumpeter advance
　　to the walls. The trumpets sound *a parley*
　　without, and an answer within; then a flourish
　　within. King Richard appeareth on the walls, with
　　the Bishop of Carlisle, the Duke of Aumerle,
　　Scrope, and the Earl of Salisbury
See, see, King Richard doth himself appear,
As doth the blushing discontented sun
From out the fiery portal of the east
When he perceives the envious clouds are bent
To dim his glory and to stain the track　65
Of his bright passage to the occident.
YORK
Yet looks he like a king. Behold, his eye,
As bright as is the eagle's, lightens forth
Controlling majesty. Alack, alack for woe
That any harm should stain so fair a show!　70
KING RICHARD (*to Northumberland*)
We are amazed; and thus long have we stood
To watch the fearful bending of thy knee,
Because we thought ourself thy lawful king.
An if we be, how dare thy joints forget
To pay their aweful duty to our presence?　75
If we be not, show us the hand of God
That hath dismissed us from our stewardship.
For well we know no hand of blood and bone
Can grip the sacred handle of our sceptre,
Unless he do profane, steal, or usurp.　80

And though you think that all—as you have done—
Have torn their souls by turning them from us,
And we are barren and bereft of friends,
Yet know my master, God omnipotent,
Is mustering in his clouds on our behalf　85
Armies of pestilence; and they shall strike
Your children yet unborn and unbegot,
That lift your vassal hands against my head
And threat the glory of my precious crown.
Tell Bolingbroke, for yon methinks he is,　90
That every stride he makes upon my land
Is dangerous treason. He is come to open
The purple testament of bleeding war;
But ere the crown he looks for live in peace
Ten thousand bloody crowns of mothers' sons　95
Shall ill become the flower of England's face,
Change the complexion of her maid-pale peace
To scarlet indignation, and bedew
Her pastures' grass with faithful English blood.
NORTHUMBERLAND *kneeling*
The King of heaven forbid our lord the King　100
Should so with civil and uncivil arms
Be rushed upon. Thy thrice-noble cousin
Harry Bolingbroke doth humbly kiss thy hand,
And by the honourable tomb he swears,
That stands upon your royal grandsire's bones,　105
And by the royalties of both your bloods,
Currents that spring from one most gracious head,
And by the buried hand of warlike Gaunt,
And by the worth and honour of himself,
Comprising all that may be sworn or said,　110
His coming hither hath no further scope
Than for his lineal royalties, and to beg
Enfranchisement immediate on his knees;
Which on thy royal party granted once,
His glittering arms he will commend to rust,　115
His barbèd steeds to stables, and his heart
To faithful service of your majesty.
This swears he as he is a prince and just,
And as I am a gentleman I credit him.
KING RICHARD
Northumberland, say thus the King returns:　120
His noble cousin is right welcome hither,
And all the number of his fair demands
Shall be accomplished without contradiction.
With all the gracious utterance thou hast,
Speak to his gentle hearing kind commends.　125
　　Northumberland and the trumpeter return to
　　Bolingbroke
(*To Aumerle*) We do debase ourself, cousin, do we not,
To look so poorly and to speak so fair?
Shall we call back Northumberland, and send
Defiance to the traitor, and so die?
AUMERLE
No, good my lord, let's fight with gentle words　130
Till time lend friends, and friends their helpful swords.
KING RICHARD
O God, O God, that e'er this tongue of mine,

That laid the sentence of dread banishment
On yon proud man, should take it off again
With words of sooth! O, that I were as great   135
As is my grief, or lesser than my name,
Or that I could forget what I have been,
Or not remember what I must be now!
Swell'st thou, proud heart? I'll give thee scope to
    beat,
Since foes have scope to beat both thee and me.   140
    Northumberland advances to the walls
AUMERLE
Northumberland comes back from Bolingbroke.
KING RICHARD
What must the King do now? Must he submit?
The King shall do it. Must he be deposed?
The King shall be contented. Must he lose
The name of King? A God's name, let it go.   145
I'll give my jewels for a set of beads,
My gorgeous palace for a hermitage,
My gay apparel for an almsman's gown,
My figured goblets for a dish of wood,
My sceptre for a palmer's walking staff,   150
My subjects for a pair of carvèd saints,
And my large kingdom for a little grave,
A little, little grave, an obscure grave;
Or I'll be buried in the King's highway,
Some way of common trade where subjects' feet   155
May hourly trample on their sovereign's head,
For on my heart they tread now, whilst I live,
And buried once, why not upon my head?
Aumerle, thou weep'st, my tender-hearted cousin.
We'll make foul weather with despisèd tears.   160
Our sighs and they shall lodge the summer corn,
And make a dearth in this revolting land.
Or shall we play the wantons with our woes,
And make some pretty match with shedding tears;
As thus to drop them still upon one place   165
Till they have fretted us a pair of graves
Within the earth, and therein laid: 'There lies
Two kinsmen digged their graves with weeping eyes.'
Would not this ill do well? Well, well, I see
I talk but idly and you mock at me.   170
Most mighty prince, my lord Northumberland,
What says King Bolingbroke? Will his majesty
Give Richard leave to live till Richard die?
You make a leg, and Bolingbroke says 'Ay'.
NORTHUMBERLAND
My lord, in the base court he doth attend   175
To speak with you. May it please you to come down?
KING RICHARD
Down, down I come like glist'ring Phaethon,
Wanting the manage of unruly jades.
In the base court: base court where kings grow base
To come at traitors' calls, and do them grace.   180
In the base court, come down: down court, down
    King,
For night-owls shriek where mounting larks should
    sing.   *Exeunt King Richard and his party*

Northumberland returns to Bolingbroke
BOLINGBROKE
What says his majesty?
NORTHUMBERLAND   Sorrow and grief of heart
Makes him speak fondly, like a frantic man.
    Enter King Richard ⌈and his party⌉ below
Yet he is come.
BOLINGBROKE   Stand all apart,   185
And show fair duty to his majesty.
    He kneels down
My gracious lord.
KING RICHARD
Fair cousin, you debase your princely knee
To make the base earth proud with kissing it.
Me rather had my heart might feel your love   190
Than my unpleased eye see your courtesy.
Up, cousin, up. Your heart is up, I know,
Thus high at least, although your knee be low.
BOLINGBROKE
My gracious lord, I come but for mine own.
KING RICHARD
Your own is yours, and I am yours, and all.   195
BOLINGBROKE
So far be mine, my most redoubted lord,
As my true service shall deserve your love.
KING RICHARD
Well you deserve. They well deserve to have
That know the strong'st and surest way to get.
    ⌈*Bolingbroke rises*⌉
(*To York*) Uncle, give me your hands. Nay, dry your
    eyes.   200
Tears show their love, but want their remedies.
(*To Bolingbroke*) Cousin, I am too young to be your
    father,
Though you are old enough to be my heir.
What you will have I'll give, and willing too;
For do we must what force will have us do.   205
Set on towards London, cousin: is it so?
BOLINGBROKE
Yea, my good lord.
KING RICHARD   Then I must not say no.
                                        Flourish. Exeunt

3.4   *Enter the Queen, with her two Ladies*
QUEEN
What sport shall we devise here in this garden,
To drive away the heavy thought of care?
⌈FIRST⌉ LADY Madam, we'll play at bowls.
QUEEN
'Twill make me think the world is full of rubs,
And that my fortune runs against the bias.   5
⌈SECOND⌉ LADY Madam, we'll dance.
QUEEN
My legs can keep no measure in delight
When my poor heart no measure keeps in grief;
Therefore no dancing, girl. Some other sport.
⌈FIRST⌉ LADY Madam, we'll tell tales.   10
QUEEN Of sorrow or of joy?

⌈FIRST⌉ LADY Of either, madam.
QUEEN Of neither, girl.
  For if of joy, being altogether wanting,
  It doth remember me the more of sorrow.   15
  Or if of grief, being altogether had,
  It adds more sorrow to my want of joy.
  For what I have I need not to repeat,
  And what I want it boots not to complain.
⌈SECOND⌉ LADY
  Madam, I'll sing.
QUEEN   'Tis well that thou hast cause;   20
  But thou shouldst please me better wouldst thou
      weep.
⌈SECOND⌉ LADY
  I could weep, madam, would it do you good.
QUEEN
  And I could sing, would weeping do me good,
  And never borrow any tear of thee.
          Enter a Gardener and two Men
  But stay; here come the gardeners.   25
  Let's step into the shadow of these trees.
  My wretchedness unto a row of pins
  They will talk of state, for everyone doth so
  Against a change. Woe is forerun with woe.
          The Queen and her Ladies stand apart
GARDENER ⌈*to First Man*⌉
  Go, bind thou up young dangling apricots   30
  Which, like unruly children, make their sire
  Stoop with oppression of their prodigal weight.
  Give some supportance to the bending twigs.
  ⌈*To Second Man*⌉ Go thou, and, like an executioner,
  Cut off the heads of too fast-growing sprays   35
  That look too lofty in our commonwealth.
  All must be even in our government.
  You thus employed, I will go root away
  The noisome weeds which without profit suck
  The soil's fertility from wholesome flowers.   40
⌈FIRST⌉ MAN
  Why should we, in the compass of a pale,
  Keep law and form and due proportion,
  Showing as in a model our firm estate,
  When our sea-wallèd garden, the whole land,
  Is full of weeds, her fairest flowers choked up,   45
  Her fruit trees all unpruned, her hedges ruined,
  Her knots disordered, and her wholesome herbs
  Swarming with caterpillars?
GARDENER   Hold thy peace.
  He that hath suffered this disordered spring
  Hath now himself met with the fall of leaf.   50
  The weeds which his broad spreading leaves did
      shelter,
  That seemed in eating him to hold him up,
  Are plucked up, root and all, by Bolingbroke—
  I mean the Earl of Wiltshire, Bushy, Green.
⌈SECOND⌉ MAN
  What, are they dead?
GARDENER   They are; and Bolingbroke   55
  Hath seized the wasteful King. O, what pity is it

  That he had not so trimmed and dressed his land
  As we this garden! We at time of year
  Do wound the bark, the skin of our fruit trees,
  Lest, being over-proud in sap and blood,   60
  With too much riches it confound itself.
  Had he done so to great and growing men,
  They might have lived to bear, and he to taste,
  Their fruits of duty. Superfluous branches
  We lop away, that bearing boughs may live.   65
  Had he done so, himself had borne the crown,
  Which waste of idle hours hath quite thrown down.
⌈FIRST⌉ MAN
  What, think you then the King shall be deposed?
GARDENER
  Depressed he is already, and deposed
  'Tis doubt he will be. Letters came last night   70
  To a dear friend of the good Duke of York's
  That tell black tidings.
QUEEN
  O, I am pressed to death through want of speaking!
          She comes forward
  Thou, old Adam's likeness, set to dress this garden,
  How dares thy harsh rude tongue sound this
      unpleasing news?   75
  What Eve, what serpent hath suggested thee
  To make a second fall of cursèd man?
  Why dost thou say King Richard is deposed?
  Dar'st thou, thou little better thing than earth,
  Divine his downfall? Say where, when, and how   80
  Cam'st thou by this ill tidings? Speak, thou wretch!
GARDENER
  Pardon me, madam. Little joy have I
  To breathe this news, yet what I say is true.
  King Richard he is in the mighty hold
  Of Bolingbroke. Their fortunes both are weighed.   85
  In your lord's scale is nothing but himself
  And some few vanities that make him light.
  But in the balance of great Bolingbroke,
  Besides himself, are all the English peers,
  And with that odds he weighs King Richard down.   90
  Post you to London and you will find it so.
  I speak no more than everyone doth know.
QUEEN
  Nimble mischance that art so light of foot,
  Doth not thy embassage belong to me,
  And am I last that knows it? O, thou think'st   95
  To serve me last, that I may longest keep
  Thy sorrow in my breast. Come, ladies, go
  To meet at London London's king in woe.
  What, was I born to this, that my sad look
  Should grace the triumph of great Bolingbroke?   100
  Gard'ner, for telling me these news of woe,
  Pray God the plants thou graft'st may never grow.
          Exit with her Ladies
GARDENER
  Poor Queen, so that thy state might be no worse
  I would my skill were subject to thy curse.
  Here did she fall a tear. Here in this place   105

I'll set a bank of rue, sour herb-of-grace.
Rue even for ruth here shortly shall be seen
In the remembrance of a weeping queen.   *Exeunt*

4.1   *Enter, as to Parliament, Bolingbroke Duke of*
Lancaster and Hereford, the Duke of Aumerle, the
Earl of Northumberland, Harry Percy, Lord
Fitzwalter, the Duke of Surrey, the Bishop of
Carlisle, and the Abbot of Westminster

BOLINGBROKE
Call forth Bagot.
        Enter Bagot, with officers
                Now, Bagot, freely speak thy mind:
What thou dost know of noble Gloucester's death,
Who wrought it with the King, and who performed
The bloody office of his timeless end.

BAGOT
Then set before my face the Lord Aumerle.   5

BOLINGBROKE (*to Aumerle*)
Cousin, stand forth, and look upon that man.
        Aumerle stands forth

BAGOT
My lord Aumerle, I know your daring tongue
Scorns to unsay what once it hath delivered.
In that dead time when Gloucester's death was plotted
I heard you say 'Is not my arm of length,   10
That reacheth from the restful English court
As far as Calais, to mine uncle's head?'
Amongst much other talk that very time
I heard you say that you had rather refuse
The offer of an hundred thousand crowns   15
Than Bolingbroke's return to England,
Adding withal how blest this land would be
In this your cousin's death.

AUMERLE   Princes and noble lords,
What answer shall I make to this base man?
Shall I so much dishonour my fair stars   20
On equal terms to give him chastisement?
Either I must, or have mine honour soiled
With the attainder of his slanderous lips.
        He throws down his gage
There is my gage, the manual seal of death
That marks thee out for hell. I say thou liest,   25
And will maintain what thou hast said is false
In thy heart blood, though being all too base
To stain the temper of my knightly sword.

BOLINGBROKE
Bagot, forbear. Thou shalt not take it up.

AUMERLE
Excepting one, I would he were the best   30
In all this presence that hath moved me so.

FITZWALTER
If that thy valour stand on sympathy,
There is my gage, Aumerle, in gage to thine.
        He throws down his gage
By that fair sun which shows me where thou stand'st,
I heard thee say, and vauntingly thou spak'st it,   35
That thou wert cause of noble Gloucester's death.

If thou deny'st it twenty times, thou liest,
And I will turn thy falsehood to thy heart,
Where it was forgèd, with my rapier's point.

AUMERLE
Thou dar'st not, coward, live to see that day.   40

FITZWALTER
Now by my soul, I would it were this hour.

AUMERLE
Fitzwalter, thou art damned to hell for this.

HARRY PERCY
Aumerle, thou liest. His honour is as true
In this appeal as thou art all unjust;
And that thou art so, there I throw my gage   45
        He throws down his gage
To prove it on thee to the extremest point
Of mortal breathing. Seize it if thou dar'st.

AUMERLE
An if I do not, may my hands rot off,
And never brandish more revengeful steel
Over the glittering helmet of my foe.   50

SURREY
My lord Fitzwalter, I do remember well
The very time Aumerle and you did talk.

FITZWALTER
'Tis very true. You were in presence then,
And you can witness with me this is true.

SURREY
As false, by heaven, as heaven itself is true.   55

FITZWALTER
Surrey, thou liest.

SURREY   Dishonourable boy,
That lie shall lie so heavy on my sword
That it shall render vengeance and revenge,
Till thou, the lie-giver, and that lie do lie
In earth as quiet as thy father's skull;   60
In proof whereof, there is my honour's pawn.
        He thows down his gage
Engage it to the trial if thou dar'st.

FITZWALTER
How fondly dost thou spur a forward horse!
If I dare eat, or drink, or breathe, or live,
I dare meet Surrey in a wilderness   65
And spit upon him whilst I say he lies,
And lies, and lies. There is my bond of faith
To tie thee to my strong correction.
As I intend to thrive in this new world,
Aumerle is guilty of my true appeal.   70
Besides, I heard the banished Norfolk say
That thou, Aumerle, didst send two of thy men
To execute the noble Duke at Calais.

AUMERLE
Some honest Christian trust me with a gage.
        He takes another's gage and throws it down
That Norfolk lies, here do I throw down this,   75
If he may be repealed, to try his honour.

BOLINGBROKE
These differences shall all rest under gage
Till Norfolk be repealed. Repealed he shall be,

And, though mine enemy, restored again
To all his lands and signories. When he is returned, 80
Against Aumerle we will enforce his trial.
BISHOP OF CARLISLE
That honourable day shall never be seen.
Many a time hath banished Norfolk fought
For Jesu Christ in glorious Christian field,
Streaming the ensign of the Christian cross   85
Against black pagans, Turks, and Saracens;
And, toiled with works of war, retired himself
To Italy, and there at Venice gave
His body to that pleasant country's earth,
And his pure soul unto his captain, Christ,   90
Under whose colours he had fought so long.
BOLINGBROKE
Why, Bishop of Carlisle, is Norfolk dead?
BISHOP OF CARLISLE
As surely as I live, my lord.
BOLINGBROKE
Sweet peace conduct his sweet soul to the bosom
Of good old Abraham! Lords appellants,   95
Your differences shall all rest under gage
Till we assign you to your days of trial.
          Enter the Duke of York
YORK
Great Duke of Lancaster, I come to thee
From plume-plucked Richard, who with willing soul
Adopts thee heir, and his high sceptre yields   100
To the possession of thy royal hand.
Ascend his throne, descending now from him,
And long live Henry, of that name the fourth!
BOLINGBROKE
In God's name I'll ascend the regal throne.
BISHOP OF CARLISLE Marry, God forbid!   105
Worst in this royal presence may I speak,
Yet best beseeming me to speak the truth.
Would God that any in this noble presence
Were enough noble to be upright judge
Of noble Richard. Then true noblesse would   110
Learn him forbearance from so foul a wrong.
What subject can give sentence on his king?
And who sits here that is not Richard's subject?
Thieves are not judged but they are by to hear,
Although apparent guilt be seen in them;   115
And shall the figure of God's majesty,
His captain, steward, deputy elect,
Anointed, crownèd, planted many years,
Be judged by subject and inferior breath,
And he himself not present? O, forfend it, God,   120
That in a Christian climate souls refined
Should show so heinous, black, obscene a deed!
I speak to subjects, and a subject speaks
Stirred up by God thus boldly for his king.
My lord of Hereford here, whom you call king,   125
Is a foul traitor to proud Hereford's king;
And, if you crown him, let me prophesy
The blood of English shall manure the ground,
And future ages groan for this foul act.

Peace shall go sleep with Turks and infidels,   130
And in this seat of peace tumultuous wars
Shall kin with kin and kind with kind confound.
Disorder, horror, fear, and mutiny
Shall here inhabit, and this land be called
The field of Golgotha and dead men's skulls.   135
O, if you rear this house against this house
It will the woefullest division prove
That ever fell upon this cursèd earth!
Prevent, resist it; let it not be so,
Lest child, child's children, cry against you woe.   140
NORTHUMBERLAND
Well have you argued, sir, and for your pains
Of capital treason we arrest you here.
My lord of Westminster, be it your charge
To keep him safely till his day of trial.
May it please you, lords, to grant the Commons' suit?
BOLINGBROKE
Fetch hither Richard, that in common view   146
He may surrender. So we shall proceed
Without suspicion.
YORK   I will be his conduct.   *Exit*
BOLINGBROKE
Lords, you that here are under our arrest,
Procure your sureties for your days of answer.   150
Little are we beholden to your love,
And little looked for at your helping hands.
          *Enter Richard and the Duke of York, ⌈with
          attendants bearing the crown and sceptre⌉*
RICHARD
Alack, why am I sent for to a king
Before I have shook off the regal thoughts
Wherewith I reigned? I hardly yet have learned   155
To insinuate, flatter, bow, and bend my knee.
Give sorrow leave awhile to tutor me
To this submission. Yet I well remember
The favours of these men. Were they not mine?
Did they not sometime cry 'All hail!' to me?   160
So Judas did to Christ. But He in twelve
Found truth in all but one; I, in twelve thousand,
          none.
God save the King! Will no man say 'Amen'?
Am I both priest and clerk? Well then, Amen.
God save the King, although I be not he.   165
And yet Amen, if heaven do think him me.
To do what service am I sent for hither?
YORK
To do that office of thine own good will
Which tired majesty did make thee offer:
The resignation of thy state and crown   170
To Henry Bolingbroke.
RICHARD (*to an attendant*)
Give me the crown. (*To Bolingbroke*) Here, cousin,
          seize the crown.
Here, cousin. On this side my hand, on that side thine.
Now is this golden crown like a deep well
That owes two buckets filling one another,   175
The emptier ever dancing in the air,
The other down, unseen, and full of water.

That bucket down and full of tears am I,
Drinking my griefs, whilst you mount up on high.
BOLINGBROKE
I thought you had been willing to resign.   180
RICHARD
My crown I am, but still my griefs are mine.
You may my glories and my state depose,
But not my griefs; still am I king of those.
BOLINGBROKE
Part of your cares you give me with your crown.
RICHARD
Your cares set up do not pluck my cares down.   185
My care is loss of care by old care done;
Your care is gain of care by new care won.
The cares I give I have, though given away;
They 'tend the crown, yet still with me they stay.
BOLINGBROKE
Are you contented to resign the crown?   190
RICHARD
Ay, no; no, ay; for I must nothing be;
Therefore no, no, for I resign to thee.
Now mark me how I will undo myself.
I give this heavy weight from off my head,
⌈*Bolingbroke accepts the crown*⌉
And this unwieldy sceptre from my hand,   195
⌈*Bolingbroke accepts the sceptre*⌉
The pride of kingly sway from out my heart.
With mine own tears I wash away my balm,
With mine own hands I give away my crown,
With mine own tongue deny my sacred state,
With mine own breath release all duteous oaths.   200
All pomp and majesty I do forswear.
My manors, rents, revenues I forgo.
My acts, decrees, and statutes I deny.
God pardon all oaths that are broke to me.
God keep all vows unbroke are made to thee.   205
Make me, that nothing have, with nothing grieved,
And thou with all pleased, that hast all achieved.
Long mayst thou live in Richard's seat to sit,
And soon lie Richard in an earthy pit.
'God save King Henry,' unkinged Richard says,   210
'And send him many years of sunshine days.'
What more remains?
NORTHUMBERLAND (*giving Richard papers*)
                    No more but that you read
These accusations and these grievous crimes
Committed by your person and your followers
Against the state and profit of this land,   215
That by confessing them, the souls of men
May deem that you are worthily deposed.
RICHARD
Must I do so? And must I ravel out
My weaved-up follies? Gentle Northumberland,
If thy offences were upon record,   220
Would it not shame thee in so fair a troop
To read a lecture of them? If thou wouldst,
There shouldst thou find one heinous article
Containing the deposing of a king

And cracking the strong warrant of an oath,   225
Marked with a blot, damned in the book of heaven.
Nay, all of you that stand and look upon
Whilst that my wretchedness doth bait myself,
Though some of you, with Pilate, wash your hands,
Showing an outward pity, yet you Pilates   230
Have here delivered me to my sour cross,
And water cannot wash away your sin.
NORTHUMBERLAND
My lord, dispatch. Read o'er these articles.
RICHARD
Mine eyes are full of tears; I cannot see.
And yet salt water blinds them not so much   235
But they can see a sort of traitors here.
Nay, if I turn mine eyes upon myself
I find myself a traitor with the rest,
For I have given here my soul's consent
T'undeck the pompous body of a king,   240
Made glory base and sovereignty a slave,
Proud majesty a subject, state a peasant.
NORTHUMBERLAND My lord—
RICHARD
No lord of thine, thou haught-insulting man,
Nor no man's lord. I have no name, no title,   245
No, not that name was given me at the font,
But 'tis usurped. Alack the heavy day,
That I have worn so many winters out
And know not now what name to call myself!
O, that I were a mockery king of snow,   250
Standing before the sun of Bolingbroke
To melt myself away in water-drops!
Good king, great king—and yet not greatly good—
An if my word be sterling yet in England,
Let it command a mirror hither straight,   255
That it may show me what a face I have,
Since it is bankrupt of his majesty.
BOLINGBROKE
Go some of you and fetch a looking-glass.
                                        Exit one or more
NORTHUMBERLAND
Read o'er this paper while the glass doth come.
RICHARD
Fiend, thou torment'st me ere I come to hell.   260
BOLINGBROKE
Urge it no more, my lord Northumberland.
NORTHUMBERLAND
The Commons will not then be satisfied.
RICHARD
They shall be satisfied. I'll read enough
When I do see the very book indeed
Where all my sins are writ, and that's myself.   265
                Enter one with a glass
Give me that glass, and therein will I read.
                Richard takes the glass and looks in it
No deeper wrinkles yet? Hath sorrow struck
So many blows upon this face of mine
And made no deeper wounds? O flatt'ring glass,
Like to my followers in prosperity,   270

Thou dost beguile me! Was this face the face
That every day under his household roof
Did keep ten thousand men? Was this the face
That like the sun did make beholders wink?
Is this the face which faced so many follies,   275
That was at last outfaced by Bolingbroke?
A brittle glory shineth in this face.
As brittle as the glory is the face,
          He shatters the glass
For there it is, cracked in an hundred shivers.
Mark, silent King, the moral of this sport: 280
How soon my sorrow hath destroyed my face.
BOLINGBROKE
The shadow of your sorrow hath destroyed
The shadow of your face.
RICHARD   Say that again:
'The shadow of my sorrow'—ha, let's see.
'Tis very true: my grief lies all within,   285
And these external manner of laments
Are merely shadows to the unseen grief
That swells with silence in the tortured soul.
There lies the substance, and I thank thee, King,
For thy great bounty that not only giv'st   290
Me cause to wail, but teachest me the way
How to lament the cause. I'll beg one boon,
And then be gone and trouble you no more.
Shall I obtain it?
BOLINGBROKE   Name it, fair cousin.
RICHARD
Fair cousin? I am greater than a king;   295
For when I was a king my flatterers
Were then but subjects; being now a subject,
I have a king here to my flatterer.
Being so great, I have no need to beg.
BOLINGBROKE Yet ask.   300
RICHARD And shall I have?
BOLINGBROKE You shall.
RICHARD Then give me leave to go.
BOLINGBROKE Whither?
RICHARD
Whither you will, so I were from your sights.   305
BOLINGBROKE
Go some of you, convey him to the Tower.
RICHARD
O good, 'convey'! Conveyors are you all,
That rise thus nimbly by a true king's fall.
                    ⌈*Exit, guarded*⌉
BOLINGBROKE
On Wednesday next we solemnly set down
Our coronation. Lords, prepare yourselves.   310
          Exeunt all but the Abbot of Westminster, the
          Bishop of Carlisle, and Aumerle
ABBOT OF WESTMINSTER
A woeful pageant have we here beheld.
BISHOP OF CARLISLE
The woe's to come, the children yet unborn
Shall feel this day as sharp to them as thorn.

AUMERLE
You holy clergymen, is there no plot
To rid the realm of this pernicious blot?   315
ABBOT OF WESTMINSTER
My lord, before I freely speak my mind herein,
You shall not only take the sacrament
To bury mine intents, but also to effect
Whatever I shall happen to devise.
I see your brows are full of discontent,   320
Your hearts of sorrow, and your eyes of tears.
Come home with me to supper. I will lay
A plot shall show us all a merry day.   *Exeunt*

5.1   *Enter the Queen, with her Ladies*
QUEEN
This way the King will come. This is the way
To Julius Caesar's ill-erected Tower,
To whose flint bosom my condemnèd lord
Is doomed a prisoner by proud Bolingbroke.
Here let us rest, if this rebellious earth   5
Have any resting for her true king's queen.
          Enter Richard ⌈*and guard*⌉
But soft, but see—or rather do not see—
My fair rose wither. Yet look up, behold,
That you in pity may dissolve to dew,
And wash him fresh again with true-love tears.—   10
Ah, thou the model where old Troy did stand!
Thou map of honour, thou King Richard's tomb,
And not King Richard! Thou most beauteous inn:
Why should hard-favoured grief be lodged in thee,
When triumph is become an alehouse guest?   15
RICHARD
Join not with grief, fair woman, do not so,
To make my end too sudden. Learn, good soul,
To think our former state a happy dream,
From which awaked, the truth of what we are
Shows us but this. I am sworn brother, sweet,   20
To grim necessity, and he and I
Will keep a league till death. Hie thee to France,
And cloister thee in some religious house.
Our holy lives must win a new world's crown,
Which our profane hours here have stricken down.   25
QUEEN
What, is my Richard both in shape and mind
Transformed and weakenèd? Hath Bolingbroke
Deposed thine intellect? Hath he been in thy heart?
The lion dying thrusteth forth his paw
And wounds the earth, if nothing else, with rage   30
To be o'erpowered; and wilt thou, pupil-like,
Take the correction, mildly kiss the rod,
And fawn on rage with base humility,
Which art a lion and the king of beasts?
RICHARD
A king of beasts indeed! If aught but beasts,   35
I had been still a happy king of men.
Good sometimes Queen, prepare thee hence for
          France.

Think I am dead, and that even here thou tak'st,
As from my death-bed, thy last living leave.
In winter's tedious nights, sit by the fire   40
With good old folks, and let them tell thee tales
Of woeful ages long ago betid;
And ere thou bid goodnight, to quit their griefs
Tell thou the lamentable fall of me,
And send the hearers weeping to their beds;   45
Forwhy the senseless brands will sympathize
The heavy accent of thy moving tongue,
And in compassion weep the fire out;
And some will mourn in ashes, some coal black,
For the deposing of a rightful king.   50
Enter the Earl of Northumberland
NORTHUMBERLAND
My lord, the mind of Bolingbroke is changed.
You must to Pomfret, not unto the Tower.
And, madam, there is order ta'en for you.
With all swift speed you must away to France.
RICHARD
Northumberland, thou ladder wherewithal   55
The mounting Bolingbroke ascends my throne,
The time shall not be many hours of age
More than it is ere foul sin, gathering head,
Shall break into corruption. Thou shalt think,
Though he divide the realm and give thee half,   60
It is too little helping him to all.
He shall think that thou, which know'st the way
To plant unrightful kings, wilt know again,
Being ne'er so little urged another way,
To pluck him headlong from the usurpèd throne.   65
The love of wicked friends converts to fear,
That fear to hate, and hate turns one or both
To worthy danger and deservèd death.
NORTHUMBERLAND
My guilt be on my head, and there an end.
Take leave and part, for you must part forthwith.   70
RICHARD
Doubly divorced! Bad men, you violate
A twofold marriage: 'twixt my crown and me,
And then betwixt me and my married wife.
(*To the Queen*) Let me unkiss the oath 'twixt thee and
   me—
And yet not so, for with a kiss 'twas made.   75
Part us, Northumberland: I towards the north,
Where shivering cold and sickness pines the clime;
My queen to France, from whence set forth in pomp
She came adornèd hither like sweet May,
Sent back like Hallowmas or short'st of day.   80
QUEEN
And must we be divided? Must we part?
RICHARD
Ay, hand from hand, my love, and heart from heart.
QUEEN
Banish us both, and send the King with me.
⌈NORTHUMBERLAND⌉
That were some love, but little policy.

QUEEN
Then whither he goes, thither let me go.   85
RICHARD
So two together weeping make one woe.
Weep thou for me in France, I for thee here.
Better far off than, near, be ne'er the nea'er.
Go count thy way with sighs, I mine with groans.
QUEEN
So longest way shall have the longest moans.   90
RICHARD
Twice for one step I'll groan, the way being short,
And piece the way out with a heavy heart.
Come, come, in wooing sorrow let's be brief,
Since, wedding it, there is such length in grief.
One kiss shall stop our mouths, and dumbly part.   95
Thus give I mine, and thus take I thy heart.
   They kiss
QUEEN
Give me mine own again. 'Twere no good part
To take on me to keep and kill thy heart.
   They kiss
So now I have mine own again, be gone,
That I may strive to kill it with a groan.   100
RICHARD
We make woe wanton with this fond delay.
Once more, adieu. The rest let sorrow say.
   Exeunt ⌈Richard, guarded, and Northumberland
   at one door, the Queen and her Ladies at
   another door⌉

5.2   *Enter the Duke and Duchess of York*
DUCHESS OF YORK
My lord, you told me you would tell the rest,
When weeping made you break the story off,
Of our two cousins' coming into London.
YORK
Where did I leave?
DUCHESS OF YORK   At that sad stop, my lord,
Where rude misgoverned hands from windows' tops   5
Threw dust and rubbish on King Richard's head.
YORK
Then, as I said, the Duke, great Bolingbroke,
Mounted upon a hot and fiery steed,
Which his aspiring rider seemed to know,
With slow but stately pace kept on his course,   10
Whilst all tongues cried 'God save thee, Bolingbroke!'
You would have thought the very windows spake,
So many greedy looks of young and old
Through casements darted their desiring eyes
Upon his visage, and that all the walls   15
With painted imagery had said at once,
'Jesu preserve thee! Welcome, Bolingbroke!'
Whilst he, from the one side to the other turning,
Bare-headed, lower than his proud steed's neck,
Bespake them thus: 'I thank you, countrymen',   20
And thus still doing, thus he passed along.
DUCHESS OF YORK
Alack, poor Richard! Where rode he the whilst?

YORK
As in a theatre the eyes of men,
After a well-graced actor leaves the stage,
Are idly bent on him that enters next, 25
Thinking his prattle to be tedious,
Even so, or with much more contempt, men's eyes
Did scowl on gentle Richard. No man cried 'God save
    him!'
No joyful tongue gave him his welcome home;
But dust was thrown upon his sacred head, 30
Which with such gentle sorrow he shook off,
His face still combating with tears and smiles,
The badges of his grief and patience,
That had not God for some strong purpose steeled
The hearts of men, they must perforce have melted, 35
And barbarism itself have pitied him.
But heaven hath a hand in these events,
To whose high will we bound our calm contents.
To Bolingbroke are we sworn subjects now,
Whose state and honour I for aye allow. 40
    Enter the Duke of Aumerle
DUCHESS OF YORK
Here comes my son Aumerle.
YORK   Aumerle that was;
But that is lost for being Richard's friend,
And, madam, you must call him 'Rutland' now.
I am in Parliament pledge for his truth
And lasting fealty to the new-made King. 45
DUCHESS OF YORK
Welcome, my son. Who are the violets now
That strew the green lap of the new-come spring?
AUMERLE
Madam, I know not, nor I greatly care not.
God knows I had as lief be none as one.
YORK
Well, bear you well in this new spring of time, 50
Lest you be cropped before you come to prime.
What news from Oxford? Hold these jousts and
    triumphs?
AUMERLE
For aught I know, my lord, they do.
YORK You will be there, I know.
AUMERLE
If God prevent it not, I purpose so. 55
YORK
What seal is that that hangs without thy bosom?
Yea, look'st thou pale? Let me see the writing.
AUMERLE
My lord, 'tis nothing.
YORK   No matter, then, who see it.
I will be satisfied. Let me see the writing.
AUMERLE
I do beseech your grace to pardon me. 60
It is a matter of small consequence,
Which for some reasons I would not have seen.
YORK
Which for some reasons, sir, I mean to see.
I fear, I fear!
DUCHESS OF YORK What should you fear?

'Tis nothing but some bond that he is entered into 65
For gay apparel 'gainst the triumph day.
YORK
Bound to himself? What doth he with a bond
That he is bound to? Wife, thou art a fool.
Boy, let me see the writing.
AUMERLE
I do beseech you, pardon me. I may not show it. 70
YORK
I will be satisfied. Let me see it, I say.
    He plucks it out of Aumerle's bosom, and reads it
Treason, foul treason! Villain, traitor, slave!
DUCHESS OF YORK What is the matter, my lord?
YORK
Ho, who is within there? Saddle my horse.—
God for his mercy, what treachery is here! 75
DUCHESS OF YORK Why, what is it, my lord?
YORK
Give me my boots, I say. Saddle my horse.—
Now by mine honour, by my life, my troth,
I will appeach the villain.
DUCHESS OF YORK What is the matter? 80
YORK Peace, foolish woman.
DUCHESS OF YORK
I will not peace. What is the matter, son?
AUMERLE
Good mother, be content. It is no more
Than my poor life must answer.
DUCHESS OF YORK   Thy life answer?
YORK
Bring me my boots. I will unto the King. 85
    His man enters with his boots
DUCHESS OF YORK
Strike him, Aumerle! Poor boy, thou art amazed.
(*To York's man*) Hence, villain! Never more come in
    my sight.
YORK
Give me my boots, I say.
DUCHESS OF YORK   Why, York, what wilt thou do?
Wilt thou not hide the trespass of thine own?
Have we more sons? Or are we like to have? 90
Is not my teeming date drunk up with time?
And wilt thou pluck my fair son from mine age,
And rob me of a happy mother's name?
Is he not like thee? Is he not thine own?
YORK Thou fond, mad woman, 95
Wilt thou conceal this dark conspiracy?
A dozen of them here have ta'en the sacrament,
And interchangeably set down their hands
To kill the King at Oxford.
DUCHESS OF YORK   He shall be none.
We'll keep him here, then what is that to him? 100
YORK
Away, fond woman! Were he twenty times my son
I would appeach him.
DUCHESS OF YORK   Hadst thou groaned for him
As I have done thou wouldst be more pitiful.
But now I know thy mind: thou dost suspect
That I have been disloyal to thy bed, 105

And that he is a bastard, not thy son.
Sweet York, sweet husband, be not of that mind.
He is as like thee as a man may be,
Not like to me or any of my kin,
And yet I love him.
YORK   Make way, unruly woman.   110
                              Exit ⌈with his man⌉
DUCHESS OF YORK
After, Aumerle! Mount thee upon his horse.
Spur, post, and get before him to the King,
And beg thy pardon ere he do accuse thee.
I'll not be long behind—though I be old,
I doubt not but to ride as fast as York—   115
And never will I rise up from the ground
Till Bolingbroke have pardoned thee. Away, be gone!
                              Exeunt ⌈severally⌉

5.3   *Enter Bolingbroke, crowned King Henry, with*
       Harry Percy, and other nobles
KING HENRY
Can no man tell of my unthrifty son?
'Tis full three months since I did see him last.
If any plague hang over us, 'tis he.
I would to God, my lords, he might be found.
Enquire at London 'mongst the taverns there,   5
For there, they say, he daily doth frequent
With unrestrainèd loose companions—
Even such, they say, as stand in narrow lanes
And beat our watch and rob our passengers—
Which he, young wanton and effeminate boy,   10
Takes on the point of honour to support
So dissolute a crew.
HARRY PERCY
My lord, some two days since, I saw the Prince,
And told him of these triumphs held at Oxford.
KING HENRY And what said the gallant?   15
HARRY PERCY
His answer was he would unto the stews,
And from the common'st creature pluck a glove,
And wear it as a favour, and with that
He would unhorse the lustiest challenger.
KING HENRY
As dissolute as desperate. Yet through both   20
I see some sparks of better hope, which elder days
May happily bring forth.
       Enter the Duke of Aumerle, amazed
                    But who comes here?
AUMERLE Where is the King?
KING HENRY
What means our cousin that he stares and looks so
       wildly?
AUMERLE (*kneeling*)
God save your grace! I do beseech your majesty   25
To have some conference with your grace alone.
KING HENRY (*to lords*)
Withdraw yourselves, and leave us here alone.
       Exeunt all but King Henry and Aumerle
What is the matter with our cousin now?

AUMERLE
For ever may my knees grow to the earth,
My tongue cleave to the roof within my mouth,   30
Unless a pardon ere I rise or speak.
KING HENRY
Intended or committed was this fault?
If on the first, how heinous e'er it be,
To win thy after-love I pardon thee.
AUMERLE (*rising*)
Then give me leave that I may turn the key,   35
That no man enter till my tale be done.
KING HENRY
Have thy desire.
       Aumerle locks the door.
       The Duke of York knocks at the door and crieth
YORK (*within*)   My liege, beware! Look to thyself!
Thou hast a traitor in thy presence there.
       King Henry draws his sword
KING HENRY (*to Aumerle*) Villain, I'll make thee safe.
AUMERLE
Stay thy revengeful hand! Thou hast no cause to fear.
YORK (*knocking within*)
Open the door, secure foolhardy King!   41
Shall I for love speak treason to thy face?
Open the door, or I will break it open.
       ⌈*King Henry*⌉ *opens the door. Enter the Duke of*
       York
KING HENRY
What is the matter, uncle? Speak,
Recover breath, tell us how near is danger,   45
That we may arm us to encounter it.
YORK
Peruse this writing here, and thou shalt know
The treason that my haste forbids me show.
       He gives King Henry the paper
AUMERLE
Remember, as thou read'st, thy promise past.
I do repent me. Read not my name there.   50
My heart is not confederate with my hand.
YORK
It was, villain, ere thy hand did set it down.
I tore it from the traitor's bosom, King.
Fear, and not love, begets his penitence.
Forget to pity him, lest pity prove   55
A serpent that will sting thee to the heart.
KING HENRY
O, heinous, strong, and bold conspiracy!
O loyal father of a treacherous son!
Thou sheer, immaculate, and silver fountain,
From whence this stream through muddy passages   60
Hath held his current and defiled himself,
Thy overflow of good converts to bad,
And thy abundant goodness shall excuse
This deadly blot in thy digressing son.
YORK
So shall my virtue be his vice's bawd,   65
And he shall spend mine honour with his shame,
As thriftless sons their scraping fathers' gold.

Mine honour lives when his dishonour dies,
Or my shamed life in his dishonour lies.
Thou kill'st me in his life: giving him breath   70
The traitor lives, the true man's put to death.
DUCHESS OF YORK (*within*)
  What ho, my liege, for God's sake let me in!
KING HENRY
  What shrill-voiced suppliant makes this eager cry?
DUCHESS OF YORK (*within*)
  A woman, and thy aunt, great King; 'tis I.
Speak with me, pity me! Open the door!   75
A beggar begs that never begged before.
KING HENRY
  Our scene is altered from a serious thing,
And now changed to 'The Beggar and the King'.
My dangerous cousin, let your mother in.
I know she is come to pray for your foul sin.   80
  Aumerle opens the door. Enter the Duchess of York
YORK
  If thou do pardon, whosoever pray,
More sins for this forgiveness prosper may.
This festered joint cut off, the rest rest sound.
This let alone will all the rest confound.
DUCHESS OF YORK (*kneeling*)
  O King, believe not this hard-hearted man.   85
Love loving not itself, none other can.
YORK
  Thou frantic woman, what dost thou make here?
Shall thy old dugs once more a traitor rear?
DUCHESS OF YORK
  Sweet York, be patient.—Hear me, gentle liege.
KING HENRY
  Rise up, good aunt.
DUCHESS OF YORK   Not yet, I thee beseech.   90
Forever will I kneel upon my knees,
And never see day that the happy sees,
Till thou give joy, until thou bid me joy
By pardoning Rutland, my transgressing boy.
AUMERLE (*kneeling*)
  Unto my mother's prayers I bend my knee.   95
YORK (*kneeling*)
  Against them both my true joints bended be.
Ill mayst thou thrive if thou grant any grace.
DUCHESS OF YORK
  Pleads he in earnest? Look upon his face.
His eyes do drop no tears, his prayers are in jest.
His words come from his mouth; ours from our
      breast.   100
He prays but faintly, and would be denied;
We pray with heart and soul, and all beside.
His weary joints would gladly rise, I know;
Our knees shall kneel till to the ground they grow.
His prayers are full of false hypocrisy;   105
Ours of true zeal and deep integrity.
Our prayers do outpray his; then let them have
That mercy which true prayer ought to have.
⌈KING HENRY⌉
  Good aunt, stand up.
DUCHESS OF YORK   Nay, do not say 'Stand up'.

Say 'Pardon' first, and afterwards 'Stand up'.   110
An if I were thy nurse, thy tongue to teach,
'Pardon' should be the first word of thy speech.
I never longed to hear a word till now.
Say 'Pardon', King. Let pity teach thee how.
The word is short, but not so short as sweet;   115
No word like 'Pardon' for kings' mouths so meet.
YORK
  Speak it in French, King: say 'Pardonnez-moi'.
DUCHESS OF YORK
  Dost thou teach pardon pardon to destroy?
Ah, my sour husband, my hard-hearted lord
That sets the word itself against the word!   120
Speak 'Pardon' as 'tis current in our land;
The chopping French we do not understand.
Thine eye begins to speak; set thy tongue there;
Or in thy piteous heart plant thou thine ear,
That hearing how our plaints and prayers do pierce,
Pity may move thee 'Pardon' to rehearse.   126
KING HENRY
  Good aunt, stand up.
DUCHESS OF YORK   I do not sue to stand.
Pardon is all the suit I have in hand.
KING HENRY
  I pardon him as God shall pardon me.
      ⌈*York and Aumerle rise*⌉
DUCHESS OF YORK
  O, happy vantage of a kneeling knee!   130
Yet am I sick for fear. Speak it again.
Twice saying pardon doth not pardon twain,
But makes one pardon strong.
KING HENRY   I pardon him
With all my heart.
DUCHESS OF YORK (*rising*) A god on earth thou art.
KING HENRY
  But for our trusty brother-in-law and the Abbot,   135
With all the rest of that consorted crew,
Destruction straight shall dog them at the heels.
Good uncle, help to order several powers
To Oxford, or where'er these traitors are.
They shall not live within this world, I swear,   140
But I will have them if I once know where.
Uncle, farewell; and cousin, so adieu.
Your mother well hath prayed; and prove you true.
DUCHESS OF YORK
  Come, my old son. I pray God make thee new.
      Exeunt ⌈*King Henry at one door; York, the
      Duchess of York, and Aumerle at another door*⌉

5.4   *Enter Sir Piers Exton, and his Men*
EXTON
  Didst thou not mark the King, what words he spake?
'Have I no friend will rid me of this living fear?'
Was it not so?
⌈FIRST⌉ MAN   Those were his very words.
EXTON
  'Have I no friend?' quoth he. He spake it twice,
And urged it twice together, did he not?   5
⌈SECOND⌉ MAN He did.

EXTON

And speaking it, he wishtly looked on me,
As who should say 'I would thou wert the man
That would divorce this terror from my heart',
Meaning the King at Pomfret. Come, let's go.   10
I am the King's friend, and will rid his foe.   *Exeunt*

5.5   *Enter Richard, alone*

RICHARD

I have been studying how I may compare
This prison where I live unto the world;
And for because the world is populous,
And here is not a creature but myself,
I cannot do it. Yet I'll hammer it out.   5
My brain I'll prove the female to my soul,
My soul the father, and these two beget
A generation of still-breeding thoughts;
And these same thoughts people this little world
In humours like the people of this world.   10
For no thought is contented. The better sort,
As thoughts of things divine, are intermixed
With scruples, and do set the faith itself
Against the faith, as thus: 'Come, little ones',
And then again,   15
'It is as hard to come as for a camel
To thread the postern of a small needle's eye.'
Thoughts tending to ambition, they do plot
Unlikely wonders: how these vain weak nails
May tear a passage through the flinty ribs   20
Of this hard world, my ragged prison walls;
And for they cannot, die in their own pride.
Thoughts tending to content flatter themselves
That they are not the first of fortune's slaves,
Nor shall not be the last—like seely beggars,   25
Who, sitting in the stocks, refuge their shame
That many have, and others must, set there;
And in this thought they find a kind of ease,
Bearing their own misfortunes on the back
Of such as have before endured the like.   30
Thus play I in one person many people,
And none contented. Sometimes am I king;
Then treason makes me wish myself a beggar,
And so I am. Then crushing penury
Persuades me I was better when a king.   35
Then am I kinged again, and by and by
Think that I am unkinged by Bolingbroke,
And straight am nothing. But whate'er I be,
Nor I, nor any man that but man is,
With nothing shall be pleased till he be eased   40
With being nothing.
     The music plays
                Music do I hear.
Ha, ha; keep time! How sour sweet music is
When time is broke and no proportion kept.
So is it in the music of men's lives.
And here have I the daintiness of ear   45
To check time broke in a disordered string;
But for the concord of my state and time
Had not an ear to hear my true time broke.

I wasted time, and now doth time waste me,
For now hath time made me his numb'ring clock.   50
My thoughts are minutes, and with sighs they jar
Their watches on unto mine eyes, the outward watch
Whereto my finger, like a dial's point,
Is pointing still in cleansing them from tears.
Now, sir, the sounds that tell what hour it is   55
Are clamorous groans that strike upon my heart,
Which is the bell. So sighs, and tears, and groans
Show minutes, hours, and times. But my time
Runs posting on in Bolingbroke's proud joy,
While I stand fooling here, his jack of the clock.   60
This music mads me. Let it sound no more,
For though it have holp madmen to their wits,
In me it seems it will make wise men mad.
     ⌜*The music ceases*⌝
Yet blessing on his heart that gives it me,
For 'tis a sign of love, and love to Richard   65
Is a strange brooch in this all-hating world.
     Enter a Groom of the stable

GROOM

Hail, royal Prince!

RICHARD   Thanks, noble peer.
The cheapest of us is ten groats too dear.
What art thou, and how com'st thou hither,
Where no man never comes but that sad dog   70
That brings me food to make misfortune live?

GROOM

I was a poor groom of thy stable, King,
When thou wert king; who, travelling towards York,
With much ado at length have gotten leave
To look upon my sometimes royal master's face.   75
O, how it erned my heart when I beheld
In London streets, that coronation day,
When Bolingbroke rode on roan Barbary,
That horse that thou so often hast bestrid,
That horse that I so carefully have dressed!   80

RICHARD

Rode he on Barbary? Tell me, gentle friend,
How went he under him?

GROOM

So proudly as if he disdained the ground.

RICHARD

So proud that Bolingbroke was on his back.
That jade hath eat bread from my royal hand;   85
This hand hath made him proud with clapping him.
Would he not stumble, would he not fall down—
Since pride must have a fall—and break the neck
Of that proud man that did usurp his back?
Forgiveness, horse! Why do I rail on thee,   90
Since thou, created to be awed by man,
Wast born to bear? I was not made a horse,
And yet I bear a burden like an ass,
Spur-galled and tired by jauncing Bolingbroke.
     Enter Keeper to Richard, with meat

KEEPER (*to Groom*)

Fellow, give place. Here is no longer stay.   95

RICHARD (*to Groom*)

If thou love me, 'tis time thou wert away.

GROOM
What my tongue dares not, that my heart shall say.

Exit

KEEPER
My lord, will't please you to fall to?

RICHARD
Taste of it first, as thou art wont to do.

KEEPER
My lord, I dare not. Sir Piers of Exton,   100
Who lately came from the King, commands the
    contrary.

RICHARD (*striking the Keeper*)
The devil take Henry of Lancaster and thee!
Patience is stale, and I am weary of it.

KEEPER Help, help, help!

Exton and his men rush in

RICHARD
How now! What means death in this rude assault? 105

He seizes a weapon from a man, and kills him

Villain, thy own hand yields thy death's instrument.

He kills another

Go thou, and fill another room in hell.

Here Exton strikes him down

RICHARD
That hand shall burn in never-quenching fire
That staggers thus my person. Exton, thy fierce hand
Hath with the King's blood stained the King's own
    land.   110
Mount, mount, my soul; thy seat is up on high,
Whilst my gross flesh sinks downward, here to die.

He dies

EXTON
As full of valour as of royal blood.
Both have I spilt. O, would the deed were good!
For now the devil that told me I did well   115
Says that this deed is chronicled in hell.
This dead King to the living King I'll bear.
Take hence the rest, and give them burial here.

*Exeunt ⌈Exton with Richard's body at one door,
and his men with the other bodies at another
door⌉*

5.6   ⌈*Flourish.*⌉ *Enter King Henry and the Duke of York,*
⌈*with other lords and attendants*⌉

KING HENRY
Kind uncle York, the latest news we hear
Is that the rebels have consumed with fire
Our town of Ci'cester in Gloucestershire;
But whether they be ta'en or slain we hear not.

Enter the Earl of Northumberland

Welcome, my lord. What is the news?   5

NORTHUMBERLAND
First, to thy sacred state wish I all happiness.
The next news is, I have to London sent
The heads of Salisbury, Spencer, Blunt, and Kent.
The manner of their taking may appear
At large discoursèd in this paper here.   10

He gives the paper to King Henry

KING HENRY
We thank thee, gentle Percy, for thy pains,
And to thy worth will add right worthy gains.

Enter Lord Fitzwalter

FITZWALTER
My lord, I have from Oxford sent to London
The heads of Brocas and Sir Bennet Seely,
Two of the dangerous consorted traitors   15
That sought at Oxford thy dire overthrow.

KING HENRY
Thy pains, Fitzwalter, shall not be forgot.
Right noble is thy merit, well I wot.

*Enter Harry Percy, with the Bishop of Carlisle,
guarded*

HARRY PERCY
The grand conspirator Abbot of Westminster,
With clog of conscience and sour melancholy,   20
Hath yielded up his body to the grave.
But here is Carlisle living, to abide
Thy kingly doom and sentence of his pride.

KING HENRY Carlisle, this is your doom.
Choose out some secret place, some reverent room   25
More than thou hast, and with it joy thy life.
So as thou liv'st in peace, die free from strife.
For though mine enemy thou hast ever been,
High sparks of honour in thee have I seen.

Enter Exton with ⌈his men bearing⌉ the coffin

EXTON
Great King, within this coffin I present   30
Thy buried fear. Herein all breathless lies
The mightiest of thy greatest enemies,
Richard of Bordeaux, by me hither brought.

KING HENRY
Exton, I thank thee not, for thou hast wrought
A deed of slander with thy fatal hand   35
Upon my head and all this famous land.

EXTON
From your own mouth, my lord, did I this deed.

KING HENRY
They love not poison that do poison need;
Nor do I thee. Though I did wish him dead,
I hate the murderer, love him murderèd.   40
The guilt of conscience take thou for thy labour,
But neither my good word nor princely favour.
With Cain go wander through the shades of night,
And never show thy head by day nor light.

⌈Exeunt Exton and his men⌉

Lords, I protest my soul is full of woe   45
That blood should sprinkle me to make me grow.
Come mourn with me for what I do lament,
And put on sullen black incontinent.
I'll make a voyage to the Holy Land
To wash this blood off from my guilty hand.   50
March sadly after. Grace my mournings here
In weeping after this untimely bier.

Exeunt ⌈with the coffin⌉

ADDITIONAL PASSAGES

The following passages of four lines or more appear in the 1597 Quarto but not the Folio; Shakespeare probably deleted them as part of his limited revisions to the text.

A. AFTER 1.3.127

And for we think the eagle-wingèd pride
Of sky-aspiring and ambitious thoughts
With rival-hating envy set on you
To wake our peace, which in our country's cradle
Draws the sweet infant breath of gentle sleep,   5

B. AFTER 1.3.235

O, had't been a stranger, not my child,
To smooth his fault I should have been more mild.
A partial slander sought I to avoid,
And in the sentence my own life destroyed.

C. AFTER 1.3.256

BOLINGBROKE
Nay, rather every tedious stride I make
Will but remember what a deal of world
I wander from the jewels that I love.
Must I not serve a long apprenticehood
To foreign passages, and in the end,   5
Having my freedom, boast of nothing else
But that I was a journeyman to grief?
JOHN OF GAUNT
All places that the eye of heaven visits
Are to a wise man ports and happy havens.
Teach thy necessity to reason thus: 10
There is no virtue like necessity.
Think not the King did banish thee,

But thou the King. Woe doth the heavier sit
Where it perceives it is but faintly borne.
Go, say I sent thee forth to purchase honour,   15
And not the King exiled thee; or suppose
Devouring pestilence hangs in our air
And thou art flying to a fresher clime.
Look what thy soul holds dear, imagine it
To lie that way thou goest, not whence thou com'st.   20
Suppose the singing birds musicians,
The grass whereon thou tread'st the presence strewed,
The flowers fair ladies, and thy steps no more
Than a delightful measure or a dance;
For gnarling sorrow hath less power to bite   25
The man that mocks at it and sets it light.

D. AFTER 3.2.28

The means that heavens yield must be embraced
And not neglected; else heaven would,
And we will not: heaven's offer we refuse,
The proffered means of succour and redress.

E. AFTER 4.1.50

ANOTHER LORD
I task the earth to the like, forsworn Aumerle,
And spur thee on with full as many lies
As may be hollowed in thy treacherous ear
From sun to sun. There is my honour's pawn.
Engage it to the trial if thou darest.   5
        He throws down his gage
AUMERLE
Who sets me else? By heaven, I'll throw at all.
I have a thousand spirits in one breast
To answer twenty thousand such as you.

KING JOHN

A PLAY called *The Troublesome Reign of John, King of England*, published anonymously in 1591, has sometimes been thought to be a derivative version of Shakespeare's *King John*, first published in the 1623 Folio; more probably Shakespeare wrote his play in 1595 or 1596, using *The Troublesome Reign*—itself based on Holinshed's *Chronicles* and John Foxe's *Book of Martyrs* (1563)—as his principal source. Like *Richard II*, *King John* is written entirely in verse.

King John (*c*.1167-1216) was famous as the opponent of papal tyranny, and *The Troublesome Reign* is a violently anti-Catholic play; but Shakespeare is more moderate. He portrays selected events from John's reign—like *The Troublesome Reign*, making no mention of Magna Carta—and ends with John's death, but John is not so dominant a figure in his play as Richard II or Richard III in theirs. Indeed, the longest—and liveliest—role is that of Richard Cœur-de-lion's illegitimate son, Philip Falconbridge, the Bastard.

King John's reign was troublesome initially because of his weak claim to his brother Richard Cœur-de-lion's throne. Prince Arthur, son of John's elder brother Geoffrey, had no less strong a claim, which is upheld by his mother, Constance, and by King Philip of France. The waste and futility of the consequent war between power-hungry leaders is satirically demonstrated in the dispute over the French town of Angers, which is resolved by a marriage between John's niece, Lady Blanche of Spain, and Louis, the French Dauphin. The moral is strikingly drawn by the Bastard—the man best fitted to be king, but debarred by accident of birth—in his speech (2.1.562-99) on 'commodity' (self-interest). King Philip breaks his treaty with England, and in the ensuing battle Prince Arthur is captured. He becomes the play's touchstone of humanity as he persuades John's agent, Hubert, to disobey John's orders to blind him, only to kill himself while trying to escape. John's noblemen, thinking the King responsible for the boy's death, defect to the French, but return to their allegiance on learning that the Dauphin intends to kill them after conquering England. John dies, poisoned by a monk; the play ends with the reunited noblemen swearing allegiance to John's son, the young Henry III, and with the Bastard's boast that

> This England never did, nor never shall,
> Lie at the proud foot of a conqueror
> But when it first did help to wound itself.

Twentieth-century revivals of *King John* have been infrequent, but it was popular in the nineteenth century, when the roles of the King, the Bastard, and Constance all appealed to successful actors; a production of 1823 at Covent Garden inaugurated a trend for historically accurate settings and costumes which led to a number of spectacular revivals.

THE PERSONS OF THE PLAY

KING JOHN of England
QUEEN ELEANOR, his mother

LADY FALCONBRIDGE
Philip the BASTARD, later knighted as Sir Richard Plantagenet, her illegitimate son by King Richard I (Coeur-de-lion)
Robert FALCONBRIDGE, her legitimate son
James GURNEY, her attendant

Lady BLANCHE of Spain, niece of King John
PRINCE HENRY, son of King John
HUBERT, a follower of King John
Earl of SALISBURY
Earl of PEMBROKE
Earl of ESSEX
Lord BIGOT

KING PHILIP of France
LOUIS THE DAUPHIN, his son
ARTHUR, Duke of Brittaine, nephew of King John
Lady CONSTANCE, his mother
Duke of AUSTRIA (Limoges)
CHÂTILLON, ambassador from France to England
Count MELUN

A CITIZEN of Angers
Cardinal PANDOLF, a legate from the Pope
PETER OF POMFRET, a prophet

HERALDS
EXECUTIONERS
MESSENGERS
SHERIFF
Lords, soldiers, attendants

The Life and Death of King John

1.1 ⌈*Flourish.*⌉ *Enter King John, Queen Eleanor, and the*
Earls of Pembroke, Essex, and Salisbury ; with
them Châtillon of France

KING JOHN
Now say, Châtillon, what would France with us?

CHÂTILLON
Thus, after greeting, speaks the King of France,
In my behaviour, to the majesty—
The borrowed majesty—of England here.

QUEEN ELEANOR
A strange beginning: 'borrowed majesty'?   5

KING JOHN
Silence, good mother, hear the embassy.

CHÂTILLON
Philip of France, in right and true behalf
Of thy deceasèd brother Geoffrey's son,
Arthur Plantagenet, lays most lawful claim
To this fair island and the territories,   10
To Ireland, Poitou, Anjou, Touraine, Maine;
Desiring thee to lay aside the sword
Which sways usurpingly these several titles,
And put the same into young Arthur's hand,
Thy nephew and right royal sovereign.   15

KING JOHN
What follows if we disallow of this?

CHÂTILLON
The proud control of fierce and bloody war,
To enforce these rights so forcibly withheld—

KING JOHN
Here have we war for war, and blood for blood,
Controlment for controlment: so answer France.   20

CHÂTILLON
Then take my king's defiance from my mouth,
The farthest limit of my embassy.

KING JOHN
Bear mine to him, and so depart in peace.
Be thou as lightning in the eyes of France,
For ere thou canst report, I will be there;   25
The thunder of my cannon shall be heard.
So hence. Be thou the trumpet of our wrath,
And sullen presage of your own decay.—
An honourable conduct let him have;
Pembroke, look to't.—Farewell, Châtillon.   30

Exeunt Châtillon and Pembroke

QUEEN ELEANOR
What now, my son? Have I not ever said
How that ambitious Constance would not cease
Till she had kindled France and all the world
Upon the right and party of her son?
This might have been prevented and made whole   35
With very easy arguments of love,
Which now the manage of two kingdoms must
With fearful-bloody issue arbitrate.

KING JOHN
Our strong possession and our right for us.

QUEEN ELEANOR (*aside to King John*)
Your strong possession much more than your right,   40
Or else it must go wrong with you and me:
So much my conscience whispers in your ear,
Which none but heaven and you and I shall hear.

Enter a Sheriff, ⌈*who whispers to Essex*⌉

ESSEX
My liege, here is the strangest controversy,
Come from the country to be judged by you,   45
That e'er I heard. Shall I produce the men?

KING JOHN Let them approach.—   ⌈*Exit Sheriff*⌉
Our abbeys and our priories shall pay
This expeditious charge.

Enter Robert Falconbridge and Philip the Bastard
⌈*with the Sheriff*⌉

What men are you?

BASTARD
Your faithful subject I, a gentleman   50
Born in Northamptonshire, and eldest son,
As I suppose, to Robert Falconbridge,
A soldier, by the honour-giving hand
Of Cœur-de-lion knighted in the field.

KING JOHN What art thou?   55

FALCONBRIDGE
The son and heir to that same Falconbridge.

KING JOHN
Is that the elder, and art thou the heir?
You came not of one mother then, it seems.

BASTARD
Most certain of one mother, mighty King—
That is well known—and, as I think, one father.   60
But for the certain knowledge of that truth
I put you o'er to heaven, and to my mother.
Of that I doubt as all men's children may.

QUEEN ELEANOR
Out on thee, rude man! Thou dost shame thy mother
And wound her honour with this diffidence.   65

BASTARD
I, Madam? No, I have no reason for it.
That is my brother's plea and none of mine,
The which if he can prove, a pops me out
At least from fair five hundred pound a year.
Heaven guard my mother's honour, and my land!   70

KING JOHN
A good blunt fellow.—Why, being younger born,
Doth he lay claim to thine inheritance?

BASTARD
I know not why, except to get the land;
But once he slandered me with bastardy.
But whe'er I be as true begot or no,   75
That still I lay upon my mother's head;

233

But that I am as well begot, my liege—
Fair fall the bones that took the pains for me—
Compare our faces and be judge yourself.
If old Sir Robert did beget us both   80
And were our father, and this son like him,
O old Sir Robert, father, on my knee
I give heaven thanks I was not like to thee.
KING JOHN
Why, what a madcap hath heaven lent us here!
QUEEN ELEANOR
He hath a trick of Cœur-de-lion's face;   85
The accent of his tongue affecteth him.
Do you not read some tokens of my son
In the large composition of this man?
KING JOHN
Mine eye hath well examinèd his parts,
And finds them perfect Richard.
(*To Robert Falconbridge*)   Sirrah, speak: 90
What doth move you to claim your brother's land?
BASTARD
Because he hath a half-face like my father!
With half that face would he have all my land,
A half-faced groat five hundred pound a year.
FALCONBRIDGE
My gracious liege, when that my father lived,   95
Your brother did employ my father much—
BASTARD
Well, sir, by this you cannot get my land.
Your tale must be how he employed my mother.
FALCONBRIDGE
And once dispatched him in an embassy
To Germany, there with the Emperor   100
To treat of high affairs touching that time.
Th'advantage of his absence took the King,
And in the meantime sojourned at my father's,
Where how he did prevail I shame to speak.
But truth is truth: large lengths of seas and shores 105
Between my father and my mother lay,
As I have heard my father speak himself,
When this same lusty gentleman was got.
Upon his deathbed he by will bequeathed
His lands to me, and took it on his death   110
That this my mother's son was none of his;
And if he were, he came into the world
Full fourteen weeks before the course of time.
Then, good my liege, let me have what is mine,
My father's land, as was my father's will.   115
KING JOHN
Sirrah, your brother is legitimate.
Your father's wife did after wedlock bear him,
And if she did play false, the fault was hers,
Which fault lies on the hazards of all husbands
That marry wives. Tell me, how if my brother,   120
Who, as you say, took pains to get this son,
Had of your father claimed this son for his?
In sooth, good friend, your father might have kept
This calf, bred from his cow, from all the world;
In sooth he might. Then if he were my brother's,   125

My brother might not claim him, nor your father,
Being none of his, refuse him. This concludes:
My mother's son did get your father's heir;
Your father's heir must have your father's land.
FALCONBRIDGE
Shall then my father's will be of no force   130
To dispossess that child which is not his?
BASTARD
Of no more force to dispossess me, sir,
Than was his will to get me, as I think.
QUEEN ELEANOR
Whether hadst thou rather be: a Falconbridge,
And like thy brother to enjoy thy land,   135
Or the reputed son of Cœur-de-lion,
Lord of thy presence, and no land beside?
BASTARD
Madam, an if my brother had my shape,
And I had his, Sir Robert's his like him,
And if my legs were two such riding-rods,   140
My arms such eel-skins stuffed, my face so thin
That in mine ear I durst not stick a rose
Lest men should say 'Look where three-farthings
       goes!',
And, to his shape, were heir to all this land,
Would I might never stir from off this place.   145
I would give it every foot to have this face;
It would not be Sir Nob in any case.
QUEEN ELEANOR
I like thee well. Wilt thou forsake thy fortune,
Bequeath thy land to him, and follow me?
I am a soldier and now bound to France.   150
BASTARD
Brother, take you my land; I'll take my chance.
Your face hath got five hundred pound a year,
Yet sell your face for fivepence and 'tis dear.—
Madam, I'll follow you unto the death.
QUEEN ELEANOR
Nay, I would have you go before me thither.   155
BASTARD
Our country manners give our betters way.
KING JOHN What is thy name?
BASTARD
Philip, my liege, so is my name begun:
Philip, good old Sir Robert's wife's eldest son.
KING JOHN
From henceforth bear his name whose form thou
       bear'st.   160
Kneel thou down Philip, but arise more great:
He knights the Bastard
Arise Sir Richard and Plantagenet.
BASTARD
Brother by th' mother's side, give me your hand;
My father gave me honour, yours gave land.
Now blessèd be the hour, by night or day,   165
When I was got, Sir Robert was away.
QUEEN ELEANOR
The very spirit of Plantagenet!
I am thy grandam, Richard; call me so.

BASTARD
Madam, by chance, but not by truth; what though?
Something about, a little from the right,   170
  In at the window, or else o'er the hatch;
Who dares not stir by day must walk by night,
  And have is have, however men do catch.
Near or far off, well won is still well shot,
And I am I, howe'er I was begot.   175

KING JOHN
Go, Falconbridge, now hast thou thy desire:
A landless knight makes thee a landed squire.—
Come, madam, and come, Richard; we must speed
For France; for France, for it is more than need.

BASTARD
Brother, adieu. Good fortune come to thee,   180
For thou wast got i'th' way of honesty.
                    Exeunt all but the Bastard
A foot of honour better than I was,
But many a many foot of land the worse.
Well, now can I make any Joan a lady.
'Good e'en, Sir Richard'—'God-a-mercy fellow';   185
And if his name be George I'll call him Peter,
For new-made honour doth forget men's names;
'Tis too respective and too sociable
For your conversion. Now your traveller,
He and his toothpick at my worship's mess;   190
And when my knightly stomach is sufficed,
Why then I suck my teeth and catechize
My pickèd man of countries. 'My dear sir,'
Thus leaning on mine elbow I begin,
'I shall beseech you—'. That is Question now;   195
And then comes Answer like an Absey book.
'O sir,' says Answer, 'at your best command,
At your employment, at your service, sir.'
'No sir,' says Question, 'I, sweet sir, at yours.'
And so, ere Answer knows what Question would,   200
Saving in dialogue of compliment,
And talking of the Alps and Apennines,
The Pyrenean and the River Po,
It draws toward supper in conclusion so.
But this is worshipful society,   205
And fits the mounting spirit like myself;
For he is but a bastard to the time
That doth not smack of observation;
And so am I—whether I smack or no,
And not alone in habit and device,   210
Exterior form, outward accoutrement,
But from the inward motion—to deliver
Sweet, sweet, sweet poison for the age's tooth;
Which, though I will not practise to deceive,
Yet to avoid deceit I mean to learn;   215
For it shall strew the footsteps of my rising.
                    Enter Lady Falconbridge and James Gurney
But who comes in such haste in riding-robes?
What woman-post is this? Hath she no husband
That will take pains to blow a horn before her?
O me, 'tis my mother! How now, good lady?   220
What brings you here to court so hastily?

LADY FALCONBRIDGE
Where is that slave thy brother? Where is he
That holds in chase mine honour up and down?

BASTARD
My brother Robert, old Sir Robert's son?
Colbrand the Giant, that same mighty man?   225
Is it Sir Robert's son that you seek so?

LADY FALCONBRIDGE
Sir Robert's son, ay, thou unreverent boy,
Sir Robert's son. Why scorn'st thou at Sir Robert?
He is Sir Robert's son, and so art thou.

BASTARD
James Gurney, wilt thou give us leave awhile?   230

GURNEY
Good leave, good Philip.

BASTARD   Philip Sparrow, James!
There's toys abroad; anon I'll tell thee more.
                    Exit James Gurney
Madam, I was not old Sir Robert's son.
Sir Robert might have eat his part in me
Upon Good Friday, and ne'er broke his fast.   235
Sir Robert could do well, marry to confess,
Could a get me! Sir Robert could not do it:
We know his handiwork. Therefore, good mother,
To whom am I beholden for these limbs?
Sir Robert never holp to make this leg.   240

LADY FALCONBRIDGE
Hast thou conspirèd with thy brother too,
That for thine own gain shouldst defend mine honour?
What means this scorn, thou most untoward knave?

BASTARD
Knight, knight, good mother, Basilisco-like!
What! I am dubbed; I have it on my shoulder.   245
But, mother, I am not Sir Robert's son.
I have disclaimed Sir Robert; and my land,
Legitimation, name, and all is gone.
Then, good my mother, let me know my father;
Some proper man, I hope; who was it, mother?   250

LADY FALCONBRIDGE
Hast thou denied thyself a Falconbridge?

BASTARD
As faithfully as I deny the devil.

LADY FALCONBRIDGE
King Richard Cœur-de-lion was thy father.
By long and vehement suit I was seduced
To make room for him in my husband's bed.   255
Heaven lay not my transgression to my charge!
Thou art the issue of my dear offence,
Which was so strongly urged past my defence.

BASTARD
Now by this light, were I to get again,
Madam, I would not wish a better father.   260
Some sins do bear their privilege on earth,
And so doth yours; your fault was not your folly.
Needs must you lay your heart at his dispose,
Subjected tribute to commanding love,
Against whose fury and unmatchèd force   265
The aweless lion could not wage the fight,

Nor keep his princely heart from Richard's hand.
He that perforce robs lions of their hearts
May easily win a woman's. Ay, my mother,
With all my heart I thank thee for my father.   270
Who lives and dares but say thou didst not well
When I was got, I'll send his soul to hell.
Come, lady, I will show thee to my kin,
And they shall say, when Richard me begot,
If thou hadst said him nay, it had been sin.   275
Who says it was, he lies: I say 'twas not.   *Exeunt*

2.1   ⌈*Flourish.*⌉ *Enter before Angers* ⌈*at one door*⌉ *Philip*
King of France, Louis the Dauphin, Lady
Constance, and Arthur Duke of Brittaine, with
soldiers; ⌈*at another door*⌉ *the Duke of Austria,*
wearing a lion's hide, with soldiers
⌈KING PHILIP⌉
Before Angers well met, brave Austria.—
Arthur, that great forerunner of thy blood,
Richard that robbed the lion of his heart
And fought the holy wars in Palestine,
By this brave duke came early to his grave;   5
And, for amends to his posterity,
At our importance hither is he come
To spread his colours, boy, in thy behalf,
And to rebuke the usurpation
Of thy unnatural uncle, English John.   10
Embrace him, love him, give him welcome hither.
ARTHUR (*to Austria*)
God shall forgive you Cœur-de-lion's death,
The rather that you give his offspring life,
Shadowing their right under your wings of war.
I give you welcome with a powerless hand,   15
But with a heart full of unstainèd love.
Welcome before the gates of Angers, Duke.
⌈KING PHILIP⌉
A noble boy. Who would not do thee right?
AUSTRIA (*kissing Arthur*)
Upon thy cheek lay I this zealous kiss
As seal to this indenture of my love: 20
That to my home I will no more return
Till Angers and the right thou hast in France,
Together with that pale, that white-faced shore,
Whose foot spurns back the ocean's roaring tides
And coops from other lands her islanders,   25
Even till that England, hedged in with the main,
That water-wallèd bulwark, still secure
And confident from foreign purposes,
Even till that utmost corner of the west
Salute thee for her king. Till then, fair boy,   30
Will I not think of home, but follow arms.
CONSTANCE
O, take his mother's thanks, a widow's thanks,
Till your strong hand shall help to give him strength
To make a more requital to your love.
AUSTRIA
The peace of heaven is theirs that lift their swords   35
In such a just and charitable war.

KING PHILIP
Well then, to work! Our cannon shall be bent
Against the brows of this resisting town.
Call for our chiefest men of discipline
To cull the plots of best advantages.   40
We'll lay before this town our royal bones,
Wade to the market-place in Frenchmen's blood,
But we will make it subject to this boy.
CONSTANCE
Stay for an answer to your embassy,
Lest unadvised you stain your swords with blood.   45
My lord Châtillon may from England bring
That right in peace which here we urge in war,
And then we shall repent each drop of blood
That hot rash haste so indirectly shed.
          Enter Châtillon
KING PHILIP
A wonder, lady: lo upon thy wish   50
Our messenger Châtillon is arrived.—
What England says, say briefly, gentle lord;
We coldly pause for thee. Châtillon, speak.
CHÂTILLON
Then turn your forces from this paltry siege,
And stir them up against a mightier task.   55
England, impatient of your just demands,
Hath put himself in arms. The adverse winds,
Whose leisure I have stayed, have given him time
To land his legions all as soon as I.
His marches are expedient to this town,   60
His forces strong, his soldiers confident.
With him along is come the Mother-Queen,
An Ate stirring him to blood and strife;
With her her niece, the Lady Blanche of Spain;
With them a bastard of the King's deceased;   65
And all th'unsettled humours of the land—
Rash, inconsiderate, fiery voluntaries,
With ladies' faces and fierce dragons' spleens—
Have sold their fortunes at their native homes,
Bearing their birthrights proudly on their backs,   70
To make a hazard of new fortunes here.
In brief, a braver choice of dauntless spirits
Than now the English bottoms have waft o'er
Did never float upon the swelling tide
To do offence and scathe in Christendom.   75
          Drum beats
The interruption of their churlish drums
Cuts off more circumstance. They are at hand;
To parley or to fight therefore prepare.
KING PHILIP
How much unlooked-for is this expedition!
AUSTRIA
By how much unexpected, by so much   80
We must awake endeavour for defence,
For courage mounteth with occasion.
Let them be welcome then: we are prepared.
          Enter, ⌈*marching,*⌉ *King John of England, the*
          Bastard, Queen Eleanor, Lady Blanche, the Earl of
          Pembroke, and soldiers

KING JOHN
  Peace be to France, if France in peace permit
  Our just and lineal entrance to our own.   85
  If not, bleed France, and peace ascend to heaven,
  Whiles we, God's wrathful agent, do correct
  Their proud contempt that beats his peace to heaven.
KING PHILIP
  Peace be to England, if that war return
  From France to England, there to live in peace.   90
  England we love, and for that England's sake
  With burden of our armour here we sweat.
  This toil of ours should be a work of thine;
  But thou from loving England art so far
  That thou hast underwrought his lawful king,   95
  Cut off the sequence of posterity,
  Outfacèd infant state, and done a rape
  Upon the maiden virtue of the crown.
  (Pointing to Arthur)
  Look here upon thy brother Geoffrey's face.
  These eyes, these brows, were moulded out of his;   100
  This little abstract doth contain that large
  Which died in Geoffrey; and the hand of time
  Shall draw this brief into as huge a volume.
  That Geoffrey was thy elder brother born,
  And this his son; England was Geoffrey's right,   105
  And this is Geoffrey's. In the name of God,
  How comes it then that thou art called a king,
  When living blood doth in these temples beat,
  Which owe the crown that thou o'ermasterest?
KING JOHN
  From whom hast thou this great commission, France,
  To draw my answer from thy articles?   111
KING PHILIP
  From that supernal judge that stirs good thoughts
  In any breast of strong authority
  To look into the blots and stains of right.
  That judge hath made me guardian to this boy,   115
  Under whose warrant I impeach thy wrong,
  And by whose help I mean to chastise it.
KING JOHN
  Alack, thou dost usurp authority.
KING PHILIP
  Excuse it is to beat usurping down.
QUEEN ELEANOR
  Who is it thou dost call usurper, France?   120
CONSTANCE
  Let me make answer: thy usurping son.
QUEEN ELEANOR
  Out, insolent! Thy bastard shall be king
  That thou mayst be a queen and check the world.
CONSTANCE
  My bed was ever to thy son as true
  As thine was to thy husband; and this boy   125
  Liker in feature to his father Geoffrey
  Than thou and John in manners, being as like
  As rain to water, or devil to his dam.
  My boy a bastard? By my soul I think
  His father never was so true begot.   130
  It cannot be, an if thou wert his mother.

QUEEN ELEANOR (to Arthur)
  There's a good mother, boy, that blots thy father.
CONSTANCE (to Arthur)
  There's a good grandam, boy, that would blot thee.
AUSTRIA
  Peace!
BASTARD Hear the crier!
AUSTRIA   What the devil art thou?
BASTARD
  One that will play the devil, sir, with you,   135
  An a may catch your hide and you alone.
  You are the hare of whom the proverb goes,
  Whose valour plucks dead lions by the beard.
  I'll smoke your skin-coat an I catch you right—
  Sirrah, look to't—i'faith I will, i'faith!   140
BLANCHE
  O, well did he become that lion's robe
  That did disrobe the lion of that robe!
BASTARD
  It lies as sightly on the back of him
  As great Alcides' shows upon an ass.
  But, ass, I'll take that burden from your back,   145
  Or lay on that shall make your shoulders crack.
AUSTRIA
  What cracker is this same that deafs our ears
  With this abundance of superfluous breath?—
  King Philip, determine what we shall do straight.
⌈KING PHILIP⌉
  Women and fools, break off your conference.—   150
  King John, this is the very sum of all:
  England and Ireland, Anjou, Touraine, Maine,
  In right of Arthur do I claim of thee.
  Wilt thou resign them and lay down thy arms?
KING JOHN
  My life as soon. I do defy thee, France.—   155
  Arthur of Brittaine, yield thee to my hand,
  And out of my dear love I'll give thee more
  Than e'er the coward hand of France can win.
  Submit thee, boy.
QUEEN ELEANOR (to Arthur) Come to thy grandam, child.
CONSTANCE (to Arthur)
  Do, child, go to it grandam, child.   160
  Give grandam kingdom, and it grandam will
  Give it a plum, a cherry, and a fig.
  There's a good grandam.
ARTHUR   Good my mother, peace.
  I would that I were low laid in my grave.
  I am not worth this coil that's made for me.   165
    He weeps
QUEEN ELEANOR
  His mother shames him so, poor boy, he weeps.
CONSTANCE
  Now shame upon you, whe'er she does or no!
  His grandam's wrongs, and not his mother's shames,
  Draw those heaven-moving pearls from his poor eyes,
  Which heaven shall take in nature of a fee;   170
  Ay, with these crystal beads heaven shall be bribed
  To do him justice and revenge on you.

QUEEN ELEANOR
Thou monstrous slanderer of heaven and earth!
CONSTANCE
Thou monstrous injurer of heaven and earth!
Call not me slanderer. Thou and thine usurp   175
The dominations, royalties and rights
Of this oppressèd boy. This is thy eld'st son's son,
Infortunate in nothing but in thee.
Thy sins are visited in this poor child;
The canon of the law is laid on him,   180
Being but the second generation
Removèd from thy sin-conceiving womb.
KING JOHN
Bedlam, have done.
CONSTANCE   I have but this to say:
That he is not only plaguèd for her sin,
But God hath made her sin and her the plague   185
On this removèd issue, plagued for her
And with her plague; her sin his injury,
Her injury the beadle to her sin;
All punished in the person of this child,
And all for her. A plague upon her!   190
QUEEN ELEANOR
Thou unadvisèd scold, I can produce
A will that bars the title of thy son.
CONSTANCE
Ay, who doubts that? A will, a wicked will,
A woman's will, a cankered grandam's will!
KING PHILIP
Peace, lady; pause or be more temperate.   195
It ill beseems this presence to cry aim
To these ill-tunèd repetitions.—
Some trumpet summon hither to the walls
These men of Angers. Let us hear them speak
Whose title they admit, Arthur's or John's.   200
     Trumpet sounds. Enter a Citizen upon the walls
CITIZEN
Who is it that hath warned us to the walls?
KING PHILIP
'Tis France for England.
KING JOHN   England for itself.
You men of Angers and my loving subjects—
KING PHILIP
You loving men of Angers, Arthur's subjects,
Our trumpet called you to this gentle parle—   205
KING JOHN
For our advantage; therefore hear us first.
These flags of France that are advancèd here
Before the eye and prospect of your town,
Have hither marched to your endamagement.
The cannons have their bowels full of wrath,   210
And ready mounted are they to spit forth
Their iron indignation 'gainst your walls.
All preparation for a bloody siege
And merciless proceeding by these French
Confront your city's eyes, your winking gates;   215
And but for our approach, those sleeping stones
That as a waist doth girdle you about,

By the compulsion of their ordinance,
By this time from their fixèd beds of lime
Had been dishabited, and wide havoc made   220
For bloody power to rush upon your peace.
But on the sight of us your lawful king,
Who painfully, with much expedient march,
Have brought a countercheck before your gates
To save unscratched your city's threatened cheeks,   225
Behold the French, amazed, vouchsafe a parle;
And now instead of bullets wrapped in fire
To make a shaking fever in your walls,
They shoot but calm words folded up in smoke
To make a faithless error in your ears;   230
Which trust accordingly, kind citizens,
And let us in, your king, whose laboured spirits,
Forwearied in this action of swift speed,
Craves harbourage within your city walls.
KING PHILIP
When I have said, make answer to us both.   235
     He takes Arthur's hand
Lo, in this right hand, whose protection
Is most divinely vowed upon the right
Of him it holds, stands young Plantagenet,
Son to the elder brother of this man
And king o'er him and all that he enjoys.   240
For this downtrodden equity we tread
In warlike march these greens before your town,
Being no further enemy to you
Than the constraint of hospitable zeal
In the relief of this oppressèd child   245
Religiously provokes. Be pleasèd then
To pay that duty which you truly owe
To him that owes it, namely this young prince;
And then our arms, like to a muzzled bear,
Save in aspect, hath all offence sealed up: 250
Our cannons' malice vainly shall be spent
Against th'invulnerable clouds of heaven,
And with a blessèd and unvexed retire,
With unhacked swords and helmets all unbruised,
We will bear home that lusty blood again   255
Which here we came to spout against your town,
And leave your children, wives, and you in peace.
But if you fondly pass our proffered offer,
'Tis not the roundure of your old-faced walls
Can hide you from our messengers of war,   260
Though all these English and their discipline
Were harboured in their rude circumference.
Then tell us, shall your city call us lord
In that behalf which we have challenged it,
Or shall we give the signal to our rage,   265
And stalk in blood to our possession?
CITIZEN
In brief, we are the King of England's subjects.
For him and in his right we hold this town.
KING JOHN
Acknowledge then the King, and let me in.
CITIZEN
That can we not; but he that proves the king,   270

To him will we prove loyal; till that time
Have we rammed up our gates against the world.
KING JOHN
Doth not the crown of England prove the king?
And if not that, I bring you witnesses:
Twice fifteen thousand hearts of England's breed— 275
BASTARD (aside) Bastards and else.
KING JOHN
To verify our title with their lives.
KING PHILIP
As many and as well-born bloods as those—
BASTARD (aside) Some bastards too.
KING PHILIP
Stand in his face to contradict his claim.   280
CITIZEN
Till you compound whose right is worthiest,
We for the worthiest hold the right from both.
KING JOHN
Then God forgive the sin of all those souls
That to their everlasting residence,
Before the dew of evening fall, shall fleet   285
In dreadful trial of our kingdom's king.
KING PHILIP
Amen, Amen! Mount, chevaliers! To arms!
BASTARD
Saint George that swinged the dragon, and e'er since
Sits on's horseback at mine hostess' door,
Teach us some fence! (To Austria) Sirrah, were I at
     home   290
At your den, sirrah, with your lioness,
I would set an ox-head to your lion's hide
And make a monster of you.
AUSTRIA   Peace, no more.
BASTARD
O tremble, for you hear the lion roar!
KING JOHN
Up higher to the plain, where we'll set forth   295
In best appointment all our regiments.
BASTARD
Speed then, to take advantage of the field.
KING PHILIP
It shall be so, and at the other hill
Command the rest to stand. God and our right!
     Exeunt ⌈severally⌉ King John and King Philip
          with their powers. The Citizen remains
                              on the walls
     ⌈Alarum.⌉ Here, after excursions, enter ⌈at one door⌉
     the French Herald, with ⌈a trumpeter⌉, to the gates
FRENCH HERALD
You men of Angers, open wide your gates   300
And let young Arthur Duke of Brittaine in,
Who by the hand of France this day hath made
Much work for tears in many an English mother,
Whose sons lie scattered on the bleeding ground;
Many a widow's husband grovelling lies,   305
Coldly embracing the discoloured earth;
And victory with little loss doth play

Upon the dancing banners of the French,
Who are at hand, triumphantly displayed,
To enter conquerors, and to proclaim   310
Arthur of Brittaine England's king and yours.
     Enter ⌈at another door⌉ the English Herald, with a
          trumpeter
ENGLISH HERALD
Rejoice, you men of Angers, ring your bells!
King John, your king and England's, doth approach,
Commander of this hot malicious day.
Their armours that marched hence so silver-bright 315
Hither return all gilt with Frenchmen's blood.
There stuck no plume in any English crest
That is removèd by a staff of France;
Our colours do return in those same hands
That did display them when we first marched forth;
And like a jolly troop of huntsmen come   321
Our lusty English, all with purpled hands
Dyed in the dying slaughter of their foes.
Open your gates and give the victors way.
⌈CITIZEN⌉
Heralds, from off our towers we might behold   325
From first to last the onset and retire
Of both your armies, whose equality
By our best eyes cannot be censurèd.
Blood hath bought blood and blows have answered
     blows,
Strength matched with strength and power confronted
     power.   330
Both are alike, and both alike we like.
One must prove greatest. While they weigh so even,
We hold our town for neither, yet for both.
     Enter at one door King John, the Bastard, Queen
          Eleanor and Lady Blanche, with soldiers; at another
          door King Philip, Louis the Dauphin, and the Duke
          of Austria with soldiers
KING JOHN
France, hast thou yet more blood to cast away?
Say, shall the current of our right run on,   335
Whose passage, vexed with thy impediment,
Shall leave his native channel and o'erswell
With course disturbed even thy confining shores,
Unless thou let his silver water keep
A peaceful progress to the ocean?   340
KING PHILIP
England, thou hast not saved one drop of blood
In this hot trial more than we of France;
Rather, lost more. And by this hand I swear,
That sways the earth this climate overlooks,
Before we will lay down our just-borne arms,   345
We'll put thee down 'gainst whom these arms we
     bear,
Or add a royal number to the dead,
Gracing the scroll that tells of this war's loss
With slaughter coupled to the name of kings.
BASTARD
Ha, majesty! How high thy glory towers   350
When the rich blood of kings is set on fire!

O, now doth Death line his dead chaps with steel;
The swords of soldiers are his teeth, his fangs;
And now he feasts, mousing the flesh of men
In undetermined differences of kings.　　　　　355
Why stand these royal fronts amazèd thus?
Cry havoc, Kings! Back to the stainèd field,
You equal potents, fiery-kindled spirits!
Then let confusion of one part confirm
The other's peace; till then, blows, blood, and death!
KING JOHN
Whose party do the townsmen yet admit?　　　361
KING PHILIP
Speak, citizens, for England: who's your king?
⌈CITIZEN⌉
The King of England, when we know the King.
KING PHILIP
Know him in us, that here hold up his right.
KING JOHN
In us, that are our own great deputy　　　　365
And bear possession of our person here,
Lord of our presence, Angers, and of you.
⌈CITIZEN⌉
A greater power than we denies all this,
And, till it be undoubted, we do lock
Our former scruple in our strong-barred gates,　370
Kinged of our fear, until our fears resolved
Be by some certain king, purged and deposed.
BASTARD
By heaven, these scroyles of Angers flout you, Kings,
And stand securely on their battlements
As in a theatre, whence they gape and point　　375
At your industrious scenes and acts of death.
Your royal presences be ruled by me.
Do like the mutines of Jerusalem:
Be friends awhile, and both conjointly bend
Your sharpest deeds of malice on this town.　　380
By east and west let France and England mount
Their battering cannon, chargèd to the mouths,
Till their soul-fearing clamours have brawled down
The flinty ribs of this contemptuous city.
I'd play incessantly upon these jades,　　　　385
Even till unfencèd desolation
Leave them as naked as the vulgar air.
That done, dissever your united strengths,
And part your mingled colours once again;
Turn face to face, and bloody point to point.　　390
Then in a moment Fortune shall cull forth
Out of one side her happy minion,
To whom in favour she shall give the day,
And kiss him with a glorious victory.
How like you this wild counsel, mighty states?　395
Smacks it not something of the policy?
KING JOHN
Now, by the sky that hangs above our heads,
I like it well.—France, shall we knit our powers,
And lay this Angers even with the ground,
Then after fight who shall be king of it?　　　400

BASTARD (to King Philip)
An if thou hast the mettle of a king,
Being wronged as we are by this peevish town,
Turn thou the mouth of thy artillery,
As we will ours, against these saucy walls;
And when that we have dashed them to the ground,
Why, then defy each other, and pell-mell　　　406
Make work upon ourselves, for heaven or hell.
KING PHILIP
Let it be so.—Say, where will you assault?
KING JOHN
We from the west will send destruction
Into this city's bosom.　　　　　　　　　410
AUSTRIA I from the north.
KING PHILIP Our thunder from the south
Shall rain their drift of bullets on this town.
BASTARD ⌈to King John⌉
O prudent discipline! From north to south
Austria and France shoot in each other's mouth.　415
I'll stir them to it. Come, away, away!
⌈CITIZEN⌉
Hear us, great Kings, vouchsafe a while to stay,
And I shall show you peace and fair-faced league.
Win you this city without stroke or wound;
Rescue those breathing lives to die in beds,　　420
That here come sacrifices for the field.
Persever not, but hear me, mighty Kings.
KING JOHN
Speak on with favour; we are bent to hear.
⌈CITIZEN⌉
That daughter there of Spain, the Lady Blanche,
Is niece to England. Look upon the years　　　425
Of Louis the Dauphin and that lovely maid.
If lusty love should go in quest of beauty,
Where should he find it fairer than in Blanche?
If zealous love should go in search of virtue,
Where should he find it purer than in Blanche?　430
If love ambitious sought a match of birth,
Whose veins bound richer blood than Lady Blanche?
Such as she is in beauty, virtue, birth,
Is the young Dauphin every way complete;
If not complete, O, say he is not she;　　　　435
And she again wants nothing—to name want—
If want it be not that she is not he.
He is the half part of a blessèd man,
Left to be finishèd by such as she;
And she a fair divided excellence,　　　　　440
Whose fullness of perfection lies in him.
O, two such silver currents when they join
Do glorify the banks that bound them in,
And two such shores to two such streams made one,
Two such controlling bounds, shall you be, Kings,　445
To these two princes if you marry them.
This union shall do more than battery can
To our fast-closèd gates, for at this match,
With swifter spleen than powder can enforce,
The mouth of passage shall we fling wide ope,　450

And give you entrance. But without this match
The sea enragèd is not half so deaf,
Lions more confident, mountains and rocks
More free from motion, no, not Death himself
In mortal fury half so peremptory,   455
As we to keep this city.
BASTARD ⌈*aside*⌉   Here's a stay
That shakes the rotten carcass of old Death
Out of his rags. Here's a large mouth, indeed,
That spits forth Death and mountains, rocks and seas,
Talks as familiarly of roaring lions   460
As maids of thirteen do of puppy-dogs.
What cannoneer begot this lusty blood?
He speaks plain cannon: fire, and smoke, and bounce;
He gives the bastinado with his tongue;
Our ears are cudgelled; not a word of his   465
But buffets better than a fist of France.
Zounds! I was never so bethumped with words
Since I first called my brother's father Dad.
QUEEN ELEANOR (*aside to King John*)
Son, list to this conjunction, make this match,
Give with our niece a dowry large enough;   470
For, by this knot, thou shalt so surely tie
Thy now unsured assurance to the crown
That yon green boy shall have no sun to ripe
The bloom that promiseth a mighty fruit.
I see a yielding in the looks of France;   475
Mark how they whisper. Urge them while their souls
Are capable of this ambition,
Lest zeal, now melted by the windy breath
Of soft petitions, pity, and remorse,
Cool and congeal again to what it was.   480
⌈CITIZEN⌉
Why answer not the double majesties
This friendly treaty of our threatened town?
KING PHILIP
Speak England first, that hath been forward first
To speak unto this city: what say you?
KING JOHN
If that the Dauphin there, thy princely son,   485
Can in this book of beauty read 'I love',
Her dowry shall weigh equal with a queen;
For Anjou and fair Touraine, Maine, Poitou,
And all that we upon this side the sea —
Except this city now by us besieged —   490
Find liable to our crown and dignity,
Shall gild her bridal bed, and make her rich
In titles, honours, and promotions,
As she in beauty, education, blood,
Holds hand with any princess of the world.   495
KING PHILIP
What sayst thou, boy? Look in the lady's face.
LOUIS THE DAUPHIN
I do, my lord, and in her eye I find
A wonder, or a wondrous miracle,
The shadow of myself formed in her eye;
Which, being but the shadow of your son,   500
Becomes a sun and makes your son a shadow.

I do protest I never loved myself
Till now enfixèd I beheld myself
Drawn in the flattering table of her eye.
    He whispers with Blanche
BASTARD (*aside*)
Drawn in the flattering table of her eye,   505
    Hanged in the frowning wrinkle of her brow,
And quartered in her heart: he doth espy
    Himself love's traitor. This is pity now,
That hanged and drawn and quartered there should be
    In such a love so vile a lout as he.   510
BLANCHE (*to Louis the Dauphin*)
My uncle's will in this respect is mine.
If he see aught in you that makes him like,
That anything he sees which moves his liking
I can with ease translate it to my will;
Or if you will, to speak more properly,   515
I will enforce it easily to my love.
Further I will not flatter you, my lord,
That all I see in you is worthy love,
Than this: that nothing do I see in you,
Though churlish thoughts themselves should be your
    judge,   520
That I can find should merit any hate.
KING JOHN
What say these young ones? What say you, my niece?
BLANCHE
That she is bound in honour still to do
What you in wisdom shall vouchsafe to say.
KING JOHN
Speak then, Prince Dauphin, can you love this lady?
LOUIS THE DAUPHIN
Nay, ask me if I can refrain from love,   526
For I do love her most unfeignedly.
KING JOHN
Then do I give Volquessen, Touraine, Maine,
Poitou, and Anjou, these five provinces,
With her to thee, and this addition more: 530
Full thirty thousand marks of English coin.
Philip of France, if thou be pleased withal,
Command thy son and daughter to join hands.
KING PHILIP
It likes us well. — Young princes, close your hands.
AUSTRIA
And your lips too, for I am well assured   535
That I did so when I was first assured.
    ⌈*Louis the Dauphin and Lady Blanche join hands
    and kiss*⌉
KING PHILIP
Now citizens of Angers, ope your gates.
Let in that amity which you have made,
For at Saint Mary's chapel presently
The rites of marriage shall be solemnized. —   540
Is not the Lady Constance in this troop?
(*Aside*) I know she is not, for this match made up
Her presence would have interrupted much.
(*Aloud*) Where is she and her son? Tell me who knows.

LOUIS THE DAUPHIN
  She is sad and passionate at your highness' tent.   545
KING PHILIP
  And by my faith this league that we have made
  Will give her sadness very little cure.—
  Brother of England, how may we content
  This widow lady? In her right we came,
  Which we, God knows, have turned another way   550
  To our own vantage.
KING JOHN   We will heal up all,
  For we'll create young Arthur Duke of Brittaine
  And Earl of Richmond, and this rich fair town
  We make him lord of. Call the Lady Constance.
  Some speedy messenger bid her repair   555
  To our solemnity. I trust we shall,
  If not fill up the measure of her will,
  Yet in some measure satisfy her so
  That we shall stop her exclamation.
  Go we as well as haste will suffer us   560
  To this unlooked-for, unprepared pomp.
                  ⌜Flourish.⌝ Exeunt all but the Bastard
BASTARD
  Mad world, mad kings, mad composition!
  John, to stop Arthur's title in the whole,
  Hath willingly departed with a part;
  And France, whose armour conscience buckled on,   565
  Whom zeal and charity brought to the field
  As God's own soldier, rounded in the ear
  With that same purpose-changer, that sly devil,
  That broker that still breaks the pate of faith,
  That daily break-vow, he that wins of all,   570
  Of kings, of beggars, old men, young men, maids,—
  Who having no external thing to lose
  But the word 'maid', cheats the poor maid of that—
  That smooth-faced gentleman, tickling commodity;
  Commodity, the bias of the world,   575
  The world who of itself is peisèd well,
  Made to run even upon even ground,
  Till this advantage, this vile-drawing bias,
  This sway of motion, this commodity,
  Makes it take head from all indifferency,   580
  From all direction, purpose, course, intent;
  And this same bias, this commodity,
  This bawd, this broker, this all-changing word,
  Clapped on the outward eye of fickle France,
  Hath drawn him from his own determined aid,   585
  From a resolved and honourable war,
  To a most base and vile-concluded peace.
  And why rail I on this commodity?
  But for because he hath not wooed me yet—
  Not that I have the power to clutch my hand   590
  When his fair angels would salute my palm,
  But for my hand, as unattempted yet,
  Like a poor beggar raileth on the rich.
  Well, whiles I am a beggar I will rail,
  And say there is no sin but to be rich,   595
  And being rich, my virtue then shall be
  To say there is no vice but beggary.

Since kings break faith upon commodity,
Gain, be my lord, for I will worship thee.   Exit

2.2   Enter Lady Constance, Arthur Duke of Brittaine,
       and the Earl of Salisbury
CONSTANCE (to Salisbury)
  Gone to be married? Gone to swear a peace?
  False blood to false blood joined! Gone to be friends?
  Shall Louis have Blanche, and Blanche those
      provinces?
  It is not so, thou hast misspoke, misheard.
  Be well advised, tell o'er thy tale again.   5
  It cannot be, thou dost but say 'tis so.
  I trust I may not trust thee, for thy word
  Is but the vain breath of a common man.
  Believe me, I do not believe thee, man;
  I have a king's oath to the contrary.   10
  Thou shalt be punished for thus frighting me;
  For I am sick and capable of fears;
  Oppressed with wrongs, and therefore full of fears;
  A widow husbandless, subject to fears;
  A woman naturally born to fears;   15
  And though thou now confess thou didst but jest,
  With my vexed spirits I cannot take a truce,
  But they will quake and tremble all this day.
  What dost thou mean by shaking of thy head?
  Why dost thou look so sadly on my son?   20
  What means that hand upon that breast of thine?
  Why holds thine eye that lamentable rheum,
  Like a proud river peering o'er his bounds?
  Be these sad signs confirmers of thy words?
  Then speak again—not all thy former tale,   25
  But this one word: whether thy tale be true.
SALISBURY
  As true as I believe you think them false
  That give you cause to prove my saying true.
CONSTANCE
  O, if thou teach me to believe this sorrow,
  Teach thou this sorrow how to make me die;   30
  And let belief and life encounter so
  As doth the fury of two desperate men
  Which in the very meeting fall and die.
  Louis marry Blanche! (To Arthur) O boy, then where
      art thou?
  France friend with England!—What becomes of me?   35
  (To Salisbury) Fellow, be gone, I cannot brook thy
      sight;
  This news hath made thee a most ugly man.
SALISBURY
  What other harm have I, good lady, done,
  But spoke the harm that is by others done?
CONSTANCE
  Which harm within itself so heinous is   40
  As it makes harmful all that speak of it.
ARTHUR
  I do beseech you, madam, be content.
CONSTANCE
  If thou that bidd'st me be content wert grim,

Ugly and sland'rous to thy mother's womb,
Full of unpleasing blots and sightless stains,   45
Lame, foolish, crooked, swart, prodigious,
Patched with foul moles and eye-offending marks,
I would not care, I then would be content,
For then I should not love thee, no, nor thou
Become thy great birth, nor deserve a crown.   50
But thou art fair, and at thy birth, dear boy,
Nature and Fortune joined to make thee great.
Of Nature's gifts thou mayst with lilies boast,
And with the half-blown rose. But Fortune, O,
She is corrupted, changed, and won from thee;   55
Sh'adulterates hourly with thine uncle John,
And with her golden hand hath plucked on France
To tread down fair respect of sovereignty,
And made his majesty the bawd to theirs.
France is a bawd to Fortune and King John,   60
That strumpet Fortune, that usurping John.
(*To Salisbury*) Tell me, thou fellow, is not France
        forsworn?
Envenom him with words, or get thee gone
And leave those woes alone, which I alone
Am bound to underbear.
SALISBURY   Pardon me, madam,   65
I may not go without you to the Kings.
CONSTANCE
Thou mayst, thou shalt; I will not go with thee.
I will instruct my sorrows to be proud,
For grief is proud and makes his owner stoop.
        ⌈*She sits upon the ground*⌉
To me and to the state of my great grief   70
Let kings assemble, for my grief's so great
That no supporter but the huge firm earth
Can hold it up. Here I and sorrows sit;
Here is my throne; bid kings come bow to it.
                ⌈*Exeunt Salisbury and Arthur*⌉

3.1   ⌈*Flourish.*⌉ *Enter King John and King Philip* ⌈*hand
        in hand*⌉; *Louis the Dauphin and Lady Blanche,*
        ⌈*married*⌉; *Queen Eleanor, the Bastard, and the
        Duke of Austria*
KING PHILIP (*to Blanche*)
'Tis true, fair daughter, and this blessèd day
Ever in France shall be kept festival.
To solemnize this day, the glorious sun
Stays in his course and plays the alchemist,
Turning with splendour of his precious eye   5
The meagre cloddy earth to glittering gold.
The yearly course that brings this day about
Shall never see it but a holy day.
CONSTANCE (*rising*)
A wicked day, and not a holy day!
What hath this day deserved? What hath it done,   10
That it in golden letters should be set
Among the high tides in the calendar?
Nay, rather turn this day out of the week,
This day of shame, oppression, perjury.
Or if it must stand still, let wives with child   15

Pray that their burdens may not fall this day,
Lest that their hopes prodigiously be crossed;
But on this day let seamen fear no wreck;
No bargains break that are not this day made;
This day all things begun come to ill end,   20
Yea, faith itself to hollow falsehood change.
KING PHILIP
By heaven, lady, you shall have no cause
To curse the fair proceedings of this day.
Have I not pawned to you my majesty?
CONSTANCE
You have beguiled me with a counterfeit   25
Resembling majesty, which being touched and tried
Proves valueless. You are forsworn, forsworn.
You came in arms to spill mine enemies' blood,
But now in arms you strengthen it with yours.
The grappling vigour and rough frown of war   30
Is cold in amity and painted peace,
And our oppression hath made up this league.
Arm, arm, you heavens, against these perjured Kings!
A widow cries, be husband to me, God!
Let not the hours of this ungodly day   35
Wear out the day in peace, but ere sun set
Set armèd discord 'twixt these perjured Kings.
Hear me, O hear me!
AUSTRIA   Lady Constance, peace.
CONSTANCE
War, war, no peace! Peace is to me a war.
O Limoges, O Austria, thou dost shame   40
That bloody spoil. Thou slave, thou wretch, thou
        coward!
Thou little valiant, great in villainy;
Thou ever strong upon the stronger side;
Thou Fortune's champion, that dost never fight
But when her humorous ladyship is by   45
To teach thee safety. Thou art perjured too,
And sooth'st up greatness. What a fool art thou,
A ramping fool, to brag and stamp, and swear
Upon my party! Thou cold-blooded slave,
Hast thou not spoke like thunder on my side,   50
Been sworn my soldier, bidding me depend
Upon thy stars, thy fortune, and thy strength?
And dost thou now fall over to my foes?
Thou wear a lion's hide! Doff it, for shame,
And hang a calf's-skin on those recreant limbs.   55
AUSTRIA
O, that a man should speak those words to me!
BASTARD
And hang a calf's-skin on those recreant limbs.
AUSTRIA
Thou dar'st not say so, villain, for thy life.
BASTARD
And hang a calf's-skin on those recreant limbs.
KING JOHN (*to the Bastard*)
We like not this. Thou dost forget thyself.   60
        Enter Cardinal Pandolf
KING PHILIP
Here comes the holy legate of the Pope.

PANDOLF
  Hail, you anointed deputies of God. —
  To thee, King John, my holy errand is.
  I Pandolf, of fair Milan Cardinal,
  And from Pope Innocent the legate here,   65
  Do in his name religiously demand
  Why thou against the Church, our Holy Mother,
  So wilfully dost spurn, and force perforce
  Keep Stephen Langton, chosen Archbishop
  Of Canterbury, from that holy see.   70
  This, in our foresaid Holy Father's name,
  Pope Innocent, I do demand of thee.
KING JOHN
  What earthy name to interrogatories
  Can task the free breath of a sacred king?
  Thou canst not, Cardinal, devise a name   75
  So slight, unworthy, and ridiculous
  To charge me to an answer, as the Pope.
  Tell him this tale, and from the mouth of England
  Add thus much more: that no Italian priest
  Shall tithe or toll in our dominions;   80
  But as we, under God, are supreme head,
  So, under him, that great supremacy
  Where we do reign we will alone uphold
  Without th'assistance of a mortal hand.
  So tell the Pope, all reverence set apart   85
  To him and his usurped authority.
KING PHILIP
  Brother of England, you blaspheme in this.
KING JOHN
  Though you and all the kings of Christendom
  Are led so grossly by this meddling priest,
  Dreading the curse that money may buy out,   90
  And by the merit of vile gold, dross, dust,
  Purchase corrupted pardon of a man,
  Who in that sale sells pardon from himself;
  Though you and all the rest so grossly led
  This juggling witchcraft with revenue cherish;   95
  Yet I alone, alone do me oppose
  Against the Pope, and count his friends my foes.
PANDOLF
  Then by the lawful power that I have
  Thou shalt stand cursed and excommunicate;
  And blessèd shall he be that doth revolt   100
  From his allegiance to an heretic;
  And meritorious shall that hand be called,
  Canonized and worshipped as a saint,
  That takes away by any secret course
  Thy hateful life.
CONSTANCE   O lawful let it be   105
  That I have room with Rome to curse awhile.
  Good Father Cardinal, cry thou 'Amen'
  To my keen curses, for without my wrong
  There is no tongue hath power to curse him right.
PANDOLF
  There's law and warrant, lady, for my curse.   110
CONSTANCE
  And for mine too. When law can do no right,

Let it be lawful that law bar no wrong.
Law cannot give my child his kingdom here,
For he that holds his kingdom holds the law.
Therefore, since law itself is perfect wrong,   115
How can the law forbid my tongue to curse?
PANDOLF
  Philip of France, on peril of a curse,
  Let go the hand of that arch-heretic,
  And raise the power of France upon his head,
  Unless he do submit himself to Rome.   120
QUEEN ELEANOR
  Look'st thou pale, France? Do not let go thy hand.
CONSTANCE ⌈to King John⌉
  Look to it, devil, lest that France repent,
  And by disjoining hands hell lose a soul.
AUSTRIA
  King Philip, listen to the Cardinal.
BASTARD
  And hang a calf's-skin on his recreant limbs.   125
AUSTRIA
  Well, ruffian, I must pocket up these wrongs,
  Because—
BASTARD   Your breeches best may carry them.
KING JOHN
  Philip, what sayst thou to the Cardinal?
CONSTANCE
  What should he say, but as the Cardinal?
LOUIS THE DAUPHIN
  Bethink you, Father, for the difference   130
  Is purchase of a heavy curse from Rome,
  Or the light loss of England for a friend.
  Forgo the easier.
BLANCHE   That's the curse of Rome.
CONSTANCE
  O Louis, stand fast; the devil tempts thee here
  In likeness of a new untrimmèd bride.   135
BLANCHE
  The Lady Constance speaks not from her faith,
  But from her need.
CONSTANCE ⌈to King Philip⌉ O if thou grant my need,
  Which only lives but by the death of faith,
  That need must needs infer this principle:
  That faith would live again by death of need.   140
  O, then tread down my need, and faith mounts up;
  Keep my need up, and faith is trodden down.
KING JOHN
  The King is moved, and answers not to this.
CONSTANCE (to King Philip)
  O, be removed from him, and answer well.
AUSTRIA
  Do so, King Philip, hang no more in doubt.   145
BASTARD
  Hang nothing but a calf's-skin, most sweet lout.
KING PHILIP
  I am perplexed, and know not what to say.
PANDOLF
  What canst thou say but will perplex thee more,
  If thou stand excommunicate and cursed?

KING PHILIP
Good Reverend Father, make my person yours,   150
And tell me how you would bestow yourself.
This royal hand and mine are newly knit,
And the conjunction of our inward souls
Married in league, coupled and linked together
With all religious strength of sacred vows;   155
The latest breath that gave the sound of words
Was deep-sworn faith, peace, amity, true love,
Between our kingdoms and our royal selves;
And even before this truce, but new before,
No longer than we well could wash our hands   160
To clap this royal bargain up of peace,
God knows, they were besmeared and over-stained
With slaughter's pencil, where Revenge did paint
The fearful difference of incensèd kings;
And shall these hands, so lately purged of blood,   165
So newly joined in love, so strong in both,
Unyoke this seizure and this kind regreet,
Play fast and loose with faith, so jest with heaven,
Make such unconstant children of ourselves,
As now again to snatch our palm from palm,   170
Unswear faith sworn, and on the marriage-bed
Of smiling peace to march a bloody host,
And make a riot on the gentle brow
Of true sincerity? O holy sir,
My Reverend Father, let it not be so.   175
Out of your grace, devise, ordain, impose
Some gentle order, and then we shall be blessed
To do your pleasure and continue friends.
PANDOLF
All form is formless, order orderless,
Save what is opposite to England's love.   180
Therefore to arms, be champion of our Church,
Or let the Church, our mother, breathe her curse,
A mother's curse, on her revolting son.
France, thou mayst hold a serpent by the tongue,
A crazèd lion by the mortal paw,   185
A fasting tiger safer by the tooth,
Than keep in peace that hand which thou dost hold.
KING PHILIP
I may disjoin my hand, but not my faith.
PANDOLF
So mak'st thou faith an enemy to faith,
And like a civil war, sett'st oath to oath,   190
Thy tongue against thy tongue. O, let thy vow,
First made to heaven, first be to heaven performed;
That is, to be the champion of our Church.
What since thou swor'st is sworn against thyself,
And may not be performèd by thyself;   195
For that which thou hast sworn to do amiss
Is not amiss when it is truly done;
And being not done where doing tends to ill,
The truth is then most done not doing it.
The better act of purposes mistook   200
Is to mistake again; though indirect,
Yet indirection thereby grows direct,
And falsehood falsehood cures, as fire cools fire

Within the scorchèd veins of one new burned.
It is religion that doth make vows kept;   205
But thou hast sworn against religion;
By what thou swear'st, against the thing thou
    swear'st;
And mak'st an oath the surety for thy troth:
Against an oath, the truth. Thou art unsure
To swear: swear'st only not to be forsworn—   210
Else what a mockery should it be to swear!—
But thou dost swear only to be forsworn,
And most forsworn to keep what thou dost swear;
Therefore thy later vows against thy first
Is in thyself rebellion to thyself,   215
And better conquest never canst thou make
Than arm thy constant and thy nobler parts
Against these giddy loose suggestions;
Upon which better part our prayers come in
If thou vouchsafe them. But if not, then know   220
The peril of our curses light on thee
So heavy as thou shalt not shake them off,
But in despair die under their black weight.
AUSTRIA
Rebellion, flat rebellion!
BASTARD   Wilt not be?
Will not a calf's-skin stop that mouth of thine? 225
LOUIS THE DAUPHIN
Father, to arms!
BLANCHE   Upon thy wedding day?
Against the blood that thou hast married?
What, shall our feast be kept with slaughtered men?
Shall braying trumpets and loud churlish drums,
Clamours of hell, be measures to our pomp?   230
    She kneels
O husband, hear me! Ay, alack, how new
Is 'husband' in my mouth! Even for that name
Which till this time my tongue did ne'er pronounce,
Upon my knee I beg, go not to arms
Against mine uncle.
CONSTANCE (*kneeling*)   O, upon my knee   235
Made hard with kneeling, I do pray to thee,
Thou virtuous Dauphin, alter not the doom
Forethought by heaven.
BLANCHE (*to Louis the Dauphin*)
Now shall I see thy love: what motive may
Be stronger with thee than the name of wife?   240
CONSTANCE
That which upholdeth him that thee upholds:
His honour.—O thine honour, Louis, thine honour!
LOUIS THE DAUPHIN (*to King Philip*)
I muse your majesty doth seem so cold
When such profound respects do pull you on.
PANDOLF
I will denounce a curse upon his head.   245
KING PHILIP
Thou shalt not need.—England, I will fall from thee.
    ⌐*He takes his hand from King John's hand. Blanche*
    and Constance rise⌐
CONSTANCE
O, fair return of banished majesty!

QUEEN ELEANOR
O, foul revolt of French inconstancy!
KING JOHN
France, thou shalt rue this hour within this hour.
BASTARD
Old Time the clock-setter, that bald sexton Time,   250
Is it as he will?—Well then, France shall rue.
BLANCHE
The sun's o'ercast with blood; fair day, adieu!
Which is the side that I must go withal?
I am with both, each army hath a hand,
And in their rage, I having hold of both,   255
They whirl asunder and dismember me.
Husband, I cannot pray that thou mayst win.—
Uncle, I needs must pray that thou mayst lose.—
Father, I may not wish the fortune thine.—
Grandam, I will not wish thy wishes thrive.   260
Whoever wins, on that side shall I lose,
Assurèd loss before the match be played.
LOUIS THE DAUPHIN
Lady, with me, with me thy fortune lies.
BLANCHE
There where my fortune lives, there my life dies.
KING JOHN (to the Bastard)
Cousin, go draw our puissance together.—   265
                        ⌜Exit the Bastard⌝
France, I am burned up with inflaming wrath,
A rage whose heat hath this condition:
That nothing can allay, nothing but blood,
The blood, and dearest-valued blood, of France.
KING PHILIP
Thy rage shall burn thee up, and thou shalt turn   270
To ashes ere our blood shall quench that fire.
Look to thyself, thou art in jeopardy.
KING JOHN
No more than he that threats.—To arms let's hie!
                        Exeunt ⌜severally⌝

3.2   Alarum; excursions. Enter the Bastard, with the
       Duke of Austria's head
BASTARD
Now, by my life, this day grows wondrous hot;
Some airy devil hovers in the sky
And pours down mischief. Austria's head lie there,
While Philip breathes.
       Enter King John, Arthur Duke of Brittaine, and
       Hubert
KING JOHN
Hubert, keep this boy.—Philip, make up!   5
My mother is assailèd in our tent,
And ta'en I fear.
BASTARD   My lord, I rescued her;
Her highness is in safety; fear you not.
But on, my liege, for very little pains
Will bring this labour to an happy end.   10
       Exeunt ⌜King John and the Bastard at one door,
       Hubert and Arthur at another door⌝

3.3   Alarum; excursions; retreat. Enter King John,
       Queen Eleanor, Arthur Duke of Brittaine, the
       Bastard, Hubert, lords, ⌜with soldiers⌝
KING JOHN (to Queen Eleanor)
So shall it be; your grace shall stay behind
So strongly guarded. (To Arthur) Cousin, look not sad;
Thy grandam loves thee, and thy uncle will
As dear be to thee as thy father was.
ARTHUR
O, this will make my mother die with grief.   5
KING JOHN (to the Bastard)
Cousin, away for England! Haste before,
And ere our coming, see thou shake the bags
Of hoarding abbots. The fat ribs of peace
Must by the hungry now be fed upon.
Imprisoned angels set at liberty.   10
Use our commission in his utmost force.
BASTARD
Bell, book, and candle shall not drive me back
When gold and silver becks me to come on.
I leave your highness.—Grandam, I will pray,
If ever I remember to be holy,   15
For your fair safety. So I kiss your hand.
QUEEN ELEANOR
Farewell, gentle cousin.
KING JOHN   Coz, farewell.
                        Exit the Bastard
QUEEN ELEANOR
Come hither, little kinsman. Hark, a word.
       She takes Arthur aside
KING JOHN
Come hither, Hubert.
       He takes Hubert aside
                        O my gentle Hubert,
We owe thee much. Within this wall of flesh   20
There is a soul counts thee her creditor,
And with advantage means to pay thy love;
And, my good friend, thy voluntary oath
Lives in this bosom, dearly cherishèd.
Give me thy hand.
       He takes Hubert's hand
                        I had a thing to say,   25
But I will fit it with some better tune.
By heaven, Hubert, I am almost ashamed
To say what good respect I have of thee.
HUBERT
I am much bounden to your majesty.
KING JOHN
Good friend, thou hast no cause to say so yet,   30
But thou shalt have; and creep time ne'er so slow,
Yet it shall come for me to do thee good.
I had a thing to say—but let it go.
The sun is in the heaven, and the proud day,
Attended with the pleasures of the world,   35
Is all too wanton and too full of gauds
To give me audience. If the midnight bell
Did with his iron tongue and brazen mouth

Sound on into the drowsy race of night;
If this same were a churchyard where we stand,   40
And thou possessèd with a thousand wrongs;
Or if that surly spirit, melancholy,
Had baked thy blood and made it heavy, thick,
Which else runs tickling up and down the veins,
Making that idiot, laughter, keep men's eyes   45
And strain their cheeks to idle merriment—
A passion hateful to my purposes—
Or if that thou couldst see me without eyes,
Hear me without thine ears, and make reply
Without a tongue, using conceit alone,   50
Without eyes, ears, and harmful sound of words;
Then in despite of broad-eyed watchful day
I would into thy bosom pour my thoughts.
But, ah, I will not. Yet I love thee well,
And by my troth, I think thou lov'st me well.   55

HUBERT
So well that what you bid me undertake,
Though that my death were adjunct to my act,
By heaven, I would do it.

KING JOHN   Do not I know thou wouldst?
Good Hubert, Hubert, Hubert, throw thine eye
On yon young boy. I'll tell thee what, my friend,   60
He is a very serpent in my way,
And wheresoe'er this foot of mine doth tread,
He lies before me. Dost thou understand me?
Thou art his keeper.

HUBERT   And I'll keep him so
That he shall not offend your majesty.   65

KING JOHN
Death.

HUBERT My lord.

KING JOHN   A grave.

HUBERT   He shall not live.

KING JOHN   Enough.
I could be merry now. Hubert, I love thee.
Well, I'll not say what I intend for thee.
Remember. (*To Queen Eleanor*) Madam, fare you well.
I'll send those powers o'er to your majesty.   70

QUEEN ELEANOR
My blessing go with thee.

KING JOHN (*to Arthur*)   For England, cousin, go.
Hubert shall be your man, attend on you
With all true duty.—On toward Calais, ho!

                    Exeunt ⌐Queen Eleanor, attended, at one door,
                    the rest at another door⌐

3.4   *Enter King Philip, Louis the Dauphin, Cardinal*
            Pandolf, and attendants

KING PHILIP
So, by a roaring tempest on the flood,
A whole armada of convicted sail
Is scattered and disjoined from fellowship.

PANDOLF
Courage and comfort; all shall yet go well.

KING PHILIP
What can go well when we have run so ill?   5

Are we not beaten? Is not Angers lost,
Arthur ta'en prisoner, divers dear friends slain,
And bloody England into England gone,
O'erbearing interruption, spite of France?

LOUIS THE DAUPHIN
What he hath won, that hath he fortified.   10
So hot a speed, with such advice disposed,
Such temperate order in so fierce a cause,
Doth want example. Who hath read or heard
Of any kindred action like to this?

KING PHILIP
Well could I bear that England had this praise,   15
So we could find some pattern of our shame.

                    Enter Constance, distracted, with her hair about
                    her ears

Look who comes here! A grave unto a soul,
Holding th'eternal spirit against her will
In the vile prison of afflicted breath.—
I prithee, lady, go away with me.   20

CONSTANCE
Lo, now, now see the issue of your peace!

KING PHILIP
Patience, good lady; comfort, gentle Constance.

CONSTANCE
No, I defy all counsel, all redress,
But that which ends all counsel, true redress:
Death, Death, O amiable, lovely Death!   25
Thou odoriferous stench, sound rottenness!
Arise forth from the couch of lasting night,
Thou hate and terror to prosperity,
And I will kiss thy detestable bones,
And put my eyeballs in thy vaulty brows,   30
And ring these fingers with thy household worms,
And stop this gap of breath with fulsome dust,
And be a carrion monster like thyself.
Come grin on me, and I will think thou smil'st,
And buss thee as thy wife. Misery's love,   35
O, come to me!

KING PHILIP   O fair affliction, peace!

CONSTANCE
No, no, I will not, having breath to cry.
O, that my tongue were in the thunder's mouth!
Then with a passion would I shake the world,
And rouse from sleep that fell anatomy,   40
Which cannot hear a lady's feeble voice,
Which scorns a modern invocation.

PANDOLF
Lady, you utter madness, and not sorrow.

CONSTANCE
Thou art not holy to belie me so.
I am not mad: this hair I tear is mine;   45
My name is Constance; I was Geoffrey's wife;
Young Arthur is my son; and he is lost.
I am not mad; I would to God I were,
For then 'tis like I should forget myself.
O, if I could, what grief should I forget!   50
Preach some philosophy to make me mad,

And thou shalt be canonized, Cardinal.
For, being not mad, but sensible of grief,
My reasonable part produces reason
How I may be delivered of these woes,   55
And teaches me to kill or hang myself.
If I were mad I should forget my son,
Or madly think a babe of clouts were he.
I am not mad; too well, too well I feel
The different plague of each calamity.   60
KING PHILIP
Bind up those tresses. O, what love I note
In the fair multitude of those her hairs!
Where but by chance a silver drop hath fallen,
Even to that drop ten thousand wiry friends
Do glue themselves in sociable grief,   65
Like true, inseparable, faithful loves,
Sticking together in calamity.
CONSTANCE
To England, if you will.
KING PHILIP   Bind up your hairs.
CONSTANCE
Yes, that I will. And wherefore will I do it?
I tore them from their bonds, and cried aloud,   70
'O that these hands could so redeem my son,
As they have given these hairs their liberty!'
But now I envy at their liberty,
And will again commit them to their bonds,
Because my poor child is a prisoner.   75
        She binds up her hair
And Father Cardinal, I have heard you say
That we shall see and know our friends in heaven.
If that be true, I shall see my boy again;
For since the birth of Cain, the first male child,
To him that did but yesterday suspire,   80
There was not such a gracious creature born.
But now will canker-sorrow eat my bud,
And chase the native beauty from his cheek;
And he will look as hollow as a ghost,
As dim and meagre as an ague's fit,   85
And so he'll die; and rising so again,
When I shall meet him in the court of heaven,
I shall not know him; therefore never, never
Must I behold my pretty Arthur more.
PANDOLF
You hold too heinous a respect of grief.   90
CONSTANCE
He talks to me that never had a son.
KING PHILIP
You are as fond of grief as of your child.
CONSTANCE
Grief fills the room up of my absent child,
Lies in his bed, walks up and down with me,
Puts on his pretty looks, repeats his words,   95
Remembers me of all his gracious parts,
Stuffs out his vacant garments with his form;
Then have I reason to be fond of grief.
Fare you well. Had you such a loss as I,

I could give better comfort than you do.   100
        ⌈She unbinds her hair⌉
I will not keep this form upon my head
When there is such disorder in my wit.
O Lord, my boy, my Arthur, my fair son,
My life, my joy, my food, my all the world,
My widow-comfort, and my sorrow's cure!   Exit
KING PHILIP
I fear some outrage, and I'll follow her.   106
                                Exit ⌈attended⌉
LOUIS THE DAUPHIN
There's nothing in this world can make me joy.
Life is as tedious as a twice-told tale,
Vexing the dull ear of a drowsy man;
And bitter shame hath spoiled the sweet world's taste,
That it yields naught but shame and bitterness.   111
PANDOLF
Before the curing of a strong disease,
Even in the instant of repair and health,
The fit is strongest. Evils that take leave,
On their departure most of all show evil.   115
What have you lost by losing of this day?
LOUIS THE DAUPHIN
All days of glory, joy, and happiness.
PANDOLF
If you had won it, certainly you had.
No, no; when Fortune means to men most good,
She looks upon them with a threat'ning eye.   120
'Tis strange to think how much King John hath lost
In this which he accounts so clearly won.
Are not you grieved that Arthur is his prisoner?
LOUIS THE DAUPHIN
As heartily as he is glad he hath him.
PANDOLF
Your mind is all as youthful as your blood.   125
Now hear me speak with a prophetic spirit,
For even the breath of what I mean to speak
Shall blow each dust, each straw, each little rub,
Out of the path which shall directly lead
Thy foot to England's throne. And therefore mark.   130
John hath seized Arthur, and it cannot be
That whiles warm life plays in that infant's veins
The misplaced John should entertain an hour,
One minute, nay, one quiet breath of rest.
A sceptre snatched with an unruly hand   135
Must be as boisterously maintained as gained;
And he that stands upon a slipp'ry place
Makes nice of no vile hold to stay him up.
That John may stand, then Arthur needs must fall;
So be it, for it cannot be but so.   140
LOUIS THE DAUPHIN
But what shall I gain by young Arthur's fall?
PANDOLF
You, in the right of Lady Blanche your wife,
May then make all the claim that Arthur did.
LOUIS THE DAUPHIN
And lose it, life and all, as Arthur did.

PANDOLF
How green you are, and fresh in this old world!   145
John lays you plots; the times conspire with you;
For he that steeps his safety in true blood
Shall find but bloody safety and untrue.
This act, so vilely born, shall cool the hearts
Of all his people, and freeze up their zeal,   150
That none so small advantage shall step forth
To check his reign but they will cherish it;
No natural exhalation in the sky,
No scope of nature, no distempered day,
No common wind, no customèd event,   155
But they will pluck away his natural cause,
And call them meteors, prodigies, and signs,
Abortives, presages, and tongues of heaven
Plainly denouncing vengeance upon John.
LOUIS THE DAUPHIN
Maybe he will not touch young Arthur's life,   160
But hold himself safe in his prisonment.
PANDOLF
O sir, when he shall hear of your approach,
If that young Arthur be not gone already,
Even at that news he dies; and then the hearts
Of all his people shall revolt from him,   165
And kiss the lips of unacquainted change,
And pick strong matter of revolt and wrath
Out of the bloody fingers' ends of John.
Methinks I see this hurly all on foot,
And O, what better matter breeds for you   170
Than I have named! The Bastard Falconbridge
Is now in England, ransacking the Church,
Offending charity. If but a dozen French
Were now in arms, they would be as a call
To train ten thousand English to their side,   175
Or as a little snow tumbled about
Anon becomes a mountain. O noble Dauphin,
Go with me to the King. 'Tis wonderful
What may be wrought out of their discontent
Now that their souls are top-full of offence.   180
For England, go! I will whet on the King.
LOUIS THE DAUPHIN
Strong reasons make strange actions. Let us go.
If you say ay, the King will not say no.   *Exeunt*

4.1   *Enter Hubert, and Executioners with a rope and*
irons
HUBERT
Heat me these irons hot, and look thou stand
Within the arras. When I strike my foot
Upon the bosom of the ground, rush forth
And bind the boy which you shall find with me
Fast to the chair. Be heedful. Hence, and watch!   5
EXECUTIONER
I hope your warrant will bear out the deed.
HUBERT
Uncleanly scruples: fear not you. Look to't!
    ⌈*The Executioners withdraw behind the arras*⌉
Young lad, come forth, I have to say with you.
    Enter Arthur Duke of Brittaine

ARTHUR
Good morrow, Hubert.
HUBERT   Good morrow, little Prince.
ARTHUR
As little prince, having so great a title   10
To be more prince, as may be. You are sad.
HUBERT
Indeed I have been merrier.
ARTHUR   Mercy on me!
Methinks nobody should be sad but I.
Yet I remember, when I was in France,
Young gentlemen would be as sad as night   15
Only for wantonness. By my christendom,
So I were out of prison and kept sheep,
I should be as merry as the day is long;
And so I would be here, but that I doubt
My uncle practises more harm to me.   20
He is afraid of me, and I of him.
Is it my fault that I was Geoffrey's son?
No, indeed is't not, and I would to God
I were your son, so you would love me, Hubert.
HUBERT (*aside*)
If I talk to him, with his innocent prate   25
He will awake my mercy, which lies dead;
Therefore I will be sudden, and dispatch.
ARTHUR
Are you sick, Hubert? You look pale today.
In sooth, I would you were a little sick,
That I might sit all night and watch with you.   30
I warrant I love you more than you do me.
HUBERT (*aside*)
His words do take possession of my bosom.
    He shows Arthur a paper
Read here, young Arthur. (*Aside*) How now: foolish
    rheum,
Turning dispiteous torture out of door?
I must be brief, lest resolution drop   35
Out at mine eyes in tender womanish tears.
(*To Arthur*) Can you not read it? Is it not fair writ?
ARTHUR
Too fairly, Hubert, for so foul effect.
Must you with hot irons burn out both mine eyes?
HUBERT
Young boy, I must.
ARTHUR   And will you?
HUBERT   And I will.   40
ARTHUR
Have you the heart? When your head did but ache
I knit my handkerchief about your brows,
The best I had—a princess wrought it me,
And I did never ask it you again—
And with my hand at midnight held your head,   45
And like the watchful minutes to the hour
Still and anon cheered up the heavy time,
Saying 'What lack you?' and 'Where lies your grief?'
Or 'What good love may I perform for you?'
Many a poor man's son would have lain still   50
And ne'er have spoke a loving word to you,
But you at your sick service had a prince.

Nay, you may think my love was crafty love,
And call it cunning. Do, an if you will.
If heaven be pleased that you must use me ill,   55
Why then you must. Will you put out mine eyes,
These eyes that never did, nor never shall,
So much as frown on you?

HUBERT   I have sworn to do it,
And with hot irons must I burn them out.

ARTHUR
Ah, none but in this iron age would do it.   60
The iron of itself, though heat red hot,
Approaching near these eyes would drink my tears,
And quench his fiery indignation
Even in the matter of mine innocence;
Nay, after that, consume away in rust,   65
But for containing fire to harm mine eye.
Are you more stubborn-hard than hammered iron?
An if an angel should have come to me
And told me Hubert should put out mine eyes,
I would not have believed him; no tongue but
     Hubert's.   70

Hubert stamps his foot

HUBERT
Come forth!

The Executioners come forth
          Do as I bid you do.

ARTHUR
O, save me, Hubert, save me! My eyes are out
Even with the fierce looks of these bloody men.

HUBERT (*to the Executioners*)
Give me the iron, I say, and bind him here.

He takes the iron

ARTHUR
Alas, what need you be so boisterous-rough?   75
I will not struggle; I will stand stone-still.
For God's sake, Hubert, let me not be bound.
Nay, hear me, Hubert! Drive these men away,
And I will sit as quiet as a lamb;
I will not stir, nor wince, nor speak a word,   80
Nor look upon the iron angerly.
Thrust but these men away, and I'll forgive you,
Whatever torment you do put me to.

HUBERT (*to the Executioners*)
Go stand within. Let me alone with him.

EXECUTIONER
I am best pleased to be from such a deed.   85
                              Exeunt Executioners

ARTHUR
Alas, I then have chid away my friend!
He hath a stern look, but a gentle heart.
Let him come back, that his compassion may
Give life to yours.

HUBERT   Come, boy, prepare yourself.

ARTHUR
Is there no remedy?

HUBERT   None but to lose your eyes.   90

ARTHUR
O God, that there were but a mote in yours,
A grain, a dust, a gnat, a wandering hair,

Any annoyance in that precious sense,
Then, feeling what small things are boisterous there,
Your vile intent must needs seem horrible.   95

HUBERT
Is this your promise? Go to, hold your tongue!

ARTHUR
Hubert, the utterance of a brace of tongues
Must needs want pleading for a pair of eyes.
Let me not hold my tongue, let me not, Hubert;
Or, Hubert, if you will, cut out my tongue,   100
So I may keep mine eyes. O, spare mine eyes,
Though to no use but still to look on you.
Lo, by my troth, the instrument is cold
And would not harm me.

HUBERT   I can heat it, boy.

ARTHUR
No, in good sooth: the fire is dead with grief,   105
Being create for comfort, to be used
In undeserved extremes. See else yourself.
There is no malice in this burning coal;
The breath of heaven hath blown his spirit out,
And strewed repentant ashes on his head.   110

HUBERT
But with my breath I can revive it, boy.

ARTHUR
An if you do, you will but make it blush
And glow with shame of your proceedings, Hubert.
Nay, it perchance will sparkle in your eyes,
And like a dog that is compelled to fight,   115
Snatch at his master that doth tarre him on.
All things that you should use to do me wrong
Deny their office; only you do lack
That mercy which fierce fire and iron extends,
Creatures of note for mercy-lacking uses.   120

HUBERT
Well, see to live. I will not touch thine eye
For all the treasure that thine uncle owes.
Yet am I sworn, and I did purpose, boy,
With this same very iron to burn them out.

ARTHUR
O, now you look like Hubert. All this while   125
You were disguisèd.

HUBERT   Peace, no more. Adieu.
Your uncle must not know but you are dead.
I'll fill these doggèd spies with false reports;
And, pretty child, sleep doubtless and secure
That Hubert, for the wealth of all the world,   130
Will not offend thee.

ARTHUR   O God! I thank you, Hubert.

HUBERT
Silence, no more. Go closely in with me.
Much danger do I undergo for thee.   *Exeunt*

4.2   ⌜*Flourish.*⌝ *Enter King John, the Earls of Pembroke*
             and Salisbury, and other lords. King John ascends
             the throne

KING JOHN
Here once again we sit, once again crowned,
And looked upon, I hope, with cheerful eyes.

PEMBROKE
This 'once again', but that your highness pleased,
Was once superfluous. You were crowned before,
And that high royalty was ne'er plucked off,   5
The faiths of men ne'er stainèd with revolt;
Fresh expectation troubled not the land
With any longed-for change or better state.
SALISBURY
Therefore to be possessed with double pomp,
To guard a title that was rich before,   10
To gild refinèd gold, to paint the lily,
To throw a perfume on the violet,
To smooth the ice, or add another hue
Unto the rainbow, or with taper-light
To seek the beauteous eye of heaven to garnish,   15
Is wasteful and ridiculous excess.
PEMBROKE
But that your royal pleasure must be done,
This act is as an ancient tale new-told,
And in the last repeating troublesome,
Being urgèd at a time unseasonable.   20
SALISBURY
In this the antique and well-noted face
Of plain old form is much disfigurèd,
And like a shifted wind unto a sail,
It makes the course of thoughts to fetch about,
Startles and frights consideration,   25
Makes sound opinion sick, and truth suspected
For putting on so new a fashioned robe.
PEMBROKE
When workmen strive to do better than well,
They do confound their skill in covetousness;
And oftentimes excusing of a fault   30
Doth make the fault the worser by th'excuse;
As patches set upon a little breach
Discredit more in hiding of the fault
Than did the fault before it was so patched.
SALISBURY
To this effect: before you were new-crowned   35
We breathed our counsel, but it pleased your
          highness
To overbear it; and we are all well pleased,
Since all and every part of what we would
Doth make a stand at what your highness will.
KING JOHN
Some reasons of this double coronation   40
I have possessed you with, and think them strong.
And more, more strong, when lesser is my fear
I shall endue you with. Meantime but ask
What you would have reformed that is not well,
And well shall you perceive how willingly   45
I will both hear and grant you your requests.
PEMBROKE
Then I, as one that am the tongue of these
To sound the purposes of all their hearts,
Both for myself and them, but chief of all
Your safety, for the which myself and them   50
Bend their best studies, heartily request

Th'enfranchisement of Arthur, whose restraint
Doth move the murmuring lips of discontent
To break into this dangerous argument:
If what in rest you have, in right you hold,   55
Why then your fears—which, as they say, attend
The steps of wrong—should move you to mew up
Your tender kinsman, and to choke his days
With barbarous ignorance, and deny his youth
The rich advantage of good exercise?   60
That the time's enemies may not have this
To grace occasions, let it be our suit
That you have bid us ask, his liberty;
Which for our goods we do no further ask
Than whereupon our weal, on you depending,   65
Counts it your weal he have his liberty.
          Enter Hubert
KING JOHN
Let it be so. I do commit his youth
To your direction.—Hubert, what news with you?
          He takes Hubert aside
PEMBROKE
This is the man should do the bloody deed:
He showed his warrant to a friend of mine.   70
The image of a wicked heinous fault
Lives in his eye; that close aspect of his
Does show the mood of a much troubled breast;
And I do fearfully believe 'tis done
What we so feared he had a charge to do.   75
SALISBURY
The colour of the King doth come and go
Between his purpose and his conscience,
Like heralds 'twixt two dreadful battles set.
His passion is so ripe it needs must break.
PEMBROKE
And when it breaks, I fear will issue thence   80
The foul corruption of a sweet child's death.
KING JOHN (coming forward)
We cannot hold mortality's strong hand.
Good lords, although my will to give is living,
The suit which you demand is gone and dead.
He tells us Arthur is deceased tonight.   85
SALISBURY
Indeed we feared his sickness was past cure.
PEMBROKE
Indeed we heard how near his death he was,
Before the child himself felt he was sick.
This must be answered, either here or hence.
KING JOHN
Why do you bend such solemn brows on me?   90
Think you I bear the shears of destiny?
Have I commandment on the pulse of life?
SALISBURY
It is apparent foul play, and 'tis shame
That greatness should so grossly offer it.
So thrive it in your game; and so, farewell.   95
PEMBROKE
Stay yet, Lord Salisbury; I'll go with thee,
And find th'inheritance of this poor child,

His little kingdom of a forcèd grave.
That blood which owed the breadth of all this isle
Three foot of it doth hold. Bad world the while.   100
This must not be thus borne. This will break out
To all our sorrows; and ere long, I doubt.
        Exeunt Pembroke, Salisbury, ⌈and other lords⌉
KING JOHN
They burn in indignation. I repent.
There is no sure foundation set on blood,
No certain life achieved by others' death.   105
        Enter a Messenger
A fearful eye thou hast. Where is that blood
That I have seen inhabit in those cheeks?
So foul a sky clears not without a storm;
Pour down thy weather: how goes all in France?
MESSENGER
From France to England. Never such a power   110
For any foreign preparation
Was levied in the body of a land.
The copy of your speed is learned by them,
For when you should be told they do prepare,
The tidings comes that they are all arrived.   115
KING JOHN
O, where hath our intelligence been drunk?
Where hath it slept? Where is my mother's ear,
That such an army could be drawn in France,
And she not hear of it?
MESSENGER   My liege, her ear
Is stopped with dust. The first of April died   120
Your noble mother. And as I hear, my lord,
The Lady Constance in a frenzy died
Three days before; but this from rumour's tongue
I idly heard; if true or false I know not.
KING JOHN
Withhold thy speed, dreadful Occasion;   125
O, make a league with me till I have pleased
My discontented peers. What, Mother dead?
How wildly then walks my estate in France!—
Under whose conduct came those powers of France
That thou for truth giv'st out are landed here?   130
MESSENGER
Under the Dauphin.
        Enter the Bastard and Peter of Pomfret
KING JOHN   Thou hast made me giddy
With these ill tidings. (*To the Bastard*) Now, what says
        the world
To your proceedings? Do not seek to stuff
My head with more ill news, for it is full.
BASTARD
But if you be afeard to hear the worst,   135
Then let the worst, unheard, fall on your head.
KING JOHN
Bear with me, cousin, for I was amazed
Under the tide; but now I breathe again
Aloft the flood, and can give audience
To any tongue, speak it of what it will.   140
BASTARD
How I have sped among the clergymen

The sums I have collected shall express.
But as I travelled hither through the land,
I find the people strangely fantasied,
Possessed with rumours, full of idle dreams,   145
Not knowing what they fear, but full of fear.
And here's a prophet that I brought with me
From forth the streets of Pomfret, whom I found
With many hundreds treading on his heels;
To whom he sung, in rude, harsh-sounding rhymes,
That ere the next Ascension Day at noon   151
Your highness should deliver up your crown.
KING JOHN
Thou idle dreamer, wherefore didst thou so?
PETER OF POMFRET
Foreknowing that the truth will fall out so.
KING JOHN
Hubert, away with him! Imprison him,   155
And on that day, at noon, whereon he says
I shall yield up my crown, let him be hanged.
Deliver him to safety, and return,
For I must use thee.
        Exeunt Hubert and Peter of Pomfret
                    O my gentle cousin,
Hear'st thou the news abroad, who are arrived?   160
BASTARD
The French, my lord: men's mouths are full of it.
Besides, I met Lord Bigot and Lord Salisbury
With eyes as red as new-enkindled fire,
And others more, going to seek the grave
Of Arthur, whom they say is killed tonight   165
On your suggestion.
KING JOHN   Gentle kinsman, go
And thrust thyself into their companies.
I have a way to win their loves again.
Bring them before me.
BASTARD   I will seek them out.
KING JOHN
Nay, but make haste, the better foot before.   170
O, let me have no subject enemies
When adverse foreigners affright my towns
With dreadful pomp of stout invasion!
Be Mercury, set feathers to thy heels,
And fly like thought from them to me again.   175
BASTARD
The spirit of the time shall teach me speed.   *Exit*
KING JOHN
Spoke like a sprightful noble gentleman!—
Go after him, for he perhaps shall need
Some messenger betwixt me and the peers,
And be thou he.   180
MESSENGER With all my heart, my liege.   *Exit*
KING JOHN My mother dead!
        Enter Hubert
HUBERT
My lord, they say five moons were seen tonight,
Four fixèd, and the fifth did whirl about
The other four in wondrous motion.   185

KING JOHN
Five moons?

HUBERT   Old men and beldams in the streets
Do prophesy upon it dangerously.
Young Arthur's death is common in their mouths,
And when they talk of him they shake their heads,
And whisper one another in the ear;   190
And he that speaks doth grip the hearer's wrist,
Whilst he that hears makes fearful action,
With wrinkled brows, with nods, with rolling eyes.
I saw a smith stand with his hammer, thus,
The whilst his iron did on the anvil cool,   195
With open mouth swallowing a tailor's news,
Who, with his shears and measure in his hand,
Standing on slippers which his nimble haste
Had falsely thrust upon contrary feet,
Told of a many thousand warlike French   200
That were embattailèd and ranked in Kent.
Another lean unwashed artificer
Cuts off his tale, and talks of Arthur's death.

KING JOHN
Why seek'st thou to possess me with these fears?
Why urgest thou so oft young Arthur's death?   205
Thy hand hath murdered him. I had a mighty cause
To wish him dead, but thou hadst none to kill him.

HUBERT
No had, my lord? Why, did you not provoke me?

KING JOHN
It is the curse of kings to be attended
By slaves that take their humours for a warrant   210
To break within the bloody house of life,
And on the winking of authority
To understand a law, to know the meaning
Of dangerous majesty, when perchance it frowns
More upon humour than advised respect.   215

HUBERT
Here is your hand and seal for what I did.
        He shows a paper

KING JOHN
O, when the last account 'twixt heaven and earth
Is to be made, then shall this hand and seal
Witness against us to damnation!
How oft the sight of means to do ill deeds   220
Make deeds ill done! Hadst not thou been by,
A fellow by the hand of nature marked,
Quoted, and signed to do a deed of shame,
This murder had not come into my mind.
But taking note of thy abhorred aspect,   225
Finding thee fit for bloody villainy,
Apt, liable to be employed in danger,
I faintly broke with thee of Arthur's death;
And thou, to be endearèd to a king,
Made it no conscience to destroy a prince.   230

HUBERT   My lord—

KING JOHN
Hadst thou but shook thy head or made a pause
When I spake darkly what I purposèd,
Or turned an eye of doubt upon my face,

As bid me tell my tale in express words,   235
Deep shame had struck me dumb, made me break off,
And those thy fears might have wrought fears in me.
But thou didst understand me by my signs,
And didst in signs again parley with sin;
Yea, without stop, didst let thy heart consent,   240
And consequently thy rude hand to act
The deed which both our tongues held vile to name.
Out of my sight, and never see me more!
My nobles leave me, and my state is braved,
Even at my gates, with ranks of foreign powers;   245
Nay, in the body of this fleshly land,
This kingdom, this confine of blood and breath,
Hostility and civil tumult reigns
Between my conscience and my cousin's death.

HUBERT
Arm you against your other enemies;   250
I'll make a peace between your soul and you.
Young Arthur is alive. This hand of mine
Is yet a maiden and an innocent hand,
Not painted with the crimson spots of blood.
Within this bosom never entered yet   255
The dreadful motion of a murderous thought;
And you have slandered nature in my form,
Which, howsoever rude exteriorly,
Is yet the cover of a fairer mind
Than to be butcher of an innocent child.   260

KING JOHN
Doth Arthur live? O, haste thee to the peers;
Throw this report on their incensèd rage,
And make them tame to their obedience.
Forgive the comment that my passion made
Upon thy feature, for my rage was blind,   265
And foul imaginary eyes of blood
Presented thee more hideous than thou art.
O, answer not, but to my closet bring
The angry lords with all expedient haste.
I conjure thee but slowly; run more fast.   270
                                    Exeunt ⌈severally⌉

4.3   *Enter Arthur Duke of Brittaine on the walls,*
       disguised as a ship-boy

ARTHUR
The wall is high, and yet will I leap down.
Good ground, be pitiful, and hurt me not.
There's few or none do know me; if they did,
This ship-boy's semblance hath disguised me quite.
I am afraid, and yet I'll venture it.   5
If I get down and do not break my limbs,
I'll find a thousand shifts to get away.
As good to die and go, as die and stay.
        He leaps down
O me! My uncle's spirit is in these stones.
Heaven take my soul, and England keep my bones!   10
                                            He dies
        Enter the Earls of Pembroke and Salisbury, and Lord
        Bigot
SALISBURY
Lords, I will meet him at Saint Edmundsbury.

It is our safety, and we must embrace
This gentle offer of the perilous time.

PEMBROKE
Who brought that letter from the Cardinal?

SALISBURY
The Count Melun, a noble lord of France,   15
Who's private with me of the Dauphin's love;
'Tis much more general than these lines import.

BIGOT
Tomorrow morning let us meet him then.

SALISBURY
Or rather, then set forward, for 'twill be
Two long days' journey, lords, or ere we meet.   20
    Enter the Bastard

BASTARD
Once more today well met, distempered lords.
The King by me requests your presence straight.

SALISBURY
The King hath dispossessed himself of us.
We will not line his thin bestainèd cloak
With our pure honours, nor attend the foot   25
That leaves the print of blood where'er it walks.
Return and tell him so; we know the worst.

BASTARD
Whate'er you think, good words I think were best.

SALISBURY
Our griefs and not our manners reason now.

BASTARD
But there is little reason in your grief.   30
Therefore 'twere reason you had manners now.

PEMBROKE
Sir, sir, impatience hath his privilege.

BASTARD
'Tis true—to hurt his master, no man else.

SALISBURY
This is the prison.
    He sees Arthur's body
                What is he lies here?

PEMBROKE
O death, made proud with pure and princely beauty!
The earth had not a hole to hide this deed.   36

SALISBURY
Murder, as hating what himself hath done,
Doth lay it open to urge on revenge.

BIGOT
Or when he doomed this beauty to a grave,
Found it too precious-princely for a grave.   40

SALISBURY (*to the Bastard*)
Sir Richard, what think you? You have beheld.
Or have you read or heard; or could you think,
Or do you almost think, although you see,
That you do see? Could thought, without this object,
Form such another? This is the very top,   45
The height, the crest, or crest unto the crest,
Of murder's arms; this is the bloodiest shame,
The wildest savagery, the vilest stroke
That ever wall-eyed wrath or staring rage
Presented to the tears of soft remorse.   50

PEMBROKE
All murders past do stand excused in this,
And this, so sole and so unmatchable,
Shall give a holiness, a purity,
To the yet-unbegotten sin of times,
And prove a deadly bloodshed but a jest,   55
Exampled by this heinous spectacle.

BASTARD
It is a damnèd and a bloody work,
The graceless action of a heavy hand—
If that it be the work of any hand.

SALISBURY
If that it be the work of any hand?   60
We had a kind of light what would ensue:
It is the shameful work of Hubert's hand,
The practice and the purpose of the King;
From whose obedience I forbid my soul,
Kneeling before this ruin of sweet life,   65
And breathing to his breathless excellence
The incense of a vow, a holy vow,
Never to taste the pleasures of the world,
Never to be infected with delight,
Nor conversant with ease and idleness,   70
Till I have set a glory to this hand
By giving it the worship of revenge.

PEMBROKE *and* BIGOT
Our souls religiously confirm thy words.
    Enter Hubert

HUBERT
Lords, I am hot with haste in seeking you.
Arthur doth live; the King hath sent for you.   75

SALISBURY
O, he is bold, and blushes not at death!—
Avaunt, thou hateful villain, get thee gone!

HUBERT
I am no villain.

SALISBURY   Must I rob the law?
    He draws his sword

BASTARD
Your sword is bright, sir; put it up again.

SALISBURY
Not till I sheathe it in a murderer's skin.   80

HUBERT (*drawing his sword*)
Stand back, Lord Salisbury, stand back, I say!
By heaven, I think my sword's as sharp as yours.
I would not have you, lord, forget yourself,
Nor tempt the danger of my true defence,
Lest I, by marking of your rage, forget   85
Your worth, your greatness and nobility.

BIGOT
Out, dunghill! Dar'st thou brave a nobleman?

HUBERT
Not for my life; but yet I dare defend
My innocent life against an emperor.

SALISBURY
Thou art a murderer.

HUBERT   Do not prove me so;   90
Yet I am none. Whose tongue soe'er speaks false,
Not truly speaks; who speaks not truly, lies.

PEMBROKE
    Cut him to pieces!
BASTARD (*drawing his sword*) Keep the peace, I say!
SALISBURY
    Stand by, or I shall gall you, Falconbridge.
BASTARD
    Thou wert better gall the devil, Salisbury.   95
    If thou but frown on me, or stir thy foot,
    Or teach thy hasty spleen to do me shame,
    I'll strike thee dead. Put up thy sword betime,
    Or I'll so maul you and your toasting-iron
    That you shall think the devil is come from hell.   100
BIGOT
    What wilt thou do, renownèd Falconbridge,
    Second a villain and a murderer?
HUBERT
    Lord Bigot, I am none.
BIGOT   Who killed this prince?
HUBERT
    'Tis not an hour since I left him well.
    I honoured him, I loved him, and will weep   105
    My date of life out for his sweet life's loss.
SALISBURY
    Trust not those cunning waters of his eyes,
    For villainy is not without such rheum,
    And he, long traded in it, makes it seem
    Like rivers of remorse and innocency.   110
    Away with me, all you whose souls abhor
    Th'uncleanly savours of a slaughter-house,
    For I am stifled with this smell of sin.
BIGOT
    Away toward Bury, to the Dauphin there.
PEMBROKE
    There, tell the King, he may enquire us out.   115
        Exeunt Pembroke, Salisbury, and Bigot
BASTARD
    Here's a good world! Knew you of this fair work?
    Beyond the infinite and boundless reach
    Of mercy, if thou didst this deed of death
    Art thou damned, Hubert.
HUBERT Do but hear me, sir.   120
BASTARD Ha! I'll tell thee what:
    Thou'rt damned as black—nay nothing is so black—
    Thou art more deep damned than Prince Lucifer;
    There is not yet so ugly a fiend of hell
    As thou shalt be if thou didst kill this child.   125
HUBERT
    Upon my soul—
BASTARD   If thou didst but consent
    To this most cruel act, do but despair;
    And if thou want'st a cord, the smallest thread
    That ever spider twisted from her womb
    Will serve to strangle thee; a rush will be a beam   130
    To hang thee on; or wouldst thou drown thyself,
    Put but a little water in a spoon
    And it shall be, as all the ocean,
    Enough to stifle such a villain up.
    I do suspect thee very grievously.   135

HUBERT
    If I in act, consent, or sin of thought
    Be guilty of the stealing that sweet breath
    Which was embounded in this beauteous clay,
    Let hell want pains enough to torture me.
    I left him well.
BASTARD   Go bear him in thine arms.   140
    I am amazed, methinks, and lose my way
    Among the thorns and dangers of this world.
        Hubert takes up Arthur in his arms
    How easy dost thou take all England up!
    From forth this morsel of dead royalty,
    The life, the right, and truth of all this realm   145
    Is fled to heaven, and England now is left
    To tug and scramble, and to part by th' teeth
    The unowed interest of proud swelling state.
    Now for the bare-picked bone of majesty
    Doth doggèd war bristle his angry crest,   150
    And snarleth in the gentle eyes of peace;
    Now powers from home and discontents at home
    Meet in one line, and vast confusion waits,
    As doth a raven on a sick-fall'n beast,
    The imminent decay of wrested pomp.   155
    Now happy he whose cloak and cincture can
    Hold out this tempest. Bear away that child,
    And follow me with speed. I'll to the King.
    A thousand businesses are brief in hand,
    And heaven itself doth frown upon the land.   160
        Exeunt ⌐severally⌐

5.1   ⌐*Flourish.*⌐ *Enter King John and Cardinal Pandolf,*
          with attendants
KING JOHN ⌐*giving Pandolf the crown*⌐
    Thus have I yielded up into your hand
    The circle of my glory.
PANDOLF (*giving back the crown*) Take again
    From this my hand, as holding of the Pope,
    Your sovereign greatness and authority.
KING JOHN
    Now keep your holy word: go meet the French,   5
    And from his Holiness use all your power
    To stop their marches 'fore we are enflamed.
    Our discontented counties do revolt,
    Our people quarrel with obedience,
    Swearing allegiance and the love of soul   10
    To stranger blood, to foreign royalty.
    This inundation of mistempered humour
    Rests by you only to be qualified.
    Then pause not, for the present time's so sick
    That present med'cine must be ministered,   15
    Or overthrow incurable ensues.
PANDOLF
    It was my breath that blew this tempest up,
    Upon your stubborn usage of the Pope,
    But since you are a gentle convertite,
    My tongue shall hush again this storm of war   20
    And make fair weather in your blust'ring land.
    On this Ascension Day, remember well,

Upon your oath of service to the Pope,
Go I to make the French lay down their arms.

⌈Exeunt all but King John⌉

KING JOHN
Is this Ascension Day? Did not the prophet   25
Say that before Ascension Day at noon
My crown I should give off? Even so I have.
I did suppose it should be on constraint,
But, heaven be thanked, it is but voluntary.

Enter Bastard

BASTARD
All Kent hath yielded; nothing there holds out   30
But Dover Castle. London hath received,
Like a kind host, the Dauphin and his powers.
Your nobles will not hear you, but are gone
To offer service to your enemy;
And wild amazement hurries up and down   35
The little number of your doubtful friends.

KING JOHN
Would not my lords return to me again
After they heard young Arthur was alive?

BASTARD
They found him dead and cast into the streets,
An empty casket, where the jewel of life   40
By some damned hand was robbed and ta'en away.

KING JOHN
That villain Hubert told me he did live.

BASTARD
So on my soul he did, for aught he knew.
But wherefore do you droop? Why look you sad?
Be great in act as you have been in thought.   45
Let not the world see fear and sad distrust
Govern the motion of a kingly eye.
Be stirring as the time, be fire with fire;
Threaten the threat'ner, and outface the brow
Of bragging horror. So shall inferior eyes,   50
That borrow their behaviours from the great,
Grow great by your example, and put on
The dauntless spirit of resolution.
Away, and glisten like the god of war
When he intendeth to become the field.   55
Show boldness and aspiring confidence.
What, shall they seek the lion in his den
And fright him there, and make him tremble there?
O, let it not be said! Forage, and run
To meet displeasure farther from the doors,   60
And grapple with him ere he come so nigh.

KING JOHN
The legate of the Pope hath been with me,
And I have made a happy peace with him,
And he hath promised to dismiss the powers
Led by the Dauphin.

BASTARD   O inglorious league!   65
Shall we, upon the footing of our land,
Send fair-play orders, and make compromise,
Insinuation, parley, and base truce
To arms invasive? Shall a beardless boy,
A cockered silken wanton, brave our fields   70
And flesh his spirit in a warlike soil,

Mocking the air with colours idly spread,
And find no check? Let us, my liege, to arms!
Perchance the Cardinal cannot make your peace,
Or if he do, let it at least be said   75
They saw we had a purpose of defence.

KING JOHN
Have thou the ordering of this present time.

BASTARD
Away, then, with good courage! *⌈Aside⌉* Yet I know
Our party may well meet a prouder foe.   *Exeunt*

5.2 *Enter, ⌈marching⌉ in arms, Louis the Dauphin, the
Earl of Salisbury, Count Melun, the Earl of
Pembroke, and Lord Bigot, with soldiers*

LOUIS THE DAUPHIN
My Lord Melun, let this be copied out,
And keep it safe for our remembrance.
Return the precedent to these lords again,
That having our fair order written down,
Both they and we, perusing o'er these notes,   5
May know wherefore we took the sacrament
And keep our faiths firm and inviolable.

SALISBURY
Upon our sides it never shall be broken.
And, noble Dauphin, albeit we swear
A voluntary zeal and an unurgèd faith   10
To your proceedings, yet believe me, Prince,
I am not glad that such a sore of time
Should seek a plaster by contemnèd revolt,
And heal the inveterate canker of one wound
By making many. O, it grieves my soul   15
That I must draw this metal from my side
To be a widow-maker! O, and there
Where honourable rescue and defence
Cries out upon the name of Salisbury!
But such is the infection of the time,   20
That for the health and physic of our right,
We cannot deal but with the very hand
Of stern injustice and confusèd wrong.
And is't not pity, O my grievèd friends,
That we the sons and children of this isle   25
Was born to see so sad an hour as this,
Wherein we step after a stranger, march
Upon her gentle bosom, and fill up
Her enemies' ranks? I must withdraw and weep
Upon the spot of this enforcèd cause—   30
To grace the gentry of a land remote,
And follow unacquainted colours here.
What, here? O nation, that thou couldst remove;
That Neptune's arms who clippeth thee about
Would bear thee from the knowledge of thyself   35
And gripple thee unto a pagan shore,
Where these two Christian armies might combine
The blood of malice in a vein of league,
And not to spend it so unneighbourly.

LOUIS THE DAUPHIN
A noble temper dost thou show in this,   40
And great affections, wrestling in thy bosom,

Doth make an earthquake of nobility.
O, what a noble combat hast thou fought
Between compulsion and a brave respect!
Let me wipe off this honourable dew   45
That silverly doth progress on thy cheeks.
My heart hath melted at a lady's tears,
Being an ordinary inundation;
But this effusion of such manly drops,
This shower blown up by tempest of the soul,   50
Startles mine eyes, and makes me more amazed
Than had I seen the vaulty top of heaven
Figured quite o'er with burning meteors.
Lift up thy brow, renownèd Salisbury,
And with a great heart heave away this storm;   55
Commend these waters to those baby eyes
That never saw the giant world enraged,
Nor met with Fortune other than at feasts,
Full warm of blood, of mirth, of gossiping.
Come, come, for thou shalt thrust thy hand as deep 60
Into the purse of rich prosperity
As Louis himself. So, nobles, shall you all
That knit your sinews to the strength of mine.
    ⌈*A trumpet sounds*⌉
And even there methinks an angel spake!
    Enter Cardinal Pandolf
Look where the holy legate comes apace,   65
To give us warrant from the hand of heaven,
And on our actions set the name of right
With holy breath.
PANDOLF   Hail, noble prince of France!
The next is this. King John hath reconciled
Himself to Rome; his spirit is come in   70
That so stood out against the Holy Church,
The great metropolis and See of Rome;
Therefore thy threat'ning colours now wind up,
And tame the savage spirit of wild war,
That like a lion fostered up at hand   75
It may lie gently at the foot of peace,
And be no further harmful than in show.
LOUIS THE DAUPHIN
Your grace shall pardon me: I will not back.
I am too high-born to be propertied,
To be a secondary at control,   80
Or useful serving-man and instrument
To any sovereign state throughout the world.
Your breath first kindled the dead coal of wars
Between this chastised kingdom and myself,
And brought in matter that should feed this fire; 85
And now 'tis far too huge to be blown out
With that same weak wind which enkindled it.
You taught me how to know the face of right,
Acquainted me with interest to this land,
Yea, thrust this enterprise into my heart;   90
And come ye now to tell me John hath made
His peace with Rome? What is that peace to me?
I, by the honour of my marriage bed,
After young Arthur, claim this land for mine;
And now it is half conquered, must I back   95

Because that John hath made his peace with Rome?
Am I Rome's slave? What penny hath Rome borne,
What men provided, what munition sent
To underprop this action? Is't not I
That undergo this charge? Who else but I,   100
And such as to my claim are liable,
Sweat in this business and maintain this war?
Have I not heard these islanders shout out
'Vive le Roi!' as I have banked their towns?
Have I not here the best cards for the game,   105
To win this easy match played for a crown?
And shall I now give o'er the yielded set?
No, no, on my soul, it never shall be said.
PANDOLF
You look but on the outside of this work.
LOUIS THE DAUPHIN
Outside or inside, I will not return   110
Till my attempt so much be glorified
As to my ample hope was promisèd
Before I drew this gallant head of war,
And culled these fiery spirits from the world
To outlook conquest and to win renown   115
Even in the jaws of danger and of death.
    A trumpet sounds
What lusty trumpet thus doth summon us?
    Enter the Bastard
BASTARD
According to the fair play of the world,
Let me have audience; I am sent to speak.
My holy lord of Milan, from the King   120
I come to learn how you have dealt for him,
And as you answer I do know the scope
And warrant limited unto my tongue.
PANDOLF
The Dauphin is too wilful-opposite,
And will not temporize with my entreaties.   125
He flatly says he'll not lay down his arms.
BASTARD
By all the blood that ever fury breathed,
The youth says well. Now hear our English king,
For thus his royalty doth speak in me.
He is prepared, and reason too he should.   130
This apish and unmannerly approach,
This harnessed masque and unadvisèd revel,
This unhaired sauciness and boyish troops,
The King doth smile at, and is well prepared
To whip this dwarfish war, these pigmy arms,   135
From out the circle of his territories.
That hand which had the strength even at your door
To cudgel you and make you take the hatch,
To dive like buckets in concealèd wells,
To crouch in litter of your stable planks,   140
To lie like pawns locked up in chests and trunks,
To hug with swine, to seek sweet safety out
In vaults and prisons, and to thrill and shake
Even at the crying of your nation's crow,
Thinking his voice an armèd Englishman;   145
Shall that victorious hand be feebled here

That in your chambers gave you chastisement?
No! Know the gallant monarch is in arms,
And like an eagle o'er his eyrie towers
To souse annoyance that comes near his nest.   150
(To the English lords)
And you degenerate, you ingrate revolts,
You bloody Neros, ripping up the womb
Of your dear mother England, blush for shame;
For your own ladies and pale-visaged maids
Like Amazons come tripping after drums;   155
Their thimbles into armèd gauntlets change,
Their needles to lances, and their gentle hearts
To fierce and bloody inclination.

LOUIS THE DAUPHIN
There end thy brave, and turn thy face in peace.
We grant thou canst outscold us. Fare thee well: 160
We hold our time too precious to be spent
With such a brabbler.

PANDOLF   Give me leave to speak.

BASTARD
No, I will speak.

LOUIS THE DAUPHIN We will attend to neither.—
Strike up the drums, and let the tongue of war
Plead for our interest and our being here.   165

BASTARD
Indeed your drums, being beaten, will cry out;
And so shall you, being beaten. Do but start
An echo with the clamour of thy drum,
And even at hand a drum is ready braced
That shall reverberate all as loud as thine.   170
Sound but another, and another shall
As loud as thine rattle the welkin's ear,
And mock the deep-mouthed thunder; for at hand,
Not trusting to this halting legate here,
Whom he hath used rather for sport than need,   175
Is warlike John; and in his forehead sits
A bare-ribbed Death, whose office is this day
To feast upon whole thousands of the French.

LOUIS THE DAUPHIN
Strike up our drums to find this danger out.

BASTARD
And thou shalt find it, Dauphin, do not doubt.   180
⌈*Drums beat.*⌉ *Exeunt the Bastard* ⌈*at one door*⌉,
all the rest, ⌈*marching, at another door*⌉

5.3   *Alarum. Enter King John* ⌈*at one door*⌉ *and Hubert*
⌈*at another door*⌉

KING JOHN
How goes the day with us? O, tell me, Hubert.

HUBERT
Badly, I fear. How fares your majesty?

KING JOHN
This fever that hath troubled me so long
Lies heavy on me. O, my heart is sick!
Enter a Messenger

MESSENGER
My lord, your valiant kinsman Falconbridge   5

Desires your majesty to leave the field,
And send him word by me which way you go.

KING JOHN
Tell him toward Swineshead, to the abbey there.

MESSENGER
Be of good comfort, for the great supply
That was expected by the Dauphin here   10
Are wrecked three nights ago on Goodwin Sands.
This news was brought to Richard, but even now
The French fight coldly and retire themselves.

KING JOHN
Ay me, this tyrant fever burns me up,
And will not let me welcome this good news.   15
Set on toward Swineshead. To my litter straight;
Weakness possesseth me, and I am faint.   *Exeunt*

5.4   ⌈*Alarum.*⌉ *Enter the Earls of Salisbury and*
Pembroke, and Lord Bigot

SALISBURY
I did not think the King so stored with friends.

PEMBROKE
Up once again; put spirit in the French.
If they miscarry, we miscarry too.

SALISBURY
That misbegotten devil Falconbridge,
In spite of spite, alone upholds the day.   5

PEMBROKE
They say King John, sore sick, hath left the field.
Enter Count Melun, wounded, ⌈*led by a soldier*⌉

MELUN
Lead me to the revolts of England here.

SALISBURY
When we were happy, we had other names.

PEMBROKE
It is the Count Melun.

SALISBURY   Wounded to death.

MELUN
Fly, noble English, you are bought and sold.   10
Unthread the rude eye of rebellion,
And welcome home again discarded faith;
Seek out King John and fall before his feet,
For if the French be lords of this loud day
He means to recompense the pains you take   15
By cutting off your heads. Thus hath he sworn,
And I with him, and many more with me,
Upon the altar at Saint Edmundsbury,
Even on that altar where we swore to you
Dear amity and everlasting love.   20

SALISBURY
May this be possible? May this be true?

MELUN
Have I not hideous death within my view,
Retaining but a quantity of life,
Which bleeds away, even as a form of wax
Resolveth from his figure 'gainst the fire?   25
What in the world should make me now deceive,
Since I must lose the use of all deceit?
Why should I then be false, since it is true

That I must die here, and live hence by truth?
I say again, if Louis do win the day,　30
He is forsworn if e'er those eyes of yours
Behold another daybreak in the east;
But even this night, whose black contagious breath
Already smokes about the burning cresset
Of the old, feeble, and day-wearied sun,　35
Even this ill night your breathing shall expire,
Paying the fine of rated treachery
Even with a treacherous fine of all your lives,
If Louis by your assistance win the day.
Commend me to one Hubert with your king.　40
The love of him, and this respect besides,
For that my grandsire was an Englishman,
Awakes my conscience to confess all this;
In lieu whereof, I pray you bear me hence
From forth the noise and rumour of the field,　45
Where I may think the remnant of my thoughts
In peace, and part this body and my soul
With contemplation and devout desires.

SALISBURY
We do believe thee; and beshrew my soul
But I do love the favour and the form　50
Of this most fair occasion; by the which
We will untread the steps of damnèd flight,
And like a bated and retirèd flood,
Leaving our rankness and irregular course,
Stoop low within those bounds we have o'erlooked,　55
And calmly run on in obedience
Even to our ocean, to our great King John.
My arm shall give thee help to bear thee hence,
For I do see the cruel pangs of death
Right in thine eye.—Away, my friends! New flight,　60
And happy newness that intends old right.　*Exeunt*

5.5　⌈*Alarum; retreat.*⌉ *Enter Louis the Dauphin, and*
　　his train
LOUIS THE DAUPHIN
The sun of heaven, methought, was loath to set,
But stayed and made the western welkin blush,
When English measured backward their own ground
In faint retire. O, bravely came we off,
When with a volley of our needless shot,　5
After such bloody toil, we bid good night,
And wound our tatt'ring colours clearly up,
Last in the field and almost lords of it.
　　Enter a Messenger
MESSENGER
Where is my prince the Dauphin?
LOUIS THE DAUPHIN　　　Here. What news?
MESSENGER
The Count Melun is slain; the English lords　10
By his persuasion are again fall'n off;
And your supply which you have wished so long
Are cast away and sunk on Goodwin Sands.
LOUIS THE DAUPHIN
Ah, foul shrewd news! Beshrew thy very heart!
I did not think to be so sad tonight　15
As this hath made me. Who was he that said

King John did fly an hour or two before
The stumbling night did part our weary powers?
MESSENGER
Whoever spoke it, it is true, my lord.
LOUIS THE DAUPHIN
Well, keep good quarter and good care tonight.　20
The day shall not be up so soon as I,
To try the fair adventure of tomorrow.　*Exeunt*

5.6　*Enter the Bastard* ⌈*with a light*⌉ *and Hubert* ⌈*with a*
　　pistol⌉*, severally*
HUBERT
Who's there? Speak, ho! Speak quickly, or I shoot.
BASTARD
A friend. What art thou?
HUBERT　　　　　Of the part of England.
BASTARD
Whither dost thou go?
HUBERT　　　　　What's that to thee?
Why may not I demand of thine affairs
As well as thou of mine?　5
BASTARD Hubert, I think.
HUBERT Thou hast a perfect thought.
I will upon all hazards well believe
Thou art my friend that know'st my tongue so well.
Who art thou?
BASTARD　　　Who thou wilt. An if thou please,　10
Thou mayst befriend me so much as to think
I come one way of the Plantagenets.
HUBERT
Unkind remembrance! Thou and eyeless night
Have done me shame. Brave soldier, pardon me
That any accent breaking from thy tongue　15
Should 'scape the true acquaintance of mine ear.
BASTARD
Come, come, sans compliment. What news abroad?
HUBERT
Why, here walk I in the black brow of night
To find you out.
BASTARD　　　Brief, then, and what's the news?
HUBERT
O my sweet sir, news fitting to the night:　20
Black, fearful, comfortless, and horrible.
BASTARD
Show me the very wound of this ill news;
I am no woman, I'll not swoon at it.
HUBERT
The King, I fear, is poisoned by a monk.
I left him almost speechless, and broke out　25
To acquaint you with this evil, that you might
The better arm you to the sudden time
Than if you had at leisure known of this.
BASTARD
How did he take it? Who did taste to him?
HUBERT
A monk, I tell you, a resolvèd villain,　30
Whose bowels suddenly burst out. The King
Yet speaks, and peradventure may recover.

BASTARD

Who didst thou leave to tend his majesty?

HUBERT

Why, know you not? The lords are all come back,
And brought Prince Henry in their company,   35
At whose request the King hath pardoned them,
And they are all about his majesty.

BASTARD

Withhold thine indignation, mighty heaven,
And tempt us not to bear above our power.
I'll tell thee, Hubert, half my power this night,   40
Passing these flats, are taken by the tide.
These Lincoln Washes have devourèd them;
Myself, well mounted, hardly have escaped.
Away before! Conduct me to the King.   44
I doubt he will be dead or ere I come.   *Exeunt*

5.7   *Enter Prince Henry, the Earl of Salisbury, and Lord
Bigot*

PRINCE HENRY

It is too late. The life of all his blood
Is touched corruptibly, and his pure brain,
Which some suppose the soul's frail dwelling-house,
Doth by the idle comments that it makes
Foretell the ending of mortality.   5
Enter the Earl of Pembroke

PEMBROKE

His highness yet doth speak, and holds belief
That being brought into the open air,
It would allay the burning quality
Of that fell poison which assaileth him.

PRINCE HENRY

Let him be brought into the orchard here.—   10
⌈*Exit Lord Bigot*⌉
Doth he still rage?

PEMBROKE   He is more patient
Than when you left him. Even now, he sung.

PRINCE HENRY

O, vanity of sickness! Fierce extremes
In their continuance will not feel themselves.
Death, having preyed upon the outward parts,   15
Leaves them invincible, and his siege is now
Against the mind; the which he pricks and wounds
With many legions of strange fantasies,
Which in their throng and press to that last hold
Confound themselves. 'Tis strange that death should
sing.   20
I am the cygnet to this pale faint swan,
Who chants a doleful hymn to his own death,
And from the organ-pipe of frailty sings
His soul and body to their lasting rest.

SALISBURY

Be of good comfort, Prince, for you are born   25
To set a form upon that indigest
Which he hath left so shapeless and so rude.
King John is brought in, ⌈with Lord Bigot attending⌉

KING JOHN

Ay marry, now my soul hath elbow-room;

It would not out at windows nor at doors.
There is so hot a summer in my bosom   30
That all my bowels crumble up to dust;
I am a scribbled form, drawn with a pen
Upon a parchment, and against this fire
Do I shrink up.

PRINCE HENRY   How fares your majesty?

KING JOHN

Poisoned, ill fare! Dead, forsook, cast off;   35
And none of you will bid the winter come
To thrust his icy fingers in my maw,
Nor let my kingdom's rivers take their course
Through my burned bosom, nor entreat the north
To make his bleak winds kiss my parchèd lips   40
And comfort me with cold. I do not ask you much;
I beg cold comfort, and you are so strait
And so ingrateful you deny me that.

PRINCE HENRY

O, that there were some virtue in my tears
That might relieve you!

KING JOHN   The salt in them is hot.   45
Within me is a hell, and there the poison
Is, as a fiend, confined to tyrannize
On unreprievable condemnèd blood.
Enter the Bastard

BASTARD

O, I am scalded with my violent motion
And spleen of speed to see your majesty!   50

KING JOHN

O cousin, thou art come to set mine eye.
The tackle of my heart is cracked and burnt,
And all the shrouds wherewith my life should sail
Are turnèd to one thread, one little hair;
My heart hath one poor string to stay it by,   55
Which holds but till thy news be utterèd,
And then all this thou seest is but a clod
And module of confounded royalty.

BASTARD

The Dauphin is preparing hitherward,
Where God He knows how we shall answer him;   60
For in a night the best part of my power,
As I upon advantage did remove,
Were in the Washes all unwarily
Devourèd by the unexpected flood.
King John dies

SALISBURY

You breathe these dead news in as dead an ear.   65
(*To King John*) My liege, my lord!—But now a king,
now thus.

PRINCE HENRY

Even so must I run on, and even so stop.
What surety of the world, what hope, what stay,
When this was now a king and now is clay?

BASTARD (*to King John*)

Art thou gone so? I do but stay behind   70
To do the office for thee of revenge,
And then my soul shall wait on thee to heaven,
As it on earth hath been thy servant still.

(*To the lords*) Now, now, you stars that move in your
    right spheres,
Where be your powers? Show now your mended
    faiths,   75
And instantly return with me again,
To push destruction and perpetual shame
Out of the weak door of our fainting land.
Straight let us seek, or straight we shall be sought.
The Dauphin rages at our very heels.   80

SALISBURY
It seems you know not, then, so much as we.
The Cardinal Pandolf is within at rest,
Who half an hour since came from the Dauphin,
And brings from him such offers of our peace
As we with honour and respect may take,   85
With purpose presently to leave this war.

BASTARD
He will the rather do it when he sees
Ourselves well-sinewed to our own defence.

SALISBURY
Nay, 'tis in a manner done already,
For many carriages he hath dispatched   90
To the sea-side, and put his cause and quarrel
To the disposing of the Cardinal,
With whom yourself, myself, and other lords,
If you think meet, this afternoon will post
To consummate this business happily.   95

BASTARD
Let it be so.—And you, my noble prince,
With other princes that may best be spared,
Shall wait upon your father's funeral.

PRINCE HENRY
At Worcester must his body be interred,
For so he willed it.

BASTARD   Thither shall it then,   100
And happily may your sweet self put on
The lineal state and glory of the land,
To whom with all submission, on my knee,
I do bequeath my faithful services
And true subjection everlastingly.   105
    He kneels

SALISBURY
And the like tender of our love we make,
To rest without a spot for evermore.
    Salisbury, Pembroke and Bigot kneel

PRINCE HENRY
I have a kind of soul that would give thanks,
And knows not how to do it but with tears.
    He weeps

BASTARD ⌜*rising*⌝
O, let us pay the time but needful woe,   110
Since it hath been beforehand with our griefs.
This England never did, nor never shall,
Lie at the proud foot of a conqueror
But when it first did help to wound itself.
Now these her princes are come home again,   115
Come the three corners of the world in arms
And we shall shock them. Naught shall make us rue
If England to itself do rest but true.
    ⌜*Flourish.*⌝ *Exeunt* ⌜*with the body*⌝

1 HENRY IV

THE play described in the 1623 Folio as *The First Part of Henry the Fourth* had been entered on the Stationers' Register on 25 February 1598 as *The History of Henry the Fourth,* and that is the title of the first surviving edition, of the same year. An earlier edition, doubtless also printed in 1598, is known only from a single, eight-page fragment. Five more editions appeared before the Folio.

The printing of at least two editions within a few months, and the fact that one of them was read almost out of existence, reflect a matter of exceptional topical interest. The earliest title-page advertises the play's portrayal of 'the humorous conceits of Sir John Falstaff'; but when it was first acted, probably in 1596, this character bore the name of his historical counterpart, the Protestant martyr Sir John Oldcastle. Shakespeare changed his surname as the result of protests from Oldcastle's descendants, the influential Cobham family, one of whom—William Brooke, 7th Lord Cobham—was Elizabeth I's Lord Chamberlain from August 1596 till he died on 5 March 1597. Our edition restores Sir John's original surname for the first time in printed texts (though there is reason to believe that even after 1596 the name 'Oldcastle' was sometimes used on the stage), and also restores Russell and Harvey, names Shakespeare was probably obliged to alter to Bardolph and Peto.

Shakespeare had already shown Henry IV's rise to power, and his troubled state of mind on achieving power, in *Richard II*; that play also shows Henry's dissatisfaction with his wayward son, Prince Harry, later Henry V. *1 Henry IV* continues the story, but in a very different dramatic style. A play called *The Famous Victories of Henry V,* entered in the Stationers' Register in 1594, was published anonymously, in a debased and shortened text, in 1598. This text—which also features Oldcastle as a reprobate—gives a sketchy version of the events portrayed in *1* and *2 Henry IV* and *Henry V*. Shakespeare must have known the original play, but in the absence of a full text we cannot tell how much he depended on it. The surviving version contains nothing about the rebellions against Henry IV, for which Shakespeare seems to have gone to Holinshed's, and perhaps other, *Chronicles*; he draws also on Samuel Daniel's poem *The First Four Books of the Civil Wars* (1595).

1 Henry IV is the first of Shakespeare's history plays to make extensive use of the techniques of comedy. On a national level, the play shows the continuing problems of Henry Bolingbroke, insecure in his hold on the throne, and the victim of rebellions led by Worcester, Hotspur (Harry Percy), and Glyndŵr. These scenes are counterpointed by others, written mainly in prose, which, in the manner of a comic sub-plot, provide humorous diversion while also reflecting and extending the concerns of the main plot. Henry suffers not only public insurrection but the personal rebellion of Prince Harry, in his unprincely exploits with the reprobate old knight, Oldcastle. Sir John has become Shakespeare's most famous comic character, but Shakespeare shows that the Prince's treatment of him as a surrogate father who must eventually be abandoned has an intensely serious side.

THE PERSONS OF THE PLAY

KING HENRY IV

PRINCE HARRY, Prince of Wales,
familiarly known as Hal ⎫
Lord JOHN OF LANCASTER ⎬ King Henry's sons
Earl of WESTMORLAND ⎭

Sir Walter BLUNT

Earl of WORCESTER ⎫
Percy, Earl of NORTHUMBERLAND, his brother │
Henry Percy, known as HOTSPUR, │
Northumberland's son │
Kate, LADY PERCY, Hotspur's wife │
Lord Edmund MORTIMER, called Earl of March, │ rebels
Lady Percy's brother ⎬ against
LADY MORTIMER, his wife │ King Henry
Owain GLYNDŴR, Lady Mortimer's father │
Earl of DOUGLAS │
Sir Richard VERNON │
Scrope, ARCHBISHOP of York │
SIR MICHAEL, a member of the Archbishop's │
household ⎭

SIR JOHN Oldcastle ⎫
Edward (Ned) POINS │
RUSSELL │
HARVEY ⎬ associates
Mistress Quickly, HOSTESS of a tavern │ of Prince
in Eastcheap │ Harry
FRANCIS, a drawer │
VINTNER ⎭

GADSHILL
CARRIERS
CHAMBERLAIN
OSTLER

TRAVELLERS
SHERIFF
MESSENGERS
SERVANT
Lords, soldiers

The History of Henry the Fourth

1.1 *Enter King Henry, Lord John of Lancaster, and the Earl of Westmorland, with other ⌐lords⌐*

KING HENRY

So shaken as we are, so wan with care,
Find we a time for frighted peace to pant
And breathe short-winded accents of new broils
To be commenced in strands afar remote.
No more the thirsty entrance of this soil   5
Shall daub her lips with her own children's blood.
No more shall trenching war channel her fields,
Nor bruise her flow'rets with the armèd hoofs
Of hostile paces. Those opposèd eyes,
Which, like the meteors of a troubled heaven,   10
All of one nature, of one substance bred,
Did lately meet in the intestine shock
And furious close of civil butchery,
Shall now in mutual well-beseeming ranks
March all one way, and be no more opposed   15
Against acquaintance, kindred, and allies.
The edge of war, like an ill-sheathèd knife,
No more shall cut his master. Therefore, friends,
As far as to the sepulchre of Christ—
Whose soldier now, under whose blessèd cross   20
We are impressèd and engaged to fight—
Forthwith a power of English shall we levy,
Whose arms were moulded in their mothers' womb
To chase these pagans in those holy fields
Over whose acres walked those blessèd feet   25
Which fourteen hundred years ago were nailed,
For our advantage, on the bitter cross.
But this our purpose now is twelve month old,
And bootless 'tis to tell you we will go.
Therefor we meet not now. Then let me hear   30
Of you, my gentle cousin Westmorland,
What yesternight our Council did decree
In forwarding this dear expedience.

WESTMORLAND

My liege, this haste was hot in question,
And many limits of the charge set down   35
But yesternight, when all athwart there came
A post from Wales, loaden with heavy news,
Whose worst was that the noble Mortimer,
Leading the men of Herefordshire to fight
Against the irregular and wild Glyndŵr,   40
Was by the rude hands of that Welshman taken,
A thousand of his people butcherèd,
Upon whose dead corpse' there was such misuse,
Such beastly shameless transformation,
By those Welshwomen done as may not be   45
Without much shame retold or spoken of.

KING HENRY

It seems then that the tidings of this broil
Brake off our business for the Holy Land.

WESTMORLAND

This matched with other did, my gracious lord,
For more uneven and unwelcome news   50
Came from the north, and thus it did import:
On Holy-rood day the gallant Hotspur there—
Young Harry Percy—and brave Archibald,
That ever valiant and approvèd Scot,
At Holmedon met,   55
Where they did spend a sad and bloody hour,
As by discharge of their artillery
And shape of likelihood the news was told;
For he that brought them in the very heat
And pride of their contention did take horse,   60
Uncertain of the issue any way.

KING HENRY

Here is a dear, a true industrious friend,
Sir Walter Blunt, new lighted from his horse,
Stained with the variation of each soil
Betwixt that Holmedon and this seat of ours;   65
And he hath brought us smooth and welcome news.
The Earl of Douglas is discomfited.
Ten thousand bold Scots, two-and-twenty knights,
Balked in their own blood did Sir Walter see
On Holmedon's plains. Of prisoners Hotspur took   70
Mordake the Earl of Fife and eldest son
To beaten Douglas, and the Earl of Athol,
Of Moray, Angus, and Menteith;
And is not this an honourable spoil,
A gallant prize? Ha, cousin, is it not?   75

WESTMORLAND

In faith, it is a conquest for a prince to boast of.

KING HENRY

Yea, there thou mak'st me sad, and mak'st me sin
In envy that my lord Northumberland
Should be the father to so blest a son—
A son who is the theme of honour's tongue,   80
Amongst a grove the very straightest plant,
Who is sweet Fortune's minion and her pride—
Whilst I by looking on the praise of him
See riot and dishonour stain the brow
Of my young Harry. O, that it could be proved   85
That some night-tripping fairy had exchanged
In cradle clothes our children where they lay,
And called mine Percy, his Plantagenet!
Then would I have his Harry, and he mine.
But let him from my thoughts. What think you, coz,   90
Of this young Percy's pride? The prisoners
Which he in this adventure hath surprised
To his own use he keeps, and sends me word
I shall have none but Mordake Earl of Fife.

WESTMORLAND

This is his uncle's teaching. This is Worcester,   95
Malevolent to you in all aspects,

Which makes him prune himself, and bristle up
The crest of youth against your dignity.

KING HENRY
But I have sent for him to answer this;
And for this cause awhile we must neglect   100
Our holy purpose to Jerusalem.
Cousin, on Wednesday next our Council we
Will hold at Windsor. So inform the lords.
But come yourself with speed to us again,
For more is to be said and to be done   105
Than out of anger can be utterèd.

WESTMORLAND I will, my liege.

Exeunt ⌈King Henry, Lancaster, and other
lords at one door; Westmorland
at another door⌉

1.2   *Enter Harry Prince of Wales and Sir John Oldcastle*

SIR JOHN Now, Hal, what time of day is it, lad?

PRINCE HARRY Thou art so fat-witted with drinking of old
sack, and unbuttoning thee after supper, and sleeping
upon benches after noon, that thou hast forgotten to
demand that truly which thou wouldst truly know.
What a devil hast thou to do with the time of the day?
Unless hours were cups of sack, and minutes capons,
and clocks the tongues of bawds, and dials the signs
of leaping-houses, and the blessèd sun himself a fair
hot wench in flame-coloured taffeta, I see no reason
why thou shouldst be so superfluous to demand the
time of the day.

SIR JOHN Indeed you come near me now, Hal, for we that
take purses go by the moon and the seven stars, and
not 'By Phoebus, he, that wand'ring knight so fair'.
And I prithee, sweet wag, when thou art a king, as
God save thy grace—'majesty' I should say, for grace
thou wilt have none—

PRINCE HARRY What, none?

SIR JOHN No, by my troth, not so much as will serve to
be prologue to an egg and butter.   21

PRINCE HARRY Well, how then? Come, roundly, roundly.

SIR JOHN Marry then, sweet wag, when thou art king let
not us that are squires of the night's body be called
thieves of the day's beauty. Let us be 'Diana's foresters',
'gentlemen of the shade', 'minions of the moon', and
let men say we be men of good government, being
governed, as the sea is, by our noble and chaste mistress
the moon, under whose countenance we steal.   29

PRINCE HARRY Thou sayst well, and it holds well too, for
the fortune of us that are the moon's men doth ebb
and flow like the sea, being governed as the sea is by
the moon. As for proof now: a purse of gold most
resolutely snatched on Monday night, and most
dissolutely spent on Tuesday morning; got with
swearing 'lay by!', and spent with crying 'bring in!';
now in as low an ebb as the foot of the ladder, and by
and by in as high a flow as the ridge of the gallows.

SIR JOHN By the Lord, thou sayst true, lad; and is not my
Hostess of the tavern a most sweet wench?   40

PRINCE HARRY As the honey of Hybla, my old lad of the

castle; and is not a buff jerkin a most sweet robe of
durance?

SIR JOHN How now, how now, mad wag? What, in thy
quips and thy quiddities? What a plague have I to do
with a buff jerkin?   46

PRINCE HARRY Why, what a pox have I to do with my
Hostess of the tavern?

SIR JOHN Well, thou hast called her to a reckoning many
a time and oft.   50

PRINCE HARRY Did I ever call for thee to pay thy part?

SIR JOHN No, I'll give thee thy due, thou hast paid all
there.

PRINCE HARRY Yea, and elsewhere so far as my coin would
stretch; and where it would not, I have used my credit.

SIR JOHN Yea, and so used it that were it not here apparent
that thou art heir apparent—but I prithee, sweet wag,
shall there be gallows standing in England when thou
art king, and resolution thus fubbed as it is with the
rusty curb of old father Antic the law? Do not thou
when thou art king hang a thief.   61

PRINCE HARRY No, thou shalt.

SIR JOHN Shall I? O, rare! By the Lord, I'll be a brave
judge!   64

PRINCE HARRY Thou judgest false already. I mean thou
shalt have the hanging of the thieves, and so become
a rare hangman.

SIR JOHN Well, Hal, well; and in some sort it jumps with
my humour as well as waiting in the court, I can tell
you.   70

PRINCE HARRY For obtaining of suits?

SIR JOHN Yea, for obtaining of suits, whereof the hangman
hath no lean wardrobe. 'Sblood, I am as melancholy
as a gib cat, or a lugged bear.

PRINCE HARRY Or an old lion, or a lover's lute.   75

SIR JOHN Yea, or the drone of a Lincolnshire bagpipe.

PRINCE HARRY What sayst thou to a hare, or the
melancholy of Moor-ditch?

SIR JOHN Thou hast the most unsavoury similes, and art
indeed the most comparative, rascalliest sweet young
Prince. But Hal, I prithee trouble me no more with
vanity. I would to God thou and I knew where a
commodity of good names were to be bought. An old
lord of the Council rated me the other day in the street
about you, sir, but I marked him not; and yet he talked
very wisely, but I regarded him not; and yet he talked
wisely, and in the street too.

PRINCE HARRY Thou didst well, for wisdom cries out in
the streets, and no man regards it.   89

SIR JOHN O, thou hast damnable iteration, and art indeed
able to corrupt a saint. Thou hast done much harm
upon me, Hal, God forgive thee for it. Before I knew
thee, Hal, I knew nothing; and now am I, if a man
should speak truly, little better than one of the wicked.
I must give over this life, and I will give it over. By the
Lord, an I do not, I am a villain. I'll be damned for
never a king's son in Christendom.

PRINCE HARRY Where shall we take a purse tomorrow,
Jack?

SIR JOHN Zounds, where thou wilt, lad! I'll make one; an
I do not, call me villain and baffle me.   101
PRINCE HARRY I see a good amendment of life in thee,
from praying to purse-taking.
SIR JOHN Why, Hal, 'tis my vocation, Hal. 'Tis no sin for
a man to labour in his vocation.   105
     Enter Poins
Poins! Now shall we know if Gadshill have set a match.
O, if men were to be saved by merit, what hole in hell
were hot enough for him? This is the most omnipotent
villain that ever cried 'Stand!' to a true man.
PRINCE HARRY Good morrow, Ned.   110
POINS Good morrow, sweet Hal. (*To Sir John*) What says
Monsieur Remorse? What says Sir John, sack-and-
sugar Jack? How agrees the devil and thee about thy
soul, that thou soldest him on Good Friday last, for a
cup of Madeira and a cold capon's leg?   115
PRINCE HARRY Sir John stands to his word, the devil shall
have his bargain, for he was never yet a breaker of
proverbs: he will give the devil his due.
POINS (*to Sir John*) Then art thou damned for keeping thy
word with the devil.   120
PRINCE HARRY Else he had been damned for cozening the
devil.
POINS But my lads, my lads, tomorrow morning by four
o'clock early, at Gads Hill, there are pilgrims going to
Canterbury with rich offerings, and traders riding to
London with fat purses. I have visors for you all; you
have horses for yourselves. Gadshill lies tonight in
Rochester. I have bespoke supper tomorrow night in
Eastcheap. We may do it as secure as sleep. If you will
go, I will stuff your purses full of crowns; if you will
not, tarry at home and be hanged.   131
SIR JOHN Hear ye, Edward, if I tarry at home and go not,
I'll hang you for going.
POINS You will, chops?
SIR JOHN Hal, wilt thou make one?   135
PRINCE HARRY Who, I rob? I a thief? Not I, by my faith.
SIR JOHN There's neither honesty, manhood, nor good
fellowship in thee, nor thou camest not of the blood
royal, if thou darest not stand for ten shillings.
PRINCE HARRY Well then, once in my days I'll be a
madcap.   141
SIR JOHN Why, that's well said.
PRINCE HARRY Well, come what will, I'll tarry at home.
SIR JOHN By the Lord, I'll be a traitor then, when thou
art king.   145
PRINCE HARRY I care not.
POINS Sir John, I prithee leave the Prince and me alone.
I will lay him down such reasons for this adventure
that he shall go.
SIR JOHN Well, God give thee the spirit of persuasion and
him the ears of profiting, that what thou speakest may
move and what he hears may be believed, that the true
prince may, for recreation' sake, prove a false thief; for
the poor abuses of the time want countenance. Farewell.
You shall find me in Eastcheap.   155
PRINCE HARRY Farewell, the latter spring; farewell, All-
hallown summer.   *Exit Sir John*

POINS Now, my good sweet honey lord, ride with us
tomorrow. I have a jest to execute that I cannot manage
alone. Oldcastle, Harvey, Russell, and Gadshill shall rob
those men that we have already waylaid—yourself and
I will not be there—and when they have the booty, if
you and I do not rob them, cut this head off from my
shoulders.
PRINCE HARRY But how shall we part with them in setting
forth?   166
POINS Why, we will set forth before or after them and
appoint them a place of meeting, wherein it is at our
pleasure to fail. And then will they adventure upon the
exploit themselves, which they shall have no sooner
achieved but we'll set upon them.   171
PRINCE HARRY Ay, but 'tis like that they will know us by
our horses, by our habits, and by every other
appointment, to be ourselves.   174
POINS Tut, our horses they shall not see—I'll tie them in
the wood; our visors we will change after we leave
them; and, sirrah, I have cases of buckram for the
nonce, to immask our noted outward garments.
PRINCE HARRY But I doubt they will be too hard for us.
POINS Well, for two of them, I know them to be as true-
bred cowards as ever turned back; and for the third,
if he fight longer than he sees reason, I'll forswear
arms. The virtue of this jest will be the incomprehensible
lies that this same fat rogue will tell us when we meet
at supper: how thirty at least he fought with, what
wards, what blows, what extremities he endured; and
in the reproof of this lives the jest.
PRINCE HARRY Well, I'll go with thee. Provide us all things
necessary, and meet me tomorrow night in Eastcheap;
there I'll sup. Farewell.   190
POINS Farewell, my lord.   *Exit*
PRINCE HARRY
I know you all, and will a while uphold
The unyoked humour of your idleness.
Yet herein will I imitate the sun,
Who doth permit the base contagious clouds   195
To smother up his beauty from the world,
That when he please again to be himself,
Being wanted he may be more wondered at
By breaking through the foul and ugly mists
Of vapours that did seem to strangle him.   200
If all the year were playing holidays,
To sport would be as tedious as to work;
But when they seldom come, they wished-for come,
And nothing pleaseth but rare accidents.
So when this loose behaviour I throw off   205
And pay the debt I never promisèd,
By how much better than my word I am,
By so much shall I falsify men's hopes;
And like bright metal on a sullen ground,
My reformation, glitt'ring o'er my fault,   210
Shall show more goodly and attract more eyes
Than that which hath no foil to set it off.
I'll so offend to make offence a skill,
Redeeming time when men think least I will.   *Exit*

1.3   *Enter the King, the Earls of Northumberland and*
      Worcester, Hotspur, Sir Walter Blunt, with other
      ⌈*lords*⌉
KING HENRY (*to Hotspur, Northumberland, and Worcester*)
   My blood hath been too cold and temperate,
   Unapt to stir at these indignities,
   And you have found me, for accordingly
   You tread upon my patience; but be sure
   I will from henceforth rather be myself,   5
   Mighty and to be feared, than my condition,
   Which hath been smooth as oil, soft as young down,
   And therefore lost that title of respect
   Which the proud soul ne'er pays but to the proud.
WORCESTER
   Our house, my sovereign liege, little deserves   10
   The scourge of greatness to be used on it,
   And that same greatness too, which our own hands
   Have help to make so portly.
NORTHUMBERLAND (*to the King*) My lord—
KING HENRY
   Worcester, get thee gone, for I do see
   Danger and disobedience in thine eye.   15
   O sir, your presence is too bold and peremptory,
   And majesty might never yet endure
   The moody frontier of a servant brow.
   You have good leave to leave us. When we need
   Your use and counsel we shall send for you.   20
                                    Exit Worcester
   You were about to speak.
NORTHUMBERLAND   Yea, my good lord.
   Those prisoners in your highness' name demanded,
   Which Harry Percy here at Holmedon took,
   Were, as he says, not with such strength denied
   As was delivered to your majesty,   25
   Who either through envy or misprision
   Was guilty of this fault, and not my son.
HOTSPUR (*to the King*)
   My liege, I did deny no prisoners;
   But I remember, when the fight was done,
   When I was dry with rage and extreme toil,   30
   Breathless and faint, leaning upon my sword,
   Came there a certain lord, neat and trimly dressed,
   Fresh as a bridegroom, and his chin, new-reaped,
   Showed like a stubble-land at harvest-home.
   He was perfumèd like a milliner,   35
   And 'twixt his finger and his thumb he held
   A pouncet-box, which ever and anon
   He gave his nose and took't away again—
   Who therewith angry, when it next came there
   Took it in snuff—and still he smiled and talked;   40
   And as the soldiers bore dead bodies by,
   He called them untaught knaves, unmannerly
   To bring a slovenly unhandsome corpse
   Betwixt the wind and his nobility.
   With many holiday and lady terms   45
   He questioned me; amongst the rest demanded
   My prisoners in your majesty's behalf.
   I then, all smarting with my wounds being cold—
   To be so pestered with a popinjay!—

   Out of my grief and my impatience   50
   Answered neglectingly, I know not what—
   He should, or should not—for he made me mad
   To see him shine so brisk, and smell so sweet,
   And talk so like a waiting gentlewoman
   Of guns, and drums, and wounds, God save the mark!
   And telling me the sovereign'st thing on earth   56
   Was parmacity for an inward bruise,
   And that it was great pity, so it was,
   This villainous saltpetre should be digged
   Out of the bowels of the harmless earth,   60
   Which many a good tall fellow had destroyed
   So cowardly, and but for these vile guns
   He would himself have been a soldier.
   This bald unjointed chat of his, my lord,
   Made me to answer indirectly, as I said,   65
   And I beseech you, let not his report
   Come current for an accusation
   Betwixt my love and your high majesty.
BLUNT (*to the King*)
   The circumstance considered, good my lord,
   Whate'er Lord Harry Percy then had said   70
   To such a person, and in such a place,
   At such a time, with all the rest retold,
   May reasonably die, and never rise
   To do him wrong or any way impeach
   What then he said, so he unsay it now.   75
KING HENRY
   Why, yet he doth deny his prisoners,
   But with proviso and exception
   That we at our own charge shall ransom straight
   His brother-in-law the foolish Mortimer,
   Who, on my soul, hath wilfully betrayed   80
   The lives of those that he did lead to fight
   Against that great magician, damned Glyndŵr—
   Whose daughter, as we hear, the Earl of March
   Hath lately married. Shall our coffers, then,
   Be emptied to redeem a traitor home?   85
   Shall we buy treason, and indent with fears
   When they have lost and forfeited themselves?
   No, on the barren mountains let him starve;
   For I shall never hold that man my friend
   Whose tongue shall ask me for one penny cost   90
   To ransom home revolted Mortimer—
HOTSPUR Revolted Mortimer?
   He never did fall off, my sovereign liege,
   But by the chance of war. To prove that true
   Needs no more but one tongue for all those wounds,
   Those mouthèd wounds, which valiantly he took   96
   When on the gentle Severn's sedgy bank,
   In single opposition, hand to hand,
   He did confound the best part of an hour
   In changing hardiment with great Glyndŵr.   100
   Three times they breathed, and three times did they
          drink,
   Upon agreement, of swift Severn's flood,
   Who, then affrighted with their bloody looks,
   Ran fearfully among the trembling reeds,
   And hid his crisp head in the hollow bank,   105

Bloodstainèd with these valiant combatants.
Never did bare and rotten policy
Colour her working with such deadly wounds,
Nor never could the noble Mortimer
Receive so many, and all willingly.   110
Then let not him be slandered with revolt.

KING HENRY
Thou dost belie him, Percy, thou dost belie him.
He never did encounter with Glyndŵr. I tell thee,
He durst as well have met the devil alone
As Owain Glyndŵr for an enemy.   115
Art thou not ashamed? But, sirrah, henceforth
Let me not hear you speak of Mortimer.
Send me your prisoners with the speediest means,
Or you shall hear in such a kind from me
As will displease you.—My lord Northumberland,   120
We license your departure with your son.
(To Hotspur) Send us your prisoners, or you'll hear of it.
              Exeunt all but Hotspur and Northumberland

HOTSPUR
An if the devil come and roar for them
I will not send them. I will after straight
And tell him so, for I will ease my heart,   125
Although it be with hazard of my head.

NORTHUMBERLAND
What, drunk with choler? Stay and pause awhile.
              Enter the Earl of Worcester
Here comes your uncle.

HOTSPUR   Speak of Mortimer?
Zounds, I will speak of him, and let my soul
Want mercy if I do not join with him.   130
In his behalf I'll empty all these veins,
And shed my dear blood drop by drop in the dust,
But I will lift the downfall Mortimer
As high in the air as this unthankful King,
As this ingrate and cankered Bolingbroke.   135

NORTHUMBERLAND (*to Worcester*)
Brother, the King hath made your nephew mad.

WORCESTER
Who struck this heat up after I was gone?

HOTSPUR
He will forsooth have all my prisoners;
And when I urged the ransom once again
Of my wife's brother, then his cheek looked pale,   140
And on my face he turned an eye of death,
Trembling even at the name of Mortimer.

WORCESTER
I cannot blame him: was not he proclaimed
By Richard, that dead is, the next of blood?

NORTHUMBERLAND
He was; I heard the proclamation.   145
And then it was when the unhappy King,
Whose wrongs in us God pardon, did set forth
Upon his Irish expedition,
From whence he, intercepted, did return
To be deposed, and shortly murderèd.   150

WORCESTER
And for whose death we in the world's wide mouth
Live scandalized and foully spoken of.

HOTSPUR
But soft, I pray you; did King Richard then
Proclaim my brother Edmund Mortimer
Heir to the crown?

NORTHUMBERLAND   He did; myself did hear it.   155

HOTSPUR
Nay, then I cannot blame his cousin King
That wished him on the barren mountains starve.
But shall it be that you that set the crown
Upon the head of this forgetful man,
And for his sake wear the detested blot   160
Of murderous subornation, shall it be
That you a world of curses undergo,
Being the agents or base second means,
The cords, the ladder, or the hangman, rather?
O, pardon me that I descend so low   165
To show the line and the predicament
Wherein you range under this subtle King!
Shall it for shame be spoken in these days,
Or fill up chronicles in time to come,
That men of your nobility and power   170
Did gage them both in an unjust behalf,
As both of you, God pardon it, have done:
To put down Richard, that sweet lovely rose,
And plant this thorn, this canker, Bolingbroke?
And shall it in more shame be further spoken   175
That you are fooled, discarded, and shook off
By him for whom these shames ye underwent?
No; yet time serves wherein you may redeem
Your banished honours, and restore yourselves
Into the good thoughts of the world again,   180
Revenge the jeering and disdained contempt
Of this proud King, who studies day and night
To answer all the debt he owes to you
Even with the bloody payment of your deaths.
Therefore, I say—

WORCESTER   Peace, cousin, say no more.   185
And now I will unclasp a secret book,
And to your quick-conceiving discontents
I'll read you matter deep and dangerous,
As full of peril and adventurous spirit
As to o'erwalk a current roaring loud   190
On the unsteadfast footing of a spear.

HOTSPUR
If he fall in, good night, or sink or swim.
Send danger from the east unto the west,
So honour cross it from the north to south;
And let them grapple. O, the blood more stirs   195
To rouse a lion than to start a hare!

NORTHUMBERLAND (*to Worcester*)
Imagination of some great exploit
Drives him beyond the bounds of patience.

⌈HOTSPUR⌉
By heaven, methinks it were an easy leap
To pluck bright honour from the pale-faced moon,   200
Or dive into the bottom of the deep,
Where fathom-line could never touch the ground,
And pluck up drownèd honour by the locks,
So he that doth redeem her thence might wear,

Without corrival, all her dignities. 205
But out upon this half-faced fellowship!
WORCESTER (*to Northumberland*)
He apprehends a world of figures here,
But not the form of what he should attend.
(*To Hotspur*) Good cousin, give me audience for a while,
And list to me. 210
HOTSPUR
I cry you mercy.
WORCESTER   Those same noble Scots
That are your prisoners—
HOTSPUR   I'll keep them all.
By God, he shall not have a Scot of them;
No, if a scot would save his soul he shall not.
I'll keep them, by this hand.
WORCESTER   You start away, 215
And lend no ear unto my purposes.
Those prisoners you shall keep.
HOTSPUR   Nay, I will; that's flat.
He said he would not ransom Mortimer,
Forbade my tongue to speak of Mortimer;
But I will find him when he lies asleep, 220
And in his ear I'll hollo 'Mortimer!'
Nay, I'll have a starling shall be taught to speak
Nothing but 'Mortimer', and give it him
To keep his anger still in motion.
WORCESTER Hear you, cousin, a word. 225
HOTSPUR
All studies here I solemnly defy,
Save how to gall and pinch this Bolingbroke.
And that same sword-and-buckler Prince of Wales—
But that I think his father loves him not
And would be glad he met with some mischance— 230
I would have him poisoned with a pot of ale.
WORCESTER
Farewell, kinsman. I'll talk to you
When you are better tempered to attend.
NORTHUMBERLAND (*to Hotspur*)
Why, what a wasp-stung and impatient fool
Art thou to break into this woman's mood, 235
Tying thine ear to no tongue but thine own!
HOTSPUR
Why, look you, I am whipped and scourged with rods,
Nettled and stung with pismires, when I hear
Of this vile politician Bolingbroke.
In Richard's time—what d'ye call the place? 240
A plague upon't, it is in Gloucestershire.
'Twas where the madcap Duke his uncle kept—
His uncle York—where I first bowed my knee
Unto this king of smiles, this Bolingbroke.
'Sblood, when you and he came back from
     Ravenspurgh. 245
NORTHUMBERLAND
At Berkeley castle.
HOTSPUR   You say true.
Why, what a candy deal of courtesy
This fawning greyhound then did proffer me!
'Look when his infant fortune came to age',
And 'gentle Harry Percy', and 'kind cousin'. 250

O, the devil take such cozeners!—God forgive me.
Good uncle, tell your tale; I have done.
WORCESTER
Nay, if you have not, to't again.
We'll stay your leisure.
HOTSPUR   I have done, i'faith.
WORCESTER
Then once more to your Scottish prisoners. 255
Deliver them up without their ransom straight;
And make the Douglas' son your only mean
For powers in Scotland, which, for divers reasons
Which I shall send you written, be assured
Will easily be granted. (*To Northumberland*) You, my
     lord, 260
Your son in Scotland being thus employed,
Shall secretly into the bosom creep
Of that same noble prelate well-beloved,
The Archbishop.
HOTSPUR   Of York, is't not?
WORCESTER   True, who bears hard
His brother's death at Bristol, the Lord Scrope. 265
I speak not this in estimation,
As what I think might be, but what I know
Is ruminated, plotted, and set down,
And only stays but to behold the face
Of that occasion that shall bring it on. 270
HOTSPUR
I smell it; upon my life, it will do well!
NORTHUMBERLAND
Before the game is afoot thou still lett'st slip.
HOTSPUR
Why, it cannot choose but be a noble plot—
And then the power of Scotland and of York
To join with Mortimer, ha?
WORCESTER   And so they shall. 275
HOTSPUR
In faith, it is exceedingly well aimed.
WORCESTER
And 'tis no little reason bids us speed
To save our heads by raising of a head;
For, bear ourselves as even as we can,
The King will always think him in our debt, 280
And think we think ourselves unsatisfied
Till he hath found a time to pay us home.
And see already how he doth begin
To make us strangers to his looks of love.
HOTSPUR
He does, he does. We'll be revenged on him. 285
WORCESTER
Cousin, farewell. No further go in this
Than I by letters shall direct your course.
When time is ripe, which will be suddenly,
I'll steal to Glyndŵr and Lord Mortimer,
Where you and Douglas and our powers at once, 290
As I will fashion it, shall happily meet,
To bear our fortunes in our own strong arms,
Which now we hold at much uncertainty.
NORTHUMBERLAND
Farewell, good brother. We shall thrive, I trust.

HOTSPUR (to Worcester)
 Uncle, adieu. O, let the hours be short   295
 Till fields and blows and groans applaud our sport!
       Exeunt ⌈Worcester at one door, Northumberland
                        and Hotspur at another door⌉

2.1 *Enter a Carrier, with a lantern in his hand*
FIRST CARRIER Heigh-ho! An't be not four by the day, I'll
 be hanged. Charles's Wain is over the new chimney,
 and yet our horse not packed. What, ostler!
OSTLER (*within*) Anon, anon!   4
FIRST CARRIER I prithee, Tom, beat cut's saddle, put a few
 flocks in the point. Poor jade is wrung in the withers,
 out of all cess.
       Enter another Carrier
SECOND CARRIER Peas and beans are as dank here as a
 dog, and that is the next way to give poor jades the
 bots. This house is turned upside down since Robin
 Ostler died.   11
FIRST CARRIER Poor fellow never joyed since the price of
 oats rose; it was the death of him.
SECOND CARRIER I think this be the most villainous house
 in all London road for fleas. I am stung like a tench. 15
FIRST CARRIER Like a tench? By the mass, there is ne'er
 a king christen could be better bit than I have been
 since the first cock.
SECOND CARRIER Why, they will allow us ne'er a jordan,
 and then we leak in your chimney, and your chamber-
 lye breeds fleas like a loach.   21
FIRST CARRIER What, ostler! Come away, and be hanged,
 come away!
SECOND CARRIER I have a gammon of bacon and two races
 of ginger to be delivered as far as Charing Cross. 25
FIRST CARRIER God's body, the turkeys in my pannier are
 quite starved! What, ostler! A plague on thee, hast
 thou never an eye in thy head? Canst not hear? An
 'twere not as good deed as drink to break the pate on
 thee, I am a very villain. Come, and be hanged! Hast
 no faith in thee?   31
       Enter Gadshill
GADSHILL Good morrow, carriers. What's o'clock?
FIRST CARRIER I think it be two o'clock.
GADSHILL I prithee lend me thy lantern to see my gelding
 in the stable.   35
FIRST CARRIER Nay, by God, soft. I know a trick worth
 two of that, i'faith.
GADSHILL (*to Second Carrier*) I pray thee, lend me thine.
SECOND CARRIER Ay, when? Canst tell? 'Lend me thy
 lantern,' quoth a. Marry, I'll see thee hanged first. 40
GADSHILL Sirrah carrier, what time do you mean to come
 to London?
SECOND CARRIER Time enough to go to bed with a candle,
 I warrant thee.—Come, neighbour Mugs, we'll call up
 the gentlemen. They will along with company, for they
 have great charge.   *Exeunt Carriers*
GADSHILL What ho, chamberlain!
       Enter Chamberlain
CHAMBERLAIN 'At hand' quoth Pickpurse.
GADSHILL That's even as fair as ' "At hand" quoth the

chamberlain', for thou variest no more from picking of
 purses than giving direction doth from labouring: thou
 layest the plot how.
CHAMBERLAIN Good morrow, Master Gadshill. It holds
 current that I told you yesternight. There's a franklin
 in the Weald of Kent hath brought three hundred
 marks with him in gold. I heard him tell it to one of
 his company last night at supper—a kind of auditor,
 one that hath abundance of charge too, God knows
 what. They are up already, and call for eggs and butter;
 they will away presently.   60
GADSHILL Sirrah, if they meet not with Saint Nicholas's
 clerks, I'll give thee this neck.
CHAMBERLAIN No, I'll none of it; I pray thee keep that
 for the hangman, for I know thou worshippest Saint
 Nicholas as truly as a man of falsehood may.   65
GADSHILL What talkest thou to me of the hangman? If I
 hang, I'll make a fat pair of gallows, for if I hang, old
 Sir John hangs with me, and thou knowest he's no
 starveling. Tut, there are other Trojans that thou
 dreamest not of, the which for sport' sake are content
 to do the profession some grace, that would, if matters
 should be looked into, for their own credit' sake make
 all whole. I am joined with no foot-landrakers, no long-
 staff sixpenny strikers, none of these mad mustachio
 purple-hued maltworms, but with nobility and tran-
 quillity, burgomasters and great 'oyez'-ers; such as can
 hold in, in such as will strike sooner than speak, and
 speak sooner than drink, and drink sooner than pray.
 And yet, zounds, I lie, for they pray continually to their
 saint the commonwealth; or rather, not pray to her,
 but prey on her; for they ride up and down on her and
 make her their boots.
CHAMBERLAIN What, the commonwealth their boots? Will
 she hold out water in foul way?   84
GADSHILL She will, she will, justice hath liquored her. We
 steal as in a castle, cocksure; we have the recipe of
 fern-seed, we walk invisible.
CHAMBERLAIN Nay, by my faith, I think you are more
 beholden to the night than to fern-seed for your walking
 invisible.   90
GADSHILL Give me thy hand; thou shalt have a share in
 our purchase, as I am a true man.
CHAMBERLAIN Nay, rather let me have it as you are a
 false thief.   94
GADSHILL Go to, 'homo' is a common name to all men.
 Bid the ostler bring my gelding out of the stable.
 Farewell, you muddy knave.   *Exeunt ⌈severally⌉*

2.2 *Enter Prince Harry, Poins, Harvey, ⌈and Russell⌉*
POINS Come, shelter, shelter!
       ⌈*Exeunt Harvey and Russell at another door⌉*
 I have removed Oldcastle's horse, and he frets like a
 gummed velvet.
PRINCE HARRY Stand close!   ⌈*Exit Poins⌉*
       Enter Sir John Oldcastle
SIR JOHN Poins! Poins, and be hanged! Poins!   5
PRINCE HARRY Peace, ye fat-kidneyed rascal! What a
 brawling dost thou keep!

SIR JOHN Where's Poins, Hal?
PRINCE HARRY He is walked up to the top of the hill. I'll
go seek him.   ⌐Exit⌐
SIR JOHN I am accursed to rob in that thief's company.
The rascal hath removed my horse and tied him I know
not where. If I travel but four foot by the square further
afoot, I shall break my wind. Well, I doubt not but to
die a fair death, for all this—if I scape hanging for
killing that rogue. I have forsworn his company hourly
any time this two-and-twenty years, and yet I am
bewitched with the rogue's company. If the rascal have
not given me medicines to make me love him, I'll be
hanged. It could not be else: I have drunk medicines.
Poins! Hal! A plague upon you both! Russell! Harvey!
I'll starve ere I'll rob a foot further. An 'twere not as
good a deed as drink to turn true man and to leave
these rogues, I am the veriest varlet that ever chewed
with a tooth. Eight yards of uneven ground is threescore
and ten miles afoot with me, and the stony-hearted
villains know it well enough. A plague upon't when
thieves cannot be true one to another!
    They whistle. ⌐Enter Prince Harry, Poins, Harvey,
    and Russell⌐
Whew! A plague upon you all! Give me my horse, you
rogues, give me my horse, and be hanged!   30
PRINCE HARRY Peace, ye fat-guts. Lie down, lay thine ear
close to the ground, and list if thou canst hear the
tread of travellers.
SIR JOHN Have you any levers to lift me up again, being
down? 'Sblood, I'll not bear my own flesh so far afoot
again for all the coin in thy father's exchequer. What
a plague mean ye to colt me thus?
PRINCE HARRY Thou liest: thou art not colted, thou art
uncolted.
SIR JOHN I prithee, good Prince Hal, help me to my horse,
good king's son.   41
PRINCE HARRY Out, ye rogue, shall I be your ostler?
SIR JOHN Hang thyself in thine own heir-apparent garters!
If I be ta'en, I'll peach for this. An I have not ballads
made on you all and sung to filthy tunes, let a cup of
sack be my poison. When a jest is so forward, and
afoot too! I hate it.
    Enter Gadshill ⌐visored⌐
GADSHILL Stand!
SIR JOHN So I do, against my will.
POINS O, 'tis our setter, I know his voice. Gadshill, what
news?   51
⌐GADSHILL⌐ Case ye, case ye, on with your visors! There's
money of the King's coming down the hill; 'tis going
to the King's exchequer.
SIR JOHN You lie, ye rogue, 'tis going to the King's tavern.
GADSHILL There's enough to make us all.   56
SIR JOHN To be hanged.
    ⌐They put on visors⌐
PRINCE HARRY Sirs, you four shall front them in the
narrow lane. Ned Poins and I will walk lower. If they
scape from your encounter, then they light on us. 60
HARVEY How many be there of them?
GADSHILL Some eight or ten.

SIR JOHN Zounds, will they not rob us?
PRINCE HARRY What, a coward, Sir John Paunch?
SIR JOHN Indeed I am not John of Gaunt your grandfather,
but yet no coward, Hal.   66
PRINCE HARRY Well, we leave that to the proof.
POINS Sirrah Jack, thy horse stands behind the hedge.
When thou needest him, there thou shalt find him.
Farewell, and stand fast.   70
SIR JOHN Now cannot I strike him if I should be hanged.
PRINCE HARRY (aside to Poins) Ned, where are our disguises?
POINS (aside to the Prince) Here, hard by. Stand close.
    ⌐Exeunt the Prince and Poins⌐
SIR JOHN Now, my masters, happy man be his dole, say
I; every man to his business.   75
    ⌐They stand aside.⌐
    Enter the Travellers, ⌐amongst them the Carriers⌐
⌐FIRST⌐ TRAVELLER Come, neighbour, the boy shall lead
our horses down the hill. We'll walk afoot a while, and
ease their legs.
THIEVES ⌐coming forward⌐ Stand!
⌐SECOND⌐ TRAVELLER Jesus bless us!   80
SIR JOHN Strike, down with them, cut the villains' throats!
Ah, whoreson caterpillars, bacon-fed knaves! They hate
us youth. Down with them, fleece them!
⌐FIRST⌐ TRAVELLER O, we are undone, both we and ours
for ever!   85
SIR JOHN Hang ye, gorbellied knaves, are ye undone? No,
ye fat chuffs; I would your store were here. On, bacons,
on! What, ye knaves! Young men must live. You are
grand-jurors, are ye? We'll jure ye, faith.
    Here they rob them and bind them. Exeunt the
    thieves with the travellers

2.3   _Enter Prince Harry and Poins, disguised in buckram_
       suits
PRINCE HARRY The thieves have bound the true men; now
could thou and I rob the thieves, and go merrily to
London. It would be argument for a week, laughter for
a month, and a good jest for ever.
POINS Stand close; I hear them coming.   5
    They stand aside.
    Enter Sir John Oldcastle, Russell, Harvey, and
    Gadshill, with the travellers' money
SIR JOHN Come, my masters, let us share, and then to
horse before day. An the Prince and Poins be not two
arrant cowards, there's no equity stirring. There's no
more valour in that Poins than in a wild duck.
    As they are sharing, the Prince and Poins set upon
    them
PRINCE HARRY Your money!   10
POINS Villains!
    Gadshill, Russell, and Harvey run away ⌐severally⌐,
    and Oldcastle, after a blow or two, ⌐roars and⌐
    runs away too, leaving the booty behind them
PRINCE HARRY
Got with much ease. Now merrily to horse.
The thieves are all scattered, and possessed with fear
So strongly that they dare not meet each other.
Each takes his fellow for an officer.   15

Away, good Ned. Oldcastle sweats to death,
And lards the lean earth as he walks along.
Were't not for laughing, I should pity him.

POINS

How the fat rogue roared!   *Exeunt with the booty*

2.4   *Enter Hotspur, reading a letter*

HOTSPUR 'But for mine own part, I could be well
contented to be there, in respect of the love I bear your
house.'—He could be contented; why is he not then?
In respect of the love he bears our house! He shows in
this he loves his own barn better than he loves our
house. Let me see some more.—'The purpose you
undertake is dangerous'—Why, that's certain: 'tis
dangerous to take a cold, to sleep, to drink; but I tell
you, my lord fool, out of this nettle danger we pluck
this flower safety.—'The purpose you undertake is
dangerous, the friends you have named uncertain, the
time itself unsorted, and your whole plot too light for
the counterpoise of so great an opposition.'—Say you
so, say you so? I say unto you again, you are a shallow,
cowardly hind, and you lie. What a lack-brain is this!
By the Lord, our plot is a good plot as ever was laid,
our friends true and constant; a good plot, good friends,
and full of expectation; an excellent plot, very good
friends. What a frosty-spirited rogue is this! Why, my
lord of York commends the plot and the general course
of the action. Zounds, an I were now by this rascal, I
could brain him with his lady's fan! Is there not my
father, my uncle, and myself? Lord Edmund Mortimer,
my lord of York, and Owain Glyndŵr? Is there not
besides the Douglas? Have I not all their letters, to
meet me in arms by the ninth of the next month? And
are they not some of them set forward already? What
a pagan rascal is this, an infidel! Ha, you shall see
now, in very sincerity of fear and cold heart will he to
the King, and lay open all our proceedings! O, I could
divide myself and go to buffets for moving such a dish
of skim-milk with so honourable an action! Hang him!
Let him tell the King we are prepared; I will set forward
tonight.

Enter Lady Percy

How now, Kate? I must leave you within these two
hours.   36

LADY PERCY

O my good lord, why are you thus alone?
For what offence have I this fortnight been
A banished woman from my Harry's bed?
Tell me, sweet lord, what is't that takes from thee   40
Thy stomach, pleasure, and thy golden sleep?
Why dost thou bend thine eyes upon the earth,
And start so often when thou sitt'st alone?
Why hast thou lost the fresh blood in thy cheeks,
And given my treasures and my rights of thee   45
To thick-eyed musing and curst melancholy?
In thy faint slumbers I by thee have watched,
And heard thee murmur tales of iron wars,
Speak terms of manège to thy bounding steed,

Cry 'Courage! To the field!' And thou hast talked   50
Of sallies and retires, of trenches, tents,
Of palisadoes, frontiers, parapets,
Of basilisks, of cannon, culverin,
Of prisoners ransomed, and of soldiers slain,
And all the currents of a heady fight.   55
Thy spirit within thee hath been so at war,
And thus hath so bestirred thee in thy sleep,
That beads of sweat have stood upon thy brow
Like bubbles in a late-disturbèd stream;
And in thy face strange motions have appeared,   60
Such as we see when men restrain their breath
On some great sudden hest. O, what portents are
     these?
Some heavy business hath my lord in hand,
And I must know it, else he loves me not.

HOTSPUR

What ho!

Enter Servant

     Is Gilliams with the packet gone?   65

SERVANT

He is, my lord, an hour ago.

HOTSPUR

Hath Butler brought those horses from the sheriff?

SERVANT

One horse, my lord, he brought even now.

HOTSPUR

What horse? A roan, a crop-ear, is it not?

SERVANT

It is, my lord.

HOTSPUR   That roan shall be my throne.   70
Well, I will back him straight.—O, *Esperance!*—
Bid Butler lead him forth into the park.

LADY PERCY

But hear you, my lord.

HOTSPUR   What sayst thou, my lady?

LADY PERCY

What is it carries you away?

HOTSPUR   Why, my horse,
My love, my horse.

LADY PERCY   Out, you mad-headed ape!   75
A weasel hath not such a deal of spleen
As you are tossed with.
In faith, I'll know your business, Harry, that I will.
I fear my brother Mortimer doth stir
About his title, and hath sent for you   80
To line his enterprise; but if you go—

HOTSPUR

So far afoot? I shall be weary, love.

LADY PERCY

Come, come, you paraquito, answer me
Directly to this question that I ask.
In faith, I'll break thy little finger, Harry,   85
An if thou wilt not tell me all things true.

HOTSPUR

Away, away, you trifler! Love? I love thee not,
I care not for thee, Kate. This is no world
To play with maumets and to tilt with lips.
We must have bloody noses and cracked crowns,   90

And pass them current, too. God's me, my horse!—
What sayst thou, Kate? What wouldst thou have
    with me?
LADY PERCY
  Do you not love me? Do you not indeed?
  Well, do not, then, for since you love me not
  I will not love myself. Do you not love me?   95
  Nay, tell me if you speak in jest or no.
HOTSPUR Come, wilt thou see me ride?
  And when I am a-horseback, I will swear
  I love thee infinitely. But hark you, Kate.
  I must not have you henceforth question me   100
  Whither I go, nor reason whereabout.
  Whither I must, I must; and, to conclude,
  This evening must I leave you, gentle Kate.
  I know you wise, but yet no farther wise
  Than Harry Percy's wife; constant you are,   105
  But yet a woman; and for secrecy
  No lady closer, for I well believe
  Thou wilt not utter what thou dost not know.
  And so far will I trust thee, gentle Kate.
LADY PERCY How, so far?   110
HOTSPUR
  Not an inch further. But hark you, Kate,
  Whither I go, thither shall you go too.
  Today will I set forth, tomorrow you.
  Will this content you, Kate?
LADY PERCY   It must, of force.   *Exeunt*

2.5   *Enter Prince Harry*

PRINCE HARRY Ned, prithee come out of that fat room,
  and lend me thy hand to laugh a little.
    Enter Poins ⌈at another door⌉
POINS Where hast been, Hal?
PRINCE HARRY With three or four loggerheads, amongst
  three or fourscore hogsheads. I have sounded the very
  bass-string of humility. Sirrah, I am sworn brother to
  a leash of drawers, and can call them all by their
  christen names, as 'Tom', 'Dick', and 'Francis'. They
  take it already, upon their salvation, that though I be
  but Prince of Wales yet I am the king of courtesy, and
  tell me flatly I am no proud jack like Oldcastle, but a
  Corinthian, a lad of mettle, a good boy—by the Lord,
  so they call me; and when I am King of England I shall
  command all the good lads in Eastcheap. They call
  drinking deep 'dyeing scarlet', and when you breathe
  in your watering they cry 'Hem!' and bid you 'Play it
  off!' To conclude, I am so good a proficient in one
  quarter of an hour that I can drink with any tinker in
  his own language during my life. I tell thee, Ned, thou
  hast lost much honour that thou wert not with me in
  this action. But, sweet Ned—to sweeten which name
  of Ned I give thee this pennyworth of sugar, clapped
  even now into my hand by an underskinker, one that
  never spake other English in his life than 'Eight shillings
  and sixpence', and 'You are welcome', with this shrill
  addition, 'Anon, anon, sir! Score a pint of bastard in
  the Half-moon!' or so. But, Ned, to drive away the time
  till Oldcastle come, I prithee do thou stand in some

by-room, while I question my puny drawer to what
end he gave me the sugar, and do thou never leave
calling 'Francis!', that his tale to me may be nothing
but 'Anon!'. Step aside, and I'll show thee a precedent.
    Exit Poins
POINS (*within*) Francis!
PRINCE HARRY Thou art perfect.
POINS (*within*) Francis!   35
    Enter Francis, a drawer
FRANCIS Anon, anon, sir!—Look down into the Pome-
  granate, Ralph!
PRINCE HARRY Come hither, Francis.
FRANCIS My lord.
PRINCE HARRY How long hast thou to serve, Francis?   40
FRANCIS Forsooth, five years, and as much as to—
POINS (*within*) Francis!
FRANCIS Anon, anon, sir!
PRINCE HARRY Five year! By'r Lady, a long lease for the
  clinking of pewter. But Francis, darest thou be so
  valiant as to play the coward with thy indenture, and
  show it a fair pair of heels, and run from it?
FRANCIS O Lord, sir, I'll be sworn upon all the books in
  England, I could find in my heart—
POINS (*within*) Francis!   50
FRANCIS Anon, sir!
PRINCE HARRY How old art thou, Francis?
FRANCIS Let me see, about Michaelmas next I shall be—
POINS (*within*) Francis!
FRANCIS Anon, sir! (*To the Prince*) Pray, stay a little, my
  lord.   56
PRINCE HARRY Nay, but hark you, Francis. For the sugar
  thou gavest me, 'twas a pennyworth, was't not?
FRANCIS O Lord, I would it had been two!
PRINCE HARRY I will give thee for it a thousand pound.
  Ask me when thou wilt, and thou shalt have it—   61
POINS (*within*) Francis!
FRANCIS Anon, anon!
PRINCE HARRY Anon, Francis? No, Francis, but tomorrow,
  Francis; or, Francis, o' Thursday; or, indeed, Francis,
  when thou wilt. But Francis.   66
FRANCIS My lord.
PRINCE HARRY Wilt thou rob this leathern-jerkin, crystal-
  button, knot-pated, agate-ring, puke-stocking, caddis-
  garter, smooth-tongue, Spanish-pouch?   70
FRANCIS O Lord, sir, who do you mean?
PRINCE HARRY Why, then, your brown bastard is your
  only drink! For look you, Francis, your white canvas
  doublet will sully. In Barbary, sir, it cannot come to so
  much.   75
FRANCIS What, sir?
POINS (*within*) Francis!
PRINCE HARRY Away, you rogue! Dost thou not hear them
  call?
    ⌈*As he departs*⌉ *Poins and the Prince both call him.*
    The Drawer stands amazed, not knowing which
    way to go.
    Enter Vintner
VINTNER What, standest thou still, and hearest such a
  calling? Look to the guests within.   *Exit Francis*

My lord, old Sir John with half a dozen more are at
the door. Shall I let them in?

PRINCE HARRY Let them alone a while, and then open the
door.   *Exit Vintner*

Poins!   86

POINS ⌈*within*⌉ Anon, anon, sir!

Enter Poins

PRINCE HARRY Sirrah, Oldcastle and the rest of the thieves
are at the door. Shall we be merry?   89

POINS As merry as crickets, my lad. But hark ye, what
cunning match have you made with this jest of the
drawer? Come, what's the issue?

PRINCE HARRY I am now of all humours that have showed
themselves humours since the old days of goodman
Adam to the pupil age of this present twelve o'clock at
midnight.   96

⌈*Enter Francis*⌉

What's o'clock, Francis?

FRANCIS Anon, anon, sir!   ⌈*Exit at another door*⌉

PRINCE HARRY That ever this fellow should have fewer
words than a parrot, and yet the son of a woman! His
industry is upstairs and downstairs, his eloquence the
parcel of a reckoning. I am not yet of Percy's mind,
the Hotspur of the North—he that kills me some six or
seven dozen of Scots at a breakfast, washes his hands,
and says to his wife, 'Fie upon this quiet life! I want
work.' 'O my sweet Harry,' says she, 'how many hast
thou killed today?' 'Give my roan horse a drench,' says
he, and answers, 'Some fourteen,' an hour after; 'a
trifle, a trifle.' I prithee call in Oldcastle. I'll play Percy,
and that damned brawn shall play Dame Mortimer his
wife. 'Rivo!' says the drunkard. Call in Ribs, call in
Tallow.   112

Enter Sir John Oldcastle, with sword and buckler,
Russell, Harvey, and Gadshill, ⌈followed by⌉
Francis, with wine

POINS Welcome, Jack. Where hast thou been?

SIR JOHN A plague of all cowards, I say, and a vengeance
too, marry and amen!—Give me a cup of sack, boy.—
Ere I lead this life long, I'll sew netherstocks, and mend
them and foot them too. A plague of all cowards!—
Give me a cup of sack, rogue. Is there no virtue extant?

He drinketh

PRINCE HARRY Didst thou never see Titan kiss a dish of
butter—pitiful hearted Titan—that melted at the sweet
tale of the sun's? If thou didst, then behold that
compound.   122

SIR JOHN (*to Francis*) You rogue, here's lime in this sack
too. There is nothing but roguery to be found in
villainous man, yet a coward is worse than a cup of
sack with lime in it.   ⌈*Exit Francis*⌉

A villainous coward! Go thy ways, old Jack, die when
thou wilt. If manhood, good manhood, be not forgot
upon the face of the earth, then am I a shotten herring.
There lives not three good men unhanged in England,
and one of them is fat and grows old, God help the
while. A bad world, I say. I would I were a weaver—I
could sing psalms, or anything. A plague of all cowards,
I say still.

PRINCE HARRY How now, woolsack, what mutter you?

SIR JOHN A king's son! If I do not beat thee out of thy
kingdom with a dagger of lath, and drive all thy subjects
afore thee like a flock of wild geese, I'll never wear hair
on my face more. You, Prince of Wales!

PRINCE HARRY Why, you whoreson round man, what's
the matter?   141

SIR JOHN Are not you a coward? Answer me to that. And
Poins there?

POINS Zounds, ye fat paunch, an ye call me coward, by
the Lord I'll stab thee.   145

SIR JOHN I call thee coward? I'll see thee damned ere I
call thee coward, but I would give a thousand pound
I could run as fast as thou canst. You are straight
enough in the shoulders; you care not who sees your
back. Call you that backing of your friends? A plague
upon such backing! Give me them that will face me.
Give me a cup of sack. I am a rogue if I drunk today.

PRINCE HARRY O villain, thy lips are scarce wiped since
thou drunkest last.

SIR JOHN All is one for that.   155

He drinketh

A plague of all cowards, still say I.

PRINCE HARRY What's the matter?

SIR JOHN What's the matter? There be four of us here
have ta'en a thousand pound this day morning.

PRINCE HARRY Where is it, Jack, where is it?   160

SIR JOHN Where is it? Taken from us it is. A hundred
upon poor four of us.

PRINCE HARRY What, a hundred, man?

SIR JOHN I am a rogue if I were not at half-sword with a
dozen of them, two hours together. I have scaped by
miracle. I am eight times thrust through the doublet,
four through the hose, my buckler cut through and
through, my sword hacked like a handsaw. *Ecce signum.*

⌈*He shows his sword*⌉

I never dealt better since I was a man. All would not
do. A plague of all cowards! (*Pointing to Gadshill,*
Harvey, and Russell) Let them speak. If they speak more
or less than truth, they are villains and the sons of
darkness.

⌈PRINCE HARRY⌉ Speak, sirs, how was it?

⌈GADSHILL⌉ We four set upon some dozen—   175

SIR JOHN (*to the Prince*) Sixteen at least, my lord.

⌈GADSHILL⌉ And bound them.

HARVEY No, no, they were not bound.

SIR JOHN You rogue, they were bound every man of them,
or I am a Jew else, an Hebrew Jew.   180

⌈GADSHILL⌉ As we were sharing, some six or seven fresh
men set upon us.

SIR JOHN And unbound the rest; and then come in the
other.

PRINCE HARRY What, fought you with them all?   185

SIR JOHN All? I know not what you call all, but if I fought
not with fifty of them, I am a bunch of radish. If there
were not two- or three-and-fifty upon poor old Jack,
then am I no two-legged creature.

PRINCE HARRY Pray God you have not murdered some of
them.   191

SIR JOHN Nay, that's past praying for. I have peppered two of them. Two I am sure I have paid—two rogues in buckram suits. I tell thee what, Hal, if I tell thee a lie, spit in my face, call me horse. Thou knowest my old ward—   196

[*He stands as to fight*]

here I lay, and thus I bore my point. Four rogues in buckram let drive at me.

PRINCE HARRY What, four? Thou saidst but two even now.   200

SIR JOHN Four, Hal, I told thee four.

POINS Ay, ay, he said four.

SIR JOHN These four came all afront, and mainly thrust at me. I made me no more ado, but took all their seven points in my target, thus.   205

[*He wards himself with his buckler*]

PRINCE HARRY Seven? Why, there were but four even now.

SIR JOHN In buckram?

POINS Ay, four in buckram suits.

SIR JOHN Seven, by these hilts, or I am a villain else. 210

PRINCE HARRY (*aside to Poins*) Prithee, let him alone. We shall have more anon.

SIR JOHN Dost thou hear me, Hal?

PRINCE HARRY Ay, and mark thee too, Jack.

SIR JOHN Do so, for it is worth the listening to. These nine in buckram that I told thee of—   216

PRINCE HARRY (*aside to Poins*) So, two more already.

SIR JOHN Their points being broken—

POINS [*aside to the Prince*] Down fell their hose.   219

SIR JOHN Began to give me ground. But I followed me close, came in foot and hand, and, with a thought, seven of the eleven I paid.

PRINCE HARRY (*aside to Poins*) O monstrous! Eleven buckram men grown out of two!   224

SIR JOHN But, as the devil would have it, three misbegotten knaves in Kendal green came at my back and let drive at me; for it was so dark, Hal, that thou couldst not see thy hand.

PRINCE HARRY These lies are like their father that begets them—gross as a mountain, open, palpable. Why, thou clay-brained guts, thou knotty-pated fool, thou whoreson obscene greasy tallow-catch—   232

SIR JOHN What, art thou mad? Art thou mad? Is not the truth the truth?

PRINCE HARRY Why, how couldst thou know these men in Kendal green when it was so dark thou couldst not see thy hand? Come, tell us your reason. What sayst thou to this?

POINS Come, your reason, Jack, your reason.   239

SIR JOHN What, upon compulsion? Zounds, an I were at the strappado, or all the racks in the world, I would not tell you on compulsion. Give you a reason on compulsion? If reasons were as plentiful as blackberries, I would give no man a reason upon compulsion, I.

PRINCE HARRY I'll be no longer guilty of this sin. This sanguine coward, this bed-presser, this horse-back-breaker, this huge hill of flesh—   247

SIR JOHN 'Sblood, you starveling, you elf-skin, you dried neat's tongue, you bull's pizzle, you stock-fish—O, for breath to utter what is like thee!—you tailor's yard, you sheath, you bow-case, you vile standing tuck—

PRINCE HARRY Well, breathe awhile, and then to't again, and when thou hast tired thyself in base comparisons, hear me speak but this.

POINS Mark, Jack.   255

PRINCE HARRY We two saw you four set on four, and bound them, and were masters of their wealth.—Mark now how a plain tale shall put you down.—Then did we two set on you four, and, with a word, outfaced you from your prize, and have it; yea, and can show it you here in the house. And Oldcastle, you carried your guts away as nimbly, with as quick dexterity, and roared for mercy, and still run and roared, as ever I heard bull-calf. What a slave art thou, to hack thy sword as thou hast done, and then say it was in fight! What trick, what device, what starting-hole canst thou now find out to hide thee from this open and apparent shame?   268

POINS Come, let's hear, Jack; what trick hast thou now?

SIR JOHN By the Lord, I knew ye as well as he that made ye. Why, hear you, my masters. Was it for me to kill the heir-apparent? Should I turn upon the true prince? Why, thou knowest I am as valiant as Hercules; but beware instinct. The lion will not touch the true prince—instinct is a great matter. I was now a coward on instinct. I shall think the better of myself and thee during my life—I for a valiant lion, and thou for a true prince. But by the Lord, lads, I am glad you have the money.—(*Calling*) Hostess, clap to the doors.—Watch tonight, pray tomorrow. Gallants, lads, boys, hearts of gold, all the titles of good fellowship come to you! What, shall we be merry, shall we have a play extempore?

PRINCE HARRY Content, and the argument shall be thy running away.   285

SIR JOHN Ah, no more of that, Hal, an thou lovest me.

Enter Hostess

HOSTESS O Jesu, my lord the Prince!

PRINCE HARRY How now, my lady the Hostess, what sayst thou to me?   289

HOSTESS Marry, my lord, there is a nobleman of the court at door would speak with you. He says he comes from your father.

PRINCE HARRY Give him as much as will make him a royal man, and send him back again to my mother.

SIR JOHN What manner of man is he?   295

HOSTESS An old man.

SIR JOHN What doth gravity out of his bed at midnight? Shall I give him his answer?

PRINCE HARRY Prithee do, Jack.   299

SIR JOHN Faith, and I'll send him packing.   *Exit*

PRINCE HARRY Now, sirs; (*to Gadshill*) by'r Lady, you fought fair—so did you, Harvey, so did you, Russell. You are lions too—you ran away upon instinct, you will not touch the true prince; no, fie!

RUSSELL Faith, I ran when I saw others run.   305

PRINCE HARRY Faith, tell me now in earnest, how came Oldcastle's sword so hacked?

HARVEY Why, he hacked it with his dagger, and said he would swear truth out of England but he would make you believe it was done in fight, and persuaded us to do the like.   311

RUSSELL Yea, and to tickle our noses with speargrass, to make them bleed; and then to beslubber our garments with it, and swear it was the blood of true men. I did that I did not this seven year before—I blushed to hear his monstrous devices.   316

PRINCE HARRY O villain, thou stolest a cup of sack eighteen years ago, and wert taken with the manner, and ever since thou hast blushed extempore. Thou hadst fire and sword on thy side, and yet thou rannest away. What instinct hadst thou for it?   321

RUSSELL (indicating his face) My lord, do you see these meteors? Do you behold these exhalations?

PRINCE HARRY I do.

RUSSELL What think you they portend?   325

PRINCE HARRY Hot livers, and cold purses.

RUSSELL Choler, my lord, if rightly taken.   [Exit]

PRINCE HARRY No, if rightly taken, halter.

    Enter Sir John Oldcastle

Here comes lean Jack; here comes bare-bone. How now, my sweet creature of bombast? How long is't ago, Jack, since thou sawest thine own knee?   331

SIR JOHN My own knee? When I was about thy years, Hal, I was not an eagle's talon in the waist; I could have crept into any alderman's thumb-ring. A plague of sighing and grief—it blows a man up like a bladder. There's villainous news abroad. Here was Sir John Bracy from your father; you must to the court in the morning. That same mad fellow of the North, Percy, and he of Wales that gave Amamon the bastinado, and made Lucifer cuckold, and swore the devil his true liegeman upon the cross of a Welsh hook—what a plague call you him?

POINS Owain Glyndŵr.

SIR JOHN Owain, Owain, the same; and his son-in-law Mortimer, and old Northumberland, and that sprightly Scot of Scots Douglas, that runs a-horseback up a hill perpendicular—

PRINCE HARRY He that rides at high speed and with his pistol kills a sparrow flying.

SIR JOHN You have hit it.   350

PRINCE HARRY So did he never the sparrow.

SIR JOHN Well, that rascal hath good mettle in him; he will not run.

PRINCE HARRY Why, what a rascal art thou, then, to praise him so for running!   355

SIR JOHN A-horseback, ye cuckoo, but afoot he will not budge a foot.

PRINCE HARRY Yes, Jack, upon instinct.

SIR JOHN I grant ye, upon instinct. Well, he is there too, and one Mordake, and a thousand blue-caps more. Worcester is stolen away tonight. Thy father's beard is turned white with the news. You may buy land now as cheap as stinking mackerel.

PRINCE HARRY Why then, it is like, if there come a hot June and this civil buffeting hold, we shall buy maidenheads as they buy hobnails: by the hundreds.

SIR JOHN By the mass, lad, thou sayst true; it is like we shall have good trading that way. But tell me, Hal, art not thou horrible afeard? Thou being heir-apparent, could the world pick thee out three such enemies again as that fiend Douglas, that spirit Percy, and that devil Glyndŵr? Art thou not horribly afraid? Doth not thy blood thrill at it?

PRINCE HARRY Not a whit, i'faith. I lack some of thy instinct.   375

SIR JOHN Well, thou wilt be horribly chid tomorrow when thou comest to thy father. If thou love me, practise an answer.

PRINCE HARRY Do thou stand for my father, and examine me upon the particulars of my life.   380

SIR JOHN Shall I? Content. This chair shall be my state, this dagger my sceptre, and this cushion my crown.

    He sits

PRINCE HARRY Thy state is taken for a joint-stool, thy golden sceptre for a leaden dagger, and thy precious rich crown for a pitiful bald crown.   385

SIR JOHN Well, an the fire of grace be not quite out of thee, now shalt thou be moved. Give me a cup of sack to make my eyes look red, that it may be thought I have wept; for I must speak in passion, and I will do it in King Cambyses' vein.   390

PRINCE HARRY (bowing) Well, here is my leg.

SIR JOHN And here is my speech. (To Harvey, Poins, and Gadshill) Stand aside, nobility.

HOSTESS O Jesu, this is excellent sport, i'faith.

SIR JOHN

Weep not, sweet Queen, for trickling tears are vain. 395

HOSTESS O the Father, how he holds his countenance!

SIR JOHN

For God's sake, lords, convey my tristful Queen,
For tears do stop the floodgates of her eyes.

HOSTESS O Jesu, he doth it as like one of these harlotry players as ever I see!   400

SIR JOHN

Peace, good pint-pot; peace, good tickle-brain.—

Harry, I do not only marvel where thou spendest thy time, but also how thou art accompanied. For though the camomile, the more it is trodden on, the faster it grows, yet youth, the more it is wasted, the sooner it wears. That thou art my son I have partly thy mother's word, partly my own opinion, but chiefly a villainous trick of thine eye, and a foolish hanging of thy nether lip, that doth warrant me. If then thou be son to me, here lies the point. Why, being son to me, art thou so pointed at? Shall the blessed sun of heaven prove a micher, and eat blackberries?—A question not to be asked. Shall the son of England prove a thief, and take purses?—A question to be asked. There is a thing, Harry, which thou hast often heard of, and it is known to many in our land by the name of pitch. This pitch, as ancient writers do report, doth defile. So doth the company thou keepest. For Harry, now I do not speak to thee in drink, but in tears; not in pleasure, but in passion; not in words only, but in woes also. And yet there is a virtuous man whom I have often noted in thy company, but I know not his name.

PRINCE HARRY What manner of man, an it like your majesty?   424

SIR JOHN A goodly, portly man, i'faith, and a corpulent; of a cheerful look, a pleasing eye, and a most noble carriage; and, as I think, his age some fifty, or, by'r Lady, inclining to threescore. And now I remember me, his name is Oldcastle. If that man should be lewdly given, he deceiveth me; for, Harry, I see virtue in his looks. If, then, the tree may be known by the fruit, as the fruit by the tree, then peremptorily I speak it— there is virtue in that Oldcastle. Him keep with; the rest banish. And tell me now, thou naughty varlet, tell me, where hast thou been this month?   435

PRINCE HARRY Dost thou speak like a king? Do thou stand for me, and I'll play my father.

SIR JOHN (standing) Depose me. If thou dost it half so gravely, so majestically both in word and matter, hang me up by the heels for a rabbit sucker, or a poulter's hare.   441

PRINCE HARRY (sitting) Well, here I am set.

SIR JOHN And here I stand. (To the others) Judge, my masters.

PRINCE HARRY Now, Harry, whence come you?   445

SIR JOHN My noble lord, from Eastcheap.

PRINCE HARRY The complaints I hear of thee are grievous.

SIR JOHN 'Sblood, my lord, they are false. ⌜To the others⌝ Nay, I'll tickle ye for a young prince, i'faith.   449

PRINCE HARRY Swearest thou, ungracious boy? Henceforth ne'er look on me. Thou art violently carried away from grace. There is a devil haunts thee in the likeness of an old fat man; a tun of man is thy companion. Why dost thou converse with that trunk of humours, that bolting-hutch of beastliness, that swollen parcel of dropsies, that huge bombard of sack, that stuffed cloak-bag of guts, that roasted Manningtree ox with the pudding in his belly, that reverend Vice, that grey Iniquity, that father Ruffian, that Vanity in Years? Wherein is he good, but to taste sack and drink it? Wherein neat and cleanly, but to carve a capon and eat it? Wherein cunning, but in craft? Wherein crafty, but in villainy? Wherein villainous, but in all things? Wherein worthy, but in nothing?

SIR JOHN I would your grace would take me with you. Whom means your grace?   466

PRINCE HARRY That villainous, abominable misleader of youth, Oldcastle; that old white-bearded Satan.

SIR JOHN My lord, the man I know.

PRINCE HARRY I know thou dost.   470

SIR JOHN But to say I know more harm in him than in myself were to say more than I know. That he is old, the more the pity, his white hairs do witness it. But

that he is, saving your reverence, a whoremaster, that I utterly deny. If sack and sugar be a fault, God help the wicked. If to be old and merry be a sin, then many an old host that I know is damned. If to be fat be to be hated, then Pharaoh's lean kine are to be loved. No, my good lord, banish Harvey, banish Russell, banish Poins, but for sweet Jack Oldcastle, kind Jack Oldcastle, true Jack Oldcastle, valiant Jack Oldcastle, and therefore more valiant being, as he is, old Jack Oldcastle,
Banish not him thy Harry's company,
Banish not him thy Harry's company.
Banish plump Jack, and banish all the world.   485

PRINCE HARRY I do; I will.

Knocking within. ⌜Exit Hostess.⌝

Enter Russell, running

RUSSELL O my lord, my lord, the sheriff with a most monstrous watch is at the door.

SIR JOHN Out, ye rogue! Play out the play! I have much to say in the behalf of that Oldcastle.   490

Enter the Hostess

HOSTESS O Jesu! My lord, my lord!

PRINCE HARRY Heigh, heigh, the devil rides upon a fiddlestick! What's the matter?

HOSTESS The sheriff and all the watch are at the door. They are come to search the house. Shall I let them in?   496

SIR JOHN Dost thou hear, Hal? Never call a true piece of gold a counterfeit—thou art essentially made, without seeming so.

PRINCE HARRY And thou a natural coward without instinct.   501

SIR JOHN I deny your major. If you will deny the sheriff, so. If not, let him enter. If I become not a cart as well as another man, a plague on my bringing up. I hope I shall as soon be strangled with a halter as another. 505

PRINCE HARRY Go, hide thee behind the arras. The rest walk up above. Now, my masters, for a true face and good conscience.   Exeunt Poins, Russell, and Gadshill

SIR JOHN Both which I have had, but their date is out; and therefore I'll hide me.   510

He withdraws behind the arras

PRINCE HARRY (to Hostess) Call in the sheriff.

Exit Hostess

Enter Sheriff and a Carrier

Now, master sheriff, what is your will with me?

SHERIFF
First, pardon me, my lord. A hue and cry
Hath followed certain men unto this house.

PRINCE HARRY What men?   515

SHERIFF
One of them is well known, my gracious lord,
A gross, fat man.

CARRIER   As fat as butter.

PRINCE HARRY
The man, I do assure you, is not here,
For I myself at this time have employed him.
And, sheriff, I will engage my word to thee   520
That I will by tomorrow dinner-time

Send him to answer thee, or any man,
For anything he shall be charged withal.
And so let me entreat you leave the house.

SHERIFF
I will, my lord. There are two gentlemen   525
Have in this robbery lost three hundred marks.

PRINCE HARRY
It may be so. If he have robbed these men,
He shall be answerable. And so, farewell.

SHERIFF Good night, my noble lord.

PRINCE HARRY
I think it is good morrow, is it not?   530

SHERIFF
Indeed, my lord, I think it be two o'clock.
                    Exeunt Sheriff and Carrier

PRINCE HARRY
This oily rascal is known as well as Paul's.
Go call him forth.

HARVEY   Oldcastle!
    ⌐*He draws back the arras, revealing Sir John asleep*⌐
                    Fast asleep
Behind the arras, and snorting like a horse.

PRINCE HARRY
Hark how hard he fetches breath. Search his pockets.
    Harvey searcheth his pocket and findeth certain
    papers. He ⌐closeth the arras and⌐ cometh forward
What hast thou found?   536

HARVEY   Nothing but papers, my lord.

PRINCE HARRY Let's see what they be. Read them.

⌐HARVEY⌐ (*reads*)
Item: a capon.   2s. 2d.
Item: sauce.   4d.
Item: sack, two gallons.   5s. 8d.
Item: anchovies and sack after supper.   2s. 6d.
Item: bread.   ob.

⌐PRINCE HARRY⌐ O monstrous! But one halfpennyworth of
bread to this intolerable deal of sack! What there is
else, keep close; we'll read it at more advantage. There
let him sleep till day. I'll to the court in the morning.
We must all to the wars, and thy place shall be
honourable. I'll procure this fat rogue a charge of foot,
and I know his death will be a march of twelve score.
The money shall be paid back again, with advantage.
Be with me betimes in the morning; and so good
morrow, Harvey.

HARVEY Good morrow, good my lord.
                    Exeunt ⌐severally⌐

3.1   *Enter Hotspur, the Earl of Worcester, Lord*
        Mortimer, and Owain Glyndŵr, with a map

MORTIMER
These promises are fair, the parties sure,
And our induction full of prosperous hope.

HOTSPUR
Lord Mortimer and cousin Glyndŵr,
Will you sit down? And uncle Worcester?
    ⌐*Mortimer, Glyndŵr, and Worcester sit*⌐
A plague upon it, I have forgot the map!   5

GLYNDŴR
No, here it is. Sit, cousin Percy, sit,
Good cousin Hotspur;
    ⌐*Hotspur sits*⌐
                    For by that name
As oft as Lancaster doth speak of you,
His cheek looks pale, and with a rising sigh
He wisheth you in heaven.

HOTSPUR   And you in hell,   10
As oft as he hears Owain Glyndŵr spoke of.

GLYNDŴR
I cannot blame him. At my nativity
The front of heaven was full of fiery shapes,
Of burning cressets; and at my birth
The frame and huge foundation of the earth   15
Shaked like a coward.

HOTSPUR   Why, so it would have done
At the same season if your mother's cat
Had but kittened, though yourself had never been
    born.

GLYNDŴR
I say the earth did shake when I was born.

HOTSPUR
And I say the earth was not of my mind   20
If you suppose as fearing you it shook.

GLYNDŴR
The heavens were all on fire, the earth did tremble—

HOTSPUR
O, then the earth shook to see the heavens on fire,
And not in fear of your nativity.
Diseasèd nature oftentimes breaks forth   25
In strange eruptions; oft the teeming earth
Is with a kind of colic pinched and vexed
By the imprisoning of unruly wind
Within her womb, which for enlargement striving
Shakes the old beldam earth, and topples down   30
Steeples and moss-grown towers. At your birth
Our grandam earth, having this distemp'rature,
In passion shook.

GLYNDŴR   Cousin, of many men
I do not bear these crossings. Give me leave
To tell you once again that at my birth   35
The front of heaven was full of fiery shapes,
The goats ran from the mountains, and the herds
Were strangely clamorous to the frighted fields.
These signs have marked me extraordinary,
And all the courses of my life do show   40
I am not in the roll of commen men.
Where is he living, clipped in with the sea
That chides the banks of England, Scotland, Wales,
Which calls me pupil or hath read to me?
And bring him out that is but woman's son   45
Can trace me in the tedious ways of art,
And hold me pace in deep experiments.

HOTSPUR ⌐*standing*⌐
I think there's no man speaketh better Welsh.
I'll to dinner.

MORTIMER
Peace, cousin Percy, you will make him mad.   50
GLYNDŴR
I can call spirits from the vasty deep.
HOTSPUR
Why, so can I, or so can any man;
But will they come when you do call for them?
GLYNDŴR
Why, I can teach you, cousin, to command the devil.
HOTSPUR
And I can teach thee, coz, to shame the devil,   55
By telling truth: 'Tell truth, and shame the devil'.
If thou have power to raise him, bring him hither,
And I'll be sworn I have power to shame him hence.
O, while you live, tell truth and shame the devil.
MORTIMER
Come, come, no more of this unprofitable chat.   60
GLYNDŴR
Three times hath Henry Bolingbroke made head
Against my power; thrice from the banks of Wye
And sandy-bottomed Severn have I sent him
Bootless home, and weather-beaten back.
HOTSPUR
Home without boots, and in foul weather too!   65
How scapes he agues, in the devil's name?
GLYNDŴR
Come, here's the map. Shall we divide our right,
According to our threefold order ta'en?
MORTIMER
The Archdeacon hath divided it
Into three limits very equally.   70
England from Trent and Severn hitherto
By south and east is to my part assigned;
All westward—Wales beyond the Severn shore
And all the fertile land within that bound—
To Owain Glyndŵr; (to Hotspur) and, dear coz, to you
The remnant northward lying off from Trent.   76
And our indentures tripartite are drawn,
Which, being sealèd interchangeably—
A business that this night may execute—
Tomorrow, cousin Percy, you and I   80
And my good lord of Worcester will set forth
To meet your father and the Scottish power,
As is appointed us, at Shrewsbury.
My father, Glyndŵr, is not ready yet,
Nor shall we need his help these fourteen days.   85
Within that space you may have drawn together
Your tenants, friends, and neighbouring gentlemen.
GLYNDŴR
A shorter time shall send me to you, lords;
And in my conduct shall your ladies come,
From whom you now must steal and take no leave; 90
For there will be a world of water shed
Upon the parting of your wives and you.
HOTSPUR
Methinks my moiety north from Burton here
In quantity equals not one of yours.

See how this river comes me cranking in,   95
And cuts me from the best of all my land
A huge half-moon, a monstrous cantle, out.
I'll have the current in this place dammed up,
And here the smug and silver Trent shall run
In a new channel fair and evenly.   100
It shall not wind with such a deep indent,
To rob me of so rich a bottom here.
GLYNDŴR
Not wind? It shall, it must; you see it doth.
MORTIMER
Yea, but mark how he bears his course, and runs
     me up
With like advantage on the other side,   105
Gelding the opposèd continent as much
As on the other side it takes from you.
WORCESTER
Yea, but a little charge will trench him here,
And on this north side win this cape of land,
And then he runs straight and even.   110
HOTSPUR
I'll have it so; a little charge will do it.
GLYNDŴR I'll not have it altered.
HOTSPUR Will not you?
GLYNDŴR No, nor you shall not.
HOTSPUR Who shall say me nay?   115
GLYNDŴR Why, that will I.
HOTSPUR
Let me not understand you, then: speak it in Welsh.
GLYNDŴR
I can speak English, lord, as well as you;
For I was trained up in the English court,
Where, being but young, I framèd to the harp   120
Many an English ditty lovely well,
And gave the tongue a helpful ornament—
A virtue that was never seen in you.
HOTSPUR
Marry, and I am glad of it, with all my heart.
I had rather be a kitten and cry 'mew'   125
Than one of these same metre ballad-mongers.
I had rather hear a brazen canstick turned,
Or a dry wheel grate on the axle-tree,
And that would set my teeth nothing on edge,
Nothing so much as mincing poetry.   130
'Tis like the forced gait of a shuffling nag.
GLYNDŴR Come, you shall have Trent turned.
HOTSPUR
I do not care. I'll give thrice so much land
To any well-deserving friend;
But in the way of bargain—mark ye me—   135
I'll cavil on the ninth part of a hair.
Are the indentures drawn? Shall we be gone?
GLYNDŴR
The moon shines fair. You may away by night.
I'll haste the writer, and withal
Break with your wives of your departure hence.   140
I am afraid my daughter will run mad,
So much she doteth on her Mortimer.   Exit

MORTIMER
Fie, cousin Percy, how you cross my father!
HOTSPUR
I cannot choose. Sometime he angers me
With telling me of the moldwarp and the ant,   145
Of the dreamer Merlin and his prophecies,
And of a dragon and a finless fish,
A clip-winged griffin and a moulten raven,
A couching lion and a ramping cat,
And such a deal of skimble-skamble stuff   150
As puts me from my faith. I tell you what,
He held me last night at the least nine hours
In reckoning up the several devils' names
That were his lackeys. I cried, 'Hum!' and, 'Well,
          go to!',
But marked him not a word. O, he is as tedious   155
As a tired horse, a railing wife,
Worse than a smoky house. I had rather live
With cheese and garlic, in a windmill, far,
Than feed on cates and have him talk to me
In any summer house in Christendom.   160
MORTIMER
In faith, he is a worthy gentleman,
Exceedingly well read, and profited
In strange concealments, valiant as a lion,
And wondrous affable, and as bountiful
As mines of India. Shall I tell you, cousin?   165
He holds your temper in a high respect,
And curbs himself even of his natural scope
When you come 'cross his humour; faith, he does.
I warrant you, that man is not alive
Might so have tempted him as you have done   170
Without the taste of danger and reproof.
But do not use it oft, let me entreat you.
WORCESTER (to Hotspur)
In faith, my lord, you are too wilful-blame,
And since your coming hither have done enough
To put him quite besides his patience.   175
You must needs learn, lord, to amend this fault.
Though sometimes it show greatness, courage, blood—
And that's the dearest grace it renders you—
Yet oftentimes it doth present harsh rage,
Defect of manners, want of government,   180
Pride, haughtiness, opinion, and disdain,
The least of which haunting a nobleman
Loseth men's hearts, and leaves behind a stain
Upon the beauty of all parts besides,
Beguiling them of commendation.   185
HOTSPUR
Well, I am schooled. Good manners be your speed!
          Enter Glyndŵr with Lady Percy and Mortimer's
          wife
Here come our wives, and let us take our leave.
          ⌈*Mortimer's wife weeps, and speaks to him in*
          Welsh⌉
MORTIMER
This is the deadly spite that angers me:
My wife can speak no English, I no Welsh.

GLYNDŴR
My daughter weeps she'll not part with you.   190
She'll be a soldier, too; she'll to the wars.
MORTIMER
Good father, tell her that she and my aunt Percy
Shall follow in your conduct speedily.
          Glyndŵr speaks to her in Welsh, and she answers
          him in the same
GLYNDŴR
She is desperate here, a peevish self-willed harlotry,
One that no persuasion can do good upon.   195
          The lady speaks in Welsh
MORTIMER
I understand thy looks. That pretty Welsh
Which thou down pourest from these swelling
          heavens
I am too perfect in, and but for shame
In such a parley should I answer thee.
          The lady kisses him, and speaks again in Welsh
MORTIMER
I understand thy kisses, and thou mine,   200
And that's a feeling disputation;
But I will never be a truant, love,
Till I have learnt thy language, for thy tongue
Makes Welsh as sweet as ditties highly penned,
Sung by a fair queen in a summer's bower   205
With ravishing division, to her lute.
GLYNDŴR
Nay, if you melt, then will she run mad.
          The lady ⌈*sits on the rushes and*⌉ *speaks again in*
          Welsh
MORTIMER
O, I am ignorance itself in this!
GLYNDŴR
She bids you on the wanton rushes lay you down
And rest your gentle head upon her lap,   210
And she will sing the song that pleaseth you,
And on your eyelids crown the god of sleep,
Charming your blood with pleasing heaviness,
Making such difference 'twixt wake and sleep
As is the difference betwixt day and night   215
The hour before the heavenly-harnessed team
Begins his golden progress in the east.
MORTIMER
With all my heart, I'll sit and hear her sing.
By that time will our book, I think, be drawn.
          He sits, ⌈*resting his head on the Welsh lady's lap*⌉
GLYNDŴR
Do so, and those musicians that shall play to you   220
Hang in the air a thousand leagues from hence,
And straight they shall be here. Sit and attend.
HOTSPUR
Come, Kate, thou art perfect in lying down.
Come, quick, quick, that I may lay my head in thy
          lap.
LADY PERCY (*sitting*) Go, ye giddy goose!   225
          Hotspur sits, resting his head on Lady Percy's lap.
          The music plays

HOTSPUR

Now I perceive the devil understands Welsh;
And 'tis no marvel, he is so humorous.
By'r Lady, he's a good musician.

LADY PERCY

Then should you be nothing but musical,
For you are altogether governed by humours.   230
Lie still, ye thief, and hear the lady sing in Welsh.

HOTSPUR I had rather hear Lady my brach howl in Irish.

LADY PERCY Wouldst thou have thy head broken?

HOTSPUR No.

LADY PERCY Then be still.   235

HOTSPUR Neither—'tis a woman's fault.

LADY PERCY Now God help thee!

HOTSPUR To the Welsh lady's bed.

LADY PERCY What's that?

HOTSPUR Peace; she sings.   240

Here the lady sings a Welsh song

HOTSPUR Come, Kate, I'll have your song too.

LADY PERCY Not mine, in good sooth.

HOTSPUR Not yours, in good sooth! Heart, you swear like
a comfit-maker's wife: 'Not you, in good sooth!' and
'As true as I live!' and   245
'As God shall mend me!' and 'As sure as day!';
And giv'st such sarcenet surety for thy oaths
As if thou never walk'st further than Finsbury.
Swear me, Kate, like a lady as thou art,
A good mouth-filling oath, and leave 'in sooth'   250
And such protest of pepper gingerbread
To velvet-guards and Sunday citizens.
Come, sing.

LADY PERCY I will not sing.   254

HOTSPUR 'Tis the next way to turn tailor, or be redbreast
teacher. (*Rising*) An the indentures be drawn, I'll away
within these two hours; and so come in when ye will.

Exit

GLYNDŴR

Come, come, Lord Mortimer. You are as slow
As hot Lord Percy is on fire to go.
By this our book is drawn. We'll but seal,   260
And then to horse immediately.

MORTIMER (*rising*)   With all my heart.

The ladies rise, and all exeunt

3.2   *Enter King Henry, Prince Harry, and lords*

KING HENRY

Lords, give us leave—the Prince of Wales and I
Must have some private conference—but be near at
hand,
For we shall presently have need of you.

Exeunt Lords

I know not whether God will have it so
For some displeasing service I have done,   5
That in his secret doom out of my blood
He'll breed revengement and a scourge for me,
But thou dost in thy passages of life
Make me believe that thou art only marked
For the hot vengeance and the rod of heaven   10

To punish my mistreadings. Tell me else,
Could such inordinate and low desires,
Such poor, such bare, such lewd, such mean attempts,
Such barren pleasures, rude society,
As thou art matched withal and grafted to,   15
Accompany the greatness of thy blood,
And hold their level with thy princely heart?

PRINCE HARRY

So please your majesty, I would I could
Quit all offences with as clear excuse
As well as I am doubtless I can purge   20
Myself of many I am charged withal;
Yet such extenuation let me beg
As, in reproof of many tales devised—
Which oft the ear of greatness needs must hear
By smiling pickthanks and base newsmongers—   25
I may, for some things true wherein my youth
Hath faulty wandered and irregular,
Find pardon on my true submission.

KING HENRY

God pardon thee! Yet let me wonder, Harry,
At thy affections, which do hold a wing   30
Quite from the flight of all thy ancestors.
Thy place in Council thou hast rudely lost—
Which by thy younger brother is supplied—
And art almost an alien to the hearts
Of all the court and princes of my blood.   35
The hope and expectation of thy time
Is ruined, and the soul of every man
Prophetically do forethink thy fall.
Had I so lavish of my presence been,
So common-hackneyed in the eyes of men,   40
So stale and cheap to vulgar company,
Opinion, that did help me to the crown,
Had still kept loyal to possession,
And left me in reputeless banishment,
A fellow of no mark nor likelihood.   45
By being seldom seen, I could not stir
But, like a comet, I was wondered at,
That men would tell their children 'This is he.'
Others would say 'Where, which is Bolingbroke?'
And then I stole all courtesy from heaven,   50
And dressed myself in such humility
That I did pluck allegiance from men's hearts,
Loud shouts and salutations from their mouths,
Even in the presence of the crownèd King.
Thus did I keep my person fresh and new,   55
My presence like a robe pontifical—
Ne'er seen but wondered at—and so my state,
Seldom but sumptuous, showed like a feast,
And won by rareness such solemnity.
The skipping King, he ambled up and down   60
With shallow jesters and rash bavin wits,
Soon kindled and soon burnt, carded his state,
Mingled his royalty with cap'ring fools,
Had his great name profanèd with their scorns,
And gave his countenance, against his name,   65

To laugh at gibing boys, and stand the push
Of every beardless vain comparative;
Grew a companion to the common streets,
Enfeoffed himself to popularity,
That, being daily swallowed by men's eyes,　70
They surfeited with honey, and began
To loathe the taste of sweetness, whereof a little
More than a little is by much too much.
So when he had occasion to be seen,
He was but as the cuckoo is in June,　75
Heard, not regarded, seen but with such eyes
As, sick and blunted with community,
Afford no extraordinary gaze
Such as is bent on sun-like majesty
When it shines seldom in admiring eyes,　80
But rather drowsed and hung their eyelids down,
Slept in his face, and rendered such aspect
As cloudy men use to their adversaries,
Being with his presence glutted, gorged, and full.
And in that very line, Harry, standest thou;　85
For thou hast lost thy princely privilege
With vile participation. Not an eye
But is a-weary of thy common sight,
Save mine, which hath desired to see thee more,
Which now doth that I would not have it do—　90
Make blind itself with foolish tenderness.

      He weeps

PRINCE HARRY

I shall hereafter, my thrice-gracious lord,
Be more myself.

KING HENRY   For all the world,
As thou art to this hour was Richard then,
When I from France set foot at Ravenspurgh,　95
And even as I was then is Percy now.
Now by my sceptre, and my soul to boot,
He hath more worthy interest to the state
Than thou, the shadow of succession;
For, of no right, nor colour like to right,　100
He doth fill fields with harness in the realm,
Turns head against the lion's armèd jaws,
And, being no more in debt to years than thou,
Leads ancient lords and reverend bishops on
To bloody battles, and to bruising arms.　105
What never-dying honour hath he got
Against renownèd Douglas!—whose high deeds,
Whose hot incursions and great name in arms,
Holds from all soldiers chief majority
And military title capital　110
Through all the kingdoms that acknowledge Christ.
Thrice hath this Hotspur, Mars in swaddling-clothes,
This infant warrior, in his enterprises
Discomfited great Douglas; ta'en him once;
Enlargèd him; and made a friend of him　115
To fill the mouth of deep defiance up,
And shake the peace and safety of our throne.
And what say you to this? Percy, Northumberland,
The Archbishop's grace of York, Douglas, Mortimer,

Capitulate against us, and are up.　120
But wherefore do I tell these news to thee?
Why, Harry, do I tell thee of my foes,
Which art my near'st and dearest enemy?—
Thou that art like enough, through vassal fear,
Base inclination, and the start of spleen,　125
To fight against me under Percy's pay,
To dog his heels, and curtsy at his frowns,
To show how much thou art degenerate.

PRINCE HARRY

Do not think so; you shall not find it so.
And God forgive them that so much have swayed　130
Your majesty's good thoughts away from me.
I will redeem all this on Percy's head,
And in the closing of some glorious day
Be bold to tell you that I am your son;
When I will wear a garment all of blood,　135
And stain my favours in a bloody mask,
Which, washed away, shall scour my shame with it.
And that shall be the day, whene'er it lights,
That this same child of honour and renown,
This gallant Hotspur, this all-praisèd knight,　140
And your unthought-of Harry chance to meet.
For every honour sitting on his helm,
Would they were multitudes, and on my head
My shames redoubled; for the time will come
That I shall make this northern youth exchange　145
His glorious deeds for my indignities.
Percy is but my factor, good my lord,
To engross up glorious deeds on my behalf;
And I will call him to so strict account
That he shall render every glory up,　150
Yea, even the slightest worship of his time,
Or I will tear the reckoning from his heart.
This, in the name of God, I promise here,
The which if he be pleased I shall perform,
I do beseech your majesty may salve　155
The long-grown wounds of my intemperature;
If not, the end of life cancels all bonds,
And I will die a hundred thousand deaths
Ere break the smallest parcel of this vow.

KING HENRY

A hundred thousand rebels die in this.　160
Thou shalt have charge and sovereign trust herein.

      Enter Sir Walter Blunt

How now, good Blunt? Thy looks are full of speed.

BLUNT

So hath the business that I come to speak of.
Lord Mortimer of Scotland hath sent word
That Douglas and the English rebels met　165
The eleventh of this month at Shrewsbury.
A mighty and a fearful head they are,
If promises be kept on every hand,
As ever offered foul play in a state.

KING HENRY

The Earl of Westmorland set forth today,　170
With him my son Lord John of Lancaster,

For this advertisement is five days old.
On Wednesday next, Harry, you shall set forward.
On Thursday we ourselves will march.
Our meeting is Bridgnorth, and, Harry, you   175
Shall march through Gloucestershire, by which
    account,
Our business valuèd, some twelve days hence
Our general forces at Bridgnorth shall meet.
Our hands are full of business; let's away.   179
Advantage feeds him fat while men delay.   *Exeunt*

3.3   *Enter Sir John Oldcastle ⌈with a truncheon at his*
        waist⌉, and Russell

SIR JOHN Russell, am I not fallen away vilely since this
last action? Do I not bate? Do I not dwindle? Why,
my skin hangs about me like an old lady's loose gown.
I am withered like an old apple-john. Well, I'll repent,
and that suddenly, while I am in some liking. I shall
be out of heart shortly, and then I shall have no
strength to repent. An I have not forgotten what the
inside of a church is made of, I am a peppercorn, a
brewer's horse—the inside of a church! Company,
villainous company, hath been the spoil of me.   10
RUSSELL Sir John, you are so fretful you cannot live long.
SIR JOHN Why, there is it. Come, sing me a bawdy song,
make me merry. I was as virtuously given as a
gentleman need to be: virtuous enough; swore little;
diced not—above seven times a week; went to a bawdy-
house not—above once in a quarter—of an hour; paid
money that I borrowed—three or four times; lived well,
and in good compass. And now I live out of all order,
out of all compass.   19
RUSSELL Why, you are so fat, Sir John, that you must
needs be out of all compass, out of all reasonable
compass, Sir John.
SIR JOHN Do thou amend thy face, and I'll amend my life.
Thou art our admiral, thou bearest the lantern in the
poop—but 'tis in the nose of thee. Thou art the Knight
of the Burning Lamp.   26
RUSSELL Why, Sir John, my face does you no harm.
SIR JOHN No, I'll be sworn; I make as good use of it as
many a man doth of a death's head, or a *memento
mori*. I never see thy face but I think upon hell-fire and
Dives that lived in purple—for there he is in his robes,
burning, burning. If thou wert any way given to virtue,
I would swear by thy face; my oath should be 'By this
fire that's God's angel!' But thou art altogether given
over, and wert indeed, but for the light in thy face, the
son of utter darkness. When thou rannest up Gads Hill
in the night to catch my horse, if I did not think thou
hadst been an *ignis fatuus* or a ball of wildfire, there's
no purchase in money. O, thou art a perpetual triumph,
an everlasting bonfire-light! Thou hast saved me a
thousand marks in links and torches, walking with
thee in the night betwixt tavern and tavern—but the
sack that thou hast drunk me would have bought me
lights as good cheap at the dearest chandler's in Europe.
I have maintained that salamander of yours with fire

any time this two-and-thirty years, God reward me
for it.
RUSSELL 'Sblood, I would my face were in your belly!
SIR JOHN God-a-mercy! So should I be sure to be heart-
burnt.   50
     Enter Hostess
How now, Dame Partlet the hen, have you enquired
yet who picked my pocket?
HOSTESS Why, Sir John, what do you think, Sir John? Do
you think I keep thieves in my house? I have searched,
I have enquired; so has my husband, man by man,
boy by boy, servant by servant. The tithe of a hair was
never lost in my house before.
SIR JOHN Ye lie, Hostess: Russell was shaved and lost
many a hair, and I'll be sworn my pocket was picked.
Go to, you are a woman, go.   60
HOSTESS Who, I? No, I defy thee! God's light, I was never
called so in mine own house before.
SIR JOHN Go to, I know you well enough.
HOSTESS No, Sir John, you do not know me, Sir John; I
know you, Sir John. You owe me money, Sir John, and
now you pick a quarrel to beguile me of it. I bought
you a dozen of shirts to your back.   67
SIR JOHN Dowlas, filthy dowlas. I have given them away
to bakers' wives; they have made bolters of them.
HOSTESS Now as I am a true woman, holland of eight
shillings an ell. You owe money here besides, Sir John:
for your diet, and by-drinkings, and money lent you,
four-and-twenty pound.
SIR JOHN (*pointing at Russell*) He had his part of it. Let
him pay.   75
HOSTESS He? Alas, he is poor; he hath nothing.
SIR JOHN How, poor? Look upon his face. What call you
rich? Let them coin his nose, let them coin his cheeks,
I'll not pay a denier. What, will you make a younker
of me? Shall I not take mine ease in mine inn, but I
shall have my pocket picked? I have lost a seal-ring of
my grandfather's worth forty mark.   82
HOSTESS O Jesu, (*to Russell*) I have heard the Prince tell
him, I know not how oft, that that ring was copper.
SIR JOHN How? The Prince is a jack, a sneak-up. ⌈*Raising
his truncheon*⌉ 'Sblood, an he were here I would cudgel
him like a dog if he would say so.
     Enter Prince Harry and Harvey, marching; and Sir
     John Oldcastle meets them, playing upon his
     truncheon like a fife
How now, lad, is the wind in that door, i'faith? Must
we all march?
RUSSELL Yea, two and two, Newgate fashion.   90
HOSTESS My lord, I pray you hear me.
PRINCE HARRY
What sayst thou, Mistress Quickly? How doth thy
    husband?
I love him well; he is an honest man.
HOSTESS Good my lord, hear me!
SIR JOHN Prithee, let her alone, and list to me.   95
PRINCE HARRY What sayst thou, Jack?
SIR JOHN The other night I fell asleep here behind the

arras, and had my pocket picked. This house is turned
bawdy-house: they pick pockets.

PRINCE HARRY What didst thou lose, Jack?   100

SIR JOHN Wilt thou believe me, Hal, three or four bonds
of forty pound apiece, and a seal-ring of my grandfather's.

PRINCE HARRY A trifle, some eightpenny matter.   104

HOSTESS So I told him, my lord; and I said I heard your
grace say so; and, my lord, he speaks most vilely of
you, like a foul-mouthed man as he is, and said he
would cudgel you.

PRINCE HARRY What? He did not!

HOSTESS There's neither faith, truth, nor womanhood in
me else.   111

SIR JOHN There's no more faith in thee than in a stewed
prune, nor no more truth in thee than in a drawn fox;
and, for womanhood, Maid Marian may be the deputy's
wife of the ward to thee. Go, you thing, go!   115

HOSTESS Say, what thing, what thing?

SIR JOHN What thing? Why, a thing to thank God on.

HOSTESS I am no thing to thank God on. I would thou
shouldst know it, I am an honest man's wife; and
setting thy knighthood aside, thou art a knave to call
me so.   121

SIR JOHN Setting thy womanhood aside, thou art a beast
to say otherwise.

HOSTESS Say, what beast, thou knave, thou?

SIR JOHN What beast? Why, an otter.   125

PRINCE HARRY An otter, Sir John? Why an otter?

SIR JOHN Why? She's neither fish nor flesh; a man knows
not where to have her.

HOSTESS Thou art an unjust man in saying so. Thou or
any man knows where to have me, thou knave, thou.

PRINCE HARRY Thou sayst true, Hostess, and he slanders
thee most grossly.

HOSTESS So he doth you, my lord, and said this other day
you owed him a thousand pound.

PRINCE HARRY (to Sir John) Sirrah, do I owe you a thousand
pound?   136

SIR JOHN A thousand pound, Hal? A million! Thy love is
worth a million; thou owest me thy love.

HOSTESS Nay, my lord, he called you 'jack' and said he
would cudgel you.   140

SIR JOHN Did I, Russell?

RUSSELL Indeed, Sir John, you said so.

SIR JOHN Yea, if he said my ring was copper.

PRINCE HARRY I say 'tis copper; darest thou be as good
as thy word now?   145

SIR JOHN Why, Hal, thou knowest as thou art but man I
dare, but as thou art prince, I fear thee as I fear the
roaring of the lion's whelp.

PRINCE HARRY And why not as the lion?

SIR JOHN The King himself is to be feared as the lion. Dost
thou think I'll fear thee as I fear thy father? Nay, an I
do, I pray God my girdle break.   152

PRINCE HARRY O, if it should, how would thy guts fall
about thy knees! But sirrah, there's no room for faith,
truth, nor honesty in this bosom of thine; it is all filled

up with guts and midriff. Charge an honest woman
with picking thy pocket? Why, thou whoreson
impudent embossed rascal, if there were anything in
thy pocket but tavern reckonings, memorandums of
bawdy-houses, and one poor pennyworth of sugar-
candy to make thee long-winded—if thy pocket were
enriched with any other injuries but these, I am a
villain. And yet you will stand to it, you will not pocket
up wrong. Art thou not ashamed?   164

SIR JOHN Dost thou hear, Hal? Thou knowest in the state
of innocency Adam fell, and what should poor Jack
Oldcastle do in the days of villainy? Thou seest I have
more flesh than another man, and therefore more
frailty. You confess, then, you picked my pocket.

PRINCE HARRY It appears so by the story.   170

SIR JOHN Hostess, I forgive thee. Go make ready breakfast.
Love thy husband, look to thy servants, cherish thy
guests. Thou shalt find me tractable to any honest
reason; thou seest I am pacified still. Nay, prithee, be
gone.   *Exit Hostess*
Now, Hal, to the news at court. For the robbery, lad,
how is that answered?

PRINCE HARRY O, my sweet beef, I must still be good angel
to thee. The money is paid back again.

SIR JOHN O, I do not like that paying back; 'tis a double
labour.   181

PRINCE HARRY I am good friends with my father, and may
do anything.

SIR JOHN Rob me the exchequer the first thing thou dost,
and do it with unwashed hands too.   185

RUSSELL Do, my lord.

PRINCE HARRY I have procured thee, Jack, a charge of
foot.

SIR JOHN I would it had been of horse! Where shall I find
one that can steal well? O, for a fine thief of the age
of two-and-twenty or thereabouts! I am heinously
unprovided. Well, God be thanked for these rebels—
they offend none but the virtuous. I laud them, I praise
them.

PRINCE HARRY Russell.   195

RUSSELL My lord?

PRINCE HARRY (giving letters)
Go bear this letter to Lord John of Lancaster,
To my brother John; this to my lord of Westmorland.
   Exit Russell
Go, Harvey, to horse, to horse, for thou and I
Have thirty miles to ride yet ere dinner time.   200
   Exit Harvey
Jack, meet me tomorrow in the Temple Hall
At two o'clock in the afternoon.
There shalt thou know thy charge, and there receive
Money and order for their furniture.
The land is burning, Percy stands on high,   205
And either we or they must lower lie.   *Exit*

SIR JOHN
Rare words! Brave world! (*Calling*) Hostess, my
   breakfast, come!—
O, I could wish this tavern were my drum!   *Exit*

4.1 *Enter Hotspur and the Earls of Worcester and*
Douglas

HOTSPUR

Well said, my noble Scot! If speaking truth
In this fine age were not thought flattery,
Such attribution should the Douglas have
As not a soldier of this season's stamp
Should go so general current through the world.   5
By God, I cannot flatter, I do defy
The tongues of soothers, but a braver place
In my heart's love hath no man than yourself.
Nay, task me to my word, approve me, lord.

DOUGLAS Thou art the king of honour.   10
No man so potent breathes upon the ground
But I will beard him.

HOTSPUR   Do so, and 'tis well.
Enter a Messenger with letters
What letters hast thou there? I can but thank you.

MESSENGER These letters come from your father.

HOTSPUR

Letters from him? Why comes he not himself?   15

MESSENGER

He cannot come, my lord, he is grievous sick.

HOTSPUR

Zounds, how has he the leisure to be sick
In such a jostling time? Who leads his power?
Under whose government come they along?

MESSENGER

His letters bears his mind, not I, my lord.   20
Hotspur reads the letter

WORCESTER

I prithee tell me, doth he keep his bed?

MESSENGER

He did, my lord, four days ere I set forth;
And at the time of my departure thence
He was much feared by his physicians.

WORCESTER

I would the state of time had first been whole   25
Ere he by sickness had been visited.
His health was never better worth than now.

HOTSPUR

Sick now? Droop now? This sickness doth infect
The very life-blood of our enterprise.
'Tis catching hither, even to our camp.   30
He writes me here that inward sickness stays him,
And that his friends by deputation
Could not so soon be drawn; nor did he think it meet
To lay so dangerous and dear a trust
On any soul removed but on his own.   35
Yet doth he give us bold advertisement
That with our small conjunction we should on,
To see how fortune is disposed to us;
For, as he writes, there is no quailing now,
Because the King is certainly possessed   40
Of all our purposes. What say you to it?

WORCESTER

Your father's sickness is a maim to us.

HOTSPUR

A perilous gash, a very limb lopped off.

And yet, in faith, it is not. His present want
Seems more than we shall find it. Were it good   45
To set the exact wealth of all our states
All at one cast, to set so rich a main
On the nice hazard of one doubtful hour?
It were not good, for therein should we read
The very bottom and the sole of hope,   50
The very list, the very utmost bound,
Of all our fortunes.

DOUGLAS

Faith, and so we should, where now remains
A sweet reversion—we may boldly spend
Upon the hope of what is to come in.   55
A comfort of retirement lives in this.

HOTSPUR

A rendezvous, a home to fly unto,
If that the devil and mischance look big
Upon the maidenhead of our affairs.

WORCESTER

But yet I would your father had been here.   60
The quality and hair of our attempt
Brooks no division. It will be thought
By some that know not why he is away
That wisdom, loyalty, and mere dislike
Of our proceedings kept the Earl from hence;   65
And think how such an apprehension
May turn the tide of fearful faction,
And breed a kind of question in our cause.
For, well you know, we of the off'ring side
Must keep aloof from strict arbitrement,   70
And stop all sight-holes, every loop from whence
The eye of reason may pry in upon us.
This absence of your father's draws a curtain
That shows the ignorant a kind of fear
Before not dreamt of.

HOTSPUR   You strain too far.   75
I rather of his absence make this use:
It lends a lustre, and more great opinion,
A larger dare to our great enterprise,
Than if the Earl were here; for men must think
If we without his help can make a head   80
To push against a kingdom, with his help
We shall o'erturn it topsy-turvy down.
Yet all goes well, yet all our joints are whole.

DOUGLAS

As heart can think, there is not such a word
Spoke of in Scotland as this term of fear.   85
Enter Sir Richard Vernon

HOTSPUR

My cousin Vernon! Welcome, by my soul!

VERNON

Pray God my news be worth a welcome, lord.
The Earl of Westmorland, seven thousand strong,
Is marching hitherwards; with him Prince John.

HOTSPUR

No harm. What more?

VERNON   And further I have learned 90
The King himself in person is set forth,

Or hitherwards intended speedily,
With strong and mighty preparation.

HOTSPUR
He shall be welcome too. Where is his son,
The nimble-footed madcap Prince of Wales,   95
And his comrades that daffed the world aside
And bid it pass?

VERNON   All furnished, all in arms,
All plumed like ostriches, that with the wind
⌐   ⌐
Baiting like eagles having lately bathed,   100
Glittering in golden coats like images,
As full of spirit as the month of May,
And gorgeous as the sun at midsummer;
Wanton as youthful goats, wild as young bulls.
I saw young Harry with his beaver on,   105
His cuishes on his thighs, gallantly armed,
Rise from the ground like feathered Mercury,
And vaulted with such ease into his seat
As if an angel dropped down from the clouds
To turn and wind a fiery Pegasus,   110
And witch the world with noble horsemanship.

HOTSPUR
No more, no more! Worse than the sun in March,
This praise doth nourish agues. Let them come!
They come like sacrifices in their trim,
And to the fire-eyed maid of smoky war   115
All hot and bleeding will we offer them.
The mailèd Mars shall on his altar sit
Up to the ears in blood. I am on fire
To hear this rich reprisal is so nigh,
And yet not ours! Come, let me taste my horse,   120
Who is to bear me like a thunderbolt
Against the bosom of the Prince of Wales.
Harry to Harry shall, hot horse to horse,
Meet and ne'er part till one drop down a corpse.
O, that Glyndŵr were come!

VERNON   There is more news.   125
I learned in Worcester, as I rode along,
He cannot draw his power this fourteen days.

DOUGLAS
That's the worst tidings that I hear of yet.

WORCESTER
Ay, by my faith, that bears a frosty sound.

HOTSPUR
What may the King's whole battle reach unto?   130

VERNON
To thirty thousand.

HOTSPUR   Forty let it be.
My father and Glyndŵr being both away,
The powers of us may serve so great a day.
Come, let us take a muster speedily.
Doomsday is near: die all, die merrily.   135

DOUGLAS
Talk not of dying; I am out of fear
Of death or death's hand for this one half year.

Exeunt

4.2   *Enter Sir John Oldcastle and Russell*

SIR JOHN Russell, get thee before to Coventry; fill me a •
bottle of sack. Our soldiers shall march through. We'll
to Sutton Coldfield tonight.

RUSSELL Will you give me money, captain?

SIR JOHN Lay out, lay out.   5

RUSSELL This bottle makes an angel.

SIR JOHN ⌐*giving Russell money*⌐ An if it do, take it for thy
labour; an if it make twenty, take them all; I'll answer
the coinage. Bid my lieutenant Harvey meet me at
town's end.   10

RUSSELL I will, captain. Farewell.   *Exit*

SIR JOHN If I be not ashamed of my soldiers, I am a soused
gurnet. I have misused the King's press damnably. I
have got in exchange of one hundred and fifty soldiers
three hundred and odd pounds. I press me none but
good householders, yeomen's sons, enquire me out
contracted bachelors, such as had been asked twice on
the banns, such a commodity of warm slaves as had
as lief hear the devil as a drum, such as fear the report
of a caliver worse than a struck fowl or a hurt wild
duck. I pressed me none but such toasts and butter,
with hearts in their bellies no bigger than pins' heads,
and they have bought out their services; and now my
whole charge consists of ensigns, corporals, lieutenants,
gentlemen of companies—slaves as ragged as Lazarus
in the painted cloth, where the glutton's dogs licked
his sores—and such as indeed were never soldiers, but
discarded unjust servingmen, younger sons to younger
brothers, revolted tapsters, and ostlers trade-fallen, the
cankers of a calm world and a long peace, ten times
more dishonourable-ragged than an old feazed ensign;
and such have I to fill up the rooms of them as have
bought out their services, that you would think that I
had a hundred and fifty tattered prodigals lately come
from swine-keeping, from eating draff and husks. A
mad fellow met me on the way and told me I had
unloaded all the gibbets and pressed the dead bodies.
No eye hath seen such scarecrows. I'll not march
through Coventry with them, that's flat. Nay, and the
villains march wide betwixt the legs, as if they had
gyves on, for indeed I had the most of them out of
prison. There's not a shirt and a half in all my company;
and the half-shirt is two napkins tacked together and
thrown over the shoulders like a herald's coat without
sleeves; and the shirt, to say the truth, stolen from my
host at Saint Albans, or the red-nose innkeeper of
Daventry. But that's all one; they'll find linen enough
on every hedge.

Enter Prince Harry and the Earl of Westmorland

PRINCE HARRY How now, blown Jack? How now, quilt?

SIR JOHN What, Hal! How now, mad wag? What a devil
dost thou in Warwickshire? My good lord of
Westmorland, I cry you mercy! I thought your honour
had already been at Shrewsbury.

WESTMORLAND Faith, Sir John, 'tis more than time that I
were there, and you too; but my powers are there

already. The King, I can tell you, looks for us all. We
must away all night.

SIR JOHN Tut, never fear me. I am as vigilant as a cat to
steal cream.   59

PRINCE HARRY I think to steal cream indeed, for thy theft
hath already made thee butter. But tell me, Jack, whose
fellows are these that come after?

SIR JOHN Mine, Hal, mine.

PRINCE HARRY I did never see such pitiful rascals.   64

SIR JOHN Tut, tut, good enough to toss, food for powder,
food for powder. They'll fill a pit as well as better. Tush,
man, mortal men, mortal men.

WESTMORLAND Ay, but Sir John, methinks they are
exceeding poor and bare, too beggarly.   69

SIR JOHN Faith, for their poverty, I know not where they
had that, and for their bareness, I am sure they never
learned that of me.

PRINCE HARRY No, I'll be sworn, unless you call three
fingers in the ribs bare. But sirrah, make haste. Percy
is already in the field.   *Exit*

SIR JOHN What, is the King encamped?   76

WESTMORLAND He is, Sir John. I fear we shall stay too
long.   ⌜*Exit*⌝

SIR JOHN
Well, to the latter end of a fray
And the beginning of a feast   80
Fits a dull fighter and a keen guest.   *Exit*

4.3   *Enter Hotspur, the Earls of Worcester and Douglas,*
and Sir Richard Vernon

HOTSPUR
We'll fight with him tonight.

WORCESTER   It may not be.

DOUGLAS
You give him then advantage.

VERNON   Not a whit.

HOTSPUR
Why say you so? Looks he not for supply?

VERNON
So do we.

HOTSPUR   His is certain; ours is doubtful.

WORCESTER
Good cousin, be advised. Stir not tonight.   5

VERNON (*to Hotspur*)
Do not, my lord.

DOUGLAS   You do not counsel well.
You speak it out of fear and cold heart.

VERNON
Do me no slander, Douglas. By my life—
And I dare well maintain it with my life—
If well-respected honour bid me on,   10
I hold as little counsel with weak fear
As you, my lord, or any Scot that this day lives.
Let it be seen tomorrow in the battle
Which of us fears.

DOUGLAS Yea, or tonight.   15

VERNON Content.

HOTSPUR Tonight, say I.

VERNON
Come, come, it may not be. I wonder much,
Being men of such great leading as you are,
That you foresee not what impediments   20
Drag back our expedition. Certain horse
Of my cousin Vernon's are not yet come up.
Your uncle Worcester's horse came but today,
And now their pride and mettle is asleep,
Their courage with hard labour tame and dull,   25
That not a horse is half the half himself.

HOTSPUR
So are the horses of the enemy
In general journey-bated and brought low.
The better part of ours are full of rest.

WORCESTER
The number of the King exceedeth our.   30
For God's sake, cousin, stay till all come in.
       The trumpet sounds a parley ⌜*within*⌝. *Enter Sir*
       Walter Blunt

BLUNT
I come with gracious offers from the King,
If you vouchsafe me hearing and respect.

HOTSPUR
Welcome, Sir Walter Blunt; and would to God
You were of our determination.   35
Some of us love you well, and even those some
Envy your great deservings and good name,
Because you are not of our quality,
But stand against us like an enemy.

BLUNT
And God defend but still I should stand so,   40
So long as out of limit and true rule
You stand against anointed majesty.
But to my charge. The King hath sent to know
The nature of your griefs, and whereupon
You conjure from the breast of civil peace   45
Such bold hostility, teaching his duteous land
Audacious cruelty. If that the King
Have any way your good deserts forgot,
Which he confesseth to be manifold,
He bids you name your griefs, and with all speed   50
You shall have your desires, with interest,
And pardon absolute for yourself and these
Herein misled by your suggestion.

HOTSPUR
The King is kind, and well we know the King
Knows at what time to promise, when to pay.   55
My father and my uncle and myself
Did give him that same royalty he wears;
And when he was not six-and-twenty strong,
Sick in the world's regard, wretched and low,
A poor unminded outlaw sneaking home,   60
My father gave him welcome to the shore;
And when he heard him swear and vow to God
He came but to be Duke of Lancaster,
To sue his livery, and beg his peace
With tears of innocency and terms of zeal,   65
My father, in kind heart and pity moved,

Swore him assistance, and performed it too.
Now when the lords and barons of the realm
Perceived Northumberland did lean to him,
The more and less came in with cap and knee,   70
Met him in boroughs, cities, villages,
Attended him on bridges, stood in lanes,
Laid gifts before him, proffered him their oaths,
Gave him their heirs as pages, followed him,
Even at the heels, in golden multitudes.   75
He presently, as greatness knows itself,
Steps me a little higher than his vow
Made to my father while his blood was poor
Upon the naked shore at Ravenspurgh,
And now forsooth takes on him to reform   80
Some certain edicts and some strait decrees
That lie too heavy on the commonwealth,
Cries out upon abuses, seems to weep
Over his country's wrongs; and by this face,
This seeming brow of justice, did he win   85
The hearts of all that he did angle for;
Proceeded further, cut me off the heads
Of all the favourites that the absent King
In deputation left behind him here
When he was personal in the Irish war.   90

BLUNT
Tut, I came not to hear this.

HOTSPUR   Then to the point.
In short time after, he deposed the King,
Soon after that deprived him of his life,
And in the neck of that tasked the whole state;
To make that worse, suffered his kinsman March—   95
Who is, if every owner were well placed,
Indeed his king—to be engaged in Wales,
There without ransom to lie forfeited;
Disgraced me in my happy victories,
Sought to entrap me by intelligence,   100
Rated mine uncle from the Council-board,
In rage dismissed my father from the court,
Broke oath on oath, committed wrong on wrong,
And in conclusion drove us to seek out
This head of safety, and withal to pry   105
Into his title, the which we find
Too indirect for long continuance.

BLUNT
Shall I return this answer to the King?

HOTSPUR
Not so, Sir Walter. We'll withdraw awhile.
Go to the King, and let there be impawned   110
Some surety for a safe return again;
And in the morning early shall mine uncle
Bring him our purposes. And so, farewell.

BLUNT
I would you would accept of grace and love.

HOTSPUR
And maybe so we shall.

BLUNT   Pray God you do.   115
Exeunt ⌈Hotspur, Worcester, Douglas, and
Vernon at one door, Blunt at another door⌉

4.4   *Enter the Archbishop of York, and Sir Michael*

ARCHBISHOP *(giving letters)*
Hie, good Sir Michael, bear this sealèd brief
With wingèd haste to the Lord Marshal,
This to my cousin Scrope, and all the rest
To whom they are directed. If you knew
How much they do import, you would make haste.   5

SIR MICHAEL My good lord,
I guess their tenor.

ARCHBISHOP   Like enough you do.
Tomorrow, good Sir Michael, is a day
Wherein the fortune of ten thousand men
Must bide the touch; for, sir, at Shrewsbury,   10
As I am truly given to understand,
The King with mighty and quick-raisèd power
Meets with Lord Harry. And I fear, Sir Michael,
What with the sickness of Northumberland,
Whose power was in the first proportion,   15
And what with Owain Glyndŵr's absence thence,
Who with them was a rated sinew too,
And comes not in, overruled by prophecies,
I fear the power of Percy is too weak
To wage an instant trial with the King.   20

SIR MICHAEL
Why, my good lord, you need not fear; there is
Douglas
And Lord Mortimer.

ARCHBISHOP   No, Mortimer is not there.

SIR MICHAEL
But there is Mordake, Vernon, Lord Harry Percy;
And there is my lord of Worcester, and a head
Of gallant warriors, noble gentlemen.   25

ARCHBISHOP
And so there is; but yet the King hath drawn
The special head of all the land together—
The Prince of Wales, Lord John of Lancaster,
The noble Westmorland, and warlike Blunt,
And many more corrivals, and dear men   30
Of estimation and command in arms.

SIR MICHAEL
Doubt not, my lord, they shall be well opposed.

ARCHBISHOP
I hope no less, yet needful 'tis to fear;
And to prevent the worst, Sir Michael, speed.
For if Lord Percy thrive not, ere the King   35
Dismiss his power he means to visit us,
For he hath heard of our confederacy,
And 'tis but wisdom to make strong against him;
Therefore make haste. I must go write again
To other friends; and so farewell, Sir Michael.   40
Exeunt ⌈severally⌉

5.1   *Enter King Henry, Prince Harry, Lord John of*
Lancaster, the Earl of Westmorland, Sir Walter
Blunt, and Sir John Oldcastle

KING HENRY
How bloodily the sun begins to peer

Above yon bulky hill! The day looks pale
At his distemp'rature.
PRINCE HARRY   The southern wind
Doth play the trumpet to his purposes,
And by his hollow whistling in the leaves   5
Foretells a tempest and a blust'ring day.
KING HENRY
Then with the losers let it sympathize,
For nothing can seem foul to those that win.
        The trumpet sounds ⌈a parley within⌉. Enter the
        Earl of Worcester ⌈and Sir Richard Vernon⌉
How now, my lord of Worcester? 'Tis not well
That you and I should meet upon such terms   10
As now we meet. You have deceived our trust,
And made us doff our easy robes of peace
To crush our old limbs in ungentle steel.
This is not well, my lord, this is not well.
What say you to it? Will you again unknit   15
This churlish knot of all-abhorrèd war,
And move in that obedient orb again
Where you did give a fair and natural light,
And be no more an exhaled meteor,
A prodigy of fear, and a portent   20
Of broachèd mischief to the unborn times?
WORCESTER Hear me, my liege.
For mine own part, I could be well content
To entertain the lag-end of my life
With quiet hours; for I protest,   25
I have not sought the day of this dislike.
KING HENRY
You have not sought it? How comes it, then?
SIR JOHN Rebellion lay in his way, and he found it.
PRINCE HARRY Peace, chewet, peace!
WORCESTER (*to the King*)
It pleased your majesty to turn your looks   30
Of favour from myself and all our house;
And yet I must remember you, my lord,
We were the first and dearest of your friends.
For you my staff of office did I break
In Richard's time, and posted day and night   35
To meet you on the way and kiss your hand
When yet you were in place and in account
Nothing so strong and fortunate as I.
It was myself, my brother, and his son
That brought you home, and boldly did outdare   40
The dangers of the time. You swore to us,
And you did swear that oath at Doncaster,
That you did nothing purpose 'gainst the state,
Nor claim no further than your new-fall'n right,
The seat of Gaunt, dukedom of Lancaster.   45
To this we swore our aid, but in short space
It rained down fortune show'ring on your head,
And such a flood of greatness fell on you,
What with our help, what with the absent King,
What with the injuries of a wanton time,   50
The seeming sufferances that you had borne,
And the contrarious winds that held the King
So long in his unlucky Irish wars

That all in England did repute him dead;
And from this swarm of fair advantages   55
You took occasion to be quickly wooed
To gripe the general sway into your hand,
Forgot your oath to us at Doncaster,
And being fed by us, you used us so
As that ungentle gull, the cuckoo's bird,   60
Useth the sparrow—did oppress our nest,
Grew by our feeding to so great a bulk
That even our love durst not come near your sight
For fear of swallowing. But with nimble wing
We were enforced for safety' sake to fly   65
Out of your sight, and raise this present head,
Whereby we stand opposèd by such means
As you yourself have forged against yourself,
By unkind usage, dangerous countenance,
And violation of all faith and troth   70
Sworn to us in your younger enterprise.
KING HENRY
These things indeed you have articulate,
Proclaimed at market crosses, read in churches,
To face the garment of rebellion
With some fine colour that may please the eye   75
Of fickle changelings and poor discontents,
Which gape and rub the elbow at the news
Of hurly-burly innovation;
And never yet did insurrection want
Such water-colours to impaint his cause,   80
Nor moody beggars starving for a time
Of pell-mell havoc and confusion.
PRINCE HARRY
In both our armies there is many a soul
Shall pay full dearly for this encounter
If once they join in trial. Tell your nephew   85
The Prince of Wales doth join with all the world
In praise of Henry Percy. By my hopes,
This present enterprise set off his head,
I do not think a braver gentleman,
More active-valiant or more valiant-young,   90
More daring, or more bold, is now alive
To grace this latter age with noble deeds.
For my part, I may speak it to my shame,
I have a truant been to chivalry;
And so I hear he doth account me too.   95
Yet this, before my father's majesty:
I am content that he shall take the odds
Of his great name and estimation,
And will, to save the blood on either side,
Try fortune with him in a single fight.   100
KING HENRY
And, Prince of Wales, so dare we venture thee,
Albeit considerations infinite
Do make against it. No, good Worcester, no.
We love our people well; even those we love
That are misled upon your cousin's part;   105
And will they take the offer of our grace,
Both he and they and you, yea, every man
Shall be my friend again, and I'll be his.

So tell your cousin, and bring me word
What he will do. But if he will not yield,   110
Rebuke and dread correction wait on us,
And they shall do their office. So be gone.
We will not now be troubled with reply.
We offer fair; take it advisedly.

Exeunt Worcester ⌈and Vernon⌉

PRINCE HARRY
It will not be accepted, on my life.   115
The Douglas and the Hotspur both together
Are confident against the world in arms.

KING HENRY
Hence, therefore, every leader to his charge,
For on their answer will we set on them,
And God befriend us as our cause is just!   120

Exeunt all but Prince Harry and Oldcastle

SIR JOHN Hal, if thou see me down in the battle, and
bestride me, so. 'Tis a point of friendship.

PRINCE HARRY Nothing but a colossus can do thee that
friendship. Say thy prayers, and farewell.

SIR JOHN I would 'twere bed-time, Hal, and all well.   125

PRINCE HARRY Why, thou owest God a death.   *Exit*

SIR JOHN 'Tis not due yet. I would be loath to pay him
before his day. What need I be so forward with him
that calls not on me? Well, 'tis no matter; honour
pricks me on. Yea, but how if honour prick me off
when I come on? How then? Can honour set-to a leg?
No. Or an arm? No. Or take away the grief of a wound?
No. Honour hath no skill in surgery, then? No. What
is honour? A word. What is in that word 'honour'?
What is that 'honour'? Air. A trim reckoning! Who
hath it? He that died o' Wednesday. Doth he feel it?
No. Doth he hear it? No. 'Tis insensible then? Yea, to
the dead. But will it not live with the living? No. Why?
Detraction will not suffer it. Therefore I'll none of it.
Honour is a mere scutcheon. And so ends my catechism.

Exit

5.2   *Enter the Earl of Worcester and Sir Richard Vernon*

WORCESTER
O no, my nephew must not know, Sir Richard,
The liberal and kind offer of the King.

VERNON
'Twere best he did.

WORCESTER   Then are we all undone.
It is not possible, it cannot be,
The King should keep his word in loving us.   5
He will suspect us still, and find a time
To punish this offence in other faults.
Supposition all our lives shall be stuck full of eyes,
For treason is but trusted like the fox,
Who, ne'er so tame, so cherished, and locked up,   10
Will have a wild trick of his ancestors.
Look how we can, or sad or merrily,
Interpretation will misquote our looks,
And we shall feed like oxen at a stall,
The better cherished still the nearer death.   15
My nephew's trespass may be well forgot;

It hath the excuse of youth and heat of blood,
And an adopted name of privilege—
A hare-brained Hotspur, governed by a spleen.
All his offences live upon my head,   20
And on his father's. We did train him on,
And, his corruption being ta'en from us,
We as the spring of all shall pay for all.
Therefore, good cousin, let not Harry know
In any case the offer of the King.   25

VERNON
Deliver what you will; I'll say 'tis so.

Enter Hotspur and the Earl of Douglas

Here comes your cousin.

HOTSPUR   My uncle is returned.
Deliver up my lord of Westmorland.
Uncle, what news?

WORCESTER
The King will bid you battle presently.   30

DOUGLAS
Defy him by the Lord of Westmorland.

HOTSPUR
Lord Douglas, go you and tell him so.

DOUGLAS
Marry, and shall, and very willingly.   *Exit*

WORCESTER
There is no seeming mercy in the King.

HOTSPUR
Did you beg any? God forbid!   35

WORCESTER
I told him gently of our grievances,
Of his oath-breaking, which he mended thus:
By now forswearing that he is forsworn.
He calls us 'rebels', 'traitors', and will scourge
With haughty arms this hateful name in us.   40

Enter the Earl of Douglas

DOUGLAS
Arm, gentlemen, to arms, for I have thrown
A brave defiance in King Henry's teeth—
And Westmorland that was engaged did bear it—
Which cannot choose but bring him quickly on.

WORCESTER *(to Hotspur)*
The Prince of Wales stepped forth before the King   45
And, nephew, challenged you to single fight.

HOTSPUR
O, would the quarrel lay upon our heads,
And that no man might draw short breath today
But I and Harry Monmouth! Tell me, tell me,
How showed his tasking? Seemed it in contempt?   50

VERNON
No, by my soul, I never in my life
Did hear a challenge urged more modestly,
Unless a brother should a brother dare
To gentle exercise and proof of arms.
He gave you all the duties of a man,   55
Trimmed up your praises with a princely tongue,
Spoke your deservings like a chronicle,
Making you ever better than his praise
By still dispraising praise valued with you;

And, which became him like a prince indeed, 60
He made a blushing cital of himself,
And chid his truant youth with such a grace
As if he mastered there a double spirit
Of teaching and of learning instantly.
There did he pause; but let me tell the world, 65
If he outlive the envy of this day,
England did never owe so sweet a hope,
So much misconstrued in his wantonness.

HOTSPUR
Cousin, I think thou art enamourèd
On his follies. Never did I hear 70
Of any prince so wild a liberty.
But be he as he will, yet once ere night
I will embrace him with a soldier's arm,
That he shall shrink under my courtesy.
Arm, arm, with speed! And fellows, soldiers, friends,
Better consider what you have to do 76
Than I, that have not well the gift of tongue,
Can lift your blood up with persuasion.

　　　　Enter a Messenger

MESSENGER My lord, here are letters for you.
HOTSPUR I cannot read them now. 　*⌜Exit Messenger⌝*
O gentlemen, the time of life is short. 81
To spend that shortness basely were too long
If life did ride upon a dial's point,
Still ending at the arrival of an hour.
An if we live, we live to tread on kings; 85
If die, brave death when princes die with us!
Now for our consciences: the arms are fair
When the intent of bearing them is just.

　　　　Enter another Messenger

MESSENGER
My lord, prepare; the King comes on apace. 　*⌜Exit⌝*
HOTSPUR
I thank him that he cuts me from my tale, 90
For I profess not talking, only this:
Let each man do his best. And here draw I
A sword whose temper I intend to stain
With the best blood that I can meet withal
In the adventure of this perilous day. 95
Now *Esperance*! Percy! And set on!
Sound all the lofty instruments of war,
And by that music let us all embrace,
For, heaven to earth, some of us never shall
A second time do such a courtesy. 100

　　　　The trumpets sound. Here they embrace. Exeunt

5.3　*King Henry enters with his power. Alarum, and*
　　　exeunt to the battle. Then enter the Earl of
　　　Douglas, and Sir Walter Blunt, disguised as the
　　　King

BLUNT
What is thy name, that in the battle thus
Thou crossest me? What honour dost thou seek
Upon my head?
DOUGLAS　　　　Know then my name is Douglas,
And I do haunt thee in the battle thus
Because some tell me that thou art a king. 5

BLUNT They tell thee true.
DOUGLAS
The Lord of Stafford dear today hath bought
Thy likeness, for instead of thee, King Harry,
This sword hath ended him. So shall it thee,
Unless thou yield thee as my prisoner. 10
BLUNT
I was not born a yielder, thou proud Scot,
And thou shalt find a king that will revenge
Lord Stafford's death.
　　　They fight. Douglas kills Blunt. Then enter Hotspur
HOTSPUR
O Douglas, hadst thou fought at Holmedon thus,
I never had triumphed upon a Scot. 15
DOUGLAS
All's done, all's won: here breathless lies the King.
HOTSPUR Where?
DOUGLAS Here.
HOTSPUR
This, Douglas? No, I know this face full well.
A gallant knight he was; his name was Blunt— 20
Semblably furnished like the King himself.
DOUGLAS (*to Blunt's body*)
A fool go with thy soul, whither it goes!
A borrowed title hast thou bought too dear.
Why didst thou tell me that thou wert a king?
HOTSPUR
The king hath many marching in his coats. 25
DOUGLAS
Now by my sword, I will kill all his coats.
I'll murder all his wardrobe, piece by piece,
Until I meet the King.
HOTSPUR　　　　Up and away!
Our soldiers stand full fairly for the day.
　　　　　Exeunt, leaving Blunt's body
　　　Alarum. Enter Sir John Oldcastle
SIR JOHN Though I could scape shot-free at London, I fear
the shot here. Here's no scoring but upon the pate.—
Soft, who are you?—Sir Walter Blunt. There's honour
for you. Here's no vanity. I am as hot as molten lead,
and as heavy too. God keep lead out of me; I need no
more weight than mine own bowels. I have led my
ragamuffins where they are peppered; there's not three
of my hundred and fifty left alive, and they are for the
town's end, to beg during life.
　　　Enter Prince Harry
But who comes here?
PRINCE HARRY
What, stand'st thou idle here? Lend me thy sword. 40
Many a noble man lies stark and stiff
Under the hoofs of vaunting enemies,
Whose deaths as yet are unrevenged. I prithee
Lend me thy sword.
SIR JOHN
O Hal, I prithee give me leave to breathe awhile. 45
Turk Gregory never did such deeds in arms
As I have done this day. I have paid Percy,
I have made him sure.
PRINCE HARRY　　　　He is indeed,

And living to kill thee. I prithee
Lend me thy sword.
SIR JOHN   Nay, before God, Hal,   50
If Percy be alive thou gett'st not my sword;
But take my pistol if thou wilt.
PRINCE HARRY
Give it me. What, is it in the case?
SIR JOHN   Ay, Hal;
'Tis hot, 'tis hot. There's that will sack a city.
     *The Prince draws it out, and finds it to be a bottle of
     sack*
PRINCE HARRY
What, is it a time to jest and dally now?   55
     He throws the bottle at him. Exit
SIR JOHN Well, if Percy be alive, I'll pierce him. If he do
come in my way, so; if he do not, if I come in his
willingly, let him make a carbonado of me. I like not
such grinning honour as Sir Walter hath. Give me life,
which if I can save, so; if not, honour comes unlooked
for, and there's an end.   *Exit ⸢with Blunt's body⸣*

5.4   *Alarum. Excursions. Enter King Henry, Prince
        Harry, wounded, Lord John of Lancaster, and the
        Earl of Westmorland*
KING HENRY
I prithee, Harry, withdraw thyself, thou bleed'st too
     much.
Lord John of Lancaster, go you with him.
JOHN OF LANCASTER
Not I, my lord, unless I did bleed too.
PRINCE HARRY (*to the King*)
I beseech your majesty, make up,
Lest your retirement do amaze your friends.   5
KING HENRY
I will do so. My lord of Westmorland,
Lead him to his tent.
WESTMORLAND (*to the Prince*)
Come, my lord, I'll lead you to your tent.
PRINCE HARRY
Lead me, my lord? I do not need your help,
And God forbid a shallow scratch should drive   10
The Prince of Wales from such a field as this,
Where stained nobility lies trodden on,
And rebels' arms triumph in massacres.
JOHN OF LANCASTER
We breathe too long. Come, cousin Westmorland,
Our duty this way lies. For God's sake, come.   15
     Exeunt Lancaster and Westmorland
PRINCE HARRY
By God, thou hast deceived me, Lancaster;
I did not think thee lord of such a spirit.
Before I loved thee as a brother, John,
But now I do respect thee as my soul.
KING HENRY
I saw him hold Lord Percy at the point   20
With lustier maintenance than I did look for
Of such an ungrown warrior.
PRINCE HARRY
O, this boy lends mettle to us all!   *Exit*

     Enter the Earl of Douglas
DOUGLAS
Another king! They grow like Hydra's heads.
I am the Douglas, fatal to all those   25
That wear those colours on them. What art thou
That counterfeit'st the person of a king?
KING HENRY
The King himself, who, Douglas, grieves at heart
So many of his shadows thou hast met
And not the very King. I have two boys   30
Seek Percy and thyself about the field;
But seeing thou fall'st on me so luckily,
I will assay thee; and defend thyself.
DOUGLAS
I fear thou art another counterfeit;
And yet, in faith, thou bear'st thee like a king.   35
But mine I am sure thou art, whoe'er thou be,
And thus I win thee.
     *They fight. The King being in danger, enter Prince
     Harry*
PRINCE HARRY
Hold up thy head, vile Scot, or thou art like
Never to hold it up again. The spirits
Of valiant Shirley, Stafford, Blunt, are in my arms. 40
It is the Prince of Wales that threatens thee,
Who never promiseth but he means to pay.
     They fight. Douglas flieth
Cheerly, my lord! How fares your grace?
Sir Nicholas Gawsey hath for succour sent,
And so hath Clifton. I'll to Clifton straight.   45
KING HENRY Stay and breathe awhile.
Thou hast redeemed thy lost opinion,
And showed thou mak'st some tender of my life,
In this fair rescue thou hast brought to me.
PRINCE HARRY
O God, they did me too much injury   50
That ever said I hearkened for your death.
If it were so, I might have let alone
The insulting hand of Douglas over you,
Which would have been as speedy in your end
As all the poisonous potions in the world,   55
And saved the treacherous labour of your son.
KING HENRY
Make up to Clifton; I'll to Sir Nicholas Gawsey. *Exit*
     Enter Hotspur
HOTSPUR
If I mistake not, thou art Harry Monmouth.
PRINCE HARRY
Thou speak'st as if I would deny my name.
HOTSPUR
My name is Harry Percy.
PRINCE HARRY   Why then, I see   60
A very valiant rebel of the name.
I am the Prince of Wales; and think not, Percy,
To share with me in glory any more.
Two stars keep not their motion in one sphere,
Nor can one England brook a double reign   65
Of Harry Percy and the Prince of Wales.

HOTSPUR
Nor shall it, Harry, for the hour is come
To end the one of us, and would to God
Thy name in arms were now as great as mine.
PRINCE HARRY
I'll make it greater ere I part from thee,   70
And all the budding honours on thy crest
I'll crop to make a garland for my head.
HOTSPUR
I can no longer brook thy vanities.
    They fight.
    Enter Sir John Oldcastle
SIR JOHN Well said, Hal! To it, Hal! Nay, you shall find
no boy's play here, I can tell you.   75
    Enter Douglas. He fighteth with Sir John, who falls
    down as if he were dead. Exit Douglas. The Prince
    killeth Hotspur
HOTSPUR
O Harry, thou hast robbed me of my youth.
I better brook the loss of brittle life
Than those proud titles thou hast won of me.
They wound my thoughts worse than thy sword my
    flesh.
But thoughts, the slaves of life, and life, time's fool, 80
And time, that takes survey of all the world,
Must have a stop. O, I could prophesy,
But that the earthy and cold hand of death
Lies on my tongue. No, Percy, thou art dust,   84
And food for—   *He dies*
PRINCE HARRY
For worms, brave Percy. Fare thee well, great heart.
Ill-weaved ambition, how much art thou shrunk!
When that this body did contain a spirit,
A kingdom for it was too small a bound,
But now two paces of the vilest earth   90
Is room enough. This earth that bears thee dead
Bears not alive so stout a gentleman.
If thou wert sensible of courtesy,
I should not make so dear a show of zeal;
But let my favours hide thy mangled face,   95
    He covers Hotspur's face
And even in thy behalf I'll thank myself
For doing these fair rites of tenderness.
Adieu, and take thy praise with thee to heaven.
Thy ignominy sleep with thee in the grave,
But not remembered in thy epitaph.   100
    He spieth Sir John on the ground
What, old acquaintance! Could not all this flesh
Keep in a little life? Poor Jack, farewell.
I could have better spared a better man.
O, I should have a heavy miss of thee,
If I were much in love with vanity.   105
Death hath not struck so fat a deer today,
Though many dearer in this bloody fray.
Embowelled will I see thee by and by.
Till then, in blood by noble Percy lie.   *Exit*
    Sir John riseth up
SIR JOHN Embowelled? If thou embowel me today, I'll give

you leave to powder me, and eat me too, tomorrow.
'Sblood, 'twas time to counterfeit, or that hot termagant
Scot had paid me, scot and lot too. Counterfeit? I lie, I
am no counterfeit. To die is to be a counterfeit, for he
is but the counterfeit of a man who hath not the life
of a man. But to counterfeit dying when a man thereby
liveth is to be no counterfeit, but the true and perfect
image of life indeed. The better part of valour is
discretion, in the which better part I have saved my
life. Zounds, I am afraid of this gunpowder Percy,
though he be dead. How if he should counterfeit too,
and rise? By my faith, I am afraid he would prove the
better counterfeit. Therefore I'll make him sure; yea,
and I'll swear I killed him. Why may not he rise as
well as I? Nothing confutes me but eyes, and nobody
sees me. Therefore, sirrah, *(stabbing Hotspur)* with a
new wound in your thigh, come you along with me.
    He takes up Hotspur on his back.
    Enter Prince Harry and Lord John of Lancaster
PRINCE HARRY
Come, brother John. Full bravely hast thou fleshed
Thy maiden sword.
JOHN OF LANCASTER   But soft; whom have we here?
Did you not tell me this fat man was dead?   130
PRINCE HARRY I did; I saw him dead,
Breathless and bleeding on the ground.
(To Sir John)   Art thou alive?
Or is it fantasy that plays upon our eyesight?
I prithee speak; we will not trust our eyes
Without our ears. Thou art not what thou seem'st. 135
SIR JOHN No, that's certain: I am not a double man. But
if I be not Jack Oldcastle, then am I a jack. There is
Percy. If your father will do me any honour, so; if not,
let him kill the next Percy himself. I look to be either
earl or duke, I can assure you.   140
PRINCE HARRY
Why, Percy I killed myself, and saw thee dead.
SIR JOHN Didst thou? Lord, Lord, how this world is given
to lying! I grant you I was down and out of breath,
and so was he; but we rose both at an instant, and
fought a long hour by Shrewsbury clock. If I may be
believed, so; if not, let them that should reward valour
bear the sin upon their own heads. I'll take't on my
death I gave him this wound in the thigh. If the man
were alive and would deny it, zounds, I would make
him eat a piece of my sword.   150
JOHN OF LANCASTER
This is the strangest tale that e'er I heard.
PRINCE HARRY
This is the strangest fellow, brother John.
(To Sir John) Come, bring your luggage nobly on your
    back.
For my part, if a lie may do thee grace,
I'll gild it with the happiest terms I have.   155
    A retreat is sounded
The trumpet sounds retreat; the day is our.
Come, brother, let us to the highest of the field
To see what friends are living, who are dead.
    Exeunt the Prince and Lancaster

SIR JOHN I'll follow, as they say, for reward. He that
  rewards me, God reward him. If I do grow great, I'll
  grow less; for I'll purge, and leave sack, and live
  cleanly, as a nobleman should do.
               Exit, bearing Hotspur's body

5.5   *The trumpets sound. Enter King Henry, Prince*
    Harry, Lord John of Lancaster, the Earl of
    Westmorland, with the Earl of Worcester and Sir
    Richard Vernon, prisoners, ⌈and soldiers⌉
KING HENRY
  Thus ever did rebellion find rebuke.
  Ill-spirited Worcester, did not we send grace,
  Pardon, and terms of love to all of you?
  And wouldst thou turn our offers contrary,
  Misuse the tenor of thy kinsman's trust?   5
  Three knights upon our party slain today,
  A noble earl, and many a creature else,
  Had been alive this hour
  If like a Christian thou hadst truly borne
  Betwixt our armies true intelligence.   10
WORCESTER
  What I have done my safety urged me to,
  And I embrace this fortune patiently,
  Since not to be avoided it falls on me.
KING HENRY
  Bear Worcester to the death, and Vernon too.
  Other offenders we will pause upon.   15
          Exeunt Worcester and Vernon, guarded
  How goes the field?
PRINCE HARRY
  The noble Scot Lord Douglas, when he saw
  The fortune of the day quite turned from him,
The noble Percy slain, and all his men
Upon the foot of fear, fled with the rest;   20
And falling from a hill he was so bruised
That the pursuers took him. At my tent
The Douglas is, and I beseech your grace
I may dispose of him.
KING HENRY With all my heart.   25
PRINCE HARRY
  Then, brother John of Lancaster,
  To you this honourable bounty shall belong.
  Go to the Douglas, and deliver him
  Up to his pleasure ransomless and free.
  His valours shown upon our crests today   30
  Have taught us how to cherish such high deeds
  Even in the bosom of our adversaries.
JOHN OF LANCASTER
  I thank your grace for this high courtesy,
  Which I shall give away immediately.
KING HENRY
  Then this remains, that we divide our power.   35
  You, son John, and my cousin Westmorland,
· Towards York shall bend you with your dearest speed
  To meet Northumberland and the prelate Scrope,
  Who, as we hear, are busily in arms.
  Myself and you, son Harry, will towards Wales,   40
  To fight with Glyndŵr and the Earl of March.
  Rebellion in this land shall lose his sway,
  Meeting the check of such another day;
  And since this business so fair is done,
  Let us not leave till all our own be won.   45
       Exeunt ⌈the King, the Prince, and their power
     at one door, Lancaster, Westmorland, and their
               power at another door⌉

2 HENRY IV

2 Henry IV, printed in 1600 as *The Second Part of Henry the Fourth*, was not reprinted until it was included in somewhat revised form in the 1623 Folio, with the same title. Shakespeare may have started to write it late in 1596, or in 1597, directly after *1 Henry IV*, but have laid it aside while he composed *The Merry Wives of Windsor*. As in *1 Henry IV*, he drew on *The Famous Victories of Henry the Fifth*, Holinshed's *Chronicles*, and Samuel Daniel's *Four Books of the Civil Wars*, along with other, minor sources; but the play contains a greater proportion of non-historical material apparently invented by Shakespeare. In this play Shakespeare seems from the start to have accepted the change of Sir John's surname to Falstaff.

Like *1 Henry IV*, Part Two draws on the techniques of comedy, but its overall tone is more sombre. At its start, the Prince seems to have regressed from his reformed state at the end of Part One; his father still has many causes for anxiety, has not made his expiatory pilgrimage to the Holy Land, and is again the victim of rebellion, led this time by the Earl of Northumberland, the Archbishop of York, and the Lords Hastings and Mowbray. Again Henry's public responsibilities are exacerbated by anxieties about Prince Harry's behaviour; the climax of their relationship comes after Harry, discovering his sick father asleep and thinking him dead, tries on his crown; after bitterly upbraiding him, Henry accepts his son's assertions of good faith, and, recalling the devious means by which he himself came to the throne, warns Harry that he may need to protect himself against civil strife by pursuing 'foreign quarrels'—the campaigning against France depicted in *Henry V*. The King dies in the Jerusalem Chamber of Westminster Abbey, the closest he will get to the Holy Land.

In this play the Prince spends less time than in Part One with Sir John, who is shown much in the company of Mistress Quickly and Doll Tearsheet at the Boar's Head tavern in Eastcheap and later in Gloucestershire on his way to and from the place of battle. Shakespeare never excelled the bitter-sweet comedy of the passages involving Falstaff and his old comrade Justice Shallow. The play ends in a counterpointing of major and minor keys as the newly crowned Henry V rejects Sir John and all that he has stood for.

THE PERSONS OF THE PLAY

RUMOUR, the Presenter

EPILOGUE

KING HENRY IV

PRINCE HARRY, later crowned King Henry V ⎤

PRINCE JOHN of Lancaster ⎫ sons of King

Humphrey, Duke of GLOUCESTER ⎬ Henry IV

Thomas, Duke of CLARENCE ⎭

Percy, Earl of NORTHUMBERLAND, of the rebels' party

NORTHUMBERLAND'S WIFE

KATE, their son Hotspur's widow

TRAVERS, Northumberland's servant

MORTON, a bearer of news from Shrewsbury

Scrope, ARCHBISHOP of York ⎤

LORD BARDOLPH ⎫ rebels against

Thomas, Lord MOWBRAY, the Earl Marshal ⎬ King Henry

Lord HASTINGS ⎪ IV

Sir John COLEVILLE ⎭

LORD CHIEF JUSTICE

His SERVANT

GOWER, a Messenger

SIR JOHN Falstaff ⎤

His PAGE ⎪

BARDOLPH ⎪

POINS ⎬ 'irregular humorists'

Ensign PISTOL ⎪

PETO ⎭

MISTRESS QUICKLY, hostess of a tavern

DOLL TEARSHEET, a whore

SNARE ⎫ sergeants

FANG ⎭

Neville, Earl of WARWICK ⎤

Earl of SURREY ⎪

Earl of WESTMORLAND ⎬ supporters of King Henry IV

HARCOURT ⎪

Sir John Blunt ⎭

Robert SHALLOW ⎫ country justices

SILENCE ⎭

DAVY, Shallow's servant

Ralph MOULDY ⎤

Simon SHADOW ⎪

Thomas WART ⎬ men levied to fight for King Henry IV

Francis FEEBLE ⎪

Peter BULLCALF ⎭

PORTER of Northumberland's household

DRAWERS

BEADLES

GROOMS

MESSENGER

Sneak and other musicians

Lord Chief Justice's men, soldiers and attendants

The Second Part of Henry the Fourth

Induction *Enter Rumour ⌐in a robe⌐ painted full of tongues*

RUMOUR

Open your ears; for which of you will stop
The vent of hearing when loud Rumour speaks?
I from the orient to the drooping west,
Making the wind my post-horse, still unfold
The acts commencèd on this ball of earth. 5
Upon my tongues continual slanders ride,
The which in every language I pronounce,
Stuffing the ears of men with false reports.
I speak of peace, while covert enmity
Under the smile of safety wounds the world; 10
And who but Rumour, who but only I,
Make fearful musters and prepared defence
Whiles the big year, swoll'n with some other griefs,
Is thought with child by the stern tyrant war,
And no such matter? Rumour is a pipe 15
Blown by surmises, Jealousy's conjectures,
And of so easy and so plain a stop
That the blunt monster with uncounted heads,
The still-discordant wav'ring multitude,
Can play upon it. But what need I thus 20
My well-known body to anatomize
Among my household? Why is Rumour here?
I run before King Harry's victory,
Who in a bloody field by Shrewsbury
Hath beaten down young Hotspur and his troops, 25
Quenching the flame of bold rebellion
Even with the rebels' blood. But what mean I
To speak so true at first? My office is
To noise abroad that Harry Monmouth fell
Under the wrath of noble Hotspur's sword, 30
And that the King before the Douglas' rage
Stooped his anointed head as low as death.
This have I rumoured through the peasant towns
Between that royal field of Shrewsbury
And this worm-eaten hold of raggèd stone, 35
Where Hotspur's father, old Northumberland,
Lies crafty-sick. The posts come tiring on,
And not a man of them brings other news
Than they have learnt of me. From Rumour's tongues
They bring smooth comforts false, worse than true
wrongs. *Exit*

1.1 *Enter Lord Bardolph at one door. ⌐He crosses the
stage to another door⌐*

LORD BARDOLPH

Who keeps the gate here, ho?
Enter Porter ⌐above⌐
Where is the Earl?

PORTER

What shall I say you are?

LORD BARDOLPH Tell thou the Earl
That the Lord Bardolph doth attend him here.

PORTER

His lordship is walked forth into the orchard.
Please it your honour knock but at the gate, 5
And he himself will answer.
*Enter the Earl Northumberland ⌐at the other door⌐,
as sick, with a crutch and coif*

LORD BARDOLPH Here comes the Earl.
⌐*Exit Porter*⌐

NORTHUMBERLAND

What news, Lord Bardolph? Every minute now
Should be the father of some stratagem.
The times are wild; contention, like a horse
Full of high feeding, madly hath broke loose, 10
And bears down all before him.

LORD BARDOLPH Noble Earl,
I bring you certain news from Shrewsbury.

NORTHUMBERLAND

Good, an God will.

LORD BARDOLPH As good as heart can wish.
The King is almost wounded to the death;
And, in the fortune of my lord your son,
Prince Harry slain outright; and both the Blunts 15
Killed by the hand of Douglas; young Prince John
And Westmorland and Stafford fled the field;
And Harry Monmouth's brawn, the hulk Sir John,
Is prisoner to your son. O, such a day, 20
So fought, so followed, and so fairly won,
Came not till now to dignify the times
Since Caesar's fortunes!

NORTHUMBERLAND How is this derived?
Saw you the field? Came you from Shrewsbury?

LORD BARDOLPH

I spake with one, my lord, that came from thence, 25
A gentleman well bred and of good name,
That freely rendered me these news for true.
Enter Travers

NORTHUMBERLAND

Here comes my servant Travers, who I sent
On Tuesday last to listen after news.

LORD BARDOLPH

My lord, I overrode him on the way, 30
And he is furnished with no certainties
More than he haply may retail from me.

NORTHUMBERLAND

Now, Travers, what good tidings comes with you?

TRAVERS

My lord, Lord Bardolph turned me back
With joyful tidings, and being better horsed 35
Outrode me. After him came spurring hard
A gentleman almost forspent with speed,
That stopped by me to breathe his bloodied horse.
He asked the way to Chester, and of him
I did demand what news from Shrewsbury. 40

He told me that rebellion had ill luck,
And that young Harry Percy's spur was cold.
With that he gave his able horse the head,
And, bending forward, struck his armèd heels
Against the panting sides of his poor jade   45
Up to the rowel-head; and starting so,
He seemed in running to devour the way,
Staying no longer question.

NORTHUMBERLAND   Ha? Again:
Said he young Harry Percy's spur was cold?
Of Hotspur, 'Coldspur'? that rebellion   50
Had met ill luck?

LORD BARDOLPH   My lord, I'll tell you what:
If my young lord your son have not the day,
Upon mine honour, for a silken point
I'll give my barony. Never talk of it.

NORTHUMBERLAND
Why should the gentleman that rode by Travers   55
Give then such instances of loss?

LORD BARDOLPH   Who, he?
He was some hilding fellow that had stol'n
The horse he rode on, and, upon my life,
Spoke at a venture.

    Enter Morton
                     Look, here comes more news.

NORTHUMBERLAND
Yea, this man's brow, like to a title leaf,   60
Foretells the nature of a tragic volume.
So looks the strand whereon the imperious flood
Hath left a witnessed usurpation.
Say, Morton, didst thou come from Shrewsbury?

MORTON
I ran from Shrewsbury, my noble lord,   65
Where hateful death put on his ugliest mask
To fright our party.

NORTHUMBERLAND   How doth my son and brother?
Thou tremblest, and the whiteness in thy cheek
Is apter than thy tongue to tell thy errand.
Even such a man, so faint, so spiritless,   70
So dull, so dead in look, so woebegone,
Drew Priam's curtain in the dead of night,
And would have told him half his Troy was burnt;
But Priam found the fire ere he his tongue,
And I my Percy's death ere thou report'st it.   75
This thou wouldst say: 'Your son did thus and thus,
Your brother thus; so fought the noble Douglas',
Stopping my greedy ear with their bold deeds;
But in the end, to stop my ear indeed,
Thou hast a sigh to blow away this praise,   80
Ending with 'Brother, son, and all are dead.'

MORTON
Douglas is living, and your brother yet;
But for my lord your son—

NORTHUMBERLAND   Why, he is dead.
See what a ready tongue suspicion hath!
He that but fears the thing he would not know   85
Hath by instinct knowledge from others' eyes
That what he feared is chanced. Yet speak, Morton.

Tell thou an earl his divination lies,
And I will take it as a sweet disgrace,
And make thee rich for doing me such wrong.   90

MORTON
You are too great to be by me gainsaid,
Your spirit is too true, your fears too certain.

NORTHUMBERLAND
Yet for all this, say not that Percy's dead.
I see a strange confession in thine eye—
Thou shak'st thy head, and hold'st it fear or sin   95
To speak a truth. If he be slain, say so.
The tongue offends not that reports his death;
And he doth sin that doth belie the dead,
Not he which says the dead is not alive.
Yet the first bringer of unwelcome news   100
Hath but a losing office, and his tongue
Sounds ever after as a sullen bell
Remembered knolling a departing friend.

LORD BARDOLPH
I cannot think, my lord, your son is dead.

MORTON (*to Northumberland*)
I am sorry I should force you to believe   105
That which I would to God I had not seen;
But these mine eyes saw him in bloody state,
Rend'ring faint quittance, wearied and out-breathed,
To Harry Monmouth, whose swift wrath beat down
The never-daunted Percy to the earth,   110
From whence with life he never more sprung up.
In few, his death, whose spirit lent a fire
Even to the dullest peasant in his camp,
Being bruited once, took fire and heat away
From the best-tempered courage in his troops;   115
For from his metal was his party steeled,
Which once in him abated, all the rest
Turned on themselves, like dull and heavy lead;
And, as the thing that's heavy in itself
Upon enforcement flies with greatest speed,   120
So did our men, heavy in Hotspur's loss,
Lend to this weight such lightness with their fear
That arrows fled not swifter toward their aim
Than did our soldiers, aiming at their safety,
Fly from the field. Then was that noble Worcester   125
Too soon ta'en prisoner; and that furious Scot
The bloody Douglas, whose well-labouring sword
Had three times slain th'appearance of the King,
Gan vail his stomach, and did grace the shame
Of those that turned their backs, and in his flight, 130
Stumbling in fear, was took. The sum of all
Is that the King hath won, and hath sent out
A speedy power to encounter you, my lord,
Under the conduct of young Lancaster
And Westmorland. This is the news at full.   135

NORTHUMBERLAND
For this I shall have time enough to mourn.
In poison there is physic; and these news,
Having been well, that would have made me sick,
Being sick, have in some measure made me well;
And, as the wretch whose fever-weakened joints,   140

Like strengthless hinges, buckle under life,
Impatient of his fit, breaks like a fire
Out of his keeper's arms, even so my limbs,
Weakened with grief, being now enraged with grief,
Are thrice themselves.
⌈*He casts away his crutch*⌉
                    Hence therefore, thou nice crutch!
A scaly gauntlet now with joints of steel   146
Must glove this hand.
⌈*He snatches off his coif*⌉
                    And hence, thou sickly coif!
Thou art a guard too wanton for the head
Which princes fleshed with conquest aim to hit.
Now bind my brows with iron, and approach   150
The ragged'st hour that time and spite dare bring
To frown upon th'enragèd Northumberland!
Let heaven kiss earth! Now let not nature's hand
Keep the wild flood confined! Let order die!
And let this world no longer be a stage   155
To feed contention in a ling'ring act;
But let one spirit of the first-born Cain
Reign in all bosoms, that each heart being set
On bloody courses, the rude scene may end,
And darkness be the burier of the dead!   160
LORD BARDOLPH
Sweet Earl, divorce not wisdom from your honour.
MORTON
The lives of all your loving complices
Lean on your health, the which, if you give o'er
To stormy passion, must perforce decay.
You cast th'event of war, my noble lord,   165
And summed the account of chance, before you said
'Let us make head'. It was your presurmise
That in the dole of blows your son might drop.
You knew he walked o'er perils on an edge,
More likely to fall in than to get o'er.   170
You were advised his flesh was capable
Of wounds and scars, and that his forward spirit
Would lift him where most trade of danger ranged.
Yet did you say, 'Go forth'; and none of this,
Though strongly apprehended, could restrain   175
The stiff-borne action. What hath then befall'n?
Or what doth this bold enterprise bring forth,
More than that being which was like to be?
LORD BARDOLPH
We all that are engagèd to this loss
Knew that we ventured on such dangerous seas   180
That if we wrought out life was ten to one;
And yet we ventured for the gain proposed,
Choked the respect of likely peril feared;
And since we are o'erset, venture again.
Come, we will all put forth body and goods.   185
MORTON
'Tis more than time; and, my most noble lord,
I hear for certain, and dare speak the truth,
The gentle Archbishop of York is up
With well-appointed powers. He is a man
Who with a double surety binds his followers.   190

My lord, your son had only but the corpse,
But shadows and the shows of men, to fight;
For that same word 'rebellion' did divide
The action of their bodies from their souls,
And they did fight with queasiness, constrained,   195
As men drink potions, that their weapons only
Seemed on our side; but, for their spirits and souls,
This word 'rebellion', it had froze them up,
As fish are in a pond. But now the Bishop
Turns insurrection to religion.   200
Supposed sincere and holy in his thoughts,
He's followed both with body and with mind,
And doth enlarge his rising with the blood
Of fair King Richard, scraped from Pomfret stones;
Derives from heaven his quarrel and his cause;   205
Tells them he doth bestride a bleeding land
Gasping for life under great Bolingbroke;
And more and less do flock to follow him.
NORTHUMBERLAND
I knew of this before, but, to speak truth,
This present grief had wiped it from my mind.   210
Go in with me, and counsel every man
The aptest way for safety and revenge.
Get posts and letters, and make friends with speed.
Never so few, and never yet more need.   *Exeunt*

1.2   *Enter Sir John Falstaff, ⌈followed by⌉ his Page*
         bearing his sword and buckler
SIR JOHN Sirrah, you giant, what says the doctor to my
   water?
PAGE He said, sir, the water itself was a good healthy
   water, but, for the party that owed it, he might have
   more diseases than he knew for.   5
SIR JOHN Men of all sorts take a pride to gird at me. The
   brain of this foolish-compounded clay, man, is not able
   to invent anything that tends to laughter more than I
   invent, or is invented on me. I am not only witty in
   myself, but the cause that wit is in other men. I do
   here walk before thee like a sow that hath o'erwhelmed
   all her litter but one. If the Prince put thee into my
   service for any other reason than to set me off, why
   then, I have no judgement. Thou whoreson mandrake,
   thou art fitter to be worn in my cap than to wait at
   my heels. I was never manned with an agate till now;
   but I will set you neither in gold nor silver, but in vile
   apparel, and send you back again to your master for
   a jewel—the juvenal the Prince your master, whose
   chin is not yet fledge. I will sooner have a beard grow
   in the palm of my hand than he shall get one off his
   cheek; and yet he will not stick to say his face is a
   face-royal. God may finish it when he will; 'tis not a
   hair amiss yet. He may keep it still at a face-royal, for
   a barber shall never earn sixpence out of it. And yet
   he'll be crowing as if he had writ man ever since his
   father was a bachelor. He may keep his own grace, but
   he's almost out of mine, I can assure him. What said
   Master Dumbleton about the satin for my short cloak
   and slops?   30

PAGE He said, sir, you should procure him better assurance than Bardolph. He would not take his bond and yours; he liked not the security.

SIR JOHN Let him be damned like the glutton! Pray God his tongue be hotter! A whoreson Achitophel, a rascally yea-forsooth knave, to bear a gentleman in hand and then stand upon security! The whoreson smooth-pates do now wear nothing but high shoes and bunches of keys at their girdles; and if a man is through with them in honest taking-up, then they must stand upon security. I had as lief they would put ratsbane in my mouth as offer to stop it with security. I looked a should have sent me two and twenty yards of satin, as I am a true knight, and he sends me 'security'! Well, he may sleep in security, for he hath the horn of abundance, and the lightness of his wife shines through it; and yet cannot he see, though he have his own lanthorn to light him. Where's Bardolph?

PAGE He's gone in Smithfield to buy your worship a horse. 50

SIR JOHN I bought him in Paul's, and he'll buy me a horse in Smithfield. An I could get me but a wife in the stews, I were manned, horsed, and wived.

Enter the Lord Chief Justice and his Servant

PAGE Sir, here comes the nobleman that committed the Prince for striking him about Bardolph. 55

SIR JOHN ⌈*moving away*⌉ Wait close; I will not see him.

LORD CHIEF JUSTICE (*to his Servant*) What's he that goes there?

SERVANT Falstaff, an't please your lordship.

LORD CHIEF JUSTICE He that was in question for the robbery? 61

SERVANT He, my lord; but he hath since done good service at Shrewsbury, and, as I hear, is now going with some charge to the Lord John of Lancaster.

LORD CHIEF JUSTICE What, to York? Call him back again.

SERVANT Sir John Falstaff! 66

SIR JOHN Boy, tell him I am deaf.

PAGE (*to the Servant*) You must speak louder; my master is deaf. 69

LORD CHIEF JUSTICE I am sure he is to the hearing of anything good. (*To the Servant*) Go pluck him by the elbow; I must speak with him.

SERVANT Sir John!

SIR JOHN What, a young knave and begging! Is there not wars? Is there not employment? Doth not the King lack subjects? Do not the rebels want soldiers? Though it be a shame to be on any side but one, it is worse shame to beg than to be on the worst side, were it worse than the name of rebellion can tell how to make it. 80

SERVANT You mistake me, sir.

SIR JOHN Why, sir, did I say you were an honest man? Setting my knighthood and my soldiership aside, I had lied in my throat if I had said so. 84

SERVANT I pray you, sir, then set your knighthood and your soldiership aside, and give me leave to tell you you lie in your throat if you say I am any other than an honest man. 88

SIR JOHN I give thee leave to tell me so? I lay aside that which grows to me? If thou gettest any leave of me, hang me. If thou takest leave, thou wert better be hanged. You hunt counter. Hence, avaunt!

SERVANT Sir, my lord would speak with you.

LORD CHIEF JUSTICE Sir John Falstaff, a word with you. 94

SIR JOHN My good lord! God give your lordship good time of day. I am glad to see your lordship abroad. I heard say your lordship was sick. I hope your lordship goes abroad by advice. Your lordship, though not clean past your youth, have yet some smack of age in you, some relish of the saltness of time in you; and I most humbly beseech your lordship to have a reverent care of your health.

LORD CHIEF JUSTICE Sir John, I sent for you before your expedition to Shrewsbury.

SIR JOHN An't please your lordship, I hear his majesty is returned with some discomfort from Wales. 106

LORD CHIEF JUSTICE I talk not of his majesty. You would not come when I sent for you.

SIR JOHN And I hear, moreover, his highness is fallen into this same whoreson apoplexy. 110

LORD CHIEF JUSTICE Well, God mend him! I pray you, let me speak with you.

SIR JOHN This apoplexy is, as I take it, a kind of lethargy, an't please your lordship, a kind of sleeping in the blood, a whoreson tingling. 115

LORD CHIEF JUSTICE What tell you me of it? Be it as it is.

SIR JOHN It hath it original from much grief, from study, and perturbation of the brain. I have read the cause of his effects in Galen. It is a kind of deafness.

LORD CHIEF JUSTICE I think you are fallen into the disease, for you hear not what I say to you. 121

SIR JOHN Very well, my lord, very well. Rather, an't please you, it is the disease of not listening, the malady of not marking, that I am troubled withal. 124

LORD CHIEF JUSTICE To punish you by the heels would amend the attention of your ears, and I care not if I do become your physician.

SIR JOHN I am as poor as Job, my lord, but not so patient. Your lordship may minister the potion of imprisonment to me in respect of poverty; but how I should be your patient to follow your prescriptions, the wise may make some dram of a scruple, or indeed a scruple itself.

LORD CHIEF JUSTICE I sent for you, when there were matters against you for your life, to come speak with me.

SIR JOHN As I was then advised by my learned counsel in the laws of this land-service, I did not come. 136

LORD CHIEF JUSTICE Well, the truth is, Sir John, you live in great infamy.

SIR JOHN He that buckles himself in my belt cannot live in less. 140

LORD CHIEF JUSTICE Your means are very slender, and your waste is great.

SIR JOHN I would it were otherwise; I would my means were greater and my waist slenderer.

LORD CHIEF JUSTICE You have misled the youthful Prince.

SIR JOHN The young Prince hath misled me. I am the fellow with the great belly, and he my dog.

LORD CHIEF JUSTICE Well, I am loath to gall a new-healed wound. Your day's service at Shrewsbury hath a little gilded over your night's exploit on Gads Hill. You may thank th'unquiet time for your quiet o'erposting that action.

SIR JOHN My lord—

LORD CHIEF JUSTICE But since all is well, keep it so. Wake not a sleeping wolf.   155

SIR JOHN To wake a wolf is as bad as smell a fox.

LORD CHIEF JUSTICE What! You are as a candle, the better part burnt out.

SIR JOHN A wassail candle, my lord, all tallow—if I did say of wax, my growth would approve the truth.   160

LORD CHIEF JUSTICE There is not a white hair in your face but should have his effect of gravity.

SIR JOHN His effect of gravy, gravy, gravy.

LORD CHIEF JUSTICE You follow the young Prince up and down like his ill angel.   165

SIR JOHN Not so, my lord; your ill angel is light, but I hope he that looks upon me will take me without weighing. And yet in some respects, I grant, I cannot go. I cannot tell, virtue is of so little regard in these costermongers' times that true valour is turned bearherd; pregnancy is made a tapster, and his quick wit wasted in giving reckonings; all the other gifts appertinent to man, as the malice of this age shapes them, are not worth a gooseberry. You that are old consider not the capacities of us that are young. You do measure the heat of our livers with the bitterness of your galls. And we that are in the vanguard of our youth, I must confess, are wags too.

LORD CHIEF JUSTICE Do you set down your name in the scroll of youth, that are written down old with all the characters of age? Have you not a moist eye, a dry hand, a yellow cheek, a white beard, a decreasing leg, an increasing belly? Is not your voice broken, your wind short, your chin double, your wit single, and every part about you blasted with antiquity? And will you yet call yourself young? Fie, fie, fie, Sir John!   186

SIR JOHN My lord, I was born about three of the clock in the afternoon with a white head, and something a round belly. For my voice, I have lost it with hallowing and singing of anthems. To approve my youth further, I will not. The truth is, I am only old in judgement and understanding; and he that will caper with me for a thousand marks, let him lend me the money, and have at him! For the box of th'ear that the Prince gave you, he gave it like a rude prince, and you took it like a sensible lord. I have checked him for it, and the young lion repents— ⌈aside⌉ marry, not in ashes and sackcloth, but in new silk and old sack.

LORD CHIEF JUSTICE Well, God send the Prince a better companion!   200

SIR JOHN God send the companion a better prince! I cannot rid my hands of him.

LORD CHIEF JUSTICE Well, the King hath severed you and Prince Harry. I hear you are going with Lord John of Lancaster against the Archbishop and the Earl of Northumberland.   206

SIR JOHN Yea, I thank your pretty sweet wit for it. But look you pray, all you that kiss my lady Peace at home, that our armies join not in a hot day; for, by the Lord, I take but two shirts out with me, and I mean not to sweat extraordinarily. If it be a hot day and I brandish anything but my bottle, would I might never spit white again. There is not a dangerous action can peep out his head but I am thrust upon it. Well, I cannot last ever. But it was alway yet the trick of our English nation, if they have a good thing, to make it too common. If ye will needs say I am an old man, you should give me rest. I would to God my name were not so terrible to the enemy as it is. I were better to be eaten to death with a rust than to be scoured to nothing with perpetual motion.   221

LORD CHIEF JUSTICE Well, be honest, be honest, and God bless your expedition.

SIR JOHN Will your lordship lend me a thousand pound to furnish me forth?   225

LORD CHIEF JUSTICE Not a penny, not a penny. You are too impatient to bear crosses. Fare you well. Commend me to my cousin Westmorland.

                    Exeunt Lord Chief Justice and his Servant

SIR JOHN If I do, fillip me with a three-man beetle. A man can no more separate age and covetousness than a can part young limbs and lechery; but the gout galls the one and the pox pinches the other, and so both the degrees prevent my curses. Boy!

PAGE Sir.

SIR JOHN What money is in my purse?   235

PAGE Seven groats and two pence.

SIR JOHN I can get no remedy against this consumption of the purse. Borrowing only lingers and lingers it out, but the disease is incurable. (*Giving letters*) Go bear this letter to my lord of Lancaster; this to the Prince; this to the Earl of Westmorland; and this to old Mistress Ursula, whom I have weekly sworn to marry since I perceived the first white hair of my chin. About it. You know where to find me.   ⌈*Exit Page*⌉

A pox of this gout!—or a gout of this pox!—for the one or the other plays the rogue with my great toe. 'Tis no matter if I do halt; I have the wars for my colour, and my pension shall seem the more reasonable. A good wit will make use of anything. I will turn diseases to commodity.   *Exit*

1.3   *Enter the Archbishop of York, Thomas Mowbray the Earl Marshal, Lord Hastings, and Lord Bardolph*

ARCHBISHOP OF YORK

Thus have you heard our cause and known our
      means,

And, my most noble friends, I pray you all

Speak plainly your opinions of our hopes.

And first, Lord Marshal, what say you to it?

MOWBRAY

I well allow the occasion of our arms,   5
But gladly would be better satisfied
How in our means we should advance ourselves
To look with forehead bold and big enough
Upon the power and puissance of the King.

HASTINGS

Our present musters grow upon the file   10
To five and twenty thousand men of choice,
And our supplies live largely in the hope
Of great Northumberland, whose bosom burns
With an incensèd fire of injuries.

LORD BARDOLPH

The question then, Lord Hastings, standeth thus: 15
Whether our present five and twenty thousand
May hold up head without Northumberland.

HASTINGS

With him we may.

LORD BARDOLPH   Yea, marry, there's the point;
But if without him we be thought too feeble,
My judgement is, we should not step too far   20
Till we had his assistance by the hand;
For in a theme so bloody-faced as this,
Conjecture, expectation, and surmise
Of aids uncertain should not be admitted.

ARCHBISHOP OF YORK

'Tis very true, Lord Bardolph, for indeed   25
It was young Hotspur's case at Shrewsbury.

LORD BARDOLPH

It was, my lord; who lined himself with hope,
Eating the air on promise of supply,
Flatt'ring himself with project of a power
Much smaller than the smallest of his thoughts;   30
And so, with great imagination
Proper to madmen, led his powers to death,
And winking leapt into destruction.

HASTINGS

But by your leave, it never yet did hurt
To lay down likelihoods and forms of hope.   35

LORD BARDOLPH

Yes, if this present quality of war—
Indeed the instant action, a cause on foot—
Lives so in hope; as in an early spring
We see th'appearing buds, which to prove fruit
Hope gives not so much warrant as despair   40
That frosts will bite them. When we mean to build
We first survey the plot, then draw the model;
And when we see the figure of the house,
Then must we rate the cost of the erection,
Which if we find outweighs ability,   45
What do we then but draw anew the model
In fewer offices, or, at least, desist
To build at all? Much more in this great work—
Which is almost to pluck a kingdom down
And set another up—should we survey   50
The plot of situation and the model,
Consent upon a sure foundation,
Question surveyors, know our own estate,

How able such a work to undergo,
To weigh against his opposite; or else   55
We fortify in paper and in figures,
Using the names of men instead of men,
Like one that draws the model of an house
Beyond his power to build it, who, half-through,
Gives o'er, and leaves his part-created cost   60
A naked subject to the weeping clouds,
And waste for churlish winter's tyranny.

HASTINGS

Grant that our hopes, yet likely of fair birth,
Should be stillborn, and that we now possessed
The utmost man of expectation,   65
I think we are a body strong enough,
Even as we are, to equal with the King.

LORD BARDOLPH

What, is the King but five and twenty thousand?

HASTINGS

To us no more, nay, not so much, Lord Bardolph;
For his divisions, as the times do brawl,   70
Are in three heads: one power against the French,
And one against Glyndŵr, perforce a third
Must take up us. So is the unfirm King
In three divided, and his coffers sound
With hollow poverty and emptiness.   75

ARCHBISHOP OF YORK

That he should draw his several strengths together
And come against us in full puissance
Need not be dreaded.

HASTINGS   If he should do so,
He leaves his back unarmed, the French and Welsh
Baying him at the heels. Never fear that.   80

LORD BARDOLPH

Who is it like should lead his forces hither?

HASTINGS

The Duke of Lancaster and Westmorland;
Against the Welsh, himself and Harry Monmouth;
But who is substituted 'gainst the French
I have no certain notice.

ARCHBISHOP OF YORK   Let us on,   85
And publish the occasion of our arms.
The commonwealth is sick of their own choice;
Their over-greedy love hath surfeited.
An habitation giddy and unsure
Hath he that buildeth on the vulgar heart.   90
O thou fond many, with what loud applause
Didst thou beat heaven with blessing Bolingbroke,
Before he was what thou wouldst have him be!
And being now trimmed in thine own desires,
Thou, beastly feeder, art so full of him   95
That thou provok'st thyself to cast him up.
So, so, thou common dog, didst thou disgorge
Thy glutton bosom of the royal Richard;
And now thou wouldst eat thy dead vomit up,
And howl'st to find it. What trust is in these times? 100
They that when Richard lived would have him die
Are now become enamoured on his grave.
Thou that threw'st dust upon his goodly head,

When through proud London he came sighing on
After th'admirèd heels of Bolingbroke,   105
Cri'st now, 'O earth, yield us that king again,
And take thou this!' O thoughts of men accursed!
Past and to come seems best; things present, worst.
⌈MOWBRAY⌉
Shall we go draw our numbers and set on?
HASTINGS
We are time's subjects, and time bids be gone.   110
                                                           Exeunt

2.1   *Enter Mistress Quickly (the hostess of a tavern),*
       and an officer, Fang ⌈followed at a distance by⌉
       another officer, Snare
MISTRESS QUICKLY Master Fang, have you entered the
    action?
FANG It is entered.
MISTRESS QUICKLY Where's your yeoman? Is't a lusty
    yeoman? Will a stand to't?   5
FANG Sirrah!—Where's Snare?
MISTRESS QUICKLY O Lord, ay, good Master Snare.
SNARE ⌈*coming forward*⌉ Here, here.
FANG Snare, we must arrest Sir John Falstaff.
MISTRESS QUICKLY Yea, good Master Snare, I have entered
    him and all.   11
SNARE It may chance cost some of us our lives, for he
    will stab.
MISTRESS QUICKLY Alas the day, take heed of him; he
    stabbed me in mine own house, most beastly, in good
    faith. A cares not what mischief he does; if his weapon
    be out, he will foin like any devil, he will spare neither
    man, woman, nor child.
FANG If I can close with him, I care not for his thrust.   19
MISTRESS QUICKLY No, nor I neither. I'll be at your elbow.
FANG An I but fist him once, an a come but within my
    vice—
MISTRESS QUICKLY I am undone by his going, I warrant
    you; he's an infinitive thing upon my score. Good
    Master Fang, hold him sure. Good Master Snare, let
    him not scape. A comes continuantly to Pie Corner—
    saving your manhoods—to buy a saddle, and he is
    indited to dinner to the Lubber's Head in Lombard
    Street, to Master Smooth's the silkman. I pray you,
    since my exion is entered, and my case so openly
    known to the world, let him be brought in to his
    answer. A hundred mark is a long one for a poor lone
    woman to bear; and I have borne, and borne, and borne,
    and borne, and have been fobbed off, and fobbed off, and
    fobbed off, from this day to that day, that it is a shame
    to be thought on. There is no honesty in such dealing,
    unless a woman should be made an ass and a beast,
    to bear every knave's wrong.
       Enter Sir John Falstaff, Bardolph, and the Page
    Yonder he comes, and that arrant malmsey-nose knave
    Bardolph with him. Do your offices, do your offices,
    Master Fang and Master Snare; do me, do me, do me
    your offices.

SIR JOHN How now, whose mare's dead? What's the
    matter?   44
FANG Sir John, I arrest you at the suit of Mistress Quickly.
SIR JOHN ⌈*drawing*⌉ Away, varlets! Draw, Bardolph! Cut
    me off the villain's head! Throw the quean in the
    channel!
       ⌈*Bardolph draws*⌉
MISTRESS QUICKLY Throw me in the channel? I'll throw
    thee in the channel!   50
       A brawl
    Wilt thou, wilt thou, thou bastardly rogue? Murder,
    murder! Ah, thou honeysuckle villain, wilt thou kill
    God's officers, and the King's? Ah, thou honeyseed
    rogue! Thou art a honeyseed, a man-queller, and a
    woman-queller.   55
SIR JOHN Keep them off, Bardolph!
FANG A rescue, a rescue!
MISTRESS QUICKLY Good people, bring a rescue or two.
    Thou wot, wot thou? Thou wot, wot'a? Do, do, thou
    rogue, do, thou hempseed!   60
PAGE   Away, you scullion, you rampallian, you
    fustilarian! I'll tickle your catastrophe!
       Enter the Lord Chief Justice and his men
LORD CHIEF JUSTICE
    What is the matter? Keep the peace here, ho!
       Brawl ends. ⌈*Fang*⌉ *seizes Sir John*
MISTRESS QUICKLY Good my lord, be good to me; I beseech
    you, stand to me.   65
LORD CHIEF JUSTICE
    How now, Sir John? What, are you brawling here?
    Doth this become your place, your time and business?
    You should have been well on your way to York.
    ⌈*To Fang*⌉ Stand from him, fellow. Wherefore hang'st
       thou upon him?   69
MISTRESS QUICKLY O my most worshipful lord, an't please
    your grace, I am a poor widow of Eastcheap, and he
    is arrested at my suit.
LORD CHIEF JUSTICE For what sum?
MISTRESS QUICKLY It is more than for some, my lord, it is
    for all, all I have. He hath eaten me out of house and
    home. He hath put all my substance into that fat belly
    of his; (*to Sir John*) but I will have some of it out again,
    or I will ride thee a-nights like the mare.
SIR JOHN I think I am as like to ride the mare, if I have
    any vantage of ground to get up.   80
LORD CHIEF JUSTICE How comes this, Sir John? Fie, what
    man of good temper would endure this tempest of
    exclamation? Are you not ashamed, to enforce a poor
    widow to so rough a course to come by her own?
SIR JOHN (*to the Hostess*) What is the gross sum that I owe
    thee?   86
MISTRESS QUICKLY Marry, if thou wert an honest man,
    thyself, and the money too. Thou didst swear to me
    upon a parcel-gilt goblet, sitting in my Dolphin
    chamber, at the round table, by a sea-coal fire, upon
    Wednesday in Wheeson week, when the Prince broke
    thy head for liking his father to a singing-man of

Windsor—thou didst swear to me then, as I was washing thy wound, to marry me, and make me my lady thy wife. Canst thou deny it? Did not goodwife Keech the butcher's wife come in then, and call me 'Gossip Quickly'—coming in to borrow a mess of vinegar, telling us she had a good dish of prawns, whereby thou didst desire to eat some, whereby I told thee they were ill for a green wound? And didst thou not, when she was gone downstairs, desire me to be no more so familiarity with such poor people, saying that ere long they should call me 'madam'? And didst thou not kiss me, and bid me fetch thee thirty shillings? I put thee now to thy book-oath; deny it if thou canst.

⌈*She weeps*⌉

SIR JOHN My lord, this is a poor mad soul, and she says up and down the town that her eldest son is like you. She hath been in good case, and the truth is, poverty hath distracted her. But for these foolish officers, I beseech you I may have redress against them.   110

LORD CHIEF JUSTICE Sir John, Sir John, I am well acquainted with your manner of wrenching the true cause the false way. It is not a confident brow, nor the throng of words that come with such more than impudent sauciness from you, can thrust me from a level consideration. You have, as it appears to me, practised upon the easy-yielding spirit of this woman, and made her serve your uses both in purse and in person.

MISTRESS QUICKLY Yea, in truth, my lord.   119

LORD CHIEF JUSTICE Pray thee, peace. (*To Sir John*) Pay her the debt you owe her, and unpay the villainy you have done with her. The one you may do with sterling money, and the other with current repentance.

SIR JOHN My lord, I will not undergo this sneap without reply. You call honourable boldness 'impudent sauciness'; if a man will make curtsy and say nothing, he is virtuous. No, my lord, my humble duty remembered, I will not be your suitor. I say to you I do desire deliverance from these officers, being upon hasty employment in the King's affairs.   130

LORD CHIEF JUSTICE You speak as having power to do wrong; but answer in th'effect of your reputation, and satisfy the poor woman.

SIR JOHN (*drawing apart*) Come hither, hostess.

She goes to him.

Enter Master Gower, a messenger

LORD CHIEF JUSTICE Now, Master Gower, what news?   135

GOWER

The King, my lord, and Harry Prince of Wales
Are near at hand; the rest the paper tells.

⌈*Lord Chief Justice reads the paper, and converses apart with Gower*⌉

SIR JOHN As I am a gentleman!

MISTRESS QUICKLY Faith, you said so before.

SIR JOHN As I am a gentleman! Come, no more words of it.   141

MISTRESS QUICKLY By this heavenly ground I tread on, I must be fain to pawn both my plate and the tapestry of my dining-chambers.

SIR JOHN Glasses, glasses, is the only drinking; and for thy walls, a pretty slight drollery, or the story of the Prodigal, or the German hunting in waterwork, is worth a thousand of these bed-hangers and these fly-bitten tapestries. Let it be ten pound if thou canst. Come, an 'twere not for thy humours, there's not a better wench in England. Go, wash thy face, and draw the action. Come, thou must not be in this humour with me. Dost not know me? Come, I know thou wast set on to this.   154

MISTRESS QUICKLY Pray thee, Sir John, let it be but twenty nobles. I'faith, I am loath to pawn my plate, so God save me, la!

SIR JOHN Let it alone; I'll make other shift. You'll be a fool still.   159

MISTRESS QUICKLY Well, you shall have it, though I pawn my gown. I hope you'll come to supper. You'll pay me altogether?

SIR JOHN Will I live? ⌈*To Bardolph and the Page*⌉ Go with her, with her. Hook on, hook on!

MISTRESS QUICKLY Will you have Doll Tearsheet meet you at supper?   166

SIR JOHN No more words; let's have her.

Exeunt Mistress Quickly, Bardolph,
the Page, Fang and Snare

LORD CHIEF JUSTICE (*to Gower*) I have heard better news.

SIR JOHN What's the news, my good lord?

LORD CHIEF JUSTICE (*to Gower*) Where lay the King tonight?

GOWER At Basingstoke, my lord.   171

SIR JOHN (*to Lord Chief Justice*) I hope, my lord, all's well. What is the news, my lord?

LORD CHIEF JUSTICE (*to Gower*) Come all his forces back?

GOWER

No; fifteen hundred foot, five hundred horse,   175
Are marched up to my lord of Lancaster
Against Northumberland and the Archbishop.

SIR JOHN (*to Lord Chief Justice*)
Comes the King back from Wales, my noble lord?

LORD CHIEF JUSTICE (*to Gower*)
You shall have letters of me presently.
Come, go along with me, good Master Gower.   180

They are going

SIR JOHN My lord!

LORD CHIEF JUSTICE What's the matter?

SIR JOHN Master Gower, shall I entreat you with me to dinner?

GOWER I must wait upon my good lord here, I thank you, good Sir John.   186

LORD CHIEF JUSTICE Sir John, you loiter here too long, being you are to take soldiers up in counties as you go.

SIR JOHN Will you sup with me, Master Gower?   190

LORD CHIEF JUSTICE What foolish master taught you these manners, Sir John?

SIR JOHN Master Gower, if they become me not, he was a fool that taught them me. (*To Lord Chief Justice*) This is the right fencing grace, my lord—tap for tap, and so part fair.   196

LORD CHIEF JUSTICE Now the Lord lighten thee; thou art
a great fool.
Exeunt ⌈Lord Chief Justice and Gower at one
door, Sir John at another⌉

2.2 *Enter Prince Harry and Poins*

PRINCE HARRY Before God, I am exceeding weary.

POINS Is't come to that? I had thought weariness durst
not have attached one of so high blood.

PRINCE HARRY Faith, it does me, though it discolours the
complexion of my greatness to acknowledge it. Doth it
not show vilely in me to desire small beer?   6

POINS Why, a prince should not be so loosely studied as
to remember so weak a composition.

PRINCE HARRY Belike then my appetite was not princely
got; for, by my troth, I do now remember the poor
creature small beer. But indeed, these humble
considerations make me out of love with my greatness.
What a disgrace is it to me to remember thy name! Or
to know thy face tomorrow! Or to take note how many
pair of silk stockings thou hast—videlicet these, and
those that were thy peach-coloured ones! Or to bear
the inventory of thy shirts—as one for superfluity, and
another for use. But that the tennis-court keeper knows
better than I, for it is a low ebb of linen with thee
when thou keepest not racket there; as thou hast not
done a great while, because the rest of thy low countries
have made a shift to eat up thy holland.

POINS How ill it follows, after you have laboured so hard,
you should talk so idly! Tell me, how many good young
princes would do so, their fathers lying so sick as yours
is?   26

PRINCE HARRY Shall I tell thee one thing, Poins?

POINS Yes, faith, and let it be an excellent good thing.

PRINCE HARRY It shall serve among wits of no higher
breeding than thine.   30

POINS Go to, I stand the push of your one thing that
you'll tell.

PRINCE HARRY Marry, I tell thee, it is not meet that I
should be sad now my father is sick; albeit I could tell
to thee, as to one it pleases me, for fault of a better, to
call my friend, I could be sad; and sad indeed too.   36

POINS Very hardly, upon such a subject.

PRINCE HARRY By this hand, thou thinkest me as far in
the devil's book as thou and Falstaff, for obduracy and
persistency. Let the end try the man. But I tell thee,
my heart bleeds inwardly that my father is so sick; and
keeping such vile company as thou art hath, in reason,
taken from me all ostentation of sorrow.

POINS The reason?

PRINCE HARRY What wouldst thou think of me if I should
weep?   46

POINS I would think thee a most princely hypocrite.

PRINCE HARRY It would be every man's thought, and thou
art a blessed fellow to think as every man thinks. Never
a man's thought in the world keeps the roadway better
than thine. Every man would think me an hypocrite

indeed. And what accites your most worshipful thought
to think so?

POINS Why, because you have been so lewd, and so much
engrafted to Falstaff.   55

PRINCE HARRY And to thee.

POINS By this light, I am well spoke on; I can hear it
with mine own ears. The worst that they can say of
me is that I am a second brother, and that I am a
proper fellow of my hands; and those two things I
confess I cannot help.   61

Enter Bardolph ⌈followed by⌉ the Page

By the mass, here comes Bardolph.

PRINCE HARRY And the boy that I gave Falstaff. A had
him from me Christian, and look if the fat villain have
not transformed him ape.   65

BARDOLPH God save your grace!

PRINCE HARRY And yours, most noble Bardolph!

POINS (*to Bardolph*) Come, you virtuous ass, you bashful
fool, must you be blushing? Wherefore blush you now?
What a maidenly man at arms are you become! Is't
such a matter to get a pottle-pot's maidenhead?   71

PAGE A calls me e'en now, my lord, through a red lattice,
and I could discern no part of his face from the window.
At last I spied his eyes, and methought he had made
two holes in the ale-wife's red petticoat, and so peeped
through.   76

PRINCE HARRY (*to Poins*) Has not the boy profited?

BARDOLPH (*to the Page*) Away, you whoreson upright
rabbit, away!

PAGE Away, you rascally Althea's dream, away!   80

PRINCE HARRY Instruct us, boy; what dream, boy?

PAGE Marry, my lord, Althea dreamt she was delivered
of a firebrand, and therefore I call him her dream.

PRINCE HARRY (*giving him money*) A crown's-worth of good
interpretation! There 'tis, boy.   85

POINS O, that this good blossom could be kept from
cankers! (*Giving the Page money*) Well, there is sixpence
to preserve thee.

BARDOLPH An you do not make him hanged among you,
the gallows shall be wronged.   90

PRINCE HARRY And how doth thy master, Bardolph?

BARDOLPH Well, my good·lord. He heard of your grace's
coming to town. There's a letter for you.

POINS Delivered with good respect. And how doth the
Martlemas your master?   95

BARDOLPH In bodily health, sir.

Prince Harry reads the letter

POINS Marry, the immortal part needs a physician, but
that moves not him. Though that be sick, it dies not.

PRINCE HARRY I do allow this wen to be as familiar with
me as my dog; and he holds his place, for look you
how he writes.   101

⌈*He gives Poins the letter*⌉

POINS 'John Falstaff, knight'.—Every man must know
that, as oft as he has occasion to name himself; even
like those that are kin to the King, for they never prick
their finger but they say 'There's some of the King's

blood spilt.' 'How comes that?' says he that takes upon him not to conceive. The answer is as ready as a borrower's cap: 'I am the King's poor cousin, sir.'

PRINCE HARRY Nay, they will be kin to us, or they will fetch it from Japhet. (*Taking the letter*) But the letter. 'Sir John Falstaff, knight, to the son of the King nearest his father, Harry Prince of Wales, greeting.'

POINS Why, this is a certificate!

PRINCE HARRY Peace!—'I will imitate the honourable Romans in brevity.'   115

POINS (*taking the letter*) Sure he means brevity in breath, short winded. (*Reads*) 'I commend me to thee, I commend thee, and I leave thee. Be not too familiar with Poins, for he misuses thy favours so much that he swears thou art to marry his sister Nell. Repent at idle times as thou mayst. And so, farewell.   121

> Thine by yea and no—which is as much as to say, as thou usest him—Jack Falstaff with my familiars, John with my brothers and sisters, and Sir John with all Europe.'   125

My lord, I'll steep this letter in sack and make him eat it.

PRINCE HARRY That's to make him eat twenty of his words. But do you use me thus, Ned? Must I marry your sister?   130

POINS God send the wench no worse fortune, but I never said so.

PRINCE HARRY Well, thus we play the fools with the time, and the spirits of the wise sit in the clouds and mock us. (*To Bardolph*) Is your master here in London? 135

BARDOLPH Yea, my lord.

PRINCE HARRY Where sups he? Doth the old boar feed in the old frank?

BARDOLPH At the old place, my lord, in Eastcheap.

PRINCE HARRY What company?   140

PAGE Ephesians, my lord, of the old church.

PRINCE HARRY Sup any women with him?

PAGE None, my lord, but old Mistress Quickly and Mistress Doll Tearsheet.

PRINCE HARRY What pagan may that be?   145

PAGE A proper gentlewoman, sir, and a kinswoman of my master's.

PRINCE HARRY Even such kin as the parish heifers are to the town bull. Shall we steal upon them, Ned, at supper?   150

POINS I am your shadow, my lord; I'll follow you.

PRINCE HARRY Sirrah, you, boy, and Bardolph, no word to your master that I am yet come to town. (*Giving money*) There's for your silence.

BARDOLPH I have no tongue, sir.   155

PAGE And for mine, sir, I will govern it.

PRINCE HARRY Fare you well; go.

Exeunt Bardolph and the Page

This Doll Tearsheet should be some road.

POINS I warrant you, as common as the way between Saint Albans and London.   160

PRINCE HARRY How might we see Falstaff bestow himself tonight in his true colours, and not ourselves be seen?

POINS Put on two leathern jerkins and aprons, and wait upon him at his table like drawers.   164

PRINCE HARRY From a god to a bull—a heavy declension—it was Jove's case. From a prince to a prentice—a low transformation—that shall be mine; for in everything the purpose must weigh with the folly. Follow me, Ned.

Exeunt

2.3   *Enter the Earl of Northumberland, Lady Northumberland, and Lady Percy*

NORTHUMBERLAND
I pray thee, loving wife and gentle daughter,
Give even way unto my rough affairs.
Put not you on the visage of the times
And be like them to Percy troublesome.

LADY NORTHUMBERLAND
I have given over; I will speak no more.   5
Do what you will; your wisdom be your guide.

NORTHUMBERLAND
Alas, sweet wife, my honour is at pawn,
And, but my going, nothing can redeem it.

LADY PERCY
O yet, for God's sake, go not to these wars!
The time was, father, that you broke your word   10
When you were more endeared to it than now—
When your own Percy, when my heart's dear Harry,
Threw many a northward look to see his father
Bring up his powers; but he did long in vain.
Who then persuaded you to stay at home?   15
There were two honours lost, yours and your son's.
For yours, the God of heaven brighten it!
For his, it stuck upon him as the sun
In the grey vault of heaven, and by his light
Did all the chivalry of England move   20
To do brave acts. He was indeed the glass
Wherein the noble youth did dress themselves.
He had no legs that practised not his gait;
And speaking thick, which nature made his blemish,
Became the accents of the valiant;   25
For those that could speak low and tardily
Would turn their own perfection to abuse
To seem like him. So that in speech, in gait,
In diet, in affections of delight,
In military rules, humours of blood,   30
He was the mark and glass, copy and book,
That fashioned others. And him—O wondrous him!
O miracle of men!—him did you leave,
Second to none, unseconded by you,
To look upon the hideous god of war   35
In disadvantage, to abide a field
Where nothing but the sound of Hotspur's name
Did seem defensible; so you left him.
Never, O never do his ghost the wrong
To hold your honour more precise and nice   40
With others than with him. Let them alone.
The Marshal and the Archbishop are strong.
Had my sweet Harry had but half their numbers,

Today might I, hanging on Hotspur's neck,
Have talked of Monmouth's grave. 46
NORTHUMBERLAND   Beshrew your heart,
Fair daughter, you do draw my spirits from me
With new lamenting ancient oversights.
But I must go and meet with danger there,
Or it will seek me in another place,
And find me worse provided.
LADY NORTHUMBERLAND   O fly to Scotland, 50
Till that the nobles and the armèd commons
Have of their puissance made a little taste.
LADY PERCY
If they get ground and vantage of the King,
Then join you with them like a rib of steel,
To make strength stronger; but, for all our loves, 55
First let them try themselves. So did your son.
He was so suffered. So came I a widow,
And never shall have length of life enough
To rain upon remembrance with mine eyes,
That it may grow and sprout as high as heaven 60
For recordation to my noble husband.
NORTHUMBERLAND
Come, come, go in with me. 'Tis with my mind
As with the tide swelled up unto his height,
That makes a still stand, running neither way.
Fain would I go to meet the Archbishop, 65
But many thousand reasons hold me back.
I will resolve for Scotland. There am I
Till time and vantage crave my company.   *Exeunt*

2.4   [*A table and chairs set forth.*] *Enter a Drawer*
⌐*with wine*¬ *and another Drawer* ⌐*with a dish of*
apple-johns¬
⌐FIRST DRAWER¬ What the devil hast thou brought there—
apple-johns? Thou knowest Sir John cannot endure an
apple-john.
⌐SECOND DRAWER¬ Mass, thou sayst true. The Prince once
set a dish of apple-johns before him; and told him,
there were five more Sir Johns; and, putting off his
hat, said 'I will now take my leave of these six dry,
round, old, withered knights.' It angered him to the
heart. But he hath forgot that. 9
⌐FIRST DRAWER¬ Why then, cover, and set them down;
and see if thou canst find out Sneak's noise. Mistress
Tearsheet would fain hear some music.
⌐*Exit the Second Drawer*¬
⌐*The First Drawer covers the table.*¬
⌐*Enter the Second Drawer*¬
⌐SECOND DRAWER¬ Sirrah, here will be the Prince and
Master Poins anon, and they will put on two of our
jerkins and aprons, and Sir John must not know of it.
Bardolph hath brought word. 16
⌐FIRST DRAWER¬ By the mass, here will be old utis! It will
be an excellent stratagem.
⌐SECOND DRAWER¬ I'll see if I can find out Sneak.
     Exeunt
Enter Mistress Quickly and Doll Tearsheet, drunk
MISTRESS QUICKLY I'faith, sweetheart, methinks now you

are in an excellent good temperality. Your pulsidge
beats as extraordinarily as heart would desire, and your
colour, I warrant you, is as red as any rose, in good
truth, la; but i'faith, you have drunk too much
canaries, and that's a marvellous searching wine, and
it perfumes the blood ere we can say 'What's this?'
How do you now?
DOLL TEARSHEET Better than I was.—Hem!
MISTRESS QUICKLY Why, that's well said! A good heart's
worth gold. 30
     Enter Sir John Falstaff
Lo, here comes Sir John.
SIR JOHN (*sings*) 'When Arthur first in court'— ⌐*Calls*¬
empty the jordan!— (*Sings*) 'And was a worthy king'—
how now, Mistress Doll?
MISTRESS QUICKLY Sick of a qualm, yea, good faith. 35
SIR JOHN So is all her sect; an they be once in a calm,
they are sick.
DOLL TEARSHEET A pox damn you, you muddy rascal! Is
that all the comfort you give me?
SIR JOHN You make fat rascals, Mistress Doll. 40
DOLL TEARSHEET I make them? Gluttony and diseases
make them; I make them not.
SIR JOHN If the cook help to make the gluttony, you help
to make the diseases, Doll. We catch of you, Doll, we
catch of you; grant that, my poor virtue, grant that.
DOLL TEARSHEET Yea, Jesu, our chains and our jewels. 46
SIR JOHN 'Your brooches, pearls, and ouches'—for to
serve bravely is to come halting off, you know; to come
off the breach with his pike bent bravely, and to surgery
bravely; to venture upon the charged chambers
bravely. 51
MISTRESS QUICKLY By my troth, this is the old fashion.
You two never meet but you fall to some discord. You
are both, i' good truth, as rheumatic as two dry toasts;
you cannot one bear with another's confirmities. What
the goodyear, one must bear, (*to Doll*) and that must
be you. You are the weaker vessel, as they say, the
emptier vessel.
DOLL TEARSHEET Can a weak empty vessel bear such a
huge full hogshead? There's a whole merchant's
venture of Bordeaux stuff in him; you have not seen
a hulk better stuffed in the hold.—Come, I'll be friends
with thee, Jack. Thou art going to the wars, and
whether I shall ever see thee again or no there is
nobody cares. 65
     Enter a Drawer
DRAWER Sir, Ensign Pistol's below, and would speak with
you.
DOLL TEARSHEET Hang him, swaggering rascal, let him
not come hither. It is the foul-mouthedest rogue in
England. 70
MISTRESS QUICKLY If he swagger, let him not come here.
No, by my faith! I must live among my neighbours;
I'll no swaggerers. I am in good name and fame with
the very best. Shut the door; there comes no swaggerers
here. I have not lived all this while to have swaggering
now. Shut the door, I pray you. 76

SIR JOHN Dost thou hear, hostess?

MISTRESS QUICKLY Pray ye pacify yourself, Sir John. There comes no swaggerers here.

SIR JOHN Dost thou hear? It is mine ensign.   80

MISTRESS QUICKLY Tilly-fally, Sir John, ne'er tell me. Your ensign-swaggerer comes not in my doors. I was before Master Tisick the debuty t'other day, and, as he said to me—'twas no longer ago than Wed'sday last, i' good faith—'Neighbour Quickly,' says he—Master Dumb our minister was by then—'Neighbour Quickly,' says he, 'receive those that are civil, for,' said he, 'you are in an ill name.' Now a said so, I can tell whereupon. 'For,' says he, 'you are an honest woman, and well thought on; therefore take heed what guests you receive. Receive,' says he, 'no swaggering companions.' There comes none here. You would bless you to hear what he said. No, I'll no swaggerers.

SIR JOHN He's no swaggerer, hostess—a tame cheater, i'faith. You may stroke him as gently as a puppy greyhound. He'll not swagger with a Barbary hen, if her feathers turn back in any show of resistance.—Call him up, drawer.   ⌈Exit Drawer⌉

MISTRESS QUICKLY Cheater call you him? I will bar no honest man my house, nor no cheater, but I do not love swaggering, by my troth, I am the worse when one says 'swagger'. Feel, masters, how I shake, look you, I warrant you.

DOLL TEARSHEET So you do, hostess.

MISTRESS QUICKLY Do I? Yea, in very truth do I, an 'twere an aspen leaf. I cannot abide swaggerers.   106

Enter Pistol, Bardolph, and the Page

PISTOL God save you, Sir John.

SIR JOHN Welcome, Ensign Pistol. Here, Pistol, I charge you with a cup of sack. Do you discharge upon mine hostess.   110

PISTOL I will discharge upon her, Sir John, with two bullets.

SIR JOHN She is pistol-proof, sir, you shall not hardly offend her.   114

MISTRESS QUICKLY Come, I'll drink no proofs, nor no bullets. I'll drink no more than will do me good, for no man's pleasure, I.

PISTOL Then to you, Mistress Dorothy! I will charge you.

DOLL TEARSHEET Charge me? I scorn you, scurvy companion. What, you poor, base, rascally, cheating, lack-linen mate! Away, you mouldy rogue, away! I am meat for your master.

PISTOL I know you, Mistress Dorothy.

DOLL TEARSHEET Away, you cutpurse rascal, you filthy bung, away! By this wine, I'll thrust my knife in your mouldy chaps an you play the saucy cuttle with me! ⌈She brandishes a knife⌉ Away, you bottle-ale rascal, you basket-hilt stale juggler, you! ⌈Pistol draws his sword⌉ Since when, I pray you, sir? God's light, with two points on your shoulder! Much!   130

PISTOL God let me not live, but I will murder your ruff for this.

MISTRESS QUICKLY No, good Captain Pistol; not here, sweet captain.   134

DOLL TEARSHEET Captain? Thou abominable damned cheater, art thou not ashamed to be called 'captain'? An captains were of my mind, they would truncheon you out, for taking their names upon you before you have earned them. You a captain? You slave! For what? For tearing a poor whore's ruff in a bawdy-house! He a captain? Hang him, rogue, he lives upon mouldy stewed prunes and dried cakes. A captain? God's light, these villains will make the word 'captain' odious; therefore captains had need look to't.

BARDOLPH Pray thee, go down, good ensign.   145

SIR JOHN Hark thee hither, Mistress Doll.

He takes her aside

PISTOL Not I! I tell thee what, Corporal Bardolph, I could tear her! I'll be revenged of her.

PAGE Pray thee, go down.

PISTOL I'll see her damned first   150
To Pluto's damned lake, by this hand,
To th'infernal deep,
Where Erebus, and tortures vile also.
'Hold hook and line!' say I.
Down, down, dogs; down, Fates.   155
Have we not Hiren here?

MISTRESS QUICKLY Good Captain Pizzle, be quiet. 'Tis very late, i'faith. I beseek you now, aggravate your choler.

PISTOL These be good humours indeed!
Shall pack-horses   160
And hollow pampered jades of Asia,
Which cannot go but thirty mile a day,
Compare with Caesars and with cannibals,
And Trojan Greeks?
Nay, rather damn them with King Cerberus,   165
And let the welkin roar. Shall we fall foul for toys?

MISTRESS QUICKLY By my troth, captain, these are very bitter words.

BARDOLPH Be gone, good ensign; this will grow to a brawl anon.   170

PISTOL
Die men like dogs! Give crowns like pins!
Have we not Hiren here?

MISTRESS QUICKLY O' my word, captain, there's none such here. What the goodyear, do you think I would deny her? For God's sake, be quiet.   175

PISTOL
Then feed and be fat, my fair Calipolis.
Come, give's some sack.
Si fortune me tormente, sperato me contento.
Fear we broadsides? No; let the fiend give fire!
Give me some sack; and, sweetheart, lie thou there.
⌈He lays down his sword⌉
Come we to full points here? And are etceteras   181
nothings?
⌈He drinks⌉

SIR JOHN Pistol, I would be quiet.

PISTOL Sweet knight, I kiss thy neaf. What, we have seen the seven stars!

DOLL TEARSHEET For God's sake, thrust him downstairs. I cannot endure such a fustian rascal.   186

PISTOL Thrust him downstairs? Know we not Galloway nags?

SIR JOHN Quoit him down, Bardolph, like a shove-groat shilling. Nay, an a do nothing but speak nothing, a shall be nothing here.   191

BARDOLPH (to Pistol) Come, get you downstairs.

PISTOL ⌈taking up his sword⌉
What, shall we have incision? Shall we imbrue?
Then death rock me asleep, abridge my doleful days.
Why then, let grievous, ghastly, gaping wounds   195
Untwine the Sisters Three. Come, Atropos, I say!

MISTRESS QUICKLY Here's goodly stuff toward!

SIR JOHN Give me my rapier, boy.

DOLL TEARSHEET I pray thee, Jack, I pray thee, do not draw.   200

SIR JOHN (taking his rapier and speaking to Pistol) Get you downstairs.

Sir John, Bardolph, and Pistol brawl

MISTRESS QUICKLY Here's a goodly tumult! I'll forswear keeping house afore I'll be in these tirrits and frights!

⌈Sir John thrusts at Pistol⌉
So!   205

⌈Pistol thrusts at Sir John⌉
Murder, I warrant now! Alas, alas, put up your naked weapons, put up your naked weapons!

Exit Pistol, pursued by Bardolph

DOLL TEARSHEET I pray thee, Jack, be quiet; the rascal's gone. Ah, you whoreson little valiant villain, you!

MISTRESS QUICKLY (to Sir John) Are you not hurt i'th' groin? Methought a made a shrewd thrust at your belly.

Enter Bardolph

SIR JOHN Have you turned him out o'doors?

BARDOLPH Yea, sir. The rascal's drunk. You have hurt him, sir, i'th' shoulder.   215

SIR JOHN A rascal, to brave me!

DOLL TEARSHEET Ah, you sweet little rogue, you! Alas, poor ape, how thou sweatest! Come, let me wipe thy face; come on, you whoreson chops. Ah rogue, i'faith, I love thee. Thou art as valorous as Hector of Troy, worth five of Agamemnon, and ten times better than the Nine Worthies. Ah, villain!

SIR JOHN A rascally slave! I will toss the rogue in a blanket.

DOLL TEARSHEET Do, an thou darest for thy heart. An thou dost, I'll canvas thee between a pair of sheets.   226

Enter musicians

PAGE The music is come, sir.

SIR JOHN Let them play.—Play, sirs!

⌈Music plays⌉
Sit on my knee, Doll. A rascal bragging slave! The rogue fled from me like quicksilver.   230

DOLL TEARSHEET I'faith, and thou followed'st him like a church. Thou whoreson little tidy Bartholomew boar-pig, when wilt thou leave fighting o'days, and foining o'nights, and begin to patch up thine old body for heaven?   235

Enter Prince Harry and Poins, disguised as drawers

SIR JOHN Peace, good Doll, do not speak like a death's-head, do not bid me remember mine end.

DOLL TEARSHEET Sirrah, what humour's the Prince of?

SIR JOHN A good shallow young fellow. A would have made a good pantler; a would ha' chipped bread well.

DOLL TEARSHEET They say Poins has a good wit.   241

SIR JOHN He a good wit? Hang him, baboon! His wit's as thick as Tewkesbury mustard; there's no more conceit in him than is in a mallet.   244

DOLL TEARSHEET Why does the Prince love him so, then?

SIR JOHN Because their legs are both of a bigness, and a plays at quoits well, and eats conger and fennel, and drinks off candles' ends for flap-dragons, and rides the wild mare with the boys, and jumps upon joint-stools, and swears with a good grace, and wears his boot very smooth like unto the sign of the leg, and breeds no bate with telling of discreet stories, and such other gambol faculties a has that show a weak mind and an able body; for the which the Prince admits him; for the Prince himself is such another—the weight of a hair will turn the scales between their avoirdupois. 256

PRINCE HARRY (aside to Poins) Would not this nave of a wheel have his ears cut off?

POINS Let's beat him before his whore.

PRINCE HARRY Look whe'er the withered elder hath not his poll clawed like a parrot.   261

POINS Is it not strange that desire should so many years outlive performance?

SIR JOHN Kiss me, Doll.

They kiss

PRINCE HARRY (aside to Poins) Saturn and Venus this year in conjunction! What says th'almanac to that?   266

POINS And look whether the fiery Trigon his man be not lisping to his master's old tables, his note-book, his counsel-keeper!

SIR JOHN (to Doll) Thou dost give me flattering busses. 270

DOLL TEARSHEET By my troth, I kiss thee with a most constant heart.

SIR JOHN I am old, I am old.

DOLL TEARSHEET I love thee better than I love e'er a scurvy young boy of them all.   275

SIR JOHN What stuff wilt have a kirtle of? I shall receive money o'Thursday; shalt have a cap tomorrow.—A merry song!

⌈The music plays again⌉
Come, it grows late; we'll to bed. Thou'lt forget me when I am gone.   280

DOLL TEARSHEET By my troth, thou'lt set me a-weeping an thou sayst so. Prove that ever I dress myself handsome till thy return—well, hearken a'th' end.

SIR JOHN Some sack, Francis.

PRINCE and POINS (*coming forward*) Anon, anon, sir.   285
SIR JOHN Ha, a bastard son of the King's!—And art not
thou Poins his brother?
PRINCE HARRY Why, thou globe of sinful continents, what
a life dost thou lead!
SIR JOHN A better than thou: I am a gentleman, thou art
a drawer.   291
PRINCE HARRY Very true, sir, and I come to draw you out
by the ears.
MISTRESS QUICKLY O, the Lord preserve thy grace! By my
troth, welcome to London! Now the Lord bless that
sweet face of thine! O Jesu, are you come from Wales?
SIR JOHN (*to Prince Harry*) Thou whoreson mad compound
of majesty! By this light—flesh and corrupt blood, thou
art welcome.
DOLL TEARSHEET How, you fat fool? I scorn you.   300
POINS (*to Prince Harry*) My lord, he will drive you out of
your revenge and turn all to a merriment, if you take
not the heat.
PRINCE HARRY (*to Sir John*) You whoreson candlemine you,
how vilely did you speak of me now, before this honest,
virtuous, civil gentlewoman!   306
MISTRESS QUICKLY God's blessing of your good heart, and
so she is, by my troth!
SIR JOHN (*to Prince Harry*) Didst thou hear me?   309
PRINCE HARRY Yea, and you knew me as you did when
you ran away by Gads Hill; you knew I was at your
back, and spoke it on purpose to try my patience.
SIR JOHN No, no, no, not so, I did not think thou wast
within hearing.
PRINCE HARRY I shall drive you, then, to confess the wilful
abuse, and then I know how to handle you.   316
SIR JOHN No abuse, Hal; o'mine honour, no abuse.
PRINCE HARRY Not? To dispraise me, and call me 'pantler'
and 'bread-chipper' and I know not what?
SIR JOHN No abuse, Hal.   320
POINS No abuse?
SIR JOHN No abuse, Ned, i'th' world, honest Ned, none.
I dispraised him before the wicked, that the wicked
might not fall in love with him; (*to Prince Harry*) in
which doing I have done the part of a careful friend
and a true subject, and thy father is to give me thanks
for it. No abuse, Hal; none, Ned, none; no, faith, boys,
none.
PRINCE HARRY See now whether pure fear and entire
cowardice doth not make thee wrong this virtuous
gentlewoman to close with us. Is she of the wicked? Is
thine hostess here of the wicked? Or is thy boy of the
wicked? Or honest Bardolph, whose zeal burns in his
nose, of the wicked?
POINS (*to Sir John*) Answer, thou dead elm, answer.   335
SIR JOHN The fiend hath pricked down Bardolph
irrecoverable, and his face is Lucifer's privy kitchen,
where he doth nothing but roast malt-worms. For the
boy, there is a good angel about him, but the devil
outbids him, too.   340
PRINCE HARRY For the women?
SIR JOHN For one of them, she's in hell already, and burns
poor souls. For th'other, I owe her money, and whether
she be damned for that I know not.
MISTRESS QUICKLY No, I warrant you.   345
SIR JOHN No, I think thou art not; I think thou art quit
for that. Marry, there is another indictment upon thee,
for suffering flesh to be eaten in thy house, contrary
to the law, for the which I think thou wilt howl.
MISTRESS QUICKLY All victuallers do so. What's a joint of
mutton or two in a whole Lent?   351
PRINCE HARRY You, gentlewoman—
DOLL TEARSHEET What says your grace?
SIR JOHN His grace says that which his flesh rebels against.
Peto knocks at door within
MISTRESS QUICKLY Who knocks so loud at door? (*Calls*)
Look to th' door there, Francis.   356
Enter Peto
PRINCE HARRY Peto, how now, what news?
PETO
The King your father is at Westminster;
And there are twenty weak and wearied posts
Come from the north; and as I came along   360
I met and overtook a dozen captains,
Bareheaded, sweating, knocking at the taverns,
And asking every one for Sir John Falstaff.
PRINCE HARRY
By heaven, Poins, I feel me much to blame
So idly to profane the precious time,   365
When tempest of commotion, like the south
Borne with black vapour, doth begin to melt
And drop upon our bare unarmèd heads.—
Give me my sword and cloak.—Falstaff, good night.
Exeunt Prince Harry and Poins
SIR JOHN Now comes in the sweetest morsel of the night,
and we must hence and leave it unpicked.   371
Knocking within. ⌈*Exit Bardolph*⌉
More knocking at the door!
Enter Bardolph
How now, what's the matter?
BARDOLPH
You must away to court, sir, presently.
A dozen captains stay at door for you.   375
SIR JOHN ⌈*to the Page*⌉ Pay the musicians, sirrah. Farewell,
hostess; farewell, Doll. You see, my good wenches, how
men of merit are sought after. The undeserver may
sleep, when the man of action is called on. Farewell,
good wenches. If I be not sent away post, I will see
you again ere I go.   ⌈*Exeunt musicians*⌉
DOLL TEARSHEET ⌈*weeping*⌉ I cannot speak. If my heart be
not ready to burst—well, sweet Jack, have a care of
thyself.
SIR JOHN Farewell, farewell!   385
Exit ⌈*with Bardolph, Peto, and the Page*⌉
MISTRESS QUICKLY Well, fare thee well. I have known thee
these twenty-nine years come peascod-time, but an
honester and truer-hearted man—well, fare thee well.
⌈*Enter Bardolph*⌉
BARDOLPH Mistress Tearsheet!
MISTRESS QUICKLY What's the matter?   390

BARDOLPH Bid Mistress Tearsheet come to my master.
⌈*Exit*⌉
MISTRESS QUICKLY O run, Doll; run, run, good Doll!
Exeunt ⌈*Doll at one door, Mistress Quickly at*
another door⌉

3.1 *Enter King Henry in his nightgown, with a page*
KING HENRY (*giving letters*)
   Go call the Earls of Surrey and of Warwick.
   But ere they come, bid them o'er-read these letters
   And well consider of them. Make good speed.
                                            Exit page
   How many thousand of my poorest subjects
   Are at this hour asleep? O sleep, O gentle sleep,   5
   Nature's soft nurse, how have I frighted thee,
   That thou no more wilt weigh my eyelids down
   And steep my senses in forgetfulness?
   Why rather, sleep, liest thou in smoky cribs,
   Upon uneasy pallets stretching thee,   10
   And hushed with buzzing night-flies to thy slumber,
   Than in the perfumed chambers of the great,
   Under the canopies of costly state,
   And lulled with sound of sweetest melody?
   O thou dull god, why li'st thou with the vile   15
   In loathsome beds, and leav'st the kingly couch
   A watch-case, or a common 'larum-bell?
   Wilt thou upon the high and giddy mast
   Seal up the ship-boy's eyes, and rock his brains
   In cradle of the rude imperious surge,   20
   And in the visitation of the winds,
   Who take the ruffian billows by the top,
   Curling their monstrous heads, and hanging them
   With deafing clamour in the slippery clouds,
   That, with the hurly, death itself awakes?   25
   Canst thou, O partial sleep, give thy repose
   To the wet sea-boy in an hour so rude,
   And in the calmest and most stillest night,
   With all appliances and means to boot,
   Deny it to a king? Then happy low, lie down.   30
   Uneasy lies the head that wears a crown.
      Enter the Earls of Warwick and Surrey
WARWICK
   Many good morrows to your majesty!
KING HENRY
   Is it good morrow, lords?
WARWICK   'Tis one o'clock, and past.
KING HENRY
   Why then, good morrow to you all, my lords.
   Have you read o'er the letter that I sent you?   35
WARWICK We have, my liege.
KING HENRY
   Then you perceive the body of our kingdom,
   How foul it is, what rank diseases grow,
   And with what danger near the heart of it.
WARWICK
   It is but as a body yet distempered,   40
   Which to his former strength may be restored

   With good advice and little medicine.
   My lord Northumberland will soon be cooled.
KING HENRY
   O God, that one might read the book of fate,
   And see the revolution of the times   45
   Make mountains level, and the continent,
   Weary of solid firmness, melt itself
   Into the sea; and other times to see
   The beachy girdle of the ocean
   Too wide for Neptune's hips; how chance's mocks   50
   And changes fill the cup of alteration
   With divers liquors! 'Tis not ten years gone
   Since Richard and Northumberland, great friends,
   Did feast together; and in two year after
   Were they at wars. It is but eight years since   55
   This Percy was the man nearest my soul,
   Who like a brother toiled in my affairs,
   And laid his love and life under my foot,
   Yea, for my sake, even to the eyes of Richard
   Gave him defiance. But which of you was by—   60
   (*To Warwick*) You, cousin Neville, as I may
      remember—
   When Richard, with his eye brimful of tears,
   Then checked and rated by Northumberland,
   Did speak these words, now proved a prophecy?—
   'Northumberland, thou ladder by the which   65
   My cousin Bolingbroke ascends my throne'—
   Though then, God knows, I had no such intent,
   But that necessity so bowed the state
   That I and greatness were compelled to kiss—
   'The time shall come'—thus did he follow it—   70
   'The time will come that foul sin, gathering head,
   Shall break into corruption'; so went on,
   Foretelling this same time's condition,
   And the division of our amity.
WARWICK
   There is a history in all men's lives   75
   Figuring the natures of the times deceased;
   The which observed, a man may prophesy,
   With a near aim, of the main chance of things
   As yet not come to life, who in their seeds
   And weak beginnings lie intreasurèd.   80
   Such things become the hatch and brood of time;
   And by the necessary form of this
   King Richard might create a perfect guess
   That great Northumberland, then false to him,
   Would of that seed grow to a greater falseness,   85
   Which should not find a ground to root upon
   Unless on you.
KING HENRY   Are these things then necessities?
   Then let us meet them like necessities;
   And that same word even now cries out on us.
   They say the Bishop and Northumberland   90
   Are fifty thousand strong.
WARWICK   It cannot be, my lord.
   Rumour doth double, like the voice and echo,
   The numbers of the feared. Please it your grace

To go to bed? Upon my soul, my lord,
The powers that you already have sent forth   95
Shall bring this prize in very easily.
To comfort you the more, I have received
A certain instance that Glyndŵr is dead.
Your majesty hath been this fortnight ill,
And these unseasoned hours perforce must add   100
Unto your sickness.
KING HENRY   I will take your counsel.
And were these inward wars once out of hand,
We would, dear lords, unto the Holy Land.   *Exeunt*

3.2 *Enter Justice Shallow and Justice Silence*

SHALLOW Come on, come on, come on! Give me your
hand, sir, give me your hand, sir. An early stirrer, by
the rood! And how doth my good cousin Silence?
SILENCE Good morrow, good cousin Shallow.   4
SHALLOW And how doth my cousin your bedfellow? And
your fairest daughter and mine, my god-daughter Ellen?
SILENCE Alas, a black ouzel, cousin Shallow.
SHALLOW By yea and no, sir, I dare say my cousin William
is become a good scholar. He is at Oxford still, is he
not?   10
SILENCE Indeed, sir, to my cost.
SHALLOW A must then to the Inns o' Court shortly. I was
once of Clement's Inn, where I think they will talk of
mad Shallow yet.
SILENCE You were called 'lusty Shallow' then, cousin. 15
SHALLOW By the mass, I was called anything; and I would
have done anything indeed, too, and roundly, too.
There was I, and little John Doit of Staffordshire, and
black George Barnes, and Francis Pickbone, and Will
Squeal, a Cotswold man; you had not four such swinge-
bucklers in all the Inns o' Court again. And I may say
to you, we knew where the bona-robas were, and had
the best of them all at commandment. Then was Jack
Falstaff, now Sir John, a boy, and page to Thomas
Mowbray, Duke of Norfolk.   25
SILENCE This Sir John, cousin, that comes hither anon
about soldiers?
SHALLOW The same Sir John, the very same. I see him
break Scoggin's head at the court gate when a was a
crack, not thus high. And the very same day did I fight
with one Samson Stockfish, a fruiterer, behind Gray's
Inn. Jesu, Jesu, the mad days that I have spent! And
to see how many of my old acquaintance are dead.
SILENCE We shall all follow, cousin.   34
SHALLOW Certain, 'tis certain; very sure, very sure. Death,
as the Psalmist saith, is certain to all; all shall die.
How a good yoke of bullocks at Stamford fair?
SILENCE By my troth, I was not there.
SHALLOW Death is certain. Is old Double of your town
living yet?   40
SILENCE Dead, sir.
SHALLOW Jesu, Jesu, dead! A drew a good bow; and dead!
A shot a fine shoot. John o' Gaunt loved him well, and
betted much money on his head. Dead! A would have
clapped i'th' clout at twelve score, and carried you a
forehand shaft a fourteen and fourteen and a half, that

it would have done a man's heart good to see. How a
score of ewes now?
SILENCE Thereafter as they be. A score of good ewes may
be worth ten pounds.   50
SHALLOW And is old Double dead?
Enter Bardolph and ⌈the Page⌉
SILENCE Here come two of Sir John Falstaff's men, as I
think.
⌈SHALLOW⌉ Good morrow, honest gentlemen.
BARDOLPH I beseech you, which is Justice Shallow?   55
SHALLOW I am Robert Shallow, sir, a poor esquire of this
county, and one of the King's Justices of the Peace.
What is your good pleasure with me?
BARDOLPH My captain, sir, commends him to you—my
captain Sir John Falstaff, a tall gentleman, by heaven,
and a most gallant leader.   61
SHALLOW He greets me well, sir. I knew him a good
backsword man. How doth the good knight? May I ask
how my lady his wife doth?
BARDOLPH Sir, pardon, a soldier is better accommodated
than with a wife.   66
SHALLOW It is well said, in faith, sir, and it is well said
indeed, too. 'Better accommodated'—it is good; yea,
indeed is it. Good phrases are surely, and ever were,
very commendable. 'Accommodated'—it comes of
'accommodo'. Very good, a good phrase.   71
BARDOLPH Pardon, sir, I have heard the word—'phrase'
call you it?—By this day, I know not the phrase; but
I will maintain the word with my sword to be a soldier-
like word, and a word of exceeding good command, by
heaven. 'Accommodated'; that is, when a man is, as
they say, accommodated; or when a man is being
whereby a may be thought to be accommodated; which
is an excellent thing.   79
Enter Sir John Falstaff
SHALLOW It is very just. Look, here comes good Sir John.
(*To Sir John*) Give me your hand, give me your worship's
good hand. By my troth, you like well, and bear your
years very well. Welcome, good Sir John.
SIR JOHN I am glad to see you well, good Master Robert
Shallow. (*To Silence*) Master Surecard, as I think. 85
SHALLOW No, Sir John, it is my cousin Silence, in
commission with me.
SIR JOHN Good Master Silence, it well befits you should
be of the peace.
SILENCE Your good worship is welcome.   90
SIR JOHN Fie, this is hot weather, gentlemen. Have you
provided me here half a dozen sufficient men?
SHALLOW Marry, have we, sir. Will you sit?
SIR JOHN Let me see them, I beseech you.   94
⌈*He sits*⌉
SHALLOW Where's the roll, where's the roll, where's the
roll? Let me see, let me see, let me see; so, so, so, so,
so. Yea, marry, sir: 'Ralph Mouldy'. ⌈*To Silence*⌉ Let
them appear as I call, let them do so, let them do so.
Let me see, (*calls*) where is Mouldy?
⌈*Enter Mouldy*⌉
MOULDY Here, an't please you.   100

SHALLOW What think you, Sir John? A good-limbed fellow, young, strong, and of good friends.

SIR JOHN Is thy name Mouldy?

MOULDY Yea, an't please you.

SIR JOHN 'Tis the more time thou wert used.   105

SHALLOW Ha, ha, ha, most excellent, i'faith! Things that are mouldy lack use. Very singular good, in faith, well said, Sir John, very well said.

SIR JOHN Prick him.   109

MOULDY I was pricked well enough before, an you could have let me alone. My old dame will be undone now for one to do her husbandry and her drudgery. You need not to have pricked me; there are other men fitter to go out than I.

SIR JOHN Go to, peace, Mouldy. You shall go, Mouldy; it is time you were spent.   116

MOULDY Spent?

SHALLOW Peace, fellow, peace. Stand aside; know you where you are?   119

⌈Mouldy stands aside⌉

For th'other, Sir John, let me see: 'Simon Shadow'—

SIR JOHN Yea, marry, let me have him to sit under. He's like to be a cold soldier.

SHALLOW (calls) Where's Shadow?

⌈Enter Shadow⌉

SHADOW Here, sir.

SIR JOHN Shadow, whose son art thou?   125

SHADOW My mother's son, sir.

SIR JOHN Thy mother's son! Like enough, and thy father's shadow. So the son of the female is the shadow of the male—it is often so indeed—but not of the father's substance.   130

SHALLOW Do you like him, Sir John?

SIR JOHN Shadow will serve for summer. Prick him, for we have a number of shadows fill up the muster book.

⌈Shadow stands aside⌉

SHALLOW (calls) 'Thomas Wart.'

SIR JOHN Where's he?   135

⌈Enter Wart⌉

WART Here, sir.

SIR JOHN Is thy name Wart?

WART Yea, sir.

SIR JOHN Thou art a very ragged wart.

SHALLOW Shall I prick him, Sir John?   140

SIR JOHN It were superfluous, for his apparel is built upon his back, and the whole frame stands upon pins. Prick him no more.

SHALLOW Ha, ha, ha, you can do it, sir, you can do it! I commend you well.   145

⌈Wart stands aside⌉

(Calls) 'Francis Feeble.'

⌈Enter Feeble⌉

FEEBLE Here, sir.

SHALLOW What trade art thou, Feeble?

FEEBLE A woman's tailor, sir.

SHALLOW Shall I prick him, Sir John?   150

SIR JOHN You may, but if he had been a man's tailor, he'd ha' pricked you. (To Feeble) Wilt thou make as many holes in an enemy's battle as thou hast done in a woman's petticoat?   154

FEEBLE I will do my good will, sir; you can have no more.

SIR JOHN Well said, good woman's tailor; well said, courageous Feeble! Thou wilt be as valiant as the wrathful dove or most magnanimous mouse. Prick the woman's tailor. Well, Master Shallow; deep, Master Shallow.   160

FEEBLE I would Wart might have gone, sir.

SIR JOHN I would thou wert a man's tailor, that thou mightst mend him and make him fit to go. I cannot put him to a private soldier that is the leader of so many thousands. Let that suffice, most forcible Feeble.

FEEBLE It shall suffice, sir.   166

SIR JOHN I am bound to thee, reverend Feeble.

⌈Feeble stands aside⌉

Who is next?

SHALLOW (calls) 'Peter Bullcalf o'th' green.'

SIR JOHN Yea, marry, let's see Bullcalf.   170

⌈Enter Bullcalf⌉

BULLCALF Here, sir.

SIR JOHN Fore God, a likely fellow! Come, prick Bullcalf till he roar again.

BULLCALF O Lord, good my lord captain!

SIR JOHN What, dost thou roar before thou'rt pricked?

BULLCALF O Lord, sir, I am a diseased man.   176

SIR JOHN What disease hast thou?

BULLCALF A whoreson cold, sir; a cough, sir, which I caught with ringing in the King's affairs upon his coronation day, sir.   180

SIR JOHN Come, thou shalt go to the wars in a gown. We will have away thy cold, and I will take such order that thy friends shall ring for thee.

⌈Bullcalf stands aside⌉

Is here all?   184

SHALLOW There is two more called than your number. You must have but four here, sir, and so I pray you go in with me to dinner.

SIR JOHN Come, I will go drink with you, but I cannot tarry dinner. I am glad to see you, by my troth, Master Shallow.   190

SHALLOW O, Sir John, do you remember since we lay all night in the Windmill in Saint George's Field?

SIR JOHN No more of that, good Master Shallow, no more of that.

SHALLOW Ha, 'twas a merry night! And is Jane Nightwork alive?   196

SIR JOHN She lives, Master Shallow.

SHALLOW She never could away with me.

SIR JOHN Never, never. She would always say she could not abide Master Shallow.   200

SHALLOW By the mass, I could anger her to th' heart. She was then a bona-roba. Doth she hold her own well?

SIR JOHN Old, old, Master Shallow.

SHALLOW Nay, she must be old; she cannot choose but be old; certain she's old; and had Robin Nightwork by old Nightwork before I came to Clement's Inn.   206

SILENCE That's fifty-five year ago.

SHALLOW Ha, cousin Silence, that thou hadst seen that
    that this knight and I have seen! Ha, Sir John, said I
    well?   210
SIR JOHN We have heard the chimes at midnight, Master
    Shallow.
SHALLOW That we have, that we have; in faith, Sir John,
    we have. Our watchword was 'Hem boys!' Come, let's
    to dinner; come, let's to dinner. Jesus, the days that
    we have seen! Come, come.   216
                        Exeunt Shallow, Silence, and Sir John
BULLCALF ⌈*coming forward*⌉ Good Master Corporate
    Bardolph, stand my friend, and here's four Harry ten
    shillings in French crowns for you. In very truth, sir,
    I had as lief be hanged, sir, as go. And yet for mine
    own part, sir, I do not care; but rather because I am
    unwilling, and, for mine own part, have a desire to
    stay with my friends. Else, sir, I did not care, for mine
    own part, so much.
BARDOLPH ⌈*taking the money*⌉ Go to; stand aside.   225
                        ⌈*Bullcalf stands aside*⌉
MOULDY ⌈*coming forward*⌉ And, good Master Corporal
    Captain, for my old dame's sake stand my friend. She
    has nobody to do anything about her when I am gone,
    and she is old and cannot help herself. You shall have
    forty, sir.   230
BARDOLPH Go to; stand aside.
                        ⌈*Mouldy stands aside*⌉
FEEBLE By my troth, I care not. A man can die but once.
    We owe God a death. I'll ne'er bear a base mind. An't
    be my destiny, so; an't be not, so. No man's too good
    to serve's prince. And let it go which way it will, he
    that dies this year is quit for the next.   236
BARDOLPH Well said; thou'rt a good fellow.
FEEBLE Faith, I'll bear no base mind.
            Enter Sir John Falstaff, Shallow, and Silence
SIR JOHN Come, sir, which men shall I have?
SHALLOW Four of which you please.   240
BARDOLPH (*to Sir John*) Sir, a word with you. (*Aside to him*)
    I have three pound to free Mouldy and Bullcalf.
SIR JOHN Go to, well.
SHALLOW Come, Sir John, which four will you have?
SIR JOHN Do you choose for me.   245
SHALLOW Marry, then: Mouldy, Bullcalf, Feeble, and
    Shadow.
SIR JOHN Mouldy and Bullcalf. For you, Mouldy, stay at
    home till you are past service; and for your part,
    Bullcalf, grow till you come unto it. I will none of you.
                        ⌈*Exeunt Bullcalf and Mouldy*⌉
SHALLOW Sir John, Sir John, do not yourself wrong. They
    are your likeliest men, and I would have you served
    with the best.
SIR JOHN Will you tell me, Master Shallow, how to choose
    a man? Care I for the limb, the thews, the stature,
    bulk, and big assemblance of a man? Give me the spirit,
    Master Shallow. Here's Wart; you see what a ragged
    appearance it is? A shall charge you and discharge you
    with the motion of a pewterer's hammer, come off and
    on swifter than he that gibbets on the brewer's bucket.

And this same half-faced fellow Shadow; give me this
    man. He presents no mark to the enemy; the foeman
    may with as great aim level at the edge of a penknife.
    And for a retreat, how swiftly will this Feeble the
    woman's tailor run off! O, give me the spare men, and
    spare me the great ones.—Put me a caliver into Wart's
    hand, Bardolph.
BARDOLPH (*giving Wart a caliver*) Hold, Wart. Traverse—
    thas, thas, thas!   269
                        ⌈*Wart marches*⌉
SIR JOHN (*to Wart*) Come, manage me your caliver. So;
    very well. Go to, very good, exceeding good. O, give
    me always a little, lean, old, chapped, bald shot! Well
    said, i'faith, Wart; thou'rt a good scab. Hold; (*giving
    a coin*) there's a tester for thee.   274
SHALLOW He is not his craft's master; he doth not do it
    right. I remember at Mile-End Green, when I lay at
    Clement's Inn—I was then Sir Dagonet in Arthur's
    show—there was a little quiver fellow, and a would
    manage you his piece thus, and a would about and
    about, and come you in and come you in. 'Ra-ta-ta!'
    would a say; 'Bounce!' would a say; and away again
    would a go; and again would a come. I shall ne'er see
    such a fellow.
SIR JOHN These fellows will do well, Master Shallow. God
    keep you, Master Silence; I will not use many words
    with you. Fare you well, gentlemen both; I thank you.
    I must a dozen mile tonight.—Bardolph, give the
    soldiers coats.
SHALLOW Sir John, the Lord bless you; God prosper your
    affairs! God send us peace! As you return, visit my
    house; let our old acquaintance be renewed.
    Peradventure I will with ye to the court.
SIR JOHN Fore God, would you would!
SHALLOW Go to, I have spoke at a word. God keep you!
SIR JOHN Fare you well, gentle gentlemen.   295
                        Exeunt Shallow and Silence
On, Bardolph, lead the men away.
                Exeunt Bardolph, Wart, Shadow, and Feeble
As I return, I will fetch off these justices. I do see the
    bottom of Justice Shallow. Lord, Lord, how subject we
    old men are to this vice of lying! This same starved
    justice hath done nothing but prate to me of the
    wildness of his youth and the feats he hath done about
    Turnbull Street; and every third word a lie, duer paid
    to the hearer than the Turk's tribute. I do remember
    him at Clement's Inn, like a man made after supper of
    a cheese paring. When a was naked, he was for all the
    world like a forked radish, with a head fantastically
    carved upon it with a knife. A was so forlorn that his
    dimensions, to any thick sight, were invisible. A was
    the very genius of famine. And now is this Vice's dagger
    become a squire, and talks as familiarly of John o'
    Gaunt as if he had been sworn brother to him, and I'll
    be sworn a ne'er saw him but once, in the Tilt-yard,
    and then he burst his head for crowding among the
    marshal's men. I saw it, and told John o' Gaunt he
    beat his own name; for you might have trussed him

and all his apparel into an eel-skin. The case of a treble
hautboy was a mansion for him, a court. And now has
he land and beeves. Well, I'll be acquainted with him
if I return; and't shall go hard but I'll make him a
philosopher's two stones to me. If the young dace be
a bait for the old pike, I see no reason in the law of
nature but I may snap at him. Let time shape, and
there an end.   *Exit*

4.1   *Enter ⌈in arms⌉ the Archbishop of York, Thomas*
        Mowbray, Lord Hastings, and ⌈Coleville⌉, within
        the Forest of Gaultres

ARCHBISHOP OF YORK What is this forest called?

HASTINGS
'Tis Gaultres Forest, an't shall please your grace.

ARCHBISHOP OF YORK
Here stand, my lords, and send discoverers forth
To know the numbers of our enemies.

HASTINGS
We have sent forth already.

ARCHBISHOP OF YORK   'Tis well done.   5
My friends and brethren in these great affairs,
I must acquaint you that I have received
New-dated letters from Northumberland,
Their cold intent, tenor, and substance, thus:
Here doth he wish his person, with such powers   10
As might hold sortance with his quality,
The which he could not levy; whereupon
He is retired to ripe his growing fortunes
To Scotland, and concludes in hearty prayers
That your attempts may overlive the hazard   15
And fearful meeting of their opposite.

MOWBRAY
Thus do the hopes we have in him touch ground
And dash themselves to pieces.
        Enter a Messenger

HASTINGS   Now, what news?

MESSENGER
West of this forest, scarcely off a mile,
In goodly form comes on the enemy;   20
And, by the ground they hide, I judge their number
Upon or near the rate of thirty thousand.

MOWBRAY
The just proportion that we gave them out.
Let us sway on, and face them in the field.
        Enter the Earl of Westmorland

ARCHBISHOP OF YORK
What well-appointed leader fronts us here?   25

MOWBRAY
I think it is my lord of Westmorland.

WESTMORLAND
Health and fair greeting from our general,
The Prince, Lord John and Duke of Lancaster.

ARCHBISHOP OF YORK
Say on, my lord of Westmorland, in peace,
What doth concern your coming.

WESTMORLAND   Then, my lord,   30

Unto your grace do I in chief address
The substance of my speech. If that rebellion
Came like itself, in base and abject routs,
Led on by bloody youth, guarded with rags,
And countenanced by boys and beggary;   35
I say, if damned commotion so appeared
In his true native and most proper shape,
You, reverend father, and these noble lords
Had not been here to dress the ugly form
Of base and bloody insurrection   40
With your fair honours. You, Lord Archbishop,
Whose see is by a civil peace maintained,
Whose beard the silver hand of peace hath touched,
Whose learning and good letters peace hath tutored,
Whose white investments figure innocence,   45
The dove and very blessèd spirit of peace,
Wherefore do you so ill translate yourself
Out of the speech of peace that bears such grace
Into the harsh and boist'rous tongue of war,
Turning your books to graves, your ink to blood,   50
Your pens to lances, and your tongue divine
To a loud trumpet and a point of war?

ARCHBISHOP OF YORK
Wherefore do I this? So the question stands.
Briefly, to this end: we are all diseased,
And with our surfeiting and wanton hours   55
Have brought ourselves into a burning fever,
And we must bleed for it—of which disease
Our late King Richard, being infected, died.
But, my most noble lord of Westmorland,
I take not on me here as a physician,   60
Nor do I as an enemy to peace
Troop in the throngs of military men;
But rather show a while like fearful war
To diet rank minds, sick of happiness,
And purge th'obstructions which begin to stop   65
Our very veins of life. Hear me more plainly.
I have in equal balance justly weighed
What wrongs our arms may do, what wrongs we suffer,
And find our griefs heavier than our offences.
We see which way the stream of time doth run,   70
And are enforced from our most quiet shore
By the rough torrent of occasion;
And have the summary of all our griefs,
When time shall serve, to show in articles,
Which long ere this we offered to the King,   75
And might by no suit gain our audience.
When we are wronged, and would unfold our griefs,
We are denied access unto his person
Even by those men that most have done us wrong.
The dangers of the days but newly gone,   80
Whose memory is written on the earth
With yet appearing blood, and the examples
Of every minute's instance, present now,
Hath put us in these ill-beseeming arms,
Not to break peace, or any branch of it,   85
But to establish here a peace indeed,
Concurring both in name and quality.

WESTMORLAND
Whenever yet was your appeal denied?
Wherein have you been gallèd by the King?
What peer hath been suborned to grate on you,   90
That you should seal this lawless bloody book
Of forged rebellion with a seal divine?
ARCHBISHOP OF YORK
My brother general, the commonwealth
I make my quarrel in particular.
WESTMORLAND
There is no need of any such redress;   95
Or if there were, it not belongs to you.
MOWBRAY
Why not to him in part, and to us all
That feel the bruises of the days before,
And suffer the condition of these times
To lay a heavy and unequal hand   100
Upon our honours?
WESTMORLAND   O my good Lord Mowbray,
Construe the times to their necessities,
And you shall say indeed it is the time,
And not the King, that doth you injuries.
Yet for your part, it not appears to me,   105
Either from the King or in the present time,
That you should have an inch of any ground
To build a grief on. Were you not restored
To all the Duke of Norfolk's signories,
Your noble and right well-remembered father's?   110
MOWBRAY
What thing in honour had my father lost
That need to be revived and breathed in me?
The King that loved him, as the state stood then,
Was force perforce compelled to banish him;
And then that Henry Bolingbroke and he,   115
Being mounted and both rousèd in their seats,
Their neighing coursers daring of the spur,
Their armèd staves in charge, their beavers down,
Their eyes of fire sparkling through sights of steel,
And the loud trumpet blowing them together,   120
Then, then, when there was nothing could have stayed
My father from the breast of Bolingbroke—
O, when the King did throw his warder down,
His own life hung upon the staff he threw;
Then threw he down himself and all their lives   125
That by indictment and by dint of sword
Have since miscarried under Bolingbroke.
WESTMORLAND
You speak, Lord Mowbray, now you know not what.
The Earl of Hereford was reputed then
In England the most valiant gentleman.   130
Who knows on whom fortune would then have
     smiled?
But if your father had been victor there,
He ne'er had borne it out of Coventry;
For all the country in a general voice
135 Cried hate upon him, and all their prayers and love
Were set on Hereford, whom they doted on   136
And blessed and graced, indeed, more than the King.

But this is mere digression from my purpose.
Here come I from our princely general
To know your griefs, to tell you from his grace   140
That he will give you audience; and wherein
It shall appear that your demands are just,
You shall enjoy them, everything set off
That might so much as think you enemies.
MOWBRAY
But he hath forced us to compel this offer,   145
And it proceeds from policy, not love.
WESTMORLAND
Mowbray, you overween to take it so.
This offer comes from mercy, not from fear;
For lo, within a ken our army lies,
Upon mine honour, all too confident   150
To give admittance to a thought of fear.
Our battle is more full of names than yours,
Our men more perfect in the use of arms,
Our armour all as strong, our cause the best.
Then reason will our hearts should be as good.   155
Say you not then our offer is compelled.
MOWBRAY
Well, by my will we shall admit no parley.
WESTMORLAND
That argues but the shame of your offence.
A rotten case abides no handling.
HASTINGS
Hath the Prince John a full commission,   160
In very ample virtue of his father,
To hear and absolutely to determine
Of what conditions we shall stand upon?
WESTMORLAND
That is intended in the general's name.
I muse you make so slight a question.   165
ARCHBISHOP OF YORK
Then take, my lord of Westmorland, this schedule;
For this contains our general grievances.
Each several article herein redressed,
All members of our cause, both here and hence,
That are ensinewed to this action   170
Acquitted by a true substantial form,
And present execution of our wills
To us and to our purposes consigned,
We come within our awe-full banks again,
And knit our powers to the arm of peace.   175
WESTMORLAND (taking the schedule)
This will I show the general. Please you, lords,
In sight of both our battles we may meet,
And either end in peace—which God so frame—
Or to the place of diff'rence call the swords
Which must decide it.
ARCHBISHOP OF YORK   My lord, we will do so.   180
                                   Exit Westmorland
MOWBRAY
There is a thing within my bosom tells me
That no conditions of our peace can stand.
HASTINGS
Fear you not that. If we can make our peace

Upon such large terms and so absolute
As our conditions shall consist upon,   185
Our peace shall stand as firm as rocky mountains.
MOWBRAY
Yea, but our valuation shall be such
That every slight and false-derivèd cause,
Yea, every idle, nice, and wanton reason,
Shall to the King taste of this action,   190
That, were our royal faiths martyrs in love,
We shall be winnowed with so rough a wind
That even our corn shall seem as light as chaff,
And good from bad find no partition.
ARCHBISHOP OF YORK
No, no, my lord; note this. The King is weary   195
Of dainty and such picking grievances,
For he hath found to end one doubt by death
Revives two greater in the heirs of life;
And therefore will he wipe his tables clean,
And keep no tell-tale to his memory   200
That may repeat and history his loss
To new remembrance; for full well he knows
He cannot so precisely weed this land
As his misdoubts present occasion.
His foes are so enrooted with his friends   205
That, plucking to unfix an enemy,
He doth unfasten so and shake a friend;
So that this land, like an offensive wife
That hath enragèd him on to offer strokes,
As he is striking, holds his infant up,   210
And hangs resolved correction in the arm
That was upreared to execution.
HASTINGS
Besides, the King hath wasted all his rods
On late offenders, that he now doth lack
The very instruments of chastisement;   215
So that his power, like to a fangless lion,
May offer, but not hold.
ARCHBISHOP OF YORK   'Tis very true.
And therefore be assured, my good Lord Marshal,
If we do now make our atonement well,
Our peace will, like a broken limb united,   220
Grow stronger for the breaking.
MOWBRAY   Be it so.
    Enter Westmorland
Here is returned my lord of Westmorland.
WESTMORLAND
The Prince is here at hand. Pleaseth your lordship
To meet his grace just distance 'tween our armies?
MOWBRAY
Your grace of York, in God's name then set forward.
ARCHBISHOP OF YORK
Before, and greet his grace!—My lord, we come.   226
    ⌈*They march over the stage.*⌉
    Enter Prince John ⌈*with one or more soldiers*
    carrying wine⌉
PRINCE JOHN
You are well encountered here, my cousin Mowbray.
Good day to you, gentle lord Archbishop;

And so to you, Lord Hastings, and to all.
My lord of York, it better showed with you   230
When that your flock, assembled by the bell,
Encircled you to hear with reverence
Your exposition on the holy text,
Than now to see you here an iron man,
Cheering a rout of rebels with your drum,   235
Turning the word to sword, and life to death.
That man that sits within a monarch's heart
And ripens in the sunshine of his favour,
Would he abuse the countenance of the King,
Alack, what mischiefs might he set abroach   240
In shadow of such greatness! With you, Lord Bishop,
It is even so. Who hath not heard it spoken
How deep you were within the books of God—
To us, the speaker in his parliament,
To us, th'imagined voice of God himself,   245
The very opener and intelligencer
Between the grace, the sanctities of heaven
And our dull workings? O, who shall believe
But you misuse the reverence of your place,
Employ the countenance and grace of heav'n   250
As a false favourite doth his prince's name
In deeds dishonourable? You have ta'en up,
Under the counterfeited zeal of God,
The subjects of his substitute, my father;
And, both against the peace of heaven and him,   255
Have here upswarmèd them.
ARCHBISHOP OF YORK   Good my lord of Lancaster,
I am not here against your father's peace;
But, as I told my lord of Westmorland,
The time misordered doth, in common sense,
Crowd us and crush us to this monstrous form,   260
To hold our safety up. I sent your grace
The parcels and particulars of our grief,
The which hath been with scorn shoved from the
    court,
Whereon this Hydra son of war is born;
Whose dangerous eyes may well be charmed asleep
With grant of our most just and right desires,   266
And true obedience, of this madness cured,
Stoop tamely to the foot of majesty.
MOWBRAY
If not, we ready are to try our fortunes
To the last man.
HASTINGS   And though we here fall down,   270
We have supplies to second our attempt.
If they miscarry, theirs shall second them;
And so success of mischief shall be born,
And heir from heir shall hold this quarrel up,
Whiles England shall have generation.   275
PRINCE JOHN
You are too shallow, Hastings, much too shallow,
To sound the bottom of the after-times.
WESTMORLAND
Pleaseth your grace to answer them directly
How far forth you do like their articles?

PRINCE JOHN
I like them all, and do allow them well,   280
And swear here, by the honour of my blood,
My father's purposes have been mistook,
And some about him have too lavishly
Wrested his meaning and authority.
(To the Archbishop)
My lord, these griefs shall be with speed redressed; 285
Upon my soul they shall. If this may please you,
Discharge your powers unto their several counties,
As we will ours; and here between the armies
Let's drink together friendly and embrace,
That all their eyes may bear those tokens home   290
Of our restorèd love and amity.
ARCHBISHOP OF YORK
I take your princely word for these redresses.
⌈PRINCE JOHN⌉
I give it you, and will maintain my word;
And thereupon I drink unto your grace.
               He drinks
⌈HASTINGS⌉ ⌈to Coleville⌉
Go, captain, and deliver to the army   295
This news of peace. Let them have pay, and part.
I know it will well please them. Hie thee, captain.
                              Exit ⌈Coleville⌉
ARCHBISHOP OF YORK
To you, my noble lord of Westmorland!
               He drinks
WESTMORLAND *(drinking)*
I pledge your grace. An if you knew what pains
I have bestowed to breed this present peace,   300
You would drink freely; but my love to ye
Shall show itself more openly hereafter.
ARCHBISHOP OF YORK
I do not doubt you.
WESTMORLAND   I am glad of it.
(Drinking) Health to my lord and gentle cousin
               Mowbray!
MOWBRAY
You wish me health in very happy season,   305
For I am on the sudden something ill.
ARCHBISHOP OF YORK
Against ill chances men are ever merry;
But heaviness foreruns the good event.
WESTMORLAND
Therefore be merry, coz, since sudden sorrow
Serves to say thus: some good thing comes tomorrow.
ARCHBISHOP OF YORK
Believe me, I am passing light in spirit.   311
MOWBRAY
So much the worse, if your own rule be true.
                              Shout within
PRINCE JOHN
The word of peace is rendered. Hark how they shout.
MOWBRAY
This had been cheerful after victory.
ARCHBISHOP OF YORK
A peace is of the nature of a conquest,   315

For then both parties nobly are subdued,
And neither party loser.
PRINCE JOHN *(to Westmorland)* Go, my lord,
And let our army be dischargèd too.
                              Exit Westmorland
(To the Archbishop) And, good my lord, so please you,
               let our trains
March by us, that we may peruse the men   320
We should have coped withal.
ARCHBISHOP OF YORK   Go, good Lord Hastings,
And ere they be dismissed, let them march by.
                              Exit Hastings
PRINCE JOHN
I trust, lords, we shall lie tonight together.
               Enter the Earl of Westmorland, ⌈with captains⌉
Now, cousin, wherefore stands our army still?
WESTMORLAND
The leaders, having charge from you to stand,   325
Will not go off until they hear you speak.
PRINCE JOHN
They know their duties.
               Enter Lord Hastings
HASTINGS ⌈to the Archbishop⌉ Our army is dispersed.
Like youthful steers unyoked, they take their courses,
East, west, north, south; or, like a school broke up,
Each hurries toward his home and sporting place. 330
WESTMORLAND
Good tidings, my lord Hastings, for the which
I do arrest thee, traitor, of high treason;
And you, Lord Archbishop, and you, Lord Mowbray,
Of capital treason I attach you both.
               ⌈*The captains guard Hastings, the Archbishop, and*
               Mowbray⌉
MOWBRAY
Is this proceeding just and honourable?   335
WESTMORLAND Is your assembly so?
ARCHBISHOP OF YORK Will you thus break your faith?
PRINCE JOHN I pawned thee none.
I promised you redress of these same grievances
Whereof you did complain; which, by mine honour,
I will perform with a most Christian care.
But for you rebels, look to taste the due
Meet for rebellion and such acts as yours.
Most shallowly did you these arms commence,
Fondly brought here, and foolishly sent hence.— 345
Strike up our drums, pursue the scattered stray.
God, and not we, hath safely fought today.
Some guard these traitors to the block of death,
Treason's true bed and yielder up of breath.   *Exeunt*

4.2   *Alarum. Excursions. Enter Sir John Falstaff and*
               Coleville
SIR JOHN What's your name, sir, of what condition are
     you, and of what place, I pray?
COLEVILLE I am a knight, sir, and my name is Coleville
     of the Dale.   4
SIR JOHN Well then, Coleville is your name, a knight is
     your degree, and your place the Dale. Coleville shall be

still your name, a traitor your degree, and the dungeon
your place—a place deep enough, so shall you be still
Coleville of the Dale.

COLEVILLE Are not you Sir John Falstaff?   10

SIR JOHN As good a man as he, sir, whoe'er I am. Do ye
yield, sir, or shall I sweat for you? If I do sweat, they
are the drops of thy lovers, and they weep for thy
death; therefore rouse up fear and trembling, and do
observance to my mercy.   15

COLEVILLE (*kneeling*) I think you are Sir John Falstaff, and
in that thought yield me.

SIR JOHN (*aside*) I have a whole school of tongues in this
belly of mine, and not a tongue of them all speaks any
other word but my name. An I had but a belly of any
indifferency, I were simply the most active fellow in
Europe. My womb, my womb, my womb undoes me.

    Enter Prince John, the Earl of Westmorland, Sir
    John Blunt, and other lords and soldiers

Here comes our general.

PRINCE JOHN
The heat is past; follow no further now.

    A retreat is sounded

Call in the powers, good cousin Westmorland.   25

               Exit Westmorland

Now, Falstaff, where have you been all this while?
When everything is ended, then you come.
These tardy tricks of yours will, on my life,
One time or other break some gallows' back.   29

SIR JOHN I would be sorry, my lord, but it should be thus.
I never knew yet but rebuke and check was the reward
of valour. Do you think me a swallow, an arrow, or a
bullet? Have I in my poor and old motion the expedition
of thought? I have speeded hither with the very
extremest inch of possibility; I have foundered nine-
score and odd posts; and here, travel-tainted as I am,
have in my pure and immaculate valour taken Sir John
Coleville of the Dale, a most furious knight and valorous
enemy. But what of that? He saw me, and yielded, that
I may justly say, with the hook-nosed fellow of Rome,
'I came, saw, and overcame.'   41

PRINCE JOHN It was more of his courtesy than your
deserving.

SIR JOHN I know not. Here he is, and here I yield him;
and I beseech your grace, let it be booked with the rest
of this day's deeds; or, by the Lord, I will have it in a
particular ballad else, with mine own picture on the
top on't, Coleville kissing my foot; to the which course
if I be enforced, if you do not all show like gilt twopences
to me, and I in the clear sky of fame o'ershine you as
much as the full moon doth the cinders of the element,
which show like pins' heads to her, believe not the
word of the noble. Therefore let me have right, and let
desert mount.

PRINCE JOHN Thine's too heavy to mount.   55

SIR JOHN Let it shine then.

PRINCE JOHN Thine's too thick to shine.

SIR JOHN Let it do something, my good lord, that may do
me good, and call it what you will.

PRINCE JOHN
Is thy name Coleville?

COLEVILLE   It is, my lord.   60

PRINCE JOHN
A famous rebel art thou, Coleville.

SIR JOHN And a famous true subject took him.

COLEVILLE
I am, my lord, but as my betters are
That led me hither. Had they been ruled by me,
You should have won them dearer than you have.   65

SIR JOHN
I know not how—they sold themselves, but thou
Like a kind fellow gav'st thyself away,
And I thank thee for thee.

    Enter the Earl of Westmorland

PRINCE JOHN   Have you left pursuit?

WESTMORLAND
Retreat is made, and execution stayed.

PRINCE JOHN
Send Coleville with his confederates   70
To York, to present execution.
Blunt, lead him hence, and see you guard him sure.

            Exit Blunt, with Coleville

And now dispatch we toward the court, my lords.
I hear the King my father is sore sick.
(*To Westmorland*) Our news shall go before us to his
     majesty,   75
Which, cousin, you shall bear to comfort him;
And we with sober speed will follow you.

SIR JOHN
My lord, I beseech you give me leave to go
Through Gloucestershire, and when you come to court
Stand, my good lord, pray, in your good report.   80

PRINCE JOHN
Fare you well, Falstaff. I in my condition
Shall better speak of you than you deserve.

           Exeunt all but Sir John

SIR JOHN I would you had but the wit; 'twere better than
your dukedom. Good faith, this same young sober-
blooded boy doth not love me, nor a man cannot make
him laugh. But that's no marvel; he drinks no wine.
There's never none of these demure boys come to any
proof; for thin drink doth so overcool their blood, and
making many fish meals, that they fall into a kind of
male green-sickness; and then when they marry, they
get wenches. They are generally fools and cowards—
which some of us should be too, but for inflammation.
A good sherry-sack hath a two-fold operation in it. It
ascends me into the brain, dries me there all the foolish
and dull and crudy vapours which environ it, makes
it apprehensive, quick, forgetive, full of nimble, fiery,
and delectable shapes, which, delivered o'er to the
voice, the tongue, which is the birth, becomes excellent
wit. The second property of your excellent sherry is the
warming of the blood, which, before cold and settled,
left the liver white and pale, which is the badge of
pusillanimity and cowardice. But the sherry warms it,

and makes it course from the inwards to the parts'
extremes; it illuminateth the face, which, as a beacon,
gives warning to all the rest of this little kingdom, man,
to arm; and then the vital commoners and inland petty
spirits muster me all to their captain, the heart; who,
great and puffed up with his retinue, doth any deed of
courage. And this valour comes of sherry. So that skill
in the weapon is nothing without sack, for that sets it
a-work; and learning a mere hoard of gold kept by a
devil, till sack commences it and sets it in act and use.
Hereof comes it that Prince Harry is valiant; for the
cold blood he did naturally inherit of his father he hath,
like lean, sterile, and bare land, manured, husbanded,
and tilled, with excellent endeavour of drinking good,
and good store of fertile sherry, that he is become very
hot and valiant. If I had a thousand sons, the first
human principle I would teach them should be to
forswear thin potations, and to addict themselves to
sack.   121
    Enter Bardolph
How now, Bardolph?
BARDOLPH
The army is dischargèd all and gone.
SIR JOHN I'll through Gloucestershire, and
there will I visit Master Robert Shallow, Esquire. I have
him already tempering between my finger and my
thumb, and shortly will I seal with him. Come, away!
    Exeunt

4.3   *Enter King Henry ⌜in his bed⌝, attended by the Earl*
    of Warwick, Thomas Duke of Clarence, Humphrey
    Duke of Gloucester, ⌜and others⌝
KING HENRY
Now, lords, if God doth give successful end
To this debate that bleedeth at our doors,
We will our youth lead on to higher fields,
And draw no swords but what are sanctified.
Our navy is addressed, our power collected,   5
Our substitutes in absence well invested,
And everything lies level to our wish;
Only we want a little personal strength,
And pause us till these rebels now afoot
Come underneath the yoke of government.   10
WARWICK
Both which we doubt not but your majesty
Shall soon enjoy.
KING HENRY   Humphrey, my son of Gloucester,
Where is the Prince your brother?
GLOUCESTER
I think he's gone to hunt, my lord, at Windsor.
KING HENRY
And how accompanied?
GLOUCESTER   I do not know, my lord.   15
KING HENRY
Is not his brother Thomas of Clarence with him?
GLOUCESTER
No, my good lord, he is in presence here.
CLARENCE What would my lord and father?

KING HENRY
Nothing but well to thee, Thomas of Clarence.
How chance thou art not with the Prince thy brother?
He loves thee, and thou dost neglect him, Thomas.   21
Thou hast a better place in his affection
Than all thy brothers. Cherish it, my boy,
And noble offices thou mayst effect
Of mediation, after I am dead,   25
Between his greatness and thy other brethren.
Therefore omit him not, blunt not his love,
Nor lose the good advantage of his grace
By seeming cold or careless of his will;
For he is gracious, if he be observed;   30
He hath a tear for pity, and a hand
Open as day for melting charity.
Yet notwithstanding, being incensed, he is flint,
As humorous as winter, and as sudden
As flaws congealèd in the spring of day.   35
His temper therefore must be well observed.
Chide him for faults, and do it reverently,
When you perceive his blood inclined to mirth;
But being moody, give him line and scope
Till that his passions, like a whale on ground,   40
Confound themselves with working. Learn this,
    Thomas,
And thou shalt prove a shelter to thy friends,
A hoop of gold to bind thy brothers in,
That the united vessel of their blood,
Mingled with venom of suggestion—   45
As force perforce the age will pour it in—
Shall never leak, though it do work as strong
As aconitum or rash gunpowder.
CLARENCE
I shall observe him with all care and love.
KING HENRY
  Why art thou not at Windsor with him, Thomas?   50
CLARENCE
He is not there today; he dines in London.
KING HENRY
And how accompanied? Canst thou tell that?
CLARENCE
With Poins and other his continual followers.
KING HENRY
Most subject is the fattest soil to weeds,
And he, the noble image of my youth,   55
Is overspread with them; therefore my grief
Stretches itself beyond the hour of death.
The blood weeps from my heart when I do shape
In forms imaginary th'unguided days
And rotten times that you shall look upon   60
When I am sleeping with my ancestors;
For when his headstrong riot hath no curb,
When rage and hot blood are his counsellors,
When means and lavish manners meet together,
O, with what wings shall his affections fly   65
Towards fronting peril and opposed decay?
WARWICK
My gracious lord, you look beyond him quite.

322

The Prince but studies his companions,
Like a strange tongue, wherein, to gain the language,
'Tis needful that the most immodest word   70
Be looked upon and learnt, which once attained,
Your highness knows, comes to no further use
But to be known and hated; so, like gross terms,
The Prince will in the perfectness of time
Cast off his followers, and their memory   75
Shall as a pattern or a measure live
By which his grace must mete the lives of other,
Turning past evils to advantages.

KING HENRY
'Tis seldom when the bee doth leave her comb
In the dead carrion.
          Enter the Earl of Westmorland
                    Who's here? Westmorland?   80

WESTMORLAND
Health to my sovereign, and new happiness
Added to that that I am to deliver!
Prince John your son doth kiss your grace's hand.
Mowbray, the Bishop Scrope, Hastings, and all
Are brought to the correction of your law.   85
There is not now a rebel's sword unsheathed,
But peace puts forth her olive everywhere.
The manner how this action hath been borne
Here at more leisure may your highness read,
With every course in his particular.   90
          He gives the King papers

KING HENRY
O Westmorland, thou art a summer bird
Which ever in the haunch of winter sings
The lifting up of day.
          Enter Harcourt
                    Look, here's more news.

HARCOURT
From enemies heaven keep your majesty;
And when they stand against you, may they fall   95
As those that I am come to tell you of!
The Earl Northumberland and the Lord Bardolph,
With a great power of English and of Scots,
Are by the sheriff of Yorkshire overthrown.
The manner and true order of the fight   100
This packet, please it you, contains at large.
          He gives the King papers

KING HENRY
And wherefore should these good news make me sick?
Will fortune never come with both hands full,
But write her fair words still in foulest letters?
She either gives a stomach and no food—   105
Such are the poor in health—or else a feast,
And takes away the stomach—such are the rich,
That have abundance and enjoy it not.
I should rejoice now at this happy news,
And now my sight fails, and my brain is giddy.   110
O me! Come near me now; I am much ill.
          He swoons

GLOUCESTER
Comfort, your majesty!

CLARENCE   O my royal father!

WESTMORLAND
My sovereign lord, cheer up yourself, look up.

WARWICK
Be patient, princes; you do know these fits
Are with his highness very ordinary.   115
Stand from him, give him air; he'll straight be well.

CLARENCE
No, no, he cannot long hold out these pangs.
Th'incessant care and labour of his mind
Hath wrought the mure that should confine it in
So thin that life looks through and will break out. 120

GLOUCESTER
The people fear me, for they do observe
Unfathered heirs and loathly births of nature.
The seasons change their manners, as the year
Had found some months asleep and leaped them over.

CLARENCE
The river hath thrice flowed, no ebb between,   125
And the old folk, time's doting chronicles,
Say it did so a little time before
That our great grandsire Edward sicked and died.

WARWICK
Speak lower, princes, for the King recovers.

GLOUCESTER
This apoplexy will certain be his end.   130

KING HENRY
I pray you take me up and bear me hence
Into some other chamber; softly, pray.
          ⌐The King is carried over the stage in his bed⌐
Let there be no noise made, my gentle friends,
Unless some dull and favourable hand
Will whisper music to my weary spirit.   135

WARWICK
Call for the music in the other room.
          ⌐Exit one or more. Still music within⌐

KING HENRY
Set me the crown upon my pillow here.
          *⌐Clarence⌐ takes the crown ⌐from the King's head⌐,
          and sets it on his pillow*

CLARENCE
His eye is hollow, and he changes much.
          ⌐A noise within⌐

WARWICK
Less noise, less noise!
          Enter Prince Harry

PRINCE HARRY   Who saw the Duke of Clarence?

CLARENCE
I am here, brother, full of heaviness.   140

PRINCE HARRY
How now, rain within doors, and none abroad?
How doth the King?

GLOUCESTER   Exceeding ill.

PRINCE HARRY
Heard he the good news yet? Tell it him.

GLOUCESTER
He altered much upon the hearing it.

PRINCE HARRY If he be sick with joy, he'll recover without
          physic.   146

WARWICK
Not so much noise, my lords! Sweet prince, speak low.
The King your father is disposed to sleep.
CLARENCE
Let us withdraw into the other room.
WARWICK
Will't please your grace to go along with us?   150
PRINCE HARRY
No, I will sit and watch here by the King.
        Exeunt all but the King and Prince Harry
Why doth the crown lie there upon his pillow,
Being so troublesome a bedfellow?
O polished perturbation, golden care,
That keep'st the ports of slumber open wide   155
To many a watchful night!—Sleep with it now;
Yet not so sound, and half so deeply sweet,
As he whose brow with homely biggen bound
Snores out the watch of night. O majesty,
When thou dost pinch thy bearer, thou dost sit   160
Like a rich armour worn in heat of day,
That scald'st with safety.—By his gates of breath
There lies a downy feather which stirs not.
Did he suspire, that light and weightless down
Perforce must move.—My gracious lord, my father!—
This sleep is sound indeed. This is a sleep   166
That from this golden rigol hath divorced
So many English kings.—Thy due from me
Is tears and heavy sorrows of the blood,
Which nature, love, and filial tenderness   170
Shall, O dear father, pay thee plenteously.
My due from thee is this imperial crown,
Which, as immediate from thy place and blood,
Derives itself to me.
    He puts the crown on his head
                Lo where it sits,
Which God shall guard; and put the world's whole
    strength   175
Into one giant arm, it shall not force
This lineal honour from me. This from thee
Will I to mine leave, as 'tis left to me.   *Exit*
    ⌈*Music ceases.*⌉ *The King awakes*
KING HENRY
Warwick, Gloucester, Clarence!
    Enter the Earl of Warwick, and the Dukes of
    Gloucester and Clarence
CLARENCE   Doth the King call?
WARWICK
What would your majesty? How fares your grace? 180
KING HENRY
Why did you leave me here alone, my lords?
CLARENCE
We left the Prince my brother here, my liege,
Who undertook to sit and watch by you.
KING HENRY
The Prince of Wales? Where is he? Let me see him.
WARWICK
This door is open; he is gone this way.   185

GLOUCESTER
He came not through the chamber where we stayed.
KING HENRY
Where is the crown? Who took it from my pillow?
WARWICK
When we withdrew, my liege, we left it here.
KING HENRY
The Prince hath ta'en it hence. Go seek him out.
Is he so hasty that he doth suppose   190
My sleep my death?
Find him, my lord of Warwick; chide him hither.
                        Exit Warwick
This part of his conjoins with my disease,
And helps to end me. See, sons, what things you are,
How quickly nature falls into revolt   195
When gold becomes her object!
For this the foolish over-careful fathers
Have broke their sleep with thoughts, their brains with
    care,
Their bones with industry; for this they have
Engrossèd and piled up the cankered heaps   200
Of strange-achievèd gold; for this they have
Been thoughtful to invest their sons with arts
And martial exercises; when, like the bee
Culling from every flower the virtuous sweets,
Our thighs packed with wax, our mouths with honey,
We bring it to the hive; and, like the bees,   206
Are murdered for our pains. This bitter taste
Yields his engrossments to the ending father.
    Enter the Earl of Warwick
Now where is he that will not stay so long
Till his friend sickness have determined me?   210
WARWICK
My lord, I found the Prince in the next room,
Washing with kindly tears his gentle cheeks
With such a deep demeanour, in great sorrow,
That tyranny, which never quaffed but blood,
Would, by beholding him, have washed his knife 215
With gentle eye-drops. He is coming hither.
KING HENRY
But wherefore did he take away the crown?
    Enter Prince Harry with the crown
Lo where he comes.—Come hither to me, Harry.
(*To the others*) Depart the chamber; leave us here
    alone.   *Exeunt all but the King and Prince Harry*
PRINCE HARRY
I never thought to hear you speak again.   220
KING HENRY
Thy wish was father, Harry, to that thought.
I stay too long by thee, I weary thee.
Dost thou so hunger for mine empty chair
That thou wilt needs invest thee with my honours
Before thy hour be ripe? O foolish youth,   225
Thou seek'st the greatness that will overwhelm thee!
Stay but a little, for my cloud of dignity
Is held from falling with so weak a wind
That it will quickly drop. My day is dim.

Thou hast stol'n that which after some few hours   230
Were thine without offence, and at my death
Thou hast sealed up my expectation.
Thy life did manifest thou loved'st me not,
And thou wilt have me die assured of it.
Thou hid'st a thousand daggers in thy thoughts,   235
Whom thou hast whetted on thy stony heart
To stab at half an hour of my life.
What, canst thou not forbear me half an hour?
Then get thee gone and dig my grave thyself,
And bid the merry bells ring to thine ear   240
That thou art crownèd, not that I am dead.
Let all the tears that should bedew my hearse
Be drops of balm to sanctify thy head.
Only compound me with forgotten dust.
Give that which gave thee life unto the worms.   245
Pluck down my officers, break my decrees;
For now a time is come to mock at form—
Harry the Fifth is crowned. Up, vanity!
Down, royal state! All you sage counsellors, hence!
And to the English court assemble now   250
From every region, apes of idleness!
Now, neighbour confines, purge you of your scum!
Have you a ruffian that will swear, drink, dance,
Revel the night, rob, murder, and commit
The oldest sins the newest kind of ways?   255
Be happy; he will trouble you no more.
England shall double gild his treble guilt,
England shall give him office, honour, might;
For the fifth Harry from curbed licence plucks
The muzzle of restraint, and the wild dog   260
Shall flesh his tooth on every innocent.
O my poor kingdom, sick with civil blows!
When that my care could not withhold thy riots,
What wilt thou do when riot is thy care?
O, thou wilt be a wilderness again,   265
Peopled with wolves, thy old inhabitants.

PRINCE HARRY
O pardon me, my liege! But for my tears,
The moist impediments unto my speech,
I had forestalled this dear and deep rebuke
Ere you with grief had spoke and I had heard   270
The course of it so far. There is your crown;
    ⌜He returns the crown and kneels⌝
And that wears the crown immortally
Long guard it yours! If I affect it more
Than as your honour and as your renown,
Let me no more from this obedience rise,   275
Which my most true and inward duteous spirit
Teacheth this prostrate and exterior bending.
God witness with me, when I here came in
And found no course of breath within your majesty,
How cold it struck my heart. If I do feign,   280
O, let me in my present wildness die,
And never live to show th'incredulous world
The noble change that I have purposèd.
Coming to look on you, thinking you dead,
And dead almost, my liege, to think you were,   285

I spake unto this crown as having sense,
And thus upbraided it: 'The care on thee depending
Hath fed upon the body of my father;
Therefore thou best of gold art worst of gold.
Other, less fine in carat, is more precious,   290
Preserving life in medicine potable;
But thou, most fine, most honoured, most renowned,
Hast eat thy bearer up.' Thus, my royal liege,
Accusing it, I put it on my head,
To try with it, as with an enemy   295
That had before my face murdered my father,
The quarrel of a true inheritor.
But if it did infect my blood with joy
Or swell my thoughts to any strain of pride,
If any rebel or vain spirit of mine   300
Did with the least affection of a welcome
Give entertainment to the might of it,
Let God for ever keep it from my head,
And make me as the poorest vassal is,
That doth with awe and terror kneel to it.   305
KING HENRY O my son,
God put it in thy mind to take it hence,
That thou mightst win the more thy father's love,
Pleading so wisely in excuse of it!
Come hither, Harry; sit thou by my bed,   310
And hear, I think, the very latest counsel
That ever I shall breathe.
    Prince Harry ⌜rises from kneeling and⌝ sits by
    the bed
                        God knows, my son,
By what bypaths and indirect crook'd ways
I met this crown; and I myself know well
How troublesome it sat upon my head.   315
To thee it shall descend with better quiet,
Better opinion, better confirmation;
For all the soil of the achievement goes
With me into the earth. It seemed in me
But as an honour snatched with boist'rous hand;   320
And I had many living to upbraid
My gain of it by their assistances,
Which daily grew to quarrel and to bloodshed,
Wounding supposèd peace. All these bold fears
Thou seest with peril I have answerèd;   325
For all my reign hath been but as a scene
Acting that argument. And now my death
Changes the mood, for what in me was purchased
Falls upon thee in a more fairer sort,
So thou the garland wear'st successively.   330
Yet though thou stand'st more sure than I could do,
Thou art not firm enough, since griefs are green,
And all thy friends—which thou must make thy
    friends—
Have but their stings and teeth newly ta'en out,
By whose fell working I was first advanced,   335
And by whose power I well might lodge a fear
To be again displaced; which to avoid
I cut them off, and had a purpose now
To lead out many to the Holy Land,

Lest rest and lying still might make them look　　340
Too near unto my state. Therefore, my Harry,
Be it thy course to busy giddy minds
With foreign quarrels, that action hence borne out
May waste the memory of the former days.
More would I, but my lungs are wasted so　　345
That strength of speech is utterly denied me.
How I came by the crown, O God forgive,
And grant it may with thee in true peace live!

PRINCE HARRY My gracious liege,
　You won it, wore it, kept it, gave it me;　　350
Then plain and right must my possession be,
Which I with more than with a common pain
'Gainst all the world will rightfully maintain.
　　Enter Prince John of Lancaster ⌈followed by⌉ the
　　Earl of Warwick ⌈and others⌉

KING HENRY
　Look, look, here comes my John of Lancaster.

PRINCE JOHN
　Health, peace, and happiness to my royal father!　　355

KING HENRY
　Thou bring'st me happiness and peace, son John;
But health, alack, with youthful wings is flown
From this bare withered trunk. Upon thy sight
My worldly business makes a period.
Where is my lord of Warwick?

PRINCE HARRY　　　　　　My lord of Warwick!
　　⌈*Warwick comes forward to the King*⌉

KING HENRY
　Doth any name particular belong　　361
Unto the lodging where I first did swoon?

WARWICK
　'Tis called Jerusalem, my noble lord.

KING HENRY
　Laud be to God! Even there my life must end.
It hath been prophesied to me many years　　365
I should not die but in Jerusalem,
Which vainly I supposed the Holy Land;
But bear me to that chamber; there I'll lie;
In that Jerusalem shall Harry die.
　　Exeunt, bearing the King in his bed

5.1　*Enter Shallow, ⌈Silence,⌉ Sir John Falstaff,*
　　Bardolph, and the Page

SHALLOW (*to Sir John*) By cock and pie, you shall not
　away tonight.—What, Davy, I say!

SIR JOHN You must excuse me, Master Robert Shallow.

SHALLOW I will not excuse you; you shall not be excused;
　excuses shall not be admitted; there is no excuse shall
　serve; you shall not be excused.—Why, Davy!　　6
　　Enter Davy

DAVY Here, sir.

SHALLOW Davy, Davy, Davy; let me see, Davy; let me
　see. William Cook—bid him come hither.—Sir John,
　you shall not be excused.　　10

DAVY Marry, sir, thus: those precepts cannot be served.
　And again, sir: shall we sow the headland with wheat?

SHALLOW With red wheat, Davy. But for William Cook;
　are there no young pigeons?

DAVY Yes, sir. Here is now the smith's note for shoeing
　and plough-irons.　　16

SHALLOW Let it be cast and paid. Sir John, you shall not
　be excused.

DAVY Sir, a new link to the bucket must needs be had;
　and, sir, do you mean to stop any of William's wages,
　about the sack he lost at Hinkley Fair?　　21

SHALLOW A shall answer it. Some pigeons, Davy, a couple
　of short-legged hens, a joint of mutton, and any pretty
　little tiny kickshaws, tell William Cook.

DAVY Doth the man of war stay all night, sir?　　25

SHALLOW Yea, Davy. I will use him well; a friend i'th'
　court is better than a penny in purse. Use his men well,
　Davy, for they are arrant knaves, and will backbite.

DAVY No worse than they are back-bitten, sir, for they
　have marvellous foul linen.　　30

SHALLOW Well conceited, Davy. About thy business, Davy.

DAVY I beseech you, sir, to countenance William Visor of
　Wo'ncot against Clement Perks o'th' Hill.

SHALLOW There is many complaints, Davy, against that
　Visor. That Visor is an arrant knave, on my knowledge.

DAVY I grant your worship that he is a knave, sir; but
　yet God forbid, sir, but a knave should have some
　countenance at his friend's request. An honest man,
　sir, is able to speak for himself, when a knave is not. I
　have served your worship truly, sir, this eight years.
　An I cannot once or twice in a quarter bear out a
　knave against an honest man, I have little credit with
　your worship. The knave is mine honest friend, sir;
　therefore I beseech you let him be countenanced.　　44

SHALLOW Go to; I say he shall have no wrong. Look
　about, Davy.　　　　　　　　　　⌈*Exit Davy*⌉
　Where are you, Sir John? Come, off with your boots.—
　Give me your hand, Master Bardolph.

BARDOLPH I am glad to see your worship.　　49

SHALLOW I thank thee with all my heart, kind Master
　Bardolph. ⌈*To the Page*⌉ And welcome, my tall fellow.—
　Come, Sir John.

SIR JOHN I'll follow you, good Master Robert Shallow.
　　　　　　　　　　　Exit Shallow ⌈with Silence⌉
　Bardolph, look to our horses.　　54
　　　　　　　　　Exit Bardolph ⌈with the Page⌉
　If I were sawed into quantities, I should make four
　dozen of such bearded hermits' staves as Master
　Shallow. It is a wonderful thing to see the semblable
　coherence of his men's spirits and his. They, by
　observing him, do bear themselves like foolish justices;
　he, by conversing with them, is turned into a justice-
　like servingman. Their spirits are so married in
　conjunction, with the participation of society, that they
　flock together in consent like so many wild geese. If I
　had a suit to Master Shallow, I would humour his men
　with the imputation of being near their master; if to
　his men, I would curry with Master Shallow that no
　man could better command his servants. It is certain

that either wise bearing or ignorant carriage is caught as men take diseases, one of another; therefore let men take heed of their company. I will devise matter enough out of this Shallow to keep Prince Harry in continual laughter the wearing out of six fashions—which is four terms, or two actions—and a shall laugh without intervallums. O, it is much that a lie with a slight oath, and a jest with a sad brow, will do with a fellow that never had the ache in his shoulders! O, you shall see him laugh till his face be like a wet cloak ill laid up!

SHALLOW (*within*) Sir John!

SIR JOHN I come, Master Shallow; I come, Master Shallow.

                                  Exit

5.2   *Enter the Earl of Warwick ⌈at one door⌉, and the*
         Lord Chief Justice ⌈at another door⌉

WARWICK
How now, my Lord Chief Justice, whither away?

LORD CHIEF JUSTICE How doth the King?

WARWICK
Exceeding well: his cares are now all ended.

LORD CHIEF JUSTICE
I hope not dead.

WARWICK   He's walked the way of nature,
And to our purposes he lives no more.   5

LORD CHIEF JUSTICE
I would his majesty had called me with him.
The service that I truly did his life
Hath left me open to all injuries.

WARWICK
Indeed I think the young King loves you not.

LORD CHIEF JUSTICE
I know he doth not, and do arm myself   10
To welcome the condition of the time,
Which cannot look more hideously upon me
Than I have drawn it in my fantasy.

    Enter Prince John of Lancaster, and the Dukes of
      Clarence and Gloucester

WARWICK
Here come the heavy issue of dead Harry.
O, that the living Harry had the temper   15
Of he the worst of these three gentlemen!
How many nobles then should hold their places,
That must strike sail to spirits of vile sort!

LORD CHIEF JUSTICE
O God, I fear all will be overturned.

PRINCE JOHN
Good morrow, cousin Warwick, good morrow.   20

GLOUCESTER *and* CLARENCE Good morrow, cousin.

PRINCE JOHN
We meet like men that had forgot to speak.

WARWICK
We do remember, but our argument
Is all too heavy to admit much talk.

PRINCE JOHN
Well, peace be with him that hath made us heavy! 25

LORD CHIEF JUSTICE
Peace be with us, lest we be heavier!

GLOUCESTER
O good my lord, you have lost a friend indeed;
And I dare swear you borrow not that face
Of seeming sorrow—it is sure your own.

PRINCE JOHN (*to Lord Chief Justice*)
Though no man be assured what grace to find,   30
You stand in coldest expectation.
I am the sorrier; would 'twere otherwise.

CLARENCE (*to Lord Chief Justice*)
Well, you must now speak Sir John Falstaff fair,
Which swims against your stream of quality.

LORD CHIEF JUSTICE
Sweet princes, what I did I did in honour,   35
Led by th'impartial conduct of my soul;
And never shall you see that I will beg
A raggèd and forestalled remission.
If truth and upright innocency fail me,
I'll to the King my master, that is dead,   40
And tell him who hath sent me after him.

    Enter Prince Harry, as King

WARWICK Here comes the Prince.

LORD CHIEF JUSTICE
Good morrow, and God save your majesty!

PRINCE HARRY
This new and gorgeous garment, majesty,
Sits not so easy on me as you think.   45
Brothers, you mix your sadness with some fear.
This is the English not the Turkish court;
Not Amurath an Amurath succeeds,
But Harry Harry. Yet be sad, good brothers,
For, by my faith, it very well becomes you.   50
Sorrow so royally in you appears
That I will deeply put the fashion on,
And wear it in my heart. Why then, be sad;
But entertain no more of it, good brothers,
Than a joint burden laid upon us all.   55
For me, by heaven, I bid you be assured
I'll be your father and your brother too.
Let me but bear your love, I'll bear your cares.
Yet weep that Harry's dead, and so will I;
But Harry lives that shall convert those tears   60
By number into hours of happiness.

PRINCE JOHN, GLOUCESTER, *and* CLARENCE
We hope no other from your majesty.

PRINCE HARRY
You all look strangely on me, (*to Lord Chief Justice*)
    and you most.
You are, I think, assured I love you not.

LORD CHIEF JUSTICE
I am assured, if I be measured rightly,   65
Your majesty hath no just cause to hate me.

PRINCE HARRY
No? How might a prince of my great hopes forget
So great indignities you laid upon me?
What—rate, rebuke, and roughly send to prison
Th'immediate heir of England? Was this easy?   70
May this be washed in Lethe and forgotten?

LORD CHIEF JUSTICE
  I then did use the person of your father.
  The image of his power lay then in me;
  And in th'administration of his law,
  Whiles I was busy for the commonwealth,   75
  Your highness pleasèd to forget my place,
  The majesty and power of law and justice,
  The image of the King whom I presented,
  And struck me in my very seat of judgement;
  Whereon, as an offender to your father,   80
  I gave bold way to my authority
  And did commit you. If the deed were ill,
  Be you contented, wearing now the garland,
  To have a son set your decrees at naught—
  To pluck down justice from your awe-full bench,   85
  To trip the course of law, and blunt the sword
  That guards the peace and safety of your person,
  Nay, more, to spurn at your most royal image,
  And mock your workings in a second body?
  Question your royal thoughts, make the case yours,   90
  Be now the father, and propose a son;
  Hear your own dignity so much profaned,
  See your most dreadful laws so loosely slighted,
  Behold yourself so by a son disdained;
  And then imagine me taking your part,   95
  And in your power soft silencing your son.
  After this cold considerance, sentence me;
  And, as you are a king, speak in your state
  What I have done that misbecame my place,
  My person, or my liege's sovereignty.   100
PRINCE HARRY
  You are right Justice, and you weigh this well.
  Therefore still bear the balance and the sword;
  And I do wish your honours may increase
  Till you do live to see a son of mine
  Offend you and obey you as I did.   105
  So shall I live to speak my father's words:
  'Happy am I that have a man so bold
  That dares do justice on my proper son,
  And not less happy having such a son
  That would deliver up his greatness so   110
  Into the hands of justice.' You did commit me,
  For which I do commit into your hand
  Th'unstainèd sword that you have used to bear,
  With this remembrance: that you use the same
  With the like bold, just, and impartial spirit   115
  As you have done 'gainst me. There is my hand.
  You shall be as a father to my youth;
  My voice shall sound as you do prompt mine ear,
  And I will stoop and humble my intents
  To your well-practisèd wise directions.—   120
  And princes all, believe me, I beseech you,
  My father is gone wild into his grave,
  For in his tomb lie my affections;
  And with his spirits sadly I survive
  To mock the expectation of the world,   125
  To frustrate prophecies, and to raze out

Rotten opinion, who hath writ me down
After my seeming. The tide of blood in me
Hath proudly flowed in vanity till now.
Now doth it turn, and ebb back to the sea,   130
Where it shall mingle with the state of floods,
And flow henceforth in formal majesty.
Now call we our high court of Parliament,
And let us choose such limbs of noble counsel
That the great body of our state may go   135
In equal rank with the best-governed nation;
That war, or peace, or both at once, may be
As things acquainted and familiar to us;
(To Lord Chief Justice)
In which you, father, shall have foremost hand.
(To all) Our coronation done, we will accite,   140
As I before remembered, all our state;
And, God consigning to my good intents,
No prince nor peer shall have just cause to say,
'God shorten Harry's happy life one day.'   Exeunt

5.3   ⌈A table and chairs set forth.⌉ Enter Sir John
       Falstaff, Shallow, Silence, Davy ⌈with vessels for
       the table⌉, Bardolph, and the Page
SHALLOW (to Sir John) Nay, you shall see my orchard,
  where, in an arbour, we will eat a last year's pippin
  of mine own grafting, with a dish of caraways, and so
  forth—come, cousin Silence—and then to bed.
SIR JOHN Fore God, you have here a goodly dwelling and
  a rich.   6
SHALLOW Barren, barren, barren; beggars all, beggars all,
  Sir John. Marry, good air.—Spread, Davy; spread, Davy.
                         ⌈Davy begins to spread the table⌉
  Well said, Davy.
SIR JOHN This Davy serves you for good uses; he is your
  serving-man and your husband.   11
SHALLOW A good varlet, a good varlet, a very good varlet,
  Sir John.—By the mass, I have drunk too much sack
  at supper.—A good varlet. Now sit down, now sit
  down. (To Silence) Come, cousin.   15
SILENCE Ah, sirrah, quoth-a, we shall
  (sings)
       Do nothing but eat, and make good cheer,
       And praise God for the merry year,
       When flesh is cheap and females dear,
       And lusty lads roam here and there   20
       So merrily,
       And ever among so merrily.
SIR JOHN There's a merry heart, good Master Silence! I'll
  give you a health for that anon.
SHALLOW Good Master Bardolph!—Some wine, Davy.   25
DAVY ⌈to Sir John⌉ Sweet sir, sit. ⌈To Bardolph⌉ I'll be with
  you anon. ⌈To Sir John⌉ Most sweet sir, sit. Master page,
  good master page, sit.
                ⌈All but Davy sit. Davy pours wine⌉
  Proface! What you want in meat, we'll have in drink;
  but you must bear; the heart's all.   30
SHALLOW Be merry, Master Bardolph and my little soldier
  there, be merry.

SILENCE (*sings*)
    Be merry, be merry, my wife has all,
    For women are shrews, both short and tall,
    'Tis merry in hall when beards wags all,   35
    And welcome merry shrovetide.
  Be merry, be merry.
SIR JOHN I did not think Master Silence had been a man
  of this mettle.
SILENCE Who, I? I have been merry twice and once ere
  now.   41
    Enter Davy ⌜*with a dish of apples*⌝
DAVY There's a dish of leather-coats for you.
SHALLOW Davy!
DAVY Your worship! I'll be with you straight. ⌜*To Sir
John*⌝ A cup of wine, sir?   45
SILENCE ⌜*sings*⌝
    A cup of wine
    That's brisk and fine,
    And drink unto thee, leman mine,
    And a merry heart lives long-a.
SIR JOHN Well said, Master Silence.   50
SILENCE And we shall be merry; now comes in the sweet
  o'th' night.
SIR JOHN Health and long life to you, Master Silence!
  He drinks
SILENCE Fill the cup and let it come. I'll pledge you a mile
  to th' bottom.   55
SHALLOW Honest Bardolph, welcome! If thou want'st
  anything and wilt not call, beshrew thy heart! (*To the
  Page*) Welcome, my little tiny thief, and welcome indeed,
  too!—I'll drink to Master Bardolph, and to all the
  cavalieros about London.   60
  He drinks
DAVY I hope to see London once ere I die.
BARDOLPH An I might see you there, Davy!
SHALLOW By the mass, you'll crack a quart together, ha,
  will you not, Master Bardolph?
BARDOLPH Yea, sir, in a pottle-pot.   65
SHALLOW By God's liggens, I thank thee. The knave will
  stick by thee, I can assure thee that; a will not out;
  'tis true-bred.
BARDOLPH And I'll stick by him, sir.
SHALLOW Why, there spoke a king! Lack nothing, be
  merry!   71
    One knocks at the door within
  Look who's at door there, ho! Who knocks?
                    ⌜*Exit Davy*⌝
    ⌜*Silence drinks*⌝
SIR JOHN ⌜*to Silence*⌝ Why, now you have done me right!
SILENCE ⌜*sings*⌝ Do me right,
    And dub me knight—   75
    Samingo.
  Is't not so?
SIR JOHN 'Tis so.
SILENCE Is't so?—Why then, say an old man can do
  somewhat.   80
    ⌜*Enter Davy*⌝

DAVY An't please your worship, there's one Pistol come
  from the court with news.
SIR JOHN From the court? Let him come in.
    Enter Pistol
  How now, Pistol?
PISTOL Sir John, God save you.   85
SIR JOHN What wind blew you hither, Pistol?
PISTOL
  Not the ill wind which blows no man to good.
  Sweet knight, thou art now one of the greatest men in
  this realm.
SILENCE By'r Lady, I think a be—but goodman Puff of
  Bar'son.   91
PISTOL Puff?
  Puff in thy teeth, most recreant coward base!—
  Sir John, I am thy Pistol and thy friend,
  And helter-skelter have I rode to thee,   95
  And tidings do I bring, and lucky joys,
  And golden times, and happy news of price.
SIR JOHN I pray thee now, deliver them like a man of this
  world.
PISTOL
  A foutre for the world and worldlings base!   100
  I speak of Africa and golden joys.
SIR JOHN
  O base Assyrian knight, what is thy news?
  Let King Cophetua know the truth thereof.
SILENCE ⌜*singing*⌝
  'And Robin Hood, Scarlet, and John.'
PISTOL
  Shall dunghill curs confront the Helicons?   105
  And shall good news be baffled?
  Then Pistol lay thy head in Furies' lap.
SHALLOW Honest gentleman, I know not your breeding.
PISTOL Why then, lament therefor.   109
SHALLOW Give me pardon, sir. If, sir, you come with news
  from the court, I take it there's but two ways: either
  to utter them, or conceal them. I am, sir, under the
  King in some authority.
PISTOL
  Under which king, besonian? Speak, or die.
SHALLOW
  Under King Harry.
PISTOL   Harry the Fourth, or Fifth?   115
SHALLOW
  Harry the Fourth.
PISTOL   A foutre for thine office!
  Sir John, thy tender lambkin now is king.
  Harry the Fifth's the man. I speak the truth.
  When Pistol lies, do this, (*making the fig*) and fig me,
  Like the bragging Spaniard.
SIR JOHN   What, is the old King dead?
PISTOL
  As nail in door. The things I speak are just.   121
SIR JOHN Away, Bardolph, saddle my horse! Master Robert
  Shallow, choose what office thou wilt in the land; 'tis
  thine. Pistol, I will double-charge thee with dignities.

BARDOLPH O joyful day!   125
  I would not take a knighthood for my fortune.
PISTOL What, I do bring good news?
SIR JOHN (*to Davy*) Carry Master Silence to bed.
                          ⌈*Exit Davy with Silence*⌉
  Master Shallow—my lord Shallow—be what thou wilt,
  I am fortune's steward—get on thy boots; we'll ride
  all night.—O sweet Pistol!—Away, Bardolph!   131
                          ⌈*Exit Bardolph*⌉
  Come, Pistol, utter more to me, and withal devise
  something to do thyself good. Boot, boot, Master
  Shallow! I know the young King is sick for me. Let us
  take any man's horses—the laws of England are at my
  commandment. Blessed are they that have been my
  friends, and woe to my Lord Chief Justice.
PISTOL
  Let vultures vile seize on his lungs also!
  'Where is the life that late I led?' say they.   139
  Why, here it is. Welcome these pleasant days.   *Exeunt*

5.4   *Enter Beadles, dragging in Mistress Quickly and
          Doll Tearsheet*
MISTRESS QUICKLY No, thou arrant knave! I would to God
  that I might die, that I might have thee hanged. Thou
  hast drawn my shoulder out of joint.
FIRST BEADLE The constables have delivered her over to
  me; and she shall have whipping-cheer, I warrant her.
  There hath been a man or two killed about her.   6
DOLL TEARSHEET Nut-hook, nut-hook, you lie! Come on,
  I'll tell thee what, thou damned tripe-visaged rascal,
  an the child I go with do miscarry, thou wert better
  thou hadst struck thy mother, thou paper-faced villain.
MISTRESS QUICKLY O the Lord, that Sir John were come!
  He would make this a bloody day to somebody. But I
  pray God the fruit of her womb miscarry!   13
FIRST BEADLE If it do, you shall have a dozen of cushions
  again; you have but eleven now. Come, I charge you
  both go with me, for the man is dead that you and
  Pistol beat amongst you.
DOLL TEARSHEET I'll tell you what, you thin man in a
  censer, I will have you as soundly swinged for this,
  you bluebottle rogue, you filthy famished correctioner!
  If you be not swinged, I'll forswear half-kirtles.   21
FIRST BEADLE Come, come, you she knight-errant, come!
MISTRESS QUICKLY O God, that right should thus o'ercome
  might! Well, of sufferance comes ease.
DOLL TEARSHEET Come, you rogue, come; bring me to a
  justice.   26
MISTRESS QUICKLY Ay, come, you starved bloodhound.
DOLL TEARSHEET Goodman death, goodman bones!
MISTRESS QUICKLY Thou atomy, thou!   29
DOLL TEARSHEET Come, you thin thing; come, you rascal.
FIRST BEADLE Very well.   *Exeunt*

5.5   *Enter* ⌈*two*⌉ *Grooms, strewing rushes*
FIRST GROOM More rushes, more rushes!
SECOND GROOM The trumpets have sounded twice.

⌈FIRST⌉ GROOM 'Twill be two o'clock ere they come from
  the coronation.   *Exeunt*
          *Enter Sir John Falstaff, Shallow, Pistol, Bardolph,
          and the Page*
SIR JOHN Stand here by me, Master Robert Shallow. I will
  make the King do you grace. I will leer upon him as a
  comes by, and do but mark the countenance that he
  will give me.
PISTOL God bless thy lungs, good knight.   9
SIR JOHN Come here, Pistol; stand behind me. (*To Shallow*)
  O, if I had had time to have made new liveries, I would
  have bestowed the thousand pound I borrowed of you!
  But 'tis no matter; this poor show doth better; this
  doth infer the zeal I had to see him.
⌈SHALLOW⌉ It doth so.   15
SIR JOHN It shows my earnestness of affection—
PISTOL It doth so.
SIR JOHN My devotion—
PISTOL It doth, it doth, it doth.   19
SIR JOHN As it were, to ride day and night, and not to
  deliberate, not to remember, not to have patience to
  shift me—
SHALLOW It is most certain.
⌈SIR JOHN⌉ But to stand stained with travel and sweating
  with desire to see him, thinking of nothing else, putting
  all affairs in oblivion, as if there were nothing else to
  be done but to see him.
PISTOL 'Tis *semper idem*, for *absque hoc nihil est*: 'tis all in
  every part.
SHALLOW 'Tis so indeed.   30
PISTOL
  My knight, I will inflame thy noble liver,
  And make thee rage.
  Thy Doll, and Helen of thy noble thoughts,
  Is in base durance and contagious prison,
  Haled thither   35
  By most mechanical and dirty hand.
  Rouse up Revenge from ebon den with fell Alecto's
          snake,
  For Doll is in. Pistol speaks naught but truth.
SIR JOHN I will deliver her.
          ⌈*Shouts within.*⌉ *Trumpets sound*
PISTOL
  There roared the sea, and trumpet-clangour sounds! 40
          *Enter King Harry the Fifth, Prince John of
          Lancaster, the Dukes of Clarence and Gloucester,
          the Lord Chief Justice,* ⌈*and others*⌉
SIR JOHN
  God save thy grace, King Hal, my royal Hal!
PISTOL
  The heavens thee guard and keep, most royal imp of
          fame!
SIR JOHN God save thee, my sweet boy!
KING HARRY
  My Lord Chief Justice, speak to that vain man.   44
LORD CHIEF JUSTICE (*to Sir John*)
  Have you your wits? Know you what 'tis you speak?

SIR JOHN
My king, my Jove, I speak to thee, my heart!
KING HARRY
I know thee not, old man. Fall to thy prayers.
How ill white hairs becomes a fool and jester!
I have long dreamt of such a kind of man,
So surfeit-swelled, so old, and so profane;   50
But being awake, I do despise my dream.
Make less thy body hence, and more thy grace.
Leave gormandizing; know the grave doth gape
For thee thrice wider than for other men.
Reply not to me with a fool-born jest.   55
Presume not that I am the thing I was,
For God doth know, so shall the world perceive,
That I have turned away my former self;
So will I those that kept me company.
When thou dost hear I am as I have been,   60
Approach me, and thou shalt be as thou wast,
The tutor and the feeder of my riots.
Till then I banish thee, on pain of death,
As I have done the rest of my misleaders,
Not to come near our person by ten mile.   65
For competence of life I will allow you,
That lack of means enforce you not to evils;
And as we hear you do reform yourselves,
We will, according to your strengths and qualities,
Give you advancement. (*To Lord Chief Justice*) Be it
     your charge, my lord,   70
To see performed the tenor of our word. (*To his train*)
     Set on!   *Exeunt King Harry and his train*
SIR JOHN Master Shallow, I owe you a thousand pound.
SHALLOW Yea, marry, Sir John; which I beseech you to
let me have home with me.   74
SIR JOHN That can hardly be, Master Shallow. Do not you
grieve at this. I shall be sent for in private to him. Look
you, he must seem thus to the world. Fear not your
advancements. I will be the man yet that shall make
you great.   79
SHALLOW I cannot perceive how, unless you give me your
doublet and stuff me out with straw. I beseech you,
good Sir John, let me have five hundred of my thousand.
SIR JOHN Sir, I will be as good as my word. This that you
heard was but a colour.
SHALLOW A colour I fear that you will die in, Sir John. 85
SIR JOHN Fear no colours. Go with me to dinner. Come,
Lieutenant Pistol; come, Bardolph. I shall be sent for
soon at night.
     Enter the Lord Chief Justice and Prince John,
     with officers
LORD CHIEF JUSTICE (*to officers*)
Go carry Sir John Falstaff to the Fleet.
Take all his company along with him.   90
SIR JOHN My lord, my lord!
LORD CHIEF JUSTICE
I cannot now speak. I will hear you soon.—
Take them away.

PISTOL
Si fortuna me tormenta, spero me contenta.
     Exeunt all but Prince John
     and Lord Chief Justice
PRINCE JOHN
I like this fair proceeding of the King's.   95
He hath intent his wonted followers
Shall all be very well provided for,
But all are banished till their conversations
Appear more wise and modest to the world.
LORD CHIEF JUSTICE And so they are.   100
PRINCE JOHN
The King hath called his parliament, my lord.
LORD CHIEF JUSTICE He hath.
PRINCE JOHN
I will lay odds that, ere this year expire,
We bear our civil swords and native fire
As far as France. I heard a bird so sing,   105
Whose music, to my thinking, pleased the King.
Come, will you hence?   *Exeunt*

     Enter Epilogue   **Epilogue**
EPILOGUE First my fear, then my curtsy, last my speech.
     My fear is your displeasure; my curtsy, my duty;
and my speech to beg your pardons. If you look for a
good speech now, you undo me; for what I have to
say is of mine own making, and what indeed I should
say will, I doubt, prove mine own marring. But to the
purpose, and so to the venture. Be it known to you, as
it is very well, I was lately here in the end of a
displeasing play, to pray your patience for it, and to
promise you a better. I did mean indeed to pay you
with this; which, if like an ill venture it come unluckily
home, I break, and you, my gentle creditors, lose. Here
I promised you I would be, and here I commit my body
to your mercies. Bate me some, and I will pay you
some, and, as most debtors do, promise you infinitely.
     If my tongue cannot entreat you to acquit me, will
you command me to use my legs? And yet that were
but light payment, to dance out of your debt. But a
good conscience will make any possible satisfaction,
and so would I. All the gentlewomen here have forgiven
me; if the gentlemen will not, then the gentlemen do
not agree with the gentlewomen, which was never
seen before in such an assembly.
     One word more, I beseech you. If you be not too
much cloyed with fat meat, our humble author will
continue the story with Sir John in it, and make you
merry with fair Katherine of France; where, for
anything I know, Falstaff shall die of a sweat—unless
already a be killed with your hard opinions. For
Oldcastle died a martyr, and this is not the man. My
tongue is weary; when my legs are too, I will bid you
good night, and so kneel down before you—but, indeed,
to pray for the Queen.
     ⌈*He dances, then kneels for applause.*⌉ *Exit*

ADDITIONAL PASSAGES

Along with some substantial additions, Shakespeare probably made a number of short excisions when preparing the finished version of the play. The following, present in the Quarto but entirely or substantially omitted in the later Folio text, are the most significant:

A. AFTER 2.2.22

And God knows whether those that bawl out the ruins of thy linen shall inherit his kingdom—but the midwives say the children are not in the fault, whereupon the world increases, and kindreds are mightily strengthened.   5

B. AFTER 'LIQUORS!', 3.1.52

       O, if this were seen,
The happiest youth, viewing his progress through,
What perils past, what crosses to ensue,
Would shut the book and sit him down and die.

C. AFTER 'FAMINE.', 3.2.309

yet lecherous as a monkey; and the whores called him 'mandrake'. A came ever in the rearward of the fashion, and sung those tunes to the overscutched hussies that he heard the carmen whistle, and sware they were his fancies or his good-nights.   5

HENRY V

THE Chorus to Act 5 of *Henry V* contains an uncharacteristic, direct topical reference:

> Were now the General of our gracious Empress—
> As in good time he may—from Ireland coming,
> Bringing rebellion broachèd on his sword,
> How many would the peaceful city quit
> To welcome him!

'The General' must be the Earl of Essex, whose 'Empress'—Queen Elizabeth—had sent him on an Irish campaign on 27 March 1599; he returned, disgraced, on 28 September. Plans for his campaign had been known at least since the previous November; the idea that he might return in triumph would have been meaningless after September 1599, and it seems likely that Shakespeare wrote his play during 1599, probably in the spring. It appeared in print, in a debased text, in (probably) August 1600, when it was said to have 'been sundry times played by the Right Honourable the Lord Chamberlain his servants'. Although this text seems to have been put together from memory by actors playing in an abbreviated adaptation, the Shakespearian text behind it appears to have been in a later state than the generally superior text printed from Shakespeare's own papers in the 1623 Folio. Our edition draws on the 1600 quarto in the attempt to represent the play as acted by Shakespeare's company. The principal difference is the reversion to historical authenticity in the substitution at Agincourt of the Duke of Bourbon for the Dauphin.

As in the two plays about Henry IV, Shakespeare is indebted to *The Famous Victories of Henry the Fifth* (printed 1598). Other Elizabethan plays about Henry V, now lost, may have influenced him; he certainly used the chronicle histories of Edward Hall (1542) and Holinshed (1577, revised and enlarged in 1587).

From the 'civil broils' of the earlier history plays, Shakespeare turns to portray a country united in war against France. Each act is prefaced by a Chorus, speaking some of the play's finest poetry, and giving it an epic quality. Henry V, 'star of England', is Shakespeare's most heroic warrior king, but (like his predecessors) has an introspective side, and is aware of the crime by which his father came to the throne. We are reminded of his 'wilder days', and see that the transition from 'madcap prince' to the 'mirror of all Christian kings' involves loss: although the epilogue to *2 Henry IV* had suggested that Sir John would reappear, he is only, though poignantly, an off-stage presence. Yet Shakespeare's infusion of comic form into historical narrative reaches its natural conclusion in this play. Sir John's cronies, Pistol, Bardolph, Nim, and Mistress Quickly, reappear to provide a counterpart to the heroic action, and Shakespeare invents comic episodes involving an Englishman (Gower), a Welshman (Fluellen), an Irishman (MacMorris), and a Scot (Jamy). The play also has romance elements, in the almost incredible extent of the English victory over the French and in the disguised Henry's comradely mingling with his soldiers, as well as in his courtship of the French princess. The play's romantic and heroic aspects have made it popular especially in times of war and have aroused accusations of jingoism, but the horrors of war are vividly depicted, and the Chorus's closing speech reminds us that Henry died young, and that hi son's protector 'lost France and made his England bleed'.

THE PERSONS OF THE PLAY

CHORUS

KING HARRY V of England, claimant to the French throne

Duke of GLOUCESTER }
Duke of CLARENCE } his brothers

Duke of EXETER, his uncle

Duke of YORK

SALISBURY

WESTMORLAND

WARWICK

Archbishop of CANTERBURY

Bishop of ELY

Richard, Earl of CAMBRIDGE }
Henry, Lord SCROPE of Masham } traitors
Sir Thomas GREY }

PISTOL }
NIM } formerly Falstaff's companions
BARDOLPH }

BOY, formerly Falstaff's page

HOSTESS, formerly Mistress Quickly, now Pistol's wife

Captain GOWER, an Englishman

Captain FLUELLEN, a Welshman

Captain MACMORRIS, an Irishman

Captain JAMY, a Scot

Sir Thomas ERPINGHAM

John BATES }
Alexander COURT } English soldiers
Michael WILLIAMS }

HERALD

KING CHARLES VI of France

ISABEL, his wife and queen

The DAUPHIN, their son and heir

CATHERINE, their daughter

ALICE, an old gentlewoman

The CONSTABLE of France }
Duke of BOURBON
Duke of ORLÉANS
Duke of BERRI } French noblemen at Agincourt
Lord RAMBURES
Lord GRANDPRÉ }

Duke of BURGUNDY

MONTJOY, the French Herald

GOVERNOR of Harfleur

French AMBASSADORS to England

The Life of Henry the Fifth

Prologue *Enter Chorus as Prologue*

CHORUS

O for a muse of fire, that would ascend
The brightest heaven of invention:
A kingdom for a stage, princes to act,
And monarchs to behold the swelling scene.
Then should the warlike Harry, like himself,   5
Assume the port of Mars, and at his heels,
Leashed in like hounds, should famine, sword, and
    fire
Crouch for employment. But pardon, gentles all,
The flat unraisèd spirits that hath dared
On this unworthy scaffold to bring forth   10
So great an object. Can this cock-pit hold
The vasty fields of France? Or may we cram
Within this wooden O the very casques
That did affright the air at Agincourt?
O pardon: since a crookèd figure may   15
Attest in little place a million,
And let us, ciphers to this great account,
On your imaginary forces work.
Suppose within the girdle of these walls
Are now confined two mighty monarchies,   20
Whose high uprearèd and abutting fronts
The perilous narrow ocean parts asunder.
Piece out our imperfections with your thoughts:
Into a thousand parts divide one man,
And make imaginary puissance.   25
Think, when we talk of horses, that you see them,
Printing their proud hoofs i'th' receiving earth;
For 'tis your thoughts that now must deck our kings,
Carry them here and there, jumping o'er times,
Turning th'accomplishment of many years   30
Into an hourglass—for the which supply,
Admit me Chorus to this history,
Who Prologue-like your humble patience pray
Gently to hear, kindly to judge, our play.   *Exit*

1.1 *Enter the Archbishop of Canterbury and the Bishop
of Ely*

CANTERBURY

My lord, I'll tell you. That self bill is urged
Which in th'eleventh year of the last king's reign
Was like, and had indeed against us passed,
But that the scrambling and unquiet time
Did push it out of farther question.   5

ELY

But how, my lord, shall we resist it now?

CANTERBURY

It must be thought on. If it pass against us,
We lose the better half of our possession,
For all the temporal lands which men devout
By testament have given to the Church   10

Would they strip from us—being valued thus:
As much as would maintain, to the King's honour,
Full fifteen earls and fifteen hundred knights,
Six thousand and two hundred good esquires;
And, to relief of lazars and weak age,   15
Of indigent faint souls past corporal toil,
A hundred almshouses right well supplied;
And to the coffers of the King beside
A thousand pounds by th' year. Thus runs the bill.

ELY This would drink deep.   20

CANTERBURY 'Twould drink the cup and all.

ELY But what prevention?

CANTERBURY

The King is full of grace and fair regard.

ELY

And a true lover of the holy Church.

CANTERBURY

The courses of his youth promised it not.   25
The breath no sooner left his father's body
But that his wildness, mortified in him,
Seemed to die too. Yea, at that very moment
Consideration like an angel came
And whipped th'offending Adam out of him,   30
Leaving his body as a paradise
T'envelop and contain celestial spirits.
Never was such a sudden scholar made;
Never came reformation in a flood
With such a heady currance scouring faults;   35
Nor never Hydra-headed wilfulness
So soon did lose his seat—and all at once—
As in this king.

ELY   We are blessèd in the change.

CANTERBURY

Hear him but reason in divinity
And, all-admiring, with an inward wish   40
You would desire the King were made a prelate;
Hear him debate of commonwealth affairs,
You would say it hath been all-in-all his study;
List his discourse of war, and you shall hear
A fearful battle rendered you in music;   45
Turn him to any cause of policy,
The Gordian knot of it he will unloose,
Familiar as his garter—that when he speaks,
The air, a chartered libertine, is still,
And the mute wonder lurketh in men's ears   50
To steal his sweet and honeyed sentences:
So that the art and practic part of life
Must be the mistress to this theoric.
Which is a wonder how his grace should glean it,
Since his addiction was to courses vain,   55
His companies unlettered, rude, and shallow,
His hours filled up with riots, banquets, sports,
And never noted in him any study,

Any retirement, any sequestration
From open haunts and popularity.   60

ELY

The strawberry grows underneath the nettle,
And wholesome berries thrive and ripen best
Neighboured by fruit of baser quality;
And so the Prince obscured his contemplation
Under the veil of wildness—which, no doubt,   65
Grew like the summer grass, fastest by night,
Unseen, yet crescive in his faculty.

CANTERBURY

It must be so, for miracles are ceased,
And therefore we must needs admit the means
How things are perfected.

ELY   But, my good lord,   70
How now for mitigation of this bill
Urged by the Commons? Doth his majesty
Incline to it, or no?

CANTERBURY   He seems indifferent,
Or rather swaying more upon our part
Than cherishing th'exhibitors against us;   75
For I have made an offer to his majesty,
Upon our spiritual convocation
And in regard of causes now in hand,
Which I have opened to his grace at large:
As touching France, to give a greater sum   80
Than ever at one time the clergy yet
Did to his predecessors part withal.

ELY

How did this offer seem received, my lord?

CANTERBURY

With good acceptance of his majesty,
Save that there was not time enough to hear,   85
As I perceived his grace would fain have done,
The severals and unhidden passages
Of his true titles to some certain dukedoms,
And generally to the crown and seat of France,
Derived from Edward, his great-grandfather.   90

ELY

What was th'impediment that broke this off?

CANTERBURY

The French ambassador upon that instant
Craved audience—and the hour I think is come
To give him hearing. Is it four o'clock?

ELY It is.   95

CANTERBURY

Then go we in, to know his embassy—
Which I could with a ready guess declare
Before the Frenchman speak a word of it.

ELY

I'll wait upon you, and I long to hear it.   *Exeunt*

1.2   *Enter King Harry, the Dukes of Gloucester,*
        ⌈Clarence⌉, and Exeter, and the Earls of Warwick
        and Westmorland

KING HARRY

Where is my gracious lord of Canterbury?

EXETER

Not here in presence.

KING HARRY   Send for him, good uncle.

WESTMORLAND

Shall we call in th'ambassador, my liege?

KING HARRY

Not yet, my cousin. We would be resolved,
Before we hear him, of some things of weight   5
That task our thoughts, concerning us and France.
        Enter the Archbishop of Canterbury and the Bishop
        of Ely

CANTERBURY

God and his angels guard your sacred throne,
And make you long become it.

KING HARRY   Sure we thank you.
My learnèd lord, we pray you to proceed,
And justly and religiously unfold   10
Why the law Salic that they have in France
Or should or should not bar us in our claim.
And God forbid, my dear and faithful lord,
That you should fashion, wrest, or bow your reading,
Or nicely charge your understanding soul   15
With opening titles miscreate, whose right
Suits not in native colours with the truth;
For God doth know how many now in health
Shall drop their blood in approbation
Of what your reverence shall incite us to.   20
Therefore take heed how you impawn our person,
How you awake our sleeping sword of war;
We charge you in the name of God take heed.
For never two such kingdoms did contend
Without much fall of blood, whose guiltless drops   25
Are every one a woe, a sore complaint
'Gainst him whose wrongs gives edge unto the swords
That makes such waste in brief mortality.
Under this conjuration speak, my lord,
For we will hear, note, and believe in heart   30
That what you speak is in your conscience washed
As pure as sin with baptism.

CANTERBURY

Then hear me, gracious sovereign, and you peers
That owe your selves, your lives, and services
To this imperial throne. There is no bar   35
To make against your highness' claim to France
But this, which they produce from Pharamond:
'*In terram Salicam mulieres ne succedant*'—
'No woman shall succeed in Salic land'—
Which 'Salic land' the French unjustly gloss   40
To be the realm of France, and Pharamond
The founder of this law and female bar.
Yet their own authors faithfully affirm
That the land Salic is in Germany,
Between the floods of Saale and of Elbe,   45
Where, Charles the Great having subdued the Saxons,
There left behind and settled certain French
Who, holding in disdain the German women
For some dishonest manners of their life,

Established there this law: to wit, no female   50
Should be inheritrix in Salic land—
Which Salic, as I said, 'twixt Elbe and Saale,
Is at this day in Germany called Meissen.
Then doth it well appear the Salic Law
Was not devisèd for the realm of France.   55
Nor did the French possess the Salic land
Until four hundred one-and-twenty years
After defunction of King Pharamond,
Idly supposed the founder of this law,
Who died within the year of our redemption   60
Four hundred twenty-six; and Charles the Great
Subdued the Saxons, and did seat the French
Beyond the river Saale, in the year
Eight hundred five. Besides, their writers say,
King Pépin, which deposèd Childéric,   65
Did, as heir general—being descended
Of Blithild, which was daughter to King Clotaire—
Make claim and title to the crown of France.
Hugh Capet also—who usurped the crown
Of Charles the Duke of Lorraine, sole heir male   70
Of the true line and stock of Charles the Great—
To fine his title with some shows of truth,
Though in pure truth it was corrupt and naught,
Conveyed himself as heir to th' Lady Lingard,
Daughter to Charlemain, who was the son   75
To Louis the Emperor, and Louis the son
Of Charles the Great. Also, King Louis the Ninth,
Who was sole heir to the usurper Capet,
Could not keep quiet in his conscience,
Wearing the crown of France, till satisfied   80
That fair Queen Isabel, his grandmother,
Was lineal of the Lady Ermengarde,
Daughter to Charles, the foresaid Duke of Lorraine;
By the which marriage, the line of Charles the Great
Was reunited to the crown of France.   85
So that, as clear as is the summer's sun,
King Pépin's title and Hugh Capet's claim,
King Louis his satisfaction, all appear
To hold in right and title of the female;
So do the kings of France unto this day,   90
Howbeit they would hold up this Salic Law
To bar your highness claiming from the female,
And rather choose to hide them in a net
Than amply to embar their crookèd titles,
Usurped from you and your progenitors.   95

KING HARRY
May I with right and conscience make this claim?

CANTERBURY
The sin upon my head, dread sovereign.
For in the Book of Numbers is it writ,
'When the son dies, let the inheritance
Descend unto the daughter.' Gracious lord,   100
Stand for your own; unwind your bloody flag;
Look back into your mighty ancestors.
Go, my dread lord, to your great-grandsire's tomb,
From whom you claim; invoke his warlike spirit,

And your great-uncle's, Edward the Black Prince,   105
Who on the French ground played a tragedy,
Making defeat on the full power of France,
Whiles his most mighty father on a hill
Stood smiling to behold his lion's whelp
Forage in blood of French nobility.   110
O noble English, that could entertain
With half their forces the full pride of France,
And let another half stand laughing by,
All out of work, and cold for action.

ELY
Awake remembrance of those valiant dead,   115
And with your puissant arm renew their feats.
You are their heir, you sit upon their throne,
The blood and courage that renownèd them
Runs in your veins—and my thrice-puissant liege
Is in the very May-morn of his youth,   120
Ripe for exploits and mighty enterprises.

EXETER
Your brother kings and monarchs of the earth
Do all expect that you should rouse yourself
As did the former lions of your blood.

WESTMORLAND
They know your grace hath cause; and means and
      might,   125
So hath your highness. Never king of England
Had nobles richer and more loyal subjects,
Whose hearts have left their bodies here in England
And lie pavilioned in the fields of France.

CANTERBURY
O let their bodies follow, my dear liege,   130
With blood and sword and fire, to win your right.
In aid whereof, we of the spiritualty
Will raise your highness such a mighty sum
As never did the clergy at one time
Bring in to any of your ancestors.   135

KING HARRY
We must not only arm t'invade the French,
But lay down our proportions to defend
Against the Scot, who will make raid upon us
With all advantages.

CANTERBURY
They of those marches, gracious sovereign,   140
Shall be a wall sufficient to defend
Our inland from the pilfering borderers.

KING HARRY
We do not mean the coursing snatchers only,
But fear the main intendment of the Scot,
Who hath been still a giddy neighbour to us.   145
For you shall read that my great-grandfather
Never unmasked his power unto France
But that the Scot on his unfurnished kingdom
Came pouring like the tide into a breach
With ample and brim fullness of his force   150
Galling the gleanèd land with hot assays,
Girding with grievous siege castles and towns,
That England, being empty of defence,
Hath shook and trembled at the bruit thereof.

CANTERBURY
She hath been then more feared than harmed, my
    liege.   155
For hear her but exampled by herself:
When all her chivalry hath been in France
And she a mourning widow of her nobles,
She hath herself not only well defended
But taken and impounded as a stray   160
The King of Scots, whom she did send to France
To fill King Edward's fame with prisoner kings
And make your chronicle as rich with praise
As is the ooze and bottom of the sea
With sunken wrack and sumless treasuries.   165

⌈A LORD⌉
But there's a saying very old and true:
    'If that you will France win,
    Then with Scotland first begin.'
For once the eagle England being in prey,
To her unguarded nest the weasel Scot   170
Comes sneaking, and so sucks her princely eggs,
Playing the mouse in absence of the cat,
To 'tame and havoc more than she can eat.

EXETER
It follows then the cat must stay at home.
Yet that is but a crushed necessity,   175
Since we have locks to safeguard necessaries
And pretty traps to catch the petty thieves.
While that the armèd hand doth fight abroad,
Th'advisèd head defends itself at home.
For government, though high and low and lower,   180
Put into parts, doth keep in one consent,
Congreeing in a full and natural close,
Like music.

CANTERBURY   True. Therefore doth heaven divide
The state of man in divers functions,
Setting endeavour in continual motion;   185
To which is fixèd, as an aim or butt,
Obedience. For so work the honey-bees,
Creatures that by a rule in nature teach
The act of order to a peopled kingdom.
They have a king, and officers of sorts,   190
Where some like magistrates correct at home;
Others like merchants venture trade abroad;
Others like soldiers, armèd in their stings,
Make boot upon the summer's velvet buds,
Which pillage they with merry march bring home   195
To the tent royal of their emperor,
Who busied in his majesty surveys
The singing masons building roofs of gold,
The civil citizens lading up the honey,
The poor mechanic porters crowding in   200
Their heavy burdens at his narrow gate,
The sad-eyed justice with his surly hum
Delivering o'er to executors pale
The lazy yawning drone. I this infer:
That many things, having full reference   205
To one consent, may work contrariously.

As many arrows, loosèd several ways,
Fly to one mark, as many ways meet in one town,
As many fresh streams meet in one salt sea,
As many lines close in the dial's centre,   210
So may a thousand actions once afoot
End in one purpose, and be all well borne
Without defect. Therefore to France, my liege.
Divide your happy England into four,
Whereof take you one quarter into France,   215
And you withal shall make all Gallia shake.
If we with thrice such powers left at home
Cannot defend our own doors from the dog,
Let us be worried, and our nation lose
The name of hardiness and policy.   220

KING HARRY
Call in the messengers sent from the Dauphin.
                                    Exit one or more
Now are we well resolved, and by God's help
And yours, the noble sinews of our power,
France being ours we'll bend it to our awe,
Or break it all to pieces. Or there we'll sit,   225
Ruling in large and ample empery
O'er France and all her almost kingly dukedoms,
Or lay these bones in an unworthy urn,
Tombless, with no remembrance over them.
Either our history shall with full mouth   230
Speak freely of our acts, or else our grave,
Like Turkish mute, shall have a tongueless mouth,
Not worshipped with a waxen epitaph.
        Enter Ambassadors of France, with a tun
Now are we well prepared to know the pleasure
Of our fair cousin Dauphin, for we hear   235
Your greeting is from him, not from the King.

AMBASSADOR
May't please your majesty to give us leave
Freely to render what we have in charge,
Or shall we sparingly show you far off
The Dauphin's meaning and our embassy?   240

KING HARRY
We are no tyrant, but a Christian king,
Unto whose grace our passion is as subject
As is our wretches fettered in our prisons.
Therefore with frank and with uncurbèd plainness
Tell us the Dauphin's mind.

AMBASSADOR   Thus then in few: 245
Your highness lately sending into France
Did claim some certain dukedoms, in the right
Of your great predecessor, King Edward the Third.
In answer of which claim, the Prince our master
Says that you savour too much of your youth,   250
And bids you be advised, there's naught in France
That can be with a nimble galliard won:
You cannot revel into dukedoms there.
He therefore sends you, meeter for your spirit,
This tun of treasure, and in lieu of this   255
Desires you let the dukedoms that you claim
Hear no more of you. This the Dauphin speaks.

KING HARRY
What treasure, uncle?
EXETER (*opening the tun*) Tennis balls, my liege.
KING HARRY
We are glad the Dauphin is so pleasant with us.
His present and your pains we thank you for.   260
When we have matched our rackets to these balls,
We will in France, by God's grace, play a set
Shall strike his father's crown into the hazard.
Tell him he hath made a match with such a wrangler
That all the courts of France will be disturbed   265
With chases. And we understand him well,
How he comes o'er us with our wilder days,
Not measuring what use we made of them.
We never valued this poor seat of England,
And therefore, living hence, did give ourself   270
To barbarous licence—as 'tis ever common
That men are merriest when they are from home.
But tell the Dauphin I will keep my state,
Be like a king, and show my sail of greatness
When I do rouse me in my throne of France.   275
For that have I laid by my majesty
And plodded like a man for working days,
But I will rise there with so full a glory
That I will dazzle all the eyes of France,
Yea strike the Dauphin blind to look on us.   280
And tell the pleasant Prince this mock of his
Hath turned his balls to gunstones, and his soul
Shall stand sore chargèd for the wasteful vengeance
That shall fly from them—for many a thousand
widows
Shall this his mock mock out of their dear husbands,
Mock mothers from their sons, mock castles down;   286
Ay, some are yet ungotten and unborn
That shall have cause to curse the Dauphin's scorn.
But this lies all within the will of God,
To whom I do appeal, and in whose name   290
Tell you the Dauphin I am coming on
To venge me as I may, and to put forth
My rightful hand in a well-hallowed cause.
So get you hence in peace. And tell the Dauphin
His jest will savour but of shallow wit   295
When thousands weep more than did laugh at it.—
Convey them with safe conduct.—Fare you well.
Exeunt Ambassadors
EXETER This was a merry message.
KING HARRY
We hope to make the sender blush at it.
Therefore, my lords, omit no happy hour   300
That may give furth'rance to our expedition;
For we have now no thought in us but France,
Save those to God, that run before our business.
Therefore let our proportions for these wars
Be soon collected, and all things thought upon   305
That may with reasonable swiftness add
More feathers to our wings; for, God before,
We'll chide this Dauphin at his father's door.

Therefore let every man now task his thought,
That this fair action may on foot be brought.   310
⌐Flourish.⌐ *Exeunt*

2.0   *Enter Chorus*
CHORUS
Now all the youth of England are on fire,
And silken dalliance in the wardrobe lies;
Now thrive the armourers, and honour's thought
Reigns solely in the breast of every man.
They sell the pasture now to buy the horse,   5
Following the mirror of all Christian kings
With wingèd heels, as English Mercuries.
For now sits expectation in the air
And hides a sword from hilts unto the point
With crowns imperial, crowns and coronets,   10
Promised to Harry and his followers.
The French, advised by good intelligence
Of this most dreadful preparation,
Shake in their fear, and with pale policy
Seek to divert the English purposes.   15
O England!—model to thy inward greatness,
Like little body with a mighty heart,
What mightst thou do, that honour would thee do,
Were all thy children kind and natural?
But see, thy fault France hath in thee found out: 20
A nest of hollow bosoms, which he fills
With treacherous crowns; and three corrupted men—
One, Richard, Earl of Cambridge; and the second
Henry, Lord Scrope of Masham; and the third
Sir Thomas Grey, knight, of Northumberland—   25
Have, for the gilt of France—O guilt indeed!—
Confirmed conspiracy with fearful France;
And by their hands this grace of kings must die,
If hell and treason hold their promises,
Ere he take ship for France, and in Southampton.   30
Linger your patience on, and we'll digest
Th'abuse of distance, force—perforce—a play.
The sum is paid, the traitors are agreed,
The King is set from London, and the scene
Is now transported, gentles, to Southampton.   35
There is the playhouse now, there must you sit,
And thence to France shall we convey you safe,
And bring you back, charming the narrow seas
To give you gentle pass—for if we may
We'll not offend one stomach with our play.   40
But till the King come forth, and not till then,
Unto Southampton do we shift our scene.   *Exit*

2.1   *Enter Corporal Nim and Lieutenant Bardolph*
BARDOLPH Well met, Corporal Nim.
NIM Good morrow, Lieutenant Bardolph.
BARDOLPH What, are Ensign Pistol and you friends yet?
NIM For my part, I care not. I say little, but when time
shall serve, there shall be smiles—but that shall be as
it may. I dare not fight, but I will wink and hold out
mine iron. It is a simple one, but what though? It will

toast cheese, and it will endure cold, as another man's
sword will—and there's an end.   9

BARDOLPH I will bestow a breakfast to make you friends,
and we'll be all three sworn brothers to France. Let't
be so, good Corporal Nim.

NIM Faith, I will live so long as I may, that's the certain
of it, and when I cannot live any longer, I will do as I
may. That is my rest, that is the rendezvous of it.   15

BARDOLPH It is certain, corporal, that he is married to
Nell Quickly, and certainly she did you wrong, for you
were troth-plight to her.

NIM I cannot tell. Things must be as they may. Men may
sleep, and they may have their throats about them at
that time, and some say knives have edges. It must be
as it may. Though Patience be a tired mare, yet she
will plod. There must be conclusions. Well, I cannot
tell.   24

Enter Ensign Pistol and Hostess Quickly

BARDOLPH Good morrow, Ensign Pistol. (*To Nim*) Here
comes Ensign Pistol and his wife. Good Corporal, be
patient here.

⌈NIM⌉ How now, mine host Pistol?

PISTOL
Base tick, call'st thou me host? Now by Gad's lugs
I swear I scorn the term. Nor shall my Nell keep
    lodgers.   30

HOSTESS No, by my troth, not long, for we cannot lodge
and board a dozen or fourteen gentlewomen that live
honestly by the prick of their needles, but it will be
thought we keep a bawdy-house straight.

⌈*Nim draws his sword*⌉

O well-a-day, Lady! If he be not hewn now, we shall
see wilful adultery and murder committed.   36

⌈*Pistol draws his sword*⌉

BARDOLPH Good lieutenant, good corporal, offer nothing
here.

NIM Pish.

PISTOL
Pish for thee, Iceland dog. Thou prick-eared cur of
    Iceland.   40

HOSTESS Good Corporal Nim, show thy valour, and put
up your sword.

They sheathe their swords

NIM Will you shog off? I would have you *solus.*

PISTOL
'*Solus*', egregious dog? O viper vile!
The *solus* in thy most marvellous face,   45
The *solus* in thy teeth, and in thy throat,
And in thy hateful lungs, yea in thy maw pardie—
And which is worse, within thy nasty mouth.
I do retort the *solus* in thy bowels,
For I can take, and Pistol's cock is up,   50
And flashing fire will follow.

NIM I am not Barbason, you cannot conjure me. I have
an humour to knock you indifferently well. If you grow
foul with me, Pistol, I will scour you with my rapier,
as I may, in fair terms. If you would walk off, I would
prick your guts a little, in good terms, as I may, and
that's the humour of it.

PISTOL
O braggart vile, and damnèd furious wight!
The grave doth gape and doting death is near.
Therefore ex-hale.   60

Pistol and Nim draw their swords

BARDOLPH Hear me, hear me what I say.

⌈*He draws his sword*⌉

He that strikes the first stroke, I'll run him up to the
hilts, as I am a soldier.

PISTOL
An oath of mickle might, and fury shall abate.

⌈*They sheathe their swords*⌉

(*To Nim*) Give me thy fist, thy forefoot to me give. 65
Thy spirits are most tall.

NIM I will cut thy throat one time or other, in fair terms,
that is the humour of it.

PISTOL *Couple a gorge,*
That is the word. I thee defy again.   70
O hound of Crete, think'st thou my spouse to get?
No, to the spital go,
And from the powd'ring tub of infamy
Fetch forth the lazar kite of Cressid's kind,
Doll Tearsheet she by name, and her espouse.   75
I have, and I will hold, the quondam Quickly
For the only she, and—*pauca*, there's enough. Go to.

Enter the Boy ⌈*running*⌉

BOY Mine host Pistol, you must come to my master, and
you, hostess. He is very sick, and would to bed.—Good
Bardolph, put thy face between his sheets, and do the
office of a warming-pan.—Faith, he's very ill.   81

BARDOLPH Away, you rogue!

HOSTESS By my troth, he'll yield the crow a pudding one
of these days. The King has killed his heart. Good
husband, come home presently.   *Exit* ⌈*with Boy*⌉

BARDOLPH Come, shall I make you two friends? We must
to France together. Why the devil should we keep
knives to cut one another's throats?

PISTOL
Let floods o'erswell, and fiends for food howl on!

NIM You'll pay me the eight shillings I won of you at
betting?   91

PISTOL Base is the slave that pays.

NIM That now I will have. That's the humour of it.

PISTOL
As manhood shall compound. Push home.

Pistol and Nim draw their swords

BARDOLPH ⌈*drawing his sword*⌉ By this sword, he that makes
the first thrust, I'll kill him. By this sword, I will.   96

PISTOL
Sword is an oath, and oaths must have their course.

⌈*He sheathes his sword*⌉

BARDOLPH Corporal Nim, an thou wilt be friends, be
friends. An thou wilt not, why then be enemies with
me too. Prithee, put up.   100

NIM I shall have my eight shillings?

PISTOL
A noble shalt thou have, and present pay,
And liquor likewise will I give to thee,
And friendship shall combine, and brotherhood.

I'll live by Nim, and Nim shall live by me.   105
Is not this just? For I shall sutler be
Unto the camp, and profits will accrue.
Give me thy hand.
NIM I shall have my noble?
PISTOL In cash, most justly paid.   110
NIM Well then, that's the humour of't.
  ⌈*Nim and Bardolph sheathe their swords.*⌉
  Enter Hostess Quickly
HOSTESS As ever you come of women, come in quickly to
 Sir John. Ah, poor heart, he is so shaked of a burning
 quotidian-tertian, that it is most lamentable to behold.
 Sweet men, come to him.   ⌈*Exit*⌉
NIM The King hath run bad humours on the knight,
 that's the even of it.
PISTOL Nim, thou hast spoke the right.
 His heart is fracted and corroborate.
NIM The King is a good king, but it must be as it may.
 He passes some humours and careers.   121
PISTOL
Let us condole the knight—for, lambkins, we will live.
          Exeunt

2.2 *Enter the Dukes of Exeter and* ⌈*Gloucester*⌉, *and the*
  Earl of Westmorland
⌈GLOUCESTER⌉
Fore God, his grace is bold to trust these traitors.
EXETER
They shall be apprehended by and by.
WESTMORLAND
How smooth and even they do bear themselves,
As if allegiance in their bosoms sat,
Crownèd with faith and constant loyalty.   5
⌈GLOUCESTER⌉
The King hath note of all that they intend,
By interception which they dream not of.
EXETER
Nay, but the man that was his bedfellow,
Whom he hath dulled and cloyed with gracious
 favours—
That he should for a foreign purse so sell   10
His sovereign's life to death and treachery.
  Sound trumpets. Enter King Harry, Lord Scrope, the
  Earl of Cambridge, and Sir Thomas Grey
KING HARRY
Now sits the wind fair, and we will aboard.
My lord of Cambridge, and my kind lord of Masham,
And you, my gentle knight, give me your thoughts.
Think you not that the powers we bear with us   15
Will cut their passage through the force of France,
Doing the execution and the act
For which we have in head assembled them?
SCROPE
No doubt, my liege, if each man do his best.
KING HARRY
I doubt not that, since we are well persuaded   20
We carry not a heart with us from hence
That grows not in a fair consent with ours,

Nor leave not one behind that doth not wish
Success and conquest to attend on us.
CAMBRIDGE
Never was monarch better feared and loved   25
Than is your majesty. There's not, I think, a subject
That sits in heart-grief and uneasiness
Under the sweet shade of your government.
GREY
True. Those that were your father's enemies
Have steeped their galls in honey, and do serve you   30
With hearts create of duty and of zeal.
KING HARRY
We therefore have great cause of thankfulness,
And shall forget the office of our hand
Sooner than quittance of desert and merit,
According to their weight and worthiness.   35
SCROPE
So service shall with steelèd sinews toil,
And labour shall refresh itself with hope,
To do your grace incessant services.
KING HARRY
We judge no less.—Uncle of Exeter,
Enlarge the man committed yesterday   40
That railed against our person. We consider
It was excess of wine that set him on,
And on his more advice we pardon him.
SCROPE
That's mercy, but too much security.
Let him be punished, sovereign, lest example   45
Breed, by his sufferance, more of such a kind.
KING HARRY
O let us yet be merciful.
CAMBRIDGE
So may your highness, and yet punish too.
GREY
Sir, you show great mercy if you give him life,
After the taste of much correction.   50
KING HARRY
Alas, your too much love and care of me
Are heavy orisons 'gainst this poor wretch.
If little faults proceeding on distemper
Shall not be winked at, how shall we stretch our eye
When capital crimes, chewed, swallowed, and
 digested,   55
Appear before us? We'll yet enlarge that man,
Though Cambridge, Scrope, and Grey, in their dear
 care
And tender preservation of our person,
Would have him punished. And now to our French
 causes.
Who are the late commissioners?
CAMBRIDGE   I one, my lord.   60
Your highness bade me ask for it today.
SCROPE
So did you me, my liege.
GREY   And I, my royal sovereign.
KING HARRY
Then Richard, Earl of Cambridge, there is yours;

There yours, Lord Scrope of Masham, and sir knight,
Grey of Northumberland, this same is yours.   65
Read them, and know I know your worthiness.—
My lord of Westmorland, and Uncle Exeter,
We will aboard tonight.—Why, how now, gentlemen?
What see you in those papers, that you lose
So much complexion?—Look ye how they change: 70
Their cheeks are paper.—Why, what read you there
That have so cowarded and chased your blood
Out of appearance?
CAMBRIDGE   I do confess my fault,
And do submit me to your highness' mercy.
GREY and SCROPE To which we all appeal.   75
KING HARRY
The mercy that was quick in us but late
By your own counsel is suppressed and killed.
You must not dare, for shame, to talk of mercy,
For your own reasons turn into your bosoms,
As dogs upon their masters, worrying you.—   80
See you, my princes and my noble peers,
These English monsters? My lord of Cambridge here,
You know how apt our love was to accord
To furnish him with all appurtenants
Belonging to his honour; and this vile man   85
Hath for a few light crowns lightly conspired
And sworn unto the practices of France
To kill us here in Hampton. To the which
This knight, no less for bounty bound to us
Than Cambridge is, hath likewise sworn. But O   90
What shall I say to thee, Lord Scrope, thou cruel,
Ingrateful, savage, and inhuman creature?
Thou that didst bear the key of all my counsels,
That knew'st the very bottom of my soul,
That almost mightst ha' coined me into gold   95
Wouldst thou ha' practised on me for thy use:
May it be possible that foreign hire
Could out of thee extract one spark of evil
That might annoy my finger? 'Tis so strange
That though the truth of it stands off as gross   100
As black on white, my eye will scarcely see it.
Treason and murder ever kept together,
As two yoke-devils sworn to either's purpose,
Working so grossly in a natural cause
That admiration did not whoop at them;   105
But thou, 'gainst all proportion, didst bring in
Wonder to wait on treason and on murder.
And whatsoever cunning fiend it was
That wrought upon thee so preposterously
Hath got the voice in hell for excellence.   110
And other devils that suggest by treasons
Do botch and bungle up damnation
With patches, colours, and with forms, being fetched
From glist'ring semblances of piety;
But he that tempered thee, bade thee stand up,   115
Gave thee no instance why thou shouldst do treason,
Unless to dub thee with the name of traitor.
If that same demon that hath gulled thee thus
Should with his lion gait walk the whole world,

He might return to vasty Tartar back   120
And tell the legions, 'I can never win
A soul so easy as that Englishman's.'
O how hast thou with jealousy infected
The sweetness of affiance. Show men dutiful?
Why so didst thou. Seem they grave and learned?   125
Why so didst thou. Come they of noble family?
Why so didst thou. Seem they religious?
Why so didst thou. Or are they spare in diet,
Free from gross passion, or of mirth or anger,
Constant in spirit, not swerving with the blood,   130
Garnished and decked in modest complement,
Not working with the eye without the ear,
And but in purgèd judgement trusting neither?
Such, and so finely boulted, didst thou seem.
And thus thy fall hath left a kind of blot   135
To mark the full-fraught man, and best endowed,
With some suspicion. I will weep for thee,
For this revolt of thine methinks is like
Another fall of man.—Their faults are open.
Arrest them to the answer of the law,   140
And God acquit them of their practices.
EXETER I arrest thee of high treason, by the name of
Richard, Earl of Cambridge.—I arrest thee of high
treason, by the name of Henry, Lord Scrope of
Masham.—I arrest thee of high treason, by the name
of Thomas Grey, knight, of Northumberland.   146
SCROPE
Our purposes God justly hath discovered,
And I repent my fault more than my death,
Which I beseech your highness to forgive
Although my body pay the price of it.   150
CAMBRIDGE
For me, the gold of France did not seduce,
Although I did admit it as a motive
The sooner to effect what I intended.
But God be thankèd for prevention,
Which heartily in sufferance will rejoice,   155
Beseeching God and you to pardon me.
GREY
Never did faithful subject more rejoice
At the discovery of most dangerous treason
Than I do at this hour joy o'er myself,
Prevented from a damnèd enterprise.   160
My fault, but not my body, pardon, sovereign.
KING HARRY
God 'quit you in his mercy. Hear your sentence.
You have conspired against our royal person,
Joined with an enemy proclaimed and fixed,
And from his coffers   165
Received the golden earnest of our death,
Wherein you would have sold your king to slaughter,
His princes and his peers to servitude,
His subjects to oppression and contempt,
And his whole kingdom into desolation.   170
Touching our person seek we no revenge,
But we our kingdom's safety must so tender,
Whose ruin you have sought, that to her laws

We do deliver you. Get ye therefore hence,
Poor miserable wretches, to your death;   175
The taste whereof, God of his mercy give
You patience to endure, and true repentance
Of all your dear offences.—Bear them hence.
                    Exeunt the traitors, guarded
Now lords for France, the enterprise whereof
Shall be to you, as us, like glorious.   180
We doubt not of a fair and lucky war,
Since God so graciously hath brought to light
This dangerous treason lurking in our way
To hinder our beginnings. We doubt not now
But every rub is smoothèd on our way.   185
Then forth, dear countrymen. Let us deliver
Our puissance into the hand of God,
Putting it straight in expedition.
Cheerly to sea, the signs of war advance:
No king of England, if not king of France.   190
                    Flourish. Exeunt

2.3   *Enter Ensign Pistol, Corporal Nim, Lieutenant*
           Bardolph, Boy, and Hostess Quickly
HOSTESS Prithee, honey, sweet husband, let me bring thee
to Staines.
PISTOL
No, for my manly heart doth erne. Bardolph,
Be blithe; Nim, rouse thy vaunting veins; boy, bristle
Thy courage up. For Falstaff he is dead,   5
And we must earn therefore.
BARDOLPH Would I were with him, wheresome'er he is,
either in heaven or in hell.
HOSTESS Nay, sure he's not in hell. He's in Arthur's
bosom, if ever man went to Arthur's bosom. A made
a finer end, and went away an it had been any christom
child. A parted ev'n just between twelve and one, ev'n
at the turning o'th' tide—for after I saw him fumble
with the sheets, and play with flowers, and smile upon
his finger's end, I knew there was but one way. For
his nose was as sharp as a pen, and a babbled of green
fields. 'How now, Sir John?' quoth I. 'What, man! Be
o' good cheer.' So a cried out, 'God, God, God', three
or four times. Now I, to comfort him, bid him a should
not think of God; I hoped there was no need to trouble
himself with any such thoughts yet. So a bade me lay
more clothes on his feet. I put my hand into the bed
and felt them, and they were as cold as any stone.
Then I felt to his knees, and so up'ard and up'ard, and
all was as cold as any stone.   25
NIM They say he cried out of sack.
HOSTESS Ay, that a did.
BARDOLPH And of women.
HOSTESS Nay, that a did not.   29
BOY Yes, that a did, and said they were devils incarnate.
HOSTESS A could never abide carnation, 'twas a colour he
never liked.
BOY A said once the devil would have him about women.
HOSTESS A did in some sort, indeed, handle women—but

then he was rheumatic, and talked of the Whore of
Babylon.   36
BOY Do you not remember, a saw a flea stick upon
Bardolph's nose, and a said it was a black soul burning
in hell-fire.
BARDOLPH Well, the fuel is gone that maintained that fire.
That's all the riches I got in his service.   41
NIM Shall we shog? The King will be gone from
Southampton.
PISTOL
Come, let's away.—My love, give me thy lips.
                    He kisses her
Look to my chattels and my movables.   45
Let senses rule. The word is 'Pitch and pay'.
Trust none, for oaths are straws, men's faiths are
                                                    wafer-cakes,
And Holdfast is the only dog, my duck.
Therefore *caveto* be thy counsellor.
Go, clear thy crystals.—Yokefellows in arms,   50
Let us to France, like horseleeches, my boys,
To suck, to suck, the very blood to suck!
BOY (*aside*) And that's but unwholesome food, they say.
PISTOL Touch her soft mouth, and march.
BARDOLPH Farewell, hostess.   55
                    He kisses her
NIM I cannot kiss, that is the humour of it, but adieu.
PISTOL (*to Hostess*)
Let housewifery appear. Keep close, I thee command.
HOSTESS Farewell! Adieu!   *Exeunt severally*

2.4   *Flourish. Enter King Charles the Sixth of France,*
           the Dauphin, the Constable, and the Dukes of Berri
           and ⌈Bourbon⌉
KING CHARLES
Thus comes the English with full power upon us,
And more than carefully it us concerns
To answer royally in our defences.
Therefore the Dukes of Berri and of Bourbon,
Of Brabant and of Orléans shall make forth,   5
And you Prince Dauphin, with all swift dispatch
To line and new-repair our towns of war
With men of courage and with means defendant.
For England his approaches makes as fierce
As waters to the sucking of a gulf.   10
It fits us then to be as provident
As fear may teach us, out of late examples
Left by the fatal and neglected English
Upon our fields.
DAUPHIN   My most redoubted father,
It is most meet we arm us 'gainst the foe,   15
For peace itself should not so dull a kingdom—
Though war, nor no known quarrel, were in
                                                    question—
But that defences, musters, preparations
Should be maintained, assembled, and collected
As were a war in expectation.   20
Therefore, I say, 'tis meet we all go forth

To view the sick and feeble parts of France.
And let us do it with no show of fear,
No, with no more than if we heard that England
Were busied with a Whitsun morris dance.　　　　25
For, my good liege, she is so idly kinged,
Her sceptre so fantastically borne
By a vain, giddy, shallow, humorous youth,
That fear attends her not.

CONSTABLE　　　　　　　　O peace, Prince Dauphin.
You are too much mistaken in this king.　　　　30
Question your grace the late ambassadors
With what great state he heard their embassy,
How well supplied with agèd counsellors,
How modest in exception, and withal
How terrible in constant resolution,　　　　35
And you shall find his vanities forespent
Were but the outside of the Roman Brutus,
Covering discretion with a coat of folly,
As gardeners do with ordure hide those roots
That shall first spring and be most delicate.　　　　40

DAUPHIN
Well, 'tis not so, my Lord High Constable.
But though we think it so, it is no matter.
In cases of defence 'tis best to weigh
The enemy more mighty than he seems.
So the proportions of defence are filled—　　　　45
Which, of a weak and niggardly projection,
Doth like a miser spoil his coat with scanting
A little cloth.

KING CHARLES　　Think we King Harry strong.
And princes, look you strongly arm to meet him.
The kindred of him hath been fleshed upon us,　　　　50
And he is bred out of that bloody strain
That haunted us in our familiar paths.
Witness our too-much-memorable shame
When Crécy battle fatally was struck,
And all our princes captived by the hand　　　　55
Of that black name, Edward, Black Prince of Wales,
Whiles that his mountant sire, on mountain standing,
Up in the air, crowned with the golden sun,
Saw his heroical seed and smiled to see him
Mangle the work of nature and deface　　　　60
The patterns that by God and by French fathers
Had twenty years been made. This is a stem
Of that victorious stock, and let us fear
The native mightiness and fate of him.

Enter a Messenger

MESSENGER
Ambassadors from Harry, King of England,　　　　65
Do crave admittance to your majesty.

KING CHARLES
We'll give them present audience. Go and bring them.

Exit Messenger

You see this chase is hotly followed, friends.

DAUPHIN
Turn head and stop pursuit. For coward dogs
Most spend their mouths when what they seem to
　　　　threaten　　　　70

Runs far before them. Good my sovereign,
Take up the English short, and let them know
Of what a monarchy you are the head.
Self-love, my liege, is not so vile a sin
As self-neglecting.

Enter the Duke of Exeter, ⌐attended⌐

KING CHARLES　　　　From our brother England?　　　　75

EXETER
From him, and thus he greets your majesty:
He wills you, in the name of God Almighty,
That you divest yourself and lay apart
The borrowed glories that by gift of heaven,
By law of nature and of nations, 'longs　　　　80
To him and to his heirs, namely the crown,
And all wide-stretchèd honours that pertain
By custom and the ordinance of times
Unto the crown of France. That you may know
'Tis no sinister nor no awkward claim,　　　　85
Picked from the worm-holes of long-vanished days,
Nor from the dust of old oblivion raked,
He sends you this most memorable line,
In every branch truly demonstrative,
Willing you over-look this pedigree,　　　　90
And when you find him evenly derived
From his most famed of famous ancestors,
Edward the Third, he bids you then resign
Your crown and kingdom, indirectly held
From him, the native and true challenger.　　　　95

KING CHARLES Or else what follows?

EXETER
Bloody constraint. For if you hide the crown
Even in your hearts, there will he rake for it.
Therefore in fierce tempest is he coming,
In thunder and in earthquake, like a Jove,　　　　100
That if requiring fail, he will compel;
And bids you, in the bowels of the Lord,
Deliver up the crown, and to take mercy
On the poor souls for whom this hungry war
Opens his vasty jaws; and on your head　　　　105
Turns he the widows' tears, the orphans' cries,
The dead men's blood, the pining maidens' groans,
For husbands, fathers, and betrothèd lovers
That shall be swallowed in this controversy.
This is his claim, his threat'ning, and my message—
Unless the Dauphin be in presence here,　　　　111
To whom expressly I bring greeting too.

KING CHARLES
For us, we will consider of this further.
Tomorrow shall you bear our full intent
Back to our brother England.

DAUPHIN　　　　　　　　For the Dauphin,　　　　115
I stand here for him. What to him from England?

EXETER
Scorn and defiance, slight regard, contempt;
And anything that may not misbecome
The mighty sender, doth he prize you at.
Thus says my king: an if your father's highness　　　　120
Do not, in grant of all demands at large,

Sweeten the bitter mock you sent his majesty,
He'll call you to so hot an answer for it
That caves and womby vaultages of France
Shall chide your trespass and return your mock   125
In second accent of his ordinance.

DAUPHIN
Say if my father render fair return
It is against my will, for I desire
Nothing but odds with England. To that end,
As matching to his youth and vanity,   130
I did present him with the Paris balls.

EXETER
He'll make your Paris Louvre shake for it,
Were it the mistress court of mighty Europe.
And be assured, you'll find a diff'rence,
As we his subjects have in wonder found,   135
Between the promise of his greener days
And these he masters now: now he weighs time
Even to the utmost grain. That you shall read
In your own losses, if he stay in France.

KING CHARLES ⌈rising⌉
Tomorrow shall you know our mind at full.   140
           Flourish

EXETER
Dispatch us with all speed, lest that our king
Come here himself to question our delay—
For he is footed in this land already.

KING CHARLES
You shall be soon dispatched with fair conditions.
A night is but small breath and little pause   145
To answer matters of this consequence.
                    ⌈*Flourish.*⌉ *Exeunt*

3.0   *Enter Chorus*
CHORUS
Thus with imagined wing our swift scene flies
In motion of no less celerity
Than that of thought. Suppose that you have seen
The well-appointed king at Dover pier
Embark his royalty, and his brave fleet   5
With silken streamers the young Phoebus fanning.
Play with your fancies, and in them behold
Upon the hempen tackle ship-boys climbing;
Hear the shrill whistle, which doth order give
To sounds confused; behold the threaden sails,   10
Borne with th'invisible and creeping wind,
Draw the huge bottoms through the furrowed sea,
Breasting the lofty surge. O do but think
You stand upon the rivage and behold
A city on th'inconstant billows dancing—   15
For so appears this fleet majestical,
Holding due course to Harfleur. Follow, follow!
Grapple your minds to sternage of this navy,
And leave your England, as dead midnight still,
Guarded with grandsires, babies, and old women,   20
Either past or not arrived to pith and puissance.
For who is he, whose chin is but enriched
With one appearing hair, that will not follow
These culled and choice-drawn cavaliers to France?

Work, work your thoughts, and therein see a siege.   25
Behold the ordnance on their carriages,
With fatal mouths gaping on girded Harfleur.
Suppose th'ambassador from the French comes back,
Tells Harry that the King doth offer him
Catherine his daughter, and with her, to dowry,   30
Some petty and unprofitable dukedoms.
The offer likes not, and the nimble gunner
With linstock now the devilish cannon touches,
           Alarum, and chambers go off
And down goes all before them. Still be kind,   34
And eke out our performance with your mind.   *Exit*

3.1   *Alarum. Enter King Harry* ⌈*and the English army,*
           with⌉ *scaling ladders*
KING HARRY
Once more unto the breach, dear friends, once more,
Or close the wall up with our English dead.
In peace there's nothing so becomes a man
As modest stillness and humility,
But when the blast of war blows in our ears,   5
Then imitate the action of the tiger.
Stiffen the sinews, conjure up the blood,
Disguise fair nature with hard-favoured rage.
Then lend the eye a terrible aspect,
Let it pry through the portage of the head   10
Like the brass cannon, let the brow o'erwhelm it
As fearfully as doth a gallèd rock
O'erhang and jutty his confounded base,
Swilled with the wild and wasteful ocean.
Now set the teeth and stretch the nostril wide,   15
Hold hard the breath, and bend up every spirit
To his full height. On, on, you noblest English,
Whose blood is fet from fathers of war-proof,
Fathers that like so many Alexanders
Have in these parts from morn till even fought,   20
And sheathed their swords for lack of argument.
Dishonour not your mothers; now attest
That those whom you called fathers did beget you.
Be copy now to men of grosser blood,
And teach them how to war. And you, good yeomen,
Whose limbs were made in England, show us here   26
The mettle of your pasture; let us swear
That you are worth your breeding—which I doubt not,
For there is none of you so mean and base
That hath not noble lustre in your eyes.   30
I see you stand like greyhounds in the slips,
Straining upon the start. The game's afoot.
Follow your spirit, and upon this charge
Cry, 'God for Harry! England and Saint George!'
           Alarum, and chambers go off. Exeunt

3.2   *Enter Nim, Bardolph, Ensign Pistol, and Boy*
BARDOLPH On, on, on, on, on! To the breach, to the
breach!

NIM Pray thee corporal, stay. The knocks are too hot,
and for mine own part I have not a case of lives. The
humour of it is too hot, that is the very plainsong of
it.   6

PISTOL

'The plainsong' is most just, for humours do abound.
Knocks go and come, God's vassals drop and die,
⌈sings⌉   And sword and shield
                In bloody field   10
                Doth win immortal fame.
BOY Would I were in an alehouse in London. I would
give all my fame for a pot of ale, and safety.
PISTOL ⌈sings⌉ And I.
                If wishes would prevail with me   15
                My purpose should not fail with me
                But thither would I hie.
BOY ⌈sings⌉ As duly
                But not as truly
                As bird doth sing on bough.   20
    Enter Captain Fluellen and beats them in
FLUELLEN God's plud! Up to the breaches, you dogs!
Avaunt, you cullions!
PISTOL

Be merciful, great duke, to men of mould.
Abate thy rage, abate thy manly rage,
Abate thy rage, great duke. Good bawcock, bate   25
Thy rage. Use lenity, sweet chuck.
NIM These be good humours!
    ⌈*Fluellen begins to beat Nim*⌉
Your honour runs bad humours.
                                        Exeunt all but ⌈the Boy⌉
BOY As young as I am, I have observed these three
swashers. I am boy to them all three, but all they three,
though they would serve me, could not be man to me,
for indeed three such antics do not amount to a man.
For Bardolph, he is white-livered and red-faced—by the
means whereof a faces it out, but fights not. For Pistol,
he hath a killing tongue and a quiet sword—by the
means whereof a breaks words, and keeps whole
weapons. For Nim, he hath heard that men of few
words are the best men, and therefore he scorns to say
his prayers, lest a should be thought a coward. But his
few bad words are matched with as few good deeds—
for a never broke any man's head but his own, and
that was against a post, when he was drunk. They will
steal anything, and call it 'purchase'. Bardolph stole a
lute case, bore it twelve leagues, and sold it for three
halfpence. Nim and Bardolph are sworn brothers in
filching, and in Calais they stole a fire shovel. I knew
by that piece of service the men would carry coals.
They would have me as familiar with men's pockets as
their gloves or their handkerchiefs—which makes much
against my manhood, if I should take from another's
pocket to put into mine, for it is plain pocketing up of
wrongs. I must leave them, and seek some better
service. Their villainy goes against my weak stomach,
and therefore I must cast it up.   *Exit*

3.3   *Enter Captain Gower ⌈and Captain Fluellen,*
        meeting⌉
GOWER Captain Fluellen, you must come presently to the
mines. The Duke of Gloucester would speak with you.

FLUELLEN To the mines? Tell you the Duke it is not so
good to come to the mines. For look you, the mines is
not according to the disciplines of the war. The concavi-
ties of it is not sufficient. For look you, th'athversary,
you may discuss unto the Duke, look you, is digt
himself, four yard under, the countermines. By Cheshu,
I think a will plow up all, if there is not better directions.
GOWER The Duke of Gloucester, to whom the order of the
siege is given, is altogether directed by an Irishman, a
very valiant gentleman, i'faith.
FLUELLEN It is Captain MacMorris, is it not?
GOWER I think it be.   14
FLUELLEN By Cheshu, he is an ass, as in the world. I will
verify as much in his beard. He has no more directions
in the true disciplines of the wars, look you—of the
Roman disciplines—than is a puppy dog.
    Enter Captain MacMorris and Captain Jamy
GOWER Here a comes, and the Scots captain, Captain
Jamy, with him.   20
FLUELLEN Captain Jamy is a marvellous falorous gentle-
man, that is certain, and of great expedition and
knowledge in th'ancient wars, upon my particular
knowledge of his directions. By Cheshu, he will
maintain his argument as well as any military man in
the world, in the disciplines of the pristine wars of the
Romans.
JAMY I say gud day, Captain Fluellen.
FLUELLEN Good e'en to your worship, good Captain James.
GOWER How now, Captain MacMorris, have you quit the
mines? Have the pioneers given o'er?   31
MACMORRIS By Chrish law, 'tish ill done. The work ish
give over, the trumpet sound the retreat. By my hand
I swear, and my father's soul, the work ish ill done, it
ish give over. I would have blowed up the town, so
Chrish save me law, in an hour. O 'tish ill done, 'tish
ill done, by my hand 'tish ill done.
FLUELLEN Captain MacMorris, I beseech you now, will
you vouchsafe me, look you, a few disputations with
you, as partly touching or concerning the disciplines
of the war, the Roman wars, in the way of argument,
look you, and friendly communication? Partly to satisfy
my opinion and partly for the satisfaction, look you, of
my mind. As touching the direction of the military
discipline, that is the point.   45
JAMY It sall be vary gud, gud feith, gud captains bath,
and I sall quite you with gud leve, as I may pick
occasion. That sall I, marry.
MACMORRIS It is no time to discourse, so Chrish save me.
The day is hot, and the weather and the wars and the
King and the dukes. It is no time to discourse. The
town is besieched. An the trumpet call us to the breach,
and we talk and, be Chrish, do nothing, 'tis shame for
us all. So God sa' me, 'tis shame to stand still, it is
shame by my hand. And there is throats to be cut, and
works to be done, and there ish nothing done, so Christ
sa' me law.
JAMY By the mess, ere these eyes of mine take themselves
to slumber, ay'll de gud service, or I'll lig i'th' grund

for it. Ay owe Got a death, and I'll pay't as valorously
as I may, that sall I suirely do, that is the brief and
the long. Marry, I wad full fain heard some question
'tween you twae.
FLUELLEN Captain MacMorris, I think, look you, under
your correction, there is not many of your nation—
MACMORRIS Of my nation? What ish my nation? Ish a
villain and a bastard and a knave and a rascal? What
ish my nation? Who talks of my nation?
FLUELLEN Look you, if you take the matter otherwise than
is meant, Captain MacMorris, peradventure I shall think
you do not use me with that affability as in discretion
you ought to use me, look you, being as good a man
as yourself, both in the disciplines of war and in the
derivation of my birth, and in other particularities.
MACMORRIS I do not know you so good a man as myself.
So Chrish save me, I will cut off your head.   76
GOWER Gentlemen both, you will mistake each other.
JAMY Ah, that's a foul fault.
    A parley is sounded
GOWER The town sounds a parley.   79
FLUELLEN Captain MacMorris, when there is more better
opportunity to be required, look you, I will be so bold
as to tell you I know the disciplines of war. And there
is an end.   *Exit*
    ⌈*Flourish.*⌉ *Enter King Harry and all his train before*
    the gates
KING HARRY
How yet resolves the Governor of the town?
This is the latest parle we will admit.   85
Therefore to our best mercy give yourselves,
Or like to men proud of destruction
Defy us to our worst. For as I am a soldier,
A name that in my thoughts becomes me best,
If I begin the batt'ry once again   90
I will not leave the half-achievèd Harfleur
Till in her ashes she lie burièd.
The gates of mercy shall be all shut up,
And the fleshed soldier, rough and hard of heart,
In liberty of bloody hand shall range   95
With conscience wide as hell, mowing like grass
Your fresh fair virgins and your flow'ring infants.
What is it then to me if impious war
Arrayed in flames like to the prince of fiends
Do with his smirched complexion all fell feats   100
Enlinked to waste and desolation?
What is't to me, when you yourselves are cause,
If your pure maidens fall into the hand
Of hot and forcing violation?
What rein can hold licentious wickedness   105
When down the hill he holds his fierce career?
We may as bootless spend our vain command
Upon th'enragèd soldiers in their spoil
As send precepts to the leviathan
To come ashore. Therefore, you men of Harfleur,   110
Take pity of your town and of your people
Whiles yet my soldiers are in my command,
Whiles yet the cool and temperate wind of grace

O'erblows the filthy and contagious clouds
Of heady murder, spoil, and villainy.   115
If not—why, in a moment look to see
The blind and bloody soldier with foul hand
Defile the locks of your shrill-shrieking daughters;
Your fathers taken by the silver beards,
And their most reverend heads dashed to the walls;
Your naked infants spitted upon pikes,   121
Whiles the mad mothers with their howls confused
Do break the clouds, as did the wives of Jewry
At Herod's bloody-hunting slaughtermen.
What say you? Will you yield, and this avoid?   125
Or, guilty in defence, be thus destroyed?
    Enter Governor ⌈*on the wall*⌉
GOVERNOR
Our expectation hath this day an end.
The Dauphin, whom of succours we entreated,
Returns us that his powers are yet not ready
To raise so great a siege. Therefore, dread King,   130
We yield our town and lives to thy soft mercy.
Enter our gates, dispose of us and ours,
For we no longer are defensible.
KING HARRY
Open your gates.   ⌈*Exit Governor*⌉
            Come, Uncle Exeter,
Go you and enter Harfleur. There remain,   135
And fortify it strongly 'gainst the French.
Use mercy to them all. For us, dear uncle,
The winter coming on, and sickness growing
Upon our soldiers, we will retire to Calais.
Tonight in Harfleur will we be your guest;   140
Tomorrow for the march are we addressed.
    ⌈*The gates are opened.*⌉ *Flourish, and they enter*
                                              the town

3.4   *Enter Princess Catherine and Alice, an old*
            gentlewoman
CATHERINE Alice, tu as été en Angleterre, et tu bien parles
    le langage.
ALICE Un peu, madame.
CATHERINE Je te prie, m'enseignez. Il faut que j'apprenne
    à parler. Comment appelez-vous la main en anglais? 5
ALICE La main? Elle est appelée *de hand.*
CATHERINE *De hand.* Et les doigts?
ALICE Les doigts? Ma foi, j'oublie les doigts, mais je me
    souviendrai. Les doigts—je pense qu'ils sont appelés *de
    fingres.* Oui, *de fingres.*   10
CATHERINE La main, *de hand*; les doigts, *de fingres.* Je pense
    que je suis la bonne écolière; j'ai gagné deux mots
    d'anglais vitement. Comment appelez-vous les ongles?
ALICE Les ongles? Nous les appelons *de nails.*
CATHERINE *De nails.* Écoutez—dites-moi si je parle bien:
    de hand, de fingres, et *de nails.*   16
ALICE C'est bien dit, madame. Il est fort bon anglais.
CATHERINE Dites-moi l'anglais pour le bras.
ALICE *De arma,* madame.
CATHERINE Et le coude?   20
ALICE *D'elbow.*

CATHERINE *D'elbow.* Je m'en fais la répétition de tous les
mots que vous m'avez appris dès à présent.
ALICE Il est trop difficile, madame, comme je pense.
CATHERINE Excusez-moi, Alice. Écoutez: *d'hand, de fingre,*
de nails, d'arma, de bilbow.   26
ALICE *D'elbow,* madame.
CATHERINE O Seigneur Dieu, je m'en oublie! *D'elbow.*
Comment appelez-vous le col?
ALICE *De nick,* madame.   30
CATHERINE *De nick.* Et le menton?
ALICE *De chin.*
CATHERINE *De sin.* Le col, *de nick;* le menton, *de sin.*
ALICE Oui. Sauf votre honneur, en vérité vous prononcez
les mots aussi droit que les natifs d'Angleterre.   35
CATHERINE Je ne doute point d'apprendre, par la grâce de
Dieu, et en peu de temps.
ALICE N'avez-vous y déjà oublié ce que je vous ai
enseigné?
CATHERINE Non, et je réciterai à vous promptement:
d'hand, de fingre, de mailès—   41
ALICE *De nails,* madame.
CATHERINE *De nails, de arma, de ilbow—*
ALICE Sauf votre honneur, *d'elbow.*
CATHERINE Ainsi dis-je. *D'elbow, de nick,* et *de sin.* Comment
appelez-vous les pieds et la robe?   46
ALICE *De foot,* madame, et *de cown.*
CATHERINE *De foot* et *de cown?* O Seigneur Dieu! Ils sont
les mots de son mauvais, corruptible, gros, et
impudique, et non pour les dames d'honneur d'user. Je
ne voudrais prononcer ces mots devant les seigneurs
de France pour tout le monde. Foh! *De foot* et *de cown!*
Néanmoins, je réciterai une autre fois ma leçon
ensemble. *D'hand, de fingre, de nails, d'arma, d'elbow, de*
nick, de sin, de foot, de cown.   55
ALICE Excellent, madame!
CATHERINE C'est assez pour une fois. Allons-nous à dîner.
                                                        Exeunt

3.5   *Enter King Charles the Sixth of France, the*
       Dauphin, the Constable, the Duke of ⌈*Bourbon*⌉,
       and others
KING CHARLES
'Tis certain he hath passed the River Somme.
CONSTABLE
And if he be not fought withal, my lord,
Let us not live in France; let us quit all
And give our vineyards to a barbarous people.
DAUPHIN
O *Dieu vivant!* Shall a few sprays of us,   5
The emptying of our fathers' luxury,
Our scions, put in wild and savage stock,
Spirt up so suddenly into the clouds
And over-look their grafters?
⌈BOURBON⌉
Normans, but bastard Normans, Norman bastards!   10
Mort de ma vie, if they march along
Unfought withal, but I will sell my dukedom

To buy a slobb'ry and a dirty farm
In that nook-shotten isle of Albion.
CONSTABLE
Dieu de batailles! Where have they this mettle?   15
Is not their climate foggy, raw, and dull,
On whom as in despite the sun looks pale,
Killing their fruit with frowns? Can sodden water,
A drench for sur-reined jades—their barley-broth—
Decoct their cold blood to such valiant heat?   20
And shall our quick blood, spirited with wine,
Seem frosty? O for honour of our land
Let us not hang like roping icicles
Upon our houses' thatch, whiles a more frosty people
Sweat drops of gallant youth in our rich fields—   25
'Poor' may we call them, in their native lords.
DAUPHIN By faith and honour,
Our madams mock at us and plainly say
Our mettle is bred out, and they will give
Their bodies to the lust of English youth,   30
To new-store France with bastard warriors.
⌈BOURBON⌉
They bid us, 'To the English dancing-schools,
And teach lavoltas high and swift corantos'—
Saying our grace is only in our heels,
And that we are most lofty runaways.   35
KING CHARLES
Where is Montjoy the herald? Speed him hence.
Let him greet England with our sharp defiance.
Up, princes, and with spirit of honour edged
More sharper than your swords, hie to the field.
Charles Delabret, High Constable of France,   40
You Dukes of Orléans, Bourbon, and of Berri,
Alençon, Brabant, Bar, and Burgundy,
Jaques Châtillion, Rambures, Vaudemont,
Beaumont, Grandpré, Roussi, and Fauconbridge,
Foix, Lestrelles, Boucicault, and Charolais,   45
High dukes, great princes, barons, lords, and knights,
For your great seats now quit you of great shames.
Bar Harry England, that sweeps through our land
With pennons painted in the blood of Harfleur;
Rush on his host, as doth the melted snow   50
Upon the valleys, whose low vassal seat
The Alps doth spit and void his rheum upon.
Go down upon him, you have power enough,
And in a captive chariot into Rouen
Bring him our prisoner.
CONSTABLE   This becomes the great.   55
Sorry am I his numbers are so few,
His soldiers sick and famished in their march,
For I am sure when he shall see our army
He'll drop his heart into the sink of fear
And, fore achievement, offer us his ransom.   60
KING CHARLES
Therefore, Lord Constable, haste on Montjoy,
And let him say to England that we send
To know what willing ransom he will give.—
Prince Dauphin, you shall stay with us in Rouen.

DAUPHIN
Not so, I do beseech your majesty.   65
KING CHARLES
Be patient, for you shall remain with us.—
Now forth, Lord Constable, and princes all,
And quickly bring us word of England's fall.
Exeunt severally

3.6 *Enter Captains Gower and Fluellen, meeting*
GOWER How now, Captain Fluellen, come you from the bridge?
FLUELLEN I assure you there is very excellent services committed at the bridge.
GOWER Is the Duke of Exeter safe?   5
FLUELLEN The Duke of Exeter is as magnanimous as Agamemnon, and a man that I love and honour with my soul and my heart and my duty and my live and my living and my uttermost power. He is not, God be praised and blessed, any hurt in the world, but keeps the bridge most valiantly, with excellent discipline. There is an ensign lieutenant there at the pridge, I think in my very conscience he is as valiant a man as Mark Antony, and he is a man of no estimation in the world, but I did see him do as gallant service.   15
GOWER What do you call him?
FLUELLEN He is called Ensign Pistol.
GOWER I know him not.
Enter Ensign Pistol
FLUELLEN Here is the man.
PISTOL
Captain, I thee beseech to do me favours.   20
The Duke of Exeter doth love thee well.
FLUELLEN Ay, I praise God, and I have merited some love at his hands.
PISTOL
Bardolph, a soldier firm and sound of heart,
Of buxom valour, hath by cruel fate   25
And giddy Fortune's furious fickle wheel,
That goddess blind that stands upon the rolling
    restless stone—
FLUELLEN By your patience, Ensign Pistol: Fortune is painted blind, with a muffler afore her eyes, to signify to you that Fortune is blind. And she is painted also with a wheel, to signify to you—which is the moral of it—that she is turning and inconstant and mutability and variation. And her foot, look you, is fixed upon a spherical stone, which rolls and rolls and rolls. In good truth, the poet makes a most excellent description of it; Fortune is an excellent moral.   36
PISTOL
Fortune is Bardolph's foe and frowns on him,
For he hath stol'n a pax, and hangèd must a be.
A damnèd death—
Let gallows gape for dog, let man go free,   40
And let not hemp his windpipe suffocate.
But Exeter hath given the doom of death
For pax of little price.
Therefore go speak, the Duke will hear thy voice,

And let not Bardolph's vital thread be cut   45
With edge of penny cord and vile reproach.
Speak, captain, for his life, and I will thee requite.
FLUELLEN Ensign Pistol, I do partly understand your meaning.
PISTOL Why then rejoice therefor.   50
FLUELLEN Certainly, ensign, it is not a thing to rejoice at. For if, look you, he were my brother, I would desire the Duke to use his good pleasure, and put him to executions. For discipline ought to be used.
PISTOL
Die and be damned! and *fico* for thy friendship.   55
FLUELLEN It is well.
PISTOL The fig of Spain.
FLUELLEN Very good.
PISTOL
I say the fig within thy bowels and thy dirty maw.
Exit
FLUELLEN Captain Gower, cannot you hear it lighten and thunder?   61
GOWER Why, is this the ensign you told me of? I remember him now. A bawd, a cutpurse.
FLUELLEN I'll assure you, a uttered as prave words at the pridge as you shall see in a summer's day. But it is very well. What he has spoke to me, that is well, I warrant you, when time is serve.
GOWER Why 'tis a gull, a fool, a rogue, that now and then goes to the wars, to grace himself at his return into London under the form of a soldier. And such fellows are perfect in the great commanders' names, and they will learn you by rote where services were done—at such and such a sconce, at such a breach, at such a convoy, who came off bravely, who was shot, who disgraced, what terms the enemy stood on—and this they con perfectly in the phrase of war, which they trick up with new-tuned oaths. And what a beard of the Generᴀ s cut and a horrid suit of the camp will do among foaming bottles and ale-washed wits is wonderful to be thought on. But you must learn to know such slanders of the age, or else you may be marvellously mistook.
FLUELLEN I tell you what, Captain Gower, I do perceive he is not the man that he would gladly make show to the world he is. If I find a hole in his coat, I will tell him my mind.   86
A drum is heard
Hark you, the King is coming, and I must speak with him from the pridge.
Enter King Harry and his poor soldiers, with drum and colours
God pless your majesty.
KING HARRY
How now, Fluellen, com'st thou from the bridge?   90
FLUELLEN Ay, so please your majesty. The Duke of Exeter has very gallantly maintained the pridge. The French is gone off, look you, and there is gallant and most prave passages. Marry, th'athversary was have possession of the pridge, but he is enforced to retire, and the

Duke of Exeter is master of the pridge. I can tell your
majesty, the Duke is a prave man.

KING HARRY What men have you lost, Fluellen?

FLUELLEN The perdition of th'athversary hath been very
great, reasonable great. Marry, for my part I think the
Duke hath lost never a man, but one that is like to be
executed for robbing a church, one Bardolph, if your
majesty know the man. His face is all bubuncles and
whelks and knobs and flames o' fire, and his lips blows
at his nose, and it is like a coal of fire, sometimes plue
and sometimes red. But his nose is executed, and his
fire's out.

KING HARRY We would have all such offenders so cut off,
and we here give express charge that in our marches
through the country there be nothing compelled from
the villages, nothing taken but paid for, none of the
French upbraided or abused in disdainful language. For
when lenity and cruelty play for a kingdom, the gentler
gamester is the soonest winner.

Tucket. Enter Montjoy

MONTJOY You know me by my habit.   115

KING HARRY
Well then, I know thee. What shall I know of thee?

MONTJOY
My master's mind.

KING HARRY   Unfold it.

MONTJOY   Thus says my King:
'Say thou to Harry of England, though we seemed
dead, we did but sleep. Advantage is a better soldier
than rashness. Tell him, we could have rebuked him
at Harfleur, but that we thought not good to bruise an
injury till it were full ripe. Now we speak upon our
cue, and our voice is imperial. England shall repent his
folly, see his weakness, and admire our sufferance. Bid
him therefore consider of his ransom, which must
proportion the losses we have borne, the subjects we
have lost, the disgrace we have digested—which in
weight to re-answer, his pettiness would bow under.
For our losses, his exchequer is too poor; for th'effusion
of our blood, the muster of his kingdom too faint a
number; and for our disgrace, his own person kneeling
at our feet but a weak and worthless satisfaction. To
this add defiance, and tell him for conclusion he hath
betrayed his followers, whose condemnation is
pronounced.'   135
So far my King and master; so much my office.

KING HARRY
What is thy name? I know thy quality.

MONTJOY Montjoy.

KING HARRY
Thou dost thy office fairly. Turn thee back
And tell thy king I do not seek him now,   140
But could be willing to march on to Calais
Without impeachment, for to say the sooth—
Though 'tis no wisdom to confess so much
Unto an enemy of craft and vantage—
My people are with sickness much enfeebled,   145

My numbers lessened, and those few I have
Almost no better than so many French;
Who when they were in health—I tell thee herald,
I thought upon one pair of English legs
Did march three Frenchmen. Yet forgive me, God,   150
That I do brag thus. This your air of France
Hath blown that vice in me. I must repent.
Go, therefore, tell thy master here I am;
My ransom is this frail and worthless trunk,
My army but a weak and sickly guard.   155
Yet, God before, tell him we will come on,
Though France himself and such another neighbour
Stand in our way. There's for thy labour, Montjoy.
Go bid thy master well advise himself.
If we may pass, we will; if we be hindered,   160
We shall your tawny ground with your red blood
Discolour. And so, Montjoy, fare you well.
The sum of all our answer is but this:
We would not seek a battle as we are,
Nor as we are we say we will not shun it.   165
So tell your master.

MONTJOY
I shall deliver so. Thanks to your highness.   *Exit*

GLOUCESTER
I hope they will not come upon us now.

KING HARRY
We are in God's hand, brother, not in theirs.
March to the bridge. It now draws toward night.   170
Beyond the river we'll encamp ourselves,
And on tomorrow bid them march away.   *Exeunt*

3.7   *Enter the Constable, Lord Rambures, the Dukes of*
       Orléans and ⌈Bourbon⌉, with others

CONSTABLE Tut, I have the best armour of the world.
Would it were day.

ORLÉANS You have an excellent armour. But let my horse
have his due.

CONSTABLE It is the best horse of Europe.   5

ORLÉANS Will it never be morning?

⌈BOURBON⌉ My lord of Orléans and my Lord High
Constable, you talk of horse and armour?

ORLÉANS You are as well provided of both as any prince
in the world.   10

⌈BOURBON⌉ What a long night is this! I will not change
my horse with any that treads but on four pasterns.
Ah ha! He bounds from the earth as if his entrails were
hares—*le cheval volant*, the Pegasus, *qui a les narines de
feu!* When I bestride him, I soar, I am a hawk; he trots
the air, the earth sings when he touches it, the basest
horn of his hoof is more musical than the pipe of
Hermes.

ORLÉANS He's of the colour of the nutmeg.   19

⌈BOURBON⌉ And of the heat of the ginger. It is a beast for
Perseus. He is pure air and fire, and the dull elements
of earth and water never appear in him, but only in
patient stillness while his rider mounts him. He is
indeed a horse, and all other jades you may call beasts.

CONSTABLE Indeed, my lord, it is a most absolute and
excellent horse.   26
⌜BOURBON⌝ It is the prince of palfreys. His neigh is like the
bidding of a monarch, and his countenance enforces
homage.
ORLÉANS No more, cousin.   30
⌜BOURBON⌝ Nay, the man hath no wit, that cannot from
the rising of the lark to the lodging of the lamb vary
deserved praise on my palfrey. It is a theme as fluent
as the sea. Turn the sands into eloquent tongues, and
my horse is argument for them all. 'Tis a subject for a
sovereign to reason on, and for a sovereign's sovereign
to ride on, and for the world, familiar to us and
unknown, to lay apart their particular functions, and
wonder at him. I once writ a sonnet in his praise, and
began thus: 'Wonder of nature!—'   40
ORLÉANS I have heard a sonnet begin so to one's mistress.
⌜BOURBON⌝ Then did they imitate that which I composed
to my courser, for my horse is my mistress.
ORLÉANS Your mistress bears well.
⌜BOURBON⌝ Me well, which is the prescribed praise and
perfection of a good and particular mistress.   46
CONSTABLE Nay, for methought yesterday your mistress
shrewdly shook your back.
⌜BOURBON⌝ So perhaps did yours.
CONSTABLE Mine was not bridled.   50
⌜BOURBON⌝ O then belike she was old and gentle, and you
rode like a kern of Ireland, your French hose off, and
in your strait strossers.
CONSTABLE You have good judgement in horsemanship.
⌜BOURBON⌝ Be warned by me then: they that ride so, and
ride not warily, fall into foul bogs. I had rather have
my horse to my mistress.
CONSTABLE I had as lief have my mistress a jade.
⌜BOURBON⌝ I tell thee, Constable, my mistress wears his
own hair.   60
CONSTABLE I could make as true a boast as that, if I had
a sow to my mistress.
⌜BOURBON⌝ 'Le chien est retourné à son propre vomissement,
et la truie lavée au bourbier.' Thou makest use of
anything.   65
CONSTABLE Yet do I not use my horse for my mistress, or
any such proverb so little kin to the purpose.
RAMBURES My Lord Constable, the armour that I saw in
your tent tonight, are those stars or suns upon it?
CONSTABLE Stars, my lord.   70
⌜BOURBON⌝ Some of them will fall tomorrow, I hope.
CONSTABLE And yet my sky shall not want.
⌜BOURBON⌝ That may be, for you bear a many super-
fluously, and 'twere more honour some were away. 74
CONSTABLE Even as your horse bears your praises, who
would trot as well were some of your brags dismounted.
⌜BOURBON⌝ Would I were able to load him with his desert!
Will it never be day? I will trot tomorrow a mile, and
my way shall be paved with English faces.   79
CONSTABLE I will not say so, for fear I should be faced out
of my way. But I would it were morning, for I would
fain be about the ears of the English.

RAMBURES Who will go to hazard with me for twenty
prisoners?
CONSTABLE You must first go yourself to hazard, ere you
have them.   86
⌜BOURBON⌝ 'Tis midnight. I'll go arm myself.   Exit
ORLÉANS The Duke of Bourbon longs for morning.
RAMBURES He longs to eat the English.
CONSTABLE I think he will eat all he kills.   90
ORLÉANS By the white hand of my lady, he's a gallant
prince.
CONSTABLE Swear by her foot, that she may tread out the
oath.
ORLÉANS He is simply the most active gentleman of France.
CONSTABLE Doing is activity, and he will still be doing. 96
ORLÉANS He never did harm that I heard of.
CONSTABLE Nor will do none tomorrow. He will keep that
good name still.
ORLÉANS I know him to be valiant.   100
CONSTABLE I was told that by one that knows him better
than you.
ORLÉANS What's he?
CONSTABLE Marry, he told me so himself, and he said he
cared not who knew it.   105
ORLÉANS He needs not; it is no hidden virtue in him.
CONSTABLE By my faith, sir, but it is. Never anybody saw
it but his lackey. 'Tis a hooded valour, and when it
appears it will bate.
ORLÉANS 'Ill will never said well.'   110
CONSTABLE I will cap that proverb with 'There is flattery
in friendship.'
ORLÉANS And I will take up that with 'Give the devil his
due.'   114
CONSTABLE Well placed! There stands your friend for the
devil. Have at the very eye of that proverb with 'A pox
of the devil!'
ORLÉANS You are the better at proverbs by how much 'a
fool's bolt is soon shot'.
CONSTABLE You have shot over.   120
ORLÉANS 'Tis not the first time you were overshot.
      Enter a Messenger
MESSENGER My Lord High Constable, the English lie within
fifteen hundred paces of your tents.
CONSTABLE Who hath measured the ground?
MESSENGER The Lord Grandpré.   125
CONSTABLE A valiant and most expert gentleman.
                              ⌜Exit Messenger⌝
Would it were day! Alas, poor Harry of England. He
longs not for the dawning as we do.
ORLÉANS What a wretched and peevish fellow is this King
of England, to mope with his fat-brained followers so
far out of his knowledge.   131
CONSTABLE If the English had any apprehension, they
would run away.
ORLÉANS That they lack—for if their heads had any
intellectual armour, they could never wear such heavy
headpieces.   136
RAMBURES That island of England breeds very valiant
creatures. Their mastiffs are of unmatchable courage.

ORLÉANS Foolish curs, that run winking into the mouth
of a Russian bear, and have their heads crushed like
rotten apples. You may as well say, 'That's a valiant
flea that dare eat his breakfast on the lip of a lion.'
CONSTABLE Just, just. And the men do sympathize with
the mastiffs in robustious and rough coming on, leaving
their wits with their wives. And then, give them great
meals of beef, and iron and steel, they will eat like
wolves and fight like devils.
ORLÉANS Ay, but these English are shrewdly out of beef.
CONSTABLE Then shall we find tomorrow they have only
stomachs to eat, and none to fight. Now is it time to
arm. Come, shall we about it?   151
ORLÉANS
It is now two o'clock. But let me see—by ten
We shall have each a hundred Englishmen.   *Exeunt*

4.0   *Enter Chorus*
CHORUS
Now entertain conjecture of a time
When creeping murmur and the poring dark
Fills the wide vessel of the universe.
From camp to camp through the foul womb of night
The hum of either army stilly sounds,   5
That the fixed sentinels almost receive
The secret whispers of each other's watch.
Fire answers fire, and through their paly flames
Each battle sees the other's umbered face.
Steed threatens steed, in high and boastful neighs   10
Piercing the night's dull ear, and from the tents
The armourers, accomplishing the knights,
With busy hammers closing rivets up,
Give dreadful note of preparation.
The country cocks do crow, the clocks do toll   15
And the third hour of drowsy morning name.
Proud of their numbers and secure in soul,
The confident and overlusty French
Do the low-rated English play at dice,
And chide the cripple tardy-gaited night,   20
Who like a foul and ugly witch doth limp
So tediously away. The poor condemnèd English,
Like sacrifices, by their watchful fires
Sit patiently and inly ruminate
The morning's danger; and their gesture sad,   25
Investing lank lean cheeks and war-worn coats,
Presented them unto the gazing moon
So many horrid ghosts. O now, who will behold
The royal captain of this ruined band
Walking from watch to watch, from tent to tent,   30
Let him cry, 'Praise and glory on his head!'
For forth he goes and visits all his host,
Bids them good morrow with a modest smile
And calls them brothers, friends, and countrymen.
Upon his royal face there is no note   35
How dread an army hath enrounded him;
Nor doth he dedicate one jot of colour
Unto the weary and all-watchèd night,
But freshly looks and overbears attaint

With cheerful semblance and sweet majesty,   40
That every wretch, pining and pale before,
Beholding him, plucks comfort from his looks.
A largess universal, like the sun,
His liberal eye doth give to everyone,
Thawing cold fear, that mean and gentle all   45
Behold, as may unworthiness define,
A little touch of Harry in the night.
And so our scene must to the battle fly,
Where O for pity, we shall much disgrace,
With four or five most vile and ragged foils,   50
Right ill-disposed in brawl ridiculous,
The name of Agincourt. Yet sit and see,
Minding true things by what their mock'ries be.   *Exit*

4.1   *Enter King Harry and the Duke of Gloucester, then*
         the Duke of ⌈Clarence⌉
KING HARRY
Gloucester, 'tis true that we are in great danger;
The greater therefore should our courage be.
Good morrow, brother Clarence. God Almighty!
There is some soul of goodness in things evil,
Would men observingly distil it out—   5
For our bad neighbour makes us early stirrers,
Which is both healthful and good husbandry.
Besides, they are our outward consciences,
And preachers to us all, admonishing
That we should dress us fairly for our end.   10
Thus may we gather honey from the weed
And make a moral of the devil himself.
         Enter Sir Thomas Erpingham
Good morrow, old Sir Thomas Erpingham.
A good soft pillow for that good white head
Were better than a churlish turf of France.   15
ERPINGHAM
Not so, my liege. This lodging likes me better,
Since I may say, 'Now lie I like a king.'
KING HARRY
'Tis good for men to love their present pains
Upon example. So the spirit is eased,
And when the mind is quickened, out of doubt   20
The organs, though defunct and dead before,
Break up their drowsy grave and newly move
With casted slough and fresh legerity.
Lend me thy cloak, Sir Thomas.
         He puts on Erpingham's cloak
                                       Brothers both,
Commend me to the princes in our camp.   25
Do my good morrow to them, and anon
Desire them all to my pavilion.
GLOUCESTER We shall, my liege.
ERPINGHAM Shall I attend your grace?
KING HARRY No, my good knight.   30
Go with my brothers to my lords of England.
I and my bosom must debate awhile,
And then I would no other company.
ERPINGHAM
The Lord in heaven bless thee, noble Harry.

KING HARRY
  God-a-mercy, old heart, thou speak'st cheerfully. 35
          Exeunt all but King Harry
    Enter Pistol ⌈to him⌉
PISTOL *Qui vous là?*
KING HARRY A friend.
PISTOL
  Discuss unto me: art thou officer,
  Or art thou base, common, and popular?
KING HARRY I am a gentleman of a company. 40
PISTOL Trail'st thou the puissant pike?
KING HARRY Even so. What are you?
PISTOL
  As good a gentleman as the Emperor.
KING HARRY Then you are a better than the King.
PISTOL
  The King's a bawcock and a heart-of-gold, 45
  A lad of life, an imp of fame,
  Of parents good, of fist most valiant.
  I kiss his dirty shoe, and from heartstring
  I love the lovely bully. What is thy name?
KING HARRY Harry *le roi.* 50
PISTOL
  Leroi? A Cornish name. Art thou of Cornish crew?
KING HARRY No, I am a Welshman.
PISTOL Know'st thou Fluellen?
KING HARRY Yes.
PISTOL
  Tell him I'll knock his leek about his pate 55
  Upon Saint Davy's day.
KING HARRY Do not you wear your dagger in your cap
  that day, lest he knock that about yours.
PISTOL Art thou his friend?
KING HARRY And his kinsman too. 60
PISTOL The *fico* for thee then.
KING HARRY I thank you. God be with you.
PISTOL My name is Pistol called.
KING HARRY It sorts well with your fierceness.
                    Exit Pistol
Enter Captains Fluellen and Gower ⌈severally⌉. King
  Harry stands apart
GOWER Captain Fluellen! 65
FLUELLEN So! In the name of Jesu Christ, speak fewer. It
  is the greatest admiration in the universal world, when
  the true and ancient prerogatifs and laws of the wars
  is not kept. If you would take the pains but to examine
  the wars of Pompey the Great, you shall find, I warrant
  you, that there is no tiddle-taddle nor pibble-babble in
  Pompey's camp. I warrant you, you shall find the
  ceremonies of the wars, and the cares of it, and the
  forms of it, and the sobriety of it, and the modesty of
  it, to be otherwise. 75
GOWER Why, the enemy is loud. You hear him all night.
FLUELLEN If the enemy is an ass and a fool and a prating
  coxcomb, is it meet, think you, that we should also,
  look you, be an ass and a fool and a prating coxcomb?
  In your own conscience now? 80
GOWER I will speak lower.

FLUELLEN I pray you and beseech you that you will.
            Exeunt Fluellen and Gower
KING HARRY
  Though it appear a little out of fashion,
  There is much care and valour in this Welshman.
    Enter three soldiers: John Bates, Alexander Court,
    and Michael Williams
COURT Brother John Bates, is not that the morning which
  breaks yonder? 86
BATES I think it be. But we have no great cause to desire
  the approach of day.
WILLIAMS We see yonder the beginning of the day, but I
  think we shall never see the end of it.—Who goes
  there? 91
KING HARRY A friend.
WILLIAMS Under what captain serve you?
KING HARRY Under Sir Thomas Erpingham.
WILLIAMS A good old commander and a most kind gentle-
  man. I pray you, what thinks he of our estate? 96
KING HARRY Even as men wrecked upon a sand, that look
  to be washed off the next tide.
BATES He hath not told his thought to the King? 99
KING HARRY No, nor it is not meet he should. For though
  I speak it to you, I think the King is but a man, as I
  am. The violet smells to him as it doth to me; the
  element shows to him as it doth to me. All his senses
  have but human conditions. His ceremonies laid by, in
  his nakedness he appears but a man, and though his
  affections are higher mounted than ours, yet when
  they stoop, they stoop with the like wing. Therefore,
  when he sees reason of fears, as we do, his fears, out
  of doubt, be of the same relish as ours are. Yet, in
  reason, no man should possess him with any
  appearance of fear, lest he, by showing it, should
  dishearten his army.
BATES He may show what outward courage he will, but
  I believe, as cold a night as 'tis, he could wish himself
  in Thames up to the neck. And so I would he were,
  and I by him, at all adventures, so we were quit here.
KING HARRY By my troth, I will speak my conscience of
  the King. I think he would not wish himself anywhere
  but where he is. 119
BATES Then I would he were here alone. So should he be
  sure to be ransomed, and a many poor men's lives
  saved.
KING HARRY I dare say you love him not so ill to wish
  him here alone, howsoever you speak this to feel other
  men's minds. Methinks I could not die anywhere so
  contented as in the King's company, his cause being
  just and his quarrel honourable.
WILLIAMS That's more than we know.
BATES Ay, or more than we should seek after. For we
  know enough if we know we are the King's subjects.
  If his cause be wrong, our obedience to the King wipes
  the crime of it out of us.
WILLIAMS But if the cause be not good, the King himself
  hath a heavy reckoning to make, when all those legs
  and arms and heads chopped off in a battle shall join

together at the latter day, and cry all, 'We died at such
a place'—some swearing, some crying for a surgeon,
some upon their wives left poor behind them, some
upon the debts they owe, some upon their children
rawly left. I am afeard there are few die well that die
in a battle, for how can they charitably dispose of
anything, when blood is their argument? Now, if these
men do not die well, it will be a black matter for the
King that led them to it—who to disobey were against
all proportion of subjection.   145

KING HARRY So, if a son that is by his father sent about
merchandise do sinfully miscarry upon the sea, the
imputation of his wickedness, by your rule, should be
imposed upon his father, that sent him. Or if a servant,
under his master's command transporting a sum of
money, be assailed by robbers, and die in many
irreconciled iniquities, you may call the business of the
master the author of the servant's damnation. But this
is not so. The King is not bound to answer the particular
endings of his soldiers, the father of his son, nor the
master of his servant, for they purpose not their deaths
when they propose their services. Besides, there is no
king, be his cause never so spotless, if it come to the
arbitrament of swords, can try it out with all unspotted
soldiers. Some, peradventure, have on them the guilt
of premeditated and contrived murder; some, of
beguiling virgins with the broken seals of perjury;
some, making the wars their bulwark, that have before
gored the gentle bosom of peace with pillage and
robbery. Now, if these men have defeated the law and
outrun native punishment, though they can outstrip
men, they have no wings to fly from God. War is his
beadle. War is his vengeance. So that here men are
punished for before-breach of the King's laws, in now
the King's quarrel. Where they feared the death, they
have borne life away; and where they would be safe,
they perish. Then if they die unprovided, no more is
the King guilty of their damnation than he was before
guilty of those impieties for the which they are now
visited. Every subject's duty is the King's, but every
subject's soul is his own. Therefore should every soldier
in the wars do as every sick man in his bed: wash
every mote out of his conscience. And dying so, death
is to him advantage; or not dying, the time was
blessedly lost wherein such preparation was gained.
And in him that escapes, it were not sin to think that,
making God so free an offer, he let him outlive that
day to see his greatness and to teach others how they
should prepare.   184

⌐BATES⌐ 'Tis certain, every man that dies ill, the ill upon
his own head. The King is not to answer it. I do not
desire he should answer for me, and yet I determine to
fight lustily for him.

KING HARRY I myself heard the King say he would not be
ransomed.   190

WILLIAMS Ay, he said so, to make us fight cheerfully, but
when our throats are cut he may be ransomed, and
we ne'er the wiser.

KING HARRY If I live to see it, I will never trust his word
after.   195

WILLIAMS You pay him then! That's a perilous shot out
of an elder-gun, that a poor and a private displeasure
can do against a monarch. You may as well go about
to turn the sun to ice with fanning in his face with a
peacock's feather. You'll never trust his word after!
Come, 'tis a foolish saying.   201

KING HARRY Your reproof is something too round. I should
be angry with you, if the time were convenient.

WILLIAMS Let it be a quarrel between us, if you live.

KING HARRY I embrace it.   205

WILLIAMS How shall I know thee again?

KING HARRY Give me any gage of thine, and I will wear
it in my bonnet. Then if ever thou darest acknowledge
it, I will make it my quarrel.

WILLIAMS Here's my glove. Give me another of thine. 210

KING HARRY There.

They exchange gloves

WILLIAMS This will I also wear in my cap. If ever thou
come to me and say, after tomorrow, 'This is my glove',
by this hand I will take thee a box on the ear.

KING HARRY If ever I live to see it, I will challenge it.   215

WILLIAMS Thou darest as well be hanged.

KING HARRY Well, I will do it, though I take thee in the
King's company.

WILLIAMS Keep thy word. Fare thee well.   219

BATES Be friends, you English fools, be friends. We have
French quarrels enough, if you could tell how to reckon.

KING HARRY Indeed, the French may lay twenty French
crowns to one they will beat us, for they bear them on
their shoulders. But it is no English treason to cut
French crowns, and tomorrow the King himself will be
a clipper.   *Exeunt soldiers*

Upon the King.

'Let us our lives, our souls, our debts, our care-full
        wives,
Our children, and our sins, lay on the King.'
We must bear all. O hard condition,   230
Twin-born with greatness: subject to the breath
Of every fool, whose sense no more can feel
But his own wringing. What infinite heartsease
Must kings neglect that private men enjoy?
And what have kings that privates have not too,   235
Save ceremony, save general ceremony?
And what art thou, thou idol ceremony?
What kind of god art thou, that suffer'st more
Of mortal griefs than do thy worshippers?
What are thy rents? What are thy comings-in?   240
O ceremony, show me but thy worth.
What is thy soul of adoration?
Art thou aught else but place, degree, and form,
Creating awe and fear in other men?
Wherein thou art less happy, being feared,   245
Than they in fearing.
What drink'st thou oft, instead of homage sweet,
But poisoned flattery? O be sick, great greatness,
And bid thy ceremony give thee cure.

Think'st thou the fiery fever will go out   250
With titles blown from adulation?
Will it give place to flexure and low bending?
Canst thou, when thou command'st the beggar's knee,
Command the health of it? No, thou proud dream
That play'st so subtly with a king's repose;   255
I am a king that find thee, and I know
'Tis not the balm, the sceptre, and the ball,
The sword, the mace, the crown imperial,
The intertissued robe of gold and pearl,
The farcèd title running fore the king,   260
The throne he sits on, nor the tide of pomp
That beats upon the high shore of this world—
No, not all these, thrice-gorgeous ceremony,
Not all these, laid in bed majestical,
Can sleep so soundly as the wretched slave   265
Who with a body filled and vacant mind
Gets him to rest, crammed with distressful bread;
Never sees horrid night, the child of hell,
But like a lackey from the rise to set
Sweats in the eye of Phoebus, and all night   270
Sleeps in Elysium; next day, after dawn
Doth rise and help Hyperion to his horse,
And follows so the ever-running year
With profitable labour to his grave.
And but for ceremony such a wretch,   275
Winding up days with toil and nights with sleep,
Had the forehand and vantage of a king.
The slave, a member of the country's peace,
Enjoys it, but in gross brain little wots
What watch the King keeps to maintain the peace,   280
Whose hours the peasant best advantages.
    Enter Sir Thomas Erpingham
ERPINGHAM
My lord, your nobles, jealous of your absence,
Seek through your camp to find you.
KING HARRY   Good old knight,
Collect them all together at my tent.
I'll be before thee.   284
ERPINGHAM   I shall do't, my lord.   *Exit*
KING HARRY
O God of battles, steel my soldiers' hearts.
Possess them not with fear. Take from them now
The sense of reck'ning, ere th'opposèd numbers
Pluck their hearts from them. Not today, O Lord,
O not today, think not upon the fault   290
My father made in compassing the crown.
I Richard's body have interrèd new,
And on it have bestowed more contrite tears
Than from it issued forcèd drops of blood.
Five hundred poor have I in yearly pay   295
Who twice a day their withered hands hold up
Toward heaven to pardon blood. And I have built
Two chantries, where the sad and solemn priests
Sing still for Richard's soul. More will I do,
Though all that I can do is nothing worth,   300
Since that my penitence comes after ill,
Imploring pardon.
    Enter the Duke of Gloucester

GLOUCESTER
My liege.
KING HARRY My brother Gloucester's voice? Ay.
I know thy errand, I will go with thee.
The day, my friends, and all things stay for me.   305
                    Exeunt

4.2   *Enter the Dukes of ⌈Bourbon⌉ and Orléans, and Lord
        Rambures*
ORLÉANS
The sun doth gild our armour. Up, my lords!
⌈BOURBON⌉ *Monte cheval!* My horse! *Varlet, lacquais!* Ha!
ORLÉANS O brave spirit!
⌈BOURBON⌉ *Via les eaux et terre!*
ORLÉANS *Rien plus? L'air et feu!*   5
⌈BOURBON⌉ *Cieux,* cousin Orléans!
    Enter the Constable
Now, my Lord Constable!
CONSTABLE
Hark how our steeds for present service neigh.
⌈BOURBON⌉
Mount them and make incision in their hides,
That their hot blood may spin in English eyes   10
And dout them with superfluous courage. Ha!
RAMBURES
What, will you have them weep our horses' blood?
How shall we then behold their natural tears?
    Enter a Messenger
MESSENGER
The English are embattled, you French peers.
CONSTABLE
To horse, you gallant princes, straight to horse!   15
Do but behold yon poor and starvèd band,
And your fair show shall suck away their souls,
Leaving them but the shells and husks of men.
There is not work enough for all our hands,
Scarce blood enough in all their sickly veins   20
To give each naked curtal-axe a stain
That our French gallants shall today draw out
And sheathe for lack of sport. Let us but blow on
    them,
The vapour of our valour will o'erturn them.
'Tis positive 'gainst all exceptions, lords,   25
That our superfluous lackeys and our peasants,
Who in unnecessary action swarm
About our squares of battle, were enough
To purge this field of such a hilding foe,
Though we upon this mountain's basis by   30
Took stand for idle speculation,
But that our honours must not. What's to say?
A very little little let us do
And all is done. Then let the trumpets sound
The tucket sonance and the note to mount,   35
For our approach shall so much dare the field
That England shall couch down in fear and yield.
    Enter Lord Grandpré
GRANDPRÉ
Why do you stay so long, my lords of France?
Yon island carrions, desperate of their bones,

Ill-favouredly become the morning field.   40
Their ragged curtains poorly are let loose
And our air shakes them passing scornfully.
Big Mars seems bankrupt in their beggared host
And faintly through a rusty beaver peeps.
The horsemen sit like fixèd candlesticks   45
With torchstaves in their hands, and their poor jades
Lob down their heads, drooping the hides and hips,
The gum down-roping from their pale dead eyes,
And in their palled dull mouths the gimmaled bit
Lies foul with chewed grass, still and motionless.   50
And their executors, the knavish crows,
Fly o'er them all impatient for their hour.
Description cannot suit itself in words
To demonstrate the life of such a battle
In life so lifeless as it shows itself.   55

CONSTABLE
They have said their prayers, and they stay for death.

⌜BOURBON⌝
Shall we go send them dinners and fresh suits
And give their fasting horses provender,
And after fight with them?

CONSTABLE
I stay but for my guidon. To the field!   60
I will the banner from a trumpet take
And use it for my haste. Come, come away!
The sun is high, and we outwear the day.   *Exeunt*

4.3 *Enter the Dukes of Gloucester, ⌜Clarence⌝, and*
      Exeter, the Earls of Salisbury and ⌜Warwick⌝, and
      Sir Thomas Erpingham, with· all ⌜the⌝ host

GLOUCESTER Where is the King?

⌜CLARENCE⌝
The King himself is rode to view their battle.

⌜WARWICK⌝
Of fighting men they have full threescore thousand.

EXETER
There's five to one. Besides, they all are fresh.

SALISBURY
God's arm strike with us! 'Tis a fearful odds.   5
God b'wi' you, princes all. I'll to my charge.
If we no more meet till we meet in heaven,
Then joyfully, my noble Lord of Clarence,
My dear Lord Gloucester, and my good Lord Exeter,
And (*to Warwick*) my kind kinsman, warriors all,
      adieu.   10

⌜CLARENCE⌝
Farewell, good Salisbury, and good luck go with thee.

EXETER
Farewell, kind lord. Fight valiantly today—
And yet I do thee wrong to mind thee of it,
For thou art framed of the firm truth of valour.
                                        Exit Salisbury

⌜CLARENCE⌝
He is as full of valour as of kindness,   15
Princely in both.
      Enter King Harry, behind

⌜WARWICK⌝   O that we now had here

But one ten thousand of those men in England
That do no work today.

KING HARRY   What's he that wishes so?
My cousin Warwick? No, my fair cousin.
If we are marked to die, we are enough   20
To do our country loss; and if to live,
The fewer men, the greater share of honour.
God's will, I pray thee wish not one man more.
By Jove, I am not covetous for gold,
Nor care I who doth feed upon my cost;   25
It ernes me not if men my garments wear;
Such outward things dwell not in my desires.
But if it be a sin to covet honour
I am the most offending soul alive.
No, faith, my coz, wish not a man from England.   30
God's peace, I would not lose so great an honour
As one man more methinks would share from me
For the best hope I have. O do not wish one more.
Rather proclaim it presently through my host
That he which hath no stomach to this fight,   35
Let him depart. His passport shall be made
And crowns for convoy put into his purse.
We would not die in that man's company
That fears his fellowship to die with us.
This day is called the Feast of Crispian.   40
He that outlives this day and comes safe home
Will stand a-tiptoe when this day is named
And rouse him at the name of Crispian.
He that shall see this day and live t'old age
Will yearly on the vigil feast his neighbours   45
And say, 'Tomorrow is Saint Crispian.'
Then will he strip his sleeve and show his scars
And say, 'These wounds I had on Crispin's day.'
Old men forget; yet all shall be forgot,
But he'll remember, with advantages,   50
What feats he did that day. Then shall our names,
Familiar in his mouth as household words—
Harry the King, Bedford and Exeter,
Warwick and Talbot, Salisbury and Gloucester—
Be in their flowing cups freshly remembered.   55
This story shall the good man teach his son,
And Crispin Crispian shall ne'er go by
From this day to the ending of the world
But we in it shall be rememberèd,
We few, we happy few, we band of brothers.   60
For he today that sheds his blood with me
Shall be my brother; be he ne'er so vile,
This day shall gentle his condition.
And gentlemen in England now abed
Shall think themselves accursed they were not here,   65
And hold their manhoods cheap whiles any speaks
That fought with us upon Saint Crispin's day.
      Enter the Earl of Salisbury

SALISBURY
My sovereign lord, bestow yourself with speed.
The French are bravely in their battles set
And will with all expedience charge on us.   70

KING HARRY
All things are ready if our minds be so.
⌈WARWICK⌉
Perish the man whose mind is backward now.
KING HARRY
Thou dost not wish more help from England, coz?
⌈WARWICK⌉
God's will, my liege, would you and I alone,
Without more help, could fight this royal battle. 75
KING HARRY
Why now thou hast unwished five thousand men,
Which likes me better than to wish us one.—
You know your places. God be with you all.
          Tucket. Enter Montjoy
MONTJOY
Once more I come to know of thee, King Harry,
If for thy ransom thou wilt now compound   80
Before thy most assurèd overthrow.
For certainly thou art so near the gulf
Thou needs must be englutted. Besides, in mercy
The Constable desires thee thou wilt mind
Thy followers of repentance, that their souls   85
May make a peaceful and a sweet retire
From off these fields where, wretches, their poor
          bodies
Must lie and fester.
KING HARRY Who hath sent thee now?
MONTJOY The Constable of France.   90
KING HARRY
I pray thee bear my former answer back.
Bid them achieve me, and then sell my bones.
Good God, why should they mock poor fellows thus?
The man that once did sell the lion's skin
While the beast lived, was killed with hunting him. 95
A many of our bodies shall no doubt
Find native graves, upon the which, I trust,
Shall witness live in brass of this day's work.
And those that leave their valiant bones in France,
Dying like men, though buried in your dunghills 100
They shall be famed. For there the sun shall greet
          them
And draw their honours reeking up to heaven,
Leaving their earthly parts to choke your clime,
The smell whereof shall breed a plague in France.
Mark then abounding valour in our English,   105
That, being dead, like to the bullets grazing
Break out into a second course of mischief,
Killing in relapse of mortality.
Let me speak proudly. Tell the Constable
We are but warriors for the working day.   110
Our gayness and our gilt are all besmirched
With rainy marching in the painful field.
There's not a piece of feather in our host—
Good argument, I hope, we will not fly—
And time hath worn us into slovenry.   115
But by the mass, our hearts are in the trim.
And my poor soldiers tell me, yet ere night
They'll be in fresher robes, as they will pluck

The gay new coats o'er your French soldiers' heads,
And turn them out of service. If they do this—   120
As if God please, they shall—my ransom then
Will soon be levied. Herald, save thou thy labour.
Come thou no more for ransom, gentle herald.
They shall have none, I swear, but these my joints—
Which if they have as I will leave 'em them,   125
Shall yield them little. Tell the Constable.
MONTJOY
I shall, King Harry. And so fare thee well.
Thou never shalt hear herald any more.
KING HARRY
I fear thou wilt once more come for a ransom.
                              Exit Montjoy
          Enter the Duke of York
YORK
My lord, most humbly on my knee I beg   130
The leading of the vanguard.
KING HARRY
Take it, brave York.—Now soldiers, march away,
And how thou pleasest, God, dispose the day.   *Exeunt*

4.4   *Alarum. Excursions. Enter Pistol, a French soldier,*
          and the Boy
PISTOL Yield, cur.
FRENCH SOLDIER *Je pense que vous êtes le gentilhomme de*
          bon qualité.
PISTOL
          Qualité? 'Calin o custure me!'
          Art thou a gentleman? What is thy name? Discuss. 5
FRENCH SOLDIER *O Seigneur Dieu!*
PISTOL ⌈*aside*⌉
          O Seigneur Dew should be a gentleman.—
          Perpend my words, O Seigneur Dew, and mark:
          O Seigneur Dew, thou diest, on point of fox,
          Except, O Seigneur, thou do give to me   10
          Egregious ransom.
FRENCH SOLDIER *O prenez miséricorde! Ayez pitié de moi!*
PISTOL
          'Moy' shall not serve, I will have forty 'moys',
          Or I will fetch thy rim out at thy throat
          In drops of crimson blood.   15
FRENCH SOLDIER *Est-il impossible d'échapper la force de ton*
          bras?
PISTOL
          Brass, cur? Thou damnèd and luxurious mountain
          goat,
          Offer'st me brass?
FRENCH SOLDIER *O pardonne-moi!*   20
PISTOL
          Sayst thou me so? Is that a ton of moys?—
          Come hither boy. Ask me this slave in French
          What is his name.
BOY *Écoutez: comment êtes-vous appelé?*
FRENCH SOLDIER *Monsieur le Fer.*   25
BOY He says his name is Master Fer.
PISTOL Master Fer? I'll fer him, and firk him, and ferret
          him.

Discuss the same in French unto him. 29

BOY I do not know the French for fer and ferret and firk.

PISTOL

Bid him prepare, for I will cut his throat.

FRENCH SOLDIER *Que dit-il, monsieur?*

BOY *Il me commande à vous dire que vous faites vous prêt,
car ce soldat ici est disposé tout à cette heure de couper
votre gorge.* 35

PISTOL

Oui, couper la gorge, par ma foi,

Peasant, unless thou give me crowns, brave crowns;

Or mangled shalt thou be by this my sword.

FRENCH SOLDIER *O je vous supplie, pour l'amour de Dieu, me
pardonner. Je suis le gentilhomme de bonne maison. Gardez
ma vie, et je vous donnerai deux cents écus.* 41

PISTOL What are his words?

BOY He prays you to save his life. He is a gentleman of a
good house, and for his ransom he will give you two
hundred crowns. 45

PISTOL

Tell him, my fury shall abate, and I the crowns will
take.

FRENCH SOLDIER *Petit monsieur, que dit-il?*

BOY *Encore qu'il est contre son jurement de pardonner aucun
prisonnier; néanmoins, pour les écus que vous lui ci
promettez, il est content à vous donner la liberté, le
franchisement.* 51

FRENCH SOLDIER (*kneeling to Pistol*) *Sur mes genoux je vous
donne mille remerciements, et je m'estime heureux que j'ai
tombé entre les mains d'un chevalier, comme je pense, le
plus brave, vaillant, et treis-distingué seigneur d'Angleterre.*

PISTOL Expound unto me, boy. 56

BOY He gives you upon his knees a thousand thanks, and
he esteems himself happy that he hath fallen into the
hands of one, as he thinks, the most brave, valorous,
and thrice-worthy seigneur of England. 60

PISTOL

As I suck blood, I will some mercy show.

Follow me.

BOY *Suivez-vous le grand capitaine.*

        Exeunt Pistol and French Soldier

I did never know so full a voice issue from so empty a
heart. But the saying is true: 'The empty vessel makes
the greatest sound.' Bardolph and Nim had ten times
more valour than this roaring devil i'th' old play, that
everyone may pare his nails with a wooden dagger, and
they are both hanged, and so would this be, if he
durst steal anything adventurously. I must stay with
the lackeys with the luggage of our camp. The French
might have a good prey of us, if he knew of it, for there
is none to guard it but boys.   *Exit*

4.5   *Enter the Constable, the Dukes of Orléans and*
      ⌈*Bourbon*⌉, *and Lord Rambures*

CONSTABLE *O diable!*

ORLÉANS *O Seigneur! Le jour est perdu, tout est perdu!*

⌈BOURBON⌉

Mort de ma vie! All is confounded, all.

Reproach and everlasting shame

Sits mocking in our plumes. 5

    A short alarum

O méchante fortune!— (*To Rambures*) Do not run away.

⌈ORLÉANS⌉

We are enough yet living in the field

To smother up the English in our throngs,

If any order might be thought upon.

BOURBON

The devil take order. Once more back again! 10

And he that will not follow Bourbon now,

Let him go home, and with his cap in hand

Like a base leno hold the chamber door

Whilst by a slave no gentler than my dog

His fairest daughter is contaminated. 15

CONSTABLE

Disorder that hath spoiled us friend us now.

Let us on heaps go offer up our lives.

BOURBON I'll to the throng.

Let life be short, else shame will be too long.   *Exeunt*

4.6   *Alarum. Enter King Harry and his train, with*
      prisoners

KING HARRY

Well have we done, thrice-valiant countrymen.

But all's not done; yet keep the French the field.

    ⌈*Enter the Duke of Exeter*⌉

EXETER

The Duke of York commends him to your majesty.

KING HARRY

Lives he, good uncle? Thrice within this hour

I saw him down, thrice up again and fighting. 5

From helmet to the spur, all blood he was.

EXETER

In which array, brave soldier, doth he lie,

Larding the plain. And by his bloody side,

Yokefellow to his honour-owing wounds,

The noble Earl of Suffolk also lies. 10

Suffolk first died, and York, all haggled over,

Comes to him, where in gore he lay insteeped,

And takes him by the beard, kisses the gashes

That bloodily did yawn upon his face,

And cries aloud, 'Tarry, dear cousin Suffolk. 15

My soul shall thine keep company to heaven.

Tarry, sweet soul, for mine, then fly abreast,

As in this glorious and well-foughten field

We kept together in our chivalry.'

Upon these words I came and cheered him up. 20

He smiled me in the face, raught me his hand,

And with a feeble grip says, 'Dear my lord,

Commend my service to my sovereign.'

So did he turn, and over Suffolk's neck

He threw his wounded arm, and kissed his lips, 25

And so espoused to death, with blood he sealed

A testament of noble-ending love.

The pretty and sweet manner of it forced

Those waters from me which I would have stopped.

But I had not so much of man in me, 30

And all my mother came into mine eyes
And gave me up to tears.
KING HARRY   I blame you not,
For hearing this I must perforce compound
With mistful eyes, or they will issue too.
 Alarum
But hark, what new alarum is this same?   35
The French have reinforced their scattered men.
Then every soldier kill his prisoners.
 ⌈*The soldiers kill their prisoners*⌉
Give the word through.
⌈PISTOL⌉ Coup' la gorge.   *Exeunt*

4.7 *Enter Captains Fluellen and Gower*
FLUELLEN Kill the poys and the luggage! 'Tis expressly
against the law of arms. 'Tis as arrant a piece of
knavery, mark you now, as can be offert. In your
conscience now, is it not?   4
GOWER 'Tis certain there's not a boy left alive. And the
cowardly rascals that ran from the battle ha' done this
slaughter. Besides, they have burned and carried away
all that was in the King's tent; wherefore the King
most worthily hath caused every soldier to cut his
prisoner's throat. O 'tis a gallant king.   10
FLUELLEN Ay, he was porn at Monmouth. Captain Gower,
what call you the town's name where Alexander the
Pig was born?
GOWER Alexander the Great.   14
FLUELLEN Why I pray you, is not 'pig' great? The pig or
the great or the mighty or the huge or the
magnanimous are all one reckonings, save the phrase
is a little variations.
GOWER I think Alexander the Great was born in Macedon.
His father was called Philip of Macedon, as I take it. 20
FLUELLEN I think it is e'en Macedon where Alexander is
porn. I tell you, captain, if you look in the maps of the
world I warrant you sall find, in the comparisons
between Macedon and Monmouth, that the situations,
look you, is both alike. There is a river in Macedon,
and there is also moreover a river at Monmouth. It is
called Wye at Monmouth, but it is out of my prains
what is the name of the other river—but 'tis all one,
'tis alike as my fingers is to my fingers, and there is
salmons in both. If you mark Alexander's life well,
Harry of Monmouth's life is come after it indifferent
well. For there is figures in all things. Alexander, God
knows, and you know, in his rages and his furies and
his wraths and his cholers and his moods and his
displeasures and his indignations, and also being a little
intoxicates in his prains, did in his ales and his angers,
look you, kill his best friend Cleitus—
GOWER Our King is not like him in that. He never killed
any of his friends.   39
FLUELLEN It is not well done, mark you now, to take the
tales out of my mouth ere it is made an end and
finished. I speak but in the figures and comparisons of
it. As Alexander killed his friend Cleitus, being in his

ales and his cups, so also Harry Monmouth, being in
his right wits and his good judgements, turned away
the fat knight with the great-belly doublet—he was full
of jests and gipes and knaveries and mocks—I have
forgot his name.
GOWER Sir John Falstaff.
FLUELLEN That is he. I'll tell you, there is good men porn
at Monmouth.   51
GOWER Here comes his majesty.
 Alarum. Enter King Harry ⌈*and the English army*⌉,
 with the Duke of Bourbon, ⌈*the Duke of Orléans,*⌉
 and other prisoners. Flourish
KING HARRY
I was not angry since I came to France
Until this instant. Take a trumpet, herald;
Ride thou unto the horsemen on yon hill.   55
If they will fight with us, bid them come down,
Or void the field: they do offend our sight.
If they'll do neither, we will come to them,
And make them skirr away as swift as stones
Enforcèd from the old Assyrian slings.   60
Besides, we'll cut the throats of those we have,
And not a man of them that we shall take
Shall taste our mercy. Go and tell them so.
 Enter Montjoy
EXETER
Here comes the herald of the French, my liege.
GLOUCESTER
His eyes are humbler than they used to be.   65
KING HARRY
How now, what means this, herald? Know'st thou
 not
That I have fined these bones of mine for ransom?
Com'st thou again for ransom?
MONTJOY   No, great King.
I come to thee for charitable licence,
That we may wander o'er this bloody field   70
To book our dead and then to bury them,
To sort our nobles from our common men—
For many of our princes, woe the while,
Lie drowned and soaked in mercenary blood.
So do our vulgar drench their peasant limbs 75
In blood of princes, and our wounded steeds
Fret fetlock-deep in gore, and with wild rage
Jerk out their armèd heels at their dead masters,
Killing them twice. O give us leave, great King,
To view the field in safety, and dispose   80
Of their dead bodies.
KING HARRY   I tell thee truly, herald,
I know not if the day be ours or no,
For yet a many of your horsemen peer
And gallop o'er the field.
MONTJOY   The day is yours.
KING HARRY
Praisèd be God, and not our strength, for it. 85
What is this castle called that stands hard by?
MONTJOY They call it Agincourt.

KING HARRY
Then call we this the field of Agincourt,
Fought on the day of Crispin Crispian.   89
FLUELLEN Your grandfather of famous memory, an't
please your majesty, and your great-uncle Edward the
Plack Prince of Wales, as I have read in the chronicles,
fought a most prave pattle here in France.
KING HARRY They did, Fluellen.   94
FLUELLEN Your majesty says very true. If your majesties
is remembered of it, the Welshmen did good service in
a garden where leeks did grow, wearing leeks in their
Monmouth caps, which your majesty know to this
hour is an honourable badge of the service. And I do
believe your majesty takes no scorn to wear the leek
upon Saint Tavy's day.   101
KING HARRY
I wear it for a memorable honour,
For I am Welsh, you know, good countryman.
FLUELLEN All the water in Wye cannot wash your
majesty's Welsh plood out of your pody, I can tell you
that. God pless it and preserve it, as long as it pleases
his grace, and his majesty too.
KING HARRY Thanks, good my countryman.
FLUELLEN By Jeshu, I am your majesty's countryman. I
care not who know it, I will confess it to all the world.
I need not to be ashamed of your majesty, praised be
God, so long as your majesty is an honest man.
KING HARRY
God keep me so.
          Enter Williams with a glove in his cap
          Our heralds go with him.
Bring me just notice of the numbers dead
On both our parts.
          Exeunt Montjoy, ⌐Gower,¬ and an English
                                        herald
          Call yonder fellow hither.   115
EXETER (*to Williams*) Soldier, you must come to the King.
KING HARRY Soldier, why wearest thou that glove in thy
cap?
WILLIAMS An't please your majesty, 'tis the gage of one
that I should fight withal, if he be alive.   120
KING HARRY An Englishman?
WILLIAMS An't please your majesty, a rascal, that
swaggered with me last night—who, if a live, and ever
dare to challenge this glove, I have sworn to take him
a box o'th' ear; or if I can see my glove in his cap—
which he swore, as he was a soldier, he would wear
if a lived—I will strike it out soundly.
KING HARRY What think you, Captain Fluellen? Is it fit
this soldier keep his oath?
FLUELLEN He is a craven and a villain else, ar't please
your majesty, in my conscience.   131
KING HARRY It may be his enemy is a gentleman of great
sort, quite from the answer of his degree.
FLUELLEN Though he be as good a gentleman as the devil
is, as Lucifer and Beelzebub himself, it is necessary,
look your grace, that he keep his vow and his oath. If
he be perjured, see you now, his reputation is as arrant
a villain and a Jack-sauce as ever his black shoe trod

upon God's ground and his earth, in my conscience
law.   14
KING HARRY Then keep thy vow, sirrah, when thou
meetest the fellow.
WILLIAMS So I will, my liege, as I live.
KING HARRY Who serv'st thou under?
WILLIAMS Under Captain Gower, my liege.   14
FLUELLEN Gower is a good captain, and is good knowledge
and literatured in the wars.
KING HARRY Call him hither to me, soldier.
WILLIAMS I will, my liege.   *Exit*
KING HARRY (*giving him Williams's other glove*) Here,
Fluellen, wear thou this favour for me and stick it in
thy cap. When Alençon and myself were down together
I plucked this glove from his helm. If any man challenge
this, he is a friend to Alençon and an enemy to our
person. If thou encounter any such, apprehend him,
an thou dost me love.   15
FLUELLEN Your grace does me as great honours as can
be desired in the hearts of his subjects. I would fain see
the man that has but two legs that shall find himself
aggriefed at this glove, that is all; but I would fain see
it once. An't please God of his grace, that I would see.
KING HARRY Know'st thou Gower?
FLUELLEN He is my dear friend, an't please you.
KING HARRY Pray thee, go seek him and bring him to my
tent.   16
FLUELLEN I will fetch him.   *Exit*
KING HARRY
My lord of Warwick and my brother Gloucester,
Follow Fluellen closely at the heels.
The glove which I have given him for a favour
May haply purchase him a box o'th' ear.   170
It is the soldier's. I by bargain should
Wear it myself. Follow, good cousin Warwick.
If that the soldier strike him, as I judge
By his blunt bearing he will keep his word,
Some sudden mischief may arise of it,   175
For I do know Fluellen valiant
And touched with choler, hot as gunpowder,
And quickly will return an injury.
Follow, and see there be no harm between them.   179
Go you with me, uncle of Exeter.   *Exeunt severally*

4.8   *Enter Captain Gower and Williams*
WILLIAMS I warrant it is to knight you, captain.
          Enter Captain Fluellen
FLUELLEN God's will and his pleasure, captain, I beseech
you now, come apace to the King. There is more good
toward you, peradventure, than is in your knowledge
to dream of.   5
WILLIAMS Sir, know you this glove?
FLUELLEN Know the glove? I know the glove is a glove.
WILLIAMS ⌐*plucking the glove from Fluellen's cap*¬ I know
this, and thus I challenge it.
          He strikes Fluellen
FLUELLEN God's plood, and his! An arrant traitor as any's
in the universal world, or in France, or in England.   11
GOWER (*to Williams*) How now, sir? You villain!

WILLIAMS Do you think I'll be forsworn?

FLUELLEN Stand away, Captain Gower. I will give treason
his payment into plows, I warrant you.   15

WILLIAMS I am no traitor.

FLUELLEN That's a lie in thy throat. I charge you in his
majesty's name, apprehend him. He's a friend of the
Duke Alençon's.

Enter the Earl of Warwick and the Duke of
Gloucester

WARWICK How now, how now, what's the matter?   20

FLUELLEN My lord of Warwick, here is—praised be God
for it—a most contagious treason come to light, look
you, as you shall desire in a summer's day.

Enter King Harry and the Duke of Exeter
Here is his majesty.

KING HARRY How now, what is the matter?   25

FLUELLEN My liege, here is a villain and a traitor that,
look your grace, has struck the glove which your
majesty is take out of the helmet of Alençon.

WILLIAMS My liege, this was my glove—here is the fellow
of it—and he that I gave it to in change promised to
wear it in his cap. I promised to strike him, if he did. I
met this man with my glove in his cap, and I have
been as good as my word.

FLUELLEN Your majesty hear now, saving your majesty's
manhood, what an arrant rascally beggarly lousy knave
it is. I hope your majesty is pear me testimony and
witness, and will avouchment that this is the glove of
Alençon that your majesty is give me, in your
conscience now.

KING HARRY Give me thy glove, soldier. Look, here is the
fellow of it.   41
'Twas I indeed thou promisèd'st to strike,
And thou hast given me most bitter terms.

FLUELLEN An't please your majesty, let his neck answer
for it, if there is any martial law in the world. 45

KING HARRY
How canst thou make me satisfaction?

WILLIAMS All offences, my lord, come from the heart.
Never came any from mine that might offend your
majesty.

KING HARRY
It was ourself thou didst abuse.   50

WILLIAMS Your majesty came not like yourself. You
appeared to me but as a common man. Witness the
night, your garments, your lowliness. And what your
highness suffered under that shape, I beseech you take
it for your own fault, and not mine, for had you been
as I took you for, I made no offence. Therefore I beseech
your highness pardon me.

KING HARRY
Here, Uncle Exeter, fill this glove with crowns
And give it to this fellow.—Keep it, fellow,
And wear it for an honour in thy cap   60
Till I do challenge it.—Give him the crowns.
—And captain, you must needs be friends with him.

FLUELLEN By this day and this light, the fellow has mettle
enough in his belly.—Hold, there is twelve pence for

you, and I pray you to serve God, and keep you out of
prawls and prabbles and quarrels and dissensions, and
I warrant you it is the better for you.

WILLIAMS I will none of your money.

FLUELLEN It is with a good will. I can tell you, it will
serve you to mend your shoes. Come, wherefore should
you be so pashful? Your shoes is not so good. 'Tis a
good shilling, I warrant you, or I will change it.

Enter ⌐an English⌐ Herald

KING HARRY Now, herald, are the dead numbered?

HERALD
Here is the number of the slaughtered French.

KING HARRY
What prisoners of good sort are taken, uncle?   75

EXETER
Charles, Duke of Orléans, nephew to the King;
Jean, Duke of Bourbon, and Lord Boucicault;
Of other lords and barons, knights and squires,
Full fifteen hundred, besides common men.

KING HARRY
This note doth tell me of ten thousand French   80
That in the field lie slain. Of princes in this number
And nobles bearing banners, there lie dead
One hundred twenty-six; added to these,
Of knights, esquires, and gallant gentlemen,
Eight thousand and four hundred, of the which   85
Five hundred were but yesterday dubbed knights.
So that in these ten thousand they have lost
There are but sixteen hundred mercenaries;
The rest are princes, barons, lords, knights, squires,
And gentlemen of blood and quality.   90
The names of those their nobles that lie dead:
Charles Delabret, High Constable of France;
Jaques of Châtillon, Admiral of France;
The Master of the Crossbows, Lord Rambures;
Great-Master of France, the brave Sir Guiscard
   Dauphin;   95
Jean, Duke of Alençon; Antony, Duke of Brabant,
The brother to the Duke of Burgundy;
And Édouard, Duke of Βar; of lusty earls,
Grandpré and Roussi, Fauconbridge and Foix,
Beaumont and Marle, Vaudemont and Lestrelles.   100
Here was a royal fellowship of death.
Where is the number of our English dead?

He is given another paper
Edward the Duke of York, the Earl of Suffolk,
Sir Richard Keighley, Davy Gam Esquire;
None else of name, and of all other men   105
But five-and-twenty. O God, thy arm was here,
And not to us, but to thy arm alone
Ascribe we all. When, without stratagem,
But in plain shock and even play of battle,
Was ever known so great and little loss   110
On one part and on th'other? Take it God,
For it is none but thine.

EXETER   'Tis wonderful.

KING HARRY
Come, go we in procession to the village,

And be it death proclaimèd through our host
To boast of this, or take that praise from God   115
Which is his only.

FLUELLEN Is it not lawful, an't please your majesty, to tell
how many is killed?

KING HARRY
Yes, captain, but with this acknowledgement,
That God fought for us.   120

FLUELLEN Yes, in my conscience, he did us great good.

KING HARRY Do we all holy rites:
Let there be sung *Non nobis* and *Te Deum*,
The dead with charity enclosed in clay;
And then to Calais, and to England then,   125
Where ne'er from France arrived more-happy men.

                                    Exeunt

5.0   *Enter Chorus*
CHORUS
Vouchsafe to those that have not read the story
That I may prompt them—and of such as have,
I humbly pray them to admit th'excuse
Of time, of numbers, and due course of things,
Which cannot in their huge and proper life   5
Be here presented. Now we bear the King
Toward Calais. Grant him there; there seen,
Heave him away upon your wingèd thoughts
Athwart the sea. Behold, the English beach   9
Pales-in the flood, with men, maids, wives, and boys,
Whose shouts and claps out-voice the deep-mouthed
     sea,
Which like a mighty whiffler fore the King
Seems to prepare his way. So let him land,
And solemnly see him set on to London.
So swift a pace hath thought, that even now   15
You may imagine him upon Blackheath,
Where that his lords desire him to have borne
His bruisèd helmet and his bended sword
Before him through the city; he forbids it,
Being free from vainness and self-glorious pride,   20
Giving full trophy, signal, and ostent
Quite from himself, to God. But now behold,
In the quick forge and working-house of thought,
How London doth pour out her citizens.
The Mayor and all his brethren, in best sort,   25
Like to the senators of th'antique Rome
With the plebeians swarming at their heels,
Go forth and fetch their conqu'ring Caesar in—
As, by a lower but high-loving likelihood,
Were now the General of our gracious Empress—   30
As in good time he may—from Ireland coming,
Bringing rebellion broachèd on his sword,
How many would the peaceful city quit
To welcome him! Much more, and much more cause,
Did they this Harry. Now in London place him;   35
As yet the lamentation of the French
Invites the King of England's stay at home.
The Emperor's coming in behalf of France,
To order peace between them ⌈
                       ⌉ and omit   40

All the occurrences, whatever chanced,
Till Harry's back-return again to France.
There must we bring him, and myself have played
The interim by rememb'ring you 'tis past.
Then brook abridgement, and your eyes advance,   45
After your thoughts, straight back again to France.

                                        Exit

5.1   *Enter Captain Gower and Captain Fluellen, with a*
         leek in his cap and a cudgel

GOWER Nay, that's right. But why wear you your leek
today? Saint Davy's day is past.

FLUELLEN There is occasions and causes why and
wherefore in all things. I will tell you, ass my friend,
Captain Gower. The rascally scald beggarly lousy
pragging knave Pistol—which you and yourself and all
the world know to be no petter than a fellow, look you
now, of no merits—he is come to me, and prings me
pread and salt yesterday, look you, and bid me eat my
leek. It was in a place where I could not breed no
contention with him, but I will be so bold as to wear
it in my cap till I see him once again, and then I will
tell him a little piece of my desires.

         Enter Ensign Pistol

GOWER Why, here a comes, swelling like a turkey-cock.

FLUELLEN 'Tis no matter for his swellings nor his turkey-
cocks.—God pless you Ensign Pistol, you scurvy lousy
knave, God pless you.

PISTOL
Ha, art thou bedlam? Dost thou thirst, base Trojan,
To have me fold up Parca's fatal web?
Hence! I am qualmish at the smell of leek.   20

FLUELLEN I peseech you heartily, scurvy lousy knave, at
my desires and my requests and my petitions, to eat,
look you, this leek. Because, look you, you do not love
it, nor your affections and your appetites and your
digestions does not agree with it, I would desire you
to eat it.   26

PISTOL
Not for Cadwallader and all his goats.

FLUELLEN There is one goat for you. (*He strikes Pistol*) Will
you be so good, scald knave, as eat it?

PISTOL Base Trojan, thou shalt die.   30

FLUELLEN You say very true, scald knave, when God's
will is. I will desire you to live in the mean time, and
eat your victuals. Come, there is sauce for it. (*He strikes
him*) You called me yesterday 'mountain-squire', but I
will make you today a 'squire of low degree'. I pray
you, fall to. If you can mock a leek you can eat a leek.
         ⌈*He strikes him*⌉

GOWER Enough, captain, you have astonished him.

FLUELLEN By Jesu, I will make him eat some part of my
leek, or I will peat his pate four days and four nights.—
Bite, I pray you. It is good for your green wound and
your ploody coxcomb.   41

PISTOL Must I bite?

FLUELLEN Yes, certainly, and out of doubt and out of
question too, and ambiguities.

PISTOL By this leek, I will most horribly revenge—   45
⌜*Fluellen threatens him*⌝
I eat and eat—I swear—
FLUELLEN Eat, I pray you. Will you have some more sauce
to your leek? There is not enough leek to swear by.
PISTOL
Quiet thy cudgel, thou dost see I eat.   49
FLUELLEN Much good do you, scald knave, heartily. Nay,
pray you throw none away. The skin is good for your
broken coxcomb. When you take occasions to see leeks
hereafter, I pray you mock at 'em, that is all.
PISTOL Good.
FLUELLEN Ay, leeks is good. Hold you, there is a groat to
heal your pate.   56
PISTOL Me, a groat?
FLUELLEN Yes, verily, and in truth you shall take it, or I
have another leek in my pocket which you shall eat.
PISTOL
I take thy groat in earnest of revenge.   60
FLUELLEN If I owe you anything, I will pay you in cudgels.
You shall be a woodmonger, and buy nothing of me
but cudgels. God b'wi' you, and keep you, and heal
your pate.   *Exit*
PISTOL All hell shall stir for this.   65
GOWER Go, go, you are a counterfeit cowardly knave.
Will you mock at an ancient tradition, begun upon an
honourable respect and worn as a memorable trophy
of predeceased valour, and dare not avouch in your
deeds any of your words? I have seen you gleeking and
galling at this gentleman twice or thrice. You thought,
because he could not speak English in the native garb,
he could not therefore handle an English cudgel. You
find it otherwise. And henceforth let a Welsh correction
teach you a good English condition. Fare ye well.   75
Exit

PISTOL
Doth Fortune play the hussy with me now?
News have I that my Nell is dead
I'th' spital of a malady of France,
And there my rendezvous is quite cut off.
Old I do wax, and from my weary limbs   80
Honour is cudgelled. Well, bawd I'll turn,
And something lean to cutpurse of quick hand.
To England will I steal, and there I'll steal,
And patches will I get unto these cudgelled scars,   84
And swear I got them in the Gallia wars.   *Exit*

5.2   *Enter at one door King Harry, the Dukes of Exeter
and ⌜Clarence⌝, the Earl of Warwick, and other
lords; at another, King Charles the Sixth of France,
Queen Isabel, the Duke of Burgundy, and other
French, among them Princess Catherine and Alice*
KING HARRY
Peace to this meeting, wherefor we are met.
Unto our brother France and to our sister,
Health and fair time of day. Joy and good wishes
To our most fair and princely cousin Catherine;
And as a branch and member of this royalty,   5
By whom this great assembly is contrived,

We do salute you, Duke of Burgundy.
And princes French, and peers, health to you all.
KING CHARLES
Right joyous are we to behold your face.
Most worthy brother England, fairly met.   10
So are you, princes English, every one.
QUEEN ISABEL
So happy be the issue, brother England,
Of this good day and of this gracious meeting,
As we are now glad to behold your eyes—
Your eyes which hitherto have borne in them,   15
Against the French that met them in their bent,
The fatal balls of murdering basilisks.
The venom of such looks we fairly hope
Have lost their quality, and that this day
Shall change all griefs and quarrels into love.   20
KING HARRY
To cry amen to that, thus we appear.
QUEEN ISABEL
You English princes all, I do salute you.
BURGUNDY
My duty to you both, on equal love,
Great Kings of France and England. That I have
laboured
With all my wits, my pains, and strong endeavours,   25
To bring your most imperial majesties
Unto this bar and royal interview,
Your mightiness on both parts best can witness.
Since, then, my office hath so far prevailed
That face to face and royal eye to eye   30
You have congreeted, let it not disgrace me
If I demand, before this royal view,
What rub or what impediment there is
Why that the naked, poor, and mangled peace,
Dear nurse of arts, plenties, and joyful births,   35
Should not in this best garden of the world,
Our fertile France, put up her lovely visage?
Alas, she hath from France too long been chased,
And all her husbandry doth lie on heaps,
Corrupting in it own fertility.   40
Her vine, the merry cheerer of the heart,
Unprunèd dies; her hedges even-plashed
Like prisoners wildly overgrown with hair
Put forth disordered twigs; her fallow leas
The darnel, hemlock, and rank fumitory   45
Doth root upon, while that the coulter rusts
That should deracinate such savagery.
The even mead—that erst brought sweetly forth
The freckled cowslip, burnet, and green clover—
Wanting the scythe, all uncorrected, rank,   50
Conceives by idleness, and nothing teems
But hateful docks, rough thistles, kecksies, burs,
Losing both beauty and utility.
An all our vineyards, fallows, meads, and hedges,
Defective in their natures, grow to wildness,   55
Even so our houses and ourselves and children
Have lost, or do not learn for want of time,
The sciences that should become our country,
But grow like savages—as soldiers will

That nothing do but meditate on blood—   60
To swearing and stern looks, diffused attire,
And everything that seems unnatural.
Which to reduce into our former favour
You are assembled, and my speech entreats
That I may know the let why gentle peace   65
Should not expel these inconveniences
And bless us with her former qualities.

KING HARRY
If, Duke of Burgundy, you would the peace
Whose want gives growth to th'imperfections
Which you have cited, you must buy that peace   70
With full accord to all our just demands,
Whose tenors and particular effects
You have enscheduled briefly in your hands.

BURGUNDY
The King hath heard them, to the which as yet
There is no answer made.

KING HARRY   Well then, the peace,   75
Which you before so urged, lies in his answer.

KING CHARLES
I have but with a cursitory eye
O'erglanced the articles. Pleaseth your grace
To appoint some of your council presently
To sit with us once more, with better heed   80
To re-survey them, we will suddenly
Pass our accept and peremptory answer.

KING HARRY
Brother, we shall.—Go, Uncle Exeter
And brother Clarence, and you, brother Gloucester;
Warwick and Huntingdon, go with the King,   85
And take with you free power to ratify,
Augment, or alter, as your wisdoms best
Shall see advantageable for our dignity,
Anything in or out of our demands,
And we'll consign thereto.—Will you, fair sister,   90
Go with the princes, or stay here with us?

QUEEN
Our gracious brother, I will go with them.
Haply a woman's voice may do some good
When articles too nicely urged be stood on.

KING HARRY
Yet leave our cousin Catherine here with us.   95
She is our capital demand, comprised
Within the fore-rank of our articles.

QUEEN
She hath good leave.
                Exeunt all but King Harry, Catherine, and Alice

KING HARRY   Fair Catherine, and most fair,
Will you vouchsafe to teach a soldier terms
Such as will enter at a lady's ear   100
And plead his love-suit to her gentle heart?

CATHERINE Your majesty shall mock at me. I cannot speak
your England.

KING HARRY O fair Catherine, if you will love me soundly
with your French heart, I will be glad to hear you
confess it brokenly with your English tongue. Do you
like me, Kate?

CATHERINE *Pardonnez-moi*, I cannot tell vat is 'like me'.

KING HARRY An angel is like you, Kate, and you are like
an angel.   110

CATHERINE *(to Alice) Que dit-il?—que je suis semblable à les
anges?*

ALICE *Oui, vraiment—sauf votre grâce—ainsi dit-il.*

KING HARRY I said so, dear Catherine, and I must not
blush to affirm it.   115

CATHERINE *O bon Dieu! Les langues des hommes sont pleines
de tromperies.*

KING HARRY What says she, fair one? That the tongues
of men are full of deceits?

ALICE *Oui*, dat de tongeus of de mans is be full of deceits—
dat is de Princess.   121

KING HARRY The Princess is the better Englishwoman.
I'faith, Kate, my wooing is fit for thy understanding. I
am glad thou canst speak no better English, for if thou
couldst, thou wouldst find me such a plain king that
thou wouldst think I had sold my farm to buy my
crown. I know no ways to mince it in love, but directly
to say, 'I love you'; then if you urge me farther than
to say, 'Do you in faith?', I wear out my suit. Give me
your answer, i'faith do, and so clap hands and a
bargain. How say you, lady?   131

CATHERINE *Sauf votre honneur*, me understand well.

KING HARRY Marry, if you would put me to verses, or to
dance for your sake, Kate, why, you undid me. For the
one I have neither words nor measure, and for the
other I have no strength in measure—yet a reasonable
measure in strength. If I could win a lady at leap-frog,
or by vaulting into my saddle with my armour on my
back, under the correction of bragging be it spoken, I
should quickly leap into a wife. Or if I might buffet for
my love, or bound my horse for her favours, I could
lay on like a butcher, and sit like a jackanapes, never
off. But before God, Kate, I cannot look greenly, nor
gasp out my eloquence, nor I have no cunning in
protestation—only downright oaths, which I never use
till urged, nor never break for urging. If thou canst
love a fellow of this temper, Kate, whose face is not
worth sunburning, that never looks in his glass for
love of anything he sees there, let thine eye be thy
cook. I speak to thee plain soldier: if thou canst love
me for this, take me. If not, to say to thee that I shall
die, is true—but for thy love, by the Lord, no. Yet I
love thee, too. And while thou livest, dear Kate, take
a fellow of plain and uncoined constancy, for he perforce
must do thee right, because he hath not the gift to woo
in other places. For these fellows of infinite tongue,
that can rhyme themselves into ladies' favours, they
do always reason themselves out again. What! A
speaker is but a prater, a rhyme is but a ballad; a good
leg will fall, a straight back will stoop, a black beard
will turn white, a curled pate will grow bald, a fair
face will wither, a full eye will wax hollow, but a good
heart, Kate, is the sun and the moon—or rather the
sun and not the moon, for it shines bright and never
changes, but keeps his course truly. If thou would have
such a one, take me; and take me, take a soldier; take

a soldier, take a king. And what sayst thou then to my love? Speak, my fair—and fairly, I pray thee.

CATHERINE Is it possible dat I sould love de *ennemi* of France? 170

KING HARRY No, it is not possible you should love the enemy of France, Kate. But in loving me, you should love the friend of France, for I love France so well that I will not part with a village of it, I will have it all mine; and Kate, when France is mine, and I am yours, then yours is France, and you are mine. 176

CATHERINE I cannot tell vat is dat.

KING HARRY No, Kate? I will tell thee in French—which I am sure will hang upon my tongue like a new-married wife about her husband's neck, hardly to be shook off. *Je quand suis le possesseur de France, et quand vous avez le possession de moi*—let me see, what then? Saint Denis be my speed!—*donc vôtre est France, et vous êtes mienne.* It is as easy for me, Kate, to conquer the kingdom as to speak so much more French. I shall never move thee in French, unless it be to laugh at me. 186

CATHERINE *Sauf votre honneur, le français que vous parlez, il est meilleur que l'anglais lequel je parle.*

KING HARRY No, faith, is't not, Kate. But thy speaking of my tongue, and I thine, most truly-falsely, must needs be granted to be much at one. But Kate, dost thou understand thus much English? Canst thou love me?

CATHERINE I cannot tell.

KING HARRY Can any of your neighbours tell, Kate? I'll ask them. Come, I know thou lovest me, and at night when you come into your closet you'll question this gentlewoman about me, and I know, Kate, you will to her dispraise those parts in me that you love with your heart. But good Kate, mock me mercifully—the rather, gentle princess, because I love thee cruelly. If ever thou be'st mine, Kate—as I have a saving faith within me tells me thou shalt—I get thee with scrambling, and thou must therefore needs prove a good soldier-breeder. Shall not thou and I, between Saint Denis and Saint George, compound a boy, half-French half-English, that shall go to Constantinople and take the Turk by the beard? Shall we not? What sayst thou, my fair flower-de-luce?

CATHERINE I do not know dat. 209

KING HARRY No, 'tis hereafter to know, but now to promise. Do but now promise, Kate, you will endeavour for your French part of such a boy, and for my English moiety take the word of a king and a bachelor. How answer you, *la plus belle Catherine du monde, mon très chère et divine déesse?* 215

CATHERINE Your *majesté* 'ave *faux* French enough to deceive de most sage *demoiselle* dat is en *Franc..*

KING HARRY Now fie upon my false French! By mine honour, in true English, I love thee, Kate. By which honour I dare not swear thou lovest me, yet my blood begins to flatter me that thou dost, notwithstanding the poor and untempering effect of my visage. Now beshrew my father's ambition! He was thinking of civil wars when he got me; therefore was I created with a stubborn outside, with an aspect of iron, that when I

come to woo ladies I fright them. But in faith, Kate, the elder I wax the better I shall appear. My comfort is that old age, that ill layer-up of beauty, can do no more spoil upon my face. Thou hast me, if thou hast me, at the worst, and thou shalt wear me, if thou wear me, better and better; and therefore tell me, most fair Catherine, will you have me? Put off your maiden blushes, avouch the thoughts of your heart with the looks of an empress, take me by the hand and say, 'Harry of England, I am thine'—which word thou shalt no sooner bless mine ear withal, but I will tell thee aloud, 'England is thine, Ireland is thine, France is thine, and Henry Plantagenet is thine'—who, though I speak it before his face, if he be not fellow with the best king, thou shalt find the best king of good fellows. Come, your answer in broken music—for thy voice is music and thy English broken. Therefore, queen of all, Catherine, break thy mind to me in broken English: wilt thou have me?

CATHERINE Dat is as it shall please de *roi mon père.* 245

KING HARRY Nay, it will please him well, Kate. It shall please him, Kate.

CATHERINE Den it sall also content me.

KING HARRY Upon that I kiss your hand, and I call you my queen. 250

CATHERINE *Laissez, mon seigneur, laissez, laissez! Ma foi, je ne veux point que vous abbaissez votre grandeur en baisant la main d'une de votre seigneurie indigne serviteur. Excusez-moi, je vous supplie, mon treis-puissant seigneur.*

KING HARRY Then I will kiss your lips, Kate. 255

CATHERINE *Les dames et demoiselles pour être baisées devant leurs noces, il n'est pas la coutume de France.*

KING HARRY (*to Alice*) Madam my interpreter, what says she?

ALICE Dat it is not be de *façon pour les* ladies of France— I cannot tell vat is *baiser en* English. 261

KING HARRY To kiss.

ALICE Your *majesté entend* bettre *que moi.*

KING HARRY It is not a fashion for the maids in France to kiss before they are married, would she say? 265

ALICE *Oui, vraiment.*

KING HARRY O Kate, nice customs curtsy to great kings. Dear Kate, you and I cannot be confined within the weak list of a country's fashion. We are the makers of manners, Kate, and the liberty that follows our places stops the mouth of all find-faults, as I will do yours, for upholding the nice fashion of your country in denying me a kiss. Therefore, patiently and yielding. (*He kisses her*) You have witchcraft in your lips, Kate. There is more eloquence in a sugar touch of them than in the tongues of the French Council, and they should sooner persuade Harry of England than a general petition of monarchs. Here comes your father.

Enter King Charles, Queen Isabel, the Duke of Burgundy, and the French and English lords

BURGUNDY God save your majesty. My royal cousin, teach you our princess English? 280

KING HARRY I would have her learn, my fair cousin, how perfectly I love her, and that is good English.

BURGUNDY Is she not apt?

KING HARRY Our tongue is rough, coz, and my condition
is not smooth, so that having neither the voice nor the
heart of flattery about me I cannot so conjure up the
spirit of love in her that he will appear in his true
likeness.

BURGUNDY Pardon the frankness of my mirth, if I answer
you for that. If you would conjure in her, you must
make a circle; if conjure up love in her in his true
likeness, he must appear naked and blind. Can you
blame her then, being a maid yet rosed over with the
virgin crimson of modesty, if she deny the appearance
of a naked blind boy in her naked seeing self? It were,
my lord, a hard condition for a maid to consign to. 296

KING HARRY Yet they do wink and yield, as love is blind
and enforces.

BURGUNDY They are then excused, my lord, when they
see not what they do.   300

KING HARRY Then, good my lord, teach your cousin to
consent winking.

BURGUNDY I will wink on her to consent, my lord, if you
will teach her to know my meaning. For maids, well
summered and warm kept, are like flies at
Bartholomew-tide: blind, though they have their eyes.
And then they will endure handling, which before
would not abide looking on.

KING HARRY This moral ties me over to time and a hot
summer, and so I shall catch the fly, your cousin, in
the latter end, and she must be blind too.   311

BURGUNDY As love is, my lord, before that it loves.

KING HARRY It is so. And you may, some of you, thank
love for my blindness, who cannot see many a fair
French city for one fair French maid that stands in my
way.   316

KING CHARLES Yes, my lord, you see them perspectively,
the cities turned into a maid—for they are all girdled
with maiden walls that war hath never entered.

KING HARRY Shall Kate be my wife?   320

KING CHARLES So please you.

KING HARRY I am content, so the maiden cities you talk
of may wait on her: so the maid that stood in the way
for my wish shall show me the way to my will.

KING CHARLES
We have consented to all terms of reason.   325

KING HARRY Is't so, my lords of England?

⌈WARWICK⌉
The King hath granted every article:
His daughter first, and so in sequel all,
According to their firm proposèd natures.

EXETER
Only he hath not yet subscribèd this: 330
where your majesty demands that the King of France,
having any occasion to write for matter of grant, shall
name your highness in this form and with this addition:
⌈reads⌉ in French, Notre très cher fils Henri, Roi
d'Angleterre, Héritier de France, and thus in Latin,
Praeclarissimus filius noster Henricus, Rex Angliae et
Haeres Franciae.

KING CHARLES
Nor this I have not, brother, so denied,
But your request shall make me let it pass.

KING HARRY
I pray you then, in love and dear alliance,   340
Let that one article rank with the rest,
And thereupon give me your daughter.

KING CHARLES
Take her, fair son, and from her blood raise up
Issue to me, that the contending kingdoms
Of France and England, whose very shores look pale
With envy of each other's happiness,   346
May cease their hatred, and this dear conjunction
Plant neighbourhood and Christian-like accord
In their sweet bosoms, that never war advance
His bleeding sword 'twixt England and fair France. 350

⌈ALL⌉ Amen.

KING HARRY
Now welcome, Kate, and bear me witness all
That here I kiss her as my sovereign Queen.

        Flourish

QUEEN ISABEL
God, the best maker of all marriages,
Combine your hearts in one, your realms in one.   355
As man and wife, being two, are one in love,
So be there 'twixt your kingdoms such a spousal
That never may ill office or fell jealousy,
Which troubles oft the bed of blessèd marriage,
Thrust in between the paction of these kingdoms   360
To make divorce of their incorporate league;
That English may as French, French Englishmen,
Receive each other, God speak this 'Amen'.

ALL Amen.

KING HARRY
Prepare we for our marriage. On which day,   365
My lord of Burgundy, we'll take your oath,
And all the peers', for surety of our leagues.
Then shall I swear to Kate, and you to me,
And may our oaths well kept and prosp'rous be.

        Sennet. Exeunt

        Enter Chorus   Epilogue
CHORUS
Thus far with rough and all-unable pen
    Our bending author hath pursued the story,
In little room confining mighty men,
    Mangling by starts the full course of their glory.
Small time, but in that small most greatly lived   5
    This star of England. Fortune made his sword,
By which the world's best garden he achieved,
    And of it left his son imperial lord.
Henry the Sixth, in infant bands crowned king
    Of France and England, did this king succeed,   10
Whose state so many had the managing
    That they lost France and made his England bleed,
Which oft our stage hath shown—and, for their sake,
In your fair minds let this acceptance take.   Exit

ADDITIONAL PASSAGES

The Dauphin/Bourbon variant, which usually involves only the alteration of speech-prefixes, has several consequences for the dialogue and structure of 4.5. There follow edited texts of the Folio and Quarto versions of this scene.

A. FOLIO

Enter the Constable, Orléans, Bourbon, the Dauphin, and Rambures

CONSTABLE *O diable!*

ORLÉANS *O Seigneur! Le jour est perdu, tout est perdu.*

DAUPHIN
Mort de ma vie! All is confounded, all.
Reproach and everlasting shame
Sits mocking in our plumes.   5
    A short alarum
O méchante fortune! Do not run away.
                                        ⌜*Exit Rambures*⌝
CONSTABLE Why, all our ranks are broke.

DAUPHIN
O perdurable shame! Let's stab ourselves:
Be these the wretches that we played at dice for?

ORLÉANS
Is this the king we sent to for his ransom?   10

BOURBON
Shame, an eternall shame, nothing but shame!
Let us die in pride. In once more, back again!
And he that will not follow Bourbon now,
Let him go home, and with his cap in hand
Like a base leno hold the chamber door,   15
Whilst by a slave no gentler than my dog
His fairest daughter is contaminated.

CONSTABLE
Disorder that hath spoiled us, friend us now,
Let us on heaps go offer up our lives.

ORLÉANS
We are enough yet living in the field   20
To smother up the English in our throngs,
If any order might be thought upon.

BOURBON
The devil take order now. I'll to the throng.
Let life be short, else shame will be too long.   *Exeunt*

B. QUARTO

Enter the four French lords: the Constable, Orléans, Bourbon, and Gebon

GEBON *O diabello!*

CONSTABLE *Mort de ma vie!*

ORLÉANS O what a day is this!

BOURBON
O jour de honte, all is gone, all is lost.

CONSTABLE We are enough yet living in the field   5
To smother up the English,
If any order might be thought upon.

BOURBON
A plague of order! Once more to the field!
And he that will not follow Bourbon now,
Let him go home, and with his cap in hand,   10
Like a base leno hold the chamber door,
Whilst by a slave no gentler than my dog
His fairest daughter is contaminated.

CONSTABLE
Disorder that hath spoiled us, right us now.
Come we in heaps, we'll offer up our lives   15
Unto these English, or else die with fame.

⌜BOURBON⌝ Come, come along.
Let's die with honour, our shame doth last too long.
                                                    Exeunt

SONNETS
AND 'A LOVER'S COMPLAINT'

SHAKESPEARE'S Sonnets were published as a collection by Thomas Thorpe in 1609; the title-page declared that they were 'never before imprinted'. Versions of two of them—138 and 144—had appeared in 1599, in *The Passionate Pilgrim*, a collection ascribed to Shakespeare but including some poems certainly written by other authors; and in the previous year Francis Meres, in *Palladis Tamia*, had alluded to Shakespeare's 'sugared sonnets among his private friends'. The sonnet sequence had enjoyed a brief but intense vogue from the publication of Sir Philip Sidney's *Astrophil and Stella* in 1591 till about 1597. Some of Shakespeare's plays of this period reflect the fashion: in the comedy of *Love's Labour's Lost* the writing of sonnets is seen as a laughable symptom of love, and in the tragedy of *Romeo and Juliet* both speeches of the Chorus and the lovers' first conversation are in sonnet form. Later plays use it, too, but it seems likely that most, if not all, of Shakespeare's sonnets were first written during this period. But there are indications that some of them were revised; the two printed in *The Passionate Pilgrim* differ at certain points from Thorpe's version, and two other sonnets (2 and 106) exist in manuscript versions which also are not identical with those published in the sequence. We print these as 'Alternative Versions' of Sonnets 2, 106, 138, and 144.

The order in which Thorpe printed the Sonnets has often been questioned, but is not entirely haphazard: all the first seventeen, and no later ones, exhort a young man to marry; all those clearly addressed to a man are among the first 126, and all those clearly addressed to, or concerned with, a woman (the 'dark lady') follow. Some of the sonnets in the second group appear to refer to events that prompted sonnets in the first group; it seems likely that the poems were rearranged after composition. Moreover, the volume contains 'A Lover's Complaint', clearly ascribed to Shakespeare, which stylistic evidence suggests was written in the early seventeenth century and which may have been intended as a companion piece. So, printing the Sonnets in Thorpe's order, we place them according to the likely date of their revision.

Textual evidence suggests that Thorpe printed from a transcript by someone other than Shakespeare. His volume bears a dedication over his own initials to 'Mr W.H.'; we do not know whether this derives from the manuscript, and can only speculate about the dedicatee's identity. His initials are those of Shakespeare's only known dedicatee, Henry Wriothesley, Earl of Southampton, but in reverse order. We have even less clue as to the identity of the Sonnets' other personae, a rival poet and the dark woman.

Shakespeare's Sonnets may not be autobiographical, but they are certainly unconventional: the most idealistic poems celebrating love's mutuality are addressed by one man to another (Sonnet 20 implies that the relationship is not sexual), and the poems clearly addressed to a woman revile her morals, speak ill of her appearance, and explore the poet's self-disgust at his entanglement with her. The Sonnets include some of the finest love poems in the English language: the sequence itself presents an internal drama of great psychological complexity.

TO.THE.ONLY.BEGETTER.OF.
THESE.ENSUING.SONNETS.
M^r.W.H. ALL.HAPPINESS.
AND.THAT.ETERNITY.
PROMISED.

BY.

OUR.EVER-LIVING.POET.

WISHETH.

THE.WELL-WISHING.
ADVENTURER.IN.
SETTING.
FORTH.

T.T.

Sonnets

1

From fairest creatures we desire increase,
That thereby beauty's rose might never die,
But as the riper should by time decease,
His tender heir might bear his memory;
But thou, contracted to thine own bright eyes, 5
Feed'st thy light's flame with self-substantial fuel,
Making a famine where abundance lies,
Thyself thy foe, to thy sweet self too cruel.
Thou that art now the world's fresh ornament
And only herald to the gaudy spring 10
Within thine own bud buriest thy content,
And, tender churl, mak'st waste in niggarding.
  Pity the world, or else this glutton be:
  To eat the world's due, by the grave and thee.

2

When forty winters shall besiege thy brow
And dig deep trenches in thy beauty's field,
Thy youth's proud livery, so gazed on now,
Will be a tattered weed, of small worth held.
Then being asked where all thy beauty lies, 5
Where all the treasure of thy lusty days,
To say within thine own deep-sunken eyes
Were an all-eating shame and thriftless praise.
How much more praise deserved thy beauty's use
If thou couldst answer 'This fair child of mine 10
Shall sum my count, and make my old excuse',
Proving his beauty by succession thine.
  This were to be new made when thou art old,
  And see thy blood warm when thou feel'st it cold.

3

Look in thy glass, and tell the face thou viewest
Now is the time that face should form another,
Whose fresh repair if now thou not renewest
Thou dost beguile the world, unbless some mother.
For where is she so fair whose uneared womb 5
Disdains the tillage of thy husbandry?
Or who is he so fond will be the tomb
Of his self-love to stop posterity?
Thou art thy mother's glass, and she in thee
Calls back the lovely April of her prime; 10
So thou through windows of thine age shalt see,
Despite of wrinkles, this thy golden time.
  But if thou live remembered not to be,
  Die single, and thine image dies with thee.

4

Unthrifty loveliness, why dost thou spend
Upon thyself thy beauty's legacy?
Nature's bequest gives nothing, but doth lend,
And being frank, she lends to those are free.
Then, beauteous niggard, why dost thou abuse 5
The bounteous largess given thee to give?
Profitless usurer, why dost thou use
So great a sum of sums yet canst not live?
For having traffic with thyself alone,
Thou of thyself thy sweet self dost deceive. 10
Then how when nature calls thee to be gone:
What acceptable audit canst thou leave?
  Thy unused beauty must be tombed with thee,
  Which usèd, lives th'executor to be.

5

Those hours that with gentle work did frame
The lovely gaze where every eye doth dwell
Will play the tyrants to the very same,
And that unfair which fairly doth excel;
For never-resting time leads summer on 5
To hideous winter, and confounds him there,
Sap checked with frost, and lusty leaves quite gone,
Beauty o'er-snowed, and bareness everywhere.
Then were not summer's distillation left
A liquid prisoner pent in walls of glass, 10
Beauty's effect with beauty were bereft,
Nor it nor no remembrance what it was.
  But flowers distilled, though they with winter meet,
  Lose but their show; their substance still lives sweet.

6

Then let not winter's ragged hand deface
In thee thy summer ere thou be distilled.
Make sweet some vial, treasure thou some place
With beauty's treasure ere it be self-killed.
That use is not forbidden usury 5
Which happies those that pay the willing loan:
That's for thyself to breed another thee,
Or ten times happier, be it ten for one;
Ten times thyself were happier than thou art,
If ten of thine ten times refigured thee. 10
Then what could death do if thou shouldst depart,
Leaving thee living in posterity?
  Be not self-willed, for thou art much too fair
  To be death's conquest and make worms thine heir.

7

Lo, in the orient when the gracious light
Lifts up his burning head, each under eye
Doth homage to his new-appearing sight,
Serving with looks his sacred majesty,
And having climbed the steep-up heavenly hill, 5
Resembling strong youth in his middle age,
Yet mortal looks adore his beauty still,
Attending on his golden pilgrimage.
But when from highmost pitch, with weary car,
Like feeble age he reeleth from the day, 10
The eyes, 'fore duteous, now converted are
From his low tract, and look another way.
  So thou, thyself outgoing in thy noon,
  Unlooked on diest unless thou get a son.

8

Music to hear, why hear'st thou music sadly?
Sweets with sweets war not, joy delights in joy.
Why lov'st thou that which thou receiv'st not gladly,
Or else receiv'st with pleasure thine annoy?
If the true concord of well-tunèd sounds 5
By unions married do offend thine ear,
They do but sweetly chide thee, who confounds
In singleness the parts that thou shouldst bear.
Mark how one string, sweet husband to another,
Strikes each in each by mutual ordering, 10
Resembling sire and child and happy mother,
Who all in one one pleasing note do sing;
  Whose speechless song, being many, seeming one,
  Sings this to thee: 'Thou single wilt prove none.'

9

Is it for fear to wet a widow's eye
That thou consum'st thyself in single life?
Ah, if thou issueless shalt hap to die,
The world will wail thee like a makeless wife.
The world will be thy widow, and still weep 5
That thou no form of thee hast left behind,
When every private widow well may keep
By children's eyes her husband's shape in mind.
Look what an unthrift in the world doth spend
Shifts but his place, for still the world enjoys it; 10
But beauty's waste hath in the world an end,
And kept unused, the user so destroys it.
  No love toward others in that bosom sits
  That on himself such murd'rous shame commits.

10

For shame deny that thou bear'st love to any,
Who for thyself art so unprovident.
Grant, if thou wilt, thou art beloved of many,
But that thou none lov'st is most evident;
For thou art so possessed with murd'rous hate 5
That 'gainst thyself thou stick'st not to conspire,
Seeking that beauteous roof to ruinate
Which to repair should be thy chief desire.
O, change thy thought, that I may change my mind!
Shall hate be fairer lodged than gentle love? 10
Be as thy presence is, gracious and kind,
Or to thyself at least kind-hearted prove.
  Make thee another self for love of me,
  That beauty still may live in thine or thee.

11

As fast as thou shalt wane, so fast thou grow'st
In one of thine from that which thou departest,
And that fresh blood which youngly thou bestow'st
Thou mayst call thine when thou from youth
    convertest.
Herein lives wisdom, beauty, and increase; 5
Without this, folly, age, and cold decay.
If all were minded so, the times should cease,
And threescore year would make the world away.
Let those whom nature hath not made for store,
Harsh, featureless, and rude, barrenly perish. 10
Look whom she best endowed she gave the more,
Which bounteous gift thou shouldst in bounty cherish.
  She carved thee for her seal, and meant thereby
  Thou shouldst print more, not let that copy die.

12

When I do count the clock that tells the time,
And see the brave day sunk in hideous night;
When I behold the violet past prime,
And sable curls ensilvered o'er with white;
When lofty trees I see barren of leaves, 5
Which erst from heat did canopy the herd,
And summer's green all girded up in sheaves
Borne on the bier with white and bristly beard:
Then of thy beauty do I question make
That thou among the wastes of time must go, 10
Since sweets and beauties do themselves forsake,
And die as fast as they see others grow;
  And nothing 'gainst time's scythe can make defence
  Save breed to brave him when he takes thee hence.

13

O that you were yourself! But, love, you are
No longer yours than you yourself here live.
Against this coming end you should prepare,
And your sweet semblance to some other give.
So should that beauty which you hold in lease   5
Find no determination; then you were
Yourself again after your self's decease,
When your sweet issue your sweet form should bear.
Who lets so fair a house fall to decay,
Which husbandry in honour might uphold   10
Against the stormy gusts of winter's day,
And barren rage of death's eternal cold?
   O, none but unthrifts, dear my love, you know.
   You had a father; let your son say so.

14

Not from the stars do I my judgement pluck,
And yet methinks I have astronomy;
But not to tell of good or evil luck,
Of plagues, of dearths, or seasons' quality.
Nor can I fortune to brief minutes tell,   5
'Pointing to each his thunder, rain, and wind,
Or say with princes if it shall go well
By oft predict that I in heaven find;
But from thine eyes my knowledge I derive,
And, constant stars, in them I read such art   10
As truth and beauty shall together thrive
If from thyself to store thou wouldst convert.
   Or else of thee this I prognosticate:
   Thy end is truth's and beauty's doom and date.

15

When I consider every thing that grows
Holds in perfection but a little moment,
That this huge stage presenteth naught but shows
Whereon the stars in secret influence comment;
When I perceive that men as plants increase,   5
Cheerèd and checked even by the selfsame sky;
Vaunt in their youthful sap, at height decrease,
And wear their brave state out of memory:
Then the conceit of this inconstant stay
Sets you most rich in youth before my sight,   10
Where wasteful time debateth with decay
To change your day of youth to sullied night;
   And all in war with time for love of you,
   As he takes from you, I engraft you new.

16

But wherefore do not you a mightier way
Make war upon this bloody tyrant, time,
And fortify yourself in your decay
With means more blessèd than my barren rhyme?
Now stand you on the top of happy hours,   5
And many maiden gardens yet unset
With virtuous wish would bear your living flowers,
Much liker than your painted counterfeit.
So should the lines of life that life repair
Which this time's pencil or my pupil pen   10
Neither in inward worth nor outward fair
Can make you live yourself in eyes of men.
   To give away yourself keeps yourself still,
   And you must live drawn by your own sweet skill.

17

Who will believe my verse in time to come
If it were filled with your most high deserts?—
Though yet, heaven knows, it is but as a tomb
Which hides your life, and shows not half your parts.
If I could write the beauty of your eyes   5
And in fresh numbers number all your graces,
The age to come would say 'This poet lies;
Such heavenly touches ne'er touched earthly faces.'
So should my papers, yellowed with their age,
Be scorned, like old men of less truth than tongue,   10
And your true rights be termed a poet's rage
And stretchèd metre of an antique song.
   But were some child of yours alive that time,
   You should live twice: in it, and in my rhyme.

18

Shall I compare thee to a summer's day?
Thou art more lovely and more temperate.
Rough winds do shake the darling buds of May,
And summer's lease hath all too short a date.
Sometime too hot the eye of heaven shines,   5
And often is his gold complexion dimmed,
And every fair from fair sometime declines,
By chance or nature's changing course untrimmed;
But thy eternal summer shall not fade
Nor lose possession of that fair thou ow'st,   10
Nor shall death brag thou wander'st in his shade
When in eternal lines to time thou grow'st.
   So long as men can breathe or eyes can see,
   So long lives this, and this gives life to thee.

19

Devouring time, blunt thou the lion's paws,
And make the earth devour her own sweet brood;
Pluck the keen teeth from the fierce tiger's jaws,
And burn the long-lived phoenix in her blood.
Make glad and sorry seasons as thou fleet'st, 5
And do whate'er thou wilt, swift-footed time,
To the wide world and all her fading sweets.
But I forbid thee one most heinous crime:
O, carve not with thy hours my love's fair brow,
Nor draw no lines there with thine antique pen. 10
Him in thy course untainted do allow
For beauty's pattern to succeeding men.
 Yet do thy worst, old time; despite thy wrong
 My love shall in my verse ever live young.

20

A woman's face with nature's own hand painted
Hast thou, the master-mistress of my passion;
A woman's gentle heart, but not acquainted
With shifting change as is false women's fashion;
An eye more bright than theirs, less false in rolling, 5
Gilding the object whereupon it gazeth;
A man in hue, all hues in his controlling,
Which steals men's eyes and women's souls amazeth.
And for a woman wert thou first created,
Till nature as she wrought thee fell a-doting, 10
And by addition me of thee defeated
By adding one thing to my purpose nothing.
 But since she pricked thee out for women's pleasure,
 Mine be thy love and thy love's use their treasure.

21

So is it not with me as with that muse
Stirred by a painted beauty to his verse,
Who heaven itself for ornament doth use,
And every fair with his fair doth rehearse,
Making a couplement of proud compare 5
With sun and moon, with earth, and sea's rich gems,
With April's first-born flowers, and all things rare
That heaven's air in this huge rondure hems.
O let me, true in love, but truly write,
And then believe me my love is as fair 10
As any mother's child, though not so bright
As those gold candles fixed in heaven's air.
 Let them say more that like of hearsay well;
 I will not praise that purpose not to sell.

22

My glass shall not persuade me I am old
So long as youth and thou are of one date;
But when in thee time's furrows I behold,
Then look I death my days should expiate.
For all that beauty that doth cover thee 5
Is but the seemly raiment of my heart,
Which in thy breast doth live, as thine in me;
How can I then be elder than thou art?
O therefore, love, be of thyself so wary
As I, not for myself, but for thee will, 10
Bearing thy heart, which I will keep so chary
As tender nurse her babe from faring ill.
 Presume not on thy heart when mine is slain:
 Thou gav'st me thine not to give back again.

23

As an unperfect actor on the stage
Who with his fear is put besides his part,
Or some fierce thing replete with too much rage
Whose strength's abundance weakens his own heart,
So I, for fear of trust, forget to say 5
The perfect ceremony of love's rite,
And in mine own love's strength seem to decay,
O'er-charged with burden of mine own love's might.
O let my books be then the eloquence
And dumb presagers of my speaking breast, 10
Who plead for love, and look for recompense
More than that tongue that more hath more
 expressed.
 O learn to read what silent love hath writ;
 To hear with eyes belongs to love's fine wit.

24

Mine eye hath played the painter, and hath steeled
Thy beauty's form in table of my heart.
My body is the frame wherein 'tis held,
And perspective it is best painter's art;
For through the painter must you see his skill 5
To find where your true image pictured lies,
Which in my bosom's shop is hanging still,
That hath his windows glazèd with thine eyes.
Now see what good turns eyes for eyes have done:
Mine eyes have drawn thy shape, and thine for me 10
Are windows to my breast, wherethrough the sun
Delights to peep, to gaze therein on thee.
 Yet eyes this cunning want to grace their art:
 They draw but what they see, know not the heart.

25

Let those who are in favour with their stars
Of public honour and proud titles boast,
Whilst I, whom fortune of such triumph bars,
Unlooked-for joy in that I honour most.
Great princes' favourites their fair leaves spread   5
But as the marigold at the sun's eye,
And in themselves their pride lies burièd,
For at a frown they in their glory die.
The painful warrior famousèd for might,
After a thousand victories once foiled   10
Is from the book of honour razèd quite,
And all the rest forgot for which he toiled.
   Then happy I, that love and am beloved
   Where I may not remove nor be removed.

26

Lord of my love, to whom in vassalage
Thy merit hath my duty strongly knit,
To thee I send this written embassage
To witness duty, not to show my wit;
Duty so great which wit so poor as mine   5
May make seem bare in wanting words to show it,
But that I hope some good conceit of thine
In thy soul's thought, all naked, will bestow it,
Till whatsoever star that guides my moving
Points on me graciously with fair aspect,   10
And puts apparel on my tattered loving
To show me worthy of thy sweet respect.
   Then may I dare to boast how I do love thee;
   Till then, not show my head where thou mayst
      prove me.

27

Weary with toil I haste me to my bed,
The dear repose for limbs with travel tired;
But then begins a journey in my head
To work my mind when body's work's expired;
For then my thoughts, from far where I abide,   5
Intend a zealous pilgrimage to thee,
And keep my drooping eyelids open wide,
Looking on darkness which the blind do see:
Save that my soul's imaginary sight
Presents thy shadow to my sightless view,   10
Which like a jewel hung in ghastly night
Makes black night beauteous and her old face new.
   Lo, thus by day my limbs, by night my mind,
   For thee, and for myself, no quiet find.

28

How can I then return in happy plight,
That am debarred the benefit of rest,
When day's oppression is not eased by night,
But day by night and night by day oppressed,
And each, though enemies to either's reign,   5
Do in consent shake hands to torture me,
The one by toil, the other to complain
How far I toil, still farther off from thee?
I tell the day to please him thou art bright,
And do'st him grace when clouds do blot the heaven;   10
So flatter I the swart-complexioned night.
When sparkling stars twire not thou gild'st the even.
   But day doth daily draw my sorrows longer,
   And night doth nightly make grief's strength seem
      stronger.

29

When, in disgrace with fortune and men's eyes,
I all alone beweep my outcast state,
And trouble deaf heaven with my bootless cries,
And look upon myself and curse my fate,   5
Wishing me like to one more rich in hope,
Featured like him, like him with friends possessed,
Desiring this man's art and that man's scope,
With what I most enjoy contented least:
Yet in these thoughts myself almost despising,
Haply I think on thee, and then my state,   10
Like to the lark at break of day arising
From sullen earth, sings hymns at heaven's gate;
   For thy sweet love remembered such wealth brings
   That then I scorn to change my state with kings'.

30

When to the sessions of sweet silent thought
I summon up remembrance of things past,
I sigh the lack of many a thing I sought,
And with old woes new wail my dear time's waste.
Then can I drown an eye unused to flow   5
For precious friends hid in death's dateless night,
And weep afresh love's long-since-cancelled woe,
And moan th'expense of many a vanished sight.
Then can I grieve at grievances foregone,
And heavily from woe to woe tell o'er   10
The sad account of fore-bemoanèd moan,
Which I new pay as if not paid before.
   But if the while I think on thee, dear friend,
   All losses are restored, and sorrows end.

31

Thy bosom is endearèd with all hearts
Which I by lacking have supposèd dead,
And there reigns love, and all love's loving parts,
And all those friends which I thought burièd.
How many a holy and obsequious tear   5
Hath dear religious love stol'n from mine eye
As interest of the dead, which now appear
But things removed that hidden in thee lie!
Thou art the grave where buried love doth live,
Hung with the trophies of my lovers gone,   10
Who all their parts of me to thee did give:
That due of many now is thine alone.
   Their images I loved I view in thee,
   And thou, all they, hast all the all of me.

32

If thou survive my well-contented day
When that churl death my bones with dust shall
   cover,
And shalt by fortune once more resurvey
These poor rude lines of thy deceasèd lover,
Compare them with the bett'ring of the time,   5
And though they be outstripped by every pen,
Reserve them for my love, not for their rhyme
Exceeded by the height of happier men.
O then vouchsafe me but this loving thought:
'Had my friend's muse grown with this growing age,   10
A dearer birth than this his love had brought
To march in ranks of better equipage;
   But since he died, and poets better prove,
   Theirs for their style I'll read, his for his love.'

33

Full many a glorious morning have I seen
Flatter the mountain tops with sovereign eye,
Kissing with golden face the meadows green,
Gilding pale streams with heavenly alchemy;
Anon permit the basest clouds to ride   5
With ugly rack on his celestial face,
And from the forlorn world his visage hide,
Stealing unseen to west with this disgrace.
Even so my sun one early morn did shine
With all triumphant splendour on my brow;   10
But out, alack, he was but one hour mine;
The region cloud hath masked him from me now.
   Yet him for this my love no whit disdaineth:
   Suns of the world may stain when heaven's sun
      staineth.

34

Why didst thou promise such a beauteous day
And make me travel forth without my cloak,
To let base clouds o'ertake me in my way,
Hiding thy brav'ry in their rotten smoke?
'Tis not enough that through the cloud thou break   5
To dry the rain on my storm-beaten face,
For no man well of such a salve can speak
That heals the wound and cures not the disgrace.
Nor can thy shame give physic to my grief;
Though thou repent, yet I have still the loss.   10
Th'offender's sorrow lends but weak relief
To him that bears the strong offence's cross.
   Ah, but those tears are pearl which thy love sheds,
   And they are rich, and ransom all ill deeds.

35

No more be grieved at that which thou hast done:
Roses have thorns, and silver fountains mud.
Clouds and eclipses stain both moon and sun,
And loathsome canker lives in sweetest bud.
All men make faults, and even I in this,   5
Authorizing thy trespass with compare,
Myself corrupting salving thy amiss,
Excusing thy sins more than thy sins are;
For to thy sensual fault I bring in sense—
Thy adverse party is thy advocate—   10
And 'gainst myself a lawful plea commence.
Such civil war is in my love and hate
   That I an accessory needs must be
   To that sweet thief which sourly robs from me.

36

Let me confess that we two must be twain
Although our undivided loves are one;
So shall those blots that do with me remain
Without thy help by me be borne alone.
In our two loves there is but one respect,   5
Though in our lives a separable spite
Which, though it alter not love's sole effect,
Yet doth it steal sweet hours from love's delight.
I may not evermore acknowledge thee
Lest my bewailèd guilt should do thee shame,   10
Nor thou with public kindness honour me
Unless thou take that honour from thy name.
   But do not so. I love thee in such sort
   As, thou being mine, mine is thy good report.

37

As a decrepit father takes delight
To see his active child do deeds of youth,
So I, made lame by fortune's dearest spite,
Take all my comfort of thy worth and truth;
For whether beauty, birth, or wealth, or wit,   5
Or any of these all, or all, or more,
Entitled in thy parts do crownèd sit,
I make my love engrafted to this store.
So then I am not lame, poor, nor despised,
Whilst that this shadow doth such substance give   10
That I in thy abundance am sufficed
And by a part of all thy glory live.
    Look what is best, that best I wish in thee;
    This wish I have, then ten times happy me.

38

How can my muse want subject to invent
While thou dost breathe, that pour'st into my verse
Thine own sweet argument, too excellent
For every vulgar paper to rehearse?
O, give thyself the thanks if aught in me   5
Worthy perusal stand against thy sight;
For who's so dumb that cannot write to thee,
When thou thyself dost give invention light?
Be thou the tenth muse, ten times more in worth
Than those old nine which rhymers invocate,   10
And he that calls on thee, let him bring forth
Eternal numbers to outlive long date.
    If my slight muse do please these curious days,
    The pain be mine, but thine shall be the praise.

39

O, how thy worth with manners may I sing
When thou art all the better part of me?
What can mine own praise to mine own self bring,
And what is't but mine own when I praise thee?
Even for this let us divided live,   5
And our dear love lose name of single one,
That by this separation I may give
That due to thee which thou deserv'st alone.
O absence, what a torment wouldst thou prove
Were it not thy sour leisure gave sweet leave   10
To entertain the time with thoughts of love,
Which time and thoughts so sweetly doth deceive,
    And that thou teachest how to make one twain
    By praising him here who doth hence remain!

40

Take all my loves, my love, yea, take them all:
What hast thou then more than thou hadst before?
No love, my love, that thou mayst true love call—
All mine was thine before thou hadst this more.
Then if for my love thou my love receivest,   5
I cannot blame thee for my love thou usest;
But yet be blamed if thou this self deceivest
By wilful taste of what thyself refusest.
I do forgive thy robb'ry, gentle thief,
Although thou steal thee all my poverty;   10
And yet love knows it is a greater grief
To bear love's wrong than hate's known injury.
    Lascivious grace, in whom all ill well shows,
    Kill me with spites, yet we must not be foes.

41

Those pretty wrongs that liberty commits
When I am sometime absent from thy heart
Thy beauty and thy years full well befits,
For still temptation follows where thou art.
Gentle thou art, and therefore to be won;   5
Beauteous thou art, therefore to be assailed;
And when a woman woos, what woman's son
Will sourly leave her till he have prevailed?
Ay me, but yet thou mightst my seat forbear,
And chide thy beauty and thy straying youth   10
Who lead thee in their riot even there
Where thou art forced to break a two-fold troth:
    Hers, by thy beauty tempting her to thee,
    Thine, by thy beauty being false to me.

42

That thou hast her, it is not all my grief,
And yet it may be said I loved her dearly;
That she hath thee is of my wailing chief,
A loss in love that touches me more nearly.
Loving offenders, thus I will excuse ye: 5
Thou dost love her because thou know'st I love her,
And for my sake even so doth she abuse me,
Suff'ring my friend for my sake to approve her.
If I lose thee, my loss is my love's gain,
And losing her, my friend hath found that loss: 10
Both find each other, and I lose both twain,
And both for my sake lay on me this cross.
    But here's the joy: my friend and I are one.
    Sweet flattery! Then she loves but me alone.

43

When most I wink, then do mine eyes best see,
For all the day they view things unrespected;
But when I sleep, in dreams they look on thee,
And, darkly bright, are bright in dark directed.
Then thou, whose shadow shadows doth make bright, 5
How would thy shadow's form form happy show
To the clear day with thy much clearer light,
When to unseeing eyes thy shade shines so!
How would, I say, mine eyes be blessèd made
By looking on thee in the living day, 10
When in dead night thy fair imperfect shade
Through heavy sleep on sightless eyes doth stay!
　　All days are nights to see till I see thee,
　　And nights bright days when dreams do show thee
　　　me.

44

If the dull substance of my flesh were thought,
Injurious distance should not stop my way;
For then, despite of space, I would be brought
From limits far remote where thou dost stay.
No matter then although my foot did stand 5
Upon the farthest earth removed from thee;
For nimble thought can jump both sea and land
As soon as think the place where he would be.
But ah, thought kills me that I am not thought,
To leap large lengths of miles when thou art gone, 10
But that, so much of earth and water wrought,
I must attend time's leisure with my moan,
　　Receiving naught by elements so slow
　　But heavy tears, badges of either's woe.

45

The other two, slight air and purging fire,
Are both with thee wherever I abide;
The first my thought, the other my desire,
These present-absent with swift motion slide;
For when these quicker elements are gone 5
In tender embassy of love to thee,
My life, being made of four, with two alone
Sinks down to death, oppressed with melancholy,
Until life's composition be recured
By those swift messengers returned from thee, 10
Who even but now come back again assured
Of thy fair health, recounting it to me.
　　This told, I joy; but then no longer glad,
　　I send them back again and straight grow sad.

46

Mine eye and heart are at a mortal war
How to divide the conquest of thy sight.
Mine eye my heart thy picture's sight would bar,
My heart, mine eye the freedom of that right.
My heart doth plead that thou in him dost lie, 5
A closet never pierced with crystal eyes;
But the defendant doth that plea deny,
And says in him thy fair appearance lies.
To 'cide this title is empanellèd
A quest of thoughts, all tenants to the heart, 10
And by their verdict is determinèd
The clear eye's moiety and the dear heart's part,
　　As thus: mine eye's due is thy outward part,
　　And my heart's right thy inward love of heart.

47

Betwixt mine eye and heart a league is took,
And each doth good turns now unto the other.
When that mine eye is famished for a look,
Or heart in love with sighs himself doth smother,
With my love's picture then my eye doth feast, 5
And to the painted banquet bids my heart.
Another time mine eye is my heart's guest
And in his thoughts of love doth share a part.
So either by thy picture or my love,
Thyself away art present still with me; 10
For thou no farther than my thoughts canst move,
And I am still with them, and they with thee;
　　Or if they sleep, thy picture in my sight
　　Awakes my heart to heart's and eye's delight.

48

How careful was I when I took my way
Each trifle under truest bars to thrust,
That to my use it might unusèd stay
From hands of falsehood, in sure wards of trust.
But thou, to whom my jewels trifles are, 5
Most worthy comfort, now my greatest grief,
Thou best of dearest and mine only care
Art left the prey of every vulgar thief.
Thee have I not locked up in any chest
Save where thou art not, though I feel thou art— 10
Within the gentle closure of my breast,
From whence at pleasure thou mayst come and part;
　　And even thence thou wilt be stol'n, I fear,
　　For truth proves thievish for a prize so dear.

49

Against that time—if ever that time come—
When I shall see thee frown on my defects,
Whenas thy love hath cast his utmost sum,
Called to that audit by advised respects;
Against that time when thou shalt strangely pass   5
And scarcely greet me with that sun, thine eye,
When love converted from the thing it was
Shall reasons find of settled gravity:
Against that time do I ensconce me here
Within the knowledge of mine own desert,   10
And this my hand against myself uprear
To guard the lawful reasons on thy part.
    To leave poor me thou hast the strength of laws,
    Since why to love I can allege no cause.

52

So am I as the rich whose blessèd key
Can bring him to his sweet up-lockèd treasure,
The which he will not ev'ry hour survey,
For blunting the fine point of seldom pleasure.
Therefore are feasts so solemn and so rare   5
Since, seldom coming, in the long year set
Like stones of worth they thinly placèd are,
Or captain jewels in the carcanet.
So is the time that keeps you as my chest,
Or as the wardrobe which the robe doth hide,   10
To make some special instant special blest
By new unfolding his imprisoned pride.
    Blessèd are you whose worthiness gives scope,
    Being had, to triumph; being lacked, to hope.

50

How heavy do I journey on the way,
When what I seek—my weary travel's end—
Doth teach that ease and that repose to say
'Thus far the miles are measured from thy friend.'
The beast that bears me, tired with my woe,   5
Plods dully on to bear that weight in me,
As if by some instinct the wretch did know
His rider loved not speed, being made from thee.
The bloody spur cannot provoke him on
That sometimes anger thrusts into his hide,   10
Which heavily he answers with a groan
More sharp to me than spurring to his side;
    For that same groan doth put this in my mind:
    My grief lies onward and my joy behind.

53

What is your substance, whereof are you made,
That millions of strange shadows on you tend?
Since every one hath, every one, one shade,
And you, but one, can every shadow lend.
Describe Adonis, and the counterfeit   5
Is poorly imitated after you.
On Helen's cheek all art of beauty set,
And you in Grecian tires are painted new.
Speak of the spring and foison of the year:
The one doth shadow of your beauty show,   10
The other as your bounty doth appear;
And you in every blessèd shape we know.
    In all external grace you have some part,
    But you like none, none you, for constant heart.

51

Thus can my love excuse the slow offence
Of my dull bearer when from thee I speed:
From where thou art why should I haste me thence?
Till I return, of posting is no need.
O what excuse will my poor beast then find   5
When swift extremity can seem but slow?
Then should I spur, though mounted on the wind;
In wingèd speed no motion shall I know.
Then can no horse with my desire keep pace;
Therefore desire, of perfect'st love being made,   10
Shall rein no dull flesh in his fiery race;
But love, for love, thus shall excuse my jade:
    Since from thee going he went wilful-slow,
    Towards thee I'll run and give him leave to go.

54

O how much more doth beauty beauteous seem
By that sweet ornament which truth doth give!
The rose looks fair, but fairer we it deem
For that sweet odour which doth in it live.
The canker blooms have full as deep a dye   5
As the perfumèd tincture of the roses,
Hang on such thorns, and play as wantonly
When summer's breath their maskèd buds discloses;
But for their virtue only is their show
They live unwooed and unrespected fade,   10
Die to themselves. Sweet roses do not so;
Of their sweet deaths are sweetest odours made:
    And so of you, beauteous and lovely youth,
    When that shall fade, by verse distils your truth.

55

Not marble nor the gilded monuments
Of princes shall outlive this powerful rhyme,
But you shall shine more bright in these contents
Than unswept stone besmeared with sluttish time.
When wasteful war shall statues overturn, 5
And broils root out the work of masonry,
Nor Mars his sword nor war's quick fire shall burn
The living record of your memory.
'Gainst death and all oblivious enmity
Shall you pace forth; your praise shall still find room 10
Even in the eyes of all posterity
That wear this world out to the ending doom.
    So, till the judgement that yourself arise,
    You live in this, and dwell in lovers' eyes.

56

Sweet love, renew thy force. Be it not said
Thy edge should blunter be than appetite,
Which but today by feeding is allayed,
Tomorrow sharpened in his former might.
So, love, be thou; although today thou fill 5
Thy hungry eyes even till they wink with fullness,
Tomorrow see again, and do not kill
The spirit of love with a perpetual dullness.
Let this sad int'rim like the ocean be
Which parts the shore where two contracted new 10
Come daily to the banks, that when they see
Return of love, more blessed may be the view;
    Or call it winter, which, being full of care,
    Makes summer's welcome, thrice more wished,
        more rare.

57

Being your slave, what should I do but tend
Upon the hours and times of your desire?
I have no precious time at all to spend,
Nor services to do, till you require;
Nor dare I chide the world-without-end hour 5
Whilst I, my sovereign, watch the clock for you,
Nor think the bitterness of absence sour
When you have bid your servant once adieu.
Nor dare I question with my jealous thought
Where you may be, or your affairs suppose, 10
But like a sad slave stay and think of naught
Save, where you are, how happy you make those.
    So true a fool is love that in your will,
    Though you do anything, he thinks no ill.

58

That god forbid, that made me first your slave,
I should in thought control your times of pleasure,
Or at your hand th'account of hours to crave,
Being your vassal bound to stay your leisure.
O let me suffer, being at your beck, 5
Th' imprisoned absence of your liberty,
And patience, tame to sufferance, bide each check,
Without accusing you of injury.
Be where you list, your charter is so strong
That you yourself may privilege your time 10
To what you will; to you it doth belong
Yourself to pardon of self-doing crime.
    I am to wait, though waiting so be hell,
    Not blame your pleasure, be it ill or well.

59

If there be nothing new, but that which is
Hath been before, how are our brains beguiled,
Which, labouring for invention, bear amiss
The second burden of a former child!
O that record could with a backward look 5
Even of five hundred courses of the sun
Show me your image in some antique book
Since mind at first in character was done,
That I might see what the old world could say
To this composèd wonder of your frame; 10
Whether we are mended or whe'er better they,
Or whether revolution be the same.
    O, sure I am the wits of former days
    To subjects worse have given admiring praise.

60

Like as the waves make towards the pebbled shore,
So do our minutes hasten to their end,
Each changing place with that which goes before;
In sequent toil all forwards do contend.
Nativity, once in the main of light, 5
Crawls to maturity, wherewith being crowned
Crookèd eclipses 'gainst his glory fight,
And time that gave doth now his gift confound.
Time doth transfix the flourish set on youth,
And delves the parallels in beauty's brow; 10
Feeds on the rarities of nature's truth,
And nothing stands but for his scythe to mow.
    And yet to times in hope my verse shall stand,
    Praising thy worth despite his cruel hand.

61

Is it thy will thy image should keep open
My heavy eyelids to the weary night?
Dost thou desire my slumbers should be broken
While shadows like to thee do mock my sight?
Is it thy spirit that thou send'st from thee   5
So far from home into my deeds to pry,
To find out shames and idle hours in me,
The scope and tenor of thy jealousy?
O no; thy love, though much, is not so great.
It is my love that keeps mine eye awake,   10
Mine own true love that doth my rest defeat,
To play the watchman ever for thy sake.
    For thee watch I whilst thou dost wake elsewhere,
    From me far off, with others all too near.

62

Sin of self-love possesseth all mine eye,
And all my soul, and all my every part;
And for this sin there is no remedy,
It is so grounded inward in my heart.
Methinks no face so gracious is as mine,   5
No shape so true, no truth of such account,
And for myself mine own worth do define
As I all other in all worths surmount.
But when my glass shows me myself indeed,
Beated and chapped with tanned antiquity,   10
Mine own self-love quite contrary I read;
Self so self-loving were iniquity.
    'Tis thee, my self, that for myself I praise,
    Painting my age with beauty of thy days.

63

Against my love shall be as I am now,
With time's injurious hand crushed and o'erworn;
When hours have drained his blood and filled his
    brow
With lines and wrinkles; when his youthful morn
Hath travelled on to age's steepy night,   5
And all those beauties whereof now he's king
Are vanishing, or vanished out of sight,
Stealing away the treasure of his spring:
For such a time do I now fortify
Against confounding age's cruel knife,   10
That he shall never cut from memory
My sweet love's beauty, though my lover's life.
    His beauty shall in these black lines be seen,
    And they shall live, and he in them still green.

64

When I have seen by time's fell hand defaced
The rich proud cost of outworn buried age;
When sometime-lofty towers I see down razed,
And brass eternal slave to mortal rage;
When I have seen the hungry ocean gain   5
Advantage on the kingdom of the shore,
And the firm soil win of the wat'ry main,
Increasing store with loss and loss with store;
When I have seen such interchange of state,
Or state itself confounded to decay,   10
Ruin hath taught me thus to ruminate:
That time will come and take my love away.
    This thought is as a death, which cannot choose
    But weep to have that which it fears to lose.

65

Since brass, nor stone, nor earth, nor boundless sea,
But sad mortality o'ersways their power,
How with this rage shall beauty hold a plea,
Whose action is no stronger than a flower?
O how shall summer's honey breath hold out   5
Against the wrackful siege of battering days
When rocks impregnable are not so stout,
Nor gates of steel so strong, but time decays?
O fearful meditation! Where, alack,
Shall time's best jewel from time's chest lie hid,   10
Or what strong hand can hold his swift foot back,
Or who his spoil of beauty can forbid?
    O none, unless this miracle have might:
    That in black ink my love may still shine bright.

66

Tired with all these, for restful death I cry:
As, to behold desert a beggar born,
And needy nothing trimmed in jollity,
And purest faith unhappily forsworn,
And gilded honour shamefully misplaced,   5
And maiden virtue rudely strumpeted,
And right perfection wrongfully disgraced,
And strength by limping sway disablèd,
And art made tongue-tied by authority,
And folly, doctor-like, controlling skill,   10
And simple truth miscalled simplicity,
And captive good attending captain ill.
    Tired with all these, from these would I be gone,
    Save that to die I leave my love alone.

67

Ah, wherefore with infection should he live
And with his presence grace impiety,
That sin by him advantage should achieve
And lace itself with his society?
Why should false painting imitate his cheek,
And steal dead seeming of his living hue?
Why should poor beauty indirectly seek
Roses of shadow, since his rose is true?
Why should he live now nature bankrupt is,
Beggared of blood to blush through lively veins,
For she hath no exchequer now but his,
And proud of many, lives upon his gains?
    O, him she stores to show what wealth she had
    In days long since, before these last so bad.

68

Thus is his cheek the map of days outworn,
When beauty lived and died as flowers do now,
Before these bastard signs of fair were borne
Or durst inhabit on a living brow;
Before the golden tresses of the dead,
The right of sepulchres, were shorn away
To live a second life on second head;
Ere beauty's dead fleece made another gay.
In him those holy antique hours are seen
Without all ornament, itself and true,
Making no summer of another's green,
Robbing no old to dress his beauty new;
    And him as for a map doth nature store,
    To show false art what beauty was of yore.

69

Those parts of thee that the world's eye doth view
Want nothing that the thought of hearts can mend.
All tongues, the voice of souls, give thee that due,
Utt'ring bare truth even so as foes commend.
Thy outward thus with outward praise is crowned,
But those same tongues that give thee so thine own
In other accents do this praise confound
By seeing farther than the eye hath shown.
They look into the beauty of thy mind,
And that in guess they measure by thy deeds.
Then, churls, their thoughts—although their eyes
    were kind—
To thy fair flower add the rank smell of weeds.
    But why thy odour matcheth not thy show,
    The soil is this: that thou dost common grow.

70

That thou are blamed shall not be thy defect,
For slander's mark was ever yet the fair.
The ornament of beauty is suspect,
A crow that flies in heaven's sweetest air.
So thou be good, slander doth but approve
Thy worth the greater, being wooed of time;
For canker vice the sweetest buds doth love,
And thou present'st a pure unstainèd prime.
Thou hast passed by the ambush of young days
Either not assailed, or victor being charged;
Yet this thy praise cannot be so thy praise
To tie up envy, evermore enlarged.
    If some suspect of ill masked not thy show,
    Then thou alone kingdoms of hearts shouldst owe.

71

No longer mourn for me when I am dead
Than you shall hear the surly sullen bell
Give warning to the world that I am fled
From this vile world with vilest worms to dwell.
Nay, if you read this line, remember not
The hand that writ it; for I love you so
That I in your sweet thoughts would be forgot
If thinking on me then should make you woe.
O, if, I say, you look upon this verse
When I perhaps compounded am with clay,
Do not so much as my poor name rehearse,
But let your love even with my life decay,
    Lest the wise world should look into your moan
    And mock you with me after I am gone.

72

O, lest the world should task you to recite
What merit lived in me that you should love,
After my death, dear love, forget me quite;
For you in me can nothing worthy prove—
Unless you would devise some virtuous lie
To do more for me than mine own desert,
And hang more praise upon deceasèd I
Than niggard truth would willingly impart.
O, lest your true love may seem false in this,
That you for love speak well of me untrue,
My name be buried where my body is,
And live no more to shame nor me nor you;
    For I am shamed by that which I bring forth,
    And so should you, to love things nothing worth.

73

That time of year thou mayst in me behold
When yellow leaves, or none, or few, do hang
Upon those boughs which shake against the cold,
Bare ruined choirs where late the sweet birds sang.
In me thou seest the twilight of such day   5
As after sunset fadeth in the west,
Which by and by black night doth take away,
Death's second self, that seals up all in rest.
In me thou seest the glowing of such fire
That on the ashes of his youth doth lie   10
As the death-bed whereon it must expire,
Consumed with that which it was nourished by.
   This thou perceiv'st, which makes thy love more
      strong,
   To love that well which thou must leave ere long.

74

But be contented when that fell arrest
Without all bail shall carry me away.
My life hath in this line some interest,
Which for memorial still with thee shall stay.
When thou reviewest this, thou dost review   5
The very part was consecrate to thee.
The earth can have but earth, which is his due;
My spirit is thine, the better part of me.
So then thou hast but lost the dregs of life,
The prey of worms, my body being dead,   10
The coward conquest of a wretch's knife,
Too base of thee to be rememberèd.
   The worth of that is that which it contains,
   And that is this, and this with thee remains.

75

So are you to my thoughts as food to life,
Or as sweet-seasoned showers are to the ground;
And for the peace of you I hold such strife
As 'twixt a miser and his wealth is found:
Now proud as an enjoyer, and anon   5
Doubting the filching age will steal his treasure;
Now counting best to be with you alone,
Then bettered that the world may see my pleasure;
Sometime all full with feasting on your sight,
And by and by clean starvèd for a look;   10
Possessing or pursuing no delight
Save what is had or must from you be took.
   Thus do I pine and surfeit day by day,
   Or gluttoning on all, or all away.

76

Why is my verse so barren of new pride,
So far from variation or quick change?
Why, with the time, do I not glance aside
To new-found methods and to compounds strange?
Why write I still all one, ever the same,   5
And keep invention in a noted weed,
That every word doth almost tell my name,
Showing their birth and where they did proceed?
O know, sweet love, I always write of you,
And you and love are still my argument;   10
So all my best is dressing old words new,
Spending again what is already spent;
   For as the sun is daily new and old,
   So is my love, still telling what is told.

77

Thy glass will show thee how thy beauties wear,
Thy dial how thy precious minutes waste,
The vacant leaves thy mind's imprint will bear,
And of this book this learning mayst thou taste:
The wrinkles which thy glass will truly show   5
Of mouthèd graves will give thee memory;
Thou by thy dial's shady stealth mayst know
Time's thievish progress to eternity;
Look what thy memory cannot contain
Commit to these waste blanks, and thou shalt find   10
Those children nursed, delivered from thy brain,
To take a new acquaintance of thy mind.
   These offices so oft as thou wilt look
   Shall profit thee and much enrich thy book.

78

So oft have I invoked thee for my muse
And found such fair assistance in my verse
As every alien pen hath got my use,
And under thee their poesy disperse.
Thine eyes, that taught the dumb on high to sing   5
And heavy ignorance aloft to fly,
Have added feathers to the learned's wing
And given grace a double majesty.
Yet be most proud of that which I compile,
Whose influence is thine and born of thee.   10
In others' works thou dost but mend the style,
And arts with thy sweet graces gracèd be;
   But thou art all my art, and dost advance
   As high as learning my rude ignorance.

79

Whilst I alone did call upon thy aid
My verse alone had all thy gentle grace;
But now my gracious numbers are decayed,
And my sick muse doth give another place.
I grant, sweet love, thy lovely argument 5
Deserves the travail of a worthier pen,
Yet what of thee thy poet doth invent
He robs thee of, and pays it thee again.
He lends thee virtue, and he stole that word
From thy behaviour; beauty doth he give, 10
And found it in thy cheek: he can afford
No praise to thee but what in thee doth live.
    Then thank him not for that which he doth say,
    Since what he owes thee thou thyself dost pay.

80

O, how I faint when I of you do write,
Knowing a better spirit doth use your name,
And in the praise thereof spends all his might,
To make me tongue-tied, speaking of your fame!
But since your worth, wide as the ocean is, 5
The humble as the proudest sail doth bear,
My saucy barque, inferior far to his,
On your broad main doth wilfully appear.
Your shallowest help will hold me up afloat
Whilst he upon your soundless deep doth ride; 10
Or, being wrecked, I am a worthless boat,
He of tall building and of goodly pride.
    Then if he thrive and I be cast away,
    The worst was this: my love was my decay.

81

Or I shall live your epitaph to make,
Or you survive when I in earth am rotten.
From hence your memory death cannot take,
Although in me each part will be forgotten.
Your name from hence immortal life shall have, 5
Though I, once gone, to all the world must die.
The earth can yield me but a common grave
When you entombèd in men's eyes shall lie.
Your monument shall be my gentle verse,
Which eyes not yet created shall o'er-read, 10
And tongues to be your being shall rehearse
When all the breathers of this world are dead.
    You still shall live—such virtue hath my pen—
    Where breath most breathes, even in the mouths of
        men.

82

I grant thou wert not married to my muse,
And therefore mayst without attaint o'erlook
The dedicated words which writers use
Of their fair subject, blessing every book.
Thou art as fair in knowledge as in hue, 5
Finding thy worth a limit past my praise,
And therefore art enforced to seek anew
Some fresher stamp of these time-bettering days.
And do so, love; yet when they have devised
What strainèd touches rhetoric can lend, 10
Thou, truly fair, wert truly sympathized
In true plain words by thy true-telling friend;
    And their gross painting might be better used
    Where cheeks need blood: in thee it is abused.

83

I never saw that you did painting need,
And therefore to your fair no painting set.
I found—or thought I found—you did exceed
The barren tender of a poet's debt;
And therefore have I slept in your report: 5
That you yourself, being extant, well might show
How far a modern quill doth come too short,
Speaking of worth, what worth in you doth grow.
This silence for my sin you did impute,
Which shall be most my glory, being dumb; 10
For I impair not beauty, being mute,
When others would give life, and bring a tomb.
    There lives more life in one of your fair eyes
    Than both your poets can in praise devise.

84

Who is it that says most which can say more
Than this rich praise: that you alone are you,
In whose confine immurèd is the store
Which should example where your equal grew?
Lean penury within that pen doth dwell 5
That to his subject lends not some small glory;
But he that writes of you, if he can tell
That you are you, so dignifies his story.
Let him but copy what in you is writ,
Not making worse what nature made so clear, 10
And such a counterpart shall fame his wit,
Making his style admirèd everywhere.
    You to your beauteous blessings add a curse,
    Being fond on praise, which makes your praises
        worse.

85

My tongue-tied muse in manners holds her still
While comments of your praise, richly compiled,
Reserve thy character with golden quill
And precious phrase by all the muses filed.
I think good thoughts whilst other write good words, 5
And like unlettered clerk still cry 'Amen'
To every hymn that able spirit affords
In polished form of well-refinèd pen.
Hearing you praised I say ''Tis so, 'tis true,'
And to the most of praise add something more; 10
But that is in my thought, whose love to you,
Though words come hindmost, holds his rank before.
    Then others for the breath of words respect,
    Me for my dumb thoughts, speaking in effect.

86

Was it the proud full sail of his great verse
Bound for the prize of all-too-precious you
That did my ripe thoughts in my brain inhearse,
Making their tomb the womb wherein they grew?
Was it his spirit, by spirits taught to write 5
Above a mortal pitch, that struck me dead?
No, neither he nor his compeers by night
Giving him aid my verse astonishèd.
He nor that affable familiar ghost
Which nightly gulls him with intelligence, 10
As victors, of my silence cannot boast;
I was not sick of any fear from thence.
    But when your countenance filled up his line,
    Then lacked I matter; that enfeebled mine.

87

Farewell—thou art too dear for my possessing,
And like enough thou know'st thy estimate.
The charter of thy worth gives thee releasing;
My bonds in thee are all determinate.
For how do I hold thee but by thy granting, 5
And for that riches where is my deserving?
The cause of this fair gift in me is wanting,
And so my patent back again is swerving.
Thyself thou gav'st, thy own worth then not knowing,
Or me to whom thou gav'st it else mistaking; 10
So thy great gift, upon misprision growing,
Comes home again, on better judgement making.
    Thus have I had thee as a dream doth flatter:
    In sleep a king, but waking no such matter.

88

When thou shalt be disposed to set me light
And place my merit in the eye of scorn,
Upon thy side against myself I'll fight,
And prove thee virtuous though thou art forsworn.
With mine own weakness being best acquainted, 5
Upon thy part I can set down a story
Of faults concealed wherein I am attainted,
That thou in losing me shall win much glory;
And I by this will be a gainer too;
For bending all my loving thoughts on thee, 10
The injuries that to myself I do,
Doing thee vantage, double vantage me.
    Such is my love, to thee I so belong,
    That for thy right myself will bear all wrong.

89

Say that thou didst forsake me for some fault,
And I will comment upon that offence;
Speak of my lameness, and I straight will halt,
Against thy reasons making no defence.
Thou canst not, love, disgrace me half so ill, 5
To set a form upon desirèd change,
As I'll myself disgrace, knowing thy will.
I will acquaintance strangle and look strange,
Be absent from thy walks, and in my tongue
Thy sweet belovèd name no more shall dwell, 10
Lest I, too much profane, should do it wrong,
And haply of our old acquaintance tell.
    For thee, against myself I'll vow debate;
    For I must ne'er love him whom thou dost hate.

90

Then hate me when thou wilt, if ever, now,
Now while the world is bent my deeds to cross,
Join with the spite of fortune, make me bow,
And do not drop in for an after-loss.
Ah do not, when my heart hath scaped this sorrow, 5
Come in the rearward of a conquered woe;
Give not a windy night a rainy morrow
To linger out a purposed overthrow.
If thou wilt leave me, do not leave me last,
When other petty griefs have done their spite, 10
But in the onset come; so shall I taste
At first the very worst of fortune's might,
    And other strains of woe, which now seem woe,
    Compared with loss of thee will not seem so.

91

Some glory in their birth, some in their skill,
Some in their wealth, some in their body's force,
Some in their garments (though new-fangled ill),
Some in their hawks and hounds, some in their horse,
And every humour hath his adjunct pleasure   5
Wherein it finds a joy above the rest.
But these particulars are not my measure;
All these I better in one general best.
Thy love is better than high birth to me,
Richer than wealth, prouder than garments' cost,   10
Of more delight than hawks or horses be,
And having thee of all men's pride I boast,
  Wretched in this alone: that thou mayst take
  All this away, and me most wretched make.

92

But do thy worst to steal thyself away,
For term of life thou art assurèd mine,
And life no longer than thy love will stay,
For it depends upon that love of thine.
Then need I not to fear the worst of wrongs   5
When in the least of them my life hath end.
I see a better state to me belongs
Than that which on thy humour doth depend.
Thou canst not vex me with inconstant mind,
Since that my life on thy revolt doth lie.   10
O, what a happy title do I find—
Happy to have thy love, happy to die!
  But what's so blessèd fair that fears no blot?
  Thou mayst be false, and yet I know it not.

93

So shall I live supposing thou art true
Like a deceivèd husband; so love's face
May still seem love to me, though altered new—
Thy looks with me, thy heart in other place.
For there can live no hatred in thine eye,   5
Therefore in that I cannot know thy change.
In many's looks the false heart's history
Is writ in moods and frowns and wrinkles strange;
But heaven in thy creation did decree
That in thy face sweet love should ever dwell;   10
Whate'er thy thoughts or thy heart's workings be,
Thy looks should nothing thence but sweetness tell.
  How like Eve's apple doth thy beauty grow
  If thy sweet virtue answer not thy show!

94

They that have power to hurt and will do none,
That do not do the thing they most do show,
Who moving others are themselves as stone,
Unmovèd, cold, and to temptation slow—
They rightly do inherit heaven's graces,   5
And husband nature's riches from expense;
They are the lords and owners of their faces,
Others but stewards of their excellence.
The summer's flower is to the summer sweet
Though to itself it only live and die,   10
But if that flower with base infection meet
The basest weed outbraves his dignity:
  For sweetest things turn sourest by their deeds:
  Lilies that fester smell far worse than weeds.

95

How sweet and lovely dost thou make the shame
Which, like a canker in the fragrant rose,
Doth spot the beauty of thy budding name!
O, in what sweets dost thou thy sins enclose!
That tongue that tells the story of thy days,   5
Making lascivious comments on thy sport,
Cannot dispraise, but in a kind of praise,
Naming thy name, blesses an ill report.
O, what a mansion have those vices got
Which for their habitation chose out thee,   10
Where beauty's veil doth cover every blot
And all things turns to fair that eyes can see!
  Take heed, dear heart, of this large privilege:
  The hardest knife ill used doth lose his edge.

96

Some say thy fault is youth, some wantonness;
Some say thy grace is youth and gentle sport.
Both grace and faults are loved of more and less;
Thou mak'st faults graces that to thee resort.
As on the finger of a thronèd queen   5
The basest jewel will be well esteemed,
So are those errors that in thee are seen
To truths translated and for true things deemed.
How many lambs might the stern wolf betray
If like a lamb he could his looks translate!   10
How many gazers mightst thou lead away
If thou wouldst use the strength of all thy state!
  But do not so: I love thee in such sort
  As, thou being mine, mine is thy good report.

97

How like a winter hath my absence been
From thee, the pleasure of the fleeting year!
What freezings have I felt, what dark days seen,
What old December's bareness everywhere!
And yet this time removed was summer's time, 5
The teeming autumn big with rich increase,
Bearing the wanton burden of the prime
Like widowed wombs after their lords' decease.
Yet this abundant issue seemed to me
But hope of orphans and unfathered fruit, 10
For summer and his pleasures wait on thee,
And thou away, the very birds are mute;
 Or if they sing, 'tis with so dull a cheer
 That leaves look pale, dreading the winter's near.

98

From you have I been absent in the spring
When proud-pied April, dressed in all his trim,
Hath put a spirit of youth in everything,
That heavy Saturn laughed and leapt with him.
Yet nor the lays of birds nor the sweet smell 5
Of different flowers in odour and in hue
Could make me any summer's story tell,
Or from their proud lap pluck them where they grew;
Nor did I wonder at the lily's white,
Nor praise the deep vermilion in the rose. 10
They were but sweet, but figures of delight
Drawn after you, you pattern of all those;
 Yet seemed it winter still, and, you away,
 As with your shadow I with these did play.

99

The forward violet thus did I chide:
Sweet thief, whence didst thou steal thy sweet that
 smells,
If not from my love's breath? The purple pride
Which on thy soft cheek for complexion dwells
In my love's veins thou hast too grossly dyed. 5
The lily I condemnèd for thy hand,
And buds of marjoram had stol'n thy hair;
The roses fearfully on thorns did stand,
One blushing shame, another white despair;
A third, nor red nor white, had stol'n of both, 10
And to his robb'ry had annexed thy breath;
But for his theft in pride of all his growth
A vengeful canker ate him up to death.
 More flowers I noted, yet I none could see
 But sweet or colour it had stol'n from thee.

100

Where art thou, muse, that thou forget'st so long
To speak of that which gives thee all thy might?
Spend'st thou thy fury on some worthless song,
Dark'ning thy power to lend base subjects light?
Return, forgetful muse, and straight redeem 5
In gentle numbers time so idly spent;
Sing to the ear that doth thy lays esteem
And gives thy pen both skill and argument.
Rise, resty muse, my love's sweet face survey
If time have any wrinkle graven there. 10
If any, be a satire to decay
And make time's spoils despisèd everywhere.
 Give my love fame faster than time wastes life;
 So, thou prevene'st his scythe and crookèd knife.

101

O truant muse, what shall be thy amends
For thy neglect of truth in beauty dyed?
Both truth and beauty on my love depends;
So dost thou too, and therein dignified.
Make answer, muse. Wilt thou not haply say 5
'Truth needs no colour with his colour fixed,
Beauty no pencil beauty's truth to lay,
But best is best if never intermixed'?
Because he needs no praise wilt thou be dumb?
Excuse not silence so, for't lies in thee 10
To make him much outlive a gilded tomb,
And to be praised of ages yet to be.
 Then do thy office, muse; I teach thee how
 To make him seem long hence as he shows now.

102

My love is strengthened, though more weak in
 seeming.
I love not less, though less the show appear.
That love is merchandized whose rich esteeming
The owner's tongue doth publish everywhere. 5
Our love was new and then but in the spring
When I was wont to greet it with my lays,
As Philomel in summer's front doth sing,
And stops her pipe in growth of riper days—
Not that the summer is less pleasant now 10
Than when her mournful hymns did hush the night,
But that wild music burdens every bough,
And sweets grown common lose their dear delight.
 Therefore like her I sometime hold my tongue,
 Because I would not dull you with my song.

103

Alack, what poverty my muse brings forth
That, having such a scope to show her pride,
The argument all bare is of more worth
Than when it hath my added praise beside!
O blame me not if I no more can write! 5
Look in your glass and there appears a face
That overgoes my blunt invention quite,
Dulling my lines and doing me disgrace.
Were it not sinful then, striving to mend,
To mar the subject that before was well?— 10
For to no other pass my verses tend
Than of your graces and your gifts to tell;
   And more, much more, than in my verse can sit
   Your own glass shows you when you look in it.

104

To me, fair friend, you never can be old;
For as you were when first your eye I eyed,
Such seems your beauty still. Three winters cold
Have from the forests shook three summers' pride;
Three beauteous springs to yellow autumn turned 5
In process of the seasons have I seen,
Three April perfumes in three hot Junes burned
Since first I saw you fresh, which yet are green.
Ah yet doth beauty, like a dial hand,
Steal from his figure and no pace perceived; 10
So your sweet hue, which methinks still doth stand,
Hath motion, and mine eye may be deceived.
   For fear of which, hear this, thou age unbred:
   Ere you were born was beauty's summer dead.

105

Let not my love be called idolatry,
Nor my belovèd as an idol show,
Since all alike my songs and praises be
To one, of one, still such, and ever so.
Kind is my love today, tomorrow kind, 5
Still constant in a wondrous excellence.
Therefore my verse, to constancy confined,
One thing expressing, leaves out difference.
'Fair, kind, and true' is all my argument,
'Fair, kind, and true' varying to other words, 10
And in this change is my invention spent,
Three themes in one, which wondrous scope affords.
   Fair, kind, and true have often lived alone,
   Which three till now never kept seat in one.

106

When in the chronicle of wasted time
I see descriptions of the fairest wights,
And beauty making beautiful old rhyme
In praise of ladies dead and lovely knights;
Then in the blazon of sweet beauty's best, 5
Of hand, of foot, of lip, of eye, of brow,
I see their antique pen would have expressed
Even such a beauty as you master now.
So all their praises are but prophecies
Of this our time, all you prefiguring, 10
And for they looked but with divining eyes
They had not skill enough your worth to sing;
   For we which now behold these present days
   Have eyes to wonder, but lack tongues to praise.

107

Not mine own fears nor the prophetic soul
Of the wide world dreaming on things to come
Can yet the lease of my true love control,
Supposed as forfeit to a confined doom.
The mortal moon hath her eclipse endured, 5
And the sad augurs mock their own presage;
Incertainties now crown themselves assured,
And peace proclaims olives of endless age.
Now with the drops of this most balmy time
My love looks fresh, and death to me subscribes, 10
Since spite of him I'll live in this poor rhyme
While he insults o'er dull and speechless tribes;
   And thou in this shalt find thy monument
   When tyrants' crests and tombs of brass are spent.

108

What's in the brain that ink may character
Which hath not figured to thee my true spirit?
What's new to speak, what now to register,
That may express my love or thy dear merit?
Nothing, sweet boy; but yet like prayers divine 5
I must each day say o'er the very same,
Counting no old thing old, thou mine, I thine,
Even as when first I hallowed thy fair name.
So that eternal love in love's fresh case
Weighs not the dust and injury of age, 10
Nor gives to necessary wrinkles place,
But makes antiquity for aye his page,
   Finding the first conceit of love there bred
   Where time and outward form would show it dead.

109

O never say that I was false of heart,
Though absence seemed my flame to qualify—
As easy might I from myself depart
As from my soul, which in thy breast doth lie.
That is my home of love. If I have ranged, 5
Like him that travels I return again,
Just to the time, not with the time exchanged,
So that myself bring water for my stain.
Never believe, though in my nature reigned
All frailties that besiege all kinds of blood, 10
That it could so preposterously be stained
To leave for nothing all thy sum of good;
  For nothing this wide universe I call
  Save thou my rose; in it thou art my all.

110

Alas, 'tis true, I have gone here and there
And made myself a motley to the view,
Gored mine own thoughts, sold cheap what is most
    dear,
Made old offences of affections new.
Most true it is that I have looked on truth 5
Askance and strangely. But, by all above,
These blenches gave my heart another youth,
And worse essays proved thee my best of love.
Now all is done, have what shall have no end;
Mine appetite I never more will grind 10
On newer proof to try an older friend,
A god in love, to whom I am confined.
  Then give me welcome, next my heaven the best,
  Even to thy pure and most most loving breast.

111

O, for my sake do you with fortune chide,
The guilty goddess of my harmful deeds,
That did not better for my life provide
Than public means which public manners breeds.
Thence comes it that my name receives a brand, 5
And almost thence my nature is subdued
To what it works in, like the dyer's hand.
Pity me then, and wish I were renewed,
Whilst like a willing patient I will drink
Potions of eisel 'gainst my strong infection; 10
No bitterness that I will bitter think,
Nor double penance to correct correction.
  Pity me then, dear friend, and I assure ye
  Even that your pity is enough to cure me.

112

Your love and pity doth th'impression fill
Which vulgar scandal stamped upon my brow;
For what care I who calls me well or ill,
So you o'er-green my bad, my good allow?
You are my all the world, and I must strive 5
To know my shames and praises from your tongue—
None else to me, nor I to none alive,
That my steeled sense or changes, right or wrong.
In so profound abyss I throw all care
Of others' voices that my adder's sense 10
To critic and to flatterer stoppèd are.
Mark how with my neglect I do dispense:
  You are so strongly in my purpose bred
  That all the world besides, methinks, they're dead.

113

Since I left you mine eye is in my mind,
And that which governs me to go about
Doth part his function and is partly blind,
Seems seeing, but effectually is out;
For it no form delivers to the heart 5
Of bird, of flower, or shape which it doth latch.
Of his quick objects hath the mind no part,
Nor his own vision holds what it doth catch;
For if it see the rud'st or gentlest sight,
The most sweet favour or deformèd'st creature, 10
The mountain or the sea, the day or night,
The crow or dove, it shapes them to your feature.
  Incapable of more, replete with you,
  My most true mind thus makes mine eye untrue.

114

Or whether doth my mind, being crowned with you,
Drink up the monarch's plague, this flattery,
Or whether shall I say mine eye saith true,
And that your love taught it this alchemy,
To make of monsters and things indigest 5
Such cherubins as your sweet self resemble,
Creating every bad a perfect best
As fast as objects to his beams assemble?
O, 'tis the first, 'tis flatt'ry in my seeing,
And my great mind most kingly drinks it up. 10
Mine eye well knows what with his gust is 'greeing,
And to his palate doth prepare the cup.
  If it be poisoned, 'tis the lesser sin
  That mine eye loves it and doth first begin.

115

Those lines that I before have writ do lie,
Even those that said I could not love you dearer;
Yet then my judgement knew no reason why
My most full flame should afterwards burn clearer.
But reckoning time, whose millioned accidents   5
Creep in 'twixt vows and change decrees of kings,
Tan sacred beauty, blunt the sharp'st intents,
Divert strong minds to th' course of alt'ring things—
Alas, why, fearing of time's tyranny,
Might I not then say 'Now I love you best',   10
When I was certain o'er incertainty,
Crowning the present, doubting of the rest?
  Love is a babe; then might I not say so,
  To give full growth to that which still doth grow.

116

Let me not to the marriage of true minds
Admit impediments. Love is not love
Which alters when it alteration finds,
Or bends with the remover to remove.
O no, it is an ever fixèd mark   5
That looks on tempests and is never shaken;
It is the star to every wand'ring barque,
Whose worth's unknown although his height be
      taken.
Love's not time's fool, though rosy lips and cheeks
Within his bending sickle's compass come;   10
Love alters not with his brief hours and weeks,
But bears it out even to the edge of doom.
  If this be error and upon me proved,
  I never writ, nor no man ever loved.

117

Accuse me thus: that I have scanted all
Wherein I should your great deserts repay,
Forgot upon your dearest love to call
Whereto all bonds do tie me day by day;
That I have frequent been with unknown minds,   5
And given to time your own dear-purchased right;
That I have hoisted sail to all the winds
Which should transport me farthest from your sight.
Book both my wilfulness and errors down,
And on just proof surmise accumulate;   10
Bring me within the level of your frown,
But shoot not at me in your wakened hate,
  Since my appeal says I did strive to prove
  The constancy and virtue of your love.

118

Like as, to make our appetites more keen,
With eager compounds we our palate urge;
As to prevent our maladies unseen
We sicken to shun sickness when we purge:
Even so, being full of your ne'er cloying sweetness,   5
To bitter sauces did I frame my feeding,
And, sick of welfare, found a kind of meetness
To be diseased ere that there was true needing.
Thus policy in love, t'anticipate
The ills that were not, grew to faults assured,   10
And brought to medicine a healthful state
Which, rank of goodness, would by ill be cured.
  But thence I learn, and find the lesson true:
  Drugs poison him that so fell sick of you.

119

What potions have I drunk of siren tears
Distilled from limbecks foul as hell within,
Applying fears to hopes and hopes to fears,
Still losing when I saw myself to win!
What wretched errors hath my heart committed   5
Whilst it hath thought itself so blessèd never!
How have mine eyes out of their spheres been fitted
In the distraction of this madding fever!
O benefit of ill! Now I find true
That better is by evil still made better,   10
And ruined love when it is built anew
Grows fairer than at first, more strong, far greater.
  So I return rebuked to my content,
  And gain by ills thrice more than I have spent.

120

That you were once unkind befriends me now,
And for that sorrow which I then did feel
Needs must I under my transgression bow,
Unless my nerves were brass or hammered steel.
For if you were by my unkindness shaken   5
As I by yours, you've past a hell of time,
And I, a tyrant, have no leisure taken
To weigh how once I suffered in your crime.
O that our night of woe might have remembered
My deepest sense how hard true sorrow hits,   10
And soon to you as you to me then tendered
The humble salve which wounded bosoms fits!
  But that your trespass now becomes a fee;
  Mine ransoms yours, and yours must ransom me.

121

'Tis better to be vile than vile esteemed
When not to be receives reproach of being,
And the just pleasure lost, which is so deemed
Not by our feeling but by others' seeing.
For why should others' false adulterate eyes   5
Give salutation to my sportive blood?
Or on my frailties why are frailer spies,
Which in their wills count bad what I think good?
No, I am that I am, and they that level
At my abuses reckon up their own.   10
I may be straight, though they themselves be bevel;
By their rank thoughts my deeds must not be shown,
  Unless this general evil they maintain:
  All men are bad and in their badness reign.

122

Thy gift, thy tables, are within my brain
Full charactered with lasting memory,
Which shall above that idle rank remain
Beyond all date, even to eternity;
Or at the least so long as brain and heart   5
Have faculty by nature to subsist,
Till each to razed oblivion yield his part
Of thee, thy record never can be missed.
That poor retention could not so much hold,
Nor need I tallies thy dear love to score;   10
Therefore to give them from me was I bold,
To trust those tables that receive thee more.
  To keep an adjunct to remember thee
  Were to import forgetfulness in me.

123

No, time, thou shalt not boast that I do change!
Thy pyramids built up with newer might
To me are nothing novel, nothing strange,
They are but dressings of a former sight.
Our dates are brief, and therefore we admire   5
What thou dost foist upon us that is old,
And rather make them born to our desire
Than think that we before have heard them told.
Thy registers and thee I both defy,
Not wond'ring at the present nor the past;   10
For thy records and what we see doth lie,
Made more or less by thy continual haste.
  This I do vow, and this shall ever be:
  I will be true despite thy scythe and thee.

124

If my dear love were but the child of state
It might for fortune's bastard be unfathered,
As subject to time's love or to time's hate,
Weeds among weeds or flowers with flowers gathered.
No, it was builded far from accident;   5
It suffers not in smiling pomp, nor falls
Under the blow of thrallèd discontent
Whereto th'inviting time our fashion calls.
It fears not policy, that heretic
Which works on leases of short-numbered hours,   10
But all alone stands hugely politic,
That it nor grows with heat nor drowns with showers.
  To this I witness call the fools of time,
  Which die for goodness, who have lived for crime.

125

Were't aught to me I bore the canopy,
With my extern the outward honouring,
Or laid great bases for eternity
Which proves more short than waste or ruining?
Have I not seen dwellers on form and favour   5
Lose all and more by paying too much rent,
For compound sweet forgoing simple savour,
Pitiful thrivers in their gazing spent?
No, let me be obsequious in thy heart,
And take thou my oblation, poor but free,   10
Which is not mixed with seconds, knows no art
But mutual render, only me for thee.
  Hence, thou suborned informer! A true soul
  When most impeached stands least in thy control.

126

O thou my lovely boy, who in thy power
Dost hold time's fickle glass, his sickle-hour;
Who hast by waning grown, and therein show'st
Thy lovers withering as thy sweet self grow'st—
If nature, sovereign mistress over wrack,   5
As thou goest onwards still will pluck thee back,
She keeps thee to this purpose: that her skill
May time disgrace, and wretched minutes kill.
Yet fear her, O thou minion of her pleasure!
She may detain but not still keep her treasure.   10
  Her audit, though delayed, answered must be,
  And her quietus is to render thee.

127

In the old age black was not counted fair,
Or if it were, it bore not beauty's name;
But now is black beauty's successive heir,
And beauty slandered with a bastard shame:
For since each hand hath put on nature's power,
Fairing the foul with art's false borrowed face,
Sweet beauty hath no name, no holy bower,
But is profaned, if not lives in disgrace.
Therefore my mistress' eyes are raven-black,
Her brow so suited, and they mourners seem
At such who, not born fair, no beauty lack,
Sland'ring creation with a false esteem.
    Yet so they mourn, becoming of their woe,
    That every tongue says beauty should look so.

128

How oft, when thou, my music, music play'st
Upon that blessèd wood whose motion sounds
With thy sweet fingers when thou gently sway'st
The wiry concord that mine ear confounds,
Do I envy those jacks that nimble leap
To kiss the tender inward of thy hand
Whilst my poor lips, which should that harvest reap,
At the wood's boldness by thee blushing stand!
To be so tickled they would change their state
And situation with those dancing chips
O'er whom thy fingers walk with gentle gait,
Making dead wood more blessed than living lips.
    Since saucy jacks so happy are in this,
    Give them thy fingers, me thy lips to kiss.

129

Th'expense of spirit in a waste of shame
Is lust in action; and till action, lust
Is perjured, murd'rous, bloody, full of blame,
Savage, extreme, rude, cruel, not to trust,
Enjoyed no sooner but despisèd straight,
Past reason hunted, and no sooner had
Past reason hated as a swallowed bait
On purpose laid to make the taker mad;
Mad in pursuit and in possession so,
Had, having, and in quest to have, extreme;
A bliss in proof and proved, a very woe;
Before, a joy proposed; behind, a dream.
    All this the world well knows, yet none knows well
    To shun the heaven that leads men to this hell.

130

My mistress' eyes are nothing like the sun;
Coral is far more red than her lips' red.
If snow be white, why then her breasts are dun;
If hairs be wires, black wires grow on her head.
I have seen roses damasked, red and white,
But no such roses see I in her cheeks;
And in some perfumes is there more delight
Than in the breath that from my mistress reeks.
I love to hear her speak, yet well I know
That music hath a far more pleasing sound.
I grant I never saw a goddess go:
My mistress when she walks treads on the ground.
    And yet, by heaven, I think my love as rare
    As any she belied with false compare.

131

Thou art as tyrannous so as thou art
As those whose beauties proudly make them cruel,
For well thou know'st to my dear doting heart
Thou art the fairest and most precious jewel.
Yet, in good faith, some say that thee behold
Thy face hath not the power to make love groan.
To say they err I dare not be so bold,
Although I swear it to myself alone;
And, to be sure that is not false I swear,
A thousand groans but thinking on thy face
One on another's neck do witness bear
Thy black is fairest in my judgement's place.
    In nothing art thou black save in thy deeds,
    And thence this slander, as I think, proceeds.

132

Thine eyes I love, and they, as pitying me—
Knowing thy heart torment me with disdain—
Have put on black, and loving mourners be,
Looking with pretty ruth upon my pain;
And truly, not the morning sun of heaven
Better becomes the gray cheeks of the east,
Nor that full star that ushers in the even
Doth half that glory to the sober west,
As those two mourning eyes become thy face.
O, let it then as well beseem thy heart
To mourn for me, since mourning doth thee grace,
And suit thy pity like in every part.
    Then will I swear beauty herself is black,
    And all they foul that thy complexion lack.

133

Beshrew that heart that makes my heart to groan
For that deep wound it gives my friend and me!
Is't not enough to torture me alone,
But slave to slavery my sweet'st friend must be?
Me from myself thy cruel eye hath taken,   5
And my next self thou harder hast engrossed.
Of him, myself, and thee I am forsaken —
A torment thrice threefold thus to be crossed.
Prison my heart in thy steel bosom's ward,
But then my friend's heart let my poor heart bail; 10
Whoe'er keeps me, let my heart be his guard;
Thou canst not then use rigour in my jail.
    And yet thou wilt; for I, being pent in thee,
    Perforce am thine, and all that is in me.

134

So, now I have confessed that he is thine,
And I myself am mortgaged to thy will,
Myself I'll forfeit, so that other mine
Thou wilt restore to be my comfort still.
But thou wilt not, nor he will not be free,   5
For thou art covetous, and he is kind.
He learned but surety-like to write for me
Under that bond that him as fast doth bind.
The statute of thy beauty thou wilt take,
Thou usurer that putt'st forth all to use,   10
And sue a friend came debtor for my sake;
So him I lose through my unkind abuse.
    Him have I lost; thou hast both him and me;
    He pays the whole, and yet am I not free.

135

Whoever hath her wish, thou hast thy Will,
And Will to boot, and Will in overplus.
More than enough am I that vex thee still,
To thy sweet will making addition thus.
Wilt thou, whose will is large and spacious,   5
Not once vouchsafe to hide my will in thine?
Shall will in others seem right gracious,
And in my will no fair acceptance shine?
The sea, all water, yet receives rain still,
And in abundance addeth to his store;   10
So thou, being rich in Will, add to thy Will
One will of mine to make thy large Will more.
    Let no unkind no fair beseechers kill;
    Think all but one, and me in that one Will.

136

If thy soul check thee that I come so near,
Swear to thy blind soul that I was thy Will,
And will, thy soul knows, is admitted there;
Thus far for love my love-suit, sweet, fulfil.
Will will fulfil the treasure of thy love,   5
Ay, fill it full with wills, and my will one.
In things of great receipt with ease we prove
Among a number one is reckoned none.
Then in the number let me pass untold,
Though in thy store's account I one must be;   10
For nothing hold me, so it please thee hold
That nothing me a something, sweet, to thee.
    Make but my name thy love, and love that still,
    And then thou lov'st me for my name is Will.

137

Thou blind fool love, what dost thou to mine eyes
That they behold and see not what they see?
They know what beauty is, see where it lies,
Yet what the best is take the worst to be.
If eyes corrupt by over-partial looks   5
Be anchored in the bay where all men ride,
Why of eyes' falsehood hast thou forgèd hooks
Whereto the judgement of my heart is tied?
Why should my heart think that a several plot
Which my heart knows the wide world's common
        place? —   10
Or mine eyes, seeing this, say this is not,
To put fair truth upon so foul a face?
    In things right true my heart and eyes have erred,
    And to this false plague are they now transferred.

138

When my love swears that she is made of truth
I do believe her though I know she lies,
That she might think me some untutored youth
Unlearnèd in the world's false subtleties.
Thus vainly thinking that she thinks me young,   5
Although she knows my days are past the best,
Simply I credit her false-speaking tongue;
On both sides thus is simple truth suppressed.
But wherefore says she not she is unjust,
And wherefore say not I that I am old?   10
O, love's best habit is in seeming trust,
And age in love loves not to have years told.
    Therefore I lie with her, and she with me,
    And in our faults by lies we flattered be.

139

O, call not me to justify the wrong
That thy unkindness lays upon my heart.
Wound me not with thine eye but with thy tongue;
Use power with power, and slay me not by art.
Tell me thou lov'st elsewhere, but in my sight,   5
Dear heart, forbear to glance thine eye aside.
What need'st thou wound with cunning when thy
    might
Is more than my o'erpressed defence can bide?
Let me excuse thee: 'Ah, my love well knows
Her pretty looks have been mine enemies,   10
And therefore from my face she turns my foes
That they elsewhere might dart their injuries.'
    Yet do not so; but since I am near slain,
    Kill me outright with looks, and rid my pain.

142

Love is my sin, and thy dear virtue hate,
Hate of my sin grounded on sinful loving.
O, but with mine compare thou thine own state,
And thou shalt find it merits not reproving;
Or if it do, not from those lips of thine   5
That have profaned their scarlet ornaments
And sealed false bonds of love as oft as mine,
Robbed others' beds' revenues of their rents.
Be it lawful I love thee as thou lov'st those
Whom thine eyes woo as mine importune thee.   10
Root pity in thy heart, that when it grows
Thy pity may deserve to pitied be.
    If thou dost seek to have what thou dost hide,
    By self example mayst thou be denied!

140

Be wise as thou art cruel; do not press
My tongue-tied patience with too much disdain,
Lest sorrow lend me words, and words express
The manner of my pity-wanting pain.
If I might teach thee wit, better it were,   5
Though not to love, yet, love, to tell me so—
As testy sick men when their deaths be near
No news but health from their physicians know.
For if I should despair I should grow mad,
And in my madness might speak ill of thee.   10
Now this ill-wresting world is grown so bad
Mad slanderers by mad ears believèd be.
    That I may not be so, nor thou belied,
    Bear thine eyes straight, though thy proud heart go
    wide.

143

Lo, as a care-full housewife runs to catch
One of her feathered creatures broke away,
Sets down her babe and makes all swift dispatch
In pursuit of the thing she would have stay,
Whilst her neglected child holds her in chase,   5
Cries to catch her whose busy care is bent
To follow that which flies before her face,
Not prizing her poor infant's discontent:
So runn'st thou after that which flies from thee,
Whilst I, thy babe, chase thee afar behind;   10
But if thou catch thy hope, turn back to me
And play the mother's part: kiss me, be kind.
    So will I pray that thou mayst have thy Will
    If thou turn back and my loud crying still.

141

In faith, I do not love thee with mine eyes,
For they in thee a thousand errors note;
But 'tis my heart that loves what they despise,
Who in despite of view is pleased to dote.
Nor are mine ears with thy tongue's tune delighted,   5
Nor tender feeling to base touches prone;
Nor taste nor smell desire to be invited
To any sensual feast with thee alone;
But my five wits nor my five senses can
Dissuade one foolish heart from serving thee,   10
Who leaves unswayed the likeness of a man,
Thy proud heart's slave and vassal-wretch to be.
    Only my plague thus far I count my gain:
    That she that makes me sin awards me pain.

144

Two loves I have, of comfort and despair,
Which like two spirits do suggest me still.
The better angel is a man right fair,
The worser spirit a woman coloured ill.
To win me soon to hell my female evil   5
Tempteth my better angel from my side,
And would corrupt my saint to be a devil,
Wooing his purity with her foul pride;
And whether that my angel be turned fiend
Suspect I may, yet not directly tell;   10
But being both from me, both to each friend,
I guess one angel in another's hell.
    Yet this shall I ne'er know, but live in doubt
    Till my bad angel fire my good one out.

145

Those lips that love's own hand did make
Breathed forth the sound that said 'I hate'
To me that languished for her sake;
But when she saw my woeful state,
Straight in her heart did mercy come, 5
Chiding that tongue that ever sweet
Was used in giving gentle doom,
And taught it thus anew to greet:
'I hate' she altered with an end
That followed it as gentle day 10
Doth follow night who, like a fiend,
From heaven to hell is flown away.
   'I hate' from hate away she threw,
   And saved my life, saying 'not you.'

148

O me, what eyes hath love put in my head,
Which have no correspondence with true sight!
Or if they have, where is my judgement fled,
That censures falsely what they see aright?
If that be fair whereon my false eyes dote, 5
What means the world to say it is not so?
If it be not, then love doth well denote
Love's eye is not so true as all men's. No,
How can it, O, how can love's eye be true,
That is so vexed with watching and with tears? 10
No marvel then though I mistake my view:
The sun itself sees not till heaven clears.
   O cunning love, with tears thou keep'st me blind
   Lest eyes, well seeing, thy foul faults should find!

146

Poor soul, the centre of my sinful earth,
⌐   ⌐ these rebel powers that thee array;
Why dost thou pine within and suffer dearth,
Painting thy outward walls so costly gay?
Why so large cost, having so short a lease, 5
Dost thou upon thy fading mansion spend?
Shall worms, inheritors of this excess,
Eat up thy charge? Is this thy body's end?
Then, soul, live thou upon thy servant's loss,
And let that pine to aggravate thy store. 10
Buy terms divine in selling hours of dross;
Within be fed, without be rich no more.
   So shalt thou feed on death, that feeds on men,
   And death once dead, there's no more dying then.

149

Canst thou, O cruel, say I love thee not
When I against myself with thee partake?
Do I not think on thee when I forgot
Am of myself, all-tyrant, for thy sake?
Who hateth thee that I do call my friend? 5
On whom frown'st thou that I do fawn upon?
Nay, if thou lour'st on me, do I not spend
Revenge upon myself with present moan?
What merit do I in myself respect
That is so proud thy service to despise, 10
When all my best doth worship thy defect,
Commanded by the motion of thine eyes?
   But, love, hate on; for now I know thy mind.
   Those that can see thou lov'st, and I am blind.

147

My love is as a fever, longing still
For that which longer nurseth the disease,
Feeding on that which doth preserve the ill,
Th'uncertain sickly appetite to please.
My reason, the physician to my love, 5
Angry that his prescriptions are not kept,
Hath left me, and I desperate now approve
Desire is death, which physic did except.
Past cure I am, now reason is past care,
And frantic mad with evermore unrest. 10
My thoughts and my discourse as madmen's are,
At random from the truth vainly expressed;
   For I have sworn thee fair, and thought thee bright,
   Who art as black as hell, as dark as night.

150

O, from what power hast thou this powerful might
With insufficiency my heart to sway,
To make me give the lie to my true sight
And swear that brightness doth not grace the day?
Whence hast thou this becoming of things ill, 5
That in the very refuse of thy deeds
There is such strength and warrantise of skill
That in my mind thy worst all best exceeds?
Who taught thee how to make me love thee more
The more I hear and see just cause of hate? 10
O, though I love what others do abhor,
With others thou shouldst not abhor my state.
   If thy unworthiness raised love in me,
   More worthy I to be beloved of thee.

151

Love is too young to know what conscience is,
Yet who knows not conscience is born of love?
Then, gentle cheater, urge not my amiss,
Lest guilty of my faults thy sweet self prove.
For, thou betraying me, I do betray   5
My nobler part to my gross body's treason.
My soul doth tell my body that he may
Triumph in love; flesh stays no farther reason,
But rising at thy name doth point out thee
As his triumphant prize. Proud of this pride,   10
He is contented thy poor drudge to be,
To stand in thy affairs, fall by thy side.
  No want of conscience hold it that I call
  Her 'love' for whose dear love I rise and fall.

152

In loving thee thou know'st I am forsworn,
But thou art twice forsworn to me love swearing:
In act thy bed-vow broke, and new faith torn
In vowing new hate after new love bearing.
But why of two oaths' breach do I accuse thee   5
When I break twenty? I am perjured most,
For all my vows are oaths but to misuse thee,
And all my honest faith in thee is lost.
For I have sworn deep oaths of thy deep kindness,
Oaths of thy love, thy truth, thy constancy,   10
And to enlighten thee gave eyes to blindness,
Or made them swear against the thing they see.
  For I have sworn thee fair—more perjured eye
  To swear against the truth so foul a lie.

153

Cupid laid by his brand and fell asleep.
A maid of Dian's this advantage found,
And his love-kindling fire did quickly steep
In a cold valley-fountain of that ground,
Which borrowed from this holy fire of love   5
A dateless lively heat, still to endure,
And grew a seething bath which yet men prove
Against strange maladies a sovereign cure.
But at my mistress' eye love's brand new fired,
The boy for trial needs would touch my breast. 10
I, sick withal, the help of bath desired,
And thither hied, a sad distempered guest,
  But found no cure; the bath for my help lies
  Where Cupid got new fire: my mistress' eyes.

154

The little love-god lying once asleep
Laid by his side his heart-inflaming brand,
Whilst many nymphs that vowed chaste life to keep
Came tripping by; but in her maiden hand
The fairest votary took up that fire   5
Which many legions of true hearts had warmed,
And so the general of hot desire
Was sleeping by a virgin hand disarmed.
This brand she quenchèd in a cool well by,
Which from love's fire took heat perpetual,   10
Growing a bath and healthful remedy
For men diseased; but I, my mistress' thrall,
  Came there for cure; and this by that I prove:
  Love's fire heats water, water cools not love.

A Lover's Complaint

From off a hill whose concave womb re-worded
A plaintful story from a sist'ring vale,
My spirits t'attend this double voice accorded,
And down I laid to list the sad-tuned tale;
Ere long espied a fickle maid full pale,   5
Tearing of papers, breaking rings a-twain,
Storming her world with sorrow's wind and rain.

Upon her head a plaited hive of straw
Which fortified her visage from the sun,
Whereon the thought might think sometime it saw   10
The carcass of a beauty spent and done.
Time had not scythèd all that youth begun,
Nor youth all quit; but spite of heaven's fell rage,
Some beauty peeped through lattice of seared age.

Oft did she heave her napkin to her eyne,   15
Which on it had conceited characters,
Laund'ring the silken figures in the brine
That seasoned woe had pelleted in tears,
And often reading what contents it bears;
As often shrieking undistinguished woe   20
In clamours of all size, both high and low.

Sometimes her levelled eyes their carriage ride
As they did batt'ry to the spheres intend;
Sometime diverted their poor balls are tied
To th'orbèd earth; sometimes they do extend   25
Their view right on; anon their gazes lend
To every place at once, and nowhere fixed,
The mind and sight distractedly commixed.

Her hair, nor loose nor tied in formal plait,
Proclaimed in her a careless hand of pride;   30
For some, untucked, descended her sheaved hat,
Hanging her pale and pinèd cheek beside.
Some in her threaden fillet still did bide,
And, true to bondage, would not break from thence,
Though slackly braided in loose negligence.   35

A thousand favours from a maund she drew
Of amber, crystal, and of beaded jet,
Which one by one she in a river threw
Upon whose weeping margin she was set;
Like usury applying wet to wet,   40
Or monarch's hands that lets not bounty fall
Where want cries some, but where excess begs all.

Of folded schedules had she many a one
Which she perused, sighed, tore, and gave the flood;
Cracked many a ring of posied gold and bone,   45
Bidding them find their sepulchres in mud;

Found yet more letters sadly penned in blood,
With sleided silk feat and affectedly
Enswathed and sealed to curious secrecy.

These often bathed she in her fluxive eyes,   50
And often kissed, and often 'gan to tear;
Cried 'O false blood, thou register of lies,
What unapprovèd witness dost thou bear!
Ink would have seemed more black and damnèd
here!'
This said, in top of rage the lines she rents,   55
Big discontent so breaking their contents.

A reverend man that grazed his cattle nigh,
Sometime a blusterer that the ruffle knew
Of court, of city, and had let go by
The swiftest hours observèd as they flew,   60
Towards this afflicted fancy fastly drew,
And, privileged by age, desires to know
In brief the grounds and motives of her woe.

So slides he down upon his grainèd bat,
And comely distant sits he by her side,   65
When he again desires her, being sat,
Her grievance with his hearing to divide.
If that from him there may be aught applied
Which may her suffering ecstasy assuage,
'Tis promised in the charity of age.   70

'Father,' she says, 'though in me you behold
The injury of many a blasting hour,
Let it not tell your judgement I am old;
Not age, but sorrow over me hath power.
I might as yet have been a spreading flower,   75
Fresh to myself, if I had self-applied
Love to myself, and to no love beside.

'But, woe is me, too early I attended
A youthful suit—it was to gain my grace—
O, one by nature's outwards so commended   80
That maidens' eyes stuck over all his face.
Love lacked a dwelling and made him her place,
And when in his fair parts she did abide
She was new-lodged and newly deified.

'His browny locks did hang in crookèd curls,   85
And every light occasion of the wind
Upon his lips their silken parcels hurls.
What's sweet to do, to do will aptly find.
Each eye that saw him did enchant the mind,
For on his visage was in little drawn   90
What largeness thinks in paradise was sawn.

'Small show of man was yet upon his chin;
His phoenix down began but to appear,
Like unshorn velvet, on that termless skin
Whose bare outbragged the web it seemed to wear;   95
Yet showed his visage by that cost more dear,
And nice affections wavering stood in doubt
If best were as it was, or best without.

'His qualities were beauteous as his form,
For maiden-tongued he was, and thereof free.   100
Yet if men moved him, was he such a storm
As oft twixt May and April is to see
When winds breathe sweet, unruly though they be.
His rudeness so with his authorized youth
Did livery falseness in a pride of truth.   105

'Well could he ride, and often men would say
"That horse his mettle from his rider takes;
Proud of subjection, noble by the sway,
What rounds, what bounds, what course, what stop
      he makes!"
And controversy hence a question takes,   110
Whether the horse by him became his deed,
Or he his manège by th' well-doing steed.

'But quickly on this side the verdict went:
His real habitude gave life and grace
To appertainings and to ornament,   115
Accomplished in himself, not in his case.
All aids, themselves made fairer by their place,
Came for additions; yet their purposed trim
Pieced not his grace, but were all graced by him.

'So on the tip of his subduing tongue   120
All kind of arguments and question deep,
All replication prompt, and reason strong,
For his advantage still did wake and sleep,
To make the weeper laugh, the laugher weep,
He had the dialect and different skill,   125
Catching all passions in his craft of will,

'That he did in the general bosom reign
Of young, of old, and sexes both enchanted,
To dwell with him in thoughts, or to remain
In personal duty, following where he haunted.   130
Consents bewitched, ere he desire, have granted,
And dialogued for him what he would say,
Asked their own wills, and made their wills obey.

'Many there were that did his picture get
To serve their eyes, and in it put their mind,   135
Like fools that in th'imagination set
The goodly objects which abroad they find
Of lands and mansions, theirs in thought assigned,
And labour in more pleasures to bestow them
Than the true gouty landlord which doth owe them.   140

'So many have, that never touched his hand,
Sweetly supposed them mistress of his heart.
My woeful self, that did in freedom stand,
And was my own fee-simple, not in part,
What with his art in youth, and youth in art,   145
Threw my affections in his charmèd power,
Reserved the stalk and gave him all my flower.

'Yet did I not, as some my equals did,
Demand of him, nor being desirèd yielded.
Finding myself in honour so forbid,   150
With safest distance I mine honour shielded.
Experience for me many bulwarks builded
Of proofs new bleeding, which remained the foil
Of this false jewel and his amorous spoil.

'But ah, who ever shunned by precedent   155
The destined ill she must herself assay,
Or forced examples 'gainst her own content
To put the by-past perils in her way?
Counsel may stop a while what will not stay,
For when we rage, advice is often seen,   160
By blunting us, to make our wills more keen.

'Nor gives it satisfaction to our blood
That we must curb it upon others' proof,
To be forbod the sweets that seems so good
For fear of harms that preach in our behoof.   165
O appetite, from judgement stand aloof!
The one a palate hath that needs will taste,
Though reason weep, and cry it is thy last.

'For further I could say this man's untrue,
And knew the patterns of his foul beguiling;   170
Heard where his plants in others' orchards grew,
Saw how deceits were gilded in his smiling,
Knew vows were ever brokers to defiling,
Thought characters and words merely but art,
And bastards of his foul adulterate heart.   175

'And long upon these terms I held my city
Till thus he gan besiege me: "Gentle maid,
Have of my suffering youth some feeling pity,
And be not of my holy vows afraid.
That's to ye sworn to none was ever said;   180
For feasts of love I have been called unto,
Till now did ne'er invite nor never woo.

'"All my offences that abroad you see
Are errors of the blood, none of the mind.
Love made them not; with acture they may be,   185
Where neither party is nor true nor kind.
They sought their shame that so their shame did find,
And so much less of shame in me remains
By how much of me their reproach contains.

'"Among the many that mine eyes have seen,   190
Not one whose flame my heart so much as warmèd
Or my affection put to th' smallest teen,
Or any of my leisures ever charmèd.
Harm have I done to them, but ne'er was harmèd;
Kept hearts in liveries, but mine own was free,   195
And reigned commanding in his monarchy.

'"Look here what tributes wounded fancies sent me
Of pallid pearls and rubies red as blood,
Figuring that they their passions likewise lent me
Of grief and blushes, aptly understood   200
In bloodless white and the encrimsoned mood—
Effects of terror and dear modesty,
Encamped in hearts, but fighting outwardly.

'"And lo, behold, these talents of their hair,
With twisted mettle amorously impleached,   205
I have received from many a several fair,
Their kind acceptance weepingly beseeched,
With th'annexations of fair gems enriched,
And deep-brained sonnets that did amplify
Each stone's dear nature, worth, and quality.   210

'"The diamond?—why, 'twas beautiful and hard,
Whereto his invised properties did tend;
The deep-green em'rald, in whose fresh regard
Weak sights their sickly radiance do amend;
The heaven-hued sapphire and the opal blend   215
With objects manifold; each several stone,
With wit well blazoned, smiled or made some moan.

'"Lo, all these trophies of affections hot,
Of pensived and subdued desires the tender,
Nature hath charged me that I hoard them not,   220
But yield them up where I myself must render—
That is to you, my origin and ender;
For these of force must your oblations be,
Since I their altar, you enpatron me.

'"O then advance of yours that phraseless hand   225
Whose white weighs down the airy scale of praise.
Take all these similes to your own command,
Hallowed with sighs that burning lungs did raise.
What me, your minister for you, obeys,
Works under you, and to your audit comes   230
Their distract parcels in combinèd sums.

'"Lo, this device was sent me from a nun,
A sister sanctified of holiest note,
Which late her noble suit in court did shun,
Whose rarest havings made the blossoms dote;   235
For she was sought by spirits of richest coat,
But kept cold distance, and did thence remove
To spend her living in eternal love.

'"But O, my sweet, what labour is't to leave
The thing we have not, mast'ring what not strives,   240
Planing the place which did no form receive,
Playing patient sports in unconstrainèd gyves!
She that her fame so to herself contrives
The scars of battle scapeth by the flight,
And makes her absence valiant, not her might.   245

'"O, pardon me, in that my boast is true!
The accident which brought me to her eye
Upon the moment did her force subdue,
And now she would the cagèd cloister fly.
Religious love put out religion's eye.   250
Not to be tempted would she be immured,
And now, to tempt, all liberty procured.

'"How mighty then you are, O hear me tell!
The broken bosoms that to me belong
Have emptied all their fountains in my well,   255
And mine I pour your ocean all among.
I strong o'er them, and you o'er me being strong,
Must for your victory us all congest,
As compound love to physic your cold breast.

'"My parts had power to charm a sacred nun,   260
Who disciplined, ay dieted in grace,
Believed her eyes when they t' assail begun,
All vows and consecrations giving place.
O most potential love: vow, bond, nor space
In thee hath neither sting, knot, nor confine,   265
For thou art all, and all things else are thine.

'"When thou impressest, what are precepts worth
Of stale example? When thou wilt inflame,
How coldly those impediments stand forth
Of wealth, of filial fear, law, kindred, fame.   270
Love's arms are peace, 'gainst rule, 'gainst sense,
              'gainst shame;
And sweetens in the suff'ring pangs it bears
The aloes of all forces, shocks, and fears.

'"Now all these hearts that do on mine depend,
Feeling it break, with bleeding groans they pine,   275
And supplicant their sighs to you extend
To leave the batt'ry that you make 'gainst mine,
Lending soft audience to my sweet design,
And credent soul to that strong-bonded oath
That shall prefer and undertake my troth."   280

'This said, his wat'ry eyes he did dismount,
Whose sights till then were levelled on my face.
Each cheek a river running from a fount
With brinish current downward flowed apace.
O, how the channel to the stream gave grace,   285
Who glazed with crystal gate the glowing roses
That flame through water which their hue encloses.

'O father, what a hell of witchcraft lies
In the small orb of one particular tear!
But with the inundation of the eyes   290
What rocky heart to water will not wear?
What breast so cold that is not warmèd here?
O cleft effect! Cold modesty, hot wrath,
Both fire from hence and chill extincture hath.

'For lo, his passion, but an art of craft,   295
Even there resolved my reason into tears.
There my white stole of chastity I daffed,
Shook off my sober guards and civil fears;
Appear to him as he to me appears,
All melting, though our drops this diff'rence bore: 300
His poisoned me, and mine did him restore.

'In him a plenitude of subtle matter,
Applied to cautels, all strange forms receives,
Of burning blushes or of weeping water,
Or swooning paleness; and he takes and leaves,   305
In either's aptness, as it best deceives,
To blush at speeches rank, to weep at woes,
Or to turn white and swoon at tragic shows,

'That not a heart which in his level came
Could scape the hail of his all-hurting aim,   310
Showing fair nature is both kind and tame,
And, veiled in them, did win whom he would maim.
Against the thing he sought he would exclaim;
When he most burned in heart-wished luxury,
He preached pure maid and praised cold chastity.   315

'Thus merely with the garment of a grace
The naked and concealèd fiend he covered,
That th'unexperient gave the tempter place,
Which like a cherubin above them hovered.
Who, young and simple, would not be so lovered?   320
Ay me, I fell, and yet do question make
What I should do again for such a sake.

'O that infected moisture of his eye,
O that false fire which in his cheek so glowed,
O that forced thunder from his heart did fly,   325
O that sad breath his spongy lungs bestowed,
O all that borrowed motion seeming owed
Would yet again betray the fore-betrayed,
And new pervert a reconcilèd maid.'

ALTERNATIVE VERSIONS OF SONNETS 2, 106, 138, AND 144

Each of the four sonnets printed below exists in an alternative version. To the left, we give the text as it appeared in the volume of Shakespeare's sonnets printed in 1609. 'Spes Altera' and 'On his Mistress' Beauty' derive from seventeenth-century manuscripts. The alternative versions of Sonnets 138 and 144 are from *The Passionate Pilgrim* (1599).

2

When forty winters shall besiege thy brow
And dig deep trenches in thy beauty's field,
Thy youth's proud livery, so gazed on now,
Will be a tattered weed, of small worth held.
Then being asked where all thy beauty lies,   5
Where all the treasure of thy lusty days,
To say within thine own deep-sunken eyes
Were an all-eating shame and thriftless praise.
How much more praise deserved thy beauty's use
If thou couldst answer 'This fair child of mine   10
Shall sum my count, and make my old excuse',
Proving his beauty by succession thine.
   This were to be new made when thou art old,
   And see thy blood warm when thou feel'st it cold.

Spes Altera

When forty winters shall besiege thy brow
And trench deep furrows in that lovely field,
Thy youth's fair liv'ry, so accounted now,
Shall be like rotten weeds of no worth held.
Then being asked where all thy beauty lies,   5
Where all the lustre of thy youthful days,
To say 'Within these hollow sunken eyes'
Were an all-eaten truth and worthless praise.
O how much better were thy beauty's use   10
If thou couldst say 'This pretty child of mine
Saves my account and makes my old excuse',
Making his beauty by succession thine.
   This were to be new born when thou art old,
   And see thy blood warm when thou feel'st it cold.

106

When in the chronicle of wasted time
I see descriptions of the fairest wights,
And beauty making beautiful old rhyme
In praise of ladies dead and lovely knights;
Then in the blazon of sweet beauty's best,   5
Of hand, of foot, of lip, of eye, of brow,
I see their antique pen would have expressed
Even such a beauty as you master now.
So all their praises are but prophecies
Of this our time, all you prefiguring,   10
And for they looked but with divining eyes
They had not skill enough your worth to sing;
   For we which now behold these present days
   Have eyes to wonder, but lack tongues to praise.

On his Mistress' Beauty

When in the annals of all-wasting time
I see descriptions of the fairest wights,
And beauty making beautiful old rhyme
In praise of ladies dead and lovely knights,
Then in the blazon of sweet beauty's best,   5
Of face, of hand, of lip, of eye, or brow,
I see their antique pen would have expressed
E'en such a beauty as you master now.
So all their praises were but prophecies
Of these our days, all you prefiguring,   10
And for they saw but with divining eyes
They had not skill enough your worth to sing;
   For we which now behold these present days
   Have eyes to wonder, but no tongues to praise.

138

When my love swears that she is made of truth
I do believe her though I know she lies,
That she might think me some untutored youth
Unlearnèd in the world's false subtleties.
Thus vainly thinking that she thinks me young,   5
Although she knows my days are past the best,
Simply I credit her false-speaking tongue;
On both sides thus is simple truth suppressed.
But wherefore says she not she is unjust,
And wherefore say not I that I am old?   10
O, love's best habit is in seeming trust,
And age in love loves not to have years told.
   Therefore I lie with her, and she with me,
   And in our faults by lies we flattered be.

When my love swears that she is made of truth
I do believe her though I know she lies,
That she might think me some untutored youth
Unskilful in the world's false forgeries.
Thus vainly thinking that she thinks me young,   5
Although I know my years be past the best,
I, smiling, credit her false-speaking tongue,
Outfacing faults in love with love's ill rest.
But wherefore says my love that she is young,
And wherefore say not I that I am old?   10
O, love's best habit's in a soothing tongue,
And age in love loves not to have years told.
   Therefore I'll lie with love, and love with me,
   Since that our faults in love thus smothered be.

144

Two loves I have, of comfort and despair,
Which like two spirits do suggest me still.
The better angel is a man right fair,
The worser spirit a woman coloured ill.
To win me soon to hell my female evil   5
Tempteth my better angel from my side,
And would corrupt my saint to be a devil,
Wooing his purity with her foul pride;
And whether that my angel be turned fiend
Suspect I may, yet not directly tell;   10
But being both from me, both to each friend,
I guess one angel in another's hell.
   Yet this shall I ne'er know, but live in doubt
   Till my bad angel fire my good one out.

Two loves I have, of comfort and despair,
That like two spirits do suggest me still.
My better angel is a man right fair,
My worser spirit a woman coloured ill.
To win me soon to hell my female evil   5
Tempteth my better angel from my side,
And would corrupt my saint to be a devil,
Wooing his purity with her fair pride;
And whether that my angel be turned fiend,
Suspect I may, yet not directly tell;   10
For being both to me, both to each friend,
I guess one angel in another's hell.
   The truth I shall not know, but live in doubt
   Till my bad angel fire my good one out.

VARIOUS POEMS

A POET like Shakespeare may frequently have been asked to write verses for a variety of occasions, and it is entirely possible that he is the author of song lyrics and other short poems published without attribution or attributed only to 'W.S.' The poems in this section (arranged in an approximate chronological order) were all explicitly ascribed to him either in his lifetime or not long afterwards. Because they are short it is impossible to be sure, on stylistic grounds alone, of Shakespeare's authorship; but none of the poems is ever attributed to anyone else.

'Shall I die?' is transcribed, with Shakespeare's name appended, in a manuscript collection of poems, dating probably from the late 1630s, which is now in the Bodleian Library, Oxford; another, unascribed version is in the Beinecke Library, Yale University. The poem exhibits many parallels with plays and poems that Shakespeare wrote about 1593-5. Its stanza form has not been found elsewhere in the period, but most closely resembles Robin Goodfellow's lines spoken over the sleeping Lysander (*A Midsummer Night's Dream*, 3.3.36-46). Extended over nine stanzas it becomes a virtuoso exercise: every third word rhymes. The strain shows in a number of ellipses, but there is no strong reason to doubt the ascription: the Oxford manuscript is generally reliable, and if the poem is of no great consequence, that might explain why it did not reach print.

Perhaps the most trivial verse ever ascribed to a great poet is the 'posy' said to have accompanied a pair of gloves given by a Stratford schoolmaster, Alexander Aspinall, to his second wife, whom he married in 1594. The ascription is found in a manuscript compiled by Sir Francis Fane of Bulbeck (1611-80).

In 1599 William Jaggard published a collection of poems, which he ascribed to Shakespeare, under the title *The Passionate Pilgrim*. It includes versions of two of Shakespeare's Sonnets (which we print as Alternative Versions), three extracts from *Love's Labour's Lost*, which had already appeared in print, several poems known to be by other poets, and eleven poems of unknown authorship. A reprint of 1612 added nine poems by Thomas Heywood, who promptly protested against the 'manifest injury' done to him by printing his poems 'in a less volume, under the name of another, which may put the world in opinion I might steal them from him . . . But as I must acknowledge my lines not worthy his patronage under whom he hath published them, so the author I know much offended with Master Jaggard that, altogether unknown to him, presumed to make so bold with his name.' Probably as a result, the original title-page of the 1612 edition was replaced with one that did not mention Shakespeare's name. We print below the poems of unknown authorship since the attribution to Shakespeare has not been disproved.

The finest poem in this section, 'The Phoenix and Turtle', was ascribed to Shakespeare in 1601 when it appeared, without title, as one of the 'Poetical Essays' appended to Robert Chester's *Love's Martyr: or Rosalind's Complaint*, which is described as 'allegorically shadowing the truth of love in the constant fate of the phoenix and turtle'. Chester's poem appears to have been composed as a compliment to Sir John and Lady Salusbury, his patron. We know of no link between Shakespeare and the Salusbury family; possibly his poem was not written specifically for the volume in which it appeared. Since the early nineteenth century it has been known as 'The Phoenix and the Turtle' or (following the title-page) 'The Phoenix and Turtle'. An incantatory elegy, it may well have irrecoverable allegorical significance.

It is not clear whether the two stanzas engraved at opposite ends of the Stanley tomb in the parish church of Tong, in Shropshire, constitute one epitaph or two, or which member (or members) of the family they commemorate. They are ascribed to Shakespeare in two manuscript miscellanies of the 1630s and by the antiquary Sir William Dugdale in a manuscript appended to his Visitation of Shropshire in 1664. Shakespeare had professional connections with the Stanleys early in his career: *Titus Andronicus* and *1 Henry VI* were performed by a theatrical company patronized by the family.

The satirical completion of an epitaph on Ben Jonson (written during his lifetime) is ascribed to Shakespeare in two different seventeenth-century manuscripts.

Shakespeare probably knew Elias James (*c*.1578–1610), who managed a brewery in the Blackfriars district of London. His epitaph is ascribed to Shakespeare in the same Oxford manuscript as 'Shall I die?'

The Combe family of Stratford-upon-Avon were friends of Shakespeare. He bequeathed his sword to one of them, and John Combe, who died in 1614, left Shakespeare £5. Several mock epitaphs similar to the first epitaph on John Combe have survived, one (on an unnamed usurer) printed as early as 1608; later versions mention three other men as the usurer. Shakespeare may have adapted some existing lines; or some existing lines may have been adapted anonymously in Stratford, and later attributed to Stratford's most famous poet. The ascription to him dates from 1634, and is supported by four other seventeenth-century manuscripts. The second Combe epitaph is found in only one manuscript; it seems entirely original, and alludes to a bequest to the poor made in Combe's will.

The lines on King James first appear, unattributed, beneath an engraving of the King printed as the frontispiece to the 1616 edition of his works. They are attributed to Shakespeare—the leading writer of the theatre company of which King James was patron—in at least two seventeenth-century manuscripts; the same attribution was recorded in a printed broadside now apparently lost.

Shakespeare's own epitaph is written in the first person; the tradition that he composed it himself is recorded in several manuscripts from the middle to the late seventeenth century.

Various Poems

A Song

1

Shall I die? Shall I fly
Lovers' baits and deceits,
  sorrow breeding?
Shall I tend? Shall I send?
Shall I sue, and not rue   5
  my proceeding?
In all duty her beauty
Binds me her servant for ever.
  If she scorn, I mourn,
I retire to despair, joining never.   10

2

Yet I must vent my lust
And explain inward pain
  by my love conceiving.
If she smiles, she exiles
All my moan; if she frown,   15
  all my hopes deceiving—
Suspicious doubt, O keep out,
For thou art my tormentor.
  Fie away, pack away;
I will love, for hope bids me venture.   20

3

'Twere abuse to accuse
My fair love, ere I prove
  her affection.
Therefore try! Her reply
Gives thee joy—or annoy,   25
  or affliction.
Yet howe'er, I will bear
Her pleasure with patience, for beauty
  Sure will not seem to blot
Her deserts, wronging him doth her duty.   30

4

In a dream it did seem—
But alas, dreams do pass
  as do shadows—
I did walk, I did talk
With my love, with my dove,   35
  through fair meadows.
Still we passed till at last
We sat to repose us for pleasure.
  Being set, lips met,
Arms twined, and did bind my heart's treasure.   40

5

Gentle wind sport did find
Wantonly to make fly
  her gold tresses.

As they shook I did look,
But her fair did impair   45
  all my senses.
As amazed, I gazed
On more than a mortal complexion.
  You that love can prove
Such force in beauty's inflection.   50

6

Next her hair, forehead fair,
Smooth and high; neat doth lie,
  without wrinkle,
Her fair brows; under those,
Star-like eyes win love's prize   55
  when they twinkle.
In her cheeks who seeks
Shall find there displayed beauty's banner;
  O admiring desiring
Breeds, as I look still upon her.   60

7

Thin lips red, fancy's fed
With all sweets when he meets,
  and is granted
There to trade, and is made
Happy, sure, to endure   65
  still undaunted.
Pretty chin doth win
Of all their culled commendations;
  Fairest neck, no speck;
All her parts merit high admirations.   70

8

Pretty bare, past compare,
Parts those plots which besots
  still asunder.
It is meet naught but sweet
Should come near that so rare   75
  'tis a wonder.
No mis-shape, no scape
Inferior to nature's perfection;
  No blot, no spot:
She's beauty's queen in election.   80

9

Whilst I dreamt, I, exempt
From all care, seemed to share
  pleasure's plenty;
But awake, care take—
For I find to my mind   85
  pleasures scanty.
Therefore I will try
To compass my heart's chief contenting.
  To delay, some say,
In such a case causeth repenting.   90

405

'Upon a pair of gloves that master sent to his
mistress'

The gift is small,
The will is all:
Alexander Aspinall

———

Poems from *The Passionate Pilgrim*

4

Sweet Cytherea, sitting by a brook
With young Adonis, lovely, fresh, and green,
Did court the lad with many a lovely look,
Such looks as none could look but beauty's queen.
She told him stories to delight his ear,   5
She showed him favours to allure his eye;
To win his heart she touched him here and there—
Touches so soft still conquer chastity.
But whether unripe years did want conceit,
Or he refused to take her figured proffer,   10
The tender nibbler would not touch the bait,
But smile and jest at every gentle offer.
     Then fell she on her back, fair queen and toward:
     He rose and ran away—ah, fool too froward!

6

Scarce had the sun dried up the dewy morn,
And scarce the herd gone to the hedge for shade,
When Cytherea, all in love forlorn,
A longing tarriance for Adonis made
Under an osier growing by a brook,   5
A brook where Adon used to cool his spleen.
Hot was the day, she hotter, that did look
For his approach that often there had been.
Anon he comes and throws his mantle by,
And stood stark naked on the brook's green brim.   10
The sun looked on the world with glorious eye,
Yet not so wistly as this queen on him.
     He, spying her, bounced in whereas he stood.
     'O Jove,' quoth she, 'why was not I a flood?'

7

Fair is my love, but not so fair as fickle,
Mild as a dove, but neither true nor trusty,
Brighter than glass, and yet, as glass is, brittle;
Softer than wax, and yet as iron rusty;
     A lily pale, with damask dye to grace her,   5
     None fairer, nor none falser to deface her.

Her lips to mine how often hath she joined,
Between each kiss her oaths of true love swearing.
How many tales to please me hath she coined,
Dreading my love, the loss whereof still fearing.   10
     Yet in the midst of all her pure protestings
     Her faith, her oaths, her tears, and all were jestings.

She burnt with love as straw with fire flameth,
She burnt out love as soon as straw out burneth,
She framed the love, and yet she foiled the framing,   15
She bade love last, and yet she fell a-turning.
     Was this a lover or a lecher whether,
     Bad in the best, though excellent in neither?

9

Fair was the morn when the fair queen of love,
⌈   ⌉
Paler for sorrow than her milk-white dove,
For Adon's sake, a youngster proud and wild,
Her stand she takes upon a steep-up hill.   5
Anon Adonis comes with horn and hounds.
She, seely queen, with more than love's good will
Forbade the boy he should not pass those grounds.
'Once,' quoth she, 'did I see a fair sweet youth
Here in these brakes deep-wounded with a boar,   10
Deep in the thigh, a spectacle of ruth.
See in my thigh,' quoth she, 'here was the sore.'
     She showèd hers; he saw more wounds than one,
     And blushing fled, and left her all alone.

10

Sweet rose, fair flower, untimely plucked, soon faded—
Plucked in the bud and faded in the spring;
Bright orient pearl, alack, too timely shaded;
Fair creature, killed too soon by death's sharp sting,
     Like a green plum that hangs upon a tree   5
     And falls through wind before the fall should be.

I weep for thee, and yet no cause I have,
For why: thou left'st me nothing in thy will,
And yet thou left'st me more than I did crave,
For why: I cravèd nothing of thee still.   10
     O yes, dear friend, I pardon crave of thee:
     Thy discontent thou didst bequeath to me.

12

Crabbèd age and youth cannot live together:
Youth is full of pleasance, age is full of care;
Youth like summer morn, age like winter weather;
Youth like summer brave, age like winter bare.
Youth is full of sport, age's breath is short.   5
Youth is nimble, age is lame,
Youth is hot and bold, age is weak and cold.
Youth is wild and age is tame.
     Age, I do abhor thee; youth, I do adore thee.
     O my love, my love is young.   10
     Age, I do defy thee. O sweet shepherd, hie thee,
     For methinks thou stay'st too long.

13

Beauty is but a vain and doubtful good,
A shining gloss that fadeth suddenly,
A flower that dies when first it 'gins to bud,
A brittle glass that's broken presently.
     A doubtful good, a gloss, a glass, a flower,   5
     Lost, faded, broken, dead within an hour.

And as goods lost are seld or never found,
As faded gloss no rubbing will refresh,
As flowers dead lie withered on the ground,
As broken glass no cement can redress,　10
　So beauty blemished once, for ever lost,
　In spite of physic, painting, pain, and cost.

14

Good night, good rest—ah, neither be my share.
She bade good night that kept my rest away,
And daffed me to a cabin hanged with care
To descant on the doubts of my decay.
　'Farewell,' quoth she, 'and come again tomorrow.'　5
　Fare well I could not, for I supped with sorrow.

Yet at my parting sweetly did she smile,
In scorn or friendship nill I conster whether.
'Tmay be she joyed to jest at my exile,
'Tmay be, again to make me wander thither.　10
　'Wander'—a word for shadows like myself,
　As take the pain but cannot pluck the pelf.

Lord, how mine eyes throw gazes to the east!
My heart doth charge the watch, the morning rise
Doth cite each moving sense from idle rest,　15
Not daring trust the office of mine eyes.
　While Philomela sings I sit and mark,
　And wish her lays were tunèd like the lark.

For she doth welcome daylight with her dite,
And daylight drives away dark dreaming night.　20
The night so packed, I post unto my pretty;
Heart hath his hope, and eyes their wishèd sight,
　Sorrow changed to solace, and solace mixed with
　　sorrow,
　Forwhy she sighed and bade me come tomorrow.

Were I with her, the night would post too soon,　25
But now are minutes added to the hours.
To spite me now each minute seems a moon,
Yet not for me, shine sun to succour flowers!
　Pack night, peep day; good day, of night now borrow;
　Short night tonight, and length thyself tomorrow.　30

Sonnets

to Sundry Notes of Music

15

It was a lording's daughter, the fairest one of three,
That likèd of her master as well as well might be,
Till looking on an Englishman, the fairest that eye could
　see,
　Her fancy fell a-turning.

Long was the combat doubtful that love with love did　5
　fight:
To leave the master loveless, or kill the gallant knight.
To put in practice either, alas, it was a spite
　Unto the seely damsel.

But one must be refusèd, more mickle was the pain
That nothing could be usèd to turn them both to gain.　10
For of the two the trusty knight was wounded with
　disdain—
　Alas, she could not help it.

Thus art with arms contending was victor of the day,
Which by a gift of learning did bear the maid away.
Then lullaby, the learned man hath got the lady gay;　15
　For now my song is ended.

17

My flocks feed not, my ewes breed not,
　My rams speed not, all is amiss.
Love is dying, faith's defying,
　Heart's denying causer of this.
All my merry jigs are quite forgot,　5
All my lady's love is lost, God wot.
Where her faith was firmly fixed in love,
There a nay is placed without remove.
　One seely cross wrought all my loss—
　O frowning fortune, cursèd fickle dame!　10
　For now I see inconstancy
　More in women than in men remain.

In black mourn I, all fears scorn I,
　Love hath forlorn me, living in thrall.
Heart is bleeding, all help needing—　15
　O cruel speeding, freighted with gall.
My shepherd's pipe can sound no deal,
My wether's bell rings doleful knell,
My curtal dog that wont to have played
Plays not at all, but seems afraid,　20
　With sighs so deep procures to weep
　In howling wise to see my doleful plight.
　How sighs resound through heartless ground,
　Like a thousand vanquished men in bloody fight!

Clear wells spring not, sweet birds sing not,　25
　Green plants bring not forth their dye.
Herd stands weeping, flocks all sleeping,
　Nymphs back peeping fearfully.
All our pleasure known to us poor swains,
All our merry meetings on the plains,　30
All our evening sport from us is fled,
All our love is lost, for love is dead.
　Farewell, sweet lass, thy like ne'er was
　For a sweet content, the cause of all my moan.
　Poor Corydon must live alone,　35
　Other help for him I see that there is none.

18

Whenas thine eye hath chose the dame
And stalled the deer that thou shouldst strike,
Let reason rule things worthy blame
As well as fancy, partial might.
　Take counsel of some wiser head,　5
　Neither too young nor yet unwed,

And when thou com'st thy tale to tell,
Smooth not thy tongue with filèd talk
Lest she some subtle practice smell:
A cripple soon can find a halt.   10
  But plainly say thou lov'st her well,
  And set her person forth to sale,

And to her will frame all thy ways.
Spare not to spend, and chiefly there
Where thy desert may merit praise   15
By ringing in thy lady's ear.
  The strongest castle, tower, and town,
  The golden bullet beats it down.

Serve always with assurèd trust,
And in thy suit be humble-true;   20
Unless thy lady prove unjust,
Press never thou to choose anew.
  When time shall serve, be thou not slack
  To proffer, though she put thee back.

What though her frowning brows be bent,   25
Her cloudy looks will calm ere night,
And then too late she will repent
That thus dissembled her delight,
  And twice desire, ere it be day,
  That which with scorn she put away.   30

What though she strive to try her strength,
And ban, and brawl, and say thee nay,
Her feeble force will yield at length
When craft hath taught her thus to say:
  'Had women been so strong as men,   35
  In faith you had not had it then.'

The wiles and guiles that women work,
Dissembled with an outward show,
The tricks and toys that in them lurk
The cock that treads them shall not know.   40
  Have you not heard it said full oft
  A woman's nay doth stand for nought?

Think women still to strive with men,
To sin and never for to saint.
There is no heaven; be holy then   45
When time with age shall them attaint.
  Were kisses all the joys in bed,
  One woman would another wed.

But soft, enough—too much, I fear,
Lest that my mistress hear my song   50
She will not stick to round me on th'ear
To teach my tongue to be so long.
  Yet will she blush (here be it said)
  To hear her secrets so bewrayed.

The Phoenix and Turtle

Let the bird of loudest lay
On the sole Arabian tree
Herald sad and trumpet be,
To whose sound chaste wings obey.

But thou shrieking harbinger,   5
Foul precurrer of the fiend,
Augur of the fever's end—
To this troupe come thou not near.

From this session interdict
Every fowl of tyrant wing   10
Save the eagle, feathered king.
Keep the obsequy so strict.

Let the priest in surplice white
That defunctive music can,
Be the death-divining swan,   15
Lest the requiem lack his right.

And thou treble-dated crow,
That thy sable gender mak'st
With the breath thou giv'st and tak'st,
'Mongst our mourners shalt thou go.   20

Here the anthem doth commence:
Love and constancy is dead,
Phoenix and the turtle fled
In a mutual flame from hence.

So they loved as love in twain   25
Had the essence but in 'one,
Two distincts, division none.
Number there in love was slain.

Hearts remote yet not asunder,
Distance and no space was seen   30
'Twixt this turtle and his queen.
But in them it were a wonder.

So between them love did shine
That the turtle saw his right
Flaming in the Phoenix' sight.   35
Either was the other's mine.

Property was thus appalled
That the self was not the same.
Single nature's double name
Neither two nor one was called.   40

Reason, in itself confounded,
Saw division grow together
To themselves, yet either neither,
Simple were so well compounded

That it cried 'How true a twain   45
Seemeth this concordant one!
Love hath reason, reason none,
If what parts can so remain.'

Whereupon it made this threne
To the phoenix and the dove,
Co-supremes and stars of love,
As chorus to their tragic scene.

Threnos

Beauty, truth, and rarity,
Grace in all simplicity,
Here enclosed in cinders lie.

Death is now the phoenix' nest,
And the turtle's loyal breast
To eternity doth rest.

Leaving no posterity
'Twas not their infirmity,
It was married chastity.

Truth may seem but cannot be,
Beauty brag, but 'tis not she.
Truth and beauty buried be.

To this urn let those repair
That are either true or fair.
For these dead birds sigh a prayer.

50

55

60

65

he gives it to Master Shakespeare to make up who
presently writes:

Who while he lived was a slow thing,
And now, being dead, is nothing.

50

———

An Epitaph on Elias James

When God was pleased, the world unwilling yet,
Elias James to nature paid his debt,
And here reposeth. As he lived, he died,
The saying strongly in him verified:
'Such life, such death'. Then, a known truth to tell,   5
He lived a godly life, and died as well.

———

An extemporary epitaph on John Combe, a noted usurer

Ten in the hundred here lies engraved;
A hundred to ten his soul is not saved.
If anyone ask who lies in this tomb,
'O ho!' quoth the devil, ''tis my John-a-Combe.'

———

Verses upon the Stanley Tomb at Tong

Written upon the east end of the tomb

Ask who lies here, but do not weep.
He is not dead; he doth but sleep.
This stony register is for his bones;
His fame is more perpetual than these stones,
And his own goodness, with himself being gone,   5
Shall live when earthly monument is none.

Written upon the west end thereof

Not monumental stone preserves our fame,
Nor sky-aspiring pyramids our name.
The memory of him for whom this stands
Shall outlive marble and defacers' hands.
When all to time's consumption shall be given,   5
Stanley for whom this stands shall stand in heaven.

———

On Ben Jonson

Master Ben Jonson and Master William Shakespeare being
merry at a tavern, Master Jonson having begun this for
his epitaph:

Here lies Ben Jonson
That was once one,

Another Epitaph on John Combe

He being dead, and making the poor his heirs, William
Shakespeare after writes this for his epitaph:

Howe'er he livèd judge not,
John Combe shall never be forgot
While poor hath memory, for he did gather
To make the poor his issue; he, their father,
As record of his tilth and seed   5
Did crown him in his latter deed.

———

Upon the King

At the foot of the effigy of King James I, before his Works
(1616)

Crowns have their compass; length of days, their date;
Triumphs, their tombs; felicity, her fate.
Of more than earth can earth make none partaker,
But knowledge makes the king most like his maker.

———

Epitaph on Himself

Good friend, for Jesus' sake forbear
To dig the dust enclosèd here.
Blessed be the man that spares these stones,
And cursed be he that moves my bones.

SIR THOMAS MORE

PASSAGES ATTRIBUTED TO SHAKESPEARE

IN the British Library is a manuscript play described on its first leaf as 'The Booke'—
that is, the theatre manuscript—'of Sir Thomas Moore'. It is a heavily revised text with
contributions in six different hands as well as annotations by the Master of the Revels. The
basic manuscript appears to have been a fair copy by the dramatist Anthony Munday of a
play that he wrote in collaboration with Henry Chettle and, perhaps, another writer.
Alterations and additions were made by Chettle, Thomas Dekker, possibly Thomas
Heywood, and the author of the pages in Addition II ascribed to 'Hand D', whom many
scholars believe to be William Shakespeare.

The theory that Shakespeare was a contributor, first mooted in 1871, has led to intensive
study of the manuscript. Our view is that the original play, dating from the early 1590s,
was submitted in the normal way to the Master of the Revels, Sir Edmund Tilney, for a
licence. But Tilney, disturbed by the play's political implications, called for substantial
revisions which, if they had been carried out, would have required that about half the play
be scrapped.

What happened next is not clear. The alterations and additions to the basic play do not
meet Tilney's objections. Perhaps they had been made before the play was submitted for a
licence. More probably (in our view) the original play was laid aside after Tilney had
objected to it, and taken up again soon after Queen Elizabeth's death, in 1603, when the
political objections would no longer be felt.

Sir Thomas More, based mainly on Holinshed's *Chronicles* and on William Roper's manuscript *Life of More*, is an episodic treatment of its hero's rise and fall, ending with his death
on the scaffold. The principal episode attributed to Shakespeare comes towards the end of
the scenes early in the play portraying events leading up to the riots of Londoners against
resident foreigners on the 'ill May Day' of 1517. The leaders are John Lincoln, Williamson
and his wife Doll, George and Ralph Betts, and Sherwin. Outraged by the illegal activities
of foreign groups in London, they have planned that 'on May Day next in the morning
we'll go forth a-maying, but make it the worst May Day for the strangers'—i.e. foreigners—
'that ever they saw'. The authorities, dismayed by the violence, have sent More as a
peacemaker. Shakespeare—if indeed he wrote the scene—seems not to have known the
rest of the play; he was probably revising an original scene, now lost, with no other
sources. The ascription of this scene to Shakespeare is based partly on comparison between
the few surviving specimens of Shakespeare's handwriting (almost entirely in signatures)
with that of Hand D; partly on spelling links with printed texts apparently deriving directly
from Shakespeare's own papers; and partly on considerations of style and imagery.

Also attributed to Shakespeare is a soliloquy by More apparently intended to show his
state of mind after having been appointed Lord Chancellor. It is written in the hand of a
professional scribe (Addition III).

Sir Thomas More

Add.II.D *John Lincoln (a broker), Doll, Betts, ⌈Sherwin (a goldsmith),⌉ and prentices armed; ⌈Thomas More (sheriff of the City of London), the other sheriff, Sir Thomas Palmer, Sir Roger Cholmeley, and a serjeant-at-arms stand aloof⌉*

LINCOLN (*to the prentices*) Peace, hear me! He that will not see a red herring at a Harry groat, butter at eleven pence a pound, meal at nine shillings a bushel, and beef at four nobles a stone, list to me.

OTHER It will come to that pass if strangers be suffered. Mark him. 6

LINCOLN Our country is a great eating country; argo, they eat more in our country than they do in their own.

OTHER By a halfpenny loaf a day, troy weight. 10

LINCOLN They bring in strange roots, which is merely to the undoing of poor prentices, for what's a sorry parsnip to a good heart?

OTHER Trash, trash. They breed sore eyes, and 'tis enough to infect the city with the palsy. 15

LINCOLN Nay, it has infected it with the palsy, for these bastards of dung—as you know, they grow in dung—have infected us, and it is our infection will make the city shake, which partly comes through the eating of parsnips. 20

OTHER True, and pumpions together.

SERJEANT ⌈*coming forward*⌉

What say you to the mercy of the King? Do you refuse it?

LINCOLN You would have us upon th'hip, would you? No, marry, do we not. We accept of the King's mercy; but we will show no mercy upon the strangers. 26

SERJEANT You are the simplest things That ever stood in such a question.

LINCOLN How say you now? Prentices 'simple'? (*To the prentices*) Down with him! 30

ALL Prentices simple! Prentices simple!

Enter the Lord Mayor, the Earl of Surrey, and the Earl of Shrewsbury

⌈SHERIFF⌉ (*to the prentices*)

Hold in the King's name! Hold!

SURREY (*to the prentices*) Friends, masters, countrymen—

MAYOR (*to the prentices*)

Peace ho, peace! I charge you, keep the peace!

SHREWSBURY (*to the prentices*) My masters, countrymen—

⌈SHERWIN⌉ The noble Earl of Shrewsbury, let's hear him.

BETTS We'll hear the Earl of Surrey. 36

LINCOLN The Earl of Shrewsbury.

BETTS We'll hear both.

ALL Both, both, both, both!

LINCOLN Peace, I say peace! Are you men of wisdom, or what are you? 41

SURREY

What you will have them, but not men of wisdom.

⌈SOME⌉ We'll not hear my Lord of Surrey.

⌈OTHERS⌉ No, no, no, no, no! Shrewsbury, Shrewsbury!

MORE (*to the nobles and officers*)

Whiles they are o'er the bank of their obedience, 45 Thus will they bear down all things.

LINCOLN (*to the prentices*) Sheriff More speaks. Shall we hear Sheriff More speak?

DOLL Let's hear him. A keeps a plentiful shrievaltry, and a made my brother Arthur Watchins Sergeant Safe's yeoman. Let's hear Sheriff More. 51

ALL Sheriff More, More, More, Sheriff More!

MORE

Even by the rule you have among yourselves, Command still audience.

SOME Surrey, Surrey! 55

OTHERS More, More!

LINCOLN *and* BETTS Peace, peace, silence, peace!

MORE

You that have voice and credit with the number, Command them to a stillness.

LINCOLN A plague on them! They will not hold their peace. The devil cannot rule them. 61

MORE

Then what a rough and riotous charge have you, To lead those that the devil cannot rule.

(*To the prentices*) Good masters, hear me speak. 64

DOLL Ay, by th' mass, will we. More, thou'rt a good housekeeper, and I thank thy good worship for my brother Arthur Watchins.

ALL Peace, peace!

MORE

Look, what you do offend you cry upon, That is the peace. Not one of you here present, 70 Had there such fellows lived when you were babes That could have topped the peace as now you would, The peace wherein you have till now grown up Had been ta'en from you, and the bloody times Could not have brought you to the state of men. 75 Alas, poor things, what is it you have got, Although we grant you get the thing you seek?

BETTS Marry, the removing of the strangers, which cannot choose but much advantage the poor handicrafts of the city. 80

MORE

Grant them removed, and grant that this your noise Hath chid down all the majesty of England. Imagine that you see the wretched strangers, Their babies at their backs, with their poor luggage Plodding to th' ports and coasts for transportation, 85 And that you sit as kings in your desires,

Authority quite silenced by your brawl
And you in ruff of your opinions clothed:
What had you got? I'll tell you. You had taught
How insolence and strong hand should prevail,   90
How order should be quelled—and by this pattern
Not one of you should live an agèd man,
For other ruffians as their fancies wrought
With selfsame hand, self reasons, and self right
Would shark on you, and men like ravenous fishes   95
Would feed on one another.

DOLL   Before God, that's as true as the gospel.

BETTS   Nay, this' a sound fellow, I tell you. Let's mark
him.

MORE
Let me set up before your thoughts, good friends,   100
One supposition, which if you will mark
You shall perceive how horrible a shape
Your innovation bears. First, 'tis a sin
Which oft th'apostle did forewarn us of,
Urging obedience to authority;   105
And 'twere no error if I told you all
You were in arms 'gainst God.

ALL   Marry, God forbid that!

MORE   Nay, certainly you are.
For to the King God hath his office lent   110
Of dread, of justice, power and command,
Hath bid him rule and willed you to obey;
And to add ampler majesty to this,
He hath not only lent the King his figure,
His throne and sword, but given him his own name,
Calls him a god on earth. What do you then,   116
Rising 'gainst him that God himself installs,
But rise 'gainst God? What do you to your souls
In doing this? O desperate as you are,
Wash your foul minds with tears, and those same
    hands   120
That you like rebels lift against the peace
Lift up for peace; and your unreverent knees,
Make them your feet. To kneel to be forgiven
Is safer wars than ever you can make,
Whose discipline is riot.   125
In, in, to your obedience! Why, even your hurly
Cannot proceed but by obedience.
What rebel captain,
As mut'nies are incident, by his name
Can still the rout? Who will obey a traitor?   130
Or how can well that proclamation sound,
When there is no addition but 'a rebel'
To qualify a rebel? You'll put down strangers,
Kill them, cut their throats, possess their houses,
And lead the majesty of law in lyam   135
To slip him like a hound—alas, alas!
Say now the King,
As he is clement if th'offender mourn,
Should so much come too short of your great trespass

As but to banish you: whither would you go?   140
What country, by the nature of your error,
Should give you harbour? Go you to France or
    Flanders,
To any German province, Spain or Portugal,
Nay, anywhere that not adheres to England—
Why, you must needs be strangers. Would you be
    pleased   145
To find a nation of such barbarous temper
That breaking out in hideous violence
Would not afford you an abode on earth,
Whet their detested knives against your throats,
Spurn you like dogs, and like as if that God   150
Owed not nor made not you, nor that the elements
Were not all appropriate to your comforts
But chartered unto them, what would you think
To be thus used? This is the strangers'. case,
And this your mountainish inhumanity.   155

⌈ONE⌉ (to the others) Faith, a says true. Let's do as we may
be done by.

⌈ANOTHER⌉ (to More) We'll be ruled by you, Master More,
if you'll stand our friend to procure our pardon.

MORE
Submit you to these noble gentlemen,   160
Entreat their mediation to the King,
Give up yourself to form, obey the magistrate,
And there's no doubt but mercy may be found,
If you so seek it.

———

Add.III   *Enter Sir Thomas More*

MORE
It is in heaven that I am thus and thus,
And that which we profanely term our fortunes
Is the provision of the power above,
Fitted and shaped just to that strength of nature
Which we are born withal. Good God, good God,   5
That I from such an humble bench of birth
Should step as 'twere up to my country's head
And give the law out there; ay, in my father's life
To take prerogative and tithe of knees
From elder kinsmen, and him bind by my place   10
To give the smooth and dexter way to me
That owe it him by nature! Sure these things,
Not physicked by respect, might turn our blood
To much corruption. But More, the more thou hast
Either of honour, office, wealth and calling,   15
Which might accite thee to embrace and hug them,
The more do thou e'en serpents' natures think them:
Fear their gay skins, with thought of their sharp
    stings,
And let this be thy maxim: to be great
Is, when the thread of hazard is once spun,   20
A bottom great wound up, greatly undone.

ALL IS TRUE

(HENRY VIII)

BY WILLIAM SHAKESPEARE AND JOHN FLETCHER

ON 29 June 1613 the firing of cannon at the Globe Theatre ignited its thatch and burned it to the ground. According to a letter of 4 July the house was full of spectators who had come to see 'a new play called *All is True*, which had been acted not passing two or three times before'. No one was hurt 'except one man who was scalded with the fire by adventuring in to save a child which otherwise had been burnt'. This establishes the play's date with unusual precision. Though two other accounts of the fire refer to a play 'of'— which may mean simply 'about'—Henry VIII, yet another two unequivocally call it *All is True*; and these words also end the refrain of a ballad about the fire. When the play came to be printed as the last of the English history plays—all named after kings—in the 1623 Folio it was as *The Famous History of the Life of King Henry the Eighth*. We restore the title by which it was known to its first audiences.

No surviving account of the fire says who wrote the play that caused it. In 1850, James Spedding (prompted by Tennyson) suggested that Shakespeare collaborated on it with John Fletcher (1579-1625). We have external evidence that the two dramatists worked together in or around 1613 on the lost *Cardenio* and on *The Two Noble Kinsmen*. For their collaboration in *All is True* the evidence is wholly internal, stemming from the initial perception of two distinct verse styles within the play; later, more rigorous examination of evidence provided by both the play's language and its dramatic technique has convinced most scholars of Fletcher's hand in it. The passages most confidently attributed to Shakespeare are Act 1, Scenes 1 and 2; Act 2, Scenes 3 and 4; Act 3, Scene 2 to line 204; and Act 5, Scene 1.

The historical material derives, often closely, from the chronicles of Raphael Holinshed and Edward Hall, supplemented by John Foxe's *Book of Martyrs* (1563, etc.) for the Cranmer episodes in Act 5. It covers only part of Henry's reign, from the opening description of the Field of the Cloth of Gold, of 1520, to the christening of Princess Elizabeth, in 1533. It depicts the increasing abuse of power by Cardinal Wolsey; the execution, brought about by Wolsey's machinations, of the Duke of Buckingham; the King's abandonment of his Queen, Katherine of Aragon; the rise to the King's favour of Anne Boleyn; Wolsey's disgrace; and the birth to Henry and Anne of a daughter instead of the hoped-for son.

Sir Henry Wotton, writing of the fire, said that the play represented 'some principal pieces of the reign of Henry 8, which was set forth with many extraordinary circumstances of pomp and majesty.' It has continued popular in performance for the opportunities that it affords for spectacle and for the dramatic power of certain episodes such as Buckingham's speeches before execution (2.1), Queen Katherine's defence of the validity of her marriage (2.4), Wolsey's farewell to his greatness (3.2), and Katherine's dying scene (4.2). Though the play depicts a series of falls from greatness, it works towards the birth of the future Elizabeth I, fulsomely celebrated in the last scene (not attributed to Shakespeare) along with her successor, the patron of the King's Men.

THE PERSONS OF THE PLAY

PROLOGUE

KING HENRY the Eighth

Duke of BUCKINGHAM

Lord ABERGAVENNY ⎫
Earl of SURREY ⎬ his sons-in-law
Duke of NORFOLK ⎭

Duke of SUFFOLK

LORD CHAMBERLAIN

LORD CHANCELLOR

Lord SANDS (also called Sir William Sands)

Sir Thomas LOVELL

Sir Anthony DENNY

Sir Henry GUILDFORD

CARDINAL WOLSEY

Two SECRETARIES

Buckingham's SURVEYOR

CARDINAL CAMPEIUS

GARDINER, the King's new secretary, later Bishop of Winchester

His PAGE

Thomas CROMWELL

CRANMER, Archbishop of Canterbury

QUEEN KATHERINE, later KATHERINE, Princess Dowager

GRIFFITH, her gentleman usher

PATIENCE, her waiting-woman

Other WOMEN

Six spirits, who dance before Katherine in a vision

A MESSENGER

Lord CAPUTIUS

ANNE Boleyn

An OLD LADY

BRANDON ⎫ who arrest Buckingham and
SERJEANT-at-arms ⎭ Abergavenny

Sir Nicholas VAUX ⎫
Tipstaves ⎪
Halberdiers ⎬ after Buckingham's arraignment
Common people ⎭

Two vergers ⎫
Two SCRIBES ⎪
Archbishop of Canterbury ⎪
Bishop of LINCOLN ⎪
Bishop of Ely ⎪
Bishop of Rochester ⎬ appearing at the Legatine Court
Bishop of Saint Asaph ⎪
Two priests ⎪
Serjeant-at-arms ⎪
Two noblemen ⎪
A CRIER ⎭

Three GENTLEMEN ⎫
Two judges ⎪
Choristers ⎪
Lord Mayor of London ⎪
Garter King of Arms ⎬ appearing in the Coronation
Marquis Dorset ⎪
Four Barons of the Cinque Ports ⎪
Stokesley, Bishop of London ⎪
Old Duchess of Norfolk ⎪
Countesses ⎭

A DOOR-KEEPER ⎫
Doctor BUTTS, the King's physician ⎬ at Cranmer's trial
Pursuivants, pages, footboys, grooms ⎭

A PORTER ⎫
His MAN ⎪
Two aldermen ⎪
Lord Mayor of London ⎪
GARTER King of Arms ⎬ at the Christening
Six noblemen ⎪
Old Duchess of Norfolk, godmother ⎪
The child, Princess Elizabeth ⎪
Marchioness Dorset, godmother ⎭

EPILOGUE

Ladies, gentlemen, a SERVANT, guards, attendants, trumpeters

All Is True

Prologue *Enter Prologue*

PROLOGUE

I come no more to make you laugh. Things now
That bear a weighty and a serious brow,
Sad, high, and working, full of state and woe—
Such noble scenes as draw the eye to flow
We now present. Those that can pity here   5
May, if they think it well, let fall a tear.
The subject will deserve it. Such as give
Their money out of hope they may believe,
May here find truth, too. Those that come to see
Only a show or two, and so agree   10
The play may pass, if they be still, and willing,
I'll undertake may see away their shilling
Richly in two short hours. Only they
That come to hear a merry bawdy play,
A noise of targets, or to see a fellow   15
In a long motley coat guarded with yellow,
Will be deceived. For, gentle hearers, know
To rank our chosen truth with such a show
As fool and fight is, beside forfeiting
Our own brains, and the opinion that we bring 20
To make that only true we now intend,
Will leave us never an understanding friend.
Therefore, for goodness' sake, and as you are known
The first and happiest hearers of the town,
Be sad as we would make ye. Think ye see   25
The very persons of our noble story
As they were living; think you see them great,
And followed with the general throng and sweat
Of thousand friends; then, in a moment, see
How soon this mightiness meets misery.   30
And if you can be merry then, I'll say
A man may weep upon his wedding day.   *Exit*

1.1 *⌐A cloth of state throughout the play.⌐ Enter the Duke
of Norfolk at one door ; at the other door enter the
Duke of Buckingham and the Lord Abergavenny*

BUCKINGHAM (*to Norfolk*)

Good morrow, and well met. How have ye done
Since last we saw in France?

NORFOLK   I thank your grace,
Healthful, and ever since a fresh admirer
Of what I saw there.

BUCKINGHAM   An untimely ague
Stayed me a prisoner in my chamber when   5
Those suns of glory, those two lights of men,
Met in the vale of Ardres.

NORFOLK   'Twixt Guisnes and Ardres.
I was then present, saw them salute on horseback,
Beheld them when they lighted, how they clung
In their embracement as they grew together,   10
Which had they, what four throned ones could have
        weighed

Such a compounded one?

BUCKINGHAM   All the whole time
I was my chamber's prisoner.

NORFOLK   Then you lost
The view of earthly glory. Men might say
Till this time pomp was single, but now married 15
To one above itself. Each following day
Became the next day's master, till the last
Made former wonders its. Today the French,
All clinquant all in gold, like heathen gods
Shone down the English; and tomorrow they   20
Made Britain India. Every man that stood
Showed like a mine. Their dwarfish pages were
As cherubim, all gilt; the *mesdames*, too,
Not used to toil, did almost sweat to bear
The pride upon them, that their very labour   25
Was to them as a painting. Now this masque
Was cried incomparable, and th'ensuing night
Made it a fool and beggar. The two kings
Equal in lustre, were now best, now worst,
As presence did present them. Him in eye   30
Still him in praise, and being present both,
'Twas said they saw but one, and no discerner
Durst wag his tongue in censure. When these suns—
For so they phrase 'em—by their heralds challenged
The noble spirits to arms, they did perform   35
Beyond thought's compass, that former fabulous story
Being now seen possible enough, got credit
That *Bevis* was believed.

BUCKINGHAM   O, you go far!

NORFOLK

As I belong to worship, and affect
In honour honesty, the tract of ev'rything   40
Would by a good discourser lose some life
Which action's self was tongue to. All was royal.
To the disposing of it naught rebelled.
Order gave each thing view. The office did
Distinctly his full function.

BUCKINGHAM   Who did guide—   45
I mean, who set the body and the limbs
Of this great sport together, as you guess?

NORFOLK

One, certes, that promises no element
In such a business.

BUCKINGHAM   I pray you who, my lord?

NORFOLK

All this was ordered by the good discretion   50
Of the right reverend Cardinal of York.

BUCKINGHAM

The devil speed him! No man's pie is freed
From his ambitious finger. What had he
To do in these fierce vanities? I wonder
That such a keech can, with his very bulk,   55

Take up the rays o'th' beneficial sun,
And keep it from the earth.
NORFOLK   Surely, sir,
There's in him stuff that puts him to these ends.
For being not propped by ancestry, whose grace
Chalks successors their way, nor called upon   60
For high feats done to th' crown, neither allied
To eminent assistants, but spider-like,
Out of his self-drawing web, a gives us note
The force of his own merit makes his way—
A gift that heaven gives for him which buys   65
A place next to the King.
ABERGAVENNY   I cannot tell
What heaven hath given him—let some graver eye
Pierce into that; but I can see his pride
Peep through each part of him. Whence has he that?
If not from hell, the devil is a niggard   70
Or has given all before, and he begins
A new hell in himself.
BUCKINGHAM   Why the devil,
Upon this French going out, took he upon him
Without the privity o'th' King t'appoint
Who should attend on him? He makes up the file   75
Of all the gentry, for the most part such
To whom as great a charge as little honour
He meant to lay upon; and his own letter,
The honourable board of council out,
Must fetch him in, he papers.
ABERGAVENNY   I do know   80
Kinsmen of mine—three at the least—that have
By this so sickened their estates that never
They shall abound as formerly.
BUCKINGHAM   O, many
Have broke their backs with laying manors on 'em
For this great journey. What did this vanity   85
But minister communication of
A most poor issue?
NORFOLK   Grievingly I think
The peace between the French and us not values
The cost that did conclude it.
BUCKINGHAM   Every man,
After the hideous storm that followed, was   90
A thing inspired, and, not consulting, broke
Into a general prophecy—that this tempest,
Dashing the garment of this peace, aboded
The sudden breach on't.
NORFOLK   Which is budded out—
For France hath flawed the league, and hath attached
Our merchants' goods at Bordeaux.
ABERGAVENNY   Is it therefore   96
Th'ambassador is silenced?
NORFOLK   Marry is't.
ABERGAVENNY
A proper title of a peace, and purchased
At a superfluous rate.
BUCKINGHAM   Why, all this business
Our reverend Cardinal carried.
NORFOLK   Like it your grace,   100
The state takes notice of the private difference

Betwixt you and the Cardinal. I advise you—
And take it from a heart that wishes towards you
Honour and plenteous safety—that you read
The Cardinal's malice and his potency   105
Together; to consider further that
What his high hatred would effect wants not
A minister in his power. You know his nature,
That he's revengeful; and I know his sword
Hath a sharp edge—it's long, and't may be said   110
It reaches far; and where 'twill not extend
Thither he darts it. Bosom up my counsel,
You'll find it wholesome. Lo, where comes that rock
That I advise your shunning.
    Enter Cardinal Wolsey, the purse containing the
    great seal borne before him. Enter with him certain
    of the guard, and two secretaries with papers. The
    Cardinal in his passage fixeth his eye on Buckingham
    and Buckingham on him, both full of disdain
CARDINAL WOLSEY (*to a secretary*)
The Duke of Buckingham's surveyor, ha?   115
Where's his examination?
SECRETARY   Here, so please you.
CARDINAL WOLSEY
Is he in person ready?
SECRETARY   Ay, please your grace.
CARDINAL WOLSEY
Well, we shall then know more, and Buckingham
Shall lessen this big look.   *Exeunt Wolsey and his train*
BUCKINGHAM
This butcher's cur is venom-mouthed, and I   120
Have not the power to muzzle him; therefore best
Not wake him in his slumber. A beggar's book
Outworths a noble's blood.
NORFOLK   What, are you chafed?
Ask God for temp'rance; that's th'appliance only
Which your disease requires.
BUCKINGHAM   I read in's looks   125
Matter against me, and his eye reviled
Me as his abject object. At this instant
He bores me with some trick. He's gone to th' King—
I'll follow, and outstare him.
NORFOLK   Stay, my lord,
And let your reason with your choler question   130
What 'tis you go about. To climb steep hills
Requires slow pace at first. Anger is like
A full hot horse who, being allowed his way,
Self-mettle tires him. Not a man in England
Can advise me like you. Be to yourself   135
As you would to your friend.
BUCKINGHAM   I'll to the King,
And from a mouth of honour quite cry down
This Ipswich fellow's insolence, or proclaim
There's difference in no persons.
NORFOLK   Be advised.
Heat not a furnace for your foe so hot   140
That it do singe yourself. We may outrun
By violent swiftness that which we run at,
And lose by over-running. Know you not
The fire that mounts the liquor till't run o'er

In seeming to augment it wastes it? Be advised.   145
I say again there is no English soul
More stronger to direct you than yourself,
If with the sap of reason you would quench
Or but allay the fire of passion.
BUCKINGHAM   Sir,
I am thankful to you, and I'll go along   150
By your prescription; but this top-proud fellow—
Whom from the flow of gall I name not, but
From sincere motions—by intelligence,
And proofs as clear as founts in July when
We see each grain of gravel, I do know   155
To be corrupt and treasonous.
NORFOLK   Say not 'treasonous'.
BUCKINGHAM
To th' King I'll say't, and make my vouch as strong
As shore of rock. Attend: this holy fox,
Or wolf, or both—for he is equal rav'nous
As he is subtle, and as prone to mischief   160
As able to perform't, his mind and place
Infecting one another, yea, reciprocally—
Only to show his pomp as well in France
As here at home, suggests the King our master
To this last costly treaty, th'interview   165
That swallowed so much treasure and, like a glass,
Did break i'th' rinsing.
NORFOLK   Faith, and so it did.
BUCKINGHAM
Pray give me favour, sir. This cunning Cardinal,
The articles o'th' combination drew
As himself pleased, and they were ratified   170
As he cried 'Thus let be', to as much end
As give a crutch to th' dead. But our count-Cardinal
Has done this, and 'tis well for worthy Wolsey,
Who cannot err, he did it. Now this follows—
Which, as I take it, is a kind of puppy   175
To th'old dam, treason—Charles the Emperor,
Under pretence to see the Queen his aunt—
For 'twas indeed his colour, but he came
To whisper Wolsey—here makes visitation.
His fears were that the interview betwixt   180
England and France might through their amity
Breed him some prejudice, for from this league
Peeped harms that menaced him. Privily he
Deals with our Cardinal and, as I trow—
Which I do well, for I am sure the Emperor   185
Paid ere he promised, whereby his suit was granted
Ere it was asked—but when the way was made,
And paved with gold, the Emperor thus desired
That he would please to alter the King's course
And break the foresaid peace. Let the King know,   190
As soon he shall by me, that thus the Cardinal
Does buy and sell his honour as he pleases,
And for his own advantage.
NORFOLK   I am sorry
To hear this of him, and could wish he were
Something mistaken in't.
BUCKINGHAM   No, not a syllable.   195

I do pronounce him in that very shape
He shall appear in proof.
     Enter Brandon, a serjeant-at-arms before him, and
     two or three of the guard
BRANDON
Your office, serjeant, execute it.
SERJEANT   Sir.
     (*To Buckingham*) My lord the Duke of Buckingham and
          Earl
Of Hereford, Stafford, and Northampton, I   200
Arrest thee of high treason in the name
Of our most sovereign King.
BUCKINGHAM ⌈*to Norfolk*⌉   Lo you, my lord,
The net has fall'n upon me. I shall perish
Under device and practice.
BRANDON   I am sorry
To see you ta'en from liberty to look on   205
The business present. 'Tis his highness' pleasure
You shall to th' Tower.
BUCKINGHAM   It will help me nothing
To plead mine innocence, for that dye is on me
Which makes my whit'st part black. The will of
          heav'n
Be done in this and all things. I obey.   210
O, my lord Abergavenny, fare you well.
BRANDON
Nay, he must bear you company.
     (*To Abergavenny*)   The King
Is pleased you shall to th' Tower till you know
How he determines further.
ABERGAVENNY   As the Duke said,
The will of heaven be dóne and the King's pleasure   215
By me obeyed.
BRANDON   Here is a warrant from
The King t'attach Lord Montague and the bodies
Of the duke's confessor, John de la Car,
One Gilbert Perke, his chancellor—
BUCKINGHAM   So, so;
These are the limbs o'th' plot. No more, I hope.   220
BRANDON
A monk o'th' Chartreux.
BUCKINGHAM   O, Nicholas Hopkins?
BRANDON He.
BUCKINGHAM
My surveyor is false. The o'er-great Cardinal
Hath showed hím gold. My life is spanned already.
I am the shadow of poor Buckingham,   225
Whose figure even this instant cloud puts on
By dark'ning my clear sun. (*To Norfolk*) My lord,
          farewell.
     Exeunt ⌈*Norfolk at one door, Buckingham and*
          Abergavenny under guard at another⌉

1.2   *Cornetts. Enter King Henry leaning on Cardinal*
     Wolsey's shoulder. Enter with them Wolsey's two
     secretaries, the nobles, and Sir Thomas Lovell. The
     King ascends to his seat under the cloth of state;
     Wolsey places himself under the King's feet on his
     right side

KING HENRY ⌜to Wolsey⌝
My life itself and the best heart of it
Thanks you for this great care. I stood i'th' level
Of a full-charged confederacy, and give thanks
To you that choked it. Let be called before us
That gentleman of Buckingham's. In person   5
I'll hear him his confessions justify,
And point by point the treasons of his master
He shall again relate.
⌜CRIER⌝ (within)
Room for the Queen, ushered by the Duke of Norfolk.
Enter Queen Katherine, the Duke of Norfolk, and
the Duke of Suffolk. She kneels. King Henry riseth
from his state, takes her up, and kisses her
QUEEN KATHERINE
Nay, we must longer kneel. I am a suitor.   10
KING HENRY
Arise, and take place by us.
He placeth her by him
                              Half your suit
Never name to us. You have half our power,
The other moiety ere you ask is given.
Repeat your will and take it.
QUEEN KATHERINE   Thank your majesty.
That you would love yourself, and in that love   15
Not unconsidered leave your honour nor
The dignity of your office, is the point
Of my petition.
KING HENRY   Lady mine, proceed.
QUEEN KATHERINE
I am solicited, not by a few,
And those of true condition, that your subjects   20
Are in great grievance. There have been commissions
Sent down among 'em which hath flawed the heart
Of all their loyalties; wherein, although,
My good lord Cardinal, they vent reproaches
Most bitterly on you, as putter-on   25
Of these exactions, yet the King our master—
Whose honour heaven shield from soil—even he
escapes not
Language unmannerly, yea, such which breaks
The sides of loyalty, and almost appears
In loud rebellion.
NORFOLK   Not 'almost appears'—   30
It doth appear; for upon these taxations
The clothiers all, not able to maintain
The many to them 'longing, have put off
The spinsters, carders, fullers, weavers, who,
Unfit for other life, compelled by hunger   35
And lack of other means, in desperate manner
Daring th'event to th' teeth, are all in uproar,
And danger serves among them.
KING HENRY   Taxation?
Wherein, and what taxation? My lord Cardinal,
You that are blamed for it alike with us,   40
Know you of this taxation?
CARDINAL WOLSEY   Please you, sir,
I know but of a single part in aught

Pertains to th' state, and front but in that file
Where others tell steps with me.
QUEEN KATHERINE   No, my lord?
You know no more than others? But you frame   45
Things that are known alike, which are not wholesome
To those which would not know them, and yet must
Perforce be their acquaintance. These exactions
Whereof my sovereign would have note, they are
Most pestilent to th' hearing, and to bear 'em   50
The back is sacrifice to th' load. They say
They are devised by you, or else you suffer
Too hard an exclamation.
KING HENRY   Still exaction!
The nature of it? In what kind, let's know,
Is this exaction?
QUEEN KATHERINE I am much too venturous   55
In tempting of your patience, but am boldened
Under your promised pardon. The subjects' grief
Comes through commissions which compels from each
The sixth part of his substance to be levied
Without delay, and the pretence for this   60
Is named your wars in France. This makes bold mouths.
Tongues spit their duties out, and cold hearts freeze
Allegiance in them. Their curses now
Live where their prayers did, and it's come to pass
This tractable obedience is a slave   65
To each incensèd will. I would your highness
Would give it quick consideration, for
There is no primer business.
KING HENRY   By my life,
This is against our pleasure.
CARDINAL WOLSEY   And for me,
I have no further gone in this than by   70
A single voice, and that not passed me but
By learnèd approbation of the judges. If I am
Traduced by ignorant tongues, which neither know
My faculties nor person yet will be
The chronicles of my doing, let me say   75
'Tis but the fate of place, and the rough brake
That virtue must go through. We must not stint
Our necessary actions in the fear
To cope malicious censurers, which ever,
As rav'nous fishes, do a vessel follow   80
That is new trimmed, but benefit no further
Than vainly longing. What we oft do best,
By sick interpreters, once weak ones, is
Not ours or not allowed; what worst, as oft,
Hitting a grosser quality, is cried up   85
For our best act. If we shall stand still,
In fear our motion will be mocked or carped at,
We should take root here where we sit,
Or sit state-statues only.
KING HENRY   Things done well,
And with a care, exempt themselves from fear;   90
Things done without example, in their issue
Are to be feared. Have you a precedent
Of this commission? I believe not any.
We must not rend our subjects from our laws

And stick them in our will. Sixth part of each?   95
A trembling contribution! Why, we take
From every tree lop, bark, and part o'th' timber,
And though we leave it with a root, thus hacked
The air will drink the sap. To every county
Where this is questioned send our letters with   100
Free pardon to each man that has denied
The force of this commission. Pray look to't—
I put it to your care.
CARDINAL WOLSEY (*to a secretary*) A word with you.
Let there be letters writ to every shire
Of the King's grace and pardon.
(*Aside to the secretary*)   The grievèd commons
Hardly conceive of me. Let it be noised   106
That through our intercession this revokement
And pardon comes. I shall anon advise you
Further in the proceeding.   *Exit secretary*
             Enter Buckingham's Surveyor
QUEEN KATHERINE (*to the King*)
I am sorry that the Duke of Buckingham   110
Is run in your displeasure.
KING HENRY   It grieves many.
The gentleman is learnèd, and a most rare speaker,
To nature none more bound; his training such
That he may furnish and instruct great teachers
And never seek for aid out of himself. Yet see,   115
When these so noble benefits shall prove
Not well disposed, the mind growing once corrupt,
They turn to vicious forms ten times more ugly
Than ever they were fair. This man so complete,
Who was enrolled 'mongst wonders—and when we
Almost with ravished list'ning could not find   121
His hour of speech a minute—he, my lady,
Hath into monstrous habits put the graces
That once were his, and is become as black
As if besmeared in hell. Sit by us. You shall hear—   125
This was his gentleman in trust of him—
Things to strike honour sad.
(*To Wolsey*)   Bid him recount
The fore-recited practices whereof
We cannot feel too little, hear too much.
CARDINAL WOLSEY (*to the Surveyor*)
Stand forth, and with bold spirit relate what you   130
Most like a careful subject have collected
Out of the Duke of Buckingham.
KING HENRY (*to the Surveyor*)   Speak freely.
BUCKINGHAM'S SURVEYOR
First, it was usual with him, every day
It would infect his speech, that if the King
Should without issue die, he'll carry it so   135
To make the sceptre his. These very words
I've heard him utter to his son-in-law,
Lord Abergavenny, to whom by oath he menaced
Revenge upon the Cardinal.
CARDINAL WOLSEY (*to the King*)
                    Please your highness note
His dangerous conception in this point,   140
Not friended by his wish to your high person.

His will is most malignant, and it stretches
Beyond you to your friends.
QUEEN KATHERINE   My learned Lord Cardinal,
Deliver all with charity.
KING HENRY (*to the Surveyor*) Speak on.
How grounded he his title to the crown   145
Upon our fail? To this point hast thou heard him
At any time speak aught?
BUCKINGHAM'S SURVEYOR   He was brought to this
By a vain prophecy of Nicholas Hopkins.
KING HENRY
What was that Hopkins?
BUCKINGHAM'S SURVEYOR   Sir, a Chartreux friar,
His confessor, who fed him every minute   150
With words of sovereignty.
KING HENRY   How know'st thou this?
BUCKINGHAM'S SURVEYOR
Not long before your highness sped to France,
The Duke being at the Rose, within the parish
Saint Lawrence Poutney, did of me demand
What was the speech among the Londoners   155
Concerning the French journey. I replied
Men feared the French would prove perfidious,
To the King's danger; presently the Duke
Said 'twas the fear indeed, and that he doubted
'Twould prove the verity of certain words   160
Spoke by a holy monk that oft, says he,
'Hath sent to me, wishing me to permit
John de la Car, my chaplain, a choice hour
To hear from him a matter of some moment;
Whom after under the confession's seal   165
He solemnly had sworn, that what he spoke
My chaplain to no creature living but
To me should utter, with demure confidence
This pausingly ensued: "neither the King nor's heirs",
Tell you the Duke, "shall prosper. Bid him strive   170
To win the love o'th' commonalty. The Duke
Shall govern England."'
QUEEN KATHERINE   If I know you well,
You were the Duke's surveyor, and lost your office
On the complaint o'th' tenants. Take good heed
You charge not in your spleen a noble person   175
And spoil your nobler soul. I say, take heed;
Yes, heartily beseech you.
KING HENRY   Let him on.
(*To the Surveyor*) Go forward.
BUCKINGHAM'S SURVEYOR On my soul I'll speak but truth.
I told my lord the Duke, by th' devil's illusions
The monk might be deceived, and that 'twas
                    dangerous   180
To ruminate on this so far until
It forged him some design which, being believed,
It was much like to do. He answered, 'Tush,
It can do me no damage', adding further
That had the King in his last sickness failed,   185
The Cardinal's and Sir Thomas Lovell's heads
Should have gone off.
KING HENRY   Ha? What, so rank? Ah, ha!
There's mischief in this man. Canst thou say further?

BUCKINGHAM'S SURVEYOR
I can, my liege.
KING HENRY   Proceed.
BUCKINGHAM'S SURVEYOR   Being at Greenwich,
After your highness had reproved the Duke   190
About Sir William Bulmer—
KING HENRY   I remember
Such a time, being my sworn servant,
The Duke retained him his. But on—what hence?
BUCKINGHAM'S SURVEYOR
'If', quoth he, 'I for this had been committed'—
As to the Tower, I thought—'I would have played 195
The part my father meant to act upon
Th'usurper Richard who, being at Salisbury,
Made suit to come in's presence; which if granted,
As he made semblance of his duty, would
Have put his knife into him.'
KING HENRY   A giant traitor!   200
CARDINAL WOLSEY (to the Queen)
Now, madam, may his highness live in freedom,
And this man out of prison?
QUEEN KATHERINE   God mend all.
KING HENRY (to the Surveyor)
There's something more would out ·of thee—what
          sayst?
BUCKINGHAM'S SURVEYOR
After 'the Duke his father', with 'the knife',
He stretched him, and with one hand on his dagger,
Another spread on's breast, mounting his eyes, 206
He did discharge a horrible oath whose tenor
Was, were he evil used, he would outgo
His father by as much as a performance
Does an irresolute purpose.
KING HENRY   There's his period—   210
To sheathe his knife in us. He is attached.
Call him to present trial. If he may
Find mercy in the law, 'tis his; if none,
Let him not seek't of us. By day and night,   214
He's traitor to th' height.   ⌐Flourish.⌐ Exeunt

1.3   Enter the Lord Chamberlain and Lord Sands
LORD CHAMBERLAIN
Is't possible the spells of France should juggle
Men into such strange mysteries?
SANDS   New customs,
Though they be never so ridiculous—
Nay, let 'em be unmanly—yet are followed.
LORD CHAMBERLAIN
As far as I see, all the good our English   5
Have got by the late voyage is but merely
A fit or two o'th' face. But they are shrewd ones,
For when they hold 'em you would swear directly
Their very noses had been counsellors
To Pépin or Clotharius, they keep state so.   10
SANDS
They have all new legs, and lame ones; one would
          take it,

That never see 'em pace before, the spavin
Or spring-halt reigned among 'em.
LORD CHAMBERLAIN   Death, my lord,
Their clothes are after such a pagan cut to't
That sure they've worn out Christendom.
          Enter Sir Thomas Louell
                              How now—
What news, Sir Thomas Lovell?
LOVELL   Faith, my lord,   16
I hear of none but the new proclamation
That's clapped upon the court gate.
LORD CHAMBERLAIN   What is't for?
LOVELL
The reformation of our travelled gallants
That fill the court with quarrels, talk, and tailors.   20
LORD CHAMBERLAIN
I'm glad 'tis there. Now I would pray our 'messieurs'
To think an English courtier may be wise
And never see the Louvre.
LOVELL   They must either,
For so run the conditions, leave those remnants
Of fool and feather that they got in France,   25
With all their honourable points of ignorance
Pertaining thereunto—as fights and fireworks,
Abusing better men than they can be
Out of a foreign wisdom, renouncing clean
The faith they have in tennis and tall stockings,   30
Short blistered breeches, and those types of travel—
And understand again like honest men,
Or pack to their old playfellows. There, I take it,
They may, cum privilegio, 'oui' away
The lag end of their lewdness and be laughed at.   35
SANDS
'Tis time to give 'em physic, their diseases
Are grown so catching.
LORD CHAMBERLAIN   What a loss our ladies
Will have of these trim vanities!
LOVELL   Ay, marry,
There will be woe indeed, lords. The sly whoresons
Have got a speeding trick to lay down ladies.   40
A French song and a fiddle has no fellow.
SANDS
The devil fiddle 'em! I am glad they are going,
For sure there's no converting of 'em. Now
An honest country lord, as I am, beaten
A long time out of play, may bring his plainsong   45
And have an hour of hearing, and, by'r Lady,
Held current music, too.
LORD CHAMBERLAIN   Well said, Lord Sands.
Your colt's tooth is not cast yet?
SANDS   No, my lord,
Nor shall not while I have a stump.
LORD CHAMBERLAIN (to Lovell)   Sir Thomas,
Whither were you a-going?
LOVELL   To the Cardinal's.   ·50
Your lordship is a guest too.
LORD CHAMBERLAIN   O, 'tis true.
This night he makes a supper, and a great one,

To many lords and ladies. There will be
The beauty of this kingdom, I'll assure you.

LOVELL
That churchman bears a bounteous mind indeed,   55
A hand as fruitful as the land that feeds us.
His dews fall everywhere.

LORD CHAMBERLAIN   No doubt he's noble.
He had a black mouth that said other of him.

SANDS
He may, my lord; he's wherewithal. In him
Sparing would show a worse sin than ill doctrine.   60
Men of his way should be most liberal.
They are set here for examples.

LORD CHAMBERLAIN   True, they are so,
But few now give so great ones. My barge stays.
Your lordship shall along. (To Lovell) Come, good Sir
      Thomas,
We shall be late else, which I would not be,   65
For I was spoke to, with Sir Henry Guildford,
This night to be comptrollers.

SANDS   I am your lordship's.
                                    Exeunt

1.4   Hautboys. ⌈Enter servants with⌉ a small table for
       Cardinal Wolsey ⌈which they place⌉ under the cloth
       of state, and a longer table for the guests. Then
       enter at one door Anne Boleyn and divers other
       ladies and gentlemen as guests, and at another door
       enter Sir Henry Guildford

GUILDFORD
Ladies, a general welcome from his grace
Salutes ye all. This night he dedicates
To fair content and you. None here, he hopes,
In all this noble bevy, has brought with her
One care abroad. He would have all as merry   5
As feast, good company, good wine, good welcome
Can make good people.
       Enter the Lord Chamberlain, Lord Sands, and Sir
       Thomas Lovell
(To the Lord Chamberlain) O, my lord, you're tardy.
The very thought of this fair company
Clapped wings to me.

LORD CHAMBERLAIN   You are young, Sir Harry Guildford.

SANDS
Sir Thomas Lovell, had the Cardinal   10
But half my lay thoughts in him, some of these
Should find a running banquet, ere they rested,
I think would better please 'em. By my life,
They are a sweet society of fair ones.

LOVELL
O, that your lordship were but now confessor   15
To one or two of these.

SANDS   I would I were.
They should find easy penance.

LOVELL   Faith, how easy?

SANDS
As easy as a down bed would afford it.

LORD CHAMBERLAIN
Sweet ladies, will it please you sit?
(To Guildford)   Sir Harry,
Place you that side, I'll take the charge of this.   20
       They sit about the longer table. ⌈A noise within⌉
His grace is ent'ring. Nay, you must not freeze—
Two women placed together makes cold weather.
My lord Sands, you are one will keep 'em waking.
Pray sit between these ladies.

SANDS   By my faith,
And thank your lordship.
       He sits between Anne and another
                                By your leave, sweet ladies.
If I chance to talk a little wild, forgive me.   26
I had it from my father.

ANNE   Was he mad, sir?

SANDS
O, very mad; exceeding mad—in love, too.
But he would bite none. Just as I do now,
He would kiss you twenty with a breath.
       He kisses her

LORD CHAMBERLAIN   Well said, my lord.
So now you're fairly seated. Gentlemen,   31
The penance lies on you if these fair ladies
Pass away frowning.

SANDS For my little cure,
Let me alone.   35
       Hautboys. Enter Cardinal Wolsey who takes his
       seat at the small table under the state

CARDINAL WOLSEY
You're welcome, my fair guests. That noble lady
Or gentleman that is not freely merry
Is not my friend. This, to confirm my welcome,
And to you all, good health!
       He drinks

SANDS   Your grace is noble.
Let me have such a bowl may hold my thanks,   40
And save me so much talking.

CARDINAL WOLSEY   My lord Sands,
I am beholden to you. Cheer your neighbours.
Ladies, you are not merry! Gentlemen,
Whose fault is this?

SANDS   The red wine first must rise
In their fair cheeks, my lord, then we shall have 'em
Talk us to silence.

ANNE   You are a merry gamester,   46
My lord Sands.

SANDS   Yes, if I make my play.
Here's to your ladyship; and pledge it, madam,
For 'tis to such a thing—

ANNE   You cannot show me.   49

SANDS (to Wolsey)
I told your grace they would talk anon.
       Drum and trumpet. Chambers discharged

CARDINAL WOLSEY   What's that?

LORD CHAMBERLAIN (to the servants)
Look out there, some of ye.   Exit a servant

CARDINAL WOLSEY   What warlike voice,

423

And to what end is this? Nay, ladies, fear not.
By all the laws of war you're privileged.
  Enter the servant
LORD CHAMBERLAIN
How now—what is't?
SERVANT   A noble troop of strangers,
For so they seem. They've left their barge and landed,
And hither make as great ambassadors 56
From foreign princes.
CARDINAL WOLSEY Good Lord Chamberlain,
Go give 'em welcome—you can speak the French
 tongue.
And pray receive 'em nobly, and conduct 'em
Into our presence where this heaven of beauty 60
Shall shine at full upon them. Some attend him.
    Exit Chamberlain, attended
All rise, and some servants remove the tables
You have now a broken banquet, but we'll mend it.
A good digestion to you all, and once more
I shower a welcome on ye—welcome all.
  Hautboys. Enter, ushered by the Lord Chamberlain,
  King Henry and others as masquers habited like
  shepherds. They pass directly before Cardinal
  Wolsey and gracefully salute him
A noble company. What are their pleasures? 65
LORD CHAMBERLAIN
Because they speak no English, thus they prayed
To tell your grace, that, having heard by fame
Of this so noble and so fair assembly
This night to meet here, they could do no less,
Out of the great respect they bear to beauty, 70
But leave their flocks, and, under your fair conduct,
Crave leave to view these ladies, and entreat
An hour of revels with 'em.
CARDINAL WOLSEY   Say, Lord Chamberlain,
They have done my poor house grace, for which I pay
 'em
A thousand thanks, and pray 'em take their pleasures. 75
The masquers choose ladies. The King chooses Anne
Boleyn
KING HENRY (*to Anne*)
The fairest hand I ever touched. O beauty,
Till now I never knew thee.
  Music. They dance
CARDINAL WOLSEY (*to the Lord Chamberlain*) My lord.
LORD CHAMBERLAIN Your grace.
CARDINAL WOLSEY Pray tell 'em thus much from me. 80
There should be one amongst 'em by his person
More worthy this place than myself, to whom,
If I but knew him, with my love and duty
I would surrender it.
LORD CHAMBERLAIN I will, my lord.
  ⌈*He whispers with the masquers*⌉
CARDINAL WOLSEY
What say they?
LORD CHAMBERLAIN Such a one they all confess 85
There is indeed, which they would have your grace
Find out, and he will take it.
CARDINAL WOLSEY ⌈*standing*⌉ Let me see then.

By all your good leaves, gentlemen, here I'll make
My royal choice.
  ⌈*He bows before the King*⌉
KING HENRY ⌈*unmasking*⌉ Ye have found him, Cardinal.
You hold a fair assembly. You do well, lord. 90
You are a churchman, or I'll tell you, Cardinal,
I should judge now unhappily.
CARDINAL WOLSEY   I am glad
Your grace is grown so pleasant.
KING HENRY   My Lord Chamberlain,
Prithee come hither.
(*Gesturing towards Anne*) What fair lady's that? 94
LORD CHAMBERLAIN
An't please your grace, Sir Thomas Boleyn's daughter—
The Viscount Rochford—one of her highness' women.
KING HENRY
By heaven, she is a dainty one. (*To Anne*) Sweetheart,
I were unmannerly to take you out
And not to kiss you ⌈*kisses her*⌉. A health, gentlemen;
 ⌈*He drinks*⌉
Let it go round.   100
CARDINAL WOLSEY
Sir Thomas Lovell, is the banquet ready
I'th' privy chamber?
LOVELL   Yes, my lord.
CARDINAL WOLSEY (*to the King*) Your grace
I fear with dancing is a little heated.
KING HENRY I fear too much.
CARDINAL WOLSEY There's fresher air, my lord, 105
In the next chamber.
KING HENRY
Lead in your ladies, every one. (*To Anne*) Sweet partner,
I must not yet forsake you. (*To Wolsey*) Let's be merry,
Good my lord Cardinal. I have half a dozen healths
To drink to these fair ladies, and a measure 110
To lead 'em once again, and then let's dream
Who's best in favour. Let the music knock it.
       Exeunt with trumpets

2.1 *Enter two Gentlemen, at several doors*
FIRST GENTLEMAN
Whither away so fast?
SECOND GENTLEMAN O, God save ye.
Ev'n to the hall to hear what shall become
Of the great Duke of Buckingham.
FIRST GENTLEMAN   I'll save you
That labour, sir. All's now done but the ceremony
Of bringing back the prisoner.
SECOND GENTLEMAN Were you there? 5
FIRST GENTLEMAN
Yes, indeed was I.
SECOND GENTLEMAN Pray speak what has happened.
FIRST GENTLEMAN
You may guess quickly what.
SECOND GENTLEMAN Is he found guilty?
FIRST GENTLEMAN
Yes, truly is he, and condemned upon't.
SECOND GENTLEMAN I am sorry for't.

FIRST GENTLEMAN So are a number more.   10

SECOND GENTLEMAN But pray, how passed it?

FIRST GENTLEMAN

I'll tell you in a little. The great Duke
Came to the bar, where to his accusations
He pleaded still not guilty, and allegèd
Many sharp reasons to defeat the law.   15
The King's attorney, on the contrary,
Urged 'on the examinations, proofs, confessions,
Of divers witnesses, which the Duke desired
To him brought *viva voce* to his face—
At which appeared against him his surveyor,   20
Sir Gilbert Perk his chancellor, and John Car,
Confessor to him, with that devil-monk,
Hopkins, that made this mischief.

SECOND GENTLEMAN   That was he
That fed him with his prophecies.

FIRST GENTLEMAN   The same.
All these accused him strongly, which he fain   25
Would have flung from him, but indeed he could not.
And so his peers, upon this evidence,
Have found him guilty of high treason. Much
He spoke, and learnèdly, for life, but all
Was either pitied in him or forgotten.   30

SECOND GENTLEMAN
After all this, how did he bear himself?

FIRST GENTLEMAN
When he was brought again to th' bar to hear
His knell rung out, his judgement, he was stirred
With such an agony he sweat extremely,
And something spoke in choler, ill and hasty;   35
But he fell to himself again, and sweetly
In all the rest showed a most noble patience.

SECOND GENTLEMAN
I do not think he fears death.

FIRST GENTLEMAN   Sure he does not.
He never was so womanish. The cause
He may a little grieve at.

SECOND GENTLEMAN   Certainly   40
The Cardinal is the end of this.

FIRST GENTLEMAN   'Tis likely
By all conjectures: first, Kildare's attainder,
Then deputy of Ireland, who, removed,
Earl Surrey was sent thither—and in haste, too,
Lest he should help his father.

SECOND GENTLEMAN   That trick of state   45
Was a deep envious one.

FIRST GENTLEMAN   At his return
No doubt he will requite it. This is noted,
And generally: whoever the King favours,
The Card'nal instantly will find employment—
And far enough from court, too.

SECOND GENTLEMAN   All the commons   50
Hate him perniciously and, o' my conscience,
Wish him ten fathom deep. This Duke as much
They love and dote on, call him 'bounteous
    Buckingham,
The mirror of all courtesy'—

Enter the Duke of Buckingham from his arraignment,
tipstaves before him, the axe with the edge towards
him, halberdiers on each side, accompanied with Sir
Thomas Lovell, Sir Nicholas Vaux, Sir William
Sands, and common people

FIRST GENTLEMAN   Stay there, sir,
And see the noble ruined man you speak of.   55

SECOND GENTLEMAN
Let's stand close and behold him.
    They stand apart

BUCKINGHAM (*to the common people*) All good people,
You that thus far have come to pity me,
Hear what I say, and then go home and lose me.
I have this day received a traitor's judgement,
And by that name must die. Yet, heaven bear witness,   60
And if I have a conscience let it sink me,
Even as the axe falls, if I be not faithful.
The law I bear no malice for my death.
'T has done, upon the premises, but justice.
But those that sought it I could wish more Christians.
Be what they will, I heartily forgive 'em.   66
Yet let 'em look they glory not in mischief,
Nor build their evils on the graves of great men,
For then my guiltless blood must cry against 'em.
For further life in this world I ne'er hope,   70
Nor will I sue, although the King have mercies
More than I dare make faults. You few that loved me,
And dare be bold to weep for Buckingham,
His noble friends and fellows, whom to leave
Is only bitter to him, only dying,   75
Go with me like good angels to my end,
And, as the long divorce of steel falls on me,
Make of your prayers one sweet sacrifice,
And lift my soul to heaven. (*To the guard*) Lead on, i'
    God's name.

LOVELL
I do beseech your grace, for charity,   80
If ever any malice in your heart
Were hid against me, now to forgive me frankly.

BUCKINGHAM
Sir Thomas Lovell, I as free forgive you
As I would be forgiven. I forgive all.
There cannot be those numberless offences   85
'Gainst me that I cannot take peace with. No black envy
Shall mark my grave. Commend me to his grace,
And if he speak of Buckingham, pray tell him
You met him half in heaven. My vows and prayers
Yet are the King's, and, till my soul forsake,   90
Shall cry for blessings on him. May he live
Longer than I have time to tell his years;
Ever beloved and loving may his rule be;
And, when old time shall lead him to his end,
Goodness and he fill up one monument.   95

LOVELL
To th' waterside I must conduct your grace,
Then give my charge up to Sir Nicholas Vaux,
Who undertakes you to your end.

VAUX (*to an attendant*)   Prepare there—

The Duke is coming. See the barge be ready,
And fit it with such furniture as suits   100
The greatness of his person.
BUCKINGHAM   Nay, Sir Nicholas,
Let it alone. My state now will but mock me.
When I came hither I was Lord High Constable
And Duke of Buckingham; now, poor Edward Bohun.
Yet I am richer than my base accusers,   105
That never knew what truth meant. I now seal it,
And with that blood will make 'em one day groan for't.
My noble father, Henry of Buckingham,
Who first raised head against usurping Richard,
Flying for succour to his servant Banister,   110
Being distressed, was by that wretch betrayed,
And without trial fell. God's peace be with him.
Henry the Seventh succeeding, truly pitying
My father's loss, like a most royal prince,
Restored me to my honours, and out of ruins   115
Made my name once more noble. Now his son,
Henry the Eighth, life, honour, name, and all
That made me happy, at one stroke has taken
For ever from the world. I had my trial,
And must needs say a noble one; which makes me   120
A little happier than my wretched father.
Yet thus far we are one in fortunes: both
Fell by our servants, by those men we loved most—
A most unnatural and faithless service.
Heaven has an end in all. Yet, you that hear me,   125
This from a dying man receive as certain—
Where you are liberal of your loves and counsels,
Be sure you be not loose; for those you make friends
And give your hearts to, when they once perceive
The least rub in your fortunes, fall away   130
Like water from ye, never found again
But where they mean to sink ye. All good people
Pray for me. I must now forsake ye. The last hour
Of my long weary life is come upon me.
Farewell, and when you would say something that is
    sad,   135
Speak how I fell. I have done, and God forgive me.
                    Exeunt Buckingham and train
    The two Gentlemen come forward
FIRST GENTLEMAN
O, this is full of pity, sir; it calls,
I fear, too many curses on their heads
That were the authors.
SECOND GENTLEMAN   If the Duke be guiltless,
'Tis full of woe. Yet I can give you inkling   140
Of an ensuing evil, if it fall,
Greater than this.
FIRST GENTLEMAN   Good angels keep it from us.
What may it be? You do not doubt my faith, sir?
SECOND GENTLEMAN
This secret is so weighty, 'twill require
A strong faith to conceal it.
FIRST GENTLEMAN   Let me have it—   145
I do not talk much.
SECOND GENTLEMAN   I am confident;

You shall, sir. Did you not of late days hear
A buzzing of a separation
Between the King and Katherine?
FIRST GENTLEMAN   Yes, but it held not.
For when the King once heard it, out of anger   150
He sent command to the Lord Mayor straight
To stop the rumour and allay those tongues
That durst disperse it.
SECOND GENTLEMAN   But that slander, sir,
Is found a truth now, for it grows again
Fresher than e'er it was, and held for certain   155
The King will venture at it. Either the Cardinal
Or some about him near have, out of malice
To the good Queen, possessed him with a scruple
That will undo her. To confirm this, too,
Cardinal Campeius is arrived, and lately,   160
As all think, for this business.
FIRST GENTLEMAN   'Tis the Cardinal;
And merely to revenge him on the Emperor
For not bestowing on him at his asking
The Archbishopric of Toledo this is purposed.
SECOND GENTLEMAN
I think you have hit the mark. But is't not cruel   165
That she should feel the smart of this? The Cardinal
Will have his will, and she must fall.
FIRST GENTLEMAN   'Tis woeful.
We are too open here to argue this.
Let's think in private more.   *Exeunt*

2.2   *Enter the Lord Chamberlain with a letter*
LORD CHAMBERLAIN (*reads*) 'My lord, the horses your
lordship sent for, with all the care I had, I saw well
chosen, ridden, and furnished. They were young and
handsome, and of the best breed in the north. When
they were ready to set out for London, a man of my   5
lord Cardinal's, by commission and main power, took
'em from me with this reason—his master would be
served before a subject, if not before the King; which
stopped our mouths, sir.'
I fear he will indeed. Well, let him have them.   10
He will have all, I think.
            *Enter to the Lord Chamberlain the Dukes of Norfolk
            and Suffolk*
NORFOLK Well met, my Lord Chamberlain.
LORD CHAMBERLAIN Good day to both your graces.
SUFFOLK
How is the King employed?
LORD CHAMBERLAIN   I left him private,
Full of sad thoughts and troubles.
NORFOLK   What's the cause?   15
LORD CHAMBERLAIN
It seems the marriage with his brother's wife
Has crept too near his conscience.
SUFFOLK   No, his conscience
Has crept too near another lady.
NORFOLK   'Tis so.
This is the Cardinal's doing. The King-Cardinal,

That blind priest, like the eldest son of fortune,   20
Turns what he list. The King will know him one day.
SUFFOLK
Pray God he do. He'll never know himself else.
NORFOLK
How holily he works in all his business,
And with what zeal! For now he has cracked the
          league
Between us and the Emperor, the Queen's great-
          nephew,   25
He dives into the King's soul and there scatters
Dangers, doubts, wringing of the conscience,
Fears, and despairs—and all these for his marriage.
And out of all these, to restore the King,
He counsels a divorce—a loss of her   30
That like a jewel has hung twenty years
About his neck, yet never lost her lustre;
Of her that loves him with that excellence
That angels love good men with; even of her
That, when the greatest stroke of fortune falls, 35
Will bless the King—and is not this course pious?
LORD CHAMBERLAIN
Heaven keep me from such counsel! 'Tis most true—
These news are everywhere, every tongue speaks 'em,
And every true heart weeps for't. All that dare
Look into these affairs see this main end—   40
The French king's sister. Heaven will one day open
The King's eyes, that so long have slept, upon
This bold bad man.
SUFFOLK And free us from his slavery.
NORFOLK We had need pray,   45
And heartily, for our deliverance,
Or this imperious man will work us all
From princes into pages. All men's honours
Lie like one lump before him, to be fashioned
Into what pitch he please.
SUFFOLK   For me, my lords,   50
I love him not, nor fear him—there's my creed.
As I am made without him, so I'll stand,
If the King please. His curses and his blessings
Touch me alike; they're breath I not believe in.
I knew him, and I know him; so I leave him   55
To him that made him proud—the Pope.
NORFOLK   Let's in,
And with some other business put the King
From these sad thoughts that work too much upon him.
(To the Lord Chamberlain)
My lord, you'll bear us company?
LORD CHAMBERLAIN   Excuse me,
The King has sent me otherwise. Besides,   60
You'll find a most unfit time to disturb him.
Health to your lordships.
NORFOLK   Thanks, my good Lord Chamberlain.
                    Exit the Lord Chamberlain
          King Henry draws the curtain, and sits reading
          pensively
SUFFOLK
How sad he looks! Sure he is much afflicted.

KING HENRY
Who's there? Ha?
NORFOLK   Pray God he be not angry.
KING HENRY
Who's there, I say? How dare you thrust yourselves 65
Into my private meditations!
Who am I? Ha?
NORFOLK
A gracious king that pardons all offences
Malice ne'er meant. Our breach of duty this way
Is business of estate, in which we come   70
To know your royal pleasure.
KING HENRY   Ye are too bold.
Go to, I'll make ye know your times of business.
Is this an hour for temporal affairs? Ha?
          Enter Cardinal Wolsey and Cardinal Campeius, the
          latter with a commission
Who's there? My good lord Cardinal? O, my Wolsey,
The quiet of my wounded conscience,   75
Thou art a cure fit for a king.
(To Campeius)   You're welcome,
Most learnèd reverend sir, into our kingdom.
Use us, and it. (To Wolsey) My good lord, have great
          care
I be not found a talker.
CARDINAL WOLSEY   Sir, you cannot.
I would your grace would give us but an hour   80
Of private conference.
KING HENRY (to Norfolk and Suffolk) We are busy; go.
          Norfolk and Suffolk speak privately to one another
          as they depart
NORFOLK
This priest has no pride in him!
SUFFOLK   Not to speak of.
I would not be so sick, though, for his place—
But this cannot continue.
NORFOLK   If it do
I'll venture one have-at-him.
SUFFOLK   I another.   85
          Exeunt Norfolk and Suffolk
CARDINAL WOLSEY (to the King)
Your grace has given a precedent of wisdom
Above all princes in committing freely
Your scruple to the voice of Christendom.
Who can be angry now? What envy reach you?
The Spaniard, tied by blood and favour to her,   90
Must now confess, if they have any goodness,
The trial just and noble. All the clerks—
I mean the learnèd ones in Christian kingdoms—
Have their free voices. Rome, the nurse of judgement,
Invited by your noble self, hath sent   95
One general tongue unto us: this good man,
This just and learnèd priest, Card'nal Campeius,
Whom once more I present unto your highness.
KING HENRY (embracing Campeius)
And once more in mine arms I bid him welcome,
And thank the holy conclave for their loves.   100
They have sent me such a man I would have wished for.

CARDINAL CAMPEIUS
Your grace must needs deserve all strangers' loves,
You are so noble. To your highness' hand
I tender my commission,
    He gives the commission to the King
(*To Wolsey*)   by whose virtue,
The Court of Rome commanding, you, my lord   105
Cardinal of York, are joined with me their servant
In the unpartial judging of this business.
KING HENRY
Two equal men. The Queen shall be acquainted
Forthwith for what you come. Where's Gardiner?
CARDINAL WOLSEY
I know your majesty has always loved her   110
So dear in heart not to deny her that
A woman of less place might ask by law—
Scholars allowed freely to argue for her.
KING HENRY
Ay, and the best she shall have, and my favour
To him that does best, God forbid else. Cardinal,   115
Prithee call Gardiner to me, my new secretary.
    Cardinal Wolsey goes to the door and calls Gardiner
I find him a fit fellow.
    Enter Gardiner
CARDINAL WOLSEY (*aside to Gardiner*)
Give me your hand. Much joy and favour to you.
You are the King's now.
GARDINER (*aside to Wolsey*)   But to be commanded
For ever by your grace, whose hand has raised me.   120
KING HENRY Come hither, Gardiner.
    The King walks with Gardiner and whispers with him
CARDINAL CAMPEIUS (*to Wolsey*)
My lord of York, was not one Doctor Pace
In this man's place before him?
CARDINAL WOLSEY   Yes, he was.
CARDINAL CAMPEIUS
Was he not held a learnèd man?
CARDINAL WOLSEY   Yes, surely.
CARDINAL CAMPEIUS
Believe me, there's an ill opinion spread then,   125
Even of yourself, lord Cardinal.
CARDINAL WOLSEY   How? Of me?
CARDINAL CAMPEIUS
They will not stick to say you envied him,
And fearing he would rise, he was so virtuous,
Kept him a foreign man still, which so grieved him
That he ran mad and died.
CARDINAL WOLSEY   Heav'n's peace be with him—
That's Christian care enough. For living murmurers 131
There's places of rebuke. He was a fool,
For he would needs be virtuous.
(*Gesturing towards Gardiner*)   That good fellow,
If I command him, follows my appointment.
I will have none so near else. Learn this, brother: 135
We live not to be griped by meaner persons.
KING HENRY (*to Gardiner*)
Deliver this with modesty to th' Queen.   *Exit Gardiner*

The most convenient place that I can think of
For such receipt of learning is Blackfriars;
There ye shall meet about this weighty business.   140
My Wolsey, see it furnished. O, my lord,
Would it not grieve an able man to leave
So sweet a bedfellow? But conscience, conscience—
O, 'tis a tender place, and I must leave her.   *Exeunt*

2.3   *Enter Anne Boleyn and an Old Lady*
ANNE
Not for that neither. Here's the pang that pinches—
His highness having lived so long with her, and she
So good a lady that no tongue could ever
Pronounce dishonour of her—by my life,
She never knew harm-doing—O now, after   5
So many courses of the sun enthronèd,
Still growing in a majesty and pomp the which
To leave a thousandfold more bitter than
'Tis sweet at first t'acquire—after this process,
To give her the avaunt, it is a pity   10
Would move a monster.
OLD LADY   Hearts of most hard temper
Melt and lament for her.
ANNE   O, God's will! Much better
She ne'er had known pomp; though't be temporal,
Yet if that quarrel, fortune, do divorce
It from the bearer, 'tis a sufferance panging   15
As soul and bodies severing.
OLD LADY   Alas, poor lady!
She's a stranger now again.
ANNE   So much the more
Must pity drop upon her. Verily,
I swear, 'tis better to be lowly born
And range with humble livers in content   20
Than to be perked up in a glist'ring grief
And wear a golden sorrow.
OLD LADY   Our content
Is our best having.
ANNE   By my troth and maidenhead,
I would not be a queen.
OLD LADY   Beshrew me, I would—
And venture maidenhead for't; and so would you,   25
For all this spice of your hypocrisy.
You, that have so fair parts of woman on you,
Have, too, a woman's heart which ever yet
Affected eminence, wealth, sovereignty;
Which, to say sooth, are blessings; and which gifts, 30
Saving your mincing, the capacity
Of your soft cheveril conscience would receive
If you might please to stretch it.
ANNE   Nay, good troth.
OLD LADY
Yes, troth and troth. You would not be a queen?
ANNE
No, not for all the riches under heaven.   35
OLD LADY
'Tis strange. A threepence bowed would hire me,

Old as I am, to queen it. But I pray you,
What think you of a duchess? Have you limbs
To bear that load of title?
ANNE   No, in truth.
OLD LADY
Then you are weakly made. Pluck off a little;   40
I would not be a young count in your way
For more than blushing comes to. If your back
Cannot vouchsafe this burden, 'tis too weak
Ever to get a boy.
ANNE   How you do talk!
I swear again, I would not be a queen   45
For all the world.
OLD LADY   In faith, for little England
You'd venture an emballing; I myself
Would for Caernarfonshire, although there 'longed
No more to th' crown but that. Lo, who comes here?
    Enter the Lord Chamberlain
LORD CHAMBERLAIN
Good morrow, ladies. What were't worth to know   50
The secret of your conference?
ANNE   My good lord,
Not your demand; it values not your asking.
Our mistress' sorrows we were pitying.
LORD CHAMBERLAIN
It was a gentle business, and becoming
The action of good women. There is hope   55
All will be well.
ANNE   Now I pray God, amen.
LORD CHAMBERLAIN
You bear a gentle mind, and heav'nly blessings
Follow such creatures. That you may, fair lady,
Perceive I speak sincerely, and high note's
Ta'en of your many virtues, the King's majesty   60
Commends his good opinion of you, and
Does purpose honour to you no less flowing
Than Marchioness of Pembroke; to which title
A thousand pound a year annual support
Out of his grace he adds.
ANNE   I do not know   65
What kind of my obedience I should tender.
More than my all is nothing; nor my prayers
Are not words duly hallowed, nor my wishes
More worth than empty vanities; yet prayers and wishes
Are all I can return. Beseech your lordship,   70
Vouchsafe to speak my thanks and my obedience,
As from a blushing handmaid to his highness,
Whose health and royalty I pray for.
LORD CHAMBERLAIN   Lady,
I shall not fail t'approve the fair conceit
The King hath of you. (*Aside*) I have perused her well.
Beauty and honour in her are so mingled   76
That they have caught the King, and who knows yet
But from this lady may proceed a gem
To lighten all this isle. (*To Anne*) I'll to the King
And say I spoke with you.   80
ANNE My honoured lord.   *Exit the Lord Chamberlain*

OLD LADY Why, this it is—see, see!
I have been begging sixteen years in court,
Am yet a courtier beggarly, nor could
Come pat betwixt too early and too late   85
For any suit of pounds; and you—O, fate!—
A very fresh fish here—fie, fie upon
This compelled fortune!—have your mouth filled up
Before you open it.
ANNE   This is strange to me.
OLD LADY
How tastes it? Is it bitter? Forty pence, no.   90
There was a lady once—'tis an old story—
That would not be a queen, that would she not,
For all the mud in Egypt. Have you heard it?
ANNE
Come, you are pleasant.
OLD LADY   With your theme I could
O'ermount the lark. The Marchioness of Pembroke? 95
A thousand pounds a year, for pure respect?
No other obligation? By my life,
That promises more thousands. Honour's train
Is longer than his foreskin. By this time
I know your back will bear a duchess. Say,   100
Are you not stronger than you were?
ANNE   Good lady,
Make yourself mirth with your particular fancy,
And leave me out on't. Would I had no being,
If this salute my blood a jot. It faints me
To think what follows.   105
The Queen is comfortless, and we forgetful
In our long absence. Pray do not deliver
What here you've heard to her.
OLD LADY   What do you think me—
                                        Exeunt

2.4   *Trumpets: sennet. Then cornetts. Enter two vergers
        with short silver wands; next them two Scribes in the
        habit of doctors; after them the Archbishop of
        Canterbury alone; after him the Bishops of Lincoln,
        Ely, Rochester, and Saint Asaph; next them, with
        some small distance, follows a gentleman bearing
        both the purse containing the great seal and a
        cardinal's hat; then two priests bearing each a
        silver cross; then a gentleman usher, bare-headed,
        accompanied with a serjeant-at-arms bearing a silver
        mace; then two gentlemen bearing two great silver
        pillars; after them, side by side, the two cardinals,
        Wolsey and Campeius; then two noblemen with
        the sword and mace. The King ⌈ascends⌉ to his seat
        under the cloth of state; the two cardinals sit under
        him as judges; the Queen, attended by Griffith her
        gentleman usher, takes place some distance from the
        King; the Bishops place themselves on each side
        the court in the manner of a consistory; below
        them, the Scribes. The lords sit next the Bishops.
        The rest of the attendants stand in convenient order
        about the stage*

CARDINAL WOLSEY
  Whilst our commission from Rome is read
  Let silence be commanded.
KING HENRY   What's the need?
  It hath already publicly been read,
  And on all sides th'authority allowed.
  You may then spare that time.
CARDINAL WOLSEY   Be't so. Proceed.   5
SCRIBE (to the Crier)
  Say, 'Henry, King of England, come into the court'.
CRIER
  Henry, King of England, come into the court.
KING HENRY Here.
SCRIBE (to the Crier)
  Say, 'Katherine, Queen of England, come into the court'.
CRIER
  Katherine, Queen of England, come into the court.   10
  The Queen makes no answer, but rises out of her
  chair, goes about the court, comes to the King, and
  kneels at his feet. Then she speaks
QUEEN KATHERINE
  Sir, I desire you do me right and justice,
  And to bestow your pity on me; for
  I am a most poor woman, and a stranger,
  Born out of your dominions, having here
  No judge indifferent, nor no more assurance   15
  Of equal friendship and proceeding. Alas, sir,
  In what have I offended you? What cause
  Hath my behaviour given to your displeasure
  That thus you should proceed to put me off,
  And take your good grace from me? Heaven witness
  I have been to you a true and humble wife,   21
  At all times to your will conformable,
  Ever in fear to kindle your dislike,
  Yea, subject to your countenance, glad or sorry
  As I saw it inclined. When was the hour   25
  I ever contradicted your desire,
  Or made it not mine too? Or which of your friends
  Have I not strove to love, although I knew
  He were mine enemy? What friend of mine
  That had to him derived your anger did I   30
  Continue in my liking? Nay, gave notice
  He was from thence discharged? Sir, call to mind
  That I have been your wife in this obedience
  Upward of twenty years, and have been blessed
  With many children by you. If, in the course   35
  And process of this time, you can report—
  And prove it, too—against mine honour aught,
  My bond to wedlock, or my love and duty
  Against your sacred person, in God's name
  Turn me away, and let the foul'st contempt   40
  Shut door upon me, and so give me up
  To the sharp'st kind of justice. Please you, sir,
  The King your father was reputed for
  A prince most prudent, of an excellent
  And unmatched wit and judgement. Ferdinand   45
  My father, King of Spain, was reckoned one
  The wisest prince that there had reigned by many
  A year before. It is not to be questioned

  That they had gathered a wise council to them
  Of every realm, that did debate this business,   50
  Who deemed our marriage lawful. Wherefore I humbly
  Beseech you, sir, to spare me till I may
  Be by my friends in Spain advised, whose counsel
  I will implore. If not, i'th' name of God,
  Your pleasure be fulfilled.
CARDINAL WOLSEY   You have here, lady,   55
  And of your choice, these reverend fathers, men
  Of singular integrity and learning,
  Yea, the elect o'th' land, who are assembled
  To plead your cause. It shall be therefore bootless
  That longer you desire the court, as well   60
  For your own quiet, as to rectify
  What is unsettled in the King.
CARDINAL CAMPEIUS   His grace
  Hath spoken well and justly. Therefore, madam,
  It's fit this royal session do proceed,
  And that without delay their arguments   65
  Be now produced and heard.
QUEEN KATHERINE (to Wolsey)   Lord Cardinal,
  To you I speak.
CARDINAL WOLSEY Your pleasure, madam.
QUEEN KATHERINE   Sir,
  I am about to weep, but thinking that
  We are a queen, or long have dreamed so, certain
  The daughter of a king, my drops of tears   70
  I'll turn to sparks of fire.
CARDINAL WOLSEY   Be patient yet.
QUEEN KATHERINE
  I will when you are humble! Nay, before,
  Or God will punish me. I do believe,
  Induced by potent circumstances, that
  You are mine enemy, and make my challenge   75
  You shall not be my judge. For it is you
  Have blown this coal betwixt my lord and me,
  Which God's dew quench. Therefore I say again,
  I utterly abhor, yea, from my soul,
  Refuse you for my judge, whom yet once more   80
  I hold my most malicious foe, and think not
  At all a friend to truth.
CARDINAL WOLSEY   I do profess
  You speak not like yourself, who ever yet
  Have stood to charity, and displayed th'effects
  Of disposition gentle and of wisdom   85
  O'er-topping woman's power. Madam, you do me wrong.
  I have no spleen against you, nor injustice
  For you or any. How far I have proceeded,
  Or how far further shall, is warranted
  By a commission from the consistory,   90
  Yea, the whole consistory of Rome. You charge me
  That I 'have blown this coal'. I do deny it.
  The King is present. If it be known to him
  That I gainsay my deed, how may he wound,
  And worthily, my falsehood—yea, as much   95
  As you have done my truth. If he know
  That I am free of your report, he knows
  I am not of your wrong. Therefore in him
  It lies to cure me, and the cure is to

Remove these thoughts from you. The which before
His highness shall speak in, I do beseech   101
You, gracious madam, to unthink your speaking,
And to say so no more.
QUEEN KATHERINE   My lord, my lord—
I am a simple woman, much too weak
T'oppose your cunning. You're meek and humble-
mouthed;   105
You sign your place and calling, in full seeming,
With meekness and humility—but your heart
Is crammed with arrogancy, spleen, and pride.
You have by fortune and his highness' favours
Gone slightly o'er low steps, and now are mounted 110
Where powers are your retainers, and your words,
Domestics to you, serve your will as't please
Yourself pronounce their office. I must tell you,
You tender more your person's honour than
Your high profession spiritual, that again   115
I do refuse you for my judge, and here,
Before you all, appeal unto the Pope,
To bring my whole cause 'fore his holiness,
And to be judged by him.
         She curtsies to the King and begins to depart
CARDINAL CAMPEIUS   The Queen is obstinate,
Stubborn to justice, apt to accuse it, and   120
Disdainful to be tried by't. 'Tis not well.
She's going away.
KING HENRY (*to the Crier*) Call her again.
CRIER
Katherine, Queen of England, come into the court.
GRIFFITH (*to the Queen*) Madam, you are called back.
QUEEN KATHERINE
What need you note it? Pray you keep your way. 125
When *you* are called, return. Now the Lord help.
They vex me past my patience. Pray you, pass on.
I will not tarry; no, nor ever more
Upon this business my appearance make
In any of their courts.
         Exeunt Queen Katherine and her attendants
KING HENRY   Go thy ways, Kate.   130
That man i'th' world who shall report he has
A better wife, let him in naught be trusted
For speaking false in that. Thou art alone—
If thy rare qualities, sweet gentleness,
Thy meekness saint-like, wife-like government,   135
Obeying in commanding, and thy parts
Sovereign and pious else could speak thee out—
The queen of earthly queens. She's noble born,
And like her true nobility she has
Carried herself towards me.
CARDINAL WOLSEY   Most gracious sir,   140
In humblest manner I require your highness
That it shall please you to declare in hearing
Of all these ears—for where I am robbed and bound,
There must I be unloosed, although not there
At once and fully satisfied—whether ever I   145
Did broach this business to your highness, or
Laid any scruple in your way which might

Induce you to the question on't, or ever
Have to you, but with thanks to God for such
A royal lady, spake one the least word that might 150
Be to the prejudice of her present state,
Or touch of her good person?
KING HENRY   My lord Cardinal,
I do excuse you; yea, upon mine honour,
I free you from't. You are not to be taught
That you have many enemies that know not   155
Why they are so, but, like to village curs,
Bark when their fellows do. By some of these
The Queen is put in anger. You're excused.
But will you be more justified? You ever
Have wished the sleeping of this business, never desired
It to be stirred, but oft have hindered, oft,   161
The passages made toward it. On my honour
I speak my good lord Card'nal to this point,
And thus far clear him. Now, what moved me to't,
I will be bold with time and your attention.   165
Then mark th'inducement. Thus it came—give heed to't.
My conscience first received a tenderness,
Scruple, and prick, on certain speeches uttered
By th' Bishop of Bayonne, then French Ambassador,
Who had been hither sent on the debating   170
A marriage 'twixt the Duke of Orléans and
Our daughter Mary. I'th' progress of this business,
Ere a determinate resolution, he—
I mean the Bishop—did require a respite
Wherein he might the King his lord advertise   175
Whether our daughter were legitimate,
Respecting this our marriage with the dowager,
Sometimes our brother's wife. This respite shook
The bosom of my conscience, entered me,
Yea, with a spitting power, and made to tremble   180
The region of my breast; which forced such way
That many mazed considerings did throng
And prest in with this caution. First, methought
I stood not in the smile of heaven, who had
Commanded nature that my lady's womb,   185
If it conceived a male child by me, should
Do no more offices of life to't than
The grave does yield to th' dead. For her male issue
Or died where they were made, or shortly after
This world had aired them. Hence I took a thought 190
This was a judgement on me that my kingdom,
Well worthy the best heir o'th' world, should not
Be gladded in't by me. Then follows that
I weighed the danger which my realms stood in
By this my issue's fail, and that gave to me   195
Many a groaning throe. Thus hulling in
The wild sea of my conscience, I did steer
Toward this remedy, whereupon we are
Now present here together—that's to say
I meant to rectify my conscience, which   200
I then did feel full sick, and yet not well,
By all the reverend fathers of the land
And doctors learned. First I began in private
With you, my lord of Lincoln. You remember

How under my oppression I did reek   205
When I first moved you.
LINCOLN   Very well, my liege.
KING HENRY
I have spoke long. Be pleased yourself to say
How far you satisfied me.
LINCOLN   So please your highness,
The question did at first so stagger me,
Bearing a state of mighty moment in't   210
And consequence of dread, that I committed
The daring'st counsel which I had to doubt,
And did entreat your highness to this course
Which you are running here.
KING HENRY (to Canterbury)   I then moved you,
My lord of Canterbury, and got your leave   215
To make this present summons. Unsolicited
I left no reverend person in this court,
But by particular consent proceeded
Under your hands and seals. Therefore, go on,
For no dislike i'th' world against the person   220
Of the good Queen, but the sharp thorny points
Of my allegèd reasons, drives this forward.
Prove but our marriage lawful, by my life
And kingly dignity, we are contented
To wear our mortal state to come with her,   225
Katherine, our queen, before the primest creature
That's paragoned o'th' world.
CARDINAL CAMPEIUS   So please your highness,
The Queen being absent, 'tis a needful fitness
That we adjourn this court till further day.
Meanwhile must be an earnest motion   230
Made to the Queen to call back her appeal
She intends unto his holiness.
KING HENRY (aside)   I may perceive
These cardinals trifle with me. I abhor
This dilatory sloth and tricks of Rome.
My learned and well-belovèd servant, Cranmer,   235
Prithee return. With thy approach I know
My comfort comes along. (Aloud) Break up the court.
I say, set on.   Exeunt in manner as they entered

❀

3.1   Enter Queen Katherine and her women, as at work
QUEEN KATHERINE
Take thy lute, wench. My soul grows sad with troubles.
Sing, and disperse 'em if thou canst. Leave working.
GENTLEWOMAN (sings)
        Orpheus with his lute made trees,
        And the mountain tops that freeze,
            Bow themselves when he did sing.   5
        To his music plants and flowers
        Ever sprung, as sun and showers
            There had made a lasting spring.
        Everything that heard him play,
        Even the billows of the sea,   10
            Hung their heads, and then lay by.
        In sweet music is such art,
        Killing care and grief of heart
            Fall asleep, or hearing, die.

Enter ⌈Griffith,⌉ a gentleman
QUEEN KATHERINE How now?   15
⌈GRIFFITH⌉
An't please your grace, the two great cardinals
Wait in the presence.
QUEEN KATHERINE   Would they speak with me?
⌈GRIFFITH⌉
They willed me say so, madam.
QUEEN KATHERINE   Pray their graces
To come near.   ⌈Exit Griffith⌉
                What can be their business
With me, a poor weak woman, fall'n from favour?   20
I do not like their coming, now I think on't;
They should be good men, their affairs as righteous—
But all hoods make not monks.
        Enter the two cardinals, Wolsey and Campeius,
        ⌈ushered by Griffith⌉
CARDINAL WOLSEY   Peace to your highness.
QUEEN KATHERINE
Your graces find me here part of a housewife—
I would be all, against the worst may happen.   25
What are your pleasures with me, reverend lords?
CARDINAL WOLSEY
May it please you, noble madam, to withdraw
Into your private chamber, we shall give you
The full cause of our coming.
QUEEN KATHERINE   Speak it here.
There's nothing I have done yet, o' my conscience,   30
Deserves a corner. Would all other women
Could speak this with as free a soul as I do.
My lords, I care not—so much I am happy
Above a number—if my actions
Were tried by ev'ry tongue, ev'ry eye saw 'em,   35
Envy and base opinion set against 'em,
I know my life so even. If your business
Seek me out and that way I am wife in,
Out with it boldly. Truth loves open dealing.
CARDINAL WOLSEY
Tanta est erga te mentis integritas, Regina serenissima—
QUEEN KATHERINE O, good my lord, no Latin.   41
I am not such a truant since my coming
As not to know the language I have lived in.
A strange tongue makes my cause more strange
    suspicious—
Pray, speak in English. Here are some will thank you,
If you speak truth, for their poor mistress' sake.   46
Believe me, she has had much wrong. Lord Cardinal,
The willing'st sin I ever yet committed
May be absolved in English.
CARDINAL WOLSEY   Noble lady,
I am sorry my integrity should breed—   50
And service to his majesty and you—
So deep suspicion, where all faith was meant.
We come not by the way of accusation,
To taint that honour every good tongue blesses,
Nor to betray you any way to sorrow—   55
You have too much, good lady—but to know
How you stand minded in the weighty difference
Between the King and you, and to deliver,

Like free and honest men, our just opinions
And comforts to your cause.

CARDINAL CAMPEIUS   Most honoured madam, 60
My lord of York, out of his noble nature,
Zeal, and obedience he still bore your grace,
Forgetting, like a good man, your late censure
Both of his truth and him—which was too far—
Offers, as I do, in a sign of peace,   65
His service and his counsel.

QUEEN KATHERINE (aside)   To betray me.
(Aloud) My lords, I thank you both for your good
   wills.
Ye speak like honest men—pray God ye prove so.
But how to make ye suddenly an answer
In such a point of weight, so near mine honour—   70
More near my life, I fear—with my weak wit,
And to such men of gravity and learning,
In truth I know not. I was set at work
Among my maids, full little—God knows—looking
Either for such men or such business.   75
For her sake that I have been—for I feel
The last fit of my greatness—good your graces,
Let me have time and counsel for my cause.
Alas, I am a woman friendless, hopeless.

CARDINAL WOLSEY
Madam, you wrong the King's love with these fears. 80
Your hopes and friends are infinite.

QUEEN KATHERINE   In England
But little for my profit. Can you think, lords,
That any Englishman dare give me counsel,
Or be a known friend 'gainst his highness' pleasure—
Though he be grown so desperate to be honest—   85
And live a subject? Nay, forsooth, my friends,
They that must weigh out my afflictions,
They that my trust must grow to, live not here.
They are, as all my other comforts, far hence,
In mine own country, lords.

CARDINAL CAMPEIUS   I would your grace   90
Would leave your griefs and take my counsel.

QUEEN KATHERINE   How, sir?

CARDINAL CAMPEIUS
Put your main cause into the King's protection.
He's loving and most gracious. 'Twill be much
Both for your honour better and your cause,
For if the trial of the law o'ertake ye   95
You'll part away disgraced.

CARDINAL WOLSEY (to the Queen) He tells you rightly.

QUEEN KATHERINE
Ye tell me what ye wish for both—my ruin.
Is this your Christian counsel? Out upon ye!
Heaven is above all yet—there sits a judge
That no king can corrupt.

CARDINAL CAMPEIUS   Your rage mistakes us. 100

QUEEN KATHERINE
The more shame for ye! Holy men I thought ye,
Upon my soul, two reverend cardinal virtues—
But cardinal sins and hollow hearts I fear ye.
Mend 'em, for shame, my lords! Is this your comfort?

The cordial that ye bring a wretched lady,   105
A woman lost among ye, laughed at, scorned?
I will not wish ye half my miseries—
I have more charity. But say I warned ye.
Take heed, for heaven's sake take heed, lest at once
The burden of my sorrows fall upon ye.   110

CARDINAL WOLSEY
Madam, this is a mere distraction.
You turn the good we offer into envy.

QUEEN KATHERINE
Ye turn me into nothing. Woe upon ye,
And all such false professors. Would you have me—
If you have any justice, any pity,   115
If ye be anything but churchmen's habits—
Put my sick cause into his hands that hates me?
Alas, he's banished me his bed already—
His love, too, long ago. I am old, my lords,
And all the fellowship I hold now with him   120
Is only my obedience. What can happen
To me above this wretchedness? All your studies
Make me accursed like this.

CARDINAL CAMPEIUS   Your fears are worse.

QUEEN KATHERINE
Have I lived thus long—let me speak myself,
Since virtue finds no friends—a wife, a true one? 125
A woman, I dare say, without vainglory,
Never yet branded with suspicion?
Have I with all my full affections
Still met the King, loved him next heav'n, obeyed him,
Been out of fondness superstitious to him,   130
Almost forgot my prayers to content him?
And am I thus rewarded? 'Tis not well, lords.
Bring me a constant woman to her husband,
One that ne'er dreamed a joy beyond his pleasure,
And to that woman when she has done most,   135
Yet will I add an honour, a great patience.

CARDINAL WOLSEY
Madam, you wander from the good we aim at.

QUEEN KATHERINE
My lord, I dare not make myself so guilty
To give up willingly that noble title
Your master wed me to. Nothing but death   140
Shall e'er divorce my dignities.

CARDINAL WOLSEY   Pray, hear me.

QUEEN KATHERINE
Would I had never trod this English earth,
Or felt the flatteries that grow upon it.
Ye have angels' faces, but heaven knows your hearts.
What will become of me now, wretched lady?   145
I am the most unhappy woman living.
(To her women) Alas, poor wenches, where are now
   your fortunes?
Shipwrecked upon a kingdom where no pity,
No friends, no hope, no kindred weep for me?
Almost no grave allowed me? Like the lily,   150
That once was mistress of the field and flourished,
I'll hang my head and perish.

CARDINAL WOLSEY   If your grace

Could but be brought to know our ends are honest,
You'd feel more comfort. Why should we, good lady,
Upon what cause, wrong you? Alas, our places,   155
The way of our profession, is against it.
We are to cure such sorrows, not to sow 'em.
For goodness' sake, consider what you do,
How you may hurt yourself, ay, utterly
Grow from the King's acquaintance by this carriage.
The hearts of princes kiss obedience,   161
So much they love it, but to stubborn spirits
They swell and grow as terrible as storms.
I know you have a gentle noble temper,
A soul as even as a calm. Pray, think us   165
Those we profess—peacemakers, friends, and servants.
CARDINAL CAMPEIUS
Madam, you'll find it so. You wrong your virtues
With these weak women's fears. A noble spirit,
As yours was put into you, ever casts
Such doubts as false coin from it. The King loves you.
Beware you lose it not. For us, if you please   171
To trust us in your business, we are ready
To use our utmost studies in your service.
QUEEN KATHERINE
Do what ye will, my lords, and pray forgive me.
If I have used myself unmannerly,   175
You know I am a woman, lacking wit
To make a seemly answer to such persons.
Pray do my service to his majesty.
He has my heart yet, and shall have my prayers
While I shall have my life. Come, reverend fathers, 180
Bestow your counsels on me. She now begs
That little thought, when she set footing here,
She should have bought her dignities so dear.   *Exeunt*

3.2   *Enter the Duke of Norfolk, the Duke of Suffolk, Lord*
       Surrey, and the Lord Chamberlain
NORFOLK
If you will now unite in your complaints,
And force them with a constancy, the Cardinal
Cannot stand under them. If you omit
The offer of this time, I cannot promise
But that you shall sustain more new disgraces   5
With these you bear already.
SURREY   I am joyful
To meet the least occasion that may give me
Remembrance of my father-in-law the Duke,
To be revenged on him.
SUFFOLK   Which of the peers
Have uncontemned gone by him, or at least   10
Strangely neglected? When did he regard
The stamp of nobleness in any person
Out of himself?
LORD CHAMBERLAIN My lords, you speak your pleasures.
What he deserves of you and me I know;
What we can do to him—though now the time   15
Gives way to us—I much fear. If you cannot
Bar his access to th' King, never attempt

Anything on him, for he hath a witchcraft
Over the King in's tongue.
NORFOLK   O, fear him not.
His spell in that is out. The King hath found   20
Matter against him that for ever mars
The honey of his language. No, he's settled,
Not to come off, in his displeasure.
SURREY   Sir,
I should be glad to hear such news as this
Once every hour.
NORFOLK   Believe it, this is true.   25
In the divorce his contrary proceedings
Are all unfolded, wherein he appears
As I would wish mine enemy.
SURREY   How came
His practices to light?
SUFFOLK   Most strangely.
SURREY   O, how, how?
SUFFOLK
The Cardinal's letters to the Pope miscarried,   30
And came to th' eye o'th' King, wherein was read
How that the Cardinal did entreat his holiness
To stay the judgement o'th' divorce, for if
It did take place, 'I do,' quoth he, 'perceive
My king is tangled in affection to   35
A creature of the Queen's, Lady Anne Boleyn'.
SURREY
Has the King this?
SUFFOLK   Believe it.
SURREY   Will this work?
LORD CHAMBERLAIN
The King in this perceives him how he coasts
And hedges his own way. But in this point
All his tricks founder, and he brings his physic   40
After his patient's death. The King already
Hath married the fair lady.
SURREY   Would he had.
SUFFOLK
May you be happy in your wish, my lord,
For I profess you have it.
SURREY   Now all my joy
Trace the conjunction.
SUFFOLK   My amen to't.
NORFOLK   All men's.   45
SUFFOLK
There's order given for her coronation.
Marry, this is yet but young, and may be left
To some ears unrecounted. But, my lords,
She is a gallant creature, and complete
In mind and feature. I persuade me, from her   50
Will fall some blessing to this land which shall
In it be memorized.
SURREY   But will the King
Digest this letter of the Cardinal's?
The Lord forbid!
NORFOLK   Marry, amen.
SUFFOLK   No, no—
There be more wasps that buzz about his nose   55

Will make this sting the sooner. Cardinal Campeius
Is stol'n away to Rome; hath ta'en no leave;
Has left the cause o'th' King unhandled, and
Is posted as the agent of our Cardinal
To second all his plot. I do assure you   60
The King cried 'Ha!' at this.
LORD CHAMBERLAIN   Now God incense him,
And let him cry 'Ha!' louder.
NORFOLK   But, my lord,
When returns Cranmer?
SUFFOLK
He is returned in his opinions, which
Have satisfied the King for his divorce,   65
Together with all famous colleges,
Almost, in Christendom. Shortly, I believe,
His second marriage shall be published, and
Her coronation. Katherine no more
Shall be called 'Queen', but 'Princess Dowager',   70
And 'widow to Prince Arthur'.
NORFOLK   This same Cranmer's
A worthy fellow, and hath ta'en much pain
In the King's business.
SUFFOLK   He has, and we shall see him
For it an archbishop.
NORFOLK   So I hear.
SUFFOLK   'Tis so.
        Enter Cardinal Wolsey and Cromwell
The Cardinal.
NORFOLK   Observe, observe—he's moody.   75
        They stand apart and observe Wolsey and Cromwell
CARDINAL WOLSEY (*to Cromwell*)
The packet, Cromwell—gave't you the King?
CROMWELL
To his own hand, in's bedchamber.
CARDINAL WOLSEY   Looked he
O'th' inside of the paper?
CROMWELL   Presently
He did unseal them, and the first he viewed
He did it with a serious mind; a heed   80
Was in his countenance. You he bade
Attend him here this morning.
CARDINAL WOLSEY   Is he ready
To come abroad?
CROMWELL I think by this he is.
CARDINAL WOLSEY Leave me a while.   *Exit Cromwell*
(*Aside*) It shall be to the Duchess of Alençon,   86
The French King's sister—he shall marry her.
Anne Boleyn? No, I'll no Anne Boleyns for him.
There's more in't than fair visage. Boleyn?
No, we'll no Boleyns. Speedily I wish   90
To hear from Rome. The Marchioness of Pembroke?
        The nobles speak among themselves
NORFOLK
He's discontented.
SUFFOLK   Maybe he hears the King
Does whet his anger to him.
SURREY   Sharp enough,
Lord, for thy justice.

CARDINAL WOLSEY (*aside*)
The late Queen's gentlewoman? A knight's daughter
To be her mistress' mistress? The Queen's queen?   96
This candle burns not clear; 'tis I must snuff it,
Then out it goes. What though I know her virtuous
And well deserving? Yet I know her for
A spleeny Lutheran, and not wholesome to   100
Our cause, that she should lie i'th' bosom of
Our hard-ruled King. Again, there is sprung up
An heretic, an arch-one, Cranmer, one
Hath crawled into the favour of the King
And is his oracle.
        The nobles speak among themselves
NORFOLK   He is vexed at something.   105
        *Enter King Henry reading a schedule, and Lovell
        with him*
SURREY
I would 'twere something that would fret the string,
The master-cord on's heart!
SUFFOLK   The King, the King!
KING HENRY ⌈*aside*⌉
What piles of wealth hath he accumulated
To his own portion? And what expense by th' hour
Seems to flow from him? How i'th' name of thrift   110
Does he rake this together? (*To the nobles*) Now, my lords,
Saw you the Cardinal?
NORFOLK   My lord, we have
Stood here observing him. Some strange commotion
Is in his brain. He bites his lip, and starts,
Stops on a sudden, looks upon the ground,   115
Then lays his finger on his temple, straight
Springs out into fast gait, then stops again,
Strikes his breast hard, and anon he casts
His eye against the moon. In most strange postures
We have seen him set himself.
KING HENRY   It may well be   120
There is a mutiny in's mind. This morning
Papers of state he sent me to peruse
As I required, and wot you what I found
There, on my conscience put unwittingly?
Forsooth, an inventory thus importing   125
The several parcels of his plate, his treasure,
Rich stuffs, and ornaments of household which
I find at such proud rate that it outspeaks
Possession of a subject.
NORFOLK   It's heaven's will.
Some spirit put this paper in the packet   130
To bless your eye withal.
KING HENRY   If we did think
His contemplation were above the earth
And fixed on spiritual object, he should still
Dwell in his musings. But I am afraid
His thinkings are below the moon, not worth   135
His serious considering.
        *The King takes his seat and whispers with Lovell,
        who then goes to the Cardinal*
CARDINAL WOLSEY   Heaven forgive me!
        ⌈*To the King*⌉ Ever God bless your highness!
KING HENRY   Good my lord,

You are full of heavenly stuff, and bear the inventory
Of your best graces in your mind, the which
You were now running o'er. You have scarce time 140
To steal from spiritual leisure a brief span
To keep your earthly audit. Sure, in that,
I deem you an ill husband, and am glad
To have you therein my companion.
CARDINAL WOLSEY   Sir,
For holy offices I have a time; a time   145
To think upon the part of business which
I bear i'th' state; and nature does require
Her times of preservation which, perforce,
I, her frail son, amongst my brethren mortal,
Must give my tendance to.
KING HENRY   You have said well. 150
CARDINAL WOLSEY
And ever may your highness yoke together,
As I will lend you cause, my doing well
With my well-saying.
KING HENRY   'Tis well said again,
And 'tis a kind of good deed to say well—
And yet words are no deeds. My father loved you. 155
He said he did, and with his deed did crown
His word upon you. Since I had my office,
I have kept you next my heart, have not alone
Employed you where high profits might come home,
But pared my present havings to bestow   160
My bounties upon you.
CARDINAL WOLSEY (aside) What should this mean?
SURREY ⌈aside⌉
The Lord increase this business!
KING HENRY   Have I not made you
The prime man of the state? I pray you tell me
If what I now pronounce you have found true,
And, if you may confess it, say withal   165
If you are bound to us or no. What say you?
CARDINAL WOLSEY
My sovereign, I confess your royal graces
Showered on me daily have been more than could
My studied purposes requite, which went
Beyond all man's endeavours. My endeavours   170
Have ever come too short of my desires,
Yet filed with my abilities. Mine own ends
Have been mine so that evermore they pointed
To th' good of your most sacred person and
The profit of the state. For your great graces 175
Heaped upon me, poor undeserver, I
Can nothing render but allegiant thanks,
My prayers to heaven for you, my loyalty,
Which ever has and ever shall be growing,
Till death, that winter, kill it.
KING HENRY   Fairly answered. 180
A loyal and obedient subject is
Therein illustrated. The honour of it
Does pay the act of it, as, i'th' contrary,
The foulness is the punishment. I presume
That as my hand has opened bounty to you, 185
My heart dropped love, my power rained honour, more

On you than any, so your hand and heart,
Your brain, and every function of your power,
Should, notwithstanding that your bond of duty,
As 'twere in love's particular, be more   190
To me, your friend, than any.
CARDINAL WOLSEY   I do profess
That for your highness' good I ever laboured
More than mine own; that am, have, and will be—
Though all the world should crack their duty to you,
And throw it from their soul, though perils did 195
Abound, as thick as thought could make 'em, and
Appear in forms more horrid—yet, my duty,
As doth a rock against the chiding flood,
Should the approach of this wild river break,
And stand unshaken yours.
KING HENRY   'Tis nobly spoken. 200
Take notice, lords, he has a loyal breast,
For you have seen him open't. (To Wolsey) Read o'er this,
         He gives him a paper
And after this (giving him another paper), and then to
         breakfast with
What appetite you have.
                Exit King Henry, frowning upon the
                Cardinal. The nobles throng after
                the King, smiling and whispering
CARDINAL WOLSEY   What should this mean?
What sudden anger's this? How have I reaped it? 205
He parted frowning from me, as if ruin
Leaped from his eyes. So looks the chafèd lion
Upon the daring huntsman that has galled him,
Then makes him nothing. I must read this paper—
I fear, the story of his anger.
         He reads one of the papers
                                    'Tis so. 210
This paper has undone me. 'Tis th'account
Of all that world of wealth I have drawn together
For mine own ends—indeed, to gain the popedom,
And fee my friends in Rome. O negligence,
Fit for a fool to fall by! What cross devil   215
Made me put this main secret in the packet
I sent the King? Is there no way to cure this?
No new device to beat this from his brains?
I know 'twill stir him strongly. Yet I know
A way, if it take right, in spite of fortune 220
Will bring me off again. What's this?
         He reads the other paper
                                    'To th' Pope'?
The letter, as I live, with all the business
I writ to's holiness. Nay then, farewell.
I have touched the highest point of all my greatness,
And from that full meridian of my glory   225
I haste now to my setting. I shall fall
Like a bright exhalation in the evening,
And no man see me more.
         Enter to Cardinal Wolsey the Dukes of Norfolk and
         Suffolk, the Earl of Surrey, and the Lord Chamberlain
NORFOLK
Hear the King's pleasure, Cardinal, who commands you

To render up the great seal presently   230
Into our hands, and to confine yourself
To Asher House, my lord of Winchester's,
Till you hear further from his highness.
CARDINAL WOLSEY   Stay—
Where's your commission, lords? Words cannot carry
Authority so weighty.
SUFFOLK   Who dare cross 'em   235
Bearing the King's will from his mouth expressly?
CARDINAL WOLSEY
Till I find more than will or words to do it—
I mean your malice—know, officious lords,
I dare and must deny it. Now I feel
Of what coarse metal ye are moulded—envy.   240
How eagerly ye follow my disgraces
As if it fed ye, and how sleek and wanton
Ye appear in everything may bring my ruin!
Follow your envious courses, men of malice.
You have Christian warrant for 'em, and no doubt 245
In time will find their fit rewards. That seal
You ask with such a violence, the King,
Mine and your master, with his own hand gave me,
Bade me enjoy it, with the place and honours,
During my life; and, to confirm his goodness,   250
Tied it by letters patents. Now, who'll take it?
SURREY
The King that gave it.
CARDINAL WOLSEY   It must be himself then.
SURREY
Thou art a proud traitor, priest.
CARDINAL WOLSEY   Proud lord, thou liest.
Within these forty hours Surrey durst better
Have burnt that tongue than said so.
SURREY   Thy ambition,
Thou scarlet sin, robbed this bewailing land   256
Of noble Buckingham, my father-in-law.
The heads of all thy brother cardinals
With thee and all thy best parts bound together
Weighed not a hair of his. Plague of your policy,   260
You sent me deputy for Ireland,
Far from his succour, from the King, from all
That might have mercy on the fault thou gav'st him;
Whilst your great goodness, out of holy pity,
Absolved him with an axe.
CARDINAL WOLSEY   This, and all else   265
This talking lord can lay upon my credit,
I answer is most false. The Duke by law
Found his deserts. How innocent I was
From any private malice in his end,
His noble jury and foul cause can witness.   270
If I loved many words, lord, I should tell you
You have as little honesty as honour,
That in the way of loyalty and truth
Toward the King, my ever royal master,
Dare mate a sounder man than Surrey can be,   275
And all that love his follies.
SURREY   By my soul,
Your long coat, priest, protects you; thou shouldst feel

My sword i'th' life-blood of thee else. My lords,
Can ye endure to hear this arrogance,
And from this fellow? If we live thus tamely,   280
To be thus jaded by a piece of scarlet,
Farewell nobility. Let his grace go forward
And dare us with his cap, like larks.
CARDINAL WOLSEY   All goodness
Is poison to thy stomach.
SURREY   Yes, that goodness
Of gleaning all the land's wealth into one,   285
Into your own hands, Card'nal, by extortion;
The goodness of your intercepted packets
You writ to th' Pope against the King; your
   goodness—
Since you provoke me—shall be most notorious.
My lord of Norfolk, as you are truly noble,   290
As you respect the common good, the state
Of our despised nobility, our issues—
Whom if he live will scarce be gentlemen—
Produce the grand sum of his sins, the articles
Collected from his life. (To Wolsey) I'll startle you 295
Worse than the sacring-bell when the brown wench
Lay kissing in your arms, lord Cardinal.
CARDINAL WOLSEY [aside]
How much, methinks, I could despise this man,
But that I am bound in charity against it.
NORFOLK (to Surrey)
Those articles, my lord, are in the King's hand;   300
But thus much—they are foul ones.
CARDINAL WOLSEY   So much fairer
And spotless shall mine innocence arise
When the King knows my truth.
SURREY   This cannot save you.
I thank my memory I yet remember
Some of these articles, and out they shall.   305
Now, if you can blush and cry 'Guilty', Cardinal,
You'll show a little honesty.
CARDINAL WOLSEY   Speak on, sir;
I dare your worst objections. If I blush,
It is to see a nobleman want manners.
SURREY
I had rather want those than my head. Have at you!
First, that without the King's assent or knowledge 311
You wrought to be a legate, by which power
You maimed the jurisdiction of all bishops.
NORFOLK (to Wolsey)
Then, that in all you writ to Rome, or else
To foreign princes, 'Ego et Rex meus'   315
Was still inscribed—in which you brought the King
To be your servant.
SUFFOLK (to Wolsey)   Then, that without the knowledge
Either of King or Council, when you went
Ambassador to the Emperor, you made bold
To carry into Flanders the great seal.   320
SURREY (to Wolsey)
Item, you sent a large commission
To Gregory de Cassado, to conclude,
Without the King's will or the state's allowance,
A league between his highness and Ferrara.

SUFFOLK (*to Wolsey*)
That out of mere ambition you have caused   325
Your holy hat to be stamped on the King's coin.
SURREY (*to Wolsey*)
Then, that you have sent innumerable substance—
By what means got, I leave to your own conscience—
To furnish Rome, and to prepare the ways
You have for dignities to the mere undoing   330
Of all the kingdom. Many more there are,
Which since they are of you, and odious,
I will not taint my mouth with.
LORD CHAMBERLAIN   O, my lord,
Press not a falling man too far. 'Tis virtue.
His faults lie open to the laws. Let them,   335
Not you, correct him. My heart weeps to see him
So little of his great self.
SURREY   I forgive him.
SUFFOLK
Lord Cardinal, the King's further pleasure is—
Because all those things you have done of late,
By your power legantine within this kingdom,   340
Fall into th' compass of a praemunire—
That therefore such a writ be sued against you,
To forfeit all your goods, lands, tenements,
Chattels, and whatsoever, and to be
Out of the King's protection. This is my charge.   345
NORFOLK (*to Wolsey*)
And so we'll leave you to your meditations
How to live better. For your stubborn answer
About the giving back the great seal to us,
The King shall know it and, no doubt, shall thank you.
So fare you well, my little good lord Cardinal.   350
                    Exeunt all but Wolsey
CARDINAL WOLSEY
So farewell—to the little good you bear me.
Farewell, a long farewell, to all my greatness!
This is the state of man. Today he puts forth
The tender leaves of hopes; tomorrow blossoms,
And bears his blushing honours thick upon him;   355
The third day comes a frost, a killing frost,
And when he thinks, good easy man, full surely
His greatness is a-ripening, nips his root,
And then he falls, as I do. I have ventured,
Like little wanton boys that swim on bladders,   360
This many summers in a sea of glory,
But far beyond my depth; my high-blown pride
At length broke under me, and now has left me
Weary, and old with service, to the mercy
Of a rude stream that must for ever hide me.   365
Vain pomp and glory of this world, I hate ye!
I feel my heart new opened. O, how wretched
Is that poor man that hangs on princes' favours!
There is betwixt that smile we would aspire to,
That sweet aspect of princes, and their ruin,   370
More pangs and fears than wars or women have,
And when he falls, he falls like Lucifer,
Never to hope again.
        Enter Cromwell, who then stands amazed
                    Why, how now, Cromwell?

CROMWELL
I have no power to speak, sir.
CARDINAL WOLSEY   What, amazed
At my misfortunes? Can thy spirit wonder   375
A great man should decline?
        ⌈*Cromwell begins to weep*⌉
                    Nay, an you weep
I am fall'n indeed.
CROMWELL   How does your grace?
CARDINAL WOLSEY   Why, well—
Never so truly happy, my good Cromwell.
I know myself now, and I feel within me
A peace above all earthly dignities,   380
A still and quiet conscience. The King has cured me.
I humbly thank his grace, and from these shoulders,
These ruined pillars, out of pity, taken
A load would sink a navy—too much honour.
O, 'tis a burden, Cromwell, 'tis a burden   385
Too heavy for a man that hopes for heaven.
CROMWELL
I am glad your grace has made that right use of it.
CARDINAL WOLSEY
I hope I have. I am able now, methinks,
Out of a fortitude of soul I feel,
To endure more miseries and greater far   390
Than my weak-hearted enemies dare offer.
What news abroad?
CROMWELL   The heaviest and the worst
Is your displeasure with the King.
CARDINAL WOLSEY   God bless him.
CROMWELL
The next is that Sir Thomas More is chosen
Lord Chancellor in your place.
CARDINAL WOLSEY   That's somewhat sudden.
But he's a learnèd man. May he continue   396
Long in his highness' favour, and do justice
For truth's sake and his conscience, that his bones,
When he has run his course and sleeps in blessings,
May have a tomb of orphans' tears wept on him.   400
What more?
CROMWELL   That Cranmer is returned with welcome,
Installed lord Archbishop of Canterbury.
CARDINAL WOLSEY
That's news indeed.
CROMWELL   Last, that the Lady Anne,
Whom the King hath in secrecy long married,
This day was viewed in open as his queen,   405
Going to chapel, and the voice is now
Only about her coronation.
CARDINAL WOLSEY
There was the weight that pulled me down. O,
        Cromwell,
The King has gone beyond me. All my glories
In that one woman I have lost for ever.   410
No sun shall ever usher forth mine honours,
Or gild again the noble troops that waited
Upon my smiles. Go, get thee from me, Cromwell.
I am a poor fall'n man, unworthy now
To be thy lord and master. Seek the King—   415

That sun I pray may never set—I have told him
What and how true thou art. He will advance thee.
Some little memory of me will stir him.
I know his noble nature not to let
Thy hopeful service perish too. Good Cromwell,   420
Neglect him not. Make use now, and provide
For thine own future safety.
CROMWELL ⌈weeping⌉   O, my lord,
Must I then leave you? Must I needs forgo
So good, so noble, and so true a master?
Bear witness, all that have not hearts of iron,   425
With what a sorrow Cromwell leaves his lord.
The King shall have my service, but my prayers
For ever and for ever shall be yours.
CARDINAL WOLSEY (weeping)
Cromwell, I did not think to shed a tear
In all my miseries, but thou hast forced me,   430
Out of thy honest truth, to play the woman.
Let's dry our eyes, and thus far hear me, Cromwell,
And when I am forgotten, as I shall be,
And sleep in dull cold marble, where no mention
Of me more must be heard of, say I taught thee—   435
Say Wolsey, that once trod the ways of glory,
And sounded all the depths and shoals of honour,
Found thee a way, out of his wreck, to rise in,
A sure and safe one, though thy master missed it.
Mark but my fall, and that that ruined me.   440
Cromwell, I charge thee, fling away ambition.
By that sin fell the angels. How can man, then,
The image of his maker, hope to win by it?
Love thyself last. Cherish those hearts that hate thee.
Corruption wins not more than honesty.   445
Still in thy right hand carry gentle peace
To silence envious tongues. Be just, and fear not.
Let all the ends thou aim'st at be thy country's,
Thy God's, and truth's. Then if thou fall'st, O
       Cromwell,
Thou fall'st a blessèd martyr.   450
Serve the King. And prithee, lead me in—
There take an inventory of all I have:
To the last penny 'tis the King's. My robe,
And my integrity to heaven, is all
I dare now call mine own. O Cromwell, Cromwell,   455
Had I but served my God with half the zeal
I served my King, He would not in mine age
Have left me naked to mine enemies.
CROMWELL
Good sir, have patience.
CARDINAL WOLSEY   So I have. Farewell
The hopes of court; my hopes in heaven do dwell.   460
                                            Exeunt

                        ✿

4.1   *Enter the two Gentlemen meeting one another. The*
        first holds a paper
FIRST GENTLEMAN
You're well met once again.
SECOND GENTLEMAN   So are you.

FIRST GENTLEMAN
You come to take your stand here and behold
The Lady Anne pass from her coronation?
SECOND GENTLEMAN
'Tis all my business. At our last encounter
The Duke of Buckingham came from his trial.   5
FIRST GENTLEMAN
'Tis very true. But that time offered sorrow,
This, general joy.
SECOND GENTLEMAN   'Tis well. The citizens,
I am sure, have shown at full their royal minds—
As, let 'em have their rights, they are ever forward—
In celebration of this day with shows,   10
Pageants, and sights of honour.
FIRST GENTLEMAN   Never greater,
Nor, I'll assure you, better taken, sir.
SECOND GENTLEMAN
May I be bold to ask what that contains,
That paper in your hand?
FIRST GENTLEMAN   Yes, 'tis the list
Of those that claim their offices this day   15
By custom of the coronation.
The Duke of Suffolk is the first, and claims
To be High Steward; next, the Duke of Norfolk,
He to be Earl Marshal. You may read the rest.
        He gives him the paper
SECOND GENTLEMAN
I thank you, sir. Had I not known those customs,   20
I should have been beholden to your paper.
But I beseech you, what's become of Katherine,
The Princess Dowager? How goes her business?
FIRST GENTLEMAN
That I can tell you too. The Archbishop
Of Canterbury, accompanied with other   25
Learnèd and reverend fathers of his order,
Held a late court at Dunstable, six miles off
From Ampthill, where the Princess lay; to which
She was often cited by them, but appeared not.
And, to be short, for not appearance, and   30
The King's late scruple, by the main assent
Of all these learnèd men, she was divorced,
And the late marriage made of none effect,
Since which she was removed to Kimbolton,
Where she remains now sick.
SECOND GENTLEMAN   Alas, good lady!   35
        Flourish of trumpets within
The trumpets sound. Stand close. The Queen is coming.
        Enter the coronation procession, which passes over
        the stage in order and state. Hautboys, within,
        ⌈*play during the procession*⌉

        THE ORDER OF THE CORONATION

        1. First, ⌈enter⌉ trumpeters, who play a lively
        flourish.
        2. Then, enter two judges.
        3. Then, enter the Lord Chancellor, with both the
        purse containing the great seal and the mace borne
        before him.

*4. Then, enter choristers singing; ⌈with them,
musicians playing.⌉*
*5. Then, enter the Lord Mayor of London bearing
the mace, followed by Garter King-of-Arms wearing
his coat of arms and a gilt copper crown.*
*6. Then, enter Marquis Dorset bearing a sceptre of
gold, and wearing, on his head, a demi-coronal of
gold and, about his neck, a collar of esses. With him
enter the Earl of Surrey bearing the rod of silver
with the dove, crowned with an earl's coronet, and
also wearing a collar of esses.*
*7. Next, enter the Duke of Suffolk as High Steward,
in his robe of estate, with his coronet on his head,
and bearing a long white staff. With him enter the
Duke of Norfolk with the rod of marshalship and
a coronet on his head. Each wears a collar of esses.*
*8. Then, under a canopy borne by four barons of the
Cinque Ports, enter Anne, the new Queen, in her robe.
Her hair, which hangs loose, is richly adorned with
pearl. She wears a crown. Accompanying her on either
side are the Bishops of London and Winchester.*
*9. Next, enter the old Duchess of Norfolk, in a
coronal of gold wrought with flowers, bearing the
Queen's train.*
*10. Finally, enter certain ladies or countesses, with
plain circlets of gold without flowers.*

*The two Gentlemen comment on the procession as it
passes over the stage*
SECOND GENTLEMAN
    A royal train, believe me. These I know.
    Who's that that bears the sceptre?
FIRST GENTLEMAN   Marquis Dorset.
    And that, the Earl of Surrey with the rod.
SECOND GENTLEMAN
    A bold brave gentleman. That should be   40
    The Duke of Suffolk?
FIRST GENTLEMAN   'Tis the same: High Steward.
SECOND GENTLEMAN
    And that, my lord of Norfolk?
FIRST GENTLEMAN   Yes.
SECOND GENTLEMAN (*seeing Anne*)   Heaven bless thee!
    Thou hast the sweetest face I ever looked on.
    Sir, as I have a soul, she is an angel.
    Our King has all the Indies in his arms,   45
    And more, and richer, when he strains that lady.
    I cannot blame his conscience.
FIRST GENTLEMAN   They that bear
    The cloth of honour over her are four barons
    Of the Cinque Ports.
SECOND GENTLEMAN Those men are happy,   50
    And so are all are near her.
    I take it she that carries up the train
    Is that old noble lady, Duchess of Norfolk.
FIRST GENTLEMAN
    It is. And all the rest are countesses.
SECOND GENTLEMAN
    Their coronets say so. These are stars indeed—   55

⌈FIRST GENTLEMAN⌉
    And sometimes falling ones.
SECOND GENTLEMAN   No more of that.
                    *Exit the last of the procession, and then
                        a great flourish of trumpets within
            Enter a third Gentleman ⌈in a sweat⌉*
FIRST GENTLEMAN
    God save you, sir. Where have you been broiling?
THIRD GENTLEMAN
    Among the crowd i'th' Abbey, where a finger
    Could not be wedged in more. I am stifled
    With the mere rankness of their joy.   60
SECOND GENTLEMAN
    You saw the ceremony?
THIRD GENTLEMAN   That I did.
FIRST GENTLEMAN How was it?
THIRD GENTLEMAN
    Well worth the seeing.
SECOND GENTLEMAN   Good sir, speak it to us.
THIRD GENTLEMAN
    As well as I am able. The rich stream
    Of lords and ladies, having brought the Queen   65
    To a prepared place in the choir, fell off
    A distance from her, while her grace sat down
    To rest a while—some half an hour or so—
    In a rich chair of state, opposing freely
    The beauty of her person to the people.   70
    Believe me, sir, she is the goodliest woman
    That ever lay by man; which when the people
    Had the full view of, such a noise arose
    As the shrouds make at sea in a stiff tempest,
    As loud and to as many tunes. Hats, cloaks—   75
    Doublets, I think—flew up, and had their faces
    Been loose, this day they had been lost. Such joy
    I never saw before. Great-bellied women,
    That had not half a week to go, like rams
    In the old time of war, would shake the press,   80
    And make 'em reel before 'em. No man living
    Could say 'This is my wife' there, all were woven
    So strangely in one piece.
SECOND GENTLEMAN   But what followed?
THIRD GENTLEMAN
    At length her grace rose, and with modest paces
    Came to the altar, where she kneeled, and saint-like 85
    Cast her fair eyes to heaven, and prayed devoutly,
    Then rose again, and bowed her to the people,
    When by the Archbishop of Canterbury
    She had all the royal makings of a queen,
    As holy oil, Edward Confessor's crown,   90
    The rod and bird of peace, and all such emblems
    Laid nobly on her. Which performed, the choir,
    With all the choicest music of the kingdom,
    Together sung *Te Deum*. So she parted,
    And with the same full state paced back again   95
    To York Place, where the feast is held.
FIRST GENTLEMAN   Sir,
    You must no more call it York Place—that's past,

For since the Cardinal fell, that title's lost.
'Tis now the King's, and called Whitehall.
THIRD GENTLEMAN   I know it,
But 'tis so lately altered that the old name   100
Is fresh about me.
SECOND GENTLEMAN   What two reverend bishops
Were those that went on each side of the Queen?
THIRD GENTLEMAN
Stokesley and Gardiner, the one of Winchester—
Newly preferred from the King's secretary—
The other London.
SECOND GENTLEMAN   He of Winchester   105
Is held no great good lover of the Archbishop's,
The virtuous Cranmer.
THIRD GENTLEMAN   All the land knows that.
However, yet there is no great breach. When it
      comes,
Cranmer will find a friend will not shrink from him.
SECOND GENTLEMAN
Who may that be, I pray you?
THIRD GENTLEMAN   Thomas Cromwell,   110
A man in much esteem with th' King, and truly
A worthy friend. The King has made him
Master o'th' Jewel House,
And one already of the Privy Council.
SECOND GENTLEMAN
He will deserve more.
THIRD GENTLEMAN   Yes, without all doubt.   115
Come, gentlemen, ye shall go my way,
Which is to th' court, and there ye shall be my
      guests.
Something I can command. As I walk thither
I'll tell ye more.
FIRST *and* SECOND GENTLEMEN You may command us, sir.
                                                    Exeunt

4.2   ⌜*Three chairs.*⌝ *Enter Katherine Dowager, sick, led*
       between Griffith her gentleman usher, and Patience
       her woman
GRIFFITH
How does your grace?
KATHERINE   O Griffith, sick to death.
My legs, like loaden branches, bow to th' earth,
Willing to leave their burden. Reach a chair.
       A chair is brought to her. She sits
So now, methinks, I feel a little ease.
Didst thou not tell me, Griffith, as thou led'st me,   5
That the great child of honour, Cardinal Wolsey,
Was dead?
GRIFFITH   Yes, madam, but I think your grace,
Out of the pain you suffered, gave no ear to't.
KATHERINE
Prithee, good Griffith, tell me how he died.
If well, he stepped before me happily   10
For my example.
GRIFFITH   Well, the voice goes, madam.
For after the stout Earl Northumberland

Arrested him at York, and brought him forward,
As a man sorely tainted, to his answer,
He fell sick, suddenly, and grew so ill   15
He could not sit his mule.
KATHERINE   Alas, poor man.
GRIFFITH
At last, with easy roads, he came to Leicester,
Lodged in the abbey, where the reverend abbot,
With all his convent, honourably received him,
To whom he gave these words: 'O father abbot,   20
An old man broken with the storms of state
Is come to lay his weary bones among ye.
Give him a little earth, for charity.'
So went to bed, where eagerly his sickness
Pursued him still, and three nights after this,   25
About the hour of eight, which he himself
Foretold should be his last, full of repentance,
Continual meditations, tears, and sorrows,
He gave his honours to the world again,
His blessèd part to heaven, and slept in peace.   30
KATHERINE
So may he rest, his faults lie gently on him.
Yet thus far, Griffith, give me leave to speak him,
And yet with charity. He was a man
Of an unbounded stomach, ever ranking
Himself with princes; one that by suggestion   35
Tied all the kingdom. Simony was fair play.
His own opinion was his law. I'th' presence
He would say untruths, and be ever double
Both in his words and meaning. He was never,
But where he meant to ruin, pitiful.   40
His promises were, as he then was, mighty;
But his performance, as he is now, nothing.
Of his own body he was ill, and gave
The clergy ill example.
GRIFFITH   Noble madam,
Men's evil manners live in brass, their virtues   45
We write in water. May it please your highness
To hear me speak his good now?
KATHERINE   Yes, good Griffith,
I were malicious else.
GRIFFITH   This cardinal,
Though from an humble stock, undoubtedly
Was fashioned to much honour. From his cradle   50
He was a scholar, and a ripe and good one,
Exceeding wise, fair-spoken, and persuading;
Lofty and sour to them that loved him not,
But to those men that sought him, sweet as summer.
And though he were unsatisfied in getting—   55
Which was a sin—yet in bestowing, madam,
He was most princely: ever witness for him
Those twins of learning that he raised in you,
Ipswich and Oxford—one of which fell with him,
Unwilling to outlive the good that did it;   60
The other, though unfinished, yet so famous,
So excellent in art, and still so rising,
That Christendom shall ever speak his virtue.

His overthrow heaped happiness upon him,
For then, and not till then, he felt himself,   65
And found the blessèdness of being little.
And to add greater honours to his age
Than man could give him, he died fearing God.
KATHERINE
After my death I wish no other herald,
No other speaker of my living actions   70
To keep mine honour from corruption
But such an honest chronicler as Griffith.
Whom I most hated living, thou hast made me,
With thy religious truth and modesty,
Now in his ashes honour. Peace be with him.   75
(*To her woman*) Patience, be near me still, and set me
lower.
I have not long to trouble thee. Good Griffith,
Cause the musicians play me that sad note
I named my knell, whilst I sit meditating
On that celestial harmony I go to.   80
Sad and solemn music. Katherine sleeps
GRIFFITH (*to the woman*)
She is asleep. Good wench, let's sit down quiet
For fear we wake her. Softly, gentle Patience.
They sit

THE VISION

*Enter, solemnly tripping one after another, six
personages clad in white robes, wearing on their
heads garlands of bays, and golden visors on their
faces. They carry branches of bays or palm in their
hands. They first congé unto Katherine, then
dance ; and, at certain changes, the first two hold a
spare garland over her head at which the other four
make reverent curtsies. Then the two that held the
garland deliver the same to the other next two,
who observe the same order in their changes and
holding the garland over her head. Which done, they
deliver the same garland to the last two who
likewise observe the same order. At which, as it
were by inspiration, she makes in her sleep signs of
rejoicing, and holdeth up her hands to heaven. And
so in their dancing vanish, carrying the garland
with them. The music continues*
KATHERINE (*waking*)
Spirits of peace, where are ye? Are ye all gone,
And leave me here in wretchedness behind ye?
Griffith and Patience rise and come forward
GRIFFITH
Madam, we are here.
KATHERINE   It is not you I call for.   85
Saw ye none enter since I slept?
GRIFFITH   None, madam.
KATHERINE
No? Saw you not even now a blessèd troop
Invite me to a banquet, whose bright faces
Cast thousand beams upon me, like the sun?
They promised me eternal happiness,   90

And brought me garlands, Griffith, which I feel
I am not worthy yet to wear. I shall,
Assuredly.
GRIFFITH
I am most joyful, madam, such good dreams
Possess your fancy.
KATHERINE   Bid the music leave.   95
They are harsh and heavy to me.
Music ceases
PATIENCE (*to Griffith*)   Do you note
How much her grace is altered on the sudden?
How long her face is drawn? How pale she looks,
And of an earthy colour? Mark her eyes?
GRIFFITH
She is going, wench. Pray, pray.
PATIENCE   Heaven comfort her.
Enter a Messenger
MESSENGER (*to Katherine*)
An't like your grace—
KATHERINE   You are a saucy fellow—   101
Deserve we no more reverence?
GRIFFITH (*to the Messenger*)   You are to blame,
Knowing she will not lose her wonted greatness,
To use so rude behaviour. Go to, kneel.
MESSENGER (*kneeling before Katherine*)
I humbly do entreat your highness' pardon.   105
My haste made me unmannerly. There is staying
A gentleman sent from the King to see you.
KATHERINE
Admit him entrance, Griffith. But this fellow
Let me ne'er see again.   *Exit Messenger*
Enter Lord Caputius ⌈ushered by Griffith⌉
If my sight fail not,
You should be lord ambassador from the Emperor,   110
My royal nephew, and your name Caputius.
CAPUTIUS
Madam, the same, ⌈*bowing*⌉ your servant.
KATHERINE   O, my lord,
The times and titles now are altered strangely
With me since first you knew me. But I pray you,
What is your pleasure with me?
CAPUTIUS   Noble lady,   115
First mine own service to your grace ; the next,
The King's request that I would visit you,
Who grieves much for your weakness, and by me
Sends you his princely commendations,
And heartily entreats you take good comfort.   120
KATHERINE
O, my good lord, that comfort comes too late,
'Tis like a pardon after execution.
That gentle physic, given in time, had cured me ;
But now I am past all comforts here but prayers.
How does his highness?
CAPUTIUS   Madam, in good health.   125
KATHERINE
So may he ever do, and ever flourish
When I shall dwell with worms, and my poor name

Banished the kingdom. (*To her woman*) Patience, is
that letter
I caused you write yet sent away?
PATIENCE   No, madam.
KATHERINE (*to Caputius*)
Sir, I most humbly pray you to deliver   130
This to my lord the King.
The letter is given to Caputius
CAPUTIUS   Most willing, madam.
KATHERINE
In which I have commended to his goodness
The model of our chaste loves, his young daughter—
The dews of heaven fall thick in blessings on her—
Beseeching him to give her virtuous breeding.   135
She is young, and of a noble modest nature.
I hope she will deserve well—and a little
To love her for her mother's sake, that loved him,
Heaven knows how dearly. My next poor petition
Is that his noble grace would have some pity   140
Upon my wretched women, that so long
Have followed both my fortunes faithfully;
Of which there is not one, I dare avow—
And now I should not lie—but will deserve,
For virtue and true beauty of the soul,   145
For honesty and decent carriage,
A right good husband. Let him be a noble,
And sure those men are happy that shall have 'em.
The last is for my men—they are the poorest,
But poverty could never draw 'em from me—   150
That they may have their wages duly paid 'em,
And something over to remember me by.
If heaven had pleased to have given me longer life,
And able means, we had not parted thus.
These are the whole contents; and, good my lord, 155
By that you love the dearest in this world,
As you wish Christian peace to souls departed,
Stand these poor people's friend and urge the King
To do me this last rite.
CAPUTIUS   By heaven I will,
Or let me lose the fashion of a man.   160
KATHERINE
I thank you, honest lord. Remember me
In all humility unto his highness.
Say his long trouble now is passing
Out of this world. Tell him, in death I blessed him,
For so I will. Mine eyes grow dim. Farewell,   165
My lord. Griffith, farewell.
(*To her woman*)   Nay, Patience,
You must not leave me yet. I must to bed.
Call in more women. When I am dead, good wench,
Let me be used with honour. Strew me over
With maiden flowers, that all the world may know 170
I was a chaste wife to my grave. Embalm me,
Then lay me forth. Although unqueened, yet like
A queen and daughter to a king inter me.
I can no more.
Exeunt ⌜Caputius and Griffith at one door;
Patience⌝ leading Katherine ⌜at another⌝

❀

5.1   *Enter ⌜at one door⌝ Gardiner, Bishop of*
         Winchester; before him, a Page with a torch
GARDINER
It's one o'clock, boy, is't not?
PAGE   It hath struck.
GARDINER
These should be hours for necessities,
Not for delights; times to repair our nature
With comforting repose, and not for us
To waste these times.
         Enter ⌜at another door⌝ Sir Thomas Lovell, meeting
         them
                         Good hour of night, Sir Thomas!
Whither so late?
LOVELL   Came you from the King, my lord?   6
GARDINER
I did, Sir Thomas, and left him at primero
With the Duke of Suffolk.
LOVELL   I must to him too,
Before he go to bed. I'll take my leave.
GARDINER
Not yet, Sir Thomas Lovell—what's the matter?   10
It seems you are in haste. An if there be
No great offence belongs to't, give your friend
Some touch of your late business. Affairs that walk,
As they say spirits do, at midnight, have
In them a wilder nature than the business   15
That seeks dispatch by day.
LOVELL   My lord, I love you,
And durst commend a secret to your ear
Much weightier than this work. The Queen's in labour—
They say in great extremity—and feared
She'll with the labour end.
GARDINER   The fruit she goes with   20
I pray for heartily, that it may find
Good time, and live. But, for the stock, Sir Thomas,
I wish it grubbed up now.
LOVELL   Methinks I could
Cry the amen, and yet my conscience says
She's a good creature and, sweet lady, does   25
Deserve our better wishes.
GARDINER   But sir, sir,
Hear me, Sir Thomas. You're a gentleman
Of mine own way. I know you wise, religious.
And let me tell you, it will ne'er be well—
'Twill not, Sir Thomas Lovell, take't of me—   30
Till Cranmer, Cromwell—her two hands—and she,
Sleep in their graves.
LOVELL   Now, sir, you speak of two
The most remarked i'th' kingdom. As for Cromwell,
Beside that of the Jewel House is made Master
O'th' Rolls and the King's secretary. Further, sir, 35
Stands in the gap and trade of more preferments
With which the time will load him. Th'Archbishop
Is the King's hand and tongue, and who dare speak
One syllable against him?
GARDINER   Yes, yes, Sir Thomas—
There are that dare, and I myself have ventured   40
To speak my mind of him, and, indeed, this day,

Sir—I may tell it you, I think—I have
Incensed the lords o'th' Council that he is—
For so I know he is, they know he is—
A most arch heretic, a pestilence   45
That does infect the land; with which they, moved,
Have broken with the King, who hath so far
Given ear to our complaint, of his great grace
And princely care, foreseeing those fell mischiefs
Our reasons laid before him, hath commanded   50
Tomorrow morning to the Council board
He be convented. He's a rank weed, Sir Thomas,
And we must root him out. From your affairs
I hinder you too long. Good night, Sir Thomas.

LOVELL
Many good nights, my lord; I rest your servant.   55
Exeunt Gardiner and Page at one door
Enter King Henry and Suffolk at another door

KING HENRY (*to Suffolk*)
Charles, I will play no more tonight.
My mind's not on't. You are too hard for me.

SUFFOLK
Sir, I did never win of you before.

KING HENRY But little, Charles,
Nor shall not when my fancy's on my play.   60
Now, Lovell, from the Queen what is the news?

LOVELL
I could not personally deliver to her
What you commanded me, but by her woman
I sent your message, who returned her thanks
In the great'st humbleness, and desired your highness
Most heartily to pray for her.

KING HENRY   What sayst thou? Ha? 66
To pray for her? What, is she crying out?

LOVELL
So said her woman, and that her suffrance made
Almost each pang a death.

KING HENRY   Alas, good lady.

SUFFOLK
God safely quit her of her burden, and   70
With gentle travail, to the gladding of
Your highness with an heir.

KING HENRY   'Tis midnight, Charles.
Prithee to bed, and in thy prayers remember
Th'estate of my poor queen. Leave me alone,
For I must think of that which company   75
Would not be friendly to.

SUFFOLK   I wish your highness
A quiet night, and my good mistress will
Remember in my prayers.

KING HENRY   Charles, good night.
Exit Suffolk
Enter Sir Anthony Denny
Well, sir, what follows?

DENNY
Sir, I have brought my lord the Archbishop,   80
As you commanded me.

KING HENRY   Ha, Canterbury?

DENNY
Ay, my good lord.

KING HENRY   'Tis true—where is he, Denny?

DENNY
He attends your highness' pleasure.

KING HENRY   Bring him to us.
Exit Denny

LOVELL (*aside*)
This is about that which the Bishop spake.
I am happily come hither.   85
Enter Cranmer the Archbishop, ushered by Denny

KING HENRY (*to Lovell and Denny*) Avoid the gallery.
⌐*Denny begins to depart.*⌐ *Lovell seems to stay*
Ha? I have said. Be gone.
What?   *Exeunt Lovell and Denny*

CRANMER (*aside*)
I am fearful. Wherefore frowns he thus?
'Tis his aspect of terror. All's not well.

KING HENRY
How now, my lord? You do desire to know   90
Wherefore I sent for you.

CRANMER (*kneeling*)   It is my duty
T'attend your highness' pleasure.

KING HENRY   Pray you, arise,
My good and gracious Lord of Canterbury.
Come, you and I must walk a turn together.
I have news to tell you. Come, come—give me your
hand.   95
⌐*Cranmer rises. They walk*⌐
Ah, my good lord, I grieve at what I speak,
And am right sorry to repeat what follows.
I have, and most unwillingly, of late
Heard many grievous—I do say, my lord,
Grievous—complaints of you, which, being considered,
Have moved us and our Council that you shall   101
This morning come before us, where I know
You cannot with such freedom purge yourself
But that, till further trial in those charges
Which will require your answer, you must take   105
Your patience to you, and be well contented
To make your house our Tower. You a brother of us,
It fits we thus proceed, or else no witness
Would come against you.

CRANMER (*kneeling*)   I humbly thank your highness,
And am right glad to catch this good occasion   110
Most throughly to be winnowed, where my chaff
And corn shall fly asunder. For I know
There's none stands under more calumnious tongues
Than I myself, poor man.

KING HENRY   Stand up, good Canterbury.
Thy truth and thy integrity is rooted   115
In us, thy friend. Give me thy hand. Stand up.
Prithee, let's walk.
Cranmer rises. They walk
                       Now, by my halidom,
What manner of man are you? My lord, I looked
You would have given me your petition that

I should have ta'en some pains to bring together   120
Yourself and your accusers, and to have heard you
Without indurance further.

CRANMER   Most dread liege,
The good I stand on is my truth and honesty.
If they shall fail, I with mine enemies
Will triumph o'er my person, which I weigh not,   125
Being of those virtues vacant. I fear nothing
What can be said against me.

KING HENRY   Know you not
How your state stands i'th' world, with the whole
    world?
Your enemies are many, and not small; their practices
Must bear the same proportion, and not ever   130
The justice and the truth o'th' question carries
The dew o'th' verdict with it. At what ease
Might corrupt minds procure knaves as corrupt
To swear against you? Such things have been done.
You are potently opposed, and with a malice   135
Of as great size. Ween you of better luck,
I mean in perjured witness, than your master,
Whose minister you are, whiles here he lived
Upon this naughty earth? Go to, go to.
You take a precipice for no leap of danger,   140
And woo your own destruction.

CRANMER   God and your majesty
Protect mine innocence, or I fall into
The trap is laid for me.

KING HENRY   Be of good cheer.
They shall no more prevail than we give way to.
Keep comfort to you, and this morning see   145
You do appear before them. If they shall chance,
In charging you with matters, to commit you,
The best persuasions to the contrary
Fail not to use, and with what vehemency
Th'occasion shall instruct you. If entreaties   150
Will render you no remedy, ⌜giving his ring⌝ this ring
Deliver them, and your appeal to us
There make before them.

    Cranmer weeps
                    Look, the good man weeps.
He's honest, on mine honour. God's blest mother,
I swear he is true-hearted, and a soul   155
None better in my kingdom. Get you gone,
And do as I have bid you.   Exit Cranmer
                    He has strangled
His language in his tears.

    Enter the Old Lady
⌜LOVELL⌝ (within)   Come back! What mean you?
    ⌜Enter Lovell, following her⌝

OLD LADY
I'll not come back. The tidings that I bring
Will make my boldness manners. (To the King) Now
        good angels   160
Fly o'er thy royal head, and shade thy person
Under their blessèd wings.

KING HENRY   Now by thy looks

I guess thy message. Is the Queen delivered?
Say, 'Ay, and of a boy.'

OLD LADY   Ay, ay, my liege,
And of a lovely boy. The God of heaven   165
Both now and ever bless her! 'Tis a girl
Promises boys hereafter. Sir, your queen
Desires your visitation, and to be
Acquainted with this stranger. 'Tis as like you
As cherry is to cherry.

KING HENRY   Lovell—

LOVELL   Sir?   170

KING HENRY
Give her an hundred marks. I'll to the Queen.   Exit

OLD LADY
An hundred marks? By this light, I'll ha' more.
An ordinary groom is for such payment.
I will have more, or scold it out of him.
Said I for this the girl was like to him? I'll   175
Have more, or else unsay't; and now, while 'tis hot,
I'll put it to the issue.   Exeunt

5.2   Enter ⌜pursuivants, pages, footboys, and grooms.
        Then enter⌝ Cranmer, Archbishop of Canterbury

CRANMER
I hope I am not too late, and yet the gentleman
That was sent to me from the council prayed me
To make great haste. All fast? What means this?
        (Calling at the door) Ho!
Who waits there?
    Enter a Doorkeeper
                    Sure you know me?

DOORKEEPER   Yes, my lord,
But yet I cannot help you.

CRANMER   Why?   5
    ⌜Enter Doctor Butts, passing over the stage⌝

DOORKEEPER
Your grace must wait till you be called for.

CRANMER   So.

BUTTS (aside)
This is a piece of malice. I am glad
I came this way so happily. The King
Shall understand it presently.   Exit

CRANMER (aside)   'Tis Butts,
The King's physician. As he passed along   10
How earnestly he cast his eyes upon me!
Pray heaven he found not my disgrace. For certain
This is of purpose laid by some that hate me—
God turn their hearts, I never sought their malice—
To quench mine honour. They would shame to make me
Wait else at door, a fellow Councillor,   16
'Mong boys, grooms, and lackeys. But their pleasures
Must be fulfilled, and I attend with patience.
    Enter King Henry and Doctor Butts at a window,
        above

BUTTS
I'll show your grace the strangest sight—

KING HENRY   What's that, Butts?

BUTTS

I think your highness saw this many a day.   20

KING HENRY

Body o'me, where is it?

BUTTS (*pointing at Cranmer, below*) There, my lord.
The high promotion of his grace of Canterbury,
Who holds his state at door, 'mongst pursuivants,
Pages, and footboys.

KING HENRY   Ha? 'Tis he indeed.
Is this the honour they do one another?   25
'Tis well there's one above 'em yet. I had thought
They had parted so much honesty among 'em—
At least good manners—as not thus to suffer
A man of his place and so near our favour
To dance attendance on their lordships' pleasures,   30
And at the door, too, like a post with packets!
By holy Mary, Butts, there's knavery!
Let 'em alone, and draw the curtain close.
We shall hear more anon.

⌜*Cranmer and the doorkeeper stand to one side.*
                    Exeunt the lackeys⌝
*Above, Butts ⌜partly⌝ draws the curtain close.
Below, a council table is brought in along with
chairs and stools, and placed under the cloth of state.
Enter the Lord Chancellor, who places himself at the
upper end of the table, on the left hand, leaving a
seat void above him at the table's head as for
Canterbury's seat. The Duke of Suffolk, the Duke of
Norfolk, the Earl of Surrey, the Lord Chamberlain,
and Gardiner, the Bishop of Winchester, seat
themselves in order on each side of the table. Cromwell
sits at the lower end, and acts as secretary*

LORD CHANCELLOR (*to Cromwell*)

Speak to the business, master secretary.   35
Why are we met in council?

CROMWELL   Please your honours,
The chief cause concerns his grace of Canterbury.

GARDINER

Has he had knowledge of it?

CROMWELL   Yes.

NORFOLK (*to the Doorkeeper*)   Who waits there?

DOORKEEPER ⌜*coming forward*⌝
Without, my noble lords?

GARDINER   Yes.

DOORKEEPER   My lord Archbishop;
And has done half an hour, to know your pleasures. 40

LORD CHANCELLOR

Let him come in.

DOORKEEPER (*to Cranmer*) Your grace may enter now.
                    Cranmer approaches the Council table

LORD CHANCELLOR

My good lord Archbishop, I'm very sorry
To sit here at this present and behold
That chair stand empty, but we all are men
In our own natures frail, and capable   45
Of our flesh; few are angels; out of which frailty
And want of wisdom, you, that best should teach us,
Have misdemeaned yourself, and not a little,

Toward the King first, then his laws, in filling
The whole realm, by your teaching and your chaplains'—
For so we are informed—with new opinions,   51
Diverse and dangerous, which are heresies,
And, not reformed, may prove pernicious.

GARDINER

Which reformation must be sudden too,
My noble lords; for those that tame wild horses   55
Pace 'em not in their hands to make 'em gentle,
But stop their mouths with stubborn bits and spur 'em
Till they obey the manège. If we suffer,
Out of our easiness and childish pity
To one man's honour, this contagious sickness,   60
Farewell all physic—and what follows then?
Commotions, uproars—with a general taint
Of the whole state, as of late days our neighbours,
The upper Germany, can dearly witness,
Yet freshly pitied in our memories.   65

CRANMER

My good lords, hitherto in all the progress
Both of my life and office, I have laboured,
And with no little study, that my teaching
And the strong course of my authority
Might go one way, and safely; and the end   70
Was ever to do well. Nor is there living—
I speak it with a single heart, my lords—
A man that more detests, more stirs against,
Both in his private conscience and his place,
Defacers of a public peace than I do.   75
Pray heaven the King may never find a heart
With less allegiance in it. Men that make
Envy and crooked malice nourishment
Dare bite the best. I do beseech your lordships
That, in this case of justice, my accusers,   80
Be what they will, may stand forth face to face,
And freely urge against me.

SUFFOLK   Nay, my lord,
That cannot be. You are a Councillor,
And by that virtue no man dare accuse you.   84

GARDINER (*to Cranmer*)

My lord, because we have business of more moment,
We will be short with you. 'Tis his highness' pleasure
And our consent, for better trial of you,
From hence you be committed to the Tower
Where, being but a private man again,
You shall know many dare accuse you boldly,   90
More than, I fear, you are provided for.

CRANMER

Ah, my good lord of Winchester, I thank you.
You are always my good friend. If your will pass,
I shall both find your lordship judge and juror,
You are so merciful. I see your end—   95
'Tis my undoing. Love and meekness, lord,
Become a churchman better than ambition.
Win straying souls with modesty again;
Cast none away. That I shall clear myself,
Lay all the weight ye can upon my patience,   100
I make as little doubt as you do conscience

In doing daily wrongs. I could say more,
But reverence to your calling makes me modest.

GARDINER

My lord, my lord—you are a sectary,   104
That's the plain truth. Your painted gloss discovers,
To men that understand you, words and weakness.

CROMWELL (*to Gardiner*)

My lord of Winchester, you're a little,
By your good favour, too sharp. Men so noble,
However faulty, yet should find respect
For what they have been. 'Tis a cruelty   110
To load a falling man.

GARDINER   Good master secretary,
I cry your honour mercy. You may worst
Of all this table say so.

CROMWELL   Why, my lord?

GARDINER

Do not I know you for a favourer
Of this new sect? Ye are not sound.

CROMWELL   Not sound?   115

GARDINER

Not sound, I say.

CROMWELL   Would you were half so honest!
Men's prayers then would seek you, not their fears.

GARDINER

I shall remember this bold language.

CROMWELL   Do.
Remember your bold life, too.

LORD CHANCELLOR   This is too much.
Forbear, for shame, my lords.

GARDINER   I have done.

CROMWELL   And I.   120

LORD CHANCELLOR (*to Cranmer*)

Then thus for you, my lord. It stands agreed,
I take it, by all voices, that forthwith
You be conveyed to th' Tower a prisoner,
There to remain till the King's further pleasure
Be known unto us. Are you all agreed, lords?   125

ALL THE COUNCIL

We are.

CRANMER Is there no other way of mercy,
But I must needs to th' Tower, my lords?

GARDINER   What other
Would you expect? You are strangely troublesome.
Let some o'th' guard be ready there.

Enter the guard

CRANMER   For me?
Must I go like a traitor thither?

GARDINER (*to the guard*)   Receive him,   130
And see him safe i'th' Tower.

CRANMER   Stay, good my lords.
I have a little yet to say. Look there, my lords—

He shows the King's ring

By virtue of that ring I take my cause
Out of the grips of cruel men, and give it
To a most noble judge, the King my master.   135

LORD CHAMBERLAIN

This is the King's ring.

SURREY   'Tis no counterfeit.

SUFFOLK

'Tis the right ring, by heav'n. I told ye all
When we first put this dangerous stone a-rolling
'Twould fall upon ourselves.

NORFOLK   Do you think, my lords,
The King will suffer but the little finger   140
Of this man to be vexed?

LORD CHAMBERLAIN   'Tis now too certain.
How much more is his life in value with him!
Would I were fairly out on't.

⌐Exit King with Butts above⌐

CROMWELL   My mind gave me,
In seeking tales and informations
Against this man, whose honesty the devil   145
And his disciples only envy at,
Ye blew the fire that burns ye. Now have at ye!

*Enter, below, King Henry frowning on them. He
takes his seat*

GARDINER

Dread sovereign, how much are we bound to heaven
In daily thanks, that gave us such a prince,
Not only good and wise, but most religious.   150
One that in all obedience makes the church
The chief aim of his honour, and, to strengthen
That holy duty, out of dear respect,
His royal self in judgement comes to hear
The cause betwixt her and this great offender.   155

KING HENRY

You were ever good at sudden commendations,
Bishop of Winchester. But know I come not
To hear such flattery now; and in my presence
They are too thin and base to hide offences.
To me you cannot reach. You play the spaniel,   160
And think with wagging of your tongue to win me.
But whatsoe'er thou tak'st me for, I'm sure
Thou hast a cruel nature and a bloody.

(*To Cranmer*) Good man, sit down.

Cranmer takes his seat at the head of the Council table

                    Now let me see the proudest,
He that dares most, but wag his finger at thee.   165
By all that's holy, he had better starve
Than but once think this place becomes thee not.

SURREY

May it please your grace—

KING HENRY   No, sir, it does not please me!
I had thought I had had men of some understanding
And wisdom of my Council, but I find none.   170
Was it discretion, lords, to let this man,
This good man—few of you deserve that title—
This honest man, wait like a lousy footboy
At chamber door? And one as great as you are?
Why, what a shame was this! Did my commission   175
Bid ye so far forget yourselves? I gave ye
Power as he was a Councillor to try him,
Not as a groom. There's some of ye, I see,
More out of malice than integrity,
Would try him to the utmost, had ye mean;   180
Which ye shall never have while I live.

LORD CHANCELLOR   Thus far,

447

My most dread sovereign, may it like your grace
To let my tongue excuse all. What was purposed
Concerning his imprisonment was rather—
If there be faith in men—meant for his trial   185
And fair purgation to the world than malice,
I'm sure, in me.
KING HENRY   Well, well, my lords—respect him.
Take him and use him well, he's worthy of it.
I will say thus much for him—if a prince
May be beholden to a subject, I   190
Am for his love and service so to him.
Make me no more ado, but all embrace him.
Be friends, for shame, my lords. (*To Cranmer*) My lord
          of Canterbury,
I have a suit which you must not deny me:
That is a fair young maid that yet wants baptism—
You must be godfather, and answer for her.   196
CRANMER
The greatest monarch now alive may glory
In such an honour; how may I deserve it,
That am a poor and humble subject to you?   199
KING HENRY Come, come, my lord—you'd spare your
          spoons. You shall have two noble partners with you—
the old Duchess of Norfolk and Lady Marquis Dorset.
Will these please you?
(*To Gardiner*) Once more, my lord of Winchester, I
          charge you
Embrace and love this man.
GARDINER   With a true heart   205
And brother-love I do it.
          ⌈*Gardiner and Cranmer embrace*⌉
CRANMER (*weeping*)   And let heaven
Witness how dear I hold this confirmation.
KING HENRY
Good man, those joyful tears show thy true heart.
The common voice, I see, is verified
Of thee which says thus, 'Do my lord of Canterbury
A shrewd turn, and he's your friend for ever.'   211
Come, lords, we trifle time away. I long
To have this young one made a Christian.
As I have made ye one, lords, one remain—   214
So I grow stronger, you more honour gain.   *Exeunt*

5.3   *Noise and tumult within. Enter Porter* ⌈*with rushes*⌉
      and his man ⌈*with a broken cudgel*⌉
PORTER (*to those within*)
You'll leave your noise anon, ye rascals. Do you take
The court for Paris Garden, ye rude slaves?
Leave your gaping.
ONE (*within*)
Good master porter, I belong to th' larder.
PORTER
Belong to th' gallows, and be hanged, ye rogue!   5
Is this a place to roar in?
(*To his man*)
Fetch me a dozen crab-tree staves, and strong ones,
⌈*Raising his rushes*⌉ These are but switches to 'em.
(*To those within*)   I'll scratch your heads.

You must be seeing christenings? Do you look   10
For ale and cakes here, you rude rascals?
MAN
Pray, sir, be patient. 'Tis as much impossible,
Unless we sweep 'em from the door with cannons,
To scatter 'em as 'tis to make 'em sleep
On May-day morning—which will never be.   15
We may as well push against Paul's as stir 'em.
PORTER How got they in, and be hanged?
MAN
Alas, I know not. How gets the tide in?
As much as one sound cudgel of four foot—
          He raises his cudgel
You see the poor remainder—could distribute,   20
I made no spare, sir.
PORTER   You did nothing, sir.
MAN
I am not Samson, nor Sir Guy, nor Colbrand,
To mow 'em down before me; but if I spared any
That had a head to hit, either young or old,
He or she, cuckold or cuckold-maker,   25
Let me ne'er hope to see a chine again—
And that I would not for a cow, God save her!
ONE (*within*) Do you hear, master porter?
PORTER
I shall be with you presently,
Good master puppy. (*To his man*) Keep the door close,
          sirrah.   30
MAN
What would you have me do?
PORTER   What should you do,
but knock 'em down by th' dozens? Is this Moorfields
to muster in? Or have we some strange Indian with
the great tool come to court, the women so besiege us?
Bless me, what a fry of fornication is at door! On my
Christian conscience, this one christening will beget a
thousand. Here will be father, godfather, and all
together.   38
MAN The spoons will be the bigger, sir. There is a fellow
somewhat near the door, he should be a brazier by his
face, for o' my conscience twenty of the dog-days now
reign in's nose. All that stand about him are under the
line—they need no other penance. That fire-drake did
I hit three times on the head, and three times was his
nose discharged against me. He stands there like a
mortar-piece, to blow us. There was a haberdasher's
wife of small wit near him, that railed upon me till her
pinked porringer fell off her head, for kindling such a
combustion in the state. I missed the meteor once, and
hit that woman, who cried out 'Clubs!', when I might
see from far some forty truncheoners draw to her
succour, which were the hope o'th' Strand, where she
was quartered. They fell on. I made good my place. At
length they came to th' broomstaff to me. I defied 'em
still, when suddenly a file of boys behind 'em, loose
shot, delivered such a shower of pebbles that I was fain
to draw mine honour in and let 'em win the work. The
devil was amongst 'em, I think, surely.   58
PORTER These are the youths that thunder at a playhouse,

and fight for bitten apples, that no audience but the
tribulation of Tower Hill or the limbs of Limehouse,
their dear brothers, are able to endure. I have some of
'em in *limbo patrum*, and there they are like to dance
these three days, besides the running banquet of two
beadles that is to come.   65
Enter the Lord Chamberlain
LORD CHAMBERLAIN
Mercy o' me, what a multitude are here!
They grow still, too—from all parts they are coming,
As if we kept a fair here! Where are these porters,
These lazy knaves? (*To the Porter and his man*) You've
     made a fine hand, fellows!
There's a trim rabble let in—are all these   70
Your faithful friends o' th' suburbs? We shall have
Great store of room, no doubt, left for the ladies
When they pass back from the christening!
PORTER   An't please your honour,
We are but men, and what so many may do,
Not being torn a-pieces, we have done.   75
An army cannot rule 'em.
LORD CHAMBERLAIN   As I live,
If the King blame me for't, I'll lay ye all
By th' heels, and suddenly—and on your heads
Clap round fines for neglect. You're lazy knaves,
And here ye lie baiting of bombards when   80
Ye should do service.
Flourish of trumpets within
                         Hark, the trumpets sound.
They're come, already, from the christening.
Go break among the press, and find a way out
To let the troop pass fairly, or I'll find
A Marshalsea shall hold ye play these two months. 85
⌈*As they leave, the Porter and his man call within*⌉
PORTER
Make way there for the Princess!
MAN   You great fellow,
Stand close up, or I'll make your head ache.
PORTER
You i' th' camlet, get up o' th' rail—
I'll peck you o'er the pales else.   *Exeunt*

5.4   *Enter trumpeters, sounding. Then enter two aldermen,*
       the Lord Mayor of London, Garter King-of-Arms,
       Cranmer the Archbishop of Canterbury, the Duke of
       Norfolk with his marshal's staff, the Duke of
       Suffolk, two noblemen bearing great standing
       bowls for the christening gifts; then enter four
       noblemen bearing a canopy, under which is the
       Duchess of Norfolk, godmother, bearing the child
       Elizabeth richly habited in a mantle, whose train is
       borne by a lady. Then follows the Marchioness
       Dorset, the other godmother, and ladies. The troop
       pass once about the stage and Garter speaks
GARTER Heaven, from thy endless goodness send
prosperous life, long, and ever happy, to the high and
mighty Princess of England, Elizabeth.

Flourish. Enter King Henry and guard
CRANMER (*kneeling*)
And to your royal grace, and the good Queen!
My noble partners and myself thus pray   5
All comfort, joy, in this most gracious lady,
Heaven ever laid up to make parents happy,
May hourly fall upon ye.
KING HENRY   Thank you, good lord Archbishop.
What is her name?
CRANMER   Elizabeth.
KING HENRY   Stand up, lord.
Cranmer rises
(*To the child*) With this kiss take my blessing—
He kisses the child
                              God protect thee,
Into whose hand I give thy life.
CRANMER   Amen.   11
KING HENRY (*to Cranmer, old Duchess, and Marchioness*)
My noble gossips, you've been too prodigal.
I thank ye heartily. So shall this lady,
When she has so much English.
CRANMER   Let me speak, sir,
For heaven now bids me, and the words I utter   15
Let none think flattery, for they'll find 'em truth.
This royal infant—heaven still move about her—
Though in her cradle, yet now promises
Upon this land a thousand thousand blessings
Which time shall bring to ripeness. She shall be— 20
But few now living can behold that goodness—
A pattern to all princes living with her,
And all that shall succeed. Saba was never
More covetous of wisdom and fair virtue
Than this pure soul shall be. All princely graces 25
That mould up such a mighty piece as this is,
With all the virtues that attend the good,
Shall still be doubled on her. Truth shall nurse her,
Holy and heavenly thoughts still counsel her.
She shall be loved and feared. Her own shall bless her;
Her foes shake like a field of beaten corn,   31
And hang their heads with sorrow. Good grows with
     her.
In her days every man shall eat in safety
Under his own vine what he plants, and sing
The merry songs of peace to all his neighbours.   35
God shall be truly known, and those about her
From her shall read the perfect ways of honour,
And by those claim their greatness, not by blood.
Nor shall this peace sleep with her, but, as when
The bird of wonder dies—the maiden phoenix—   40
Her ashes new create another heir
As great in admiration as herself,
So shall she leave her blessèdness to one,
When heaven shall call her from this cloud of darkness,
Who from the sacred ashes of her honour   45
Shall star-like rise as great in fame as she was,
And so stand fixed. Peace, plenty, love, truth, terror,
That were the servants to this chosen infant,

Shall then be his, and, like a vine, grow to him.
Wherever the bright sun of heaven shall shine,   50
His honour and the greatness of his name
Shall be, and make new nations. He shall flourish,
And like a mountain cedar reach his branches
To all the plains about him. Our children's children
Shall see this, and bless heaven.

KING HENRY   Thou speakest wonders.

CRANMER
She shall be, to the happiness of England,   56
An agèd princess. Many days shall see her,
And yet no day without a deed to crown it.
Would I had known no more. But she must die—
She must, the saints must have her—yet a virgin,   60
A most unspotted lily shall she pass
To th' ground, and all the world shall mourn her.

KING HENRY O lord Archbishop,
Thou hast made me now a man. Never before
This happy child did I get anything.   65
This oracle of comfort has so pleased me
That when I am in heaven I shall desire
To see what this child does, and praise my maker.
I thank ye all. To you, my good Lord Mayor,
And your good brethren, I am much beholden.   70

I have received much honour by your presence,
And ye shall find me thankful. Lead the way, lords.
Ye must all see the Queen, and she must thank ye.
She will be sick else. This day, no man think
He's business at his house, for all shall stay—   75
This little one shall make it holiday.

⌈*Flourish.*⌉ *Exeunt*

Epilogue *Enter Epilogue*

EPILOGUE
'Tis ten to one this play can never please
All that are here. Some come to take their ease,
And sleep an act or two; but those, we fear,
We've frighted with our trumpets; so, 'tis clear,
They'll say 'tis naught. Others to hear the city   5
Abused extremely, and to cry 'That's witty!'—
Which we have not done neither; that, I fear,
All the expected good we're like to hear
For this play at this time is only in
The merciful construction of good women,   10
For such a one we showed 'em. If they smile,
And say ''Twill do', I know within a while
   All the best men are ours—for 'tis ill hap
   If they hold when their ladies bid 'em clap.   *Exit*

INDEX TO FIRST LINES OF
SONNETS

The Sonnets are to be found on pp. 371–396. The numbers refer to their position in the sequence.

INDEX TO FIRST LINES OF SONNETS